ONE • THOUSAND • ONE

PAPUA • NEW • GUINEAN • NIGHTS

ONE • THOUSAND • ONE

PAPUA • NEW • GUINEAN • NIGHTS

FOLKTALES • FROM
WANTOK • NEWSPAPER

VOLUME • 2 • TALES • FROM • 1986-1997,
INDICES, • GLOSSARY, • REFERENCES, • AND • MAPS

TRANSLATED • AND • EDITED • BY
THOMAS • H • SLONE

PUBLISHED • BY
MASALAI • PRESS
OAKLAND • CALIFORNIA
2001

This book is dedicated to Qiron Adhikary, my loving wife.

Published by
MASALAI PRESS
368 Capricorn Avenue
Oakland, California 94611-2058
U. S. A.

First Edition, 2001

Publisher's Cataloging-in-Publication Data
Slone, Thomas H., 1960-
One thousand one Papua New Guinean nights :
ancestor stories from Wantok newspaper.
Volume 2 : Tales from 1986-1997, indices,
glossary, references, and maps / by Thomas H. Slone.
p. cm.
Includes bibliographical references and index.
ISBN 0-9714127-0-7 (Volume 1, pbk.)
ISBN 0-9714127-1-5 (Volume 2, pbk.)
ISBN 0-9714127-2-3 (2 Volume Set)
1. Tales — Papua New Guinea.
2. Folklore — Papua New Guinea.
3. Mythology — Melanesian — Papua New Guinea
4. Legends — Papua New Guinea
I. Thomas H. Slone II. Title III. Papua New Guinea Folklore Series 2

Papua New Guinea Folklore Series
1. One Thousand One Papua New Guinean Nights: Folktales from Wantok Newspaper.
    Volume 1: Tales from 1972-1985
2. One Thousand One Papua New Guinean Nights: Folktales from Wantok Newspaper.
    Volume 2: Tales from 1986-1997, Indices, Glossary, References, and Maps (this volume)

"I know of no part of the world, the exploration of which is so flattering to the imagination, so likely to be fruitful in interesting results, whether to the naturalist, the ethnologist, or the geographer, and altogether so well calculated to gratify the enlightened curiosity of an adventurous explorer, as the interior of New Guinea. New Guinea! The very mention of being taken into the interior of New Guinea sounds like being allowed to visit some of the enchanted regions of the 'Arabian Nights,' so dim an atmosphere of obscurity rests at present on the wonders it probably conceals."

(Jukes, 1847: 291)

"'Am I to understand that you [Pandit Gananath Sastri] have translated the works of Molière, Rabelais, and Boccaccio into Sanskrit?' I asked, laughing at the outrageousness of the very idea... 'Who publishes the translations?'... 'No one,' he smiled with pleasure... 'Doesn't it bother you that nobody publishes your work, that nobody reads it?' He laughed again, flowers of laughter, 'What if you write this book on Indian comedy and nobody publishes it? What if somebody publishes it, but nobody reads it? What if somebody reads it, but nobody likes it? What if you knew your book would not be published? Would you write the book anyway? If your answer is 'no,' then you should not write this book. If the answer is 'yes,' then nothing can stop you from writing it. The only things that are important are necessities — eating, sleeping, breathing, defecating, urinating — these things our bodies compel us to do. Writing has to be like that. I have no choice in doing these translations. I have no choice,' he laughed, 'and if you have a choice about your book on humor, then don't write the book.'"

(Siegel, 1987: 90)

Table of Contents

List of Folktales — Volume 1

How the Stone Axe Came About

(Wantok 603, January 11, 1986, page 20)

Long ago, before there were stone axes in the Highlands, there was an old man and woman who lived in Kunjin Village. The old man's name was Timbe and the old woman's name was Doimbe.

One day, they went to work in the garden. While they were working in the garden, the old woman told her husband that she would go look for bamboo shoots and gather small pieces of firewood to carry back to the village. She finished talking to her husband, then she departed.

The old woman gathered bamboo shoots and put them in a pile. Then she searched for and gathered firewood. Old man Timbe cut and tied up wild sugarcanes (*pitpit*) and sugarcanes.

The old woman put the bamboo shoots into a net bag, then she saw a stone on the ground. Only the top of the stone was visible. The old woman noticed that it was a very unusual stone. She had never seen any stones like this before. Quickly, she called out to her husband to come and see it.

Her husband, Timbe, went to the place where the stone was located. He looked there and he was surprised. He told his wife, "It's probably a *masalai* stone or something like that."

Timbe took a piece of wood and began digging the earth under the stone. The top of the stone was like an axe. Timbe and his wife dug down into the earth. They found that it was a very unusual stone inside the hole. They removed the stone, then they sat and talked. They tried to think of what kind of thing they could make with this stone.

In the afternoon, they left their garden and went back to the village. They carried the stone and put it in their house. At night, after they cooked and ate, they called out for their kin to come. They showed them their unusual stone.

After their kin came and saw the stone, they talked about making a house at the place where they had found the stone. They wanted to sleep by that place and to remove more stones like the one that the old woman had found.

After the people made the house, they had a party for raising more stones. All of the men gathered and gave a name to this stone, and to the work of the special stone that they found at this place. They gave a name to the place where the stones come from. In the **Nii** Language, the name of this stone is "*tui kunjin*," meaning "stone axe."

The men of the other villages heard the story of this stone axe and they also liked this stone. They sent the women to go marry at the place where the people cut the stones. The women just married without getting a big bride price, because the people of the other villages wanted to get the stone axes.

After that, the stone axes of the people of the Kunjin [**Kunjip**] area went to all of the places in **Western Highlands** Province. Now, the other villages of the Highlands also use these stones to cut trees or to do their other hard work.

Simon Yesim
World Vision
P. O. Box 409
Hagen
Western Highlands Province

A1446.2. Origin of the axe; P210. Husband and wife; T52. Bride purchased

Salahmo [Salahamo] Killed the Old *Masalai*s

(Wantok 604, January 18, 1986, page 24)

Long, long ago, in the time of the ancestors, there were three brothers who lived in **Giviseveka** Village. The name of the first brother was Maniho, the name of the second brother was Siofe, and the third brother was named Salahamo.

One day, they did not have meat in the house, so the brothers sat and talked about going to hunt for wild game. There was other work to be done too, so the big brother, Maniho, told his two little brothers to stay in the village while he went alone to hunt for game in the forest.

Maniho straightened his bow and arrows well, then he slept. In the early morning, he awoke, took his three dogs and went into the forest.

They walked and walked until they passed some big mountains, then they went down to a flat area. The area that they arrived at was the home of an old *masalai* and his wife. The old *masalai* caught wind of a man coming to his home, so he explained to his wife that he would go watch the trail.

The *masalai* saw Maniho and asked, "Kinsman, where do you want to go that you're walking on the trail so hard?"

Maniho listened then lied to the old man, "No. I'm trying to find vines to fence the house, so I came around here."

The old man said, "I found a tree hole that is jam-packed with marsupials (*kapul*) inside of it."

The old man told Maniho that his house was nearby and that he could sleep in his house until morning. Then they would wake up and hunt the marsupials in the tree hole.

They arrived at the old man's house and they slept. When it was nearly dawn, the *masalai* woke up very quietly and defecated at the door of the house. After he defecated, he pretended to sleep.

When dawn broke, he went down and waited for Maniho. Maniho awoke and went outside. Then the old man said, "Was that your dogs or maybe it was you yourself who shat at my doorstep?"

The old man berated poor Maniho and shamed him terribly. He told the old man that he did not know who had defecated by the house.

The old man insisted that Maniho remove the pile of feces. So, poor Maniho listened and went down to remove the feces. While he was bending down to remove the feces, the old man came quietly behind his back and struck his head with a piece of wood. Maniho fell down and the old man killed him.

The old man took Maniho, then the two of them [the husband and wife] butchered and cooked him. When their meat [Maniho] was ready, they ate. They killed Maniho's three dogs and cooked them too. When they finished eating, they carried the bones to the back of the house where a clump of bamboo was growing, and they threw the bones there.

One week passed and Maniho did not return to the village, so his two brothers at the village began to worry. They were worried because Maniho could not stay for very long in the forest. They knew that if one of them went to the forest, he would stay for only two days then return to the village.

So, the second brother, Siofe, told his little brother that he would go look for Maniho. They thought that it was bad if Maniho had become lost in the forest or if he had become injured, he would not return home.

Siofe took his bow and arrows. He called for his dogs to come, then they left to find Maniho. The dogs sniffed the trail that Maniho had followed, and they walked away. They walked and walked until they arrived at the place where Maniho had met the old *masalai* man.

The old *masalai* caught Siofe's scent, so he went down to watch the trail. When Siofe arrived at this place, the old man asked him, "Kinsman, who are you looking for, that you've come to my home?"

Soife [Siofe] listened and said, "My big brother went hunting for game and he didn't return home. I was looking for him and I came here. Have you seen him or not?"

The old man said, "I'm very sorry, kinsman, I haven't seen him. It's only me who usually goes around this part of the forest. Never mind, come and we'll go sleep in my house. It's nearly dark now. Tomorrow morning you can go look for him."

When they arrived, the old woman saw Siofe and was very happy. She knew that she and her husband would have good meat for themselves. The old woman quickly cooked some food, then they finished eating and slept.

Near dawn, the old man woke up and did the same thing again. He went outside very quietly and defecated right at the front of the door. Soife and his dogs were dead asleep, and did not hear a thing.

In the morning, the old man went outside first, then he called out to Soife, "Kinsman, wake up and come look. I think that your dogs have just defecated right by my house gable."

Soife listened and went outside. He saw a huge pile of feces right by the house gable.

The old man said, "I don't know but it looks like this is human shit, not dog shit. The two of us don't have a baby. I think it was just you that shat there."

Poor Soife was speechless. He told the old man that he never did that sort of thing. However, he was ashamed, so he said that he would remove the feces.

When Soife was bending down to remove the feces, the old man hit him, knocking him down. Then he killed him. The old woman saw this, so she happily sang and danced.

The two of them carried Soife and cut him into little pieces, then they cooked him. Later, the old man also killed Soife's dogs.

The poor last brother, Salahamo, was waiting and waiting. His two brothers had not returned home. He was very worried, so he left to look for them.

Salahamo gave some good food to his dogs, then he scolded them. He said, "When we go to the forest to look for my two brothers, you must not become confused or fall dead asleep. If I sleep, you must stay awake."

After he finished teaching his dogs, they left the village. The dogs went first and showed the way that the two brothers had followed into the forest.

Just like before, the old man was sitting by the trail. When they arrived, he saw Salahamo and he called out, "Hey kinsman, why are you and your dogs walking around here?"

Salahamo just listened and did not reply to what the old man said. He walked further and the old man called out again, "Kinsman, I know a place where there are many, many marsupials. If you'd like, I'll show you this place."

Salahamo spoke angrily to the old man, "You asked me what I was doing. I didn't come to see you or to hunt marsupials."

The old man listened and he lied sweetly to Salahamo, "I told you this because two young men came here. I showed them this place and they hunted marsupials there."

Salahmo listened and turned back to the place where the old man was sitting. He interrogated the old man. Then the old man lied to him, "The two men went to a place that is much farther. If you walk that way, you'll get confused on the trail."

The old man told him to sleep and eat with them, but Salahamo said that the dogs had already eaten. They finished eating, then Salahamo slept.

He slept very well, but his dogs did not sleep. They watched over him because he had instructed them to do so.

They slept until it was nearly dawn, then the old *masalai* woke up very quietly and went to defecate by the house door. It was dark, so he did not see one of Salahamo's dogs lying there. The dog thought that the old man wanted to kill Salahumo [Salahamo], so it jumped up and bit the old man's [face] and arms.

The old man screamed terribly and went to wake Salahamo. He said, "Kinsman, your bad dog is biting me."

Salahamo listened and said, "It's still dark. What were you looking for that the dog bit you? This is a dog that bites men, women and children."

The old man went to sleep and thought that Salahamo and his dogs were also asleep. Then he got up very quietly again. He went down and wanted to go outside, but the dog jumped and finished him off.

Salahamo heard this and he went outside to look. He told the dog to watch the old man. Then he needed to urinate, so he went outside to urinate behind the house. When he went to the base of the bamboos, he saw his two brothers' bones and their dogs' bones lying there.

Then he went back quietly, taking his bow and arrows. He shot the old man dead. The old man's wife came and heard the noise. She came to look, then Salahamo killed her too.

Salahamo put their bodies inside their house. Then he took his two brothers' bones. He burned the old *masalai*s' house along with their two bodies.

Goramo Ariti
P. O. Box 2095
Rabaul
East New Britain Province

B212. Animal understands human speech; F490+. Masalai; G405. Man on hunt falls into ogre's (witch's) power; G512.1+. Ogre killed with spear/arrow; K800+. Dupe killed after being persuaded to bend down; P210. Husband and wife; P251.3.1. Brothers strive to avenge each other; P251.6.1. Three brothers; Q211. Murder punished; Q215. Cannibalism punished; Q411. Death as punishment; S110. Murders; S139.2. Slain person dismembered; S139.2.2+. Corpse put into cooking pot or cooked; W157. Dishonesty; X716.1H+. Befouling with excrement

A Wild Cat Found Kewa's Wife

(Wantok 605, January 25, 1986, page 20)

Long ago, in the time of the ancestors, there lived a man named Kewa. He lived in a place called **Kuare**, in the Kagua area of **Southern Highlands** Province [**Kewa** People].

Kewa lived by himself because there were no other people in the area. This did not concern him because he was a very hard worker. He always worked in his garden, and he went by himself into the forest to hunt for wild game.

He did this for a while, and the food just rotted at his house. He worked so hard that the food from his garden just piled up and rotted.

One time, there was no meat in the house, so Kewa carried his bow and arrows then went into the forest. He walked and walked until he arrived at a place where there was a huge tree that had fallen and was rotting. He saw a big wild cat sleeping at the base of the tree.

Kewa drew back his bow and prepared to shoot the cat. However, the cat awoke and said, "Kewa, don't shoot me."

Kewa was shocked and afraid. He stopped thinking about hunting for game in the forest. He took his arrows and ran back home. When he arrived at his house, Kewa went inside and shut the door. He thought hard about the wild cat that had spoken to him. He was afraid and hid.

He stayed inside the house, then he heard the cat arrive and cry outside the house, "*Meo, meo*." In the language used at Kagua, this means, "Fetch me."

Kewa listened and was sorry for the cat, so he opened the house door, letting the cat inside. The cat lay quietly in the house. Kewa made a fire and cooked some food, then they ate and slept.

In the morning, the cat awoke, went into the forest and killed some game for themselves, then the cat carried it back home. The next morning, it did the same thing.

From then onwards, Kewa would stay home and just go to work in the garden. The cat would travel the forest and kill game for themselves. The cat was content because it had no more worries. It had found a good owner. However, the cat always worried about Kewa who was alone and without a wife to care for him.

Time passed. One day the cat told Kewa, "I'm leaving you to travel the forest. The place where I want to go is very far away, so I can't return quickly."

The cat finished speaking to Kewa, then they slept. In the early morning, the cat left home and walked into the forest. The cat walked and walked until it arrived at a place where women were working and making much noise. The cat heard this and walked very quietly. Then the cat saw that there were many women by a pond.

They were fishing in the pond, so they had removed their "grass" skirts and put them on top of their net bags. They were fishing intensely, so they did not see the cat hiding and watching them.

The sun set, so the women came outside the water to tie on their skirts. The cat inspected the young women carefully, and decided which woman was the leader.

Very quietly, the cat took the skirt and net bag of this woman. The cat carried them away and hid them. When this woman came out of the water, she could not find her skirt or bag. She looked around, then the cat came outside its hiding place, and the woman saw it.

The woman called out to the other women, then all of them came and surrounded the cat. However they could not grab it, so the other women gave up and went back home because it was getting very dark.

Their leader tried to chase the cat to get back her skirt. Whenever she came close to catching the cat, the cat would run away and hide. They did this for a while, then the woman became completely confused about where the forest cat had taken her.

The woman gave up completely and called out to the cat, "If you so desire, take me to your home. However, you must leave my skirt so that I can tie it on first."

The cat left the woman's skirt. The woman came, took her skirt and tied it on. When she finished, they walked and walked, arriving at Kewa's home.

When they arrived, the cat told the woman to hide near the house, while the cat went there alone. Kewa saw the cat and was ecstatic to see it. However, the cat jumped on top of Kewa and scratched him, then walked to the area where the banana plants grew. Kewa went to see what was at the base of the banana plants.

When he approached, he was surprised to see a very beautiful woman standing there. The woman was terrified, but Kewa went and took her, then they were happy together.

He asked the woman, "How did you get here?" The woman told him what the cat had done, pulling her skirt through the forest. Kewa listened and just laughed quietly because he knew that the cat had thought of him and went to find this woman to bring there.

Kewa married this woman and they lived together. The cat stayed with them until it became very old, then it died.

Mathias Asuma
Wakunai Police Station
P. O. Box 28
Wakunai
North Solomons Province

B211.1.8. Speaking cat; B422. Helpful cat; B582.1.1. Animal wins wife for his master (Puss in Boots); K401.1.1. Trail of stolen goods made to lead to dupe; P210. Husband and wife; T100. Marriage

[The ancestor story in *Wantok* #606 is very similar to the one in #450.]

The Ghost Women of Damugoi

(Wantok 607, February 8, 1986, page 20)

Long, long ago, there was a married couple who lived in a village by **Okapa**, in **Eastern Highlands** Province [**Fore** People]. The man's wife was pregnant. They lived for a while, then the woman gave birth.

One day, the man told his wife that he would go hunting for wild game in the forest. He took his bow and arrows and dog too, then went into the forest.

The man walked and walked, then arrived at a place in the forest where he erected a small forest hut. He left a little food and some of his things in the hut, then he traveled in the forest. He hunted for game until evening, then he went back to the little hut, sat and cooked his food.

He did not think about going home quickly because he wanted to hunt for game the next day. After that, he would return to his wife and baby.

The man sat and cooked his food. When it was nearly ready and he was about to sit and eat, his wife and baby arrived. Oh my, was he surprised to see his wife and newborn baby.

He trembled and thought, "Is this really my wife, or who is it?"

He thought that his real wife must have died at the village, and that it was just her ghost who had come to fool him.

The man was very troubled, so he asked the woman, "Why did you come here?"

The ghost woman said, "You came alone into the forest, so we were sorry for you and followed you here."

The man told the woman, "I've been hunting marsupials (*kapul*), and my body is very tired. It's nearly dark too, so I think I'll sleep here. Tomorrow morning, I'll hunt for some more game, then in the afternoon I'll go back home."

The woman listened and wanted to sit with him, but he already knew that the woman was a ghost.

He told her, "Go fetch some water for me, but fetch it from the second stream. Men don't drink from the first stream."

The ghost woman took a bamboo tube and went to fetch water. She returned very quickly to him. The man saw this and asked her where she really had fetched the water.

The ghost woman replied, "I just fetched it nearby."

The man told the ghost woman to spill out the water because it was forbidden for men to drink from that stream. He sent the woman back again to fetch water from the second stream.

When the woman left, the man tied up his dog, then quickly carried the dog with him up a wild pandanus tree (*karuka*). However, the woman returned. She saw the dog and man on top of the big wild pandanus tree.

The woman was completely furious. Late that night, she removed the vines from the base of the pandanus tree [to prevent his descent]. The man saw this and knew that she was a ghost, not a real woman.

The woman continued to remove the vines until it was nearly dawn and there was just one route down. When dawn broke, the ghost woman disappeared.

The man saw this, took his dog, and went back to the village. When they arrived at the village, they saw that the woman had died. He mourned and was very troubled about his wife. His kin in the village took his baby and looked after it.

Later, the man thought, "It was true that the woman's ghost had followed me into the forest."

This is not an ordinary story. This forest, called Damugoi, is in the Okapa area of Eastern Highlands Province. This forest is filled with ghost women.

Before, in the time of the ancestors, whoever went to the forest called Damugoi never returned to the village. They would just be lost, or some kind of enemy would intercept them.

Sipha Tusuke
Port Moresby
National Capital District

C260. Tabu: drinking at certain place; C612. Forbidden forest; E221+. Dead wife's malevolent return; E425.1.4. Revenant as woman carrying baby; E276+. Ghosts haunt forest; E452. Ghost laid at cockcrow (dawn); K1910. Marital impostors; P210. Husband and wife; P230. Parents and children; R311. Tree refuge; T570. Pregnancy; T580. Childbirth

Sape Tricked the *Masalai* of Vokopoan

(Wantok 608, February 15, 1986, page 24)

Long, long ago, in a village called **Lebam**, there lived a man and his wife. The man's name was Sape, and his wife's name was Solem.

One afternoon, Sape told his wife, "Very early, tomorrow morning, I'll leave the village and go hunt for wild game in the very deep forest. I'd like you to cook two pieces of sweet potato for me, then put them aside."

His wife listened to him, so that night she cooked for themselves. Then she cooked two pieces of sweet potato for her husband and put them aside.

In the very early morning when all of the other people were still sleeping, Sape awoke. He took his bow, arrows and axe. He covered up his sweet potatoes and left the village. The village was far from this part of the forest, so he walked swiftly until he approached a big mountain. The name of this mountain is Vokopoan.

The sun rose strongly, so Sape put his things down at the base of Mount Vokopoan and rested a little. This was because he wanted to cut across the mountain to go to the other side and hunt for game. While he sat and rested, he saw a huge tree standing there. The tree looked as if it was filled with [edible] insects [probably beetle grubs], so Sape took his axe and began to cut it. While he was cutting the tree, the noise of the axe exploded through the forest.

There was a *masalai* who lived in a cave in this area. The *masalai* was sleeping and heard the sound of the man cutting the tree. Oh my, was the *masalai* happy because he knew that there was wild game [i.e., the man] for himself going around the forest.

The *masalai* got up, pricked up his ears, and listened carefully. The *masalai* finished listening, left his cave and followed the forest to the place from where the noise was coming. He walked and went quietly until he arrived at the place where Sape was cutting the tree.

When the *masalai* arrived, the tree was fallen and broken. Sape turned to put down his axe and was surprised to see a man standing behind him.

Sape trembled fiercely because he knew that no other man came to this part of the forest. He knew that the man must be a *masalai*.

The *masalai* said, "If you don't let me also take insects from this tree, I'll kill you now."

Sape listened and whispered, "That's OK, you can take the insects."

After Sape said this, he began to break open the tree. The *masalai* just stood and watched. When Sape finished breaking the tree apart, the *masalai* began to gather the insects with Sape.

While they gathered the insects, Sape carefully gathered his, but the *masalai* ate his. After a while, he asked the *masalai*, "Why are you eating the raw insects?"

The *masalai* listened and lied to the man, "If you eat the raw insects, you'll become a very strong man. You'll be able to see things that are hidden as well as things that are not hidden."

Sape listened to what the *masalai* said, but he did not believe it. He knew that the *masalai* would kill him if he did not escape from this place. He gathered his insects, then he thought of a way that he could escape from the *masalai*.

After a while, he saw the *masalai* begin to eat his insects too. He knew that he now had little time. He was furious, so he took his axe and broke a piece of wood that was not well dried.

He lied to the *masalai*, "Kinsman, there's plenty of insects still in the tree. Come put your hand inside and remove them."

The *masalai* thought that it was true. Quickly, he put his two hands inside the place where the axe had opened the tree. When Sape saw this, he immediately removed the axe, causing the tree shut again and trapping the *masalai*'s two hands.

The *masalai* shouted for Sape to come remove his hands by opening the tree again with his axe. However, Sape had already thrown the insects into his net bag and had gone back towards the village. He did not turn back or think about resting. He left nothing inside the forest, then he arrived at the village.

The *masalai* twisted and turned. He shouted inside the forest, but who would hear him? The place was far away and there was no one who traveled that part of the forest.

When the man arrived in the village, he told his wife what had happened in the forest. The man did not return to the forest. He just stayed in the village and helped his wife do their other work.

After some months, the man traveled in the forest and he arrived at the place where he had trapped the *masalai*'s hands. Oh my, when he arrived at this place, he saw many kinds of food growing.

He saw this and turned back to tell the villagers. They followed him to see the excellent and abundant foods. The people removed them and brought them to plant in their gardens by the village.

After this, there were many kinds of foods that grew in the villagers' gardens. Now if you go there, you will see the foods just rotting there [because they are so plentiful].

This story comes from Musim [**Misim**] Village, in the Salamaua area of **Morobe** Province [**Misim** People]. My maternal kin told me this, and I wrote it down.

Nickson Yana
Yansom
Kerema High School
Gulf Province

A1420.1+. Origin of food from body of slain ogre; F419.4K. Spirits eat food raw; F490+. Masalai; G512. Ogre killed; G642K. Ogres eat raw flesh; H46.1+. Cannibal recognized when it devours raw flesh; K1111. Dupe puts hand (paws) into cleft of tree (wedge, vise); P210. Husband and wife; S110. Murders

The *Tatavebuki* Snakes of Magarina [Margarima]

(Wantok 609, February 22, 1986, page 24)

Long, long ago, in my village, Magarima, there lived an old woman. The old woman had twelve sons. Her twelve sons just stayed there because their father had died.

Their mother made a huge sweet potato garden, so they always ate sweet potatoes. There was no man to go hunt for wild game in the forest, so they were always short of food [meat].

After a while, the children became fed up. One day, the eldest brother awoke then told his mother and little brothers, "Tomorrow morning I'll awake and go to the forest to hunt for game for us. Look, we're just staying in the village and eating sweet potatoes. I'm tired of this." In the early morning, he awoke and went to the forest. In the evening, he did not return. His mother and brothers ate sweet potatoes and slept. The next day, they waited and waited, the sun set and it became completely dark, but the eldest son did not return.

Then on the third day, another brother awoke then told his mother and little brothers that he would go find his big brother. He too left the village and went to the forest.

The mother and the other brothers waited. But no, their two brothers did not return to the village. They thought that an enemy probably had found them in the forest and that they had died.

However, this was not true. The second brother walked and walked then entered the very deep forest. When he was in the deep forest, he saw smoke rising from a fire. He went up a mountain and looked more carefully.

After he looked carefully, he followed the smoke. He walked and walked then arrived at this place. He saw his big brother cutting the forest and trees to make a garden. The second brother called out to his big brother to turn and look at him.

The second brother said, "What are you doing in the forest? All of us were waiting for you to bring marsupials (*kapul*) back home. When you did not return, we thought that you probably had died, so I came to look for you."

The big brother listened and said, "I've tired of returning home. I want to stay in the forest, make my garden and plant food. Also, it's easy to hunt game in this area."

His younger brother told him, "I don't want to go back either. I'll stay with you here in the forest."

So, the second brother stayed in the part of the forest that the big brother had cleared and made his house. The kin in the village thought that the two children had died. Their mother cried and was worried for her two children.

They lived there a fairly long time, then the third brother followed his brothers into the forest. He too did not return. Then the fourth brother also went and did not return.

It went like this until the only the last brother was with his mother. They thought that the big brothers had died in the forest. Many years had passed and their mother was old. The last brother had also become a man.

One day, the last brother told his mother, "Mother, I want to travel the forest. I think that I'll go so that I can see what happened to my lost brothers in the forest. Don't worry about me, I'll return to see you."

His mother was very troubled, but she just agreed. Then in the early morning, the son woke up, left home, and walked into the forest.

He walked and walked until he entered the very deep forest. However, inside the deep forest there was a place that was completely clear. He knew that there must be men who lived in this place who had cut the trees to make this clearing.

Very quietly, he walked closer to the house and saw his brothers sitting there. He was angry because they had come

to live very well in the forest. They had completely forgotten him and their poor mother.

Then he entered the clearing and shouted at them, "Man! Mom and I thought that all of you had died in the forest, but you're living happily in this big house of yours, and you haven't thought of us."

His big brothers listened and were terribly troubled. They held him and cried.

They said, "We lived in this forest where there are various foods in the garden. The game is also very plentiful, and we did not think about returning home."

The little brother listened and was not very happy. He thought that his big brothers had acted greedily.

His big brothers looked at him and said, "Brother, there is another important thing that happened, so we didn't return home. Come inside the house and we'll show you."

His brothers stood in a row and each went to hold the [house] posts. The first brother went to hold a post and he turned into a snake. Then he slithered up the post and came down again. When he coiled on the house floor, he became a man again.

After him, the other brothers also did this. Oh my, the little brother saw this and wanted to try it too. He went and held the post then turned into a snake. Later, he became a man again.

Afterwards, the last brother did not want to return home. He wanted to live with his big brothers in the forest and celebrate with them.

However on the second night that he slept in the house, he thought hard about their old mother. So in the early morning, he awoke very quietly and left his brothers' house. He had not told them that he wanted to return to the village and see their mother. He just ran through the forest until he arrived at the village.

His mother was very happy to see him again because when he had not returned, she had thought that her last son probably had died in the forest too. The last brother told the story to his mother about the other brothers.

The mother listened and was terribly troubled. Her last son saw this and told her, "I'll take you to see them at their home."

So, the two of them left the village and walked into the forest. They walked and walked until they arrived at the big brothers' home.

The brothers saw that their mother was old now. They cried terribly for her. The mother saw that her big sons had white hair and she was also very troubled.

Later, the sons told their mother about the wooden post that they used to transform their bodies and become snakes.

The mother also saw her sons transform their bodies and she was very troubled.

These snake children are called *tatavebuki*, and they lived in the place called **Tatave**, near Magarima [**Margarima**] in the [**Southern**] **Highlands** [Province, **Huli** People].

Nick S. Avene

Wakunai

North Solomons Province

A1617. Origin of place-name; D191M. Transformation: man to serpent (snake); D391M. Transformation: serpent (snake) to man; D565. Transformation by touching; D956+. Magic house post; P231. Mother and son; P251.6.7. Twelve brothers; R260. Pursuits; W151. Greed

A Brother and Sister Tricked the *Masalai*

(Wantok 610, March 1, 1986, page 21)

Long, long ago, in the time of the ancestors, the village children often decided to go together to search for Malay apples when they were in season.

In the village, there lived a brother and his sister. One day, the brother traveled by the river and saw that the Malay apples were very ripe. After he went back to the village and told his sister.

They decided to go pick the Malay apples. In the very early morning, when the other people were still sleeping, they awoke very quietly and went to the place where the Malay apple trees stood.

The trees stood on the other side of the river, where the people of the village never went. There was a ghost man and his wife who lived in this area.

The brother and sister climbed a tree, picked Malay apples and filled their net bags. After a while, they saw a wild pig going around the base of the tree. The pig wanted to eat the ripe Malay apples that had fallen around the base of the tree.

The brother and sister saw this and began to throw Malay apples down to the pig. The pig gorged itself. Then they tricked the pig. The sister took traditional nails and shoved three of them inside a ripe Malay apple. She threw it down to the pig.

The pig swallowed the Malay apple, and the nails became caught in its throat. Oh my, it squealed, and turned about, then it fell down dead.

The pig died, then the brother and sister went down to the ground and left the tree. However when they trampled the ground, the ghost man also arrived, right at the base of the Malay apple tree.

The two of them saw this and they thought that it was a real man, so the brother told the ghost, "Come help us carry this pig to the village."

However the ghost lied to them and said, "Never mind that. Don't worry, we'll carry the pig to my house. It's very close."

The brother and sister listened and said, "That's alright. We'll go to your home first, butcher the pig, then later we can go to our village."

The brother told the ghost, "Go cut some vines. When you return we'll tie the pig and carry it to your home."

The ghost listened then said, "If you give me your sister to marry, I'll go cut the vines."

The brother listened and lied to the ghost, "That's alright. You'll marry my sister."

The ghost was ecstatic. Immediately, he went inside the forest, cut vines, and carried them back. They tied up the pig and carried it. The ghost man walked in the back, while the real man and his sister went first.

However while they walked along the trail, the ghost man cut the vines and the pig fell down. The real man told him to go inside the forest and cut new vines again.

The ghost again said, "If you give me your sister, I'll cut the vines." The man lied and said, "She's your woman, so you'll marry her."

The ghost was happy, so he went to cut new vines again and bring them back. They tied up the pig and carried it away. They walked and walked until they arrived at the ghost's home. They saw his old wife sitting there. When the brother and sister saw her, they began to think hard.

The brother told the ghost to cut some coconut fronds to bring back. The ghost went up a coconut palm, cut the fronds, and descended. They made a fire [with the fronds], then cooked and carved the pig.

The ghost man took the pig guts and told them, "I'll go clean the pig guts in the river."

However, he did not go to wash them. He carried the pig guts away, sat by the river and gobbled them down.

The ghost man's wife told the real man's sister to go fetch water and clean the pig blood. When the woman went down to the river, she saw the ghost man gobbling the pig guts.

The woman ran back and told her brother. The old woman heard this and told them, "Take your meat and run away now. The bad man is coming back to eat you too."

They took the meat, filled the net bags, and fled. They ran and ran. The things in their net bags were heavy, so they climbed a tree that was near the trail.

The brother took his gourd [trumpet], blew it, and the tree shot up very high. Then they saw the ghost man running behind them on the trail.

The ghost arrived at the tree, looked up at them and said, "Where do you two want to run away to? Now you'll be soup."

Then he began to climb the tree. He tried and tried, but he was unsuccessful. He gave up and shouted at them, "How did you get up there?"

The brother called down, "Go look for a piece of vine in the forest, then tie it to the tree and you'll come up."

The ghost ran inside the forest, cut a vine, then returned. He tied up the vine, then began to climb the tree again. However, the vine broke and he fell to the ground again. He went into the forest, cut another kind of vine, and returned to try again. However, this vine also broke.

He did this for a while, then the brother sat down and told him to go cut a very strong vine. The ghost did this, then began to climb the tree.

The brother asked the ghost man, "Do you have some traditional ring money or not?"

The ghost replied and said that there was an enormous amount of money.

The brother told him, "Go get the money, make a big fire, then burn it. When it's bright red, throw it at the base of the tree and the tree will break."

The poor ghost listened and thought it was true. Immediately, he ran back to his house and took the ring money. He carried it back, made a fire and burned it. When he threw it at the base of the tree, something bad happened.

He was furious, so he climbed the tree. The ghost climbed and climbed, then he arrived at the branch where the brother and sister were sitting. Immediately, they cut the vine and the ghost fell down to the ground and rolled around. When he stopped moving, the brother told his sister that he would go down to the ground and look.

The brother went down very quietly until he trampled the ground. He walked and went closer. He saw that the ghost was dead. He called up to his sister and his sister came down.

They shoved a spear up the ghost's rectum until the spear came out of his mouth. Then they left this area and ran back to their village.

Rakom Gomba
Arawa
North Solomons Province

D1221. Magic trumpet; D1576. Magic object causes tree to spring up; E425.1. Revenant as woman; E425.2. Revenant as man; E440+. Walking ghost laid from fall; E541. Revenants eat; F54.1. Tree stretches to sky; F419.4K. Spirits eat food raw; G11.10. Cannibalistic spirits; G530.1. Help from ogre's wife (mistress); G642K. Ogres eat raw flesh; H46.1+. Cannibal recognized when it devours raw flesh; K897.1+. Dupe killed by putting thorns in food it is about to swallow; K983. Dupe persuaded to climb tree; K1400. Dupe's property destroyed; P210. Husband and wife; P253. Sister and brother; R220. Flights; R260. Pursuits; R311. Tree refuge; S139.2.2.1+. Corpse impaled

The Boys Tricked the Greedy *Masalai*
(Wantok 611, March 8, 1986, page 23)

Long, long ago, in the time of the ancestors, there lived a group of boys. The twelve boys did not have parents, but they lived in a huge house.

The boys never worked. They never gardened or hunted for food. Their activities consisted of playing in the mud, then running down to the river and washing off well. When it was nearly dark, they would run inside the forest, look around for leafy greens and tree fruits, then carry them back to the house to eat.

The next morning, they would wake up and do their activities again. One afternoon, they returned to the house with leafy greens and tree fruits. They were surprised to see a big leg of pork lying in the house.

They were ecstatic. They cut and cooked it, then they ate until their bellies were bloated and they went to sleep happily. In the morning, they awoke and left their house to play. When they returned in the afternoon, they found another leg of pork lying in the house. They cooked and ate the pork.

Henceforth they only ate pork. After a while, all of them became strong and stout boys. They did not know who it was that put pork in their house, and they did not think about finding out who it was. They were just happy to see the meat because before they had only eaten leaves and tree fruits, then slept.

One afternoon, the boys sat and ate the pork, then the man who had given them the pork arrived. They were surprised to see him because no one else lived in this area.

The man told them, "Children, eat well and sleep. I'll come to see you tonight."

Oh my, the boys trembled fiercely when they heard this. They did not think any more about eating pork. They just left it there and sat trembling. They talked about how they could find a way to kill this bad man. They recognized that he was a *masalai*.

The boys dug up a house post, then went inside [the hole] and hid. At night they heard the *masalai* arrive at their house. He went inside the house very quietly and looked for them, but not one boy was in the house.

The *masalai* did not find them, so he went back to his house. In the morning, the boys were not in the house. He carried the leg of pork and again put it in their house.

In the afternoon, the boys arrived at the house and saw the pork. They sat and ate, then the *masalai* arrived at the house. He told them, "Children, last night I came to see you, but you were not at home."

The boys lied to him, "We slept by the stones that surround the fireplace, so you probably didn't see us."

The *masalai* listened to this and returned to this house. The boys quickly finished their food, then they all went inside the posthole and slept. When it was becoming late, they heard the *masalai* coming to their house.

He went directly to the kitchen and looked for them. The *masalai* broke the stones of the fireplace, but the children were not there. He did not find them, so he was completely furious and went back.

In the afternoon, he returned and said to the boys, "At night I came to look for you in the kitchen, but you weren't there."

The boys told him, "We were too hot, so we went to sleep by the post near the door where the cool wind would find us."

The *masalai* was very angry, but he did not speak. He returned to his house and waited until it was dark. At night, the boys went to hide again, and the *masalai* returned to their house. He cut the doorpost, but no one was there.

In the afternoon, he came and asked them again. The boys told him that they had slept on the roof. The *masalai* came that night and cut the roof of the house, but he did not find a single boy there either.

The *masalai* was completely irate now because his pigs were almost gone and he had not yet eaten one of them. In the afternoon, they came back to see the pork. They cooked and ate it. Then the *masalai* arrived at the house.

He said, "I always come to look for you, but you're never home."

The boys told him, "If you call out, we'll hear you because we'll slept at the base of a big post in the middle of the house. We didn't know that you were looking for us."

The *masalai* then went to his house. At night, the boys made a hole in the big post at the middle of the house. They went inside the post and slept well.

The *masalai* arrived and cut the big post, then the house also fell down. Oh my, he was terrified and ran out-side. Then he quickly looked for the boys, but he did not see them because they were well hidden.

The *masalai* was furious, so he carried all of the posts and planks of the house and threw them into the river. The river carried the posts down and down. The boys drifted inside the post in the river until they arrived at a place where women were washing.

The women saw the good firewood coming downriver, and they went to pull out the wood. They finished washing, then they went up and cut the firewood. They started with the little pieces of wood, leaving the big post in which the boys were staying for last.

When the women wanted to cut the last log, the men called out to them. The women wanted to see the boys come out of the log. Oh my, were they surprised to see the very handsome boys.

The women each took a boy, returned to the village and married them. They lived together and raised children in their village.

The boys did not want to return to the old place because they knew that the *masalai* would watch for them, then kill and eat them.

Barkley Koi
P. O. Box 1133
Panguna
North Solomons Province

F490+. Masalai; G82. Cannibal fattens victim; G572. Ogre overawed by trick; K1892. Deception by hiding; L111.4. Orphan hero; P210. Husband and wife; P230. Parents and children; T100. Marriage; W151. Greed

Nime Became a Bird of Paradise
(Wantok 612, March 15, 1986, page 23)

Long, long ago, there was a married couple that lived in a village. The man's name was Daga and his wife's name was Elekina. They had a little son whose name was Nime.

One day, the father told the mother, "Tonight you should cook sweet potatoes and put them aside. In the early morning, I'll take Nime and we'll go hunt for wild game in the forest."

In the very early morning, the father and Nime, his son, awoke. They carried a bow and arrows and their food, then they left for the forest. They walked and walked until they arrived at the base of a big mountain. They sat and rested, then they went inside the forest and began to hunt for marsupials (*kapul*).

The father walked and walked, then he saw a giant tree standing there. The tree had a huge hole in the middle of it. The father saw this and thought there would be many marsupials piled inside the tree.

He climbed the tree. He went up to the crown of the tree and saw the hole. However, he was afraid to go inside the hole, so he went back down to the ground and told his son to climb it.

Nime listened and said, "Give me the axe and spear, then I'll climb." However his father said, "No. Just go up and look, then come down again."

Nime persisted, so his father gave him the spear and axe, then Nime went up the tree. He climbed and climbed, then he arrived at the crown.

When he looked inside the hole, he saw a beautiful house inside the tree. There was also a good place to sleep there. When Nime saw this, his thoughts were confused, so he went down to the last branch of the tree and began to cut the tree branch.

His father saw this and called out for Nime to come down. However Nime called down to his father, "Papa, you can go back to your home now. I'll stay here."

The father called out and tried to coax him, but to no avail. Nime went inside the tree hole and stayed there. The father kept calling out, then gave up and cried. Afterwards, he returned to the village.

When he arrived, his wife saw him and asked, "You came alone. Where's Nime?" Poor Daga heard this and cried. He told his wife what had happened to their son.

The next day, Daga awoke in the very early morning. He carried ripe bananas and some other good food, then he returned to the place where his son had gone inside the tree hole.

He arrived at the tree, then he took a piece of wood and struck the base of the big tree. Oh my, when Daga looked up, he saw that his son had completely changed. His skin was bright red and he did not look like his son, Nime.

The second day, the father again went to this place and again struck the base of the tree. When Nime appeared, the father saw that his son had changed completely and become a bird of paradise. The father was very troubled, so he returned to the village and never went back to see his son.

Nime's mother was troubled about her son for a long time. One day, her husband, Daga, traveled to another place. The mother followed the trail that her husband had taken to the place where Nime lived.

The mother walked and walked until she arrived at the big tree. She saw that the base of the tree was completely clean from where her husband had beaten the base of the tree.

The mother was surprised to see this. She took a stick by the base of the tree and beat the tree hard. When she looked up, she saw that her son had become a bird of paradise and was perched at the crown of the tree.

The mother cried terribly and called out Nime's name. Nime had become a bird, so he was afraid when he heard his mother's crying. He removed his feathers and tail then threw them down to his mother. He flew to the mountains by **Bundi** Village in **Madang** Province [**Gende** People].

When Nime's father went and saw that his son was not there, he was very troubled and began to look around for Nime. The father followed him until he arrived at a mountain. He stood on this mountain, looked down, and saw their son, Nime, going around with the other birds.

Agare Kon
P. O. Box 115
Goroka
Eastern Highlands Province

D150+B. Transformation: boy to bird of paradise; D681. Gradual transformation; D2000+. Magic confusion; F771+. House inside tree; P210. Husband and wife; P231. Mother and son; P233. Father and son; R260. Pursuits

Men Killed *Masalai* Sobili
(Wantok 613, March 22, 1986, page 22)

Long, long ago, in a village named **Ianipe**, there lived a *masalai*. The name of the *masalai* was Sobili. *Masalai* Sobili often ate men.

Near Ianipe, there was another village. This village was in the very deep forest. The name of this village was **Firuf**. The group of men from Firuf Village often went into the deep forest to see who was eating men and finishing them off. In this village, there were two brothers who usually went with the men into the forest to watch this *masalai* Sobili.

One time, they went into the forest and the big brother made a house just for shooting birds. He did not finish it because a sore pained him, so he left it just half-finished. While they were still there, his little brother heard thunder. A little later, while they were still there, stones crashed.

Oh my, the little brother thought hard. The little brother watched, and a huge white-haired man came down to the top of the house that they had made for shooting birds.

The man went completely inside the house, and pointed at the beds in which the men slept. He said, "I'll eat this man." He did this until he had gone to all of the beds inside the house.

When he went out of the house, he took breadfruit leaves and covered the top of the house. Later, he went to his own home, which was in a huge cave.

When the men returned from the forest, the little brother told them about the *masalai*.

The men said, "Oh my, we're not girls and he won't chase us away. We must stay and fight with him."

The men made their decision, and they stayed. They cooked breadfruits and ate, then they heard the *masalai* Sombili [Sobili] approaching. When the *masalai* came to the house, they told him, "You must come to the door."

When he came close to the door, the men told him, "If you want to come inside, then your belly and head must come in first."

The *masalai* came to the exact center of the house, then they tied him up well with the door and he was stuck. This was because the men of the village had tricked Sobili by tying his legs and arms so that he did not have the strength to do anything.

When the breadfruit was ready, they gave some to the *masalai*. They kept giving him food until all of the food was gone.

Then they fetched water and they also tossed it down the *masalai*'s mouth. When the *masalai* had plenty of food in his belly, he felt unable to move. His belly was completely bloated and he lay there awkwardly.

Then the men decided to take a bamboo [knife] and cut the *masalai*'s neck. They cut until the bamboo came to the other side of his neck. *Masalai* Sobili was immobilized and did not feel anything. When he got up, he took the bamboo and fled to his cave. The *masalai* took the bamboo that they had used to cut his neck and he planted it in the opening of his house inside the cave.

When the *masalai* arrived at the cave, all his strength was gone because all of his blood had spilled out when the men had cut him. So, the poor *masalai* died inside the cave.

The bamboo that he planted grew large. Before, there was not much bamboo that grew in my area, but now the bamboo is everywhere.

Noel Sonu
Mukili Community School [**Beli** People]
Nuku
West Sepik Province

512

A2770+. Why bamboo is plentiful; F490+. Masalai; F531.3+. Giant's walking causes earthquake; F531.3+. Giant's walking causes thunder; F1041.14+. Beheaded person runs; G100. Giant ogre; G512.1. Ogre killed with knife (sword); G514. Ogre captured; G572+. Ogre immobilized by stuffing with food; K914. Murder from ambush; P251.5. Two brothers; Q215. Cannibalism punished; Q421.3. Punishment: cutting throat; S118.2. Murder by cutting throat

The Stars Helped a Man
(Wantok 614, March 26, 1986, page 26)

Long, long ago, a man took his bow and arrows then went to hunt for wild game in the forest at night. The man walked a very long distance to a mountain.

He worked hard, but he did not find any game, so his eyes became sleepy. When he was about to sleep, he put his bow and arrows at his side then fell dead asleep.

The man was dead to the world, so he did not know what was happening about him. A *masalai* man was also looking for game. He hunted and hunted, but did not find any game.

While he was walking along, he smelled the man nearby. When the ghost [*masalai*] man looked, he saw the man but he thought that a piece of tree had broken and was lying there. The *masalai* stood and watched carefully, then he saw the man there.

The *masalai* was very happy. He said, "Oh my, I tried hard to find game and now it's come to me."

So, he dumped the man into his net bag and carried him towards his home. However it was too bad that the *masalai* dwelled on an island.

When the *masalai* arrived on the beach, he put the man in the net bag on his back and began to swim to the island. The *masalai* swam and swam, and the waves rose and fell very strongly.

The man inside the net bag felt cold and thought, "Oh my, where am I now?" When he opened his eyes, he saw the waves.

The man had a good idea because when he was running through the forest, he had put a small piece of sharp bamboo into his loincloth. So when the *masalai* was still carrying him, he removed the bamboo and began to cut the net bag.

When they approached the island, the man saw a log drifting in the sea and coming towards them. He took the log and put it inside the net bag, then he swam back to the beach.

The poor *masalai* thought that the man was still sleeping in the net bag, so he kept swimming. When he arrived as the house, he quickly told his daughters, "Go and quickly make a fire. Then heat some stones and get some vegetables for us to cook the meat."

Oh my, when the *masalai*'s kin heard this, they were very happy and immediately prepared the things for the earth oven. When all of the things were ready, the *masalai* went to get the net bag. However, it was too bad. The real meat was not there. It was just a piece of wood lying in the net bag.

The *masalai* was furious because the man had tricked him. He told his kin to stay there and he would begin to swim back to the beach.

The man was completely out of breath and could not run away any further, so he climbed up a coconut palm tree. He stayed there and thought that the *masalai* could not follow him.

He stayed there for a little while, but the *masalai* arrived on the beach and began to sniff for the man's odor. He sniffed and sniffed, then he found the man on top of the coconut palm.

The *masalai* took his axe and began to cut the coconut palm. It was too bad for him that the man thought of something. When the coconut palm was about to fall, he jumped to another coconut palm. They did this for a long time until many of the coconut palms on the beach were gone.

The stars looked at the man going around and they were sorry for him. Quickly, they made a ladder and threw it down to the man on top of a coconut palm. The man was happy for this, so he went up the ladder, and the stars pulled him up.

The stars helped him, but the *masalai* did not know it. The *masalai* kept cutting the coconut palm and when the palm fell, he quickly ran to kill the man. However it was too bad, the man was not there.

When the *masalai* looked up, he saw the man with the stars. The *masalai* called out to the stars, "Hey! Friends, help me too. I want to get my game, but you took him up there."

The stars made a decision and sent a ladder that was not very strong. When the stars took him up near their home, they made it shake. The ladder broke and the *masalai* fell down dead.

The stars took the man and carried him directly to his home. The man told the stars, "I'll prepare some food and I'll send a message for you to come and celebrate with me."

The man prepared everything, then he told all of the men of the village to come and gather with him. He told them, "I'll call out to some men to come and meet me. They'll come, but you men will not be able to see them. I alone will see them and talk with them."

When everything was ready, he sent a message to the stars. Then they descended to meet with him. They ate, then the stars went back to their places. When the stars returned, they lit up the night. Before, they never lit up the night. However after this party, they began to light up the night. When the men of the village saw this, they thought that this time the stars helped a man.

Chicky Decklan
Pes Village [**Olo** People]
Aitape
West Sepik Province

A769. Origin of stars' shining; E425.2. Revenant as man; F52. Ladder to upper world; F490+. Masalai; F961.2. Extraordinary behavior of stars; G441. Ogre carries victim in bag (basket); G512. Ogre killed; K525+. Escape by substituting log; K1034. Dupe persuaded to climb rope for food: rope breaks; P234. Father and daughter; P252. Sisters; Q53. Reward for rescue; Q215. Cannibalism punished; Q411. Death as punishment; R11. Abduction by monster (ogre); R169+. Rescue by stars; R210. Escapes; R260. Pursuits; R311. Tree refuge; S127. Murder by throwing from height

Two Sisters Killed a *Masalai*
(Wantok 615, April 12, 1986, page 24)

Long, long ago, there were two women who lived in my village. Today, the two women are still there.

One time, the two women wanted to go hunt for crayfish in the river. They began at the mouth of the river and went up towards the headwaters.

When they arrived at the middle of the river, a *masalai* man heard their noises and tried to see who was making the noises in the river. The *masalai* saw the two women, quickly turned into a herring and went into the water.

The two sisters worked at fishing, then the big sister held a fish in her net. She took it and threw it to her sister to kill. When the little sister tried to bite the fish head to kill it, it slipped and went inside her belly.

The little sister was very worried and asked the big sister, "What should I do now?"

Her big sister replied, "Don't worry. When you shit, you'll get rid of the herring."

The two sisters finished looking for crayfish and herring, then they went back home. When they arrived at the house, it was dark. They went to sleep, and in the morning the little sister felt that her belly was very full. She got up and told her big sister that her belly was full.

The big sister said, "It's bad that you've tangled with men and now you're pregnant."

The little sister replied, "I've never traveled with men."

Before long, the little sister gave birth to a baby. The big sister was very happy and said, "Oh, this is a good baby for us."

However, it was not a real baby. It was a *masalai* man. He was terribly old. When he lived with his mother, he did not cry for milk. No, he just slept quietly.

One time, the two sisters said, "Oh, this baby is very good. He never cries for milk." Then they decided to go to the garden and leave the baby in the house.

When they left the baby and went to the garden, the baby got up, left its net bag and turned into an old man. He called for the pigs to come and eat, then instead, he killed and ate them. Later, he turned back into a baby, went to sleep in the net bag, and defecated.

That afternoon, the two sisters returned from the garden and saw the baby sleeping on top of his feces. The baby's feces smelled terrible.

Then the big sister said, "This baby's shit smells awful."

The little sister replied, "That's just baby shit."

Whenever they left the baby to go to the garden, they would see that the number of their pigs was lessened. The two sisters thought hard and said, "What is it that's eating and finishing off our pigs?"

One day, they made a decision to hide. They wanted to find out who it was that was finishing off their pigs. One time, they put the baby down and went to the garden. The little sister told the big sister, "You hide and I'll go to the garden to look for food for ourselves."

The little sister went to the garden while the big sister hid and watched. Then the old man got up, left the net bag and descended. He called out for the pigs to come, he killed them and ate.

When the big sister saw this, she quickly ran to her sister in the garden and told her what had happened. They were terrified. They decided to run away from the *masalai*. They made one hundred net bags, then they rested. They took the baby and put him in the net bags that they had made.

The sisters had planned out their idea, and they told the baby, "Stay here, we're going to the garden then we'll return."

When they were about to leave, they killed two pigs and took them with them. However they did not go to the garden, they ran away from the baby *masalai*.

The sisters shared the pork at each place that they went. When they gave the pork to the men of the villages, the sisters told them, "When an old man comes and asks for us,

you must tell him that you don't know about the two sisters."

They did this until they went to all of the places along the beach. Then they approached Walinga [**Walingai** Village, **Migabac** People, **Morobe** Province]. All of the meat from the two pigs was gone. There were just bones left, and they gave them to Titina.

When they gave the pig bones to him, they asked him, "Can you take us to Siasi?" [**Siassi** Island, **Mutu** People] He replied and agreed.

While they were doing this, the old *masalai* had gotten up and followed them. He asked all of the villages about them and he did not find them. When the *masalai* came to the man who had taken the pig bones, he asked him too. He replied, "I took the two sisters to Siasi."

The man told the *masalai*, "I can take you there too."

While he was taking the *masalai* there, the man said something to ruin the *masalai*. The man said, "*Laiwa tumbic jafalawa tumbic tukawa tumbic Siasiwa tumbic*." After the man said this, they arrived on the island.

The two women and the old man killed the man [*masalai*] then they ran away to another place. They stayed there a little while, then they returned to see various vegetables and foods growing where they had killed the *masalai*.

If you go to this area on Siasi, you will still see these things there.

Tanni Gemeng
Keboki Trade Store
East Taraka
Lae
Morobe Province

A1420.1+. Origin of food from body of slain ogre; D56.1. Transformation to older person; D1880+. Transformation to young man to escape recognition; D1881. Magic self-rejuvenation; D1890. Magic aging; D170+M. Transformation: man to herring; D1774. Magic results from speaking; E631.5. Reincarnation as plant; F321.1. Changeling; F490+. Masalai; P231. Mother and son; P252.1. Two sisters; P294. Aunt; R220. Flights; R260. Pursuits; S110. Murders; T511.5.1. Conception from eating fish; T570. Pregnancy; T580. Childbirth

A Ghost Killed Muli
(Wantok 616, April 19, 1986, page 24)

Long, long ago, there was a man who lived in a village. His name was Kowa. He lived for a little while, then he died. When Kowa died, the people of the village beat the signal drum then sang and danced mournfully for Kowa. Afterwards, they went to the cemetery. The men cried over Kowa's body, then they went back to their village. The village men stopped crying then walked back to their village. Their village was not nearby; they walked a very long way.

While they were still walking, a man named Muli became famished. When he felt that his stomach was empty, he lied to the men that his belly was in pain and that he wanted to defecate. However, this was just a lie because he was famished.

Muli went inside the forest. When he went, oh my, he saw that the fruits of a fig tree with edible leaves were ripe and plentiful. He climbed the tree and picked the food. He ate and ate until he was completely sated from eating the fig fruits.

While Muli was eating, Kowa's ghost came along the trail and heard Muli spitting the seeds from his mouth. Then the ghost went inside the forest, looked up the tree and saw Muli sitting there. Kowa's ghost looked up and, oh my, he itched to eat some of the fig fruits.

He called up to Muli, "Hey! Kinsman, throw some down to me and I'll eat. I'm also hungry."

Muli took some and threw them down to Kowa's ghost. After the ghost ate, he called out again. Then Muli had a thought, "He's probably not a man. He must be just Kowa's ghost."

Muli thought of a way that he could kill the ghost. Fortunately, Muli had thought long ago to shove the bone of a flying fox into his hair. So, he tried to find where it was by shoving his hand around his head and getting the flying fox bone. He shoved the flying fox bone inside a fruit and threw it down to the ghost.

Before that, he had called out to the ghost, "Friend, open your mouth and I'll throw this fruit to you."

So the ghost opened his mouth and Muli said, "*Yumkof*," in the language of the **Lumi** area [**Olo** People, **West Sepik** Province]. This is a kind of ghost talk.

The ghost opened his mouth, then Muli took the good fruit and threw it down the ghost's mouth. When the ghost tried to swallow, the bone became stuck in his throat. Muli just jumped down the tree and sped away, going directly home.

At night, they sat and he told his wife, "Stay here, I'm going out to shit." Then he got up, lit a bamboo torch and went to the toilet.

Oh my, Muli thought that the ghost was dead. But no, the ghost was waiting for Muli at the toilet. When Muli wanted to defecate at the toilet, the ghost jumped on top of him and held him fast. Then he began to eat Muli.

Muli's wife and children waited and waited for him, but he did not return quickly. So, they lit a bamboo torch

and ran down to the toilet. They looked inside and, oh my, they saw that the ghost's belly was greatly distended as he was sitting there.

The ghost was completely bloated and sitting awkwardly. He could not escape. Muli's wife saw this, so she ran to get an axe, then ran back down to the toilet to kill the ghost.

Before, when she had chewed betel nuts, the betel nuts had knocked her out. So, she ran off and cut Kowa's belly. Oh my, the blood spilled all over. The woman took all her children and ran away to another place.

Now, wild taro grows on top of the place where these two men are decaying. This place is called **Kowa Lalo Muli**.

Augustine N. Wolfu

c/- Anis Wolfu

Moem Barracks

Wewak

East Sepik Province

A1617. Origin of place-name; E261.4. Ghost pursues man; E631.5.4K+. Reincarnation as wild taro; E425.2. Revenant as man; E440+. Ghost laid by axe; E541. Revenants eat; G11.10. Cannibalistic spirits; K897.1+. Dupe killed by putting thorns in food it is about to swallow; P210+. Wife avenges husband's death; P230. Parents and children; Q260+. Attempted poisoning punished; Q211. Murder punished; Q215. Cannibalism punished; Q429.1. Punishment: culprit eaten by cannibals; R220. Flights; R260. Pursuits; S139.4. Murder by mangling with axe; W157. Dishonesty

From Where Did the Insects in House Posts Come?

(Wantok 617, April 26, 1986, page 23)

Long ago, there lived an old man. One time, he went to the forest to hunt for wild game. While he walked around in the forest, he heard a noise from a small bird. He listened and felt that something was coming towards him.

This thing came very strongly and told the old man, "Tomorrow, you'll find something in your house."

The old man thought hard. He told himself, "This sort of thing never happened to me before. Now what will happen?"

In the morning, he again went to the forest to hunt for game. While he was going along, he saw a bird turn into a girl. The girl was very beautiful.

When he saw the girl, he went completely crazy. He quickly took the girl to his house. When he arrived at his house, he trembled when he saw the plentiful pigs at his house. He sat and thought, "Who gave these pigs to me?

People never come to my home, but now what's happened?"

While he was thinking, an old man came and told him, "You were living alone, so I gave these things to you. You're old too, so it's bad if you work hard at hunting for game." When the old man left them, he took his girl and went to the house.

The girl and the old man went into the house. He took care of the girl until she grew up, then they married. They gave a big party. They ate, sang, danced and celebrated their new marriage.

The newlyweds lived for a long time, the woman's old father was close to dying. When he was about to die, he told his daughter, "Now, go and live with your husband. When I die, I'll return as insects beneath your house. When you see me, you can't remove me."

So then the woman's father died and the married couple buried him. After a week passed, they saw the insects coming and working on the house posts.

If you travel to some areas of Papua New Guinea by the beach, you can see insects in the house posts.

Ricky M.

Goroka

Eastern Highlands Province

A2070. Creation of miscellaneous insects; D350G. Transformation: bird to girl; E616. Reincarnation as insect; P210. Husband and wife; P234. Father and daughter; P261. Father-in-law; P265. Son-in-law; T100. Marriage; V61.3+. Dead buried

Avebam's Mistake

(Wantok 618, May 3, 1986, page 27)

Nowadays, men of Usung [**Isung** Village] in the Bogia area still chase wild pigs and shoot them with spears [**Igom** People, **Madang** Province]. Some of these pigs turn around and chase the men, barely missing them as they run away. So, do these pigs have some kind of strength and knowledge?

Long ago, there lived two brothers. Their names were Avebam and Buam. Avebam was the big brother and Buam was his little brother.

Avebam was a man who was good and hunting pigs in the forest. He would cut sago palm trees and leave them to rot, then the pigs would come and eat them. Every night, he would go to watch the sago palms then shoot four or five pigs. His poor brother, Buam, was not like this. He would shoot pigs by the sago just one at a time.

One time, Avebam was terribly sick and could not go to the forest to hunt for pigs. Furthermore, the two brothers' kin were hungry for meat.

After a while, Buam told his big brother, "You've been sick and you've not hunted for game, so our kin are very hungry for meat now. If there are secret words that you use to hunt for pigs, please explain them to me."

So Avebam told him, "If you go to my house, you'll see a pig skin there. You must take this pigskin and carry it to the place where your sago palms are. When you arrive there, you must cover yourself with this pigskin, then walk like a pig and call out like the pigs. When you call, they'll approach. Then you can take your spears and shoot them. You must call out to the pigs one at a time so that the other pigs don't know what you're doing."

However, Avebam made a very big mistake. He did not explain to Buam about the coconut oil. Before putting on the pigskin, one must rub the oil on one's skin. This is so that one can remove the pigskin to shoot the pigs.

So, poor Buam just took the pigskin and went into the forest. When he arrived at the place where his sago palms were, he put on the pigskin and called out to the pigs. He did as his brother had told him to do, and he shot some pigs.

However, when he wanted to remove the pigskin from his body... there was a problem for the poor brother. The pigskin was completely stuck! He could not remove it. He tried to remove his skin, but it broke and blood flowed, causing him pain. He did this for a very long time in the forest.

At this time Avebam knew that something had happened to his brother. Quickly, he took the coconut oil and went to the place where his brother was. When he arrived, he saw his brother trying hard to remove the pigskin from his body.

Avebam spilled the coconut oil on the pigskin to try to remove it, but it did not work. Buam had turned completely into a pig.

Avebam was very worried about his brother, so he cried and told his Buam, "I ruined you, my brother. In your lifetime you'll stay as a pig, but you're different than the other pigs of the forest. Your thoughts will be like that of a man."

Avebam wanted to help his brother fight his enemies, that is men. He took two pieces of bamboo and put them into his brother's mouth. These two pieces of bamboo are the two long tusks that one sees in boars' mouths.

With these two teeth that Avebam gave his pig brother, he warned him, "When men chase you, don't just run. You must listen carefully to their calls and noises to avoid them.

When you go stealing in men's gardens, don't go back and forth alone lest men put something bad there or dig a hole for you to fall into. However if some men trap you and try to kill you, try to fight back. I have given you these two tusks."

Avebam finished talking to his pig brother, then much later he said good-bye to him and left for the village. Poor Buam stayed in the forest.

So now, the men of Usung believe that wild pigs that fight men and carefully avoid their enemies are not real pigs. They are men who are blood relatives of Buam, Avebam's pig brother.

Alphonse Ariasi
D. W. I.
Madang
Madang Province

A2345+. Where boar got his tusks; D114.3.2M. Transformation: man to boar; D450+. Transformation: bamboo to tooth; D531. Transformation by putting on skin; D1242.4+. Magic coconut oil; P251.5. Two brothers

Two Brothers Were Enemies
(Wantok 619, May 10, 1986, page 23)

Long, long ago, there lived two brothers. The name of the big brother was Kimal and the little brother was Puio.

One day, they decided to go to the very deep forest to hunt for wild game. First, they went to the garden and picked various foods. Then they returned to the house and straightened their bows, arrows and axes.

In the very early morning, they awoke, carried their loads and walked into the forest. They walked and walked until they arrived in the very deep forest where men of the village did not travel.

They put their things down, cut some tree branches and erected their forest hut. They finished working on their hut, then they went inside, put their things there, sat and rested.

When it was nearly dark, they got up, carried their bows and arrows, and went to hunt for marsupials (*kapul*). Oh my, at this time, they did not fool around with killing marsupials. They did very well. Their net bags were completely filled with marsupials, so they took their two net bags of marsupials and returned to their hut.

They arrived and threw the marsupials down, then they slept. In the morning, they awoke and cooked the marsupials in an earth oven with sweet potatoes that they had brought with them. They left one net bag of marsupials uncooked.

They waited until the afternoon, then Kimal told Puio to go remove the marsupial guts from the other net bag. When Puio went to clean the marsupials, Kimal watched their earth oven. When the earth oven was ready, Kimal removed the fire and uncovered it.

Kimal removed the sweet potato and marsupial skins then put them aside. He filled a net bag with the marsupial meat and sweet potatoes, then carried it into the deep forest.

When Puio returned to their forest hut, he saw that his big brother had uncovered the earth oven. When he saw that the skins were just in a heap, he called out to his brother. However there was no reply, so he ate the marsupial and sweet potato skins. He cried as he was eating.

He held some, then he followed his brother and called out. He did this until the sun set and it was becoming dark. When it became dark, he started to become afraid. He found a big tree, then he took a vine, tied it around his legs and climbed the tree.

While he was climbing the tree, Puio thought that he was really going up the tree, but he was actually going to another place. When he arrived at the crown of the tree, he was lost. He had arrived at a place with wild sugarcanes (*pitpit*).

Puio saw this and was terrified, so he hid at the base of the wild sugarcanes. While he was hiding, he saw a very beautiful woman approaching. The woman was carrying various kinds of birds and marsupials to a house.

Another woman came and followed her. This woman saw Puio hiding at the base of the wild sugarcanes. Quietly, the woman pulled Puio's leg and called out to the other woman. The woman ran towards them, then the first woman held Puio's legs while the second woman held his head, and they carried Puio to their house.

They took him to their house, then quickly cooked food in an earth oven and gave it to Puio. He ate and they told him that they lived alone at this place.

They held Puio there and he married the two women. These two women were *masalai* women, so when Puio married them, he became a *masalai*. They lived together on this big tree in the deep forest.

Kimal ran away through the deep forest until he arrived at a big river. The river was flooded, so Kimal sat and waited for the water to subside. He ate the marsupials and sweet potatoes near the river.

Puio and his two wives on top of their tree looked down and saw him. So, they descended and followed him there. When they arrived, they called out to him. Kimal turned, saw them and was terrified. He wanted to run away, but he made a misstep, fell into the river and drowned.

Issu Londari
P. O. Box 140
Arawa
North Solomons Province

D94+M. Transformation: man to spirit; F54. Tree to upper world; F490+. Masalai; P210. Husband and wife; N339+. Accidental drowning; P251.5. Two brothers; P251.5.3. Hostile brothers; P263. Brother-in-law; P264. Sister-in-law; R220. Flights; R260. Pursuits; S143. Abandonment in forest; T111. Marriage of mortal and supernatural being; T145.0.1. Polygyny

Tukai Found a Beautiful Woman

(Wantok 620, May 17, 1986, page 23)

One time, there lived a boy named Tukai who followed a river upriver, looking for crayfish. The name of this river is Wib. Trukai [Tukai] speared many, many crayfish. After he looked in the water, he strung them up. He looked and looked, then he speared a huge fish. When he speared the fish, he shouted with joy.

Oh my, an old man on the mountain heard his shouting and thought hard. He was a man or something. The man called out, "Grandson, the fish head belongs to [me] and the good meat belongs to you."

The boy listened and was very sorry for the old man, so he rose quickly and took the fish to the old man. The old man's name was Pira. The old man watched Tukai bring the fish up to the house and he was very happy because of Tukai.

They stayed there and the old man asked him, "Are you hungry too or not?"

Tukai replied, "Please, old man, I'm famished." So, old Pira thought of Tukai and quickly carved the food. He cooked it and gave it to Tukai.

They ate, then old Pira asked Tukai to climb a coconut palm tree. Pira said, "Old man I've never climbed a coconut palm." The old man said, "When you climb up, your head should go first, and then your legs after that. When you come down, your head must come first, then your legs. You just have to listen to me."

Tukai climbed the coconut palm. After he climbed it, he called down to Pira, "How many coconuts should I fetch?"

The old man replied, "Just four." So, Tukai followed Pira's wishes.

After Tukai did everything, the old man was very happy and told Tukai, "Grandson, come live with me and you'll help me very much. I have nothing to give to you, but what would you like?"

Tukai said, "The thing that I want is hard for me to tell you, but since you're my good grandpa, I'll tell you. I want a woman."

Pira said, "Don't worry. Just do as I tell you. Now go to the village and sleep. Tomorrow, when it's still in the middle of the night, go to the beach and watch the waves breaking. While you're watching, a big wave will break. You must run and jump inside of it."

Tukai listened and went back to the village. He slept, and in the early morning, he ran to the beach. He watched and a wave was about to break. He ran and jumped inside.

When he wanted to come up and catch his breath, he arrived on an island called Balis [**Unea**]. While Tukai was walking on Balis Beach, he smelled *purpur* shrubs. Oh my! The smell of the *purpur* was very nice, and it completely confused his thinking.

Then a beautiful young woman came and saw Tukai. She said, "Who's the man that's playing in my *purpur*?" [*Purpur* also means "grass" skirt.]

The woman asked Tukai, "What have you come here to do?" The lazy boy was not worried, he replied, "I came to get you." Then the woman's thoughts were confused, and she went back to the house. She took her things and followed the man to the beach. They waited then a big wave came. They jumped in and went back to the beach by Tukai's village.

When they arrived at the village, the people saw the woman and said, "Oh my, that's not an ordinary woman, she's very beautiful." Some men asked Tukai, "Where did you get this woman?" However Tukai said, "You won't be able to find this kind of woman."

Tukai and the woman married in the customary way of the village. They were happy and lived together. Their descendants lived in **Mai** Village [**Xarua** People, **West New Britain** Province].

Wangy Gamuna
Lamtub Village
Saidor
Madang Province

D911.1. Magic wave; D2125.1.1. Magic transportation by waves; J2244+. Climb down tree head first; P210. Husband and wife; P291.1+. Foster grandfather; Q40. Kindness rewarded; T100. Marriage

A Wild Woman Tricked a Real Man

(Wantok 621, May 24, 1986, page 23)

Long, long ago, in the time of the ancestors, there were many wild women. They always went around looking for men, women or children then killed them.

One day, two boys decided to go fishing at night by the sea. Afterwards, they took coconut leaves and fastened torches for themselves with them. Then they hid the torches by the beach and walked towards the village. While they were walking, they decided which one of them would wake up first to wake the other.

The two boys were talking when a wild woman had come and hidden by the forest to listen to them. The wild woman finished listening, then very quietly went back to her home.

The two boys slept that night, then very early in the morning, the wild woman came to the house of one of them and woke him. It was still dark, so the boy saw the woman and thought that it was really his friend that was waking him. So he got up, took his hooks and followed the woman to the beach.

They pulled the canoe with the things inside, then they paddled out to sea. The wild woman told the boy to fish while she continued to paddle. The wild woman paddled and paddled until they came to the middle of the sea. She threw the anchor down, and the boy began to fish.

The boy caught fish and put them inside the canoe. He had his back turned, so he did not see behind him. The wild woman at his back cut the fish heads and ate them.

They fished until the boy had caught many fish. It was nearly four o'clock when the boy turned around and saw the woman gorging on the fish heads. The boy collected his thoughts. He thought that he must have come with a ghost. So he lied to the woman, "We've caught many fish. We should probably go back now."

The wild woman listened and paddled back to the beach. They paddled and paddled until about five o'clock when they went ashore. They pulled the canoe up to the beach and the boy told the wild woman, "You take care of the fish. I'll go inside the forest and cut some leaves for us to bundle up the fish."

The boy lied to the wild woman, then he went inside the forest. When he was fairly far away, the good-for-nothing began to run. He ran and ran until he arrived at the base of a tall tree. This was the kind of tree that if you removed the bark, it was very slippery and impossible for people to climb.

Quickly, the man cut the tree bark at its base, after he cut it, he climbed the tree until he arrived at the crown. Then he just sat there.

The wild woman was waiting at the beach. She waited and waited, then dawn broke. She knew that the boy must have tricked her and run away to the village. So, she just followed his scent until she arrived at the base of the slippery tree. She looked up and saw the boy sitting at the crown.

The wild woman called up, "How did you get up there?" It looked as if all of the tree bark was gone and there was no way to climb the tree.

The boy lied to the woman, "Go bathe first, then climb the tree."

The wild woman listened and thought that what he had said was true. Quickly, she ran back and bathed in the sea. She sped back and tried to climb the tree. The poor woman tried and tried but was unsuccessful. The tree was still slippery, so she fell back down to the base of the tree.

She called up again to the boy. The boy replied, "Go get a tall tree and stand it up here. I'll hold it while you climb on it."

The woman listened then quickly went and cut a tall tree. She came and shoved the top far up to where the boy was sitting. When she climbed the tree, the boy was ready and waiting. The woman climbed and climbed until she approached to him. Then the boy pushed it back, and the wild woman had a terrible fall to the ground.

She was furious. She stood the tree up again and climbed it. Again, the man pushed the tree back and the wild woman fell down. They did this until the sun rose strongly. At about seven o'clock, the wild woman became afraid and ran back to her house. As she ran, the boy sat well on the tree crown so that he could see the place where the wild woman was running. The woman ran and ran, then went down a hole.

The interior of the hole was filled with other wild women. The man saw the place where the wild woman went into the hole, then he took a vine, tied it to a branch of the tree and went down slowly to the ground. When he landed on the ground, he ran to the beach, took his canoe and paddled back to his village.

His friend in the village waited and waited until morning, then he saw that the boy did not meet him. The poor boy thought that his friend had lied to him and had gone with another boy from the village. He went down to the beach and saw that the canoe was not there, so he stood and thought.

Then he saw his friend's canoe coming. When the canoe came to shore, his friend jumped out. He ran to hold him and to tell him the story of how the wild woman had tricked him at night into going fishing.

They left the canoe, ran to the village and beat the signal drum. The people of the village heard it and all gathered to hear what had happened. The boy told the story of what had happened to him that night and morning. He told them that he had seen the place where the wild women hid.

The men of the village listened and decided to go kill the wild women. All of them carried their big earthen pots. The men carried bows and arrows then followed the boy to the place where he had seen the wild woman go inside the hole.

When they arrived at this place, they made a fire, filled the pots with water, and put them in the fire. When the water was boiling fiercely, they removed the pots from the fire and began to spill the water into the hole. The women began to run out of their hole.

Each woman came outside and ran into the deep forest. They did this until the last woman came outside the hole. It was the woman who had tricked the boy. When she came out, the boy shouted and the men grabbed her. They cut her into little pieces and burned the pieces in the fire.

The other wild women ran about in the deep forest. Now, this hole where the wild women lived is still by **Erima** Village in **Madang** Province [**Erima** People]. The name of this place is *Bobolu*. It means, "The place of wild women."

Munia Lukson
National Forest Products
Port Moresby
National Capital District

A1617. Origin of place-name; F567.1. Wild woman; K983. Dupe persuaded to climb tree; K1930. Treacherous impostors; P310. Friendship; Q262. Impostor punished; Q429.3. Cutting into pieces as punishment; R210. Escapes; R220. Flights; R260. Pursuits; R311. Tree refuge; S139.7. Murder by slicing person into small pieces

Worpowei Brought Yams (*Yam* and *Mami*)
(Wantok 622, May 31, 1986, page 23)

This is a story of long ago when our ancestors obtained yams (*yam* and *mami*). Long ago, among the Wapei [**Olo** People] in [**West**] **Sepik** [Province], there was a big ghost festival for a big fish. People carried food with them from far away and gathered together. Many people left their villages and walked for two days to go to this place.

They approached the Wapei area, then they prepared their things well. The men did this kind of work, and the women cooked. On the day of the festival, the Wapei area became entirely different. They young people, the old people, and the children dressed very finely.

Everyone carried various foods: meats such as pork, taros, bananas, and sago. These were piled high at this place. The leaders of the area adorned the fish with bird feathers and *tanget* leaves, then they trembled. The leaders prohibited the women and children from approaching. They stood the fish in the middle of where the leaders were gathered.

At this time, there lived a man. His wife had just had a baby and was staying at home. The man was worried because everyone would be going to the festival for three days and two nights.

The man told the woman that there was food that they had cooked that was ready to be eaten. There was enough food to last three days and two nights. The man finished speaking, then he went out of the house and tied the door tightly with rattan. After that, he barricaded the house door with ironwood logs.

Everyone had departed. Only the pigs and dogs stayed in the village. The woman and her baby stayed quietly, so that whoever came by would think that there was no one in the village.

The woman sat inside the house. She just listened to the sound of hand drums and signal drums coming from very far away. The woman heard the faint sounds of the festival.

Very late at night, a flying fox ate bananas near their house. These bananas are called *reikel* in my language [*rikël* is a very small banana]. When it is ripe, it is very delicious.

The flying fox did not rest quietly. It made much noise, waking the mother and child. The woman heard the noise and was angry. She called out to the flying fox, "Hey, who is it that's finishing off my ripe bananas? When did you plant them? You're finishing off my ripe bananas."

The flying fox listened, rested quietly, and ate the bananas. The woman scolded the flying fox again, and the flying fox listened. The third time, the woman was angry and scolded the flying fox. However it was not an ordinary flying creature, it was a ghost man. It listened and sped down to the ground.

He went and stood by the door that the woman's husband had barricaded, and he worked at removing the rattans and ironwood logs. When the woman saw this, she was happy. She thought that her husband had returned from the festival. The flying fox (or ghost man) told the woman to open the house door so that he could enter.

The woman asked, "Why did you come so late at night?" The flying-fox man replied, "Poor me, I thought of you alone, so I left the festival and came back." The ghost man asked the woman for food, and the woman told him that all of the food was still there.

The man took all of the food and finished it. The woman saw this and was worried. She thought hard because her husband never ate that much. The woman decided that it must be a ghost that was fooling her.

The ghost finished all of the food, then told the woman that they would sleep together. The woman told the ghost, "Man, are you crazy or what? I just gave birth to this baby."

The ghost told the woman that if she did not want to sleep with him, he would eat her and the baby. The woman was afraid, so she slept with the ghost flying-fox man. That night, the flying fox put his hands on top of the baby. Quickly, the baby got up, sat down, and walked on hands and knees.

The flying-fox man told the woman that the people of the village would not live with them. On the third day, they left and walked away. The woman's kin were ready to go back to their village.

The ghost man told the woman, "My name is _Worpowei_. This is the name of a kind of yam. When daylight comes, your kin will come to the village. I'll just leave the area of the house. Some days later, you'll see a red sprout coming up from the ground that I've left. You'll look for a stick or wild sugarcane (_pitpit_) and stand it near the sprout. I'll grow on this stick like yams. After I grow on the tree or stick, and all my leaves are dead and dry, dig the root of the vine and you'll find food in the ground. Remove me and cut my head, then plant me again. Cook my body in a fire and eat it. Then share it with everyone in the village." After the flying fox (or ghost man) finished speaking to her, he just disappeared.

The woman was worried and cried for the flying fox (or ghost man). Her baby stood up near her like a young man. The mother was surprised.

The child told her, "Mother, don't be surprised. I'm the baby that you bore three days ago. Flying fox, my foster father, gave me powers and made me a big boy now."

When the woman's husband returned to the village, everything had changed. The man was speechless. He thought that a _masalai_ had ruined the village, his wife and his child.

His wife carefully told him the story about everything that had happened. They lived there until the yam sprout came up, then they followed the flying fox's instructions. This is our story of how the yam arrived.

Arthur Mopin

Wewak

East Sepik Province

A132.13. Fish-god; A2686.4.3. Origin of yams; B611+. Flying fox paramour; D310+M. Transformation: flying fox to man; D210+M. Transformation: man to yam; D1720+. Magic power from spirit; D1890. Magic aging; D2095. Magic disappearance; E423.2+. Revenant as flying fox; E425.2. Revenant as man; E541. Revenants eat; G11.10. Cannibalistic spirits; K1910. Marital impostors; P210. Husband and wife; P230. Parents and children; P271. Foster father; T91.3. Love of mortal and supernatural person; T471. Rape; T580. Childbirth; V1.8.11. Fish worship; Z71.1. Formulistic number: three

The Last Boy Killed Masalai Bululung
(Wantok 623, June 7, 1986, page 23)

Long, long ago, there was a village with five brothers. The name of this village is Gemeng [**Gemaheng** Village, **Kube** People, **Morobe** Province]. The father and mother of these five brothers had died, so the brothers often worked hard at finding food, cutting firewood, and doing other work.

One day, the brothers decided to go cut some forest to make a garden for themselves. So in the very early morning, all five brothers woke up and went to the forest together.

The big brother told the younger ones, "Hey, you brothers go first. I'll go to the sword grass hill first, then I'll follow you."

This sword grass hill was the home of a _masalai_. The name of the _masalai_ was Bululung. He was very old, and all of the hair on his head and body were completely white.

When the brothers were ready to go to the forest, they carried their axes with them. The big brother also carried his axe and went to the _masalai_'s home.

The _masalai_ saw the big brother coming and hid. When the big brother approached, the _masalai_ called out, "_Pa ire ire_!" Oh my, the boy was surprised and threw the axe. He ran away and told his little brothers what had happened.

When the brother told them, they all went to find the big brother's axe. They searched and searched until their eyes were pained. Then the brothers went back home and told their last brother what had happened. All of the brothers went and tested the *masalai*. They went and went, then the little brother said that he too would test the *masalai*.

He told his brothers, "I think that you have often given your axes to him."

The big brothers told him, "You can't go." But he said, "That's not so. I'm still going."

The big brothers were angry and struck him. They told him, "You're just a boy. The *masalai* will simply [swallow] you up." The last brother listened to this and cried.

Before it was light out, he carried his stone axe and went to bathe. While he had gone to bathe, he sharpened his axe. He sharpened his axe on top of a hill. The name of this hill is Wameusucka. This hill is where the *masalai* dwelled.

While he hid, he heard a great noise on the side of the hill. He sat then the *masalai* came and did the same thing. The *masalai* called out, "*Pa ire ire*!" Then the last brother got up and called the name of the *masalai*. He called, "*Aha tangama nono gone*."

Then the last brother spun around and tricked the *masalai*. He took his axe and cut the old *masalai*, Bululung. When he cut the *masalai* and the *masalai* fell down. Then the boy ran back to the village to tell his brothers.

When he arrived at the village, he told his brothers, "Hey, hey, hurry up! Go butcher your pigs. It's you who gave your axes to him, and I who shall eat."

The big brothers ran and ran to see the *masalai*. They buried him, then the boys grew and turned into pigs that lived in Gemeng Village.

If you go to Sialum in Morobe Province, you will hear the name of a youth group and sports club.

Anis Tanni

Mangata Soccer Club

Sialum

Morobe Province

D136B. Transformation: boy to swine; F490+. Masalai; G512.1+. Ogre killed with axe; L31. Youngest brother helps elder; P251.6.2+. Five brothers; R220. Flights; S139.4. Murder by mangling with axe; V61.3+. Dead buried

Two Women Became Bananas

(Wantok 624, June 14, 1986, page 31)

Long, long ago, in the time of the ancestors, there lived two brothers. The first brother was Bang and the other was Mankebung. They still lived together and made yam gardens.

One time they worked in the garden for a while, then Monkebung felt hungry. He told his big brother, "Bang, I feel hungry. I'll cook some bananas for ourselves."

The big brother, Bang, listened and said, "Go make a fire at the base of the fig tree, then cook the bananas."

Bang was not thinking too much about eating. He kept working and left his little brother to cook the bananas. When all of the bananas were ready, Monkebung called out for his brother to come, then they ate.

Afterwards, they continued to work until it was evening. When it became evening, it was time to quit working, so the brothers walked back to the village.

They went to sleep, and in the very early morning they awoke and went to the garden again. When they arrived at the garden, they heard the voices of two girls. The girls were sitting at the place where the little brother had made the fire, right at the base of the fig tree.

The big brother told his little brother, "Let's go closer. You hold the little sister and I'll hold the big one."

The brothers went very quietly. When they came close, they did as they had decided. The big brother held the big sister and the little brother held the little sister.

The brothers asked the girls, "Hey, how did you get here?"

The sisters replied, "Many of us came, but you cooked us in the fire and ate us. We're just the ones that you didn't eat. We stayed here in the ashes of the fire." They finished their story then the brothers took them back to the house. The big brother married the big sister, Ambak. Monkebung married the little sister, Nani.

The brothers and their wives lived well for a while, then the sisters became pregnant. They gave birth to two baby boys. Bang's son was Tuk-Bang. Monkebung's was called Tuk-Monkebung. They lived well in their village, then the two boys became big men.

One day, all of them together were removing grasses from the garden. They removed the grasses, then the two sons felt hungry. Their parents told them to cut some bananas.

The two brothers [cousins], Tuk-Bang and Tuk-Monkebung took their knives and went to cut bananas. After they cut them, they shared them with their parents. When they arrived at the garden, their parents told them to cook the bananas at the base of the fig tree.

The brothers cooked the bananas and called out to their parents, then they ate together. After they ate, they went to the village. When they arrived at the village, the brothers Tuk-Bang and Tuk-Monkebung decided to go hunting for wild game in the forest. So, in the early morning, the brothers awoke and went to hunt for game.

They walked and went on the trail towards the garden. When they approached the garden, they heard the voices of two girls sitting by the ashes of the fire in which they had cooked the bananas.

The girls talked and did not hear the brothers walking towards them. Their talking blocked their ears, so the brothers grabbed both of them.

The brothers' eyes were opened wide when they saw these girls because they were just like angels. Their breasts stood out straight like kapok thorns.

The brothers took the girls and hid them by the village, then they went to talk to their parents. The parents assented and the girls went to the village.

Afterwards, the two brothers married the two girls. Tuk-Bang married one and Tuk-Monkebung married the other. They lived together and raised large families in Mumengtaen [**Mumengtein** Village]. This village is in the Mumeng District of **Morobe** Province [**Mumeng** People].

Bang and Monkebung told their family, "Let's begin to cut the bananas and throw them around." So, the families threw the bananas into the river.

The water carried them down along the shores of the Makham [Markham] Valley. So now throughout the Makham Valley, there are many bananas. These are just *kalapua* bananas [a kind of small banana].

Sae Gwae
Motupore Island
Magi Highway
Central Province

A2687.5+. Distribution of kind of banana; D431.4+G. Transformation: banana to girl; P210. Husband and wife; P231. Mother and son; P233. Father and son; P251.5. Two brothers; P252.1. Two sisters; P261. Father-in-law; P262. Mother-in-law; P263. Brother-in-law; P264. Sister-in-law; P265+. Daughter-in-law; P293. Uncle; P294. Aunt; P295. Cousins; P297. Nephew; T100. Marriage; T570. Pregnancy; T580. Childbirth

A Woman Married a Signal Drum *Masalai*

(Wantok 625, June 21, 1986, page 23)

Long, long ago, in **Kaiwokir** Village, there lived two brothers. The big brother was married and the little brother was still single.

They lived well together for a while, then the little brother grew to be a big man. Henceforth, his big brother often thought badly about him, and his wife did too. The poor little brother saw this, so he was often worried about his brother's stupid thoughts.

Because of this, the little brother thought of leaving the two of them. One day, he told his big brother that he would leave them and live in the forest because he was clearing the forest to make a new garden.

The big brother listened and said, "My wife and I will also go to the forest, but to process sago. We'll probably stay about a week."

The little brother listened to this and was very happy because no one would be at the house. He wanted to return and get his belongings, then leave the village very quietly when his big brother and sister-in-law were still in the forest.

He arranged his things for working, then he left the village when his brother and sister-in-law were still at the village. The man arrived at the place where he would cut his forest and stay to work.

He pretended to clear the area, but really there would be no garden. No, he cut one big tree and left it. Then he began to cut a good tree and carve it into a signal drum.

He worked until sunset. He made a fire and carved the tree until it became a signal drum. He sat and caught his breath, then he ate and slept.

In the very early morning, he returned to the village. He saw that his brother and sister-in-law were gone. He went and killed a big boar of theirs, then he quickly butchered it and divided the meat. He left a hind leg for his brother and a foreleg for his sister-in-law. He put the other pieces [into a net bag] and carried them away.

He took betel nuts and betel peppers then put them with the two pieces of pork that he left for his big brother and his wife. He took some ashes from the fire and put them near the door. He went outside, took a he-dog and returned to the place where he had made the signal drum.

He put all of the things inside the signal drum and tried to sleep inside. He saw that all of the things fit inside the drum, then he went outside and performed a song and dance for rain and wind.

As he sang and danced, he put his nose into a crab's hole. Then he went inside the signal drum and waited. The clouds thundered, then a heavy rain and strong wind arose. Water came out of the crab's hole and flooded the place where the signal drum lay. Water ran and took the signal drum directly to the Bilap River. The name of this stream is Paimuruf Kutnuv.

The flood carried the signal drum away, which then became stuck by a huge bay. In the early morning, women carried their nets and lines for killing fish, then went to dam the river. They fished until the afternoon when they arrived at the bay where the signal drum was stuck. They saw the drum and thought that it was just a piece of wood.

They continued to fish, then one woman felt back pain, so she sat on top of the drum. She sat and felt as if something was stabbing her. She got up and nothing was there, so she continued to sit. The other women called to her, but she pretended that she was sick and sitting in the sun.

It was getting dark, so the other women want back to the village. The woman got up to leave, but she played a trick by leaving her fishing line on top of the signal drum. They walked and walked for a long distance, then she told the other women that she had left some fish at the place where she had sat.

She told the women that she would go back and get the fish. The woman ran back to the log. When she arrived at the opening of the signal drum, she saw the handsome man inside. The man came out and they talked. Afterwards, the woman went back to the village.

In the morning, she told the men of the village that they should go carry the log and put it by her house. So, the men brought it. They did not know that there was a man inside the log.

The log was by the house, and the woman would always go to sit on top of it to make net bags. After a while, the woman became pregnant. The men of the village gathered and asked her about this. She told them about the man who lived inside the signal drum. Then the woman married the signal drum *masalai*, and they lived together.

When the woman gave birth, the baby was a ghost fish, or <u>*malankar*</u>. The woman beat the signal drum and the sound went, "Kirili Kirili. Tupum Tupum." This was the name of the place where the signal drum came from, and where it is now.

One day, the man's big brother heard this and told his wife, "We should go take a look. I think that it's just my little brother who's sending this message."

So, the two of them followed the signal drum until they arrived at the place where the little brother was. The names of these villages are Tupum [**Tubum**] and **Lelyekel** [**Autu** People, **West Sepik** Province].

Rirchard [Richard] W. Kinou

c/- C. M. L. Temeni

Lumi

West Sepik Province

A1011. Local deluges; A1617. Origin of place-name; D94+M. Transformation: man to spirit; D270+M. Transformation: man to drum; D1781. Magic results from singing; D1781+. Magic results from dancing; D2142.1. Wind produced by magic; D2143.1.2. Rain produced by singing; D2143.1.2+. Rain produced by dancing; D2149.1. Thunderbolt magically produced; E617. Reincarnation as fish; F490+. Masalai; P210. Husband and wife; P251.5. Two brothers; P251.5.3. Hostile brothers; P263. Brother-in-law; P264. Sister-in-law; R220. Flights; R260. Pursuits; T100. Marriage; T518+. Impregnation from spirit; T554.0.4K. Woman gives birth to fish; T590+. Woman gives birth to revenant; T570. Pregnancy; T580. Childbirth; W181. Jealousy

A Father Ruined His Family

(Wantok 626, June 28, 1986, page 23)

Long, long ago, in the time of the ancestors, there lived a man and his wife in a place called **Kleai**, in the **Madang** Province area. This place was just filled with wild pigs, and there were no other people who lived there.

The married couple just made their house and burned the forest to make a huge garden. Before long, the food in the garden was ready. They ate it, then planted more food.

They lived for a while, then the woman became pregnant and gave birth to a baby girl. After this, she did not give birth to any more children. They just had one child.

Whenever they ate, they would just eat the garden food, so the woman began to scold her husband. One day, she scolded her husband terribly and told him to carry his multi-pronged spear down to the stream and spear some fish.

The man just sat and listened. The woman continued her scolding, then they went to sleep. At dawn, the woman began scolding again. After a while, the man became completely furious. He told his wife, "I'll go find some fish for you and the child, then I'll bring it back."

The man woke up in the very early morning and went up to the source of the stream. He went to defecate, then followed the stream down to the place where he had started. He waited, then his feces turned into a huge fish and came downstream. The man just speared it and carried it back to the house.

He arrived at the house, then threw the fish at his wife and said, "Here's your fish. You two always cry for fish, now your bellies will be stuffed with this big fish."

Very Happy

The woman was very happy for the fish. She took it and quickly cut it, then cooked it with other food from the garden. When the fish was ready, her husband said that he did not feel like eating. So, only the woman and child ate the fish.

It was too bad that they did not know that they were eating the father's feces. So, whenever they spoke about eating fish, the man would go to defecate, then later he would bring the feces-turned-fish to his wife and daughter.

One day, the woman wanted to find out where the good place was that her husband found the big fish. So one morning, the woman told her daughter to look after the house. Then she got up quietly and followed her husband to the stream.

She went and hid, then saw her husband defecate at the source of the stream. He walked down and waited for the fish to descend. The woman followed him down and saw him spear the feces-turned-fish.

The woman saw this and was very troubled. She thought of the feces-fish that she and her daughter had been eating, and she was furious. She thought of getting revenge at her husband.

She returned to the house, then the man brought the fish and gave it to her. The woman just looked at the fish and told her daughter that they could not eat it.

The next day, she told her daughter that her father did something disgusting by giving his feces for them to eat. She told her daughter that they must get revenge, then they would flee him.

Looking for Leafy Greens

The father went into the forest, and the mother took the daughter to look for edible fig leaves. They arrived at a fig [tree], then the woman left a small piece of her loincloth and put it on top of a sprout. Quickly, the insects from the tree arrived.

She tied them up carefully in a leaf, then she and her daughter carried them back to the house. They cooked the food well and also put the insects in it, then they waited for the father.

When the father returned, the woman told him, "We've always been concerned that you work so hard at catching fish for us, so we went and got a little bit of leafy greens and insects for you [to eat]."

The man listened to this and salivated. He sat down and took all of the food that the woman had cooked. He ate, then he got up and went to sleep.

He slept that night, and his belly began to swell. In the morning, he could not get up. He just lay there. His wife saw this, and she knew that something bad was inside her husband's belly.

She lied to him, "Stay in the house. Daughter and I will go plant food in the garden." After she lied to her husband, she took her things in a net bag and brought her daughter to the garden.

They arrived at the garden and began to remove the food. After they finished, they filled their net bags, then followed the trail to the beach. They walked and walked until they arrived at the beach, then they stayed there. Later, they made a house for themselves, cleaned the area and planted food in a garden.

Thinking Hard

The father waited and waited until dark, then he thought hard. In the morning, he saw that they had not returned to the house, so he just got up and left, but he did not go far. He stayed in the garden hut because his belly was too big. It was just like that of a pregnant woman.

He just stayed in the garden hut, then he gave birth. The baby was a boy. The father took the baby and hid him in the garden hut. The child just stayed there until he became a man.

The child's skin was red, and he looked very handsome, so the father was very happy to have him. The father slept in his house and the boy just stayed in the garden hut.

The girl's mother stayed in their new place at the beach. The mother always told her daughter that she could not look back at the mountains. The mother said that this was because she did not want her to think of her father. They lived well, and the daughter became a woman.

One day, they went to the forest to look for *tulip* leaves. They walked and walked a very long distance from the beach. They arrived at a mountain where there were many *tulip* trees. The mother told the daughter to climb the tree and pick the *tulip* leaves.

The daughter climbed up and picked the *tulip* leaves. Then she turned and looked to the place where her father lived. She saw smoke from a fire. When she saw this, she thought of her father and began to cry. Her tears fell down on her mother's breasts.

The mother saw this and called up to her, "Hey, what did you do to make yourself cry?" When the daughter heard this, she cried harder. The mother tried to stop her but to no avail. She kept crying. After a while, the mother called for her to come down. They walked to the place where the smoke was rising.

Seeing Father

They walked and walked until they arrived at the place where the father lived. Then they saw the father. The poor man was old. The father also saw them and was surprised, but he was extremely happy.

The mother and daughter slept in the house. In the early morning, the father told them to just stay there while he went to the garden to get a little food. He told them to kill a big pig and to wait for him to bring the food back, then they would cook it in an earth oven.

The father went to the garden and called out for his son to come. He explained to him that his mother and sister had returned and were staying there. The father told the boy to hide and not to come to the clearing where they could see him.

After he told him this, the father took some food and returned. The mother and daughter helped him. They made an earth oven, then they sat and waited. When the food was nearly ready, the father sent his daughter to fetch some water for them to drink while they ate the food from their earth oven.

The daughter listened and brought bamboo tubes to fill with water. When she arrived at the stream, she bent over to fetch the water and she saw a man's shadow. She saw a very handsome man and was surprised.

Fetching Water

She turned then searched and searched for the man, then she looked up and saw her brother sitting on a tree. The woman forgot about fetching water. She ran up to the tree and called up for him to come down. The man knew that this woman must be his sister.

The man told her that she was his sister, but the woman insisted that he come down because she wanted to marry him. They went on like this for a while, and then the woman stopped thinking about bringing the water back.

The parents waited and waited for a very long time. The father got up to see what was happening and to bring his daughter back quickly. He arrived to see his two children arguing.

The father was angry and scolded his daughter, "What do you want to do with this man? He's your true brother."

However, the father's scolding and talking was all for nothing. The woman was persistent, and the man came down from the tree. The woman saw this and ran to wait at the base of the tree. When the man came down to the last branch of the tree, he told the woman to go stand far away.

The woman did not listen to him. She went directly to the base of the tree and waited. Then when he jumped down, he jumped on top of the woman. Oh my, the woman just fell to the ground, dead. The father and son saw this and were speechless.

The son turned into a bird and flew into the deep forest. The father carried his daughter's body back home. The mother saw this. She was troubled and cried for her

daughter. Then they buried their daughter's body. They stayed at this place until they died.

Robinson Soksok

P. O. Box 445

Kieta

North Solomons Province

D150M. Transformation: man to bird; D440+. Transformation: excrement to fish; F527.1. Red person; N320.1+. Man unwittingly causes death of sister; P210. Husband and wife; P232. Mother and daughter; P233. Father and son; P234. Father and daughter; P253. Sister and brother; Q200+. Feeding excrement punished; Q200+. Nagging punished; Q478+. Punishment: eating excrement; Q550+. Punishment: male impregnation; R213. Escape from home; R227.2. Flight from hated husband; R227.2. Flight from hated husband; S62. Cruel husband; S11. Cruel father; T253. The nagging wife; T415.2. Brother repels incestuous sister; T511+. Male conception from eating woman's loincloth; T511.5.3+. Conception from eating insects; T570. Pregnancy; T578. Pregnant man; T580. Childbirth; V61.3+. Dead buried; W111. Laziness; X716H+. The escoumerda

Togogu Ran Away with Mumegi
(Wantok 627, July 5, 1986, page 27)

Long, long ago, in **Emegari** and Bogaie [**Bogai**] Villages, there lived few people who lived [**Gende** People, **Madang** Province]. At this time, there was a young woman who lived in Bagaie [Bogaie] Village. Her name was Mumegi.

This woman was very beautiful, so men from **Bundi** always competed aggressively to try to marry her. All of their hard work was for nothing because the woman was very strong and did not want to marry quickly.

In Emegari Village, there was a poor man whose legs and arms were crooked. The men of the village never treated him well, so he lived alone. The men of the village always told stories about the young woman Mumegi. He would go to hear them curse him and talk secretly about him, that the young woman would not look at him.

The poor man's name was Togogu. He never worried about the secretive talk of the young men of the village. But he always tried to hear the stories about the young woman Mumegi and he tried to see her.

A Big Festival

One day, there was a big festival at Bogaie Village. All of the young men of Emegari Village brought their hand drums and fineries then went to the festival.

The poor man Togogu walked slowly behind them to Bogaie. He was ashamed that the people of the village would talk secretly about him when he arrived at Bogaie, so he sat at the house of a man named Kanive.

When it was almost dark, he went outside Kanive's house and walked to the festival site. Togogu stood nearby and watched the young men dancing and singing fervently. They beat their hand drums and performed magic with betel nuts, betel peppers and smoke, then they gave them to the young woman. However, the young woman Mumegi did not take the things that the young men tried to give her.

Poor Togogu stood and watched, then he took a piece of ginger and called the woman's name, Mumegi, then he shot it. Afterwards, he went and sat by the fire.

Leaving the Festival

Before long, Mumegi left the festival site, walking directly to Togogu. She sat and asked Togogu, "If you have betel nuts or peppers, can you give me one?"

Togogou listened and said, "Sorry, I'm not handsome like the young boys who compete to get you. I just have one betel nut and one betel pepper."

Mumegi listened and said, "That's alright. Don't worry. I'd like us to run away from Bogaie to Emegari. I want to take you right to Orombi Wait Ston."

The woman finished talking, then she took the betel nuts and betel peppers that poor Togogu gave her. The other young men of the village saw this and were furious. Some of them came and castigated Togogu.

Kanam Dance

In the afternoon, the young men passionately performed the Kanam, Yawiyawi, Geke Imbadi Muri, and Kago songs and dances. They excelled at their singing and dancing. While they were doing this, Mumegi ran away with Togogu.

They ran away and jumped in the Imbrum River, then they turned to look back. They saw the young men of the festival running behind them.

The men of the festival carried bows, arrows and fighting clubs. They ran after Mumegi and Togogu, so the two of them began to run.

When the men came and jumped in the Imbum [Imbrum] River, the two of them had arrived at **Bedum** Village. When the two of them arrived at **Kuraini** Village, the men had arrived at Bedum Village.

Becoming Stones

The men came closer, then when the two of them came to Orimbiouo [Orombi] Village, they turned into stones that stood there. The men from the festival followed their footprints and arrived at the base of these stones where they no longer saw their footprints.

When they looked up to the top of the stones, they saw two white marsupials [probably the spotted cuscus, *Spilocuscus maculatus maculatus* (Flannery, 1995a: 181-182)] sitting high upon the pinnacles. The men saw this, but they did not have a way to kill the marsupials. They tried and tried, but they were unsuccessful, so they left them there and went back to their villages.

After the men returned to their villages, the two of them became human again and lived at this place. At this place, they raised children who married and gave birth to more children.

Now this village is called Emegari Koinaraua. This place, *Orimbiouo* means **Wait Ston** in Tok Pisin [or White Stone in English].

Gabriel and Sisilia Doa [Andbruk]

Wait Ston Village, Emegari

Bundi

Madang Province

A1617. Origin of place-name; D179.6K+M. Transformation: man to marsupial; D179.6K+W. Transformation: woman to marsupial; D231M. Transformation: man to stone; D231W. Transformation: woman to stone; D310+M. Transformation: marsupial to man; D310+W. Transformation: marsupial to woman; D967+. Magic ginger; D985.5. Magic betel-nut; D985.5+. Magic betel-pepper; D1271+. Magic smoke; D1900. Love induced by magic; F610.0.1. Remarkably strong woman; L161+. Deformed man marries beautiful woman; P210. Husband and wife; P230. Parents and children; R220. Flights; R260. Pursuits; T10. Falling in love; T50. Wooing; T100. Marriage; T580. Childbirth

A Brother Snubbed His Sister
(Wantok 628, July 12, 1986, page 23)

Long, long ago, in the time of the ancestors, there lived a brother and his sister. The brother's name was Afinuniva and his sister was Tumeriya.

Afinuniva was married in the village and lived with his wife. When his sister had married, she married in a village that was far away, so the sister left the village and went to live in her husband's village.

They lived like this for a while, then one day Afinuniva wanted to make big party for his first child. He slaughtered pigs and gathered food, then he sent out a message about the party.

All of the villages received the message, and the people went to leave for Afinuniva's party. Finally, the message went to his sister, Tumeriya, to come to the party.

Tumeriya received the message, put her baby in a net bag and walked off to her brother's village. The village was far away, so while she was still walking on the trail, her brother began dividing the food among the others in their tribe.

They were eating, celebrating and sharing the food when Tumeriya arrived at the village. Her brother Afinuniva did not see her. He was busy giving food to the other people. He did not think about his sister and giving food to her.

Tumeriya saw this and just sat quietly with her baby. Afinuniva and his wife did not speak with her or tell her to go to their house and catch her breath. No, they were busy celebrating.

It was nearly dark, and the people who had come from faraway villages went to the houses of their kin. Poor Tumeriya and her baby just sat there. It became completely dark, and Tumeriya saw that Afinuniva's kin had not called for them to go into their house, so she carried her baby and found a place to sleep.

They looked for a place and saw her brother Afinuniva's pigsty, so the woman went inside the hut and sat down with her baby. The baby was hungry, so Tumeriya took some fresh sweet potatoes that had been put there for the pigs to eat. She took the sweet potatoes, broke them into small pieces with her teeth and gave them to her baby. She also ate some.

After they ate, they tried to sleep. However, the pig fleas bit their skin. They just stayed there in the pigsty until dawn, then Tumeriya awoke and carried her baby in the net bag, leaving the village. They walked back to their village.

While they were walking, the men of the village saw them and spoke to Afinuniva. He listened and ran off to see his sister. He went to hold her and ask her to go to the house to take some of his food. However, Tumeriya did not speak. She just cried and walked away. Afinuniva asked her why she did not want to take some food, and Tumeriya told him that the day before she and her baby had sat in hunger in the pigsty.

Ainuniva [Afinuniva] listened and was very troubled. He asked Tumeriya to turn and go back with him to the village, but Tumeriya did not listen to him. She kept walking away.

They continued to do this until they left the village behind. Tumeriya carried her baby and walked first, while her brother Afinuniva went behind her. When they arrived at a big cave, Tumeriya jumped inside with her baby.

Afinuniva saw this then screamed and cried. He ran towards the cave. His sister had gone inside. He was very troubled, so he cut his ear off and threw it inside the cave. When he went back to the village, Afinuniva just went and killed his wife and baby.

Defston Doe

Kainantu

Eastern Highlands Province

M451.1. Death by suicide; P210. Husband and wife; P230. Parents and children; P253. Sister and brother; P681+. Mourning customs: self-mutilation; S11.3. Father kills child; S12.2. Cruel mother kills child; S63+. Husband kills wife; S110. Murders; S160.1. Self-mutilation; S168. Mutilation: tearing off ears

A *Masalai* with Three Kinds of Faces
(Wantok 629, July 19, 1986, page 23)

Long, long ago, in the time of the ancestors, there lived an old woman. Before, when she was still young, she did not marry, so she did not have any children either.

One time, she was working at cutting up taros to be cooked. Her bamboo knife missed and cut one of her fingers.

The poor woman's blood just spilled out. The old woman put her finger on top of a coconut shell and the blood fell into the shell. Later, she bandaged her finger well with a string to stop the blood.

The old woman forgot this and did not remove the blood or spill it into the river. She left it there in the coconut shell on top of the firewood near the fireplace.

That night, the old woman went to sleep. Some time that night, near morning, she heard the cry of a baby coming from inside the house. She woke up completely and listened carefully. Then she heard the cry of a newborn baby. The old woman heard the cry coming from her fireplace.

Quickly, she got up to look, and oh my, was she surprised. Two little babies had come from the blood from her finger. They were lying on top of the firewood and crying.

The old woman trembled fiercely and carried the two babies with her. She washed them well and went to find some sweet liquid to give to them as milk.

The old woman took good care of them. She always gave them ripe bananas that she chewed and mashed up well. The old woman looked after them, and they grew up. They were boys. They called the old woman their mother.

When they became big, their old mother told them stories for them to follow. She told stories about the land, the garden, and the places to find food when they became big men and had families.

The mother told them which land they could use and which places were forbidden. She told them which trails to use and which not to use.

One day, the two young men traveled in the forest. They walked and searched for food and wild game for their old mother. They traveled and arrived at a place that was filled with mangos. The mangos were ripe and falling about. These mangos were right in front of the house of a *masalai* and his family who lived underground. The trail to their house went down through the ground. The house was slightly open, but by the base of a mango tree there was hard earth, like a big stone.

The two youths did not know this, so they went up the mango tree and gorged themselves. They left food at the base of the mango tree. After a short time on top of the mango tree, the two men saw a pig sniffing around the base of the tree.

Quickly, they left the tree and went down very quietly to kill the pig. They came down awkwardly because their spears were at the bottom of the tree. They had gone up the tree empty-handed.

When they came down, one brother quietly took his spear. When the pig was about to flee, the man speared and killed it. This was not an ordinary pig, like a wild pig from the forest. No, it was a pig that belonged to the *masalai*. The pig often went around the house, looking for food. The two poor young men did not know this. They thought that it was an ordinary pig, so they had killed it.

They wanted to carry it back home, but it was too heavy. They did not have the strength because it was a *masalai* pig too. If it were an ordinary pig, it would have been easy for them to tie it with vines to a pole and carry it on their shoulders.

The *masalai* had heard his pig's squeals. Quickly, he left his house beneath the ground and ascended. The ground trembled when the *masalai* wanted to come out. The two youths felt the trembling. When they turned around, they saw the mango tree shaking too. Oh my, they were terrified and just stood quietly, but they saw something coming now.

They thought of the stories that their old mother had told them. One thing that she had told them was to stand strong and not be afraid to fight with enemies.

When the *masalai* arrived, his face was the same as a pig in the front. In the back, he had the face of a man. On the two sides were the faces of snakes. The two men trembled a little, but they stood strong. He went close to them and the ground kept trembling.

One brother held the other's hand. They stood until the *masalai* came close, then the big brother pulled back his bow and shot an arrow right into the pig-face. The arrow

went to the other side where one of the man's eyes came out of the back of the *masalai*.

The other brother drew back his bow and arrow too, shooting the snake-faced side. The arrow also went through to the other side. Then the two brothers took their arrows and shot the *masalai*'s liver or heart. They killed him and cut him up, then tied him with vines to the trees in the forest.

After this, they went home and explained to their mother what had happened. Their mother was very happy because this part of the forest was the place where people never traveled because they were afraid of the *masalai*.

Their mother was ecstatic and sent a message to the nearby villages. The mother was very old, so the people of the nearby villages came and gathered at the home of the two boys and their old mother. This was because it was time for a big festival.

This marked them as two men. They were no longer boys. They were ready to marry because they had finished off the people's great enemy from this land.

Thereafter, the people who lived far away and the people who lived nearby were not afraid. They had often walked very quietly through this part of the forest where it was forbidden to travel. The *masalai* from this place was dead, so they were happy and they traveled there as they pleased.

Bill Ivung
Rabaul
East New Britain Province

A515.1.1. Twin culture heroes; C612. Forbidden forest; F401.3.10K. Spirit in form of boar; F490+. Masalai; F511.1.3+. Human-snake-pig face; F531.3+. Giant's walking causes earthquake; G100. Giant ogre; G512.1+. Ogre killed with spear/arrow; P251.5. Two brothers; P231. Mother and son; S110. Murders; T534. Conception from blood; T587. Birth of twins; T685. Twins; Z210. Brothers as heroes

Two Brothers Killed the Devil Eagle

(Wantok 630, July 26, 1986, page 23)

I am Tombias Kanji from **Aibom** Village by the Sepik River [**Iatmul** People, **East Sepik** Province]. This is my story.

Long ago, in the time of the ancestors, in my village, there lived a huge eagle. This eagle would eat men, women and children. People could not leave their hiding places and go to the river or to clearings. They always just hid. The eagle's eyes were very sharp. The people were terrified of this eagle because it was like a [devil]. They searched very hard for food and wild game because they only traveled at night.

When the eagle saw a man, woman or child, it would quickly fly around and snatch the person up with its two talons, then go up to a huge tree to perch eat them. The eagle's aerie was very high, hidden by the clouds, where men could not see.

The eagle often did this sort of thing, so many people of the village died. There were few people left in the village. The eagle was very happy because the people of the village were afraid of it and it and they did not think of trying to kill the eagle.

After a while, the little group that was left in the village was angry and decided to kill the eagle. They went to cut a pandanus tree (*karuka*). They all worked at night when the eagle was sleeping on top of the huge tree. They cut the pandanus tree and fashioned it like a small house. The inside of it looked like a house. They arranged it well and sent two brothers inside the pandanus tree.

When all of the work was finished, they gathered that night and had a festival. The men gathered in the spirit house where they sang, danced and spat ginger to give strength to the two young men.

The leaders gave them a knife from their forefathers that they had sharpened on sago palm tree bark. The mother of the two young men was very worried. She thought about whether they would be all right or whether they would meet their enemy, the big devil eagle, at this place.

Before dawn, the people put the two of them inside the pandanus house. The men tied a long vine to the pandanus. They carried them while it was still night and put them near the Sepik River by a clearing.

They pushed the two of them out into the water. The pandanus with the two men drifted downriver. The eagle saw this and immediately flew downwards. They had not covered the pandanus well, so the eagle saw that men were inside. The eagle flew down, smelled them and was very happy. The eagle flew around and around, singing, then flew down.

The eagle wanted to snatch the whole pandanus and fly upwards, but the pandanus was too heavy. The eagle turned and flew up, passing the white clouds, then caught its breath. The devil flew down and snatched the pandanus with the two men, then flew up and put them on a branch of the eagle's huge tree. The eagle's tree was huge, taller than any other was. The eagle perched very happily on the side. It knew that it would eat the people inside.

Near the door of the pandanus were two big boulders. The eagle sat and caught its breath, then it began to open up the pandanus. The village men stood firmly because of the strong rattans. The eagle worked at removing all of the rattans, then it saw the two boulders. It was furious and broke the two stones. This was because the eagle thought that the people from the ground had tricked it and had only sent stones.

Darkness came, and the eagle left the pandanus tree with the two men inside. They did not have a way to escape. The tree was very high, and there were no branches where they could get down and escape. They knew that if they made a wrong move, they would slip and fall to their deaths.

That night while the eagle slept, the men sat inside the pandanus house up in the clouds where the villagers could not see them or the eagle.

Late at night, the two brothers sat and listened. The eagle was asleep, so they heard it break wind. At about two o'clock in the morning, it broke wind again. The third time, at about four o'clock, they really believed that the devil eagle was dead asleep.

Dawn broke, and the eagle wanted to awake, but too bad, it was too late. The two brothers had cut the pandanus with their sago knives. They went out and cut the eagle's neck. That was the end. Blood spilled all about. Its head and body were huge, bigger than that of a human. The eagle's head fell down and landed at the base of the tree down by the village.

The body, neck, legs and wings also fell down to the ground. The leaders of the village gathered and took the eagle's head to the spirit house.

They took the pieces of the eagle's body and its blood too, putting them inside bamboo tubes. They closed up the tubes and carried them to the spirit house.

The men up on the tree tied the long vine that the people had put inside the pandanus with them to the tree branch high on the tree. One brother went down first on the vine, and then the other followed. Meanwhile, the villagers were still celebrating.

We, the people of Aibom Village, call the vine that the two brothers used *dumakua*. The brothers sang happily while they descended the vine. The singing that the two brothers performed is called *wandapanban*.

They had no more troubles. During the day, morning or afternoon, the men went into the forest, the women looked for food by the river, and the children played around the village. The devil eagle was dead, so the people were no longer afraid. The people have multiplied at Aibom Village until this day.

Tobias Kanji
Aibon [Aibom] Village
East Sepik Province

A515.1. Culture heroes brothers; B163+. Devastating eagle killed; B33. Man-eating birds; B872.1. Giant eagle; D967+. Magic ginger; D1001. Magic spittle; D1781. Magic results from singing; D1781+. Magic results from dancing; D1830. Magic strength; F54.1. Tree stretches to sky; G303.3.3.3+. Devil in form of eagle; G510.4. Hero overcomes devastating animal; K750. Capture by decoy; P251.5. Two brothers; V112.1. Spirit huts; Z71.1. Formulistic number: three; Z210. Brothers as heroes

A Flying Fox Won over a Woman
(Wantok 631, August 2, 1986, page 20)

Long ago, in the time of the ancestors, a man and his wife were working in a garden. They were newlyweds who wanted to start a new garden for themselves.

They began to make their big garden. The man did the big work of cutting trees. The woman began far away, cutting the branches of small trees and clearing the area to make a garden.

On this day, another man was hunting for wild game on top of a mountain when he saw smoke rising. This was the smoke that was coming from the fire that the woman had made.

The mountain where the man was walking was very far away. The smoke from the fire that the woman had made only rose a little. The mountain was the home to flying foxes. They completely filled the mountains that stood near this area.

The man on the mountain was not an ordinary man. He was a flying fox. Sometimes he would turn into a man and travel the forest, then later he would turn back into a flying fox again.

When he saw the smoke from the fire, he sat and thought, "I'll turn into a flying fox and fly down to see who's making the fire that is causing the smoke to rise."

He thought and thought, then his heart went out to the woman. He turned into a flying fox and went to the place where the smoke was rising. When he arrived, he saw the young woman working in the garden. The woman was putting some food on the fire and sitting by it. The flying fox approached the woman and perched on top of a tree. He saw a marsupial (*kapul*) on a tree.

The flying fox told the marsupial, "Don't tell the other marsupials. I'm going to steal that woman now."

The flying fox went down very quietly after making the agreement with the marsupial. The woman's husband was still working, so he did not know what was happening. The flying-fox man flew down and snatched the woman. The woman wanted to scream, but it was too late. She flew up with the flying fox.

Her husband looked and ran quickly to get his bow and arrows. He drew back his bow to shoot down the flying fox, but he missed. The flying fox flew and hid in the trees. The man could not see his wife and the flying fox anymore.

The flying fox carried the woman to a nearby mountain, then put the woman down. The woman was afraid, so she just stood there. The flying fox flew to the nearby forest.

A little later, there was a noise, so the woman turned around and saw the rotten good-for-nothing walking towards her. He arrived as a very handsome young man.

He came closer and told her, "Don't be afraid. I don't look like you first saw me. I'm not your husband, but I'm also a man. I can't steal you from your husband, so I'll carry you back. I didn't see what kind of woman you were. You're an excellent woman in my eyes."

The woman replied, "Oh my, when I look at you, I feel at ease too. I thought that you were going to kill me or eat me. I've never seen a man like you before."

The woman told the man that she was a newlywed, that she and her husband had begun living together and doing work together. So, her husband and the people of his village would be searching for her in every corner of the forest, every river and every mountain.

The woman's husband looked in every part of the forest, but he could not find his wife. He cried and cried, then he went to the village and explained to his kin what had happened.

It was nearly dark when the flying-fox man turned into a flying fox again. Then he carried the woman back. Before they flew back, the man straightened something out with the woman, "When you go to the village and live with your husband, you must not forget about me. If you feel this way, that you want me, then you must go to the garden by the village where you made the fire. Then I'll come to see you again."

That night, the flying fox left the woman in a small forest near her house in the village. The woman walked up to the house, then her real husband came and held her.

The woman told him the story, but it was hard for him to kill the flying-fox man because he had flown away. The woman was completely hooked on the flying fox because he was really a man.

They slept, then in the morning, the woman woke up and did not eat. She thought about the flying-fox man. She was very troubled because she did not know if she would see him again. She always worried about this. Some months passed and the married couple were still together. The man was much afraid that his wife would be raped, so he told her that they would leave the old garden and go to clear some forest at a new place to make another garden.

The man saw that the woman had changed her ways. She was always very troubled about the flying-fox man. Her real husband was angry and he beat her. He always beat her, and the poor woman lost her appearance.

The flying fox often flew to the village, hid on top of the trees, and saw the man beating her. The flying fox saw this and was furious.

One night, he flew to the house when the woman's husband was not there. He told the woman that he would take her away. The woman was very happy and said that they could meet at the fireplace in the old garden. After they made their decision, the flying fox flew back to his home.

In the morning, the woman told her husband that she would go looking for food in the garden. She took all of her nice adornments and other things, then she filled a net bag with them and hid them somewhere in the forest.

She took only a small net bag and a stone knife, then she left the house. Her husband asked about what she would be doing. She lied to him that she was going to their new garden.

She did not go there, but to the old garden where she made a small fire. The smoke rose. The flying fox and four of his kin saw the smoke from the mountain. Immediately, they flew down to the garden. The man flew down and grabbed the woman.

He told her, "That's the end. Your body will no longer be in pain. You won't have troubles, your heart won't be heavy. Your new life begins now."

He carried the woman away, and the other flying foxes joined them in flight. They arrived at the home of the flying foxes. Her real husband no longer troubled the woman. She ignored him completely.

Later, her flying-fox husband fetched the things that she had hidden in the forest near the house. They married and lived happily.

Jeffery Sombe

Kieta

North Solomons Province

B552+. Person carried by flying fox; B650+. Marriage to flying fox in human form; D117.5KM. Transformation: man to flying fox; D310+M.

532

Transformation: Flying fox to man; P210. Husband and wife; R10+. Abductee returned; R13.1+. Abduction by flying fox; R100. Rescues; R150+. Animal rescues woman from cruel husband; R227.2. Flight from hated husband; S62. Cruel husband; T100. Marriage; W181. Jealousy

A Woman Ruined Two Brothers
(Wantok 632, August 9, 1986, page 20)

Long ago, there were two brothers. The first brother was married and the second brother still lived alone. The brothers' parents had died. They were by themselves for a while, then the big brother married.

One day, the big brother went to the forest to hunt for wild game. After he left for the forest, the little brother stayed with his sister-in-law. When the big brother was in the forest, his wife never treated his little brother well. She was very mean to him.

The woman would give a lot of work to her brother-in-law. When it was time to cook, she would tell her brother-in-law to cook food too. When the food was ready, the woman would take it and go inside the house, then she would eat alone. The poor little brother would not have food.

The woman would carry the food, then go to sit and eat inside the house. Then the little boy would be hungry. When the woman saw that her husband was about to return to the village, she would come down from the house and pretend to give food to the little brother.

When the man returned from the forest, he would give the meat to his wife to smoke. On other days that the man traveled in the forest, his wife would do the same thing as she had done before. She would not give food to the little brother. No, she would take the food up to the house, lock the door, and eat by herself.

The woman would do this kind of thing many times. The little brother would tell his big brother, but the big brother never did anything. One time, the woman did it again.

The little brother cried and cried, then his mother's ghost came and asked him, "Why are you crying?"

The little brother replied, "Big brother's wife never treats me well."

So his mother's ghost told him, "Don't worry. I'll come get you."

She marked one day to come and get the little brother. The time for the mother's ghost to get the little brother approached. The little brother told his big brother, "You and [your] wife come then we'll go to the beach." Their mother's ghost said that she would come to take the little brother at the beach.

When he went to the house, the big brother scolded him, "What are you looking for?" However, he did not tell his big brother what had happened.

The day that their mother had marked [arrived] and the little brother left the house.

At this time, the big brother and his wife tried to find the little brother. They searched and searched for a long time. They searched for him, then the little brother returned to the village. In the afternoon, they all went to the beach. The little brother saw their mother's ghost and he began to cry.

The big brother asked him, "Why are you crying?"

The little brother revealed all of his little stories, "It's because of the bad things that your wife did to me that I'm crying. Now I'll leave you."

Then the little brother turned into a fish and swam away. The big brother saw this. He was troubled and cried.

He scolded his wife, then he sped off towards the sea and turned into a bird. The woman just stayed there for a long time. She became old and died.

So when you go to the beach, you'll see birds flying above the sea. These seagulls are the big brother, and the fish are the little brother.

Peter Rewi

Goroka

Eastern Highlands Province

A1945. Creation of gull; A2100. Creation of fish; D170B. Transformation: boy to fish; D154.4M. Transformation: man to gull; E323. Dead mother's friendly return; E545. The dead speak: P210. Husband and wife; P251.5. Two brothers; P263. Brother-in-law; P264. Sister-in-law; S55. Cruel sister-in-law

Nokondi and His Kin

(Wantok 633, August 9-16, 1986, page 23)

Long, long ago, there were no people who lived at **Nokolakolato** or **Watabung** Villages [**Siane** People, **Eastern Highlands** Province]. These are villages that we know and think of as pleasant, but before in the time when Nokondi was alive, they were not like that.

In the time of Nokondi, these places did not look like villages. No, there was very dense forest growing there, and Nokondi lived on top of [Mount] Aiambo.

He was a man who was excelled at hunting wild game. When he made a fire, he did not know to break branches to make a fire. No, he threw marsupials (*kapul*) inside and lit the fire on them like firewood.

One day, the young people of **Sinasina** Village traveled to a mountain [**Sinasina** People, **Simbu** Province]. They stood and watched. They saw smoke coming from very far away at Watabung. They were very troubled by this. They said, "Oh dear, who is it that's so far away making that fire?"

After they said this, they fetched some firewood and went back to the village. Some of them made a fire and said, "Whoever saw the smoke from the fire will know that we've seen him."

Among them, there was a young woman who was very beautiful. Her name was Aiambowena. When she went back to the village, she could not sleep at night. She thought hard about the smoke from the fire that she had seen rising from the Watabung area.

She was very troubled. She just lay there thinking until dawn broke and the light shone in her eyes. That morning, the woman got up and went up to the mountain to look at the Watabung area. She saw the smoke still rising. She just sat there and looked at this place. She became very troubled.

When it was getting dark, she went back to the house. Her parents saw her and asked, "Where did you go that you've just come back home?"

The woman replied, "No, papa. Yesterday we traveled to the [forest], then we arrived at the source of the Maia River. So this morning, I went back to see. I saw smoke still rising and I'm very troubled. I want to go [find out] who the man is who lives there and who made the fire that made the smoke that we saw."

The woman's father listened and was sorry for his daughter. He saw that she wanted very much to find out who the man was that lived there and always made fire on top of the mountain.

So in the very early morning, the father awoke and went to kill a huge pig. He cooked it, then he cut sugarcanes and bananas in the garden, and carried them back to the village. The father arranged everything, then the daughter woke up and put them inside her net bag.

At about five o'clock in the morning, the woman awoke and carried her net bag of food. She left Sinasina Village and went down to the Suave [**Chuave**] area. She followed the Mai [Maia] River until she arrived at Nokolakolato. She looked up the mountain and saw smoke billowing forth.

The Sinasina woman saw this and was ecstatic. However she said, "Never mind. I'll take my time, I'll plant some sweet potatoes and sugarcanes first."

So, she planted these foods at Nokolakolato. After she finished, she continued to follow the Keveanoku River until she arrived at Aiambo. The woman saw the firelight, but she did not see a man there, so she sat and waited.

The man was Nokondi. He arrived, carrying many, many marsupials. He put the marsupials down and went to get the old ones to make a fire with them.

His nose caught the smell of the woman, so he immediately turned into a snake. Later, he changed again into a tree. He thought that when he performed his tricks, the woman would be afraid and run away. But this was not the case. The woman had a strong desire to marry Nokondi, so when she saw these things happen, she did not tremble at what was supposed to make her afraid.

Nokondi saw this and turned back into a man. However, the man was missing one leg, one arm, one ear, and one eye. The woman sat and saw this, but she was not afraid of him in the slightest.

She got up and took her bamboo knife, then went to cut the man's leg. Immediately, he became a real man again. He knew that the woman must have a strong desire for him, and that she was not the slightest afraid of the various tricks that he had performed.

Nokondi married this Sinasina woman, Aiambowena, and the two of them lived at this place. They lived for a while, then one day the woman told her husband Nokondi, "We'll go down to Watabung. I planted some food there. Let's see whether it's grown or not."

So, they left this place and went to Watabung. They made a garden and house, and lived there for many years. Later, they left Watabung and went to live at **Kulefu** because when they lived at Watabung, they would see the sun rise and shoot directly towards Kulefu. They left Watabung and went to live at Kulefu.

Then they left Kulefu and went back to Watabung. When they arrived at Watabung, they made a house and garden again. They went back and forth, then some other people also came to Watabung.

The woman told them, "I'm a Sinasina and my husband is Nokondi, a wild man from this forest."

They were happy to see this group come with them because they had no other people living with them until that point. They lived well, and many children grew up at Watabung. These children married and raised more children.

One day, they were cooking their food in an earth oven and they sent two women to go fetch some water. The women carried the bamboo tubes down to the river. When they arrived, they saw two Guhikwe [**Gohikave**] men from Nokolalo [Nokolakolato Village, **Gahuku** People, Eastern Highlands Province].

They left these men and played around, then [the men] broke the two women's bamboo tubes. When the women wanted to fill them with water, the water spilled out because the bases had been broken.

The men had finished cooking the food in the earth oven and were waiting for the women to bring the water back. The women did not return, so the men called out in vain for them. Then they went to see what had happened to them that caused them to take so long to fetch the water.

When they arrived at the river, the women told them, "We came to fetch the water, then two Guhikwe men came and broke our bamboo."

The men listened to this, then they went to fight with the group from Nokolalo. Everyone broke off and left this place, so there are few people at Watabung.

Some of them know that if Nokondi's kin raise more children, they will come back and fight then take back all of their land. Then they will finish off all of Nokondi's family.

There are some people who live at Watabung who say that all of the land at Watabung belongs to the Yakono Clan, or Yamofe Kofoufa Nokondi.

This ancestor story is from the Kofoufa Nokondi Clan from **Yamofe** Village near Watabung, Eastern Highlands Province.

John Noko

B871.1.2.1. Giant hog; D50+M. Transformation to man with half of a body; D50+M. Transformation to whole man from man with half a body; D191M. Transformation: man to serpent (snake); D215M. Transformation: man to tree; D610. Repeated transformation; F490+. Nokondi; F525. Person with half a body; F567. Wild man; H360. Bride test; H1400. Fear test; J1813+. Cooking processes misunderstood: using animal flesh as firewood; P210. Husband and wife; P230. Parents and children; P232. Mother and daughter; P234. Father and daughter; T100. Marriage

A Spear Became a Dog
(Wantok 634, August 16-23, 1986, page 23)

Long, long ago, on Maluen Mountain, there lived a man. This mountain stands in what is now the Finschhafen area. Before, in the time of the ancestors, there was no area called Finschhafen. The ancestors still lived as they wished and they had their own [place] names.

The man of Mount Maluen had nothing, such as a dog, for companionship. No, he lived alone.

One early morning, he carried his bow and arrows then walked into the forest. While he was going around, he saw a beautiful and young, wild bamboo growing. The name of this wild bamboo is _zongon_.

The man cut the wild bamboo and carried it to the house. He sharpened the little wild bamboo well and made a spear. Then he put it on top of the roof of the house.

In the morning, the man awoke and went to the garden. When the man had left the house, the spear turned into a huge dog. The dog walked into the forest and found a big marsupial (_kapul_). The dog killed the marsupial, carried it in its mouth, and went to put it on the house.

The dog turned back into the spear again and went up to the roof of the house. However, the marsupial's blood was still stuck to the spear.

The old man did not know what his spear had done. He worked in the garden until the afternoon. Afterwards, he cut two pieces of firewood, put them on his shoulder and carried them back to the house.

The old man put the firewood outside the house and went inside. He looked around the house, then he saw blood falling down to the house floor.

The old man looked up to his spear and saw the blood stuck to it. He was completely furious. He took the spear and held it in his hand. Then various things happened.

[He thought,] "Some men must have come inside my house, taken my spear, and used it to kill a pig, marsupial, cassowary or something." He was furious.

His anger caused him to break the spear and put it into the fire. However, he did not check around the house where the spear-dog had carefully hidden the marsupial.

Later, he calmed down a little and smelled the fresh marsupial blood. When he checked, the marsupial was lying in the house.

His thoughts were confused about the spear, "How did the marsupial get into the house?" The old man cooked it on the fire and ate it.

That night, he slept and dreamt that his spear had become a dog then had gone into the forest to kill the marsupial.

In the morning, the old man woke up and looked at the fireplace. He looked at where the spear was. He was very troubled. He sat and cried because he was wrong to have broken the spear.

That night, he saw a huge dog approaching the house. He had never seen the dog before because he lived alone in this mountain area.

When the old man went closer to call out to it, the dog walked closer and circled the old man. The dog sniffed him, jumped and barked. After the dog finished barking, it walked off into the darkness.

When the man went to hold the dog, it was too late, the dog had run away into the forest. The man never saw the dog's face again. This dog was the spear that the old man had broken and burned in the fire. If he had not burned the spear, it would have turned into a dog and lived with him forever.

After many months passed, the old man walked into the forest and looked for some young, wild bamboo. However, he could not find the wild bamboo along the trails that he walked. The poor old man continued to live alone.

Gabriel Sapore
Zengaring [**Zengaren**] Village [**Burum** People]
Finsafen [Finschhafen]
Morobe Province

B871.1.7. Giant dog (hound); D422.2+. Transformation: dog to spear; D440+. Transformation: spear to dog; D1810.8.2. Information received through dream; P426.2. Hermit; R220. Flights

Two Brothers Slew Masimura
(Wantok 635, August 23-30, 1986, page 20)

Long, long ago, there was a _masalai_ named Masimura. This _masalai_ Masimura ate everyone in the area. All of them died except for some who escaped and went to other places.

However, there was one old woman who stayed. The old woman often hid in her house among the vines. During the day, she would hide until it was dark, then she would go cook her food and do other work. Afterwards, she would hide again.

The old woman's husband was afraid of the _masalai_, so he left her and canoed to the other side of the island. When he arrived on the other side, the people had died. He saw this and fled.

The old woman stayed there and ran out of food. So one day, she went to the old gardens to look for various foods. She only saw sugarcanes there.

The old woman quickly broke the sugarcanes and the leaves cut her hands. She saw this and quickly dug a hole in which to let the blood spill. She was terrified that the blood would fall about and that the _masalai_ Masimura would smell it and follow her.

The old woman went back to her house and stayed there. About three weeks passed, then she returned to the place to look for more sugarcane. When she took some sugarcane, she looked at the place where she had hidden the blood and she saw four human legs. The old woman saw this and was shocked, but she did not approach them.

After one week, she returned to this place and saw human trunks. After another week, she went and saw four human arms coming out.

On the fourth week, the old woman went back and saw two little boys playing in the garden. The old woman went close to them and saw that they were indeed two boys.

She was very happy to see the two children. She took them and they went to her house among the vines. She lived in the house, and the old woman told the boys about the *masalai* Masimura.

The old woman told them, "When it is day, it is completely forbidden to go out because Masimura is going around and hunting for his meat. If he sees you two, he'll kill you."

The two boys lived with the old woman and she looked after her children very well. At night, they would leave the house and travel, looking for food in the gardens or killing bandicoots and other nocturnal game.

They lived like this until the boys became big men. One day, their mother told them, "Go fetch some banana leaves."

The boys became birds then flew away. One of them went directly to get banana leaves, and the other just fetched ordinary leaves then returned.

After a while, their mother sent them to cut small bamboos to make bows and arrows. They listened and went to fetch them. Afterwards, the old mother showed them how to make bows and arrows. She taught them how to shoot the bows. The brothers practiced and practiced then they became marksmen.

Then the old woman told them that they could try to kill Masimura, the *masalai*. She told them to flatter the *masalai*'s assistant to help them kill the *masalai*.

The name of the *masalai*'s assistant was Gende. The two men listened, then went down to the *masalai*'s assistant. They called out to Gende and told him, "We want you to get Masimura's tooth and burn it. When you do this, we'll give you a big present."

Gende was very happy about this. He knew that the *masalai* did not have any more people to kill so he removed one of his teeth and just put it in the house.

Gende took some bamboo and carried it home. Masimura was sleeping there, so Gende very quietly went and took his tooth then burned it.

While Masimura slept there, he smelled the smoke and called out, "Gende, what are you cooking?" Gende told the *masalai* that he was just burning bamboos.

The *masalai* listened and went back to sleep. After the tooth was in the fire with the bamboo, Gende quietly went and told the two men that he had burned the *masalai*'s tooth. They gave him a pig. Gende sat and ate it, then returned.

The brothers made four big fences around the house, then they prepared everything for fighting. They stood by Masimura's house and called out to him. The *masalai* heard this and awoke.

He turned and called to Gende, "Fetch some water for me, then we'll go hunt the game that's calling out over there." Gende listened and brought Masimura's water, then they stretched and departed.

Masimura went and saw the two men standing inside the fence. They called for him to come and fight with them. The *masalai* saw this and ran to try to break the fence. He tried and tried, then the fence broke down. The brothers jumped inside the second fence and fought with the *masalai*.

When the *masalai* nearly broke the fence, they pummeled the *masalai*'s body with their bows and arrows. They did this until the third fence broke and only one fence was left.

One of the *masalai*'s teeth was not there, so he had only one tooth to use. When his tooth broke, the brothers gave it to him good and he fell down. He called out for water, so Gende carried water to give to him. However when *masalai* Masimura wanted to drink, the water just spilled down.

When the water spilled down Masimura's belly, he became a stone. This is the place where he died, where the water flows. This stone still stands there, and the water always flows from holes in it.

These holes are the marks from the spears that the two brothers made when they fought with Masimura, the *masalai*.

Lepot Galo

Arawa

North Solomons Province

[See the ancestor stories in *Wantok* #520, 672 and 721. These stories have a *masalai* with the same name. These stories probably come from the **Kâte** People, **Morobe** Province.]

A941.0.1. Origin of a particular spring; D150M. Transformation: man to bird; D231+. Transformation: ogre to stone; D350M. Transformation: bird to man; F490+. Masalai; F490+. Masumura; F513.1+. Removable teeth; G346. Devastating monster; G510.4+. Hero overcomes devastating ogre; G512.1+. Ogre killed with spear/arrow; G530+. Help from ogre's assistant; P210. Husband and wife; P231. Mother and son; P251.5. Two brothers; Q114. Gifts as reward; Q211. Murder punished; Q551.3.4. Transformation to stone as punishment; R213. Escape from home; R260. Pursuits; S62. Cruel husband; S110. Murders; S140.1. Abandonment of aged; S371+. Abandoned woman's son becomes hero; S433. Cast-off wife abandoned on island; T541.1. Birth from blood; T545. Birth from ground; T587. Birth of twins; T685. Twins; Z71.2. Formulistic number: four; Z210. Brothers as heroes

Enemies Killed Segiyo

(Wantok 636, August 30 — September 6, 1986, page 20)

Long, long ago, there was an old man who lived in a village. The name of this old man was Segiyo. Segiyo had children. All of them had grown and had their own children. His wife had died, and he lived alone in his own little house. If his sons' wives thought of him, they would give him food. If they did not think of him, he would go to sleep hungry.

When the women wanted to go the forest or work in the gardens, they would leave their children with their old grandfather, Segiyo. When they returned to the village, they would take their children and go back to their own houses.

One day, all of the women wanted to travel in the forests and gardens. The first woman left her children there, then departed. Then the other woman also left her children there and she departed. Old Segiyo took care of his grandchildren in the village.

In the afternoon, the women returned, took their children and just went back to their houses. The first son's wife came to get her children and told the old man, "Sorry dad, I didn't go to the garden. I went to make a new garden, so I came back empty-handed."

The second son's wife came to take her child and said, "Dad, I only brought food for the pigs. It's not good to give you. Those behind me will give you good food." After she said this, she took her child and the two of them left.

All of the other women came to get their children, and they did not give food to poor old Segiyo either. When his last son's wife arrived, she thought that the other women had already given food to the old man, so she just carried her child away.

Hunger was killing poor old Segiyo. He had no food in his house, nor did he have any water. He was very thirsty and the hunger was killing him.

He went to sleep, but the hunger was killing him, so he could not sleep well. Near dawn, he awoke and sat down. He worried and sang a mournful song as he cried until dawn broke.

He got up, took his ragged net bag and a piece of stick that he used to dig sweet potatoes, then he walked down to find an old garden.

The forest had covered up the garden, but the old man went inside. He searched and searched, then he saw some sweet potato sprouts. He removed the sprouts, made a fire and cooked them. Hunger was killing the poor man, so he removed the sweet potatoes quickly and ate them.

Enemies were around this area. They saw the smoke rising from this part of the forest, so they very quietly went to see whom it was making the fire. They arrived and saw the old man by himself. They surrounded him well, put arrows into their bows, and then came into the clearing.

The old man saw this and was not afraid. He told them, "It's good that you've come to see me. I have no bow or arrows to fight back with, so wait a little until I finish the sweet potato sprouts."

After the old man said this, he ate all of the sweet potato sprouts that he had cooked. Then he turned and told his enemies, "Now you can do as you like with me."

After he said this, he began to sing a song in the language of the Kamano-Kafe [**Kamano** People, **Kafe** Village] from the **Eastern Highlands** Province. The song goes, "*Krisae yarinanto kofre nafre krisse yarinanto yarinanto.*"

The meaning of this song is, "Why did you not take care of me? I looked for food in the forest garden and they killed me."

He sang like this, then the enemies killed him. Later, they burned him in the fire that he had made to cook the sweet potatoes.

This land where the enemies had killed Segiyo is called Segiyonte. This is a true story. My father always told me this story and cry, then I too would be very troubled when I heard it. If the Kamano-Kafe Clan heard this, they would be troubled because it is my story.

Daniel Ludin

P. O. Box 442

Kieta

North Solomons Province

A1617. Origin of place-name; K914. Murder from ambush; P210. Husband and wife; P230. Parents and children; P233. Father and son; P261. Father-in-law; P265+. Daughter-in-law; P291. Grandfather; S54. Cruel daughter-in-law; S110. Murders

Yirinketif Fooled the Women

(Wantok 637, September 6-13, 1986, page 19)

Long, long ago, in the time of the ancestors, in **Maugilam** Village, there was a *masalai* [**Olo** People, **West Sepik** Province]. The name of this *masalai* was Yirinketif.

One day, the young women of Maugilam Village gathered together and decided to go sleep by the stream, then beat poisonous vines to kill fish. They also said that they would break big bamboos to look for the grasshoppers that lived inside [the bamboos and eat them]. While the women talked, Yirinketif, the *masalai*, heard everything that they said.

Yirinketif usually lived inside the base of a wild *limbum* palm tree, called *foyol yenkil* [*foiyol yenkil*] in my language. Men in the village had cut this *limbum*, and only the stump was left. The *masalai* made a house inside of it.

The next day, the women with their little sisters prepared to leave the village. They told their parents that they would sleep by the Warri Stream and look for fish and grasshoppers.

The parents assented because the stream was near the village and they were not worried about their children sleeping there. All of the women gathered, then they walked away. On the trail, they gathered the vines for killing fish. In my language, we call these vines, *fape*.

They arrived at the Warri Stream, put their things down, then they arranged things and sat to rest. The women told their little sisters, "We'll live here for about a week, then we'll go back to the village." The girls listened to this and were happy.

They ate, then they sat and told stories and went to sleep. In the morning, some women carried the vines and walked to the source of the stream. They crushed the vines and put them in the stream, then they sat and waited for the fish to die.

The women who went to break the big bamboos found many grasshoppers. Later, they returned to the stream to help the other women gather fish. Oh my, the fish were big and plentiful.

That night, they [cooked] the fish and ate. Afterwards, they sat and talked. All of them talked about going to search for grasshoppers in the morning. When they finished talking, they went to sleep.

In the morning, they awoke and all of them went to the forest to hunt for grasshoppers. They worked at breaking the bamboos, then one woman saw the *masalai*, Yirinketif, who had turned into a little crying baby.

The woman saw this and called out to the other women. All of them saw the baby and were very sorry for him. They took the baby and went back to the place where they slept by the stream. They did not know that it was the *masalai* who had become the baby.

They returned to their hut and cooked some food, then all of them sat and ate together. They finished eating and they were happy. They ran back and forth like a little baby would do. The woman who had found the baby carried him.

When it was time to sleep, all of the women joined their sisters and slept. When they were dead asleep, the *masalai* awoke, turned back into a real *masalai*, and then looked at the women.

He needed to defecate, but he went near where one girl was sleeping. Oh my, did he make a huge pile of feces. After he defecated, he went back to sleep with his mother.

In the morning, the women woke up and smelled the feces. They looked around and saw the pile of feces near the girl. They scolded her and told her big sister to remove the feces.

The *masalai* pretended to sleep like a little baby while he listened to the women scold the poor girl. He laughed when he heard the women's scolding. The women saw this and thought that he was just laughing at nothing in particular, as babies do.

The next morning, the women awoke and saw a huge pile of feces near the place where the little girl slept. They scolded her again, and her big sister removed the feces.

On the third night, the same thing happened. In the morning, the women scolded the two sisters. The big sister was angry because she saw that the pile of feces was too big. It looked as if a big man must have defecated there, not her little sister.

On the fourth night, they cooked and ate, then went to sleep. The *masalai* slept very well with his mother. The other women and their sisters were really asleep, but [one woman] just pretended to snore while she kept watch.

Very late at night, she saw the baby wake up, leave her mother and go to the place where her little sister was sleeping. However, he had become a huge, muscular man. His hair swayed about, and his teeth were huge. The woman saw this and trembled terribly, but she did not make a noise. She kept pretending to sleep.

The *masalai* went by the sister, then sat and defecated. Afterwards, he rose and went back to his mother. He became a little baby again and just slept quietly.

In the morning, the women awoke and saw the huge pile of feces and were angry again. The big sister did not talk, she just kept quiet and removed the pile of feces.

Very quietly, she told the women what had happened that night. The women listened and were afraid. However, the woman told them to stay quiet lest the *masalai* find out that the women knew that he was a *masalai*, not a little baby.

The women decided to get rid of the *masalai*. In the morning, they told their little sisters that they would go back to the village because it looked as if a heavy rain would fall and cause the stream to flood.

The women decided to make rain so that a flood would arise. They [planned] to fool the *masalai* and throw him into the stream. Some of them went to the place of the rain then cut the brush and trees near the place where the rain dwells. Afterwards, a heavy rain began to fall.

The rain fell and the stream began to flood. The woman saw this and took their belongings quickly. They prepared to walk by the stream, back to the village.

When they were about to turn around the corner, the women exchanged glances. The woman who was carrying the *masalai* turned to the others and said, "Hold the boy, I have to shit."

She raised the *masalai* to give to another woman. The woman did not hold the baby and he left her hands. The *masalai* fell directly into the stream, and the flood carried him away.

The *masalai* called out to the women, "You knew and you got rid of me!"

The women ran away and arrived at the village. They told the story of the *masalai* and the smart trick that they had played upon him.

So, near Maugilam Village, in the place where the deep forest stands, we have named this place after Yirinketif, the name of this *masalai*. The place is called Alol Yirinketif — *alol* is land that is broken that has become mountainous and bad.

This place is by Lumi in West Sepik Province. This is a story that my old maternal kin told and that I heard when I still lived there.

William Sabien
c/- Kevin T.
P. O. Box 385
Lae
Morobe Province

A1011. Local deluges; A1131+. Rain from certain part of forest; A1617. Origin of place-name; D94+B. Transformation: boy to spirit; D94+B. Transformation: spirit to boy; D2143.1+. Rain produced by cutting trees in certain part of forest; F321.1. Changeling; F490+. Masalai; F544.3.5. Remarkably long teeth; K650+. Escape by throwing enemy into river; P230. Parents and children; P252. Sisters; P252.1. Two sisters; P272. Foster mother; P275. Foster son; Q262. Impostor punished; X716H+. Feces as gift

A Boy Stole an Old Man's Meat
(Wantok 638, September 11, 1986, page 25)

This is an ancestor story from the **Kewa** [People] of **Southern Highlands** Province. A little boy lived with his mother. One day, his mother sent him to cut firewood. The boy carried the pieces of wood that were by the house then went to work at cutting them.

While he worked at cutting the firewood, the sun was very hot, so he left off work and went down to the stream. Then he followed the stream.

He thought of bathing and looking for fish too, but he knew that if he only bathed, his mother would think about finding fish too.

He searched and searched for fish, but he did not find any. He kept following the stream, then he saw pig guts lying in the water.

The pig guts looked as if some man had removed them and thrown them into the stream. He looked further and also saw some pig fat lying nearby.

The boy went to break some bamboo with which to carry the fat. He cut a piece of bamboo, then he began to clean the pig guts. After that, he carried the pig guts and fat then went back to the house.

He took some leafy greens, called *wakia*, covered the meat with them, and made a fire outside of the house. Then he sat and cooked.

His mother returned from the garden and saw the boy cooking. His mother carried sweet potatoes to feed to the pigs.

They gave the sweet potatoes to the pigs, then the boy told his mother, "Mama, I want to tell you what happened to me."

The mother listened and told her son that after they ate, he could tell his story. They returned the house. The mother saw the meat in the fire and asked her son, "Where did you get this meat? I thought you went fishing in the stream."

The boy told his mother that he had found the meat by the stream. His mother listened and told him to be very careful when he traveled to the stream.

They ate, then went to sleep. They ate the meat until all of it was gone. Then the boy thought about going around again to the forest, finding more meat for his mother and himself.

He told his mother, "I'm going to the place where I found the meat. If I don't return, you'll know that enemies killed me."

The boy went down and followed the stream until he arrived at the place where he saw some _rupi_ stones lying by the water. He went closer and saw a small trail.

He followed the trail for a while, then he saw casuarina trees standing. There were many banana plants growing there, and other food plants too.

He hid and watched, then he saw an old man sitting there. The old man was huge. The man only had legs, arms and a head. He did not have eyes, ears or a mouth. The old man sat and heated stones for cooking pork in an earth oven.

The boy hid and watched him work. He thought, "That man has no mouth. How will he eat that meat?"

The old man had killed many, many pigs, and he was cooking the pig livers while he sat and waited for the food in the earth oven to be ready to eat. When the pig livers were ready, the old man put them inside the hole on top of his head, then he ate them. Because he did not have eyes either, he did not see that much of the pig liver fell down to the ground.

When the boy saw this, he ran quickly to get some then he ate them. When the old man uncovered the earth oven, he also put this food inside his mouth and a lot of it fell about. The boy saw this and ran quickly to scavenge the pork, pig guts and other food. After he gathered it, he ran away back to his house. He arrived at the house and gave the food to his mother.

His mother saw the food and asked the boy, "Where did you get this food?"

The boy told his mother about the old man who did not have a face, mouth or eyes. His mother listened and told him that he could [not] return to this place. The boy listened but did not reply to his mother.

They ate until all of the food was gone. Then the boy thought about going back again and stealing more food from the man. However the old man was thinking, "Why did my food disappear so quickly? A man must have stolen my food."

Then the old man thought about making a trap and holding whomever it was that had stolen his food. He made a hole, then he put a piece of net bag inside the hole. After that, he tied one end of a rope to the piece of net bag and the other end to his leg.

When the food was gone, the boy very quietly went back to the place where the old man lived. He went inside to steal some food, but he did not see the trap that the old man had made.

When the boy went inside the fence, he fell inside the old man's trap. When he was stuck in the net bag, the rope around the old man's leg became taut. The old man knew that the thief had fallen down into the hole that he had made. The old man removed the boy from the hole. He carried him back to the house, then he put the boy into a net bag and put him inside another net bag. He did this until the boy was inside about ten net bags. The old man carried the net bags down and hung them up on a very tall tree above the stream.

The poor boy slept inside the net bags because he did not have a means of escape. He stayed there for a while and became famished. He began to eat the strings on his loincloth. After he ate them, he ate his fingernails and toenails. Then the first net bag broke. He fell down very slowly, and he was close to dying from hunger. He was skin and bones, and he just lay there waiting to die. His poor mother thought that he had died.

One day, a group of flying foxes flew by and saw the poor boy lying there. They were carrying some bananas, and threw them down to him. The boy took the bananas and ate. At night, the _sai_ birds flew by and gave him bananas too.

The poor boy gained strength. He lay in the net bag until it was about to break. One night, the flying foxes flew by and carried him to his mother's house.

His mother saw him and was very happy. She asked the flying foxes, "What can I give you?"

The flying foxes told her, "Just get ready. We'll return."

The boy's mother went and killed a pig. She took shell money, oil, and food and put them aside. The flying foxes returned and she wanted to give these things to them, but the flying foxes told her that they did not want these things.

So, the mother went and took some vines for making net bags. She asked the flying foxes [if they wanted them]. They took the vines and they told the old woman that they would return to ask her for more later.

The boy lived with his mother until he became strong again. Then he went down to the stream to look for the old man.

He went closer and saw smoke rising from the old man's home. He went closer still and saw the old man heating stones. Quickly, the boy approached, took a stone and heated it too.

The old man did not have eyes, so he did not see the boy. When the stone was red hot, the boy rose quietly and put the stone inside the hole on top of the old man's head.

The old man felt the tremendous heat and ran down to the stream. The stone was red hot and killed the old man. When the old man went inside the stream, smoke rose.

[Anonymous]

B211.2.11K+. Speaking flying fox; B449.3+. Helpful flying fox; B450. Helpful birds; B542.1.2+. Flying fox rescues person from height; F511.1.0.1. Person without features (with flat face); F511.2.4. Person without ears; F512.5. Person without eyes; F513+. Person with mouth on top of head; F513.0.3. Mouthless people; F531.1.1.3. Blind giant; F531.6.12.6. Giant slain by man; K333. Theft from blind person; K951.1. Murder by throwing hot stones in the mouth; P231. Mother and son; Q53. Reward for rescue; Q212. Theft punished; Q414. Punishment: burning alive; Q433. Punishment: imprisonment; R4. Surprise capture; R49+. Captivity in bag; R49.1. Captivity in tree; R51.1. Prisoners starved; R110. Rescue of captive; S112. Burning to death; W126. Disobedience

Tuk and Moon Fooled the Ghost Woman
(Wantok 639, September 18, 1986, page 21)

Long, long ago, there was an old man and his wife. They had only two sons. The name of the elder son was Tuk and the little boy was named Moon. They lived at Ptumni Village.

When Moon was still a little baby, their father died, and only their mother cared for them until the time when they became big men. Then their mother died and they buried her in Ptumni Village.

The two brothers did not want to leave the village. They decided to just stay there, so later their descendants would fill Ptumni Village.

The name of this village is Ptumni, but the white men usually call it **Katumani** [**Manga Buang** or Mumeng People, **Morobe** Province]. The descendants of Tuk and Moon became very plentiful, so they fought with the other villages in the Mumeng area and with the villages on the Middle Watut [River].

The descendants of Tuk and Moon fought very strongly, so they conquered the other villages and took their land. Their descendants now live in six villages in the **Wau** [**Biangai** People] and **Bulolo** areas [**Mumeng** People]. Their real origin is still the **Mumeng** area [Mumeng People].

This story has a true origin. One of the three parts of this story is in the village of the two ancestors, Tuk and Moon. One part of Tuk and Moon's stories goes like this. One day, Tuk told his brother Moon, "Let's just stay in the village, I'm tired. Later, we'll probably travel the forest a little and kill some wild game."

In the early morning, they awoke and began to walk. They walked and walked, going past two big mountains. When they arrived at the third mountain, they saw a mango tree standing.

It was mango season too, so the mangos were ripe and falling on the ground. Wild pigs were eating the mangos that lay about. The brothers gorged themselves on the mangos [on top of the tree].

While they ate, the wild pigs came. The brothers saw this and thought about killing a pig to carry back to their house. However, they did not have anything with which to kill pigs.

Tuk asked Moon, "Is there a piece of bamboo inside your net bag or not?"

Moon looked for his bamboo knife and gave it to his brother. Tuk took the knife, shoved it inside a ripe mango and threw it down to a huge pig.

The huge pig just swallowed the mango. When it went down, the knife cut its belly and killed it. The brothers saw this and were ecstatic. They went down the tree and wanted to tie the pig up to carry to the village, but they were unable to lift it because it was incredibly heavy.

They realized that they could not lift it, so Tuk asked his brother for a knife. However, neither of them had a knife to butcher the pig. Tuk told his brother to climb the tree and look around for smoke from a fire. He came down and told Tuk [that he had seen smoke]. Tuk told him to go that place and ask for a knife and for fire.

Moon listened and walked away. He arrived there and saw an old woman and her child who had ringworm working in a garden. The place where the old woman had made a fire is called Guraval. This area is a bad place, but Moon did not know it.

When he approached, the old woman saw him and asked, "Grandson, where did you come from?" Moon told the old woman about the pig that they had killed and that they did not have a knife or fire, so he had come to ask for assistance.

The old woman listened and said, "That's OK. We'll all go back and I'll help you two butcher the pig." The old woman told Moon to carry her child, then they walked back to the place where Tuk was.

They arrived, and the old woman told the brothers to make a fire and singe off the pig hair. They made a fire, and when they had burned off all of the pig hair well, Tuk asked the old woman to give him the knife so that he could begin to butcher the pig.

The old woman listened and told them, "I have no knife. I usually butcher game with my finger." When the men heard this, they knew that the old woman was a ghost.

The brothers listened and were speechless. They just sat quietly. The old woman began to cut the pork with her finger. Oh my, when she put her finger into the pork, it just fell apart as if a machine was cutting it.

When she finished the butchering, she told the two boys [that she would] carry the pig entrails down and wash them in the stream. When the ghost woman went down to the stream, the ghost of the men's mother arrived and made the stream dry up. The ghost woman had to walk very far to wash the pig guts. While she was walking to find water, the men cooked the pork and gathered it.

When all of the meat was done, they carried it up the mango tree and put it there carefully. Then they descended, killed the ghost woman's child, cooked it, and made some good soup.

The old woman cleaned the pig guts, then she returned to see that some terrific soup was ready. The boys lied to her, "Grandma, here's your soup."

The old woman ate the meat and drank the excellent soup, then sat at the base of the tree. The boys climbed the mango tree and sat there. They called out to the old woman, "Granny, when you finish eating, come on up." The old woman said, "I'm sitting first, my belly's bloated and I can't come up."

The two boys called down, "A woman ate her own child." When the old woman heard this, she got up to look for her child. The brothers told her, "The meat was not pork. It was just the meat of her child." The old woman was furious.

She ran and tried to go up the tree, but her belly was too swollen and she could not climb. Then she began to eat the base of the tree. The brothers saw this and began to throw down the pig fat. The old woman worked on the fat and did not quit. She kept at it.

Then Tuk told Moon to throw the pieces of pork down towards the old woman's back. When the tree was about to break, the brothers jumped down to the pork and they became [birds].

Moon became a white cockatoo [sulphur-crested cockatoo (Beehler *et al.*, 1986: 117)] and Tuk became a bird of paradise. Moon told Tuk, "I'll follow the stream down to the deep forest (Ce-Cee) in the Middle Watut [River]." If you go to this place, you will find many white cockatoos in the deep forest.

Tuk became a bird of paradise and just stayed at Ptumni Village. So today if you go to Katumani Village, you will see birds of paradise there. This is a true story that comes from Katumani Village in the Mumeng District of Morobe Province.

Steven Moon
Yanioc
P. O. Box 6039
Boroko
National Capital District

A1611+. Origin of Mumeng People; A1611+. Origin of Biangai People; A1620. Distribution of tribes; A1970+. Creation of bird of paradise; A1998K+. Creation of white cockatoo; B871.1.2. Giant boar; D150+M. Transformation: man to bird of paradise; D150+M. Transformation: man to cockatoo; D642.2. Transformation to escape death; D671. Transformation flight; D996.1. Magic finger; D1564. Magic object splits or cuts things; D2095. Magic disappearance; E323. Dead mother's friendly return; E425.1.4. Revenant as woman carrying baby; E425.3. Revenant as child; E446. Ghost killed and thus finally laid; E541. Revenants eat; G61. Relative's flesh eaten unwittingly; K897.1+. Dupe killed by putting thorns in food it is about to swallow; P210. Husband and wife; P230. Parents and children; P231. Mother and son; P233. Father and son; P251.5. Two brothers; R311. Tree refuge; S110. Murders; S139.2.2+. Corpse put into cooking pot or cooked; V61.3+. Dead buried

A Woman Got Revenge upon a Bad Man
(Wantok 640, September 25, 1986, page 27)

Long, long ago, in the time of the ancestors, there were two brothers who lived in the place that is now called the mid-Waghi [Mid-Wahgi River, **Wahgi** People, **Western Highlands** Province]. They lived with some of their clan. This clan was divided into two groups. One group was the kin of these brothers, and the other group was their enemy.

One brother was a good and smart man. The men of the village liked him very much, but his brother was bad. He was a bad man whom the people never liked. The good man was the first brother and the second brother was the bad man.

One day, the brothers' group picked a woman from the enemy group to marry the first brother. At this time, the second brother was still competing to get this woman. He had ruined himself trying to marry this woman, but she did not like him. The woman liked the first brother.

They picked the woman for the big brother, so the big brother often went to the woman's house to see her. The man also helped her kin, but something bad happened to this situation. The woman was happy with the good man, but during the engagement, the situation was ruined.

The good brother, who was picked to marry the woman, became very sick. The sickness destroyed him completely and he died. The woman's kin and the two brothers' kin were very sorry for the good, smart man. The woman was sorry. She cried for many days and did not eat. She was completely upset and she also became sick.

The bad brother did not care that his big brother was dead. He was delighted because he was very eager to marry the woman that had been picked for his big brother. When his big brother died, he was very happy.

They buried the body of the good man, then they sat and mourned for him. Many people did not work in the gardens, and each person found their own food. After about a week, the bad man tried to find various ways to make the woman covet him.

One morning, he took his bow and arrows then went to the forest. He killed a marsupial (*kapul*) in the forest. He cooked it and ate the marsupial, but he carefully attached the marsupial feces to some tree leaves. He put this into his net bag and carried it to the young woman's house.

When the man went inside the house, a heavy rain fell. The man could not leave the house now. He was in the house with the woman and her mother. They stayed there until late at night, then the woman's mother prepared things for sleeping.

When the young woman was dead asleep, the man removed the marsupial feces from the vines [leaves] and rubbed them all over the woman's face and body. Later, he slept near the young woman. In the morning, the woman's mother awoke and made a fire. She saw that the man's skin and her daughter's skin were defiled with the marsupial feces.

The mother saw the bad man lying with her daughter and she was speechless. She called out for the woman's father to come and see the man with her.

They were speechless. The woman's kin took a pig then just gave the pig and the woman to the man. The man was happy and brought the woman with the pig to his house. The woman became his wife. They lived there for a while, then they had a son.

Later, the bad man went to make a garden by a river. They call this river, Waki. One time, the married couple went to the garden with their little son.

The mother and son stayed in the garden while he sprang up a tree and worked at cutting the branches. While he was standing on top of the tree, he sang as he cut. This is how he sang to his wife, "I didn't just marry you. You [thought that] you shat upon me, but I rubbed marsupial shit on you so that you would like me. Then I married you!"

When the woman heard this, she was furious. She hid the baby well, then she took her net bag and filled it with all kinds of things. The baby went into another net bag.

She went and stood near the man, "Is that so, huh? You sang that you rubbed marsupial shit [on me] so that you would marry me, huh? Now look at your son."

After she said this, she threw a net bag with a piece of wood inside of it, which made it look as if there was a baby inside. She threw the net bag with the heavy wood into the Waki River. The man was surprised and thought that the woman had thrown the baby, so he jumped down the tree and into the water to get the baby.

The water was flooded because it had rained for many days. The man went down and drowned. The woman was ecstatic. She took her baby that she had hidden in the forest and went back home. Later, the woman married another man.

Before, the man had tricked the woman by rubbing marsupial feces upon her so as to marry her. The woman did not like this man. Her true heart went to his big brother who had died. So, she did not want to marry this bad man.

Later, it was time for the woman to get revenge and trick the bad man. The man thought that the woman had really thrown away the baby, so he jumped into the river and died.

Robert Nants
Catholic Mission, **Ambang**
Banj [Banz]
Western Highlands Province

K891. Dupe tricked into jumping to his death; K1350. Woman persuaded (or wooed) by trick; P210. Husband and wife; P231. Mother and son; P232. Mother and daughter; P233. Father and son; P234. Father and daughter; P251.5.4. Two brothers as contrasts; Q260. Deceptions punished; Q428. Punishment: drowning; T10. Falling in love; T80. Tragic love; T100. Marriage; V61.3+. Dead buried; W181. Jealousy; X716.1H+. Befouling with excrement

A Man Married a *Masalai* Women

(Wantok 641, October 2, 1986, page 23)

Long, long ago, there were two *masalai* women. During the day, they would walk above the forest and by the rivers. They would appear before people as two real women.

This is true. They were young *masalai* women. One morning, an old woman from the village was looking for string to make net bags. She was looking for some *mangas* tree bark in the forest. The old woman arrived at a small stream and saw the two young women bathing. Very quietly, the old woman walked and hid. She looked carefully at them.

The two youths put their "grass" skirts on top of a stone then went down to bathe. The old woman saw this and thought, "Oh my, I've never seen their faces before. What village are they from? Whose children are they? Oh my, one of my sons could marry them."

She looked at their skirts and spied upon them. The skirts were not like those usually found in the old woman's village. She hid well. The young *masalai* women played, talked and laughed together, then they bathed in the water. Because they appeared as real women and because they were in the water, they had not smelled the old woman.

Later, they wanted to go back on the dry ground and put on their skirts. The old woman quickly went to hide completely. When they put on their skirts, they turned back into *masalai*s. They looked like short, fat snakes with multicolored skins. Then they could smell when there were people near them.

The old woman quickly left the area and fled so that they did not smell her. If they had found her, they would have quickly hidden.

When they smelled a sorcerer, they would bite him so that the snakes would put their mark upon a real man. Later, the man would die in the village.

When they saw good people going around the forests, the streams, or their gardens, they would just glance at them. In days past, they would hide in a tree hole or cave then they would just watch.

When they saw young men, they would go very close to the open forest. They would hide and lust for the young men. But the men could not see them because they looked like snakes.

When they removed their skirts, they became real women. When they held their skirts and put them on, they became big fat snakes and lay upon the ground.

When they became real women, they would walk around the streams and clearings, or go very far away from people. When people approached them, they would hide. Sometimes, they would just disappear and become snakes if they saw men approaching them.

This day, the old woman fled and forgot to carry a bundle of *mangas* string. The bundle was where she was hiding. This was near where the two women were.

After bathing, the young women went up to a stone. They saw the bundle of *mangas* lying there. They began to look for whomever it was who had hidden it there.

They decided that the next day, they would sit and bathe near the stream. They wanted to find out who had left the bundle of *mangas*.

The day before, the old woman went to the village and told the story to her son. The son listened, then quietly took his bow and arrows and pretended to go to the forest. However, he wanted to go find the two women.

His mother told him, "When you arrive at this stream, don't make a noise, you must hide very quietly. Don't trample the dry tree leaves or dry sticks. Just be quiet."

The man went then stood and watched, but he stood far away. The two women waited and waited, then they grew tired. They removed their skirts and became real women. They went down to bathe in the stream. The water was terribly cold, so they talked and laughed and played.

Their skirts were like snakeskins. When they [removed] them from their bodies, they looked like "grass" skirts.

The man stood and watched, then he saw them and thought, "Gosh! Mama's story is true. There are no women like that in the village."

The women bathed vigorously while the man quickly took their skirts and held them at the base of a tree. The women finished bathing and wanted to go back. When they went up, they did not see the skirts on the stone. They searched and searched to no avail. They were worried and began to cry. They could not just put on leaves like skirts because then they could not become *masalai*s. They continued to search near the base of the tree. Then the man came out to the clearing.

He told them, "Here are your two skirts." Quickly, he burned their skirts in a fire that he held. The women saw this and were ashamed.

The man told them, "Don't be ashamed." Then he held their hands. One woman held the right hand and became his first wife. The other woman held his left hand and became his second wife.

He held them and told them, "I've married you now. You're my wives."

The women were speechless. They were ashamed and just cried. The man took them to the village. The first wife carried the bundle of *mangas* from the man's mother. Then they departed.

At the village, the old woman dressed up then sang and danced happily for his son's two young wives. They did not know that the women were *masalai* women. They decided that the women were from very far away.

Kaupa Lukas
Sua Community School [**Chuave** People]
Simbu Province

B656.2. Marriage to serpent in human form; D191W. Transformation: woman to serpent (snake); D391W. Transformation: serpent (snake) to woman; D530+. Transformation by removing skirt; D531+. Transformation by removing skin; F401.3.8. Spirits in form of snake; F401.6. Spirit in human form; F490+. Masalai; P210. Husband and wife; P231. Mother and son; P262. Mother-in-law; P265+. Daughter-in-law; R220. Flights; T111. Marriage of mortal and supernatural being; T145.0.1. Polygyny

Women Took the *Salam* Festival

(Wantok 642, October 9, 1986, page 27)

Long ago, in the time of the ancestors, a family lived in a village called **Wanu** [**Olo** People, **West Sepik** Province].

The family consisted of the two parents and their two daughters. The father was a man who performed the fish song and dance, called *salam* in my language.

The daughters often saw their father perform this song and dance, and coveted their father's style. Of all those who performed the fish song and dance, or *salam*, their father was the best. Their father was worried because he had no son to teach this song and dance.

One time, there was a big *salam* festival. Many, many people from villages near and far gathered on this great day. The women's father was always the leader of the fish singing and dancing.

All of the leaders of the villages appointed him to go first. He was dressed completely differently. The other men were also dressed differently so that their daughters could not recognize them.

The two women and their mother could not recognize their father either. However when he sang and danced, they recognized his voice. When the daughters saw their father, they were very worried for him.

The little sister turned to look at her mother and said, "Mama, why didn't I become a man? Who will take papa's place when he dies?"

Her mother held her and said, "Don't worry. Papa's renown will remain. He's a leader and he's famous for the *salam*. People will think of him and tell stories about him."

The daughters knew the *salam* well. Their mother was also renowned. The people called her the mother of the *salam*. This was because the father went first, and the mother also went first to sing and dance with the women.

However, there were many things that the women did not know. They did not know how to make adornments. Sometimes the men would perform the *salam* to confuse the thoughts of the young women. Sometimes the married women would leave their husbands and jump to a new man.

When it was the time of the *salam* festival, they would send the father of the fish to kill the enemies. The father of the two women had all of these powers within him.

When the gathering at the big festival was over, everyone went his or her separate ways. Another time, the two women were just walking through the forest. The little sister saw some tree leaves. Her father would gather these leaves to make the fish. She asked her big sister whether these were the leaves that their father would gather. The big sister told her that it was true.

Another day, the women again went together to this part of the forest. They decided that they would gather the leaves, feathers and many other adornments to make the *salam* fish. They sat and tried to make it. They prepared all of the markings for the fish to appear. Then they put the decorations on top of the fish.

It was still morning when they were sitting in this part of the forest. In the evening, the fish appeared. The two of them hid by a tree. They tried to hold it and sing and dance, but the fish was terribly heavy because they had made a huge fish.

The fish's power took hold of them and their eyes spun around a little, then they fell asleep. The fish spirit approached them. They saw the spirit of *salam* as a dream.

The fish told them, "You two were worried about your father's power, so you just left, huh? You've found me. I'm not just Salam. Now you've made me become a real man. Before I only stayed in your father's head and thoughts. However, you women have broken the law. Now you shall hold me in your thoughts, so you'll do all of my work as men. You two women will become completely different. You will become muscular women. The men will die for you during the *salam* festival. You shall hold me and know the entire song and dance. However, you cannot marry. So, only one of you must take all of the powers and the real meaning of *salam*."

The spirit of the fish held the hand of the little sister in the dream. Then he told her, "Here, I give you my powers. Then at night, your father will give you all of his powers too. When he dies, you will get the village. You will become the leader of the *salam* festival. Many men will die to have you, but you cannot marry them. You will stay single. Only your big sister will marry. Her husband will become your assistant when you do the work of the *salam* festival."

Late that evening, near nighttime, they hid the fish at the base of a big tree. Underneath the tree, it looked like a house. The rain and wind could not take the fish away.

When they arrived at the village, their father knew what had happened. He felt inside that some people wanted to steal his power.

The little sister went directly to him and cried. She said, "Papa, I'm sorry for you. There's no son to take your place."

The father turned quickly and told his wife, "Some people want to take my power."

His wife laughed and said, "The _salam_ festival no longer belongs just to men. Now, women also hold the _salam_."

The father looked sternly at his daughter and said, "Daughter, you're talking crazily."

The daughter turned her head a little, in the style of the _salam_ dance. Then she tried to sing. But no, the daughter trembled and so did the father. Together they trembled from the heat. Perspiration fell down their bodies. The fish spirit made the powers jump from the father to the daughter.

Later, the father said, "I have no strength now." The father held his second daughter, then he called out to his wife.

The father told his daughter, "Now you are my son. Your big sister will marry, but you won't. Take my place."

The daughter became the leader of the _salam_ festival. Everything that the spirit fish and the father had said became true. While it was still at night, the father and daughter went to the forest. They took the fish and went to the house to hide it in a secret location.

The mother and big sister were forbidden to look at it. The big sister did not have strong powers thereafter. She became an ordinary woman. Later, she married. Her husband also became a participant in the _salam_ festival. However, the _salam_ was right in the heart of the young woman.

William Sabien

P. O. Box 385

Lae

Morobe Province

B874. Giant fish; C311.1.8. Tabu: looking at deity; D370M. Transformation: fish to man; D1275. Magic song; D1275+. Magic dance; D1726. Magic power from deity; D1731. Magic power received in dream; D1781. Magic results from singing; D1781+. Magic results from dancing; D1810.8.2. Information received through dream; D1964.6. Magic sleep induced by deity; D2000+. Magic confusion; F401.6. Spirit in human form; F420.1.3.2. Water-spirit as fish; F610.0.1. Remarkably strong woman; J157.0.1. Deity appears in dream and gives instructions or advice; P210. Husband and wife; P232. Mother and daughter; P234. Father and daughter; P252.1. Two sisters; P263. Brother-in-law; P264. Sister-in-law; T100. Marriage; W195. Envy

A Snake Swallowed a Man

(Wantok 643, October 16, 1986, page 29)

Long, long ago, there was a man who lived in a village called **Bunam** [**Banaro** People, **East Sepik** Province]. The name of this man was Budul. He lived with his two dogs. The names of the two dogs were Tupil and Mapil.

His dogs had learned well how to kill wild game in the forest. When Budul took the dogs and went to the forest, they would kill many animals, then they would carry them back to the village.

One day, Budul took the two dogs and they went to hunt for game in the forest. They killed many, many animals, then they walked back to the village. While they were walking along the trail, a heavy rain began to fall.

They looked for place to hide, then Budul saw the base of a big tree that had a hole in it. He took the two dogs and went inside the hole. The hole was quite large, so Budul put the game inside, made a fire and began to smoke the meat.

They sat by the fire and Budul cooked some meat, then he ate and gave some to the dogs. The rain continued to fall through the night, so after Budul smoked the meat he went to sleep. His dogs kept watch.

They did not know that a lake was near this tree, and that there was a gigantic snake that lived inside the lake.

While Budul slept soundly, he also snored loudly. The snake heard this and knew that it had game for itself nearby. Very quietly, it came out of the water. It heard the noise coming from the base of the tree.

The snake smelled him, quickly encircled the tree and swallowed Budul. In the time of the ancestors, men did not have knives. They sharpened bamboo until it was as sharp as a razor. Budul had used his knife to butcher the meat, then he had put it in his armband.

He was dead sleep, so he did not know that the snake had swallowed him. When he wanted to turn, he felt cold and could not turn because there was no space in which to do so. He woke up completely and saw that he must be inside something's belly.

Slowly, he felt for his knife and he knew that his knife was still in his armband. He felt that whatever had swallowed him was moving, so he knew that he must by lying in a snake's belly.

The snake began to move into the water. Budul lay inside the snake's belly and he felt like a pig moving [inside the belly], so he knew that he must cut the snake's belly immediately. Slowly, he put his hand down his armband and removed his bamboo knife.

Slowly, he cut the snake's belly, and it began to break open. The snake felt that something was turning in its belly, so it went down into the water.

It turned again and went to lie in the water. The man stretched and gave it to the snake once more with the bamboo knife. The snake's belly broke open and spilled him out. The man got up and ran to get his two dogs and the meat. Then they fled back to the village.

After this, the people of the village decided that whoever goes to sleep in the forest must not snore strongly, lest a snake hears your snoring and swallowed you.

Robin Peter Napi

P. O. Box 40

Kimbe

West New Britain Province

B875.1. Giant serpent; C735+. Tabu: snoring in forest; F911.7. Serpent swallows man; F912.2. Victim kills swallower from within by cutting; R210. Escapes

Three Brothers Killed the *Baratok*s

(Wantok 644, October 23, 1986, page 24)

Long, long ago, there was a family that lived in their own area. Long before this, when the parents were newlyweds, they left the big village and went very far away to live by themselves. They had a large pig fence. The woman husbanded the pigs and the man hunted for food.

Later, the woman gave birth to children. They had just five sons. The boys never saw people from other villages because they were too far away.

The eldest brother knew that there were people in faraway villages because when he was little, his parents took him with them to a huge festival that happened in a village. They walked for many days and nights to arrive at this village. It was on the other side of the mountain and forest, which was completely forbidden for traveling.

Their parents told them that it was a bad place on that side. They believed that whoever traveled to that part of the forest would never return home. They never found the bodies of people lost in that forest. So, their sons never went to that place when they traveled in the forest.

The brothers were no longer little boys now. The three elder brothers had become men. The two little ones still stayed with their parents.

One time, the elder brothers decided that the next day they would travel the forbidden forest. The three of them did not explain to their parents that they would travel there.

They carried their bows and arrows, then they left home when it was still morning. They followed the trail to the place where they always went, to the gardens and forests.

When they entered the deep forest, they decided to walk to the place where their parents forbade them to go. They had not seen men disappear, and they did not know that some men disappeared in this place.

They went to find out what it was that dwelled in this place, an ancestral ghost, a *masalai*, or a demon. They just went, but they did not find any place that was the slightest different which looked as if *masalai*s dwell there.

They found tree fruits and ate them, then they continued to walk. They walked and walked up a mountain, then they continued and one brother saw something like smoke rising from far away.

He stood and looked very carefully, then he called his two brothers. The brothers asked their elder, "Are there people there too or not?" The two of them pointed to the place where the smoke was rising.

The big brother replied, "That place is unknown. Papa and mama never took me there." The three brothers stood and watched the smoke rise high into the clouds.

The smoke came from very far away, so they just watched. They thought about going there, but if they walked there, it would take many days and nights on the trail.

They stopped looking, then they went back home. They walked and decided that they would work for a while, then they would lie to their parents that they would go and live for about a week in the forest to hunt for more wild game for themselves to eat. When they went to the forest, they would try to walk to the place where the smoke rose.

They stayed for a [week] at home, and prepared everything. They helped with the food for their parents and two little brothers, then they prepared to leave home and go to the forest.

They told the two old parents that they would travel the forest for a week. In the very early morning, they left home and walked away. They were gone for many days and nights on the trail. They walked and walked until they arrived at this place. They were all exhausted because they had no good food.

When they arrived, they did not see anyone. It was dark, so they just made do and slept in the forest on the side of the mountain. The next day, the brother who had seen the smoke still rising in the early morning walked around, near the place where they had slept.

This brother saw that below the mountain, there was another small, treeless mountain. It was covered only with sword grasses. He saw that fire was burning the grasses.

He thought, "It must be that it was only the sword grass when we saw the smoke."

He stood and watched, then he walked a little farther and saw the houses. However, there were no people. Quickly, he ran to tell his two brothers. They got up, made a little fire and cooked their food.

He called out, "I've seen the village over there. The smoke that we saw came from the sword grass down below."

Quickly, they carried their things and went towards the sword grass. They arrived and hid in a small patch of forest that the fire had not burned.

They saw two women attaching breadfruits to strings and hanging them from sticks. Another woman carried the breadfruits in a net bag.

The two women were very big. Their muscles were like those of men. When the three men saw the two women walking to the village, they got up and walked closer to the village too.

Then they just looked at the women. The men hid because they wanted to find out what kind of men and women lived in this place.

They saw that there were only women there. Their parents had not told them that this part of the earth had a different kind of woman living there.

These women often ate the flesh of men. In my language, this kind of woman is called *baratok*.

The tall women had big bones and many muscles. Men had never lived in this place before because the women's ancestors had eaten them. They would walk for many days and nights to villages that were very far away, take little girls, then carry them back to this place. Later, they would become big like the *baratok*s.

The three brothers stayed until the evening, then two women went to a small stream to fetch water. The three brothers surrounded the two women there, surprising them.

The brothers told the women that they would not fight or kill them, that they lived very far away, that they were looking for food in the forest and that they had come to this place. They lied to the two women.

That night, the two women took the men and hid them inside the house, [lest] the other women see them, kill them and eat their flesh.

The two women sent a message to the other women who were afraid to go looking for girls. They were afraid because people from the villages had killed many of their women.

They decided that they would just hide the three men in the house and they would take care of them. However, the other women who often ate human flesh could not know. These women supported the idea of marrying the three men.

They all made their decision, but some women were not happy. These were the women who patrolled around, looking for girls and killing men. These women did not like this idea.

The good women became angry and a great fight ensued. The women made a decision with the three men, and they killed the *baratok* women who strongly desired to eat the flesh of men.

The three brothers divided the women among themselves and married them. One brother married about ten women, the other two brothers did the same.

The ones who were girls, whom the bad women had stolen and whom the old women cared for, were marked for the two little brothers who lived with their parents.

Many months passed, and the three brothers with of their young women walked and arrived at the home of the mother, the father and the two little brothers.

They took the whole family and arrived at the place where the women lived. This became their home, with streams, sword grasses, and ponds, where there was much wild game and food.

The old father also married some of the old women for whom he lusted. Now, there are no longer *baratok*s who eat the flesh of men because these three brothers had killed them.

Steven Sangi

Wewak

East Sepik Province

A515.1. Culture heroes brothers; C612. Forbidden forest; C612+. Forbidden mountain; F112. Journey to Land of Women; F565.2. Remarkably strong women; G11.6. Man-eating woman; G34. Human child brought up by ogress becomes a man-eater; G346. Devastating monster; G510.4+. Hero overcomes devastating ogre; P210. Husband and wife; P231. Mother and son; P233. Father and son; P251.6.1. Three brothers; P251.6.2+. Five brothers; P261. Father-in-law; P262. Mother-in-law; P263. Brother-in-law; P264. Sister-in-law; P265+. Daughter-in-law; P294. Aunt; P297. Nephew; R10.3. Children abducted; R11. Abduction by monster (ogre); S110. Murders; T100. Marriage; T145.0.1. Polygyny; T580. Childbirth; W126. Disobedience; W157. Dishonesty; Z210. Brothers as heroes

A *Masalai* Was Caught in a Bandicoot Trap

(Wantok 645, October 30, 1986, page 24)

Long, long ago, in the time of the ancestors, there was a village called **Pependaug** in the Pindiu area of **Morobe** Province [**Kube** People?]. In this village, there lived a man named Honewec. His wife's name was Rosiwec.

Honewec excelled at making animal traps. He always made traps and killed wild game for himself and his wife, so they were never short of meat.

The Forest

One morning, Honewec awoke to go to the forest to place his traps. The name of this part of the forest is called Sipusec, and Honewec always went to this part of the forest to place his traps.

Honewec arrived at this part of the forest and set traps for bandicoots. The very last trap that he set was where a huge fig had broken and fallen down. This was a bandicoot trail, so Honewec prepared the last trap well, then he returned to the village.

In the evening, Honewec returned to his house. He arrived at the house and called for Rosiwec to open the house door. Honewec told his wife that he had set many traps, and that he would check on them in the early morning.

There were other people who lived near them in Pepedaug [Pependaug] Village. The two of them ate, then they went to sleep.

Near dawn, Honewec awoke then took his bow and went to check on his traps in the forest. He arrived at the first trap and saw a bandicoot stuck in it. He took the bandicoot and put it into his net bag.

He went to the second trap and he saw another bandicoot stuck in that one. He took it and put it in his net bag. Then he walked to the third trap

The Last Trap

He found a bandicoot stuck in that trap too, so he took it. He kept doing this until he came close to the last of his traps. When Honewec arrived at the last trap at the base of the fig tree, he saw a gigantic bandicoot stuck in his trap.

Honewec was ecstatic and said, "I've always made traps and taken small bandicoots. Now, I've won big and I've gotten this huge bandicoot."

Honewec did not look carefully at the bandicoot. Its body was like a bandicoot, but the bandicoot's face and nose looked like those of a frog.

He was just happy, so he took the bandicoot and put it in his net bag, then he turned back towards the village. He arrived in the village and told his wife Rosiwec to cook some pandanus fruit (*marita*).

His wife cooked the pandanus and drank some of the pandanus soup. Honewec arrived at the house, left the bag of bandicoots on the verandah, then went inside.

Honewec entered the house, then took the pandanus soup and drank it. He told his wife, "Go remove the bandicoots from the net bag, then remove the guts and cook them."

Rosiwec went outside and saw that the net bag was filled with bandicoots, so she was very happy. She worked at removing the marsupials. She worked and worked, then she pulled out the gigantic bandicoot that Honewec had taken by the base of the fig tree.

The Giant Bandicoot

When Rosiwec saw the face of the huge *masalai* bandicoot, she was terrified and screamed to Honewec, "What kind of bandicoot did you bring here?"

Honewec listened and said, "Just look at it. Do you kill game too?"

Rosiwec listened and did not say anything more. She butchered the marsupials, removed their guts and cooked them.

Honewec wanted to sit. He felt pain in his two knees. Later, he felt pain in his two elbows. Honewec then called out and his wife came to see what it was that was causing pain to her husband's arms and legs.

Honewec stood up. He wanted to take a step, but his legs missed and became very long. When he wanted to move his arms, the same thing happened. His two arms became very long.

Trembling Fiercely

Rosiwec saw her husband's legs and arms trembling fiercely. She went outside the house. She traveled to the other places and called people to go see her husband.

The people listened and went to see Honewec. They too were surprised to see that his legs and arms were very long. They asked him, and he told them about the bandicoot that he had taken at the base of the fig tree.

Then they knew that Honewec must have taken a *masalai* in his trap. They knew that it was not a real bandicoot because the bandicoot's face was like that of a frog.

The people of the village said that when a man goes to place a trap to catch bandicoots, he must check carefully where he puts the trap. Also, he must look carefully at the bandicoot before carrying it to the house.

This story comes from Pepedaug Village in the Pindiu area.

Belgut Ningki
Vunakabi Plantation
Rabaul
East New Britain Province

B90+. Frog-faced bandicoot; B871.2+. Giant bandicoot; D55.1+. Person's limbs grow larger; F401.3+. Spirit in bandicoot form; F490+. Masalai; P210. Husband and wife; Q228+. Punishment for killing animal spirit; Q551.3. Punishment: transformation

Why Is the Moon in the Sky?

(Wantok 646, November 6, 1986, page 28)

In the time of the ancestors, there was no moon in the sky. There lived a man and his wife who controlled the moon inside an earthen pot. This pot lay in their cooking hut.

The name of the old man was Labu, and his wife was Tuma. This old couple had two children. The son was Toka and the daughter was Raika.

At this time, the children did not know that their parents hid the moon inside a pot. The pot in which the old couple put the moon inside was very tall.

Whenever the parents wanted to go to the garden, or process sago, they would tell their two children, "Just don't open the tall pot because the food is inside the short pot."

One day, the parents left for the forest. The two children were playing around and became famished. They went inside the cooking hut and opened the lid of the tall one.

They looked inside and saw the incredibly bright moon inside the pot. When they saw this, they wanted to put their hands inside to get it, but the moon rose very quickly and jumped outside.

When the moon went outside, it escaped through the hut window. When the children wanted to grab it, the moon leapt up a coconut palm tree.

The little boy, Toka, saw this and followed the moon, up the coconut palm. However, the moon very quickly went to the crown of the palm tree, then it went all of the way up to the sky.

When it was in the sky, it had escaped completely. The children saw this and were speechless. They were afraid because they knew that their parents would be very angry when they returned to the village.

The old couple was processing sago in the forest and did not know that the moon had escaped the earthen pot.

When they went to the stream to rinse the sago, they saw the moon's reflection in the stream. They turned and saw it up in the sky.

The old mother cooked some food, then ate. The children were terribly afraid. They did not tell their parents that they had opened the pot and that the moon had escaped.

The children finished eating, then they fell dead asleep. Very quietly, the old couple went to them and killed them. After they killed them, the old couple made a bonfire and threw the bodies of their children, Toka and Raika, into the fire.

Poor Toka and Raika were dead, but because of them, the moon is up in the sky. Before, the old man and woman hid the moon carefully inside the pot and people on the earth always looked up in darkness.

Alois Yaman Biku
Tambunum [**Tambanum**] Village [**Iatmul** People]
Middle Sepik
East Sepik Province

A750+. Moon escapes to sky from captivity in pot; A754. Moon kept in box; P210. Husband and wife; P231. Mother and son; P232. Mother and daughter; P233. Father and son; P253. Sister and brother; Q325. Disobedience punished; Q411. Death as punishment; R210. Escapes; R260. Pursuits; S11.3. Father kills child; S12.2. Cruel mother kills child; S110. Murders; W126. Disobedience

A Marsupial's (*Sikau's*)
Sorrow Helped a Man

(Wantok 647, November 13, 1986, page 23)

Long, long ago, a marsupial (*sikau*) stole a sleeping baby along with the baby's net bag. The marsupial carried the baby and ran away into the forest. It was a very nice, sunny day.

The name of the baby's mother was Tauaire. She had just given birth to the baby. Afterwards, she had carried the baby in a net bag into the forest while she looked for food.

She had hung up the net bag on the branch of a tree, then Tauaire worked at cutting the forest for a new garden.

While the mother had been working, the baby cried and cried for milk, then the baby fell dead asleep. He had also lost his voice completely. While he had been crying, his mother was unable to hear his voice.

At this time, there was a marsupial who flew down to where the baby was. The marsupial heard the baby quietly crying, as if he had lost his voice. This was because he had been crying for so long and his mother had been working very hard and did not hear the baby. The marsupial thought that the baby was sleeping quietly.

The marsupial approached to look at the baby. She was sorry and said, "So, mama doesn't care about her baby. I'll carry him and give him milk."

The marsupial went and hid, then saw the baby's mother working. The marsupial went back to the baby and thought of stealing him. She went back a second time and hid. The marsupial saw the mother working very hard and not thinking about her baby.

The marsupial went to the baby and said, "So, your mama doesn't care about you. Come, I'll carry you and take good care of you."

The marsupial quickly pulled the sling of the net bag, making it shorter and very tight. Then she hung the net bag on her neck and departed.

The marsupial carried him past mountains and rivers, and went very far. When the marsupial arrived home, her child and her child's father were shocked. The father marsupial was elated and treated the baby very well.

The mother marsupial sang to the baby that night, and the baby slept very well. He did not cry at all for milk, either.

The poor real mother of the baby tried very hard to find her baby by the garden. She went back to the village and told her husband. The people of the village traveled the whole forest, mountains and rivers, day and night, to find the baby. They searched for the baby for many weeks. Later, they decided that a wild pig or *masalai* must have carried the baby away, then killed and eaten him.

Some months passed, then the villagers made a big feast to remove their sorrows and troubles about the baby. Afterwards, they forgot completely about the baby.

The marsupial became the baby's mother. When he cried for milk, the marsupial would pour water from a tree leaf and performed her powerful songs and dances to the baby. The baby would drink the water and sleep quietly. His belly was always full.

The she-marsupial took care of the baby, and he became completely grown. The son grew up and helped his [foster] parents work in the garden and look for food. The she-marsupial quickly thought of things.

She hung the net bag upon her neck and went to a nearby village. She flew down then stole axes and knives that people had left outside their houses. She carried them back to her home. Before long, the son began to use these things to cut trees in the forest and to find food too.

The marsupial mother told the story to her son about how he had arrived. The son listened to this story and was very troubled. He wanted to see his real parents.

However, he could not go yet because his marsupial mother wanted him to become a real man and to marry first. Afterwards, he could go to his parents.

The marsupial mother traveled to villages. She found a very beautiful young woman. She watched this woman until the woman walked around. When she went to one place, the marsupial quickly went and blew in her ear. This was the signal that the marsupial mother made to mark the woman for her son.

Another time, the marsupial mother went to another place that was far away from where she had found the beautiful young woman. Quickly she put a mark upon her face. It was another signal.

Later, she returned and told her son, "It's time now for you to leave me to find a good life for yourself. Until now, I've taken care of you. I want you to walk along this trail until you arrive at a village that has a woman. At another village, there is another young woman with a mark on her face."

The marsupial told him about the marks on the two women in the two villages, "They can't marry another man. Never mind if they don't see you, they'll have thoughts of a man who lives in a faraway place. When they see you, they'll love you completely."

The mother marsupial told him stories on another morning, then he walked away. He slept many nights. During the days, he was in villages.

One day, he arrived at a village and found a woman who had the mark on her ear that had been put there by his marsupial mother. The man took the woman and walked to another village that was still farther away.

At this village, he immediately met the other woman. The man took the two young women and again walked for days and nights, back to his marsupial mother.

The marsupial mother explained to him that he must return to the life of real people in his own village. The marsupial mother gave him all of her stories and powers. Some time later, the two women both had children.

The man thought about walking to his village. They walked day and night for many, many months, leaving the trail. Then they approached the village.

The marsupial mother had told him that near the village there was a mark like a breadfruit garden and there was a stream that the people often used. These things were there. One day, they met some women and children bathing in a stream, so they also went to bathe.

Some of the people of the village saw them. The villagers had never seen these types of faces before, this family that was [now] in their garden. A woman in the garden saw them first and ran to tell her husband in the garden that there was a different kind of people from another village bathing in their stream.

The man went and asked the two women and their children. They said that they were the wives of a man looking for his village. However, the two people in the garden did not understand that the marsupial had taken him. They went about crazily.

Later, the real man arrived and told the story to the two people. They were shocked and immediately went to tell the old couple, the man's parents. The parents went to hold their son. They held the two wives and their children, then they cried and were happy.

Later, the man told the real story of his life. Afterwards, the man lived in his village with his family.

[Anonymous]

B40+. Flying marsupial; B211.2.12K+. Speaking marsupial; B535.0.16K+. Marsupial as nurse for child; D1355.13. Love-spot; D1737.1. Magic power from mother; D1781. Magic results from singing; D1781+. Magic results from dancing; D1900. Love induced by magic; K300. Thefts and cheats — general; P210. Husband and wife; P230. Parents and children; P231. Mother and son; P233. Father and son; P271. Foster father; P272. Foster mother; P275. Foster son; P291. Grandfather; P292. Grandmother; R13.1+. Abduction by marsupial; S110. Murders; T10. Falling in love; T145.0.1. Polygyny; T580. Childbirth

A Ghost Helped the Little Sister

(Wantok 648, November 20, 1986, page 30)

Long, long ago, in the time of the ancestors, the mountains and forests of **Pindiu** were not quiet [**Kube** People, **Morobe** Province]. The ancestral men often fought and fought. The fights between tribes were huge. It was in the ancestors' hearts at this time.

In one village, there lived two sisters. When they were young girls, their parents had died, so they lived by themselves. This was before they had gone to work in gardens, hunt for wild game, burn sword grasses, or do other work that people usually did. When their house was wrecked or broken down, they would cut new trees and leaves then fix the house.

The young men of their village often [coveted] them, but the men were afraid to tell them of their desires. This was because the two women were very strong. They were as strong as men were, with big bones and real muscles, be-cause they never just did the work of women. They often did the work of men, and they excelled at it.

One day, a message came from a faraway village that a man from another village would come to see the two of them. On this day, the two of them did not work, they just rested in the house.

One sister sat and made a net bag. The other sister did some work around the house. Then the man arrived for them. This man looked very similar to their father. The man held their hands and cried. He told them, "I'm your paternal uncle, your father's little brother. Another woman brought me to a faraway village as her son."

He said, "I no longer belong to this village. I often thought of your father. Not long ago, I heard that you are my brother's daughters. You're not sons, but you work very hard. I heard this kind of story and I walked from very far away to find you. I want you to come with me to my village. I have three grown sons, and they also have two sisters. All of you can live together in one place."

The two women thought hard about their work, their food garden, their father's land, and all of the parts of the forest that they controlled that their father had left them.

He told them that a brother would return later with them to take care of them until they married. But now, he wanted them to go see their cousins.

The next day, in the early morning, the two women and their uncle walked away then arrived at the faraway village. The uncle's kin, the mother, the three brothers, and the two sisters met them.

They were sorry for the two young women. They celebrated and welcomed them. They held the two of them and prevented them from returning to their village.

Their lives were very good with the father of the five children. The father told stories about the two women's father and himself who had the same mother and father. Another woman, his foster mother, had taken him and gone to another village.

The two women did not leave. They stayed for a very long time. The big sister was attracted to a young man from the village. They arranged to be married. The big sister married this young man from the village. The other sister had not found a man yet.

Some time passed, then the big sister, the little sister and one of their uncle's sons went to the two sisters' real village. The uncle sent another small man [uncle?] to take the place of the two women's father. They raised their family, and became well known. When the two women married, they went to the man's family.

There was a man who was ruined with desire to marry the big sister. He was furious at the other man from the other village who had married her.

He said, "Why is there no good man from this village? She found a man from very far away and married him."

The man revealed his feelings to his kin about this. They wanted to start a fight with the big sister's husband. The man's kin from the other village heard this. They quickly prepared all of their things for fighting. They decorated themselves well for the fight.

Talk went back and forth, then the fight broke out. This was because the two women married far away rather than marrying a man from their own village. The men from their own village who liked them had been too spineless to ask them to marry.

So, the courageous men of the other village took the big sister. Not long after that, the other sister also married in the faraway village.

A great fight broke out. The lustful man who had hidden was furious. He killed the big sister and her husband together. Afterwards, there was a great mourning. The man had been jealous because the big sister had married a man from the other village and because he had not married her.

The little sister was very troubled. She cried day and night. She put the bodies of her sister and brother-in-law on top of a tree branch.

Some weeks passed and the worrying overcame the little sister. She went and sat under the place where the bodies were. The liquid from her big sister's body fell on top of her skin.

Every day, she would put mud on top of her skin and sit underneath her sister's body. Time passed. Then one day, the big sister's ghost appeared as a woman and told her little sister, "I speak to you, little sister, you must leave this village and go far away. You cannot return. Go very far away and marry a good man, then make your family. That is the complete way of life. Forget about this village. If you ignore what I say, you'll die like me. The men of this village are jealous and will kill you."

The little sister was troubled and cried. Some time later, she quietly took her big belongings and walked back to her uncle's village. Later, she left this village and went far away. She married and lived there entirely.

John Komas
Kieta
North Solomons Province

E325. Dead sister's friendly return; E363.3. Ghost warns the living; E425.1. Revenant as woman; E545. The dead speak; F565.2. Remarkably strong women; J1050. Attention to warnings; P210. Husband and wife; P233. Father and son; P234. Father and daughter; P252.1. Two sisters; P253.0.3+. Two sisters and three brothers; P263. Brother-in-law; P264. Sister-in-law; P272. Foster mother; P275. Foster son; P295. Cousins; P293. Uncle; P298. Niece; P681+. Mourning customs: earth on body; Q200+. Exogamy punished; Q411. Death as punishment; R213. Escape from home; S110. Murders; T10. Falling in love; T80. Tragic love; T100. Marriage; V61.10. Corpses exposed in tree; W181. Jealousy

Ninah and Omabarara

(Wantok 649, November 27, 1986, page 29)

Long, long ago, there was a village called Yame [**Iame**]. In this village, there lived many men, women and children.

The men of the village made a big spirit house for themselves. They took a man from another village, and he was like their laborer.

They gave the name Ninah to this young man because he belonged to another village. He was a worthless, small-boned man. Ninah's tasks were to cut firewood, cook food and fetch water for the spirit house. He also often went to the forest and fetched leaves for the men to smoke.

Laborer

The men of the village often made Ninah do their labor and they were not the slightest bit sorry for him. When they killed a pig, all of the men of the village would sweat to plant sticks at the gable of the long house where they would kill the pigs [tethered to the sticks].

They gathered the firewood and stones, then made a platform for the big feast. When the men did this work, poor Ninah did the housework.

One day, Ninah tired of working in the men's house and ran away to the forest. Poor Ninah was very troubled and rested from the men's work in the village.

One day, Ninah went looking for leaves to smoke, but he could not find any. He searched and searched until he entered the very deep forest. He kept going until he left the places that men knew of, and went deeper still into the deep forest.

Exhausted

Ninah arrived at the base of a tree and was exhausted, so he sat and rested. His eyes shut and he fell asleep. He fell dead asleep, then when he awoke, he saw that he was in a part of the forest where he had never been before.

When he looked around, he saw that a gigantic pig was lying at the base of a tree. They pig was dead asleep, so Ninah quietly went and held the pig.

He rubbed the pig's skin back and forth, then the pig woke up and opened her eyes. When the pig saw Ninah, she spoke to Ninah in a special language.

The pig told Ninah that her name was Omabarara. Ninah sat and listened to the pig's story. Later, Ninah told Omabarara about how the men of Yame Village had treated him. He also told the story of how all of the men from the village were preparing for a great day of pig killing. He said that he was searching for leaves for smoking, and he had arrived at this part of the forest.

Omabarara told Ninah that while the men were working at fixing the long [ceremonial] house, he must also make a house and then [there would be] many sticks for killing pigs.

Get Up and Go

Ninah listened to the huge pig, then he returned to the village. When he arrived, he saw that the men were finishing their work of planting the sticks. Quickly, Ninah also prepared some sticks then planted two hundred, just as the pig Omabarara had told him to do.

When the men saw that Ninah was planting many, many sticks, they laughed hysterically at him and spat at him. However, Ninah did not care. He kept planting the sticks until he finished all of his work.

Later, he went back to the spirit house and did his work. When Ninah finished all of the work in the spirit house, he returned to the forest and found Omabarara, the pig, waiting for him. He asked the pig to follow him to the village. While they were walking on the trail, Omabarara told Ninah to tie her to the one hundred ninety-ninth stick.

When they arrived at the village, Ninah tied the pig to the one hundred ninety-ninth stick. The pig was huge, like a cow, so the people of the village were shocked to see the pig. They were terrified of the pig and Ninah too.

When the time approached to slaughter the pigs, Ninah took everything that he had prepared. The other men of the village looked at him.

Pig Slaughter

It was close to the time for slaughtering the pigs. Ninah prepared everything, then just waited. The other men of the village saw this and they asked him whether he could repay all of his debt with just the one pig.

Ninah replied, "I can."

At night, all of the men laid down two hundred pigs, tethered to the sticks that Ninah had planted. However the big pig, Omabarara, was no longer there. She had just disappeared.

Ninah saw this and was very happy. He killed all of the pigs, then shared it with everyone who had gathered in the village for the pig slaughter. The people were very happy and spoke to him. They asked him to become the leader of the village.

The people told Ninah that he was the leader of Yame because he had many more pigs than the other men of the village did. After this, Ninah lived well as the leader of the village, and of the Yame Clan.

Rimba Nipa
Yame Village [**Kewa** People]
Kaugua [Kagua]
Southern Highlands Province

B184.3.1. Magic boar; B211.2+. Speaking boar; B215+. Pig language; B216. Knowledge of animal languages; B443.5. Helpful wild hog (boar); B871.1.2. Giant boar; L113.1. Menial hero; L300. Triumph of the weak; P160. Beggars; R210. Escapes; V112.1. Spirit huts; Z71.16+. Formulistic number: one hundred ninety-nine

A Pond Arose at the Place Where the *Masalai* Died
(Wantok 650, December 4, 1986, page 25)

Long ago, in **Kogaru** Village, in the Bena [Benabena] area inside **Eastern Highlands** Province, there was a huge tree [**Benabena** People]. A big *masalai* owned the huge tree. This *masalai* only ate children.

The tree was near a trail on which people often traveled to fetch drinking water and to bathe. When the big people went to the gardens, the children would go to bathe at this stream. Then the *masalai* would come and kill one or two of them then eat them. The men of the village were worried because they saw that many of their little children had disappeared.

One day, the men gathered in the village. They decided that when the little boys went to bathe, a man would go to hide and watch. This was because they had discovered that the children were disappearing there.

In the morning, the children went to bathe and one man followed them. The man hid in the grasses and watched. Then he saw the big *masalai* come outside of the tree and [… Then the men took] all of their spears and axes and went to the tree.

They stood around and began to cut. The tree fell down and they cut it again in the middle. When the tree fell, it broke in the middle. They saw the *masalai* lying there. The *masalai* saw these men and said, "I know you'll kill me, but I want to talk to whoever saw me kill the children and told you."

When the man approached the *masalai*, the *masalai* said, "Take all of my good things that you like and give some to your kin."

The men of the village heard this and were very sorry for the *masalai*. Many of them did not want to kill the *masalai*. When they cut the *masalai*, they saw that the *masalai* did not have much muscle, but was full of fat. They left him there and went away.

One week passed and some young men traveled to the place where they had killed the *masalai*. They saw a clean pond there.

Today, this pond is still there. Even when there is drought, the pond never dries up.

This story comes from Kogaru in the Bena area of Eastern Highlands Province. Daniel Igo sent this story. He is a student at Dauli Teachers' College in Tari, Southern Highlands Province.

A920.1.0.1. Origin of particular lake; E636. Reincarnation as water; F490+. Masalai; G312.3. Flesh-eating spirits live in trees; G346. Devastating monster; G512. Ogre killed; S110. Murders

Two Brothers Were Angry over Pandanus
(Wantok 651, December 11, 1986, page 25)

Long ago, in the time of the ancestors, there lived two brothers. Their names were Ailina and Ko'aku.

One day, Ailina was cutting some pandanus (*karuka*) nuts in the forest. Afterwards, he went and put them in the house. The pandanus nuts were ripe, and Ailina called out for his brother Ko'aku to remove the bad pandanus nuts, put them in one place, then put the good ones in another place.

After that, Ailina went to look for more pandanus. Ko'aku sat quietly, removing the pandanus nuts and dividing them between good and bad.

However, the good-for-nothing did not work correctly. He looked at the good pandanus nuts and desired them. He ate some of the good pandanus nuts. Ko'aku kept at it. That day, his belly became bloated from the pandanus nuts.

In the afternoon, Ko'aku thought that his brother Ailina would be coming back to the house soon. So, Ko'aku quickly removed the skins and rubbish from the pandanus, then he pretended to work. When Ko'aku saw his big brother Ailina, he pretended to straighten his back and throw out his arms and legs like a man who had worked for a long time whose body was stiff. But no, he just felt tired because his belly was bloated with pandanus nuts.

Ailina went and looked at Ko'aku's work, then he asked him, "Where did you put the good pandanus nuts?"

Ko'aku replied, "It's just these. Many were bad and I threw them away."

Ailina listened and said, "You're lying. I know you finished all of the pandanus. When I arrived, you quickly arranged everything then pretended to sit and work."

Ailina then he slapped his brother, Ko'aku. He said, "I'm your mother and father, and you just live here. I hunt for food and you just swallow it."

Ko'aku wanted to reply with his hand, but Ailina beat him and down he went.

Ailina told Ko'aku, "Mom and dad are dead. So when I go hunting for food, you must stay and take care of everything in the house because you're not big enough to walk in the forest with me to find food. I always work hard and you just finish off the food."

Ailina finished talking, then he went inside the house. Blood flowed from Ko'aku's nose. He cried and took all of his things then he began to walk away.

Ailina did not know that Ko'aku had run away from him, his brother. He looked for Ko'aku, but he did not find him. So, he thought that his brother had just gone away to cry. He thought that when he cooled off, he would return to the village.

However that night, and the next day and night, Ko'aku did not return to the village, so Ailina began to worry. He searched and searched, but Ko'aku was very far away.

Ko'aku walked and walked. At night, he slept at the bases of big trees or in caves. At night, he would rest and during the day, he walked swiftly on the trails. He went up mountains and climbed tall trees to see where he was going. He walked to the plains.

When he arrived at the plains, he followed mountains and went to a river. He walked on the flat side, then he went to a very big body of water. When he saw that he had arrived at this water, his vision shortened because there was no way around it.

This body of water was the sea. Ko'aku had carried some pandanus fruits and other things while he was walking. He had thrown big pieces of pandanus on the trail. The pandanus arrived at the beach.

However, this pandanus did not bear nuts. It only gave good leaves, leaves that people use to make mats and baskets nowadays.

Ko'aku had arrived at the beach and lived there henceforth. He no longer thought about returning to his village and seeing his brother.

It was just the anger over the pandanus that made the big brother beat the little brother. Then the little brother ran away to find a good, new place to live henceforth. He was no longer a mountain man. The big brother, Ailina, was a mountain man. Ko'aku became a shore-dweller.

Vincent Haihi
Burauta Village
Tairora [People]
Kainantu
Eastern Highlands Province

A2681.15K2. Origin of pandanus tree; P251.5. Two brothers; P251.5.3. Hostile brothers; Q272. Avarice punished; Q325. Disobedience punished; R213. Escape from home; W126. Disobedience; W151. Greed

Mombi Kula's Child

(Wantok 652, December 18, 1986, page 21)

Long, long ago, in the time of the ancestors, there were two old women who lived in a village. The names of the old women were Kula and Mombi. Kula had a little daughter named Nakas, but Mombi did not have children.

Mombi was older than Kula, so when Kula went looking for food for the two of them, Mombi would take care of the little daughter, Nakas.

They lived very happily for a while, then one time they decided to search for crayfish in the river. At night, the two women took a canoe and paddled away.

Kula carried her daughter Nakas. When they went inside the canoe, Mombi paddled. She paddled and paddled until they arrived at the place where they wanted to search for crayfish. When they arrived, Kula told Mombi to watch the girl while she went into the water to search for crayfish. Mombi watched Nakas, while her mother Kula went into the water and searched for crayfish.

When the girl cried, she came out and gave her breast to her. Then Mombi went down again and searched for crayfish. After that, Kula told her to keep an eye on Nakas while she went inside the water.

When Kula went inside to search for crayfish, Mombi broke off Nakas' hand and began to eat it. The girl cried and screamed for her mother, Kula. Mombi lied and said that a mosquito must have bitten her and caused her to cry.

She said, "You search for crayfish and I'll put her to sleep again." Mombi said this, then continued to eat the hand of poor baby Nakas.

Then when her mother went fairly far away, Mombi ate the baby's two legs. The poor baby cried. Her mother heard her and called out to her.

Mombi heard this and lied by shouting to Kula, "Nakas must be hungry. Don't worry, I'll give her some food now." This old ghost Mombi said this, then quickly killed the baby.

The baby stopped crying and her mother, Kula, thought that her baby was asleep. The poor mother thought this and continued to search for crayfish. At this time, Mombi feasted on the flesh of the baby, Nakas, then she hid the baby's head inside a basket and shoved it inside the canoe.

Poor Kula finished searching for crayfish, then she went up to the canoe, rested and smoked. She put her basket inside and did not see her baby, so she asked Mombi about her.

Mombi lied, "I put the baby inside the canoe." Kula listened to this and sat well, then she wanted to look inside the canoe at a basket. She opened the basket and saw her baby's head.

She was furious but she did not say anything. She lied to Mombi. They spoke of paddling to another place and searching for crayfish. Kula took the paddle and paddled right in the middle of the river. She told Mombi to go down and search for the crayfish.

Mombi went out and Kula paddled back. She left the ghost woman, Mombi, stuck in the middle of the water. Kula left Mombi there and paddled back to the village.

Mombi stayed in this place because she did not have a way to return to the village. Then a big crocodile came ashore at this place. The crocodile went up and slept with Mombi. The name of this crocodile was Mandagu.

Every day, the crocodile would do this. After a while, Mombi gave birth to two eggs. When the two eggs broke open, one was a crocodile and the other was an eagle. In my language we call [this bird], _kawi_.

The crocodile child went down to the water and became the ruler of the river. The eagle child flew up to the sky where it was the king of birds. It made its aerie on top of a huge tree. Later, it went down and carried its mother up with itself.

The father crocodile, Mandagu, often traveled in the water, killing fish and other kinds of wild game. Then the eagle child would fly down and take the game to give to its mother, Mombi.

John Wangi
Popondeta [Popondetta]
Northern [Oro] Province

B240.15+. Crocodile as king of river animals; B242.1.1. Eagle king of birds; B552. Man carried by bird; B613.2. Crocodile paramour; B632. Animal offspring from marriage to animal; E425.1+. Revenant as old woman; G11.10. Cannibalistic spirits; P230. Parents and children; P232. Mother and daughter; Q211.4. Murder of children punished; Q215. Cannibalism punished; Q467K+. Abandonment in river as punishment; S110+. Eaten alive; S142. Person thrown into the water and abandoned; T565. Woman lays an egg; T587. Birth of twins; T685. Twins

Eagles Took the Marsupial's (*Kapul*'s) White Skin

(Wantok 653, December 25, 1986, page 22)

Long, long ago, there were two married brothers who lived in their small village. Their marriages were not very good because the big brother coveted the little brother's wife.

Oh my, the little brother did not know that the big brother lusted for his wife. No, he was usually friendly and helpful to his big brother. He helped with various kinds of work.

One time, the big brother asked the little brother to travel the deep forest with him to hunt for wild game. The little brother agreed. They met and then set off for the deep forest.

They hunted for game from the early morning until the afternoon. However, they did not kill a single animal. It was getting a little dark.

They went back towards the village. They walked a little farther then the big brother saw a white marsupial (*kapul*) [probably the spotted cuscus, *Spilocuscus maculatus maculatus* (Flannery, 1995a: 181-182)] sitting on top of a *galip* tree branch. The tree's base was very large. The tree went up very high before there were any branches.

The big brother told the little brother, "Climb the *galip* tree and kill that white marsupial. The base of the tree is too big, so you must hold this vine to climb the tree."

The little brother held the vine very firmly and climbed up to the *galip* tree branch. He looked down and saw that his big brother had cut off the way that he had used to climb the tree. The poor little brother was troubled by this and cried terribly.

He stayed on top of the tree branch for a very long time. He was completely famished. He ate the *galip* tree bark, then he used his spear to kill the white marsupial. The big brother left him and walked back home.

The little brother used a strong bamboo razor to carefully remove the marsupial's skin. He hung the marsupial's skin on a small branch of the tree. Then he ate all of the marsupial meat.

He ignored that the flesh was bloody. He was hungry and just ate it. He did not have a way to descend to the ground, so he stayed for a little while and saw a bird come to perch on another branch of the tree.

The bird cast its eyes upon the white skin of the marsupial. The bird also saw the man near the marsupial's skin. Then the bird spoke to the man.

The bird said, "Please, I'd like that marsupial skin." However the man said, "No, that's my marsupial skin. You can't take it." They argued back and forth, then the man had a good idea.

The man told the bird, "Friend, if you help me, I'll give you the white marsupial skin."

The bird replied, "Friend, how do you want me to help you?" The man said, "I want you to carry me down to the ground." The bird said, "OK, my friend, stay here. I'll call my bird sisters and brothers. Then we'll gather together and help you."

The bird flew and called out for the other birds, big and small to come. The bird explained that there was a man on top of the *galip* tree with something nice. If all of the birds helped this man, they could take pieces of this nice thing.

All of the birds followed the first bird and flew up to the tree branch. They explained to the man that they were ready to help because he had something desirous. The man told them to fly down to the river and carry a broad stone back to him.

All of the birds flew together down to the river. They gathered, took a broad stone and flew it back to the man. The birds asked him what else he wanted.

The man said, "Can you carry me and bring me to my home?" The birds said, "Don't worry. This broad stone was very heavy. We'll put you on the stone and carry you directly to your door."

The birds really believed this. He sat well and the birds carried him down with the white marsupial skin. They dropped him off directly at the door of his house.

The birds wanted to fly back, but the man called to them to wait a little. This was because he wanted to make a small [feast] for them first.

The little brother was there now. The big brother was shocked to see him again because he had thought that the little brother was dead. The big brother had befouled the little brother's wife. However, the little brother did not know about this sin and he was untroubled.

The little brother told his wife and his big brother's wife to go to the garden. The two women went and told the other women from the other villages too. They each went to their gardens and took sweet potatoes, taros, bananas, leafy greens, papayas, ripe bananas and other foods.

The foods arrived. Then they had a huge feast. The birds were very happy to swallow so much food. Later, they thanked the little brother and prepared to fly back.

However, the little brother stopped them again. He wanted to show them his great gratitude. He cut the white marsupial skin into many small pieces. He fastened a piece of marsupial skin to the neck of each bird.

The number of pieces came up short for the last two birds. These birds were troubled and furious. They went to the little brother's new garden. They took soot from the fire and rubbed it upon their necks and bodies. All of the other birds were happy with their presents, and they flew away. They left the wide stone with the little brother.

Today, we can see many eagles with white marks on their necks. These are on one group of eagles. The other group has black necks and bodies. These are the kin of the two birds who missed receiving the marsupial skin.

The wide stone that the birds had carried to the village is there now at Nokori [**Nungori**] Village, near Sassoya [Sassoia] Catholic Mission Station in Wewak, **East Sepik** Province [**Boiken** People]. It looks as if Nokori Village is the old village of the big and little brothers from long ago.

The custom of fighting also arose between the brothers of this area by Sassoya [Sassoia]. The custom of the big brother lusting for the wife of the little brother also arose in this area, and also in many other areas of Papua New Guinea today. We probably still follow these ancestral customs, just like this, do we not?

Arnold Wafi

Arawa

North Solomons Province

[Mr. Wafi also wrote the ancestor story in *Wantok* #345, which is similar to this one.]

A977.5. Origin of particular rock; A1556.3. Origin of adultery; A1599.11.1. Origin of war; A2411.2. Origin of color of bird; A2411.2.2. Origin of color of falconiformes; B211.3. Speaking bird; B450. Helpful birds; B455.3. Helpful eagle; B542.1. Bird flies with man to safety; B542.1.1. Eagle carries man to safety; B552. Man carried by bird; D1520.36. Transportation by magic stone; K2211.0.1. Treacherous elder brother(s); P210. Husband and wife; P251.5. Two brothers; P251.5.3. Hostile brothers; P263. Brother-in-law; P264. Sister-in-law; Q53. Reward for rescue; R49.1. Captivity in tree; R51.1. Prisoners starved; R110. Rescue of captive; S73.1.4. Fratricide motivated by love-jealousy; S143.2. Abandonment in tall tree; T10. Falling in love; T92.10. Rival in love killed; T481. Adultery; W27. Gratitude; W181. Jealousy

Two Brothers Were Angry Over Beans

(Wantok 654, January 8, 1987, page 19)

Long ago, in the time of the ancestors, two brothers lived near Mount Agakamatasa by **Okapa** [Village, **Fore** People, **Eastern Highlands** Province]. They were still together because they could not find their family.

Close to their house, there was a lot of trash that the two of them had piled up. One day, a small vine grew on top of the trash. The brothers saw this vine and thought that it was just an ordinary vine, like the kinds that grew around in the forest. Another morning, the big brother awoke and saw that the vine had a different kind of leaf on it. He had never seen this kind of vine before.

The big brother thought hard, "It would be better if I attached a long stick nearby so that the vine could hold onto it and grow on it." The big brother did this. The vine grabbed the stick and grew upwards.

Some weeks later, the vine grew to be a tree, and four bean pods hung from it. The four pods were edible. The big brother saw this first. He told his little brother not to take the beans that hung there. They took good care of the bean plant, and it bore more pods. Many more pods hung from this big bean plant.

One day, the big brother told the little brother that he would go looking for some food and also do some work in the forest. He told the little brother not to take a single pod, that he must watch the bean plant carefully.

It was a new thing in the life of these two of them, taking care of the vine that bore pods. The vine was very unusual compared to the vines of the forest.

However, the little brother broke his promise. Before, he had never cared about breaking open a bean pod and eating it. He wanted to know if it would be sweet or if it was just a forest vine growing near their house.

When the big brother was in the forest, the little brother went quietly and broke a pod, then he cooked it in the fire. He tried eating just a little and he swallowed it. Oh my, it was delicious. He wanted to cook the bark of the bean plant in the fire. He just threw the bark in, then he went to the clearing. The little brother was terrified now.

A Brother Falls Down

When the big brother arrived at the house, he saw that the fire had bark from the bean plant in it. He went to check on the bean vine and he saw that the leaves had fallen.

The big brother was furious. He was angry and beat his little brother. Then they fought until the big brother turned and cut the little brother's leg with an axe.

The little brother fell down and rolled around. He was in great pain. He took all of his things. He looked for vines and tied them to his leg. Then he took all of his little things and left the village.

Two Women

He held a stick and walked away slowly. He slept in the forest for days, looking for forest medicine and affixing it to the big wound that he had on his leg. Later, he felt a little better. He held a wooden stick and walked slowly until it was dark, then he slept in the middle of the trail.

He did this for a while, then he went very far away. He saw a house with two women living by themselves. The house stood in the middle of the very deep forest, but their house was in the center of a big garden that was just packed with bean plants.

The man went towards them. The women looked at him and were very sorry for him. They took some more forest medicine and affixed it to the leg that the axe had cut. They gave him food. After he ate, he sat and told the story of the fight with his big brother.

The little brother saw that that there were many, many beans outside, like a plantation. When he saw this, he was troubled. He cried terribly. It was just because of this that he carried great shame and because of this that he had become an enemy of his brother.

Later, the women told him that the bean that grew at the brothers' house must have been carried there by the wind from their plantation.

The little brother did not return to the big brother. He married the two women and lived at this place where the bean garden was.

Kuta Patoro

Okapa Community School

Goroka

Eastern Highlands Province

P210. Husband and wife; P251.5. Two brothers; P251.5.3. Hostile brothers; Q325. Disobedience punished; R213. Escape from home; T100. Marriage; T145.0.1. Polygyny; W126. Disobedience

Urahi Befouled the Snake's Hand Drum

(Wantok 655, January 15, 1987, page 23)

Long, long ago, in the time of the ancestors, there was a man and his child who lived in a village. The name of the man was Urahi. He and the child lived in Yakwal [**Wegior**] Village [**Abelam** People, **East Sepik** Province].

One day, Urahi told his child that the two of them would go to sharpen stone axes by the river. So in the morning, they awoke and went to the Wolmtombom River.

They arrived there and worked at sharpening their stone axes. Urahi worked at sharpening his axes for a while, then an axe fell into the river.

Very Deep

The water where they sat was very deep, so Urahi could not see where his axe had fallen. He worried a lot about his axe, so he sat and thought hard.

He told his child that he would go to cut a long piece of bamboo [to breathe with], then he would return to try to find his stone axe. Urahi rose slowly and went to cut a long piece of bamboo, then he returned to the river.

Urahi put the bamboo down into the river, held the bamboo and prepared to descend. He told his child, "Don't worry. I'll go down and get my axe, then I'll come up."

The father said this, then he went down into the river. When he went down, he saw the axe handle stuck to a fig tree with edible leaves. He put his hand down to get it, but he had arrived at a special place underneath the water.

The Snakes' Lair

The place where Urahi had arrived was the snakes' lair. When he arrived, they were sleeping about, because it was at night that they sang and danced until dawn broke.

Urahi traveled very quietly to this place. He saw the snakes lying there dead asleep. Their hand drums were lying about there too. He took his axe, but he coveted the hand drums.

He walked and walked then he saw a very handsome hand drum. Quietly, Urahi went and took the hand drum, then he quickly went back up to the dry ground. He took his child, then they returned to the village.

When they arrived at the village, he dried the hand drum well, then put it away. They cooked some food, then they ate. Urahi took the snake's hand drum down and tried beating it. Oh my, the hand drum's sound was sweet and loud. All of the men of the other villages heard the sound of the hand drum.

Hearing the Hand Drum

The snakes, down below in their home, also heard the hand drum's sound, so they went to look for their hand drum. The snake that Urahi had stolen the hand drum from could not find its hand drum. The other snakes helped this snake at searching, but they could not find it because Urahi had taken the drum.

The snakes searched unsuccessfully for the hand drum, then they thought of asking the others in the lake to help them. They killed a big boar and butchered it. They sent the pork to all in the lake who were near their home, the Wolmtombom River.

Then the snakes explained that those of the lake must come gather with those of Wolmtombom to look for the lost hand drum. In the evening, all of the small denizens of the lake came and gathered, then they began to move towards Yakwal Village.

The water swelled and rose. The people saw this and were terrified. The leaders of the village saw this and asked, "You people who live by the water, what did you do to cause this to happen?"

There was no man who knew that Urahi had done wrong, causing the enemies to come to the village. The water swelled and came up, then Urahi saw this. He ran up a tall coconut palm tree. But the water followed him up further.

When the hand drum fell down, the water quickly subsided. All of the little tributaries of the water moved back to their places. Then the snakes carried the hand drum and went back inside the Wolmtombom River.

Augustine Walombak
Yangoru
East Sepik Province

A1011. Local deluges; B211.6.1. Speaking snake (serpent); B214.1.10. Singing snake; B225.1.1+. Snake kingdom underwater; B293.5+. Dance of snakes; D915.6. Magic flood; F725.2. Submarine cities; K423. Stolen object magically returns to owner; P230. Parents and children; R311. Tree refuge; R260. Pursuits; W195. Envy

How Did the *Pimates* Tree Originate?

(Wantok 656, January 22, 1987, page 23)

Long, long ago, in the time of the ancestors, there were two brothers who lived in my village. The first brother was Sembo Teakali. The second brother was Sembo Paupia. They lived on top of a mountain called Kamanda.

The brothers were grown men, but they were not married, so they did all of their work together. When the big brother went to the garden to remove food, his little brother would go and cut firewood. They made many gardens, so their house was packed with various kinds of food.

Very Far Away

One day, the second brother, Sembo Paupia, wanted to hunt for marsupials (*kapul*) in the forest. He arranged all of his things, then in the early morning of the next day, he awoke and told his brother that after two days, he would return to the village. He left the village and walked into the deep forest.

This forest was very far away, so he walked and walked until it was becoming late at night, then he arrived in the forest. He made a fire underneath the base of a big tree, then he slept.

In the very early morning, he woke up and made a fire, then he cooked some sweet potatoes. He sat and waited for the sweet potatoes to be ready, then he heard a man calling.

Sembo Paupia left his food and ran to see who was calling. He went and saw a short man standing at the base of a tree.

This man saw Sembo Paupia and said, "Good man, I found many, many marsupials on this tree. Go up there and kill them."

Paupia was very happy and climbed the tree very quickly. He worked at killing the marsupials. When the marsupials fell down to the base of the tree, the man gathered them. Then he saw the last marsupial on the tree.

Paupia aimed his bow and shot, but he missed and the marsupial jumped down to the ground then ran away. When the marsupial jumped down and ran away, the man who was standing on the ground took his bow and shot Paupia directly in the testicles.

Poor Paupia was in pain and blood was flowing, so he came down the tree. The man saw this and pretended to be sorry for Paupia.

The man told Paupia, "Carry this bag of marsupials and we'll go back to the village."

They walked and walked, then they arrived at a river. The man told Paupia, "Rest a little and I'll carry the bag of marsupials."

The man walked a little, but he quickly became a standing tree. Paupia finished resting then followed, but he did not find the man. Poor Paupia searched and searched, but to no avail, so he went empty-handed to the village.

When he arrived, his brother Sembo Teakali, was surprised to see him in his condition. Paupia told the story of what had happened to him inside the forest.

Teakali listened and was very angry with the man who had tricked his brother. He told him that in the morning, he would go to the forest to search for the short man.

They slept then in the early morning, Teakali awoke, carried his bow and arrows, and walked off to the place where his brother had gone. He arrived at the place at night, then he made a fire, arranged his things, and went to sleep.

In the very early morning, he woke up, made a fire, sat and cooked some sweet potatoes. Then he heard a man calling out. Teakali heard this, took his bow and arrows and ran to see him.

The Short Man

He arrived, then he saw a short man standing at the base of a tree. The man saw Teakali and said, "Good man, I found many, many marsupials on this tree, but I can't go up and kill them."

Teakali listened and lied to the man, "My good brother, I have a sore on my leg, so you go up and kill the marsupials. I'll watch down here and gather the marsupials that you shoot down."

The short man listened and leapt up the tree. However he turned back and told Teakali, "You must gather the marsupials. If one is lost, I can't share any with you."

Killing the Marsupials

The short man said this, then went up the tree and worked at killing the marsupials. He killed them and when they fell down, Teakali gathered them.

After a while, the very last marsupial was on the tree. The short man aimed and shot, but the arrow missed and the marsupial fell down then ran off into the forest. When Teakali saw this, he took his bow and shot the short man directly in the testicles.

The poor man screamed terribly and blood spilled out, then he came down to the ground. Teakali lied to him, "I'm so sorry, I wanted to help you kill the marsupial, but I missed. That's OK, let's go to my village."

After he said this, the short man followed him. Teakali told the short man to carry the marsupial bag, then they walked away.

A Big River

They walked and walked, then they arrived at the big river. When they arrived there, the short man became a tree. Teakali searched and searched for him until it became dark.

He slept in this place, then in the early morning he woke again and continued searching for him. Teakali saw a hole at the base of a tree, and he knew that the man must have gone inside the tree hole.

Teakali went inside the tree hole. The hole went down very deeply. Teakali followed and followed, then he arrived at the other side of the mountain.

Teakali stood on the mountain and looked down. He saw a village down below, so he went down the mountain and arrived at the village.

When he arrived, he saw many people cooking marsupials and having a party. Teakali took his axe, ran inside and killed them. Only one man was very strong, so the two of them fought and fought until the short man completely lost his breath.

Then he told Teakali, "Brother, I'm tired now. You can kill me, but you must carry my head to your village and bury it."

Teakali listened to this and killed the man. He cut off the man's head, carried it back to his village, and buried it. In the morning, he woke up and saw a new sprout growing.

A Small Tree

After about four weeks, Teakali went to check on it again and saw a little tree growing in the place where he had buried the man's head. This kind of tree is now called *pimates*, and it only grows in my village.

Ipa Yatapaki
Yakadaesia [**Enga** People?]
Enga Province

A2611.3.1K+. *Pimates* tree from head of human; D215M. Transformation: man to tree; F123. Journey to land of little men (pygmies); F451. Dwarf; F562.7K. People live in mountain top; F610. Remarkably strong man; F721.1. Underground passages; K419+. Thief escapes detection through transformation; P251.5. Two brothers; Q411. Death as punishment; Q583. Fitting bodily injury as punishment; S139.4. Murder by mangling with axe; S176.1. Mutilation: emasculation; V61.3+. Dead buried; X712.3.1H. Injury to testicles

Kangaroo Fooled Dog

(Wantok 657, January 29, 1987, page 19)

Long, long ago, there was a place where Dog and Kangaroo lived. They lived very well because they were like real brothers. Dog was the elder brother and Kangaroo was the younger brother.

Dog was the bigger brother because he fought with their enemies, and because he also killed various kinds of wild game that he brought to the house.

The little brother, Kangaroo, was a true loafer. When the enemies would come to fight, he would have already run away into the forest. He was a fearful man, so poor Dog would work hard at taking care of their livelihood.

One day, they sat. Dog asked Kangaroo, "Brother, can you help me?"

Kangaroo listened and said, "How can I help you?"

Dog replied, "Can you give me your two long arms? Then I'll give you my two short arms. My two arms are too short. When I go chasing the pigs and cassowaries, my arms are too short, so the forest dwellers often escape."

When Dog spoke to Kangaroo, Kangaroo sat with his head turned. He told Dog, "OK, we can exchange arms. You take my arms and I'll take yours. When I travel the forest and the enemies chase me, my arms just get stuck on the trees."

Dog listened and was very happy for this. They got up and exchanged arms. Dog gave his two short arms to Kangaroo, and Kangaroo gave his two long ones to Dog.

Kangaroo put on Dog's two arms, then he turned to look for Dog, but Dog had already run off into the forest to hunt for game for themselves. He killed a huge pig that one person alone could not carry back home.

Dog left the pig there in the forest, then went back home to tell Kangaroo. Kangaroo listened and thought that Dog must have tricked him.

Dog said, "Before, I never killed pigs because my arms were too short and the pigs escaped. However now I have long arms, so I can kill game such as pigs and cassowaries."

Kangaroo did not believe it, but he followed Dog and they went to the place where Dog had killed the pig. They arrived and Kangaroo was surprised to see the huge pig lying there. He was happy, so he jumped and sang.

Kangaroo calmed down, then they tied up the pig and carried it back to the village. They butchered it, cooked some meat and smoked the rest.

This time, the two brothers were not short of meat. Their house just stank from the game that Dog had killed. Now, he had good arms and he often found game. Before, he had short arms and chased game by jumping, just as a kangaroo would do nowadays.

The brothers were quite content. When Dog traveled in the forest, Kangaroo would also travel. He did not go to hunt for food for themselves. No, Kangaroo would travel, looking for tree sprouts in the forest and eating them. When his belly was bloated, he would return home.

Dog always brought game back, cooked it and sat to eat. Afterwards, he would smell a nice smell in Kangaroo's mouth. He thought hard and did not ask Kangaroo about this.

One day, Dog asked Kangaroo, "What is it that you often eat that causes your mouth smells so good?" Kangaroo tricked Dog and said, "I often travel to other places. When men go into the forest, I follow them and eat something that they leave in the forest."

Dog listened and thought that Kangaroo was telling the truth. He thought that in the morning, he would go find this nice thing that Kangaroo often went to eat.

In the very early morning, Dog awoke and left the house. He went directly to the village and waited. He saw a man come and go inside the forest. Dog watched and saw the man return to the house. Dog ran into the forest and smelled the pile of feces that the man had left.

Dog ate the feces, then he went back to the house. He arrived and saw Kangaroo sitting there. Dog was very happy and told Kangaroo that he had eaten the thing that the man had left in the forest.

Kangaroo listened to this and laughed. He told Dog, "You went and ate a man's shit then you returned... I lied to you and you thought it was the truth." Dog listened to this and was angry. He told Kangaroo, "You lied to me, huh? Now you're soup."

Dog got up and held Kangaroo, but Kangaroo jumped down the house and ran off into the forest. He was terrified and did not want to go back.

Now after this, these two men have become complete enemies.

Willia [William] J. Sabien
Kamkumun Block
West Taraka
Lae
Morobe Province

[Mr. Sabien also wrote the ancestor stories in *Wantok* #510, 513, 517, 581, 637, 642, and 771. He is probably from the **Olo** People, **West Sepik** Province.]

A2435.3.1+. Why dog eats excrement; A2494.4+. Enmity between dog and kangaroo; B211.1.7. Speaking dog; B211.2.12K. Speaking kangaroo; B214.1+. Singing kangaroo; B871.1.2. Giant boar; F517+. Removable legs; J1772.9+. Excrement thought to be food and therefore eaten; K1044. Dupe induced to eat filth (dung); P251.5. Two brothers; P251.5.3. Hostile brothers; R213. Escape from home; W111. Laziness; W157. Dishonesty; X716H+. The escoumerda

A Brother and Sister Created Kiyadi Village

(Wantok 658, February 5, 1987, page 19)

Long, long ago, in the time of the ancestors, there was a boy and his sister who lived on Mount Kilikafo, on the **Labogai** side of Lufa [**Yagaria** People, **Eastern Highlands** Province]. The boy's name was Motode and the girl's name was Havamato.

At this time, there was much fighting among enemies, so people fled. The brother and sister left Mount Kilikafo and fled to Kiyadi [**Kiari**] Village, in the **Simbu** [Province] area [**Nomane** People]. They went to this place, and they just hid in a cave.

Famished

The people of this village did not know that the brother and sister were hiding there. The cave in which they stayed was in a big garden that belonged to the people of the village.

After the people went to the garden, removed food, and then went back the village, the brother and sister would follow and look for food scraps. They would remove them and carry them back to the cave.

One day, they were famished, so they removed the good taros and sweet potatoes that belonged to the villagers. They carried them off, then cooked, ate and slept. In the morning, they got up to go back and watch by the garden.

The people returned to the garden to work and they saw that their garden food was not there. They were furious. They went back and forth angrily. They spread the word that they would hide and grab the thieves who were coming to their garden and stealing the food.

They Returned to the Village

The leader [lit., "renowned one"] of the village told the other people to take the food back to the village. He told them that he would [hide] and see who it was that was taking their food. The people listened, took the food and went back to the village. Their leader hid in the garden.

When everyone left, he saw the two children carrying their huge net bag and running out of the cave. They went into the garden and began to remove the food.

The leader saw this, quietly rose, and went over to hold the two children. They were shocked and they trembled.

Stealing Food

The leader told them, "We've always been losing garden food, and you two have stolen our food. Now I've found you, and I'll kill you."

The children were speechless. They were afraid and began crying. The leader saw that they were children, and that they were terrified and trembling.

He asked them, "Where did you come from?"

The children both cried and told the leader, "We're from Labogai, by Lufa. The place that we came from is the Kilikafo Stone."

Hearing the Story

The leader listened to their story and was very sorry for them. He told the children that he would take them to his village, Kiyadi. The leader took the two children back to his village and hid them. Later, he lied to the people of the village. He told them that he had not found the men who had stolen food from the garden. The people listened and told him that it must have just been their enemies that had been stealing food from the garden. The children stayed with the leader as if they were his own. The men asked him about them. He told them that they were the children of a brother from another village, and that he was taking care of them as if they were his own children.

Looking for a Husband

When the children grew up, it was time to find a husband and wife for them to marry. However, there were no young people in this village. Everyone in the village was quite old. The youths saw this and they just stayed there.

They stayed with the old people of the village for a while, then all of the old people died. The two of them were alone for a while, then they married and raised children in Kiyadi Village. Their children married and raised more children, then there were many people in this village.

So, from this ancestor story that we tell, the people of Kiyadi Village came from a brother and sister, Motode and Hawamato.

Simon Kefo
Kakemuto Village
Lufa
Eastern Highlands Province

A991+. Origin of particular village; K300. Thefts and cheats—general; P210. Husband and wife; P230. Parents and children; P253. Sister and brother; P271. Foster father; P275. Foster son; P275+. Foster daughter; R213. Escape from home; R315. Cave as refuge; T100. Marriage; T415.5. Brother-sister marriage; W157. Dishonesty

The Greedy In-Laws Ruined Lives
(Wantok 659, February 12, 1987, page 21)

Long, long ago, a marsupial (*sikau*) lived in a place near where men made their gardens. When the marsupial felt hungry, he would walk around the gardens and take food.

One day, the marsupial walked off to look for food in an old garden. At this time, there was a woman from the village who was pregnant and was working in the garden. The woman toiled and toiled, then a tree fell down and killed her. She was dead, but her baby came out and lay on the ground, crying.

The marsupial traveled and heard the noise, then went to this place. When the marsupial arrived to check, he saw the newborn baby lying there. The baby's mother lay there dead. The marsupial was terrified and ran away. The marsupial thought that he would return to look at the baby.

The marsupial saw the poor little baby crying, and he felt very sorry for him. So, he took the baby and went to his house, bathed him well and put him to sleep.

Every day, the marsupial would take sugarcanes from the gardens, then return, remove the skins and give them to the baby to drink. When baby grew a little bigger, the marsupial would look for ripe bananas, then mash the food and give it to the baby. The marsupial took very good care of the baby, and the baby grew to be about two years old.

Long Hair

When the marsupial went to hunt for food in the forest, he would put the baby on his back and they would travel in the forest. They lived like this for a while until the baby became a man. His hair was very long and went down his back.

The boy had grown up and his father, the marsupial, told him that they would make a big house for themselves. They cut the trees and gathered grasses to tie onto the roof of the house. They worked on this house for a while and it became a huge house. When the house was finished, they lived well inside of it.

While they lived there, the fire in the house never died because the marsupial always put pieces of firewood on the fire. If the fire died, there would not be a way for them to cook their food.

Looking for Food

One day, the father marsupial wanted to go to the garden to look for food. He told the boy to carefully watch the fire. He told the boy to put more firewood on the fire if it looked as if the fire would die.

The marsupial finished explaining, then he went inside the forest to look for food for themselves. His son stayed at the house and worked at tying grasses. Because of this, he did not see that the fire had died out completely.

The father marsupial returned to see that the fire was completely dead, so he scolded his son terribly. The boy listened and was ashamed. He told his father that he would go find fire and carry it back to their house.

Looking for Smoke

He climbed a tree, then he stood and looked around. He saw smoke from a fire coming from a faraway place. Quickly, he went down and told his father that he had seen light from a fire that was very far away. He said that he would go to bring it back.

The boy went down and followed the smoke. He walked and walked, then he arrived at a garden in the forest. He went quietly, then hid and watched. He saw a mother and her daughter working in the garden. They were burning rubbish, and the fire was bright.

The boy waited, but the mother and daughter did not go very far. They lived very close to where the fire was burning. The mother cleaned the garden, while the daughter burned the rubbish and sat close to the fire.

The boy waited and waited and became very angry. Then he spoke, "Smoke, block the eyes of that girl." He spoke like that, then the smoke blocked the eyes of the young girl.

Quickly, the boy jumped up and took a piece of fire. Then he immediately jumped into the forest. However, he did not aim well. A piece of wood burned his long hair, removing some. The girl saw this and ran there, but the boy had already run away towards his home. Only his hair was left, and the girl went to get it.

The girl took the man's hair and held it, then she cried. When she and her mother returned to their house, she put down the young boy's nice hair. She always looked at it, worried and cried.

Telling Them

One day, the parents asked her about this. She told her parents that it was the hair of a young man. The parents listened and called out to the young men of the village to come gather, then they compared it to their hair. They all compared their hair, but it did not match any of their heads. After a while, the right young boy came and tried the hair. The hair matched perfectly on his head.

The girl's kin gave her to him and they married. The man took the woman away. They lived together for a while, then the woman became pregnant. When the woman's kin heard this, they came and asked for meat. The man listened, then left to tell his father, the marsupial.

The two of them went inside the forest and killed many, many marsupials (*kapul*). The man carried the game, and gave it to his wife's kin.

The man's kin were very happy, but his wife spoke quietly to her brother, "I often see the man taking care of a marsupial (*sikau*), but he says that the marsupial is his father."

A Marsupial (*Kapul*)

The woman's brother became angry. He said, "You two have killed all of those marsupials (*kapul*), but there is one that I desire very much."

The man listened to this then slowly left the house to tell his father what his brother-in-law had said to him. The father listened and was speechless. He thought and thought, then he told his son, "Never mind, kill me and give me to your in-laws."

His son was very troubled by this and he cried. He took a rope, tied it around the marsupial's neck and killed him. Then he carried him to give to his in-laws.

His in-laws were very happy. They carried the marsupial back to their village. The man cried for his father, then he took his bow and put it in the fire. The bowstring broke and whipped back, killing him. The man was dead. Later, his wife came and saw that her husband was dead.

That is the end of our story. So, the woman's kin were greedy and ruined the lives of the woman, her husband, and his marsupial father.

Samo Penavi

Okapa [Village, **Fore** People]

Eastern Highlands Province

B211.2.12K+. Speaking marsupial; B535.0.16K+. Marsupial as nurse for child; D1774. Magic results from speaking; D2062.2. Blinding by magic; F555.3. Very long hair; H75.6. Recognition by missing hair; N331+. Killed by treefall; N337. Accidental death through misdirected weapon; P210. Husband and wife; P232. Mother and daughter; P233. Father and son; P234. Father and daughter; P253. Sister and brother; P261. Father-in-law; P262. Mother-in-law; P263. Brother-in-law; P265. Son-in-law; P265+. Daughter-in-law; P271. Foster father; P275. Foster son; R220. Flights; S22+. Patricide; S55+. Cruel brother-in-law; S113. Murder by strangling; T52. Bride purchased; T100. Marriage; T570. Pregnancy; T584.2. Child removed from body of dead mother; W28.2+. Man sacrifices life for son's honor; W151. Greed

Kewul Ruined His Friend, the Lizard

(Wantok 660, February 19, 1987, page 21)

Long, long ago, in the time of the ancestors, Wawuyonk lived at the mouth of the Sepik River [**Kopar** or **Watam** People, **East Sepik** Province]. Wawuyonk was a lizard.

He always lived alone and was not very happy, so he befriended Kewul, a man who was always catching fish. They lived together in a house that Wawuyonk had made.

Kewul often went fishing in the river, then Wawuyonk would go inside the forest and hunt for wild game. Their house was packed with meat and other foods, so they always lived well.

One day, they heard that there would be a big contest to find out who was the handsomest man in the village. This man would marry the very beautiful woman from the Bird-of-Paradise Clan.

Big Contest

The lizard, Wawuyonk, and his friend, Kewul, wanted to compete in the contest. However, Wawuyonk died laughing when he heard that his friend wanted to join contest.

He told Kewul, "Your nose is too long. No one would think that you're a handsome man."

Poor Kewul listened to this and was very troubled, but he did not speak. He just kept quiet. Then the lizard, Wawuyonk, prepared to go to the contest alone. Kewul kept just kept quiet when Wawuyonk said that he would go alone to the contest.

The day before the contest was to begin, Wawuyonk asked his friend, Kewul, to help him dress. However, they did not have any good adornments.

Wawuyonk asked, "What should we do? We don't have oil, feathers or paint to adorn my skin."

Gathering Shells

When Kewul heard this, he told his friend, "We can gather shells on the beach, then adorn your body with them. I'll go find them, then return and decorate you. You'll be very handsome."

Wawuyonk listened to this and was very happy, so he sat and waited for his friend. Kewul went down to the beach and searched for shells.

Kewul traveled to the mouth of the river and scavenged shells, but he was still angry that his friend had said that his nose was too long to win the contest.

Kewul thought of this and wanted to get revenge, so he did not take the good, pretty shells that were there. He took those that were plain and put them inside the basket.

Kewul took the trashy shells and searched the ground until he obtained the shells for his friend's body. He carried all of these things to their house, then he began to adorn Wawuyonk's body.

When Kewul was finished adorning his friend, he lied to Wawuyonk, "Friend, you look handsomer. I think the young woman will swoon on your shoulder."

Poor Wawuyonk listened to this and thought that his friend was telling the truth. There was no pond nearby, so he could not see his reflection. He believed Kewul, but Wawuyonk looked very bad. Kewul had put a line of trashy shells on his back and his body looked very badly.

Very Bad

Wawuyonk did not know that he looked very bad. He was very happy that his friend had helped him, so he left home and walked to the village of the Bird-of-Paradise [Clan]. He went to sleep. He awoke in the morning and stood with the other handsome men who had come to vie for the marriage to this young woman.

When the people of the village saw Wawuyonk standing among the handsome men of the village, they were very angry. They thought that he had come to inflame their tempers.

Some of them laughed terribly because he looked so bad. However, many of them were angry and evicted him back to his home. They threw sticks and stones at him.

The Two Fought

Wawuyonk arrived at their house and he saw Kewul sitting there. He went and scolded Kewul, "You lied to me and you made me look terrible, you long-nosed man, you."

Wawuyonk spoke like this, then they fought. They fought and fought. Kewul felt as if all his strength was sapped, so he fled to the sea. He swam out to the sea, then he turned into a fish.

Kewul escaped, then his friend, Wawuyonk, sat and caught his breath. He wanted to remove the shells that Kewul had put on his body. He tried and tried, but he could not remove them. The shells were stuck fast to his body.

Wawuyonk saw this and ran away to hide in the marsh. He was ashamed of his body because the men of the village had said that he was ugly and because they had chased them.

Then Wawuyonk just hid there by the rivers and marshes by the Sepik River. He was ashamed to show his face to the men up on the ground because of his body. Wawuyonk stayed in this area, then he became a crocodile.

This is the end of the story. Now, crocodiles go around and hide when they see men because they are still ashamed of the time when the villagers ridiculed them. Whenever crocodiles see fish, they chase and kill them.

Hyacinth Y. Kasi
P. O. Box 1052
Boroko
National Capital District

A2146. Creation of crocodile; A2435.6+. Food of crocodiles; A2494.15+. Enmity between fish and crocodile; A2520+. Why crocodile hides from people; B211.6.2K. Speaking lizard; D170M. Transformation: man to fish; D418+. Transformation: lizard to crocodile; F543.1. Remarkably long nose; H300. Tests connected with marriage; H1596. Beauty contest; K1840. Deception by substitution; P310. Friendship; Q263. Lying (perjury) punished; Q288. Punishment for mockery; R210. Escapes; R220. Flights; R260. Pursuits; W157. Dishonesty

Why Ant and Lizard Are Enemies

(Wantok 661, February 26, 1987, page 21)

Long, long ago, Ant and Lizard were two very good friends. They lived well together and often ate together. They lived like brothers.

They were good friends for a while until the time when food was very scarce in the area. Ant was not too concerned because he was a small man. However, his friend, Lizard, found this time difficult because he was always famished.

One morning, they awoke and carried their nets and spears, then they went to the forest to hunt for pigs. They arrived in the forest, then they arranged the nets. Lizard told Ant, "Go chase the pigs to the base of the mango tree here. I'll climb up to sit and wait on a mango tree branch."

Ant listened to this and agreed. He would go hunt for a pig and chase it towards the tree. Ant went into the forest, then he found a pig. He chased the huge pig towards the base of the mango tree. Ant bit the pig on its buttocks. The pig ran and ran until it came to the base of the tree.

Lizard sat on top of the tree branch. When the pig went directly underneath the tree, he jumped down onto the back of the pig. The pig felt it and turned back and forth, then Lizard flew off and fell badly into the sword grass. Ant followed them. When he saw that the pig had pushed his friend down, he died laughing.

He jokingly said to Lizard, "Oh my, you're a real hunter, you fell right onto the spears." The sword grass was very sharp, and it had cut Lizard's skin badly when he had fallen on it.

Ant stopped laughing, then he told his friend, Lizard, "That's OK, we'll try again. Go chase a pig like that, then I'll watch from here and kill it."

Lizard listened to Ant, then got up to hunt for a pig. He went into the forest and walked around. He found a pig eating wild taros. Lizard chased the pig and then came towards the base of the mango tree.

The pig ran towards the tree, then Ant jumped down right on the pig's head. Ant shot the pig's eye and the pig fell down [dead].

The two friends tied the pig up and carried it back to the village. They butchered the pig and made huge earth oven. While they waited for the pork to become ready, Lizard told Ant that they should go to bathe and that when they return, they would eat the pork that would then be ready.

Ant listened to what his friend said, then they went down to the beach and jumped into their canoe. They paddled and paddled out to sea. Lizard said, "Let's try jumping down very far into the sea, grabbing some sand and coming up again." Ant thought this was a great idea of Lizard's, so he jumped down first.

Poor Ant jumped down, then tried to swim down, but he was unable to do so, so he came up again to catch his breath. When Ant rose to catch his breath, Lizard tried to beat his head with the canoe paddle. Lizard said, "Oh my, this man can't do it. Why doesn't he want to give up?" Then lizard said, "Now it's my turn."

Then he jumped down into the sea, but he went down, turned and swam back to the beach. He arrived at the beach and ran to uncover their earth oven, then he began to eat.

His friend, Ant, waited for a very long time, then he thought hard. He said, "I think we can't be friends anymore." Then he paddled back to the beach. He arrived and put the canoe away, then he walked back to the village.

He arrived and saw his friend, Lizard, gorging himself on the pork. Ant saw this and said, "Lizard, it looks like we can't be good friends any more, but that's OK. Now we'll eat this pork together, then we'll go our separate ways."

Lizard listened and did not say anything. Ant sat with him. They ate until their bellies were bloated and all of the food was gone.

Ant said, "Now is the day that our good relations are finished. Blow your conch trumpet, and I'll blow mine to call our kin here. When they come and gather, we'll fight until one of us wins."

After Ant said this, he blew his conch trumpet. When the ants heard this, all of them filed towards the village. Then Lizard blew his conch trumpet. The lizards heard this and they also came to gather.

When all of them gathered, a great fight occurred. The ants bit the lizards and the lizards trampled the ants, killing them. The two groups fought and fought until the ants won. After this great fight, the ants and lizards were no longer

friends. They live by themselves, but if you see a dead lizard, the ants will file over and clean its body well until there are just bones left.

H. [Hyacinth] Y. Kasi
P. O. Box 1052
Boroko
National Capital District
[See the ancestor stories in *Wantok* #660, 684, 687 and 701. H. Y. Kasi also wrote these stories. She is probably from the **Kopar** or **Watam** People, **East Sepik** Province.]

A2494.16+. Enmity between lizard and ant; B211.4.1. Speaking ant; B211.6.2K. Speaking lizard; B263+. War between ants and lizards; K16. Diving match won by deception; K650+. Escape by swimming away underwater; P310. Friendship; R220. Flights

Kep Killed Kumasi
(Wantok 662, March 5, 1987, page 21)

Long, long ago, in the time of the ancestors, there lived a man and his wife by Mount Lumusa in the **Baiyer River** area [**Kyaka** People, **Western Highlands** Province].

The man's name was Waiye and his wife's name was Kumasi. They were married for a long time, but they had no children, so they lived alone in this place.

One time, Waiye wanted to go hunting for wild game in the forest, so he told his wife, "It's daylight now, so I'll go to hunt for game in the forest. At night, there will be a good moon, so I'll hunt for marsupials (*kapul*) on the trees."

Kumasi agreed. She told Waiye that she would go get some vines for making net bags. These vines usually grow by rivers.

When Waiye left, Kumasi took some sweet potatoes and sugarcanes, then she went to search for vines to make net bags. She followed a big river and took vines as went up towards the river's source.

When she arrived at the source, she heard a baby crying and rolling in the sand by the stream. Kumasi went and saw the baby. She thought that his mother was nearby, but nobody was there.

Kumasi saw this and was very happy because she was childless. She was happy and cried at the same time, then she carried the baby towards the village.

Kumasi put the baby on top of her neck, and they walked back home. When they came close to the village, Kumasi thought of going to get some sweet potatoes before going home.

When they arrived at the garden, Kumasi wanted to put the baby down, but the baby held her neck tightly and started to cry. The woman saw this and left the baby on her neck, then she worked at digging up sweet potatoes.

After she removed the sweet potatoes, they went back to the village. When they arrived at the house, she wanted to put the baby down, but baby held tightly and started to cry.

The woman carried the baby into the house, then she put her things away and went to the cooking hut. When Kumasi wanted to cook, she tried again to remove the baby and put him down. But no, the same thing happened as before.

Kumasi was unsuccessful and left the baby sitting on her neck. Afterwards, she worked at cooking food. When the food was ready, the baby still did not want to be removed from Kumasi.

Kumasi left the baby there, then she ate and sat and waited. She wanted the baby to sleep first, so she very slowly tried to remove the baby from her neck and put him to sleep on the mat.

When she tried to remove the baby, the baby began to cry and scream terribly. Kumasi saw this and was afraid now. She just sat and sat, then her eyes shut and she slept.

While she slept, the baby quietly left Kumasi's neck. The baby went down and cut her neck and her two breasts too, then he carried them away.

Waiya [Waiye] went to hunt for game, and returned very late to the village. It was late at night, so he went directly to the spirit house and slept. He did not check on his wife.

In the morning, Waiye awoke and went to the house. He saw that Kumasi had not awoken yet. He called out, but there was no answer, so he went inside. When he stood at the door, he saw blood all over the house. Waiye went inside and saw his wife's body lying there, headless and without breasts.

Waiye screamed, then ran to get spears and an axe. He began to follow the man's trail. He went and went until he arrived at the source of the river. He looked around and saw a small hut by the water.

Waiye went in quietly and stood at the back of the hut. He heard a man start to talk. The man said, "Long, long ago, I would take it like that and eat it. No one could find me because they did not know about this place where I live."

The man said this, then he burned the hair from poor Kumasi's head. Waiye listened, then opened the door. The man was surprised and threw Kumasi's head at his back.

Waiya saw this and asked, "What are you cooking?" The man lied and said, "No, I'm not cooking anything."

The wild man was short and very hairy. Waiye saw this and he knew that this man had killed Kumasi. Waiya cut the man with the axe.

The man screamed, "Kinsman, why did you cut me?" Then he ran and grabbed Waiye. They began to fight inside the house.

They fought and fought, but neither of them fell. They were both completely out of breath, but they kept fighting. Then Waiye saw that there was a beautiful red *tanget* plant growing outside the wild man's house.

Waiye ran and removed the *tanget*. Then the wild man, Kep, screamed terribly and fell down dead. Waiye carried Kumasi's head and two breasts, then he returned to the village and buried her.

The wild man, Kep, was dead. He had lived alone in this area and often killed and eaten people who traveled to the headwaters. This place where the wild man, Kep, made his house is still there. We often look at it and think of this story.

Mai Pushow

Arawa

North Solomons Province

D91+. Transformation: baby to wild man; D1402.1+. Picking tanget plant (*Taetsia fructicosa*) kills person; E761.3+. Life token: tanget plant (*T. fructicosa*); F321.1. Changeling; F451. Dwarf; F555+. Exceptionally hairy man; F567. Wild man; G11+. Wild man as cannibal; G241.2. Witch rides on person; P210. Husband and wife; P272. Foster mother; P275. Foster son; Q211. Murder punished; Q411. Death as punishment; S133. Murder by beheading; S176+. Mutilation: breasts cut off; V61.3+. Dead buried; V112.1. Spirit huts

The Ghosts Killed Their Own Children
(Wantok 663, March 12, 1987, page 18)

Long, long ago, there was a village where some people lived. In this village, there lived an old woman with her two grandchildren.

One grandchild was grown and the other was still little. They were both boys. One time, the little brother's age-mates wanted to go to the forest to search for breadfruits. They made their decision and they departed.

These boys searched for breadfruits and gathered them together. In the afternoon, they returned to the village. The boys who had mothers carried the breadfruits to give to them. This boy, carried the breadfruits to give to his grandmother.

The boy went to play, then he became very hungry. The poor boy thought that the breadfruits would be ready, so he ran back to his grandmother's house.

He asked his grandmother, and his grandmother lied to him, saying that the breadfruits were ruined and that she had thrown them away. The boy was troubled by this and began to cry.

His big brother came back to see this and asked, "Why are you crying?"

The little brother told him that their grandmother had eaten all of the breadfruits that he had taken from the forest in the morning. The big brother listened and told his little brother that they would go back to the forest in the morning and find some more.

In the early morning, the two of them awoke and went to the forest to search for breadfruits. They went very far into the forest until they arrived at the base of a huge breadfruit tree.

The big brother saw this and told his little brother to make a bonfire at the base of the tree. The little brother made a fire and the big brother climbed the breadfruit tree.

He went up the tree, cut the breadfruit stems, and the breadfruits fell. His brother told him to eat all of the breadfruits and not to leave any. The poor boy listened and ate the breadfruits until they were all gone.

His brother went down and asked him if he had eaten his fill of breadfruits. He said that he had eaten enough. Then the big brother told him to get up and they would go back to the village.

The poor little boy got up and wanted to walk, but he was too heavy, the walking stick broke and he fell down. His big brother had already left and arrived at the village. The little boy could not make it, so he sat at the base of the breadfruit tree.

Late at night, a ghost man and his wife walked through this area. The ghost man went and saw that all of the breadfruits on the tree were gone. He was furious and yelled, "Who came and stole the breadfruits from my tree?"

The little boy who was still sitting there trembled fiercely. He called back, "It was just me and my brother who took your breadfruits."

The ghost man listened to this and looked for the boy. He found him sitting near the base of the breadfruit tree.

The ghost man grabbed the poor boy, then his wife carried the boy in her giant net bag. They dumped the boy inside the net bag and carried him back to their village.

The two ghosts arrived at the house. They put the boy inside a room, then they slept. In the morning, they awoke and went to the forest to look for leafy greens and other foods with which to garnish the boy.

They told the children of the village that they must watch their wild game [i.e., the boy] very carefully and not to let him go outside the house.

They departed and only the children were left in the village. While the children were in the village, they played with tree fruits.

They played and played, then one of them threw a tree fruit inside the house. When the child went inside the house, the child saw the boy lying there.

The other ghost children heard this, so they all ran inside the house to see the boy lying there. They began to eat all of the breadfruits that were inside the boy's body.

While the ghost children ate the breadfruits inside the boy, his belly became lighter and he stood up. He told the boys that he would teach them a song and dance.

He performed a traditional song and dance. The ghost children were very happy to hear and see this. He told them that if they dressed finely, he would sing and dance some more.

The ghost children listened and ran to the house. They carried their parents' adornments. They gave some to the boy and they themselves dressed up. Then they followed the boy in singing and dancing fervently.

When the boy sang and danced, he jumped in the house until he stood towards the village. Then he jumped and flew up, escaping to his village. The ghost children saw that their game had escaped, and they were terrified.

All of the ghost children ran away to hide in the forest. In the afternoon, the parents returned to the village. There was not a single child in the village.

They began to call out to the children, and the children replied from the forest. The parents heard this, so they knew that something must have been wrong that their children were hiding in the forest.

They went to check and they saw that their game had escaped. They were furious, but they hid their fury and called out again to the children that they must return home.

When the children heard this, they returned to the village. They arrived and the parents asked them why they were hiding in the forest. The children said that the game had escaped and that they were afraid, so they went to hide in the forest. When the parents heard this, they were furious and killed their children.

Steve Suaka
Teobuhine [**Teobuhin**] Village [**Teop** People]
P. O. Box 32
Tinputz
North Solomons Province

D670. Magic flight; E425.1. Revenant as woman; E425.2. Revenant as man; E425.3. Revenant as child; E541. Revenants eat; G11.10. Cannibalistic spirits; G441. Ogre carries victim in bag (basket); K300. Thefts and cheats—general; K606.0.1. Pursuer persuaded to sing while captive escapes; K810. Fatal deception into trickster's power; P210. Husband and wife; P230. Parents and children; P251.5. Two brothers; P292.1. Grandmother as foster mother; Q212. Theft punished; Q325. Disobedience punished; Q411. Death as punishment; R11. Abduction by monster (ogre); R210. Escapes; S11.3. Father kills child; S12.2. Cruel mother kills child; S41. Cruel grandmother; S70+. Cruel brother; S110. Murders; S143. Abandonment in forest; W126. Disobedience

A Man Married a Woman from the Water
(Wantok 664, March 19, 1987, page 21)

Long, long ago, there lived an old woman. She lived in **Gurependa** Village in the Enga area [**Enga** People, **Enga** Province]. She had a son, and they lived alone.

One night, the son wanted to go to the men's house to sleep. He was approaching the door of the men's house when he heard some noises coming from the pond that was near his house. He turned and looked down at the pond.

The man saw some young women making a fire by the water, then sitting and singing. The man was speechless. He thought, "Where did these singing women come from?" He just watched, then he went inside the house and slept.

The next night, he again went inside the house to sleep. When he approached the house, he looked down and saw a bonfire. The women had lit the fire and made it brighter. The light took his two eyes.

The man could not sleep because the women were singing intensely. He just tossed and turned, then he walked back to his mother's house.

He asked her, "Mama, do you know who the women are that have come and made a fire by the pond down below?" The house that belonged to the two of them was on top of a mountain.

The mother replied that she did not know. She also got up and went outside the house. She looked down and saw the young women singing.

The mother was also confused. She asked, "Where did these young women come from? I didn't know that so many young women were nearby."

The son told his mother, "Mama, don't worry. I have an idea. You must follow what I say because I want to find out if those are real women. I'll lie in the middle of the house and pretend that I'm dead. You must cry and scream loudly so that the women can hear you. When they come to help you mourn, you must carefully pick a beautiful young woman and sit close to her. Then you must perform some songs, dances and speeches. After that, I'll open my eyes, get up and grab the young woman who is sitting close to you. Then she'll tell us where they really came from."

The old woman followed her son's instructions. The son lay as if he were dead. The old woman cried and the young women heard her. They went up to the house with much food, such as taros, yams, leafy greens, and bananas.

They also mourned and cried for the young man. They said that they were also women of this village, but that they never sat in the house of the old woman and her son.

After a fairly long time, the man who was pretending to be dead moved. This happened after his mother's unusual speech. The man rose quickly and grabbed the young woman who was sitting near his mother. The women saw this and ran away in fear. They said, "The bad dead man has revived and will eat us!"

The mother also got up, but quietly. She went to see where the women where fleeing. She saw them jump down into the water. The woman and her son knew that the young women were *masalai* women from the pond.

One of their friends, a man, held her. This man's mother gave them various things from the village and she forgot her kin in the pond. The woman married this man. Some time later, the man wanted to pay the bride price. The mother and the two of them took some pigs and left them by the water.

Another morning, the three of them returned and the pigs were gone. They had gorged themselves where the pigs had been left. The woman's kin had taken the pigs and repaid them with food. The two of them lived together and the wife gave birth to a boy. Some time passed and the power of the old mother lost its strength. The woman often went down to the water to see her kin, then she would return again.

Benjamin Mayo
Sirunki Lutheran Church
Wabag
Enga Province

D1710. Possession of magic powers; F421. Lake-spirit; F490+. Masalai; K700. Capture by deception; K1860. Deception by feigned death (sleep); P210. Husband and wife; P231. Mother and son; P233. Father and son; P262. Mother-in-law; P265+. Daughter-in-law; P310. Friendship; R220. Flights; T52. Bride purchased; T111. Marriage of mortal and supernatural being; T192. Marriage by force; T580. Childbirth

Two Brothers Married
Green Coconut Women

(Wantok 66[5], March 26, 1987, page 21)

Long, long ago, there were two brothers who lived by a mountain. The name of this mountain is Sagaluti. The name of the big brother was Saga and the name of the little brother was Moos.

One day, the big brother told his younger brother, Moos, that the next day he would go to the forest to hunt for wild game. Moos listened and asked Saga how many days he would be in the forest. Saga said that he would probably sleep there for about two nights.

That night, Saga arranged all of his things, then he went to sleep. In the very early morning, he awoke, carried his belongings, and walked off into the deep forest. He walked and walked, then it became dark on the trail and he slept.

In the morning, he awoke and walked off again. He walked briskly, then he saw a house by the trail. Saga walked towards the house.

The house belonged to an old woman. When Saga arrived, the old woman saw him and asked, "Where did you come from?" Saga told his story to the old woman, that he and his brother lived in their own house, and that he wanted to hunt for game so he walked around and arrived there.

The old woman listened to Saga's story and was very sorry for the two brothers. She told Saga, "Climb up the coconut palm and take down a green coconut."

Saga went up, took a green coconut, and came down again. The old woman told him, "Carry this coconut away, but you must take good care of it. Don't throw it down on the ground."

Saga listened to the old woman and carefully carried the green coconut back home. When he approached the village, he saw a marsupial (*kapul*) by the trail.

He quickly dropped the coconut and chased the marsupial into the forest. He killed the marsupial and carried it back to the place where he had thrown the coconut.

When he arrived, he saw a woman sitting there. Saga saw this and asked, "Did you see a green coconut that I put here or not?"

The woman told him, "The coconut that you took was just me." Saga listened and did not reply. He told the woman to follow him to the village. When the woman got up to walk, Saga saw that she had a bad leg.

This happened because Saga had not thought when he dropped the coconut on the trail. The two of them walked until they arrived at the village. The little brother, Moos, was shocked to see them.

Saga told the story to Moos about the old woman who had met him in the forest. Moos listened and trembled with excitement. He too wanted to go and get a woman, then return to the village.

In the very early morning, Moos awoke and walked briskly on the trail into the forest. He slept on the trail until the morning, then he woke up and walked away, arriving at the old woman's house.

The old woman saw Moos and she asked him why he was there. Moos told her that he was going around the forest and arrived at this place. The old woman told Moos to sleep, then in the morning, he could return to the village.

In the morning, she told Moos to climb up the coconut palm and take a green coconut. He listened and went up to get a coconut. The old woman told him to take good care of the coconut and not to throw it down hard on the ground. Moos listened and carried his coconut back to the village.

Moos walked on the trail and then he saw a lizard. He put the coconut down gently, chased the lizard and killed it. He took the lizard and went back to carry his belongings. However when he arrived, he saw a very beautiful woman sitting there.

Moos was shocked to see the woman and he asked her whether she had seen his coconut. The woman just laughed and told Moos that it was just she who was the coconut. Moos was ecstatic and took her to the village.

They arrived, and Saga saw Moos' wife. He was troubled because his wife's leg was bad and Moos' wife was truly beautiful. However, he knew that it was because he had not listened to the old woman that his wife's leg was bad.

The brothers, Saga and Moos, and their two wives lived in **Sagaluti** Village until their wives gave birth, then later many people grew up in this village.

Yana Bey

Mekok Village

Morobe Province

[Yana Bey also wrote the ancestor story in *Wantok* #724. This story has a village named Saga Moos (**Sawetmove**) from the **Safeyoka** People.]

D222+W. Transformation: woman to coconut; J652. Inattention to warnings; J1050. Attention to warnings; P210. Husband and wife; P230. Parents and children; P251.4+. One brother acts wisely, another acts unwisely; P251.5. Two brothers; P263. Brother-in-law; P264. Sister-in-law; T100. Marriage; T580. Childbirth

The People Who Were Lost in a Cave

(Wantok 666, April 2, 1987, page 21)

Long, long ago, in **Nubuni** Village, among the **Chuave** [People], there were two clan houses [**Simbu** Province]. There were two men's houses and the leaders of these two houses were Kuman and Kamare.

One time, there was a young woman who was menstruating, and they put her inside a hut. The custom of the ancestors in this place was that women must just stay in the [menstrual] hut. When she was ready to come outside, they had to kill pigs and find wild game in the forest, then have a big feast so that the woman could come into the clearing [probably for menarche].

At this time, the men of the clan house decided to go to a big cave. This cave was huge and also very wide. They knew that there must be plentiful game inside.

In the morning, everyone in the village prepared to leave. They searched for torches. The young men and women went to search for dry, wild sugarcane (*pitpit*). They fastened these into torches and carried them with them. The women carried sweet potatoes and some other foods in their net bags too. There were just two men left in the village.

The clan arrived at the cave. They lit the torches and went inside. When the light went inside, the flying foxes alit and flew about. The men were very happy and shot the flying foxes. When the lights went by the sides of the cave, they [saw] many, many marsupials (*kapul*).

The marsupials did not have a way to escape, so the men finished them off. They walked further and continued killing the marsupials until they arrived at the end of the cave. They looked up and saw a stone that was like a table above them.

The men were surprised to see two marsupials (*sikau*) sitting on this stone. The people saw that the marsupials were also staring at them.

The marsupials imitated our language and said, "*Ku, ku, ku*." This means, "Enough, enough, enough," or "stop fighting."

The men listened to this, but their eyes were opened to kill these two animals, so they did not think.

They said, "They're just marsupials. Kill them and we'll carry them back to the village. The men will be shocked to see this kind of marsupial."

They threw spears at the marsupials. The poor marsupials screamed when the spears hit them, then they fell to their deaths. When they died, the entrance of the cave shut completely, and the people did not have a way to escape.

There was one young woman who was cooking sweet potatoes outside the cave who had not followed her kin inside. When she saw the cave shut, she was afraid and she cried. She ran back to the village and explained to the men in the village what had happened.

The two men ran to this place, but there was no way for them to go inside the cave because it was completely blocked. The poor people who were inside the cave did not have a way to get outside again, but they could hear the men's shouting outside.

They stayed there for a while, then each of them began to die. When one of them died, they would shout to the men outside and explain that a man or woman had died. They did this until no one else inside spoke. Then those who were outside knew that the people must have all died.

Afterwards, the men returned to the village. There were just two women there because all of the other women had gone with the men into the cave and died.

Later, the two women married and raised children. These children married and raised more children, then there were again many people in Nubuni Village.

John Karana
Star Earth Moving
P. O. Box 25
Kiunga
Western Province

B211.2.12K+. Speaking marsupial; C141. Tabu: going forth during menses; D1552. Mountains or rocks open and close; D1724. Magic power from Death; J652. Inattention to warnings; P210. Husband and wife; P230. Parents and children; P600+. Customs associated with menarche; Q211.6. Killing an animal revenged; Q411. Death as punishment; R45.3. Captivity in cave; T100. Marriage

Two Sisters Ruined Their Brother

(Wantok 667, April 9, 1987, page 21)

Long, long ago, in the time of the ancestors, there were three families that lived on a mountain called Sanumbieng. This mountain was between two villages called Sakalang [**Sokelen**] and **Mogom** [**Nabak** People, **Morobe** Province].

There were two women and their little brother, Andibona. The two sisters were grown and close to marriage age. They often took care of their little brother.

They lived there for a while, then the two sisters married a man. The man came and lived with them at their home. They lived there, and the man with his little brother-in-law built two houses. One house belonged to them and the other house belonged to the two women.

They lived well. There were no arguments between them. During daylight, they cleared the forest and made a huge garden. They planted food and then the rain began to fall.

The rain came forth, and there was no more food in the houses, so they were famished. The sisters' husband told his little brother-in-law to go see his sisters and ask them for food.

The boy, Andibona, listened to this and went to ask his sisters. The sisters were angry and cursed him. Poor Andibona listened to them and was very troubled. He went back to the house that he shared with his brother-in-law.

Andibona arrived and his brother-in-law asked him what had happened. He told him what his sisters had said. His brother-in-law listened to him, then he too cursed Andibona. Poor Andibona listened to this and was very troubled.

When the rain ended, the two sisters and their husband got up and carried their net bags. They wanted to go to the garden. They called out to Andibona to go with them, but he did not reply. He just kept quiet. When he came out of the house, he saw that his two sisters and their husband had left.

After Andibona saw this, he killed a big pig. He butchered it and cleaned it. Then he cooked the pig. When the pork was ready, he sat and ate. He ate and ate until he finished the whole pig and only bones were left.

He carried the bones and put them in the house of his two sisters, then he went to get his net bag. He carried his bow, arrows and knife, then he left this place.

Andibona walked and walked into the forest, then he saw a marsupial (*kapul*), and he shot it. He cut a piece of wood, then stood it in the ground. He speared the marsupial on the wood and left it there.

He kept walking into the forest. When he killed marsupials, he put them on stakes and left them by the trail. Andibona did this until he entered the very deep forest and was completely lost.

His two sisters and their husband returned home in the afternoon. They saw that no one was there. They went inside to put away the food, then they saw the pig bones just lying there inside their house. They knew that their brother, Andibona, must have killed the pig, cooked it, and left home.

The sisters were very troubled by this. They began to look for their brother, Andibona. They shouted and shouted to no avail, then they searched and searched for him. They saw the first marsupial that he had killed and stood by the

trail. Then they followed and followed until they came to the last mark.

Andibona had shot a bird, then he had put it down on the ground. He had climbed a huge tree and sat on a branch.

His sisters followed him until they arrived at the base of the tree. They looked up and saw their brother sitting there. They both cried and shouted for him to come down, then they would return home. However, Andibona just listened and sat.

They cried and talked and talked, then they removed the arrow with which he had shot the bird. Blood flowed from the bird down to the ground and became a pond. Andibona sat on the tree branch and saw his two sisters become stones. One went down to the bottom of the water and the other was at the top of the water.

Buka Nasate
Niugini Kompaun
Oro Province

D231W. Transformation: woman to stone; D457.1+. Transformation: blood to lake; P210. Husband and wife; P253.0.2+. Two sisters and one brother; P263. Brother-in-law; R213. Escape from home; R260. Pursuits; T100. Marriage; T145.1.3. Man married to several sisters

The Old Man Ended His Worries
(Wantok 668, April 16, 1987, page 21)

Long, long ago in the Poka area, in a small village called **Palagao**, there lived an old man [**Solos** People, **Buka** Island, **North Solomons** Province]. This old man did not have wife. He often worried about why he did not have a wife to help him work and to be his companion.

One day, the old man sat down and thought. He told himself, "How can I find a woman? My face is ulcerated and the women don't like me."

The old man sat mournfully, then a boy came to him. He asked the old man, "What's happening?" The old man replied, "Nothing. I have a big sore upon my soul. I'm very worried because I don't know how I'll get a wife."

The young man replied, "Old man, don't worry. I'm still small and my grandparents gave me something to attract women, something they call a love charm. You'll use this and it will help you."

When the old man heard this, his eyes popped open. The old man said, "Go on boy, now you must make a love spell for me."

The boy told the old man, "Tomorrow, you must come and see me at the *masalai* place. You must come when it is high noon. Don't come in the morning or the afternoon. You must bathe very carefully, then come."

Then next day, when it was still early in the morning, the old man awoke. He followed the instructions of the young boy. He bathed very carefully, then he walked up to meet the young boy at the *masalai* place.

However, the boy had another love charm with him. The boy thought that he would tell the old man to walk off to a place where there were wild taros. These wild taros would stick to the old man's skin. It would make his buttocks and other parts of his skin scratched.

The young boy took the taro leaves and placed them. When the old man arrived, the boy told the old man to take the wild taro leaves and rub them on his skin.

The old man thought that it was really a love charm, so he rubbed his skin vigorously. The young boy stood there then told the old man, "Go ahead, after you've finished rubbing your skin and your skin is very hot, scrape it with *salat* and the sap of the wild taros. Then slowly the women will lust for you."

He told the old man, "You can choose whichever woman you want because many women will fall for you after the wild taro leaves are stuck to your skin."

The old man kept at it. Later, he felt his as if his skin was burning, and he kept scraping his skin. The old man scraped his skin until he screamed and cried. He spread his two legs, then ran and jumped back and forth to get air on them.

But no, the boy had performed a prank on the poor man. The poor man had ruined his skin and was in great pain. The old man was furious at the boy, but the boy had already run away from the old man, never to show his face again.

Because of the old man's anger, he stopped worrying about women. This was because thinking about women had nearly made him completely ruin his skin.

Israel Kout
Buka
North Solomons Province

D1355.3. Love charm; F490+. Masalai; K1014+. Stinging plants given for beautification; K1963.2. Sham magician promises to induce love by magic; R220. Flights; T10. Falling in love; T24.1. Love-sickness

Two Women Ran Away
from Their Old Husband

(Wantok 669, April 23, 1987, page 21)

Long ago, in the time of the ancestors, there was an old man who lived in Toloro Village [**Tolofon** Village, **Urat** People, **East Sepik** Province]. He had two wives. When they worked in their garden, only the two women would work hard while their husband would just sleep.

At night, the women would eat then go to sleep. The old man never slept then. He would turn into a young man and travel. The women did not know that he always did this because during the day, they worked hard in the garden then fell dead asleep at night.

When there was a festival or gathering at another village, the man would tell his two wives that they could go to the festival if they wanted to, but that he would stay in the village.

He would say, "Go ahead. If you see our kin, tell them I'm here. I'm too old to travel, but you must bring the food and meat back to me."

When they departed, the old man also left the house. He would hide carefully in the forest then turn into a very handsome young man.

The old man would dress very finely, so that the women would die when they saw him. When he arrived at the village of the festival, he would stand by and wait. When the singing and dancing began, he too would sing and dance fervently.

He would be terrified that his two wives would recognize him, but they did not. The man changed and became a young man so that he did not look like the old man.

When the man saw the two of them, he would hide in the crowd so that they did not see him. They would dance and dance until it was close to dawn, then he would leave the festival grounds and run back home.

He would remove the adornments and quickly perform a song and dance that made him an old man. Afterwards, he would pretend to sleep.

Later, when the two women would return to the house, the old man would trick them and ask them what had happened at the festival. They would tell the story to him.

One day, there was a big festival in a village. The old man again sent off his two wives. When it was dark, he changed into a young man. Then he went and danced at this festival, but this time he did not hide well.

The two women saw this young man and they lusted for him. They did not know that he was really their husband. They just stared at him longingly.

They said, "Why did we marry that old lazy good-for-nothing? He always just sits in the house and we work hard at doing everything. When it's time for festivals, he never takes us like the other men do with their wives."

So at another time, the two of them went to another festival. This time, they did not dance at the festival. They just stood and watched. They waited and saw the young man.

They asked people which village this man came from. They asked everyone, and nobody knew where the young man had come from. No one knew.

Another time, the two of them went to watch the trailhead where they thought that the man would go. They held a big rope and hid. Then they saw him coming.

When the man came close, they pulled the rope and the good-for-nothing fell on top of the sword grasses. The two women held him and said, "You're just the man that we've lusted for every time that we've seen your face."

However, when the women held him, the young man quickly changed into their old husband. They were furious. They wanted to kill him. They left him and went back to get all of their things, then they told the man, "We're too young to marry an old man like you."

They told him, "Why did we work so hard for you? All of this time, you've tricked us and acted conceitedly. Now we'll get revenge, then you'll feel like we do."

The two of them went home and performed a song and dance. The first woman saw feathers grow upon her first hand. She looked and laughed, "I think I'm changing into a bird." It was true, she became a bird of paradise. The second wife turned into a Victoria crowned pigeon [*Goura victoria*]. They flew away and perched on a tree branch and made noises.

When the old man went by the house, he saw the two birds. The birds looked down at the old man and squawked at him. The old man was very troubled because he knew that the birds were just his wives. He looked up at the tree and cried. He cried and said, "I was at fault. Who will look after an old man like me now?"

But the bird of paradise and the Victoria crowned pigeon flew away.

William Wokumel
Raval Settlement
New Ireland Province

[Mr. Wokumel retold this story in *Wantok* #405.]

D56.1. Transformation to older person; D150+.W. Transformation: woman to bird of paradise; D154.2+W. Transformation: woman to Victoria crowned pigeon; D1781. Magic results from singing; D1781+. Magic re-sults from dancing; D1880+. Transformation to young man to escape recognition; D1881. Magic self-rejuvenation; K1814+. Man in disguise wooed by his faithless wife; K2213+. Treacherous husband; P210. Husband and wife; Q261. Treachery punished; R227. Wife flees from husband; T10. Falling in love; T145.0.1. Polygyny; W111. Laziness

A Cockatoo Taught People How to Make Fire
(Wantok 670, April 30, 1987, page 21)

Long, long ago, in the time of the ancestors, there lived a cockatoo. This cockatoo was the leader of all of the other birds. He and his servants lived on an island.

The cockatoo often just sat in the house while the other birds would work very hard doing all of the cockatoo's work. When the cockatoo wanted to go asea, the cockatoo's servants would paddle while the cockatoo would sit quietly and chew betel nuts. If the cockatoo felt that the other birds were not paddling fast enough, the cockatoo would pelt them with betel nut husks.

They lived like this for a while, then one day the cockatoo told the other birds that he desired to go to an island that was far from their island. The cockatoo told his servants to prepare his food, betel nuts, and tobacco, then they would sleep.

In the very early morning, the cockatoo's servants pulled the cockatoo's big canoe down to the sea and waited for the cockatoo. The cockatoo went down and sat in the chair, then the cockatoo's servants paddled away.

They paddled and paddled, then the sun rose strongly. The sun baked them. Many of them tired and did not paddle strongly. The cockatoo lay there and asked why they were not paddling strongly.

The poor birds paddled harder. The cockatoo removed the betel nut husks and chewed the nuts. He took the husks and pelted the birds' backs, telling them to paddle quickly. When he did this, all of the birds became very angry. The birds talked about escaping from the cockatoo when they arrived at the island.

When they approached the island, the birds were completely exhausted from paddling. The cockatoo saw this and asked them what was happening. The birds told the cockatoo that the sun was baking them terribly and their throats were parched.

The cockatoo listened and told them, "OK, go drink some water. When you return, I'll go and drink."

The birds were very happy upon hearing this. They went ashore to the island. They jumped down and went to find some water. After they drank, they went back to the canoe. Then the cockatoo went down to find some water.

When he left, the other birds quickly got up and paddled the canoe back to sea.

The cockatoo drank some water, then returned to the beach, but he did not see the canoe. The cockatoo shouted loudly and went up a tree, only to see that the birds were very far away in the deep sea.

The cockatoo saw that they had escaped him. The cockatoo had a [bad] thought, then it went down to the ground and looked for a trail. The cockatoo walked and walked, then he saw a fruit tree standing near the trail. The cockatoo jumped up the tree, perched and ate the tree fruits.

Later, the cockatoo heard a person walking towards the tree. When the cockatoo looked down, he saw a young woman walking along the trail.

The cockatoo took a tree fruit and threw it down at the woman, but it missed. Then the cockatoo took a second tree fruit and threw it, hitting the woman directly. The woman turned and looked up to see the cockatoo perched upon the tree branch.

The cockatoo called down, "I like you."

The woman replied, "Come down."

The cockatoo jumped down to the ground. The cockatoo told the woman that they would marry and live on this island. The woman agreed, then they went to the woman's village.

In the afternoon, the cockatoo said that he was hungry, so his wife took some taros and gave them to the cockatoo. The cockatoo saw the taros and was very happy. He sat and broke the taros then tried to eat. However when he put the taro inside his mouth, he found out that the taro was raw. So, he told his wife to cook the taro well.

The woman took it and put it back in the sun. The sun heated it, then she carried it to give to the cockatoo. The cockatoo wanted to eat, but he again tasted that the taro was raw, so he was angry.

He said, "Oh my, you don't know how to cook food? I'll make a fire and cook the taro myself." However when he got up to cook the taro, he found that there was no fire. The woman had heated her food in the sun.

The cockatoo asked the woman, "Where's the fire?"

The woman asked, "What's fire?"

The cockatoo told her to go fetch some dry sword grasses and then he would show her. The woman fetched the grasses and some dry wood, then the cockatoo rubbed two pieces of wood until smoke arose. He put the dry sword grasses there and the fire lit. His wife was terrified and stood far away.

While the fire was burning, the cockatoo told the woman to put her hand there and feel it. The woman went and put her hand there. The fire burned her hand, so she screamed loudly and ran away. Her kin heard this and came to look.

They were afraid and stood far away. When the taro was cooked, the cockatoo called out for the people to come and try the food. They ate it and it was delicious. They asked the cockatoo to show them how to make fire.

The cockatoo showed them, then everyone on the island understood how to make fire. They cooked food on a fire and no longer heated it in the sun.

Titus Namaeanato

Wau

Morobe Province

A1414. Origin of fire; A1455. Origin of cooking; B211.3. Speaking bird; B211.3+. Speaking cockatoo; B242.1+. Cockatoo as king of birds; B295.2.1K. Animals make voyage in canoe; B602+. Marriage to cockatoo; J1813+. Cooking processes misunderstood: cooking with the sun; P210. Husband and wife; R210. Escapes; S145. Abandonment on an island; T100. Marriage

A Dog Helped a Woman
(Wantok 671, May 7, 1987, page 25)

Long, long ago, there was a man and his sister who lived in a village. They had a he-dog. The man always went with his dog into the forest. They would hunt for marsupials (*kapul*) and bring them back to the village. The man's sister often liked to eat just the marsupials' heads.

One time, the man took his dog and they went into the forest to hunt for wild game. They walked and walked, then they arrived at the base of a tree.

The man saw this and told his dog to watch the base of the tree while he climbed it. The man climbed the tree, and approached a marsupial. When he was about to kill the marsupial, the tree branch broke and he fell down to the stones underneath the tree, breaking his head off.

The dog was underneath the tree when he saw this. The dog thought that a marsupial had fallen, so he ran over and was surprised to see his master lying at the base of the tree. The dog carried his master's head back to the village, then he placed it by the fireplace.

The man's sister had gone to work in the garden. When she returned home, she put her things away, then she sat and made a fire in the cookhouse. The fire did not light quickly, so she lay down and blew on the fire. Her eyes looked up to the rack for some smoking meat. She saw the head of her brother lying there.

When she saw this, she was terrified. She got up, then took her net bag and other belongings. She left the village and ran away. Her dog followed her and they ran away to the forest. While they were fleeing, the brother's head also followed them.

The woman and her dog kept fleeing, and the man's head kept following them. They went and went until they approached a cave, then they saw a vine hanging there. The woman carried her dog and they jumped on the vine up into the cave.

They turned and saw the head coming up the vine too. Quickly, the woman cut the vine. Then the brother's head fell back to the ground and fell apart completely.

When the woman fled from her brother's head, she had not thought about bringing food. They sat there, and the woman felt terribly hungry. She checked inside the net bag, and there was not a single piece of food for her to cook and eat.

She told her dog, "If you're a real man, you'll go find some food for us."

The dog lay there and listened, but the woman did not know that the dog could hear what she had said. While the woman was dead asleep, the dog got up very quietly and went into the mountain. The dog began to dig the earth.

The dog dug and dug the earth until he arrived at the other side of the mountain. The dog saw a huge garden. He removed food and carried it back to the place where the woman was sleeping.

The woman heard a noise and thought that she must be dreaming, then she saw the food piled up. She asked the dog, but the dog did not reply. He just wagged his tail. The woman was very happy and cooked the food, then they ate and stayed there. After a while, their food was gone.

The woman told the dog, "Where did you go to get the food that you brought here?"

The dog walked off to the place where he had dug the hole and gone out of the mountain. The woman followed him and saw the hole. She followed the dog outside and arrived at the big garden where the dog had taken the food.

They hid and watched. They saw a man walking towards them. He went into the garden. The woman watched the man and was slightly afraid because she thought that the man was a *masalai*.

The woman called out, "Are you a real man or a *masalai*?"

The man replied that he was not a *masalai*. The woman also said that she was not a *masalai*. Then the man told the woman that he would marry her. The woman was

happy to hear this, but it made the dog angry so the dog chased the man up a tree.

The man sat on the tree while the dog barked and barked. The man did not have a way to get down. The woman said that the dog was worried because he was like her husband and had taken very good care of her when they were hiding on the mountain.

The man listened and told the dog that he would kill a pig to settle for the very hard work that he had done taking care of her. The man's kin heard this and helped obtain a pig. They killed the pig and made a huge earth oven for the dog.

Afterwards, the man, his wife and the dog lived well in this village. When the dog died, they were very saddened for him. They lived for a while, then they raised many children. The children also married and raised more people. This village became very big. The name of this clan is Yowibiri.

Mark Niama
Bobe Village [**Mikaru** or **Pawaia** People]
South Karimui
Simbu Province

A1640+. Origin of Yowibiri Clan; B212. Animal understands human speech; B421. Helpful dog; D1641.7. Severed head moves from place to place; F639.1.1. Mighty digger of tunnels; F721.1. Underground passages; N339+. Person falls to death from tree; P210. Husband and wife; P230. Parents and children; P253. Sister and brother; Q42. Generosity rewarded; R220. Flights; R261.1. Pursuit by rolling head; T100. Marriage; W181. Jealousy

Two Young Men Killed Masmuri [Masmura]

(Wantok 672, May 14, 1987, page 21)

Long, long ago, there was a *masalai* who lived by a village. The name of this *masalai* was Masmura. Masmura, the *masalai*, killed everyone in the village until there was not one man left in the village.

There was just one woman from this village who had hidden carefully. Masmura, the *masalai*, had not found her because she had hidden on a mountain called Kombu. She was very careful when she searched for food in the forest and when she cooked the food because she was terrified that the *masalai* would smell her, then come to kill her.

One time, the old woman was sitting down when two young men arrived at this place. The men were from **Muvandan** Village, but they had searched for this woman and come to her home.

The woman saw then and said, "Why did you two come here? This place has a *masalai* who killed everyone."

The young men told her, "Don't worry. If this *masalai* comes here, we'll kill him." The woman gave them food and the men stayed with her. However, they saw that the woman was terrified of this *masalai*, so they told her that they would try to kill the *masalai*.

The men carried *limbum* arrows. They sharpened the arrows and [straightened] the bows to kill the *masalai*. They sharpened and sharpened, then each had six bundles of arrows were ready. They put all of their things in the woman's home, then they decided to go find Masmuri, the *masalai*.

The woman told them that the *masalai* usually slept in a cave. They told the old woman that the next day, they would go and call out for the *masalai* to come, and then they would kill the *masalai*. The woman listened and was afraid. She told them that if they missed, the *masalai* would kill them both and then kill her too.

In the evening, the woman cooked food then they ate and slept. The woman did not sleep well because she was thinking too much about the *masalai* killing the men then coming to kill her too. Dawn broke, then the men carried their arrows and went to look for the *masalai*.

They arrived outside the cave and began to call to the *masalai*. They shouted and shouted to the *masalai*. The *masalai* heard them, then went outside. When he saw the two men, he sharpened his teeth well, then ran to kill them.

When the *masalai* went outside, the two men fought and fought. The men chewed ginger and spat at the *masalai*. The *masalai*'s eyes spun around, then they planted arrows into his belly. The *masalai* fell down at the base of a fig tree and died.

The men called for the woman to come. She came and saw that the *masalai* was dead. She was happy, so she jumped about and sang. The men married her and they lived together at **Kombu Jengaring** Village in the Finschhafen area of **Morobe** Province.

Omsa Masang

Kombu, Finsafen [Finschhafen]

Morobe Province

[See the ancestor stories in *Wantok* #520, 635 and 721. These stories have a *masalai* of the same name. This story probably comes from the **Kâte** People.]

F490+. Masalai; F490+. Masumura; G346. Devastating monster; G510.4+. Hero overcomes devastating ogre; G512.1+. Ogre killed with spear/arrow; P210. Husband and wife; S110. Murders; T100. Marriage; T146. Polyandry; Z356. Unique survivor

How Flying Foxes Arose
(Wantok 673, May 21, 1987, page 25)

Long ago, in the time of the ancestors, there lived a man and his wife in a village called **Gogona** near Angoram [**Angoram** or **Buna** People, **East Sepik** Province].

One time, they wanted to make a new garden, so they went to cut some forest. They worked very hard and cut all of the forest, clearing the trees. When it was almost dark, they returned to the village. They cooked some food, then went to sleep.

In the morning, they awoke, carried the work tools and went back to this place. They wanted to sweep the garden clean, then prepare to plant food. However, when they arrived at this place that they had cut, they saw that dense forest had covered up the area. It did not look as if anyone had cut the trees and cleared it.

The man turned to tell his wife, "We must have gone to the wrong place. This is not the place where we worked yesterday." However, his wife was adamant and said, "No, this is the part of the forest that we cut yesterday."

They argued and argued. Then they cut the forest again, clearing the detritus and tree branches. In the morning, they awoke and went back to this part of the forest. They saw the same thing. It looked as if no one had cut the trees and cleared the forest. The trees stood firmly in place, and the forest covered the entire area. They were furious. They decided to cut the forest again and clear the area, but they would try to find out who had made the trees and forest regrow in this area.

They cleared the area, then they returned to the village. They arrived at the village, fastened some torches and prepared to go back to this part of the forest.

Late that night, they awoke very quietly, lit the torches, and walked off to the part of the forest that they had cut. When they approached, they extinguished the torches and walked very quietly to the new garden.

When they came close to the garden, they heard a *masalai* woman singing. Her voice was like a loudspeaker and sang, "*Tambumeri, klung, klung*." In English, this means, "Tree, grow, grow."

The *masalai* woman sang like this, then the trees stood back in their places. The grasses and other things also grew again, standing as if the man and his wife had never cut them. When all of the forest covered the area, the *masalai* woman held the branch of a small, wild *limbum* palm tree.

The couple watched and saw the *masalai* woman hold the wild *limbum* palm, then the ground opened up and the woman went inside.

In the morning, everyone carried axes, knives, and digging sticks. They followed the married couple back to this part of the forest. They arrived and the couple showed them the place where the *masalai* woman had descended. The men gathered around this wild *limbum* palm and began to dig the earth.

They dug and dug, then they found the *masalai* woman's clay pot. When they took it out, she called out, "Yo, who took my pot, huh?"

The men heard this, but they were not afraid. They continued to dig the ground. They dug and dug, then they found the *masalai* woman's chicken. When they took the chicken, they heard her shout again, "Yo, who took my chicken, huh?"

They kept digging the earth until they removed everything and brought it all up. When they removed the things, they heard the *masalai* woman shouting angrily.

The last thing that they took from inside the hole was the *masalai*'s dog. The men knew that the *masalai* woman must be close now. They kept digging the hole, then they found her too. They held her and took her to the village. The men told her, "You'll live as our shaman."

They arrived at the village, and the men made a spirit house. They did this work, but they no longer thought of their wives and children. The house was ready, and the men began to cut *limbum* palms from the forest. They carried them and put them in the house.

Whenever they carried a *limbum* palm and threw it, the *masalai* woman would be happy. She would shout and sing. They did this for a while, then one man carried a *limbum* palm and threw it. He did not hear the *masalai* woman shout. He went inside to check. He saw blood splattered in the spirit house.

The men's wives had been angry and killed the *masalai* woman. They had cut her into small pieces. Each of the women had cut her flesh and taken it back to their houses. They cooked sago and they cooked the flesh of this *masalai* woman too, then they carried it back to the spirit house.

The men spilled all of the sago, then they went back inside the spirit house. They stayed there and made flying fox skins. They finished, then they put them away carefully. They lied to their wives and told them to go fishing. They told the women to take all of the girls too and to leave only their sons in the village with their fathers. The skins fit very well, like shirts. Afterwards, they began to fly around, trying out their bodies. All of them felt as if they could fly, so they went outside the spirit house and flew away.

They saw that two young women were menstruating and staying at home. They flew and brought sago sprouts, then put them on the two women who then turned into birds of paradise and flew away into the deep forest. All of the men and the boys became flying foxes and flew away to find caves and branches of big trees in the forest.

Just one old man was too heavy to fly, so he fell back down to the ground. He gave up and went back to the village. When the women returned to the village, he explained what had happened to their husbands and sons. The women listened and were speechless. They knew that they were wrong, and that their husbands had fled them.

Afterwards, the old man married some of the women and they lived there. Now if you go to this village, you can see the ditch where the men of the village had dug to find the *masalai* woman who ruined the garden of the couple from the village.

Pius Dambui
P. O. Box 256
Wewak
East Sepik Province

C141. Tabu: going forth during menses; C962.2. Transformation to bird for breaking tabu; D117.5KM. Transformation: man to flying fox; D150+W. Transformation: woman to bird of paradise; D310+M. Transformation: flying fox to man; D531. Transformation by putting on skin; D950.19+. Magic *limbum* palm tree (Caryota spp.); D1711. Magician; D1781. Magic results from singing; F450. Underground-spirits; F490+. Masalai; H1115.1+. Task: cutting down forest, which is magically, replanted; P210. Husband and wife; P231. Mother and son; P232. Mother and daughter; P233. Father and son; P234. Father and daughter; Q211. Murder punished; R213. Escape from home; R220. Flights; S139.2.2+. Corpse put into cooking pot or cooked; S139.7. Murder by slicing person into small pieces; T100. Marriage; T145.0.1. Polygyny; V112.1. Spirit huts; W181. Jealousy

A Woman Killed the Leader of the *Masalai*s

(Wantok 67[4], May 28, 1987, page 21)

Long, long ago, in the time of the ancestors, there was a married couple who lived in the **Kandep** area of **Enga** Province [**Enga** People]. The man's name was Menakali Lesa and the woman's name was Tambun Ipali.

One day, they wanted to walk into the forest to hunt for marsupials (*kapul*). They dug up some sweet potatoes, broke some sugarcane, and prepared everything. When dawn broke, they awoke and walked off into the forest.

As they walked along, they worked at killing marsupials. After a while, they had killed many, many marsupials. When it was nearly dark, they made a hut and put their things inside.

The man, Menakali Lesa, told his wife, Tambun Ipali, "Cook some marsupials and sweet potatoes in an earth oven. I'll go out again and hunt for some more marsupials."

The man said that he would carry his bow and arrows then go into the forest. The woman cooked the food in an earth oven, then she sat and waited. She sat there and heard a noise from the forest that sounded like a man walking towards her.

It was dark, and she could not see the man's face clearly. The man approached and the woman was surprised to see that the man was a *masalai*.

The *masalai* asked her, "Where did my kinsman go, so that you're all alone here?" The woman replied that her husband had gone to hunt for marsupials inside the forest.

The *masalai* listened and said, "OK, when your husband returns, I'll return too."

The *masalai* then departed. The woman, Tambun Ipali, took a stick and went fairly far away into the forest to dig the earth. She dug a hole that went up inside the hut. She took some rubbish and blocked up the hole, then she sat. Her husband, Menakali Lesa, returned, then they removed the food from the earth oven and ate.

They ate, then the woman told her husband about the *masalai* who had come looking for him. When they were about to go to sleep, the woman told her husband to sleep in a corner of the hut. She would sleep inside the hole in the other corner.

When the man was dead asleep, the woman went inside the hole that she had dug. She put back the rubbish, covered the hole well, and sat there.

Very late at night, she heard very loud noises, as if many men were walking towards the hut. Her husband, Menakali Lesa, heard this and pretended to be dead asleep. The woman, Tambun Ipali, sat quietly inside the hole.

These noises were the sounds of the footsteps of hundreds of *masalai*s walking towards the hut that the married couple had made in the forest. They were following their leader who had spoken with the woman, Tambun Ipali.

This group of *masalai*s only followed their leader. If he told them to go somewhere, they would just follow him.

The *masalai*s went inside the house where the man, Menakali Lesa was lying. The man heard the *masalai*s enter his house, then he woke up and loudly broke wind.

When the *masalai* leader heard this, he spoke, "This place stinks." The man heard this and kept breaking wind because he had eaten plenty and his belly was bloated.

The *masalai* leader looked around the place, then he sat firmly on top of the hole where the woman, Tambun Ipali

was hiding. When the woman saw this, she quietly put her hands up and pulled the *masalai*'s testicles. Then she began to cut them.

The *masalai* was in pain and screamed. The other *masalai*s heard this, so they got up and shouted. It was nearly dawn, so the *masalai* shouted loudly that that they would die now. The other *masalai*s heard this and fled. The woman cut the testicles off of the *masalai* leader, then he fell down dead.

Dawn broke, and the man and his wife saw the *masalai* lying there. His hair was very long, and his two teeth were also very long. They saw that the *masalai* was finished, so they returned to their house.

However, the *masalai*'s kin returned and asked the two of them to straighten out the death of their leader. The man and his wife said that they would straighten out the death of their leader.

The married couple went back to this place. They killed a pig and gathered things together. They gave them to this group of *masalai*s. If they had not done this, the group of *masalai*s would have come and finished off everyone in Kandep Village.

Paul Ipan [Ípane is an Enga clan name (Lang, 1973: 215).]
P. O. Box 193
Arawa
North Solomons Province

C752.2.1. Tabu: supernatural creatures being abroad after sunrise; F252.1. Fairy king; F389.4. Fairy killed by mortal; F490+. Masalai; F544.3.5. Remarkably long teeth; F555.3. Very long hair; F585.2. Magic phantom army; F639.1.1. Mighty digger of tunnels; K910+. Dupe sits on trap, is killed from below; P210. Husband and wife; P600+. Payment of goods to kin as recompense for murder; Q211. Murder punished; Q595. Loss or destruction of property as punishment; R220. Flights; S110. Murders; S176.1. Mutilation: emasculation; X712.3.1H. Injury to testicles; X716.6H. Smell of breaking wind

People Arose and Filled the Earth

(Wantok 675, June 4, 1987, page 25)

Long, long ago, in the time of the ancestors, there were a man and his two wives who lived someplace. There were no other people who lived in this place, so they were by themselves. They had a big piece of land and forest, and they were never short of food.

One time, the man made some traps to catch wild game. He surrounded two mountains and two streams. He put the traps where the game could be caught. Afterwards, he sent the two women to go check on the traps and get the game.

The two of them went and saw many animals stuck in the traps. Oh my, when they saw this, their eyes popped open, and they became like children again.

One of them worked at bagging the animals, and they raced to get the animals. They did not care that it was a bad place, they just raced to get the animals and fill their net bags.

It was nearly evening when they carried the net bags and began to walk back home. Oh my, was the game very plentiful. So, they walked slowly towards the house. When they put the bags down, the ground shook because there was so much [game] in the bags.

The women wanted to rest, but their husband said, "I already prepared the firewood, but there are no leafy greens or other food to mix with the meat."

The women listened, then they got up to go the garden to fetch some leafy greens and other food to mix with the meat. They carried the food back, then they removed the skin from the food, cleaned the meat and removed the guts.

The earth oven was ready, and they covered it up. The women's husband made a fire and put the food inside. Afterwards, their husband told them to straighten their backs and sleep a little, that he would watch the earth oven.

When the earth oven was ready, the man uncovered it. Then he sat and ate. He did not wake his two wives. They awoke by themselves and saw him eating the food.

The man said to them, "What are you looking at? I left some for you." However, he was lying. The good-for-nothing had eaten all of the food and had not left any for them. The women saw this and were very troubled, so they cried.

The man finished all of the food, and his belly was bloated. He could not move, so he went into the house and fell down dead asleep.

The women saw that he was dead asleep. They decided to kill him. They were furious because he had often done this kind of thing. When there was food in the house, he ate it and just gave them the scraps.

They decided to burn the house with him inside. They took some large bamboo and wood, then piled these around the house. They put some strong logs on the house door to stop him from escaping.

They shut the door and they began to light the fire. They stood on two sides and lit it. They saw a bonfire arise and they stood far away, watching the house burn.

They heard the man shouting inside the house. They heard him say, "Birds, sing." The fire burned the house, then they heard a loud noise and they knew that the man's belly had broken.

Before long, they heard another noise. They knew that the man's head was burning. They were very happy because the man was dead. They returned to see that the house was completely burnt. The man was also incinerated and only his bones were left with the ashes of the fire.

The women went to get the bones then they put them inside of a water hole. After some time, they returned to look and they saw many little fish with tails inside the water hole. They went back home and prepared "grass" skirts, loincloths, stone axes, spears, headdresses and other things. They knew that when they had put the man's bones inside the water hole, many people would come and fill the land.

Much later, they returned to the water hole and looked. They did not see a single fish there. They saw the legs of many men, women and children by the water hole.

They followed the legs and saw that the legs were at the base of a big tree. The two women shouted and heard men who were nearby. They took the stone axes and cut a piece of tree about five feet long. Afterwards, a man came outside. When a man or woman came outside this tree, the two women would give clothing to them, and they would go away. Some were short people, others were tall people. They went to various places and populated their villages, so that now there are many people on the earth.

This ancestor story is from us, the Kame'a [**Hamtai**] People. It is a very long story, so I have shortened it and sent it to *Wantok* newspaper.

Steven Diano
Hawabango [**Hauabongo**] Village
Kaintiba
Gulf Province

A1600. Distribution and differentiation of peoples—general; D370C. Transformation: fish to child; D370M. Transformation: fish to man; D370W. Transformation: fish to woman; D447.8+. Transformation: bone to fish; D681. Gradual transformation; K812. Victim burned in his own house (or hiding place); K2213+. Treacherous husband; P210. Husband and wife; Q261. Treachery punished; Q272. Avarice punished; Q414. Punishment: burning alive; S62. Cruel husband; S112.0.2. House (hostel) burned with all inside; T145.0.1. Polygyny; T543.1. Birth from a tree; W151. Greed

Cassowary Treated Crab in a Nasty Manner

(Wantok 676, June 11, 1987, page 21)

Long ago, in the time of the ancestors, there lived a cassowary and a chicken in a village. They had become very good friends. One time, they felt terribly hot because for two months, there was only bright sun. The area had become too hot and it was completely dry.

The two of them felt that the sun was too hot, so they decided to get some air and to cool their bodies with some water. They found a canoe and jumped into it.

Quickly, the wind took them out into the deep sea. When the big waves jumped over the canoe it turned them around. The chicken's tail feathers were also turned by the wind. The cassowary's feathers stood straight.

The cassowary wanted its feathers to dance and twist in the wind like those of the chicken. However, the cassowary did not have long tail feathers.

The cassowary was jealous and angry. The cassowary asked the chicken about its tail feathers. The cassowary coveted the feathers on the chicken's tail very much.

The cassowary said to the chicken, "Give me your tail feathers, and I'll put my tail feathers on you for just a short time. I want to see them dance nicely in the wind from the sea."

The chicken replied, "I can't give them to you. They're stuck on my body. I can't remove them. They're still part of my body."

The chicken said, "How did you grow up without any tail feathers? I still have a few. You don't have any feathers standing up."

The cassowary was furious at what the chicken had said. The cassowary told the chicken, "If you don't give me your tail feathers, I'll break this canoe and we'll swim in the water. Then we won't have a way back to the beach."

However, the chicken was unconcerned by what the cassowary had said. The chicken repeated what it had said to the cassowary, that the tail feathers were stuck to its body. It was not something that could be removed and sent back and forth.

The cassowary was furious and gave a hard kick to the canoe. Their canoe broke into two pieces. The sea carried the pieces away, but the cassowary's anger got the best of it.

The chicken was not worried when the canoe broke; it flew back to the beach. The cassowary did not have a way back to the village; it nearly drowned. At this time, a gigantic crab went up to the place where the cassowary was.

The cassowary asked the crab, "Please, can you carry me on your back and swim to the shore?"

The crab replied, "Don't worry, I can help you."

The crab carried the cassowary and swam to the mainland. The crab said, "Now you won't die. Don't be afraid anymore." However, the cassowary ignored the crab and did not show gratitude or happiness towards the crab. The crab stopped saying good things and wanted to return to the

sea, but the cassowary put its leg right upon the crab's head. The crab broke into two pieces and died.

We, the people from Finschhafen, have this story of the place where crab and cassowary became enemies. This place is now called Satelbek [**Sattelberg**] Bible School [**Kâte** People, **Morobe** Province].

Gering Azeher
Kavui Oil Palm [Plantation]
Kimbe
West New Britain Province

[See the ancestor stories in *Wantok* #249,289 and 1184, which are similar.]

A2494.13+. Enmity between cassowary and chicken; B211.3.2.1. Speaking chicken; B211.3.17K. Speaking cassowary; B211.8.1K. Speaking crab; B295.2.1K. Animals make voyage in canoe; B296.2K. Animal (who is land-dweller) crosses water on back of another animal; B336+. Helpful crab killed by ungrateful cassowary; B876.2.1. Giant crab; J2133.11+. Cassowary destroys boat in anger, but almost drowns while chicken flies away; P310. Friendship; S110. Murders; W154. Ingratitude; W195. Envy

The Daughter Who Arose
From Her Father's Leg
(Wantok 677, June 18, 1987, page 21)

Long, long ago, in Gupagin (now called Angisi), there lived a man. This man's name was Katinpri. This man lived alone and never spoke. He was mute.

One time, Katinpri went to the forest to carve a signal drum. He cut a tree down, then he sat and carved the drum. After a while, a piece of firewood debris jumped up and struck his leg. Katinpri did not think too much about this small accident. He kept working at carving the drum.

Afternoon came, and he went back to his house. He cooked food, then he slept. When he awoke in the morning, he felt a pain in his leg. His leg swelled slowly and became huge. Poor Katinpri thought that his leg was just swelling for no reason, so he heated water and washed it, but his leg did not shrink.

Later, his leg broke open and a baby girl came out. Katinpri took the baby, washed her, and put her to sleep. He took care of the girl well, and the girl grew to be woman.

The leg sore did not dry, so Katinpri tied a bandage around it. They lived there for a while, and the girl became a woman. Katinpri made a house for her, and she lived there. Then one day, Katinpri went to the forest to hunt for wild game. His daughter was alone at home. She was sitting by the house when a bird with an arrow stuck in it flew down by the house and died. When the woman saw the bird, she knew that a man must have shot it and that he would be coming to retrieve his arrow.

Before long, the woman saw a young man arrive. The man saw the woman and was surprised. He asked about her parents. The woman replied that she did not know her mother, that she only had a father.

The man inquired further and the woman said that her father was mute, that he had gone hunting, and that she was there alone. The young man looked at this beautiful woman lustfully.

The young man told the woman that he wanted to marry her, but the woman said that she must ask her father first. The man listened and told the woman that the next day, he would return to hear her father's reply. The man gave the bird that he had shot to the woman, then he went back to his village.

In the afternoon, the father returned to the house. The woman told him about the young man who had come to their home. The father listened and was happy that his daughter would marry. He was not strong enough to always take care of her anymore.

The next day, the man went back to this place and made arrangements with the woman's father. Afterwards, he married her. The man and his wife lived happily. The man often told stories to his mute father-in-law and he often thought about finding a way to make him speak again.

One day, the young man went to the forest and cut the arm [or branch] of a ghost woman who in the form of a fig tree. He carried it and put it inside his father-in-law's signal drum. He knew that his father-in-law, Katinpri, was someone who beat the signal drum.

The man hid the ghost woman's arm inside the drum, then he called out for his father-in-law to beat the drum. Katinpri came and put his hand inside to get the stick for beating the drum, but his hand held the ghost woman's arm. The arm was icy cold, so he knew that he was holding an arm. He trembled and screamed.

His mouth was completely open, and he began to speak and laugh. All were happy that he was not mute anymore. They lived well at this place. Katinpri and his son-in-law often went hunting for game in the forest, and the woman would work in the garden. Because of this, they had plenty of food and they lived well in their little home.

One day, the young woman and her husband were angry. The man told her, "You did not come from a woman, you came from your father's leg."

The woman listened to this and was very troubled. She asked her father, and her father told her that what her husband had said was true. The father was terribly ashamed about what his son-in-law had said and done, so he thought hard and ran away from them.

In the morning, the married couple awoke and went to the forest to process sago. The father had pulled his signal drum and put it in the river. He took sago and spilled it in the house and everywhere that he had put the signal drum. Afterwards, he jumped into the signal drum and left this place.

The river carried him and his signal drum away. The *masalai*s of the Keram River took him and gave him spirit [or wind]. The river carried him down and he went down to their village.

After that, Katinpri lived on the shores of the Keram River in the village called Simudu [**Chuimondo**], in the region of the **Angoram** [People], **East Sepik** [Province]. We often go by motorboat to Angoram, and we often see Katinpri's signal drum there on the sand when the Keram River is dried up.

The married couple lived there for a while. They had children who all lived in **Angisi** Village [**Banaro** People].

Shirley D. Loweng
Church of Christ Mission
Bunam
Angoram
East Sepik Province

D950.8. Magic fig tree; D1298. Magic firewood; E422.1.3. Revenant with ice-cold hands; E293. Ghosts frighten people (deliberately); E426+. Revenant as fig tree; F121. Journey to world of spirits; F420.2.2. Water-spirits live in village under water; F424. River-spirit; F490+. Masalai; F954. Dumb person brought to speak; P210. Husband and wife; P230. Parents and children; P234. Father and daughter; P261. Father-in-law; P265. Son-in-law; R213. Escape from home; T100. Marriage; T541.5. Birth from man's thigh

The Banana Women Created Gurakor Village
(Wantok 678, June 25, 1987, page 21)

Long, long ago, in Gurakor [**Gurukor** Village], there lived a man who was married to two women [**Mumeng** People, **Morobe** Province]. The man was very lazy at making gardens, so when the women wanted to go to the garden, he would just go to the forest and hunt for wild game.

When he went to the forest, he never returned home quickly. He would go and go until about seven o'clock at night, then he would return home. He always did this sort of thing, and his wives grew tired of it. The two of them decided to find out what their husband really did when he did not return home.

In the morning, their husband left for the forest, then they went to the garden. They returned to the village in the afternoon, then they cooked food and went back to hide by the trail.

They hid by the trail and waited for their husband. One of them hid on one side of the trail, and the other hid on the other side. Later, they saw their husband walking towards them. He was carrying game and walking briskly.

When he came close to where the two women were hiding, they went behind him and followed him. The man turned and looked. He screamed terribly, threw the game away, and went back to the village.

The women turned down another trail. They ran back to the village and pretended to sleep. Before long, they heard their husband panting hard and arriving at the house. The women asked him what had happened, but he did not speak. He just fell down asleep quietly because he knew that it was just them who had fooled him and broken through the forest.

The two women just laughed quietly and slept. In the morning, the man did not speak. He just helped his wives doing the gardening. The women were happy because they thought that their trick had changed his thinking and that he would not go into the forest anymore.

They lived there for a long time, then the women forgot about this. However, the man was still angry. After a while, he thought about getting revenge. He went into the deep forest and cleared a small piece of forest. Afterwards, he went back to the village and told his two wives about their new garden.

In the morning, they all awoke to go to the deep forest. They walked and walked to the new garden. They arrived and the two women worked at cutting the forest, clearing the area to plant food. The man sat and sharpened his axe.

When the axe was very sharp, he walked over very quietly and gave a whack to the back of the first wife. The woman fell down dead. Then the man butchered her body into little pieces. He cooked them in an earth oven with leafy greens and sweet potatoes. Then he told his other wife to eat.

The woman was afraid to eat, but the man said that he would kill her if she did not eat the food. The poor woman fearfully ate the food. The man held the axe and told the woman to finish all of the food. The woman listened and finished all of the food. Her belly was completely bloated; she could not move.

Then the man told her, "Now is the time for each of us. See if you can find the way back home." The man left her there and went back to the village.

The poor woman could not walk because her belly was terribly bloated, so she rolled and rolled. She went past the fence of a house belonging to some young men, and she slept there.

The woman slept, then her belly burst and she died. The young men of this place smelled something, searched around and saw her there dead. They carried her body and buried it by their house.

After some weeks, they saw a banana plant bearing fruit. They saw that the bananas were edible. When the bananas were ripe, there were six young women inside the six ripe bananas. When the men went away to the forest, the women went outside and cleaned the area around the house. They cut firewood and straightened everything up, then they went back inside the bananas.

The young men returned to the house in the afternoon. They saw that the place was organized, so they thought hard. The next day, they went back to the forest. The women came and cleaned the house, then went back into the bananas. The men returned and saw the same thing. They decided to find out who it was that was cleaning their house.

The next day, the men pretended to go to the forest, but they went and hid. Afterwards, they saw the beautiful young women come down from the bananas and go into their house. The women cleaned up, cut firewood, fetched water, and organized everything. Later, they sat in the house.

The men came very quietly, went inside the house and held the women. Later, they married these women. They all lived in this village and raised children. Many people were raised there, and this village enlarged. The name of this village is Gurakor.

Tom Philimon
P. O. Box 1333
Bulolo
Morobe Province

A991+. Origin of particular village; E631.5.7K. Reincarnation as banana plants; F562.4+. Women live in banana; G61. Relative's flesh eaten unwittingly; K2320. Deception by frightening; P210. Husband and wife; P230. Parents and children; Q411. Death as punishment; Q260. Deceptions punished; Q438. Punishment: abandonment in forest; Q478+. Punishment: eating dead relative; R210. Escapes; R260. Pursuits; S62. Cruel husband; S62.1. Bluebeard; S63+. Husband kills wife; S139.2. Slain person dismembered; S139.2.2+. Corpse put into cooking pot or cooked; S139.4. Murder by mangling with axe; S143. Abandonment in forest; S183.1. Person forced to eat hearts (flesh) of relatives (draw blood); S441. Cast-off wife and child abandoned in forest; T100. Marriage; T145.0.1. Polygyny; V61.3+. Dead buried; W111. Laziness

The Old Woman Scared the Vain Women

(Wantok 679, July 2-9, 1987, page 21)

Long, long ago, in the time of the ancestors, there was a big problem that occurred on **Petats** Island [**Petats** People, **North Solomons** Province]. The rain had not fallen for a long time, and there was no water on the island.

One day, the women of the island decided to go to the mainland [**Buka** Island] and find water. They awoke in the morning and took their canoes, then they paddled and paddled until they arrived on the mainland. They tied up the canoes well, then they carried pots and things to fill with water, and they went searching.

Big River

They searched and arrived at a big river. The women saw the water and were very happy. They jumped inside then washed, laughed and played in the water.

They saw an old woman with ringworm coming down to the water. The woman was not an ordinary woman. This river belonged to her and her *masalai* snakes.

When the women saw this old ringworm woman, they scolded her and mocked her. They did not want her to go inside the water, lest her ringworm ruin the river and they bring it back to their home.

They shouted, "Hey, old woman, don't go inside the water and ruin it. We want to fetch the water."

The old woman listened to these young women boast, mock and scold her. She was very troubled. Then she called out to her *masalai* snakes

Ringworm Woman

She called out, "Monotegin! Monotengin! Come and hear what the women are doing to me. They're calling me scab-woman. I want you to come and show them."

When the old woman called out like this, the clouds thundered and the little *masalai* snakes flew down to the river.

Escape

The women saw this and were terrified. They got up with their containers of water, but the snakes went inside and ruined all of the water. The women cried and trembled because they thought that the woman had told the snakes to finish them off.

However, the old woman left the snakes and just gave a good scare to the women. Afterwards, she was sorry for them. She spoke again, then her *masalai* snakes left the water and went back to their home. The women were terrified. They quietly took their water containers to their canoes and paddled back to the island.

They knew that they had been wrong and that this was why they had been punished. However, they also knew that the old woman was sorry for them. She had only scared them and not killed them.

The snakes lived in the deep forest. They always helped this old woman at the river. These *masalai*s never did anything else because the mission came to this place and eliminated such behavior.

Jonathan Manin and Israel Kout

Arawa

North Solomons Province

B91.4. Sky-traveling snake; D1774. Magic results from speaking; D2074.1. Animals magically called; D2149.1. Thunderbolt magically produced; D2156+. Magic control over snakes; D2176.3. Evil spirit exorcised; F420.1.3.9. Water-spirit as snake; F490+. Masalai; Q288. Punishment for mockery; Q304. Scolding punished; Q331.2. Vanity punished; Q552.11. Punishment: meeting frightful apparition; R210. Escapes; V331. Conversion to Christianity; W116. Vanity

The Five Brothers Killed a *Masalai*

(Wantok 680, July 9-16, 1987, page 22)

Long, long ago, in the time of the ancestors, there was a big *masalai* pig that lived by a place called Rubawa. Rubawa was the name of a big river that had many, many crocodiles.

Near this river, there was a huge sword-grass land. The *masalai* pig lived inside this sword-grass land. This *masalai* pig never traveled around, it just slept. When the pig was hungry, it would get up and go to a village, then eat all of the men, women, pigs, dogs, and whatever kinds of animals it could find.

It would eat everything, then go to sleep in the grasslands for about two months. Afterwards, it would wake up and look for food again. This *masalai* pig did this until it finished off everyone in eight villages. Then there was just one village left.

The people of this last village knew about the habits of this *masalai*, so they decided to flee their village. They did not want this *masalai* pig to eat them too. The people cut large trees in the forest, carved canoes from them, then made houses on top of the canoes.

The men of the village tried to surround the pig and shoot it with spears, but it would not die. They bound it with nets, but it was very strong and it broke their nets.

When the pig squealed, its voice was like the sound of thunder, and the ground would shake with it.

When the *masalai* pig finished everyone in the ninth village, it went to sleep for two months. The people of the last village decided to flee then. All of them went into the big canoes that they had carved and prepared for their flight.

One woman who was pregnant was there at this time. When she and her husband left the village and went out, their canoe turned over. They told her to try another canoe. She wanted to go on top of the other canoes, but she was too heavy and nearly tipped the other canoes, making these people angry.

The woman's husband saw this and was very worried about his wife. Quickly, he dug into the sand and made a big hole where his wife could hide. After he did this, he jumped on the last canoe, then all of them left the village and paddled out to the deep sea.

The woman hid inside the hole and listened to the *masalai* pig squeal and come towards their village. When the pig walked, the earth shook. The pig came to the village and searched for everyone who had fled. The pig was angry and broke all of the houses, ruining everything in the village. Then it went back to sleep in the grasslands.

Later, the woman just stayed in the hole. At night, she would come outside and look for food quickly, then she would go back into her hole. She did this for a while, then she gave birth to five babies. Her first two babies were boys, the third was a cockatoo, the fourth was a vine called *wasimara*, and the fifth was a crocodile.

The woman took care of her children until they became big. She would always tell them the story of the *masalai* pig that had killed everyone, and of the people of the village who had fled the *masalai*. The children listened and said that they would not go far, that they would just stay near the hole where they lived with their mother.

One day, the two boys told their mother that they would try to kill the *masalai* pig. They told their little brothers to take care of their mother, then the two of them left for the forest to cut *limbum* palm trees and sharpen them into spears.

The two brothers entered the forest. They cut *limbum* palms, then they began to sharpen them into spears. They sharpened twenty spears, ten for the big brother and ten for the little brother. After they finished, they carried them back home.

At night, they sat and talked about going to kill the *masalai* pig. Their mother was happy to hear that her children would kill this *masalai*. But she told them to be very care-

ful lest the *masalai* kill them. They finished talking, then went to sleep.

The next day, the five brothers all woke up in the very early morning. They carried the spears and surrounded the grasslands where the *masalai* pig slept. When they arrived there, the big brother divided the work among his little brothers.

He sent the crocodile to watch by the river. Then he sent Wasimara to put his branches all around the grasslands, and he sent to cockatoo up a tree. He told the little brother to go stand in back of the pig. He himself stood right in front of the *masalai* pig's face.

The brothers were ready, and the eldest threw a spear at the pig. The spear stuck to the pig's body. The pig got up and went to eat the big brother, but the little brother was ready in the rear and he shot the pig. The cockatoo flew down and shot the pig's eye. Then Wasimara got up and tied the pig's four legs.

All of the brothers gathered together and pummeled the *masalai* pig. They pulled the pig slowly towards the place in the river where the crocodile was waiting. That afternoon, they went to the river and the big brother called out to the crocodile.

The crocodile came and began to fight with the *masalai* pig. They fought and fought, then the crocodile knocked out the *masalai*. The crocodile put the pig on his back and swam in the water until he arrived at their home.

Their mother saw this and was ecstatic because her sons were strong and they had killed the pig. She sang and danced and was happy. When the other sons came, the mother cooked food. They celebrated, sat and ate together.

Later, the big brother divided their home. He told the crocodile to go live in the water, Wasimara to live in the forest, and the cockatoo to live on top of trees. The two brothers with their old mother would live in the village. The name of this village is Rubawa.

Now, if you go to Rubawa [**Radava**] Village, you will see many crocodiles in the river, and in the forest there will be many cockatoos and *wasimara* vines. This ancestor story is from the Matagara Clan in the Rabaraba District of **Milne Bay** Province [**Boianaki** People].

Rod Willis Kopa

P. O. Box 2070

Madang

Madang Province

A515.1.1+. Quintuplet culture heroes; B16.1.4.1. Giant devastating boar; B871.1.2. Giant boar; F401.3.10K. Spirit in form of boar; F531.3+. Giant's walking causes earthquake; F531.3+. Giant's walking causes thunder; F490+. Masalai; G346. Devastating monster; G352.2. Wild boar as ogre;

G510.4. Hero overcomes devastating animal; K914. Murder from ambush; P210. Husband and wife; P231. Mother and son; P251.6.2+. Five brothers; Q211. Murder punished; Q411. Death as punishment; R213. Escape from home; R315+. Hole as refuge; S110. Murders; T554.0.3K+. Woman gives birth to crocodile; T554.10+. Woman bears cockatoo; T555+. Woman gives birth to a vine: T570. Pregnancy; T580. Childbirth; Z71.16.2. Formulistic number: ten; Z210. Brothers as heroes

A *Masalai* Ate Her Own Child

(Wantok 681, July 16-23, 1987, page 18)

Long, long ago, in the time of the ancestors, there were two brothers who lived in a village. They had a huge garden, and the two men were excellent hunters.

One day, they wanted to eat pork, so the big brother told his little brother that they would go to the forest and hunt for some wild pig. In the early morning, they awoke, left the village and walked off to the forest. They walked and walked until they arrived at the base of a mango tree. They knew that pigs always came to this area, so they had gone there directly.

They saw that the mango tree was bearing plenty of ripe mangos. The wild pigs often came and gathered in this area, eating the mangos that fell about on the ground.

They saw the ripe mangos lying there, so they took stones and put them inside the mangos. After they finished, they went up the tree to sit and wait. Afterwards, they saw a huge wild pig walking around. The pig came and began to eat mangos.

The brothers watched the pig and they sat quietly. The pig was famished, so it just gobbled the mangos. A piece of stone inside a mango became stuck in the pig's throat, and the pig collapsed.

The pig turned and turned until it died. When the brothers saw that the pig was dead, they were very happy and they jumped down the tree quickly. They found vines, tied up the pig's legs and left it at the base of the tree.

They went up the tree again and made a platform. When they finished, they sat and looked at the faraway places. They saw smoke rising near a river.

The big brother told his little brother, "Go to that place and bring some fire back, then we'll make a fire and singe off the pig's hair."

The little brother listened and descended. He went through the forest to the place where the smoke was rising. He arrived there and saw a ghost woman and her baby sitting by the fire.

The *masalai* woman saw him and asked, "Why did you come here?"

The little brother said, "I came to get some of your fire to bring to my big brother to light his tobacco."

The *masalai* woman knew that the boy was lying, so she said, "You must tell the truth or I'll eat you."

The little brother listened and was terrified. He told the *masalai* that he wanted to take some fire so that they could singe off the hair of a pig that they had killed. The *masalai* listened and told the boy that they would all go together to the place where he and his brother had killed the pig.

The *masalai* woman gave her baby to the boy to carry, while she held a piece of firewood as they walked back. While they walked on the trail, the boy smelled the awful aroma of the baby *masalai*, and he wanted to vomit.

He was afraid of the *masalai* woman, so he did not speak. However, he hit the baby. So when the baby cried, his mother asked the boy what was happening. The boy replied, "Oh, it's nothing. I think the baby's afraid of me and is crying."

He kept doing this until they arrived at the base of the mango tree. They saw the big brother arranging the firewood and waiting. He saw his brother carrying the baby, and the woman walking with the fire. He knew that this woman was a *masalai*.

They made a big fire and singed off the pig's hair, then the big brother butchered the pig and removed the guts. The *masalai* woman was very happy because she thought that she would eat the pig then kill the brothers and eat them too.

She told the brothers, "Sons, I'll take the pig guts to the river and wash them well, then I'll bring them back. You two watch your little brother [the baby]."

The *masalai* carried the pig guts to the river, then the brothers quickly killed the *masalai*'s baby and cooked him well in an earth oven. Then they fled up to the platform on the mango tree.

The brothers sat and ate a pig leg on the tree. While they ate, the *masalai* woman returned with the pig guts. They called down to the *masalai* and told her that her food was ready and by the fire. The *masalai* listened and forgot her son. She uncovered the earth oven then sat and ate.

The *masalai* ate one arm, then she ate another arm, and then she arrived at the baby's fingers. The brothers had filled up all of the pork into a basket and they were ready to fly.

They watched and watched. They saw that the *masalai* was eating her son's fingers. They shouted to her, "Hey mama, that's not pork. You're eating your own son's bones!"

The *masalai* woman heard this and threw away the bones. She called out for her kin to help her kill the two brothers. The *masalai* clan spilled out and surrounded the base of the mango tree. They circled the tree and began to cut it with their teeth. After a while, the tree was about to fall.

When the mango tree was ready to fall, the brothers became birds and flew back to their home. The mango tree fell and killed the *masalai* woman. Her kin thought it was the two brothers, so they ate her.

The brothers returned to their village and lived well. The *masalai* woman was dead, so she could not follow them and try to kill them to avenge the death of her son.

Anuma Kay

P. O. Box 3906

Lae

Morobe Province

B871.1.2. Giant boar; D642.2. Transformation to escape death; D150M. Transformation: man to bird; D642.6. Transformation to escape ogress; D671. Transformation flight; E425.1.4. Revenant as woman carrying baby; E425.3. Revenant as child; E588. Ghost leaves stench behind; F544.3. Remarkable teeth; F687. Remarkable fragrance (odor) of person; F490+. Masalai; G11.10. Cannibalistic spirits; G61. Relative's flesh eaten unwittingly; K897.1+. Dupe killed by putting thorns in food it is about to swallow; N331+. Killed by treefall; P231. Mother and son; P251.5. Two brothers; R210. Escapes; R311. Tree refuge; S110. Murders; S139.2.2+. Corpse put into cooking pot or cooked; W157. Dishonesty

Two Brothers Fought Over Women

(Wantok 682, July 23-30, 1987, page 18)

Long ago, in the time of the ancestors, two brothers lived in a village. One day, the brothers decided to go hunt for wild game in the forest. They prepared their bows and arrows, then they departed.

They went all around the forest, but they did not find a single animal, so they turned and walked back to the village. They walked and walked, then they saw a hornbill eating tree fruits. They walked quietly towards the tree. They approached, then one brother aimed his bow carefully and shot down the hornbill.

However, the hornbill did not fall to the ground; it flew away with the arrow. The brothers saw this and followed the bird. The hornbill flew down to the house of an old woman.

The old woman saw the hornbill come down with the arrow and she scolded her hornbill. After she finished, she killed the hornbill and sat waiting to see who would follow the bird.

The brothers arrived and asked the old woman whether she had seen the bird that they had shot. The old woman listened and asked, "What kind of bird did you shoot?"

They replied that they had killed a hornbill. The old woman told them that it was her bird that they had shot. The brothers listened and were speechless. They just sat quietly.

The old woman went up into the house and called to the brothers that they should rest first, then they could return to their village. She gave them green coconuts to drink, then she told them that she would go to the garden and bring some food back. After she cooked it, they could return.

The old woman went to the garden and removed some food, then she took some leafy greens and returned home. She told the two boys [men] to scrape the coconuts. The two of them took shells, then sat and scraped coconuts. The old woman oiled the food and leafy greens. They ate, then the men told her that they would go back to their village.

The old woman told them, "It's too dark now and you have very far to walk. Never mind that, you'll sleep here. In the morning, you'll go back home."

The boys listened and thought hard. They told the old woman, "No, we can walk. We know the trail."

The old woman was persistent, "I want you to sleep here tonight because I want you to see something that will happen here tonight."

The boys listened and told the old woman that they would sleep there. The old woman told them, "Tonight when you hear singing, you must not go outside and look. You must just sit inside the house and look."

The old woman told them this, then they arranged things for sleeping and went to sleep. They did not hear anything because their bodies were bloated and their bellies were completely filled, so they were dead asleep. When something was happening that night, the old woman awakened them. They awoke and heard a loud noise.

The old woman told them, "It's the coconuts singing tonight. They're not people. No, the coconuts came down to the ground. They're passionately singing and dancing."

The coconuts sang and danced intensely until it was close to dawn, then they all went back and hung onto their stems. In the morning, the boys awoke and went outside. They saw the coconuts hanging there.

They ate, then they wanted to return to their village. The old woman told them, "Never mind that. You can't go empty-handed. Go up this white coconut palm, then each of you bring one down. Fetch green coconuts, and don't throw them down. Carry them down carefully and place them on the ground."

The brothers listened to what the old woman said, then they climbed up the white coconut palm. They each took a green coconut, then descended. The old woman told them again to carry the coconuts carefully, and not to throw them down on the ground. The two boys thanked the old woman and walked back to their village.

They walked and walked, then they saw a big lizard lying on the trail. When the big brother saw the lizard, he nervously anticipated killing it, so he forgot what the old woman had said. He threw down his coconut.

The little brother still remembered what the old woman had said, so he placed his coconut down gently on the ground. The brothers chased the lizard up a tree. The two of them stood at the base of the tree and heard two women talking and laughing.

They came out and saw two beautiful women standing, talking and laughing. The women saw them and asked, "Husbands, did you kill the lizard too or not?"

The men listened and were surprised. They said, "We don't have wives." Then the women told them that it was just them whom they had carried from the old woman's home.

The big brother's wife had a bad leg because he had forgotten and thrown the coconut down on the ground. However, the little brother's wife was truly beautiful.

The big brother saw that his wife's leg was bad, so he was jealous of his little brother. He told his little brother that they would keep following the lizard. They told the women to just wait on the trail.

The brothers arrived at the base of the big tree. The big brother told the little brother to climb it. The little brother looked and saw a rattan. He carried it up a small tree. He tied the rattan, then he jumped to the big tree.

The big brother saw this and quickly went up the small tree, cutting down the rattan. The rattan broke, and the poor little brother did not have a way to get down to the ground.

He killed the lizard, then when he turned to come down, he saw that the rattan was broken. He shouted to his big brother to help him.

The big brother listened and said, "You're still strong. Go find a way down. I'll go marry your wife too."

The poor little brother listened to this and was very troubled. He shouted, but his big brother had already gone back to get the women and go back to the village. The big brother married both of the women.

The little brother sat on top of the tree for about six months. His body was emaciated because he did not have

food or water. Birds always came to eat the tree fruits, so he would kill them and eat them because he had asked the birds to help him but they did not want to do so.

The poor little brother kept sitting on the tree. All of his strength was gone, and he thought that he would die on top of the tree. However one day, a group of birds flew by and ate the tree fruits. The little brother asked them if they could help carry him down to the ground.

The birds saw that the man was close to death, and were sorry for him. They told him that they would help him. The man asked them to carry him and put him in his garden.

The birds listened to him. They all gathered together, raised him up and flew away. The man did not have any more strength, so he was not heavy. The birds carried him gently and put him in his garden.

The man did not move when they put him down on the ground, so they were worried and [did not leave]. They sat and watched him.

That day, his wife went to the garden and was surprised to see many birds filling the garden. The birds saw her and said, "We carried your husband here. He's lying in the garden."

The woman listened and went to see the poor man who was unconscious. When she saw this, she cried terribly. Her husband opened his eyes and saw her. Then he too was troubled and cried. Her husband told her what his brother had done to him. He told of the little birds who had helped him.

The woman listened and told the birds, "I'll take care of my husband. When he's strong again, we'll reward you for the great work that you have done."

The birds listened and were happy, but they did not go too far. They stayed close to the garden and him. The man told his wife not to tell his brother that he was in the garden. He said that when he became strong again, he would get revenge. The woman just listened, then she went back to the village.

Every day, the woman would go back to the garden, stay with her husband and give him food. When her husband's body became a little stronger, he told her to get a bow for him. The woman brought a bow to her husband. He straightened it and practiced shooting until he became accurate.

The man told his wife that he was ready to get revenge. He told her, "Go back to the village and break a hole in the side of the house where I can go inside. Then you must prepare to light a fire. When you hear a noise, light the fire so I can see well and shoot him."

The woman listened to her husband and went back to the village. She pretended to work around the house, then she broke a hole in the wall of the house. When the big brother and his bad-legged wife returned, the woman told them that forest debris had come close to the house, so she was working at cleaning it up.

That night, they ate and went to sleep. The man slept at the far edge and his two wives slept in the center. However, the little brother's wife did not really sleep. She kept an ear out for her husband. Then she heard a noise and she knew that her husband had arrived.

She got up and blew on the fire quickly. The fire lit up, and her husband saw his brother dead asleep. Very quietly, he aimed at his brother's chest and let the arrow fly. The arrow shot his big brother right in the liver, killing him.

The little brother told the two women to carry their belongings, then the three of them would flee this village, and go to live far away. The little brother married the two women, and they lived in their new home.

My story is too long, so I have shortened it a little.

Justin Moaitz
Gabsonkeg [**Gabsonkek**] Village [**Wampar** People]
Norobe [**Morobe**] Province

B211.3. Speaking bird; B450. Helpful birds; B542.1. Bird flies with man to safety; B552. Man carried by bird; D431.11+W. Transformation: coconut to woman; D1615.3+. Singing coconut; D1646.1+. Dancing coconut; J652. Inattention to warnings; J1050. Attention to warnings; K2211.0.1. Treacherous elder brother(s); P210. Husband and wife; P251.4+. One brother acts wisely, another acts unwisely; P251.5. Two brothers; P251.5.3. Hostile brothers; P263. Brother-in-law; P264. Sister-in-law; Q261. Treachery punished; Q285. Cruelty punished; Q411. Death as punishment; R130. Rescue of abandoned or lost persons; R213. Escape from home; S70+. Cruel brother; S73.1. Fratricide; S110. Murders; S143.2. Abandonment in tall tree; T100. Marriage; T145.0.1. Polygyny; W27. Gratitude; W181. Jealousy

Kaun and Weibaru, Two Men [Who Created] the Simbrien Song and Dance

(Wantok 683, July 30-August 6, 1987, page 18)

This ancestor story is about two brothers, Kaun and Weibaru. Kaun lived in his village, **Polu**, and Weibaru lived in **Abua**. These two brothers excelled at composing various songs, and everyone in the various villages knew them well.

One day, they received a message that a big festival would happen, so they began to prepare for the big festival. The man who wanted to make this big festival was Selmien from Yepura [**Yapunda**?] Village [**Yapunda** People?].

Selmien sent a message to all of the villages to come to his festival. He asked his friend, Kaun, and his brother Weibaru to come and perform the Simbrien. The two brothers were the first to have performed this song and dance.

After the brothers received the message, they also sent the message to other villages to go to the festival when the sun set. However, many did not come because they were not happy. Only one of their leaders went to see Kaun and his little brother, Weibaru.

The man went to see the brothers, and the brothers prepared to go to the festival. The man wanted to chew betel nuts, so he asked Kaun, "Brother, your lime [calcium oxide] comes first, then I'll chew betel nut."

Kaun was still preparing things for the festival, so he told him, "Go inside the house and ask the in-law."

The man went inside the house and asked Kaun's second wife for lime, but the woman showed her body to the man and completely confused him.

The man thought of abducting Kaun's wife, so he played a trick. He went out of the house, removed his lime and began to chew betel nuts. When he finished, he spat upon his [leg]. Then he took some grass from the forest, tied up his leg and pretended to walk back awkwardly.

Kaun saw this and asked him about it. He lied, "Bamboo cut my leg." Kaun listened and said, "That's OK. Stay in the village and look after things. Your in-law is menstruating and sleeping."

Then Kaun, his first wife, and his brother, Weibaru, went to the festival at Yapura [Yapunda]. They went close to Yapura. Oh my, the place was hot! However when Kaun and Weibaru with their kin went there, oh no, the Simbrien was hotter still.

All of the women were "wounded" by his kin. They passionately sang and danced, not thinking about what was happening to their village. The hand drums were beaten, and the signal drums too. The voices of the men made the fire bright.

Kaun was singing and dancing. He heard the sound of signal drum at his spirit house. At this time, the man who had lied and was staying in the village had sex with Kaun's wife, then prepared to abduct the signal drum and Kaun's wife to his village.

He chewed a vine and spat upon the signal drum, then the signal drum was ready to go. He took Kaun's second wife and put her someplace. Then he took a yam and put it in another place, and took them to his village. This yam is called _opoi_ in my language.

Kaun heard his signal drum, so he immediately left his first wife at the festival grounds and ran back to the village. He sped off and arrived at Polu. He saw that his wife and his signal drum were not there. Then Kaun sped off again, following their trail. He ran and ran until he arrived at the man's village.

The next day, he went back again and took back his wife. However, he could not take back his signal drum. He chewed a vine and spat and spat, but the signal drum was stuck at a post that belonged to the clan called Palu. Palu is the name of the signal drum that belonged to Kaun of Polu Village.

The Simbrien song and dance is very popular among everyone in Palai [Palei/**Kayik** People?]. Mount Polu is near Suning [**Suninga**] Village in the Nuku District of **West Sepik** Province.

August S. Nick
P. O. Box 8
Vanimo
West Sepik Province

A1464.2.1. Origin of particular song; A1542.2. Origin of particular dance; D965+. Magic vine; D1001. Magic spittle; K1326. Seduction by feigned illness; P210. Husband and wife; P251.5. Two brothers; P260. Relations by law; P263. Brother-in-law; P264. Sister-in-law; P310. Friendship; R10. Abduction; R151.1. Husband rescues stolen wife; R260. Pursuits; T145.0.1. Polygyny; T471. Rape; V112.1. Spirit huts; X743H. Humor concerning exhibitionism

Why Cassowaries Do Not Fly Anymore

(Wantok 684, August 6-13, 1987, page 18)

Long, long ago, Cassowary flew around in the forest, while poor Hornbill walked on the ground. At this time, the two birds were very good friends, so they lived together.

Hornbill would make a house underneath the tree in which Cassowary slept. One day, Cassowary searched for a new place in the forest where there was much food. There was wild game for each of them at this place, so Cassowary thought that they would go there to live. Cassowary flew around and examined this place carefully, then went back to tell Hornbill.

Hornbill replied, "We have a good home. Why should we leave for this new place?"

Cassowary replied, "This new place is much nicer than where we live now."

Cassowary tried to talk Hornbill into moving, but Hornbill was not very happy. Hornbill told Cassowary, "It's easy for you to talk because you can fly there easily.

However, I must walk and I'll have to do so for a very long time to get there."

Cassowary persisted and Hornbill eventually agreed. They finished the arrangements, then they slept. Cassowary had convinced Hornbill into it by saying that they would walk there, so Hornbill felt a little better.

In the morning, the two of them awoke and began to walk to their new home. They walked and walked, then Cassowary tired and told Hornbill that it would fly up to see the new place.

However, Cassowary took a shortcut and arrived at the new place. Cassowary [flew] well, going up to the mountains, crossing a river, and arriving at their new home.

When Hornbill arrived at this place, it was completely dark. Hornbill was completely out of breath. Its two legs were in pain and its neck was dry. Hornbill was furious at its friend, Cassowary.

Cassowary saw Hornbill arrive, then Cassowary said, "We've come close to the place, so I'll leave you and fly there first. You'll walk there very slowly and you'll get there."

When Hornbill heard this, it was even angrier and thought of getting revenge upon its friend. Hornbill began to think of a way to ruin its friend.

The next day, Hornbill got up to see an insect that was very knowledgeable. Hornbill told the insect what Cassowary had done. The insect listened and told Hornbill that it would take care of Hornbill's worries.

Cassowary slept on a tree branch and did not know what its friend, Hornbill, was thinking. The tree insect walked up the tree and began to make a hole in the tree branch where Cassowary was sleeping.

The tree branch broke and Cassowary fell down very badly to the base of the tree, breaking its two wings. Hornbill saw this and was very sorry. Hornbill saw the insect taking some medicine to help Cassowary.

The insect gave the medicine to Cassowary to make it better, but the insect told Hornbill that Cassowary could not fly again. The insect gave medicine to Hornbill and Hornbill flew up to a tree branch, while poor Cassowary slept at the base of the tree.

After this, the two birds were no longer friends. Cassowary traveled by itself underneath the trees in the forest and Hornbill flew above among the tree branches.

Today, if you see a tree hole where a hornbill is nesting, you will see a cassowary sleeping at the base of the tree.

Hyacinth Y. Kais [Kasi]
P. O. Box 1052
Boroko
National Capital District

[See the ancestor stories in Wantok #660, 661, 687 and 701. H. Y. Kasi also wrote these stories. This story is probably from the **Kopar** or **Watam** People, **East Sepik Province**.]

A2442.2+. Hornbill's flight; A2442.1.1.1K+. Why cassowary is flightless; A2494.13+. Enmity between cassowary and hornbill; B211.3+. Speaking hornbill; B211.3.17K. Speaking cassowary; B211.4. Speaking insects; B296. Animals go a-journeying; B299.14K. Animals build house; B480. Helpful insects; D670. Magic flight; D1241. Magic medicine (= charm); K2297. Treacherous friend; P310. Friendship; Q263. Lying (perjury) punished; W157. Dishonesty

A *Masalai* Blocked a Cave
Entrance and Killed a Family

(Wantok 685, August 13-20, 1987, page 22)

Long, long ago, in the time of the ancestors, there was a family that made a huge garden in the forest. The place that they made the garden was very far away, so they had to walk and walk a long way to get there.

This new garden was very far, so the parents took their children and went to this place. They thought that they would sleep and work in their new garden for some days.

Near the garden was a big cave. This cave was not an ordinary one. No, it was the home of a *masalai*, but the family did not know this.

The family arrived at this place, organized all of their things and made beds inside the cave. The mother took the girls and went down to the river to catch fish. The father took the boys and went to hunt for game in the forest. They left two little children inside the cave.

The two children sat and played, then the *masalai* arrived. The *masalai* hit the stone and blocked the cave, then the *masalai* hit the stone again and the cave entrance was clear. The two children saw this and were terrified. They trembled and sat there.

In the afternoon, the parents returned. The children cried terribly and told them about what had happened when they were in the cave. The parents listened to the story, but they did not believe it. The children were persistent and said that they did not want to sleep inside the cave.

The mother cooked food and they all gathered to eat. Then they went to sleep. However, the two little children did not want to try sleeping inside, so they went outside.

Their father was furious, so he beat them and pulled them back inside the cave.

They slept there, then late at night, the *masalai* came and hit the stone, blocking the entrance of the cave where the family was sleeping. They did not have a way to get out, but they did not know that their way was blocked.

One child defecated, so the mother got up to remove the feces. She saw that the stone was blocking the cave entrance. She awakened her husband and the other children. They tried to remove the stone, but the stone was stuck fast.

They just stayed inside the cave. After a while, the children began to die. The little children died first. Then some of the bigger children died. Then their father died. Finally, only the mother, a daughter and their dog were left.

The mother told the daughter, "I am also close to dying. You must keep your eyes upon the entrance. When you see the stone clear from the entrance, you must send the dog out first. The dog will chase the *masalai*, then you can go outside."

The daughter listened to her mother, then they stayed there for a while and the mother died too. Only the daughter and the dog were left in the cave. They just sat and watched the cave entrance.

One day, the woman saw the cave open slowly. She knew that the *masalai* must be outside. Immediately, she shoved her dog outside. The dog chased the *masalai* away, and the woman went outside the cave.

She took her dog, then they walked and walked, looking for food because they were half-dead from hunger. They walked and walked, then they arrived at a garden. This was the garden of an old woman. The woman went directly to the sugarcanes. She was about to break some and drink the juice, but the old woman also arrived in the garden. The [young] woman was afraid and hid among the canes.

The old woman arrived at the garden and just wanted to work. She saw that there were many flies in the sugarcanes, so she went to check on them.

Then the woman shouted to her, "Grandma, my family and I came to the garden and slept in the cave. The *masalai* killed all of us except me, so I escaped and went here."

The old woman listened and was very sorry for her. She removed some food from the garden, made a fire, and cooked the food. Then the woman and her dog ate. After they ate, the old woman took them to her village.

They lived there for a while, then the woman married the old woman's son, and they continued to live there. The other young men of the village saw the beautiful woman and were jealous of her husband. One time, the man went to the forest, and the other men killed him.

The woman revived him because she was not an ordinary woman, she was an authority [at magic]. Then the man and his wife had children and lived well in their village.

[Anonymous]

D1552. Mountains or rocks open and close; D1711. Magician; E50. Resuscitation by magic; F490+. Masalai; G580+. Ogres chased away by dog; J652. Inattention to warnings; P210. Husband and wife; P231. Mother and son; P232. Mother and daughter; P233 Father and son; P234. Father and daughter; P250. Brothers and sisters; P262. Mother-in-law; P265+. Daughter-in-law; R45.3. Captivity in cave; R220. Flights; R51.1. Prisoners starved; S110. Murders; T75.2. Scorned lover kills successful one; T100. Marriage; W181. Jealousy; Z356. Unique survivor

A Woman Burned Her Husband

(Wantok 686, August 20, 1987, page 18)

Long, long ago, in the time of the ancestors, there lived an ancestor who excelled at trapping marsupials (*kapul*), pigs and birds.

One day, he went and placed many, many traps in the forest, then he went back to sleep in his house. The next day, he woke up and went to check on the traps. He was very happy to see that all of his traps had animals in them. Not one was empty.

He put the pigs in three net bags and he put the marsupials in three net bags, then he carried them back to his village. He arrived and called out for his wife to come. He told her to go to the garden and fetch a certain kind of banana. He gave the name of the banana, then the poor woman went to the garden and worked very hard finding these bananas that her husband had asked for.

While the woman was looking for the bananas in the garden, her husband was singeing the marsupial's skins and cleaning them. Afterwards, he singed off the pig hair then butchered and cleaned them too.

The woman found the bananas, then she brought them back to the village. Her husband told her to remove the peels and put them aside. Then he sent her to the forest to find a certain kind of leafy green. He gave the name of the leafy green.

The poor woman searched without finding any, so she took some other kind and went back to the village. She arrived there, and her husband had butchered all of the meat. He saw the greens and scolded his wife.

He told his wife to go to his kin. The woman went to his kin. Later, she went back to where her husband was.

She saw that her husband was cooking the food with [hot] stones.

The old man gathered all of the food, including the food that his wife had found, *aibika* and bananas, with the pork from the pigs that he had trapped.

The woman arrived at her kin's mountain village. She asked all of her kin to go with her. When they arrived, the old man carried the food inside the house, shut the door, sat quietly and ate. The woman was furious. They went to the old man's house, but the old man did not reply to them when they called.

When they arrived at the house, they just heard the sound of bones breaking. These were the bones of the game that the man had killed and was eating. The angry woman quickly locked the house door, quietly lit a fire and ran away.

They arrived at a river, and they heard the bones of the man burning and crackling. They just listened and said, "Now the old man's bones are crackling."

When they went fairly far away, they heard a rather loud noise. This was when the man's head burned and cracked.

They kept walking, and passed another river. Then they arrived at their mountain village. They sat and made it rain. They made a tremendous downpour come forth.

The heavy rain fell at the place where the fire had burned the old man. The heavy rain fell and the flood washed away all of the old man's bones.

After this, the woman returned to the place where she and her old husband had lived. She stopped thinking about her old husband's bones.

She saw the place where the house had stood. She was sorry now and felt troubled. She cried and she always said, "You ruined me and my kin, so we killed you."

The old woman went to her kin's village. She made armlets and put them on the ground. Then she put a ragged "grass" skirt there.

Thomas Miapamango
Aseki Village [**Hamtai** People]
Morobe Province

A1011. Local deluges; D2143.1. Rain produced by magic; K812. Victim burned in his own house (or hiding place); P210. Husband and wife; P260. Relations by law; Q276. Stinginess punished; Q414. Punishment: burning alive; S50. Cruel relatives-in-law; S62. Cruel husband; S63+. Wife kills husband; S112.0.2. House (hostel) burned with all inside; W151. Greed

The Men Who Became Women

(Wantok 687, August 27, 1987, page 18)

One time, long ago, there were two brothers who lived in a village. One day, the big brother told his little brother that the next day he would go to the forest and make a bird blind.

The little brother listened and wanted to follow his big brother, but his big brother told him to stay in the village. So, the big brother carried his things and went to the forest. He entered the forest, climbed a big tree, and made a bird blind. Then he sat and watched for birds.

The little brother did not listen to his big brother. He was stubborn, so when his big brother had left, he quietly followed his big brother into the forest. He [arrived] and saw his big brother sitting on the tree, so he climbed another tree. He sat quietly and just watched.

Afterwards, a gigantic snake went up the tree where the little brother was sitting. The snake encircled him and was about to eat him when the little brother shouted and his big brother heard him. The big brother saw what was happening, got up, took his bow and shot the snake. The snake was knocked out and fell down to the ground.

The big brother went down quickly and finished off the snake. He told his little brother, "Let's butcher the snake, then cook and eat it."

The little brother was afraid and did not want to do this. So, the big brother told him that they would carry it back to the village, then divide it among the young men at the spirit house.

The brothers carried the snake back to the village and carried it all the way into the spirit house where the young men usually slept. That night, the men cooked the snake and ate their fill. After they ate, their bellies were bloated, so they slept awkwardly.

Late that night, one of the young men needed to urinate, so he woke up and went outside. When he stood to urinate, no, he felt as if the urine was running down his leg. The man looked down and was shocked to see that his genitals had changed to that of a woman.

The man went inside, awakened all of the men in the spirit house, and told them what had happened. The men checked themselves, and they too had turned into women. They were terribly ashamed, so they sat and talked about what they must do. They made their decision. That same night, they would get up and cut sago palm shoots then bring them to make "grass" skirts for themselves.

They made the skirts, then they fastened them and quietly ran away from the spirit house, following the beach.

They hid and saw some canoes. They saw a big canoe and they decided to kill all of the men in the canoe, take the canoe and go into hiding very far away.

When the canoe came ashore, the men quickly came out of the forest and killed all of the men in the canoe. Then they all jumped into the canoe and paddled very far away.

However, they had not seen one man on this canoe. He had quickly jumped into the sea and swam to the shore where he hid. After the men who had become women killed all of the men of the canoe and fled, this man walked into the forest.

He walked and walked until dawn broke. He was afraid and went to hide in a garden. He saw sugarcanes growing, so he hid among the yams and sat quietly. The sun was terribly hot and his throat was dry, so he broke some sugarcane to chew.

Afterwards, the owner of this garden arrived. She cleaned around the banana plants and removed some food. She felt thirsty, so she went to get some sugarcane. When she went to the base of the sugarcanes, she saw that someone had taken her sugarcanes.

The woman was angry and cursed. The man in hiding was among the yams. He heard the woman cursing, so he came out and told the woman that it was just he who had eaten the sugarcane.

The woman was surprised to see such a handsome young man. She asked him, "How did you get here?" The woman asked him this, but she did not think of anything. She was just very nervous because she had never seen such a man before.

The woman took this man, and they went back to her village where they married. They lived in this village and raised children. Later, their children married and raised children, so many people live in this village.

Hycinth [Hyacinth] Y. Kasi
P. O. Box 1052
Boroko
National Capital District

[See the ancestor stories in *Wantok* #660, 661, 684 and 701. H. Y. Kasi also wrote these stories. This story is probably from the **Kopar** or **Watam** People, **East Sepik** Province.]

B875.1. Giant serpent; D12. Transformation: man to woman; D551.3+. Transformation by eating snake; K914. Murder from ambush; P210. Husband and wife; P230. Parents and children; P251.5. Two brothers; Q211.6. Killing an animal revenged; Q551.3. Punishment: transformation; R100. Rescues; R213. Escape from home; R260. Pursuits; S110. Murders; T100. Marriage; V112.1. Spirit huts; W126. Disobedience; X712.1H. Female genitals; X712.2H. Male genitals; W167. Stubbornness; Z356. Unique survivor

The Greedy Brother's Time Came

(Wantok 688, September 3-10, 1987, page 18)

Long, long ago, in the time of the ancestors, there were two brothers who lived on an island. Their parents had died and they lived alone.

They made their garden on one side of the island. They always took food from the garden, and they took their meat from the sea because they excelled at fishing. The brothers always would fish in the sea or work in their garden until dark, then they would go back home.

They lived on just one side of the island. They never traveled to the other side. One day, the little brother told the big brother that he wanted to travel to the other side of the island and see what was over there.

In the very early morning, he awoke, pulled his canoe down, and paddled away. He paddled and paddled, then he met a big crab in the sea.

The crab spoke to him, "Be careful because there is a ghost woman who lives there." The little brother listened and paddled off, leaving the crab behind. Then he met a long-legged bird.

The bird saw him and said, "Good morning friend, where are you going?" The little brother told the bird that he wanted to go see who lived on the other side of the island.

The bird told the little brother to be very careful about the ghost woman with long hair and with scabs all over her skin. This woman sat on the beach. When the little brother arrived and paddled the canoe up to the beach, the woman told him, "Listen, I'm going down to the sea, so wash me well."

The boy listened to the ringworm woman and carried her down. He washed her well, then carried her back to the beach. Afterwards, the woman told him to sweep around the house. The boy listened and swept by the house, then he did other work that the woman told him to do. When all of the work was done, he sat down.

The woman told him, "You've done all the work that I asked you to do very well. Now, the last thing that you must do is climb the coconut palm, take a nice, green coconut, and carry it gently down. Don't throw it down to the ground like trash."

The little brother listened to the ringworm woman. He went up the coconut palm, took a green coconut, then came down gently. The woman told him to put the coconut in the stern of the canoe, then paddle back home.

He told the little brother that when he heard a noise in the stern that he must not turn and look. The little brother listened to the woman. He carried the green coconut, put it in the stern of the canoe, and paddled back home. While he paddled, he heard noises, but he did not turn around. He just kept paddling. After a long time, he turned and saw a very beautiful young woman sitting in the stern of the canoe.

They went ashore, then he took the woman up to the house. When the big brother saw the beautiful young woman, he coveted her very much, so he quietly asked the little brother about her. The little brother told the story to him.

The big brother listened and was very eager to go get a woman for himself. He slept, then before dawn broke, he awoke, pulled the canoe down and paddled away to the place where the ringworm woman lived.

He paddled and paddled, then he met the big crab. The crab asked him what he was doing, but the big brother scolded the crab and paddled away.

He paddled very quickly, then he met the long-legged bird. The bird said good-morning and also asked him what he was doing. However, the big brother scolded the bird, "Have you no shame for your bony legs? Go hide them."

When the bird heard this, it was terribly ashamed and flew away. The big brother just laughed and kept paddling. He saw the woman sitting on the beach. He paddled ashore, then pulled the canoe up and put it on the beach. He walked towards her. He went close and saw that scabs covered the woman's skin.

The woman told the big brother to carry her down to the sea and wash her. The big brother listened and was very angry. He carried the woman down and washed her. Then the woman told him to sweep around the house, so the man picked up the broom quickly and did not sweep very well.

After that, the woman told him to climb the coconut palm and bring down a green coconut. The man sped up the coconut palm, took a dry [brown] coconut and carried it down. The old woman told him to put the coconut in the stern of his canoe and not to turn around when he heard a noise. The man took the ripe coconut and put it in his canoe, then he began to paddle back to his home. When he heard a noise, he turned around quickly.

Oh my, he saw an ugly, ringworm woman sitting in his canoe. He was angry and tried to oust her, but the woman told him, "You yourself wanted me and you took me. Now you've married me."

The man was furious, so they argued and fought in the canoe. Then the outrigger of the canoe turned and they drowned. The little brother and his wife lived well on the island. Later, they had many children.

Wendy Kungkei
Tusbab High School
P. O. Box 2034
Madang
Madang Province

B211.3. Speaking bird; B211.8.1K. Speaking crab; E425.1. Revenant as woman; H310+. Suitor tests: kindness; J652. Inattention to warnings; J1050. Attention to warnings; N339+. Accidental drowning; P210. Husband and wife; P230. Parents and children; P251.4+. One brother acts wisely, another acts unwisely; P251.5. Two brothers; Q40. Kindness rewarded; Q280. Unkindness punished; T100. Marriage; W151. Greed; W181. Jealousy

An Old Couple Killed Four Brothers

(Wantok 689, September 10-17, 1987, page 18)

Long, long ago, there was an old man and his wife. There were no other people near them. There was another place nearby that had five young men [brothers].

One day, the first brother left his brothers and went into the forest. He walked and walked, then he arrived at the old couple's home. The old couple saw him and was happy. They called out for him to come up to the house.

The old man told his wife, "Grandson walked here on a long trail and he's hungry. Go to the garden, get some food and cook it. After he eats, he can return home."

The woman listened to him, went to the garden, and pulled up some sweet potatoes that rats had eaten. She carried them back to the house. She arrived and told her husband that a big bandicoot was in the garden eating sweet potatoes.

The old man told the young man to help them kill the bandicoot. They arrived in the garden, then the old man lied, saying that the bandicoot climbed a tree and was hiding in a hole by a branch. He climbed the tree and made a noise to chase down the bandicoot.

He broke a tree branch, took the sap and threw it down on the man's head. His wife tricked the man. She shouted and shot his head. The poor man fell down dead.

The old couple quickly carried him to the river, cleaned him, and cut him into little pieces. Then they heated stones and cooked him in an earth oven. They ate him, then they carried his bones to the house.

The brothers at home were waiting and waiting, but their big brother did not return. They thought hard. The second brother told the others that he would go to look for their big brother.

In the early morning, he woke up and left home. He walked and walked into the forest. He traveled and traveled, then he arrived at the place where the old couple lived. When he saw the couple, he told them that one of his brothers was lost and that he was searching for him. The old couple told him, "We're very old, and no one ever comes to see us."

The old man told his wife to go get some food from the garden, then to cook it so that their grandson could eat. The old woman listened and left. However, she did the same thing as before. She removed the sweet potatoes that a rat had eaten and took them back.

She lied to the boy, saying that she had seen a huge bandicoot that was up a tree. Her husband listened and told the second brother to watch the base of the tree while he climbed it. The old woman stood behind the brother, at the ready.

The old man went up the tree branch and threw sap down at the boy's head, then he shouted and said that the bandicoot was jumping down. The old woman quickly shot the boy's head, killing him.

The three brothers did not see their two brothers return home, so the third brother also left to find them. He arrived at the old couple's house and they killed him too. Then the fourth brother came to look for his three brothers, and the old couple tricked and killed him too.

The last brother left home and went into the forest to look for his four brothers. The last brother went to the old couple and asked them about his brothers. The old couple lied to him, that they had not seen his brothers.

The old man sent his wife to get some food from the garden. The woman removed the bad sweet potatoes and brought them back. She told them that a bandicoot had eaten the sweet potatoes in the garden. The old man listened and told the boy that they would go make some noise and kill the bandicoot.

They arrived there, and the old man went up the tree while his wife was at the ready, behind the boy. The old man threw sap down and the boy quickly jumped to the side. The old woman was about to kill him, but the boy took his knife and killed her. The woman fell into the river and became a frog. The old man jumped down to the ground and became a bandicoot.

The last brother chased and shot him. Then he saw his brothers' bones in the couple's house. He took the bones and put them at the base of a tree.

This tree rotted and fell down. Its detritus turned into fish. The man saw this and went back to his home. After some time, he returned and saw that the fish had become big and were playing. Later, he went back again and saw that they had become children and were playing.

The little brother saw this and was happy, so he went back to the house and made nice spears and "grass" skirts to give to them. When he finished these things, he carried them back there. When he arrived, he did not see anyone there. He shouted and heard them call back.

He went closer and saw a tree with a hole in it. There was a big path inside the tree. The man cut the tree down and many people appeared. The man gave the spears and skirts to them.

The little brother brought the men towards him. He told the women to sing and dance, and to hold *tanget* leaves. The women [carried] *tanget* leaves and enticed the people inside. They sang, "*Yamakeki, Yamak Waiki ditol apemaga apekue*."

Mark Hiwikawo
Koakaka [**Kwagaga**] Village [**Menya** People]
P. O. Box 84
Menyamya
Morobe Province

D117.3.1M. Transformation: man to bandicoot; D370C. Transformation: fish to child; D440+. Transformation: tree to fish; E615.1. Reincarnation as frog; E617. Reincarnation as fish; G10. Cannibalism; K917. Treacherous murder during hunt; P210. Husband and wife; P251.6.2+. Five brothers; Q211. Murder punished; Q411. Death as punishment; Q551.3.2+. Punishment: transformation into marsupial; S110. Murders; S139.2. Slain person dismembered; W157. Dishonesty

ToVup — The Crippled Thief

(Wantok 690, September 17, 1987, page 15)

Long ago, in Turagunan [**Turaguna**] Village, near Kokopo in **East New Britain** Province, there was a woman who gave birth to a baby boy [**Tolai** People]. They gave him the name of ToVup.

When ToVup became a big boy, his parents noticed that their son's legs were ruined and that he could not walk. ToVup would just sit, he could not get up or move around the house.

When his parents went to the garden, or to other places, they would carry him with them. They sat him down, then they did their work. However when ToVup grew bigger, he was too heavy, so his parents could not carry him around anymore. When they wanted to go someplace, they would leave him at home.

They always left ToVup at home and they thought that he was alone there. But no, the bad *masalai*s would go to ToVup. They would teach him various kinds of love spells and ways to perform sorcery. His parents and the other people of the village did not know about this.

One thing that the *masalai*s taught ToVup to do was to make himself grow very tall. When ToVup knew how to do this well, he became very tall and stole food from the houses in the village. He would always do this, and the people of the village then knew that there was a thief going amongst themselves.

One day, they gathered and argued. One man told them to ask ToVup because he was always in the village. When they asked him, ToVup scolded them and said that he could not go around and see who it was that was stealing food from their houses.

The people thought that he was telling the truth, so they left him. They went back and decided to grab the thief. They put some food in a banana leaf, and tied it to a very tall tree in the middle of the village. Then they pretended to go to the gardens.

They left the village and went into the forest. Some turned and came back to hide and watch. Before long, ToVup performed a song and began to grow. He grew and became very tall, then he put his hand up to the tree and pulled down the food bundle. He removed the food, sat comfortably and ate.

The men saw this, got up and went to chase ToVup. ToVup saw the men carrying spears and coming towards him, so he ran away to another place. He turned and saw the men still chasing him. ToVup kept going until he arrived at the beach. There was nowhere else to run, so he went into the sea.

One man aimed and threw his spear. The spear stuck into ToVup's back, but he kept walking into the sea until he left completely.

The people saw this, jumped into their canoes, and paddled off to find him. But they could not find him, ToVup was gone completely.

Julian Waninara
Ulaulatava Village
East New Britain Province

D55.1. Person becomes magically larger; D55.2. Person becomes magically smaller; D1711. Magician; D1721. Magic power from magician;

D1781. Magic results from singing; D1830+. Cripple walks by magic; D2165. Escapes by magic; F490+. Masalai; K420. Thief loses his goods or is detected; P210. Husband and wife; P231. Mother and son; P233. Father and son; Q212. Theft punished; R213. Escape from home; R260. Pursuits; T580. Childbirth

How Did Fire Arise?

(Wantok 691, September 24, 1987, page 15)

Long, long ago, in **Maprik**, there was no fire [**Abelam** People, **East Sepik** Province]. Two brothers lived there, their names were Sendegen and Nolumu. Sendegen was the big brother and Nomulu [Nolumu] was the little brother.

They always ate food that was not cooked because they had no fire. One morning, they awoke and sat in the sun. While they sat, the big brother saw white smoke rising from a small mountain. Behind the trees, up on this mountain, there lived an old woman.

The old woman originated fire. Her name was Wangonomais. She did not have a man with her. The big brother saw the smoke and showed his little brother. They saw the smoke rise into a big cloud and break apart towards all of the parts of the forest.

The big brother talked to the little brother about these sights. They talked to themselves about what this could be. The big brother told the little brother, "Be quiet, and we'll go see what it is."

When they approached, they saw a fire that looked like nothing they had seen. It was red and terribly hot. They watched, then the old woman came outside her house and saw them. She asked them, "Where did you come from? What village do you belong to?"

They told the old woman, "We saw the smoke from the fire and we came here."

They told the old woman their story, then she showed them how to light a fire and cook food. She took a bamboo tube and put some fire inside. Then she took some coconut husk and closed the end of the bamboo tube so that the fire could not exit.

She told them not to try to open the bamboo lest all of the forest burn. They listened and began to walk back to their home. While they walked, the big brother needed to defecate, so he told the little brother, "Hold the fire while I go and shit."

The big brother sat by a vine and defecated. The little brother tried to pull the coconut husk out and look at the fire. When he opened the tube, it exploded and burned all of the forest. The big brother turned into a butterfly. The little brother jumped down into the water and turned into a river eel.

Now if you want to go to Maprik, you will see that one side of the mountain has forest, whereas the side by the Sepik River is just sword-grass land. This is because of what happened in this story, where the fire burned all of the forest.

Lawrence Winau
Paradise Bakery
Lae
Morobe Province

A990+. Why one area is grassland; A1415.0.2. Original fire property of one person (animal); D173M. Transformation: man to eel; D186.1M. Transformation: man to butterfly; D1271. Magic fire; J652. Inattention to warnings; P251.5. Two brothers

A Man Married a Ghost Woman

(Wantok 692, October 1-8, 1987, page 14)

Long, long ago, in Su [**Sua**] Village, at the source of the Wani River, there was a huge tree that grew on a hill. There was a very beautiful ghost woman that lived on this big tree. The ghost woman just lived on the tree, she never went down to travel the forest.

There was a man who lived in a village near this place. His wife gave birth to a baby boy. The man was ecstatic, and went to the forest to hunt for wild game. He took his dog, and they followed the Wani River towards its source.

When the man approached the hill, he heard a woman singing. When he heard this, he began to search for her. He searched everywhere in the forest and did not find her. He approached the base of the big tree, then he heard the woman's voice clearly. Oh my, his heart went out completely, and he forgot entirely about his wife and newborn son.

The man knew that there was a woman on top of the tree, but he did not have a way to climb the tree because it was huge. All of the tree's branches were too high. The man thought that he could not climb it, then he sat at the base of the tree and made a ladder going up the tree. For three whole days, he cut small trees, then sat and made a ladder.

The ladder was ready, so he attached it to the tree and began to climb. He climbed, then he held a tree branch and went up very slowly until he arrived at the ghost woman's house. When the man saw the ghost woman, he trembled and urinated.

The ghost woman saw him and asked, "Why did you come up to my house? It's completely forbidden for men to come here. I'll call out for my kin to finish you off."

The man trembled and said, "I heard your beautiful song and I came to see you." The ghost became angry and said, "I wasn't singing. I was mourning for my dead parents and crying."

The man listened and he too began to cry. Then he cut [off] a finger on his hand. He cried hard as if it were his own family that had died.

The ghost woman saw this and said, "You're mourning with me and you cut [off] one of your fingers, so I'll marry you."

The man listened and was ecstatic. He married the woman, then they lived in the house on top of the forest. They lived there for many months, then the people of the village thought that he must have become lost in the forest.

One day, the man told his ghost wife that they must return to the village and live with the other people. The woman listened to her husband and they left. They arrived in the village, then they lived well with the man's first wife and son.

The other people of the forest were jealous of him because he was married to a very beautiful woman. The men thought that if they killed him, one of them could marry the beautiful ghost woman.

One day, they enticed him to go into the forest with them to hunt for game. While they were in the forest, they killed him. Afterwards, the men returned to the village. When the man did not return, his ghost wife asked them about him. They told her that they had not seen her husband.

The woman waited and waited for three days, then she just left. She knew that the men of the village must have killed her husband. The woman was very troubled, so she tied a rope to a tree branch and hanged herself.

After this, whenever men travel the forest and arrive at the base of the big tree near Su Village, they become terribly sick and die. However, there [is one] thing that can be done for those who travel this place.

Whoever goes around this part of the forest and becomes ill, should immediately kill a black pig, then give it to the owner of this place. The man should cook the pig at the base of the big tree, then just leave it there and return home.

People believe that the woman's ghost dwells on top of this tree, and that she comes down to eat the pigs that are put at the base of the tree. The people of this village did this until the mission came and revealed the word of God. After that, this custom ended.

Today, people no longer believe in this custom, so they travel the forest as they please. This story comes from the area of Kabera [**Kabari**] Village, South **Simbu** [Province, **Chuave** People].

Willey Brown

P. O. Box 114

Arawa

North Solomons Province

C621. Forbidden tree; C929.2. Death from specific disease for breaking tabu; D2176.3. Evil spirit exorcised; E276. Ghosts haunt tree; E425.1. Revenant as woman; E440+. Ghost commits suicide; E495.2. Marriage (ceremony) to a ghost; E541. Revenants eat; K917. Treacherous murder during hunt; M451.1. Death by suicide; P214.1. Wife commits suicide (dies) on death of husband; P231. Mother and son; P233. Father and son; P681+. Mourning customs: self-mutilation; S110. Murders; S161.1. Mutilation: cutting off fingers; T75.2. Scorned lover kills successful one; T100. Marriage; T111. Marriage of mortal and supernatural being; T145.0.1. Polygyny; T580. Childbirth; V12.4.3. Pig as sacrifice; V331. Conversion to Christianity; W181. Jealousy

Marsupial (*Kapul*) and Dog Tricked a Woman
(Wantok 693, October 8-15, 1987, page 18)

Long, long ago, there was a man who lived in Kauwo Village. The man's name was Tiabali Lapa. He had no wife or kin. He lived alone in this place. Tiabali had a dog and a marsupial (*kapul*) that lived with him.

One time, there was a food shortage. They ate very slowly so that the food would not disappear right away and so that they would not die of hunger. One day, there were only two sweet potatoes in the house. They had finished all of the other food.

Tiabali saw this and cooked the two sweet potatoes. When the sweet potatoes were ready, he broke off a piece and gave it to the marsupial. He gave the other piece to the dog. He himself ate the other sweet potato.

The dog saw that the sweet potato was too small, so it became angry and pushed its piece towards the marsupial. The marsupial was also angry at its little piece, then it pushed its piece towards the dog.

Tiabali Lapa saw this and thrashed the two of them, then he said, "Where's the woman who will cook your food? You're always too angry about food."

They listened and were terribly ashamed. The marsupial quietly went outside and the dog followed it out of the house. The two of them left home and walked away.

They walked and walked, then arrived at a mountain. The name of this mountain is Pangowai. They stood on Mount Pangowai and looked into Lombiyo Forest. They saw smoke rising there.

They looked at the smoke, then they walked off to see who had made the fire and smoke. They went closer and were surprised to see young women at work.

Oh my, the young women were filled with laughter and talking while they cleaned the garden. Some of them worked at burning the rubbish.

The two of them sat there, quietly watching the women. Then they heard one woman tell the others that she was thirsty and that she would go down to the river. The marsupial quickly ran there first and waited for her by the river.

The young woman arrived there and bent down to drink the water. When she was about to drink, the marsupial jumped down into the water, making it very murky.

The woman saw this and got up to find what it was that was making the water murky. She searched and looked up to see a gigantic marsupial rolling in the water.

The woman salivated and tried to grab the marsupial, but the marsupial quickly jumped up. The woman chased and chased the marsupial, forgetting completely about the other young women.

While she was catching her breath, the marsupial sat and cleaned its nose and face. Then it tried to look at the woman.

The woman saw this and said, "Aiyo! Where is there a dog that will help me kill this marsupial?"

When the woman said this, the dog came quickly and jumped on top of the marsupial, pretending to kill it. The marsupial pretended to die and made the noise that marsupials make when dogs kill them.

The woman saw this and was ecstatic. She got up to take the marsupial. The dog left, then the marsupial got up and ran away. The dog came and chased the marsupial and pretended to kill it again. The marsupial made the dying noise again. The woman listened and went to get the marsupial, but the dog left again and the marsupial got up and fled.

They kept doing this, tricking the poor young woman until they were very far away. The woman was furious and she scolded them, "You're probably not a dog and marsupial. A man must have taught you to do what you're doing. That's alright. Wait for me and I'll go with you."

The two of them listened and waited for the young woman to catch her breath. She caught her breath, then they walked off to their home. They walked and walked until they arrived at the house.

The marsupial told the dog and woman, "Wait for me here. I'll go alone to see papa."

Then the marsupial broke off a piece of the woman's "grass" skirt, hid it and carried it away. Their father, Tiabali Lapa, had been terribly worried when the marsupial and dog had left him, so he had rubbed dirt on his skin [a sign of mourning] and just sat there, crying in the house.

When the marsupial arrived at the house, Tiabali Lapa got up and ran to hold the marsupial. He cried terribly because he had thought that they were dead. The marsupial gave the piece of the woman's skirt to Tiabali Lapa. Tiabali Lapa saw this and did not say anything. He followed the marsupial.

When he saw his dog, he ran to hold the dog and he cried terribly. Then he turned to see the woman, and he stopped thinking about his dog and marsupial. Tiabali Lapa held this beautiful woman and they all went back home.

They lived in Kauwo Village for a while, then the woman gave birth to children. Afterwards, these children married and gave birth to more children. This has happened until now, 1987, when the number of people in Kauwo Village is over six hundred.

This story comes from my own village, **Kauwo** 1, by Pangia, **Southern Highlands** Province [**Wiru** People].

Nelson Pege
Punu Video House
P. O. Box 1223
Hagen
Western Highlands Province

B211.2.12K+. Speaking marsupial; B421. Helpful dog; B430+. Helpful marsupial; B582.1.1. Animal wins wife for his master (Puss in Boots); B871.2+. Giant marsupial; K1860. Deception by feigned death (sleep); P210. Husband and wife; P230. Parents and children; P681+. Mourning customs: earth on body; R260. Pursuits; T100. Marriage; T580. Childbirth

Duku Tricked Gargariva and He Died

(Wantok 694, October 15, 1987, page 14)

There was a sorcerer who lived in the forest. His name was Gargariva. This sorcerer often knocked off the people of the village. The men tried to kill him, but they were completely unsuccessful. One time, there was a son in the village whose parents had died. The sorcerer had killed both of them.

The son's name was Duku. One time, Duku wanted to travel the forest. He took his spears, then walked and walked until he arrived at a *galip* tree in the very deep forest, far from the village.

When he found the *galip* tree, he did not fool around at picking nuts. He looked up and saw that some *galip* nuts were very black, and some were still green, so he raised his desires and climbed the tree.

This *galip* tree belonged to the old sorcerer who had finished off the villagers. Duku went up the tree and did not think of anything else but the *galip* nuts in the forest. He gorged himself on the *galip* nuts.

Then a leaf from the *galip* tree flew towards the sorcerer. Gargariva saw this and asked the *galip* leaf, "Who took you? Did the birds take you?" No, the leaf did not make the slightest sound. He called all of the names of the birds, then he said, "A man must have taken you, huh?" Then the leaf turned back and departed.

Gargariva quickly ran to the base of the *galip* tree, then said, "Very good. You're my meat. How will you get down from there?"

Duku thought and thought. Then he found a way that he could trick Gargariva. He spoke, "Hey, you're looking to see how I'll come down, huh? I'll pull all your spears here and go down on them."

When Gargariva heard this, he broke all his spears. Then he asked again, "Now how will you get down?" Duku said, "I'll take all your dogs and go down on them." The man listened and killed the dogs.

Then he asked again, "Now how will you get down?" Duku said, "I'll pull all your coconut, betel nut, breadfruit, and Malay apple trees, then I'll go down on them." He listened to this and cut down all of these trees.

He asked again, "Now, how will you get down?" Duku said, "I'll go down on your house." He went and broke his house, and it fell down. He asked again, "How will you get down?"

Duku knew that all of his things were gone, so he said, "I'll pull the hair on your head, then I'll come down upon it." So Gargariva cut off the hair on his head. He asked again, "How will you get down now that all my things are gone?"

Duku said, "I'll pull your head and I'll come down on it." Gargariva listened and pulled up one of his broken spears, then he jabbed it into his head and he died.

Duku went down, then he took all of the *galip* nuts and went to the village. He told the people about what he had done. The men went to see the sorcerer. They were very happy about what Duku had done, so they made a huge feast.

They chose a wife for Duku. He married and they lived happily. Then there were no more sorcerers to ruin the people of the village.

Cat Gabriel Simo, Anton Biu
Garu [**Garua**] Catholic Church [**Bola** People]
P. O. Box 304
Kimbe
West New Britain Province

D955. Magic leaf; D1311. Magic object used for divination; D1711. Magician; D2061. Magic murder; G10. Cannibalism; G346. Devastating monster; G510.4+. Hero overcomes devastating ogre; K890. Dupe tricked into killing himself; K1400. Dupe's property destroyed; K1440. Dupe's animals destroyed or maimed; L111.4. Orphan hero; P210. Husband and wife; P231+. Son avenges mother; P233.6. Son avenges father; Q53. Reward for rescue; R311. Tree refuge; S110. Murders; T100. Marriage

Repe Was a Little Trickster

(Wantok 695, October 22-29, 1987, page 21)

Long, long ago, in Bibine [**Bimbienye**] Village, by Ialibu in **Southern Highlands** [Province], there lived a man named Welali Repe [**Hagen** People].

The men of Bibine Village did not like him very much because he never wore nice things and because he did not have a wife to cook his food. Also, the women often spat at him. One time, the men sat at the festival grounds and told a story about a young woman and her mother who walked and walked on a trail with net bags of pork. Repe quickly cut across another trail and watched them. When they came, Repe appeared like a crazy man.

The mother and young daughter did not have a way to escape. He chased them and took their good net bags, then he ran away with the bags of pork.

He told them, "*Ripora wen wen konapu piri pa pamu ma mea pua lape*." This means, "I'm a *masalai* of this forest. I don't have a loincloth and I carry it away. Tell them this if men ask you."

Repe quickly went to his house and sat there. After a little while, the mother and daughter came crying. The men asked them what had happened, and they said, "A *masalai* man carried away the bags of pork and our other things." The men said, "All of us were here, but Repe was not here."

They went to find Repe who was sleeping in his house. They gave him the story about the mother and daughter. Repe said, "You think that I'm a small man and you want to humiliate me, huh? I've been sleeping in the house and I don't know what you're talking about."

He spoke sternly and they left him. Later, he used the same net bags as his loincloth, and the men became angry with him.

One time, his age-mates went to fight with another clan. They only left the women in the village. When they went to the gardens, Repe put on the decorations that the enemies used for fighting. He stood with his bow, and all of the women trembled and ran away, leaving all of their things. He took their possessions and hid them back at his house.

Another time, the men of Bibine Village went to Mount Giluwe to hunt for marsupials (*kapul*) and bandicoots. This time, Repe told them, "I've never eaten sweet potatoes that have been planted in mounds. I just eat sweet potatoes that have been planted on the flat ground."

They lived on Mount Giluwe for some months, then all of Repe's sweet potatoes were finished. He would eat tree leaves and marsupial guts for some weeks, but his kin's sweet potatoes were still there. When they went to hunt for wild game, Repe lay asleep half-dead and did not move at all.

In the afternoon, the brothers returned to find that Repe was dead because he had not eaten sweet potatoes. The brothers cried for him, then they removed tree bark, made a platform and carried him to the village. They approached the village and told people that Repe had died. The news traveled to the other villages too.

At the same time, a big festival was occurring at Kongibul [**Kongibugl**] Village, so the men said, "Tomorrow, we'll bury Repe's body. We'll go to the festival first." They dressed up and left.

The bad man, Repe, very quietly cut the ropes that bound him and went outside. Quickly, he bathed and changed. He put on nice clothing and became a handsome man. Then he followed his brothers and went to the festival.

Oh my, the men were shocked because he had died and they were about to bury him when they put him by the house. He had tricked them well in the deep forest so that they would carry him to the village.

This is a true story. One of my old paternal figures told me this story and I wrote it down.

Eke I Ukeye
Y. M. C. A. [Young Men's Christian Association]
P. O. Box 1463
Lae
Morobe Province

[The ancestor story in *Wantok* #726 is also about Welali Repe.]

J1110. Clever persons; K335. Thief frightens owner from goods; K1861. Death feigned in order to be carried; P232. Mother and daughter; P251. Brothers; R260. Pursuits

Two Brothers Divided Their Work
(Wantok 696, October 29 — November 5, 1987, page 16)

Long, long ago, there were two brothers who lived in a village called **Muagamanda** [Enga People, **Enga** Province]. Their parents had died and they lived alone. They planted their own food.

The big brother's work was to hunt for wild game in the forest. The work of the little brother was to husband the pigs, to dig sweet potatoes, to look for leafy greens, and then to cook the food at the house.

The little brother became like a woman. He did all of the gardening and housework, and he took care of the pigs. The big brother would go to the forest to hunt for marsupials (*kapul*), cassowaries, and other kinds of game in the forest. Their house was always filled with various kinds of meat. They lived at Mongamanda [Muagamanda] Papatale Village. One time, the big brother told the little brother, "I'm going into the deep forest, so go find a little bit of sweet potato for me to bring to the forest."

The little brother went to remove some sweet potatoes called *pore mapu* [*póte mapú* (Lang, 1973: 66, 89)], which are red sweet potatoes. He dug the sweet potatoes and brought them to his big brother. The big brother put the sweet potatoes in a small net bag. He carried a bow and arrows, and an axe on his shoulder. Then he sped off towards a mountain. In the afternoon, at about three o'clock, he arrived directly at the place called Yapopaus Sword-Grass Lands. He heard a dog barking and whining. The man went closer and looked around. He saw a small black dog sitting there. The man went there and the poor dog wagged its tail. It barked and whined, then it attached itself to the man. The man walked behind the dog, and the dog barked again.

The dog looked at the man, then it looked at a breadfruit tree. The dog barked and stared at the tree. The man climbed the tree, picked the young breadfruits and descended. The poor dog looked at various kinds of leafy vegetables, then just barked. The man knew this, then they kept walking and arrived at a house.

The dog showed the man that he must wait there. Then the man looked for leafy greens and gathered them. He heard a big pig squealing on the mountain, then he saw the poor dog pulling a black pig on a rope. When the pig wanted to go another way, oh my, the darn dog would bite the nose and ears of the pig. Then the dog would keep chasing it down the trail, until they went directly up to the man.

The man killed the pig, then the two of them cooked it in an earth oven. Later, the dog went into the forest and brought a big net bag back. The dog picked ginger with its teeth.

The dog filled the net bag and gave it to the man. Then he uncovered the earth oven. The dog just came and pulled the pig's head and liver.

The dog took these, then told the man, "Stay for two days. Then on the third day, you must return." The dog broke off its little finger for the man, then they left the forest and returned to each of their homes.

The man went up to the house. His pal [brother] was happy and jumped about, then the two of them ate. After they were done, the big brother returned and the dog did the same thing. The dog took a white pig, then the two of them cooked it in an earth oven and divided the meat as before. They went back to each of their homes again.

The big brother and his little brother ate the pork, then the next day, he [the big brother] went back again. The dog brought a red pig, then they cooked it in an earth oven and divided the pork. The big brother carried the pork home. The little brother said, "I don't like the food. Eat it yourself because you never let me go hunt for game." The man told his brother, "OK, tomorrow you'll go. You must eat now."

The big brother finished all of the pork. In the morning, the big brother taught him and told him, "There is no man or woman when you arrive. A dog will come and you must follow it." The little brother told him, "Don't worry, I'll do that." He left and arrived there. He saw the dog barking. The good-for-nothing just took his arrow and whipped the dog's groin. Oh my, the poor dog yelped awfully, then it fell down and got up again. After that, the two of them left. The dog went to get a big pig, as it had done before. The dog brought the pig and they cooked it in an earth oven.

When they uncovered the earth oven, the man did not give a portion to the poor dog. No, he put all of the pork into the net bag. The dog just tried to put its teeth on the pig's head, but the man took a big stick and broke the [dog]'s head. The dog died, then the man carried all of the pork to the house. The big brother saw his friend carrying the pig's head and coming towards him, so he slipped outside and sped off to the place where the dog lived. He saw that the dog was dead, so he followed the blood. Later, the good-for-nothing saw that a woman was hanging up a man. She was shouting and crying, "Brother, brother, when you

called for a white pig, I gave you a white one. When you called for a black one, I gave you a black one, but now there is trouble and you're dead..."

The woman cried like this, then the big brother arrived at his house, raised his spear and killed his little brother. The boy [man] went back, then two women took a tree leaf called *liok* and a green snake. They put these into a fire, then the man arose as a man again and lived with them.

Upu Anton Wea [Wéa is an Enga place name (Lang, 1973: 215).]

Panguna

North Solomons Province

B176.1. Magic serpent; B211.1.7. Speaking dog; B421. Helpful dog; D955. Magic leaf; D1787. Magic results from burning; E15. Resuscitation by burning; E64.18. Resuscitation by leaf; E122.2. Resuscitation by snake; P251.4+. One brother acts wisely, another acts unwisely; P251.5. Two brothers; P253. Sister and brother; P681+. Mourning customs: self-mutilation; Q211.6. Killing an animal revenged; Q411. Death as punishment; S73.1. Fratricide; S110. Murders; S161.1. Mutilation: cutting off fingers; W126. Disobedience

A Boy Tricked the *Masalai* Thief
(Wantok 697, November 5-12, 1987, page 20)

Long, long ago, in the time of the ancestors, there was an old man and his son who lived in a place by a river. On the other side of the river, there lived an old *masalai*.

This *masalai* was a true loafer. He never worked. He always just slept in his house. At night, he would wake up and travel, stealing food from the old man and his son.

The *masalai* always did this, and the food in their garden was decimated. However, the two of them could not find out who it was that was stealing the food in their garden.

The old father thought that his son was hungry and had just taken the food, but when the father asked his son, the son said that it was not he who had taken the garden food. They tried every way to find out who was the thief, but they were unsuccessful.

The old father and the son excelled at making traps for marsupials (*kapul*). They often killed many, many marsupials and brought them to the house. They would smoke the meat and put it away.

One day, the boy saw that the meat in their house was almost gone. He knew that the thief must have come to the house and taken the marsupial meat when they had been in the forest.

The boy saw this and was terrified. He knew that when his father entered the house, he would see this, then scold and beat him. He was afraid, so he ran away and hid in the forest.

His father returned from the forest, carrying more marsupials that he had killed. He saw that his son was not at the house, so he called out and searched for him.

He found the boy and asked him what had happened. The boy told his father that he was scared that the meat in the house was gone, so he went to hide in the forest. The father listened and lectured his son.

The father was angry, so he took a big stick and gave the boy a good one. The boy fell down, half-dead on the ground. The father let him cry there and he fell asleep. When the food was ready, the father called for his son to eat, but the boy was dead asleep. He did not hear his father calling.

In the morning, the father told his son to watch the meat very carefully. He said that if some of the meat were lost again, he would kill him. After the father explained this, he left for the forest.

The boy was afraid to walk around, so he sat and watched the meat in the house. He sat and sat, then near noon, his body became tired. He got up and walked near the garden.

While he was gone, the old *masalai* came there. He did not hear a noise, so he did not know that there was someone nearby. Very quietly, he went closer to the house and began to look for a way to go inside and steal the meat.

He searched and searched, then he saw a hole high up on the roof. The *masalai* went up the side of the house, then into the hole. Slowly, he began to descend. When he went down, he became stuck in a trap that the boy had made and put inside the house.

The trap stuck to his testicles, so he screamed terribly. The boy was around the garden and heard the screaming, so he ran back to the house. He knew that a thief must be stuck and screaming in the trap that he had made.

The boy went into the house and saw the old *masalai*. The *masalai* was hung up and screaming. When he looked at the *masalai*, he was angry and laughed at the same time.

He said, "So you're the bad one that stole the food, causing my papa to beat me. Now you'll feel it too."

In the afternoon, his father returned home. The boy turned to him and told him about the old *masalai* that had always stolen their food.

His father listened and was furious. He threw the meat down and ran inside the house. He cut the rope, and the *masalai* fell down. Then the two of them began to fight. They fought and fought, but neither of them won because

both of them were old and not strong enough to fight effectively.

It became dark, and they kept at it. The boy sat watching and grew very tired. He took his bow and shot the old *masalai*'s belly, killing him. Then the father and son cut up the *masalai* into small pieces and burned him in the fire.

R. Joe
P. O. Box 2270
Lae
Morobe Province

F419.2. Thieving spirit; F490+. Masalai; K437+. Thief falls into trap; P233. Father and son; Q212. Theft punished; Q411.13. Death as punishment for thievery; R213. Escape from home; R260. Pursuits; S11. Cruel father; S110. Murders; S139.2. Slain person dismembered; W111. Laziness; X712.3.1H. Injury to testicles

A Man Tricked the Ghosts and Took Their Hand Drum

(Wantok 698, November 12-19, 1987, page 20)

Long, long ago, in the time of the ancestors, there was a man from **Yakalu** Village who was traveling around the forest. He went around and around, then he arrived at the base of a tree where there were plenty of wildfowl feces.

The tree was a *ton* tree. Birds always went to perch upon its branches and to defecate. The man saw this and was happy, so he said that the next day, he would go to the tree then watch and kill many birds. Afterwards, he went back to his house.

Later, on the third day, the man thought about returning to the forest to check upon the traps that he had put there. In the afternoon, he cooked his food, then he left the village and walked into the forest. He walked until he arrived at his forest hut. He put his things inside the hut, then he carried his bow and arrows and checked on his traps.

He checked on the traps until he arrived at the base of the *ton* tree where the wildfowls rested. When he went closer, he saw a bird flying up to the tree and resting there.

The man took his bow and arrows then quietly climbed a tree that was near the *ton* tree. He went up and sat well, then he aimed his arrow and shot at a bird. However, the bird turned to look and immediately flew into the forest.

The poor man went down again, took his things and went back to the hut. He had not taken other things to the hut, so he lit a torch and walked back to the village.

He walked and approached **Kapu** Village, then he heard ghosts eating mangos and singing around the base of a mango tree. The man saw this and was afraid, but he did not have another way to get back home. He was alone on the trail and the ghosts had surrounded him.

The man stood and stopped thinking. He went to hide his things in the forest. Then he went down to wash himself in smelly water at the base of a sago palm tree. He went back, and his skin smelled terrible like the ghosts' smell.

He went out and walked very slowly. He arrived at the place where the group of ghosts were passionately singing and dancing. He stood for a little while, then he saw a ghost that was exhausted from dancing. Stealthily, he took the ghost's hand drum.

The ghost heard him, then turned and looked at him. The ghost asked, "Where did you come from?"

The man lied to the ghost, "I live in my village. I heard the hand drums, so I came to help you sing and dance."

The ghost listened, then thought that the man was one of them, so the ghost gave him the hand drum. They passionately sang and danced. They kept going and going, then the man heard a bird calling, a bird that sings at dawn. He knew that it was almost dawn.

The ghosts kept singing and dancing passionately, and the man kept going with them. The bird called out again. The man saw that each ghost was leaving the base of the mango tree, they were beginning to return to their houses.

He watched carefully, and he saw one go inside the base of a pandanus tree (*aran*), one go inside the base of a wild banana plant, and one go inside a hole in the ground. The others ran away into the forest to their homes.

When dawn arrived, the man saw that all of the ghosts had left for their homes. He took his things that he had hidden in the forest. He carried the ghost's hand drum that he had taken that night, then he walked back towards his village.

When he arrived at a mountain, he beat the hand drum. The ghosts heard the sound of the drum, so they beat their drums and said, "There must have been a ghost that tricked us who came to the festival with us. He carried our drum away."

The ghosts call us, the real people, "ghosts." The man took the hand drum to his house, then he took rattans and tied the drum to the first post of his house.

That night, the ghosts followed him to the village. They put him soundly asleep, then they untied the hand drum that he had tied up and they carried it back to their home.

August Nick
P. O. Box 8
Vanimo
West Sepik Province

[August S. Nick wrote the ancestor story in *Wantok* #683. He is probably from the **Kayik** or **Yapunda** People.]

D1960. Magic sleep; E238.1. Dance with the dead; E261.4. Ghost pursues man; E276. Ghosts haunt tree; E352. Dead returns to restore stolen goods; E425. Revenant in human form; E493. Dead men dance; E541. Revenants eat; E545. The dead speak; E546. The dead sing; E587.3. Ghosts walk from curfew to cockcrow; E588. Ghost leaves stench behind; F687. Remarkable fragrance (odor) of person; K300. Thefts and cheats — general; K1833. Disguise as ghost; R260. Pursuits

A River Ruined Oipo [Oibo] Village
(Wantok 699, November 19-26, 1987, page 20)

Long, long ago, in the time of the ancestors, there was a river called Oipo. At the source of this river, there lived a man who husbanded pigs.

Below him on the river was a very big village. The people of this village always traveled in the forest to hunt for wild game. When they killed a pig or cassowary, they would make a huge festival in the village.

When they hunted for game, they would follow the river down until they approached the beach and found game. They never followed the river up to its source.

One day, a man from the village wanted to go hunt for game. He took his dogs and followed the river up towards its source. The dogs left him and ran in front. Before long, he heard his dogs barking.

The man listened and ran quickly. He looked, and oh my, the place was filled with pigs. He shot a huge pig down and he was happy. He ran to look, and was surprised to see that the pig had two heads. One was its real head and the other was on its buttocks.

The man left the pig there in the forest. He ran back to the village and told the other men of Oipo Village [**Oibo** Village, **Guhu-Samane** People, **Oro** Province]. The men listened to him, then they followed the river upwards. They tied up the pig and carried it back to the village.

When the men arrived there, the sun had set and it was dark. They carried the pig away, then put it down. They decided to go to the forest and garden the next day, then gather food and leafy greens to cook the pig.

In the morning, all of the men, women and children of the village left for the forest. Some fetched firewood, some went to find leafy greens, and others picked food from the gardens.

One old man left his grandson in the village. He went alone, following the other people into the forest. The little boy stayed in the house while everyone left. He saw an old man fastening his loincloth, carrying his spear towards him and crying. The boy saw this and was afraid, so he hid.

The old man went to the village. He cried and called the names of all his pigs. The boy listened to the man talk, "Tiopo Khaina _nini_ _mai_."

Tiopo Khaina was the name of the pig that the man from the village had killed. _Nini_ _mai_ means, "Just you, huh?"

When the man said this, the pig replied. The man went and saw his pig where the people of the village had tied and placed it. Then he also saw the little boy who was in hiding.

The man told the boy, "I see you. When your grandfather returns, you two must leave this place and go elsewhere."

The man said this, then left the village and went to the headwaters. He dammed the water up and waited for the people to return to the village.

In the afternoon, all of the men, women and children returned to the village. They made a fire, then singed off the pig's hair. They butchered the pig and began to cook it. When all of the food was in the fire, they sang and danced intensely.

The boy waited for his grandfather. When he saw the grandfather arrive, he told him what had happened, that a man had told them that they must leave the village and flee far away.

The boy told his grandfather that they must go up a small mountain that was near the village. His grandfather listened and scolded him, but the boy was persistent and cried. So, his grandfather took him up the mountain and made a hut there.

When the hut was finished, they sat and caught their breath. The old man scolded his grandson, "Oh, you're so wrong. Look at the old folks down there eating the good meat while we're hungry up here."

The people of the village sang and danced passionately. They ate the good pork. It was the Oipo people's custom that when they killed game, they sang and danced until dawn broke.

The men sang and danced, and the boy told his grandfather, "You covet the pork, so you can't sleep. OK, sit and watch the firelight, and listen to their singing."

He went to sleep. His old grandfather sat and looked down at the village. Before long, the old man said, "Hey, what was that noise at the head of the Oipo [River]?"

The boy listened and replied, "That was just what I told you about."

The pig's owner had removed the pieces of _limbum_ wood that he had used to dam the river. All of the men, women, and children who were happily eating the pork, singing and dancing were washed down by the water and finished off. The water carried all of them away, and the noise of the water covered the area.

In the morning, the two of them awoke and went to see what had happened, but they did not see anything. They only saw the house posts standing there. All of the men, women and children of this village had been carried away by the water.

This story is from the area of the Papuan Waria [River].

Biary Oga

Panguna

North Solomons Province

A1011. Local deluges; A1018. Flood as punishment; B15.1.2.1+. Two-headed pig; B871.1.2.1. Giant hog; E521.5. Ghost of hog; E545. The dead speak; J1050. Attention to warnings; P291. Grandfather; Q211.6. Killing an animal revenged; Q428. Punishment: drowning; R220. Flights; S131. Murder by drowning; W195. Envy

A Man Married a Fish-Woman

(Wantok 700, November 26 — December 3, 1987, page 20)

Long, long ago, in the time of the ancestors, all of the men of a certain village went to plant food in the garden. They worked until it was nearly dark, then they took their things and walked back to the village.

However, one boy with ringworm stayed in the garden. He said that he would sleep in the garden, then in the early morning, he would continue to work.

Everyone returned to the village, then he was by himself in the garden and he felt terribly hungry. He went to the river and fished using his cold sago.

He fished and fished, then he speared a fish that is called _welmow_ (grouper or cod) in my language. When he shot the fish, he saw that it went inside a stone. This was not an ordinary fish, it was a fish-woman, but the man did not know it. After the boy saw that the fish was hiding, he searched for other fish using his sago as bait.

He followed the river upwards, then he sat and rested. He did not know that the fish-woman was following him. The woman arrived and called out to the boy.

The boy was surprised. He looked downriver and saw the fish-woman. He asked her, "Where did you come from? You must go back now or your kin will come to find you and then beat me."

The fish-woman just laughed and said, "I don't have kin. I just live alone."

The ringworm boy was afraid and tried to get rid of the woman, but the woman did not want to return to her home. After a while, the boy tired and told the woman that he would go to his garden.

The fish-woman listened and said that she would go with him to the garden. He thought that she could not do this, so he consented. They arrived at the garden, then the fish-woman performed a song and dance, and the boy fell dead asleep.

The boy slept there, then the fish-woman returned to her house inside the river. She brought much meat and sago back. She made a fire, cooked the food, and the awakened the boy.

The boy awoke and they ate the food that the fish-woman had [cooked]. After the boy ate, his skin changed. He was no longer scabrous, and his body became big, like that of his big brother.

In the village, the ringworm boy's big brother thought of him. So, after his wife had cooked and they finished eating, the two of them tied up some food and carried it back to the garden. They arrived there and saw the handsome man with the fish-woman. They thought that they were from another group of people because the boy had changed and he looked like a real man.

The married couple looked at the two of them and asked, "We're looking for a boy. Have you seen him or not?"

The fish-woman listened and told them that the boy had left the garden. The married couple listened and just sat quietly. The fish-woman let them sit there, then she went to get some betel nuts. She chewed the nuts. Then she told them, "The boy that you're looking for is here. You two did not take care of him well because he was a scabrous boy. I myself made him become a handsome man. Now I shall marry him."

When the ringworm boy's big brother heard this, he was shocked. He ran to hold his brother, then he cried. He was very happy to see that his brother had become a handsome man. They took the fish-woman back to their village. The boy married the fish-woman and they lived together.

The woman told them, "When you go fishing, you can catch all kinds of fish, but don't take one fish with bad eyes. It is forbidden to take that kind of fish."

The men of the village listened to this and they never killed this kind of fish. The fish-woman and her husband lived well in the village. One day, the boys went fishing, and the big brother's son killed the kind of fish that the woman had told them not to kill.

This boy killed the fish, then he carried it back in a *limbum* basket of water. The basket was placed in the house.

The fish-woman felt very strongly that something must be wrong. She went around the house and was very troubled because her husband's family had killed one of her own.

She went to the house and lied to her husband, that she would go to fetch water. She said that she would carry the basket down to the river. However, when she arrived at the river, she jumped inside and went back to her home.

Her husband waited and waited, and it became dark. When his wife did not return, they went to find her. They saw the basket by the river. When they looked inside the basket, they saw the dead fish inside.

Then they knew that the woman must have been troubled about the fish, and must have returned to her underwater home. The man was very troubled but he could not get back his wife. The woman had gone back to her home for good.

That is the end of our story from the **West Sepik** Province.

Anton Waipey
P. O. Box 959
Madang Province

B81.2. Mermaid marries man; C841.9. Tabu: killing certain fish; D56.1. Transformation to older person; D551.2+. Transformation by eating sago; D551.3. Transformation by eating flesh; D1719.7. Magic power of mermaid; D1781. Magic results from singing; D1781+. Magic results from dancing; D1862.1. Magic beauty bestowed by supernatural wife; D1960. Magic sleep; P210. Husband and wife; P251.5. Two brothers; P233. Father and son; P260. Relations by law; P263. Brother-in-law; P264. Sister-in-law; R227. Wife flees from husband; R260. Pursuits; S110. Murders; T100. Marriage; T111. Marriage of mortal and supernatural being

A Marsupial (*Kapul*) Tricked a Dog and Ruined the Dog's Hair

(Wantok 701, December 3-9, 1987, page 23)

Long, long ago, the birds and the wild game of the forest lived as people. There were two very good friends, a marsupial (*kapul*) and a dog.

The two friends lived inside a cave in the deep forest. At this time, the marsupials lived on the ground, like dogs. They never went up on trees. Near the place where the friends lived, there was a big water hole. The marsupial and dog always went there to bathe.

When they went inside the water, they would play around. When they tired, they would go up to the stones and dry their bodies. In the afternoon, they would walk back to their home in the cave.

One day, the sun was terribly hot, so the two friends went to bathe in the water hole. They played around inside the water, then they went out and sat to dry their bodies. They said, "Oh my, it's been a long time since we've combed our hair."

The marsupial could not comb its own hair, so it told the dog to comb it. The dog said that the marsupial should comb its hair too. The dog ran to their home and brought out its bamboo comb.

The dog returned and told its friend, the marsupial, to sit quietly while it combed its hair. The dog combed the marsupial's hair from its ears to its tail, and marsupial looked very nice.

When the dog finished combing the marsupial's hair, the marsupial looked very handsome. The marsupial's hair stood nicely in the sunlight, and the marsupial looked completely different. Then the dog told the marsupial to go to the water and look at its reflection.

The marsupial ran quickly and looked down into the water. Oh my, when the marsupial saw its reflection in the water, it was shocked. The marsupial stood for a very long time admiring itself. It was very happy looking at its nice hair and skin.

When the marsupial finished looking at itself, it went back to help its friend, the dog. The dog jumped up and down, then sat quietly and waited for its friend, the marsupial, to comb its hair. The marsupial took the comb and began to comb the dog's hair. However, the marsupial had a malicious thought and did not comb the dog's hair well.

While the marsupial combed the dog's hair, the marsupial thought, "I can't comb the dog's hair well. It would be bad if the dog looked nice like me."

The marsupial completely ruined the poor dog's hair. The dog thought that its friend was doing its hair well, so the dog just sat quietly. The marsupial pretended to comb and comb, then it told the dog to go look in the water.

When the poor dog got up, the marsupial began to laugh. The marsupial almost died laughing because the poor dog's hair was a mess and looked hilarious.

The dog asked the marsupial, "Friend, what are you laughing about?"

The marsupial did not say. The dog went and stood to look down in the water. The dog saw its hair shooting in all directions, and it looked terrible. The dog knew that the marsupial had played a trick and had not combed its hair well.

The dog was furious at the marsupial. The dog returned and told its friend, the marsupial, "I know about you now. You played a trick and ruined my hair, so now you're laughing."

The marsupial wanted to speak, but no, it laughed again because the poor dog looked hilarious. The dog was furious, so it got up and chased the marsupial. The marsupial thought that the dog was just pretending to chase it, so it laughed and ran away from the dog. However, when the marsupial saw that the dog was trying to kill it, it was afraid and ran up a tall tree that was by the pond.

The dog saw this and shouted up to the marsupial, "You must watch carefully when you travel. If I catch you, you'll die."

The marsupial listened and trembled fiercely. Later, the marsupial jumped to another tree and fled this area where they had lived in the cave. The marsupial never came down because it was afraid that the dog would find and kill it.

Hyacinth Y. Kasi
P. O. Box 1052
Boroko
[National Capital District]

[H. Y. Kasi also wrote the ancestor stories in *Wantok* #660, 661, 684 and 687. She is probably from the **Kopar** or **Watam** People, **East Sepik** Province.]

A2433.2.1+. Why marsupial lives in forest; B211.1.7. Speaking dog; A2494.4+. Enmity between dog and marsupial; B211.2.12K+. Speaking marsupial; K1200. Deception into humiliating position; P310. Friendship; R220. Flights; R260. Pursuits; R311. Tree refuge; W116. Vanity

A *Masalai* Tricked a Man

(Wantok 702, December 10-16, 1987, page 23)

Long, long ago, in the time of the ancestors, there were two friends. Their names were Puim and Mila. Puim was from **Koen** Village, and Mila was from **Wantenda** Village [**Mendi** People, **Southern Highlands** Province]. The two men were very good friends, so they always worked well with each other and went around doing things together.

One day, there was no rain and the moon was very bright, so the two friends decided to go to the forest and hunt for some wild game. They sat in the afternoon and made their decision, then they went to their villages.

Puim told Mila that they would meet on the trail, then decide which part of the forest they would travel. They finished speaking, then they went to prepare their things to carry into the forest.

However, Puim changed his mind, so he did not meet his friend, Mila. Poor Mila carried his bow and arrows, put some food in his net bag, and went to the meeting place on the trail.

He arrived and saw his friend, Puim, waiting there. However, it was not really his friend. This man was a *masalai*. In the afternoon, the *masalai* had been scavenging trash and had heard the two friends make their decision, so the *masalai* had come quickly to wait for them.

Mila did not know this. He saw the man from faraway and thought that it was his friend, Puim, waiting there. Mila arrived, and the *masalai* tricked him, saying that he had been waiting there for a long time.

They arrived somewhere in the forest and the *masalai* lied to Mila, "There's plenty of marsupials (*kapul*) in this part of the forest, so we should make a hut and sleep."

They cut tree branches, [gathered] leaves, and erected their hut. When they finished, they sat and caught their breaths. Before long, it was dark. They cooked the food that Mila had brought.

They ate and waited for the light of the moon. When the moon was bright and everything was clear, they carried their bows and arrows, then went out to prepare for marsupial hunting.

Mila told the *masalai* to follow the stream downwards while he went upwards, but the *masalai* did not want to do this. The *masalai* wanted them to go together. Mila listened to him and they went upstream. They walked and walked, and they killed seven marsupials.

They shot another marsupial, then the marsupial got up and ran up a tree. Mila saw this and told the *masalai* to climb the tree then kill the marsupial. The *masalai* said that he felt terribly cold, so he could not climb the tree.

Milai [Mila] listened and told the *masalai* to find a rope so that he could climb the tree and kill the marsupial. The *masalai* listened and removed a tendon [lit., "rope"] from his leg, then gave it to Mila. Mila tied the tendon, climbed the tree, and followed the marsupial.

When he was very high, by the crown of the tree, he turned to look down to the ground. Oh my, he was surprised to see that the eyes of the *masalai* were bright, like the light of a fire. When poor Mila saw this, he knew that he had not come with his friend, Puim, but with a *masalai*.

Mila sat on a branch and tried to think of a way to escape from this *masalai*. He knew that if stayed there, the *masalai* would eat him. The poor man thought and thought, then he thought of a way to trick the *masalai*.

He broke a dry tree branch, and called down to the *masalai*. He said that the marsupial was jumping down, so that he must go fairly far away and wait. When he saw the *masalai* go far away from the base of the tree, he broke another branch.

The tree crackled, so he lied to the *masalai* that the marsupial had jumped down to the ground. The *masalai* listened and ran to the place where the man had thrown the tree branch. When Mila saw this, he jumped down and ran back to his village.

Mila crashed through the forest. He went down then he got up again and ran away. He did not know that the *masalai* had heard him and was following behind. However, the *masalai* could not run very strongly because he had given his leg tendon to Mila, so he took his time at running.

Milai ran and ran until he arrived at his village and dawn had broken. The *masalai* saw that it was dawn, so he turned back towards his home. Mila was half-dead and fell down by his house. When he felt better, he got up and killed one of his big pigs. After this, he felt better still, and just rested.

In the afternoon, he saw his friend, Puim, and he told the story about the *masalai* who had tricked and nearly killed him. Mila was furious at Puim because it was Puim who had talked about hunting for game in the forest. Mila had listened to him and almost died in the hands of the *masalai*.

After this, the two men were no longer friends. They lived by themselves and no longer traveled together as they had done before.

If you go to this area near Mendi, you will see two stones. One is named Puim that we now call it Mount Clancy [Clancy's Knob]. We call the other one Mila. These are fairly far from town.

Robert Pipik

Mendi

Southern Highlands Province

A1617. Origin of place-name; F490+. Masalai; F541.1.1. Eyes flash fire; G572. Ogre overawed by trick; G636. Ogres powerless after cockcrow; K525+. Escape by substituting log; K1930. Treacherous impostors; P310. Friendship; R210. Escapes; R260. Pursuits

A Woman Became a Bird of
Paradise and Left Her Husband

(Wantok 703, December 16-21, 1987, page 23)

Long, long ago, in the time of the ancestors, there were two girls. The two women [girls] lived in the very deep forest on a mountain where no other people lived.

The parents of these two girls had died, so they lived by themselves. They often worked in the garden and husbanded their pigs, so they did not lack any food. They lived at this place for a while. The elder sister became a woman and after some more years, she began to think hard about leaving her sister and going to marry.

One day, the big sister told her little sister, "I'm leaving you to go to a place that is very far away. You must take care of the house and garden well. It is completely forbidden for you to break the sugarcanes that grow behind the house."

After the big sister explained this to the little sister, she carried her belongings and went to find a man in a village who was far from their little home. She spent very many days on the trail.

The little sister stayed by herself at their home. She took care of the food in the garden and of their house well. She gave good food to their pigs, too. She always thought about what her big sister had told her about the sugarcanes growing behind the house.

One day, the little sister was famished, so she went behind the house, broke some sugarcane and drank the juice. Nothing happened to her, so she thought again about what her big sister had explained to her.

The big sister searched and searched for a husband, then she thought back to her little sister, and she felt sorry for her again. She turned back towards their home. She arrived and her little sister held her. They cried because they were very happy. The big sister told the story of her journey to faraway villages, while the little sister just sat quietly and listened.

That night, they ate then they slept. In the very early morning, the big sister awoke and went down to look around carefully at their things. She saw that all of the things were in order, then she walked behind the house. She looked at the place where the sugarcanes grew and saw that the canes were not there.

The big sister went to ask her little sister about the sugarcanes. The little sister answered that she had been hungry, that she had broken the sugarcanes and had drunk the juice.

The big sister listened and was furious. She took a rattan and beat her little sister, then she took [another] thorny vine, tied her sister to the house post and left her there. The girl was in pain. She screamed and cried, but her big sister was unconcerned, she beat her soundly.

The big sister stood by the forest, then began to call out to the *nokondi masalai*s of the forest.

She called out, "If you *nokondi*s of the forest hear me, then come and take your game-meat that I have tied up." After the woman called to the *nokondi*s, she took all of her belongings, then she ran away to marry a man that she desired.

The *nokondi*s are *masalai*s who only have one hand, one leg and the left part of the head. When the big sister stood and shouted, one of them heard her shouting, saw the little sister, and was sorry for her. Immediately, the *nokondi* arrived and removed the thorny vines from her hands and legs, then carried her away and hid her well.

Then the other *nokondi*s heard the big sister's shouting and ran. They went in a group towards the place where the two sisters lived, [gnashing] their teeth together. However when they arrived, they did not see their game [the sister] at the house.

The good *nokondi* who had carried the girl off and hidden her, told her, "I'll show you the way to follow to escape from this place. You must follow this trail until you come to a pond where a tree stands. You must climb the tree and sit there."

After the *nokondi* explained this, the girl put a feather headdress on her head. Then the girl followed the trail that the *nokondi* had shown her.

She cut through the deep forest, walking and walking, until she arrived at the pond. She climbed the tree by the water, and sat there.

When the sun was setting, a young boy came to fetch water. While the boy was lying down to fetch water, he saw the girl's shadow in the water. The feathers that the *nokondi* had put on her head moved back and forth.

The boy saw this and searched for her, but he did not see the girl sitting there in the tree. While he was searching, the *nokondi* arrived and told him to look up on the tree.

The boy looked up and saw the girl sitting there. Quickly, he climbed the tree and took the girl down to the ground. He removed the thorns that were stuck in the girl's skin. Then he carried his bamboo tube of water, and the two of them walked to his village.

When they arrived at the house, the boy hid the girl in the place where the firewood was kept. Then he went inside the house. He did not tell his mother about the girl.

Whenever they cooked and ate, he would stealthily carry some food to give to the girl.

After the boy did this for a while, his mother began to think. She saw that her child never helped her work in the garden or hunt for game in the forest as they had done before.

One day, the two of them went to work in the garden. The boy left the garden and went back to the house. The mother saw this and pretended to work a little, then she carried her things and walked back very quietly to the village.

She arrived and was surprised to see her son sitting with a beautiful longhaired girl. The mother was ecstatic that her son had found a girl. They lived together, and the two youths married.

Not much later, the mother died, and the boy lived with his wife there alone. When they fought, the man would beat the woman and ridicule her. He would say, "You're a wild woman from the bush."

The woman would listen to this and be very troubled, but she never did anything. She would just stay there. However, she thought hard about leaving this man.

One day, they went to work in the garden. The woman climbed a tree and called down to her husband, "I live well with you, but you always beat and ridicule me. I'm leaving you for good. If you want to find me, then come look for me in the deep forest."

After the woman said this, she changed into a bird of paradise and flitted among the tree branches. Her husband saw this and was shocked. He wanted to catch the woman, but the woman tricked him and jumped among the tree branches, then she left completely for the deep forest.

This story belongs to the people of Goroka.

T. Fotu
Seigupi [**Seigu**] Village [**Gahuku** People]
P. O. Box 271
Goroka
Eastern Highlands Province

D150+W. Transformation: woman to bird of paradise; D642. Transformation to escape difficult situation; F525. Person with half a body; F490+. Masalai; F490+. Nokondi; G550. Rescue from ogre; P210. Husband and wife; P231. Mother and son; P252.1. Two sisters; P262. Mother-in-law; P265+. Daughter-in-law; Q325. Disobedience punished; Q429.1+. Punishment: culprit sacrificed to cannibals; Q458. Flogging as punishment; R100. Rescues; R213. Escape from home; R227.2. Flight from hated husband; R260. Pursuits; R311. Tree refuge; S62. Cruel husband; S70+. Cruel sister; S211. Child sold (promised) to devil (ogre); T100. Marriage; W126. Disobedience

Why the Enemies Finished Off Suwena Village

(Wantok 704, December 24, 1987 — January 7, 1988, page 23)

Long, long ago, in the time of the ancestors, the clans of the Waria River were enemies [**Morobe** Province]. The clans of the beach were enemies with the clans that lived on the middle and headwaters of the Waria River.

There lived a man named Konokabio who was married to a woman from the beach. For a long time, the people of Waria did not fight. They lived well because of this marriage. The name of the woman's homeland was **Suwena** [Village, **Suena** People].

Konokabio was a hard worker who always hunted for wild game, but he often beat his wife. One time, he beat his wife and the woman fled back to her kin. She told them that her husband always beat her, so she grew tired of it and fled back to them.

The woman's kin listened and were furious. They decided to kill Konokabio. Before long, Konokabio went to the woman's village. When he arrived, no one was there. Everyone had gone to the forest or to the gardens.

There was only an old man who was sitting in the spirit house. He saw Konokabio and told him, "Eat some taro, then go to sleep in my pigsty. In the early morning, wake up and go back to your village."

However Konokabio thought that he was smarter, so he did not listen to what the old man had said. He sat well in the spirit house and waited for the people to return to the village.

In the afternoon, the people returned to the village. The men went to the spirit house and saw Konokabio sitting there. They began to speak in their language [which was unintelligible to him].

The old man listened and told Konokabio, "You've made a mistake. I told you to leave this spirit house long ago, and you did not listen to what I said. Your enemies have arrived."

The men surrounded Konokabio, bound his legs and arms, and then tied him up inside the house. All of the leaders of the village gathered and argued.

All of the men wanted to kill and eat him. They asked each other how they should kill and cook Konokabio. Some said to cook him in an earth oven, some said to let him live and to cut off small pieces of flesh from his body to cook.

Many men said that Konokabio was a stubborn man, so they would let him live while they would cut small pieces of flesh from his body to eat.

Poor Konokabio listened to the men decide what they would do to him the next day. They made their decision, then they left their house and told the women to prepare food to eat with Konokabio's flesh.

Konokabio listened to the men going about, then he spoke to himself, "Oh poor Konokabio, will dawn bring something good or not?"

Before long, he saw the men bring a plate of food. Poor Konokabio just sat and watched. The old man who had told Konokabio to flee and hide in the pigsty had gone back to his house. He called out for all of his family to gather. He told them not to do as the other people of the village and eat Konokabio.

The old man's family listened to him and just stayed in their house. In the early morning, the men awoke and went to the spirit house. They cut flesh from Konokabio's body, brought it to cook, ate it, then they sang and danced. When all of the flesh from Konokabio's legs and arms was gone, they cut the other parts of his body.

When they cooked the flesh from Konokabio's left arm and ate it, they sang, "Konokabio, he's delicious!" They gorged themselves, sang and danced.

The old man broke off a *tanget* plant, then sent it up to Konokabio's kin. They sent a message up to all those in the Waria headwaters. When the men of these villages received this message, they became furious and prepared to go fight. They told the old man to take his kin and hide in the forest because they would come to Suwena Village to avenge the death of Konokabio.

The old man returned to his village. He explained to his family what had happened, then they hid in the pigsty. The old man hid alone by a huge tree, where he sat and watched. The vines on the tree clapped on one side, so when the men came by, they would clap the tree vines and follow the trail to Suwena Village.

At about eight o'clock, he saw the men of Konokabio's village spilling down. They crumpled the tree vines, then the tree broke and fell down.

The old man cried and said, "Suwena, You have wronged. The enemies are coming now."

The enemies spilled down and surrounded Suwena Village. The people saw this and were surprised. They ran inside the big house. All of their singing, dancing and happiness was over. The men were not prepared to fight with their enemies. The enemies had surrounded them well. One of them stood in the front door and another stood in the back. The two of them called inside, "Hey Suwena, where is Konokabio?"

The people of Suwena replied, "Go back, have your last party, then come back and we'll fight."

When they said this, the two enemies put a fire to the doors of the house. The hand drums beat loudly inside the house where the people of Suwena were packed.

The fire was ruining everyone inside the house. When they ran outside, the enemies were ready and shot them with spears. However, one man was strong. He broke through the house and stood on top of it. He called out to the enemies that he was a champion fighter and that no one could kill him.

The enemies threw their spears, but they kept missing. One man, named Sopera, killed this strong man of Suwena. Then everyone inside the house died, and the enemies went back to their villages.

Only the old man and his family were not killed in the big battle between the people of Suwena and their enemies from the headwaters of the Waria. After the enemies left the village and went back, the old man with his family returned to the village where they lived. The children and the grandchildren of the old man married. More people were raised there, reforming Suwena Village.

They lived well with their enemies and no more troubles arose. Now, we people of the Waria River have this story of how the enemies finished off Suwena Village.

Nga Biary [Oga]
Panguna
North Solomons Province

G10. Cannibalism; J652. Inattention to warnings; K812. Victim burned in his own house (or hiding place); K914. Murder from ambush; K2210+. Man betrays village to save family; P210. Husband and wife; Q211. Murder punished; Q215. Cannibalism punished; Q285. Cruelty punished; Q411. Death as punishment; Q414. Punishment: burning alive; Q429.3. Cutting into pieces as punishment; R213. Escape from home; R227.2. Flight from hated husband; S62. Cruel husband; S112.0.2. House (hostel) burned with all inside; S139.7. Murder by slicing person into small pieces; T100. Marriage; V112.1. Spirit huts; W167. Stubbornness

Kulele Tricked the Villagers

(Wantok 70[5], January 7-14, 1988, page 23)

Long, long ago, in the time of the ancestors, a woman and her child who lived in the **Baniara** area of **Milne Bay** Province [**Gapapaiwa** People]. The boy's name was Kulele. He lived with his mother on a mountain.

Kulele was not very handsome because various sores ruined his skin. Everyone in the village was tired of Kulele because his body smelled horrible. Only his mother was concerned about him, so she took care of her son well.

Kulele always just sat in the ashes of the fire and blew his bamboo flute. When he blew his flute, beautiful music came forth. His mother would scold him, but Kulele did not care, he would just blow the flute.

One day, he was sitting and blowing the flute when a woman from **Goodenough** Island [**Bwaidoka** People?] heard the sound. She was enraptured by the beautiful music from Kulele. Whenever she heard the beautiful music, she would want to know who was blowing the flute. The woman told her father that she wanted to go to the mainland and see who was making the beautiful flute music.

The woman's father was the leader of Goodenough Island. When his daughter told him this, he told the men to carve a big canoe. When the canoe was ready, they tied the sail and paddled to the mainland.

At about four o'clock in the afternoon, the canoe went ashore on Baniara Beach. They slept on the shore, then in the early morning, the men awoke and walked until they arrived at Kulele's home. When they were still on the trail, they smelled Kulele's festering sores, so they spat and vomited as they approached the home.

Kulele's mother saw the men approaching their home, and she was terrified. She just wanted to flee and hide, but the leaders among the men told her that they were searching for a man or woman, and that was why they had come.

The men asked, "Do you know which man or woman has been blowing a flute and making beautiful music?"

The mother's heart jumped, and she replied that the man who had been blowing the flute was her son, Kulele.

The leaders told her, "We've come to take him. The daughter of our leader wants him."

Kulele's poor mother listened and was speechless. Then she told the men that her son was a bad man, so they could [not] take him away. However the men were insistent, so the mother agreed.

The men made a platform and carried Kulele down to the beach. They put him in the canoe and sailed back to Goodenough Island. When they arrived, everyone from the village was waiting on the shore. A woman stood at the very front of them. It was the daughter of the leader, the one who had fallen for Kulele's music.

The canoe went ashore. When the woman saw that Kulele was sore infested, she was furious. She told the men to bring him back to the deep sea and drop him overboard.

However the woman's little sister was sorry for Kulele, so she took him back to their house. The big sister arrived at the house and saw Kulele there. She became angry and chased the two of them. The little sister took Kulele to live in another house.

The little sister took good care of Kulele, as his mother had done before. Poor Kulele did not have a way to return to his home, and the people of the village did not want to go near him because his skin was putrefying and he smelled horrible.

One day, they received a message from **Kalo Kalo** Village in West Fergusen [**Fergusson**] Island, that there would be a huge festival, and that the people of Goodenough should come [**Kalo Kalo** People]. The woman heard this, so she went to tell Kulele that they would go together to sing and dance at Kalo Kalo.

Kulele listened and told the woman, "I'm a bad man, so I won't go. It's alright if you go to the festival. I'll stay in the village and take care of the house. Follow your kin and go."

The woman listened to Kulele and followed her kin to the festival at Kalo Kalo. Very late at night, Kulele got up from the ashes of the fire, removed the nasty stores from his skin, and became a very handsome man. He went down to get his canoe on the beach, then he paddled to the place where everyone was singing and dancing.

When he arrived at Kalo Kalo, the women were ruined with lust for him. He sang and danced like no one else, so everyone coveted his style.

Kulele sang and danced passionately for a while, then at about two o'clock in the morning, he got up quietly and went back to the house where he pretended to sleep in the ashes of the fire. In the morning, the people went back to the village. The woman returned to the house and told the story of the man who had gone to the festival with them.

Later, there was another festival and Kulele did the same thing. He told the woman to go with her kin. Later, he removed the nasty sores, and then went to sing and dance. When dawn was about to break, he left the festival site and ran back to sleep.

Three times he did this, then the woman had the idea that the handsome man must just be Kulele. So, she wanted to play a trick and find out if it was really Kulele who always fooled them.

One time, there was another festival on the side of West Fergusen Island, so the woman lied to her parents that she was sick and could not go to the festival. However, she did not tell Kulele. She lied to Kulele that she was going to the festival with the other people of the village.

Everyone left, then the woman hid well inside her father's house. Kulele slept until late at night, then when it was very quiet, he thought that no one was in the village. He removed his nasty skin and became a very handsome man. The woman saw this and nearly fainted, but she did not make a sound. She kept quiet.

Kulele arrived at the festival site, then he went inside where he sang and danced passionately. After a while, he looked around to see whether the woman was there too, but he did not see her. Kulele then knew that the woman must have been in the village. She must have seen him remove his nasty skin and become a handsome man.

He left the festival site immediately and paddled back to Goodenough Island. However, the woman had burned the nasty skin that Kulele had removed, the skin that he had used to trick people. When Kulele arrived, the woman ran down to hold him. She told him that she knew about his trick.

When villagers returned, the woman ran to tell her father that she would marry Kulele because he was the handsome man who had always gone to the festivals. However, the woman's big sister said that Kulele was her husband because she had taken Kulele to their island.

The little sister was persistent, and told her big sister that when she had seen the sores on Kulele's skin, she had told the men to carry Kulele away and throw him into the ocean. So, the little sister married Kulela [Kulele], and the two of them lived very happily on Goodenough Island.

This story is from the people of Goodenough Island in Milne Bay Province.

Irebaeus Moses

Lae

Morobe Province

D52.2. Ugly man becomes handsome; D531+. Transformation by removing skin D793.2. Disenchantment made permanent by burning cast-off skin; D1223.1. Magic flute; D1275.1+. Magic music travels great distance; D1337.2.5. Magic skin makes person appear ugly; D1355.1.1. Love-producing song; F687. Remarkable fragrance (odor) of person; P210. Husband and wife; P231. Mother and son; P234. Father and daughter; P252.1. Two sisters; P261. Father-in-law; P264. Sister-in-law; P265. Son-in-law; R100. Rescues; T10. Falling in love; T100. Marriage; W181. Jealousy

A Mother Worried about Her Child then She Turned to Stone

(Wantok 706, January 14-21, 1988, page 23)

Long, long ago, in the time of the ancestors, there was a boy who lived with his mother. The name of the boy was Gelam, and the name of his mother was Usar. The two of them lived in **Bulbul** Village, on **Moa** Island [**Kala Lagaw Ya** People]. This is an island in the **Torres Strait**, between the Australian mainland and Western Province.

When Gelam was still small, he did not have many worries because he just lived happily with his mother. But when he was big, he saw that it was just he and his mother there. He did not have a father, and his mother never spoke about his father.

One day, he asked his mother, "Where does my papa live?"

Searching for Father

The mother replied that she did not know where Gelam's father lived. Gelam listened and began to think hard. He thought very hard about trying to find his father.

Then Gelam went down to the beach. He looked for a nice piece of wood, then he began to carve a dugong (or dolphin). He carved the wood until his carving was finished and it looked beautiful, like a dugong (or dolphin).

When the carving was ready, Gelam pulled it down to the sea, sat on top of it, and swam out to the ocean. He swam and swam until he arrived at Mer [**Maer**] Island, another island in the Torres Strait.

Gelam went to the island, pulled the carving up to the beach, then sat and caught his breath. However, the carving had its own power. It could speak.

When they sat on the beach, the carving told Gelam that his father's house was nearby and that he must go quickly to this house. Geram [Gelam] listened to the carving and walked directly to his father's house.

Everyone was dead asleep, so they did not hear them arrive. He went inside the house, then he went directly to the first room of the house. He looked inside the room and he saw two sisters sleeping. He went to sleep between them.

Gelam Slept

That night, one sister saw Gelam sleeping. She was afraid and awakened her sister. She asked, "Who's that man who came to sleep between us? He's a very tall man."

Gelam heard the sisters talking, then told them, "Don't be afraid. I'm your brother."

However, the sisters did not believe this. They replied to him, "You lie! You're not our brother. You're completely nuts. The two of us are short."

Real Brother

Gelam was persistent, and told the two women that he really was their brother. They kept talking until dawn broke. In the morning, the two sisters told their father about Gelam. Their father was also surprised, so he told the two women to bring Gelam so that he could see him.

When Gelam arrived, his father recognized him and then went to hold him. He asked Gelam about his mother. Gelam replied that his mother was living well on Moa Island.

Return

The father told Gelam, "Go back to Bulbul, take your mama, then return with her and we'll all live in this village."

Gelam listened to his father. That same day, he went back towards Moa Island to fetch his mother. He jumped on his carving, and swam to Moa Island. Then he walked up towards his mother's house.

He arrived at the house and saw his mother, Usar, sitting there. He said, "Mama, I've found papa. He's living on Mer Island. He sent me back to get you. We'll live with him."

However, his mother spoke angrily, "I absolutely can't go to live with your father. He left us when you were still small. He didn't think any more of us, so why should I go to live with him now?"

Talking to Mother

Gelam was persistent. He told his mother that his father truly wanted her to go to Mer Island. However, Usar absolutely did not want to go, so she told Gelam, "You want to go? OK, go by yourself. I absolutely won't leave my island."

Gelam saw that his mother truly did not want to follow him back to the place where his father was now living. He talked and talked, then he gave up completely.

He told his mother, "If you don't want to come with me, OK, I'll go back alone to live with papa."

Gelam then went down to the beach. He jumped on his carving, then he began to swim out to the sea. His mother, Usar, saw this and ran after him down to the beach. She told him not to go, but Gelam did not listen. He just thought of returning to his father.

The Mother Cries

The mother cried and shouted, then followed him into the sea. Gelam ignored her, and kept swimming toward Mer Island. The mother did not care about the sea, she kept walking, crying and shouting for Gelam to return.

The mother stood crying until Gelam left completely for the deep sea. She kept standing there. The tide returned, but she did not care, she kept crying there. The water came up to her middle, then up to her shoulders, then only her neck was above water.

Then the sea covered her completely. When the sea covered Usar, she became a stone. This stone is still there, and the people of Moa Island believe that this stone is just Usar who is still crying for her son, Gelam.

This ancestor story is from the shores of Western Province, and the people of Torres Strait Islands in Australia. Grace Ware of Saint Paul's Station on Moa Island, Torres Strait and Kobeda Kare of **Masingara** Village, **Western** Province wrote this ancestor story [**Bine** People].

A974. Rocks from transformation of people to stone; A977.5. Origin of particular rock; D231W. Transformation: woman to stone; D1620.2. Automatic statue of animal; P231. Mother and son; P233. Father and son; P234. Father and daughter; P253.0.2+. Two sisters and one brother

How Did the Two Toaripi Clans Arise?
(Wantok 707, January 21-28, 1988, page 23)

Long, long ago, in the time of the ancestors, a man and his wife who lived with their two children. They lived in the forest by **Kakoro** Village in the **Gulf** Province.

The name of the man was Akara. The name of the son was Ikui and the name of the daughter was Siari. Ikui was five years old and Siari was eight years old.

One day, they left the village and went to make sago in the swamp. The father worked hard and the two children played. They worked and worked until the sun was setting. Then the parents gathered their things to carry back to the village.

Many Things

They saw that there were too many things to carry, so the father told them that he and the mother would carry the belongings and put them in the village. Later, they would return to fetch the children.

The parents carried the belongings and put them in the village, then they turned back to get the two children. However, it was completely dark and they became disoriented on the trail. The children waited and waited, then they went to sleep.

They stayed in this place for a while, waiting for their parents. Many months passed. They ate sago beetle grubs and other food that they found in the swamp.

A Long Time

The two of them lived for a long time in this swamp and stopped looking for their parents. They knew that their parents could not return to get them. The big sister, Siari, saw this, and thought of a way for them to leave the swamp.

One day, she began to gather fallen bamboos from the area. Siari told her little brother to help her carry the bamboos to the water. Siari took vines and began to tie up the bamboos.

Ikui asked Siari, "What are you making?"

Siari replied to her brother that she was making a raft for them to drift down the water to find other people.

Ikui asked again, "How will we drift? The water is dried up. There's just a little water there."

Siari replied that she knew the song to make a flood arise. After she finished making the raft, she would sing, then the water would rise again.

When the bamboo raft was finished, Siari told Ikui to carry their belongings. They would go and sit on top of the raft. Siari began to sing to make the water flood:

> *Tivu i Tivu*   [*ma taiva* = flood, *i* = to call]
> *Tivu i ete tapa* [*ete* = female genitals, *tapare* = oil]
> *Momo ete tapa.*   [*omoi* = to talk]

Before long, the flood spilled down and carried their raft downriver. They drifted and drifted until they approached a village called Kapui [**Kapuri**].

They went ashore at the village, then they sat and waited. A man and his wife walked towards them. They saw Siari and Ikui, and they asked them why they had come to Kapui.

Very Sorry

Siari told their story to the married couple, and they were very sorry. They took the two of them to their house. They arrived at the house, then the man's wife cooked some sago and gave it to them.

While Siari and Ikui ate, the man of the house told them that they must just stay inside the house. He told them that the people of the village often killed people who came there, so they could not go outside and play with the other children.

The brother and sister listened, then they just lived inside the house. After a while, some boys of the village had heard the children talking inside the house, so the thought hard. They knew that the married couple must have hidden some children inside the house because the couple was childless.

The boys went and told their parents. Afterwards, the people of the village decided to kill Siari and Ikui. They picked a day to kill the two children. The first day, they would go to process sago. The second day, they would go to the garden and harvest some food. Then on the third day, they would kill the two children.

Hidden Children

They did not tell the couple who had hidden Siari and Ikui in their house. The first day, the people awoke in the very early morning, then went to process sago.

There was one woman who had just given birth and was sleeping in a house. She had heard the people make their decision, so she waited until everyone left then she went to tell the married couple.

She told them that the people of the village were processing sago, that the next day they would go to get food from the garden, and that on the third day, they would kill Siari and Ikui. After the woman explained this, she went back to her house.

The couple listened, then took all Siari and Ikui's belongings and put them in one place. The woman tied up some sago and fish, fetched some water, then put all of the things inside a net bag. It was dark now, so they took Siari and Ikui down very quietly to the river. Ikui asked the man of the house, then he gave him a hand drum and a dog named Aia.

The brother and sister jumped on the raft that they had made with palms [*limbum* or sago?], then they drifted downriver. They drifted until they arrived at **Moriuari** Village where the water swirled. Ikui beat the hand drum and sang:

> Kapui *o ivai vani o*   [*o auai* = to talk]
> Kapui *opo pani o, ivai vani o.*

At Kapui Village, the people heard the singing, then they knew that their two "animals" had escaped [implying intended cannibalism]. They did not have a way to follow them and kill them.

When the brother and sister approached the village, Siari told her brother that she would go ashore because she wanted to go to Apanipa [**Apanaipi**] Village and find a husband. Ikui cried and did not want his sister to go. However Siari insisted, so her brother just listened.

Siari left Ikui who drifted alone on the raft until a man and his wife, Vitapara and Uapara, found him. The married couple was from **Moveave** Village. They took him to their village and cared for him as their own son.

Ikui became a big man, then they put him in the *elavo* spirit house. [*Elavo* is a men's house or ceremonial club house (Brown, 1986: 19).] Ikui stayed an entire year. When he left the spirit house, his foster father and mother, Vitapara and Uapara, had died.

He stole a canoe belonging to the Moveave people, then he paddled back upstream from whence he had come. He arrived at a village on a bay, then he left the canoe and went up to the village. The name of this village is **Popoaitave**.

In Popoaitave Village, he met Koko, his little brother Ope Parauka, and their wives, Uravita and Toropeauvita. The two women were sisters.

Koko was worried about Ikui, so he took him and cared for him. He changed the name of Ikui, giving him the name Ikui Koko. Ikui stayed in Popoitave [Popaitave] Village. Later, he married a woman named Horere.

His sister, Siari, had arrived at Apainaipi [Apanaipi] Village and married a man named Maura Leoava. After some years, she became pregnant and gave birth to a daughter, whom she named Siari. She had followed the custom of her people from Kovio [**Kovu**] Village.

When the baby, Siari, grew up, her mother sent her to live with her uncle, Ikui in Popoatiave [Popoaitave] Village. Siari went to live with her uncle there, then she married a man named Popoe Fareova. Afterwards, Sairi [Siari] gave birth to a girl and again gave name Siari to the baby.

Now, from this brother and sister, Siari and Ikui, arose the two clans of the **Toaripi** People. Ikui Avosa told the story and I, Joe Martin, wrote it.

Joseph Martin

Gerehu

National Capital District

A1011. Local deluges; A1640. Origin of tribal subdivisions; D1781. Magic results from singing; D2151.8. Magic flood; G10. Cannibalism; J1050. Attention to warnings; K300. Thefts and cheats—general; N825.1. Childless old couple adopt hero; P210. Husband and wife; P231. Mother and son; P232. Mother and daughter; P233. Father and son; P234. Father and daughter; P251.5. Two brothers; P252.1. Two sisters; P253. Sister and brother; P263. Brother-in-law; P264. Sister-in-law; P271. Foster father; P272. Foster mother; P275. Foster son; P275+. Foster daughter; P293. Uncle; P298. Niece; R210. Escapes; S110. Murders; S143. Abandonment in forest; T100. Marriage; T570. Pregnancy; T580. Childbirth; T596. Naming of children; V112.1. Spirit huts; X712.1H. Female genitals

Nokondi Helped Kamusi

(Wantok 708, January 28 — February 4, 1988, page 23)

Long, long ago, in the time of fighting among the ancestors, there was a clan house. The name of this clan house was Kamusi [**Kamus** Village, **Gahuku** People, **Eastern Highlands** Province].

At this time, there was also a wild man of the forest who lived near the clan house. The name of this man was Nokondi. Nokondi had one hand, one leg, one eye, one ear, and there was only one of everything else on his body.

Bringing Food

He never went inside the clearings when he traveled. He often just went near the village and looked at people, but he was strongly attached to my ancestral clan.

When he went by the village, the men would say, "The old man of the forest has come. Bring some food."

Then they would bring food, put it on the branch of a tree, and call out for him to come and eat. He would eat, then return quietly to his home in the forest.

One time, the men received a message that the enemies would come to fight with themselves. They sent two men to the forest to explain this to Nokondi. Some people of the village killed a pig, cooked it an earth oven, and ate. Then they waited for Nokondi.

That night, Nokondi arrived at the men's house. The men gave food to him. After he ate, they began to query him. They wanted to know whether they would win the battle or not.

No One Left

Nokondi did not speak. He rose and blasted a spear into the forest. The men saw this and knew that they would lose the battle. When it was still at night, they awakened all of the women and children, then they left the village, fleeing into a cave on the side of a mountain.

Losing the Battle

Before, Nokondi would sleep in this cave, but he left and slept in another place. They arrived at this place, then sat and looked down at their village.

Dawn was about to break. The enemies arrived in the village. They surrounded the village and prepared to burn it. They thought that everyone was still sleeping, but the people were sitting on the mountain, laughing at their enemies.

The enemies went inside the village and searched everywhere. There were no people or pigs, the village was empty. They were angry with this, so they burned every house and completely wrecked the gardens. After the enemies ruined the village, they went back. The people saw this and were very sorry. Nokondi was also sorry for his clan.

Some days later, the people returned to the village, made houses and replanted the food in their gardens. They stayed in the village for a while, then they again received a message that the enemies would return to fight with them.

They again sent two men into the forest to explain this to Nokondi. That night, Nokondi went to the village and ate at the men's house. They asked him whether they would win or not.

Singing and Dancing

Nokondi rose, took a bow and shot towards the area of their enemies. The men saw this and were ecstatic. They sang and danced. They knew that they would win the battle.

The Kamusi Clan ran to get their bows and arrows. They awoke in the very early morning, left the village and watched from Mount Hulorige.

They saw their enemies begin to spill out. There were many more of them than there were Kamusi men. The enemies approached the mountain and the Kamusi began to shoot the arrows. They shot and shot, then their enemies began to fall. Old Nokondi was helping them.

They fought and fought until the sun was bright and all of their enemies were dead. Not one of them returned to their village. The Kamusi Clan won the battle. They carried old Nokondi. They sang, danced and shouted back to the village.

They told the other clans that the Kamusi Clan was very strong at fighting, so they could take out the big clan houses [in battle]. After that, the other clan houses were afraid and no longer fought with the Kamusi Clan.

The Enemies Were Dead

Today, we, the Kamusi, often tell stories about Nokondi, the man who helped our ancestors. We have a rugby team in the village named the Nokondi Rugby Club.

Robin Lusoho
P. O. Box 206
Goroka
Eastern Highlands Province

D1092. Magic arrow; D1712. Soothsayer (diviner. oracle, etc.); F349.2. Fairy aids mortal in battle; F490+. Nokondi; F525. Person with half a body; F567. Wild man; L310. Weak overcomes strong in conflict; R213. Escape from home; R315. Cave as refuge

The Story of Lalafaremori

(Wantok 709, February 4, 1988, page 27)

Long, long ago, there was a tree that was similar to a mangrove, which grew in the water. The name of this tree is *lala* in the **Toaripi** Language of the **Gulf** Province. One of the tree fruits was ripe and ready to fall.

It was daylight, and a crab left her hole in the swamp. She went to rest underneath this tree. The crab was not an ordinary one. No, she was an old woman who had turned into a crab.

After the crab rested, she alit and gathered threads from the branches of a wild sago palm tree to make a net bag. While she was working hard gathering string for the net bag, she heard the voice of the tree fruit, "Crab, I want to fall, but you've blocked the place. Can you move back a little?"

The crab listened and said, "That's OK. Go ahead and fall. I don't want to get up and sit elsewhere."

So the fruit fell and blasted the poor crab's back. Oh my, the crab was furious, so she moved back up to the fruit and broke it in the middle. After the crab finished, the two halves of the fruit joined together again.

After a long time, the fruit became a girl who called herself Lalafaremori. She went looking around and arrived at a river. Near the river, there was a cave in a mountain where the girl made her home.

In the morning, she gathered threads from the branch of a wild sago tree, and made a net for catching fish. When the net was finished, she took it down to the water and caught small fish.

After she caught the fish, she heated them in the sun and later ate them. Another day, she did the same thing. However this time, she caught big fish. She knew that the big fish would not cook well in the sun.

She knew that she must find a fire to cook the fish so that she could eat well. Lalafaremori climbed a tall tree and looked for smoke from a fire. She looked towards the place where the sun sets, then she looked towards the place where the sun rises and she saw smoke rising.

Lalafaremori jumped down the tree and followed the smoke from the fire. When she arrived at this place, she saw a house that had its door open. Quickly, Lalafaremori jumped inside and saw a boy asleep. The boy's legs were very short.

Lalafaremori saw some bananas and sago, and she knew that it was food. When she was about to leave the house, she took a piece of firewood and a net bag. She filled the net bag with sago and bananas, then she carried it away.

The short-legged boy, Mikaekapo, was sleeping soundly, so he did not know that the girl had these things and that she had carried them away. In the afternoon, Mikaekapo's parents returned to the house. They found that some things were missing, so they scolded Mikaekapo terribly.

Another day, the same thing [happened...]

One time, Mikaekapo pretended to sleep as he kept watch. Before long, the girl arrived and went inside the house. Quickly, Mikaekapo grabbed her.

Lalafaremori cried and told Mikaekapo to leave her alone, but the boy took her and put her inside a big, traditional pot. Then he covered the pot.

When the parents returned from the garden, they saw Mikaekapo crying, so they asked him what had happened. He told them that he was hungry.

His mother listened, cooked sago and gave it to him. However when the boy saw just the one plate, he cried for another. So, the mother gave him another plate. He got up and took Lalafaremori, then the two of them went to his room and hid the food.

Mikaekapo told his parents that it was just the girl who had stolen the food. The parents said that they must take care, so that a baby comes. While Mikaekapo was sleeping, Lalafaremori went to steal some bananas and sago, then carried it away. When the parents arrived at the house, they again scolded Mikaekapo.

[...] Then Lalafaremori stayed with them and became a grown woman.

One time, Lalafaremori followed the desires of her foster father and mother. She took them to her home. They lived at her home, then her foster mother would always take her and go to the beach. Lalafaremori would play at trying to balance her breasts.

One time, Mikaekapo's parents wanted to go back to their home, so they told Mikaekapo to stay and watch Lalafaremori while she played at the beach.

One time, Mikaekapo watched then he slept. Lalafaremori finished playing, then she went down to wash her face. A man turned into a butterfly, then flew towards her and struck her face. Lalafaremori scolded the butterfly, then ran to the beach and played.

Another time, Lalafaremori was playing then the butterfly, Pipi, flew by. The butterfly carried Lalafaremori to his home, where he married her.

Mikaekapo waited and waited. When Lalafaremori did not return, he followed Lalafaremori's footsteps and went to the sea. When he saw that there were no footsteps returning from the beach, he cried terribly.

His parents came, and Mikaekapo told them that Lalafaremori had gone. The parents were furious, so they beat poor Mikaekapo. They told him to stay until he found Lalafaremori.

After about a year, Lalafaremori came one night in a dream to her foster mother. She told her foster mother to send a man down, then wait for her with her husband and child on the beach.

In the early morning, Mikaekapo went down to the beach to wait. When it was nearly noon, Mikaekapo saw a canoe. When Mikaekapo saw this, he jumped and ran away, calling for his parents. The three of them went to the beach and they saw Lalafaremori. Her husband and their child came ashore and waited. Then Mikaekapo and his parents took them to the house.

Some months passed, then Pipi saw that his two in-laws often worked very hard at finding food. So, he asked them to go with them to the place where the sun sets, where there is much food. So, Mikaekapo and his parents arranged their things, and they went with Pipi, Lalafaremori and their child.

Mehari Avosa
Port Moresby
National Capital District

B170+. Flight on butterfly; B211.8.1K. Speaking crab; B643+. Marriage to person in butterfly form; D175W. Transformation: woman to crab; D186.1M. Transformation: man to butterfly; D431.4G. Transformation: fruit to girl; D1602.2+. Cut fruit rejoins itself again; D1610.10. Speaking fruit; D1810.8.2. Information received through dream; F17. Visit to land of the sun; F166.11. Abundant food in otherworld; F517.0.2+. Short-legged people; J1813+. Cooking processes misunderstood: cooking with the sun; K331. Goods stolen while owner sleeps; K420. Thief loses his goods or is detected; K1868. Deception by pretending sleep; P210. Husband and wife; P230. Parents and children; P231. Mother and son; P233. Father and son; P260. Relations by law; P271. Foster father; P272. Foster mother; P275+. Foster daughter; Q325. Disobedience punished; Q458. Flogging as punishment; R4. Surprise capture; T100. Marriage; W126. Disobedience

The Big Brother Killed
the Little Brother's Dog

(Wantok 710, February 11-18, 1988, page 22)

Long, long ago, there were two brothers who lived in the Enga area. The name of the first brother was Wapona and his little brother was Huli. When the brothers were still little, their parents had died when they were still living together.

The two brothers cooked food, made gardens, and straightened things around the house. The big brother, Wapona, was an excellent hunter. His little brother, Huli, did the housework. He would look after the house and do the gardening.

When the first brother traveled in the forest, he would kill three or four marsupials (*kapul*). The little brother would just stay in the house and take care of a little dog. The dog became grossly fat.

One time, the two brothers sat and argued about the work that they would do in the following days.

The big brother sat and told the little brother, "I'll take your dog with me to the forest to hunt for wild game. It's bad that the dog just stays in the village. It won't be able to kill or smell game."

The big brother, Wapona, wanted to teach the little dog to kill big game, such as cassowaries, marsupials, and pigs. When the little dog grew up, it would become strong at chasing and killing game.

The little brother listened and was very worried because the dog was very dear to him. However, he told his brother Wapona, "Everything that you said is true, so I'll let the little dog follow you."

In the very early morning, Wapona and the little dog awoke, then left the village. They went into the deep forest to hunt for game. They sat in a hut in the forest, then they left their things.

The big brother took the dog, then the two of them went past all of the marks of the forest. They went to find the thorny rattans and big tree holes. This was because the terrestrial marsupials [probably the ground cuscus, *Strigocuscus gymnotis*] often hid in the tree holes.

Wapona and the dog kept hunting for marsupials until it started to become dark. They returned to the forest hut, made a fire, and cooked some sweet potatoes. After the big brother ate, he slept with the dog near the fire.

On the second morning, Wapona called for the dog to go to the very deep forest to hunt for marsupials or other game. They hunted and hunted, but they did not see a single tiny marsupial, so they returned to the hut and slept.

When they arrived at the hut, Wapona was a little angry because when he usually traveled in the forest, he would kill marsupials. However when he took the dog, he had not killed a single tiny marsupial.

Wapona became very angry. He drew back his bow and shot his little brother's dog. He removed all of the hair from the dog and smoked it well so that it looked like a marsupial.

Wapona spoke to himself, "I traveled with the dog and the marsupials were afraid of the dog, so I didn't kill a single one."

He cooked the dog in an earth oven, then ate some meat. Later, he carried some for his brother and went back to the village. Huli opened the package and took a piece of leg, then ate it. While he was eating, he saw that it was not a marsupial's leg. It was a dog's leg.

Huli said to his brother, "This does not look like a marsupial leg."

However, his big brother insisted that it was a marsupial leg. Wapona said, "This is the marsupial that I killed. Later, the dog got lost in the forest. I searched and searched for the dog, then I tired and just carried the marsupial back to the house."

Poor Huli knew that his brother had killed his dog, so he was very troubled. He was angry and ran away from his big brother.

He told his big brother, "This dog was very dear to me, so now you will not be able to see me. You can stay here by yourself. I'll run away to another place."

So, the little brother, Huli, ran very far away to another place. This place is **Tari** [**Huli** People, **Southern Highlands** Province]. He lived there, made his house, and raised his family with the others of Tari.

This is a little story that we often hear about Tari and the **Enga** [People, **Enga** Province]. These two areas often work very well together and never get angry with each other.

Mai Pushow [Mái is a place name for Wabag and westward in Enga Province (Lang, 1973: 62).]
Panguna
North Solomons Province

A1611+. Origin of Huli People; A1680+. Friendship between Huli and Enga Peoples; P251.5. Two brothers; P251.5.3. Hostile brothers; R213. Escape from home

Where Did the Coconut Come From?
(Wantok 711, February 18-24, 1988, page 18)

Long, long ago, there lived two brothers. One time, they decided to go hunt for game in the forest and in the water. The big brother told the little brother, "Go to the river and fish. I'll go to the forest to hunt for wild pigs, marsupials (*sikau*), and terrestrial marsupials (*kapul*) [probably the ground cuscus, *Strigocuscus gymnotis*]."

In the very early morning, the brothers went hunting for game. The big brother went to the forest, and his little brother went to the river.

They hunted and hunted, then afternoon came and they returned to the house. The poor big brother had not killed a single pig. No, he returned with nothing. The little brother had raked-in the fish, and he carried them back to the house.

The brothers were not angry. The big brother was very happy for the little brother, who had caught the fish. They sat quietly, cooked the fish with other food and ate that night. After they ate, the brothers slept.

The next day, they awoke again and went to do other work in and around the garden.

While they did this, the big brother thought hard and said, "Why did my little brother beat me at hunting game?"

So, the big brother planned to spy upon his little brother. That night, the two brothers sat by the fire and decided what they would do the next day.

They would do the same thing again. The little brother would go to the river, and the big brother would go to the forest. However, the big brother lied because later he would spy upon his brother.

In the morning, the brothers departed. The little brother went to the river, and the big brother went to the forest. The big brother did not go directly to the forest. He turned back and followed his little brother to the river to spy upon him.

He hid while the little brother went and stood near the river. The little brother removed his head and he put it aside, then he went into the river.

When his big brother saw this, he spoke to himself, "Little brother does this, so he often catches more game." The big brother walked very quietly. He went and took his brother's head, then ran back to the house.

He thought that when the little brother caught fish, he would come looking for his head, and then he would follow him to the village. However when the little brother finished catching fish, he did not see his head, so he was ashamed. He removed the fish and left them in the water.

The big brother waited and waited for his little brother, then he said, "Hey, what is my brother doing, wasting time?" Then, he went to search for his brother.

The big brother left the head at the house and he walked to the river. When he arrived at the river, no one was there. He called and called to the little brother, but he did not hear a reply. He was very worried for his little brother, then he went back to the village.

He took his little brother's head and planted it by their house.

He was very troubled about his brother, so he sat by himself in the house. Later, after some months and years, he went to see that the grave of his little brother's head had a tree sprout growing there. He said that something was growing at his brother's grave, so he would take care of it. He took care of it well, then the tree grew big and bore food.

The big brother lived there for a while, then said, "This tree has good food." He went up the tree and took food from the tree, then he cut and ate it.

He cut one, then drank and ate it. The food was delicious to him, so he waited and all of the food on the tree ripened. He took it and planted it by his forest. Now, there are many of these trees. They are coconuts.

Philip Xoxal

Wewak

East Sepik Province

A1423.3. Origin of coconut; A2611.3.1K. Coconut tree from head of human; D2150+. Catching fish by removing one's head and letting fish enter body; F511.0.4+. Person with removable head; P251.5. Two brothers; R260. Pursuits; V61.3+. Dead buried; W195. Envy

The *Masalai* Snake Tricked the Little Sister
(Wantok 712, February 25 — March 2, 1988, page 18)

Long, long ago, in **Marili** Village, there lived two sisters. Their father and mother had died. They lived in this village with the other people. Near the village, there was a big river. The name of this river is Mare.

One time, the people of **Arumut** Island, near Siasi [Siassi], wanted to go to the mainland and give fish to the people at Marili [**Mutu** People, **Madang** Province]. When they would give fish, the Marili Clan would reply with garden foods, such as taros, bananas, sweet potatoes and leafy greens.

They heard that they were coming. So the little sister, Aro Babuk, with the others villagers went to their gardens to gather these foods. When the little sister was in the garden harvesting foods, there was a *masalai* snake, Palru, in the big river Mare. Palru, the *masalai* snake, saw them and turned into her boyfriend. Then he went to flirt with the woman. They flirted, then the snake had sex with Aro Babuk. The poor woman did not know that the man was a *masalai*. She thought that it was her boyfriend, so she just gave her body to him. Afterwards, the snake asked her, "Do you know me or not?" When the snake asked this, she recognized that he was a *masalai* snake that lived in the big Mare River.

The woman was terribly ashamed, so she began to cry. The snake left her and went back to the river. Then the little sister got up and walked to the house. She told her big sister what had happened to her, "I didn't know. I think I should leave you." When the little sister finished her story, the two of them carried the food and walked to the meeting place.

They crossed the river, then they arrived and sent their food to the others. When they had taken enough fish in exchange for their taros, sweet potatoes and bananas, they walked back to the village. [The big sister said], "You swim first and when you arrive at the other side, stand and watch me swim there."

Her sister listened, so she swam first. She went to the other side of the river. When she arrived, she stood and watched her sister swimming. When her sister came to the middle of the river, the snake turned into a flood and carried the little sister away, placing her on top of a reef. The name of this reef is Ansimo.

The big sister saw this and cried as she went to the village. When she told the people of the village, they fetched the little sister's body and buried her.

Today if you travel to Arumut, you will see a reef in this part of the deep sea. The reef often breaks off and goes into the mouth of the Mare River.

Manaseh Aikan

PNG Forest Products

Lae

Morobe Province

A935.1K+. Origin of particular current; B613.1. Snake paramour; D191M. Transformation: man to serpent (snake); D283.3. Transformation: water-sprite to flood; D391M. Transformation: serpent (snake) to man; F402.1.11. Spirit causes death; F420.1.3.9. Water-spirit as snake; F490+. Masalai; K1311+. Seduction by masking as woman's boyfriend; K1910. Marital impostors; P252.1. Two sisters; S131. Murder by drowning; V61.3+. Dead buried

How Did Lake Kutubu Arise?

(Wantok 713, March 3-9, 1988, page 21)

Long ago, in Wasami [**Wasemi**] Village in the **Southern Highlands** Province, there lived ten women and one dog [**Foe** People]. When the women felt hungry, five of them would go hunting for wild game, while the other five would process sago.

Every day, they would do this, but one thing that they did not have was drinking water. They would cook the food, then when they finished eating, they would begin to search for water.

When the food was gone, they never saw their dog. The dog would quickly finish their food, then leap away. The dog would always do this. One time, the women got the idea that the dog must be eating its fill, then running to hide and drink water. Only this dog knew where the water was.

So, the women tried to watch and follow the dog into the forest. However every time the dog would run into the deep forest, the poor women would become lost and turn back towards the house.

One time, the women decided that they would cook some good food and give it to their dog to eat. After the dog ate, they would take a long vine from the forest and tie the dog's leg. When the dog was satiated, it would want to run and drink water, so they would slowly follow it and see where the dog drank.

One morning, the women did as they had discussed. The dog ate its fill. Then it ran away to drink from a water hole that was at the base of a big tree. The women followed the vine and arrived to see the dog drinking water.

When the dog was finished, it rose and ran back home. The women saw this, took a stone axe, and began to cut the tree. They cut and cut until it was evening, then the tree fell.

Oh my, when the tree fell down, they saw the hole at base of the tree break open. Water began to flow. When the women saw this, they ran away, but the water followed them, trying to take them down. They knew that they could not escape, so they told the water, "*Ira kabero waeo fari fario ibu laik kutbuo Na'a ha bera's*."

When they said this, the water stayed near the place where they had stood and became a lake. The water drowned the ten women. The women turned into fish, and their dog became wild in the deep forest.

Now, this place has many, many wild dogs that live in caves. Many people never go by this area because they are terrified that the dogs would eat them. This lake is called Kutubu.

B. [Boncy] K. [Kay] Masene

Lake Kutubu

Southern Highlands Province

[For a variant of this story from Manu Village (Fasu People), see Busse *et al.* (1993: 5-6).]

A920.1.0.1. Origin of particular lake; A1111. Impounded water; D522. Transformation through magic word (charm); D921.1. Lake (pond) produced by magic; D928. Magic water-hole; D1774. Magic results from speaking; E617. Reincarnation as fish; F402.1.10. Spirit pursues person; F402.1.11. Spirit causes death; F420. Water-spirits; R260. Pursuits; S131. Murder by drowning

Dogs Still Search for Their Tails: They Often Smell Each Other when they Meet

(Wantok 714, March 10-16, 1988, page 21)

Long, long ago, the leader of the dogs lived on an island with his wife and child. One time, the leader sent a message to the mainland that all of the dogs of the area should come and gather at his home. The dogs of the mainland were very happy because many of them had many troubles, so they wanted to bring them to their leader.

The leader sent his big canoe to the mainland and fetched the dogs. Oh my, the canoe was not a toy, it was packed with dogs when it arrived on the island. When the dogs arrived, they walked directly to the big council house used for holding meetings with their leader.

While they walked, many of them argued among themselves. Before they could hold their meeting, their leader asked all of them to remove their tails and put them in a hut that was near the meetinghouse.

They all listened and removed their tails. When they removed their tails, the meeting began. However before long, they all smelled the strong smell of something burning. All of them got up and left the meetinghouse, then ran out to sniff about the area.

Oh my, when they looked around, they saw that the hut where they had left their tails was on fire. They ran over there, broke down the door and tried to go inside to get their tails.

The dogs were not clear about which tails they took or which were in front of them. They did not care whether they took their own tails or not.

The next day, the dogs were troubled. They jumped into the canoe and went back to their home on the mainland. Not one of them had its own tail, and some of them had no tail at all.

So now, if you look carefully, you will see that all of the dogs on the earth will try to find their own tails. When one dog meets another, the first thing it will do is to sniff the other's tail to see if it is its own or not.

Sellan Pose and Steven Sangi

Nuigo [Nuigo is a squatter settlement of Wewak.]

Wewak

East Sepik Province

[This folk tale resembles the Ozark song in Randolph (1992: 490-491), "The Dogs' Convention."]

A2471.1. Why dogs look at one another under tail; A2378.1.7+. Why some dogs have no tail; B211.1.7. Speaking dog; B241.2.7. King of dogs; P210. Husband and wife; P230. Parents and children

A Son Was Helped by His Father's Ghost

(Wantok 715, March 17-23, 1988, page 21)

Long, long ago in Kamusi [**Kamus**] Village, in the Goroka area, there lived a young man [**Gahuku** People, **Eastern Highlands** Province]. The man's name was Givonimo. One early morning, he awoke, took a piece of rattan and walked down to the river to remove the bad things [lit., "trash"] inside of himself.

He arrived at the water, took the rattan and pushed it into his stomach, then removed the bad things that were there inside. Afterwards, this bad boy felt cold. He removed his *tanget*-leaf buttock covering and the bird-of-paradise feathers from his head, then he exposed his chest to the sun on top of a rock. Oh my, he was knocked out by sleep. He snored very loudly.

While Givonimo snored, he did not know that a group of enemies from another village had surrounded his village. They had killed his father and mother. His brother, Monefa, escaped with some others to **Wosan** Village.

When all of them arrived at Wosan, Monefa thought of his brother, Givonimo, and quickly turned back down to the river. When he arrived at the river, he saw his brother who was sleeping soundly. He went quietly and awakened his brother. He told his brother what had happened.

Givonimo just listened. He did not think about his *tanget* buttock covering or his bird-of-paradise feathers. No, he just got up and held his brother, then they sped off to Wosan Village.

Not long after they fled, the enemies came to the river and saw Givonimo's things there. They took the things and carried them back to their village to give to their strongman to use to kill the owner of these things.

The people of Wosan lived and Givonimo died. While they cried for him, his ghost came and ran down the trail to a river. The ghost did not have a way to get to the other side, but when he looked down at his legs, he saw a stick used for harvesting sweet potatoes lying there.

He took this stick and beat the water, then the river broke right in the middle like a trail. When Givonimo's ghost saw this, he ran to the other side of the river and kept running.

He ran and ran, then he arrived at a place where there was a very long row of houses. He looked and saw his father and mother, and his ancestors from long ago making an earth oven. They just looked at him and did not speak to him. When they finished the earth oven, his father took an axe and asked, "What are you doing? Why do you want to watch the old people so carefully?"

After his father spoke, he took the axe and tried to cut Givonimo. When the boy saw that his father was trying to cut him with the axe, the poor boy ran as fast as he could. His legs went up so far that they hit his buttocks.

He sped off and his father sped off too. They arrived at the river, jumped to the other side, then kept running. They ran and ran, then arrived at the house where the enemies were burning Givonimo's possessions, so as to kill him. When the two of them went up to the house, the enemies saw them and were terrified. They left the things there and fled.

Then Givonimo's father took Givonimo's adornments and gave them back to him. He said, "Look at me." When Givonimo turned to look at his father, the father took the axe and broke his son's head open.

While the people of Wosan Village were crying, they saw Givonimo begin to move his arms and legs. Oh my, when they saw this, they were afraid and ran out, shouting. Givonimo got up and went out of the house. He told them what had happened between his father and himself.

Robin Inee [Inwee] Lusoho

Goroka

Eastern Highlands Province

D956. Magic stick of wood; D1551. Waters magically divide and close; D1711. Magician; D2061.2.2. Murder by sympathetic magic; E12+. Resuscitation by decapitation in otherworld; E425.1. Revenant as woman; E425.2. Revenant as man; F1. Journey to otherworld as dream or vision; F6. Departure to otherworld (fairyland) attributed to death; F141.1. River as barrier to otherworld; K914. Murder from ambush; P210. Husband and wife; P231. Mother and son; P233. Father and son; P251.5. Two brothers; P600+. Cane swallowing as purgative; R213. Escape from home; R260. Pursuits; S139.4. Murder by mangling with axe

Two Brothers Found Wives

(Wantok 716, March 24-30, 1988, page 21)

Long, long ago, there were two young boys. Their father and mother had died. The names of the boys were Hakambo and Siheremba. They lived on top of a mountain in the forest.

One morning when they were sleeping, Hakambo heard birds calling from very close to their house. He awoke, opened the door and very quietly walked outside. When he went out, he saw the birds perched on top of a tree and calling. When he went to the base of the tree, the birds saw him and flew away. Hakambo saw this and quickly made a platform underneath the base of the tree so that he could watch and shoot the birds.

When he went back to the house, his brother asked him what had happened when he had gone and returned. Hakambo replied to Siheremba, "I went to shit. Then I returned." Whenever the sun rose, the two of them would wake up, take their things, and go to their garden. In the afternoon, they would return to the house, cook, then go to sleep after they ate. In the early morning, while Siheremba slept, Hakambo woke up very quietly, took his bow and arrows, and then went to the platform that he had made. He readied himself then the birds flew to the tree and ate the tree fruits. While they were eating the tree fruits, he drew back the bow and shot one directly in the breast.

However the bird did not fall, it flew off, carrying Hakambo's arrow. It fell down exactly where an old woman was working in her garden. The old woman was removing trash and grasses. Hakambo searched for his arrow and went directly to the place where the old woman was working. He stood outside the garden and called to the old woman, "Hey, old woman, have you seen my arrow or not? I shot a bird and it carried it away." The old woman told him, "I put your arrow here with the bird. I wanted to cook and eat the bird, but I was still working so I left it here."

After the old woman spoke, Hakambo just talked to her about the arrow. The old woman listened and asked the boy whether he could climb a tree, cut a branch, and carve it into a stick for removing [digging] sweet potatoes. The boy listened as if he were a man. He did as the old woman had asked him to do.

The old woman looked again and asked Hakambo to go remove the stones from her earth oven. After he did this, the old woman told him to go inside the big house, shut the door and sleep. He could not get up or come outside if he heard much noise coming from outside. After she spoke, Hakambo went inside the house, shut the door and slept. Before long, he heard two women laughing and talking outside. When Hakambo heard them, his heart went out for them but he did not do a thing.

When the three women removed the food from the earth oven, the old woman sent the two young ones into hiding, then she awakened Hakambo. They went and prepared to eat the food. When they were about to eat the food, the old woman rose and called out for the two young women to come, sit and befriend Hakambo. This was so that he would take them with him as his wives. Oh my, when Hakambo heard this, he was speechless and he stopped thinking. The old woman jumped on top of the house, took two nice net bags, and went to give them to the two women. She told them to fill the bags with some food, then to carry them to their husband's home.

Hakambo took the two women and they went to his house. When they arrived, Siheremba saw the women and asked his brother, "Where did you get these two women?" Hakambo told the story to his brother about what had happened to him that he had found the two women. His brother listened and said that he would try this. When he said this, Hakambo told him not to ask the old woman questions, just to follow what the old woman would ask him to do.

In the very early morning of the next day, Siheremba awoke, took his bow and arrows then went outside the house very quietly. He walked to the platform at the base of the tree. He sat then the birds flew by and perched on the tree. The birds called out. He put an arrow on the bow, drew back and shot a bird. The bird took his arrow and flew down directly to the place where the old woman was working hard in her garden. The old woman saw this, took the bird with the arrow, put them aside and continued to work. Before long, Siheremba arrived at the old woman's garden. He asked her for his arrow and the bird. When the old woman told him that she had found these things, the boy did not fool around with her. He berated her terribly and said, "Where's your good mouth that you want to eat the meat?" When the old woman asked the boy to do some of her work, the boy did not want to do it. So, the old woman did all of the work until the food in the earth oven was ready to be eaten. When the two of them sat to eat, the old woman called out for two women to come and eat the food with them.

When Siheremba saw the two women, he was speechless. He was completely stunned because the faces of the women looked like *masalai*s from the deep forest. He got up quietly, took the two of them and brought them towards his home. Because he was ashamed to take the women to his brother, he took them into the deep forest where they made their own house in a completely different place.

Robin Inee [Inwee] Lusoho
Lamus [**Kamus**] Village [**Gahuku** People]
P. O. Box 167
Goroka
Eastern Highlands Province

F562.7K. People live in mountain top; J652. Inattention to warnings; P210. Husband and wife; P251.4+. One brother acts wisely, another acts unwisely; P251.5. Two brothers; P263. Brother-in-law; P264. Sister-in-law; Q10. Deeds rewarded; Q325. Disobedience punished; T145.0.1. Polygyny; W31. Obedience; W126. Disobedience

Flying Foxes Helped a Man
(Wantok 717, March 30 — April 6, 1988, page 20)

Long, long ago, there was a man named Lama who lived on Mount Karikonamu, in the **Southern Highlands** Province area. He always sat and looked down at the home of a man who was completely blind that lived below the mountain. The name of this man was Topa. Whenever Lama would look down at Topa's home, he would see smoke rising from a fire.

One time, Lama sat there and saw smoke rising, so he walked down the mountain towards the place where the smoke was rising. When he arrived, Lama finished all of poor, blind Topa's food. Topa thought that his food was still there, but when he went to check, there was not a single scrap. The blind man said, "I cooked plenty of food, so why did it disappear just like that? Who came and stole my food then ate it?"

The same thing always happened. The poor Topa's food would disappear whenever he would make his fire and the smoke rose high.

One time, Topa thought of a trick to catch the man who often came to steal his food. He made a hole right in the trail. Then he put a big, traditional net bag inside the hole and covered it over. Afterwards, he made a fire. Before long, Lama saw the smoke from the fire and followed the trail down the mountain. He walked along and did not see the hole, so he fell directly into the net bag in the hole. When Topa arrived and heard Lama screaming inside the hole, he laughed hysterically. He told Lama, "So, it was just you who came and stole my food. Now it's your turn."

He carried Lama inside the net bag and went to the Polu [Poru] River. He hung him [in the bag] upon the branch of a tree that stuck out over the water. Poor Lama did not have a way to escape, so he just hung there. When it was nearly dark, he looked up to the moon and saw a flying fox flying towards him. He saw the flying fox throw five ripe bananas into the net bag in which Lama was hanging.

After the flying fox did this, it flew to its home and told all of the other flying foxes what it had seen. They all decided to come help Lama, to remove him from the tree branch and to put him on the ground.

After the flying foxes made their decision, they went and carried the man in the net bag, then placed him on the ground. When Lama went out of the bag, he told the flying foxes that he would cook some food for them because they had helped him. However, they did not want food. Lama asked them if he could give them a pig, but they did not want one.

Lama thought hard, then took a vine parcel from his mother. He asked them to take it. When the flying foxes saw this, they were ecstatic and they took the vine parcel.

So now, if you kill a flying fox and remove its guts, you will see this vine parcel inside its belly. Also nowadays, this vine parcel blocks the flying foxes so they never defecate because it is inside of them.

Kondo L. Kelo
Taikopini [**Taukapini**] Village [**Wiru** People]
Pangia
Southern Highlands Province

A2270+. Origin of nature of flying fox's internal organs; B449.3+. Helpful flying fox; B542.1.2+. Flying fox rescues person from height; B552+. Person carried by flying fox; K333. Theft from blind person; K420. Thief loses his goods or is detected; K735. Capture in pitfall; P231. Mother and son; Q53. Reward for rescue; Q212. Theft punished; Q433. Punishment: imprisonment; R49+. Captivity in bag; R49.1. Captivity in tree; R51.1. Prisoners starved; R110. Rescue of captive

Hapara-Ura-Ura-Vila

(Wantok 718, April 7-13, 1988, page 20)

Very long ago, there were five brothers and their sister who lived in the **Gulf** Province. The name of their sister was Marirevo and their last brother was Hurua-Tamora.

Not far from where they lived, towards the east, there was a pandanus tree. The name of this tree is *hapara* [actually, the fishtail palm, *Caryota* spp. (Brown, 1986: 26)]. Inside the pandanus, there was a man who killed and ate people. This man had a huge sore on his leg. His name was *Hapara-Ura-Ura-Vila*, meaning, "The Man from the Hole in the Pandanus Tree." [*Ura* means "hole" and *vila* means "man" in the Orokolo Language (Brown, 1986: 103, 106).]

The eldest four brothers often enjoyed fishing, hunting, and working in their garden. When they had plenty of meat or fish, they enjoyed going to other villages and trading with other people for things that they did not have.

When they did this, Morirevo [Marirevo] and little Hurua-Tamora stayed there by themselves. The brothers never forgot to explain to the sister about the cannibal, Hapara-Ura-Ura-Vila. They would tell them Marirevo and Hurua-Tamora] not to try to make a fire when the wind blew towards the east. This was because he [Hapara-Ura-Ura-Vila] would see or smell the smoke from the fire. He would think that they were cooking, then he would come to

eat them. So, whenever the wind blew towards the east, Morirevo never cooked or made a small fire because she was afraid.

One time, the sun rose very high. At the beach, the sea was calm [lit., "sleeping sadly"], so the four big brothers wanted to go to a faraway village towards the east. They took sago and some garden foods, then they carried the food to their canoe on the beach. When everything was ready, the eldest called for their sister to come.

He told her, "Little sister, your other three brothers and I will leave you and our little brother for one or two weeks. We're going to the east to trade the things that we are bringing with other people. Also this time, we shall try to find wives for ourselves. Now, be very careful. Don't make a fire when the wind blows eastward lest the cannibal will come to kill you and little Hurua-Tamora. Then he'll eat the two of you." After he said this, they all went to sleep.

In the very early morning when the birds of dawn sang, the four brothers woke up, raised the canoe's sail and left home towards the villages to the east.

The poor woman and her little brother were there alone. Four days later, the sun was very hot, so Hurua-Tamora sped down to the beach where he played. He played for a while. When it was almost noon, the poor boy was famished. His stomach was growling. Hurua-Tamora ran back to the house and asked his sister for food.

His sister told him, "I'm not cooking because the bad man will come to kill and eat us." The little boy said, "Please, sister, I'm famished. Can you cook some sago for me to eat?" Morirevo listened and was worried about her brother, so she made a fire and cooked sago for him to eat.

When the sago in the fire was almost ready, they heard a man singing and walking towards their house. The song that they heard was:

> Hapara-Ura-Ura-Villa [Hapara-Ura-Ura-Vila] *va*,
> > Morirevo *ve*
> *Pai aro mou koa,*
> *Ere a'urai a,*
> *Ape a'urai a.*

In English, this means:
> Hapara-Ura-Ura-Villa smells the sago
> Of Morirevo in the fire.
> His belly is burning,
> His mouth is burning.

[In the **Orokolo** Language, *pai* means "sago", *a* means "fire", *muo* means "smell", *ape* means "mouth", *koa* means "to hit", *ere* means "belly", and *a uru* means "flame" (Brown, 1986).]

When Morirevo heard this, she told her brother, "I'm very sorry, my little brother, we've made a big mistake. The cannibal is coming."

Then, they heard Harapa-Ura-Ura-Vila [Hapara-Ura-Ura-Vila] call up to them at the house, "Morirevo, is the little boy there or not?"

Morirevo replied, "Big man, he's finishing his sago now. Why are you asking for him?"

Harapa-Ura-Ura-Vila replied, "No, I just thought he was there. I wanted him to come with me so that we could go catch some fish."

When Morirevo heard this, she let her little brother go outside with the man because the two of them had not eaten fish or meat for a very long time.

At the beach, while the two of them were fishing with hooks, the man told Hurua-Tamora that he must always sit near him. The man would cut a piece of flesh from his sore, put it on a string, and then throw it out for the fish to eat.

He did this, and oh my, they caught a huge amount of fish. Then the bad man, Harapa-Ura-Ura-Vila, told the little boy to go find a piece of firewood. When the boy left and was about to take a piece of firewood, he told him, "Leave that firewood there, and come here. That firewood is your pal."

The boy listened and returned to Harapa-Ura-Ura-Vila. Harapa-Ura-Ura-Vila just took the fish and broke their spines on top of the poor boy's head. He did this until he had finished all of the fish, then he divided the fish between himself and the boy.

The poor boy was in pain and cried when he arrived at his sister's house. His sister saw this and was very sorry for him. She heated some water in a fire and washed her little brother's head. The next day, Hapara-Ura-Ura-Vila came to fetch the little boy to do the same thing again. When Hura-Tamora's [Hurua-Tamora's] sister asked him to let the two of them live in peace, the man told her that if she did not let her little brother come with him, he would kill both of them.

This entire time, they only thought of when their brothers would come and get revenge. While they were thinking like this, one of the brothers ran back and [arrived] at the house. Morirevo told him what had happened to their little brother.

After her brother heard this, he ran back to the beach and called for his other three brothers to come to the house. When they heard the story, they took their bows, arrows and axes then ran directly to the base of the big pandanus tree.

When they arrived, their big brother called inside to Hapra-Ura-Ura-Vila [Hapara-Ura-Ura-Vila], "Come out, do you think you can escape after what you did to our brother?"

The eldest finished speaking, then the four of them took their axes and cut down the pandanus tree. The man tried to escape, but they grabbed him quickly and killed him. After they killed him, they made a bonfire and threw his body on top of the fire.

They went back home and celebrated with their sister and little brother. After this time, they never worried about the bad man.

Joe [Joseph] Martin
National Capital District

[Mr. Martin also wrote the ancestor story in *Wantok* #707 about Toaripi clans, but the words in this story are from the Orokolo Language (Brown, 1986).]

F540+. Person fishes using own flesh as bait; G234. Witch resides in tree; G440. Ogre abducts person; G512. Ogre killed; J652. Inattention to warnings; P253.0.3+. One sister and five brothers; Q213. Abduction punished; Q411. Death as punishment; R11. Abduction by monster (ogre); R155.2. Elder brother rescues younger; S110. Murders; S160.1. Self-mutilation; S186. Torturing by beating; W126. Disobedience

*Masalai*s Chased the People of Lupamanda towards the Sepik: Are the Sepik People Related to the Wabag People?

(Wantok 719, April 14-20, 1988, page 21)

Long, long ago, in **Lupamanda** Village, there was an old man, his wife, and their child [**Enga** People, **Enga** Province]. The name of the old man was Dulin, his wife's name was Imalawana, and their child's name was Karape.

One time, old Dulin became very ill, and was near death. His wife and child saw this and cried. Dulin told his child, Karape, to call out for his brother, Sabal, to come see him. Karape listened and sped off to explain what was happening to Dulin's brother.

When Sabal and his kin came to Dulin's house, they saw Imalawana crying at her husband's legs, and Karape was crying at Dulin's head. They thought that Dulin was dead, but Sabal told them that Dulin was not dead yet.

Dulin was asleep, and when he heard them talking like this, he tried very hard to open his eyes and to move his arms and legs. He tried very hard, then his eyes opened.

His kin, who had come to see him, told Dulin, "We saw you sleeping and thought that you had died, so we were crying for you."

Dulin listened, rose, and told them, "I'm not dead yet. When I shut my eyes and sleep, I dream and see some men. They're the same as us, but their skins are white. On their skins and legs are fastened something that looks like tree bark. In their hands are long sticks that they hold."

His kin listened to him and were surprised. Sabal told them, "Then, they'll come to take you away now."

The next morning, Dulin told the same story to them. After he slept and woke up, he just told them what kinds of dreams he had had. Sabal and all of the others who heard this thought very hard.

On the second night, all eyes were asleep except for Dulin who did not sleep. He shut his eyes and just pretended to sleep. Before long, four *masalai*s came and saw that everyone in the house was asleep. They tried to carry Dulin away.

They apportioned Dulin's weight upon their shoulders, then carried him away. They did not know that Dulin was not dead, but that he was just lying there. He knew that if he tried to shout or do something, they would kill him, so he just lay quietly.

They carried him up to a place called Taitesa. They carried him and put him on top of a wild pandanus tree (*karuka*). He thought hard and was afraid that he would fall down to the ground.

When old Dulin looked down, he saw many, many *masalai*s sitting and talking. His primary thought was that the group of *masalai*s would soon kill and eat him. However, they sat talking until it was nearly daybreak. Then one of them rose and told the other four, "What did you bring this man here for? Take him quickly and put him in his house."

The four listened and immediately carried old Dulin away, putting him back in his house. Later, [he] told them what had happened to him. All of them woke up and tried to hold his body, but it was completely cold.

He told them that when he was in the wild pandanus tree, he saw the place where the sun rises. The name of this place is Lakemanda. Not long after he spoke, they heard screams, as if the *masalai*s had killed children, pigs and dogs.

When they heard this, they were afraid and ran up to Mount Lakemanda. They stood and looked down at Lakemanda Village. They saw the houses burning, and the awful screams of men, women and children. They shouted and shouted for their Tribe [Clan] Apo, but they did not hear anything.

At this time, old Dulin's kin made a house, then they lived at this place near Mount Lupamanda. This mountain is by Wabag, near the Sepik side.

Lanekepa K. Manda
Lupamanda Village
Wabag
Enga Province

D1810.8.2. Information received through dream; F17. Visit to land of the sun; F490+. Masalai; F527.7K+. White person; G440. Ogre abducts person; J1050. Attention to warnings; K1868. Deception by pretending sleep; P210. Husband and wife; P230. Parents and children; P251.5. Two brothers; P260. Relations by law; P263. Brother-in-law; P264. Sister-in-law; P293. Uncle; R11. Abduction by monster (ogre); R220. Flights; S110. Murders

How Did Saure [Sauri] Village Arise?
(Wantok 720, April 21-27, 1988, page 25)

Long, long ago, in Saure [**Sauri Number 1**] Village, near Wewak Town, there was a *masalai* eel that lived in a pond called Paltou [**Boiken** People, **East Sepik** Province]. The poor people of Saure often worked hard in the gardens, but the eel always turned into a pig and completely ruined their gardens.

When they would see the *masalai* and try to kill it, the *masalai* would escape to Paltou Pond. This same thing would happen all of the time. One time, they chased the pig, and they arrived at the pond. When they looked into the water, they saw a huge eel moving back into the stones.

When they saw this, they decided to kill the eel. They went into the forest, cut vines and tree bark used to kill fish, then they brought them to the water. They beat and beat the vines and bark [to release the poisons], then they threw them into the water. When they did this, the sun was setting, so they went home.

In the very early morning, when the birds of dawn were singing, the people of Saure woke up and went down to the pond to see what had happened that night. When they arrived at the water, they saw the massive eel lying on top of the water. However, the poor people of Saure did not know that this eel was a *masalai*.

They cut a long stick and carried the eel to the village. When they arrived at the village, they butchered the eel and divided it among all of the houses in Saure Village. That same day when the sun was setting, the clouds began to thunder. The clouds thundered and thundered, then a tremendous downpour began. The water in Paltou Pond began to swell and spill the banks.

The people of Saure were sitting tight in their houses. They saw many, many grasshoppers jumping about inside the village, but they did not know what was happening. Before long, they saw a marsupial (*sikau*) jump and play in the rain.

On the marsupial's tail was a tree fruit. The people saw it there and shouted, but the marsupial did not run away. It kept playing in the rain. The rain poured and poured, then before long the water rose up to the village. All of the people, everything they owned, and their houses went under water.

There were only two sisters who were not drowned. They had taken a hand drum, a chicken, a net called <u>uaurahuana</u>, and the pot in which the two of them had cooked the eel. They had climbed a tall coconut palm tree that stood by the village. It was only the two of them there. The other people were lost in the water.

When the water took everyone with all of eel pieces that they had cooked, the water receded. However, when the pieces of eel began to rejoin, some of them were not there, so the water swelled and rose up again.

When the water rose close to the coconut palm, the two youths took a piece of eel from the pot and threw it into the water. When they threw the first piece, the water receded and went down again.

When the pieces of the eel wanted to rejoin again, they found that some were still missing, so the water swelled again. The two sisters threw down another piece. They kept doing this until all of the eel pieces in the pot were gone.

However, the water swelled and rose again, so they spilled the eel soup from the pot into the water too. When they did this, the water receded entirely. They broke off one coconut leaf and threw it down, but his leaf hit the water. They heard this, then a little later, they threw down another leaf. This time, it went directly to the ground.

The sisters heard this and jumped down to the ground. They carried the hand drum, the chicken and the net, then ran up towards a mountain. The walked and walked, then they arrived at a stream branch and followed it. They walked a little, then they threw away the chicken. They followed the stream. They walked a little further, then they did the same thing with the hand drum.

After they did this, they arrived at Homproure [**Hamberauri**] Village and they called it **Saure Number 2**. They went and saw a cave on the side of the mountain, so the sisters wanted to rest there.

The sisters did not know that a ghost man lived in the cave. The name of this ghost man was Wamahailo. The sisters met him and asked, "Are you a ghost or a real man?" Wamahailo lied to them and said that he was a real man. Then he asked them the question. The big sister, Nahin,

told him, "We're stone women." Nahin told Wamahailo to remove his net, so that they could hang themselves up.

Wamahailo removed his net, then the two sisters hung themselves up. Nahin told her little sister, "Go outside and turn into a flying fox, then fly back and attach to the net." Her poor little sister listened and did what her big sister told her to do.

When she flew back and attached to the net, Wamahailo quickly jumped up and held her. Nahin saw this and told Wamahilo [Wamahailo], "Don't kill her. She's just my little sister." But Wamahailo did not listen to her. He killed the little sister (flying fox) and broke her down the middle. He gave half to Nahin and he put the entire other half into his mouth along with the blood.

When Nahin saw this, she knew that this man was just a ghost. He had lied to them that he was a real man and he had killed her little sister. Nahin knew that this man would try to kill her too, so she thought of fleeing. She thought and thought, then Wamahailo asked her why she had not eaten her piece of flying fox flesh yet. Nahin told him that there was no fire for cooking her meat to make it edible.

Wamahailo told her that he would go to another place to fetch some fire to cook her meat. He departed, but he did not leave completely. Along the trail, he went back and hid in the forest near the cave and watched. Nahin knew that the bad man was hiding and watching, so she did not do a thing.

Wamahailo saw this and got up to leave again. However along the trail, he did the same thing. He turned back and spied upon her. However, she still knew that Wamahailo was hiding, so the poor woman still did not do anything.

The ghost saw this and believed strongly that the woman would not flee, so he walked away to fetch the fire. While he was walking on the trail, the woman quickly jumped up and removed her net. She took a leaf and covered the piece of her sister's flesh, then she fled this place.

When the ghost man returned to his home with the fire, he saw that Nahin was no longer there. When he saw this, he burned inside. He threw away the fire that he had carried, then he sped off, following the poor woman. However, Nahin had already arrived at the headwaters. Nahin was about to jump to the other side.

Wamahailo came to the source of the stream and saw this. He called out to a ghost on the other side of the stream, "Pal, if you see one of my wild animals fleeing, hold her and wait for me."

When the woman heard this, she was terrified, so she quickly jumped across the water to the other side. When she arrived on the other side, she met Bouromo, the other ghost man who was standing there.

Bourmo [Bouromo] told the woman, "Don't be afraid. You wanted to come here. The cannibal called out, telling me to grab you and wait for him, but I'll help you escape. When I open my hand, you must go inside it."

Nahin listened and did as Bouromo had told her. Wamahailo went to that side of the water, then Bouromo just took his spear and planted it right inside the bad man's chest. Wamahailo fell down and died.

So, in Saure Village, the bones of Wamahailo are still there. Also, there is a tree leaf that looks like human blood. This is because Nahin had covered the piece of her sister's flesh with this leaf, and it changed the color from green to red. So, in Saure Village and in the nearby forests, there is still something there from the stories of yore from the Saure People.

Steven Sangi

Hambraure Village

Wewak

East Sepik Province

A991+. Origin of particular village; A1011. Local deluges; A2760+. Why certain tree has red leaves; B750+. Eel rejoins itself; B874.2. Giant eel; D117.5KG. Transformation: girl to flying fox; D410+. Transformation: eel to swine; D412.3.2+. Transformation: swine to eel; D2143.1. Rain produced by magic; D2149.1. Thunderbolt magically produced; D2151.8. Magic flood; E32.0.2K. Eel cooked and eaten comes to life; E168. Cooked animal comes to life; E300. Friendly return from the dead; E425.2. Revenant as man; E440+. Ghost laid by spear/arrow; E467. Revenants fight each other; E541. Revenants eat; F405+. Spirit killed by poisoning; F419.4K. Spirits eat food raw; F420.1.3.2+. Water-spirit as eel; F490+. Masalai; G11.10. Cannibalistic spirits; G642K. Ogres eat raw flesh; H46.1+. Cannibal recognized when it devours raw flesh; P252.1. Two sisters; Q211.6. Killing an animal revenged; Q428. Punishment: drowning; R100. Rescues; R210. Escapes; R220. Flights; R260. Pursuits; R311. Tree refuge; S131. Murder by drowning; W157. Dishonesty

Two Brothers Killed the *Masalai* Masumura

(Wantok 721, April 28 — May 4, 1988, page 18)

Long, long ago, near **Nanduo** Village on the Finschafen [Finschhafen] Peninsula, there was a *masalai* [**Kâte** People, **Morobe** Province]. The name of this *masalai* was Masumura. Masumura had killed all of the men, women and children in this village except for an old woman and her two young children. The three of them hid inside a cave, and the *masalai* had not found them.

They lived there for a while, then the two young boys grew big and strong. When the two of them went around outside the cave, their old mother would tell them not to go far. However, they did not know why their mother stopped them from going far. They always asked their mother why, and she just stopped them because she was afraid and never told them.

One time, the three of them sat outside the cave. The elder brother asked his mother, "Why is there no one else in this area with us?" Their old mother shouted for them to go inside the cave, then she told the story about what had happened before in the time of their grandparents.

When the youths heard this, oh my, they were furious. They told their mother that they would kill Musumura [Masumura]. They asked their mother again where the grandparents made bows and arrows. Their old mother sent them into the deep forest to cut *limbum* palm. After they cut it and returned, she showed them how to make bows and arrows, then they asked her where the grandparents made fences. Their old mother again showed them.

The two of them went back into the deep forest, cut very strong trees and returned. They made a huge fence around their home. Inside this fence, they made another fence. When they finished this fence, they made another, smaller fence inside the others.

The two of them carried their bows and all of their arrows, then they went inside the third fence that they had made. When they were ready, their mother ran out of the cave and told her two children, "You're all that I have now. If you kill Masumura, then we'll live. If Masumura kills you, then I'll kill myself too."

Then the two of them shouted loudly to Masurumu [Masumura], "Masumuru [Masumura], you're a rotten ghost man. You think you're great, huh? You killed all our kin. Come here and we'll kill you."

Not long after they said this, they heard Masumura laughing and replying, "Where have you two been hiding such that just now you want to come and fight with me? I killed and ate all of your kin. Now, I'll do the same with you two and your mother." The two of them heard this but were unafraid.

Before long, they saw him walking towards them and standing by the first fence. When he saw the youths, he laughed hysterically. His teeth were long and terribly sharp. In his hand was a very long spear. He tried to break the fence that they had made.

They did not wait. They began to shoot him with arrows. He was in pain, but he broke the first fence. When he jumped to the second fence, he tried to shoot the two brothers, but he missed. His spear stuck to a post that they had erected. When they saw that they had a chance, they did not rest. They blasted him. They did this, then they saw that Masumura's strength was fading. They kept at it, then Masumura jumped inside the second fence, but the youths were unafraid. They kept shooting him.

He tried to break the third fence, but his strength was gone and he fell to the ground. The blood flowed from his skin and he trembled. Quickly, they jumped out and cut off Masumura's head with a stone axe. Poor Masumura was dead. They circled him, singing and dancing. Their old mother was also ecstatic, so she came out and joined them.

They made a big fire and were about to burn Masumura's body, but it quickly turned into a huge boulder. This boulder is still there in Nanduo Village, in the Finschafen area. The brothers married and repopulated Nanduo.

Nombri Miaba
Kimbe
West New Britain Province

A515.1. Culture heroes brothers; A977.5. Origin of particular rock; E642. Reincarnation as stone; F490+. Masalai; F490+. Masumura; F544.3.5. Remarkably long teeth; G214.1. Witch with long teeth; G346. Devastating monster; G510.4+. Hero overcomes devastating ogre; G512.1.2. Ogre decapitated; P210. Husband and wife; P231. Mother and son; P251.5. Two brothers; Q211. Murder punished; Q421.0.4. Beheading as punishment for murder; R315. Cave as refuge; Q211. Murder punished; Q421. Punishment: beheading; S133. Murder by beheading; T100. Marriage; Z71.1. Formulistic number: three; Z210. Brothers as heroes

Why Are There No People in Yuka Village? A Brother Killed Them

(Wantok 72[2], May 5-11, 1988, page 22)

Very long ago, in **Yuka** [Yúkuá? (Lang, 1973: 215)] Village in **Enga** Province, there only lived a boy and his sister [**Enga** People]. All of the other people of the village had died. The boy always awoke in the very early morning to go to the deep forest to hunt for marsupials (*kapul*) for themselves to eat. When he went into the forest, he would kill many marsupials. He was usually in the forest until the sun set completely, then he would return to the house.

Marsupial Hunting

When the boy would go into the forest, his sister would work in their garden. In the afternoon, she would finish in the garden, then quickly go to the house to cook food for themselves. They always did this.

One time, the boy told his sister, "Last night, I dreamt that I killed the big king of the marsupials, so now you must go to the garden and prepare plenty of food."

After the boy told his sister this, he took his bow and arrows, then walked swiftly on the trail into the deep forest. He walked and walked along the trail, then he saw a little marsupial playing on a tree branch. Without waiting, he bombed it with something and it fell down to the ground. He quickly removed the marsupial's guts and hung it upon a tree branch. Then he walked completely into the deep forest. While he was walking, the marsupial turned into a man. Its face was exactly like the boy's face. He left this place and walked to the garden where the boy's sister was working.

When the marsupial-man entered the garden, the woman saw him and asked, "You told me that you were going into the forest, so what are you doing here?" The marsupial-man did [not] reply, he just walked towards her and grabbed her. The woman asked him again, "Why are you holding me?" He still said nothing. He slept with the woman, going down to the ground, and performing an immoral act upon her.

The marsupial-man then fled into the deep forest and completely disappeared. The woman forgot entirely about the garden. She cried and ran to the house. She thought that it was her brother who had done this to her, but it was not. It was just the little marsupial-man.

Bearing Snakes

The woman arrived at the house. She took various kinds of tree bark and tied them together, making a very long rope. After she did this, she got up, tied one end of the rope to the house, and held the other end. She took all of her belongings and walked until she arrived at the home of an old woman.

When she arrived at this place, the rope was very short and then it ended. She left this place and kept walking. She walked and walked, then arrived at the home of a man who often turned into a snake. She met this man, then they married. They lived there for a while, then the woman became pregnant and gave birth to many little baby snakes.

When her brother returned to the house, he found that his sister was not there, so he waited and waited. He waited for five months, but his sister did not return.

One time, the boy took his knife, bow and arrows, then he followed the trail to find his sister. He walked and walked, then he arrived at the place where the old woman lived. He saw the old woman sitting there, so he asked her about his sister. [She said], "Your sister came here, but she's not here now. She walked to another place on that side. She married a man who turns into a snake." The boy listened, then walked swiftly on the trail to the place where his sister and her snake-children lived. He arrived at his sister's house and went inside. When he went into the house, the little snakes jumped upon his body. He was terrified, so he shouted to his sister.

His sister did not say anything. She completely ignored her brother. The woman told her brother, "Stay with your little kin [the snakes]. I'm going to the garden to tell their father that you've come to the house." The woman left them and walked on the trail to the garden. The boy told the little snakes, "Stay here, I'm going out to cut some firewood for cooking food."

Killing the Snakes

After he said that, he followed his sister and arrived at a big mountain. He hid and saw his sister take a rope and throw it down the mountain. The woman then followed the rope down the mountain. When the boy saw this, he ran and cut the rope. After he did this, he turned back and went to his sister's house.

He told the little snakes that there was no firewood in the forest, so he had returned to the house. The snakes told him, "Never mind the firewood, tell us some stories." So, the boy told the little snakes, "OK, if all of you close your eyes, I'll tell you stories. I won't tell stories to anyone who opens their eyes."

When the little snakes shut their eyes, he took his knife and cut off all of their heads, killing them. He made a big fire in the house, then fled back to his home at Yuka. He alone lived at Yuka, then he too died.

Now, if you go to Yuka Village in Enga Province, you will not see anyone there. Yuka Village is completely deserted.

Tokopitani E. Nalia
P. S. M.
P. O. Box 1423
Arawa
North Solomons Province

B211.6.1. Speaking snake (serpent); B656.2. Marriage to serpent in human form; B611.10K+. Marsupial paramour; D191M. Transformation: man to serpent (snake); D391M. Transformation: serpent (snake) to man; D1810.8.2. Information received through dream; E656+. Reincarnation: marsupial to man; F766+. Deserted village; K1930. Treacherous impostors; P210. Husband and wife; P230. Parents and children; P253. Sister and brother; P253+. Hostile sister and brother; P293. Uncle; Q211.6. Killing an animal revenged; R213. Escape from home; R220. Flights; R260. Pursuits; S71.1+. Murderous uncle; S75.1K2. Sororicide; S133. Murder by beheading; T100. Marriage; T415. Brother-sister incest; T471. Rape; T554.7. Woman gives birth to a snake; T580. Childbirth

A Man Tricked His Wife, She Hid His Eyes

(Wantok 723, May 12-18, 1988, page 16)

Long, long ago, in **Yaikua Kinns**, in the Sta [Star] Mountain area of the **Chuave** [People], **Simbu** Province, there lived a man named Kawo and his wife. The woman's name was Gomena. They also had a dog.

One day, Kawo told Gomena that he would go into the forest to hunt for marsupials (*kapul*) and other game. Gomena knew that he would kill many marsupials, so she was ecstatic because she would use the marsupial fur to make net bags and she would use the meat for food. She awoke in the very early morning and went to dig sweet potatoes from the garden.

She returned to the house, cut the sweet potatoes, making them completely white. Later, she filled a net bag with them, and gave the bag to her husband to eat in the forest when he became hungry.

Kawo took his bow and arrows and his bag of sweet potatoes, then he walked swiftly along the trail into the forest with his dog. Oh my, the two of them did not fool around. They wiped out the marsupials in the forest. It was nearly afternoon when they walked back towards home.

They approached home, then Kawo spoke to the dog, and they rested near a mountain. Kawo walked further on the side of the mountain and took a wild taro leaf. He put this leaf on the ground, and sang, "*Piri-gin piri-gin*." While he sang, his two eyes fell directly upon the taro [leaf]. Blinded, he began to eat the marsupials and the blood. He gave the livers and guts to the dog. He left the legs, arms and heart (or liver) to take home.

They arrived home, then Kawo lied to his wife. He told her that they went to the forest, but their dog [...] some men had killed marsupials and eaten them, and that he only had found the legs, arms and heads, then he had brought them home. His wife, Gomena, listened to this and was furious, but she did not reply because Kowa [Kawo] would beat her.

Another day, Kawo awoke and went back into the forest to hunt for marsupials. This day, he and the dog killed many, many marsupials. When they returned home, the man did the same thing. However, this time he did not win. He sent [?] directly to his wife.

The bad woman, Gomena, was hiding and watching. Quietly, she came out and took the taro leaf on which Kawo's eyes rested. Then she sped back home.

Kawo was searching for them. He sang, "*Koru-gen Koru-gen*," meaning that his eyes must return again, but they did not. Where were they? He searched for them, then he held the ground and walked very slowly like a blind man, arriving at a stream with a ditch.

This ditch had two logs over it that men had placed as a bridge. Poor Kawo missed holding the two logs and fell flat on the rocks. The rocks [caused him to] fall into the water, then he arrived at another village.

The people there saw him and took him to his wife, but his wife was not sorry and did not cry. She told them, "Why did you work hard for this worthless man?" She tied up a pig, gave it to them, and they left.

Gomena was still angry, so she took a long rope, tied it to Kawo's neck, and then pulled it around the house. Kawo was in terrible pain, so he said, "I'm your husband, pity me and let go of the rope." Gomena replied, "You're going to die. You're a bad man and I'm tired of you."

But later, the woman felt sorry for her husband. She let go of the rope and put Kowa's eyes back. Afterwards, Kowa never did this sort of thing. When he went to the forest, he would bring the meat directly home.

John Kamana
P. O. Box 318
Tabubil
Western Province

D1781. Magic results from singing; F541.11. Removable eyes; K2213+. Treacherous husband; P210. Husband and wife; Q53. Reward for rescue; Q261. Treachery punished; Q276. Stinginess punished; Q451.7. Blinding as punishment; S62. Cruel husband; W152. Stinginess; W157. Dishonesty

Why Are Dog and Marsupial (*Kapul*) Enemies?

(Wantok 724, May 19-25, 1988, page 24)

Long, long ago in a place called Saga Moos [**Sawetmove**] in **Morobe** Province, there lived a dog and a marsupial (*kapul*) [**Safeyoka** People]. They were very good friends, and they always traveled together. Whatever food they found, they would eat together. If the dog found something, it would eat part of it and leave part of it for the marsupial. They did this all of the time.

Because of this kind of behavior, they were friends. They traveled well together and were like blood relatives. However, one day the dog thought about two of them often sharing food, but that the dog was never full.

Another day, the dog told the marsupial, "Go into the forest and find some meat for us to eat. I'll stay at the house and wait for you."

The marsupial listened, then in the very early morning, it awoke and went into the deep forest. The poor marsupial worked hard at hunting for food for themselves in the deep forest. The dog stayed at the house and thought hard. The dog tried to find a way to break their friendship. The dog thought and thought then had an idea.

The dog got up and did not wait. It broke its two ears and the two ears flopped down. Then it sat well and waited for its friend, the marsupial, to return to the house.

When the marsupial arrived, the dog told it, "Look, I cut off my two ears." The marsupial thought that its friend was telling the truth, so it asked, "Why do you feel no pain?"

The dog told it, "The pain is mild, so I don't feel it. Cut your own ears, then you'll see."

The marsupial believed what its friend had said, so it did what the dog said. The marsupial took a knife and cut off its two ears. Oh my, when it cut off the ears, it felt a terrible pain and screamed loudly.

The dog saw this and laughed hysterically at its friend, "Oh my, you're a lunatic. You cut your own ears off. I didn't cut off my ears, I just broke them in back and made them lie down."

After the dog said this, it made its two ears stand up again. The marsupial saw this and its stomach churned, "Why is it that when we were such good friends before, you never did such a thing, but now you tricked me and I cut my two ears off. So, now I'm leaving you to live by myself."

The dog told the marsupial, "OK, if you leave me to live on your own, we can no longer be blood relatives. We'll always be enemies. I'll live with men in villages. When we meet you in the deep forest, I'll eat you."

The marsupial told the dog, "That's if you can catch me up on the tall trees of the deep forest."

They finished talking, then they went their separate ways. So nowadays, you can see that dogs and marsupials are archenemies. Dogs travel with their owners because they know that they cannot kill marsupials on their own. Marsupials are afraid of them, so they always live on top of tall trees in the deep forest. Also, you can see that some dogs' ears flop down and that other dogs' ears stand up.

Yana Bey
Buang
Morobe Province

[There is a similar ancestor story in *Wantok* #587. Yana Bey also wrote the ancestor story in *Wantok* #665. In that story, there are two brothers named Saga and Moos.]

A2284. Origin of animal characteristics: animal persuaded into self-injury; A2325+. Why some dogs have floppy ears; A2325+. Why marsupials have short ears; A2433.2.1+. Why marsupial lives in forest; A2494.4+. Enmity between dog and marsupial; B211.1.7. Speaking dog; B211.2.12K+.

Speaking marsupial; K1065+. Dupe persuaded into mutilating ears; K2297. Treacherous friend; P310. Friendship; W157. Dishonesty

A Man Became a Flying Fox

(Wantok 725, May 26 — June 1, 1988, page 20)

Long, long ago, there was a man who lived in a village in **Eastern Highlands** Province. The man's name was Paroko. No one in the village ever liked him. The young women did not like him either. When they saw him, they would curse and spit at him.

One time, there was going to be a festival in a village, so everyone went to make adornments for themselves. Paroko also made adornments for himself.

He made a very long head adornment. Then he cut some nice *tanget* leaves to affix to his body. When it was still that day, he went to the forest, killed a marsupial (*kapul*), and brought it back. He skinned the marsupial, then tied it to the top of a hand drum. After Paroko finished his decorations, he waited for the other men of the village.

The day of the festival came, then all of the men and women of the village went to the festival with their children. They would sing and dance at the village called **Sirumpa** on the other side of the mountain [**Kamano** People]. They passed over the mountain, to the village. Poor Paroko followed them.

They arrived at Sirumpa Village, then the people began to sing and dance. After the festival had gone for a long time, they rested and then Paroko got up to sing and dance.

He went into the festival grounds, then beat his hand drum. The sound of the drum went, "Mini troviyo vivi vivi." Everyone listened and stood to look at him.

Paroko was not an ordinary man, he had tree bark too. When he sang, the place was hot. Everyone rose and sang with him. The women took fire and circled around him, putting the fire very close to his legs.

There was one very beautiful woman at this village. Her name was Kimidi. She was absolutely gorgeous. All the men of the village just died for her, but she did not like them.

The bad man, Paroko, kept singing and dancing. He sang, "*Saiye-e saiye-e Kimidi saiye-e*."

This beautiful woman, Kimidi, heard this and replied singing, "*Saiye-e saiye-e Paroko Naroko saiye*."

The two of them sang like this until it was almost daybreak. All of the men sat and just watched them, but many of them felt tired and went to sleep. The two of them kept at it.

When the light of the sun shone very strongly, Paroko's eyes began to spin. He finished singing, put his hand drum down as a pillow, and fell dead asleep. Kimidi was also tired and she slept.

When the people awoke in the afternoon, they thought that Paroko was gone. They checked all of the trails to bring Paroko back to the festival. Kimidi also thought that Paroko had left, so she followed the other men to bring Paroko back. However, in the middle of the trail, Kimidi had a thought and went back to check the place where the two of them had sung and danced.

When she arrived at this place, she saw Paroko there dead asleep. She shot a thorn into Paroko's body, but he did not awake. He was dead asleep and he did not feel it.

Kimidi tied the thorn to Paroko's body. She tied the other end to her own body, then she slept. Parako [Paroko] wanted to turn in his sleep. The rope stretched and broke. He ran away on the trail.

The woman, Kimidi, woke up and followed Paroko. When Paroko took another trail, the woman also took the trail. They did this until they were both short of breath.

Paroko still had a little strength, so he made a hole and went down it. Kimidi looked down and could not follow him. She shouted down to him.

She shouted, "I love you and I came for you, but you ran away. I'll go to **Undite** and become a tree. Then you'll eat the fruits of this tree in back of me."

Then the woman became a tree. The man became a flying fox and would go to eat the fruits of this tree. The cave that Paroko made is still at this place. Many flying foxes live inside this cave. Also, many tourists go to see it.

Jossie H. Manuo
Yohotegave Village
Goroka
Eastern Highlands Province

A999.1K. Origin of caves; D117.5KM. Transformation: man to flying fox; D215W. Transformation: woman to tree; R220. Flights; R260. Pursuits; T10. Falling in love

A Snot-Nosed Man Married
a Beautiful Woman

(Wantok 726, June 2, 1988, page 19)

Long, long ago, there was a man who lived in a village called Bibine [**Bimbienye**], near Mount Giluwe [**Hagen** People]. This is in the Ialibu area of **Southern Highlands** Province. The name of the man was Welali Repe.

Near Bibine, there is another village. The name of this village is Kongibul [**Kongibugl**]. In this village, there lived a gorgeous woman. Many young men tried to win the hand of this woman, but not one of them was able to do so.

Young men from Bibine would often stroll to Kongibul just because of this woman. [They] would pretend to look at her, ask her desires, and grill her [with questions].

Every night, the young men of Bibine Village would go to Kongibul Village. They would turn their heads (*tanim het*), or rub their noses (*kukim nus*) in courtship with the young women of this village. This was where young people sat and sang at night.

Rebe [Repe] was not a good man. Mucus completely filled his nose, so many women did not want him. However, he befriended the other young men of the village and went with them.

This woman would turn heads with the other men, but when Rebe wanted to turn heads with her, the woman did not want to do so. Poor Rebe would just sit near her.

The woman would spit at him and say, "Who wants to turn heads and rub noses with you? Your nose is full of snot."

This woman always mocked Rebe, and poor Rebe would feel terribly ashamed. He felt terrible inside, so he thought of making a trick. One time, the youths wanted to turn heads with the women again, so Rebe followed them. On the trail, the youths told Rebe, "The woman doesn't like you, so why do you work so hard and come with us? You must go back to the village and take care of our girls."

However, Rebe was not troubled by what they said. He followed them and went to the woman's village. The other men turned heads with her, then it was Rebe's turn. Rebe was the very last man. When he wanted to turn heads with her, she said the same thing to him. Because of this, poor Rebe was ashamed and did not turn heads with her.

When they wanted to return to their village, the woman told them, "Tomorrow, my papa and I will go mushroom hunting near Mount Giluwe, so you must stay and rest. Come back another day." Rebe heard this and put it well inside his head.

In the very early morning, Rebe awoke silently, then he went to the place where the woman and her father would go mushroom hunting. He arrived there and waited. He waited and waited, then he saw the father and daughter coming. The two of them picked many, many mushrooms, filling their bag. When it was nearly afternoon, the two of them wanted to return to the village.

However the bad man, Rebe, had performed his magic, and a heavy rain and strong wind arose. The river flooded and carried all of the bridges away, so the father and daughter did not have a way back to the village. They would sleep in a hut in the forest. Rebe already knew this, so he went to wait close to the hut.

There was a boulder in back of the hut, so Rebe went to hide behind the boulder. He shoved a long piece of bamboo close to the hut, then he waited very quietly. The gorgeous woman and her father arrived and went into the hut. The two of them made a fire, sat and dried their bodies. It was nearly dark, so they prepared to sleep.

Afterwards, Rebe put his mouth to the bamboo and said, "I'm a *masalai* from here. I'm going to eat you two now. If you don't want me to eat you, then you must fuck each other."

The gorgeous woman heard this and told her father. Rebe spoke into the bamboo again, "I'm going to pluck your eyes and eat you now, so hurry up and fuck each other."

They heard this and were terrified. The father was completely afraid, so he told his daughter that they should sleep together, "Do you want this *masalai* to eat us or what do you think?"

The daughter said, "Papa, no one will know if we sleep together. It's alright if we do as the *masalai* says, otherwise he'll eat us."

The bad man, Rebe, heard this and gnashed his teeth. That night, the father and daughter held each other until dawn.

Rebe was not an ordinary man. He performed magic again, and the rain stopped. Then in the morning, the father and daughter went back to the village. Rebe found their adornments in the forest, then followed them to the village that afternoon.

That night, the other men returned to Kongibul Village to turn heads with this gorgeous woman. The rotten snot, Rebe, was dressed finely and went with them.

The other men turned heads with her, then it was Rebe's turn again. Rebe was the very last man. He went to sit close to her, and the woman wanted to flee. Quickly, Rebe told her that he had seen her with her father acting immorally in the forest. The woman was terribly ashamed, but what could she do? She just sat and turned heads with Rebe. The other men saw this and were very angry with Rebe. They just left Rebe with her and returned to the village.

Afterwards, Rebe told the story to the woman of what she had done with her father in the forest. The woman felt like complete trash and she told Rebe not to tell the other men of the village. That night, Rebe and the gorgeous woman slept together until dawn.

In the morning, the woman went and told her father that Rebe had seen them in the forest. She told her father what Rebe had told her. The father listened and also felt terribly ashamed.

That same day, the father killed a pig and made a huge feast in the village. He rubbed pig fat on his daughter, then told her to marry Rebe. He did this to shut Rebe's mouth, so that he would not tell the other men. The scoundrel, Rebe, was elated and married the gorgeous woman.

When the two of them went to Rebe's village, the men could not believe their eyes. Their eyes just popped out. Many of the young men of the village were angry with Rebe, but what could they do? Rebe had won.

Before, the gorgeous woman would spit upon Rebe for his mucous, but now, she cleaned off his mucous. They lived together until they were old and they died.

This is a true story that comes from the Bibine area.

Potter McKing

Bibine Village

Ialibu

Southern Highlands Province

[The ancestor story in *Wantok* #695 is also about Welali Repe.]

D1711. Magician; D2142. Wind produced by magic; D2143.1. Rain produced by magic; D2151.8. Magic flood; K1271.1. Threat to tell of amorous intrigue used as blackmail; K1350. Woman persuaded (or wooed) by trick; L161. Lowly hero marries princess; P210. Husband and wife; P234. Father and daughter; P261. Father-in-law; P265. Son-in-law; P600+. Courtship customs: *kukim nus*; P600+. Courtship customs: *tanim het*; R260. Pursuits; T50. Wooing; T100. Marriage; T411. Father-daughter incest

A Man Stole a *Masalai*'s Baby
(Wantok 727, June 9-15, 1988, page 16)

Long, long ago, there was a village. The name of this village was Slang [**Siang**]. This village is inside the Kabwun [Kabwum] District of **Morobe** Province [**Komutu** People].

One time, there was a man from this village who went into the forest to hunt for marsupials (*kapul*). He went around and around, but he did not find a single marsupial. He was furious, so he wanted to return to the village.

He turned to go back to the village and he saw a wild banana plant. This was a plant that marsupials often ate. He was very happy and thought that he would watch for marsupials at the base of the plant.

He said, "Now I'll watch from the base of this wild banana. When the marsupials come to eat the bananas, I'll kill them and take them back home."

He was very happy. He made a hut near the banana plant and he went to sleep. He slept until it was almost evening, then he awoke to watch for marsupials. He watched until late at night, but not one marsupial ate the bananas.

His eyes grew sleepy, but he did not care. He just kept sitting, then he heard a *masalai* woman with her daughter walking towards him. The *masalai* woman's daughter was crying as they approached.

The man thought that the *masalai* woman and her daughter were going somewhere else, but no, they were going directly towards the banana plant.

The man stayed quiet and heard them come closer. He thought that the *masalai* woman and her daughter had come to eat the wild bananas.

Quickly, he took two coconut shells and put them on his two knees, then he pretended to sleep. The *masalai* woman came to where he was sleeping and she saw the man's knees. The *masalai* took her stone axe and beat the man's knees.

The *masalai* beat and beat and beat him. She felt that the man's knees were strong, so she thought that he was a tree. It was very dark, so the poor *masalai* could not see well and she could not see if it really was a tree. She hung up her daughter [in a net bag] on the man's knees, then she went up the wild banana plant and ate bananas.

The baby kept crying. Then she told the baby, "Don't cry, I'll bring some bananas down and we'll eat." After she said this, she kept eating bananas.

Very quietly, the man got up, took the *masalai* woman's baby and ran away to the village. After the *masalai* woman finished eating bananas, she went down and saw that her daughter was not there. She was worried and wailed terribly for her daughter. Then she followed the trail that the man had taken.

You know, *masalai*s are faster. She followed and approached him. The man was not afraid of the *masalai* woman, so he did not leave the *masalai*'s baby.

The *masalai* shouted to him, "That's not a human baby. That's a *masalai* baby. Leave her and I'll get her."

However, he did not listen to the *masalai* woman. He kept carrying the ghost child, running directly to his village, Slang. He arrived at the village, told everyone, and just went into a house. They shut the door tightly and got ready. They took a stone and heated it in the fire. The stone became bright red.

Afterwards, the *masalai* woman arrived in the village. She shouted for them to give back her baby. She shouted, "Give me back my baby. She's not a human baby. She's a *masalai* baby."

The people listened and shouted for her to come and stand at the house ladder that they had hidden, then they would give her the baby. The ghost [*masalai*] woman went and stood at the house ladder. They told her to open her mouth and they would throw her baby inside. The poor *masalai* woman thought it was true, so she opened her mouth.

When she opened her mouth, they took the stone from the fire and threw it into her mouth. The stone burned the ghost woman's innards, and she rolled on the ground.

While she rolled on the ground, the water rose up to this place. So now at Slang Village, this water is called, *Utniya Aramiuk*, meaning, "A Ghost Broke It."

Robert Tiwung
Kurum Plantation
Karkar Island
Madang Province

A920.1.0.1. Origin of particular lake; A1617. Origin of place-name; E261.4. Ghost pursues man; E425.1.4. Revenant as woman carrying baby; E425.3. Revenant as child; E437.4. Ghost laid under stone; F402.1.10. Spirit pursues person; F490+. Masalai; K951.1. Murder by throwing hot stones in the mouth; K1868. Deception by pretending sleep; P232. Mother and daughter; R10. Abduction; R220. Flights; R260. Pursuits; S112. Burning to death

How Did Nusi [Nguzi] Village Arise?
(Wantok 728, June 16-22, 1988, page 22)

Long, long ago in Nusi [**Nguzi**] Village, in the Upper Waria River area of **Morobe** Province, there lived two brothers [**Weri** People]. Only the big brother had a wife. They lived alone in this place, there were no other men or women who lived with them.

One morning, the big brother went to the forest to hunt for wild game. He told his wife to stay with her brother-in-law, then he went alone.

He arrived at a mountain and he saw a huge cassowary. He did not know that this was a *masalai* cassowary. He took out his spear and planted it directly into the *masalai* cassowary. You know, *masalai*s have many powers. The cassowary's *masalai* [spirit] turned back and killed the big brother. The *masalai* took the big brother's body and put it behind a tree.

The big brother was dead and his ghost returned to the village alone. His ghost arrived at the house and saw the little brother with his sister-in-law. The two of them saw the big brother's ghost and thought that it was the big brother who had returned from the forest. However, the big brother's ghost had come to take the two of them away to bring his body home.

The woman saw her husband's ghost and thought that it was her husband. She told the ghost, "Hey, you told us that you were going to the forest to hunt for game, but the sun hasn't set yet and you've returned home quickly. You didn't bring any game either."

The poor woman did not know that the cassowary's *masalai* had killed her husband in the forest. She thought that the ghost was really her husband.

The woman asked, "Have you killed a big animal, so that you came to fetch me and little brother to go help you?"

The ghost man told her, "Yes, what you say isn't wrong. It's the truth." The ghost man lied to his wife and brother.

He said, "I wanted to go into the very deep forest, but at Mount Komurtomuk I saw a huge cassowary and I killed it. I could not carry the cassowary back by myself, so I came to get the two of you. Let's go bring the cassowary back home."

The ghost man also said that he had killed a wild pig, "I came to fetch you to help me. Let's get the cassowary and pig." He lied to them and they thought that it was really true, so they were elated.

The woman and the little brother took some things, then walked swiftly along the trail with the ghost man to Mount Komurtomuk. They walked and walked, then it started to become dark. The woman began to scold the ghost man, "We've come a long way and it's almost dark now. Where did you really put the cassowary and pig?"

The ghost man replied to the woman that they had nearly arrived at the mountain where he had killed the pig and cassowary. It was nearly dark when they arrived at the mountain. The ghost man told them to look down the side of the mountain.

When they looked down, they were frozen. Then they jumped for joy. They went down, tied up the cassowary and took it up to the top of the mountain.

On top of the mountain, the woman asked the ghost man where he had put the pig. She did not know yet that he was a ghost. She thought that it really was her husband.

The ghost man told her that the wild pig was below the mountain. They would go a little further to get it. They went down and down a very long way. The woman became very angry because it was almost completely dark.

She asked the ghost man again, "We've come a long way, where's the wild pig?" The ghost man told her to be quiet and just walk, then he would show them.

The woman listened and walked down. They approached a tree and the ghost told them to look behind it. The woman and her brother-in-law went to the other side of the tree. Oh my, they were shocked to see the woman's husband there, dead.

When the two of them saw this, they were terrified and wanted to run away. Quickly, the man's ghost, who was on one side of the mountain, told them not to be afraid.

He said, "Don't be afraid of my body. I killed the cassowary, then the cassowary's *masalai* killed me. Leave the cassowary there and take my body home."

The woman followed the ghost's instructions, and with her brother-in-law she took her husband's body home. When they arrived, they cried terribly. Later, they buried the body there.

That night, the big brother came and told the little brother in a dream that he should not worry. He told the little brother to marry his sister-in-law and to live there. When it was still that night, the little brother awoke and told this to his sister-in-law. The woman listened and followed the instructions from the dream. She married the little brother and they lived together.

They lived there and raised two children, a boy and a girl. The two children married and raised two children, a boy and a girl. They did this until now when many people live in Nusi Village.

Joe Epi
Murray Barracks
National Capital District

A991+. Origin of particular village; B872+. Giant cassowary; D1810.8.2. Information received through dream; E231. Return from dead to reveal murder; E321. Dead husband's friendly return; E326. Dead brother's friendly return; E425.2. Revenant as man; F401.3.7+. Spirit in form of cassowary; F490+. Masalai; P210. Husband and wife; P231. Mother and son; P232. Mother and daughter; P233. Father and son; P234. Father and daughter; P251.5. Two brothers; P253. Sister and brother; P263. Brother-in-law; P264. Sister-in-law; Q211.6. Killing an animal revenged; Q411. Death as punishment; T100. Marriage; T415.5. Brother-sister marriage; V61.3+. Dead buried; W157. Dishonesty

A Cassowary Killed the Big Brother

(Wantok 729, June 23-29, 1988, page 19)

Long, long ago, in a village called **Sala**, there lived two brothers. The little brother's name was Neum. One day, they decided to go hunt for wild game. The next day, they prepared their bows and arrows, and some food for the forest.

In the early morning, they awoke and walked into the forest. They arrived at a forest hut that they had made. They made a fire, then cooked some sweet potatoes and ate.

While they ate, the big brother told Neum, "Stay and cut firewood to make a fire. I'll go check on some trees. If the marsupials are eating the tree fruits, we'll go to watch tonight."

After the big brother told Neum this, he took his bow and arrows, then went alone. He walked swiftly along the trail, then he saw two cassowary eggs. Quickly, he cleared some forest and made a path for the two of them to watch at night.

After he arranged everything, he went back and told his little brother, "I saw two cassowary eggs, then I made a path. Tonight I'll go first. If I see a cassowary sleeping there, I'll tie a rope on the cassowary's leg. After I tie the rope, I'll whistle for you. Then light a torch and come running."

The little brother listened and was very happy. They prepared the firewood, then sat. That night, the big brother took a rope and went first to the place where the cassowary eggs were lying. He went directly there and saw a huge cassowary asleep. Quietly, he tied the rope around the cassowary's leg. However, he did not want to tie the other end of the rope to a tree, he thought wrongly and tied the other end to his own leg.

After he tied the rope, he whistled to Neum. Neum heard the whistle, lit the torch, and ran to the place where the cassowary was sleeping.

The light from the torch awakened the cassowary. The cassowary pulled the big brother and ran away into the very deep forest. The cassowary pulled the big brother away into the forest. The big brother's legs were still tied with the rope to the cassowary's leg.

Neum returned to the forest hut, thinking and mourning. He worried for a while, then he went to sleep. That night, the big brother marked a place, then told the little brother in a dream, "Tomorrow morning, go to a big fig tree and kill the cassowary. This cassowary sleeps underneath this big fig tree."

In the morning, the little brother ran back and told the men of the village. All of the men took their bows and arrows, then they went to this place. They killed the big cassowary and carried it back to the village with the big brother's legs.

They arrived at the village, then made a huge feast. Later, they buried the big brother's legs.

The little brother lived alone for a while, then he married a woman. The name of this woman was Mawe. He lived well with her and they raised three children, two boys and one girl.

This story comes from the Finschhafen Peninsula of **Morobe** Province.

Dix Hendeng
P. O. Box 931
Boroko
National Capital District

B872+. Giant cassowary; D1810.8.2. Information received through dream; J2132.1+. Man ties himself to cassowary and is dragged to death; P210. Husband and wife; P231. Mother and son; P232. Mother and daughter; P233. Father and son; P234. Father and daughter; P251.5. Two brothers; P253.0.2. One sister and two brothers; T100. Marriage; V61.3+. Dead buried

The Big Brother Killed the Little Trickster

(Wantok 730, June 30 — July 6, 1988, page 16)

Long, long ago, in **Yopopaus** Village, in the swordgrass lands, there lived two brothers [**Enga** People, **Enga** Province]. They lived well and their house was packed with various kinds of meats.

They were never short of food, so they lived happily in the village. The little brother often stayed at home. Only the big brother went to the forest to hunt for game.

One time, the little brother told the big brother that he wanted to go hunt for wild game in the forest. He told the big brother that he would take some sweet potatoes to eat in the forest. The big brother brought some long and red sweet potatoes. The little brother put them in a net bag then prepared to go. The long sweet potatoes are called _taita mapu_ [_taitáá mapú_ (Lang, 1973: 66, 97)], and the red ones are called _pore mapu_ [_póte mapú_ (Lang, 1973: 66, 89)].

The little brother took the bag of sweet potatoes, an axe, and a bow and arrows, then he walked swiftly along the trail towards a huge mountain in the deep forest.

He walked and walked, then some birds, called _kusit_ [_kusíti_, a kind of small bird (Lang, 1973: 49)], sang. They called to him, "Hey, why are you walking so hard towards the big mountain? Your papa and mama never came this way."

The little brother replied, "Swallow some tree sap and your mouths will shut. It's too bad you live on this side, but I'm still going." After he said this, he sped on up the mountain.

Oh my, when he arrived in the dense forest, he killed many, many marsupials (_kapul_) and birds. He packed them into his net bag. When he had killed enough game, he walked swiftly back to the village. He walked along, then he felt stiff and rested inside a pandanus (_karuka_) hut.

He burned the hair from some of the marsupials and the feathers from some of the birds in a fire. Then he cooked some in an earth oven. Some were to be carried back to the village and he ate some. After he ate, he slept under the pandanus hut. While he slept, a bird called _alua_ [_aluá_, a kind of black bird (Lang, 1973: 4)] came and sang near him. This bird has white eyes and a long beak. This bird can speak like people.

The _alua_ called and told the good-for-nothing, "Man, get up! It's time! It's dawn now."

The little brother heard the bird's cry and woke up to look around. Quickly, he took the bag of meat, then walked towards the village. While he was walking on the trail, he was surprised to see a short man from the forest. They call this kind of short man a _purutuli_. [_Pututuli_ is a kind of non-human ghost (Lang, 1973: 90).] These _purutuli_s are sorcerers of the forest or ghosts of the trees.

This short man saw the little brother with his big bag of meat and [laughed] hysterically at him. He told the little brother, "Oh my, oh my, the two of us are true brothers because our papa made a big feast, then we ate plenty of food and lived happily. However, now papa is dead and we have each grown up. Now, we don't have this sort of enjoyment and life together."

He asked the little brother, "Oh my, that's a big bag of meat. You must feel terrible. Can I help you?"

The little brother was terrified, so he gave the bag of meat to the short man. Then they both walked swiftly towards the village. While they walked, the short man saw a good piece of firewood. He told the little brother to cut it so that they could cook the meat. The little brother went down the side of the mountain and cut the wood. After he cut it, he told the short man to help him carry it.

While he spoke, the short man's face became completely different. The little brother was terrified, so he just followed what he said. The firewood was too big, so when he went down to carry it, the firewood knocked him out and he passed wind. The little man heard the little brother's noise and laughed hysterically.

The little man jumped on top of the firewood with the bag of meat, then he finished all of the songs that he knew. The little brother was terrified and thought that the short man would eat him at once. He was furious, but he did not worry. He was still strong and carried the firewood, going with the little man towards the village.

When they approached a row of wild sugarcanes (*pit-pit*), the short man jumped into the base of the wild sugarcanes then he fled with the bag of meat.

The little brother shouted and wailed because he alone could not carry the large firewood with the ghost man. He cried, then told his big brother what had happened.

In the morning, the big brother told the little brother to stay at the house, then he would go alone into the forest to look for this short man. He took some sweet potatoes with his bow and arrows, then he walked swiftly into the forest.

He arrived in the forest, then he too killed many animals and filled his net bag. When it was nearly evening, he went to sleep in the pandanus hut in which his little brother had slept. In the morning, he awoke and walked very quietly towards home, thinking that he would meet the short man. Immediately, the short rogue stood by the trail. The big brother met him and pretended that he was surprised to see him.

The big brother told the little man, "Go cut a big piece of firewood then bring it here. We'll cook this meat in an earth oven, then we'll eat it."

The little man replied, "Ha! Never mind that. You go and cut the firewood, and I'll watch the meat."

However, the big brother was wise to this and wanted to cut the little man's neck. The little man was afraid, so went to cut the firewood. When he tried to carry the firewood, it knocked him out and he passed wind. The big brother heard this and laughed hysterically.

The little man brought the firewood, then the big brother did as the little man had done to his little brother. He jumped on top of the firewood with the bag of meat, then he finished all of the songs that he knew.

When they approached the row of wild sugarcanes, he let the big brother fall badly with the firewood and bag of meat. Quickly, he took the bag of meat and ran into the wild sugarcanes.

The big brother chased and chased him, then he ran out of breath. He stood and saw him go into a stone house. Quietly, he walked there and stood behind the stone house.

He heard the little man tell his kin, "Oh my, yesterday I took some marsupials from the forest and brought them here. Now I've brought some too. Does your papa hunt like this or is it just me?"

The big brother then sped over and stood at the door of the stone house. He went inside and grabbed the short man. The two of them fought and fought. Before long, the little man beat the big brother because all of the little man's kin helped him. However, the big brother was stronger still.

They fought and fought, then the big brother looked at the house fence. The house fence was their strength. He wanted to trample the house fence, then the little man told him, "Friend, let's fight here. Men can't trample that fence." The big brother ignored him. He moved back to the fence and trampled the fence [like a] flower.

He was surprised to see the little man and his family kick out their arms and legs, then die. Quickly, he cut them into little pieces, then ran back to the village with the bag of meat.

He arrived at the village, then he told his little brother what he had done. The two of them lived very happily in the village.

Anton Upu Wea [Wéa is an Enga place name (Lang, 1973: 114).]
P. O. Box 1106
Panguna
North Solomons Province

B143.1. Bird gives warning; B211.3. Speaking bird; D52. Magic change to different appearance; D1335. Object gives magic strength; D1711. Magician; E422.3.1. Revenant as small man; E446. Ghost killed and thus finally laid; E461. Fight of revenant with living person; E761.7+. Life token: fence; F451. Dwarf; J652. Inattention to warnings; J1110. Clever persons; K335. Thief frightens owner from goods; P251.5. Two brothers; Q212. Theft punished; Q411. Death as punishment; R220. Flights; R260. Pursuits; S110. Murders; S139.2. Slain person dismembered; X716.6H+. Humor concerning breaking wind

The Birds of the Sword-Grass Lands Are Enemies with the Birds of the Deep Forests
(Wantok 731, July 7-13, 1988, page 19)

Long, long ago, on Mount Ambra in **Western Highlands** Province, there lived a little bird [**Hagen** People]. His name was Miniga. There were no other birds in this area.

One day, Miniga wanted to make a men's house for himself on this mountain. So, he went around searching for vines to make a house. However, near Mount Ambra there were only sword-grass lands. There were no real trees where he could take things for making a house.

Miniga saw this and thought hard about going into the deep forest to find things for making a house. So, in the early morning, he awoke, left Ambra and walked into the deep forest. He arrived in the deep forest and began to gather vines and other things for making a house.

After he had all of the things, he tied them up well, then prepared to carry them back to his house. After he tied the things up, a heavy rain began to fall. Oh my, it poured and poured.

The heavy rain was ruining poor Miniga, so he looked for a place to hide. However there was no place to hide, so he sat and trembled at the base of a big tree.

He trembled and trembled at the base of the tree, then a cassowary walked towards him. The rain pounded the tree fruits down to the ground, so the cassowary was searching for them and eating them. The cassowary arrived at the base of the tree and thought that Miniga was a fruit too, so the cassowary swallowed Miniga.

After that, the cassowary kept walking and searching for food. Poor Miniga was inside, lying in the cassowary's belly. When the cassowary defecated, Ambra Miniga came out too.

Oh my, the cassowary's feces completely ruined Miniga's skin and feathers. He looked at himself, then he went down to the river and bathed thoroughly. He removed all of the trash from his skin and went up again. When his feathers were dry, he walked back to the place where he had put the vines and things.

Miniga was furious at the cassowary. He carried the house materials and walked back to his home. While he was walking on the trail, he thought about killing the cassowary.

He arrived at his house, put the things there, and sat to catch his breath. After he rested, he began to make his men's house. He worked very quickly until the house was finished, then he rested again.

One week later, Miniga sent a message for all of the birds to come and eat at his big party. The message went to all of the birds of the forest and of the sword-grass lands. They listened and all came to Mount Ambra.

Every bird arrived on the day of the party. They saw that it was packed and they were happy. When it was time to eat, Miniga told all of the birds to wait first because he had some speeches to make.

Miniga took a spear and put to his shoulder, then he began to talk. He spoke and spoke, then he went to the place where cassowary was sitting. He raised the spear and broke it on top of cassowary's head. Oh my, blood gushed out of the cassowary. The poor cassowary fell to the ground and counted stars.

The birds saw this and got up to fight. They broke into two halves. The birds of the sword-grass lands gathered on one side, and the birds of the deep forest gathered on the other side, then they battled.

They fought and fought. The little birds of the grasslands were stronger and won the battle. They chased all of the other birds into the deep forest.

Today, if you go towards Mount Hagen and arrive at Mount Ambra, you will see various ditches going down the mountain. These ditches are from when the birds fought. Also, you will see that the cassowaries are bald. They are bald because the little bird, Miniga, broke a spear over the cassowary's head.

Today, you will see that the birds of the grasslands only live in the grasslands. They never meet with the birds of the forest. If the birds of the forest go to the grasslands, the birds of the grasslands will cry and make much noise, and men will come kill them.

Jacob Mun
Ramu Sugar
P. O. Box 2183
Lae
Morobe Province

[A similar story was told in *Wantok* #112, involving a bird named Miniga.]

A983. Origin of valleys or hollows; A2320+. Why cassowary is bald; A2433.4+. Why bird lives in forest; A2433.4+. Why cassowary lives in forest; A2494.13. Enmities of birds; B211.3. Speaking bird; B263.5. War between groups of birds; B299.7.1K. Birds hold a feast; B299.14K. Animals build house; F911.2+. Cassowary swallows bird and defecates it alive; R260. Pursuits

A Ghost Tricked a Man

(Wantok 732, July 13-21, 1988, page 19)

Long, long ago, in a village called Nusi [**Nguzi**], there lived a man and his wife. Nusi Village is on the Upper Waria River of **Morobe** Province [**Weri** People].

The two of them lived together for a while, then one time, the man's wife became pregnant. The woman told her husband to go find some wild game from the forest.

However, the man said, "I hear what you say, but I'm thinking of you. It would be bad if I go to the forest and other men work hard when you give birth."

Not Ready

The woman replied to her husband, "I'm not ready to give birth, so you can go to the forest and sleep for three nights, then find some game. However, you must come back to the village quickly."

The man agreed with what his wife thought. He told her to go find some sweet potatoes for him to cook and eat in the forest. The woman took a net bag and went to get sweet potatoes from the garden. The man prepared his bow and arrows and other things for the forest.

Speeding Away

The guy took his things with some sweet potatoes, then sped off to the forest with his five dogs. He followed the Waria River to a small mountain. He left the mountain and arrived at a big and narrow sword-grass land. He followed the grassland, then he approached the very deep forest.

A Marsupial

He prepared his bow and arrows, then walked very quietly into the forest. Before long, his dogs met some game and barked. He heard them and sped off to where they were.

Oh my, he was surprised to see a marsupial (*kapul*) there on a tree. Quickly, he aimed his bow and shot down the marsupial.

He tied up the marsupial, put it in a basket, and then walked farther into the forest. When it was nearly evening, he arrived at a place where he thought he would sleep that night.

Swiftly Along the Trail

He made a hut, then prepared some firewood for making a fire. Later, he cooked the marsupial in an earth oven, then he ate it with some sweet potatoes. After he ate, he slept until dawn.

In the morning, he ate a piece of marsupial with sweet potatoes, then he prepared to go hunt for some game in the forest. He took his bow and arrows, then sped off into the deep forest. When he entered the deep forest, the marsupials were plentiful. He killed many of them and his net bag was full of them. He found it hard to carry the marsupials, so when it was still noontime, he went back quickly to the forest hut where he had slept.

Forest Hut

He arrived at the forest hut, then he began to cook the marsupials. He removed their guts, then he began to singe off their hair and skin.

It was nearly dark when he heard the cry of a baby coming along the trail. He thought that it was some man from the village who knew that he had come alone into the forest, and had come for him. So, he looked down the trail and waited.

He heard the voice of his wife, then he was surprised to see her carrying a little baby. The woman approached him and said, "Oh my, you've been in the forest a long time and haven't thought a bit about me. So, I brought the baby and came looking for you."

The Meat

Her husband replied, "I wanted to go tomorrow, so I was preparing the meat. It's OK that you came with the baby. Let's sleep, then tomorrow we'll go back to the village."

The man did not know that this was not really his wife. What had really happened was that in the village, his wife had died in childbirth, so the woman's ghost had followed him into the forest to test his strength.

The ghost woman hung up the baby [in a net bag] and helped her husband cook the marsupials. The man broke the tail of a marsupial and gave it to the ghost woman to cook. The ghost woman pretended to cook it, then just ate the bloody marsupial tail.

When the man turned around, oh my, he was shocked to see that the ghost woman's eyes had completely changed. The ghost woman's eyes became bigger than her head and became very long.

He was terrified, so he lied and told her to fetch water. When the ghost woman went to fetch water, he killed her ghost baby, then sped back towards the village.

He ran and ran, then he approached the sword-grass lands. You know, ghosts have powers. Quickly, the ghost woman followed him and approached him. She told him, "I can't do anything to you, so go to the house first, then you must return. I'll wait for you at night."

Ghost Woman

The poor man listened to the ghost woman, then he thought hard and ran to the village. Quickly, he ran into the house and was surprised to see his real wife lying dead.

His heart went out and he cried, holding his wife's body. When he held his wife's body, he died too. Later, the people of the village found them and buried them together.

Joe Epi
Trade Training Unit (T. T. U.)
Murray Barracks
National Capital District

E261.4. Ghost pursues man; E425.1.4. Revenant as woman carrying baby; E425.3. Revenant as child; E446. Ghost killed and thus finally laid; F512+. Unusually large eyes; E541. Revenants eat; F419.4K. Spirits eat food raw; H46.1+. Revenant recognized when it devours raw flesh; P210. Husband and wife; P230. Parents and children; R220. Flights; R260. Pursuits; S110. Murders; T211.9.2+. Man dies in dead wife's arms; T570. Pregnancy; T580. Childbirth; V61.3+. Dead buried

Lime (Calcium Oxide) For
Making Love-Magic

(Wantok 733, July 21-27, 1988, page 19)

Long, long ago, there was a man and his wife who lived in a village in **East Sepik** Province. The man was not a good man. His skin was very mangy and he was terribly old.

He always just slept by the fire. His poor wife worked hard. She worked alone in the garden and she hunted for food for themselves to eat.

One time, there was a festival in a village, so the woman told her old husband to stay while she went alone to the festival. However, the old man was not an ordinary man. When the woman left the house for the festival, he rose and performed a little magic, then he removed his old skin. Oh my, he became a truly handsome man. Quickly, he hid his skin and followed her to the festival grounds.

When he arrived at the festival grounds, all of the bad and good women looked at him. They were completely knocked out by him. Some of their hearts fell for him, and they completely forgot about the festival. They just watched the scoundrel and lusted for him.

He bided his time, however. When the festival was almost over, he quickly went first to the house, then he changed back to his old skin. He did this all of the time, and his wife did not know it.

One time there was a festival again in a village. The woman told her old husband, "Sleep here. I'll go to the festival, then I'll return in the morning."

The woman had lied to her husband. She returned quietly and hid in the hut where they kept firewood. Oh my, her heart jumped when she saw her husband remove his old skin and become a completely handsome man. The good-for-nothing looked young and completely handsome.

Finished Looking

Immediately, the woman ran first to the festival grounds, then waited. The scoundrel did not know that his wife had seen him. He sped away and arrived at the festival grounds. This time too, the beautiful young women of the village went crazy for him. Some of them wanted to go directly to him and ask him about his desires.

However, his real wife was waiting before them. Quietly, she went and held her husband's hand, then she told him, "You're really my husband. You've always tricked to me, but now I've tricked you." The scoundrel was surprised, but what could he do?

They stayed at the festival grounds until dawn, then in the morning the two of them went back together. In the house, the woman took the old skin and burned it in the fire.

The man saw this and was very troubled about his old skin. He took white lime (calcium oxide) from a bamboo container, then he put it on his face. After he applied the lime, he turned into a parrot. He flew a very long distance into the forest, then he went down into a hole in an ironwood tree. This ironwood tree was by a stream near a village. The people of the village always went there to fetch water.

One time, a very young woman went down to the stream to fetch water. Then the parrot went out of the ironwood tree hole and had sex with her. The parrot always had sex with this young woman, and after a while she became pregnant.

Pregnancy

The people of the village asked her who it was who had impregnated her, so she told them, "It was a man who lives in the big ironwood tree near the place where we fetch water. He had sex with me when I went to fetch water, so now I'm pregnant."

When they heard this, they were furious, so they decided to cut the ironwood tree. One morning, they took their stone axes and went to cut the tree. They cut and cut until it was close to evening, then they stopped and returned to the houses.

In the morning, they awoke and went back to cut the tree. However when they arrived, they were surprised to see that there were no marks on the tree because the tree bark had grown back again.

They were furious and cut the tree again until it fell down. Later, they found the tree hole and met the parrot. They killed him savagely and burned him in a fire. Later, they took the red ashes from the fire and they each filled a bamboo tube with them. They carried the ashes back to their houses.

Now if you go to the two big villages called **Witupe Number One** and **Witupe Number Two**, you will find this red lime [**Abelam** People]. The young men of these villages use this lime to perform magic on the young women, so the men of these villages often pull in many, many young women.

Isaac Wamakuara

A978+. Origin of lime (calcium oxide); B614. Bird paramour; D157M. Transformation: man to parrot; D642. Transformation to escape difficult situation; D671. Transformation flight; D793.2. Disenchantment made permanent by burning cast-off skin; D931.1.4. Magic lime; D950+. Magic ironwood tree; D1355+. Love-produced by lime (calcium oxide); D1711. Magician; D1866.2. Beautification by removal of skin; D1880+. Transformation to young man to escape recognition; D1889.6. Rejuvenation by changing skin; D1900. Love induced by magic; H1115.1. Task: cutting down huge tree which magically regrows; K1814+. Man in disguise wooed by his faithless wife; K1930. Treacherous impostors; P210. Husband and wife; Q254+. Punishment for impregnating girl; Q411. Death as punishment; R213. Escape from home; R260. Pursuits; S110. Murders; T10. Falling in love; T570. Pregnancy; W111. Laziness

Masalai Weimbemi Changed His Mind

(Wantok 734, July 28 — August 3, 1988, page 18)

Long, long ago, there was a *masalai*. The name of this man was Weimbemi. Weimbemi always traveled in the forest, hunting for wild game, and bringing it back to his house. When he would arrive home, he would beat the meat on stones, then put it in the sun to dry. When the meat dried, he would take it and eat it.

He would also do this to the food from his garden. He did this for a while, then one time he met a *masalai* woman, Sembami, and they married.

The *masalai* woman lived on a mountain near where the sun rises. The name of this mountain is Sembawo. When Sembami came and married Weimbemi, she carried a piece of firewood with her and made a fire in Weimbemi's area.

When Sembami would cook food in the fire, she alone ate it. Poor Weimbemi would eat his own food from the sun. They did this until one time, Sembami told her husband to make a house for themselves. Weimbemi listened and began to make their house. When he went up to the top of the house and worked at putting on the thatch shingles, his wife made a fire inside the house. When the smoke from the fire rose to the top of the house, oh my, her poor husband had a bad time of it.

The smoke went inside his nose, mouth and ears, and he did not have a way to breathe. He fell down to the ground and vomited all of the food that he had eaten. The food was uncooked.

His wife saw this and boiled some water, then gave her husband some to drink. After he drank the water, his wife cooked some taros and pork in the fire, then gave it to him

to eat. Her husband ate and ate; it was delicious. He finished it all.

So now, we all know to cook food in a fire and to eat it after it is cooked.

Augusta Engehile
Aresili [**Arisili**] Village [**Wom** People]
P. O. Box 46
Maprik
East Sepik Province

A1455. Origin of cooking; F490+. Masalai; J1813+. Cooking processes misunderstood: cooking with the sun; P210. Husband and wife; T100. Marriage

The Third Wife Ruined Their Lives

(Wantok 735, August 4-10, 1988, page 18)

Long, long ago, there was a man who lived in a village. He was married to two wives. The first wife gave birth to a boy, and the second wife had no children.

The two women lived well together. They never fought as with other marriages. Their husband was not an ordinary man, he was an excellent hunter. The people of the village were happy for him. The man and his family lived well in the village. They had plentiful food and were never short of meat.

They lived well for a while, then a great drought came. The sun was strong, so the wild animals searched for water and fled into the very deep forest. Whenever the men went into the forest, they did not find game.

For a long time, they did not have good meat, so the two women's [husband] told them that he would go into the very deep forest to hunt for wild game. In the early morning, he awoke and left the village, walking into the deep forest. He walked and walked, until he entered the deep forest, but he did not find the smallest animal.

The man walked away from the streams, and hiked over a mountain. He walked and walked until he arrived at a huge river. He rested a little, then he took his multi-pronged spear and fished in the river. He kept fishing until he had enough, then he followed the river back to the village.

He walked and walked, then he saw a woman. Oh my, she was not just a woman, she was angelic. The woman's hair was very long, and she wore a nice "grass" skirt, too. The good-for-nothing fell down when he saw this.

He approached her, then she asked him for fish. He listened and quickly gave the fish to her. She was happy for the fish, so she told him to follow her to her house. They walked and walked until they arrived at the base of a big tree. Then the woman told the man that her house was on top of the tree.

There was a rope ladder at the base of the tree. The woman pulled the ladder and told him to follow her. They went up to the house, then went inside. She cooked food and they ate. After they ate, he asked her to make love and she agreed.

They stayed until evening, then he told her that he must return to the village. He took just one fish, then he left her. She told him that if he returned again, he must beat the base of the tree three times, then she would lower the ladder. He understood and went back towards the village.

When he arrived at the village, he lied to his wives that there were no animals, and that he had found just one fish that he had brought back. The women believed what he said because he was not a liar. They cooked the fish, then they ate and slept.

In the morning, the man told them that he would return to hunt for game again, but the good-for-nothing did not go to hunt for game. He went to see his new wife. He followed the forest until he arrived at the base of the tree, then he beat the tree three times. The woman lowered the ladder, and he ascended.

He had found some game too, so he gave it to her, then they cooked, ate and stayed there. In the evening, he left her and went to pretend that he [only] found some small game to bring back to the village.

He did this all of the time His son grew tired of this because he was a meat-eater. One day, the father wanted to go into the forest and his son told him that he wanted to go too. The father said no, but the boy was persistent and cried. The father said no, but he was sorry for the boy and took him with him.

When they were far from the village, he told the boy that they would go to see a new mother. The boy just listened and followed his father. They arrived at the base of the big tree, then he saw his father beat the base of the tree three times. The house ladder came down, then the boy followed his father up it.

The two of them went into the house, and the good-for-nothing told the new lady that the boy was his son. She already knew because he had been sorry for his two wives. She was happy to see the little boy. The father told the boy to stay with the new mother, then he would go to hunt for game for themselves.

The man went hunting, and he found many, many animals, then he brought them back. The woman cooked them and they ate. In the evening, the man took his son and left her.

The man took a small marsupial (*kapul*) to bring to the two mothers in the village. They walked and walked along the trail, then he told the little boy, "Don't tell your two mothers about this new mother."

The boy listened and told his father that he would keep his mouth shut. They arrived in the village, and gave the marsupial to the mothers to cook. The father lied to them that there was not much game, and that they were lucky to have this little marsupial.

The next day, the man quickly went back to the forest. The boy and the mothers just stayed in the house. The boy's mother asked him about his travels with his father. Then the little boy revealed what had happened.

He told exactly what his father had done. The women listened and were furious. They said, "He always brings meat to that woman, then the two of them cook and eat it. When he comes here, he lies and says there are no animals in the forest."

The women decided to go find this woman and kill her. They stayed there. After the man returned, they did not say anything, they just stayed quiet. Because they did this, the man did not know that the women were wise to him.

In the morning, the women lied to him that they wanted to go find *talis* trees in the forest. He told them that he would stay in the village and do other work. The women took the little boy and went into the forest. The boy showed them the trail. They followed it until they arrived at the base of the big tree.

They beat the base of the tree three times, then the ladder of the house descended and they went up it. They went inside the woman's house. The poor woman saw them and did not think that they had come to kill her. She cooked food and gave it to them.

While they ate, she sat, and the women said that they would like to braid her hair. The two of them worked at braiding her hair. They played with her hair for a while, then she fell dead asleep. The two women saw this and shot her ear, killing the poor woman.

After they saw that she was dead, they quickly carried her down to the river and threw her body into it. Then they took the little boy and pretended to look for some *talis* trees. Afterwards, they went back to the village. The two of them lied to the man that they did not find many *talis* nuts.

The women just lived quietly in the village. The man did not travel the forest for a fairly long time. Then one morning, he woke up, took his bow and arrows, and then went into the forest to see his wife. However, the poor woman was rotting and insects were laying waste to her body.

The man walked and walked, then he arrived at the base of the tree. He beat the tree, but the house ladder did not descend. He waited, then he beat it again. Nothing happened, so he thought hard. He turned and looked up, then he saw the house ladder hanging from the other side.

Quickly, he went up to the house, but his wife was not there. He searched to no avail, then he went down again. He shouted and shouted, but no one replied.

He searched and searched, then he smelled something rotting. He went there and saw the woman's body by the river. When he saw this, he was troubled and he wailed. He cried for her, but then he thought that it was just his wives who must have killed the poor woman. He also knew that the boy must have told his two mothers.

The man cleared his eyes, then he went back to the village. He arrived there and just lived quietly. The women saw this and they thought that he did not know yet. They cooked, ate and slept.

In the morning, the man lied to his wives and son, telling them that they must go into the forest. They walked and walked, then they arrived at the place where the women had thrown the other woman's body. He told them to keep walking until they arrived at the place where the woman's body lay.

The women were terrified now. They did not speak. Then he revealed his anger. He asked them why they had killed her. The women did not speak, they kept their mouths shut.

He told the women and the boy to eat the woman's corpse, then and there. The women did not want to do this, but he told them that he would kill them if they did not heed him.

They listened and ate her corpse. The little boy saw this and became a bird, then he flew and pecked at his mother's breasts. His mother cried terribly, then she became a turtle. The second wife became a trevally fish [*Caranx* spp.]. The two of them jumped into the water and fled.

The man saw this and shouted, "Come back. I was just fooling." He kept shouting like this, but it was too late. His two wives and son had already fled.

Vincent Kiki
Morabang
Bogia
Madang Province

646

[Mr. Kiki also wrote the ancestor story in *Wantok* #740. The story in *Wantok* #740 came from the **Manam** and **Aris** islands, **Manam** People.]

D150B. Transformation: boy to bird; D179+W. Transformation: woman to trevally fish; D193W. Transformation: woman to tortoise (turtle); D642. Transformation to escape difficult situation; D671. Transformation flight; F555.3. Very long hair; K1500. Deception connected with adultery; P210. Husband and wife; P231. Mother and son; P233. Father and son; Q211. Murder punished; Q241. Adultery punished; Q411. Death as punishment; Q580+. Murderer forced to eat corpse; R220. Flights; S11. Cruel father; S62. Cruel husband; S110. Murders; T10. Falling in love; T145.0.1. Polygyny; T481. Adultery; T580. Childbirth; W157. Dishonesty; Z71.1. Formulistic number: three

Juarguandu Took His Father's Place
(Wantok 736, August 11-17, 1988, page 18)

Long, long ago, in the time of the ancestors, there lived a man who excelled at fighting with spears. The man's name was Bautipma, and he was from Saikisi [**Sagasi**] Village in the Maprik area, **East Sepik** Province [**Abelam** People]. Bautipma was married and had a son. His wife's name was Mikarguande, and their son's name was Juarguadu [Juarguandu].

Fight
Bautipma was very strong at fighting with the enemies from other villages. One time, he went to fight with the enemies from Swambukim [**Suambukum**] Village. The guy fought very hard in this battle and he killed two strong fighters from Swambukim Village.

He took the blood from these two men and rubbed it on his face, then he went back to the village. He would do this with many men from Swambukim Village, so the people of that village were furious with him. One time, they decided to kill him.

Hiding
One night, they went to hide in the forest. The bad guy did not know that he would meet his enemies like this. That night, he went back to the battle and met these enemies.

The man was shocked when a spear stuck to his side. The poor guy held his side and fell to the ground. Bautipma was not an ordinary man. He was a fighter, so he still had plenty of strength.

Fleeing Back
Quickly, he got up and fled back to the village. He ran into his house and died there. His poor wife, Mekarguandu

[Mikarguande] saw him and cried terribly. She put her son, Juarguandu, on top of Bautipma's chest, then Juarguandu drank his father's blood.

The other men of the village also arrived. They were very troubled about Bautipma's death. In the morning, the men of the village took Bautipma's body and buried it under his house. Then Mikarguande and her son, Juarguandu, slept in another house that the Bautipma had made.

The Baby Grows Up

Mikarguande and the baby just lived there, then the baby grew to be a very big boy. Oh my, the young man, Juarguandu, became very different, and very strong like his father.

Two Men

One time, they heard that there would be a huge festival in Swambukim Village. The two of them heard this, so the mother told her son to go and cut two pieces of bamboo from the forest. His mother sharpened the bamboos into two spears and taught her son how to use them.

She told Juarguandu, "When you arrive at the festival grounds, you'll see two men with spears. They will run outside to the platform, then dance. After them, two other men will come out. These two men will dress in cassowary feathers. These are the two men who killed your father. When they want to run up to the platform, shoot each of them with the spears. Then you must run back quickly to the village."

Juarguandu absorbed his mother's instructions. He took the spears and followed the other leaders to Swambukin [Suambukum] Village.

The leaders scolded him and told him to stay in the village. They said, "Whom are you following, that you want to go to the festival? You're too little. Go back and stay in the village with your mother, otherwise the enemies will kill you."

Father's Death

Juarguande [Juarguandu] replied, scolding them too, "You probably killed my father, so you want to stop me from going to see the festival."

After he said such things, the leaders let him go with them. When they arrived at the festival grounds, Juarguande left the leaders and stood very close to the platform where they would sing and dance.

He stood and watched two men come out and dance up to the platform. After them, he saw another [two] men come out. Quickly, Juarguandu took his spear and buried it

in one of the men. The man that Juarguandu had speared died right there.

Escape

Quickly, Juarguande ran under the legs of the men, speeding back to the village. He told his mother, and the two of them were elated. However, many of the men who were at the festival fought among themselves and many of them died.

The leaders of Saikisi Village returned and were surprised to hear this story. Later, they were elated and appointed Juarguande to be their leader.

Peter Thieodore
P. O. Box 301
Kieta
North Solomons Province

[For a similar story, see *Wantok* #758.]

D1041. Blood as magic drink; F610. Remarkably strong man; K914. Murder from ambush; P210. Husband and wife; P231. Mother and son; P233.6. Son avenges father; Q211. Murder punished; Q411. Death as punishment; R210. Escapes; S110. Murders; V61.3+. Dead buried

A Stone Became a Man and Tricked a Woman
(Wantok 737, August 18-24, 1988, page 18)

Long, long ago, there was a gorgeous woman who lived in a village inside the Markham Valley area [**Morobe** Province]. This woman lived with her parents.

This family had a stone that the father used to sharpen and cut wood. When he was not doing anything, he would hang it up in the back of the house. This stone would turn into a man and spy upon the young woman.

Spying

One time, the father told his daughter to clean the area, wash things, and cook food at the house. The father, mother, and the other men of the village went to hunt for food in the forest.

Afterwards, the stone saw the young woman alone in the village, so he turned into a real man. The man looked unusual and very handsome. If a woman had seen him, she would just die for him.

The woman was surprised to see him and asked, "Hey! Where did you come from?"

The guy replied, "I often come to the village and see you alone here, so I came to bring you to another village."

Very Handsome

She did not know what to say. She just followed what the stone-man said because the stone-man looked very handsome and cut straight to her heart.

The two of them went up to the house, then the woman took all of her belongings. After she took them, they walked swiftly along the trail to another village.

They walked and walked then they arrived at a river. They put their things down then they rested by the river. The guy found a tree and made a raft for themselves to drift downriver. After he made the raft, they drifted downriver.

They drifted down, then became stuck on some snags in the water. The raft turned about, so the woman quickly jumped on top of the snags. The stone-man went underwater. Then he went up on the other side of the snags and ran back to the village.

The poor woman searched for him, but he was not there. What could she do there, now that she was alone? She made a hut, then slept by the river. She lived there for a while, then one time she found a bird's egg. The bird's egg was among some wild sugarcanes (*pitpit*) near the river.

The Egg Hatches

She took care of the egg for a while, then the bird's egg hatched. She would always go fishing and then give food to the bird. She did this until the bird became very big.

The woman taught the bird to talk like a human. When the bird was big, it told the woman that it would travel and look at the village.

One time, the bird flew right down to the woman's village. The bird took a banana leaf and brought it back to show her. She saw this and was elated.

The two of them lived for a while, then the bird itself went fishing. It also learned to carry things. The poor bird would also listen to its mother then quickly find food and bring it back to her.

One time, the woman told the bird to try to carry a big stone. The bird replied, "Mama, that's OK. I'll just try because the stone isn't little. It's huge."

The bird carried the stone and flew very high, then it went down and put the stone in the river. The woman saw this and was elated for her bird-child.

Later, she told the bird, "I'll prepare some things, then take me to the village."

Carrying the Belongings

Two days later, the bird began to carry each of the belongings to the village. Much later, after it had carried everything, it carried the woman to the village too.

Oh my, the people of the village and her parents saw her and were shocked. Many of them thought that they were seeing the woman's ghost because they thought that she was dead.

Later, she was sorry for what had happened to her. She told them about the young man who had tricked her into marriage. Her father listened and was furious, but he did not know that the man was really his stone.

A thought came to him that one day he would tell everyone to go to the forest. Then he told his daughter, "We're all going to hunt for wild game. We'll sleep two nights in the forest. You'll be alone here. If this man returns to flatter you, you must tell him, 'I first went with another man, but he was lost in the river. The people of the village told me that if another man comes to flatter me, I must not go with him.'"

That same day, the villagers prepared to go to the forest, then departed. However, the woman's father hid by the village and waited.

The Stone Transformed

The poor young woman was alone in the village. She was there for just a little while when the stone-man saw this and turned back into a very handsome man. The scoundrel fixed his body very nicely, then walked very quietly towards her.

The woman's father performed magic for her. This magic was to turn the woman's thoughts so that she could not be shaken into marriage if she saw a handsome man.

The scoundrel came and told the woman that he would marry her if she went with him to another village. However, the woman was very strong and said no to his plans.

She told him, "One time, a man came and tricked me. Later, he left me alone somewhere, but I was strong and I returned to the village."

The stone-man was persistent about taking her with him, but she was also persistent and did not listen to what he said. The two of them talked and talked, then the woman's father came out from his hiding place. The stone-man saw her father and jumped back, turning to a stone inside the house. However it was too late, the father had seen him.

He told everyone in the forest to return to the village, then he told them what had happened. Oh my, the daughter was also surprised to hear this. She had thought that the man who had spoken to her was a real man.

Every man of the village gathered together in the spirit house, then the woman's father told them his plan to kill the stone-man. All of them followed what he said, and they made a house in just one day. They constructed it very strongly, then they fenced the house in very well.

Later, the woman's father took the stone and left it inside this house. The poor stone-man did not know their plan. The house did not have a door in it because they had fenced in the walls very strongly.

Later, they decided to make food in the house, but they only pretended to cook food inside the house. They burned the house with the stone-man. He was in pain and screamed. The poor stone-man screamed and screamed as he burned inside the house.

The woman's bird-child went and perched on top of the river where the men, women and children usually bathed. The bird did something wrong when the children would go to bathe in the river. The bird would call the children, then they would go up the tree and be bitten. The children became angry at this and they killed the bird.

This is a very long story. I forgot some parts and just shortened it.

Moaitz Justin

Markham [Valley]

Morobe Province

[Justin Moaitz wrote the ancestor stories in *Wantok* #682 and 745. He is from **Gabsonkek** Village, **Wampar** People.]

B31.6. Other giant birds; B211.3. Speaking bird; B317. Helpful bird hatched by hero; B542.1+. Bird flies with woman to safety; B552+. Woman carried by bird; D231M. Transformation: man to stone; D432.1M. Transformation: stone to man; D1908. Love lost by magic; D2000+. Mind control; F610.0.1. Remarkably strong woman; H1562.2.2+. Before undertaking rescue, bird tests strength by lifting stone; P210. Husband and wife; P232. Mother and daughter; P234. Father and daughter; Q213. Abduction punished; Q411. Death as punishment; Q414. Punishment: burning alive; R16+. Abduction by stone-person; R130. Rescue of abandoned or lost persons; R225. Elopement; S112.0.2. House (hostel) burned with all inside; S143. Abandonment in forest; V112.1. Spirit huts

Two Women Turned to Stone

(Wantok 738, August 25-31, 1988, page 18)

Long, long ago, in a place called Mount Oka [Moogoga], in the **Hagen** [People's] area, there lived two women [**Western Highlands** Province]. Their names were Tekal and Mikal. They listened to their parents, made gardens and husbanded pigs. The two of them lived very well together and were never angry. They were very good friends.

They lived very well for a while, then a great drought arose. No rain had fallen for a very long time, so Tekal told Mikal that they should ask their parents for permission, then go to the forest to look for vines to make net bags.

Permission

They asked their parents, and the parents agreed. They went to the garden, took some bananas and sweet potatoes, then carried them back to the village. They arranged everything, then they slept. In the morning, when it was still dark, they awoke, took their little dog and walked swiftly into the forest.

They walked and walked along the trail until they arrived at a stream. They drank water and ate, then they continued to walk swiftly. They walked until they arrived at a forest hut where the men of the village would go to sleep when they traveled in the forest. The sun was beginning to set, so they quickly arranged things and cooked food. They ate then they slept. In the early morning, they awoke and went up the mountain.

Many Vines

They saw many, many vines there, so they put down their net bags and worked at cutting the vines. They cut and cut, then when it was nearly dark, Tekil [Tekal] told Makil [Mikal], "We should stop sister, it's nearly dark now. Let's go back to the hut, then at dawn, we'll come and get some more."

They carried the net-bag vines, then they walked back to the forest hut. They arrived, cooked food, ate and slept. In the morning, they awoke and went back to the place where they had cut the vines.

They arrived, then they cut vines until noon when they rested. They sat, rested, and ate. Tekil saw a boulder standing among the trees.

Tekil quickly left her sister, then climbed to the top of the boulder. She stood on the boulder, looked at faraway villages, and was very happy.

When she saw the villages, she called to her sister, Mikal, to come up and look at the villages too. Mikal listened and jumped behind her sister. She went up and sat well on the boulder, then she began to pound sweet potatoes.

They sat watching the other places, then when they wanted to turn and look from the other side of the boulder, it was too bad. They could not move. They were stuck to the stone where they had sat.

Tekil saw this and told her sister, "Oh dear, we left our parents and came here. Now we'll die in the forest." Her sister, Mikal, was also troubled. She cried and spoke mournfully.

The sisters were stuck fast to this stone. The men of the village saw the stones and called them Tekil and Makil.

Lawrence Lomorok

Hagen

Western Highlands Province

A974. Rocks from transformation of people to stone; A977.5. Origin of particular rock; A1617. Origin of place-name; D231W. Transformation: woman to stone; D1413.17. Magic adhesive stone; P210. Husband and wife; P232. Mother and daughter; P234. Father and daughter; P252.1. Two sisters; W31. Obedience

Kimala Shot His Own Sister

(Wantok 739, September 1-7, 1988, page 16)

Long, long ago at **Kandep** inside **Enga** Province, there lived a man and his sister, Ipaliowian [**Enga** People]. The name of the man was Kimala. A dog also lived with them. The name of this dog was Pulyan. They lived in the very deep forest where no men went to hunt for wild game.

Kimala and his sister never gardened. They only ate game from the forest. Every day, Kimala and his dog, Pulyan, would go to hunt for marsupials (*kapul*) in the forest. The sister, Ipaliowan [Ipaliowian], would stay alone in the house.

Hunting Marsupials

One afternoon, Kimala told his sister that he would go to hunt for marsupials in the forest. He told Ipaliowan, "Tomorrow morning, the dog and I will go far away to hunt for marsupials, so I'd like you to prepare some food for me to bring into the forest." Ipaliowan listened and prepared food for her brother.

The next day, Kimala awoke in the early morning, then prepared his bow and arrows. Ipaliowan wanted to go with him, but he said no. Kimala took his belonging and walked into the forest with his dog.

A Great Desire

The sister, Ipaliowan, wanted very much to go with Kimala, so she cried and followed her brother. Kimala did not know that his sister was crying and coming behind him. He thought that his sister was at home.

Kimala and his dog walked and walked until it became dark on the trail. They slept underneath a big tree. That night, Kimala dreamt of his sister. He dreamt that Ipaliowan came and held his bow and arrows.

Thinking Hard

In the morning, he awoke and thought very hard about the dream. He thought that it was just a dream, so he sped off into the forest with his dog. The two of them walked and walked, then entered the very deep forest.

There, the two of them rested and began to make a hut. He put the food inside the hut and began to hunt for marsupials in the forest.

They hunted for marsupials, but they did not kill even a small one. Oh my, Kimala's eyes were completely red and it was almost dark. Quickly, they went back to the forest hut, then they ate the food that his sister had cooked and prepared for him. Later, they slept.

Hunting Marsupials

In the morning, the two of them awoke and went to hunt for marsupials on another side of the forest. That day, they also did not find the smallest marsupial. Kimala was furious, so he took the dog and went back to the forest hut.

Along the trail, Kimala told his dog, "We've worked at hunting marsupials to no avail, so tomorrow we can't come back again. We'll go back home." After he told his dog this, they walked very quietly back to the hut.

When they arrived at the forest hut, his dog saw a marsupial and barked loudly. Kimala looked up and was surprised to see a giant marsupial hanging upon a tree.

One Arrow

His heart jumped and he was very happy. Quickly, he removed an arrow and shot the marsupial straight down. He laughed and told his dog, "We've hunted fruitlessly for marsupials. Now, there's just this one, so we'll bring it home. Sister Ipaliowan must see it first."

After he spoke to the dog, they slept. That night, Kimala again dreamt of his sister. Ipaliowan told Kimala in the dream, "Brother Kimala, don't be sorry for me. You shot me with your arrow. The marsupial that you killed yesterday was not really a marsupial. It was just me. I had followed you here and you killed me. Now you want to carry me back home. Tomorrow morning, you'll be surprised to see that the marsupial is not there and that I'm dead."

Surprise

Kimala was shocked by his dream, so he checked on the marsupial while it was still night, but the marsupial was not there. Immediately he awakened his dog and they raced back home.

Oh my, when they arrived home, Kimala's heart jumped [because] Ipaliowan had died and was inside the house. He cried terribly and buried his sister.

This is a true ancestor story. The meaning of this story is as follows. If Kimala had just told his sister that he wanted to go hunting for game, it would have been all right. However, he had clearly said that he was going hunting for marsupials, so his sister's spirit turned into a marsupial and followed him into the forest. The brother, Kimala, did not know this and killed his own sister.

So, in our area of Kandep and **Laiagam**, if we men want to go hunting for marsupials in the forest, we never tell the women of the house. We just hide and go hunting for marsupials in the forest.

Panda Minapi [Pándane is an Enga male name (Lang, 1973: 214).]

Aipilama Lyokati Village

Mulisos Community School, P. O. Box 68

Wabag

Enga Province

B871.2+. Giant marsupial; C490+. Tabu: telling specific hunting plans; C920+. Death of sister for breaking tabu; D179.6K+W. Transformation: woman to marsupial; D1810.8.2. Information received through dream; D1812.3.3. Future revealed in dream; F401.3+. Spirit in marsupial form; P253. Sister and brother; R260. Pursuits; S75.1K2. Sororicide; S110. Murders; W126. Disobedience; V61.3+. Dead buried

Tears Became Mountains

(Wantok 740, September 8-14, 1988, page 18)

Long, long ago, when all of the places on the earth were still new, there were no mountains and everything was completely flat. If a person stood up, he could see very far away.

At this time, there was a man who lived in a place on **Manam** Island [**Manam** People, **Madang** Province]. The poor man was afraid of snakes, so he never went close to places where snakes lived. In this place, there was a small area where he lived. He would use just one spot to urinate.

At the spot where he urinated, there lived a big snake. The poor man did not know that there was a snake there. This snake was also a *masalai*.

The man always went to urinate there, so after a while, his urine impregnated the snake. The poor man did not know this. After a very long time, the snake's belly became very big, then the snake gave birth to two boys. Oh my, the snake took care of the two boys very well, and they grew very stout. The snake took care of them until her two sons

walked and talked. They listened carefully to their mother, so when they grew up, they made a house and took care of her. They lived there for a while, then one time the snake told her sons that their father was still alive.

One time, in the very early morning the man went to urinate. When he wanted to return, the snake told her boys that this man was their father. The snake told them to go and bring the man to the house with them. Before the two of them followed him, they took their mother and put her in a *galip* basket.

When the man went inside his house, he [went] and sat down then stretched his body by the fire. The boys came and knocked on the door. The poor man got up and opened the door. The boys called him, "Papa." When he heard this, oh my, he was shocked. He told them that he was not their father, but the snake-children insisted that he was their father because their mother had told them so. He trembled and thought hard, "Why did these boys call him father?"

The boys were persistent and the poor man followed them to the house. When they arrived at the house, the man asked the boys for their mother. Slowly, the boys went inside the house and took their snake-mother out and put her directly before his face. He was fearful of snakes, so when he saw the snake inside the *galip* basket, oh my, he trembled terribly and jumped. The poor man did not stand near the *galip* basket. He stood far away and asked the snake how he had become the father of the boys. The snake told the story to him of how she had given birth to the children.

The snake told the story of how she had slept in the place where the man urinated, and that the man's urine had made her pregnant. When he heard this, he agreed that he was the father of the boys. However the poor man was still afraid of snakes, so he never went any closer to the snake-woman.

They lived for a very long time, then one time the snake told her sons that their father was fearful of snakes and that before long he would burn her with the house. The snake told the boys that when she was destroyed, they must leave this place.

One time when it was good for torch fishing, the brothers took some fishing gear and a canoe, then they paddled away to Boisa [**Aris**] Island. The boys went torch fishing directly between Boisa and Manam islands. It was dark and a good time for fishing. The brothers used the torches and caught many fish.

When they wanted to paddle a little farther, towards Boisa Island, they looked back to Manam Island and they saw a big fire with smoke rising from their home. Quickly, they thought that their mother was in trouble. The brothers quickly paddled toward shore. They arrived at a ditch at **Yassa** Village [Manam Island] and ran up to help their mother.

When they arrived home, they were too late. The house was completely burned and their snake-mother was burned with it. When the poor boys saw this, they cried terribly. They both cried, then they left home and followed the ditch back to the place where they had left the canoe.

They arrived at the canoe, then the big brother told the little brother that they must go to the mainland. So, they paddled towards the mainland.

When the brothers arrived on the mainland, the big brother told the little brother that they could no live together. The little brother must go to the place where the sun sets, and the big brother would go to the place where the sun rises. Before each of them departed, the big brother told the little brother not to worry or to think too much of him. The big brother said that he would do the same.

However, when they began to go their separate ways, the big brother was very worried about his little brother. He cried and walked away. His tears fell and turned into mountains.

The little brother did not worry about his brother or think about him. He walked and walked, then when the sun was setting, he thought of his big brother and two tears fell, turning into two mountains. These two mountains are still there in **East Sepik** Province.

Vincen [Vincent] A. Kiki
Bogia
Madang Province

A960. Creation of mountains (hills); B154. Animal as soothsayer; B211.6.1. Speaking snake (serpent); B754.6.1. Unusual impregnation of animal; B875.1. Giant serpent; D457.18+. Transformation: tears to mountains; D1712. Soothsayer (diviner, oracle, etc.); F401.3.8. Spirits in form of snake; F490+. Masalai; K812. Victim burned in his own house (or hiding place); M341. Death prophesied; P231. Mother and son; P233. Father and son; P251.5. Two brothers; R220. Flights; S112.0.2. House (hostel) burned with all inside; T512.2.1. Child develops from man's urine; T566. Human son of animal parents; T570. Pregnancy; T587. Birth of twins; T685. Twins; X717.1H+. Urination on animal

A Sister Killed the *Masalai* Nokotise

(Wantok 741, September 15-21, 1988, page 16)

Long, long ago in **Mando** Village, in the Asaro District of the **Eastern Highlands** Province, there was a mountain [**Asaro** People]. The name of this mountain is Muvola. Three brothers and a sister lived on this mountain. They had four dogs that lived with them.

They lived for a while, then one time the eldest brother told them that he wanted to go hunting for wild game in the forest. So, he took his bow and arrows then he went alone into the forest. His dog accompanied him and they went away. The name for dog [in my language] is *mondu kandu*.

Deep Forest

He walked and walked until he was in the very deep forest. Along the trail, the dog left him and went first. The dog arrived on a small mountain. This was a mountain where no people had ever traveled. A *masalai* and his wife lived on this mountain. The name of this ghost man was Nokotise.

Only the two of them traveled this part of the forest. They would take care of the marsupials (*kapul*) in this forest and call them their "pigs."

One House

The big brother arrived there later. Before long, he arrived at the marsupials' dwelling. The people of Mando Village usually call this kind of marsupial dwelling a *mosupo*.

Quickly, the big brother went and rattled a vine to make the marsupials come out so that he could kill them. Oh my, when he pulled the vine, the marsupials came out and jumped all over the vines and the branches of the trees.

The big brother saw this and was very happy. He took out his bow and slaughtered the marsupials. It was nearly afternoon, so he wanted to return to the village, but he thought of his dog and called to it. He called, "Usa *mondu kandu*." He called and called, but the dog did not come.

Then the ghost man heard his calling and replied, "Usa *mondu kandu lanimo yowane gulokama yalaka minaiye anomo*."

The big brother heard this and ran a little closer to the mountain to see who it was that was replying to him. He arrived at the mountain and was shocked to see the ghost man (Nokotise) with his dog.

The ghost Nokotise had only one leg and his wife also only had one leg, but the big brother was not afraid of this ghost man. He went directly up to him and berated him for grabbing and holding his dog.

The ghost man replied, "I'm very sorry brother. Why did you want to kill my pigs?"

The big brother replied, "Those weren't your pigs. They were marsupials from the forest."

Ghost Man

The ghost man replied to the big brother, "These marsupials here are my pigs. I take care of them as if they were my pigs."

The big brother said, "Those aren't your pigs. They're from the forest."

They argued and argued, then the sun set and it was nearly dark. The ghost man told the big brother to stay with him, then in the morning they would straighten this out.

The big brother listened and went with the ghost man to his house. The poor big brother did not know that the ghost was lying to him.

The ghost man's wife usually slept in her own house. That night, the ghost man snored very loudly to fool the big brother that he was asleep. The big brother listened and thought that the ghost man was really sleeping, so he fell dead asleep.

However, late at night, the ghost awoke and took a big boulder that he used for killing men. He threw the boulder directly on top of the big brother's head, killing him.

When it was still at night, he went and told his wife. Then the two of them cooked the big brother in an earth oven and ate him. Afterwards, they took the bones and threw them at the base of some bamboos.

Three days passed, and the two brothers and sister at the village had not seen their brother return. They waited and waited, then the second brother told the little brother and the sister to stay, while he went alone to find the big brother in the forest.

He took his dog and went towards the place where the big brother had killed marsupials. He too arrived there and killed many, many marsupials. Later, he searched and searched for his big brother, then he called out for his dog because the dog had left him and gone ahead.

The ghost man heard this and replied. Later, the two of them argued and argued until it became dark. Then they went to the ghost's house.

That night, the ghost killed the second brother and cooked him in an earth oven. The husband and wife ate the second brother, then they took the bones and threw them at the base of the bamboos.

Last Brother

The last brother and the sister saw that the second brother and the big brother had not returned. They thought that something must have happened in the forest, so the last brother told his sister to stay. He took his bow and arrows, then he raced off into the forest with his dog.

He went and went, then he arrived at the place where the two brothers had killed marsupials. Later, the ghost arrived and met him. The last brother saw the ghost and thought that this ghost man must have killed his two brothers, so he was unafraid.

He was angry, then later he fought with the ghost man. They fought and fought, then the ghost man became afraid of the last brother. You know though, ghosts have many powers. So, the ghost won the fight with the little brother and killed him.

He took the little brother's body to the house and told his wife to make a big earth oven again. They ate the little brother, then threw his bones at the base of the bamboos.

Oh my, this time they just slept and ate meat. They never worked hard at hunting small game, so the ghost man's wife was fat, just like a cow. She just stayed in the house. Only the ghost man hunted for game and then brought it home. The woman just slept and ate.

The Sister Waited

The sister waited and waited at the village, but her three brothers did not return. She thought very hard, and she became depressed. She took her net bag, then followed the three brothers into the forest. She had sharpened a stick used for digging sweet potatoes into a fine point and carried it with her. Her dog also came with her. Her dog was not like that of her brothers. Her dog listened to speech.

They followed the trail that the brothers had used. They walked swiftly and arrived at the place where the brothers had killed the marsupials. When the sister arrived at this place, she did as her brothers had done. The dog left her and traveled in the forest.

Searching For the Dog

She searched for the dog, but she did not find it, so she called out, "Lisa _mondu_ _kandu_." The ghost Nokotise heard this and replied, "Usa _mondu_ _kandu_ _lanimo_ _yovane_ _gulokama_ _yalaka_ _malaka_ _minaye_ _anomo_."

The bad sister heard this shouting, then shouted back angrily at the ghost man to let her dog come back to her. The ghost man listened and was terrified. He thought that before, it was just dead men's bodies who had come and that he was lucky to have killed them, but that now a wicked woman had come. This made him terrified.

The sister went closer to the ghost man and began to argue with him, "That isn't your dog that you're holding there."

The ghost man replied to her, "Then why did you kill my pigs?"

Talking To the Ghost

The sister told the ghost, "Those weren't your pigs, they were marsupials from the forest." The ghost man told the sister that he took care of the marsupials as if they were his pigs, but the sister berated the ghost terribly and he was completely dumbfounded.

The sister thought that the ghost man had killed her brothers, so she was not the slightest bit afraid to berate the ghost. They argued and argued, then the ghost became terrified. It was nearly dark, so the ghost told her to go back to his house.

Talking To the Dog

That night, the sister told her bad dog, "I'll fall dead asleep tonight, so you can't sleep. You must watch over me. If the ghost man awakes tonight and tries to kill me or tries to make a fire, you must bite him right in his balls." After she spoke to the dog, she slept.

During the night, the ghost awoke and wanted to take his boulder to kill the sister. However before he could do this, the dog got up and bit both of the wild man's testicles. The ghost man screamed and collapsed.

Quickly, the sister ran to the ghost woman's house and buried the digging stick directly into her belly. Then she took the ghost woman's body down and put it in the ghost man's house. She made a fire and burned the two of them inside the house.

Seeing the Bones

Later, she went to the base of the bamboos and was shocked to see the bones of her three brothers. She took the bones and carried them back to the village.

Beaten Together

She arrived at the village and shoved the bones of her three brothers into bamboo tubes. She performed a song and dance, then all of the brothers came to life again and they all lived with her. Later, they married and gave birth to many children.

Peter Kara Haiyo

Mando Village, Asaro [District]

Goroka

Eastern Highlands Province

B212. Animal understands human speech; B421. Helpful dog; E55.1. Resuscitation by song; D1781. Magic results from singing; D1781+. Magic results from dancing; E55.1. Resuscitation by song; E55.1+. Resuscitation by dance; E440+. Ghost laid by spear/arrow; E446.2. Ghost laid by burning body; F490+. Masalai; F490+. Nokondi; F517.0.1. Person with one leg; G11.10. Cannibalistic spirits; G512. Ogre killed; G512.1+. Ogre killed with spear/arrow; K1868. Deception by pretending sleep; P210. Husband and wife; P230. Parents and children; P253.0.3+. One sister and three brothers; P253.5. Sister avenges brother's death; Q211. Murder punished; Q211.6. Killing an animal revenged; Q411. Death as punishment; Q422. Punishment: stoning to death; S110. Murders; S176.1. Mutilation: emasculation; T100. Marriage; W157. Dishonesty; X712.3.1H. Injury to testicles

Wamati Found a Real Man

(Wantok 742, September 22-28, 1988, page 22)

Long, long ago, in the Maprik [area] of **East Sepik** Province, the women only lived with he-dogs. So at this time, the women only married the he-dogs and lived in the village.

They lived like this for a while, then one morning, a young woman took the pots and went to put them in the river. She took her dog husband and they went to the garden.

They returned to the village in the afternoon, then went down to the river to wash the pots. When they arrived at the river, she was shocked to see that bottoms of the pots had holes.

She was furious and took the pots back to the house. The second time that she took the pots to the river, the same thing happened.

Every time that she put the puts in the river, the pots would get holes in their bottoms. She never told her little sister, or the other women of the village about this. She thought hard and she just left the pots alone.

One time, she took the pots and went to put them in the river. Later, she pretended to go back to the house, but she went to hide in the forest instead. She hid and saw an eel come out from a tree hole. Oh my, her heart jumped. This tree stood in the river.

The eel came out and broke all of the bases of the pots. Immediately, she ran back to the village and beat the signal drum. She called out for all of the women to come, then she told them what she had seen.

Oh my, the village women heard this and their hearts jumped too. That night, they met and decided to dam the river. They pretend to go fishing. They wanted to grab the eel and kill it.

In the morning, they all awoke and went to the river. They dammed the river well, then they gathered many fish. They grabbed the eel and brought it to the village. At the village, they made a bonfire and cooked the eel.

Later, they divided the eel meat and ate. They gave pieces to their dog husbands. All of the women and their dog husbands ate the eel.

Only one woman was given the eel's head. The name of this woman was Wamati. The eel's head did not have much good meat on it, so Wamati was not very happy about this. She took a coconut shell and used it as a basket. She put the eel's head down in it, then put it up in the house.

Later, the eel rejoined and became a very handsome man. Whenever Wamati would sleep with this man, her skin would stay very clean.

This was not so with the other women who slept with their dog husbands. Their bodies had a lot of dust and looked very white. The village women saw this and thought very hard.

One time they asked her, "Wamati, what do you do to keep your skin so clean? We always sleep with our dog husbands and get plenty of dust on our bodies."

Wamati replied, "I don't do anything. I just wake up every morning and bathe, so my skin is clean."

Every morning, when Wamati wanted to go the garden, she would lock up her house carefully before she left. One time, the other village women gathered and talked.

At this meeting, they decided to find out why Wamati's skin was always so clean. Wamati had a little sister who lived with her. The name of the little sister was Sila. They told Sila to go inside her big sister's house and find out what happened.

One morning, Wamati wanted to go the garden so she told her little sister to go with her. However, Sila lied to the big sister, telling her that she was sick.

She said, "Big sister Wamati, I have a headache, so I'll stay in the village and fetch your water."

Wamati agreed to this, then told Sila that she could not open the door and bring the water into the house. She must leave the water just outside the house. After she told Sila this, she gave her one of her pots, then she went to the garden.

[Before] she went to the garden, she went back into the house and took out the ashes from the fire, then she shut the house. Wamati thought that her little sister had listened to her and would do as she had said, so she did not think much about it. However, when she was at the garden, Sila fetched the water and went into the house.

Oh my, her heart jumped right out when she saw this handsome man. The scoundrel was sitting on the bed and [laughing]. Sila asked him, "Hey! How did you get here? It's alright. Come down and fuck me."

The scoundrel went down and had sex with Sila. Later, Sila went out of the house and walked right on top of the ashes that Wamati had removed. When she went out, her footprint was close to the door. She was afraid that her big sister would scold her, so she went out quickly and did not shut the door well.

When Wamati returned, she was shocked to see that the door was not shut well and that a footprint was at the place where one opened the door. Quickly, she called for Sila to come. She asked her, "Who opened my house door?" Sila replied that it was just she who had opened the door and had gone inside the house.

When Wamati heard this, she beat Sila terribly with a knife, making her bloody. Later, she was sorry for her sister and told her that the two of them could both marry this man and live together.

However, at this time all of the village women also knew. All of them wanted to marry this handsome man. Wamati and the little sister wanted to take him and escape to somewhere else, but the two of them thought hard and changed their minds.

Wamati beat the signal drum, then all of the women of the village spoke their thoughts. All of the women were happy. They met with their dog husbands and killed them.

This handsome man married all of the good and bad women of this village and they all lived together. So now, you can see that there are many people in Maprik, East Sepik Province.

I am from **Utamup** Village, by Maprik [**South Arapesh** People], but now I live in Kimbe, West New Britain Province.

Robert Nailabel
P. O. Box 150
Kimbe
West New Britain Province

A1280+. First man; B601.2. Marriage to dog; E32.0.2K. Eel cooked and eaten comes to life; E168. Cooked animal comes to life; E656+. Reincarnation: eel to man; F566.1+. Village of women only; J1146. Detection by strewing ashes (sand); P210. Husband and wife; P252.1. Two sisters; P263. Brother-in-law; P264. Sister-in-law; Q325. Disobedience punished; Q458. Flogging as punishment; S63+. Wife kills husband; S110. Murders; T100. Marriage; T145.0.1. Polygyny; T425. Brother-in-law seduces (seeks to seduce) sister-in-law; W126. Disobedience; W157. Dishonesty

How Did Two Lakes Arise?

(Wantok 743, September 29, 1988, page 19)

Long, long ago, in Yaro [**Iaro**] Village in **Southern Highlands** Province, there lived an old man and his wife [**Wiru** People]. They had two daughters who lived with them. Their names were Ekar and Pepa. The old couple was happy with their daughters, and they lived well.

One day, all of them awoke in the very early morning and went to work in the garden. In the garden, the old father felt ill and told his two daughters that he would go back to the house to rest.

He said, "Take me back to the house, then I'll rest. Leave mama here. She'll take some food from the garden and come in the afternoon.

The two girls listened and took their old father to the house. When they arrived, the old man fell right down at the house door and died.

The girls cried terribly at their father's side and waited for their mother. In the afternoon, the mother returned and was shocked to see the girls crying. When the girls asked why their father had died like that, the mother was very troubled and hanged herself with a rope. She died too.

The girls cried and went into the house. They were shocked to see that their mother was also dead. Their hearts went out. That night, they cried over their parents' bodies until dawn. In the morning, they dug a hole, then buried their mother and father together. Afterwards, they just lived in the village, searching for their own food.

They lived for a while, then one morning they awoke and went to work in the garden. Ekar told her sister that the next day, she would go to sleep in the forest, then hunt for some marsupials (*kapul*). She told her sister to find some sweet potatoes for herself to bring and eat in the forest for when she would become hungry.

Pepa slept that night while Ekar sat alone and prepared the bow, arrows and other things to take into the forest. After she finished, her eyes shut and she too slept.

In the very early morning, Pepa awoke first, took some sweet potatoes and put them into a net bag. She gave it to Ekar, telling her that she must return quickly to the village.

Pepa said, "I'll stay alone in the village, so don't be gone for four or five days in the forest. Go to sleep there, then the next day you must hunt for marsupials and return the day after that."

Ekar took the bow, arrows and bag of sweet potatoes, then she sped off into the forest. She went and went, then when the sun was setting, she arrived at a deep-forest hut. She ate some sweet potatoes then she prepared to sleep.

She awoke in the morning, then she went a little farther into the forest and wiped out a marsupial nest. When it was nearly evening, she took the marsupials back to the forest hut. She was exhausted, so she quickly ate some sweet potatoes and prepared to sleep.

The little sister was alone in the village. She was near the house and she made a stack of sweet potatoes. The poor girl did not know that a *masalai* was spying upon her.

Pepa was a beautiful young woman, so the *masalai* was dying for her. The *masalai* took a piece of detritus [seed?] from a tree, then aimed carefully at Pepa. He threw it and hit Pepa's breast.

Pepa was surprised and looked around, but she did not see anything. She was afraid, then she thought that her big sister, Ekar, had returned to trick her.

After she thought this, she went into the house and waited. It was nearly dark and her big sister had not returned home. Pepa thought hard for a while, then her eyes hurt and she slept.

Ekar, you know, had killed many marsupials so her body was pained. That night, her ears were shut and she was dead asleep. In the very early morning, she awoke before the birds, then she quickly went back to the village with her huge bag of marsupials.

When she arrived at the village, she saw her little sister crying. She asked her why she was crying. She replied that she was just crying.

Ekar began to prepare the food for an earth oven, then she told her sister to help her. Ekar said, "Never mind that 'just crying.' Find some leafy greens and sweet potatoes, then bring them here and we'll make an earth oven and eat. I'll cut some firewood."

The little sister did not want to do this, so Ekar prepared the earth oven by herself. When the food was ready, she removed it and served the sweet potatoes, greens, and marsupials to Pepa. Ekar took it to her little sister, then she told her to stop crying and to eat. The little sister did not want to eat and she kept crying.

Pepa cried and cried, then Ekar became furious. She said, "OK! I think you'll like living by yourself here, so you can keep crying, and you won't be hearing from me. I'll leave you and climb Mount Gilluwe [Giluwe], away from you."

After she said this, she took all of her things and began to walk towards Gilluwe. Pepa saw this and stopped her big sister, then told her that she was not angry with her. Pepa said, "I'm not angry anymore. Come back."

However, Ekar did not listen to her little sister. She ignored her and sped off towards Gilluwe. Pepa followed Ekar and cried along the trail. Pepa kept following her until she caught up to her. The big sister had already gone very far.

Pepa followed her big sister until they arrived at Mount Gilluwe. It was nearly evening and a heavy rain arose. Ekar hugged the base of a tree and the little sister hugged the base of another tree while they hid from the rain. The rain soaked them for a while, then their tears fell. [Two] big lakes arose at this place where the two of them stood.

Now, if you go to this place, you will still see these two lakes there. The names of the lakes are Ekar and Pepa.

Sweeney Unda

Kimbe

West New Britain Province

A920.1.0.1. Origin of particular lake; A1617. Origin of place-name; D457.18.2+. Transformation: tears to lake; F490+. Masalai; M451.1. Death by suicide; P210. Husband and wife; P214.1. Wife commits suicide (dies) on death of husband; P232. Mother and daughter; P234. Father and daughter; P252.1. Two sisters; R213. Escape from home; R260. Pursuits; V61.3+. Dead buried

A Woman Became a Turtle

(Wantok 744, October 6-12, 1988, page 19)

Long, long ago, in the time of the ancestors, there lived a married couple with only three children who lived in a village called **Rempi** in **Madang** Province [**Rempi** People].

The first child was a girl of about twelve years old. The other two were boys. The eldest boy was about seven years old, and the youngest was still a baby.

The parents and their children lived very well together, but the father never hunted for wild game or other food for the household. He just watched the children like a woman, while his wife went hunting for food.

Every day, when the mother went to the garden, she would remove her "grass" skirt, then put it under a banana plant before she worked in the garden. In the afternoon, she would go back to trample the banana leaves, then the skirt would transform itself and become a bandicoot. She would kill the bandicoot and carry it back to the house.

At the house, she would cook some very nice soup, then they would eat. However, the father and children did not know that the mother tricked them. The mother always did this, so the father would think very hard about it.

One day, the mother went to work in the garden and the father stayed at home with the children. That day, the father revealed his thoughts to the children.

He told the children, "You know, we always eat bandicoot. How does mama manage to kill them everyday? She never misses a single day. That's OK, one time I'll find out how she does it."

One day, the father told the eldest boy to follow his mother into the garden to find out what she did. He told the boy, "When mama goes to the garden, you must follow her. Mama likes to go to the garden by herself, so she'll burn you with fire or *salat*, so don't be afraid and come back. You must be strong and follow her to see what she does."

Another day, the mother wanted to go the garden, so the boy followed her. On the trail, the mother took fire and *salat*. She burned him, but the boy did not care.

He was strong and followed his mother. Later, the mother was sorry for him and they walked together towards the garden. They walked to the garden, then the boy pretended that he was sleeping. The mother was very happy and put him into a net bag. Then she put the net bag into another net bag.

The mother did this until the boy could not see her, but the boy thought of what his father had said, so he pretended to sleep as he spied upon his mother.

He watched and saw his mother remove [her] skirt, then hide it under the banana leaves. Then she went to work in the garden. When it was afternoon, the mother prepared to go back to the village. She thought that her son was still asleep.

Quickly, she went to the base of the banana plant and trampled the banana leaves. Oh my, the skirt fell down and became a bandicoot, then the mother killed it. The boy had seen everything that the mother had done.

After the boy saw this, he pretended that he was still sleeping. The mother went to awaken him, then she gave him the bandicoot to hold while they went back home. The little boy did not waste time, he straightened his legs and began to run back first to the village.

The boy arrived at the house, then he went directly to his father and told him what he had seen. He waited for his mother to arrive at the house.

The mother cooked the bandicoot, then put it on plates for the father and children. She left some hot soup waiting in the pot. The poor mother did not know that the father and children had decided to kill her.

They ate, then the father pretended to throw a food-spearing pin down under the house. He told the mother to go underneath and fetch it. The mother did not want to do this. She wanted to send a child down to get it.

She said, "I'm still eating. Send a child down to get it."

The father insisted that the mother must go down and fetch the pin. The poor mother did not know, so she went down. While the mother was under the house, the father quickly took the hot soup in the pot and spilled it on top her.

The soup burned her. She cried out and ran towards the sea to cool her skin. However, she turned into a turtle, then swam out to the sea. Afterwards, the father and three children lived alone.

Every day, the big sister would take the little baby to the beach and call for the mother to come and give her breasts to him. When the mother heard the call, she would swim back and give her breasts to the child.

One time, she told the big sister, "When I travel to other places and men kill me, you'll hear the clouds thunder. This will show that I've died." After she explained this to the girl, she returned to the sea.

The father and children lived alone for a while, then they heard the clouds thunder. The children listened and said, "Oh, mama's dead now." They said this and cried.

Now if you kill a turtle, you will see that it has markings on its back. These marks are from the hot soup that had burned her. Also, in my village, we youths never eat bandicoots because the fathers have tabooed them to us. They say that they are not really bandicoots, but women's skirts.

This story comes directly from my village, Rempi, in Madang Province.

Fidelis and Herman

A2411.5.1. Color of turtle; B211.6.3K. Speaking turtle; C221.1+. Tabu for children: eating flesh of bandicoot; D193W. Transformation: woman to tortoise (turtle); D440+. Transformation: skirt to bandicoot; D642.2. Transformation to escape death; D671. Transformation flight; D688. Transformed mother suckles child; D2074.1. Animals magically called; F960+. Thunder announces death; K1868. Deception by pretending sleep; P210+. Husband and wife perform each other's duties; P231. Mother and son; P232. Mother and daughter; P233. Father and son; P234. Father and daughter; P253.0.2. One sister and two brothers; Q260. Deceptions punished; Q469.10. Scalding as punishment; R260. Pursuits; S63+. Wife kills husband; S110. Murders; T611. Suckling of children

The Turtle Broke the Cockatoo's Head
(Wantok 745, October 13-19, 1988, page 18)

Long, long ago, in the time of the ancestors, a cockatoo that we call _naragemo_, and a turtle were very good friends. They lived in a house and ate together.

One time after they ate in the house, they decided to go hunting for some wild game in the forest. That night, they prepared their bows and arrows.

At the time of first cockcrow, they awoke, took their belongings and some food, and then began to walk into the forest. They walked and walked, then they entered the very deep forest.

In the deep forest, they hunted for wild game, but they did not see any. They became angry and thought of re-turning home. They were also famished, so they were in very bad shape.

However, they were fairly strong, so they walked further into the forest. Oh my, they regained their strength when they saw a breadfruit tree.

This tree was filled with fruits. The branches of the tree were sagging and almost touching the ground. They both felt hungry, so they decided who should climb and fetch the breadfruits. The turtle was completely famished, and so told the cockatoo to climb the tree.

The cockatoo said, "That's alright, poor you, under the base of the tree. Find some firewood to cook the breadfruits. You feel hungry too, huh? I'm a little stronger, so I'll go up." Then the cockatoo raced up to a tree branch. The cockatoo sang and went up the tree.

It went up to the crown of the tree, then began to check on the tree branches. The cockatoo cut down some fruits with its mouth, then it began to rain.

The cockatoo's friend, the turtle, had cut firewood and was ready at the base of the breadfruit tree. The turtle had gathered the firewood and was making a fire, waiting for the cockatoo.

Cockatoos, you know the scoundrels, love to sing. So, the cockatoo was singing on top of the tree. The turtle called out for the cockatoo to come down, but the cockatoo did not listen.

The turtle waited and waited, then became very angry. The turtle was famished, so it quickly threw some breadfruit onto the fire and waited. When the breadfruit was ready, the turtle removed it from the fire.

The turtle was still angry, so it quickly took the good, strong breadfruits and put them by the turtle's side. The turtle put the young, soft ones by the cockatoo's side.

The cockatoo was still singing on top of the tree and did not know what the turtle was doing down below. The cockatoo sang and sang, then it felt terribly hungry. The cockatoo sped down and saw its friend, the turtle.

The cockatoo asked the turtle, "Hey, my good friend, I sang and sang, then I became terribly hungry. Is there some breadfruit ready or not?" Then the cockatoo went to check.

The turtle replied, "Don't worry a bit. Your breadfruits are there. Eat your fill." The turtle told the cockatoo this, but the poor cockatoo did not know what the turtle had done and it ate the soft breadfruits.

The cockatoo filled its belly, then told the turtle that it would go to wash in the stream, "Friend, stay here. I'm going to wash and drink some water, then I'll come back." The cockatoo sped off to the stream near the base of the breadfruit tree.

The poor cockatoo did not know about the turtle's stomachache [hunger] and thoughts. The cockatoo went to the stream and bathed well, then it went back to the base of the tree.

The cockatoo arrived at the base of the tree, then the turtle said that it would go to bathe, "Wait for me here, I'm going to drink water and bathe." The turtle left the cockatoo and went to the stream.

At the stream, the turtle bathed for a very long time, then began to dig a hole in the stream. The poor cockatoo waited for a very long time and became furious.

However, the turtle knew this and quickly went back to the base of the tree. "Pal, I'm very sorry. My body was very hot, so I bathed for a very long time," the turtle lied to the cockatoo. Then the turtle ate some more breadfruit.

However, the cockatoo knew in its heart and mind that the when the turtle bathed, it must have done something while it was there for such a long time.

They talked about looking for lice, so the cockatoo told the turtle, "You have no hair or feathers, so how will I find lice on you? You'll find lice on me because I have feathers."

The turtle replied, "That's alright. I don't have feathers like you, so I'll look for lice on you." The turtle began to look for lice on the cockatoo.

The cockatoo fell dead asleep while the turtle was looking for lice. While the cockatoo was sleeping, the turtle took a piece of wood and bashed the cockatoo's head.

Quickly, the turtle left the cockatoo, fleeing into the stream. The poor cockatoo's eyes spun around, and the cockatoo was half-dead. Later, the cockatoo felt better and got up. The cockatoo thought of what the turtle had done to it, so it was very troubled and cried. The turtle had already fled and was hiding in the hole that it had dug in the stream.

The cockatoo saw that its face was full of blood, so it was furious. Immediately, it called out to its kin and they arrived. Large and small birds both came to the gathering. They decided to begin to search for the turtle and to kill it. None of them knew that the turtle was in the water.

The other birds searched for the turtle at the base of the breadfruit tree, while the cockatoo alone walked away to the stream to see whether the turtle was there. When the cockatoo arrived at the stream, it was shocked to see the turtle digging the hole.

Immediately, the cockatoo called for the other birds to come and surround the turtle. The turtle saw this and called out to its kin, then they too came.

Oh my, a great battle began between the cockatoos and the turtles. They gave it to each other, then the cockatoo's group showed that they had more power and they defeated the turtles.

The turtle was alone now, and they surrounded it in the water. So now, turtles usually live in the water. At this time, the cockatoos and turtles broke apart and they are no longer friends.

You can now see the blood that the _naregemo_ cockatoo received on its head as a red mark on top of its head. [_Naregemo_ is probably the palm cockatoo (Beehler _et al._, 1986: 117).]

Moaitz Justin

Lae

Morobe Province

[Justin Moaitz wrote the ancestor stories in _Wantok_ #682 and 737. He is from Gabsonkeg (**Gabsonkek**) Village, **Wampar** People.]

A2411.2.6.11+. Color of cockatoo; A2433.6.1.3K. Why turtle is water animal; A2494.13+. Enmity between cockatoo and turtle; B211.3+. Speaking cockatoo; B211.6.3K. Speaking turtle; B263.4+. War between cockatoos and turtles; P310. Friendship; Q551.8.7. Punishment: face distorted; R220. Flights; R260. Pursuits; W157. Dishonesty

How Did Lake Dunu Arise?

(Wantok 746, October 20-26, 1988, page 22)

Long, long ago, in the Lake Kutubu area of **Southern Highlands** Province, there only lived a man and his wife in one part of the forest [**Foe** People]. This area has two big mountains on each side that go down very far. The place that the couple lived was a very nice one, but what this place did not have was water.

The area was filled with various kinds of wild game, and they were always sated. However, the meat would become stuck in the poor wife's throat, and she would [practically] die of thirst.

Only the man knew where there was water. So every evening after they had eaten, the man would lie to the woman that he was going to defecate, but what he really did was to go and drink water.

When he arrived at the place where the water was, he would drink and drink, then his belly would become completely bloated. He would take just a little water in a bamboo tube and bring it back to his wife.

The woman would drink the little bit of water and she would still be thirsty. You know, there would still be plenty of meat that would be stuck in her craw. This would happen to the poor woman all of the time. So she would be angry with her husband, but what could she do?

One time the woman made a decision and said, "That man fetches water to give to me every day. Where does he always get the water when he tricks me? Tomorrow morning when he goes to the forest to hunt for game, I'll find out where he gets the water."

In the morning, her husband took his bow and arrows, then sped off into the forest. Before he went into the forest, she told him, "My husband, look carefully and find some game. Don't get lost in the forest." You know what this was: she said various kinds of women's flattery.

She waited very quietly. Then when the sun was in the middle of the sky, she began to look for the trail to the place where the man fetched water.

She followed a small trail for a while, then she saw a tree that was short but large in girth. The name of this tree is _yira_. She went close to it and saw the place where her husband drank water. She saw something black that was stuck on top of the tree.

She was elated and said, "Now I know. This black thing is what that good-for-nothing husband uses to block up the water."

She held it tight and removed it. Oh my, the water poured out, and she drank and drank. Her belly became completely bloated. She wanted to block the opening of the water again, but she was unable to do so. The water shot out strongly, and the black thing would not go into the opening. She tried and tried, but the sun was nearly setting. She was unsuccessful, so she let the water go out like that, then she ran back home and waited for her husband.

Her poor husband had killed many animals, and was walking back home very slowly. The poor man did not know about his wife's mistake.

He arrived at the house, then they made a huge earth oven. They cooked the game, then sat and waited. When the food was ready, they uncovered the oven and removed the food.

They ate, then they began to take the trash from dinner out of the house. They cleaned the house, then the man heard some trash fall on top of the water.

Oh my, he was shocked and asked his wife what the noise was. Then he went to look underneath the house. Oh my, every place was filled with water, and it was rising towards the house. They saw this and wanted to flee, but they were too late. They were completely surrounded by water.

Before long, the water came right up to the house, so they jumped up to the very top of the house. The water kept rising and they jumped to a very tall tree that stood by the house.

But you know, the water made the ground soft. So, the tree broke and fell down into the water. They just hung on to a piece of the tree. The water took them to two different places, then they arrived at a huge lake.

We now call this water Lake Dunu, or _Ibu_ Dunu.

Boncy Kay Masene
Port Moresby
National Capital District

A920.1.0.1. Origin of particular lake; A1011. Local deluges; A1111. Impounded water; P210. Husband and wife; R311. Tree refuge; S62. Cruel husband; W157. Dishonesty

A Ghost Tricked a Mother and Child
(Wantok 747, October 27 — November 2, 1988, page 24)

Long, long ago, there was a woman and her two children who lived someplace. The father had died. The woman's daughter was grown and her son was still nursing.

Only the three of them lived there. One time, they were very hungry for meat. So, the mother told her daughter, "You must take good care of your little brother at home. I'm going to go fishing in the river."

After she said this, she just left them there and sped off into the forest. She walked and walked, then arrived at a river.

A Branch of the River
She fished in the river, then she arrived at a small branch of the river. She followed the stream upwards and did not find many fish. She only found one fish.

The sun was still high, so she kept following the stream, then she met an old man. The old man was not really a man, he was a ghost.

The ghost was shocked to see her, so he asked, "How did you get here? Did you catch many fish or not?"

The woman replied, "No, old man. I think the fish went to hide somewhere else. Why, did you want some?"

The ghost was famished, so the woman was sorry for him and she gave him a fish.

Raw
You know the custom of ghosts, they gobble raw fish. The old man just swallowed the fish as a dog would. When the woman turned past the bend in the stream, the ghost man ate the fish. Then he took his pile of stones and quickly cut through the forest, coming to the other side of the stream.

He sat quietly and sharpened his [stone] knife, waiting for her. When she turned the bend, she was again surprised to see the old man.

He asked her again for fish. She said, "You're just the man whom I saw down below. I already gave you a fish. How many fish do you want?"

The old man replied, "No, that was another man. You didn't give me a fish yet."

The woman thought that the old ghost was telling the truth, so she gave a fish to him. The old man just swallowed it, as he had done with the first fish that the woman had given to him.

He ate the fish, then the woman went past him, fishing as she went towards the source of the stream. When she turned the bend, the old ghost did the same thing. He had cut through the forest and was waiting for her. The poor woman fished, then was surprised to see the old man again. The old ghost asked her for fish again.

Angry

However, this time the woman was furious and told him, "You can't fool me again. You're the just the old man that I met before who pretended that he was another old man. I can't give you any more fish."

The old man insisted, "No, the old men that you met were other old men. I'm a completely different man."

They argued and argued, then the old man told her, "OK, never mind this arguing. What should we do now? Will you follow me or shall I follow you?"

She thought and thought, then she followed the old man. The poor woman did not yet know that the old man was a ghost. They walked and walked, then they arrived at the old man's garden. You know, ghosts' gardens are filled with various kinds of foods. The old man pointed and told the woman to remove the yam that he was pointing to, then he would remove another.

Before she began to remove the yam, the old man told her that she must not break it. She must dig the earth down far, then remove the yam carefully.

She listened, then began to dig down around the yam. She dug and dug, but the old man sang and danced, so the yam went very far down into the ground. The woman kept digging and digging, then she became completely exhausted and broke the yam in the middle.

The old man saw this, and was furious. Quickly, he removed his knife and cut off the woman's head into the yam hole. He took her body and performed a song and dance again, then she came back to life. Quickly, "she" looked for a way to race back home. However, it was not really

the woman. The old ghost had played a trick and taken the form of the real woman.

On the trail, he saw a small, round stone. He took the stone, then he met the woman's two children. The children saw him and thought that it was really their mother who had returned, so they were elated.

He lied to the girl, "Give the boy to me, then go fetch some water for cooking."

He took the baby and sat. He removed a fake breast and gave it to the baby. He took a bamboo tube and made a small hole in the bamboo. Then he gave it to the girl to fetch water.

However, when he sat down, his testicles came out and the girl saw them. She quickly thought that it was not really her mother. She took the bamboo and went to the stream. She cried and fetched the water. The poor girl did not know that the bamboo had a hole in the bottom, so the water did not fill quickly.

At the house, the old man heated the stone that he had taken on the trail. The stone was red and terribly hot, so he opened the little boy's mouth and threw it in. The poor little baby cried and cried, then died. Quickly, he took the little boy and put him in the sleeping place, then he waited.

The poor girl tried to fill and fill the bamboo with water, but she just took the bamboo back to the house. When she arrived at the house, the old man lied to her, "Baby's sleeping. Go to sleep, then I'll sleep too."

The girl went to the sleeping place and saw that her little brother was dead. She cried very loudly, then quickly took some fire and put it to the old man's legs. The old man did not feel any pain or get up.

She carried the little brother's body and raced up a mountain. When she arrived at the top of the mountain, she looked back at the house.

Oh my, fire had engulfed the house. The old man's broken leg exploded. When she heard this, she said, "That's for my mama." Then the other leg exploded and the girl said, "That's for my brother." Later, she was troubled, and carried her brother's body, walking into the forest. She walked and walked, then arrived at a big garden. Her legs were completely stiff, so she slept.

In the morning, the owner of the garden with his dog came and saw the two of them lying there. He awakened the girl, then she told him the story of what had happened. The man was very sorry for her and helped her to bury her little brother's body.

Later, he took the girl to the house and married her. They were happy together and raised many children.

Jossie H. Manua

P. O. Box 262

Goroka

Eastern Highlands Province

[Jossie Manua (or Manuo) wrote the ancestor stories in *Wantok* #372, 725, 799, and 1048. He is from the **Kamano** People.]

D983.2. Magic yam; D1781. Magic results from singing; D1781+. Magic results from dancing; E55.1. Resuscitation by song; E55.1+. Resuscitation by dance; E261.4. Ghost pursues man; E425.2.1. Revenant as old man; E446.2. Ghost laid by burning body; E541. Revenants eat; F419.4K. Spirits eat food raw; H46.1+. Revenant recognized when it devours raw flesh; H1023.2.4. Task: filling a bottomless water tube; H1100+. Task: digging a long yam without breaking it; K1930. Treacherous impostors; P210. Husband and wife; P230. Parents and children; P231. Mother and son; P232. Mother and daughter; P253. Sister and brother; Q211. Murder punished; Q325. Disobedience punished; Q414.0.12. Burning as punishment for murder; Q421. Punishment: beheading; R213. Escape from home; R260. Pursuits; S112. Burning to death; S133. Murder by beheading; T100. Marriage; T611. Suckling of children; V61.3+. Dead buried; W11. Generosity; W126. Disobedience; W157. Dishonesty; X712.3H. Testicles; X743H. Humor concerning exhibitionism

A Woman Married a Snake

(Wantok 748, November 3-9, 1988, page 20)

Long, long ago, in the Kabum [Kabwum] area of **Morobe** Province, there was a village called Sambayo [**Sambori**], near Malandum [Melandum] Village [**Komba** People]. A beautiful young woman lived in this village with her parents.

The young woman often liked to travel the forest, hunting for marsupials (*kapul*). Every day, she would go alone, hunting for marsupials in the forest. However, she never killed a marsupial.

One night, she dreamt of a river called Puleng. This dream told her to go very high up, to the source of the river, then she would find many marsupials.

Still Asleep

In the early morning when her parents were still asleep, she awoke, took her net bag, and followed the trail. She walked and walked, then she arrived at the Puleng River.

She followed the river upwards until she arrived at a pond. She went around the pond, then she climbed to the source of the Puleng River. It was then that she found that her dream was true.

Oh my, there were many, many marsupials, just lying dead in the water. She was ecstatic, and she put the marsupials into her bag.

The net bag was completely packed, so she quickly sped off back towards the village. Her parents saw the many marsupials and they were shocked. The two of them asked, "Who killed those marsupials and gave them to you?"

The woman was just happy about the marsupials and she did not want to explain it to her parents. Quickly, she gave the marsupials to them, then she wanted to return to take some more.

However the parents told her, "Don't shake so much. It's OK. Go and sleep, then tomorrow morning you can return and get some more." She listened to her parents and stayed there.

That night, she did not sleep well. She thought hard, then in the early morning, she woke up and cooked herself some food. She ate, then she left the house, speeding back towards the source of the river.

She walked and walked, then she arrived back to the Puleng River. There were no people who lived by this river. She followed the river upwards, then she met an old woman working in a garden by the river. The old woman was surprised to see her, so she asked, "Who showed you the way here?"

She told the old woman that she had followed the river to this place.

Old Woman

It was nearly evening, so the old woman took her and they went towards her house. The old woman's house was in a cave. They went into the cave home. Then the old woman told her, "I have many snake children. They return in the evening. When they come to hold you and shake your hand, don't be afraid." The young woman listened, and they stayed there.

It was nearly evening, then the snake children streamed back to the house. Oh my, when they approached, the house and the ground shook. Their hearts stopped when they saw this gorgeous woman. All of them held her and shook her hands.

That night, the old woman told the young woman to marry her first son. This first snake child looked exactly like a python. The poor woman was afraid, but she did as the old woman wished. She married the snake and they all lived together.

They lived there for a while, then the old woman died. After that, only she lived with her snake husband inside this house. The two of them lived for a while, then the woman became pregnant. Later, she gave birth to a boy.

The boy grew big, then he traveled with his father, hunting marsupials. The mother's duty was to work in the garden by the river.

One time, the father left the boy with the mother, then he went alone to hunt for marsupials. That day, the mother worked in the garden, while the boy went up to the source of the river and dammed it. When the water was swollen, he removed the dam and the water sped down, ruining the garden.

The mother was angry and scolded her son, "You're the son of a snake. Has your papa planted various foods and given them to you? Will you grow up or not?"

The boy listened and was completely ashamed. He cried and waited for his father. In the evening, the father returned. He told his father what his mother had said to him. The snake father listened and was very troubled. Quickly, he ran out and jumped into the river, turning into a real man.

He carried his son, and the two of them went past Mount Kirin, fleeing the mother. They walked and walked, then it became dark and they slept by the mountain.

Before dawn broke, they awoke and kept going. However, the mother was crying and following them. She kept crying and following them. Then she cried and shouted, "You two stand there, then I'll come and we'll all go together."

The boy heard his mother's voice and told his father, "Hey, papa, I heard mama's voice. I think mama's following us."

The father lied to him, "No, don't worry about mama. That's a _ningon kotingon_ bird calling."

After the father had fooled the boy, they kept speeding away. They walked and walked, then they arrived at a place called Kumba [**Kumbip**]. At that time, the sun had set and it was nearly dark.

Still Following

The boy put his hand on a stone, and it turned into a stone house. He and his father went inside and slept in the house. The next morning, they awoke and kept fleeing.

The poor mother was worried and kept following them. She followed and followed, then she arrived at the stone house. She saw her son's hand marks on top of the stone house, and she cried terribly. The mother slept [there], then in morning she awoke and kept following the father and son's footsteps.

However, the father and son had already arrived at Mount Sarawaget [Saruwaged] in the area of the cold Kabum Mountains. At this time, the mother also arrived near them and cried with them in the [Komba] language.

The father heard her voice and immediately told his son to become a fuzzy-leafed tree that we call _sago_ [fig]. Then the father became the sun.

Edible Fig Leaves

Before long, the mother arrived at the base of the fig tree. The mother cried terribly. She took the stick that she had used for walking up the mountain. She shot the stick up into her head, then she turned into a tree. Her breasts became stones. Water would always fall from these stones. These two trees and the stones are still at this place. It is from this origin that now the sun shines upon them first, then later it rises to us.

I am a boy from Morobe Province who now lives at Badili in Port Moresby.

Wipsy Seru
M/Painting Construction, P. O. Box 4249
Boroko
National Capital District

[See _Wantok_ #516 for a similar story.]

A711. Sun as man who left earth; A726+. Why sun shines at particular point first; A941.0.1. Origin of a particular spring; A974. Rocks from transformation of people to stone; A977. Origin of particular stones or groups of stones; B604.1. Marriage to snake; B631.9. Human offspring of marriage of person and snake; D215B. Transformation: boy to tree; D215W. Transformation: woman to tree; D391M. Transformation: serpent (snake) to man; D450+. Transformation: breast to stone; D452.1.1. Transformation: rock to hut; D562. Transformation by bathing; D566. Transformation by striking; D1810.8.2. Information received through dream; D2148. Earth magically caused to quake; P210. Husband and wife; P231. Mother and son; P232. Mother and daughter; P233. Father and son; P234. Father and daughter; P262. Mother-in-law; P265+. Daughter-in-law; R213. Escape from home; R260. Pursuits; T100. Marriage; T570. Pregnancy; T580. Childbirth; W157. Dishonesty

Anger Arose over a Pig

(Wantok 749, November 10-16, 1988, page 20)

Long, long ago, there lived a man named Sukawo. He was from Kamusi [**Kamus**] Village in area of the **Eastern Highlands** [Province, **Gahuku** People].

One time, Suwako [Sukawo] was famished, so he went to his garden to get some sweet potatoes. While he was digging the sweet potatoes in the garden, he thought about going to cook them in an earth oven by the river.

Suwako took the sweet potatoes, then he took some fire from the house of an old man and he began to walk towards the river. When he approached the river, he heard pigs grunting. He pricked up his ears and listened to the pigs digging the earth.

He went closer and saw the pigs, then he salivated about eating pork. The pigs belonged to his brother. Suwako thought that his brother would not become angry, so he took a stone and threw it directly at a big, fat pig. He did not know that his brother loved this pig.

Suakawe [Suwako] killed the pig, then he carried it to the river. He cut firewood and made a fire to heat some stones. He skinned the sweet potatoes, then he butchered the pig and removed its guts. He cooked it with the sweet potatoes.

He finished making the earth oven, then he climbed a tree and sat there, singing. He sang and sang until the afternoon, then he went down to uncover his food.

While he was removing the food, his big brother was going around the headwaters of the river, looking for vines to make a fence. He cut some vines and trees, then he followed the river downwards.

Sukawo took out the food, then he began to gorge himself. Afterwards, his big brother arrived. His brother was famished, so when he arrived, he was elated to see the good food. He also sat down and ate the pork and sweet potatoes. He did not know that he was eating his own pig.

When the big brother asked Sukawo about the pig, Sukawo lied, saying that river had carried the pig down then he killed and cooked it. Sukawo cut the pig, then gave the head and forelegs to his brother. His brother was happy and ate a little, then he carried some to the house. He gave a piece to his wife, then he took another piece to his own house.

The food was very good and their bellies were full, so they sat quietly. That night, all of the pigs returned to the house. However, the nice, fat pig was not among them. The big brother saw this, so he and his wife got up to search for it. They went around calling out for the pig until late at night, but the pig did not return.

The big brother sat and worried about his pig, then he thought about the pork that Sukawa [Sukawo] had given to him. He got up very quietly and went to Sukawo's house to ask about the pig. Sukawo listened and did not speak because he knew that he had done wrong.

His big brother was angry, so he took a rope and bound Sukawo's hands and legs. Then he pulled him up before the leaders' eyes. The leaders saw this and asked what was the matter. The big brother told them that Sukawo had killed his pig. Sukawo was a smart man. He told the leaders that he had given the head and forelegs for his brother to carry away to eat.

The leaders listened and told the Sukawo's big brother not to kill him. Because he had already eaten the pig's head, he could say no more. The big brother listened to the leaders and let Sukawo go free.

This man, Sukawo, was a man of renown in this area. This was because he was a trickster. He lived for a very long time, and he died not long ago.

Robin Inwee Lusoho
Kamusi Village
Goroka
Eastern Highlands Province

J1110. Clever persons; K330+. Thief escapes punishment by feeding owner his own stolen food; K420. Thief loses his goods or is detected; P210. Husband and wife; P251.5. Two brothers; P251.5.3. Hostile brothers; W157. Dishonesty

The Story of the Mundakiring Song and Dance
(Wantok 750, November 17, 1988, page 20)
(Wantok 751, November 24-30, 1988, page 20)

Long, long ago, many, many people lived in an old village called **Kamuar** in **Madang** Province [**Saki** People]. This village is in the Alamani [Almami] Council area of the Bogia sub-District.

One time, a young man thought of going to hunt for wild game, so he took his bow and arrows. He walked and walked, and then he came close to a river. The name of this river is Suanakanam.

At this place, he saw a tree that was bearing many, many fruits. Many of these fruits were ripe, and some were falling to the ground.

The man did not wait. He found some wood and vines, and then he made a platform near the tree. After he finished, he went back to the house.

In the afternoon, when the sun was setting, the man walked away very quietly and arrived at the place where the tree stood. He sat on the platform and just waited until the insects of the evening began to sing, and it became completely dark.

The man sat quietly and waited. Before long, he heard water crashing. He just sat quietly, and then he saw some black things coming out of the Suanakanam River.

The man did not say anything; he just opened his mouth and watched. While he stood near the platform, one of his hands held onto a *tulip* tree and the other hand was at his side.

Later, he wanted to have a better look. He was shocked to see the things coming out of the water and walking near him.

The man's heart jumped right out. "Aaie-e-e-e-ye, the [big?], young tits [lit., "kapok thorns"] are lined up and walking towards me now," he whispered as he trembled. This was because he saw the beautiful women.

All of them held coconut shells in each of their hands as they carried net bags. They arrived, and then each of them hung their net bags on small trees that stood near them.

One woman looked directly at him and went towards him. She hung her bag on his arm. She actually thought that his arm was a tree branch, so she hung up her bag there. This woman and the others held the coconut shells, then looked around, gathering tree fruits.

You know, the women were from a cold place, the river. So, the tree fruits warmed their hands when they held them. Because of this, they blew on them and shook them before putting them in the coconut shells. The man up on the platform did not make a noise. He sat very quietly, just watching.

It was nearly dawn, and almost time for them to return to the river, to their home. They walked back and took their little bags, then jumped back into the water.

The woman who had hung her net bag on the man's arm went to get hers. When she put her hand out to get the bag, the man quickly grabbed her hand. The woman was shocked and shouted. The other women heard her shouting and making noise. They were afraid too, so they sped back down into the water.

The woman tried to escape, so she became various kinds of things, such as a snake, a bandicoot, a [breadfruit], a bird, and many other things. She wanted the man to become afraid and to leave her alone. However, the scoundrel thought intently about marrying this gorgeous woman, so he kept his strength and held onto these things.

The woman kept at it, and then she became exhausted and turned back into a real woman again. The man was elated and he took the woman with him to his house.

At the house, the woman put her two legs straight, and laid them on top of the man's legs. The man's little brother took his bow and played around, searching for little insects on the ground [to eat].

When he approached his big brother's house, he looked inside a little hole in the house. Oh my, he was shocked to see the big brother with this woman inside the house.

Immediately, he sped back to his house and told his parents. The mother listened and did not wait. She cut some food and made some excellent soup, then she brought it to her new daughter-in-law.

The man took the food and gave it to the woman, but she just smelled the food and vomited out the tree fruits that she had eaten. The man was persistent, so later she ate some food. After this, she lived in his house.

One time, the man's mother took her, and then the two of them went to the garden. The old mother searched for food and the young woman searched for firewood.

The young woman finished preparing the firewood, then she went on top of a stick. She sat well on top of this yam stick, then she sang passionately.

The old mother fetched the food. She told her daughter-in-law to carry the firewood, and then they went back to the village. When they arrived at the village, the woman just left the firewood and went back to her husband's house.

The old woman thought hard about what her daughter-in-law had done in the garden. Afterwards, she went to ask her son to tell her the whole story about this woman.

Her son said that the woman did not come from a village near them, that she was from the river. The old woman just listened.

They lived for a while, then one time they made a new garden. After a while, all of the food in the garden was ready to be eaten. The sugarcanes were very plentiful and blocked their way.

At this time, the woman told her husband that she wanted to see her parents. She asked her husband to go with her to her home in the river.

He listened to her, then they went towards the river. They arrived at the river, and then he stood by, while she went into the middle of the river. She turned her net bag into the river, and then she too went down into the river. Before long, she arrived at her village.

She left the bag at the house, then took a *tanget* leaf. She broke a palm leaf shingle from the house, and then she held them together. She went out of the river and saw her husband there, waiting.

She showed the *tanget* leaf and the piece of palm leaf to him. Then she told him that they would go underwater, but he was afraid. She insisted. She told her husband to shove his hand to her side and hold on strongly to her "grass" skirt while they swam.

They swam a little, and then they quickly went down and stood in her village. She went to the house, and explained to her parents that she had come with her husband.

Her father brought a coconut frond mat outside and placed it on the ground. The two of them sat and told their story. Before long, some others from the village ran towards them in battle dress. They drew back their bows and raised their arrows as they approached.

They arrived and scolded the man, "You men from outside think that we're fish, so you often shoot us eels. It's you people who often kill our kin, huh!"

They argued like that, then drew back their bows. The arrows went very close to the man's body, but they did not kill him. They were happy for him, but they did this to show their troubles.

The man trembled and was fearful as he sat by the woman's father. Later, the men decreased their belligerence and went back to their houses. They returned with various foods.

They sang and danced together, and then they brought these things to the man and his wife. The man listened to the singing and he much enjoyed it. So, he told them to teach him this singing and dancing.

The woman's maternal kin listened and told him that in the evening, they would return and teach him. The man listened, and then he broke some dry bamboos and waited.

In the evening, the woman's maternal kin came and gathered, then they began to sing and dance. When they finished singing one part of the song, the man would break a little piece of bamboo and make a mark. He kept doing this until his two hands were filled. From this method, he knew how many parts of the song the woman's maternal kin had performed.

The two of them lived there for a while, then one time, they prepared to return to the man's village, Kamuar. They decided with her kin that when they ate food from the gardens of his village gardens, they must come and sing. They also decided that one group of women must go up and look around. If the food were ready, all of them would go out of the water to sing and dance.

The married couple shook hands with them, then they went up to Kamuar Village. Before long, the food from the garden was ripe, so the two of them planted a tall tree in the middle of the village. They hung up the various foods that they had planted in the garden. The other people of the village also helped them. One man from the woman's village also went to look, and then he returned and explained what he had seen to the woman's kin.

The clan from the Suanakauni [Suanakanam] River dressed very finely, then they came out to sing and dance at Kamuar Village. In the evening, they went out of the water, walking in a line. When they wanted to sing and dance, their in-law filled a bamboo tube with water then spilled it around where they would sing and dance. The in-law did this, following their custom.

At this time too, the woman had a son. This boy was grown a little, so he could walk and talk. His mother dressed him very finely, then they sat watching the mother's kin singing and dancing.

The place was "on fire" when the singing began. They kept at it until it was nearly dawn. They kept singing and dancing, then each of them took some food and left Kamuar, returning to their village in the river.

The other kin had left, then the woman's brother and maternal kin kept singing and dancing. While they were still singing and dancing, the woman told her son to draw back a bow and shoot her brother with an arrow. The boy drew back the bow and watched. When his uncle danced towards him, he just shot his uncle right in his armlet.

When the poor uncle saw this, he left his hand drum and shell cup that he had held during the singing and dancing. The uncle told him, "The story that you have taken will stay with you. I can't take it back to my village."

Then he left the little drum and the shell cup in Kamuar Village. So after this, when people looked at these objects, they would remember that the clan from Suanakanani [Suanakanam] had brought the Mundakiring Song and Dance to the people of Kamuar.

This story and the Mundakiring Song and Dance came to the ancestors of Kamuar Village and it is still there now. So, this story is still there for us. Some villages near Kamuar, such as **Undangokanam** and **Pariakinam**, know this song and dance.

The ancestors and father told me this story, then I wrote it for some friends and kin who wanted an ancestor story that they could read.

Paul B. Mekiah
Auipa Village
c/- L. C. Kabak
P. O. Bogia
Madang Province

A1464.2.1. Origin of particular song; A1542.2. Origin of particular dance; B631. Human offspring from marriage to animal; B654.1K. Marriage to eel in human form; D117.3.1W. Transformation: woman to bandicoot; D191W. Transformation: woman to serpent (snake); D150W. Transformation: woman to bird; D173M. Transformation: man to eel; D211.7K+W. Transformation: woman to breadfruit; D373M. Transformation: eel to man; D610. Repeated transformation; D2126. Magic underwater journey; F725.5.1. Visit to people of village under lake; P210. Husband and wife; P231. Mother and son; P232. Mother and daughter; P233. Father and son; P234. Father and daughter; P251.5. Two brothers; P260. Relations by law; P261. Father-in-law; P262. Mother-in-law; P265. Son-in-law; P265+. Daughter-in-law; P290+. Maternal kin; P293. Uncle; S110. Murders; T192. Marriage by force

A *Masalai* Marsupial (*Kapul*)
Had Sex with a Woman

(Wantok 752, December 1-7, 1988, page 20)

Long, long ago, on Mount Tsaka [Tsak] in **Enga** Province, there lived a man and his sister [**Enga** People]. Their parents had died, so they lived alone.

They had one pig that they cared for very well. The pig never traveled with other pigs. It just slept by the house, and it became very big.

One day, the brother told his sister that he would go to hunt for some wild game in the forest. The sister listened and prepared some food for him. They prepared everything, then slept. In the very early morning, the brother woke up and went into the forest.

He walked and walked, then in the middle of the trail, he was surprised to hear a noise from on top of a tree. He looked up and saw a small marsupial (*kapul*). Quickly, he removed his bow and arrows, then he shot down the marsupial. The little marsupial is called *agata* in my language because the marsupial is very small. [*Angátá* is a tree kangaroo (Lang, 1973: 160).]

The brother saw this and said, "It's very small. Never mind, I'll put it under this tree. If I don't kill any more game, I'll take it back home."

He put the marsupial under the tree, then he kept going into the forest. He walked and walked, then when evening came, he arrived at an old hut. He had made this hut before and whenever he traveled in the forest he would sleep in the hut. He put his things inside the hut, then he cut firewood and cooked food. After he ate, he went to sleep.

He slept until the very early morning, then he woke up and cooked some food. He ate quietly and waited for dawn. Dawn broke, then he took his bow and arrows and left to hunt for game.

The brother was not an ordinary man. He was a terror in the forest, so he killed many, many animals. The next day, he killed more animals. He never gave the slightest chance to the animals. He was elated and thought of staying four whole days in the forest.

The little marsupial that he had killed on the trail had turned into a very handsome man, and went back to the village to see the brother's sister. The marsupial changed his face to be exactly like that of the brother. He walked and walked, then arrived at their home.

He went to the house and told the sister, "I went to hunt for marsupials, but I tired and returned." After he said this, he went on top of the woman and had sex with her. The woman tried to remove him, but she was unable to do so.

The poor sister thought that it was really her brother doing this to her. The man finished having sex with her, then he ran back into the forest and turned back into the dead marsupial under the tree.

The brother did not know that this had happened to his sister. He was very happy that he had killed many animals, so he wanted to return home quickly to show his sister. Quickly, he filled a net bag with the animals and went back home.

He walked and walked, then when he approached home, he did not see his sister. He thought hard and quickly went into the house with the game.

The sister was not in the house. He began to shout, "*Monag! Monag! Monag!*" *Monag* [*Móna* in the Enga Language means "heart" or "liver", i.e., "dear" (Lang, 1973: 70)].

The brother did not hear a reply, so he kept shouting. He shouted and shouted, then he heard a crying sound coming from the place where their pig slept.

The brother knew that something must be wrong with his sister. "*Monag!* Come out quickly and tell me what has happened to you." He told his sister to come out, but the sister did not listen to him. He waited until it was dark. The poor brother's body felt stiff, so he slept.

In the morning, he awoke and did not say anything. Very quietly, he took a stone axe and began cutting firewood to make an earth oven.

He killed their pig too and cooked it with the other meat. When the meat was under the [hot] stones, he went into the house and took all of his clothing. He took these things and dressed very finely, then he began to uncover the earth oven.

He divided the meat well for his sister and himself. He took some of the pig's legs for himself, and placed some for his sister. He did the same with the pig's guts. He cut the head in the middle, then he divided the other meat right down the middle.

After he divided the food, he put his in a net bag. He left his sister's share outside. Then he took a spear and began to walk towards another place.

The sister saw this and went out of the house. She shouted to him, "*Monag, monag!* Come back, come back. Look at me eat the pork! Look at me eat the marsupials!"

However, the brother did not listen to his sister's shouting. He put his head down and walked away. The sister saw this. She took a piece of pork and a piece of marsupial meat, then she followed her brother. Shed cried and shouted, but her brother was already standing on the other side of a river that is near the forests of Laigam [**Laiagam**], Kadep [**Kandep**] and Mount Tsak.

He stood and rested a little, but the fat from the pig and the marsupials was plentiful. It fell down and covered him. He stood and watched his sister approaching the other side of the river.

He wanted to run away farther. He wanted to get the spear that he had planted by the river while he had been resting, but his hand missed and he fell down into a pond.

So now if you travel to this pond, you will see the spear still standing there.

Martin Ratu

Mingondi Health Centre

Simbu Province

A990+. Origin of particular stick; D179.6K+M. Transformation: man to marsupial; E656+. Reincarnation: marsupial to man; K1930. Treacherous impostors; P253. Sister and brother; P253+. Hostile sister and brother; Q211.6. Killing an animal revenged; R213. Escape from home; R260. Pursuits; T415. Brother-sister incest; T471. Rape

The Story of Two Brothers, Muna and Dat

(Wantok 753, December 8-14, 1988, page 20)

Long, long ago, many people lived in a village inside **Morobe** Province, called Lalan [**Lalang** Village, **Tobo** People]. There were also two brothers who lived there. The name of the big brother was Dat and the name of the little brother was Muna. Their parents had already died, so the two of them lived on a hill called Kuigu. This hill is near the big village.

The people of the village often killed wild game for themselves to eat. They were never sorry for the two brothers and they never gave them a piece of meat. The big brother, Dat, did not care about this. But the little brother, Muna, always worried and cried in front of his big brother.

One day, the big brother prepared a bow and arrows, then he told the little brother, "Muna, you're always crying too much. What are you crying about?"

Muna replied, "Dat, Mama and Papa have died. The people of the village often do bad things to us. They kill game and don't think of us, so I think of this and I cry."

Dat was troubled too and told his little brother, "That's OK, don't worry too much about this. Do you think that your big brother is an ordinary man? I'm fairly big now. Tomorrow we'll go hunting for some game in the forest."

The two of them slept, then in the very early morning, they woke up and sped off into the forest. The poor broth-

ers walked and walked, then they entered the very deep forest. At this time, it was nearly dark.

They saw that it was getting dark, so they quickly constructed a hut in which to sleep. They slept, then in the early morning, Dat awoke first. After he woke up, he began cutting and hauling wood. Muna, you know, was a little boy, so he was still asleep.

Dat had already tied a ladder for killing flying foxes [by climbing up to their perches]. Later, he awakened his little brother Muna, "Muna, Muna, wake up and watch me kill the flying foxes." Muna listened and got up to watch, then Dat worked at killing the flying foxes.

The poor brother killed the flying foxes for a while, then he stood on a stone. However, this stone was slippery, so he fell straight down into a bad place and he died.

The little brother, Muna, heard the sound of his big brother falling, so he shouted, "Dat! Oh no, you've fallen."

However, he did not hear a reply. He did not know that his big brother was dead. He thought that maybe it was water, or something big that had fallen and made a noise. He sat and waited for Dat.

Dat's ghost arose and replied, "Muna! Don't worry. I can't worry, I haven't fallen. I brought some flying foxes here, so we'll return home."

Dat's ghost brought the flying foxes and Muna helped him, then they returned to Kuiyu [Kuigu]. Poor Muna did not know that his big brother's ghost was doing this.

When they arrived home, Dat's ghost lied to Muna that he wanted to go urinate. He went to the place where he had fallen and he carried his body back home.

Dat's ghost arrived home, then put his body nearby. Later, he went inside the house to tell Muna that his big brother had died, "Muna, sit down and I'll tell you a story. Don't think that I'm really your brother." Dat's ghost told Muna this, then Muna listened and heard the story.

The ghost said, "Muna, I stood on a stone and was about to kill some flying foxes, but the stone was slippery, so I fell down into a bad place and died. Don't think that I'm really your brother. No, I'm his ghost. You've heard that I fell, but I was tired of you so I hid from you because it would have been bad for you to cry in the deep forest."

Poor Muna cried as he listened. Dat's ghost said, "Stay here and look, I'll go bring my body here." Then Muna stayed and watched as Dat's ghost brought his body and stood it near him.

When Muna saw this, he cried terribly. However, Dat's ghost said, "Don't worry about me or cry. Leave my body here. Cook the flying foxes, then throw a party for me." Afterwards, Dat's ghost blessed Muna.

After he blessed Muna, he took a log and drifted down a river called Borap. He drifted around the bend, then just disappeared. The little brother listened to what Dat's ghost had told him. He tried to be strong and not to worry too much, then he threw a party.

This party drew in everyone from the big village, Lalan. Everyone gathered together and was happy at the party. After the party, they buried the big brother's body. Later, the little brother lived alone for a while, then he too died at this little place where he and his brother had lived alone.

One time, on the hill that they call Kuiyu, my little brother made a garden and found the bones of these two brothers, Dat and Muna. So, my little brother and I strongly believe this ancestor story.

Saliwong Wasiong
P. O. Box 93
Wau
Morobe Province

C612+. Tabu: crying in the forest; E231. Return from dead to reveal murder; E326. Dead brother's friendly return; E425.2. Revenant as man; E545. The dead speak; K1900. Impostures; N339+. Death from slipping; P251.5. Two brothers; V61.3+. Dead buried; W151. Greed

The *Masalai* of Owedelga Wont Pina

(Wantok 754, December 15-21, 1988, page 24)

Long, long ago, there was a man who lived on a mountain near Hagen. The name of the mountain is Owedelga Wont Pina, and the name of the man was Owedelga Mulg Tembi.

This man was not a real man, he was a *masalai* man. His backside had wood growing out of it, and his front had a face, just as we men do.

The *masalai* only lived on this mountain. He often confused people who wanted to cross Mount Owedelga Wont Pina and go to the other side to hunt for wild game or something. Many people who cut across the mountain just became confused in the forest and arrived at another place.

When the place was dark, the *masalai* would go to the gardens of the men who lived near the mountain, and then he would steal their food. He did not just steal food from the gardens, he also often stole pigs from villagers.

You know how *masalai*s are, so the people of the village never found him. When he stole things, he would quickly turn his back, and people would think that he was a tree. They would go around him then leave. After they de-

parted, he would very quietly walk back to his house on Mount Owedelga Wont Pina.

One time, a man went to make a new garden near Mount Owedelga. His new garden was completely filled with various kinds of food plants.

Masalai Owedelga Mulg Tembi had already smelled the plants in this new garden. At night, he woke up very quietly, sniffed around, and then arrived at the new garden.

He began to remove the food plants. After he removed all of the plants, he brought them back and planted them in his own garden.

In the morning, the owner of the garden thought that his plants were still there, so he went to remove the grasses and weeds in the garden.

Oh my, when he arrived at the garden, he was surprised to see that there was not one plant standing there. He was furious. He sat in the middle of the garden and thought hard.

He thought, "Who came and stole my plants?" When he finished brooding, he began to replant the food in the garden. After he finished, he walked back to the village.

When he arrived in the village, he called out for everyone to come and gather. He told them what had happened in his garden. The people of the village listened and they too were furious.

"Which man does this selfish thing? There must be a man who steals food and ruins our gardens. Let's go hide by the garden and see who it is that does this."

They spoke like this, then when it was dark, they gathered and went to hide and wait by the garden. They waited and waited, but they did not see anyone. Later, they heard something crashing towards them from the forest. They waited a little longer, then they were surprised to see the *masalai* man coming. Oh my, their hearts stopped.

They could not believe it when they saw that the back of this *masalai* had grass and wood growing out of it. All of them saw this and were terrified. When the *masalai* turned, they were surprised to see that his face was like that of a real man.

When the men saw this and they immediately ran into the garden, and grabbed him. They tied up his hands and legs well, then they took him to the village.

The *masalai* looked very strange, so they were afraid to beat or mistreat him. Instead, they scolded him, "A man is always stealing pigs and food from our gardens. It must be you who steals these things." After they scolded him, they let him be.

They did not mistreat him. They held him there, then the first Hagen Show [a regular cultural exhibition] was about to happen. At this time, I was still a little boy.

They took *masalai* Owedelga Mulg Tembi to the show and they received money for him. Later, they took him back to the village.

This time, *masalai* Owedelga was furious at what they had done to him. He thought, "I used to hide in the deep forest and stay there, but because of what the people of this village have done, people from all over have seen me." After he thought this, he was very angry.

That night, he broke through the ropes and the fence in which they had put him. He killed all of the pigs of the village. Later, he ran back to his house on Mount Owedelga Wont Pina.

In the very early morning, he took his things and ran away further, to the other side of the mountain. That morning, the people of the village woke up and saw that things had changed a little. They did not hear the sound of pigs.

Immediately, they went outside the houses and were surprised to see that all of the pigs in the village were dead and that the *masalai* was no longer there. They were furious, so they followed the *masalai* up the mountain.

Where would they see him? The scoundrel had made a new home on the other side of Mount Owedelga Wont Pina.

Masalai Owedmulg [Owedelga Mulg] Tembi lived in his new home, and he never stole as he had done before. He lived quietly at his new home.

The story also says that this *masalai* still lives at his home. Possibly, he is finished with this earth. This is a true ancestor story.

John Keka Yaiya
Moika Village [**Hagen** People]
Mt. Hagen
Western Highlands Province

D2000+. Magic confusion; F490+. Masalai; F529.3+. Man with grass growing on body; F521.5K+. Spirit with human front, tree backside; K400. Thief escapes detection; K420. Thief loses his goods or is detected; Q212. Theft punished; Q433. Punishment: imprisonment; R9+. Spirit captured; R210. Escapes; R260. Pursuits

An Ancestor Story from Ikana Village

(Wantok 755, December 22-28, 1988, page 20)

Long, long ago, in the time of the ancestors, in the **Ikana** area, by Kainantu, **Eastern Highlands** Province, there lived two men [**Gadsup** People]. Their names were Karo and Aputa.

Karo was married and had five children. The name of his wife was Uyae. His friend, Aputa, was also married, but he had no children. Karo and Aputa lived very happily in this village. However, one time Karo was jealous of Uyae, so he shot his mouth off about her to the other men of the village.

Uyae replied angrily to Karo, "I never sleep around with men and you just shot your mouth off about me. What you're doing isn't very nice. I think you should just stop this jealousy."

However, Karo did not believe what Uyae had said. He thought that Uyae was lying. Before long, he lifted up Uyae and beat her terribly. Poor Uyae was in pain and cried.

Whenever Karo had this thought and was jealous, he would beat Uyae. He would always do this, so poor Uyae became exhausted and thought of fleeing.

One time, Uyae gathered her five children and told them that she would leave them, "Your papa often beats me night and day for no reason. He also broke my hand, so I don't think I'll live with you anymore. I'll leave you."

Uyae told the children that she would leave the house before Karo arrived. Before long, Uyae met Karo's friend, Aputa. Then the two of them married. Oh my, Aputa was ecstatic and forgot completely that Karo was his friend. Aputa had had a great desire to marry Uyae because he wanted children. His first wife had never had children.

Later, Karo found out that Uyae had married Aputa, so he was furious. He asked Uyae to return, but Uyae would spit upon him as if he were utter trash. This put a fire in Karo's belly, so he wanted to kill Aputa, but Aputa already knew this, so he would hide from Karo.

One morning, Karo took his bow and arrows, then he went to hide by Aputa and Uyae's garden. Aputa thought that Karo could not come in the morning, so he went to the garden with Uyae. However, Karo had already arrived there and was lying in wait by the garden. Aputa told Uyae to remove the grasses, then he walked around the garden, standing up the fence.

Karo saw Aputa go fairly far away, then very quietly he went to stand close to Uyae. He whistled to Uyae, then Uyae turned and saw him standing with his fighting gear. Quickly, he told Uyae to come out of the garden, but Uyae got up and called out to Aputa.

Aputa heard her and knew that Uyae must have seen Karo. Quickly, Aputa went there, then Uyae told him that Karo had whistled to her.

Aputa was angry, so he took his bow and arrows. He drew back his bow to shoot Karo, but Karo jumped about inside the rows of wild sugarcanes (*pitpit*).

Aputa did not know that Karo was hiding inside the rows of wild sugarcanes. He walked quietly to shoot Karo, but Karo was watching very carefully from the wild sugarcanes.

Karo was a very muscular man, so when Aputa drew back his bow and walked close to where Karo was hiding, Karo quietly jumped like a frog and grabbed Aputa's hands.

Then the fight between the two Highlanders began. Aputa tried to remove Karo's hands and shoot him with the arrow, but Karo held him very tightly.

They held on to each other, then fell about in the forest, killing the grasses of the forest and making them dry out completely. Oh my, it was very hot, so they bathed in a stream. They fought until it was afternoon.

You know, Karo was a strong man, so when Uyae saw that Karo was about to beat Aputa, she quickly broke a tree branch and knocked Karo right on the head.

Uyae kept beating Karo's head, but Karo did not care about this. He kept holding onto Aputa because he thought that if he let go of Aputa so that he could beat Uyae, Aputa would take an arrow and shoot him. Because he thought this, he did not worry about his head. A woman from the village came and saw that the tree seedlings were moving. This woman's name was Awa.

Awa walked closer to see and she was shocked to see these two guys. Oh my, they were fighting fiercely. Quickly, she fetched some water and spilled it on top of Karo. Karo was furious, and shooed Awa, "Go away! Don't spill water on me or I'll slip and lose Aputa, then he'll shoot me."

They fought until evening, then their muscles became completely exhausted and they let each other go. Their throats were completely blocked, so they could not speak.

Karo thought that Aputa would shoot him now with an arrow, so he fled to the village. Aputa thought the same of Karo, so he went down another trail to the village.

Karo found out that Aputa was not an ordinary man either, so Aputa kept living with Uyae and he married her for good.

Kura Lao

Ikana Village

Kainantu

Eastern Highlands Province

P210. Husband and wife; P230. Parents and children; P310. Friendship; Q458. Flogging as punishment; R213. Escape from home; R227.2. Flight from hated husband; R260. Pursuits; S62. Cruel husband; T100. Marriage; T145.0.1. Polygyny; T201. Marriage destroys friendship; W181. Jealousy

Two Brothers Killed a *Masalai*

(Wantok 756, December 29, 1988 — January 4, 1989, page 18)

Long, long ago, on **Manubada** Island, just outside Port Moresby [**National Capital** District], there were two brothers who lived with their parents [**Motu** or **Koiari** People].

Before, Manubada Island had many, many people on it, but a big *masalai* snake often came to this island. Every night, it would kill and eat people on the island.

Oh my, this *masalai* snake was not small. It was immense and it had four heads. One head was that of a snake, one was that of a dog, one was that of a pig, and the fourth was that of a man.

The *masalai* snake would use the man's head to look for food and other things. The three other heads were used for killing people. The men of this island always tried to kill the *masalai* snake, but they were unable to do so.

You know, this snake was not an ordinary one, it was a *masalai*. Because of this, when the men tried to kill it, it would quickly run away and hide, so they never found it. Whenever the *masalai* snake would do this, the number of people on the island declined.

One night, the two brothers were asleep. They both dreamt of an old woman. They saw in their dream that the old woman was sitting on top of a grave.

While they were still dreaming, the old woman told them, "Tomorrow in the early morning, you two must kill one of your own large pigs. Cook it well in an earth oven, then bring the meat to the cemetery and give it to me."

In the morning, the big brother woke up first and thought very hard about this dream. He asked his little brother, and the little brother told him that he also had had exactly the same dream. Oh my, their two hearts jumped right out. They did not tell their parents about this dream. They kept it to themselves. Afterwards, they did as the old woman had told them to do in their dream.

The big brother took his spear and killed one of their pigs. Later, they cooked the pig in an earth oven, then they brought the meat to the cemetery.

They arrived in the cemetery. Then they put the pig on top of the old woman's grave and waited. They had not known where the old woman's grave was, but the old woman's ghost took them directly there.

The little brother was afraid and the big brother bolstered him as they waited. Before long, they were shocked to see their pig just disappear. They wanted to flee, but the old woman's ghost came and appeared as a real woman, then she stood in back of them.

The old woman said, "Don't be afraid. I want to help you and the other people of the island, so you must follow me and we'll go to a mountain."

The brothers followed her. They walked and walked, then they arrived at the mountain. Inside the mountain, there was a cave. Quietly, they walked into the cave. Before long, they arrived at the place where the *masalai* snake slept.

The brothers saw this and their hearts jumped right out. Quickly, they turned back and wanted to run out of the mountain, but the old woman blocked their way. The old woman walked close to the snake's fourth head, the one that was human, then she blocked the snake's eyes.

The *masalai* was completely exhausted and was dead asleep. The old woman performed a little magic, then the snake did not think of anything. It was dead asleep like a piece of firewood.

The old woman helped the two brothers, then they cut off the heads of the pig and the dog. Quickly, the little brother also cut off the snake's head.

The *masalai* was in pain and tried to wake up, but it was too late. Three of its heads were already off, so it did not have any strength with only its one head, the one that was human.

Quickly, the old woman left the big brother, then he cut the last head of the *masalai* snake. Oh my, the two brothers were elated that they had slain this *masalai* snake, so they jumped and sang together. They wanted to turn around and give thanks to the old woman, but she had just disappeared.

They took the snake's head that was human, then they returned to the village. A strong rain and wind arose and the ground also trembled. It is the custom of *masalai*s that when a *masalai* dies, this sort of thing will happen.

The people of the village also saw the strong wind and rain, and they were terrified. They thought that the *masalai* snake was coming back to kill them. This was the [same] kind of signal that it was coming.

They were afraid, so they fled into the houses and spied out through the house walls. Before long, the two brothers arrived at the village. When they arrived, the rain and wind stopped completely.

The brothers just ran into the [leader's] house and showed them the snake's head. Later, the two of them told the story of how they had killed the snake. The leader saw the snake's head and believed their story.

He was elated, so the next day, he called out for everyone on the island to gather in the middle of the village. He told them what the two brothers had done, and all of them were ecstatic.

That day, they made a huge party to celebrate the two brothers. Oh my, the young, gorgeous women of the island lusted for the two brothers.

They lived there for a while, then the leader of the village died. The big brother took his place, and the little brother became his assistant.

William Muingnepe
c/- Ruino Brothers
P. O. Box 170
Bulolo
Morobe Province

A515.1. Culture heroes brothers; B15.1.2.2.2+. Four-headed serpent: snake, dog, pig and man; B16.5.1. Giant devastating serpent; B875.1. Giant serpent; D1810.8.2. Information received through dream; D2095. Magic disappearance; D2148. Earth magically caused to quake; D2142.1. Wind produced by magic; D2143.1. Rain produced by magic; D2000+. Mind control; E363.1. Ghost aids living in emergency; E425.1+. Revenant as old woman; F401.3.8. Spirits in form of snake; F490+. Masalai; G346. Devastating monster; G354.1. Snake as ogre; G510.4+. Hero overcomes devastating ogre; G512.1.2. Ogre decapitated; G510.4. Hero overcomes devastating animal; P210. Husband and wife; P231. Mother and son; P233. Father and son; P251.5. Two brothers; Q211. Murder punished; Q421.0.4. Beheading as punishment for murder; S133. Murder by beheading; W27. Gratitude; V61.3+. Dead buried; Z210. Brothers as heroes

The Story of Waifo and the Sago Bundle
(Wantok 757, January 5-12, 1989, page 17)

Long, long ago, a man lived in a village called **Tamrdamaf** in **East Sepik** Province [**Bisis** People]. The name of this man was Waifo. Waifo was not an ordinary man, he excelled at hunting pigs and marsupials (*kapul*).

He never slept with his wife and child lest they counteract his powers at killing wild game. He usually slept in the spirit house with the other men.

The rainy season ended, and it was the time of drought. All of the streams in the forest were dry. Only the big stream had a little water. The meat was also gone from the wife and child's house, so Waifo thought of going to hunt for some game in the forest.

He took his spear and basket into the forest. Inside the basket was his bundle of sago. Wafio [Waifo] walked a long way into the very deep forest, then he arrived at his forest hut. He put all of his things into the hut, then he went to bathe in a stream that was near the hut.

After he bathed, he went back to the hut. Later, he took the basket, turned and smoked. He did not yet feel hungry, so he put the sago bundle on top of a piece of *lim-bum*.

He smoked quietly and waited. When it was dark, he got up to go into the forest to check the bases of sago trees. Waifo had cut the sago trees before and let them lie there. At night, the game would smell the sago trees and come to eat.

He went to check on the first sago tree. There was nothing, so he went back to check on another. He traveled to the bases of all of the sago trees.

However, he did not know that the sago bundle that he had left on top of the *limbum* had turned into a real man. This sago man did not fool around at singing. He sang, "That man, come back to the house and I'll kill him." Then the sago man spoke and sang, and waited.

Near the forest hut, there was a tree that is called *bodohus* in my language. The tree heard the things that the sago man said and waited for Waifo.

Waifo checked on the sago trees, but he did not kill a single animal. He felt hungry, so he walked back to eat the sago bundle. When he approached the forest hut, Bodohus stopped him and asked, "Hey pal! Did you leave something in the forest hut?" Waifo thought and replied, "Uh yes, just some sago that I thought I would go to eat now."

"Pal, your sago bundle is not really sago. It turned into a man. If you go there, he'll kill [you]. I heard him talking, then I waited to explain this to you. If you want me to help you then I will. However, you must pay for my hard work first. Afterwards, I'll take you and leave you at the trail, then you'll go back quickly to the village. Around your neck is a shell. Remove this shell and tie it to me."

Waifo was afraid and just listened. Bodohus took Waifo and left him on the part of the trail where he could arrive quickly at the village.

Waifo told Bohudus [Bodohus], "Don't go back quickly. Explain to me the way back to the village now, then wait until I arrive at the village first. After that you can tell him."

Waifo left Bodohus on the trail, and Wafio went back towards the village. When Wafio arrived at the village, he ran directly into the spirit house and took the ghost masks made of rattan, the wooden masks, and those with one leg [?] that they had sharpened before and put away.

He told them, "If a man follows me here tonight, then eat him. He's your meat." He performed this small song, then he lined them up outside the door of the spirit house, and he went to sleep.

In the forest, Bodohus, the tree, arrived later and asked the sago man, "Pal, what are you doing here?"

The sago man replied, "I'm waiting for the man who came and just left me here, then went to capture game. When he returns, I'll eat him."

Bodohus said, "Never mind wasting your time. The man already went back to the village."

The sago man was furious, so he got up and followed Waifo to the village. He arrived in the village and walked directly up to the door of the spirit house.

Three ghostly guardians had already heard Waifo and were waiting. When the sago man wanted to go inside the house, they quietly pushed him back. He went down to the ground and fell apart, turning into sago.

In the morning, the leaders of the spirit house awoke, made a fire, then sat and told stories. They were surprised to see that a sago bundle had broken apart outside the door of the spirit house. Waifo went outside the spirit house and told the story to them of what had happened to him in the forest.

That is the end of the story, so today we people of Tamrdamaf Village eat good sago and never waste it. This is because sago has a story. All of the leaders with the women and children know this story, so this story is still there.

Paul Le [Lee] Tommy
Shanghai Village
East Sepik Province

C181.2+. Tabu: man not to sleep in same house as women or children prior to hunting; C933.1. Luck in hunting lost for breaking tabu; D215.11K+M. Transformation: man to sago; D431+M. Transformation: sago to man; D950. Magic tree; D1067.4. Magic mask; D1610.2. Speaking tree; D1781. Magic results from singing; E363.1. Ghost aids living in emergency; E384+. Ghost summoned by singing; G10. Cannibalism; N815.0.1. Helpful tree-spirit; P210. Husband and wife; P230. Parents and children; Q53. Reward for rescue; R260. Pursuits; V112.1. Spirit huts

Dukuami Got Revenge against the Enemies
(Wantok 758, January 12-18, 1989, page 16)

Long, long ago, there lived two brothers named Wapindu and Kuyandu. They had a sister who was married and lived in **Saikuare** Village [**East Sepik** Province, **Abelam** People]. Their sister's name was Yaruse.

One time, their [brother]-in-law Suakin went to his wife's village [where the two brothers lived], Saikisi [**Sagasi**], to obtain some sago. Suakin was away for two whole days with his two brothers-in-law from Saikisi. On the third day, he took the sago and returned to Saikuare. Before he left the village, he told his brothers-in-law, "If you want some tobacco, then come see me and I'll give you some."

His brothers-in-law were very happy because they were often short of tobacco. So, the two of them decided to wait until their brother-in-law arrived at his village first, then they would go see him and get the tobacco.

However, when their brother-in-law arrived at the village, he decided with his kin to kill the two in-laws, Wapindu and Kuyandu. They waited for the two men.

Wapindu and Kuyandu waited for one week, then they went to see their brother-in-law, Suakin, at Saikuare Village. They arrived and their brother-in-law was waiting for them. They rested, then their brother-in-law took them to cut tobacco.

When they gathered enough tobacco, they returned to the village. When they arrived, their sister Yaruse was cooking food and waiting for them.

After they sat and ate, she told them, "Eat, then your brother-in-law will take you to the trail and you'll return home."

Their brother-in-law pretended to walk with them to the trail, however the enemies were already waiting. They came out and chased the two of them, killing the big brother Wapindu.

After they killed Wapindu, they chased the little brother Kuyandu down a row of sago palm trees. While Kuyandu was running, he saw women working at rinsing sago, so he went and fell close to them. The women saw this and were sorry for him. They got up and covered him with sago pulp.

After the women hid Yukandu, they pretended to rinse the sago. Before long, the enemies ran and arrived there. They saw the women and asked, "Did you see a man running here or not?"

The women lied, "No one came here. He must have gone another way."

The enemies listened and followed another trail. When they were fairly far away, Kuyandu got up and fled back to his village. While he was running, he turned and saw his brother, Wapindu, following him. This was Wapindu's ghost. The enemies had killed the real man.

When they approached the village, Kuyandu turned and saw Wapindu's ghost hanging from a vine on a tree. Kuyandu saw that Wapindu's ghost was angry. The ghost said, "What are you looking at? Go to the house now and get some facial adornments to put on."

Kuyandu listened and went to the village. When he arrived, their father asked him, "Where is Wapindu? You've come back alone."

While the father was talking, some people from Mambaure [**Mambauro**] Village carried Wapindu's body back. They arrived in the village and called out for his kin to come and take his body.

They were surprised and went to take Wapindu's body to the house, where they put him on a bed. Wapindu's wife took her baby and lay him on top of his father's body to drink his blood. The baby, Dukuami, drank his father's blood until dawn.

When dawn broke, they buried Wapindu's body. They lived for a while, then the baby, Dukuami, grew up until he was about thirteen.

One day, they heard that there would be a big festival happening at Saikuare Village. When the time of the festival was near, everyone in the village straightened out their adornments and got ready.

When the time of the festival approached, Dukuami's grandfather called to him. He told him to go to the forest and cut a piece of bamboo. Dukuami listened and cut a piece of bamboo, then he returned to the village. Afterwards, his grandfather made a spear for him.

They sat and heard the men calling, "Tomorrow, we'll go to the festival." Then the old grandfather sent Dukuami to go get ginger with which he would spit upon Dukuami's spear.

After the grandfather applied the ginger onto his spear. He told Dukuami, "If you stand up, you'll see two men who will come outside and go around a platform, then they'll bring another two men outside. These two men will go back, and another two men will come out to sing and dance. It is these two men who killed your father."

Dukuami listened to what his grandfather told him, then he carried his spear and followed the people to the festival. However, the people saw him and said, "Little boy, where do you want to go? Don't you want to stay in the village?"

They scolded Dukuami, but he was persistent and he followed them away. They arrived at the festival grounds. Dukuami took a good position and stood watching.

Two men held their spears and came outside. They went around the platform, then they went inside again. Next, two other men came outside then sang and danced. They went inside to fetch two other men. When Dukuami saw these men, he knew that they were the men who had killed his father.

They sang and danced around the platform. When they were about to go back, Dukuami threw his spear, shooting one of them. The man fell down and died. When Dukuami saw this, he went underneath the legs of the people, fleeing back to the village.

Dukuami arrived at the village, and his grandfather asked him, "What happened? Did someone die?"

Dukuami replied affirmatively. The old man listened and was very happy. Dukuami cut wild taro leaves and put them on all of the big marks [?]. His grandfather beat the signal drum.

The people who were at the festival grounds heard this and said, "His son killed him, so he returned to the village to beat the signal drum."

Later, Dukuami's grandfather tied up pigs, and then he prepared a feast. Dukuami became a strong man at fighting with spears in this village. Never mind where there was a big fight, he could go alone to the fight. Dukuami was the king of fighting with spears in Siakisi [Sagasi] Village.

Lawrence Wapindu told this ancestor story and I, Peter Theodore, wrote it down. We are from Saikisi Village, in the Maprik area of East Sepik Province. Now we live in Kieta, North Solomons Province.

Peter Theodore, Jack Kumun and Lawrence Wapindu
P. O. Box 301
Kieta
North Solomons Province

[For a similar story, see *Wantok* #736.]

D967+. Magic ginger; D1041. Blood as magic drink; E226. Dead brother's return; E261.4. Ghost pursues man; E545. The dead speak; K914. Murder from ambush; K2211.1. Treacherous brother-in-law; P210. Husband and wife; P233.6. Son avenges father; P253.0.2. One sister and two brothers; P263. Brother-in-law; P291. Grandfather; Q211. Murder punished; Q411. Death as punishment; R100. Rescues; R210. Escapes; R220. Flights; R260. Pursuits; S55+. Cruel brother-in-law; S110. Murders; V61.3+. Dead buried

Ganeme Thought that a Net Bag Was a Woman

(Wantok 759, January 19-25, 1989, page 25)

Long, long ago, there was a man who lived in **Sipulda** Village, in **Eastern Highlands** Province [**Yagaria** People]. This man's name was Ganeme.

He had no kin and he lived alone in this place. This place was on top of a mountain, so he made his garden below in the sword-grasslands.

He always wanted to go to the garden, so he would leave his home and walk past the house of an old couple along the trail. Then he would arrive at his garden.

When Ganeme walked down the mountain, he would carry a piece of firewood too. When he passed the old couple's house, he would throw it by the house and shout, "Hey old folks, here's a piece of firewood."

In the afternoon, he would take some food from his garden. He did not have a net bag, so he would make a basket from wild sugarcane leaves (*pitpit*), and put the food inside. When he walked back to his home, he would leave some food by the old couple's house.

He would always do this, so the old man told his wife, "You must make a net bag for him. He always carries food in a basket, and the food falls about on the trail."

The old woman listened and made a very nice net bag, then she put it away. Ganeme arrived at his garden, then in the afternoon, he brought food to give to them. When he was about to leave, the old woman called out for him to come, so that she could give the net bag to him.

The old woman said, "You always bring food in the basket and the food falls on the trail. Now you have a net bag and the food won't fall."

Ganeme was very happy with his new bag and he carried it away. He thought the old woman had given a woman to him because he had never seen a net bag before. He hauled the net bag and basket of food up the mountain, then arrived as his house.

He put down the net bag and basket of food, then he caught his breath and told the net bag, "Take the food basket up to the house. I'll go fetch some firewood for us to cook."

After he said this, he went to search for firewood. He was very happy and fetched the firewood, then he walked back. He arrived back at the fence to see that the net bag and food basket were still lying on the ground.

He thought, "What kind of woman is this, that she didn't listen to me?"

Ganeme spoke to the net bag again, "You don't want to go up to the house, huh? That's OK, we'll go inside together." He lifted the net bag and food basket, then he carried them into the house.

Ganeme made a fire, then he cooked sweet potatoes. He spoke to the net bag, but the net bag did not reply at all. He went outside and stood, thinking.

He said, "Oh my, what kind of woman is that? The old couple must have tricked me and given me the skin of a dead woman."

After he ate, Ganeme told the net bag to sleep close to the fire, and he would go to sleep in another room. In the morning, he awoke and saw that the bag was still in the same place where he had put it on the previous day.

Ganeme made a fire and cooked sweet potatoes. He told the net bag, "Watch the sweet potatoes. I'm going to check on some of my traps."

He left the house and went to check on his traps. He returned to the house and smelled the sweet potatoes burning. When he went inside the house, he saw the net bag lying there and the sweet potatoes burning in the fire.

When Ganme [Ganeme] saw this, he was furious and he shouted at the net bag, "What kind of woman are you? If you want to go back to your parents, OK you can go now." Then he went inside, pulled the net bag and threw it outside of the house. Ganeme found some parts of the sweet potatoes that were not burned and he ate them. He got up and went outside. He pulled the net bag on the ground and walked down the mountain. He pulled it through the mud, and the poor new bag became ruined on the ground.

He arrived at the old couple's house [and said], "You're a crazy woman. Why did you give this trashy woman to me?"

The old woman went to look. She said, "That's not a woman. That's a net bag. You can fill it with things and carry it around."

The old woman talked and shouted, then the old man came. He heard this and asked Ganeme, "You want a woman, huh? OK, go prepare a bride price, then bring it here."

Ganeme listened and went back to his house. He tied up five of his large pigs. He took bird feathers, bird-of-paradise feathers, and traditional shell wealth. Then he brought them back to the old couple.

The old couple were very happy with these things, but the old man told Ganeme, "Go back and kill a huge pig, then bring it here in the afternoon."

The poor man listened and went to kill a pig. He carried it back to their house. They butchered it, then they made a big earth oven and they ate.

In the morning, the old man told Ganeme to go back and kill two pigs, then carry them there. He did this, then the old couple also killed two pigs and they made a big feast again. The old man fetched his daughter and gave her to Ganeme. They married and lived together.

Dugweri Nicklas

P. O. Box 2067

Boroko

National Capital District

B871.1.2.1. Giant hog; F562.7K. People live in mountain top; J1770+. Net bag mistaken for woman; P210. Husband and wife; P232. Mother and daughter; P234. Father and daughter; P261. Father-in-law; P262. Mother-in-law; P265. Son-in-law; Q40. Kindness rewarded; T52. Bride purchased; T100. Marriage; W11. Generosity

Kumanyagl Died near Bundi

(Wantok 760, January 26, 1989, page 18)

A big moon was lit very brightly and there was a gentle breeze. The little birds celebrated the day by singing their last songs, then they went to their nests. The young children of Siako [**Siago** Village] were just sitting by an earth oven that still had hot stones [**Kuman** People, **Simbu** Province]. Each of them held a pig bone and was eating, telling stories, and celebrating a good month.

When they heard a noise from behind the sword-grass house, some of them pricked up their ears. "Hooray, Kuagle has arrived!" They shouted and were happy that it really was their mother. Kuagle came closer. She had a piece of tobacco in her hand. She smoked it, then told the children this ancestor story.

In the time of yore, there was a village. The name of this village was *Endinaigigugl*. The meaning of this word is, "Tree Bark." This was because near this village, there were huge casuarina trees growing. At night, the place was pitch black. Before, this place was very well known because people always went there to make huge feasts and festivals. People from various villages would file in and celebrate together there.

There was a leader who lived in this village. His name was Kumanyagl. He was renowned for killing many pigs and cassowaries. Because of this, the people were often happy for him and recognized him as one of their leaders.

Kumanyagl did not have enough adornments for a festival. This was because he had many sons and he had shared the adornments with them until there were no more. He saw this and thought of going hunting for marsupials (*kapul*) and birds in the forest [to use the skins and feathers as adornments].

He awoke in the very early morning. He carried his bow and arrows, and some sweet potatoes too, then he left the village. His two dogs got up and followed him into the forest. Kumanyagl went through the forest until he arrived in the area by Kidrupamaglm [**Kindarupa** Village, **Gende** People, **Madang** Province]. This village is near Bundi.

The poor man, he traveled for two whole weeks in the forest, but he did not find a single marsupial or bird. The sweet potatoes that he had brought with him were gone and he was famished. The cold was also ruining him in this part of the forest.

The dogs tried to kill some game, but the hunger and cold were ruining them too, so they did not act smartly. They just whined and went close to each other.

Kumanyagl saw this and gave up. He went to try again on another mountain. They went towards another mountain and hunted for game, but they did not find anything. It was dark, and Kumanyagl and the two dogs were famished, so they fell down asleep on the grass. The dogs howled for a while, then they tired and just slept by their master.

They slept for a while, then a cold wind arose and braced Kumanyagl's body. He opened his eyes and saw a man standing there. He turned his head and looked in another direction, but when he turned again he saw the old man still there standing and watching.

Kumanyagl was not afraid. He got up and asked the man for some food. He said, "Friend, we've come a very long way. Our food is gone and we're famished."

He did not know that this was not a real man, but a ghost. The man confused Kumanyagl's thinking, then he told them to follow him to his house. Kumanyagl and the dogs followed him away.

They arrived at the house, then the ghost made some very nice soup and gave it to them. The ghost had taken Kumanyagl's belly and made soup with it, but poor Kumanyagl did not know it. He thought that he was eating game meat, so he swallowed it.

When Kumanyagl finished eating, he wanted to feel his belly, but it was not there. He was surprised to see this, so he tried to run away but he missed and fell into a pond and died.

His dogs stood by the water and waited to see their master come out of the water, but he did not come out again. They stayed by the water for three whole days.

The dogs followed the water away. They walked and walked, then darkness fell on them on the trail. The next day, they kept walking and they arrived at a small village. The children of the village often hunted for frogs in the moonlight. Six months had passed, and the moon was very bright, making the area quite clear. The children went to the river and hunted for frogs. The two dogs saw them and barked a little.

The children quickly saw the dogs and ran to tell their parents. The parents listened and followed their children there. They arrived at the river and saw the two dogs. The two dogs whined a little, and ran back and forth. They wanted the men to follow them back to the forest. So, two strong men followed the two dogs on the trail from which they had come.

When they arrived at the pond, the two dogs barked very loudly. Kumanyagl's body drifted and came up to the surface of the water.

The next day, there was a big festival occurring at **Sikindiwai**. So late at night, this group of people from the Bundi area took Kumanyagl's body to Skindiwai [Sikindiwai]. Oh my, when the people of the village heard that their leader was dead, they were frightened and ran away. However, they returned together and were very sorry for their leader. They also cried and mourned for the two dogs, and for the people from Bundi who had found Kumanyagl's body.

They made a huge feast for the group from Bundi and for the two dogs. After this, there was no more fighting between these two places.

John Mays Bonma
Simbu Province

A1670+. Origin of peace between two peoples; B301+. Faithful dog leads to recovery of master's body; D2000+. Magic confusion; E250. Blood-thirsty revenants; E425.2. Revenant as man; G51. Person eats own flesh; G60. Human flesh eaten unwittingly; P230. Parents and children; P233. Father and son; Q53+. Reward for retrieval of body; R220. Flights

A Man Married a Marsupial (*Kapul*) Woman
(Wantok 761, February 2, 1989, page 20)

Long, long ago, in the time of the ancestors, there lived a married couple. The husband's name was Wakosa and his wife's name was Huya. They lived in **Matakiripa** Village, in the Lufa [sub-]District.

They lived there for a while, and they had a boy named Inivide. After a while, the father, Wakosa, died and only the two of them were there.

Inivide and his mother lived for a while, then he became a big boy. One time, the men of the village decided to go to the forest to hunt for marsupials (*kapul*). In the very early morning, the men awoke and left the village for the deep forest.

Little Inivide saw this and went to ask his mother, because he also wanted to go hunting for marsupials. His mother said no because Inivide was too little and could not kill marsupials. However, Inivide persisted, so his mother agreed. The mother prepared sweet potatoes and a [bow] and arrows, then Inivide left the village and followed the men into the forest.

The men had already left and Inivide could not find them, so he went by himself on another trail. When he arrived in the deep forest, he made a place to sleep, then he made some traps. He made many, many traps. When darkness came, he returned to the place where he had prepared to sleep for the night.

Inivide ate, then he slept and waited. He heard a loud noise that was from far away, so he thought hard. The noise came close and Inivide was surprised to see a very beautiful woman.

Inivide was terrified. He thought that it was a *masalai* who had come to eat him. The woman saw Inivide's fear, so she told him not to be afraid.

She said, "Go to sleep. I'll watch over you." However Inivide was still afraid, so he just pretended to sleep with his eyes half-open so that he could watch her.

She sat down and watched Inivide while she made something nice for Inivide to put on his body. She made a Jew's harp, a comb, armbands, and other adornments until dawn broke.

When dawn broke, she told Inivide to climb up a tree and fetch a bird. The little bird was perched upon the branch of a tree that was very high.

Inivide listened and went up the tree. He climbed and climbed, then he arrived at the branch where the bird was perched. He was afraid though, because the tree branch was too small. If he moved, it would break and he would fall down.

She shouted and shouted up to Inivide that he could not come down. When Inivide wanted to get the bird, he fell down directly to the place where she was standing.

He fell down and he became a very handsome man. He put on the adornments that she had made at night. She told him to go check on the traps. Then he saw many, many marsupials hanging in them. He brought the marsupials back and she was very happy.

The woman told Inivide that they would marry. She explained to him, "When we live in your village and the men give you marsupials for you to butcher, you must not use this knife to cut anything else. Then you must give it to me."

She explained this, then they walked back to the village. They arrived there in the evening. Inivide's mother was watching the trail and she asked all of the men who returned from the forest, "Have you seen my son or not? He went to the forest and has not returned yet, so I'm trying to find him."

Every man replied that he had not seen her son. The mother was very troubled, so she began to cry. When Inivide and his wife approached the village, he told his wife, "You must go down to the back of the house and wait. I'll play the Jew's harp and go down to mama's house."

When his mother saw the two of them, she cried and asked whether they had seen her little son, Inivide. The man replied, "That's just me, Inivide. Whom are you looking for that you're crying?"

The mother heard this and said, "Don't try to fool me. You're a big man, and my son is just a little boy."

Inivide replied again, "It's just me. Look at the marks from sores upon my body. They're from when I had cried for sweet potatoes and you burned me in the fire. Those marks are here."

The mother saw the marks and believed him. She went and held her son, crying terribly. They arrived at the house, then Inivide told the story of what had happened to him. They made a big party with the marsupials that they had brought from the forest.

Inivide and his wife lived in the village for a while, then she gave birth to a son. The baby's name was Iraiko. They lived well together in this village. When Invide [Inivide] butchered a marsupial with the knife, they would eat and never use the knife, then the knife would be given to the wife.

One time, the man forgot his promise. He butchered a marsupial, then he butchered a pig and gave it to the wife.

When she ate the pork, her skin jumped and she knew that Inivide had broken his promise by butchering a pig with the knife that he had used to cut the marsupial.

Inivide left for the garden to fetch some food. The wife took the baby and told Inivide's old mother, "My breasts hurt. We're going up a little ways to bathe in a forest stream." Then she walked with her son into the forest.

When Inivide returned to the house, he saw that his wife was not there, so he asked his mother. His mother told him that his wife's breasts were pained, so she had gone to find some water to put on them.

Inivide listened and followed his wife. He followed and followed, then he saw the two of them and shouted, "I know that I was wrong. OK, if you want to go, then give the baby to me and you can go alone."

She replied, "Come and we'll go up the Haeroto Stream, then I'll put water upon my breasts. Later, we'll go back to the village."

After she said this, she went up a mountain called Kopami. The little baby cried, and she nursed him. Then she took a thorn used for making net bags, and she cut the baby's tongue a little. She told him, "Go to a small tree and try to cry."

Then the little baby turned into a bird and flew away, perching on a small tree. The bird cried, "Iraiko kori kori."

The mother told him, "OK, come back and sleep in the net bag."

The two of them sped away, up a mountain called Hairasero, and then the mother hung up the net bag with the baby. She turned into a marsupial called _hama_. [_Hamú_ is a rodent or small animal.] Then she went inside a cave.

When Inivide arrived at the mountain, he saw the net bag hanging there, so he went up and took it. When he took the bag down, the little baby turned into a bird and flew away. It perched on a tree and sang out, "Irako [Iraiko], kori kori."

The father was very troubled, so he cut his hands and feet then threw them down into the cave where the mother had turned into a marsupial.

If you go to **Litipinaga** Village, you will see the cave where the mother had become a marsupial. You will also see the place where the mother gave her breast to the baby. You will also see the footprints, the mother's skull, and the tree where she had hung her net bag.

This bird still calls and its cry is very beautiful. It is sweet like music. The men of this village never kill this bird, and we never kill the marsupial either because she is our ancestor.

This is an ancestor story from us, the people of Litipinaga, from the Lufa [sub-]District of **Eastern Highlands** Province [**Yagaria** People].

Benson Konofaro

P. O. Box 437

Badili

Central Province

B2+. Marsupial totem; C200+. Tabu: cutting wrong animals with special knife; C841+. Tabu: killing certain marsupial; C841.12K. Tabu: killing certain birds; C841.7. Tabu: killing totem animal; D56.1. Transformation to older person; D179.6K+W. Transformation: woman to marsupial; D150B. Transformation: boy to bird; D350B. Transformation: bird to boy; D560+. Transformation by falling; D958. Magic thorn; D1860. Magic beautification; D1890. Magic aging; P210. Husband and wife; P231. Mother and son; P233. Father and son; P262. Mother-in-law; P265+. Daughter-in-law; P292. Grandmother; P681+. Mourning customs: self-mutilation; R213. Escape from home; R260. Pursuits; S160.1. Self-mutilation; S161. Mutilation: cutting off hands (arms); S162. Mutilation: cutting off legs (feet); T100. Marriage; T580. Childbirth; T611. Suckling of children

A Snake Swallowed Hullywa

(Wantok 762, February 9, 1989, page 24)

Long, long ago, there lived a man named Hullywa. One time, in the very early morning, he awoke, took his canoe, and went to look at the basket traps that he had placed in the stream. This stream was in a bad place. There was a huge snake that lived in the place where Hullywa had put his baskets.

Poor Hullywa did not know that the snake lived in this stream. He arrived there and put the canoe aside. He went down into the water to fetch the baskets.

When Hullywa went down into the water, he trampled the snake's back. He felt the snake's skin and he thought that he had trampled a fish.

The snake rose and surrounded Hullywa's legs, then they began to fight in the water. They fought and fought, then the snake won and swallowed him. However, Hullywa did not die. He went down and lay in the snake's belly.

The snake left the water and went onto the ground. It came up slowly, pulling its huge belly up to the base of a tree, where it slept.

Hullywa stayed inside the snake's belly. He felt terribly cold, so he opened his eyes. His thoughts returned to him and he recognized that he must have been lying inside the snake's belly. He lay there and thought of a way to get out again. Then he thought of a piece of _kina_ shell that he had put in his ear [as an earring].

He took out the _kina_ shell and cut the snake's belly. He went out and fled back to the village. He arrived and explained to the people about the snake that had swallowed him.

His wife and children had thought that he had slept in the forest that night. They were surprised to hear his story. They were very troubled and said, "Oh my, you died and came back again."

Timothy Banje

Gaigorobi [**Gaikarobi**] Village [**Iatmul** People]

Pagwi

East Sepik Province

B875.1. Giant serpent; F911.7. Serpent swallows man; F912.2. Victim kills swallower from within by cutting; P210. Husband and wife; P230. Parents and children; R210. Escapes

A Man Married Flying Fox Women

(Wantok 763, February 16, 1989, page 20)
(Wantok 764a, February 23, 1989, page 20)

Long, long ago, in the time of the ancestors, in **Tofungu** Village, there lived an old woman with her son his wife. The couple had a baby boy.

When the man and his wife went to hunt for wild game in the forest, they would leave the little baby with his grandmother. Their house had two rooms. One room was for the man, his wife and son. The other room was for his old mother.

The man had cut a hole in the sago-palm thatch wall between their rooms. Whenever they cooked, his wife would put some food there for the old woman to take and eat. It was too bad though, the old woman never took this food.

The food would just fall down the hole. They thought that the old woman was taking it. The old woman thought that they never thought of her when they ate by themselves.

One time, the man went to the forest and killed a huge pig. He butchered it and carried it back to the village. The old woman saw this and was very happy because she had not eaten pork in a very long time.

They cooked the pork. The man's wife divided the meat and other food for the old woman, then she put it in the hole. She thought that the old woman took the food. Afterwards, they sat down and ate.

The poor old woman waited and waited, then she called out, "Why haven't you two given me any meat? You're always doing this sort of thing to me."

They listened and the woman asked, "I just put your portion there. Didn't you get it?"

The old woman went to check and she saw that the food was not there. So, her son had an idea and he said, "Wait there. I'll put some food inside. If you get it, then call out and I'll hear you." He put a piece of meat inside the hole. Quickly, a hand shot out and pulled the meat.

He did not hear his old mother call out, so he called to his mother, "Did you get it?" The old woman replied that she did not.

It was then that they recognized that a man was hiding inside the hole and was stealing the old woman's food. The man told his mother that when he put the meat inside the hole again, he would cut the hand of whoever tried to get the meat.

He put a piece of pork inside the hole. Quickly a hand shot out to take it, but he was ready with his sharp bamboo knife. He cut the man's hand, then the man went down and ran away.

When he arrived at a clearing, they saw that "he" was a cassowary. The cassowary ran and ran, down to a small stream, then escaped completely.

At dawn, the man told his wife and mother that he would take the two dogs and follow the cassowary. The name of his he-dog was Noku and the name of his bitch was Muni.

They wanted to go, so he told his mother and wife, "If men kill me when I leave, the two dogs will return to tell

you. However, if women befoul me, the dogs will still return to explain this to you."

After he explained this, he left them and followed the forest. He walked and walked until he arrived at a stream named Yolluwom. He left this stream and kept going, then he arrived at Sawyelef. He left that stream entirely until he arrived at the big Weni [Gweinif] River. He went down very close and saw the cassowary lying by the water.

He carried the cassowary and put it down, then he butchered it and made a fire. He heated stones and cooked the cassowary in an earth oven. He took leafy greens from the forest and cooked them with the cassowary.

Then he began to dam the river. He dug the sand up, damming the river. He called for his dogs to come, then he put them on top of a tree and told them, "When men come, you must not fight. Just be quiet. If they try to kill me, then I'll tell you and you can chase and kill them."

After he explained this to the dogs, they lay quietly and waited for the earth oven to become ready. The man removed his betel nuts and betel peppers, then he chewed them and spat about. He spat on stones that were by the river.

At this time, there were some young women who were fishing and coming towards them on the river. They approached the place where there was a fork in the river. Two sisters decided to follow the small branch of the river. The other women followed the main river. The sisters followed the stream upwards.

The two of them caught many, many fish. They kept at it as they went and did not look around. They approached the place where the man had made the earth oven and was resting. They stood and caught their breath, then they saw the spittle from the betel mixture splattered on the stones.

The little sister saw this and told her big sister. The big sister said, "That's bird shit." However, the little sister was persistent and said, "Smell it first. It doesn't smell like shit. It smells very nice."

The man and his dogs saw this. The dogs wanted to jump down and fight, but he tied them up, so they just lay there quietly watching. The women finished speaking, then they went back to fishing.

When they went fairly far away, the man stood up and the little sister saw his shadow in the water. When she told her big sister, the man hid again. The women did not find him, so they kept fishing. Then he got up again and showed his face. When the little sister told her big sister, he hid again.

The two of them both saw him on the third time. Oh my, they were terrified. He jumped down a tree and went up to them, asking, "Are you real women or ghosts?" They also asked him, "Are you a real man or a ghost?"

He said that he was a real man, and the women told him that they were real women. He asked the women, "Give me some betel nuts and we'll chew first." The women listened and gave him the betel nuts and peppers. However, they were not really women, they were flying foxes. The betel nuts that they had given him were wild betel nuts, and the betel peppers were from the forest [i.e., uncultivated].

He saw this, so when he wanted to chew betel nut, he took real betel nuts and chewed them with betel peppers and lime (calcium oxide). They chewed the betel mixture and the man told them, "Let's spit and see whose spittle is reddest."

They women's spittle was not very red, but his was. He told them, "You two did not chew real betel nuts and peppers. You chewed something from the forest, so your betel mixture is not very red."

He gave them real betel nuts and peppers and they chewed them. It tasted good and the betel mixture was very red. He also saw that their teeth were too long, so he told them that he would straighten them out. He filed their teeth shorter, then he gave them betel nuts to wash out their mouths.

He told them to dam the river, then they would eat the cassowary that he had cooked. The women did not want to do this because they had never eaten cassowary. The man dammed the river himself, then he went up and uncovered the earth oven.

He gave a piece of cassowary meat and some leafy greens to the women, but they said that they had never eaten this food. The man insisted and the two of them tried it. Oh my, it was delicious and they finished it all.

He asked them whether their home was near or far. They replied and asked him about his home. The women insisted that they must go to their home.

He tied a bundle for his mother and put it on his dog Noku's back. He told Noku, "Carry this meat for mama back home. When you get there, you must go directly to her "grass" skirt and bark. When you do this, mama will know that women have befouled me."

He tied a bundle on the back of his dog Muni's back and said, "This is meat for my wife. When you arrive at the village, you must go and bark at the bamboo used for heating hot water for sago. She will know that I've gone with women."

The dogs listened to their master and went back to the village. They arrived and did as he had told them. His mother and wife saw this and said, "Oh my, women must have taken him away, so the dogs came to tell us."

The man followed the women back to the home of the flying foxes. When they arrived there, the two of them hid him in a kitchen. The food was ready, so the two of them told their parents and brothers, "Go inside the room and take our fork used for holding food. If you see something, don't move it all around. That's forbidden. Bring it here and we'll eat."

They took the man inside who then sat with them to eat. The flying foxes broke some mushrooms and gave them to him to eat. He saw this and told them, "We've never eaten this kind of mushroom before."

The flying foxes told him that it was their meat. He removed the cassowary flesh and gave it to them to eat. However, they did not want it. He insisted and they ate it. It was delicious, so they finished it all.

He lived with them henceforth. He married the two flying foxes and they lived together. They lived for a while, then when it was breadfruit season, the flying foxes prepared to fly away to find breadfruits. The women's kin flew directly to **Fairu** and perched directly upon the breadfruit tree that belonged to the old mother. They ate there.

The old mother heard the flying foxes coming and making noises on the breadfruit tree, so she went outside and scolded them. She said, "Leave those breadfruits alone. Those belong to my son. Some women drew him to their home. I'm watching them for him."

They flying foxes listened. They left and flew back to their home. In the morning, they told stories and spoke of the old woman who had scolded them at her son's breadfruit tree.

The man listened and knew that they must have gone to eat breadfruits in his area. He told them, "If you go again tonight, I want you go carry some breadfruit seeds back for me to look at."

At night, the flying foxes went and took the breadfruit seeds, then returned. They showed him the seeds in the morning, then he asked them whether the tree was near a house. They said that it was, so the man told them that it was his mother who had scolded them.

At night, his two wives and his in-laws gave him a flying fox skin, then they told him to try to fly around. The man was very happy. He attached the skin, then flew back and forth until he learned how to fly well.

Another night, he told them that he would follow them. They flew off, then they arrived and ate. His old mother went outside and scolded them. She said the same thing as she had said before. When the son heard this, he was very troubled. He thought of his mother, wife and son, then he wanted to return to his home.

One day, his in-laws said that there was a big festival approaching. The man listened and told his wives, "We must go back to my home and find some meat for the festival."

The women listened and followed him. They stayed in the village and cut sago palm trees and wild sago palm trees, then they left them for the insects [to eat, which would then be harvested later]. The man also killed some wild game to carry back to the home of the flying foxes.

He took his adornments for the festival and brought them back. He straightened out all his adornments, then put them away carefully. When it was time for the festival, his wives and in-laws were dressed and ready to go first.

He stayed in the house and dressed very finely, then he went outside. When he went to the festival, all of the men were surprised. They came and looked and talked about his adornments. This was because his adornments were the finest. Tree leaves, flowers and things were tied around him.

They sang and danced, then he showed his in-laws how to make fine adornments. He gave adornments to them so that they could see how to make them too. His in-laws were very happy, so they let him take the two flying foxes back to his home.

They lived in his village for a while, then it was the season when the fruiting trees were in bloom. The men of the village were ready to go watch the trees and kill the flying foxes.

He wanted to go watch with the other men and kill flying foxes. His wives told him, "If you watch and you see our maternal kin, you must not kill this flying fox. You will see that one of its eyes is bad."

He went and watched. They killed the maternal kin of the two flying-fox women. The man did not know this. The men butchered the flying fox and carried its head to him. He took it to the house and put it in a *limbum* [basket].

In the morning, his wives wanted to go to rinse sago. One sister went and took the *limbum* basket. When she looked inside, she saw their maternal kin's head inside.

The sisters saw this and they cried terribly for their kin. They thought of leaving their husband and running back to their home. The big sister thought hard because she already had a baby, but the little sister did not have one.

The sisters did not speak, so their husband did not know that they now wanted to leave him. In the morning, he woke up and went with the men to look for pigs. After he departed, the sisters took the flying fox skin that they had given him and that they had hidden. They wanted to carry it back to their home.

Their husband went hunting for pigs in the forest, so he came back at night to eat and sleep. When the women saw that he was dead asleep, they got up very quietly, put on their flying fox skins and flew back to their home.

In the morning, he woke up and searched for the women, but they were not there. He went and checked on the flying fox skin, but it was not where he had hidden it. Then he and his son cried and were troubled.

After this, the son grew up and married, raising his children and grandchildren. Now, this clan lives in Tofungu in the Lumi area of **West Sepik** Province [**Olo People**].

Daniel K. Wilai

West Sepik Province

B211.2.11K+. Speaking flying fox; B630+. Human offspring of marriage to flying fox; B650+. Marriage to flying fox in human form; B871.1.2. Giant boar; D117.5KW. Transformation: woman to flying fox; D169.4M. Transformation: man to cassowary; D310+W. Transformation: flying fox to woman; D531. Transformation by putting on skin; D642. Transformation to escape difficult situation; K400. Thief escapes detection; K400. Thief escapes detection; K420. Thief loses his goods or is detected; P210. Husband and wife; P230. Parents and children; P231. Mother and son; P232. Mother and daughter; P233. Father and son; P234. Father and daughter; P250. Brothers and sisters; P252.1. Two sisters; P260. Relations by law; P261. Father-in-law; P262. Mother-in-law; P265. Son-in-law; P265+. Daughter-in-law; P290+. Maternal kin; P292. Grandmother; P600+. Tooth filing; Q212. Theft punished; Q411. Death as punishment; R210. Escapes; R260. Pursuits; T100. Marriage; T145.0.1. Polygyny

Two Snakes from Pangia

(Wantok 764b, February 23, 1989, page 20)

Long, long ago, a man lived in a village called Yaro [**Iaro**]. This village is in the Pangia area inside **Southern Highlands** Province [**Wiru People**].

The man was very handsome. He was married to a woman. This woman was from **Ialibu** Village, also in the Southern Highlands Province [**Kewa People**].

One time the two of them were in the village, then he told her, "Hey, we don't have meat in the house. What will we eat now? Take care of the house and stay in the village. Tomorrow I'll go alone to hunt for some marsupials (*kapul*) in the forest."

In the very early morning, he awoke and arranged his things. The woman also woke up and cooked his food to be eaten in the forest. He ate some sweet potatoes, and he tied some up and put them in a net bag. He took a bow and arrows, then he went off into the forest.

He leapt over mountains, then he entered the very deep forest and began to hunt for marsupials. He hunted and hunted until the afternoon, but he did not see a single marsupial nest. He was furious, so he began to walk back to the village. While he was walking back, he saw a big python sleeping in the middle of the trail.

Oh my, when he saw this, his heart stopped. This was because he thought that the snake would eat him. However, the python was asleep and did not do anything to him.

Very quietly, he walked closer to the snake, then he grabbed the snake right around its neck. He took a tree leaf and bound up the snake's head tightly.

He put the snake inside his net bag and took it back to the village. He arrived at the village, and his wife was also surprised to see this snake.

Later, he told his wife, "Tomorrow, carry this snake to give to your kin at Ialibu." After he told her this, they slept. Then in the very early morning, she awoke and put the snake in her net bag.

She left her husband and walked towards her village. She walked and walked, then she came to the middle of the trail. At this place, there was a long boulder near the trail. Underneath the boulder was a cave. She walked very quietly by the cave and she heard something singing mournfully.

This thing sang in the language of the Kagua [Kewa Language], "*Nogo nakinume ralomere gopiare*." ["*Nogo naaki-nu-me na-lo-me-re go pia-re*."] This song means, "People often eat it. If you are inside the net bag, then reply to me." ["The children who are sitting here are wanting to eat." (Karl Franklin, personal communication)]

Then the snake inside the net bag heard this and replied, singing, "*Mandali pale roliro*." The meaning of this song is, "Something people often eat it [sic]. I'm inside the net bag." [*Manda-li* means, "you will carry it" (Kewa). The rest is possibly Wiru (K. Franklin, personal communication)]

The woman heard this and was shocked. Quickly, she removed the net bag from her head and threw it down to the ground. She left the net bag with the snake on the trail, then she sped back to her husband. The snake went out and then into the cave. The snake saw one of its friends and they were happy in this cave.

The name of this boulder is Kuepalo Kue. This boulder is near Pangia Station. This is a true story. I wanted this story to appear in *Wantok Newspaper* so that other people from the Pangia area would see it and know.

Sweeney Unda Wiepe
Walala Trading Company
P. O. Box 237
Kimbe
West New Britain Province

B214.1.10. Singing snake; P210. Husband and wife; P310. Friendship; R100. Rescues; R220. Flights

Women Married Breadfruit Men
(Wantok 765, March 2, 1989, page 19)

Long, long ago, in the Wasu area of **Morobe** Province, there were breadfruit brothers who lived in **Kalalo** [**Selepet** People]. Today, Kalalo Community School stands at this place. There are women who live by the side of the Kalalo River, at the place they call **Horon Keban**.

During the day, these brothers would hang up like real breadfruits on a tree. When people saw them, they would think that they were just breadfruits hanging there. At night, they would leave the tree, then descend to sing and dance. They would beat their hand drums while they sang and danced passionately until daybreak. Then they would return to the tree.

Every night, the women of Horon Keban Village would hear the beating of the hand drums and the voices of the young men who were passionately singing. So, they would think hard. One day, they decided to go see who it was that often sang at night.

They fastened their torches then they waited. At night, the breadfruits changed and became real men. Then they descended and sang and danced passionately.

The youths heard this and lit their torches, then they walked towards the sounds. When they jumped into the Kalalo River and arrived there, it was too bad. The men had already fled and returned to the tree where they hung as breadfruits.

The women arrived there and saw that no one was singing. Only the adornments and the dance site were there. There were no men there. The men were hanging from the tree and watching the women. The poor women did not find them, so they left this place and returned to their home.

Another night, the women heard the hand drums beating and the men singing passionately. They jumped into the water, going back to Kalalo. However, there were no men at the place of the singing. This sort of thing always happened, so the women tired of it and decided to go hide and see who it was that sang at Kalalo.

When it was still daylight, they went to hide and watch. When it became dark, they saw the breadfruits descend the tree then sing and dance passionately. They did not know that the women were hiding and watching them.

When the women saw the young men, they each quickly picked one. When they finishing singing and dancing, the women went out into the clearing and held the men, blocking their path of escape.

The women married these breadfruit men and lived with them. The last brother married a very beautiful woman, so his big brothers were angry with him.

When they traveled in the forest and they saw wild game in a bad place, they would send the little brother to go kill it. They wanted him to fall to his death so that they could marry his wife.

However, the boy knew how to avoid these obstacles. When he would shoot the marsupial (*kapul*) down, they would take the marsupial or other animal that he had shot and run away back home. When he descended, he would not find the animal.

One day, the brothers found an animal down in the area of the Kalalo River rapids. At this place, there was a very tall tree. This place was a very bad place called Monin. If you take a ship and leave Sialum, then go to Gidua [**Gitua**], you can see water cascading down [**Gitua** People]. The people from here are always afraid to go down to this place.

The brothers went to this place and saw that this tall tree was filled with marsupials, so they made a very tall ladder. When they finished, they told the little brother to go up and kill the marsupials on the tree.

The little brother killed marsupials, then his brothers gathered them as they fell. After they gathered them, they cut the rope and removed the ladder from the tree. The little brother did not have a way to return to the ground.

The big brothers ran back to the village. The poor little brother finished killing the marsupials, then he tried to go down, but there was no way down because it was a tall tree. That night, he was freezing cold, so he hid among the tree leaves and slept. In the morning, he woke up and tried to get down again, but he was unable to do so. This was because the tree branches were very far apart.

At night, the flying foxes would come to the tree and he would shoot them. There was no one there to get these flying foxes, so they would just fall down into the Kiari River.

One time, two sisters were searching for salt and went up to this river. They saw the flying foxes lying about in the water, so they followed the river. They saw the man's shadow in the water. When they looked up, they saw him sitting on the tree.

They called out for him to come down, but he told them that there was no way down. The women listened and returned to the village to tell their father. He went to see this, then he made a ladder up to the tree.

However, the man could not get down because it had been a long time since he had eaten and his body was no longer strong. The women's father saw this, so he himself went up the ladder and carried him down.

They carried him back to their village, which was on the side of a stream. They gave food to him. He ate and rested well until his body became strong again. Then he married the two women.

They lived together for a while, then they made a garden and husbanded pigs. The food in the garden ripened and the pigs became very large. Then the brother made a decision with his two wives and their father. He wanted to get revenge on his brothers.

He sent a message for his brothers to come to his festival. He tied up a huge pig and he bundled plenty of food. Then he cooked a pig with some wild taros and wild bananas in an earth oven. He prepared the festival food, then he waited for his brothers to come.

His brothers arrived and pretended that they were happy to see him. They sang and danced until dawn, then he gave food to them. They ate, then he gave them the huge pig. They were very happy, so they carried the pig back to their village.

While they were walking on the trail, the brother who was carrying the pig wanted to urinate. He told the other brothers to come and change places with him, so that he could go urinate. After he urinated, he became a wild taro plant.

Another brother needed to defecate, so he went into the forest to defecate, then he became a wild banana plant. After a little while, another brother said that he wanted to urinate. When he went to urinate, he became a wild taro plant.

This went on for a while, then only two brothers were carrying the pig. They went up to a mountain, then they put the pig down, rested and talked. One brother said, "I think men have performed sorcery upon us, huh?" Then he felt the need to urinate too.

He went to urinate then he became a wild taro plant. The other brother needed to defecate, so when he wanted to go to defecate, he became a wild banana plant.

The pig lay there, rubbing its legs until the rope became loose. Then it got up and went back to its owner's house.

Nelson Dapepe
P. O. Box 357
Rabaul
East New Britain Province

D211.7K+M. Transformation: man to breadfruit; D213.6+M. Transformation: man to banana plant; D213.8KM. Transformation: man to taro plant; D431.4+M. Transformation: breadfruit to man; D560+. Transformation from defecation; D560+. Transformation from urination; K2211.0.1. Treacherous elder brother(s); P210. Husband and wife; P234. Father and daughter; P251.5.3. Hostile brothers; P252.1. Two sisters; P261. Father-in-law; P263. Brother-in-law; P264. Sister-in-law; P265. Son-in-law; Q285. Cruelty punished; Q551.3. Punishment: transformation; R100. Rescues; S70+. Cruel brother; S143.2. Abandonment in tall tree; T100. Marriage; T145.0.1. Polygyny; W181. Jealousy

Two Friends Went to the Ghosts' Village
(Wantok 766, March 9, 1989, page 20)

Long ago, in the time of the ancestors, there lived two men named Palik and Pana. They were always very good friends, so they would travel together, doing any kind of work, such as hunting for wild game.

One time, they promised to travel and gather tree sap for using to trap birds. They went and cut the sap from breadfruit trees and brought the sap to the village.

That night, they sat and talked about going to gather sap at Ganbage. They finished talking, then they slept. In the early morning, they awoke and went to Ganbage where they gathered tree sap. Afterwards, they waited for birds to come and become stuck.

They finished gathering tree sap, then they climbed a huge tree and watched. They watched and saw ghosts come out of a wild *limbum* palm tree. This *limbum* tree was their trail.

The two of them were still there. It was as if it was a dream and they were seeing ghosts coming out, carrying nets for catching pigs. When they saw this, they lay there very quietly and watched.

All of the men came out and went to chase pigs. The very last man to come out of the door was an old man. He wanted to shut the door, but the *limbum* door was very hard. He tried unsuccessfully to shut it, so he left it open and followed the other ghosts to hunt for pigs.

Palik and Pano saw this, so they left the sap there and went down to the ground. They went inside the trail of the ghosts, and then they went to a spirit house.

They went into the spirit house, where they saw beautiful hand drums and bamboo flutes. They beat the hand drums and blew the flutes inside the spirit house.

When the hand drums were beaten, two very beautiful women heard them and came to see. When they saw the two men, they blocked their way.

The men turned and saw this, so they asked, "Whose wives are you?" The women replied, "We're your wives." The two friends listened and were very happy. They did not want to return to their village now. They wanted to stay at this place with the two women.

However, the women said, "Two of your fingernails are not black, so you must return to your village. If you stay, the men will come and kill you."

The two men were very troubled, but they knew that the ghosts would kill them if they stayed there. So, they followed the women back the way they had come, and they left of the village of the ghosts.

The women went back inside the spirit house. They took a hand drum, a bamboo flute, and a yam. Then they gave these to the two men. This yam had a nice aroma.

Pano [Pana] and Palik carried these things and walked along the trail. They said, "What should we do? Should we return to this ghost village?" They kept talking as they walked back to the village.

They tried to think of a way, but they were unable to do so. They decided to kill themselves. They said that if they died, they could then arrive at the ghost village and see the two women.

When they arrived at the village, they killed pigs. Palik killed a pig to give to Pano, and Pano killed a pig to give to his friend Palik.

They butchered the pigs, then they cooked them well with other food. When the food was ready, they sat and ate. The other men of the village saw this, so they came and gathered to see the two of them.

The two men ate meat and drank soup, then they went outside and picked some young ginger (*gorgor*). Pano went around to one side of the spirit house, while Palik went to the other side. They ran to the other side and threw the ginger at each other, just as men would throw spears.

Then they went back and sat down. They finished all of their meat and soup. Their bellies were bloated, so the got up, took their real spears and went outside.

They went around the spirit house again, then they did as before. However when they met, Palik threw a spear, shooting Pano. Then Pano shot Palik. They both fell and died. The men gathered and saw that the two friends had killed each other. They carried their bodies away and buried them.

I want to explain about the three things that the two men had brought from the ghost village. Only the hand drum is rotting. The flute and the yam are still there in **Kalabu** Village, in the **East Sepik** Province area [**Abelam** People]. Whoever goes around to Kalabu Village can see that these things are still there.

Jason Yalikua
P. O. Box 97
Kimbe
West New Britain Province

A1461.7+. Origin of flute; A2824. Origin of drum; E276. Ghosts haunt tree; E425.1. Revenant as woman; E425.2. Revenant as man; E425.2.1. Revenant as old man; E495.2. Marriage (ceremony) to a ghost; F81. Descent to lower world of dead (Hell, Hades); F81.5. Journey to lower world to get treasures; F87. Journey to otherworld to secure bride; F91. Door (gate) entrance to lower world; F765. City inside a tree; M451.1. Death by suicide; P210. Husband and wife; P310. Friendship; S110. Murders; V61.3+. Dead buried; V112.1. Spirit huts

A Woman Hid inside a Snake's Skin

(Wantok 767, March 16, 1989, page 19)

Long, long ago, in the time of the ancestors, there lived two brothers. Their names were Sisirue and Konia. Sisirue was the big brother and Konia was the little brother.

Their parents had died, so they lived with other people. Their maternal kin and their sister and brother had tired of them, and they always beat them. They often spat upon them too.

One time, food was short, so they beat the two of them and told them to go find food for themselves. This was because there was not enough food to give to them. The big brother, Sisirue, listened and told his little brother Konia that they would leave the village and go into the forest.

They took their belongings and left the village. They walked and walked. They cried together because the people of the village had always treated them badly.

They arrived in the forest and made a small house. They lived in this house and made a huge garden. They planted various foods inside their garden.

One day, they went fishing in the stream. When they went upstream, they saw a huge snake lying in the water. Konia took a stick to stab the snake, but the snake did not move. It just lay there in the water.

Sisrue [Sisirue] saw this and told his brother, "Look out, that snake will kill you." However, Konia ignored what Sisrue said and kept stabbing the snake with the stick.

Then the snake rose up and told them, "I want to go to my house now. If you so desire, you may come with me."

The brothers listened and followed the snake to her house. They arrived and stayed with the snake at her house. They lived there for a fairly long time, then the big brother, Sisirue, said that he wanted to go check on their garden.

He told his little brother Konia to stay at the house, then he would go alone. After Sisirue departed, Konia stayed there very quietly, not making a noise. The snake noticed that it was silent, so she thought that the house must be empty. Immediately, the snake removed her skin and became a real woman. She went down and did housework, then she put on the snakeskin again and slept.

Konia was hiding quietly in his room when he saw what had happened. He was surprised to see that this very beautiful woman was hiding inside the body of a snake, and that she had tricked him and his brother.

He went down very quietly and ran to explain this to his brother. He just ran and ran until he entered their garden, then he told Sisrue.

The big brother listened and said that they must hide and burn the snake's skin. The brothers went back, then they saw the snake lying there. They played a trick and made noises here and there.

One day, they pretended to go to the forest. However, they returned and went inside, where they hid in their room. They did not make a noise. They sat very quietly.

The snake was lying there and did not hear any more noises. She thought that no one was in the house, so she got up and went inside her room, removing her skin. Then she went out and became a real woman.

When she went far away, the brothers went inside her room and saw the snake's skin lying there. The big brother, Sisirue, took it outside and burned it. While the skin burned, the two brothers laughed and made much noise.

She heard this and knew that the men had returned. She ran back quickly to put her skin on again. She arrived and saw the brothers sitting there.

There was no place to hide now. The big brother, Sisirue told her, "You're a real woman and you were hiding inside the snakeskin. Now you don't have a way to hide anymore. I'll marry you now."

Sisirue married her and they lived together. The brothers took their food from their garden and made a huge festival. They called out for their clan to come gather and celebrate with them. They also killed various animals from the forest and their clan was happy. They ate their fill of the good food.

Dowton Viresi
North Solomons Province

B211.6.1. Speaking snake (serpent); B656.2. Marriage to serpent in human form; B875.1. Giant serpent; D191W. Transformation: woman to serpent (snake); D391W. Transformation: serpent (snake) to woman; D531. Transformation by putting on skin; D531+. Transformation by removing skin; D793.2. Disenchantment made permanent by burning cast-off skin; P210. Husband and wife; P250. Brothers and sisters; P251.5. Two brothers; P263. Brother-in-law; P264. Sister-in-law; P290+. Maternal kin; R213. Escape from home; S70+. Cruel brother; S70+. Cruel sister; S70+. Cruel maternal kin; T100. Marriage

Two Friends Raised Clan Houses

(Wantok 768, March 23, 1989, page 19)

Long, long ago, in the time of the ancestors, there were two friends who lived in **Yombaliyi** Village, in the Goroka area [**Eastern Highlands** Province]. Akekuwe was black-skinned and Agiyi Kuwe was red-skinned.

They lived very well in their village. Akekuwe made a huge garden on one side of **Huwa** that went all of the way down to the river [**Yagaria** People]. Agiyi Kuwe made a garden that went down one side of **Olen Numugu**.

They only gathered their food in these two gardens to eat. In Akekuwe's garden, there were no red-colored foods. He had only planted foods of other colors. Agiyi Kuwe had only planted red-colored food in his garden.

One day, they had no meat, so they just ate the food from the gardens. After a while, they grew tired of this, so they talked about going to hunt for wild game.

They talked for a while, then Akekuwe said, "Friend, I know what. The men say that they often make a little bow and arrow, then shoot their leg or arm veins. When the blood flows, they take a tree leaf to catch the blood. Then they cook leafy greens in the blood and eat it."

After he told this story, he flattered his friend, then they tried this method to see whether their food would taste delicious. Agiyi Kuwe sat and thought for a while, then they tried this method.

Agiyi Kuwe told his friend Akekuwe, "You make a little bow and arrow, and shoot my leg. Then we'll catch the blood and cook it with our leafy greens."

Akekuwe listened and was very happy. He quickly went into the forest, took some rattan and bamboo, made a little bow, and sharpened some arrows. He also cut a banana leaf for catching the blood.

He shot Agiyi Kuwe's leg. Oh my, the blood shot out and down the banana leaf. The blood filled it and nearly overflowed. Poor Agiyi Kuwe's eyes spun around and he fell down, prostrate.

Then he told his friend Akekuwe, "My eyes are spinning. You've done well, so cook and we'll eat."

Akekuwe carried the banana leaf with the blood into the house. He quickly peeled the food, then prepared the leafy greens too. He cooked two packets in the blood.

Agiyi Kuwe was still asleep while his friend Akekuwe was cooking. When the food was ready, he took out a flying fox bone and opened a packet with it. A delicious smell wafted into his nose, so he tried a piece on his tongue. Oh my, it was more delicious than any food.

Akekuwe turned and saw that his friend was still asleep. Immediately, he removed the food packets, then he hid and swallowed some food. After he ate, he hid the leaves under the house, by a rat's hole. He returned, woke up his friend Agiyi Kuwe, and they ate. Oh my, was it delicious. They cleaned up every scrap.

After they ate, they went to the gardens. Akekuwe went to work in his garden, but poor Agiyi Kuwe still felt hungry. He took some bananas and ate them, then he dug up some taros, took some leafy greens and returned to the house. Agiyi Kuwe cooked at the house, then he saw ants swarming under the house.

He took a piece of firewood and burned them. The ants died and he thought that the ants would not return. He continued to cook, then he saw the ants swarming again. He took a piece of fire and shoved it roughly at the hole where the ants were swarming.

When Agiyi Kuwe shoved the fire inside the hole, he saw the banana leaf inside it. He pulled it out and he looked carefully. He saw that it was a banana leaf, so he knew that his friend Akekuwe had tricked him and eaten a packet of food by himself. He was furious, so he waited for his friend.

In the afternoon, his friend Akekuwe arrived. Agiyi Kuwe asked him, "Friend, why did you trick me? You ate a whole packet, then hid it underneath the house."

Agiyi Kuwe then threw up his hands to fight Akekuwe. A tremendous fight broke out between the two friends. They fought and fought, then Agiyi Kuwe took an axe and put it right to Akekuwe.

The axe went into Akekuwe's body, and he fell onto the fire. An earthen pot containing leafy greens spilled onto him, burning his chin badly.

When Agiyi Kuwe saw the fire burning Akekuwe, he was very sorry, so he ran and lifted up his friend. He took Akekuwe to wash the blood and trash from his body, then he told him to sleep.

Agiyi Kuwe took care of his friend Akekuwe until the sores on his body and chin had healed completely. How-

ever, his body was ruined because the axe had cut his uri-
nary tract, so when he urinated, the urine exited the hole
where the axe had cut him.

They lived for a while, then Akekuwe became a
woman. They married and lived in this village. Their children grew up and married. Some of them lived on the side
where Akekuwe had made his garden. They made a clan
house, and they lived there. They are the first Kownigi
Clan.

The other went came to live in the place where Agiyi
Kuwe had made his garden. They also made a clan house.
This is where the Miruma Clan now lives. This story is
from long ago, and has been told until now.

Duwgeri Niklas [Dugweri Nicklas]
Boroko
National Capital District

A1640+. Origin of Kownigi Clan; A1640+. Origin of Miruma Clan; D12.
Transformation: man to woman; D560+. Transformation by cutting;
F527.1. Red person; F527.5. Black man; G51. Person eats own flesh;
K2297. Treacherous friend; P210. Husband and wife; P230. Parents and
children; P310. Friendship; Q261. Treachery punished; Q272. Avarice
punished; Q451.10.1. Punishment: castration; Q551.3+. Punishment: trans-
formation to woman; S176.1. Mutilation: emasculation; T100. Marriage;
W151. Greed

A Real Woman Married a Python
(Wantok 769, April 5, 1989, page 19)

Long, long ago, some people lived in a village named
Kondulap [**Kondolop**, **Selepet** People, **Morobe** Province].

One time, there was a huge party approaching, so the
clan house tied up a pig and cooked food. The young
women carried the pig guts to a body of water and cut them.
They cut and washed them, then they carried them back to
the village. The water where they had gone was not a bab-
bling brook, it was a pond.

A young woman carried some pig guts down to the
water, then she worked at washing them. While she sat
doing this, she did not know that there was a man who was
spying upon her.

This young man was from a place below the pond. He
saw the woman, and he went very quietly to see her face,
then he went back.

The young woman did not know what was happening
inside the water. She removed the feces from the pig guts,
then she washed them well and put them away. She took
some water in a bamboo tube, then she headed back to the
village.

The young man turned into a snake. When it became a
little dark, the clouds blocked the sky and a little rain began
to fall. Everyone saw this and fled into their houses. Some
of them beat hand drums, sat and sang.

The man who had become a snake had become a huge
python. His kin had become little snakes. The snakes left
the water, then they went up to the ground. They followed
the trail that the men of the village used when they went to
the pond.

The big python rubbed red paint onto his eyes and then
upon his head. The little snakes followed him and they arrived at the village.

When the snakes arrived at the village, the people were
terrified. They thought hard, "Oh my, where did these
snakes come from? Who will go to the water now?" The
people asked themselves this, then they waited for the
snakes to speak.

The big python and all of the others went directly to the
house where the men were sitting and arguing. They sat
and waited, then the village leaders gathered their thoughts.

They got up and then went to beautifully adorn a
woman who had ringworm. They brought her and showed
her to the snakes, but the python looked carefully at her,
then shook his head. They took her back and brought another woman to show to the snakes.

The python looked at her, then shook his head again.
He did this until they had shown all of the young women of
the village. When the snake shook his head, the parents of
these women were happy because they knew that the snake
did not like their daughters.

The parents of the very last woman were terribly worried because they knew that the snakes had come to take
their children. They cried terribly and adorned their
daughter finely, then they got ready.

When they took their daughter, oh my, the big python
nodded his head vigorously for this woman alone. The little snakes jumped about and were elated.

However, the woman's poor parents wailed. They
watched her walking away. The little snakes followed her
and the big python went last.

When they approached the water, the little snakes scat-
tered, then just the two of them were there. The python told
the young woman, "Jump down into the water." The
woman was terrified and did not want to do this, so the
snake spoke sternly to her, "Jump down into the water."

She jumped down, then she arrived at a huge underwater village. When the python jumped down after her, he
turned back into a man. Oh my, the woman saw this very

handsome man and she was very happy that she had followed him to his home.

The man took her and they went to his house. His old mother saw the woman and scolded her son. She said, "Why did you bring this woman here. The men will come and kill us." However, he told his mother that the woman's parents had given her to him.

They lived together for a while, then she gave birth to two handsome boys. He and his wife were elated for their two children.

The boys grew up to be about seven years old. One day, they went to work in the garden by the water. They worked and worked, then the boys worked at damming the water. When the water was full, they broke the earth and the water flowed again. They did this until the water was full once more. When the water was completely filled, they broke the earth again and the water shot directly to their mother's garden, removing all of the food.

Their mother saw this and was furious. She scolded and yelled, "You two aren't human children. You're a python's children and you're obstinate."

Her husband heard this and was furious, so he killed her and ate her. Then he said, "I can't listen to the language of the Kondolop." He went to the **Kulavi** area and made a big lake, and he lived there.

So today, the people of Kondolop usually keep quiet when they go to this lake. They do not want the snake to hear them speak. That is the end of our ancestor story from the Kabwum Clan.

Rex Mingi
P. O. Box 2322
Boroko
National Capital District

A920.1.0.1. Origin of particular lake; B211.6.1. Speaking snake (serpent); B631.9. Human offspring of marriage of person and snake; B656.1. Marriage to python in human form; B875.1. Giant serpent; C400. Speaking tabu; C615.1. Forbidden lake (pool); D191M. Transformation: man to serpent (snake); D391M. Transformation: serpent (snake) to man; F725.5.1. Visit to people of village under lake; G77. Husband eats wife; P210. Husband and wife; P231. Mother and son; P232. Mother and daughter; P233. Father and son; P234. Father and daughter; P251.5. Two brothers; P262. Mother-in-law; P265+. Daughter-in-law; Q411. Death as punishment; S63+. Husband kills wife; S110. Murders; T100. Marriage; T587. Birth of twins; T685. Twins

Nawalok and Dan Turned into Stones
(Wantok 770, April 6, 1989, page 19)

Long, long ago on **Karkar** Island, there was a village. The name of this village was **Katom** [**Takia** People, **Madang** Province]. There was an old man named Nawalok who lived in this village.

This old man was the kind of man to display his body to young women, even the married women. His wife had died, so he lived alone. In Katom Village, there also lived an old woman. Her name was Dan. Her husband had also died, and she too lived alone.

The old man Nawalok often tried his luck with young women, the married women, and even this old woman. However, the women usually disparaged and shamed him by saying, "That man's so close to death that his children are about to bury him, but he's still trying to find a wife."

Poor old Nawalok heard this and was terribly ashamed. He left the village and fled into the forest. He went to live in the forest for a very long time. He lived there, and he was furious that the women had shamed him like that. He thought of a way to grab one of these women.

He was still living in the forest when he heard the old woman, Dan, searching for one of her sows. The pig had given birth in the forest and had not returned to get her food, so the old woman was very troubled about her pig and was trying to find her.

One afternoon, Nawalok returned to the village and slept. In the very early morning, before it was light, he awoke and went down to his house, then he went to Dan's house.

The old woman had not yet awoken, so Nawalok stood and waited, then he pretended to cough. The old woman heard this and asked, "Who's there?" The old man replied, "It's me, Nawalok."

When old Dan heard this, she was furious and shouted, "You're that bad man. Go away!"

However the old man ignored what Dan said. He stood for a little while, then he replied to Dan, "Hey, I didn't come to molest you, so don't be angry. I just live in the forest. I heard that your sow gave birth and that you were working hard to find her, so I came to help you find her."

When Dan heard this, all of her anger disappeared. She went outside and they chewed betel nuts, then spat. The sun rose and old Nawalok fooled around, loosening his loincloth.

The old woman turned and saw this from the corner of her eye. She began to think, "What can I do to trick this old man?" The old woman kept thinking like that.

689

She gathered her thoughts and lied to old Nawalok, "Nawalok, stay here. I'll go find some more betel peppers for us first."

Nawalok listened and said, "OK, but hurry because we'll go find your pig too."

Old Dan lied and ran into the forest. Before long, she came back, completely out of breath. She called out to old Nawalok, "Hurry and take your spears, then go to the scrub forest. You'll see a gigantic old wild pig lying there. This pig must have been with my sow and impregnated her. Now, this pig has confused her and she doesn't think of returning to the village anymore."

Old Dan was not really talking about a wild pig. She had seen something of old Nawalok's and she lied. Poor Nawalok listened and thought that the old woman was telling the truth.

He ran and carried spears into the forest, but he did not see a wild pig. So, he returned to the village and asked Dan, "Where's this big wild pig that you spoke of? I went to find it and there were none there."

The old woman saw that poor Nawalok was completely out of breath as he was speaking, so she died laughing. She said, "Oh my, you fell for my trick, huh!"

When Nawalok heard this, it put his belly on fire. He returned to his house, then he stayed there and thought of getting revenge on old Dan.

He thought, "Oh my, this old woman wanted to play with me. Now I'll see her."

He took his stone axe and he went into the forest. He arrived in the woods, then he began to cut the trees and make a nest that looked as if pigs had made it. He finished, then he returned to the village.

He arrived at Dan's house, then he shouted, "Oi, oi, Dan, are you there?"

Dan listened and went outside, then asked, "Yes, old man, why?"

Nawalok lied, "I found your mother pig. She gave birth in the forest and is sleeping in a nest that she made at the base of a big *galip* tree."

Old Dan listened and thought that this was true, so she was elated. She went into the house and quickly cooked some food to carry and give to her mother pig. After she cooked it, she packed it and brought it into the forest.

Old Nawalok was hiding and watching. When he saw Dan coming down and leaving the house, he ran ahead and hid at the base of the *galip* tree.

When he saw old Dan approaching, he went into the nest and lay there very quietly. The old woman arrived, then sat at the front of the nest and began to call her pig.

Old Nawalok answered in the voice of a pig. The old woman heard this and thought that it was really a pig inside the nest, so she called back.

The old woman kept calling, but the pig did not come out. It just called back to her. After a while, Nawalok jumped out and grabbed the old woman.

He said, "You women of the village are short, but we men are taller. So, now I'm tricking you back."

When he said this, a big cloud thundered and the two of them turned to stone. Now if you go to Katom Village, you will see these two stones, Nawalok and Dan, still holding each other.

Tamie Abeck
Gaubin Hospital
Karkar Island
Madang Province

A974. Rocks from transformation of people to stone; A977. Origin of particular stones or groups of stones; D231M. Transformation: man to stone; D231W. Transformation: woman to stone; D2149.1. Thunderbolt magically produced; Q263. Lying (perjury) punished; Q551.3.4. Transformation to stone as punishment; R213. Escape from home; W157. Dishonesty; X743H. Humor concerning exhibitionism

A *Masalai* Pretended that She Was a Real Woman
(Wantok 771, April 13, 1989, page 19)

Long, long ago on a mountain, there lived a man, his wife and their children. They lived well in this, their home. One time, the woman told her husband that she would go into the forest to gather *tulip* leaves.

In the morning, she awoke and went towards the place where a *tulip* tree was growing. She arrived there and saw that some people had taken the *tulip* leaves. She was angry and tied a taboo sign to the *tulip* tree, then she returned home.

She explained to her husband that other people had taken their *tulip* leaves. They stayed there for a fairly long time, then she went back to the forest to check on their *tulip* tree.

She arrived there, then she saw that the taboo sign that she had placed on the tree was no longer there. Another taboo sign was there. She was furious, so she went and removed the taboo sign. She put back her own taboo sign and returned home.

This real woman did not know that there was a *masalai* woman who always would come to gather the leaves of this *tulip* tree. This taboo sign belonged to the *masalai* woman.

The real woman kept returning to gather *tulip* leaves for a very long time. One day, she traveled and saw that the *tulip* tree was filled with leaves. She saw that the taboo sign was also there, so she removed it, climbed the tree, and began gathering leaves.

The *masalai* woman left her house and went to gather *tulip* leaves. When she arrived, she saw the woman sitting nicely on the tree, gathering *tulip* leaves. The ghost was furious and shouted, "So you've come to gather your *tulip* leaves, huh? Did you put a taboo on this tree or did I?"

The real woman was angry and shouted, "These are my *tulip* leaves and I placed the taboo. Why did you just come to argue? This *tulip* tree is on our land."

The two women argued back and forth. The real woman did now know that this woman was a *masalai*. The *masalai* told her, "That's OK, take the leaves from your *tulip* tree. I'm leaving now."

The *masalai* then went to her house and she brought a stick with a hook on it. She returned to the base of the *tulip* tree and began removing the leaves. When she finished, she began to cut the tree branches.

When the woman fell down, the *masalai* took her and threw her down a hole at the base of a New Guinea walnut tree. Then the *masalai* took the woman's face and skin and carried the net bag of *tulip* leaves back to her home.

The poor real mother had fallen down a hole and did not have a way to get out because the hole was very deep and there was no place for her to grab and go back out. She tried calling out, but there was no one who could hear her because the hole was so deep.

Her husband and the children lived very well with the *masalai*. They thought that she really was their mother, but the *masalai*'s habits were different. Sometimes, she would just beat and scold the children if they did not want to eat. She would do this when the food that she had cooked did not come out well.

When the children cried, their father would ask her about it. She would lie and say that the children were stubborn so she had beaten them. They lived like this for a while, then she gave birth to a boy.

When the son was fairly strong, she would leave him there with his father. She would then go to process sago, but she never brought back any sago. She would leave the sago, then take clay for making pots and carry it back home. Afterwards, she cooked the clay and gave it to the man and the children.

The man and children ate and ate, but it did not taste good at all. He complained, and she said, "If you don't like the food that I cook, alright, get up yourself, find your own food, then carry it back and cook it."

His poor real wife was still lying inside the hole and she no longer had any strength. With what little strength she had, she would use to eat rootlets and mud.

One time, a flying fox flew into the hole, and it was surprised to see her. It asked her why she was there, then she told her story.

The flying fox went to find some ripe bananas, then it brought them to give to her. The poor woman ate just a little, then she slept. When she woke up, she ate some more, then a little strength began to come back to her body.

When she had regained her strength, the flying fox said, "I'll carry you back to your brothers' village, but you must not return to your husband's village."

The flying fox lifted her and carried her to the house of her two brothers. It put her down on the ground, then she went and knocked on the house door. When the men opened the door, they saw their sister with the flying fox.

Their sister cried and cried, then she told the story of what had happened to her when she went to look for *tulip* leaves. The brothers took traditional ring money, then they put it around the flying fox's neck. They paid the flying fox for the hard work of helping their sister.

However, this was not a flying fox. It was really their ancestor who had become a flying fox to help their sister. The flying fox's neck was now white because the two brothers had put the ring money around its neck. This ring money was bright white, and very clean. In my language, we call this *molem* [*mole*].

She stayed with her brothers for a very long time. One day, the brothers sent a message to their brother-in-law. They asked him to come and help them make a house.

The next day, the man left his family and walked to his in-law's village. He arrived, then he went to sit and chew betel nuts with his brothers-in-law. They did not yet tell him about his wife.

He saw his real wife and thought, "That woman looks exactly like my wife, but she's at home. That must be her sister."

He sat, still chewing betel nuts with his brothers-in-law, telling stories. They chewed and chewed, then one of the brothers was feeling the effects of the betel nuts and asked him, "Brother-in-law, do you see that woman who came here and lives with us?"

The man replied, "Brother-in-law, your sister lives in the village with the children. I came alone. That woman must be her little sister."

Then the two brothers told him about what the *masalai* had done to their sister. He listened and was speechless. He was furious and wanted to go kill the *masalai* woman, but his brothers-in-law told him that he must wait a little first lest the *masalai* find out and kill him instead. He left his real wife and went back to the village where the *masalai* woman and children lived.

One time, he lied to the *masalai* woman, saying that he was sick. He told her to go fetch some *salat*. She listened and took a net bag. She was about to leave for the forest. When she turned her back, he took a spear and stabbed her right in the back, killing her.

He took the real woman's children along with the *masalai* woman's two children and ran away to live in his in-law's village.

William Jimmy Sabien
P. O. Box 323
Lae
Morobe Province

[Mr. Sabien also wrote the ancestor stories in *Wantok* #510, 513, 517, 581, 637, 642, and 657. This story comes from the **Olo** People, **West Sepik** Province.]

B211.2.11K+. Speaking flying fox; B449.3+. Helpful flying fox; B540+. Flying fox rescuer; B552+. Person carried by flying fox; D117.5K. Transformation: person to flying fox; E320. Dead relative's friendly return; F405+. Spirit killed by spear/arrow; F490+. Masalai; K1900. Impostures; K1910. Marital impostors; K2213. Treacherous wife; P210. Husband and wife; P230. Parents and children; P231. Mother and son; P233. Father and son; P253.0.2. One sister and two brothers; P263. Brother-in-law; Q53. Reward for rescue; Q262. Impostor punished; Q411. Death as punishment; Q458. Flogging as punishment; R45.1. Man confined under roots of tree; R110. Rescue of captive; S12. Cruel mother; S62. Cruel husband; S110. Murders; W167. Stubbornness

The Animals Helped Esengi Clan House

(Wantok 772, April 20, 1989, page 19)

Long, long ago, in the Okapa area of **Eastern Highlands** Province, there was a clan house. The clan house was by a big river. The name of the clan house was Esengi. Near the house and the river was a mountain. Only one old man lived on this mountain. The name of the old man was Wainu.

Wainu was not like the other men of this time. He was a *masalai* who ate people, so he lived alone on the mountain. There were no men who went to the mountain to search for food, or anything else, because they were afraid of him.

The old man decimated the men, women and children of the Okapa area, so few people lived by Okapa at this time. At this time, people would use just one fire to cook food. This fire was in the Esengi House and it was always lit.

One time, the men forgot about putting on more firewood, so the fire died. That completely ruined their lives because there was no fire to cook food. They all knew that only old Wainu had a fire in his house, but they were afraid to go and take it lest he eat them.

The leaders of the clan house argued at a big meeting. They called for all of the wild animals of the forest to come to the meeting. In the time of the ancestors, people often spoke with various forest animals. At this meeting, they talked about a way that they could take the fire from old Wainu's house.

They met for a while, then a dog said that it would help the men of the clan house to get the fire.

Quickly, a pig replied, "OK, go get the fire. I'll stay at old Wainu's fence gate to help you."

Then came a frog from the river saying, "No problem. I'll watch from the river and give a little, just in case."

By the river, on the side of the mountain, there was a marsupial (*kapul*) and a bird who said that they would watch. All of them agreed what they would do, then the dog sped away to old Wainu's house.

The dog walked and crossed the river, then went up the mountain. The dog walked and walked up the mountain, then approached the old man's house. As the dog approached, it pretended to eat food scraps, then it went very close to old Wainu's house.

That night, old Wainu had killed some men. He was gorging himself upon them, so he had forgotten completely about watching his house. This gave an excellent chance for the dog. The dog walked very quietly into the house, then circled old Wainu's fire.

Quickly, the dog took a piece of fire, then ran out of the house. Old Wainu was surprised to see the dog stealing his fire. He left the meat there, took his multi-pronged spear, and followed the dog out of the house. However, the dog and the other animals had carefully planned to confuse old Wainu.

Old Wainu thought that the dog had come alone to steal his fire, but the dog ran quickly to old Wainu's fence gate. Then the dog gave the fire to the pig.

The pig took the fire and sped away to the river. The dog followed another trail, racing into the forest. However, old Wainu did not worry about the dog, he followed the pig down to the river.

The pig arrived at the river and was completely out of breath. The frog was already standing by the river. Quietly, the pig handed off the fire. The pig followed another trail, and sped into the forest.

Before, in the time of the ancestors, frogs had tails on their behinds, so the frog quickly put on its tail. The frog swam and swam to the other side of the water. Oh my, the fire was lit strongly and burned its tail, but it did not care. Old Wainu approached, but the frog kept swimming.

When the frog arrived at the other side of the river, the marsupial was standing by, waiting for the frog. However, by then the frog's tail was ablaze. So today, you will see that frogs have no tails. This is because the fire burned off its tail.

It felt a pain on its tail and quickly gave the fire to the marsupial. The marsupial took the fire, then raced up a tree. However, old Wainu had already arrived and grabbed the marsupial.

The two of them began to pull each other. Old Wainu held the marsupial by the tail, pulling it down, but the marsupial was strong and kept climbing. They did this for a while, then all of the hair on the marsupial's tail came out. So today, you will see that marsupials do not have hair on their tails. This is because old Wainu removed the tail hair at this time.

Old Wainu and the marsupial kept at it, but the marsupial was strong and raced to the top of the tree. The poor marsupial was in great pain, so it gave the fire to the bird. The bird took the fire and flew away to the clan house. Poor old Wainu was completely out of breath, so he could not follow them. He turned and walked very slowly back to his house.

Oh my, the men, women and children of the clan house saw the bird coming with the fire, and they were elated. So from this time until today, this clan house at Okapa has many, many people.

Jenop Oveo
Yasubi Village [**Fore** People]
Okapa
Eastern Highlands Province

A1415. Theft of fire; A2317.12. Why opossum has bare tail; A2378.2.6. How frog lost tail; B210.3. Formerly animals and man spoke the same language; B211.1.4. Speaking hog; B211.1.7. Speaking dog; B211.2.12K+. Speaking marsupial; B211.3. Speaking bird; B211.7.1. Speaking frog; B421. Helpful dog; B430+. Helpful marsupial; B443.5. Helpful wild hog (boar); B450. Helpful birds; B493.1. Helpful frog; F490+. Masalai; G346. Devastating monster; G610. Theft from ogre; K300. Thefts and cheats—general; R260. Pursuits; S110. Murders

A Man Grabbed a Ghost Woman from a Hole

(Wantok 773, April 27, 1989, page 19)

Long, long ago, there was a man who lived in a village called **Sumi**, in the Kagua area [**Kewa** People, **Southern Highlands** Province].

One day, he awoke, left the village and traveled in the forest. He went around and around, then he approached a big hole. There was paint affixed to the leaves and forest of this area [i.e., paint was derivable from these plants]. In our language, we call this _ambu_. When it was time for a festival, they would adorn themselves with this paint.

He stood watching and thinking. He walked closer and saw handprints. He knew that there must have been people who came around to this area; it was filled with paint.

He made a hut there. He worked very quickly, then he returned to the village. He arrived at the village, then he ate and rested. In the afternoon when the sun was setting, he got up and went back to the forest.

He arrived at the hut, then he went inside and put his things down. He sat and he did not want to sleep. He wanted to see who came around to this part of the forest.

He sat for a while, then his eyes grew sleepy, but he endured and just sat there. After a while, when it was close to dawn, he heard a crashing sound outside. He went out very quietly and saw women coming down from a huge tree.

The women descended and went directly to the hole where they gathered paint. They carried it away, back up the tree. The man's eyes spun around as he watched the very beautiful women fetching the paint.

He just stayed there, quietly watching for a while, then dawn was almost breaking. He saw a woman who was more beautiful than the others. This woman descended and called out for the other women to get some paint for her, but the other women said, "Get it yourself. Dawn's breaking now and we can't wait."

She went down and stood at the very end of the line. When she was about to go inside and get the paint, the man went outside and grabbed her. She wanted to flee, but he held her firmly.

While he was still holding her, she turned into a snake. However, he was unafraid. He kept holding on to her. She turned into something else, but he kept holding her firmly. The woman kept this up, then she gave up and became a woman again.

She told him, "You're stronger and you've won, so I'll go with you. However, you must always listen to what I say."

He was happy and took her back to his village. They married and lived well. She told her husband, "If you want to make a house, then go cut only the posts. Then bring them here and prepare them."

He brought the posts and put them down. They slept that night, then in the morning he saw a house standing there.

She asked him, "Do you have pigs too?" He replied that he only had one. She told him to go make a pigsty. He listened and erected a pigsty. In the morning, they awoke and he saw that there were pigs packed into the pigsty. She made a big garden for themselves that was filled with various foods. He was elated and always let his wife do the various chores to help their livelihood.

One time, there was a festival about to happen in a nearby village. He wanted to go to the festival. His wife listened and said, "It's OK for you to go to the festival, but it's completely forbidden for you to dance or sing with women. If you ignore this and return, you will not see me. There will be no house, no garden, and no pigsty. There will be just forest here."

He listened and said that he would not sing and dance with other women. He dressed very finely and prepared to go to the festival. She cut a piece of string and tied it to his *tanget*-leaf buttock covering. She held the other end. He left the village and went to the festival grounds.

When he arrived, the women raced to go pull him and dance. He saw the young women and forgot the promise that he had given to his wife. He went inside the festival grounds then sang and danced with them passionately.

His wife in the village felt the piece of string in her hand tighten. Then she knew that her husband was singing and dancing with the women. She was furious, so she left the village. When she left, the forest covered it over. The house broke and went down and the pigs ran off in different directions.

She left the village and went to live on top of a *limbum* palm tree. Her husband had his fill of the festival, then he went back to the village. When he arrived, he saw forest. He knew that his wife had fled.

He searched for his wife in the forest. He walked and walked, then he saw a woman's reflection in the water. She was making a net bag. He thought that it was really his wife, so he tried to grab the water. Then he turned and looked around. He saw her sitting on top of the *limbum* tree, making a net bag.

The tree upon which she was sitting was very tall. He saw this and cut [notches in] the tree, making a ladder ascending it. He finished the ladder, then he climbed the tree.

He went up and up, then he approached her. The *limbum* tree began to move back and forth, then he climbed further. It did this for a while, then he came close to holding her. The ladder began to shake a little, then he fell down and died.

The name of this man was Sumi Sama and his bones are still at this place. For those of us in this village, if enemies ensorcell a man and kill him, we will go and sleep at this place. In our dreams, Sumi Sama will reveal whoever performed the sorcery.

If the men of the village are sick, they will also go to sleep at this place, then they will become well again. This is still a strong custom at our village.

This ancestor story comes from the Kagua area of Southern Highlands Province.

David Warea
Kapiura Plantation
P. O. Box 451
Kimbe
East New Britain Province

D191W. Transformation: woman to serpent (snake); D610. Repeated transformation; D941. Magic forest; D941.1. Forest produced by magic; D1133.1. House created by magic; D1184.2. Magic string; D1500.1.3. Magic tree heals; D1810.8.2.3. Murder made known in a dream; D2106.1.2. Animals miraculously multiplied; D2136.9. Magic house removed; F54.1. Tree stretches to sky; P210. Husband and wife; Q325. Disobedience punished; Q386. Dancing punished; Q595. Loss or destruction of property as punishment; R213. Escape from home; R260. Pursuits; T100. Marriage; T111. Marriage of mortal and supernatural being; T192. Marriage by force; W126. Disobedience

Before, Giniambu and Witupe Were Enemies
(Wantok 774, May 4, 1989, page 19)

Long, long ago, in the Yangoru area of **East Sepik** Province, the people of **Witupe Number One** and **Witupe Number Two** Villages [**Abelam** People] would gather together and fight the people of **Giniambu** [**Kiniambu** Village, **Boiken** People].

One day, the people of Witupe did not travel the forest to hunt for game, or do any other work. All of them rested and just stayed in the village.

That day, they were shocked to see a big black cloud of smoke rising up into the sky from a fire. This smoke came from a sword-grass area that the people of Giniambu Village were burning. The name of this sword-grass area is Kutwi. [*Wy* means "sword grass" in the Abelam and Boiken Languages (Laycock, 1965: 160).]

The men of the two Witupe villages saw this and they knew that the fire must be coming directly from their sword-grass lands, and that the people of Giniambu had begun this fire.

Quickly, they took their spears and ran to surround all of the areas near the sword-grass land. However, the people of Giniambu had fled to their village.

Only one man and woman were there, catching fish from a small stream. The people of Witupe saw them and killed them. Afterwards, they threw their bodies into the sword grass and the fire burned them.

Later, they sent a message to Giniambu Village, explaining that they had killed a man and a woman from their village. "If you are troubled about this, then come and we'll fight in the sword-grass lands." Then they sang and danced together, and they returned to their villages.

When the people of Giniambu heard this, oh my, they were very troubled. They were furious and they said that they would get revenge.

One day, the men of Giniambu decided to fight with the men of Witupe. The Witupe heard this, so they prepared all of their fighting gear and just waited. In the morning, all of them met in the sword-grass lands. The men of Giniambu came with just their little boys.

They threw spears back and forth, and began to fight. They fought and fought, then one man from Witupe Number One shot a man from Giniambu directly in his eye. The name of this man was Kapmandu. The poor man fell down. The men of Giniambu saw this and all of them fled back to their village.

After they fled, the men from Witupe checked carefully all around. They checked and saw little boys from Giniambu hiding. They took the little boys and killed all of them.

They lived for a fairly long time, then one man from Witupe Number One went to Giniambu. He went there and saw men, women and children singing and dancing.

He climbed a coconut palm tree where there was a good view [lit., "big mark"]. Then he took some green coconuts.

He took the coconuts and threw them down to the ground, killing the men, women and children. When the other people saw this, they told a man to climb the coconut palm. The name of this man was Sasavi.

Sasavi was furious and said that he would go up the tree and throw down the man from Witupe Number One.

"Wait here. I'll go up, kill this man, and throw him down. The Witupe want to fool around with us, huh? That man is marked for me. I'll kill him." After he said this, he climbed the coconut palm.

Sasavi called out, then he raced up the coconut palm. When he climbed the tree, he called out in the language of the Giniambu, "Sasavi *Unire! Kambu kambu*!" In English, this means, "That's my target! That's my target!"

Sasavi called out as he climbed the tree, but the scoundrel at the top of the tree put some green coconuts into a net bag and prepared to give it to him good.

When Sasavi approached, he took the bag of coconuts and put it around Sasavi's neck. Oh my, the weight of the coconuts made Sasavi fall down to the ground. Sasavi's kin thought that Sasavi had beaten this man down, but it was Sasavi who had fallen badly to the ground and died.

The scoundrel from Witupe Number One went down very quietly and fled back to his village. When he arrived at the village, he told the other men what he had done and all of them were elated.

This is the end of the ancestor story. In the time of ancestors, the people from the two Witupe villages were great enemies with the people of Ginuambu [Kiniambu]. So at this time, great fights in the forest and on the ground always arose between them.

However, today we children never argue or fight like this. We are usually friendly and we have forgotten these things from the days of yore.

Isaac Wamakuara
Witupe No. 2 Village
Sepik Plain, Patrol Post Yangoru, Wewak
East Sepik Province
P551.5. Boy corps; P555. Defeat in battle; R210. Escapes; R220. Flights; S110. Murders

A Snake-Man Married a Real Woman
(Wantok 775, May 11, 1989, page 19)

This story comes from the time before our grandfather, Arike, was born. Long, long ago, in the Okapa area, at the Ibusa-Etasena Clan House [**Ibusa** and **Etesena** Villages], there was a tall mountain [**Fore** People, **Eastern Highlands** Province]. On this mountain, there lived a huge snake. This was not an ordinary snake, it was part-man too.

His house was very long, big enough to fit his body. The inside of the house was filled with many kinds of meats, such as from marsupials (*kapul*) and birds. He would use the marsupials to make fire.

One time, he heard that there was a big festival happening at a village called **Yasubi** in the southern part of the Okapa District. He transformed his body and became a very handsome young man.

He dressed himself very finely with bird feathers and marsupial fur. He went to the place where the festival was happening. When he arrived there, the people were shocked because his adornments were so fine, better than those of all of the other men.

The women could not sit quietly. They asked him [to dance]. He beat his hand drum as he sang and danced passionately. He sang and danced until it was nearly four o'clock in the morning, then he got up very slowly and left the festival grounds. He walked and walked, back to his home. However, he was surprised to see that a young woman was following him.

When he saw this, he changed and became a huge snake. He tried to scare her, but she was persistent and said, "I'm not afraid. You're a real man." Then she kept following the snake.

The snake turned into a pond, but she was unafraid and did not run back to the village. She said the same thing and kept following him. The snake performed various tricks to frighten her, but she was persistent and kept following. Later, the snake gave up and turned back into a man.

He told her, "OK, if you want to follow me, then you can come. However, don't be afraid when you see something in my house."

They arrived at his house, then she went inside and was surprised to see the marsupials in the fire. Immediately, she removed them and began to eat. She continued to eat, then he went inside and said, "Don't eat the firewood. The edible marsupials are in the forest."

The snake-man divided his room into two parts. He slept in one room and his wife slept in the other room. They lived well and every day they would go to hunt for wild game in the forest.

After a while, his wife became pregnant. It was nearly time for her to give birth, so the snake told her, "If you give birth and they're snakes, then you must put them in a bamboo tube. If the children are human, then you must put them in a net bag."

When she gave birth, they were all snakes. There were about ten of them, so she put them inside bamboo tubes and that is where they lived.

One day, her old mother came to see them. The married couple had gone to the forest when the old woman arrived. No one was there, so she opened the door and went inside the house. Immediately, the snakes jumped out of the bamboo tubes and attached themselves to her breasts.

The old woman was surprised and terrified. She grabbed them and threw them on top of the fire, killing them. However, one of the snakes fell down and went to hide near the stones by the fireplace.

In the afternoon, the old woman's daughter returned to the house. She saw her mother and was happy, but she was surprised to see that the snake-children were dead in the fire. The child who was hiding by the stones came out very quietly and said, "_Aio taku tagu_." This means, "The old mother burned the others in the fire."

She listened and cried terribly. She told her mother that her husband was not a real man, that he was a snake. Their children had come out as snakes too, so she had been mistaken to burn them in the fire.

She told her mother to go back to the village quickly, lest her husband return and hear the news, then he would be angry and kill her. She gave a ripe banana to her mother, then said, "When you arrive at the village, you must eat this banana before you go inside the house." The old mother took the ripe banana and left her daughter, going back to the village.

When the snake-man arrived at his house, his little child came out and told him, "_Alo tagu tagu_."

His wife told him what had happened. The snake listened and said, "I'll just follow mother, then I'll leave her in the village and return." However, he really wanted to kill the old woman.

The snake left the house and sped off into the forest, searching for the old woman. However, when he arrived at the village, he saw the old woman standing outside her house, eating the ripe banana. The snake went into the old woman's house. He ate all of her belly, then he went back to his home.

His wife knew that he had killed her old mother, so she took a round stone and heated it in the fire. She took the stone and shoved it into a bamboo tube with leafy greens. Then she shoved in more leafy greens with the hot stone.

When the snake arrived at the house, she took the bamboo and gave it to him. The snake thought that it just contained leafy greens, so he swallowed all of it. The stone went inside and blocked the snake's throat, killing him. She took her belongings and went outside. She burned the house and the snake too, then she fled back to her village.

This mountain is still there. It is called, _Nagintayanadi_ or "A Snake Swallowed a Stone." The baby snake is still there, inside the hole of a tree called _nabu_.

Nason, Joel, Jerry, Betty, Jeffrie, and father and mother
   Smith
P. O. Box 1217
Arawa
North Solomons Province

A1617. Origin of place-name; B211.6.1. Speaking snake (serpent); B632. Animal offspring from marriage to animal; B646.1. Marriage to person in snake form; B875.1. Giant serpent; D191M. Transformation: man to serpent (snake); D391M. Transformation: serpent (snake) to man; D425.1+. Transformation: snake to pond; G71+. Son-in-law eats mother-in-law; J1813+. Cooking processes misunderstood: using animal flesh as firewood; P210. Husband and wife; P230. Parents and children; P232. Mother and daughter; P262. Mother-in-law; P265. Son-in-law; P292. Grandmother; Q211. Murder punished; Q411. Death as punishment; Q414. Punishment: burning alive; R260. Pursuits; S41. Cruel grandmother; S56. Cruel son-in-law; S63+. Wife kills husband; S110+. Eaten alive; S112. Burning to death; S112+. Murder by throwing hot stones down throat; T100. Marriage; T554.7. Woman gives birth to a snake; T570. Pregnancy; T586.1. Many children at a birth; Z356. Unique survivor

Wosungku Tricked the Enemies

(Wantok 776, May 18, 1989, page 19)

Long, long ago, in a village by **Maprik**, **East Sepik** Province, there lived a woman [**Abelam** People]. The name of this woman was Wosungku. Wosungku was a very beautiful woman. Her father and mother had died, so she lived alone.

Every day, people would wake up in the very early morning and go to work in the gardens. In the evening, they would return to the village.

One morning, before cockcrow, everyone awoke and went to the gardens. Wosungku felt a little lazy and was still sleeping. She woke up much later and prepared her food. Later still, she took her things for working in the garden, then she walked away slowly.

Along the trail, some sorcerer men saw her and wanted to kill her. They performed a song and dance to knock her out, then later, they would kill her.

However, the ghosts of Wosungku's parents were watching over her, so the powers of these sorcerers did not work. The magic just followed her and she arrived at the garden.

Near the garden, there was a river named Kepma. She went down by the river and took a crab. She tied up the crab well, then she put it in her net bag.

Later, she jumped across the river and walked to her garden. She arrived at the garden, put all of her things in the garden hut, and began removing grasses in the garden.

She removed the grasses, then she cut her hand on a sugarcane leaf. The poor woman lost plenty of blood from her hand. Quickly, she ran to the garden hut and took a stick. She dug a hole and placed her hand down into the hole. She did this to stanch the flow of blood from her hand. Later, she tied up her hand with leaves and went to sit in the garden hut.

The sorcerers had followed her to the garden and were watching carefully. They had forgotten completely about killing her. They only thought of having sex with her. However, there were big, black clouds in the sky, and rain and wind came. The other people had seen this and gone back to the village.

Wosungku took her things and was about to walk back to the village too, but when she arrived at the Kepma River, she saw that the flooded water had carried the bridge away.

She went down to the river and tried to cross, but the water was too strong. She turned back to her garden and slept there. While she slept, she dreamt that some enemies had come towards her body. She was surprised in the dream and was terrified. A good thought came to her. She removed all of the firewood and went to hide among the firewood.

The rain also drenched the enemies, so they looked for a place to hide. They went to the other garden huts, but these had no firewood.

They went to all of the garden huts. Then they arrived at Wosungku's garden hut. They were elated when they saw the firewood inside. Wosungku was dead asleep and did not know that the sorcerers had arrived at her hut.

The sorcerers made a bonfire, then prepared to sleep. One of them walked away to fetch some more firewood, then he was surprised to see Wosungku sleeping there.

He was elated and did not tell the other sorcerers. His heart jumped. He thought that this would be an excellent chance for himself.

The other sorcerers were preparing to sleep and they told each other to keep watch when the others slept. The sorcerer who had found the woman stood up quickly and told the others that he would take first watch while the others slept.

He waited for the other sorcerers to sleep, then he very quietly walked away to fetch firewood. He removed the firewood, then he tried to grab Wosungku.

However, Wosungku saw him and pretended to be dead asleep. When the sorcerer put out his hand to grab her, she quietly untied the crab that she had taken from the water. She untied the crab's two claws and put them right at the sorcerer's testicles.

Oh my, the crab pinched the sorcerer and he screamed terribly. The pain was greater than any other, so the poor sorcerer jumped about and cried terribly like a little boy.

The other sorcerers heard this and woke up. They thought that some enemy had come and grabbed their watchman. They got up and ran about inside the forest. Wosungku also followed them, fleeing back to the village.

She arrived at the village and was surprised to see a very handsome man waiting at the house. The man told her that he had arisen from her blood, the blood that she had buried in the ground when she had cut her hand on the sugarcane leaf. They married and they lived happily together in this village.

Willie Wanda

Maprik Station

Wewak

East Sepik Province

D1711. Magician; D1781. Magic results from singing; D1781+. Magic results from dancing; D1810.8.3. Warning in dreams; D2061. Magic murder; E327+. Dead father returns to aid child; E323.2+. Dead mother returns to aid child; J1050. Attention to warnings; P210. Husband and wife; P231. Mother and son; P232. Mother and daughter; P234. Father and daughter; Q244.1. Punishment for attempted rape; Q451.10.1+. Punishment: attack on testicles; R220. Flights; R260. Pursuits; T100. Marriage; T412+. Mother-son marriage; T541.1. Birth from blood; W111. Laziness; X712.3.1H. Injury to testicles

A Boy Became a Bird

(Wantok 777, May 25, 1989, page 19)

Long, long ago, in the Frigano [**Firigano**] area of **Eastern Highlands** Province, there was a small mountain [**Yagaria** People]. The name of this mountain was Avokokopa.

One night, a father told his son that they would leave the village in the very early morning and go to hunt for wild game in the forest. The father told his son that he must wake up quickly in the morning, then cook some sweet potatoes for themselves for when they are in the forest.

They awoke in the very early morning and the boy cooked the sweet potatoes. They carried their bows and arrows, then they walked away into the forests of Avokokopa.

They arrived in the forest, then they searched and searched for game, but they did not see a single animal. They went to the other side of the mountain, then they searched and arrived at the place where their forest hut was located.

They began to kill some animals at this time. They put them in a net bag and the boy carried them. His father continued hunting for animals and he climbed trees. He wanted to fill the net bag with animals before they returned to the forest hut and rested.

By this time, the boy was famished. He had not eaten in the morning before they had left the village. The sun was very hot too, so the boy had lost his strength. His father was also hungry, but he was a big man so he ignored his hunger. He wanted to find marsupials (*kapul*) first, then he would worry about eating.

The father was still up on a tree, and the boy tried some sweet potato skin. He ate and the skin was delicious, so he broke off a piece of sweet potato and ate it. It was even more delicious, so he finished a whole sweet potato.

The father descended the tree and the boy thought that they would then rest. However, the father went up another tree and continued to hunt for marsupials. The boy waited and waited, then he ate another sweet potato. He finished this sweet potato, then he ate another one. He did this until all of the sweet potatoes were gone.

The father hunted for marsupials for a while, then he was dying of hunger and about to faint. He went down to the ground very slowly, then he found a very good place (**Kumadama**). He asked his son for sweet potato. The boy listened and did not speak.

The father spoke sternly and the boy told him, "I was famished and I finished all of the sweet potatoes."

His father did not speak because he was famished. The father was furious and he sat there. After a while, he lied to the boy, "Stay here. I'll go down the mountain and check on a tree. I always find marsupials on this tree."

The father went down, but he ran back to the village. He did not care about his son. The poor boy sat waiting and waiting until it was nearly dark, then rain began to fall. He was afraid. He cried and shouted for his father. In my language, "father" is *avo* [*ávo'a*].

The boy cried and cried. His eyes became completely red, then his tears became red too. He kept calling out, "*Avo, avo*." However, his father was already in the village.

It was completely dark and the rain had stopped. The boy was afraid and climbed a big tree, where he slept. He slept and dreamt that he was in his house. When he turned, he fell down. He put his hand out and grabbed at the tree branches, but he turned into a bird and flew up to the trees.

This bird is still there in our very deep forests of Lufa. When you travel the forest there, you will hear the bird's call, "Avo o, avo o, avo o." The place where his tears fell has become a lake. You can still see this lake. The name of this place now is Avokokopa.

Yanuvi Mode

Herea Mart

Badili

National Capital District

A1617. Origin of place-name; D150B. Transformation: boy to bird; D457.18.2+. Transformation: tears to lake; P233. Father and son; Q272. Avarice punished; Q438. Punishment: abandonment in forest; S11. Cruel father; S143. Abandonment in forest; W151. Greed; W157. Dishonesty

A Sister Turned into a Marsupial (*Kapul*)

(Wantok 778, June 1, 1989, page 19)

Long, long ago, in the time of the ancestors, there was a boy and his sister who lived in **Bomai Kiari**, in southern **Simbu** Province. [Bomai Village has **Golin** and **Mikaru** speaking people. Kiari Village has **Nomane** speaking people.]

One time, there was a great drought in the Kiari area. All of the grasses were dry, and all of the food plants in the gardens had died. The rivers and streams dried up and dust swirled about.

The boy saw this and told his sister that they would leave this place and go to live somewhere else. His sister asked, "Where shall we go?"

The brother replied, "Come and I'll show you."

He took his sister and they climbed the mountain at **Nubuni** [**Chuave** People]. The brother showed her a fog-covered mountain. The girl saw this and told her brother that they must go there to find water at the base of a boulder. The name of the boy was Moiwa and the name of the girl was Gorai.

They killed a big pig and cooked it. Then they butchered the pig and packed it with taros, sweet potatoes, and salt. They left the village and walked to the mountain.

They went to a mountain named Gun Sta, then they went to see the nearby Kinns Sta whose peak was covered in fog. They were very happy to see this cold place.

When they wanted to see Gul Glas, they descended the mountain. Little Gorai carried her brother's little dog. Her legs were cramped and she was in pain. She could not walk well. Moiwa let his sister stay there while he sped away to the stone base of Mount Kinns Sta. He grabbed at the grasses and tried to drink the water.

When little Gorai and the dog arrived at the base of the mountain, the cold water began to come out of the hole in the mountain. The water was freezing, and the brother and sister drank their fill. When they finished drinking, Moiwa told his sister that they would climb to the top of the mountain and look around. He wanted to see if someone had made a fire that they could use to warm their cold food so that they could eat.

When Moiwa went to the top of the mountain, he saw a big tree. He went directly to it. He climbed the tree and looked around, then he saw smoke rising from the side of the mountain.

He looked carefully, then he saw a round house. He went down and went to the house. The door was open, so he went inside. He saw two beautiful young women sitting there who were cooking sweet potatoes. The women were also surprised to see Moiwa.

They asked about him. He told them that he was from Bomai and that his name was Moiwa. The women told him that their names were Kai and Mokomane.

Moiwa took some fire from them. When he was about to return to his sister, a heavy rain began to fall, so they told him to wait until the rain stopped. He listened to them, went inside the house and sat comfortably.

While he was sitting in the house, he saw that the house floor was filled with marsupial (*kapul*) furs and bird feathers. There was a wonderful smell inside the house, like perfume. Then Moiwa thought of his sister, Gorai.

He looked up towards the place where the trees came together and he saw a marsupial sitting there. Gorai looked down at her brother and said, "If you want me to stay here, then I'll stay. Come and take your dog. Then I'll return."

Gorai said this, then she put her hand to her belly, removed Moiwa's dog, and threw it down. She walked and held a tree branch, then jumped to hold another. She did this for a while until she was completely hidden.

Moiwa's brother saw this cried mournfully. He raised an axe and cut off his first finger, then he cried and went to the two women. When they asked him why he was crying, he told them that his sister had become a marsupial.

They listened and scolded him, "That's your own fault. Why didn't you want to take her with you?"

So now, we see that female marsupials have their own net bags [i.e., their pouches]. This began at the time of Moiwa and his sister Gorai in the Nubuni Kinns Sta Mountain.

John Kamana

Ok Tedi Mining Ltd., P. O. Box 25

Kiunga

Western Province

A2380+. Origin of marsupial's pouch; D179.6K+G. Transformation: girl to marsupial; P253. Sister and brother; P681+. Mourning customs: self-mutilation; S160.1. Self-mutilation; S161.1. Mutilation: cutting off fingers

Two Friends from Simbu and Bundi

(Wantok 779, June 8, 1989, page 19)

Long, long ago, in the time of the ancestors, there was a man who lived in a village called Gueyui [**Gueibi**] in the Bundi area of the Highlands of **Madang** [Province, **Gende** People]. The name of this man was Tawi Mundua.

Mundua had a very good friend. This friend was from another village, one called **Siago** in **Simbu** Province [**Kuman** People]. The name of the good friend was Yari. Their two villages were not near each other. Mundua always traveled to see Yari and Yari also traveled to see his friend.

One day, Mundua thought of going to Siago to see Yari. Siago Village was very far, so he walked for three whole days and nights. On the fourth day, he arrived at Siago Village.

Yari was very happy when he saw his friend Mundua. He quickly called out for the women and their daughters to cook food to give to his friend. The two of them ate, then they sat and told stories. Yari told him to stay for a fairly long time in Siago.

Mundua stayed for a long time with Yari and he forgot about returning to his village. One day, he thought hard that he must return to Gueyui. He was very worried that his wife and four daughters were short of food.

So one afternoon, he told Yari that in the morning he would return to Gueyui. The next day, Yari took seven yellow pandanus (*marita*) fruits and gave them to Mundua.

Mundua said, "Friend, bring me to the trail, then you can return." Yari replied, "That's OK. There's nothing to it. We'll go together and then I'll leave you on the trail."

They walked and walked, then they arrived at a village called Kavamukey [**Karamukei**]. Yari said, "OK, I'll leave you here." However Mundua was not happy about this. He said, "No, leave me at **Tumuanogoi** Village, then return."

They kept walking until they arrived at Tumuanogoi Village. When they arrived there, it was night. Yari did not have time to return, so they slept in Tumuanogoi Village and they awoke in the very early morning.

Yari said good-bye to Mundua, then he wanted to return to Siago, but Mundua stopped him. Mundua wanted Yari to leave him at the border between Simbu and Bundi.

They walked and walked, then they approached the Simbu-Bundi border. Before long, they heard a man calling from inside the deep forest. Mundua heard this and thought that it was his friend from Simbu calling, so he quickly asked his friend, "Yari! Did you year that shouting or not? Who was it?"

Yari replied, "No! That was a man from Tumuanogoi Village hunting for marsupials in the forest and shouting. It wasn't me."

They walked a little further, then the birds of the forest called about. The birds came and pulled Yari's hair. At first, just individual birds came, but later many, many birds came and removed all of his hair.

Oh my, the birds were plentiful and their singing blocked the Simbu man's hearing completely. He felt like collapsing as he walked because the pandanus weighed him down as he walked swiftly.

He sat in the middle of the trail and told Yari, "Oh Yari, my good friend! I feel like I can't walk now, so can you carry these pandanus fruits along the trail? Later, you can return and carry me. I'm very sorry but I'm old now and all of my strength is gone."

Yari saw that his friend Mundua was completely out of breath, so he was very worried for him.

Mundua told Yari, "My good friend, never mind. Leave me and go back lest you think badly of me. I'm old now and very soon I'll leave you, so you should leave me." After he said this, Yari was completely upset.

They arrived exactly at Mount Willem [Wilhelm]. Mount Willem is exactly at the border of Simbu and Bundi. Mundua was worried and began to tell a story to Yari, "I have no son who could give you a present or fete you for the hard work that you've done. However, I have four daughters. They'll think of you and give you some presents. Now, don't worry about me any more because you've carried me a long ways. Leave me and go first to the village with these seven pandanus fruits. Explain to my wife and four daughters what has happened, then in the morning you can return to get me."

Yari cut some trees and removed some sword grass. Then he made a nice bed outside and placed Mundua on top of it. After he did this, he went to the village.

He arrived at Gueyui. Mundua's wife and four daughters were shocked to see him, "Hey! Our papa went to see you. Why have you come here?"

Quietly, Yari took them into the house and explained to them what had happened. They were very sorry. Yari had cried terribly as he walked to the village. He told Mundua's wife and four daughters. All of them were very troubled. He stayed there for a while, then he married one of Mundua's daughters and lived permanently at Gueyui Village.

Benny Tawi
P. O. Box 918
Lae
Morobe Province

B17.2.3+. Hostile bird; P210. Husband and wife; P232. Mother and daughter; P234. Father and daughter; P252.2+. Four sisters; P310. Friendship; T100. Marriage

Simbonga, a Man Who Searched for Wildfowl Eggs

(Wantok 780, June 15, 1989, page 16)

Long, long ago, in the time of the ancestors, there was a man who lived in Bongkiman [**Bonkiman**] Village [**Bonkiman** People, **Morobe** or **Madang** Province]. The man's name was Simbonga.

He was a man who searched for wildfowl eggs. After wildfowls went to his forest and he found their eggs, he would go to others' forests to search for eggs there.

He did this all of the time, so he was better at it than everyone else in the village. They knew that when it was wildfowl season, Simbonga would finish off all of the eggs. They tried to beat him, but they were unable to do so because he was the best at finding wildfowl eggs.

After a while, the people of the village began to become angry because Simbonga always finished off the eggs and they had none. The men went to the spirit house and argued. They decided to perform sorcery and teach Simbonga a lesson.

It was wildfowl season now and Simbonga awoke in the very early morning to go to the forest. He arrived in the forest, then he searched for eggs until he filled his net bag. He leapt towards another forest and kept searching for eggs. After a while, his second net bag was also full.

It was nearly dark, and he carried the net bags of eggs to his forest hut. He wanted to sit, rest and sleep, then in the morning he would awake and return to the village.

He arrived at the hut, then he put the net bags down and searched for firewood to make a fire. There were some dry leaves, so he took them and lit a fire. The poor man did not know that the men had performed sorcery on these dry leaves and placed them there.

Before long, a dog arrived. Simbonga saw the dog and thought that the men of the village had come and that their dog had run ahead of them. However, no one came. He kept sitting there, then he heard babies crying and men talking in the forest. However, they did not come to the hut.

Then Simbonga went outside to look. When he went to the door, he saw a giant hanging from the door of the hut. His tongue was hanging down, but his eyes looked at Simbonga. He tried to jump and grab Simbonga, but Simbonga was not an ordinary man either. He had a little trick.

He performed a song and dance, then he beat the man who was hanging from the door. The man descended and disappeared. Simbonga saw this and pulled out his net bags, then he walked down the mountain.

It was completely dark, but Simbonga did not take the mountainous terrain into account. He ran a little, then he walked a little. He kept doing this, then he fell at various points along the trail. He went and went, then he became completely out of breath. He could not stand and catch his breath because he heard various ghosts making noises behind him and following him.

He heard the babies crying, men shouting, and various screams. He knew that if he rested along the trail, the ghosts would meet up with him and kill him.

Simbonga was completely out of breath and he thought that a big stone was lying on the trail. He went up to it and tried a little [trick] of his. He shoved the stone to the side of the mountain and it tumbled down.

Simbonga removed his loincloth, then he climbed a big *galip* tree. He went to the very top of the tree, then he made a bed from his loincloth and he slept.

The ghosts began to climb the *galip* tree. They went up and surrounded poor Simbonga, chasing him up further. They did this until the sun rose. When the sun rose, the ghosts descended the tree. When they arrived on the ground, they turned into pieces of ginger, stones and logs, then they fell down.

Simbun [Simbonga] stayed on top of the *galip* tree until the sun was very strong. At about ten o'clock, he descended very slowly until he trampled the ground. He saw the pieces of ginger, stones, and logs lying there. He knew that the people of the village must have performed sorcery or something for him to be surrounded that night.

He left this place, then he ran to the village and explained to his clan what had happened. He went back with them to the base of the *galip* tree. They made a bonfire, and burned the things upon which the people had performed sorcery. After they burned them, they returned to the village.

After this, Simbonga never went around gathering wildfowl eggs in the forests of other clans. When it was wildfowl season, he would go directly to his own forest, gather the eggs there, then return to the village.

Hora Bare

Bonkiman

Tapen Seket

[Morobe or Madang Province]

D955. Magic leaf; D1421.4. Magic object summons giant; D1781. Magic results from singing; D1781+. Magic results from dancing; D2095. Magic disappearance; E261.4. Ghost pursues man; E380. Ghost summoned; E446.2. Ghost laid by burning body; E553. Ghost becomes log during day; E553+. Ghost becomes ginger during day; E553+. Ghost becomes stone during day; E587.3. Ghosts walk from curfew to cockcrow; F531. Giant; K420. Thief loses his goods or is detected; Q212. Theft punished; Q272. Avarice punished; Q551. Magic manifestations as punishments; R260. Pursuits; R311. Tree refuge; V112.1. Spirit huts; W151. Greed

Why Dogs and Marsupials (*Kapul*) Have Been Enemies Until Today

(Wantok 781, June 22, 1989, page 20)

Long, long ago, in a village inside **Eastern Highlands** Province, the dogs and marsupials (*kapul*) were very good friends. They erected a huge house, and they lived together in this village. At this time, the dogs and the various kinds of marsupials lived as very good brothers and sisters.

The dogs would go searching for food during the day. They would sleep at night, then the marsupials would go searching for food. During the day, the marsupials would sleep and the dogs would go to work again. This is what they did while they lived together.

One day, in the very early morning, all of the dogs awoke and went to search for food in the garden. One poor dog was terribly sick, so it stayed alone in its room.

The dog lay there and heard the marsupials returning. The dog took a big stick. It did not go outside to tell stories with marsupials when they returned. The dog lay there very quickly and listened to the marsupials telling various stories about what they had done that night.

The marsupials thought that all of the dogs had gone into the forest, so they began to speak behind their backs and say bad things about the dogs.

Oh my, they said various shameful things and completely disparaged the dogs. A marsupial said, "Those dogs think that they're better. Oh my! Daylight is the time for sleeping, but they go to do things in the garden."

They told stories like that, and they joked around. Later, the sun rose higher and they all slept. However, they did not know that the sick dog had heard the things that they had said. The dog heard everything that they said behind the dogs' backs, and this dog was furious.

The dog did not do a thing because it was alone and felt ill. The dog did not have enough strength to fight if the marsupials teamed together, so the dog stayed there quietly and waited for the other dogs to return in the afternoon.

In the afternoon, all of the dogs returned to the house. Then the marsupials each went into the forest because it was time for them to search for food.

The sick dog waited for all of the marsupials to leave, then it got up and called for all of the dogs to gather. The dog told them about what the marsupials had said behind their backs.

Oh my, the dogs were furious. Some dogs wanted to run into the forest and find the marsupials, but others stopped them and they stayed.

The dog leader said, "Let's live well together as good brothers and sisters. However, if they want us to break apart, then that's OK. We'll leave them and become enemies."

The dogs prepared their things for fighting, then they went to sleep. They slept and slept, then when it was nearly [morning] they woke up quickly. This time the marsupials would not return alone.

Quickly, they took their fighting gear and went into the forest. They waited in the forest for all of the marsupials to come and enter the house.

Then it was time. They ran into the village and began to call out. The marsupials inside the house were shocked. They wanted to flee outside, but the dogs had surrounded the door.

They killed and ate the marsupials. Some marsupials were strong and fled into the forest, but the dogs kept following them into the forest. However, those marsupials were lucky and jumped up on the trees.

The leader of the dogs told the leader of the marsupials, "We had lived well as good brothers and sisters. We ate in one house and we slept in one house, but you turned on us and spoke behind our backs. So now, we've become enemies. We'll return to the village and live with men. You'll live in the forest."

The leader of the marsupials replied, "That's OK because you've killed and eaten some of us. At some time, we'll scratch your noses."

After this, the dogs went back to the village. The marsupials stayed in the forest. It was because of this that dogs and marsupials are enemies. This story comes from Irakea [**Ilakia**] Village in the Okapa [sub-]District [**Awa** People].

Mote Wi

P. O. Box 4042

Boroko

National Capital District

A2433.2.1+. Why marsupial lives in forest; A2494.4+. Enmity between dog and marsupial; B211.1.7. Speaking dog; B211.2.12K+. Speaking marsupial; B241.2+. King of marsupials; B241.2.7. King of dogs; K914. Murder from ambush; P310. Friendship; Q288. Punishment for mockery; Q411. Death as punishment; R213. Escape from home; R260. Pursuits; S110. Murders

A Ghost Woman Confused a Real Woman

(Wantok 782, June 29 — July 5, 1989, page 19)

Long, long ago, in the time of the ancestors, there lived a man and his wife. They lived in a village near the sea in **East Sepik** Province. The man and woman were newlyweds, so they did not have children yet. They lived very happily with the other people of the village.

Later, the woman was pregnant and she was staying alone in the village. Her husband and the other people had gone to the forest. While she was there, a ghost woman came to her. The ghost woman tricked her and they went down to bathe in the sea.

The woman bathed for a while, then she swallowed some seawater. The baby in her belly was heavy, and she was very short of breath. The ghost woman saw this and fled.

The poor woman did not have the strength to swim back to shore. The current was strong and carried her out to an island. This island was in the middle of the sea, so there was no one who lived on this island.

She slept on the beach, then she woke up in the early morning. Oh my, she was shocked to see that she was on the shore of this island.

Quickly, she walked around the island. She thought that there were some people on the island, but she did not hear a single noise and she did not hear anyone shouting. Birds and other animals only populated this island. Later, she made a hut. She lived alone on the island. After some weeks, she gave birth to a baby boy.

She was elated for her baby and took good care of him. The baby grew up quickly and became strong like his father. The boy had grown, so one time the mother told the story of what had happened to her. The boy listened and was very troubled.

One time, the boy told his mother, "Mama! Mama! I want to make a canoe." However, the mother told her son, "I'm very sorry my son. I know what you're thinking, but we have no knife or axe to make a canoe."

They lived there for a while, then one time the sea current brought an axe and a knife to the beach. Oh my, they saw these and were elated. The boy chose a good tree and began to carve a canoe. In the afternoon, the canoe was ready and the mother arrived.

The mother encouraged him and said, "Oh my! You're an excellent son. You made this canoe just like your father made them. Son! I'll stay on this island. You're a big man now. You'll take this canoe by yourself, then paddle to the village. At the village you'll tell the story to the people and they'll find your papa. Your papa knows that I was lost when I was pregnant with you. So, he knows that if I'm still alive and that his son will come. He's waiting for you there, so don't worry. Go ahead."

The next day, the boy took all of the food to give him strength, then he jumped into the canoe. He cried terribly that he was leaving his mother because he did not know what kind of adversity he would encounter. He was terrified of the sea ghosts. However, his mother gave him courage, so he did not worry about this.

During the day, the boy rested on top of the canoe. At night, he followed the stars in the sky and paddled. He did this for some weeks, then he arrived at the village. Some men saw him and took him to the leader of the village.

They gave him food, then he revealed the story that his mother had told him. His father heard the story and held his son. They hugged and cried terribly.

The father showed him foods such as taro, banana, sugarcane, and yam. The boy took these foods and put them on top of the canoe.

The father jumped in with him, then they paddled back towards the island. They paddled and paddled, then they approached the island.

The mother saw the canoe out in the sea. She knew that her son must have returned. Oh my, she jumped and sang and danced on the beach. Her husband jumped down onto the beach, then they hugged. They cried and cried until all of the tears in their eyes were gone.

The three of them held each other and sang as they went to the house. The mother cooked all of the food, then the father and son carried the food ashore. The food was ready, so the three of them had a big party by themselves. This was to celebrate their son's first adventure.

They stayed on the island for a little while, then they prepared to return to the village. They put all of their belongings on top of the canoe, then they paddled to the village. At the village, everyone gathered and had a huge party.

Daniel Yaul
Witupe Number Two [**Abelam** People]
East Sepik Plain
Patrol Post Yangoru, Wewak
East Sepik Province

E271. Sea-ghosts; E299.5+. Ghost causes person to be lost at sea; E425.1. Revenant as woman; P210. Husband and wife; P231. Mother and son; P233. Father and son; R154.1. Son rescues mother; T570. Pregnancy; T580. Childbirth

Gawe [Gowe] and Kuagle Became Rivers

(Wantok 783, July 6, 1989, page 19)

The clouds arrived and covered Mount Wilhelm. The children of Siako [**Siago**] Village knew that today there would be a heavy downpour, so each of them ran inside their sword-grass huts [**Kuman** People, **Simbu** Province].

I also ran quickly into my sword-grass hut near the Kuaglenigle River. This time, I had not forgotten the ancestor story that mother had told me. I heard this story on November 2, 1975 when I was in fourth grade. At that time I wrote it in my book, which I still have.

When I was in twelfth grade at Kerevat [Keravat] National High School, I translated this story into English. I won first prize for this story.

The story goes as follows. Long, long ago, in the time of the ancestors, there was a village. The name of this village was Irugl Torogl. "*Irugl Torogl*" in the language of those of us who live near Mount Wilhelm means, "The Rainy Place." [*Irugl* is a kind of tree (Nilles, 1969: 85). *Torogl* means, "is lit" (Nilles (1969: 230).]

There was a small clan house in this village. Inside the village, there lived a boy and a girl. The boy's name was Gowe and the girl's name was Kuagle. Their father and mother had died when they were still little, so they lived alone in the house that their father and mother had made when they were still alive.

They lived for a while, then one time the little sister, Kuagle, had a strong desire to eat meat. She talked and cried. Gowe saw this, so he was very worried about his sister. The nearby clan house never cared about them or gave them any kind of meat or food.

When they ate meat, they would just give the bones with a little meat to the two of them. The two children were unfortunate. The other children often gathered and talked about what kinds of meat they had eaten. They would tell stories and draw pictures of the animals on the ground. The two children would just stay nearby and listen to their stories.

Gowe saw this and was in great pain because of it. He was also very sorry for his little sister. He wanted to take a spear and go into the forest, but he was not a big man yet and he did not have the strength to kill a pig.

His father had not died when he was a big man, when he could have shown him how to kill animals. His father had died when he was still young.

One time, strong thoughts came to him that he must go into the forest. He slept for a while, then in the very early morning, when the birds were singing, he awoke. Quickly, he prepared his things and walked into the forest with his bow and arrows. He walked and walked, then he entered the very deep forest, on the side of Irugl Torogl.

Oh my, before long, he saw a nice pig walking towards him. He thought that his eyes must be shut and that he was dreaming. Later, he was surprised to see that the pig was coming closer to him. He tensed his muscles and shot an arrow directly at the pig's body. The pig threw out its legs and fell to the ground.

Gowe was elated and carried the pig back to his sister. This time, they had plenty of meat to eat. Kuagle was very happy for Gowe. However, they did not know that this was a ghost's pig.

They lived there for a while, then one night, the ghost was searching and calling for his pig to come home. They heard the ghost's calling and noises, and they were terrified.

The ghost man knew that it was Gowe who had killed his pig, but he explained to the people of the village that whoever had killed the pig must speak out. When he said the color of the pig, Gowe knew that he had killed this pig. Quickly, Gowe spoke out and said that he had killed the pig. Oh my, the ghost man was furious and walked back to his cave.

Two days later, the ghost returned. The ghost killed Gowe and Kuagle late at night. The people of the village saw this and trembled fiercely.

When it was still that night, they saw two lights following the side of the mountain, going to the two headwaters on top of Mount Wilhelm, then the lights stayed there.

Today, if you go to Toromambuno [**Toromambuna**] Village, where there is a small Catholic Mission under Mount Wilhelm, you will see two streams. The name of one stream is Gowe and the other is Kuagle.

The people gave the names of the brother and sister two these two rivers. Gowe River and Kuagle River meet at Niglguma Village. *Niglguma* in the language of the people who live near Mount Wilhelm means, "Mouth of the River." [*Nigl* means "river" (Nilles (1969: 171) and *guma* means "nose" (Nilles (1969: 76).]

John Mays Bonma

C. M. [Congregation of Mission] Toromambuno

P. O. Box 34

Gembogl

Simbu Province

A934.11. River from transformation. A1617. Origin of place-name; E423.1.5. Revenant as swine; E425.2. Revenant as man; E636+. Reincarnation as river; E722.1.3. Soul leaves body as small point of light; P253. Sister and brother; Q211.6. Killing an animal revenged; Q411. Death as punishment; S110. Murders; W151. Greed

A Snake Created the Kipurepa Tribe

(Wantok 784, July 13-19, 1989, page 19)

Long, long ago, in the time of the ancestors, there lived a married couple. The man's name was Kipu. The woman's name was Yawinu.

At this time, men always fought with enemies from other villages. Only Kipu never went to fight. He would follow the men into battle, but he would turn around on the trail and go back to the house. He did this because he was afraid of fighting. He did not want to die and not have anyone to take care of his wife.

Kipu would flee back to the house, where he would wait for Yawinu. This was because Yawinu would be in the garden until the afternoon.

Kipu would always look at Yawinu's "grass" skirt when she returned to the house to determine whether the fringes of the skirt were broken or crooked.

One day, he pretended to go fighting, and Yawinu went into the garden. Along the trail, Kipu fled back to the village. Then he followed Yawinu into the garden. He wanted to find out what Yawinu actually did in the garden. Quickly, he arrived at the garden, then hid by a tree, and watched.

Yawinu worked very hard in the garden. It was nearly noon, and Yawinu left a corner of the garden, then walked to the rubbish pile in the middle of the garden.

Then Kipu's eyes popped open to see what his wife would do. Oh my, a big snake came out of the big rubbish pile. It surrounded Yawinu, then they went to the ground and had sex. Yawinu had sex with the snake for a while and she forgot about everything.

Kipu's heart was burning up inside, so he could not wait. He took out his stone axe and ran into the garden. Yawinu saw Kipu and was shocked.

Then Kipu shamed his wife in front of the snake, "Your skirt is never straight. Now I know that you've done sinful things with this snake husband of yours."

Kipu pulled the snake and cut it into seven whole pieces. The pieces turned into seven whole men. These seven men later married and created seven whole villages.

The head of the snake turned into a little lizard. It told Kipu, "You must think carefully when you come to my area. Don't call the name of your mama or papa if you're surprised to see me. If you call your mama, someone from your mama's clan will die. If you call your papa's name, someone from your father's clan will die."

After the lizard said this, it went to a part of the earth that people did not know about. Some time later, Kipu took his bow and arrows and went hunting for wild game in the place where the lizard lived. The man was shocked to see something that was incredibly bright at the base of a tree. He went closer and saw a lizard attached to the base of this tree.

This lizard had swallowed a tree fruit, but the fruit was stuck in its neck and it was about to die. Kipu went very close. He saw that the middle of the lizard was swollen terribly. He felt very sorry for the lizard.

Kipu aimed his arrow and shot the lizard right in its belly. The lizard felt better and thanked Kipu, "I almost died and you came to save my life. So, I'll help you later when you are in trouble." Kipu listened to this and then went back to the village.

One time, the men went to fight with the enemies. This time, Kipu also went into battle. The enemies shot Kipu on his side. He returned to the village and was ill because the arrow was still inside his body. He was ill for a long time and was close to dying.

One day, all of the men went to fight. Yawinu and the other women of the village had gone to the gardens, so this time Kipu sent a man to go explain to friends in another village that he was dying. The man called out along the trail as he went and the lizard heard him.

Quickly, the lizard turned into a huge snake. The snake followed the trail and arrived at Kipu's house. The snake went inside, but Kipu was not there.

The snake went around the house and saw Kipu tossing and turning, near death. Quickly, the snake surrounded Kipu and squeezed his body. The piece of arrow came out of Kipu's body.

Kipu felt better and the snake told Kipu, "You went to help me. So when I heard about you, I came to help."

The seven pieces of the snake today mark seven villages. The names of these villages are **Wakua**, **Wama**, **Waluaperepa**, **Rupiali**, **Keloa**, **Rakili** and **Perepe**. Collectively, these are called **Kipurepa**.

That is all that the man and woman did, so we of the small villages of Aropa [**Aboba**], **Riwi**, **Kondeali**, Yamanda [**Iamanda**], Lakire [**Lagira**], **Isale** and **Ropore** have arisen [**Kewa** People]. This story comes from the Ialibu area of **Southern Highlands** Province.

[Anonymous]

A991+. Origin of particular village; B19.4.2+. Glowing lizard; B211.6.2K. Speaking lizard; B380. Animal grateful for relief from pain; B491.1. Helpful serpent; B491.2. Helpful lizard; B511.1. Snake as healer; B520+. Snake saves person's life by squeezing out arrow;. B613.1. Snake paramour; B875.1. Giant serpent; C920+. Death of relative for breaking tabu; C435+. Tabu: uttering parent's name; D391M. Transformation: serpent (snake) to man; D418+. Transformation: lizard to snake; E614.2. Reincarnation as lizard; E656+. Reincarnation: snake to man; P210. Husband and wife; P310. Friendship; Q53. Reward for rescue; Q241. Adultery punished; Q411. Death as punishment; R100. Rescues; R220. Flights; R260. Pursuits; T100. Marriage; T481. Adultery; W27. Gratitude; W121. Cowardice; Z71.5. Formulistic number: seven

A Ghost Woman Killed the Men of Raungwe

(Wantok 785, July 20-26, 1989, page 19)

This ancestor story comes from **Raungwe** in the Nuku District of **West Sepik** Province. This is a story of a ghost man and woman who lost their child and then found their child again.

Long, long ago, there were many people who lived in Raungwe Village. One afternoon, they gathered and spoke about hunting pigs in the forest. They agreed then went to sleep in the spirit house.

At this time, the married men and the big boys did not sleep with women. The men slept by themselves in the spirit house. This was because the men had various powers. If they had slept with the women, they would have lost their powers.

They slept and slept, then in the very early morning, they awoke. Then they went to eat with the women and children. Later, they walked into the forest.

They walked and walked, then they arrived in the very deep forest. The place where they stayed had very tall sword grass. All of them gathered and began to surround the sword grass.

They surrounded it well, then they burned the sword grass. They shouted, sang and danced in their language. They had sharpened their spears well. They prepared to shoot any pigs that fled from the sword grass. However, there were no pigs inside the sword grass. They waited and sang for nothing. They were furious.

Afternoon approached, and a heavy downpour fell. Quickly, they each fled to find a place to hide. One man ran and ran away, then saw a cave. He looked into the cave and he saw that it was a good place to sit. He was elated and wanted to go inside.

He heard a noise coming from the forest. He looked and saw a ghost woman with her daughter approaching. The ghost woman carried her daughter and walked towards the cave because this was their home. She saw him and thought that it was her husband who had come first and was waiting for them.

Quickly, she put the girl in his hands then she went inside the cave. He did not speak. He waited for the ghost woman to go inside the cave, then he sped away with the ghost woman's daughter and went to the village.

The other men had already arrived in the village and were waiting for him. They were surprised to see him arrive with the ghost girl. They put her in the middle of the playground and played with her.

The ghost woman was alone in the cave for a while, then her real husband arrived. She asked her husband for the girl, "Hey, where's the baby? You were standing outside and I gave her to you."

Her husband was shocked, "Ah! You didn't give the baby to me. I've just arrived. You must've given her to another man. OK, find her quickly. I'll stay at home and wait for you."

The ghost woman made her spell. She took ashes from the fire and blew on them. She blew the ashes out of the cave. Then she followed the man's footsteps and arrived at the village.

Oh my, she was furious to see the men playing with her daughter. The men of the village did not know that the ghost girl's mother had arrived.

The ghost woman beat all of the men with a stick. They fell about and died. She took her daughter and went back into the forest.

Tony Gedi
Mukili Catholic Mission [**Beli** People]
Raungwe Village
Nuku [District]
West Sepik Province

D931.1.2. Magic ashes; E261.4. Ghost pursues man; E425.1.4. Revenant as woman carrying baby; E425.2. Revenant as man; E425.3. Revenant as child; K1910. Marital impostors; P210. Husband and wife; P232. Mother and daughter; P234. Father and daughter; Q213. Abduction punished; Q411. Death as punishment; R10. Abduction; R153.4+. Mother rescues daughter; R260. Pursuits; S110. Murders; V112.1. Spirit huts

Two Sisters Tricked a *Masalai* Woman

(Wantok 786, July 27 — August 2, 1989, page 19)

The name of this ancestor story is Kobisi. This story is from the Maprik area of **East Sepik** Province. Kobisi is the story of two sisters fishing in a river. They met a *masalai* woman, then the *masalai* woman wanted to kill them.

Long, long ago, there were two sisters who lived in **Kuminibis** Village in the Maprik area [**Abelam** People]. One time, they thought of going fishing in the river. The name of this river is Watipik.

They prepared their nets, then slept. In the very early morning, they woke up and cooked some food. They ate, then they walked into the forest.

They walked and walked, then arrived at the bottom of the Watipik River. They fished there, then they went up-river. They fished and fished, then they arrived at the source of the river. A *kombi* fruit drifted down towards them. The little sister took it. The fruit was perfectly ripe.

She broke it and gave half to her big sister, then they ate. The *kombi* fruit was delicious. They tasted its sweetness and said, "Oh my! Where did this *kombi* fruit come from?"

They spoke, then they looked up and around. Oh my, they were shocked to see a tree by the water that was completely filled with *kombi* fruits. The *kombi* fruits were perfectly ripe and hanging down.

They were elated, so the big sister told the little sister to go climb the tree. The little sister went up the tree and gathered the fruits.

She threw some down to her big sister. She threw some down for the pigs because the pigs would smell the *kombi* fruits and gather at the base of the tree.

The sisters did not know that a *masalai* woman was spying upon them. This *masalai* woman lived on the side of the mountain by the river.

The *masalai* woman called out to the sisters, "Hey! You two! Give some *kombi* fruits to my pig too." Then the sisters replied, "Ah! *Wokitawa*." In English, this means, "Ah! It belongs to just us two."

Later, the *masalai* woman called out again, "Hey! Tie up a boar, then bring it here. We'll make an earth oven, then eat together."

The sisters listened, and the little sister took a rope. The big sister cut a tree. They grabbed a boar, then carried him up for their earth oven.

When the earth oven was ready, they uncovered it. After they removed the fire, the ghost woman began to divide the pork, "This is for papa. This is for mama. This is for the grandparents. This is for the maternal kin." The ghost woman said this as she divided the pork. Then she gave some meat to the sisters.

The sisters took their piece of meat and lied to the ghost woman, "Hey! Stay there. We'll go very close to the sword grass, give some pieces of meat to our dog, then we'll return."

However, the *masalai* woman knew that they were lying. She got up and chased the two sisters. The sisters ran and ran, then they met some men along the trail. They told the men to help them, "Please help us. A *masalai* woman is chasing us. We'll give you some pork and coconut if you help us."

They gave them some pork and coconut, but the *masalai* woman arrived. Then the sisters fled. The men saw the *masalai* woman and they ran off in various directions.

The sisters ran and ran, then they met two birds, a hornbill and a dove (or pigeon). The sisters were completely out of breath. They asked the birds to help them, "If you are really men, then help us. A *masalai* woman is chasing us."

The hornbill and the dove saw the sisters. They were very sorry for the two of them. Quickly, the big sister jumped up on the hornbill, tying a rope between herself and the hornbill. The little sister jumped up on the dove.

The *masalai* woman arrived later and was too late to hold them. The big sister flew with the hornbill towards the east. The little sister flew with the dove towards the west.

Theo Tom
Kuminibis Number One
P. O. Box 111
Maprik
East Sepik Province

B457.2. Helpful pigeon; B469+. Helpful hornbill; B542.1+. Bird flies with woman to safety; B552+. Woman carried by bird; E261.4. Ghost pursues man; F490+. Masalai; P252.1. Two sisters; R210. Escapes; R100. Rescues; R260. Pursuits

Why Dogs are the Enemies of Kangaroos

(Wantok 787, August 3, 1989, page 23)

This ancestor story comes from **Kenemomo** Village in the Frigano [Firigano] area of **Eastern Highlands** Province [**Yagaria** People].

Long, long ago, in Kenemomo Village, there lived a dog and a kangaroo. They were very good friends. They were like brothers. They slept in the small house and they hunted for food together.

In the early morning, they would wake up and go to hunt for wild game in the forest. One day, before dawn had broken, they woke up and went hunting for food in the forest.

When they approached a men's clan house in a village, the kangaroo would go first, then the dog would follow. In the forest, the dog would try to go first to hunt for good food, and the kangaroo would follow. They did this all of the time when they went hunting for game.

After a while, they arrived at the base of a breadfruit tree. This time, the kangaroo wanted to go first. The kangaroo noticed that the breadfruits were rotting badly. The area was filled with breadfruits that had fallen onto the ground. The kangaroo was elated and sated itself.

The kangaroo worried as it finished the rotting breadfruits, "Why does the dog always go first and finish all of the good food? Poor me, I always follow and I never find good food."

The dog arrived, saw the kangaroo, and asked, "Friend, what are you eating? Is there some for me too?"

The kangaroo replied, "You always go first and eat the good meat. Poor me, I come later and I'm famished. The men came and shat here, and I'm eating it."

The dog said, "Can I try some?"

The kangaroo replied, "Never mind that! Go look around and see if there's any. There must be some shit around somewhere. Cast your eyes about first, then I'll give you a piece."

So the dog began searching and searching, then it saw a big pile of feces. The dog was elated and gulped the pile right down.

The kangaroo finished the breadfruit and went to meet the dog. The kangaroo saw the dog eating the feces and laughed hysterically. The kangaroo told the dog, "Pal, I was eating breadfruit and I tricked you well, so now you've eaten that shit."

Oh my, the dog was completely furious, but it did not say anything. The dog just said, "The shit that I swallowed was alright." Then the dog walked ahead. The dog walked and arrived at a river. The name of this river is Kamaguta.

Quickly the dog removed some sand and dug two big holes. The dog dug until its front paws went down and were well hidden. Later, the dog looked around and saw a piece of pig bone. The river had brought it along and put it on the sand. The dog took the pig bone and put it close to the holes that it had dug. Later, the dog threw its two front paws down into the holes and covered them well with sand. Then the dog began to break the pig bone and chew it.

Before long, the kangaroo arrived and saw this. The kangaroo asked, "Hey, brother! What's that you're eating?"

The dog replied, "What are you asking? I didn't find game, I cut off my two paws and ate them." The kangaroo was shocked.

Quickly, the kangaroo cut off one of its front paws and began to eat it. Later, it cut off the other paw and ate it too. The dog saw this and very slowly raised its two front paws up to the top of the sand. The dog said, "Ha! I tricked you. Now you've cut off your two paws. This is because you played a prank on me and I ate shit. You didn't want to tell me that you were eating breadfruit or something. We were friends for a long time until now, but you ruined our friendship. So now, I'll live in a house and eat shit. You can't go close to me. If I see you, I'll kill you."

The dog chased the kangaroo off into the forest. Later, the dog went back to the men's clan house. So, today you can see that kangaroos have short front paws, and that dogs are no longer friends with kangaroos.

Eron M. Salii
Herea Mart
P. O. Box 768
Boroko
National Capital District

A2284. Origin of animal characteristics: animal persuaded into self-injury; A2371.2.10. Why kangaroo has short front legs; A2435.3.1+. Why dog eats excrement; A2494.4+. Enmity between dog and kangaroo; B211.1.7. Speaking dog; B211.2.12K. Speaking kangaroo; K1065+. Kangaroo persuaded into cutting off its front legs; K2297. Treacherous friend; P310. Friendship; S160.1. Self-mutilation; S161. Mutilation: cutting off hands (arms); W157. Dishonesty; X716H+. The escoumerda

An Old Couple Called Out for Water

(Wantok 788, August 16, 1989, page 19)

Long, long ago, in the time of the ancestors, there lived an old man and his wife. They lived in a village called **Murifa-aya** in the Fayantina Balintina Balint area of **Eastern Highlands** Province.

They did not have children, so they lived alone and did all of their own work with their own small strength. One time, they made a winged-bean garden. When the winged beans were ripe, they prepared to harvest them.

They woke up in the very early morning and went to the garden. They harvested all of the winged beans, then they went back to the village.

At the village, they cut firewood, then they prepared things to make an earth oven. They made a bonfire, and when the fire was terribly hot, they threw stones into the fire. Oh my, the stones were red and terribly hot.

They wanted to cool the stones, so the old man asked the woman to fetch some water and bring it to him. However, there were no nearby streams.

Everything was ready except for the water that they had forgotten. The old man was furious. He sent the old woman into the forest to find some water and bring it back, but the old woman did not find any water so she just returned.

Quickly, the old man told her, "Run into the house and fetch my stick."

This stick had power and bad *masalais* dwelled inside of it. The man would use this stick when he wanted something. He took the stick, then he told the old woman to follow him. They left everything there, then they went into the forest. They searched and searched for water, but there was no water nearby.

They were befuddled and went into the very deep forest. They walked and walked, then they arrived somewhere. They did not make a sound.

They stood quietly and put their ears towards the forest. They heard water falling from the base of a tree. It crashed and jumped out of the base of this tree. This tree is called *nupa* in my language.

They followed the sound and arrived at the base of this tree. Quietly, the man held his *masalai* stick. He beat the base of the *nupa* tree.

Before long, the water began to emerge. They were elated. They held each other and jumped about. They walked back to the village, and the *masalais* of the stick made the water follow them.

Before long, they arrived at the village. The water also arrived at the village. They drew some water, then they spilled it on top of the earth oven and much steam rose into the sky.

They celebrated together and sang this song:

> *Murifana karuruhe karuruhe marufana karuruhe*
>
> *Karuruhe aehe-e murifana aehe-ea*
>
> *Waeya-o-o waeya-o-o aehe-ea*

After they sang this song, they sang another:

> *Hagave o kehave fakainade-e*
>
> *Kinadeve-eo kekaveo*

After they sang this, they uncovered the earth oven. They divided the food, then they called out for all of the *masalais* to come and eat with them. All of the *masalais*

ate, then each went back to their homes and the old couple was by themselves.

That is the end of the story. Today you will see many, many trees growing in the area where the old couple made this earth oven.

[Oruso] Fero Wayasa
Aropa Sawmill
P. O. Box 20
Kieta
North Solomons Province

A1111. Impounded water; D1242.1. Magic water; D1254.1. Magic wand; D1314.2.2. Divining rod (twig) locates underground water supply; F473.6.4. Spirit eats food; F490+. Masalai; N813. Helpful genie (spirit); P210. Husband and wife; Q93. Reward for supernatural help

Ende Yomba Stole Babies
(Wantok 789, August 23, 1989, page 19)

Long, long ago, in a small village in the Kerowagi area of **Simbu** Province, there lived two women [**Kuman** People]. One day, in the very early morning, they woke up, took their two babies and went to the garden.

They arrived at the garden, hung up their babies [in net bags] on the branch of a casuarina tree, then they went to work in the garden.

They worked and worked, until it was nearly afternoon. The poor babies were dying for milk, so they began to cry, but the mothers did not worry about them.

Near this casuarina tree, there was a huge tree. The name of the tree was Ende Yomba. A *masalai* dwelled on top of this tree. The name of the *masalai* was Duakua Yumba. This *masalai* heard the cries of the two babies and went down to check on them. Quickly, the *masalai* took the two babies and carried them up to the *masalai*'s house.

The mothers worked and worked, and then noticed that the babies were not crying anymore. They went to check, but their babies were not there. Later, they heard the babies crying from the top of the Ende Yomba tree. They looked up, but the tree was very tall so they did not see anything.

They knew that the *masalai* of this tree had taken their babies. They cried terribly, then ran quickly to the village. They arrived at the village and told their husbands.

Immediately, all of the men of the village gathered, took their stone axes, and sped off to the garden. They arrived at the garden, then they saw that the tree was immense. They could not do anything. They just cried underneath the tree, then returned to their village.

Many months and years passed, so they forgot completely about the babies. One time, there was a big festival in **Amdi** Village. All of the men went into the forest to search for adornments, such as *tanget* leaves, to decorate their bodies. Two men went into the forest together. Their names were Kurumba and Kawage.

They went into the forest, then heard a woman's cry. The woman had seen that men had killed her father, so she was crying.

This woman's father was Suakua Yomba. He had wanted to go to a place to kill a pig, so he told his daughter, "Daughter, I'm going somewhere to kill a pig. If the men see and kill me, you'll see a dry leaf blocking the place where the sun rises. If no enemies come to me, then you'll see a wet leaf blocking the place where the sun sets. This will show that I'm taking game to you."

The daughter stayed and saw a burned leaf blocking the place where the sun rises, so she knew that men had killed her father. Kurumba and Kawage heard the woman's crying up on the Yomba tree, so they thought hard. Quickly, they arrived at the base of the tree, then Kawage climbed it. He went up very high, to the top of the tree, then he saw a hole.

Oh my, his heart jumped. Suakua Yomba's daughter was sitting inside and crying. She was not a girl, she was grown and ready for marriage.

Later, he moved inside slowly and sat close to her. By the woman's sides, there were many marsupial (*kapul*) furs. Kawage asked her why she was crying. She told him her story, and Kawage was very sorry for her.

They told stories for a little while, then Kawage asked her, "Do you want to go down the tree?" She replied sweetly, "My papa carried me and put me in this tree, so I've never gone down."

Kawage said, "That's alright, I'll carry you down. Then you'll come and live with me in my village." She agreed and Kawage was elated.

Kawage took all of the marsupial furs and put them in a big net bag. Then he told the woman to jump on his back. They went down very slowly and then arrived at the base of the tree.

They rested for a little while, then Kawage asked her to walk first. He would carry the net bag, then walk behind her, but the woman said, "I've never walked. My papa would carry me."

Quietly, Kawage gave the bag of marsupials to Kurumba, then he carried her. They went over many mountains and through many forests, then they approached the village. Kawage felt exhausted, so he told her, "Please, can you walk a little. I've carried you a long ways and I'm winded." She replied, "Papa and I would travel for a very long ways, but he never lets me walk."

You know, this woman was big, but none-the-less Kawage carried her again and they walked away. When they arrived at the village, it was evening. He took her and carried her directly to his house.

When they arrived at the house, he divided the marsupial furs. He gave some to Kurumba and he took some to his house.

Then Kawage lived with her in the house. They lived for a very long time. Kawage thought that he had taken a gorgeous woman, so he just let her stay inside the house. He always worked by himself cooking food and doing other things. When she wanted to urinate or defecate, Kawage would carry her to the latrine.

Many years passed, and Kawage was furious because he alone did all of the work. One time, he was angry and was removing banana peels.

He was furious and he told her, "What are you? You always just sit there. I alone work hard, taking care of you." He said this as he walked outside the house.

The poor woman felt ashamed, so she went and took a knife. It was there for cutting the banana peels. However, she missed and cut her hand. Oh my, blood gushed out and she wailed.

She took the banana peels and the knife then walked back to her father's home. Her father's home had a pond. Quietly, she put the banana peels and knife on the side, then she jumped down and died in this pond.

Kawage did not know about this. He was going around, speaking with the other men. Later, he went to the house and was surprised to see her blood at the doorway. He went inside the house, but his wife was not there.

His heart went out. He cried and followed her blood, then arrived at the pond. He checked by the pond, then saw some banana peels and the knife. When he saw this, he was very troubled. He cried terribly, then he jumped into the pond. He died with his wife.

Giu Bolonga
P. O. Box 293
Kundiawa
Simbu Province

E761.7+. Life token: leaf blocks sun; F54.1. Tree stretches to sky; F441.2. Tree-spirit; F490+. Masalai; F562.1+. Person who never walks; F562.2. Residence in a tree; M451.1. Death by suicide; M451.2. Death by drowning; P214.1+. Husband commits suicide (dies) on death of wife; P230. Parents and children; P232. Mother and daughter; P234. Father and daughter; P271. Foster father; R10.3. Children abducted; R14+. Abduction by spirit; S110. Murders

A Fight Regarding Dogs Caused
Sambe to be Evicted from Sirunki

(Wantok 790, August 30, 1989, page 19)

This ancestor story is about two brothers. They lived very well, but one time they fought. So, the big brother went his own way and the little brother went another way. The story goes as follows.

Long, long ago, in the time of the ancestors, there was a village called **Sirunki**. This village was in **Enga** Province [**Enga** People].

The names of the two brothers who lived in the village were Kunarini and Sambe [Sámbé (Lang, 1973: 214)]. The big brother was Kunarini and the little brother was Sambe. Their father and mother had died when they were babies, so they lived by themselves.

They were still young, so they were unmarried. One time, they found two dogs. Kunarini took care of the big dog and Sambe took care of the little dog.

The dogs each had a rope around their necks. Our ancestors used to do this. They would put a mark on each dog and they would also decorate the dogs.

They would take a strong stick and make a hole on each end of the stick. Then they would put the stick near the dog's neck. They would put a rope through the two holes and tie it together. This strong stick would be close to the dog's neck and it would prevent the dog from chewing off the rope. We Enga People call this _yana kola_ in our language. [_Yána_ means "dog" and _kóla_ means "cane" (Lang, 1973: 117).]

One time, the brothers were in the house. The two dogs were going around outside. By the afternoon, their dogs had not come home. The brothers thought that their dogs must have encountered an enemy or something.

When it was nearly dark, the two dogs arrived and the brothers were elated. Sambe's dog did not have a rope around its neck though. Sambe saw this and was shocked. Only Kunarini's dog returned with a rope.

Sambe saw this and thought that Kunarini had stolen his rope. Quickly, he asked Kunarini, "Hey! Why did my dog lose its rope? Kunarini! You must have removed the rope and put it on your dog."

Kunarini replied that had not stolen it, "Sambe! Don't get the wrong idea. Your dog left its rope in the forest. Get up and we'll go find it."

However, Sambe did not believe what Kunarini had said. He was burning up inside and he wanted to fight badly because he thought that Kunarini must have been lying to him.

The brothers began to argue. Before long, they used their spears and threw them at each other. They fought and fought, then the people who slept close to them awoke. They helped the big brother, Kunarini, because they believed that the fight was caused by the little brother's error.

There were two big clans that lived near the Sirunki area. The names of these two clans were Lyaini and Sakarini. They supported the big brother, Kunarini.

They evicted Sambe who went to a faraway place at the head of the Lagaip River in Enga Province and he lived there. Sambe lived alone for a while, then he married. He raised many, many children.

Apetami A. Lyaini
P. O. Box 396
Panguna
North Solomons Province

K2127. False accusation of theft; P210. Husband and wife; P230. Parents and children; P251.5. Two brothers; P251.5.3. Hostile brothers; Q431. Punishment: banishment (exile); T100. Marriage

Why Eagles and Chickens are Enemies

(Wantok 791, September 6, 1989, page 18)

This ancestor story is about the origin of why the other animals are enemies with chickens. Before, they all lived together. But now, they do not.

Long, long ago, all of the animals of the earth such as pigs, dogs, chickens, eagles, _kapul_ marsupials, snakes, lizards, and _sikau_ marsupials, never argued or fought among themselves. They would eat, walk and sleep together. At this time, there was also only one language.

One time, all of them gathered and appointed Eagle as their leader. Whatever Eagle would say, they would do. One day, Eagle called all of the other animals of the forest to come and meet. At the meeting, they decided that another day, they would go hunting for grasshoppers in the forest.

The next day, Eagle woke up first and called out, "Everybody wake up now. Today, all of us will go hunting for grasshoppers in the forest." All of the animals listened and awoke.

Eagle and the other birds flew. The other animals of the ground walked. They went and entered the very deep forest where there was a big area with sword grass.

This sword grass had many, many grasshoppers. They did not waste time. They went into the sword grass and gathered all of the grasshoppers, both big and small.

They took all of the grasshoppers and put them in one spot. They looked for a fire to cook the grasshoppers, but not one animal had brought fire.

The poor animals were furious, so they all met together. They appointed Chicken to return and fetch some fire from their village. Their village was very far away. Chicken did not want to do this, but all of them wanted Chicken to return to the village. So Chicken just did what they said.

Chicken took off and arrived at the village. You know, the village had much trash there. Chicken saw this and ate the trash because Chicken was racked by hunger. Chicken ate and ate, then forgot completely about bringing the fire back into the forest.

The other poor animals were waiting and waiting, and they were terribly famished. They were burning up inside at Chicken. Eagle said, "What's that crazy Chicken doing that it hasn't returned quickly?"

It was nearly dark and all of them just waited to see what Eagle would tell them to do. They all kept quiet when Eagle stood and spoke, "That bad Chicken did not listen to us. That's OK, but when Chicken lays eggs or has chicks, these children will not become big. I'll take the children and eat them."

Dog and Snake also supported Eagle, "Let it be! Chicken was conceited towards us. We'll also finish off Chicken's eggs and chicks."

They spoke like this, then they just ate the grasshoppers because they were famished and could not wait. After they ate, they went back to the village. Chicken was bloated and sleeping. Chicken did not know that the other animals had arrived in the village.

The other animals were not too angry at this, but Eagle, Dog and Snake were completely furious. They surrounded and chased Chicken. From that time until now, there is great enmity between chickens and eagles, snakes and dogs.

Tumby Gembiong

Lae

Morobe Province

[Tumby Gembey and Siwi Gole wrote the ancestor story in *Wantok* #842. This story is probably from **Avenggu** Village (**Tobo** People, **Morobe** Province) or **Komban** Village (**Komba** People, Morobe Province).]

A2494.4.11. Enmity between dog and rooster; A2494.13+. Enmity between eagle and chicken; A2494.16+. Enmity between snake and chicken;

B211.3.11K. Speaking eagle; B211.1.7. Speaking dog; B211.6.1. Speaking snake (serpent); B240+. Eagle as king of animals; Q325. Disobedience punished; R260. Pursuits; W111. Laziness; W126. Disobedience

Wakaia Became a Place of Rats

(Wantok 792, September 13, 1989, page 19)

Long, long ago, there were many people who lived in a village called Wakaia in the Garaina area of **Morobe** Province [**Guhu-Samane** People]. This village had two *masalai*s. Their names were Uberi and Tangori.

One time, everyone wanted to leave the village and create a new village in another place. They made a huge party so that they could later leave Wakaia.

One day, their leader called out for everyone to come and gather. Then he told them to gather plenty of food from the gardens.

They all slept, then they woke up in the very early morning. They divided themselves into two big groups. One group would go into the forest to hunt for animals. This group consisted of men. The other group, the women and children, would go to get food from the gardens, such as leafy greens, taros, sweet potatoes, wild sugarcanes (*pit-pit*), bananas, and yams.

The men went into the forest and collected all of the pigs. When it was nearly noon, they all met back at the village. The women and children had finished [gathering] all of the food in the garden. The food was not ripe yet, but they took it anyway because they would be leaving the village.

They put all of the food in the fire and cooked it. The next day, they would all gather and eat the food, then they would leave the village.

They cooked the pigs in the fire and just left them there. In the morning, they would butcher them and divide them among each clan house.

That night, there was a tremendous festival. All of the men, women and children sang and danced. Those who were not singing and dancing were preparing the food.

Before the festival began, their leader stood and shouted, "Tomorrow after the big feast, all of us will leave this village and make a new village on another piece of land. You must prepare everything of yours now."

The festival went until dawn. In the very early morning, their leader stood in the middle of the festival grounds and called for everyone to gather. Each clan house brought their pigs and put them in the middle of the grounds. They began to butcher the pigs.

However, the two *masalai*s, Uberi and Tangori, were not happy about what the people were doing. They did not want them to leave Wakaia. So, all of the pigs that the men butchered became rats. The people saw this and were terrified. They immediately left Wakaia and fled to a new place. They lived at this new village for a very long time.

One time, a man and his wife traveled to Wakaia. Their dog also went with them. The name of this dog was Monire. They arrived at the village and saw much blood from the pigs that they had butchered. They were terrified and wanted to flee, but the dog stayed and lapped down the pig's blood.

They shouted, but their dog did not come. The *masalai*s, Uberi and Tangori, had taken their dog. They shouted, "*Hao* Monire *he Sinna gegemaho pitita gate onita, bote dzairami ma* Uberi Tangori *niipe noo kokora et garare*."

In English, this means, "How terrible. We've lost our dog, Monire, at this place. So please, you bad ghosts, Uberi and Tangori, you must take care of our dog."

They shouted like this, then they ran back to the place where their clans had fled, back to the new village. Later, they gave the name **Garaina** to this village, so today, that is what we call it.

Today, if the people travel to Kawaia [Wakaia], where the ancestors had butchered the pigs, you will hear a dog barking. Also, this place is just filled with rats. My father told me this story.

Em Tee

Lae

Morobe Province

A1854.1+. Why particular place is filled with rats; D412.3+. Transformation: swine to rat; F419.2. Thieving spirit; F490+. Masalai; P210. Husband and wife; Q551.3. Punishment: transformation; R213. Escape from home

Yamarai Helped the Dog and Its Friends

(Wantok 793, September 14-20, 1989, page 15)

Long, long ago, in the time of the ancestors, there was just one man who lived in the Purimanda area inside **Enga** Province. This area is now where **Wabag** High School is located [**Enga** People]. The name of this man was Yamarai. He lived alone and he owned Purimanda.

One time, he wanted to go into the forest, so he prepared his bow and multi-pronged arrows. He also prepared some sweet potatoes to eat in the forest, then he slept.

He awoke in the very early morning, then he took all of his things and walked into the forest. He walked and walked, then he arrived in the very deep forest.

However this was not a good day for him, so he did not kill any wild game. The sun was about to set, so he felt very tired. He sat by the base of a tree and smoked quietly.

Before long, he saw a dog approaching. Oh my, when he saw this dog, he was elated. Yamarai thought, "Now I'm going to kill that dog and carry it back home." He readied his bow and multi-pronged arrow, then he just quietly waited.

However, the dog approached Yamarai and told him, "Yamarai! Don't kill me. I'm your friend. Two friends, ant and blow fly [Sarcophagidae family], and I have a big problem, so we came to see you. Can you straighten out this problem of ours or not?"

Yamarai replied, "Could you say what kind of problem you have?"

The dog did not give him an answer. The dog just told him to follow. Yamarai listened to the dog and followed. Yamarai and the dog arrived at a house. Inside the house, there lay a gigantic pig. The dog, the ant and the blowfly had killed this pig. Yamarai was shocked when his eyes fixed upon the pig. Quickly, he asked the dog, "How did you kill this pig?"

The dog replied, "That's a little thing. What do you want to know about? Just cut the pig and divide it among us. You yourself can take some to your home."

Yamarai was elated. Quickly, he removed the skin with a bamboo [knife], then he cut the pig and divided it into four piles, for himself, the dog, the ant, and the blow fly.

Yamarai put all of the bones together in one pile, the meat in another pile, the urine [i.e., clear fluids] in another pile. He affixed the blood and fat to leaves where he butchered the pig.

Yamarai took all of the meat of this pig. He filled his net bag with it. He straightened everything out, then he called for the dog, the ant, and the blowfly to come.

He pointed to the pile of pig bones and told the dog, "I know that bones are your favorite food, so I have apportioned the bones to you."

The ant and the blow fly came, then he told them, "All of the piss there is for you, ant. And blow fly, the fat and blood that is stuck to the leaves is for you to sate yourself."

All of them were very happy, so dog spoke, "Yamarai, you're a very good man because you had two ideas. All of the bones are mine because bones are my favorite food."

The ant also spoke, "I very much like the piss that you apportioned." The blowfly also spoke happily to Yamarai, "You had two good ideas. I like blood and fat, because I don't have teeth with which to eat meat. I just have a proboscis on my mouth to suck up the blood. So, I give great thanks to you."

So today, you will see that animal bones are the favorite food of dogs, and that ants' favorite food is urine. And, you know what the blowfly's favorite food is.

Paul Kai Ipara
Mountain of Purimanda
Laita-Kaipu Parange
Wabag
Enga Province

A2435.3.1+. Why dog favors bones; A2435.5+. Food of ant; A2435.5+. Why blow fly favors blood and fat; B211.1.7. Speaking dog; B211.4.4K2. Speaking fly; B211.4.1. Speaking ant; B392.1. Animals grateful for being given appropriate food; B871.1.2. Giant boar; W27. Gratitude

A Ringworm Man Won over the First Woman

(Wantok 794, September 21-27, 1989, page 23)

Long, long ago, in the time of the ancestors, there were very many men who lived in a village called Emegari in the Bundi area of Madang Province [Gende People]. At this time, only men lived in the village. There were no women.

There was another village near Emegari Village, named Bogaie [Bogai]. This village was also composed of men only. There was a man who lived in this village. His name was Pubari Kidari. One time, Kidari felt his belly swelling. His belly became big and he was shocked.

The men of the village found out that Kidari was pregnant and about to give birth, so they put him in a small house of his own. Kidari gave birth to a baby girl. The girl's name was Mumegi. Mumegi was gorgeous.

All of the men of the nearby villages would come and try to make Mumegi marry them. Mumegi did not like the young men of Bogaie Village or the other nearby villages, so their black magic [lit., "black power"; the author probably meant "love magic"] was for naught.

At Emegari Village, there was a young, scabby man who had ringworm. His name was Togugu Izokugua. The young men would always go back and tell stories about this woman.

Many times, Izokugua wanted to follow the other young men to see the woman from Bogaie, but the young men would shame him and say, "You don't have good skin. You're a scabby man. Why do you want to come with us? Mumegi couldn't possibly like you. Never mind that. Stay and watch the village."

They would tell him this, then they would go to Bogaie to compete at singing and dancing to win her over. How-

ever, one time Izokugua followed them with his hand drum. He approached Bogaie and he hid by the village. When it was nearly dark, he went into the festival grounds.

Oh my, all of the young men of Bogaie and the other nearby villages were [dancing fervently] at the festival. The scabby boy, Izokugua, went and sat near a man from Bogaie Village. This man's name was Kaniwe Duava.

They sat and told stories. Later, Izokugua took out some honey and put it on his hand drum. Izokugua sang and danced, then he went inside the festival grounds and joined the other men.

It was too bad for the others, the sound of Izokugua's drum cut right to the heart of the gorgeous woman, Mumegi. Mumegi looked at Izokugua for a while, then her tears fell. She had a strong desire to marry the scabby scoundrel.

Quietly, she told her father, "Papa! Papa! That man over there, he did not beat the hand drum but he called my name, so I want to go marry him now."

After Mumegi told her father this, she walked into the area where the men were singing and dancing. She grabbed the scabby man's hand, then she sang and danced with Izokugua.

They other young men saw this and were furious, "That rotten scab! We told him to stay. Why did he come here?" Slowly, the men began to leave the festival grounds.

Izokugua saw this and held her tightly. He pulled the hand of his new wife, Mumegi. The two of them ran away. They jumped over a fence. Some men saw them and called out, "That rotten scab man, Izokugua, took that Mumegi woman."

They shouted like this, then they took their bows and arrows. They chased them, but Izokugua and Mumegi had already gone. They ran and ran, then they arrived at a place called Wait Ston Orimbi. Then they became two white marsupials (*kapul*) [probably the spotted cuscus, *Spilocuscus maculatus maculatus* (Flannery, 1995a: 181-182)].

Gabriel Doa Andbruk
Emegari Village
Bundi-Upper Ramu [River]
Madang Province

A1280+. First woman; D179.6K+M. Transformation: man to marsupial; D179.6K+W. Transformation: woman to marsupial; D1900. Love induced by magic; F566.1. Village of men only; H310+. Suitor test: dancing; H310+. Suitor test: singing; P210. Husband and wife; P234. Father and daughter; R220. Flights; R260. Pursuits; T578. Pregnant man; T580. Childbirth; W181. Jealousy

Masalai Beleko's Wife

(Wantok 795, September 28 — October 4, 1989, page 21)

Long, long ago, in the time of the ancestors, there were many people who lived in a village called Sola in the Noru area of North Solomons Province.

A young man and his wife lived in this village. Their names were Beleko and Waluame. They were newlyweds and did not have children yet.

One time, the married couple thought of going to sleep in the forest. Beleko thought of killing some wild game and bringing them to the woman's clan.

They arrived in the forest and made a hut near a big mountain. They stayed there for three whole days. On this mountain, there lived a *masalai*, but the married couple did not know this. Waluame would stay in the hut while Beleko would go alone into the forest to hunt for wild game.

On the first day, Beleko went into the forest and killed many marsupials (*kapul*), pigs and cassowaries. He brought these back to the hut, then they butchered the animals and smoked the meat in the fire.

On the second day, Beleko took his bow and arrows then went into the forest again. Waluame stayed alone in the hut, and continued to smoke the meat.

The *masalai* of the mountain saw what the two of them were doing. Beleko was killing many, many animals and was still in the forest.

The *masalai* transformed himself and became like Beleko. He went and stood outside the hut, then called out, "Hey Waluame! I just shot at the animals and my arrows didn't hit a single one. Come and we'll climb the mountain to see if there are some animals up there."

The *masalai* had taken Beleko's face exactly, so Waluame thought that it really was her husband. She listened, then they climbed the mountain. This mountain was very high, but the *masalai* performed his magic and they arrived quickly at the top of the mountain.

He took Waluame and hid her in a cave. They stayed there for a little while, then Waluame found out that this man was a *masalai* and not really her husband.

However, what could she do? She did not have a way to go back. Her husband, Beleko, could not get up there either because this mountain was so high that a person could not climb it.

It was nearly evening, and Beleko again arrived at the hut with many, many animals. He called out, but Waluame did not reply. Then he checked carefully and found that Waluame was not there.

Oh my, he was enraged because he knew that the *masalai* of the mountain must have taken his wife. He shouted up the mountain and Waluame heard him. Waluame cried and replied down to him, "Beleko! Help me! I'm up here, but there's no way to come down."

Beleko cried terribly. He knew that he could not do anything. Quickly, he took all of the meat, then ran back to the village. He went to all of the houses of his in-laws, telling them what had happened.

The people of the village took their bows and arrows. They sped away and arrived at the mountain, but they found it very hard to climb.

They could not do it, and they just cried and walked slowly back to the village. Beleko was terribly worried and did not want to follow the people back to the village.

He made a house and a big garden by the mountain, and he lived there. Beleko lived there for a while, then one time he heard the cry of a baby on top of the mountain.

Beleko called up the mountain and Waluame replied down to him, "That's the cry of your son. I gave birth to him."

Beleko heard this and was furious at the *masalai*. Every day, he would think of his wife and son, so he would just cry. Many times, he would not eat well.

He continued to live there, then one time he heard Waluame calling down, "Beleko! Beleko! The *masalai* is taking us to another place now, so your son and I are leaving this mountain now. We're going to another place."

Beleko listened and cried terribly. The next morning, the *masalai* took Waluame and the boy to another place. Beleko thought that his wife would return. He waited and waited but to no avail. He was furious, so he cut down [the house] and burned it.

He cried and walked back to the village. He told the people what had happened. All of them cried and cried. Beleko was still a young man, but he did not have a wife so many people of the village were very worried for him. Some years passed, and then a young man died, leaving his wife. Beleko married this man's wife, and the two of them were happy.

Eri Okane Yoyope

Arikua Plantation

P. O. Box 108

Kieta

North Solomons Province

D2122. Journey with magic speed; F55. Mountain reaches to sky; F401.6. Spirit in human form; F460. Mountain-spirits; F490+. Masalai; K1910. Marital impostors; P210. Husband and wife; P231. Mother and son; P233. Father and son; P260. Relations by law; R14+. Abduction by spirit; R45.3.

Captivity in cave; T100. Marriage; T111. Marriage of mortal and supernatural being; T192. Marriage by force; T580. Childbirth

Girinde's Garden Brought in the *Masalai*s

(Wantok 796, October 5-11, 1989, page 27)

Long, long ago, in the time of the ancestors, there was a man who lived in Tumua [Naratumwa] Village, in the Ramu Sugar area of Morobe Province [Adzera People]. His name was Sayu Girinde.

Girinde was an excellent farmer. He was better than all of the others in the village were because he had many gardens. One day, Girinde walked into the very deep forest to make a garden. He cut all of the trees, leaving just one big fig tree there.

This fig tree was immense. He thought that he would sleep, then in the early morning he would awake and cut down the fig tree.

It was nearly evening, so he made a hut. He made a bonfire and he slept inside of the hut. A heavy rain and wind arose that night. There was a stream that was near this new garden. This stream filled quickly and flooded strongly.

The big fig tree that Girinde wanted to cut in the morning was actually the home of *masalai*s. Poor Girinde did not know this. He thought that the fig must be just an ordinary tree.

When it was nearly midnight, the fig tree opened up. All of the *masalai*s went outside and smelled Girinde's body. Quickly, they gathered and surrounded the forest hut where Girinde was sleeping.

Poor Girinde was dead asleep, so he did not know what the *masalai*s were doing. He was shocked when the *masalai*s broke down the forest hut and tried to eat him.

Girinde saw the *masalai*s and he was terrified. He did not wait. He immediately jumped over the *masalai*s and ran outside. He sped like lightning and jumped down to the stream.

He saw a log in the flooded water and grabbed onto it. He drifted with the log downstream, but the *masalai*s smelled him and found him still in the water.

The flood took Girinde quickly to another little village called **Asial**. The *masalai*s saw that Girinde had approached this village, so they went back into the forest.

Girinde slept at Asial until the sun rose. His body was strong, so later he walked slowly back to his village. Girinde arrived at the house and his wife asked him, "Did you make the new garden?" Girinde replied, "Yes! I made

it and I've returned." Girinde lied to his wife because he did not want her to make a joke or to laugh at him.

They talked, then Girinde thought of one of his other gardens. He told her that the next day, he would go and tie up the bananas that were ready in this garden.

She told him that he must awake in the middle of the night to go to that garden. Girinde listened to her and quickly went to sleep. When it was still in the middle of the night, he walked to the garden.

He arrived at the garden and he was shocked to see a man inside his garden. This man had the exact face and body of Girinde. Girinde saw him and knew that he must be a *masalai*.

Girinde gathered his thoughts and quickly called out to him, "Girinde! Did you tie up your bananas?" The *masalai* heard this and turned to look at Girinde. Oh my, he sped directly to where Girinde was. Girinde's buttocks exploded, "Puf-f-pu-ba", then he flew up into the sky like a rocket. He fell to the ground and knocked his head very hard. Oh my, he was half-dead, and he slept until dark.

When it was nearly midnight, he awoke. He thought that he had had a big accident. He laughed and laughed, then he went back to the village. The men of the village saw him and laughed hysterically, then they asked him, "Hey Girinde! Why are you laughing? You've never done that before."

Girinde told the story of what had happened to him and they all laughed hysterically.

Gidi Noah

P. O. Box 1010

Arawa

North Solomons Province

D670. Magic flight; D1002+. Magic flatulence; D2142.1. Wind produced by magic; D2143.1. Rain produced by magic; D2151.8. Magic flood; F441.2. Tree-spirit; F490+. Masalai; F1021. Extraordinary flights through air; G570. Ogre overawed; K1900. Impostures; P210. Husband and wife; R210. Escapes; R260. Pursuits; X716.8H. Fortuitous breaking wind

The Crocodile Men of Noran Abducted a Young Woman

(Wantok 797, October 12-18, 1989, page 19)

Long, long ago, in the time of the ancestors, the women of **Malol** Village would finish off all of the fish in the river [**Sissano** People, **West Sepik** Province]. The women would arrive at the river, then divide themselves into two groups. Some women would hold baskets and follow the other women who would go first with nets.

The women with the nets would surround the fish that went down into the nets. By doing this, they would gather many, many fish, big and small.

One day, all of the women decided to go to the river again. They gathered fish and they caught many of them. However, before long, a he-crocodile came out of the water and took a woman underwater. The crocodile took the woman to his underwater home.

The other women saw this and were terrified. They wanted to flee, but they were worried about this woman. They searched for her, but they did not find her. They cried and returned to the village. The men saw the women and were shocked.

The women told about the enemy that had come. The men listened and were furious. They all returned and went down to the river where the crocodile had taken the woman. They searched and searched, but they did not see a mark or blood or anything.

Their main thought was that a *masalai* of the river must have taken her. The poor people were very troubled, so they walked slowly back to the village. Many months and years passed and they forgot completely about her.

The crocodile had taken her to his home and the other crocodiles were very happy to see her. You know, human flesh is the preferred meat of crocodiles, so they were elated.

They did not want to kill her quickly. They wanted to take care of her and give her plenty of food so that she would become obese, then they would eat her.

They all gathered and made a strong hut. They finished the hut, then they put her inside. The hut was fenced in well, so the poor woman did not have a chance to break out.

The one place that she could break out and flee was the window. They did not make this window very strong, but she was afraid to flee.

One day, all of the he-crocodiles, she-crocodiles and crocodile children gathered. They met and marked the next evening as the time to kill and eat her.

They slept, then in the very early morning they awoke and went to the gardens. They arrived at the gardens and took many leafy greens and other kinds of food from the gardens to cook and eat with the woman's flesh.

At the village, there was only an old she-crocodile. She was nearly blind, so she did not see well. They had left her alone in the village to keep watch on the woman.

The poor woman knew when the crocodiles would kill her. She sat inside the hut and thought hard. She wanted to flee, but she was afraid.

This was because she thought that some he-crocodiles must have been keeping watch on her. However, this was not the case. She cried quietly and sat in the corner of the hut.

All of the crocodiles went into the forest. Before long, the woman heard a shout coming from outside the hut. This shout came directly from the mouth of the old she-crocodile.

"Sister! Are you inside or not! Listen carefully to what I say. All of the crocodiles have gone to the gardens to find food. In the evening, they'll return to kill you. Then they'll make a big party. Break the window and come out quickly. I've prepared a canoe by the river. Take the canoe and paddle quickly to your village lest they return quickly and kill you. If the adult crocodiles return and ask me, I'll lie that I didn't see you because my eyes are shut and I can't see well."

The woman listened and was elated. Quickly, she tightened all of her muscles that she had and she broke the window. She jumped out of the house and the old crocodile woman took her to the river. She jumped into the canoe and paddled towards her village. This time, the canoe ran just like a motorboat.

The people of the village saw her paddling towards them and they were shocked. They asked her what had happened and she told them everything that had happened to her.

Quickly, all of the men of the village gathered. They prepared their bows and arrows, then they waited to fight with the he-crocodiles if they followed her.

When it was nearly evening, all of the crocodiles returned from their gardens. They cooked the food, then they sent some men to the hut in which the woman had lived. However, they were very sorry. They were surprised to see the window broken and to find that she was not there.

They castigated the old crocodile woman, but the old woman lied to them, "Why are you angry at me? You saw beforehand that I don't have good eyesight."

They ran by the river and saw that a canoe was not there. They knew that she must have fled in the canoe back to her village.

The he-crocodiles did not wait. They took their bows and arrows, then they each jumped into canoes. They paddled and paddled, then before long, they arrived at the woman's village.

They fought and fought. The men killed many he-crocodiles. Some he-crocodiles saw that they were losing, so they jumped back into the canoes and fled back to their village. We now call this place Noran.

Francis Swaki

Malol Village

Aitape

West Sepik Province

B29+. Crocodile-person; B211.6.4K. Speaking crocodile; B225+. Kingdom of crocodiles; D2122. Journey with magic speed; F401.3+. Spirit in crocodile form; F490+. Masalai; G82. Cannibal fattens victim; G354.2. Crocodile as ogre; G512.1+. Ogre killed with spear/arrow; G550. Rescue from ogre; R4. Surprise capture; R13.4+. Abduction by crocodile; R110. Rescue of captive; R210. Escapes; R260. Pursuits; S110. Murders

A Father Fled and a *Masalai* Killed a Boy: There Is a Pond Where the *Masalai* Killed the Boy

(Wantok 798, October 19-25, 1989, page 8)

Long, long ago, in **Kaiap** Village, inside **Enga** Province, there lived a man and his son [**Enga** People]. The man's wife had died long ago after she had given birth to their son, so only the man and his son lived there.

One day, the two of them were short of meat, so they took their bows and arrows then they walked into the forest. The father also took some sweet potatoes to bring into the forest for themselves to eat.

They arrived in the very deep forest. The father believed that there would be many marsupials (*kapul*) to kill there. They rested at a good spot, then they made a hut.

Later, the father told his son, "Stay and watch the hut. Don't eat the sweet potatoes inside the net bag. You must wait until I've returned, then we'll eat together."

The father went into the forest with his bow and arrows. However, the boy did not listen to his father. He removed a post from the house and took a sweet potato. He cooked it in the fire and ate it.

Before long, a man arrived and asked him, "Hey boy! You're alone. Where's your papa?"

The boy replied to him that his father had gone to hunt for marsupials and that he was alone at the hut. The boy thought that this was a real man, but it was not really a man. It was a *masalai* from this part of the forest.

The man checked his net bag, then he took two pig livers. He gave them to the boy, saying, "Eat one piece and leave the other for your father. When your father comes, give it to him."

After the *masalai* man said this, he quickly left and went into the forest. The boy gulped down the pig liver with the sweet potato that he had cooked.

The *masalai* man hid in the forest and spied upon the boy. He was elated when the boy ate the sweet potato with the pig liver. He knew that he would now eat the boy because he had performed a song and dance upon the sweet potato and pig liver.

However, he also wanted the father to eat the sweet potato and pig liver so that he could eat both of them. The *masalai* man waited there and before long the little boy's father returned.

Oh my, the father was shocked when he saw the boy eating the sweet potato with the pig liver. He knew that a *masalai* had put a watch over them to kill them. He stopped thinking about the boy.

Quietly, he left his bow and arrows, then he ran back to the village. The *masalai* man saw this and came out to grab the boy's father.

The boy saw this and shouted for his father to wait. The father did not wait, so he cried and followed his father. However, the boy had eaten the *masalai*'s poison. The boy's legs were too heavy to run, so the *masalai* grabbed him.

The *masalai* held the poor boy and began to eat him. He shouted to his father that he was dying and that the *masalai* was eating his liver.

A pond is now at this part of the forest where the *masalai* killed the boy. The color of pond water is black and white. The black is from the meat and the white is from the blood of the little boy.

This pond does not look nice. If you look at it, you will be terrified. Today, we are never disobedient when we hunt for wild game or travel this part of the forest.

We cannot curse or ignore what other men say. If we do that, the clothes that we have put on will just burn up. This is a true story that comes from my village, Kaiap.

Pius Lungupin

P. O. Box 193

Wabag

Enga Province

A920.1.0.1. Origin of particular lake; C494. Tabu: cursing; C612. Forbidden forest; C836. Tabu: disobedience; C927. Burning as punishment for breaking tabu; D1015.4. Magic liver of animal; D1039. Magic sweet potato; D1781. Magic results from singing; D1781+. Magic results from dancing; F408.3. Spirits dwell at tabu place; F490+. Masalai; G312+. Ogre tricks victim into eating ensorcelled food, then eats victim; P233. Father and son; Q325. Disobedience punished; Q411. Death as punishment; Q438. Punishment: abandonment in forest; R210. Escapes; R260. Pursuits; S110. Murders; S110+. Eaten alive; S143. Abandonment in forest; W126. Disobedience

A Friend Helped a Blind Man

(Wantok 799, October 26 — November 1, 1989, page 13)

Long, long ago, two men lived in a village inside the **Yohotegave** area, by Goroka, **Eastern Highlands** Province [**Kamano** People]. One man lived on one side of a mountain, and the other lived on the other side with his dog.

When one man made a fire, the smoke would rise and the other would also make a fire to reply to the smoke signal. They would do this to show whether they were all right or not.

The man with the dog had a tree that was near him. This tree was always just filled with marsupials (*kapul*). One night, the moon was very bright. He prepared his bow and arrows, then he called his dog and they kept watch at the tree. This tree had a *masalai* man, but the poor man did not know this.

The man saw a marsupial and was about to shoot it, but the *masalai* man of the tree sent a bright light directly from the marsupial's eyes. The man drew back his bow to shoot, but the light came and removed [his] eyes.

The poor man found it very difficult to return home because the *masalai* had taken his eyes. He just stumbled through the forest, and fled back to the house. When he arrived at the house, he just slept. He never did any work because he could not see.

Some days later, his friend on the other side of the mountain made a fire. The smoke from the fire rose very high. He waited for his friend on the other side to reply, but he did not see any smoke. He thought very hard. He knew that his friend must have encountered an enemy or died.

Immediately, he took some things, then he walked towards the other side of the mountain. He approached his pal's house, then he saw ripe beans there. He took one and called into the house.

Then he went into the house and saw that his friend was in very bad shape inside the house. Oh my, he was terribly sorry when he heard the story of what had happened.

He stayed with his friend that day. At night, he prepared his bow and arrows well, then he walked off to the base of the tree. Before long, a light shone very brightly at his face. He drew back his bow and shot at the light. The *masalai* man fell down. He went to check on the *masalai* man's net bag. He took his friend's eyes and returned to his home.

In the very early morning, he awoke and called his dog. He told the dog to go bring a pig to the fence. The dog followed his owner's instructions and brought a pig.

The man butchered the pig and gathered all of the pig's blood. Later, he took his friend's eyes and washed them well in the pig's blood. He also removed some rubbish from inside the eyes.

His poor friend screamed terribly when he wanted to put his eyes back. Some days later, he felt better and could see again. Oh my, he was terribly happy.

They lived together for a while, then one day he regained his strength. Quickly, he took a bow and arrows, then he went into the forest with his dog. Oh my, they collected all of the pigs inside the forest and brought them home.

They made a bonfire and began to cook the pigs in an earth oven. They gathered the pig guts together in a pile, then they made them into a bundle. He gave this to his friend who had saved his life.

When he gave him this, he said, "Go back home and call out to your tribe, then cook this on stones and eat it."

He returned to his home and slept. In the morning, he awoke and called out for everyone in the village to gather and hold a party. They asked for the meat, and he showed them the bundle that his friend had made of the pigs' guts.

The people thought that he was lying, but he put the bundle on the ground and they turned into many, many pigs. They butchered the pigs and divided the meat well among the houses.

Some days later, they held a meeting again. The man called for his friend to come. The two of them celebrated each other at this meeting.

The people of the village gathered and gave him a woman. He married this woman and took her back to his village. They raised many children there.

Jossie H. Manuo

YHV Bros of Nega

Goroka

Eastern Highlands Province

D1016. Magic blood of animal; D2062.2. Blinding by magic; D2161.3.1.1. Eyes torn out magically replaced; E168. Cooked animal comes to life; F441.2. Tree-spirit; F490+. Masalai; P210. Husband and wife; F541.1.1. Eyes flash fire; F969.3. Marvelous light; P230. Parents and children; P310. Friendship; Q53. Reward for rescue; Q451.7. Blinding as punishment; S165. Mutilation: putting out eyes; T100. Marriage

Hunger for Bandicoots Killed an Old Woman

(Wantok 800, November 2-8, 1989, page 23)

This ancestor story comes from **Yasubi** Village in the **Eastern Highlands** Province [**Fore** People]. This is the story of Yasubi Village when an old woman still lived there. She died when she was hunting for bandicoots on a mountain. Everyone in Yasubi Village knows this story.

Yasubi Village is at the base of a big mountain called Yasonandi. At the top of Mount Yasonandi, there lived just one man. This man was from Yasubi Village, but he tired of living with the other people. So, he ran away to live by himself at the top of Mount Yasonandi.

The crest of this mountain had a very tall *limbum* palm tree. Near this *limbum* tree, there was a gigantic cave. Inside the cave, there lived a bad *masalai*.

One time, the food was gone in the house of the man who lived on top of the mountain. He was too lazy to hunt for game. An idea came to him to burn the sword grass by the mountain, then the bandicoots would run out and he could kill them easily.

He made a fire on one side of the mountain. The mountain was just filled with sword grass on all sides. A great fire arose. The wind blew strongly and the fire raced just like a jet plane.

At Yasubi Village, all of the men and women had gone into the deep forest. There were only four young women who were menstruating that were staying in the village on this day. Oh my, they saw the smoke from this fire at the top of the mountain, and they were shocked.

They stopped thinking about staying inside the house and went outside. All of them had the idea that it was a great opportunity to hunt for bandicoots in the sword grass because the people of the village had forbidden them to eat and they were famished.

They took their net bags and sped off to the place where the fire was located. They hunted for bandicoots on the top of the mountain. The four women did not know that an old woman was also staying in the village on this day. The old woman saw the fire and had the same thought as the young women. She began to hunt for bandicoots on the other side of the mountain, where the cave was.

The four women did not think of being ashamed if the people of the village saw them. They put their heads down and kept vigilant watch for bandicoots fleeing the sword grass. Oh my, they caught many bandicoots.

The poor old woman hunted for bandicoots for a while, then she arrived at the cave. The sword grass by the cave did not burn well, so she trampled upon the grass. Before long, she fell down into the cave.

However, she was very lucky that some sword grass by the cave entrance had not burned well, so she grabbed it tightly and shouted for help.

The sound of the fire prevented the four women from hearing her. The poor old woman kept holding on tightly to the sword grass, then she came out.

The bad *masalai* of the mountain saw her. Quietly, the *masalai* got up and blew its wind. Oh my, a strong wind arose and planted the old woman on top of the mountain. She went to the very top of the *limbum* tree. The wind was very strong, so it pummeled the old woman onto the tree and she was stuck there.

The poor old woman was hanging from the top of the *limbum* tree and shouting. The four women heard her. They sped up to the top of the mountain.

Oh my, they were shocked to see the old woman stuck on top of the *limbum* tree. They shouted and cried together at the base of the *limbum* tree. The man who had made the fire heard their cries.

He sped up there and met the four women. They showed him the old woman on top of the *limbum* tree and he raced up the tree. He approached the old woman and saw that she was half-dead. Slowly, he put the old woman on top of his shoulders then he carried her down.

When she came to the ground, the poor old woman was dead. They were very troubled, and they carried the old woman's body back to the village. That night, everyone gathered and cried terribly. The next morning, they buried her body and gave a huge party.

They killed six big pigs and called for all of the men, women and children to gather. They ate the pork, then sang and danced until dawn.

Tasalit Meuzo
PNG C. C. R. I., P. O. Box 1846
Rabaul
East New Britain Province

C141. Tabu: going forth during menses; C200+. Tabu: eating during menstruation; D906. Magic wind; D1402.26. Magic wind kills; F402.1.11. Spirit causes death; F460. Mountain-spirits; F490+. Masalai; F562.7K. People live in mountain top; F963. Extraordinary behavior of wind; F1021. Extraordinary flights through air; P426.2. Hermit; V61.3+. Dead buried; W111. Laziness; W126. Disobedience

Guipe Left Sirunki and Went to Live at Birip
(Wantok 801, November 9-15, 1989, page 19)

Long ago, in the time of the ancestors, there were two ponds in the **Sirunki** area of **Enga** Province [**Enga** People]. The names of these two ponds are Ipae and Guipe. They have been there from the time of the ancestors until now.

One time, Pond Ipae told Pond Guipe, "We've been here and we've heard the cries of many pigs, men, and children. I'm tired of smelling their shit, so it's not good for us to stay here. I'd like us to leave this place and find a better one."

So one time in the afternoon, the ponds decided to leave Sirunki. Ipae told Guipe, "You must wake up in the very early morning and prepare some food. Later, you'll come meet me at the Mamaites Trail junction. Then we'll go down to the Wabag side." That is the place where **Wabag** Town is now located.

Guipe listened carefully and prepared some sweet potatoes, then went to sleep and awoke in the very early morning. Guipe walked away and waited for Ipae at the Mamaites Trail junction.

Poor Guipe waited and waited until it was nearly noon, but Ipae did not arrive. Guipe stayed there and thought, "Ipae must have come before me, so Ipae waited for me then left. That's OK, I must follow Ipae."

Guipe got up and followed the trail down towards the area of Wabag Town, where Guipe is now located. Guipe met some streams along the trail and asked them, "Did you see Ipae or not?" They replied that they had not seen Ipae.

Guipe then knew that Ipae must have lied. Guipe was furious and followed the trail all of the way down to a village called **Birip**. Guipe met some streams there and asked them whether they had seen Ipae, but they replied that they had not. Guipe was now convinced that Ipae had lied. Guipe stood on the trail and looked towards where Birip Mission Station is now located. Guipe walked slowly and arrived at a good place. This place is now the site of Birip Lutheran Seminary. Before, in the time of the ancestors, some people lived there.

Guipe put the sweet potatoes down and made a village at this site. The people of this area often used Guipe's water to wash their things, to make their gardens and such. Guipe had found a good place.

One time, Guipe sent a message to Ipae at Sirunki, "You lied to me and I came to live at a faraway place, but this is a good place that is better than where you live now. I never smell shit like we used to smell it at Sirunki."

Ipae heard this message and was furious. This caused Ipae to jump about and kill many men, women and children who had come to bathe in the pond.

So today, many people are afraid to bathe in Ipae Pond. This is because the water often kills many people. Today, if you go to Sirunki, you will see that Ipae Pond is still there. You will also see the place where Guipe Pond was formerly located. This place is dry and has no more water. This ancestor story is from our people from Sirunki.

Ben Yopo Benjamin [Yópó is a clan name (Lang, 1973:
215).]
Yalomale Village
Enga Province

A920.1.0.1. Origin of particular lake; F713+. Speaking lake; F713+. Walking lake; F932.12. Speaking river (brook); K1600+. Dupe tricked into leaving home, but arrives at better home; N339+. Accidental drowning; R213. Escape from home; S110. Murders; X716.4H. Fastidiousness regarding excrement; W157. Dishonesty

Surinangu [Sirunangu] Married Yakandua's Wife

(Wantok 802, November 16-22, 1989, page 19)

Long, long ago, in the time of the ancestors, there were two brothers who lived in a village in the east Yangoru [**Boiken** People, **East Sepik** Province]. The big brother's name was Yakandua and the little brother's name was Sirunangu.

Sirunangu was still a baby when the enemies had come and killed their parents. Yakandua was a big boy, so he alone took care of his brother.

Many months and years passed, then Sirunangu became a big man, but he did not yet have a beard like his big brother Yakandua. They lived very well and traveled together in the forest. They never argued or fought between themselves. They were both very handsome. When young women saw them, they would just follow them and try to marry them.

They lived for a while, then one time they did not have meat in the house. Yakandua told Sinrunangu [Sirunangu], "Stay and look after the house. It would be bad if both of us went to the forest and the enemies ruined the place. I'm going very far into the deep forest to find some wild game. I'll return when it is nearly evening."

After Yakandua said this, he prepared his bow and arrows. Later, he filled up his net bag with wild taros, then he sped off into the forest. At this time, it was still very early in the morning.

He walked and walked, then he came to a lake. He rested there, then he heard the sound of birds. Today, these birds are called doves (or pigeons).

The meat of these birds is very good to eat. Oh my, the birds were scrambling to eat the ripe fruits on the tree. Quietly, Yakandua readied his bow and arrows, then he climbed up the mountain. Before long, he arrived at the base of the tree.

He sat well and waited for the doves to gather on a tree branch so that he could shoot many of them with just one arrow. Quietly, he drew back the bow and shot it up to the place where the birds were gathered. He shot just one, but the bird carried the arrow and flew away, falling up by the headwaters of a stream.

He went back to the stream, then he ran up to the headwaters, where he met an old woman. The old woman was sitting on top of a stone and making a net bag. He said to the old woman, "Good afternoon, old woman. I was shooting at doves and one brought my arrow down here. Did you see it or not?"

The old woman replied, "Oh son, the arrow and the bird fell exactly where I'm sitting. You know that it was edible, so I cooked and ate it."

Yakandua was not angry at the old woman. He told her, "That's OK, it doesn't matter. See you later. I'm going back home."

However, the old woman told him not to go, that he should sleep with her because it was nearly dark and he would not be able to see well on the trail. Yakandua agreed, so they stayed there.

Yakandua wanted to sleep, and the old woman told him, "At night, you must not wake up if you hear a noise. You must just sleep." Yakandua listened to what the old woman said.

That night, young and gorgeous women spilled out of the old woman's house. Yakandua saw them and he strongly wanted to hold one of them, but he followed the old woman's instructions and fell dead asleep.

In the early morning, the old woman awoke first and sharpened a stick. She sharpened the stick very finely. Then she gave it to Yakandua and said, "You can go now. Thank you very much for the dove and for staying with me. You'll take this stick back home and think of me."

Yakandua took the stick and walked back towards the village. On the trail, he wanted to defecate, so he went into the forest. He placed the stick by the side of the trail with his bow and net bag.

After he defecated, he came out and, oh my, was he shocked. A gorgeous woman had taken the place of the stick. Yakandua was a big man, so he thought of taking her to the village, then they would marry and live together.

However, the little brother, Sirunangu had a great desire to have a wife like this. So one time, Yakandua told him what he must do.

One day, Sirunangu awoke and went to this place. He knocked out a dove and the dove fell down at the old woman's home. However, when he arrived there, he was furious and scolded the old woman, "Who told you to take my dove, you nasty old lady!" They argued, then at night they slept. The same thing happened as with Yakandua.

However, the old woman was not happy with Sirunangu, so she gave him a stick that she had not sharpened well. On the trail, the stick became an old woman. Sirunangu was furious and killed the old woman on the trail. Later, he arrived at the village, killed his big brother and married his wife.

[Anonymous]
Box 1359
Wewak
E. S. P. [East Sepik Province]

D431.2+W. Transformation: stick to woman; P251.5. Two brothers; P251.4+. One brother acts wisely, another acts unwisely; P263. Brother-in-law; P264. Sister-in-law; Q40. Kindness rewarded; Q280. Unkindness punished; Q411. Death as punishment; S73.1. Fratricide; S110. Murders; T100. Marriage; T425. Brother-in-law seduces (seeks to seduce) sister-in-law; W27. Gratitude; W181. Jealousy

Kasulege Pond Arose at Kimala

(Wantok 803, November 23-29, 1989, page 17)

Long, long ago, there lived a man and his sister. The man's name was Ipatokos Kimala and his sister's name was Takuan Ipali. They lived in **Kamatatopemandak** Village, near Kandep, in **Enga** Province [**Enga** People]. They husbanded a pig whose name was Supi Meok.

They never slept together in the same house. Kimala stayed by himself in the spirit house, and Ipali stayed in the women's house with the pigs. Every morning, Kimala would awake and erect the garden fence. Sometimes, he would help his sister take care of the pig.

One afternoon, Kimala thought of going to hunt for marsupials (*kapul*) in the forest. He told Ipali, "Tomorrow in the very early morning, I'm going to the forest to hunt for some wild game. So, I'd like you to prepare some sweet potatoes and such for me to take into the forest."

After he said this, he returned to the spirit house. He prepared all of his things for hunting game, such as bows and arrows, then he slept for a while. He awoke in the very early morning.

He left the village and walked away, into the very deep forest. He walked and walked, then in the afternoon, he arrived at a place that we call **Yopopaus**.

He made a forest hut, then he made a fire. Later, he slept by the fire until the birds cried out in the early morning. He awoke, cooked some sweet potatoes and ate. When it was still dark, he took his bow and arrows, then he went to check the trees where the marsupials often ate fruits.

Kimala was a champion at hunting game, so he ruined the lives of many marsupials. At the village, his sister Ipali was working and feeling hot. so she walked towards a nearby stream to bathe.

By the stream there lived a *masalai* marsupial. This marsupial lived on a tree and was spying upon Ipali. The name of this tree is *kupidi*. [*Kúpí* means "breadfruit" (Lang, 1973: 190).]

Afterwards, the marsupial became exactly like Kimala. He took a tree fruit and shot it down at Ipali's breast. Ipali was surprised. She looked up and saw Kimala.

Ipali thought that it was her brother, Kimala, who had done this. However, it was really the *masalai*, pretending to be Kimala, who had done this.

Poor Ipali felt ashamed and ran away to the house, crying. Kimala was killing many marsupials in the forest, for four whole days. During these days, Ipali slept in the house and just cried.

Kimala returned to the village and prepared a fire to make an earth oven for the meat. Afterwards, he called out for Ipali to come and help him, "Ipali, come help me make the earth oven, then we'll eat this meat."

However, he did not hear a reply. Later, he walked over there quietly and heard Ipali crying. He asked Ipali, "Why are you crying?" However, Ipali did not reply. This made him furious.

She did not reply, so he went back and heated the stones [for the earth oven]. Later, he killed his pig and put in inside the earth oven with the marsupial meat. After the meat was ready, he removed it.

He put some meat in his net bag, and he put some on Ipali's side. He divided all of the meat along with taros and bananas, then he went into the spirit house.

He went outside and dressed himself. Afterwards, he took his bow and arrows and his pig fat in a net bag, then he left the village and walked to another place.

Ipali saw that Kimala must have been angry with her, so she wanted to run away with him. Ipali cried and ran behind Kimali [Kimala]. She called for Kimala to return, but Kimala did not listen to her. Ipali called out, "Kimala! Kimala! I'll eat the marsupial meat and pork now. Come back, don't leave me."

Kimala walked and walked, then he arrived at **Kasumandaka**. Along the trail, the pork juices fell down and covered his legs. Kimala kept walking farther, then the pork juices rose high and covered him.

Today, this pond is still there. The name of this pond is Kasulege. Then Ipali transformed and became like the *masalai* marsupial that had tricked her. In my language, we call this *masalai* marsupial, *katiniamundu*.

Kandaki Salipen

Tinjipaka Village

Enga Province

A920.1.0.1. Origin of particular lake; D179.6K+W. Transformation: woman to marsupial; D310+M. Transformation: marsupial to man; D476+. Transformation: grease to lake; F401.3+. Spirit in marsupial form; F490+. Masalai; K1930. Treacherous impostors; P253. Sister and brother; P253+. Hostile sister and brother; R213. Escape from home; R260. Pursuits; V112.1. Spirit huts

A Man Stole a *Masalai* Baby

(Wantok 804, November 29 — December 6, 1989, page 20)

Long, long ago, in the time of the ancestors, there was a village called **Siriwai**. This village was on the Rai Coast, by Saidor, inside **Madang** Province.

In this village, there lived a man who was a champion at hunting for wild game at night. This man's name was Amudang. He never missed when he went into the forest. When he went into the forest, he would just return with game, then he would divide it among everyone in the village.

However, one night something happened to him when he went into the forest. He tried very hard to kill pigs or bandicoots, but he did not kill a single one. He tired then he stood up his bow and arrows at the base of a tree. Then he straightened his back by the side of the tree.

Fruits

It was the custom of leaders to stand on a single leg when they slept, like a short post to support themselves as they slept. Amudang did this and slept.

He was just going to pretend to sleep to straighten his back, but he fell soundly asleep instead. He did not know that the tree under which he slept had ripe fruits on top of it. Every night, a *masalai* woman would come and eat the fruits of this tree.

That night, the *masalai* woman carried her baby boy in a net bag, and came to eat some more tree fruits. The *masalai* woman arrived at the base of the tree, then searched for a place to hang the baby in the net bag. She looked around, then she saw Amudang's leg standing like a post. She thought that Amudang's leg was part of the tree.

So, she hung the baby on Amudang's leg while she went up the tree to eat the fruits. Amudang slept for a while, then he wanted to turn. However, he felt that his leg was very heavy. He opened his eyes and saw the *masalai* baby hanging from his leg.

He heard a noise on top of the tree and gathered his thoughts. He did not make a sound. Very quietly, he carried the *masalai* woman's baby and ran away, back to the village. Then he put the baby inside his house.

Later, he went out and fenced his house in tightly. He knew that the *masalai* woman would follow him to get her baby. He fenced in the house so that *masalai* woman could not go on top of it. This was because *masalai* women never jump over logs.

The *masalai* woman thought that her baby was still underneath, at the base of the tree. When it was nearly dawn, she went down to get her baby and go back to her home.

She checked all of the places by the base of the tree, but the baby was not there. Oh my, she was furious. She caught Amudang's scent and followed him towards the village. She arrived at the village and went directly to Amudang's house. However, she found it very difficult to jump over the logs to get inside the house and fetch her baby.

Youth

She was unsuccessful, so she shouted for Amudang to take good care of her baby. The poor *masalai* woman cried and cried, then returned to the forest, where she went completely crazy.

After this, Amudang no longer traveled in the forest. He just stayed at home and took good care of the *masalai* woman's baby boy.

Many months and years passed, and the baby grew up. Later, Amudang found a young woman in the village. The *masalai* man married her, and they raised many babies. Something that was slightly wrong with the *masalai* man was that he had a very long nose. So, all of his children had long noses.

This is a true ancestor story because the *masalai* man's families are still there. These clans are the descendants of this *masalai* man.

Koss Kipsie
Hohola
N. C. D. [National Capital District]

A1641+. Clan with long noses descended from supernatural being; F401.6. Spirit in human form; F402.1.10. Spirit pursues person; F490+. Masalai; F543.1. Remarkably long nose; P210. Husband and wife; P230. Parents and children; P231+. Mother becomes insane when she loses son; P261. Father-in-law; P265+. Daughter-in-law; P271. Foster father; P275. Foster son; R10.3. Children abducted; R260. Pursuits; T111. Marriage of mortal and supernatural being

How the People of Kizeng [Kwenzenzeng] Arose

(Wantok 805, December 7, 1989, page 20)

Long, long ago, in Pindu [**Pindiu** Village], in the Finschaffen [Finschhafen] District of **Morobe** Province, there lived a man who traveled in the forest [**Kube** People]. He traveled in the forest and arrived at the base of a tree. He saw the footprints of ghosts. We call this tree *kizeng*.

Ghosts, who threw parts of them down to the base of the tree, were eating the tree fruits. The man saw this and returned to the village.

He stayed for a while, then in the afternoon, he walked back to the base of the tree. He climbed the tree, then waited and waited until it was very late at night.

While he waited, he heard the crying of a baby ghost girl whose mother was carrying her towards the tree. They went directly to the base of the tree. The man saw them and sat exactly as if he was part of the tree, not making a noise.

The ghost woman carried the baby and climbed the tree. The ghost woman saw him and was shocked. She approached and scratched his skin, but he did not make a sound. The ghost woman took some ants and put them on his skin, but he stood firmly like a tree branch.

The ghost woman saw this and thought that it was a tree branch, so she hung up her daughter [in a net bag] on his arm. Then she ate tree fruits.

Before long, she went far up where the tree leaves blocked her view and she could not see the baby. Very quietly, he took the baby, then sped away like a lizard to the base of the tree.

He carried the baby inside the net bag, not thinking of anything. [His] legs [flew] back to his buttocks, while he raced as fast as possible towards the village.

He approached the village, then he shouted as he went, "I'm bringing a ghost baby, so hide all of the axes, knives, bows, arrows and other fighting gear."

The people heard this and hid all of these things. They blocked the doors and hid inside their houses. The poor ghost woman finished eating, then descended to get her baby so that they could go back to their hole. However, she saw that the baby was not there, so she wailed terribly. She sniffed around, then she followed the man towards the village.

She ran directly to his house and shouted inside to get her baby. However, the man replied that he could not give back the baby girl, "I can't send her away. She's my baby now. I took her and she belongs to me." The ghost woman cried and cried, then she shouted for him to give back her baby until dawn arrived.

He did not return the baby, so she shouted to him, "Dawn is breaking, so I'm giving up. You're very strong, so the baby belongs to you people. You yourselves will own and take care of her." She shouted and cried as she returned to her home.

The people of the village took the ghost baby girl and washed her well in very hot water. Later, they cut off the long hair from her legs and arms, and cut off her long finger and toenails. Afterwards, they took care of her. They taught her their language and customs. The ghost's baby girl grew up, then they gave her a man and they married. She lived with him for a while, then she became pregnant and gave birth to a baby girl.

After she gave birth, she called out to her ghost mother. The ghost mother heard this and explained something to her other families. All of them gathered and brought to the village all of the foods that the ghost usually ate, foods such as wild sugarcanes (*pitpit*), taros, bananas, leafy greens, and *aibika*s.

The people of the village also prepared and killed a very large pig. They all gathered in the village, then the human clan gave the pig to the ghost woman's clan.

You know, ghosts often eat pigs with the hair still on them. They ate, then the woman's ghost mother gave wild sugarcanes, bananas, and other food to the people of the village.

Before they ate, the ghost mother told her daughter, "This food and the leafy greens are for you and your husband to eat. However, you cannot throw away the tops or roots of these foods. You must plant them in the ground, so that they will bear food later. We'll go back now, so we'll put you by your husband's hand. You can live with him and raise your baby. We're going to a mountain that has a cave. When you see that this cave is dark, you must know that [we]'re standing and blocking the space. When the hole is light again, it shows that we've left the cave and gone to our home."

Tese B. Suanku

E422.1.8+. Revenant with long nails; E425.1.4. Revenant as woman carrying baby; E425.3. Revenant as child; E261.4. Ghost pursues man; E495.2. Marriage (ceremony) to a ghost; E541. Revenants eat; F402.6.4.1. Spirits live in caves; F515.2.2. Person with very long fingernails; F555.3. Very long hair; K1810. Deception by disguise; K1860. Deception by feigned death (sleep); P210. Husband and wife; P232. Mother and daughter; P234. Father and daughter; P262. Mother-in-law; P265. Son-in-law; P271. Foster father; P275+. Foster daughter; P290+. Maternal kin; P292. Grandmother; P600+. Custom: birth payment; R10.3. Children abducted; R24. Abductor in disguise; R260. Pursuits; T111. Marriage of mortal and supernatural being; T580. Childbirth

Kiwalema Arose from Clay
(Wantok 806, December 14, 1989, page 18)

Long, long ago, in the Lake Murray area of **Western** Province, there only lived women. These women lived by themselves because their husbands had died many years before.

They never worried about finding good meat to eat because they had many strong dogs to do this work. However, among these women, there lived a very old woman. The old woman did not have the strength to hunt for wild game in the forest.

When the young women returned from the forest, they never gave meat or game to her. The old woman became very troubled because she just ate sago every day while the others had meat to eat with it.

However one day, a good idea came to the old woman's head. She thought of taking some clay and making a young man. This man would hunt game for her.

One day, all of the women returned into the forest. The old woman was alone and went down to Lake Murray. She gathered some clay and made something like a human head.

However, the head looked like a woman. This was because it had been a very long time since the old woman had seen a man and she had forgotten what a man's head looked like.

On the second day, she made the body, the arms, and the legs. She also made the other parts of the body that a man has, such as muscles, a nose, a face, and a mouth. She also planted a cassowary feather on top of the clay-man's head. Later, she left it in the sun to dry, then she walked back to the long house where she and the other women slept.

On the third day, she went back down to bring up the clay body and put it inside the house on top of a mat. That night, she performed a traditional song and dance, then she put various kinds of love charms into the clay body.

When she awoke the next morning, she was surprised to see a young man sitting on top of the mat. She was elated because of her thoughts about fetching food. Also, she would no longer worry about eating meat.

The young man woke up and spoke to the old woman, "Don't be afraid of me. I'm the man that you yourself made."

The old woman was very happy and gave the name Kiwalema to this young man. Some weeks later, the old woman made some spears, a bow, and other things for killing game. She told Kiwalema that he would use these things for hunting game in the forest.

Kiwalema was extremely happy to hunt for game, but the old woman told Kiwalema that he could not touch water or wash in the rain lest he became clay again.

The next day, Kiwalema went into the forest and returned with a pig and a cassowary. He and the old woman cooked the meat well, then just the two of them ate it.

However some days later, the other women found out that a young man was living with the old woman. They were shocked at how the young man had arisen. Quickly, they asked the old woman to show them the method that she had used to create the young man.

The old woman replied that she had made the man from clay. The next day, all of the women went down by Lake Murray and tried to make a man from the earth. However, it was very hard for them and they had not brought food. This was because they did not have the traditional song and dance, or the love charms that the old woman had used.

The women were furious and they thought badly of the old woman. This was because all of them had a strong desire to marry Kiwalema so that he could hunt game for them.

The old woman knew that the other women were furious at her. So, she told them that the next day Kiwalema would go with them to an island in the middle of Lake Murray to hunt for some game.

That night, all of the women were elated and went to sleep. In the very early morning, all of them awoke at cockcrow. Kiwalema and the women jumped into their canoe, then paddled off to the island.

When it was nearly noon, they arrived at the island. All of them decided to hunt for game in the Lake Murray fashion that is called "blocking" (*blokim*) or "tying up the point" (*pasim poin*).

So, the women went to the middle of the island and began making noises to scare the animals. Kiwalema with his bow and arrows shut off the point or place where the animals would flee. There were no men who had hunted on this island, so there was plentiful game. Kiwalema killed two animals for each woman.

Later, they all gathered and Kiwalema asked his old mother where they would make a party with the animals. The old mother replied that they would paddle to another nearby island to make a party there.

They paddled and paddled, then they arrived on the island and made a huge party. When the meat was on top of the fire, the women made jokes, laughed, sang, and danced. They said that the clay-man, Kiwalema, was the best at killing animals, so he would still hunt for game for themselves.

However, Kiwalema was very troubled and shouted to the women, "No! Wait a little first! Can't you see the heavy rain coming?"

"Ha! You're not a soul of the forest who would just disappear if the rain touched you. The rain is still far away. We can paddle quickly and arrive at the long house before the rain comes," a woman said.

Kiwalema was not very happy. Quietly, he took the bow and arrows, then he sat at the front of the canoe and helped the women paddle.

However, they were still in the lake when the rain caught them. Kiwalema shouted for the women to hide him in the black sago leaves, but the women laughed and told him to just sit quietly.

The women put their heads down and paddled very hard. They did not see that the rain was washing Kiwalema away into nothing but clay.

When they arrived at the front of the long house and prepared to go down, they were surprised to see that Kiwalema was not there. They just saw the place where the clay was in the front of the canoe.

One woman shouted, "Where is he?" They searched everywhere. Later, the old woman came outside and shouted to them, "That hunk of clay on the front of the canoe is Kiwalema!" All of the women were shocked.

Francis Topa
Miwa Village [**Zimakani** People]
Western Province

A1280+. First man; D230+M. Transformation: man to clay; D435.1.1. Transformation: statue comes to life; D562.1. Transformation by application of water; D1355.3. Love charm; D1781. Magic results from singing; D1781+. Magic results from dancing; F566.1. Village of men only; J652. Inattention to warnings; P231. Mother and son; W151. Greed; W181. Jealousy

Entap Killed a Snake with His Teeth

(Wantok 807, December 21, 1989, page 16)

Long, long ago, [in the time of the] ancestors, there lived a man named Entap. Entap lived with his family in a small village called **Wampit** in **Morobe** Province [**Wampar** People].

This village also had many other people and Entap's family lived with them. Of all the people in the village, Entap excelled at hunting wild game in the forest. He hunted for game both day and night.

However, he never did the slightest garden work. His wife and children did the garden work. Entap only worked at filling the house with meat.

One very early morning, Entap took his bow and arrows, and his multi-pronged spear, then he sped off into the forest. He arrived somewhere and he kept watch at a pig trail. The pig trail went directly into a big group of sago palm trees that was in a *masalai* place called Ngarochopang. So, Entap went on his hands and knees, and then he followed the pig trail.

You know, pigs are very good food for snakes too. So in the middle of the trail, a gigantic snake was doing the same kind of work that Entap was doing amidst the sago palms.

The snake was lying in wait for the pigs. Entap did not know that there was an enemy on the trail. Oh my, he worked hard and he sped along to kill a pig. Before long, Entap approached the place where this bad thing was waiting.

The snake smelled Entap and was quite ready at the trail opening. When Entap went under a sago tree branch, the snake immediately encircled Entap and took him down to the ground.

The snake encircled Entap's body very well, but missed Entap's right arm. All of Entap's things, such as arrows and the spear, flew about as if a man had taken them and thrown them away.

Entap tensed his body, but all of his strength was gone. However, Entap then pretended that he was dead and he stopped tensing his body. The snake moved its head back towards Entap's nose and mouth to determine whether he was dead or not. Immediately, Entap grabbed the snake's head with his right hand and cut the snake's throat with his teeth.

The snake twisted about, but Entap still held the snake's head tightly and bit the snake's throat. Before long, he broke a bone then the snake twisted and died, letting go of Entap.

Poor Entap got up and ran awkwardly like a dog to the village. When he arrived at the village, his kin were shocked to see him walking awkwardly towards them like a dog, banging his sides as he walked. Oh my, the people laughed hysterically.

However, Entap did not care about them. He sped directly to his eldest son, Fose, and his wife, Hocco. Quickly, the two of them washed his body in hot water because he smelled awful. Later, he felt well and told them what had happened to him.

Geoffrey Elias

Box 3500

Lae

M. P. [Morobe Province]

B875.1. Giant serpent; F490+. Masalai; F628.1.3. Strong man kills great serpent; K1860. Deception by feigned death (sleep); P210. Husband and wife; P230. Parents and children; P231. Mother and son; P233. Father and son

A Fish Transformed and Married the Little Sister

(Wantok 808, December 28, 1989, page 14)

Long, long ago, two sisters lived in a place near **Wela** and **Selni** Villages, by Drekikir [Dreikikir] in **East Sepik** Province [**Wom** People]. One time, the two sisters went to fish in the river. Two brothers noticed this and followed them to the river.

The two [brothers] went to the source of the river. They covered their genitals with vines. Later, they drank plenty of juice from sugarcanes that they had taken with them from the garden.

They drank and drank, then their bellies became remarkably swollen. Later, they let go of the vines and urinated into the river. The river was fouled, and the sisters saw that the river was flooding. However, it was not a real flood.

You know, in the time of yore, if you saw a little man, you could not think that he was an ordinary boy. He would have been a grown man with evil powers to transform into various things. So, the two [brothers] turned into fish.

The big brother turned into a fish and went into the big sister's net. The little brother went into the little sister's net. The little sister carefully put her fish into her *limbum* bucket. The big sister tried to kill the fish that she had caught, but it did not die. They continued to search for fish, then when it was nearly afternoon, they returned to the village.

The big sister went directly to the house and cooked her fish. However, the fish did not cook at all. She was furious and ate the raw fish.

The little sister cooked the other fish and pretended to put the one fish into an earthen pot. She ate the other fish, then she slept. In the very early morning, she awoke and saw an extremely handsome man sitting by the earthen pot. You know, the little brother had turned in a real man.

The little sister saw this and did not speak to the big sister. At night, she often slept with and had sex with him. Before long, the little sister was pregnant.

The big sister asked the little sister why her belly had enlarged. The big sister already thought that the little sister had been hiding a man in the house, and that this man had impregnated her.

One day, the sisters went to look for firewood near the village. The big sister quickly found some firewood and told the little sister, "Stay and find some more firewood. I'll carry some firewood back first. Look at that part of the trail; that is where I'll come back to get you. Afterwards, we'll return to the village."

The big sister had lied and she sped back to the village. The little sister waited for a long time, then she followed the big sister back to the village.

She arrived in the village and saw that the house door was open. She knew that her big sister had found out. The big sister saw this and was about to come outside. However, the little sister took a piece of bamboo and beat her on the head, telling her, "When it's your time to give birth to a baby, who shall make your [birthing] hut?" The big sister listened and did not scold the little sister.

She made a hut, then helped the little sister give birth inside this hut. They lived for a while, then they heard that a big festival would be happening at Wela Village. The big sister and the little sister's husband went. Only the little sister and the baby stayed to take care of the village.

The little sister went to the latrine. She returned and saw that a *masalai* man had swallowed the baby and was sitting there. Oh my, she cried and took her *limbum* bucket, then she sped away to the festival site.

However, the *masalai* followed her towards the Amuk River. The little sister took some stones and ran with them. When the *masalai* approached, she shot the *masalai* with stones.

She did this for a while, but they were small stones, so the *masalai* swallowed the stones and kept following her. The little sister ran and ran, then they arrived at the top of a mountain where there were no more stones. So, she pushed a boulder down towards the *masalai*.

The *masalai* man swallowed the boulder, and his belly became leaden. He twisted and turned, then he went down to the Wambriel River, which the ancestors named after this story.

The little sister sped away and arrived at the festival grounds. She found her husband with her sister, then she broke open both of their heads with a piece of bamboo. This was because she was irate from the enemy having come to her.

The other people took wild taro leaves and let the blood go inside and wash them. The man turned into a bird of paradise and flew away.

The little sister cried and cried, then she turned into a black bird of the sword-grass lands. They left the bamboo that the little sister had used to beat her husband and sister in Selni Village. The bamboo grew, so now there is a big grove of bamboos growing in this area.

Imelda Engime

Wewak

East Sepik Province

A1012.2. Flood from urine; A1617. Origin of place-name; D150W. Transformation: woman to bird; D150+M. Transformation: man to bird of paradise; D170M. Transformation: man to fish; D370M. Transformation: fish to man; D1724. Magic power from Death; F535. Pygmy; F490+. Masalai; F529.6. Person with enormous belly; F910. Extraordinary swallowings; G512.3.1+. Ogre tricked into eating hot stones; P210. Husband and wife; P230. Parents and children; P251.5. Two brothers; P252.1. Two sisters; P263. Brother-in-law; P264. Sister-in-law; P294. Aunt; Q211.4. Murder of children punished; Q411. Death as punishment; Q458. Flogging as punishment; R260. Pursuits; S110. Murders; T570. Pregnancy; T580. Childbirth; X712.2H. Male genitals

Hunger Caused a Brother's Death

(Wantok 809, January 4, 1990, page 16)

In the time of the ancestors, there were seven brothers who lived in a village called Powung [**Pobung**] in the Kabwum District of **Morobe** Province [**Timbe** People].

This village had no food, so the brothers often just ate ashes from the fire. They would burn firewood, then carefully gather up all of the black ashes and prepare them to be eaten in the morning and afternoon.

When they wanted to defecate, they would sit on top of a tree, then defecate onto the ground. One morning, they all went to go defecate. They went in a group up a tree, starting with the youngest brother up to the eldest brother. They defecated, and all of their feces were black. Only the last brother's feces were yellow.

All of the brothers knew that the last [youngest] brother had eaten some kind of food so that his feces had come out yellow. The little brother frightened the elder brothers by saying that he often stole food from a *masalai* man's garden.

They followed what he had done. Every day they would tie on ropes and descend to an area near a mountain where the *masalai*'s garden was located. They would steal the food from this garden.

One day, they all awoke and went to steal from this garden. They stole food, and then the *masalai* arrived with his wife. All of the elder brothers jumped quickly onto the rope and sped up to the top of the mountain, then they fled.

The last brother jumped up too, but the rope broke and he fell to the ground. The poor brother searched hard for a place to hide. He could not find one, so he removed a ginger plant (*gorgor*). He held the ginger stem and dug the earth, then he went to hide underneath it.

The *masalai* and his wife had been searching for food, and they wanted to return. They jumped over the garden fence, then they were about to go back to the house, but the last brother whistled and the two of them returned.

They searched to find out who had whistled to them. They could not find anything, so they jumped over the garden fence and just went back. The last brother whistled again.

This time, the *masalai* man was furious. He returned and removed all of the ginger and wild sugarcane roots (*pitpit*). He went to the base of the ginger plant where the little brother was hiding. He tried to remove it too, but the ginger was very strong, so his wife came to help him and they pulled very hard at the base of the ginger plant. However, the last brother was biting hard on the ginger stem with his teeth as he lay there. The *masalai* and his wife used all of their strength and they saw the white of the little brother's teeth. The *masalai* took a spear and killed the last brother, then he carried him to the house.

The *masalai*'s children saw this and were happy. They shouted, "*Ju nenne ju nenne*." Their father cooked the brother's body, then in the afternoon they made a huge party.

The next day, the *masalai* and his wife went to hunt for wild game in the forest. The elder brothers went to the *masalai*'s house and only the children were there.

They asked the children, "Did you also eat an animal yesterday or not?" The children replied that they had eaten a huge animal that their father had killed in the garden and brought home. They took all of the little brother's bones and brought them out to show the brothers. The brothers saw these and were furious. They knew that the *masalai* man had killed their little brother.

Later, they lied to the children and asked them, "How do you sleep at night?" The children showed them how they lay in a row. Immediately, the brothers took a rope and bound them. Afterwards, they blocked the house door tightly and set the house on fire.

The *masalai* man and his wife saw the smoke rising from the house, and they sped back home. However, the brothers were well prepared, and they killed the *masalai* and his wife with their bows and arrows.

Later, they carried the *masalai* bones back to the village. They filled a net bag with them and with dry (or large) banana leaves. They took ants and put them inside the net bag.

The ants joined all of the *masalai*'s bones, which then became a baby. The brothers took care of the baby who then grew up and lived with them.

Konilias Nango
Box 275
Kimbe
West New Britain Province

E607.1+. Reincarnation by collecting bones of dead and placing with ants and banana leaves; F490+. Masalai; F969.7. Famine; G512.1+. Ogre killed with spear/arrow; G610. Theft from ogre; K400. Thief escapes detection; K713.1. Deception into allowing oneself to be tied; K812. Victim burned in his own house (or hiding place); K2061.10+. Banana detected from color of excrement; P210. Husband and wife; P230. Parents and children; P251.6.3+. Seven brothers; Q211. Murder punished; Q212. Theft punished; Q215. Cannibalism punished; Q402. Punishment of children for parents' offenses; Q411. Death as punishment; Q414. Punishment: burning alive; R4. Surprise capture; R210. Escapes; S110. Murders; S112.0.2. House (hostel) burned with all inside

Wando Killed Rande and Became the Ancestor of the People of Pambal [Pangal]

(Wantok 810, January 11, 1990, page 16)

Long, long ago, in Pambal [**Pangal** Village] in **Southern Highlands** Province, there lived just two young brothers [**Mendi** People].

Their names were Naki Wando and Naki Rande. The big brother's work was to hunt for wild game in the forest. The little brother would just stay at home and work in the garden every day.

One time, Wando went to hunt for game in the deep forest. Oh my, he killed many, many animals, and his bag was packed with them. When it was nearly afternoon, he heard the howl of a dog on top of Mount Hari Wopa.

He followed the sound and climbed the mountain. He met the dog and the dog came to lick him. Wando rested at this place and made a bonfire to cook the meat in an earth oven. Then the dog went into the forest and brought a gigantic pig.

Wando saw this and was shocked. He was happy and he killed the pig, then he cooked it in the fire with the other meat. When the earth oven was [ready], he divided all of the meat. He gave some to the dog and he took some. He and the dog were very good friends, to the point where they [almost] could not leave each other.

When it was nearly dark, he shook hands with the dog, then he went back home. The dog also went back to its home. Before it left, the dog told him, "You must return tomorrow."

The little brother, Rande, packed the house with food from the garden and waited. Before long, the big brother came with plenty of meat. They cooked the food well, then they ate. Afterwards, their bellies were terribly bloated and they slept.

The next day, Wando returned to the forest and met the dog. Oh my, they killed many, many animals and Wando took them home. Rande knew that something was happening because every day Wando would pack his bag with various kinds of game and return home.

One day, Rande told Wando that he wanted to try going to the forest, but Wando said, "No", because the little brother could not follow the things that he did. However, Rande insisted that he would follow everything that the big brother did to kill so many animals. So, Wando let him go.

Rande went to the forest and did not kill many animals. He was tired and he had not killed the various kinds of animals that Wando usually did. He only killed animals that he looked in the eyes and his bag was not full.

Later, he went up to the mountain and heard the dog's howl. He was completely furious. He screamed curses and said, "You're a crazy dog. What are you looking for that you came to howl here?"

He walked away a little, then he looked at the dog. Oh my, he took a stick and gave it good directly upon the dog's behind. The poor dog yelped terribly and ran away into the forest.

Before long, the dog brought a piglet in its mouth. Rande saw this and was furious. He took the piglet, and he took a stone. He gave it to the dog again, directly upon its head.

Blood flowed down from the poor dog, and the dog sped off into the forest, leaving for good. Wando had followed and heard everything. Then he returned home and waited.

Rande just cooked the small game in an earth oven, and brought it home. He arrived and the big brother told him, "Your meat bag is not very heavy. You look as if you didn't do what I had told you to do." Rande replied, "I did everything. That dog didn't bring a big pig, so I didn't bring much meat."

Wando was furious. Quickly, he went out of the house and tied the door to Rande. Later, he put a fire to the house and fled into the forest to find the dog. Poor Rande was burning inside the house.

Wando followed the trail and arrived at the place where he and the dog usually met. He saw much blood, blood that the dog had lost, and he was terribly worried. He cried and cried, then he followed the dog's blood and arrived at a hill.

When he arrived, he heard a woman crying. Wando was afraid and he wanted to turn back, but his concern for the dog made him push forward.

He approached, then he heard the woman talking and crying terribly, "My brother. I gave you the things that you liked. Why have you encountered death? I often gave you multicolored pigs."

Wando listened and cried terribly. Then he went closer and was shocked. He saw a young woman sitting near a corpse and crying.

Wando gathered his thoughts. The poor man who had died wanted to give his sister to Wando, so he had pretended to turn into a dog and make good friends with Wando. However, Rande had beaten him with a large stone, so he had lost much blood and died.

Wando thought this and was very troubled. Oh my, he grabbed the man's sister and they cried terribly. Later, Wando helped and they buried the man's body.

He took her and they went back home. They married and raised many, many children. So, Wando and the woman are the true ancestors of the people who now live in Pumbul [Pangal] Village.

Edward Ipne

Box 179

Aitape

West Sepik Province

A991+. Origin of particular village; B211.1.7. Speaking dog; B871.1.2.1. Giant hog; D141M. Transformation: man to dog; D341M. Transformation: dog to man; K812. Victim burned in his own house (or hiding place); P210. Husband and wife; P230. Parents and children; P251.4+. One brother acts wisely, another acts unwisely; P251.5. Two brothers; P253. Sister and brother; P310. Friendship; Q285.1. Cruelty to animals punished; Q414. Punishment: burning alive; R220. Flights; R260. Pursuits; S73.1.

Fratricide; S112.0.2. House (hostel) burned with all inside; T100. Marriage; V61.3+. Dead buried

Naroyats Originated from Three Women

(Wantok 811, January 18, 1990, page 20)

Long, long ago, in the time of the ancestors, there were three married women who were good friends and traveled together. They lived in a village in the Makam [Markham] area of **Morobe** Province.

[When] they worked at hunting for wild game by the river, or eating, you would see the three women together. One day, they agreed to hunt for little frogs at a river called Mpo Moae.

They woke up in the very early morning. They left the children with their husbands and walked to the river. Before long, they arrived and began to lift stones, and to catch the little frogs. They hunted for a while, then they went to the source of the river.

It was daylight when they reached this place. The leaders of the village had decided to burn the sword grass of the area where the three women were hunting for frogs.

The leaders did not know that they had put fire to the places around the women because the Mpo Moae River went inside a large sword grass area.

The three poor women had not known about the men's plans. Oh my, they were shocked to see the smoke from the fire. They knew that the men of the village must have placed the fire so that they could grab the animals [that fled]. Immediately, they went as fast as they could back down to the river.

The fire fenced them in and they could not return to the source of the river. The fire blocked them from above. They knew that they did not have anywhere else to go.

They looked around and saw a hill by the river. They climbed it and looked down to see if there was a place where they could escape before the fire encircled them completely.

They looked around and saw that the smoke and fire and surrounded them. Their spirits sank. They just stood on the hill and began to call their children and husbands. However, the sound of the wind and fire prevented their voices from carrying.

Afterwards, the fire approached and the smoke went in their eyes. They wanted to flee, but the fire blocked them. They were lost, and they died inside the fire.

The poor women's bodies were burnt to a crisp. Their heads rolled and went down to the other side of the hill, then went to a river called Leron.

The three heads went to a boulder and turned into two tall mountains. We **Wampar** [People] call these mountains Naroyuata [Naroyats]. There is a Naroyats One and a Naroyats Two. They stand near Leron Bridge.

The tears and blood of the third woman turned into three big river branches. The names of these branches are Buzampung Eran, Binum Ampo, and Rereb.

Their breasts became the Susu [lit., "breast" or "milk"] Mountains. In the Wampar Language, we call them the Mountains of the Young Women's Breasts.

Now, if you drive in an automobile and leave Lae, then follow the Markham Highway, then arrive at a large group of sword grass by Lero River, look to the right. You will see the Susu Mountains standing there. The three little river branches are beneath the Susu Mountains. Then drive a little further, up the mountain near Leron Bridge and look again to the right. You will see the two Naroyats Stones.

The Mpo Moae River is to the north of the Susu Mountains. The women of the village often cut sago sprouts at this river and make "grass" skirts. So, now they have given another name to this river. The new name that they gave is Azira, similar to the Sasiang River.

Meano Bair
Markham Valley
Morobe Province

A934.11. River from transformation; A965. Origin of mountain chain; A1617. Origin of place-name; D450+. Transformation: breast to mountain; D450+. Transformation: head to mountain; D457.1+. Transformation: blood to river; D457.18.2. Transformation: tears to river; N330. Accidental killing or death; P210. Husband and wife; P230. Parents and children; P310. Friendship

Kiwame and Kawame Turned into Stones

(Wantok 812, January 25, 1990, page 16)

Long, long ago, in **Maimapi** Village, in **Eastern Highlands** Province, there lived very many people. In this village, there lived a man and his son. The man's name was Magupia, and his son's name was Kiwame. Magupia's wife had died, so Magupia and his son lived alone.

Kiwame was Magupia's only child, so Magupia took very good care of him. Their lives were very good and they were always happy.

They lived for a while, then Kiwame grew up to be a big, strong man in this village. The two of them killed many animals when they traveled in the forest.

Father Magupia was the best man because he was better than every other village man was at hunting for wild game. The son, Kiwame, followed after him, and they lived together. After a long time, Magupia became old. However, his strength at hunting animals was not gone yet.

Every year, there is a season when the pandanus trees (*karuka*) bear nuts, and the people go to find them. This is because if you break the pandanus fruits open and eat them, they are excellent.

One day, the two of them went to search for pandanus in the forest. They walked and walked, then they approached a village called **Kanemolo**. Near Kanemolo Village, there stood a huge pandanus tree.

They rested a little under the tree, then they made a hut. Afterwards, they collected all of the pandanus nuts and put them inside the forest hut. Oh my, they took very many pandanus nuts and cut them open. They smoked some in the fire and filled the net bags. When the net bags were completely packed, they returned to the village.

At night, Magupe [Magupia] told Kiwame that the next day, they would hunt for game such as marsupials (*kapul*). They would go cook them in an earth oven and eat them with pandanus. They would share some of them with the people of the village.

They slept, then in the very early morning, they awoke. They had prepared their things, such as bows and arrows, and food the night before. They just carried these things and walked into the forest.

Later, they rested a little, then they kept walking. Before long, they arrived at Mount Kilua. This part of the forest has many kinds of animals, such as marsupials, pigs and cassowaries..

You know, the father and son were champions at killing animals. Their arrows never missed an animal. So, they ruined the lives of many kinds of animals, and their net bags were packed.

Near noon, they straightened out their net bags and walked back towards the village. The net bags were completely full, and they just wanted to defecate.

In the afternoon, they arrived at the village and called out for everyone to come gather. Oh my, they made a huge earth oven and ate the meat with pandanus nuts.

The people of the village saw this and brought their food to the gathering too. That night, they had a huge gathering. The leaders of the village gathered and gave a gorgeous woman to Kiwame. This woman's name was Kawame.

Many young men of the village had fought to marry this woman, but the boy without a mother, Kiwame, took her heart. Kiwame was elated and married this woman that same night. Afterwards, they very well.

One day, just the two of them went to the forest with a dog. They went and went, then they arrived at the same place where Kiwame and his father had killed the game before. That day, Kiwame killed a big pig and a cassowary

Kiwame did not know that he had killed a *masalai* pig and cassowary. They carried the animals and walked back to the village. The woman carried the pig in a net bag, and Kiwame carried the cassowary.

They arrived at a place on the trail and rested. Later, they left the game on the trail and went into the forest to defecate. They heard a shout and wanted to return, but the pig and cassowary had gotten up and fled.

Their dog went off and chased the pig and the cassowary. They followed and arrived at the same place that Kiwame had killed the two animals.

They had the idea that these were not really animals. They wanted to turn back and flee. But no, you know the powers of *masalai*s. The *masalai*s held them and transformed them into stones. The *masalai*s multiplied their dog many-fold.

So, today if you travel to the Kilua area, you will see these two big stones. The two stones are in the same place. Also, at Kilua, there are very many dogs.

David Ruma
Box 5695
Boroko
National Capital District

A974. Rocks from transformation of people to stone; A977. Origin of particular stones or groups of stones; A2433.2+. Why there are plentiful dogs at particular place; D231M. Transformation: man to stone; D231W. Transformation: woman to stone; D2106.1.2. Animals miraculously multiplied; E3. Dead animal comes to life; F401.3.10K. Spirit in form of boar; F401.3.7+. Spirit in form of cassowary; F490+. Masalai; P210. Husband and wife; P233. Father and son; Q211.6. Killing an animal revenged; Q551.3.4. Transformation to stone as punishment; R210. Escapes; R260. Pursuits; T10. Falling in love; T100. Marriage

Atopang's Wife Found Him in Her Dream

(Wantok 813, February 1, 1990, page 19)

Long, long ago, in the time of the ancestors, there was a man who lived in **Yuraseng** Village in **Madang** Province. The man's name was Jigen. Jigen was not an ordinary man; he was the best hunter.

He would always dig a pitfall for killing pigs and marsupials (*kapul*). He often killed very many animals, so his house was just packed with marsupial and pig meat.

One day, Jigen took his bow and arrows, then he walked into the very deep forest. The deep forest was near another village called **Dudun Atoung**.

In this place, there was a big pitfall that Jigen had dug before. Jigen arrived and kept watch by the pitfall. That day, there was not one pig or marsupial that fell into the pitfall. Jigen waited until it was nearly afternoon, then he returned to the village.

The next day, he went back to check the pitfall. He took his bow and arrows then walked into the forest. He walked and walked, then he approached the pitfall. He raised his head and saw that that mouth of the pitfall trap was open. He knew that the day before, some animals must have fallen down into the hole.

He was elated, so he readied his bow and arrows. He crouched and walked quietly towards the hole. His hand was fixed to the bow and the arrow was at the ready.

However, Jigen did not see a marsupial or a pig. He saw that there were only marsupial and pig guts filling the pitfall. A man had killed marsupials and pigs in his pitfall. Oh my, he was completely furious.

Quietly, he shut the pitfall trap and returned to the village. The next day, he stayed in the village and did other work. On the second day, he thought of the hole and went back to check on it.

Jigen arrived and was surprised to see the same thing. He belly was burning up and he shouted, "Which shitty man came and killed animals in my hole?"

He stood for a while and thought of a way to find out who it was that had stolen animals from his pitfall. Later, he closed the trap and walked back towards the village. However along the trail, he quickly turned around and went back. He approached the hole and went to spy out of a forest hut.

Before long, two pigs came and fell into the hole. Jigen waited and heard the sound of a man walking closer. Oh my, he was shocked to see Wabang Atopang. Atopang was a man who lived with him in the village. Jigen's belly was burning in anger.

Quietly, he waited and watched Atopang go down to the hole, then kill the pigs. Jigen walked stealthily towards the hole opening.

Atopang was shocked and shouted, "_Hei Gande! Sa gukung-be mogoti ga-mun._" Jigen took a big, traditional piece of rope and went down into the hole.

He grabbed Atopang and tied his arms and legs with the rope. Then he pulled him up through the hole opening. He just pulled Atopang by the ropes and carried him close

to the village. Jigen was an authority, so no man in the village would fool around with him.

He tied Atopang to the base of a tree. The name of this tree is _gadung wagalt_. When Atopang was hungry, Jigen would just give him garbage to eat. After a while, Atopang was nearly dead.

In the village, Atopang's wife tried to find out what had happened to her husband. She asked around the village, but the people did not know.

Atopang's wife also had an authority on her chest. At night, she slept and followed her dream. She went to **Lagohbongong**, then she followed a hill and went down to **Vissoh Malun**. Afterwards, she walked a little and arrived at **Vissoh Haven**, then she went to the far side.

She knew that her husband, Atopang, must be there. Still in her dream, she called to Atopang, "_Biyenk hama nee nee – e - e - Biyenk hama nee nee - e - e - Biyenk tna nee nee nee - e - e - e - Biyenk hama gyangong tna nee nee nee - e - e._"

She met her husband and cried terribly. Quickly, she loosened the ropes and they returned to the village, still in the dream. They did not follow another trail. They returned the way that she had come.

In the very early morning, Jigen awoke and went to the base of the tree where Atopang was tied, but Atopang was not there. Oh my, he was completely irate. He just ran back to the village. Atopang and his wife had fled to another village.

That is the end of my story. D. Atoung told this story and I wrote it.

Dairus Bonny

Box 131

Madang

Madang Province

D1810.8.2. Information received through dream; D1976.1. Transportation during magic sleep; K420. Thief loses his goods or is detected; P210. Husband and wife; Q212. Theft punished; Q418. Punishment by poisoning; Q433. Punishment: imprisonment; R49.1. Captivity in tree; R51.1. Prisoners starved; R152. Wife rescues husband; R220. Flights

Waipetro Found the Voice of the Simbu
(Wantok 814, February 8, 1990, page 20)

Long, long ago, in the time of the ancestors, in the **Simbu** [Province] area, there lived a man and his wife. The man's name was Waipetro and the woman's name was Maume Madarina. One day, they went into the forest, near the base of the stone mountain called Elimbari [Erimbari] to hunt for wild game. This mountain is near a village called **Megan Kobu** [**Siane** or **Chuave** People].

They arrived at the base of the mountain, then the woman went to the far side to look for vines that are used to make rope. The man went to the other side and hunted for game.

Madarima [Madarina] went to the base of a big bamboo grove, and then she heard something crying. Quickly, she shouted to her husband, "Waipetro! Waipetro! I heard a man approaching and talking on this side. Come and see."

Waipetro went to check, but he did not see a man. He waited a little, then he saw the wind blowing all of the bamboo leaf litter. Later, he looked at the base of a bamboo plant and saw that an [insect] was chewing it and making a hole.

The sound came from this bamboo. The sound was exactly like a bird's cry. He followed its singing very well. Quietly, he took his axe and cut down the bamboo. Later, he arranged his axe carefully and told his wife to go to the village first.

She arrived at the village and called out for all of the men to just come and gather at the spirit house. Waipetro showed the bamboo and told them, "I traveled in the forest and took something back. We'll try out this thing's sound. It sounded like a bird and I brought it here. Let's all try it and see."

After he said this, he called for his friend to come hold the other side of the bamboo. They began to blow the bamboo flute and they followed the bird's cry. They did this exactly and it really happened that way.

All of the men were speechless. They all tried the bamboo, then they decided to hide the bamboo inside the spirit house. They put a taboo against the women and children of the village seeing the flute.

The men would kill women or children who would see the flute, and their bodies would be hidden. Henceforth, the women would be terrified. After a while, they gave the name Yalbai to this flute. They would only blow it very late at night when the women [and] children were asleep.

During the day, when they would go out to work in the gardens, they would dress very finely and return in the afternoon. The flute would also be adorned very finely.

When they wanted to go out of the spirit house first, the men would call out beforehand, "All of the mothers, women and children, you must shut your house doors tightly. You can't look outside. Turn your heads inside to the fire. Shove sweet potatoes onto sticks and throw them outside. Whichever women look shall die."

At this time, the spirit house was packed with various foods. They would do this to ruin the women with sweat and hard work, searching for many sweet potatoes.

After a while, all of the men decided to burn the flute, and to follow the true and good life like other people. Everyone brought many pigs, and cooked food upon the flute. When the food was ready, the men cut a tree, then they brought it and made a big platform that was very high.

Waipetro himself jumped up to the platform and spoke. He shouted and cried. The leaders of the mission also came and gathered at this time with the women and children. They made a bonfire under the platform and burned the flute. The flute burned up completely. All of the men went to become baptized, and changed their beliefs to be Christian.

Another flute was still hidden by the men to be used during the times of traditional festivals. Afterwards, many white men arrived and built Kundiawa Town. They built a radio station and gave it the name, "Radio Simbu, the Voice of the Simbu."

Kiage Duon
Chuave
Simbu Province

A1461.7+. Origin of flute; C181. Tabu confined to women; C310+. Tabu: looking at sacred flute; K2370+. Sacred flute hidden from missionaries; P210. Husband and wife; P230. Parents and children; P310. Friendship; S110. Murders; V112.1. Spirit huts; V150+. Discovery of sacred flute; V331+. Sacred flute destroyed upon conversion to Christianity

A Brother Married an Old Women
(Wantok 815, February 15, 1990, page 16)

Long, long ago, there were two brothers who lived in a village. The big brother gave all of the hard work to his little brother. They did this often, but the little brother became tired of it.

One day, he took a canoe and paddled away towards the other side of an island. On this island, there lived an old woman who did not bathe, not even a little.

While the boy was paddling the canoe, a small bird flew towards him and told him, "Why are you going to this side of the island? It's a very bad place."

The little brother replied to the bird, "My big brother never treats me well. He usually leaves all of the house and garden work for me to do, so I became tired of it and I ran away here."

They finished speaking, then the bird left the boy and flew away. When the boy paddled close to the beach, he saw the old woman sitting there. He went ashore and asked the old woman, "Why are you sitting on the beach like that and why do you never bathe?"

However, the old woman did not reply, so the boy carried her down to the sea and bathed her well. Later, he carried her and brought her to the house. The old woman was elated.

The old woman cooked food and they ate. Afterwards, they went to sleep. In the very early morning, they woke up and the old woman told him to climb a coconut palm tree and to fetch some green coconuts.

She explained to him, "You must look at the coconuts very carefully and take two very nice ones. When you take the coconuts, bring them down to the ground." So, the boy took two nice, green coconuts and carefully brought them back down to the ground.

Later, the old woman told him to put the coconuts in the back of the canoe and paddle back to his village, "When you hear the coconuts making noises in the back, you can't turn and look."

The boy listened to everything that the old woman taught and he paddled back to the village with the coconuts. When he went to the very deep sea, he heard something making noises in the back of the canoe. However, he did not turn to look back.

He kept paddling, then he heard the voices of two women speaking and laughing in the back of the canoe. The little brother listened and his heart went out. Quickly, he turned and saw two very beautiful women sitting in back of the canoe.

He asked them, "How did you get here?"

They replied, "It was just you who called out to us, then we came."

The boy listened and did not say anything. He was elated. A little later, they paddled and arrived at the village. When they arrived, the big brother saw the women and he asked his little brother, "Exactly where did you get these two women? Can you give me one?"

However, the little brother replied, "I'm very sorry. I can't give you one. These are my wives."

Then he told the story to his big brother of what he had done to obtain the young women. The big brother pushed the canoe down to the sea and paddled away. Midway, he met the bird. However when the bird wanted to come sit on the canoe and talk with him, the big brother got up and killed the bird. Afterwards, he paddled and paddled, then he arrived at the old woman's home.

He arrived at the beach and saw the old woman sitting there. The big brother got up and asked her, "Why do you never bathe? Oh my, your body smells horrible."

The old woman replied to the youth, "Can you carry me down to the sea and wash me?"

He replied, "I didn't come to wash you. I came for you to give me two women."

They went to the house, cooked food and went to sleep. In the very early morning, they awoke and the old woman told him, "Climb the coconut palm and look for two coconuts that are not yet hardened, then fetch them. When you pick them, don't throw them down. You must carry them down carefully."

However, the man leapt up the tree and tossed down to the ground two coconuts that were already hard. Then he leapt back down, took them and put them in the back of the canoe. The old woman explained to him again that he could not turn and look when there was a noise in the back of the canoe.

The man jumped into his canoe and paddled back towards the village. When he went to the deep sea, he heard a noise in the back of the canoe. Oh my, he immediately turned and looked behind.

The man's stomach was uneasy when he saw two nasty old women in the back of the canoe who were talking and laughing. He was furious and scolded them, "Who told you to come here?"

They replied, "You yourself went and brought us here with you."

He listened and became irate. He got up and beat the women. They fought and fought, then their canoe capsized in the middle of the sea. They tried to swim away, but the sea conquered them and they all drowned. They died and became big stones in the sea.

Nelson Batanii

Kieta

North Solomons Province

A974. Rocks from transformation of people to stone; B143.1. Bird gives warning; B211.3. Speaking bird; E642. Reincarnation as stone; D431.11+W. Transformation: coconut to woman; J652. Inattention to warnings; J1050. Attention to warnings; P210. Husband and wife; P251.4+. One brother acts wisely, another acts unwisely; P251.5. Two brothers; P251.5.3. Hostile brothers; P263. Brother-in-law; P264. Sister-in-law; Q40. Kindness rewarded; Q280. Unkindness punished; Q325. Disobedience punished; Q428. Punishment: drowning; R213. Escape from home; T145.0.1. Polygyny; W31. Obedience; W126. Disobedience

Kozaga Boys Won over Magamito Women

(Wantok 816, February 22, 1990, page 20)

Long, long ago, there were two brothers who lived in a small village called **Kozaga**. This village was in the Henganofi area of **Eastern Highlands** Province [**Kamano** People]. Near Kozaga, there was a big village called Magamito [**Nakamito**]. This village had very many people.

One time, the brothers heard that the people of this village would be holding a huge festival. So, they prepared their feather headdresses, various bundles, and decorations.

On the night of the festival, they went towards Magamito. They arrived in Magamito Village and saw that the festival had begun. They put on their adornments and went inside to join the other people at the festival. Their two voices were excellent and everyone cast their eyes upon them.

Magamito had two young and gorgeous women. All of the young men of this village lusted to marry them, but the women did not have any desire for them.

The two brothers were also very [handsome]. The two women loved the brothers' voices and they began to lust for them. The women's hearts stopped and they stopped thinking. They just thought about the two brothers that [their godfather?] pointed towards.

The brothers sang and danced until dawn. After the festival, the brothers walked back towards their village a little. The brothers approached the village and saw the two gorgeous women following them. They did not speak. Quietly, they held the women's hands and went to the village. Later, the women married the brothers and they lived together.

The young men of Magamito were not in agreement with the two brothers. Their bellies were on fire and they just wanted to kill the brothers. However, they held off and decided to perform sorcery upon the big brother.

They ensorcelled the big brother so that he would go to the place where his wife lived. He would take her to the forest and he would die.

When it was nearly dawn, the big brother went to the place where his wife was living. He told her, "Come and we'll go into the forest to hunt for some wild game. Then you'll bring it to the house."

However, the woman was ashamed and said, "Never mind that, I'm ashamed of this behavior that you've never done it before. It's daylight. We'll go back to your house."

The sorcery made the big brother insistent, so she followed his desires. They went into the forest and the big brother hunted for game. The sun went down and it was nearly dark. However, the big brother was not worried about the darkness. He kept hunting for game.

The woman was completely furious and she told her husband, "Hey! It's dark. Let's return home now."

He replied, "Let's go a little longer."

The sun set completely and it was dark. The big brother went and stood at the base of a big tree. He looked up and saw a huge marsupial (*kapul*). The marsupial was hanging and about to jump to another tree branch.

Immediately, the big brother spoke quietly to his wife, "Don't look around the forest. You must only cast your eyes upon me. I'm going to take out the last marsupial. We'll sleep at the base of this tree until dawn, then we'll return to the village."

The big brother said that he would climb the tree, to the very top. The woman would keep watching him. The big brother climbed up the tree very high, then he put his back to a tree branch. Insects had gone inside this branch, so it was not strong, but the big brother did not notice this.

He lay well upon the branch and called down to his wife, "This is our last marsupial. Put the net bag down on the ground and find a stick. Get ready to kill it when I shoot it down."

He drew back the bow and shot the marsupial. At the same time, the tree branch broke. He fell down and broke his back on a stone and died.

His wife was shocked and ran to hold his body. She cried terribly until dawn. In the morning, she cried and went down to Kazaga [Kozaga] Village. She told the people that her husband had died and was in the forest. Everyone in the village, including the little brother and his wife, gathered and went to the place where the big brother's body was located.

They carried the body back to the village. That night, they cried over the body until dawn when they buried it. The big brother's wife lived with the little brother and his wife.

Itoto Jumao

Kieta

North Solomons Province

B871.2+. Giant marsupial; D2061. Magic murder; P210. Husband and wife; P251.5. Two brothers; P263. Brother-in-law; P264. Sister-in-law; R260. Pursuits; S110. Murders; T10. Falling in love; T92.10. Rival in love killed; T100. Marriage; T145.0.1. Polygyny; V61.3+. Dead buried; W181. Jealousy

How Did the *Yamu* Bird Arise

(Wantok 817, March 1, 1990, page 16)

Long, long ago, there were two brothers who lived in a village. The brothers husbanded two large pigs in the village. They took such good care of the pigs that it was as if they were human and the pigs lived with them.

The pigs spoke like men, so they lived very well. When the brothers went to the forest or to another place, they would tell the pigs to cut firewood and prepare things. When the brothers returned, they would just cook and eat.

One day, the pigs told the brothers, "You must mark us so that we won't just die."

The brothers listened and did as their pigs said. Before long, the pigs fell to the ground and passed out.

Clouds Thundered

The brothers finished off the pigs with spears, then they began to butcher them. They cut the pigs into halves and entirely filled four large net bags.

Before long, the clouds thundered and a tremendous rain fell. Inside the clouds, there was a ghost woman. Oh my, her teeth were very long, exactly like those of a cow.

The brothers saw the ghost woman and were terrified. They fled into the house and shut the door. They stayed inside until the rain finished.

The big brother opened the door to check and he saw the ghost woman standing outside. The brothers cried and urinated just like babies. Immediately, the ghost woman went into the house and grabbed the big brother. She killed the big brother and began to eat him.

The little brother saw this and carried the four bags containing the two pigs. He took some arrows and a bow, then he jumped out of the house, fleeing into the forest.

However, the ghost woman had great powers of smell. She finished eating the big brother, then she smelled the little brother and went into the forest.

The little brother ran and thought that he was very far from the ghost woman, but the she quickly approached and ran behind him.

The ghost woman wanted to grab the little brother, but he was removing pork from the bags and throwing it into her mouth. They did this for a while as they ran, then the ghost woman became completely out of breath.

The little brother took a stone axe and began to cut around the ghost woman's body. The ghost woman was pained, but her body did not expire. You know, ghosts have much strength.

The ghost woman grabbed the little brother and shouted, "If you cut my armpits, I shall die. If you don't, you'll go the same way as your big brother."

Forgot

They kept holding onto each other and fighting. The ghost woman forgot and raised her arm. Quickly, the little brother aimed his multi-pronged arrow at the ghost woman's armpit and shot her.

The ghost woman fell down, rolled on the ground, and died. The place where the ghost woman fell and rolled has become a lake now. The little brother turned into a bird. He flew up to a tree.

So today, when people sing and dance in the village, they adorn their bodies with the feathers of this bird. We call this bird *yamu*.

Gabita Lobe
Sogeri Red Shield Farm
Port Moresby
National Capital District

A920.1.0.1. Origin of particular lake; A1970. Creation of miscellaneous birds; B211.1.4. Speaking hog; D150M. Transformation: man to bird; D2143.1. Rain produced by magic; D2149.1. Thunderbolt magically produced; E261.4. Ghost pursues man; E425.1. Revenant as woman; E440+. Ghost laid by spear/arrow; E461. Fight of revenant with living person; E636+. Reincarnation as lake; F544.3.5. Remarkably long teeth; F652. Marvelous sense of smell; G11.10. Cannibalistic spirits; P251.5. Two brothers; R213. Escape from home; R260. Pursuits; S110. Murders; Z311.4. Man can be injured only in armpits

How Did Kuimbu Village Obtain Love Magic?

(Wantok 818, March 8, 1990, page 19)

Long, long ago, in the time of the ancestors, there were a man and his wife who lived in a place near the big village of **Kuimbu** in the Kokopo area of **East New Britain** Province [**Tolai** People].

The man's name was Sawigu and the woman's was Sagiltakua. They were married for a long time, but they did not yet have a child. This was because every night, Sagiltakua was afraid to sleep with Sawigu.

When they wanted to sleep, Sagiltakua would take a net bag and cover her genitals. This would make Sawigu terribly angry. One early morning, Sawigu told Sagiltakua that they would go to the garden to get some taros, bananas and sweet potatoes.

Making an Earth Oven

They arrived at the garden and gathered the foods, then they returned home. They left the food, then some days later the bananas were ripe. Sawigu told Sagiltakua that they would make an earth oven the next day and cook the foods.

In the very early morning, they woke up and gathered stones. Afterwards, they made a bonfire and began heating the stones. When the stones were terribly hot, Sawigu told Sagiltakua to remove them from the fire and put them aside. Sagiltakua listened and did as her husband had told her to do.

When Sagiltakua removed the stones from the fire, Sawigu took a forked stick and pushed Sagiltakua into the fire. The food was ready. Sawigu immediately took the food and cooked it in the earth oven with his wife's flesh. When the food was done, he tied it into bundles.

He prepared some bundles to carry to her kin in Kuimbu Village. He took the bundles and went to her kin. Sagiltakua's father and mother saw this and asked, "Hey son-in-law! It's very good that you've come. Where's your wife, Sagiltakua?" Sawigu lied that she was at the house.

He gave some bundles of food to Sagiltakua's brothers, sisters, and maternal kin. Then he spoke a little and quickly went back towards his home.

Some families were hungry and immediately ate their bundles of food. Sagiltakua's father and mother left their bundle for the morning.

In the very early morning, the father and mother awoke and opened their bundles to eat. Oh my, they were shocked to see human fingers inside with the bananas and taros.

They knew that Sawigu must have killed their daughter and cooked her with the other food. They asked the other families to check their bundles, but they had already eaten them.

Wild Taro

Sawigu, the scoundrel, had already returned to his little home and eaten his yams (*yam* and *mami*). Later, he took Sagiltakua's bones and sharpened them well, like bayonets.

Before long, the warriors of the big village arrived and surrounded his house. However, the rotten scoundrel knew that they would come and he had already gone crazy in the forest.

He just stayed in the forest and when it rained, he would cut wild taro leaves [for shelter]. He would go stand by people's houses in the big village.

When men heard a noise and went outside to check, he would kill them and flee. He did this all of the time and he killed very many people with his stone axe and his bayonets.

The men of the big village were inflamed to kill him, but they never found him. This was because he hid very carefully. One time, there was a huge festival in the village. All of the men, women and children held hands and sweated while they sang and danced.

Sawigu heard the sound of hand and signal drums, so he approached the village. He went on top of a tall coconut palm tree, then he began to throw coconuts down to the festival grounds.

Oh my, the people saw this and began to run around. Before long, some leaders gathered and sent a man to go up and kill him. The rotten scoundrel saw this and held a big coconut at the ready. The man approached, then he hit him with the coconut. The poor man lost his grip and fell down.

His kin on the ground saw this and thought that he had beaten down Sawigu. Oh my, they pulverized their own kinsman. Later, they turned the man's body over and saw that they had beaten one of their own. Sawigu went down quickly from the coconut palm and fled into the forest.

All of the men gathered and prepared their spears. They went into the forest, but they did not find Sawigu. Sawigu just lived in the forest for a while, then one time he returned to the village to meet his two maternal kin. He thought that they could not kill him.

However, they grabbed him and killed him. They put his body inside a big signal drum and burned it. Later, they took his bones and made paint for fighting and for love magic or black magic to attract women. This is how the villagers obtained the powers for fighting and for attracting women.

Martin Rogi

Box 150

Kokopo

East New Britain Province

D1007. Magic bone (human); D1355.3. Love charm; G61. Relative's flesh eaten unwittingly; G61.1+. Parent recognizes child's flesh when it is served to be eaten; K840. Deception into fatal substitution; K914. Murder from ambush; L116. Insane hero (heroine); P210. Husband and wife; P231. Mother and son; P232. Mother and daughter; P233. Father and son; P234. Father and daughter; P250. Brothers and sisters; P260. Relations by law; P261. Father-in-law; P262. Mother-in-law; P263. Brother-in-law; P264. Sister-in-law; P265. Son-in-law; P290+. Maternal kin; Q211. Murder punished; Q251+. Punishment for withholding sex from spouse; Q414. Punishment: burning alive; R210. Escapes; R213. Escape from home; R260. Pursuits; S63+. Husband kills wife; S112. Burning to death; X712.1H. Female genitals

Muyen Stole the Pig Liver

(Wantok 819, March 15, 1990, page 20)

Long, long ago, in the time of the ancestors, there were two brothers who lived in a village called **Nupkuluf Bau** in **West Sepik** Province.

The brothers' names were Numolou and Muyen. Muyen was the big brother. They lived by themselves because their father and mother had died long ago when they were children.

The big brother, Muyen, was the best man at hunting for wild game in the forest. So, he often went into the forest to hunt for game for themselves. Numolou would stay in the village and work at the garden because he was afraid of malevolent sorcery and of forest ghosts.

One time, the big brother, Muyen, told his little brother that they must go together and watch the base of a sago palm tree, "We'll go together to watch the base of a sago palm tree. The pigs often go there to eat. Yesterday, I saw pig tracks all over the sago. We'll go together and kill two or three. It'll be good."

The next day, near evening, they took their multi-pronged spears and walked into the forest. When it was nearly dark, they arrived at the base of the sago palm.

Muyen told Numolou to stand fairly far away under the base of a huge tree. Muyen backed up slowly and stood near the base of the sago palm.

Numolou, you know, was afraid to travel the forest. He went and stood by the big, dry tree, and a branch fell down. Numolou thought that a ghost was coming at him or that there was malevolent sorcery in the forest. Quietly, he left his big brother and sped off to the village and waited. Muyen did not know that his little brother had returned to the village.

Muyen watched and saw a gigantic pig sniffing the sago and walking closer. He was completely ready and watching. The pig came closer, then he took the bamboo multi-pronged spear and buried it directly into the pig's side. You know, it was a big pig, it turned, then went and pulled one of Muyen's legs.

Muyen shouted for Numolou to come help him, but he did not hear anything because his little brother had not explained that he had gone back to the village.

The poor brother fought hard with the pig for a while, then the pig ran away. Oh my, he was burning up at his little brother. It was nearly midnight when he walked slowly back to the village.

He arrived in the village and did not scold Numolou. He just kept his pain to himself. Numolou knew that his big brother was angry with him, so he pretended that he was sorry, "I watched for a long time and thought that you had returned, so I returned. I came here shortly before you did. So, did you kill some pigs or not?"

Muyen was completely furious and did not reply. Quietly, he went to his bed by the fire and slept. They lived for a long time, then Muyen went back alone into the forest. This time, he killed a gigantic pig. He butchered it when he was still in the forest and carried the meat back to the village.

They ate all of the meat, then there were just the pig guts which Muyen then put in the fire. Muyen went back to the forest, and Numolou went to work in the garden. Before long, Numolou returned to the house and saw the pig guts, which he looked at longingly to eat.

He quickly ate the pig guts. Afterwards, he took the rubbish from the fire and he put it on top of the platform on which the pork lay.

Numolou did this so that Muyen would see it and think that the dog had eaten it, and so that he would not lay the guilt upon him. After he did this, Numolou just stayed there quietly.

It was nearly dark when Muyen arrived at the house. Muyen knew that it was just Numolou who had eaten the pig guts and then had played a trick.

Oh my, he was completely furious. They argued and argued, then he took a small stone knife and buried it directly into Numolou's belly.

You know the customs of yore, they never worried too much about kin. Muyen eviscerated Numolou, and his feces shot out. Then Numolou was dead.

Felix Eddy

Vanimo

West Sepik Province

B871.1.2. Giant boar; K2211.0.2. Treacherous younger brother(s); P251.5. Two brothers; P251.5.3. Hostile brothers; Q261. Treachery punished; Q263. Lying (perjury) punished; Q272. Avarice punished; Q469.7. Punishment: twisting entrails from body; R220. Flights; S73.1. Fratricide; S139.1. Murder by twisting out intestines; S143. Abandonment in forest; W151. Greed; W157. Dishonesty

A *Masalai* Attracted a Real Woman

(Wantok 820, March 22, 1990, page 13)

Long, long ago, in the big village of Supa, there were very many people. So the people broke into two halves, and formed three small villages, together called **Iwam** [**Iwam** People, **East Sepik** Province].

In Iwam Number Three, there was a gorgeous young woman. Her name was Oilmill. Many young men would ask Oilmill if she wanted to marry, but Oilmill did not like them.

Oilmil [Oilmill] liked a young man inside the village, but she did not reveal her thoughts. Many months passed, and the man grew up. Oilmill asked the man what his desires were. Oh my, the man's heart leapt out.

The man did not wait, he immediately told his family and they prepared a huge feast. They took it to Oilmill's kin. That night, he married Oilmill and they had a huge party until dawn.

Before, in the time of the ancestors, the *masalai*s of the forest would walk in the clearings. The people of the village would see them. The *masalai*s had various powers.

Near the village, there was a *masalai* man who lived by Bakraleh Pond. The *masalai* was named after this pond. This *masalai* man also had kept eye on Oilmill, and he very much wanted to marry her.

He did not care that Oilmill had married another man. You know the customs of the *masalai*s, they had terrible powers to attract women.

One day, everyone in the village gathered and wanted to make a big party. Before, in the time of the ancestors, the parties would come close in close succession.

Oilmill was menstruating (or had women's sickness) at this time. She went alone into the forest to search for wild banana leaves. Afterwards, she would go back to the house.

The bad *masalai* man saw her and followed her. He followed her to the village, then changed his appearance to that of the woman's husband. At this time it was dark.

Quietly, he went inside the house and slept with Oilmill. Oilmill thought that it was her husband. After this, the *masalai* man would come to Oilmill every night because Oilmill's husband usually slept in the spirit house with the other men.

After a while, Oilmill became pregnant. Every night, when Oilmill's husband wanted to sleep with her, she would scold him, "Man, aren't you tired of this too? Every night you slept with me, and I'm tired of it. After all that, I've become pregnant."

Oilmill's husband listened and was shocked. He scolded Oilmill and beat her terribly. Afterwards, he left the house and went to sleep in the spirit house.

The next day, he carefully prepared his traditional bow and arrows, and his stone axe. When he finished, he waited for darkness. When it was dark, he quietly went and kept watch at the house where his wife lived alone. He pricked up his ears and heard Oilmill with a man.

He stood at the door and opened it. Oh my, he was shocked to see the head of a big snake watching. The tail of the snake was having sex with her.

He trembled and left his bow, arrows, and axe. He sped away to the spirit house and woke up all of the men. They came back, but the *masalai* man who had turned into a snake had gone.

Quietly, they went back to sleep. In the morning, Oilmill woke up and felt terribly ashamed. She knew that a *masalai* man had come to sleep with her, and that he was not really her husband.

All of the leaders of the village made a decision and gathered food. Afterwards, they took Oilmill and the food to the pond where the *masalai* dwelled.

They put all of the food there, then they gave a red ball from a wild tree. In our language, we call this tree, *pandi*.

Everyone went back to the village. Just one man stayed back. This man went up a tree and watched. Oilmill held the red wild ball, and stood by the pond.

She stood for a while, then before long a flood came and took her. The wild ball drifted on top of the pond. The man on top of the tree saw this and knew that the *masalai* man had taken Oilmill.

He came down slowly, walked back to the village and told the people what had happened.

Thomas Kere
Box 21
Kimbe
West New Britain Province

B613.1. Snake paramour; D191M. Transformation: man to serpent (snake); D391M. Transformation: serpent (snake) to man; D1355.3. Love charm; F420.1.3.9. Water-spirit as snake; F420.5.3+. Water spirit takes woman away; F421. Lake-spirit; F441. Wood-spirit; F490+. Masalai; K1910. Marital impostors; P210. Husband and wife; Q458. Flogging as punishment; R260. Pursuits; S62. Cruel husband; S185. Cruelty to pregnant woman; T10. Falling in love; T91.3. Love of mortal and supernatural person; T100. Marriage; T570. Pregnancy; V112.1. Spirit huts

Ramingihan's Troubles
Killed the People of Wosera
(Wantok 821, March 29, 1990, page 16)

Long, long ago, in the time of the ancestors, many people lived in a village in the **Wosera** area of **East Sepik** Province [**Abelam** People]. In this village, there was a *ma-*

salai woman named Ramingihan. This *masalai* dwelled with her child.

One day, the men of the village wanted to have a festival, so they went hunting for lizards in the forest. They killed the lizards and use their skins for the hand drums that they would beat during the festival.

They adorned themselves with ashes from the fire until they were completely black. Afterwards, they took their bows and arrows then went into the forest. Oh my, they killed very many lizards.

The *masalai* woman's child was a lizard. The men killed this lizard too, and they carried it back to the village. Ramingihan, the *masalai* woman, had gone to another place in the forest at this time, so the men had not killed her.

Poor Ramingihan arrived at the house and saw that her child was not there. She searched and searched, then she knew that the men of the village must have killed her child. Oh my, she was both troubled and furious.

Quietly, she performed a small song and dance, then she turned herself into a dog. She walked and walked towards the village, then she saw them preparing the hand drums. She took a hand drum and saw that it was her child's skin.

She cried and walked back to her house inside the forest. Along the trail, she met two brothers who were breaking apart sago and taking the sago beetle grubs [for food].

The parents of the brothers had died, so they just lived by themselves. They hunted for their own food with their own strength.

The ghost woman was still a dog. She went up to the brothers and they gave her some grubs. She ate some, then she waited for them.

The brothers thought that it was a dog from the village. They did not know that the dog was a ghost woman. It was nearly afternoon and the dog followed them to the village.

They cooked the grubs, then when they were about to eat, the brothers were surprised to see the same dog sleeping by the house. They called out and the dog came up to them. They gave the dog some grubs, and they ate together.

They ate, then the dog turned back into the ghost woman with long fingers and hair. Oh my, the two brothers were terrified and tried to find a way to escape.

However, the ghost woman told them, "Don't be afraid of me. You gave me food and took care of me, so I can't ruin you. The people of this village killed my child, so I want to kill them. You must prepare something for yourselves. Then make a house on a tall coconut palm tree inside the village. Take all of the things you want, then climb tomorrow night when they are about to sing and dance."

After the *masalai* woman said this, she disappeared. In the very early morning, they awoke and did as the ghost woman had told them to do.

The villagers worked at cooking and gathering food. It was completely dark. They began beating the new hand drums, singing, and dancing.

The brothers wanted to talk, but they shut their mouths because the villagers had never treated them well. The *masalai* woman heard the sound of the hand drums and the singing, then she arrived in the village. She turned into a dog, then she lay at the base of the coconut palm on top of which the two brothers were sitting.

She lay there for a while, then she began to sing and dance to raise a flood. Before long, a woman went to the base of the coconut palm to throw away some garbage. The woman's leg missed and hit a big coconut leaf. Then the water shot up and began covering everyone.

The people left the festival and the food, then they ran about. That night, the flood rose and killed everyone in the village. The *masalai* woman stood at the base of the coconut palm, jumping back and forth. She removed the water that would have swallowed the coconut palm. When it was nearly dawn, the two brothers descended.

Oh my, the brothers were surprised to see that everyone in the village was gone. Only they were left, so they built a new village.

Mathew Bawi

Wosera

East Sepik Province

A1011. Local deluges; A1015.2. Spirit causes deluge; A1018. Flood as punishment; D141W. Transformation: woman to dog; D341W. Transformation: dog to woman; D1781. Magic results from singing; D1781+. Magic results from dancing; E425.1. Revenant as woman; E541. Revenants eat; F401.3.13K2. Spirit in form of lizard; F401.6. Spirit in human form; F441. Wood-spirit; F490+. Masalai; F515.1+. Remarkably long fingers; F555.3. Very long hair; L111.4. Orphan hero; P230. Parents and children; P251.5. Two brothers; Q40. Kindness rewarded; Q151. Life spared as reward; Q211.6. Killing an animal revenged; Q428. Punishment: drowning; S110. Murders

A Cassowary Helped a Child
(Wantok 822, April 5, 1990, page 16)

Long, long ago, in the time of the ancestors, a man and his wife lived in **Sangriman** Village [**Bisis** People, **East Sepik** Province]. The man's name was Loloh, and the woman's was Bunta. They were married for a long time, and they had a daughter. This daughter had grown to be a woman. In this village, they would make a party for a woman when she had her menarche. All of the women of the village would sing and dance for many days.

Loloh and his family had no more food, so one night Loloho [Loloh] told his wife and daughter, "Tomorrow, in the very early morning, I'll go to the river and cut sago for us. When you awake, follow me. I'll put marks on the trail that I take so that you can find me cutting sago. Look carefully at the marks at the two trailheads." The mother and daughter agreed with what the father said.

Loloh awoke in the very early morning. The women of the village were still singing and dancing. He took an axe, a knife, an iron blade for scraping sago, and his basket, then he left the house. At the trailhead, Lolohoi [Loloh] took [the trail] with the large fig tree. A ghost woman was hiding there. She often chased people who went on this trail or she would trick them.

When the sun rose, Bunta and her daughter took their things and went to follow her husband. They saw the marks that Loloh had made when he went in the very early morning. They went and went, then they arrived at a house in the deep forest. They approached and saw that no one was there.

Unfortunately for them, they did not see Loloh. What had happened to him? They were terrified and went down the side of the mountain a little, then they hid under the ginger (*gorgor*). They thought hard. What had happened to the father? Who had tricked the two of them?

Loloho had not tricked them. It was the ghost woman who was hiding in the fig tree. She had seen Loloh put the marks at the trailhead in the early morning for his wife and daughter to follow him. The ghost woman followed and changed all of the marks, then she put them on another trail. This trail went to the house inside the deep forest.

Poor Loloh cut a sago palm down, then he cut and scraped the tree too. He thought that his wife, Bunta, and his daughter would come and rinse the sago. He waited, but they did not come, so he went back to look for them on the trail. He did not find on them on the trail, not at all. He arrived at the village. The women were sleeping because they had sung and danced until dawn. The men had gone into the forest to look for pigs or wild game in the forest to make a party. He went to the house and saw that his wife and daughter were not there. They had taken all of their things for processing sago and had left the house. Oh my, Loloh was terribly worried. He returned to the forest to the place where he had cut the sago palm. He did not see them, so he went back to the village again.

The mother and daughter were hiding. They heard some noises approaching the house. They watched and they saw a big cassowary carrying a basket with a bundle of sago hanging from its mouth. The cassowary arrived and went into the house. The cassowary put its things down, then collapsed and slept. The mother and daughter were terrified that the cassowary would kick them with its legs, so they stayed very quietly and did not make a sound.

The sun was setting at about four o'clock. The cassowary felt hungry and awoke. The cassowary tied up sago and fish into a leaf bundle, then cooked the food. The cassowary went down the side of the mountain to fetch some ginger at the place where the two women where hiding. The cassowary raised a ginger leaf, then saw them trembling and in shock. They screamed terribly.

Afterwards, the cassowary took them up to its house. The cassowary asked them which village they were from and about their family. They gave the name of their village and their clan. The cassowary heard this and was very happy because it was also from this clan: the three of them were from the same family. The cassowary cooked the sago and fish, then gave it to them to eat. The cassowary told them that they could live there. The mother and daughter forgot completely about returning to their village.

In the village, Loloh waited and waited for many days and weeks. He thought that they had died, so he wanted to forget them.

The cassowary treated the two of them very well, like its own family. One day, the cassowary told Bunta, "Go into the forest and scrape sago for us. I'll take care of your little girl at the house."

The woman listened, and in the very early morning she awoke and went into the forest. The cassowary and its grandchild were there. The cassowary tricked the girl and she slept. The cassowary took betel nuts, betel peppers, and lime (calcium oxide). The cassowary chewed the betel mixture and filled fifty plates with spittle. The cassowary spilled the betel spittle upon the girl's skin. Oh my, the girl grew very quickly, and her skin became beautiful.

When her mother was about to return from the forest, the cassowary told the young woman to hide in the corner, "When your mama comes to the house and asks for you, I'll make a sign. Then throw these two ginger stalks at her and come out of there."

When Bunta came into the house carrying two [bundles of] sago, the young woman watched her grandmother [the cassowary] and did as she was told.

The mother was surprised to see this new, young woman. She was elated. She held the young woman and her grandmother jumped about. However, the cassowary did not speak much.

The three of them stayed there for a while, then one day they heard singing from the women's village. The cassowary told them, "Come, we'll go see the festival in your village." They arrived there and went inside a house. Before long, the cassowary took a stick for the signal drum and began singing with them. When the cassowary finished, it was time for Bunta. She beat the signal drum and sang her husband Loloh's song. Bunta did not know whether he was there or not. She finished, then it was time for the young woman. Everyone stared at her. They asked, "Who's that? Whose child is it?" She finished, then they returned home. In the morning, the clan asked the women, "Who was it that had sung with them?" The women replied that they did not know.

The next night, the three of them returned to sing again. When they sang, the men of the village surrounded them and held them.

Paul Lee Tommy

East Sepik Province

B211.3.17K. Speaking cassowary; B469+. Helpful cassowary; D931.1.4. Magic lime; D985.5. Magic betel-nut; D985.5+. Magic betel-pepper; D1001. Magic spittle; D1860. Magic beautification; D1890. Magic aging; E276. Ghosts haunt tree; E425.1. Revenant as woman; P210. Husband and wife; P232. Mother and daughter; P234. Father and daughter; P292. Grandmother; P600+. Customs associated with menarche

How Did Wobima Village Originate?

(Wantok 823, April 12, 1990, page 20)

Long, long ago in the Warawaka [**Marawaka**] area in **Eastern Highlands** Province, there lived a man [**Baruya People**]. His name was Wobima. Wobima had a dog that lived with him. He took very care of his dog well, and they were very good friends when they went into the forest.

One day, he took the dog and they went into the deep forest to hunt for marsupials (*kapul*). They walked and walked. When it was close to noon, they arrived in the deep forest.

Wobima left his things and made a forest hut. When he finished, he put the food and other things inside. Afterwards, he took his bow and arrows then called to the dog. They went into the forest and began hunting marsupials. This was not their day, so they did not even see a small marsupial.

Wobima was furious. He called the dog and they walked back to the forest hut. They arrived at the place where Wobima had put logs for killing marsupials [as a trap]. Quietly, he walked there and saw that the logs had killed a marsupial. Oh my, he was elated.

However, this was a *masalai* marsupial, so its neck had a red rope (or artery or vine) around it. Wobima was ravenous to eat the flesh of this animal, so he did not worry or think about this.

He carried the marsupial to the trail and he took some wild leafy greens from the forest. When it was nearly afternoon, he arrived at the forest hut. He rested a little, then he began removing the fur and butchering the marsupial.

After he removed the marsupial guts, he got up and went out to fetch some leaves. Quickly, his dog went inside and took the marsupial, then threw it out.

The dog smelled that this was not a real marsupial, and it did this so that its master would get this idea into his head and understand.

However, Wobima did not understand the meaning of what the dog had done. He was completely furious. He took a small stick and gave it good to the dog.

The poor dog fled, then returned to lie and watch by the side of the fire. Wobima continued to prepare the marsupial. Quietly, the dog went behind, pulled the marsupial, carried it out and threw it away.

Wobima took a gigantic stick and gave it right to the dog's behind. The poor dog howled and ran out again. Before long, the dog returned to see its master taking the marsupial back into the hut and cooking it on the fire. The dog just lay and watched by the side of the fire.

Wobima cooked the marsupial well with the leafy greens from the forest, then he ate. After he ate, his belly was bloated. Before long, it was dark.

He made a bonfire and slept by it. That night, the other *masalai* marsupials smelled the two of them and approached the hut. They jumped about on the tree branches, then they came and shouted together, "That's the man who killed our baby. The baby is inside his belly. We'll go kill him."

Then all of the *masalai* marsupials shouted and began surrounding the hut. The marsupial that Wobima had eaten heard the other marsupials and cried from within his belly.

Wobima noticed this and was terrified. He was a big man, but he defecated and urinated because he knew that his time was up. Wobima's dog was sleeping and he did not hear a thing. Later, he was surprised when the leader of the *masalai* marsupials began to remove the leaves of the forest hut.

The leader of the marsupials was as big as a gigantic pig. The dog awoke and barked, then ran out of the hut.

The dog opened its mouth and sunk its teeth right into the leader of the *masalai* marsupials.

The *masalai* marsupial jumped down and ran to the river. However, the dog kept following and biting the marsupial's tail. They fought and fought, then the dog killed the leader of the *masalai* marsupials.

After the dog killed the marsupial, it ran back to the hut. The dog checked on its master and Wobima felt terribly sorry. Wobima cried terribly.

That night, they slept together by the fire until dawn. In the morning, they tied up the *masalai* marsupial and carried it back to the village. When he arrived at the village, he blew the flute.

Everyone came and gathered, then he told them the story. Later, they butchered the *masalai* marsupial and divided it among all of the clan houses.

That night, they made a huge party and celebrated Wobima's dog. This village is now called **Wobima**, after this man's name.

Lukas Upawaka

Goroka

Eastern Highlands Province

A1617. Origin of place-name; B211.2.12K+. Speaking marsupial; B241.2+. King of marsupials; B340+. Helpful dog beaten; B421. Helpful dog; B871.2+. Giant marsupial; E32. Resuscitated eaten animal; E168. Cooked animal comes to life; F401.3+. Spirit in marsupial form; F490+. Masalai; J652. Inattention to warnings; P230. Parents and children; R260. Pursuits; S110. Murders

A Real Man Married a *Masalai* Woman
(Wantok 824, April 19, 1990, page 16)

Long, long ago, there were seven brothers who lived in the **Maibana** Village area, by Bundi, in **Madang** Province [**Gende** People]. These brothers were good farmers.

One day, the brothers worked in the garden until the sun set completely. They took their things, then walked back home. The six younger brothers went first, and the eldest followed behind.

The eldest brother walked and saw a very beautiful woman sitting on top of a fuzzy tree. This woman was cutting fruits of the fuzzy tree with a bamboo [knife], then eating them. When the big brother saw this, he did not speak or make a sound. Quietly, he jumped up the tree and tried to hold her.

However, the woman had already gotten wind of him and jumped down to a pond. The leader [brother] jumped down and tried to find her, but he was unsuccessful. The woman had disappeared. The boy [brother] was terribly worried, then he went to the house.

When his little brothers wanted to give him food, he went directly to his bed by the fire and lay there. Then his six little brothers asked, "Why don't you want to eat?" He replied that he was sick.

The big brother acted like this for a whole week. There was not the slightest food in his stomach. After one week, he told his brothers what had happened to him, so all of the brothers held a meeting and decided what to do.

After one day, they told their youngest brother, "Cook some food, then stay and wait for us in the house. We're going to bring mother here."

The little brother listened and prepared all of the food, then he sped after his big brothers. The big brothers surrounded the whole pond and watched for the woman. The last brother arrived at the pond, but the others did not see him.

He went down and followed the pond up to its source. He arrived at a corner and saw a big leaf lying on top of the side of the stream. He lifted the leaf and saw a bed. Then the boy just had the idea that the bed belonged to the woman, so he sat and waited.

When his big brothers chased the woman, she wanted to come inside and hide, but she became caught up on the little brother's arm. The bad boy took her and they went to the village. The two of them arrived at the house, then the little brother put her on top of his big brother's bed. He cooked food and waited.

The sun set completely, and the big brothers arrived. The boy asked them, "Hey... you're here, where's Mama?" They replied that the mother had fled.

The big brother gave up completely and wanted to go to sleep. When he cast his eyes up to the bed, he was shocked to see the woman sitting and laughing, "Aiyo... little brother found mama." All of the brothers heard this, gathered and feted their little brother.

The big brother and the woman married, then the woman gave birth to a son. When the baby was three years old, his father made a small bow and some arrows for the little boy to shoot lizards by the house.

One day, a big boil grew under the father's armpit (or groin). So, he slept during the day, and his wife went to the garden. The little boy took his bow and hunted lizards by the house. He chased one and it went directly to the place where his father was sleeping. He looked and saw that an insect was lying directly on top of his father's boil.

The boy just drew back the bow and let go. Oh my, the arrow went deep inside the father's boil, causing excruciating pain. The father awoke. His eyes were red and he gave it good to the boy. He beat him and told the boy, "You're the son of a *masalai* woman. Your mother traveled to the stream and she ate fuzzy tree fruits. Leave with her now."

The boy was still crying when his mother arrived at the house. She saw the little boy and asked him what had happened. The little boy told everything that his father had done. Then the mother told him, "Don't worry. You and I shall leave."

Late that night, the mother awoke, cooked some taros, and then filled her net bag. She took some [taros] that were still new and filled a [bag] with these. Afterwards, she took her son and put him on top of her shoulders. She jumped down from the house and followed the Imbrum River.

The boy held an axe in his left hand, and a bow and arrow in his right hand. They wanted to go to Mount Kungo. This was in the Mount Wilhem [Wilhelm] area. While they walked along the trail, the side on which the boy held his bow became flat ground, and the boy's left side became mountainous. This was the side on which he held the axe.

Also at this time, the father was searching for them, and following their footsteps. The mother and son arrived at a good place, then they sat to rest. They ate and the boy defecated in that area. They stayed there for a while, then a rattan vine fell down. On top of this vine were some ripe bananas. The boy saw this and began eating the ripe bananas.

After just a short while, another rattan fell down. When the boy was about to take the bananas, the rattan quickly pulled him up. The mother was surprised and shouted for her son, but no, the boy was completely hidden. When the mother tried to call for her son, a bird replied, singing, "*Ki-kolg-kolg*-mama-*o*, *ki-kolg-kolg*-mama-*o*." The mother screamed and cried, but no, she too disappeared.

When the father arrived at this place, he just saw the taro peels and the boy's feces. He tried shouting, but they did not reply. He cried terribly and rubbed the boy's feces on his face. When he did this, he heard a bird singing on top of a tree, "*Ki-kolg-kolg*-papa-*o*, *ki-kolg-kolg*-papa-*o*."

The father heard this and he was completely destroyed inside. He kept shouting, then he became a boulder. At this place, the taros that the mother and son had left propagated and are still growing there. The boulder is also still at this place and the bird usually sings, making this song fill the area. We of Bundi usually call this bird *mori*.

Freddy Angia
Pacific Security Monitoring
Arawa
North Solomons Province

A965. Origin of mountain chain; A974. Rocks from transformation of people to stone; A977. Origin of particular stones or groups of stones; B211.3. Speaking bird; D231M. Transformation: man to stone; D2095. Magic disappearance; F401.6. Spirit in human form; F421.1. Lady of the Lake; F424. River-spirit; F490+. Masalai; P210. Husband and wife; P231. Mother and son; P233. Father and son; P251.6.3+. Seven brothers; P263. Brother-in-law; P264. Sister-in-law; Q458. Flogging as punishment; R10. Abduction; R213. Escape from home; R260. Pursuits; T111. Marriage of mortal and supernatural being; T580. Childbirth

A Pauper Founded the Peri-Kali [Hagen-Wiru] Tribes

(Wantok 825, April 26, 1990, page 20)

Long, long ago in **Tungili** Village in **Southern Highlands** Province, there was a big clan house. Their houses were in a very long line [thus forming a single house]. These people lived very well.

Among these people, there lived a very poor man. No one was satisfied with him. None of the women wanted to marry him either. However, the pauper excelled at playing sad flute music during times of mourning. The style of flute music that he played cut directly to people's hearts during times of death.

One afternoon, this pauper walked up to Mount Tali, then he blew the flute. A woman heard the sound of the flute going forth and she was very troubled. This was because her husband had died, so she was crying and thinking hard.

The woman was greatly troubled, so she left the garden and followed the trail back to the village. However, when the flute music came to her, she changed her mind and wanted to see the face of the man who was playing this nice, mournful music.

The woman approached and the flute music became louder, then the music cut directly to her heart. Her heart stopped and she felt short of breath. She walked up a little further, then she saw the pauper sitting on top of a stone and blowing the flute. The woman cried and told the pauper, "Please, I love you, so let's go to your house."

However, the pauper replied, "I'm very sorry. That's nice of you to ask, but I'm afraid of your husband's clan, so I can't take you to my house."

The woman persisted, ignoring whatever he said. She overcame his fears and the flute-blowing pauper took her to his house. When they arrived in the village, the men saw them and were furious. They beat him terribly and told him, "Where's the good man who brought this woman to his house? Such a man cannot marry her. You can no longer stay with us in this village. You must leave now."

The poor pauper got up, took his things, and went into the deep forest where no one went. He made a hut and stayed there. At this place, he made a big garden and planted various foods. However, he was a man who liked marsupials (*kapul*), so much of the food just rotted in the garden. When he wanted to walk, he would just trample marsupial fur [i.e., he was very successful at hunting].

One day, when the sun was bright, two women from the village went fishing and followed a stream branch up a mountain. They followed this branch, then they arrived at another branch. One woman followed this branch, and her friend followed the other branch as they continued to fish.

The first woman followed the stream into the forest. When she wanted to return to the main stream, she became confused and went aimlessly in the deep forest. The other woman followed the stream and went directly to the pauper's garden. The man was working at tying sugarcanes to sticks. When he saw this woman, his heart stopped and he thought hard, "Is this a real woman or a ghost woman?" This was because no man or woman ever came to this part of the forest.

He was terrified and he walked quietly towards the woman. She saw him coming and she was also afraid, so she sat on the ground. He asked her, "Are you a ghost or a real woman?" She replied that she was a woman from the village. Then she told the story of what had happened to her friend and herself.

He took her to his house and told her to wait. He went to find some food in the garden. He returned from the garden and they ate. After they ate, he and told her, "Now let's sleep. Tomorrow, I'll bring you to the village." However, she replied, "Sorry, I don't want to return to the village because you saved my life. If you weren't here, I'd probably be dead. Let's marry and live here."

They married and she gave birth to two sons. The names of these children were Peri and Kali. They also married, and they raised large families. Peri's tribe lived in Kokola [**Kogoga**] Village, by Ialibu [**Hagen** People]. Kali's tribe went to live in Yaro [**Iaro**] Village in the Pangia area [**Wiru** People].

I, myself, came from the blood of Kali and we have a very large tribe now.

Sweeney Unda
Walala Trading
P. O. Box 237
Kimbe
West New Britain Province

A527.4. Culture hero as poet (musician); A1611+. Origin of Hagen People; A1611+. Origin of Wiru People; D1355.1. Love-producing music; L123. Pauper hero; P210. Husband and wife; P231. Mother and son; P233. Father and son; P251.5. Two brothers; P310. Friendship; P428. Musician; Q431. Punishment: banishment (exile); R130. Rescue of abandoned or lost persons; T10. Falling in love; T100. Marriage; T580. Childbirth

A Lazy Man Married a Leader's Daughter
(Wantok 826, May 3, 1990, page 20)

Long, long ago, a man lived in a village called **Guala** in **Southern Highlands** Province [**Huli** People]. This man had very many kinds of things. He had two hundred pigs and a young daughter. In the same area, there lived a pauper. He did not own anything and he was very lazy.

One time, the pauper saw the rich man with his daughter going to hunt for wild game in the forest. The pauper thought of doing something because he was jealous when he saw the girl going with her father.

He waited and waited, then in the late afternoon he followed them. He carried a traditional spade for digging the earth. He arrived at the place where the two of them wanted to sleep and prepare a hut. He wanted to clear a hole to go very close to the place where they wanted to sleep.

The pauper worked hard at digging the hole, then he went very close to the place where they wanted to sleep. It was nearly dark when he finished his work and waited for them. Before long, it was dark and the father and daughter returned to prepare food and sit.

Quickly, the pauper jumped into the hole that he had cleared. He walked and went very close to them underneath the place where they were sitting. The poor father and daughter were fearful as they sat there.

This was because out in the forest, there was not the slightest light, and there was no moon either. While they sat on top of the pauper, the pauper shouted exactly like an ancestral ghost.

When they heard this, they were terrified. He said, "Now is my time."

The father replied, "Please, don't kill us. We'll give you whatever you want."

So, the pauper said, "You must give your daughter to a pauper who lives in your village. Then you must share all of your pigs, giving half to the pauper. If you ignore me you'll die."

The father replied, "I'll go do everything that you've told me to do."

Before dawn, the pauper went out of the hole and returned to the village. Afterwards, the father sent the girl to marry the pauper. The pauper said, "Yes leader, it's nice that you're giving your daughter to me, but you know I don't have any pigs to pay for her." So, the woman's father gave one hundred pigs to this pauper.

Later, the pauper became an important leader. At first, he did not have much, but then he became our ancestor. The hole is still there now. It is about fifty meters long.

We call the hole Gamiabi Pango. Our ancestors gave it this name and now some tourists know about this hole too. It is located near Guala Village, in the South Koroba area of Southern Highlands Province.

Paul Porawa Mandiligo
Box 21
South Koroba
Southern Highlands Province

A983+. Origin of holes in ground; F639.1.1. Mighty digger of tunnels; K1315. Seduction by impostor; K1833. Disguise as ghost; L114.1. Lazy hero; L161.1. Marriage of poor boy and rich girl; L123. Pauper hero; P210. Husband and wife; P234. Father and daughter; P261. Father-in-law; P265. Son-in-law; T52.6+. Father pays for bride rather than suitor; T100. Marriage; W111. Laziness; W181. Jealousy

A Boy Became a Bird of Paradise

(Wantok 827, May 10, 1990, page 20)

Long, long ago, a man, Aina Kama, and his son, Ounokorokumugl, lived in **Kalandigl** Village, in the Kembogl [Gembogl] District of **Simbu** Province [**Kuman** People?].

One day, Aina Kama told his son that they would go hunt for wild game. They prepared all of their bows and arrows, then they left the village in the afternoon. They entered the forest and they kept walking. They passed all of the signs [of humanity] and went very far into the dense forest.

They walked and walked, then they arrived at a place where a big tree stood. Aina Kama made a fire, and they put their things there. Then Aina Kama and his son, Ounokorokumugl, took their bows and arrows and tried to find some game to eat.

However, they did not find any and they returned to just sleep until dawn. In the very early morning, Aina

Kama awakened Ounokorokumugl and they walked again, arriving at a mountain. They wanted to find the place where the marsupials (*kapul*) lived. Aina Kama walked and walked, then he arrived at the base of a gigantic tree.

You know, the Highlands have many marsupials on the big trees. Aina Kama called out for Ounokorokumugl to come climb the tree to see if there were marsupials there.

Ounokorokumugl listened to his father and jumped up the big tree. When he was up there, Ounokorokumugl looked around and did not see a single marsupial.

However, on top of this tree, he saw a house. There was a place to cook food, to sleep, and to sit. There was also a rope to hold and jump to another nearby tree. When young Ounokorokumugl saw this, his thoughts became confused.

He forgot his father, Aina Kama, who was below. He played fervently, going back and forth [on the rope]. Aina waited and waited, then he called up to his son, "Ounokorokumugl, what are you doing on the tree? Come down now and we'll leave." However, his son did not want to do this.

The father asked Ounokorokumugl, "What are you doing that you don't want to come down?" When he told him to come down this time, Ounokorokumugl still did not want to descend. The father was angry and shouted up the tree, "You're a crazy boy. Your head must be confused. Your ancestors never lived, slept or ate on top of trees. Now, what are you doing?"

They [would] walk hard and leave, but Ounokorokumugl insisted on sleeping on the tree that night. Even though the father had variously bribed and threatened Ounokorokumugl, the boy was still insistent. They kept at it, but then the sun set completely. When the father saw this, he left his son on top of the tree and returned to the village. He stopped thinking about hunting for game.

Aina Kama arrived in the village and did not explain to anyone that his son, Ounokorokumugl, was sleeping on top of a big tree in the deep forest. In the very early morning, Aina Kama awoke and took some food from the village, then he brought it to his son. When he arrived, he was shocked to see that Ounokorokumugl's skin had changed and become completely black. Aina Kama just gave him food then returned to the village.

The next day, the same thing happened, but this time Aina Kama did not see his son, Ounokorokumugl. He saw a very beautiful bird perched on the branch of the tree. Aina Kama gave it some ripe bananas and told the bird, "Tomorrow, I can't come to see you. I have some work to do in the village."

Aina Kama finished speaking, then he sped away to Kalandigl. Ounokorokumugl's grandmother had seen the boy until the third day. On the fourth day, she followed Aina Kama's footsteps and arrived at this big tree. She looked up and shouted very loudly at the beautiful bird. The bird was also surprised and flew into the deep forest.

This bird is just the blue bird of paradise of Papua New Guinea [*Paradisaea rudolphi*? (Beehler *et al.*, 1986: 233)]. This bird is well known as the mark of our country, PNG.

Johnson Enny
Goroka
Eastern Highlands Province

A1970+. Creation of bird of paradise; D57.4. Transformation to black man; D150+B. Transformation: boy to bird of paradise; P233. Father and son; P292. Grandmother; W126. Disobedience

A Sister Was Troubled and Became a Bird

(Wantok 828, May 17, 1990, page 16)

Long, long ago, in Balaiye Village, there lived a man and his sister. One day, they decided to go fishing in the river. In the very early morning, they awoke and walked towards the garden to get some food. Afterwards, they walked swiftly on the trail down to the river. They followed the river and they fished towards the river's source. The brother used goggles underwater, spearing the fish. When he shot one, he would throw it to his sister above on the shore. The sister would take it and put it in a coconut basket. They just did this and followed the river upwards.

Feeling Cold

They kept at it, then the brother got up and told his sister, "Take these fish in the basket and cook them, then wait for me. I'll find some more and come later." The sister felt very cold and she was completely famished. She listened to her brother and let him go.

The sister arrived at a nice place, then she cooked the fish. Then she sweated profusely. The ashes from the fire flew about on her skin and face, making her look completely black. At this time, her brother was still fishing in the river and going upstream.

The brother fished and fished, then he too felt hungry and cold. So, he left the river and walked back to find his sister. When he arrived at the place where his sister was, he saw that his sister's face and mouth were terribly black. He said to his sister, "You must have eaten some food already. Your mouth is black."

However, his sister replied, "No. My mouth and skin are black because I cooked the food, and the ashes rubbed on my skin and mouth. I cleaned the sweat from my skin, and that made my skin and mouth black."

The brother insisted that his sister was lying. They argued heatedly for a while, then the brother wanted to beat his sister. He and the sister cried together, then they cooked and scraped the food. Later, she told her brother, "Stay here, I'm going to pee, then I'll return."

After the sister said this, she went into the forest. When she hid, she went to find wild *limbum* palm trees, which are called <u>*piriri*</u> in my language. She removed the tree seedlings and tied them to her legs, arms and head. After she did this, she walked back to her brother.

Crying Terribly

When she went close to her brother, she shouted, "You berated me about your food, so you can eat now because I'm ready for you. I'm leaving you now." After the woman said this, she turned into a bird of paradise and flew into the deep forest. The brother saw this and cried terribly for his sister, [then he] went to the village.

At this time, the birds of paradise looked better because they had arisen from a woman. This story comes from Balaiye [**Balaia**] Village in the Bugaty area of **Madang** Province [**Kwato** People].

Jackson Ijana Gajila
Balaiye Village
Madang Province

A1970+. Creation of bird of paradise; D150+W. Transformation: woman to bird of paradise; D642. Transformation to escape difficult situation; D671. Transformation flight; P253. Sister and brother; P253+. Hostile sister and brother; R220. Flights

The Enga Area Is Filled with Pandanus (*Karuka*) Trees

(Wantok 829, May 24, 1990, page 15)

Long, long ago, in the Yandaipia [**Yandapo**] area of **Enga** Province, there lived a man and his sister [**Enga** People]. This man's name was Minakal Les and his sister's name was Tambwan Ipali.

They lived very well in Yandaipia. Tambwan Ipali was a woman who excelled at gardening, so their garden was always packed with food.

Tambwan Ipali usually took care of their garden. She lived in the women's house. Her brother, Minakal Les, was a man who excelled at hunting wild game in the forest.

Every day, he would leave the village and travel the deep forest.

When Minakal Les would return to the village, he would carry various kinds of animals, such as cassowaries, and various kinds of marsupials (*kapul*) from the trees and the ground) [probably the ground cuscus, *Phalanger gymnotis* (Flannery, 1995a: 166-168)]. His net bag would be packed with various animals.

When Minakal Les would return to the village, he would carry firewood, and breadfruit and *tanget* leaves from the forest that he would lay directly on top of the firewood. When he walked back, he would walk like a wild man. His sister in the village would hear the pounding of his legs while Minakal Les was still coming from the deep forest. This was because the ground would tremble as he walked.

When she heard this, Tambwan Ipali would prepare her brother's food. When he arrived at the men's house, he would cut the firewood and make a big fire to heat stones and cook the meat in an earth oven.

After Minakal Les cooked all of the meat, he would go into his men's house, take a traditional flute (*pupe* [Lang, 1973: 146]), then lie down and blow it. When the earth oven was ready, he would divide it in the middle and give half to his sister.

They did this for a while, then one time, Minakal Les told his sister, Tambwan Ipali, that he had killed all of the marsupials that were nearby. So, they must go kill marsupials on a big stone mountain. The name of this stone mountain is Yanakal Kan. He told his sister to prepare some food to carry for themselves.

Tambwan Ipali listened and went to the garden to fetch and prepare some food to bring. In the very early morning, they awoke and walked swiftly along the trail to the big stone mountain.

They arrived at the mountain, then made a big fire. Afterwards, they slept until morning. Later, they walked just a little farther and arrived at Yanakol [Yanakal] Kan, a cave in the mountain. The man told his sister, "Stand at the mouth of the cave. I'll go inside and chase the marsupials outside. You must kill all of the marsupials that I chase out. Kill the little ones too."

After his said this, Minakal Les went inside to chase the marsupials. Tambwan Ipali worked at killing the marsupials. She killed all of them, then a tiny one came out last. She felt sorry for the little marsupial, so she let it go.

Minakal Les went outside the cave and counted the marsupials. He discovered that one was not there. He asked his sister, "Why did you let one of the marsupials go?" The sister replied, "No. It was tiny, so I felt sorry for it and let it go." He spoke again, "I told you to kill all of the marsupials, but you let the little one go. One time, there will be a big famine in the village. At this time, you must come here because only I will be here."

Then he told his sister to return to the house with the net bag of marsupials. Tambwan Ipali went to the village, and one day there was a big famine. She thought about what her brother had told her, to go to the place where he had told her to stand. She arrived at this place and saw an unusual kind of tree standing there. She had never seen it before.

The fruits of this tree were very large. One was ripe and fell to the ground. She took it and tried to eat it. Oh my, the tree fruit was delicious. As she stood there, she thought back to what her brother had told her. Tambwan Ipali knew that it was just her brother who had become a pandanus tree (*karuka*). She cried passionately, then went back to the village.

So now, the Enga area is filled with pandanus trees.

Jackson Kaimanda
Morobe Province

A2681.15K2. Origin of pandanus tree; D215.10KM. Transformation: man to pandanus tree; D2148. Earth magically caused to quake; F969.7. Famine; M359.9. Prophecy of famine; P253. Sister and brother; Q325. Disobedience punished; Q552.3.1. Famine as punishment; W126. Disobedience

A Woman Gave Her Breasts to Marsupials (*Kapul*)
(Wantok 830, May 31, 1990, page 16)

Long, long ago, in the time of the ancestors, there was an old couple who lived in a small village. In this village, there also lived two youths, a boy and a girl.

The youths lived there for a while, then they grew up. When they were big enough, they left the old couple and went to live in their own place. They made a garden and lived by themselves. After a while, they married and slept together.

One day, the old woman told her husband, "Stay here, I'm going to see the children in the other place." So in the very early morning, before dawn had broken, she awoke and sped along the trail to see her two grandchildren.

She arrived there, and they saw her. The boy shouted to the old woman, "Hey granny, good morning. Did you just come around, or is there something that you came for?"

The old woman replied, "I came to see you two because I have a little story to tell you."

Then the old woman told the story to the boy, "Tomorrow, in the very early morning, take your wife and go to the forest. You must carry a *kina* shell. When you arrive at the base of a betel nut palm, then tell her to climb it."

The old woman finished the story, then she went back home. The next day, the young couple awoke in the very early morning and went into the forest. On the trail, they arrived at the base of a betel nut tree, then the boy told his wife to climb it.

When the woman was on top, the boy quickly nailed the *kina* shell in the middle of the betel nut tree. He shouted for his wife to descend. When the woman sped down, she cut herself upon the *kina* shell. They got up and went back home. This was like the woman's signal that has become important now [i.e., menstruation].

The young couple went hunting for tree mushrooms, and filled bamboo tubes with them. Afterwards, they sped back home. When they arrived home, the man told his wife to cook the mushrooms in the bamboo. When she put the mushrooms and bamboos on the fire, he told her, "When the mushrooms and bamboos boil, you must put the bamboo opening right at the place on your skin where the *kina* had cut you." The woman did this, then her sore dried up completely. From that time onward, they never slept together.

The man's work was hunting for wild game, cutting the forest to make gardens, and going around the deep forest. The woman just worked in the garden and cooked food. She took care of the baby marsupials (*kapul*) that her husband would bring from the deep forest. She would give her breasts to the baby marsupials and her breasts became completely ruined.

One day, their old grandmother thought of them and wanted to go see them. She told her old husband that she would go check on the grandchildren. In the very early morning, the old woman woke up, slung a little net bag on her side, then walked swiftly along the trail. She arrived at the young couple's home and the man saw her. He shouted, "Aiyo granny, you've returned, huh?"

They waited for the man's wife to cook all of the food, then they sat and ate. They ate then the old woman saw that the woman's breasts were completely ruined. She asked her, "Hey, what did you do to your breasts?" The young woman replied, "No, the little marsupials drank my milk and their teeth bit my breasts."

The old woman told the young man, "Tomorrow, you'll go into the forest. When you encounter a spider, you must poke it with your finger. Look carefully at what it does."

The man listened and went into the deep forest, then he found a spider. He poked the spider with his finger. Shortly after this, the spider returned and kept watch. The man saw everything and returned home.

He arrived home and he did not wait. The boy just jumped up into the house and had sex with his wife. Henceforth, they slept together. One day, the woman was pregnant, and she gave birth to two children, a boy and a girl.

Joshua Reresere M.
Tuvituvin Village
P. O. Box 12
North Solomons Province

A1352. Origin of sexual intercourse; A1355+. Origin of menstruation: cutting; D1500.1.19. Magic healing salve; P210. Husband and wife; P253. Sister and brother; P291.1. Grandfather as foster father; P292.1. Grandmother as foster mother; T100. Marriage; T570. Pregnancy; T587. Birth of twins; T685. Twins

Bananas Brought the Goroka Women
(Wantok 831, June 7, 1990, page 16)

Long, long ago, in the time of the ancestors, many women lived on Kipi Mountain, in the Frigano [**Firigano**] area, by Goroka in **Eastern Highlands** Province [**Yagaria** People].

The Kipi women were very gorgeous. They always would gather and go searching for firewood, mushrooms, and edible grasses in the forest.

They would follow Mount Korua into the forest where an old couple lived. The old man was named Kosuta and the woman was named Hitene. Inside the forest, there was a big ditch. The old couple's house was close to this ditch.

When the women arrived at the ditch, they would hang up their net bags on the trees and shout in my language, "*Hae-e-ae-aee-aee.*" The meaning of this is, "Old couple, you sleep on each other's legs." Then they would laugh hysterically and lie on the ground. Afterwards, they would go into the forest. When they returned, they would just do the same thing again. Every day that they went into the forest, they would do this.

One morning, they all woke up, took their net bags, and followed the same trail into the forest. They arrived at the ditch and stood in a row. Then they shouted, "*Buga Itotolio Luto Aiyo-aiyo lato aiyo hae-e-aee.*" After they said this, they went into the forest.

In the afternoon, they returned and did the same thing. The old couple listened and thought that their kin were shouting. They went outside the house, but no, it was just the young women of Kipi.

They were completely furious. So, one day they decided what they would do. The old man had a good idea and told his wife, "Hitene! Never mind our confused thinking. The women of Kipi often give it to us mercilessly, but tomorrow will be a first."

In the early morning, he awoke and cut bananas, then he planted them in the ground. Some days later, the bananas were terribly ripe. Old Hitene did not know what old Kosuta wanted to do. She just worked at helping him. Then Kosuta told his wife, "Hitene! Give me your ass." The old woman replied, "Kosuta! Why?" The man said, "Just follow me." The woman sent her buttocks toward him and the old man plugged them up well. Then the old man turned and Hitene plugged his buttocks too.

After that, they ate the ripe bananas and finished them all. Oh my, their bellies were terribly swollen because they had blocked their anuses.

The next day, the women of Kipi went into the forest and shouted by the ditch. Later, they went down to the Damaguta River, searching for edible grasses and mushrooms as they went towards **Fevegota** and **Kamiepa**.

When it was nearly afternoon, the old couple sped off to the ditch. The old woman turned her buttocks, then Kosuta cut the rope from her buttocks. All of the feces came out and completely filled the ditch.

Afterwards, Hitene turned and loosened the rope from Kosuta's buttocks. He too filled the ditch with feces. Immediately, they cut some banana leaves and covered the opening of the ditch.

When they finished, they sped back to the house and just kept watch on the trail. All of the women came back and were about to stand in a row and shout. After they shouted, they went down to the ditch. The poor women, they all sat directly on top of the pile of excrement.

One emaciated woman was the last to descend. She jumped up again and cleaned herself off, then pulled up the others. They knew that the old couple must have been furious and done this. They were speechless. They just shut their mouths and walked back to the village. When they arrived at the village, it was dark.

The next day, all of the women went to each of the houses and asked for ripe bananas. They all ate and ate, then their bellies became bloated as if they were pregnant.

Late at night, all of them gathered and walked into the forest. They arrived at the house where the old couple was sleeping. They defecated around the house, then fled back to the village. Near dawn, the feces turned into mushrooms.

The old couple awoke in the morning and saw very many mushrooms. Oh my, they were elated and they began gathering them. They finished, then made a huge earth oven. They cooked some of them in bamboo tubes.

However, when they removed the leaves from the earth oven and bamboos, they just saw feces. They were completely furious. They knew that the women had gotten revenge upon them.

Hitene was not too angry, but Kosuta was completely enraged. So the next day, he took an axe and went to cut a big tree. When he finished, he made a giant drum. He let the water carry it down to the Hagavi River. Late at night, he performed some sorcery and the women slept very deeply.

Afterwards, he took each of them and put them inside the big drum. He closed off the base of the drum with a live pig. The mouth of the drum was blocked with various kinds of garden foods, ropes, net bags, and women's walking sticks. Then he left and the water carried them down to **Anitokepa**.

The young women thought that they were sleeping at home. When it was nearly dawn, the pig went out and into the forest. The women each went out of the drum's mouth and were surprised that they were not sleeping in the house.

Later, they all lived and married at Anitokepa. Today, if you go to this area, you will see various kinds of foods growing there. Also, you will only see big, gorgeous women.

Yanuvi Mode

Boroko

National Capital District

D450+. Transformation: excrement to mushroom; D450+. Transformation: mushroom to excrement; D1964.3. Magic sleep induced by abductor; K735. Capture in pitfall; P210. Husband and wife; Q288. Punishment for mockery; Q470+. Befouling as punishment; R10. Abduction; T100. Marriage; X716H+. Feces as gift; X716.1H+. Befouling with excrement

A Crab Helped a Woman Chase Away Evil Sorcerers
(Wantok 832, June 14, 1990, page 16)

Long, long ago in Wapindumaka [**Wabindumga**] Village, in the Maprik District of **East Sepik** Province, there was a woman who was pregnant and about to give birth [**Abelam** People].

One time, she went to the garden and worked at removing the grasses. She worked and worked, then she saw a crab hole. She dug and dug, then she saw a crab.

She grabbed the crab tightly, then she tied its legs with rope and put it inside her net bag. She was elated because in the afternoon, she would cook it well and eat it.

When it was nearly afternoon, a heavy rain and wind arose. She noticed this and ran to hide inside the garden hut. She made a big fire, then cooked bananas and ate. She waited for the rain to end so that she could return to the village because the afternoon was ending and it was becoming dark.

However the rain was still strong, so she went outside and walked by the river. Oh my, the river was strongly flooded, so she did not have a way to cross and get back to the village.

She was stranded, so she walked back to stay at the garden hut. By this time, darkness had arrived. The garden hut had plenty of firewood. She took some more and made a bonfire, then she sat. The poor woman sat and was afraid of evil sorcery. Our village has very much evil sorcery.

An idea came to her to remove all of the firewood. She went beneath it and put the firewood on top of herself, then she slept. At this time, some evil sorcerers were going around the forest and searching for a house in which to hide. The rain drenched them terribly, so they raced and came to this garden hut.

She heard them and was terrified. She did not make a sound. She sat very quietly and just listened to them. The sorcerers saw the fire and were elated. They sat around the fire and spoke in their language.

When the firewood was gone, they would go and fetch some more, then put it on top of the fire. However, they did not see her because she was lying far below.

She lay there for a while, then she broke wind. They heard this and removed all of the firewood. When they saw her, oh my, their hearts stopped completely.

Immediately, they put some of themselves on watch, while others had sex with her. They did this for a while, then all of them had sex with her. The poor woman could not do a thing. This was because the men were stronger than she was and because they just followed their desires.

Near midnight, the sorcerers wanted to sleep. They told one of themselves to watch while the others slept. The sorcerer who watched was elated. He knew that it would be a good chance to sleep with her.

When all of the other sorcerers were asleep, he asked her to sleep with him. She agreed, then they slept together. However, the sorcerer did not know what she was thinking.

They slept together for a while, then the sorcerer wanted to remove the woman's "grass" skirt and have sex with her.

At this time, she thought of the crab that she had taken from the garden. Very quietly, she loosened the ropes around the crab's legs. She put the crab on top of the man's two testicles. The crab bit the man terribly, and he shouted like nothing else.

The other sorcerers were shocked and thought that enemies had grabbed one of themselves. Their eyes were still sleepy, but they got up and sped out into the rain.

They went their own ways into the forest. At this time, the woman got up and followed them, then ran to the river. Quite luckily, the water had subsided, so she crossed. She went to the other side, then fled to the village. The poor woman returned to the village. When she gave birth, the baby was dead.

Collines Patiken

Kieta

North Solomons Province

[For a similar story, see *Wantok* #894.]

D1711. Magician; F547.1.1. Vagina dentata; Q244. Punishment for ravisher; Q451.10.1+. Punishment: attack on testicles; Q583. Fitting bodily injury as punishment; R220. Flights; S185. Cruelty to pregnant woman; T471+. Gang rape; T580+. Stillbirth; X712.1H. Female genitals; X712.3.1H. Injury to testicles; X716.7H. Disastrous breaking wind

Pictures of the Vanimo Masked Dance
(Wantok 833, June 21, 1990, page 20)

This ancestor story comes from the **Vanimo** area in **West Sepik** Province [**Vanimo** People]. This story is about origin of the masked dance, which is an important song and dance in West Sepik Province.

Long ago, in the time of the ancestors, there lived a man. This man's name was Tulipe. Tulipe had a dog, and they lived together. The dog's name was Waune. Tulipe and Waune lived well together and were pals. They lived for a while, then their house became short of meat.

One day, Tulipe prepared things for hunting wild game, such as a bow and arrows. He also prepared some food to fill his belly in the forest.

He knew that the next day, he would beat his body at hunting for game, so that night he slept very well and prepared his body for the next day.

In the very early morning, he awoke, then took his bow and arrows and the food that he had previously prepared. He called for his dog to come, and they followed the trail into the forest.

Tulipe had a very strong desire to eat bandicoot. He was tired of eating the other animals, such as pig and marsupial (*kapul*). So, they went to a place that had a large area of sword grass, which they could surround and then grab some bandicoots.

Dawn had not yet broken when they arrived at a stream. The name of this stream is Manim Etingi. They jumped over the stream, then went up a hill. When they were nearly at top of the hill, there was a large sword grass area. When they arrived there, dawn broke.

They rested a little, then they began to surround the sword grass. After they surrounded it, they made noises around it so that the bandicoots would flee to just one side where the two of them could kill many of them.

They killed many bandicoots, then Tulipe chased a huge one. The bandicoot ran and ran, then it went down into a big crab's hole in the ground.

Tulipe was unconcerned. He followed and began to break the earth. He dug and dug, but the hole kept descending. He did not see the bandicoot either. The bandicoot went down and just disappeared into the earth.

His dog, Waune, also helped dig the earth with its paws. Poor Tulipe did not know that this bandicoot was a *masalai* bandicoot. He kept digging the earth. Then the bandicoot turned into a ground lizard that we call *touprine* in my language.

Tulipe kept digging, then he was surprised to see the lizard. The *masalai* lizard jumped and knocked out Tulipe. It was nearly dark when the lizard performed various kinds of traditional songs and dances, then Tulipe awoke. Tulipe rose and felt as if his head was still confused. He had the idea that the bandicoot was a *masalai*.

Quickly, he took his bow and arrows, and called for Waune to come. Then they ran back to the village. It was after midnight when they arrived at the house.

Tulipe felt as if his body was dead, so he sped away to the place for making fires, then he fell dead asleep. At night, Tulipe dreamt and saw the *masalai* come to him. The *masalai* performed a song and dance for Tulipe. The *masalai* drew a picture of the wooden mask and showed it to Tulipe.

The *masalai* also drew a picture of the bandicoot that was itself. The *masalai* showed Tulipe that the bandicoot's image must stay on the face of the mask and that the lizard must stay on the back side.

Later, the *masalai* taught Tulipe all of the traditional songs and dances. In the morning, Tulipe awoke and thought of all of these songs and dances. The people of the village listened and were shocked.

He taught them and today the masked dance is important in West Sepik Province. Some villages in East Sepik Province know how to sing this too. Only the men go inside the wooden masks to sing and dance.

John Wikiye

Vanimo

West Sepik Province

A1464.2.1. Origin of particular song; A1542.2. Origin of particular dance; A1465.6. Origin of masks; B214.1.10+. Singing lizard; B293.5+. Dance of lizards; B871.2+. Giant bandicoot; D411+. Transformation: bandicoot to lizard; D1781. Magic results from singing; D1781+. Magic results from dancing; D1810.8.2. Information received through dream; E55.1. Resuscitation by song; E55.1+. Resuscitation by dance; F401.3+. Spirit in bandicoot form; F401.3.13K2. Spirit in form of lizard; F490+. Masalai; R220. Flights

Nehemaiiah Burned Baby Nema with a Stone
(Wantok 834, June 28, 1990, page 24)

Long, long ago, there was a man and his wife who lived on top of a small mountain. The name of this mountain is Mussy. The man's name was Nehemaiiah and the woman's name was Maren.

Nehemaiiah made a big, round house on top Mount Mussy and they lived there. Their garden was very close to a river. However, the couple had a great problem that made them depressed. They had lived together for a very long time, but Maren had not given birth to a baby. Nehemaiiah told Maren that they must have a child to take care of themselves and to do work. This was because their time for being able to work was nearing an end.

One day, they sat for a while, then Nehemaiiah shouted to Maren, "Maren, why is it that you've not given birth? I've slept with you many times, but you're not pregnant." After Nehemaiiah spoke out, they went to sleep.

At night, Maren slept and felt a pain in her belly. She woke up and went outside the house, then she gave birth to a baby girl. Maren took the baby back inside the house and put her on top of the bed.

When dawn was about to break, Nehemaiiah woke up from the bed. At the same time, the baby girl awoke and cried. When Nehemaiiah heard this, he moved back his *tanget* leaves above his knees and he sped over to see what it was that was crying in the early morning. When he arrived, oh my, Nehemaiiah was very happy to see the little baby girl sleeping on top of Maren's bed.

He turned back to look at his wife and he said, "Oh my, exactly how did you give birth to this baby girl? You weren't the slightest bit pregnant." Maren replied to her husband, "What kind of question is that for you to ask me? My belly was in pain just yesterday, and I went outside of the house. It was then that I gave birth."

So, the couple thought of a name to give to the baby girl. They thought for a while, then Maren told her husband, "You're the father of the house and family, so it's your job to find a name and give it to this little baby girl."

Old Nehemaiiah listened to this and racked his brain. He sat thinking by the fire, then it was clear. He would take the first part of his name, "ne", and the first part of his wife's name, "ma." So, he would give the name, "Nema" to the baby.

The three of them lived very well until the time when the baby was two years old. Then one day, Maren left little Nema with her father and went to the garden to look for food. This was because all of the food in the house was gone. Maren put Nema to sleep in a net bag and hung her up on a tree branch near the house. Then she sped away to the garden. Only father Nehemaiiah and the baby were there. Before long, little Nema woke up and cried.

Nehemaiiah tried to stop his little daughter from crying, but he was unsuccessful. Little Nema wailed. Father Nehemaiiah kept at it to no avail, so he became furious. Quickly, he made a fire, then he heated a stone. When the stone was very hot, he took it and pushed it down little Nema's throat. Father Nehemaiiah took a little water, then spilled it on top of the stone. The smoke rose from the stone and shot all of the way into little Nema's innards, killing her.

Later, Nehemaiiah put little Nema into the net bag and hung her on the place on the tree branch where mother Maren had left her when she had gone to the garden.

When the mother returned to the house, she looked and thought of the baby, "Nema is just sleeping well there." Mother Maren threw the net bag of food on top of the house, then she sped down to get little Nema. However, when she approached the net bag and looked inside, little Nema did not make a sound or breathe. Maren tried to wake the baby for a while, but to no avail. She looked inside at the baby again and she saw the stone with which the father had burned his daughter.

Maren was very troubled and cried until morning. When dawn was about to break, Maren carried little Nema's body up to a hill that was near the house, then she jumped down. Now the two of them were dead. Nehemaiiah saw this and was terribly ashamed. He took a rope and hanged himself.

Many people from **Kainantu** in the **Eastern Highlands** Province know about Mount Mussy and its story [**Agarabi** People]. This little place is still there, but the deep forest has covered it over now.

Ali Tom
P. O. Box 2385
Boroko
National Capital District

F562.7K. People live in mountain top; M451.1. Death by suicide; P214.1+. Husband commits suicide (dies) on death of wife; P232+. Mother commits suicide on death of daughter; P234. Father and daughter; S11.3.3+. Father kills daughter; S112. Burning to death; T573. Short pregnancy; T580. Childbirth

Marsupial (*Kapul*) and Dog are Enemies
(Wantok 835, July 5, 1990, page 20)

Long, long ago, in **Aipau** Village, in the Kandep [sub-]District of Western Highlands [**Enga**] Province, there lived an old woman and her little baby [**Enga** People].

One night, they were short of forest vines for making net bags, so in the very early morning they awoke and went to the forest. They went and went, then they arrived at a mountain called Aipau Pau.

They were famished, so they sat and rested there, then they ate some sweet potatoes. Before long, they heard various songs coming from the middle of the mountain.

The songs were unusual, so they went closer to try to look. They arrived and saw various animals of the forest jumping and singing. Oh my, their hearts jumped.

All of the dogs made a line. The marsupials (*kapul*) stood in another line. All of the birds sang and jumped in another line. So, the various animals sang and danced like this. The mountain was forested too, and much of it looked very nice. The two of them were very happy there, so they sat and watched.

They watched and forgot about returning home. It was nearly dark, so they searched for the trail. The animals were still singing and dancing. The two stayed for a little, then they saw a dog singing, and its throat became completely dry. It walked near the water and drank.

The water was delicious, so the dog quenched its thirst. Afterwards, the dog followed the river up to the source. The dog arrived at the source of the river and it saw a dead marsupial by the river.

Oh my, when it ate, it was delicious, like nothing else. The dog finished the whole marsupial. After the dog ate, it quickly followed the river downstream. It arrived at the place where the dogs and other animals were singing and dancing.

It arrived and just killed a marsupial, then ate it. Just then, it told the other dogs that the marsupial meat was very good. Then all of the dogs followed suit, grabbed the marsupials, killed and ate them.

The leader of the marsupials saw this and began singing, "*Pole tamble pee kanden kala up lep mendai lo yokap*." [*pée* means "time" and *mendá:* means "one" (Lang, 1973: 68, 84)] This means, "It's a good time now and you can't kill me. I'm jumping on the vine and climbing the tree."

The old mother and the girl sat and continued to watch. The leader of the marsupials and the dog pranced belligerently back and forth (*samsam*), then went to fight. They fought and fought. They opened their eyes and looked at themselves, then they turned to stone. The mother and daughter saw this and fled to the village.

The marsupial and dog just became stones. These stones are still there on Mount Aipau Pau. Many people often see them today. Today, you see that the dog is the enemy of the marsupial.

Paul Ipan and Mole Mauwi [Ípane is an Enga clan name
    (Lang, 1973: 215)]

Lae

[Morobe Province]

A977. Origin of particular stones or groups of stones; A2494.4+. Enmity between dog and marsupial; B214.1+. Singing marsupial; B214.1.4. Singing dog; B293.6K. Dance of birds; B293+. Dance of dogs; B293+. Dance of marsupials; B241.2+. King of marsupials; B263+. War between dogs and marsupials; D420+. Transformation: marsupial to stone; D422.2.4K. Transformation: dog to stone; P232. Mother and daughter; R220. Flights; S110. Murders

Old Koe Stole a Baby

(Wantok 836, July 12, 1990, page 20)

Long, long ago, in Hambuke [**Haumbugwe**], in the Kubalia area of **East Sepik** Province, there lived two women and an old man [**Boiken** People]. The old man's name was Koe. The names of the two women were Yrok and Jiraun. Jiraun had a daughter, and Yrok did not have children yet.

They lived for a while, then Jiraun had a second baby, a boy. Jiraun was a woman who worked very hard. Food was often found in the house. Old Koe and the other sister, Yrok, would just sleep in the house.

Jiraun was furious at old Koe and his sister. One time, she scolded them terribly, "You two just sleep in the house. My two children and I work hard finding food for you." Yrok was ashamed and ran away to live in another house far from her sister. Koe was unconcerned about the scolding, so he just lived with Jiraun and the two children.

One day, Jiraun and the two children went fishing in the river. That day, they took very many fish as well a crab. They returned to the house, and old Koe asked, "Did you kill some game or not?"

Jiraun was furious, but she did not to reveal her anger. She just replied, "*A Muanto Tuo*, don't worry, take it easy. We'll cook now."

When the food was ready, Jiraun placed all of the fish for just herself and the two children. On the old man's carved wooden plate, Jiraun put just the crab.

Jiraun and the two children just ate the fish, so their mouths did not make loud noises. The poor old man worked at breaking the crab. His mouth made crunching sounds like nothing else.

The old man asked them, "Why is it just my mouth making noises and not yours?" Jiraun looked at his plate and replied, "It's bad that you chew betel nuts and such in the sun, or that sometimes you men often talk about playgrounds or whichever gatherings are approaching. Come and we'll cook. What kind of noise does the fish you're eating make?"

Old Koe listened and did not say anything. Quickly, he finished eating and went to sleep. The next day, Jiraun and the two children went back to fishing. Koe waited until they went fairly far away, then he followed them. They arrived at the river, then Jiraun put the youngest child in a net bag. She hung the net bag on a *ton* tree branch. She and the elder child went down to the river and fished.

Quietly, the old man approached the place where the baby was sleeping. He broke a *ton* tree branch and put it inside the net bag. He took the baby and ran back to the village.

He arrived at the village, then gave the baby to Yrok to take care of. He told Yrok that he had found this baby by the river and that she could not tell the other people if they were looking for the baby.

Jiraun fished for a while, then she thought of giving milk to the baby. She raised the net bag and was surprised to see the *ton* tree branch inside.

Oh my, her heart stopped completely. She grabbed her daughter, then they cried and returned to the village. They arrived at the house and told the story that an enemy had come. Old Koe listened and spoke deceitfully.

Many months and years passed, then Jiraun forgot her son. Yrok was taking care of the baby in another house. She would always just give bananas to the baby, so the baby grew quickly.

One day, Yrok taught a song and dance to the child. They worked at it passionately. Yrok taught the song as follows, "_Kuruo Kuruk nu Hru ni Te nien yiafi ampowi ni Hra ni de mark ma_." In English, the song is, "This baby was taken from the river."

They sang loudly at the house and Jiraun heard it from her house. She thought that this must just be her child. She took spears with her and went to Yrok's house. She looked inside and saw her child's face. Oh my, she was furious.

She just held a spear and buried it inside her sister's belly. Poor Yrok died, and the child fled to another village.

Paul Hama

Yangoru

East Sepik Province

P231. Mother and son; P232. Mother and daughter;P252.1. Two sisters; P253. Sister and brother; P275. Foster son; P293. Uncle; P294. Aunt; P294+. Aunt as foster mother; P297. Nephew; P298. Niece; Q288. Punishment for mockery; Q411. Death as punishment; R10.3. Children abducted; R213. Escape from home; R260. Pursuits; S71. Cruel uncle; S75.1K2. Sororicide; S110. Murders; T611. Suckling of children; W111. Laziness; W157. Dishonesty

A Pig Had Sex with A Woman and Created Kambaram Village in Enga [Province]

(Wantok 837, July 19, 1990, page 20)

This ancestor story is from **Kambaram** Village in **Enga** Province and goes as follows [**Enga** People]. Long, long ago, in the time of the ancestors, there was only an old woman who lived in Kambaram Village. There were no other people who lived in this place at this time. This was because they had all died and some had died in a fight.

This woman lived by herself. She searched for food to strengthen herself. She was old, but she still had enough strength. She had a garden that was fairly far from the village. She always went to the garden to work.One day, the food was in short supply in the house. Also, she had not weeded the food plants for a long time, so she thought about going to the garden and doing some work.

That evening, she ate and went to sleep quickly. In the early morning, she awoke and cooked some food. She ate some food and she bundled some food in leaves to take to the garden in case she became hungry.Dawn had not broken yet when she walked towards the garden. When she arrived at the garden, the sun was rising. The birds of dawn were also singing.

She went by the garden and heard a sow and her piglets digging the earth. She was elated. She put her net bag and other things quietly on the ground. Then she walked quietly towards the group of pigs.She made a noise, then the sow and her children heard her. The mother pig did not think of her piglets. The mother pig thought of her own life and fled first into the forest. The piglets went around crazily, fleeing in their own directions.

Some followed their mother and some fled towards where the old woman was standing. The old woman was strong and grabbed a he-piglet, while some ran away. She put the piglet inside her net bag, then worked in the garden. When it was nearly evening, she took some food and walked back to the house.

She took care of the pig for a while and the pig grew larger. She did not have a husband with whom to have sex. So, when she thought of having sex with a man, she had sex with this pig. She would do this every night. She slept with the pig for a while, then the pig impregnated her.

Before long, she gave birth to two children, a boy and a girl. Oh my, her heart stopped. She was elated because she now had a son and a daughter with whom to talk. She took good of the children well and they grew up. She taught them the things to do to find wild game, to make gardens, and to speak.

Some months and years later, the pig died. The poor family cried terribly and buried his body. Before long, the mother died too. Only the brother and sister lived in this place. Later, they had sex together and raised more children. These children married among themselves.

So, this is the way that the people of Kambaram Village arose. This is a true story. If you read this story and want to receive more, I will give it to you quickly.

Kelly Yukuti Sau [Sáu is an Enga clan name (Lang, 1973: 215)]

Wabag

Enga Province

A991+. Origin of particular village; B611.9K. Pig paramour; B631. Human offspring from marriage to animal; P210. Husband and wife; P231. Mother and son; P232. Mother and daughter; P233. Father and son; P234. Father and daughter; P253. Sister and brother; R220. Flights; T415. Brother-sister incest; T570. Pregnancy; T587. Birth of twins; V61.3+. Dead buried

How Did the Cockatoo Get Its Crown?

(Wantok 838, July 26, 1990, page 16)

Long, long ago in the time of the ancestors, there were two gorgeous sisters who lived in Hambuke [**Haumbugwe**] Village, in the Kubalia area of **East Sepik** Province

[**Boiken** People]. Their names were Wama and Sengi.
Wama was the elder and Sengi was the younger.

Their father and mother had died when they were still
little. However they lived in a small village called Anumbo
Sahi Wia [**Abauia**]. They looked very nice, and many
young and old men tried their luck with them. Wama was a
strong-headed woman, so she never trembled at the men's
questions.

Whenever she would act strongly, the little sister,
Sengi would do as her sister did. She would not shake
quickly at the men. The women were excelled at finding
food. There was no man or family to find food for them.

Every day, they would go to the forest by themselves,
kill wild game, and cook the game in an earth oven with taros and other foods. The sisters were never angry with one
another, and they lived very well.

One time, Sengi told her big sister, "We just eat taros
and bananas, and I'm tired of it. Let's go beat some sago,
then turn it and eat it too, OK?"

Wama replied that this was a good idea. She said that
the next day, they would go to the swamp to look for a sago
palm tree and cut it down.

They slept, then in the early morning, they awoke, took
their things for beating sago and some food. Then they
sped into the sago swamp.

They found a good sago tree, quickly made a platform
and prepared things. Then the big sister, Wama, took an
axe and went to cut the sago tree down to the ground.

Quickly, they cut the vines, then removed the bark and
spines of the sago palm. Later, they made a platform from
the sago tree rubbish where the tree had fallen, to be used
later when they would pulverize the sago.

They scraped the sago diligently. They worked very
quickly scraping the sago until they finished. They rested a
little, then carried all of the pulverized sago pith to the platform for rinsing the sago with water so that it would be edible.

All of the sago lay on top of the platform, then Wama
told her little sister to rinse the sago. The little sister replied, "That's alright. You rinse the sago. I'll go cook
some bananas for us to eat because in the evening we'll
have killed [our] bodies from [processing] the sago."

Sengi went to cook the bananas in a fire that they had
made long before. Wama made a shell from [*limbum*] to
fetch water for rinsing sago. Then she went to fetch the
water. She returned to rinse the sago and a young boy arrived.

The boy saw the sisters and was very sorry for them
because they were alone doing hard work that only men

usually did. The boy walked close to Wama and told her,
"Yes, I'm very sorry for you. All of the hard work that
you've done is good. I'll just help you at rinsing."

Then he took Wama's [*limbum*] and began rinsing the
sago. The boy worked very hard at rinsing the sago. The
sisters ate bananas, then they came and stood nearby. They
looked down at the [*limbum*] on the ground where the sago
was going.

Sengi saw that the water and sago were at the same
point. She said, "I'd like the water to come up and still stay
there. The sago must stay by itself." However, the big sister, Wama, wanted all of the water and sago to stay at the
same point.

The little sister changed and so did the big sister. They
did this for a while, then they fought. This was the first
time that they had fought like this.

Sengi was completely furious and took a knife used for
scraping sago. She gave a good one right on top of her big
sister's head. Blood spilled out of the big sister's head and
splashed upon Sengi.

They broke apart and the big sister turned into a white
cockatoo [sulphur-crested cockatoo (Beehler *et al.*, 1986:
117)]. At the place where the little sister had beaten her,
you can see red grasses. The big sister's blood had
splashed the little sister, so the little sister turned into a red
cockatoo [the palm cockatoo, *Probosciger aterrimus*, which
has a red cheek patch (Beehler *et al.*, 1986: 117)].

The bad boy who had rinsed the sago pulled a piece of
sago and put it on his head. He turned into a brown-colored
bird. Sometimes you will see that this bird's tail feather is
long, like a vine.

Paul Hama
Kubalia
East Sepik Province

A1998K. Creation of black cockatoo; A1998K+. Creation of white cockatoo; A2321.12K. Origin of comb of white cockatoo; D150B. Transformation: boy to bird; D150+W. Transformation: woman to cockatoo; D566.
Transformation by striking; F610.0.1. Remarkably strong woman; P252+.
Hostile sisters; P252.1. Two sisters; T50. Wooing

A *Masalai* Killed Wokimboli and Ate Him
(Wantok 839, August 2, 1990, page 20)

This ancestor story comes from **Urindogum** Village in
East Sepik Province [**Boiken** People]. It is the story of two
brothers, one of whom was eaten by a ghost. The other fled
to the village.

Long, long ago, two brothers lived in this village. The name of the big brother was Wokimboli. The name of the little brother was Wasuru.

They lived alone in this village because their mother and father had died when they were still little. They usually lived very well with the other people of the village. They did not fight among themselves.

One day, the food was in short supply in the house, so the big brother, Wokimboli, asked the little brother to catch some fish. He said, "We've eaten the other meat and I'm tired. Tomorrow, we'll go to big river and beat tree bark [to kill the fish with poison]. Then we'll eat a little fish. Oh my, it's been a very long time since we've eaten any fish."

The little brother, Wasuru, replied, "Wokimboli! You speak of eating fish! That's great! It's been a very long time since we've eaten it. Early tomorrow morning, we'll annihilate the fish."

They made their decision. In the evening, they prepared all of their things and some food to eat in the forest. When they finished, they went to sleep.

They slept, then Wokimboli heard the first cock's crowing. He awakened Wasuru, then they cooked some sweet potatoes. They ate, then took their things and walked into the forest.

They walked and walked, then they arrived at the big river. They rested a little, then cut trees to make a forest hut. They thought they would stay inside the forest for a whole week.

After they finished the hut, they searched for the kind of tree that has bark that they could put at the source of the river. This kind of tree has poison that kills fish.

They found it, then Wokimboli removed the bark. He carried the bark up a little to the source of the river, then he began to beat it.

Wasuru stayed at the hut and cooked some sweet potatoes. You know, when it was nearly noon, they were racked with hunger. Wosuru [Wasuru] cooked the sweet potatoes, then shouted for Wokimboli to come. Afterwards, they would play around and eat.

The place where they had made a hut was the home of *masalai*s and ghost women. The two poor brothers did not know this. They were eating when a *masalai* bird saw them. The *masalai* bird called out that the other *masalai*s were living in the area. The big brother heard this.

He thought that it was an ordinary bird, and he replied, "Are you a bird that comes to take meat to eat with sweet potatoes? You're just an ordinary bird! Come down and eat my shit until you're sated!"

The *masalai* bird listened and was furious. Before long, the other *masalai*s and ghost women came and gathered, and the bird spoke to them.

The two brothers ate while the high water rose. They did not know this. The big brother, Wokimboli, turned and looked down at the river. Oh my, his heart stopped. He had the idea that all of the river *masalai*s must be angry with them.

Quickly, they saw a tall mango tree standing nearby. Wasuru went up first, then Wokimboli followed. They went up very high, to the crown of the mango tree.

At this time, a very heavy rain fell, and it started to become dark. They knew that they would not see another day.

The *masalai*s came down to the tree and tried to kill them. They were terrified and cried together. After a while, all of their strength was gone.

Wokimboli was a little bit lower on the mango tree, so the ghosts carried him away to eat. The little brother saw this and cried terribly.

You know, he was still a boy. He used the little strength that he had and jumped down into the river. The river took him down towards his home, then he ran and ran, and arrived at the village.

He lived alone for a while, then he died. This mango tree that the two brothers climbed is still there.

John Tom

Wewak

East Sepik Province

A1011. Local deluges; A1015.2. Spirit causes deluge; A1018. Flood as punishment; B143.1. Bird gives warning; B211.3. Speaking bird; D2143.1. Rain produced by magic; D2151.8. Magic flood; E425.1. Revenant as woman; F401.3.7. Spirit in form of a bird; F424. River-spirit; F490+. Masalai; G11.10. Cannibalistic spirits; G440. Ogre abducts person; J652. Inattention to warnings; P251.5. Two brothers; Q288. Punishment for mockery; R10. Abduction; R210. Escapes; R311. Tree refuge; S110. Murders

A *Masalai* Stone Killed Men

(Wantok 840, August 9, 1990, page 20)

This ancestor story comes from Tomaura [**Omaura**] Village in the Kainantu District of **Eastern Highlands** Province [**Gadsup** People]. It is the story of the *masalai* stone that killed some men.

Long, long ago, in the time of the ancestors, there was a village behind a mountain called Nonorata. The name of the village is Tomaura.

One day, some men from this village gathered together and went to hunt for marsupials (*kapul*) and other wild game. They walked and walked, then they arrived at Mount Nonorata. By this mountain there was a *masalai* stone, and by this stone there was a big cave.

The men arrived there, then they thought of making a forest hut where they could sleep, and then hunt for game. Then they divided up. Some went to hunt for game and some arranged a place to sleep.

The men who arranged the sleeping place went into a big cave, then straightened it out well. They did not know that this was a *masalai* place. Among these men, there was a short man. This man was afraid to sleep inside the cave, so he made a little house of stone.

In the evening, they all gathered and cooked food. They ate, then they told stories. When it was nearly midnight, they went to sleep. They did not know what would happen to them when they slept.

Very late at night, the stone *masalai* awoke and spoke in my language, "*Viti orio pepu, ma orio pepu, ula ula vaim*."

After this, the cave shut with all of the men inside. The short man who had slept outside saw this and was terrified. He thought that the other men had died.

However in the morning, the *masalai* stone spoke again and the cave opened. The men inside the cave had been sleeping, then they awoke. They did not know that the cave had shut that night.

The short man had awoken first and was waiting for the other men to come outside the cave. He told them what he had seen and heard.

However, they said, "You're just a runt. You're always afraid of forest *masalais*. Never mind lying to us and scaring us."

All of the men went into the forest, then they returned in the afternoon. The short man spoke sternly and some of them listened to him. So, when it was nearly dark, each of these men went out and slept with him.

Late at night, they listened carefully for what the *masalai* stone would say and do. Then the stone spoke again in my language and the cave shut. All of the other men who were sleeping inside did not know anything.

The short man and the others who were outside saw this and were terrified. They waited for the cave to open in the morning. However, the cave was completely shut.

They knew that the other men had been killed and eaten by the *masalai*. They got up and fled back to the village where they told the other people.

The next day, they all gathered food, including pigs and marsupials. They carried these and met outside the stone, then they made a huge party.

They did this to propitiate the *masalai* stone so that it would open its cave again and let the men come out and live. The *masalai* was happy for the people's food and it opened the cave again. However not one man was alive. All had been eaten by the *masalai*. The people saw that only the men's bones were left, so they fled back to the village.

Now, the cave is open. Inside it, people often see the bones of the men who were eaten by the *masalai*. The people of Tomaura Village have made the Inau Cargo Cult by this cave. They often use the bones of the men who died in the cave for their cargo cult beliefs.

Jackson T. Pata

Kainantu

Eastern Highlands Province

D1552.2. Mountain opens to magic formula (Open Sesame); D1610.18. Speaking rock (stone); D1774. Magic results from speaking; F406. Spirits propitiated; F490+. Masalai; G371+. Stone ogre; J652. Inattention to warnings; J1050. Attention to warnings; R220. Flights; S110. Murders; V140+. Sacred bones; V450+. Cargo cult

The Sasaura Burned their In-Law
(Wantok 841, August 16, 1990, page 20)

This ancestor tale is the story of a boy who was grabbed and burned inside a house by the people of **Sasaura** Village in the Kainantu area of **Eastern Highlands** Province [**Gadsup** People]. This was because he had spied upon young women inside their own clan house. The boy belonged to another village near Sasaura. The story goes as follows.

Long, long ago, in the time of the ancestors, there was a young, gorgeous woman. The woman lived with just her little brother. This was because their parents had died when they were still young. The mother and father had encountered enemies when their village was fighting with warriors from another village.

The woman and her brother lived very well. They never fought between themselves, and they would search for food to strengthen themselves.

She lived for a while, then she loved a young man from Sasaura Village. They were friends for a while, then she married him. She went to live with him at his village. She cried terribly for her little brother, then she left him.

The little brother lived by himself. By this time, he was a big man. He had a little strength to find food and hunt for wild game for himself.

Whenever he traveled to Sasaura Village, he would see his sister. This village had many gorgeous women who slept in a clan house.

One day, he traveled to Sasaura Village to see his sister. He told stories with his sister and brother-in-law until it was dark. Later, he wanted to return home, but it was dark so he slept with his sister and brother-in-law that night.

He had seen the women during the day, so he waited for everyone to be asleep. Then, very quietly, he went to the women's clan house. He went up and opened the door, then his heart stopped.

He saw the women's tits [lit., "kapok thorns"] standing up like nothing he had seen. He ran towards a woman who was sleeping by the door, but she saw him and shouted.

The rotten scoundrel jumped out and ran back to his village. Another night, he did the same thing, but the women called for their fathers, mothers and brothers to come chase him. His legs [flew up] to his buttocks while he was running back home.

The next day, all of the parents held a big meeting. They spoke about preparing to grab this man. They did not yet know that his sister had married among themselves. The poor sister and her husband did not know that the brother had done this bad thing.

They met and talked, then the men spoke, "What kind of man is that? If he still comes at night, all of you must get up quickly and come stand at the house door. Shout and we'll come open the door to take you outside. Then we'll burn him with the house."

They finished speaking, then they prepared for the night. That night, nothing happened. The next day, the man went back to see his sister. They told stories for a while, then it became dark.

He said goodnight to his sister and her husband, then he walked back towards his village. However, along the trail, he turned and walked quietly back to Sasaura Village.

When he arrived at the village, many people were asleep, but the young women were not asleep yet. They were telling stories and joking around.

The rotten scoundrel went and opened the house door. He walked inside and the women saw him. Slowly, they got up and shouted, then they ran for the door. They ran out of the house, then the fathers and mothers came with fires and blocked the house door.

The poor man was inside the house, and they burned [the house]. He found it difficult to escape, so he shouted

the name of his big sister. His sister heard this and knew that it was her brother who had done this.

She shouted and cried for them to stop the fire, but the fire was blazing and the little brother died inside. This is a true story.

Maru Jim

Kainantu

Eastern Highlands Province

C312. Tabu: man looking at woman; J651. Inattention to danger; P210. Husband and wife; P230. Parents and children; P231. Mother and son; P232. Mother and daughter; P233. Father and son; P234. Father and daughter; P250. Brothers and sisters; P253. Sister and brother; P260. Relations by law; P263. Brother-in-law; R220. Flights; R260. Pursuits; Q240+. Spying on woman in bedroom punished; Q414. Punishment: burning alive; S112.0.2. House (hostel) burned with all inside; T10. Falling in love; T100. Marriage; X743H+. Humor concerning voyeurism

A Man from Komban Became a Sow
(Wantok 842, August 23, 1992, page 16)

Long, long ago, in Awengu [**Avenggu**] Village in the Finschhafen area of **Morobe** Province, there lived two brothers [**Tobo** People].

One time, they wanted to go to **Komban** in the Kabwum District area [**Komba** People]. They prepared all of the food, then the next day they met in the very early morning.

They walked and walked, then they arrived at a mountain and it became dark. They looked around and saw a forest hut. They arranged the sleeping places, then an old man arrived.

The old man was the owner of this hut. He asked them what they were doing. They replied, "We came here wanting to go to the other side, but it became dark and we wanted to rest here. Tomorrow we'll walk away."

The old man replied, "That's OK. We'll sleep together, then tomorrow I'll show you the way to leave."

After they made their plans, they sat and rested. Later, they prepared food, ate and were about to sleep by the fire. When they were about to sleep, the old man told them, "Brothers! If tonight you sleep and see something turn into a pig, you can't lust to catch it as food."

They listened to this and thought very hard. They thought for a while, then they fell dead asleep late at night. The brothers slept soundly while the old man became a pig. He smashed and kicked strongly like a pig as he slept on the other side of the fire.

His smell made the little brother awake. He saw the pig and salivated. Then he went to get a get a piece of the pig's bone. When it was [cooked], he ate it.

After he ate, he went back to sleep. The poor brother did not know that this was not really a pig. It was really the old man who had turned into a pig. The old man did this whenever he went to sleep.

Near dawn, the big brother awoke. He saw what had happened and he was quite fearful. Quickly, he awakened his little brother and they walked away. They sped off past the mountain, then dawn broke.

At this time, the old man awoke. He took the bones of his body and rejoined them, but he discovered that something was missing. The little brother had awoken at night and eaten his backbone.

The brothers kept walking, then they arrived at Komban Village. It was then that the little brother felt a pain in his belly. His saliva also began to spill out. Shortly thereafter, he wanted to eat grass. Before long, his mouth changed into that of a pig. Later, all of the parts of his body turned into a sow.

The big brother saw this and was terribly worried for his little brother. He knew that the little brother must have ignored the old man. He had made a mistake and this is what had happened.

Slowly, the big brother gathered large tree leaves and made a pigsty. The big brother made another hut for himself to sleep and live.

He thought strongly that he would not see his little brother again. He was very troubled by this. Before long, he heard the squeals of piglets. He got up and looked into the hut where his transformed brother was sleeping.

Oh my, he was surprised to see the ten little pigs that the mother pig had born. He was furious and removed the piglets. All of the pigs were multicolored.

He cried and told everyone in Komban Village to come. They met, then chased all of the little pigs and their mother. They beat the signal drum and the hand drums at the same time, then the little pigs fled throughout Finschhafen. You know, the little pigs were afraid of the sound of hand and signal drums, so they sped away quickly.

They ran and went through Finschhafen, but they kept hearing the sound of the hand drums, so they sped away and arrived in **Madang** [Province]. They still heard it, so they left Madang and went to the Ramu [River]. However, the sound of the hand and signal drums was still strong, so they fled completely and went up to the Highlands.

So today, if you travel the Highlands, you will see that the pigs listen to and follow the speech of the people who husband them. If you go to Finschhafen or Kabum [Kabwum], you will see that the pigs do not listen. Regardless of whether a fence is tall, they will jump over it and steal the garden food.

If the people of Kabum in the time of the ancestors had not chased the pigs, the pigs would have become nice and would have listened to them just like the pigs in the Highlands.

Tumby Gembey and Siwi Gole

Wabag

Enga Province

A2490+. Why pigs from one area do not listen to what people say; B212. Animal understands human speech; D136M. Transformation: man to swine; D136+M. Transformation: man to sow; D551.3. Transformation by eating flesh; D681. Gradual transformation; D696. Transformation during sleep; J652. Inattention to warnings; P251.5. Two brothers; Q551.3.2+. Punishment: transformation into pig; R220. Flights; R260. Pursuits

The Short *Masalai* Men Killed Fubut
(Wantok 843, August 30, 1990, page 16)

This ancestor story comes from Wangat [**Wongat**] Village, inside the Markham Valley, in the Kaiapit District of **Morobe** Province [**Ngariawan** People].

Long, long ago, in the time of the ancestors, there was a man who lived in this village. His name was Fubut. Fubut had some kin who lived in a village on top of a mountain. One day, he thought of going and seeing his kin. The village on top of the mountain is called **Simpok**. It is by the Leron River.

He took his things, then walked away. He followed the Leron River, then he met some short men, women and children who were bathing.

The short men were arranging their stone axes. They were speaking their language among themselves. They spoke in a language called **Muim** [**Wantoat** People?].

Poor Fubut did not know that these [were] *masalai* people. The name of these short *masalai* people in my language is *Mamalie Puibie*.

They were only about one meter tall. These *masalai*s came from a red river. The river runs down from a stone and meets the big River Leron.

Fubut saw them and thought that they were little boys. He did not see a big person like a father or mother, so he asked them, "Hey boys, where are your parents? Are your parents working in the gardens? Have you taken your brothers and sisters to bathe?" The *masalai*s said, "Yes."

However in their thoughts, they were not happy with Fubut's question. A short *masalai* man whispered to his wife, "Hey! He thinks that we're his boys. What kind of a way to talk is that?"

Then a *masalai* man asked Fubut, "Where are you going and what time will you return?" Fubut replied, "I'm going to stay with my kin in Wangat Village for just one week. After that, I'll return."

The *masalai*s listened and Fubut walked up to Simpok. Then the *masalai*s prepared their fighting equipment so as to kill Fubut when he returned. When they were done, they waited for Fubut's return.

One week passed, then Fubut walked back towards his village. The short *masalai* men were already standing by the trail and they blocked the way.

Fubut arrived, then they began shooting his legs with spears. You know, he was a tall man and he found it difficult to shoot at their bellies or heads.

There were very many of them, they blocked his way with ropes and trees. Fubut wanted to flee, but the ropes blocked his legs and he fell down. Then they jumped on top of him and killed him.

They immobilized Fubut, then they carried him up to their village on the red river. They arrived at the source of the river, then they blew their sails (or shells), carrying Fubut down to their village.

They arrived at the village, then many people came and gathered. They made a huge party. They made an earth oven with Fubut's body and divided him up among each house. That night, they [partied] until dawn.

The people of Simpok Village never again saw Fubut. Some warriors went to Wangat Village and saw that it had turned to forest.

They followed the trail back and saw the marks from ropes and spears that the short men had used to kill Fubut. They knew that Fubut must [have become] food for the bad *masalai*s.

Kemsie Kepu

Lae

Morobe Province

F424. River-spirit; F460. Mountain-spirits; F490+. Masalai; F451.4.1.11. Dwarfs live in hills and mountains; F535. Pygmy; F562.7K. People live in mountain top; F715.9. Red river; G11.1. Cannibal dwarfs; K914. Murder from ambush; P210. Husband and wife; P230. Parents and children; Q395. Disrespect punished; Q411. Death as punishment; S110. Murders

A Woman Came from a Coconut

(Wantok 844, September 6, 1990, page 21)

Long, long ago, in the time of the ancestors, there were two brothers who lived in a village inside the Lumangurun [**Zumanggurun**] area of the Makam [Markham, or Kaiapit] District of **Morobe** Province [**Adzera** People].

The big brother grew strong and often hunted for wild game for themselves. The little brother was still young, so he usually just stayed in the village.

However, one day he sweet-talked his big brother. The big brother agreed for him to go game hunting. He took his bow and arrows then went into the very deep forest.

He walked and walked, then he rested at the base of a tree. While he was resting, an old woman came with a big bundle of firewood on her back. The little brother saw this and threw away his bow and arrows. He quickly ran and helped the poor old woman.

They walked for a little while, then they arrived at the old woman's house. They rested well and ate some food that the old woman had prepared. After they ate, the old woman sent him up to fetch a green coconut. The old woman told the little brother that he must fetch the coconut carefully, then carry it down.

The little brother listened and followed her instructions. He brought it down, then put it on the trail as the old woman had instructed him to do. When he turned and looked, a young, gorgeous woman had taken the place of the coconut and was standing there.

The bad boy married this woman and they went back to the village. The big brother saw the little brother's wife and was [shocked]. He asked the little brother about her, and the little brother told him what had happened.

The next day in the very early morning, the big brother awoke and went to wait at the same place where the little brother had waited. He waited for a while, then he saw the old woman arrive.

By this time, the big brother felt famished so he rushed her, and they went towards the house. He did not think of helping the old woman.

They arrived at the house, then the old woman sent the big brother up to fetch a ripe coconut. The big brother sped up the tree and threw down a ripe coconut.

Afterwards, he carried it and left it on the trail. Then he turned to see whether a gorgeous woman appeared as had happened to his little brother. He was surprised to see an old woman with ringworm standing and laughing at him. Oh my, he was completely furious.

He was very angry, but he shut his mouth and took the woman to the village where he married her. However, every day he thought badly of his little brother. He wanted to kill his brother and marry his brother's young wife.

One day, he lied to his little brother and the two of them went into the forest. They entered the forest, then he sent his little brother to tie on a rope and climb a tree. [He would] keep watch for striking birds.

When the little brother was on top of the tree, the big brother shouted for him to look down. He looked down, then the big brother immediately cut the rope. He left the little brother there, then he told him that he would marry his young wife.

The little brother was irate, but he was a young boy and did not have strength. He sat on the tree and cried. Before long, a bird came and sat on his head. The bad boy just knew that the bird must be the old woman. Slowly, he held the bird's legs, then they flew to the old woman's home.

The old woman took care of the boy and he grew up. He became a strong man and excelled at spear throwing. One day, he told the old woman that he must return to the village and fight to get back his wife.

The next day, he took his spears and walked away. He walked and walked, then he arrived at the village and shouted for his brother to come outside. Then they began to fight. The big brother threw spears, but the little brother dodged them. Afterwards, the little brother threw his spears and killed his big brother. He took his wife, then they fled back to the old woman's home where they lived.

Kila Karawak

Makam [Markham]

Morobe Province

[William Mai wrote an ancestor story in *Wantok* #1069, which is nearly identical to this one.]

B450. Helpful birds; B542.1. Bird flies with man to safety; B552. Man carried by bird; D150W. Transformation: woman to bird; D350W. Transformation: bird to woman; D431.11+W. Transformation: coconut to woman; J1050. Attention to warnings; K2211.0.1. Treacherous elder brother(s); P210. Husband and wife; P251.4+. One brother acts wisely, another acts unwisely; P251.5. Two brothers; P251.5.3. Hostile brothers; P263. Brother-in-law; P264. Sister-in-law; P272. Foster mother; P275. Foster son; Q40. Kindness rewarded; Q280. Unkindness punished; Q285. Cruelty punished; Q411. Death as punishment; R130. Rescue of abandoned or lost persons; R151.1. Husband rescues stolen wife; R220. Flights; S73.1. Fratricide; S110. Murders; S143.2. Abandonment in tall tree; T100. Marriage; T145.0.1. Polygyny; W10. Kindness; W181. Jealousy

Two Brothers Killed a *Masalai* Man

(Wantok 845, September 13, 1990, page 17)

This ancestor story comes from a little village in **Morobe** Province. Long, long ago, in the time of the ancestors, there was a man who killed and ate the village men. When he killed men, he would carry them to his house. At the house, he would make a huge festival.

After the festival, he would make a big fire, then cook them on the fire and eat them. When he took boys, he would put them in an enclosure and take care of them. When the boys grew up, he would kill and eat them.

He would do this sort of thing every day. One time, he held two brothers. Their names were Pai and Karevino. Pai was the elder and Karevino was the younger brother.

The brothers were still small, so he did not want to eat them because their bodies did not have much flesh. He put them inside an enclosure and took care of them. He took care of them very well and they became big men.

One day, the man gave food to the brothers. After he fed them, he told them, "Stay here and look after the house. I'm going to the garden to find some food, then I'll return."

After he said this, he took his things and went into the forest. Then the two brothers looked after the house alone. However, the big brother, Pai, knew that the man was lying to them.

Pai had the bright idea that he must have gone to the garden to find some leafy greens, and that when he returned, he would kill them. He would eat them with the edible grasses and other garden food.

[He thought this] because many other men of the village had been carried away, and then had disappeared. So, the two of them knew that he just killed and ate men.

Pai did not reveal his thought to his little brother, Karevino. He knew that it would be bad if his little brother heard this and became afraid. If that happened, he would not be of much help with what he wanted to do.

He shouted for Karevino to come, then he told him everything to do. He said, "When that man returns, I'm going to trick him into giving me fire. Then you trick him and ask him to give you some stones. We'll heat the stones in the fire and make them terribly hot. When everything is ready, trick him into coming to the enclosure to see something. When he comes, we'll grab him and push him into the red-hot fire. This is because he has killed too many people. Before long, he'll do the same to us."

Karevino listened and aided his big brother. Then they decided to just wait quietly. Near afternoon, the big man returned home. He checked the enclosure because he thought that the brothers had fled.

He told them, "It's good that you did not run away. I'll go to the house and cook some food, then we'll all eat together."

He was about to walk to the house when Pai asked him, "We'd like some fire to burn some rubbish." The big man listened to him and gave him some fire.

Later, the little brother, Karevino, asked him for some stones. The big man listened and followed what the two brothers were thinking.

The big [man] went to cook in the house and the two brothers made a bonfire by the enclosure where they slept. The stones inside the fire were red and terribly hot.

The big man was in the house and he saw the smoke from the fire. He ran out and saw the bonfire by the fence. He was furious and wanted to pummel the brothers. He ran and went to begin putting out the fire. At the same time, he scolded the brothers.

The brothers saw this then they quickly grabbed the big man and put him into the fire. At this time, the fire was roaring, and it burned the big man to a crisp.

Pai called for his little brother to come, then they went into the big man's house. They took everything that they wanted, then they burned the house.

They walked back to the village. The people of the village saw them and were elated. They thought that they had died.

Jacob Lile

Lae

Morobe Province

A515.1. Culture heroes brothers; G82. Cannibal fattens victim; G440. Ogre abducts person; G512.3. Ogre burned to death; K925. Victim pushed into fire; P251.5. Two brothers; Q211. Murder punished; Q414. Punishment: burning alive; R4. Surprise capture; S112. Burning to death; W157. Dishonesty

A Ghost Woman Died from the Axe
that She Herself Had Sharpened

(Wantok 846, September 20, 1990, page 21)

This ancestor story tells of an old ghost woman who often killed and ate people. One time she grabbed two boys and wanted to do this to them.

Long, long ago, in the time of the ancestors, there was an old ghost woman who dwelled near a village. The name of this village was **Dowaeta**.

The ghost woman would sleep inside a cave. The cave was in a small part of Ningalimbi [**Ningaumbi** Village, **South Arapesh** People, **East Sepik** Province]. In the cave, she sharpened a cassowary bone like an axe. She would always smoke it in a fire and leave it there.

Many times, she would go to hide by the village and grab people. Then she would put them inside a big basket and carry them to the cave. Later, she would go to her garden and find some leafy greens and other garden food, such as taros and bananas, then carry them back home.

She would cook them well with stones. Then she would kill the people that she had grabbed, and she would make an earth oven with them and the other food. She would always do this and people were terrified of her.

Once, there was no rain for a long time. Then after a while, a tremendous downpour fell. All of the streams and rivers of the forest filled up high with water. Amuk was the name of the big river in the Dowaeta area.

One day, no one thought of going to the river except for just two boys. They took nets and fishing spears, then they went down to the river.

That day, the ghost woman also went to keep watch at the river. She hid and saw the boys fishing and coming towards the source of the river.

Immediately, the ghost woman jumped into a hole in a big tree. She hid and waited for the boys to approach to her. You know, ghost women have various kinds of black magic. She performed a song and dance, then a strong wind arose.

The boys left all of their fish and ran to the base of the tree where the ghost woman was hiding. The boys hid for a while, then they felt sleepy. Before long, they were dead asleep. You know, the old woman's evil powers had taken them.

The old ghost saw this and was elated. She took a huge basket and dumped them inside. After she put them in the basket, she carried them to the cave where she slept.

In the very early morning, the ghost woman awoke. She took her net bag and walked towards the garden to find some leafy greens.

She wanted to cook the boys in an earth oven with the garden food, then eat. However, she was still in the garden when the boys awoke.

Oh my, they were surprised that they were sleeping in another place. They looked around, but there was no place for them to escape.

They were stuck, so they took the stone axe that the old woman had sharpened with the cassowary bone [cassowary bone axe?], then they waited. They stood waiting by the cave entrance. Afterwards, the old woman arrived.

They did not waste time. The old woman was about to go inside when they threw the axe directly at her head. She fell down to the ground with her net bag of food and died then and there. Before long, she transformed into a huge boulder.

The boys saw this and immediately jumped over her. They went outside and ran back to the village. They arrived in the village and told everyone what had happened. Everyone listened and was elated. This boulder is still there at Ningalimbi Village.

Wilson Job

Kwagiatama Community School

P. O. Box 78

Maprik

East Sepik Province

A974. Rocks from transformation of people to stone; A977.5. Origin of particular rock; A515.1. Culture heroes brothers; D1781. Magic results from singing; D1781+. Magic results from dancing; D1964.3. Magic sleep induced by abductor: D2142.1. Wind produced by magic; E425.1. Revenant as woman; E440+. Ghost laid by axe; E642. Reincarnation as stone; G11.10. Cannibalistic spirits; G441. Ogre carries victim in bag (basket); G519.2+. Ogre killed with own weapon; R11. Abduction by monster (ogre); R45.3. Captivity in cave; S110. Murders

Why are Cassowaries and Dogs Enemies?

(Wantok 847, September 27, 1990, page 20)

Long, long ago, in the time of the ancestors, dogs and cassowaries were very good friends. In one place inside **Simbu** Province, there lived a cassowary and her three children.

They lived with a dog inside a house. They lived very well. There was no anger or anything that came to break this friendship. They lived for a while, then one day, the dog went to the garden and fetched some food.

Covetousness

The dog cocked the food well, then left it in the house. The dog walked and walked into the forest to find some wild game to eat with the food.

When the dog left the house, only the cassowary and her three children were there. The mother cassowary saw the food on the fire and desired it greatly. Quietly, she walked towards the fire and took the food. She gave it to her children, and they ate.

She thought that the dog would not be angry because they had lived together for a long time and the dog would not get angry over this small thing.

However, this thinking did not bring forth food when the dog arrived. The dog returned from the forest when it was nearly afternoon. The dog had not eaten in the morning and it felt famished.

The dog went up the house and saw that the food on the fire was not there. The dog was completely furious. The dog knew that it was just the cassowary and her three children who had eaten the food.

Killing You

The dog did not speak. The dog lay very quietly in the corner of the house, waiting for the mother cassowary and three children to come. Afterwards, they arrived. They argued and argued, then they were about to fight.

The cassowary told the dog, "That's OK. I'll run away with my three children into the forest. You can live alone here. Now you know. When you come to the forest, I'll chase and kill you."

However, the dog was not troubled by what the cassowary had said. The cassowary and the three children walked into the forest, then the dog shouted behind them, "Do you hear this? You're vain about those damn long legs of yours."

The cassowary did not forget what the dog said. So now, we see that when dogs chase cassowaries, the cassowaries use their long [legs] to kick the dogs. Also, dogs and cassowaries are great enemies nowadays. Today, dogs rule the village and cassowaries rule the forest.

Sali Yuika

Simbu Province

A2433.4+. Why cassowary lives in forest; A2494.4.12+. Enmity between cassowary and dog; B211.1.7. Speaking dog; B211.3.17K. Speaking cassowary; P230. Parents and children; P310. Friendship; R213. Escape from home; W116. Vanity; W195. Envy

A Brother and Sister Committed Incest

(Wantok 848, October 4, 1990, page 17)

Long, long ago, there was a brother and sister who lived by Kimbe, in the area of a big mountain [**Xarua** People, **West New Britain** Province]. The name of the big brother was Kauringi, and the sister's name was Saumbali. They lived by themselves because no one thought of them.

They usually did things for themselves. The young men would look at Saumbali and they would lust for her.

However, they were afraid of her because she was a strong woman, as strong as her own brother was.

One time, her brother asked her to go make a new garden with him. The sister agreed with him. When it was still early morning, they awoke and cooked some sweet potatoes for themselves to eat. They took these for when they would be hungry in the garden.

Working Hard

When it became lighter, they went out of their house quietly and walked towards the place where they wanted to make the garden. They arrived and worked hard at cutting trees and clearing scrub. They burned the brush, then the garden area became a very good place for planting food.

While they were working in the garden, Kauringi had a bad thought about his sister. Because his sister was very beautiful, men often lusted for her. So, he thought of marrying his sister. Saumbali worked and worked, then she became very thirsty for water. She asked her brother if he would let her go down to the stream to drink.

Her brother agreed, then she walked to where the stream was. When she arrived at the stream, she removed her "grass" skirt and put it down. She went down to the stream and bathed enthusiastically.

Before long, her brother arrived at the stream and saw his sister bathing. He told her that they would marry. Saumbali just got up and went out of the stream. She told her brother that it was all right, that they could marry.

After this, they married and lived very well together. They raised many children. The children married among themselves, and multiplied. Then this village became very large and it is still there.

Daniel Togi
Kimbe
West New Britain Province

A991+. Origin of particular village; F610.0.1. Remarkably strong woman; P210. Husband and wife; P230. Parents and children; P253. Sister and brother; T415.5. Brother-sister marriage

Tears Turned into the Porap River

(Wantok 849, October 11, 1990, page 21)

Long ago, in the Awangu [Avenggu] area on the Finschhafen [Peninsula] of **Morobe** Province, there lived two brothers [**Tobo** People]. Their names were Glon and Molonget. The brothers lived in a village called **Zamolo**, near Awangu.

One time, the bright sun rose in the sky, and the little brother spoke about eating wild game. So the big brother told him, "Don't worry. Tomorrow morning, we'll go hunting for game for you."

At night, a bright moon rose. They began to prepare their bows and arrows, and their food to eat in the forest. In the early morning, they awoke, took their things, and walked into the forest. In the forest, they began to hunt for wildfowl eggs at the bases of all of the banana plants and trees where they thought there would be wildfowls.

Stolen Baby

They hunted for a while, then they arrived at the home of a ghost woman. They approached and heard the sound of water. They saw the ghost woman bathing and putting up her baby.

The little brother saw the baby and told his big brother, "I'll steal her baby, then we'll run back to the house." However, the big brother insisted that he could not take the baby. They spoke for a while, then the little brother took the baby and they turned back towards the house.

The ghost woman finished bathing, then she went up to get her baby. She searched, but the baby was not there. The ghost woman sniffed everywhere, then followed the brothers and arrived at their house.

The poor woman cried terribly, then she told the brothers to give back her baby. However, the little brother did not want to do this. He blocked her, then the big brother became angry, took a marsupial (*kapul*) bone and killed the baby. Afterwards, they sent the baby down, and the mother took the baby to her house.

When she was about to give her breast to the baby, she saw that the baby was dead. The poor woman wailed and wailed. Her tears became a big river. This river is called Porap.

Later, she took her kin and went to fight with the two brothers, and to ruin everything of theirs. The water ran and ran, then arrived at **Puleng** and Malandung [**Melandum**] villages, in the Kabwum area [**Komba** People].

Pelle M. Levo
Boroko
National Capital District

A934.11. River from transformation; D457.18.2. Transformation: tears to river; E261.4. Ghost pursues man; E425.1.4. Revenant as woman carrying baby; P230. Parents and children; P251.5. Two brothers; Q211. Murder punished; Q595. Loss or destruction of property as punishment; R10.3. Children abducted; R260. Pursuits; S110. Murders

Kwasia Gave Birth to the Wantoat People

(Wantok 850, October 18, 1990, page 18)

Long, long ago, there were no men who lived in a small village called **Yopbukan** in the **Wantoat** [People's] area, **Morobe** Province. In this village, there was no one except two brothers who lived there after all of the other people had died.

The big brother's name was Kwano and the little brother's was Ngasi. At this time, the brothers were farmers. In their garden, there was much grass growing, and there was no one to weed.

Whenever they would see this, they would be sorry for themselves because the grass was growing closer to the house. The grass was growing in their garden and every place that was theirs.

Beginning at this time, they talked about who would clean all this trash and grass. One time, they went and stayed in the garden until the afternoon.

They walked on the trail for a while, then the little brother told his big brother, "We often work hard, but who will clean of all our land?" The big brother replied, "That's true. Brother, I'm sorry for us because there are no women to help and to clean all of these places."

That night, they cooked, ate and slept. A bird-woman *masalai* was there at this time and she heard everything that they had said. They slept that night, then the *masalai* woman went and told all of her woman pals, and then she went to clean the brothers' garden.

In the early morning, the brothers cooked sweet potatoes and ate. Later, they walked and walked to the garden to finish off the grass that they had left there on the previous afternoon.

When they arrived in the garden, their eyes popped open because everything was cleaned. Oh my, were the brothers happy. They did not think of doing any work that day. In the afternoon, they went to the trail and said the same thing about who would clean the house.

In the evening, they ate and slept. Late at night, the *masalai* women came and did all of the work of cleaning the house, washing the plates, and cooking the food.

In the very early morning, they awoke and saw that the house was completely different. Everything was ready for them to eat. They stayed there for a while, then the little brother told the big brother, "Let's pretend to go home, then we'll turn back to the garden and see who it is that does our work."

They thought that it would be bad if their kin who had died heard what they had said and that the kin had come to help them. The little brother hid carefully. He saw little birds come and sit on top of a tree in the middle of the garden. Before long, they flew down and changed into young women, then they did the brothers' work.

He saw a nice woman approach. He wanted to grab her but he thought hard because he had to tell his big brother first. It was very dark and he just lay there looking at her. He kept his eyes open until dawn. In the very early morning, the bad boy ran back to the house and told his brother what had happened.

The next day, the big brother told him, "Stay here so I can go see."

Oh my, when the big brother saw this, his eyes also opened wide and he thought, "How can I take one of them?" He sat there and a woman walked towards him, then she left her wings nearby.

The scoundrel got up and took her wings. Near dawn, all of the women took their wings and flew away. The poor woman could not find her wings, so she cried. The cad held her and took her to the house in the early morning. His little brother saw this and was very happy.

The little brother asked her, "What's your name?" She said that her name was *Kwasia*, meaning "bird of paradise." Now, if you go there, you will see very many people in this little village of Yopbukan. This is because Paradise [Kwasia] scavenged [gave birth to] real children who went out to the other areas, such as Wantoat.

Ya-ap Bunning
Morobe Province

A1611+. Origin of Wantoat People; B631. Human offspring from marriage to animal; B652. Marriage to bird in human form; D150+W. Transformation: woman to bird of paradise; D350+W. Transformation: bird of paradise to woman; F401.3.7. Spirit in form of a bird; F490+. Masalai; P251.5. Two brothers; P310. Friendship; R10. Abduction; T111. Marriage of mortal and supernatural being; T192. Marriage by force

A *Masalai* Baby Killed Pigs

(Wantok 851, October 25, 1990, page 23)

Long ago, there was a good family that lived in **Munum** Village in the Markham [Valley] of **Morobe** Province [**Wampar** People].

In this family, there were two young sisters. One nice afternoon, the sisters talked about getting bamboo tubes to fill with water. The stream was in the forest, fairly far from the village.

So, they fetched some bamboos. They filled the bamboos with water, then they walked back to the village. At the trail midpoint, they saw an old man sitting in the middle of the trail and waiting for them.

They approached him, then the old man asked for a drink of water. The old man finished off all of the water in the two bamboos. So, they turned back to the stream to fill the bamboos with water again.

They went back to the midpoint and saw an old man again. This old man looked like the first man that they had met who had finished their water.

This old man also asked to drink the water. They did not turn. They looked at the old man and just told him, "You just drank our water."

The old man told them, "That old man who asked you before must have been your grandpa. I myself just came from the garden and caught my breath sitting on the trail."

The two women listened and were sorry for the old man, and then they gave the bamboos of water to him again. The old man finished both bamboos, then they returned to the river.

This time, they did not meet any more men. They walked back towards the house and saw a yam (*mami*) growing by the trail. They put their water down, then they began to dig the yam.

Before long, they heard a baby crying underneath the ground. They dug and dug, then they saw a baby. Oh my, their hearts were elated.

They took this boy and went to the house, then they hid him well inside their room. When they wanted to eat, they would give time to one of them to check on the baby.

They did this for a while, then one time, their father found out what was happening. By then, then baby had grown bigger, so they took the baby out and they all ate together.

One day, they all woke up in the very early morning. They cooked food, ate, and then prepared to go work in the garden. They walked and walked, to the garden, but the baby did not want to do this. He cried and wanted to stay back at the house.

The two sisters were furious. They grabbed the baby and carried him, then they all went to the garden. They hung the baby up in a net bag, then they worked in the garden. The sun rose higher. Then they removed the net bag and went outside.

He went out and turned into a big man who was strong enough to do work. He ran back to the village and killed all of the pigs that they husbanded.

Later, he sped back and jumped into the net bag as a little child, then he went to sleep. In the afternoon, they all returned to the village. The father went first and found out

that all of the pigs in the village were dead. Oh my, he was completely furious.

At night, they ate then he told his family, "We'll hide one of us back at the village to see who it is that killed and ate our pigs."

They made their decision then they went to sleep. In the early morning, they awoke and sent the little brother up a tree. The little brother would hide and see who would kill their pigs.

The sisters, their baby, and the other members of the family took their things and began walking to the garden. However, the baby in the net bag did not want to go the garden and he began to cry.

This time, the baby cried very loudly. The sisters relented and hung him up in a net bag inside the house, then they went to the garden. The baby stayed inside the house alone.

They all went to work in the garden and the baby did the same thing. He went out of the net bag and out of the house. This time, he looked just like a big man. He killed the pigs and ruined everything in the village. The little brother sitting on top of the tree saw everything that happened.

When it was nearly afternoon, the big man went into the house, turned into a little boy and jumped into the net bag. He heard the sound of the people of the house returning, so he pretended to sleep.

That night, after eating, the little brother told the story of what he had seen during the day. He told the father and the other members of the family, such as the mother, the brother and the two sisters.

The other members of the family were furious at the two sisters because the sisters had brought the baby, and now he had caused them many problems.

The next morning, they all awoke and took the deceitful big baby to the garden. He cried, but they did not care about this. They took him to a bad place, and tricked him onto a seesaw or rope swing. The two women pretended to push him back and forth, then they pushed him right down into the bad [i.e., rocky] place. The trick baby died in this bad place.

All of them were happy and they went back to the village. After this, all of the pigs lived well and no enemies came to them.

Robert Jang
Lae
Morobe Province

D213+M. Transformation: man to yam; D431.9+C. Transformation: yam to child; D1880. Magic rejuvenation; D1890. Magic aging; F321.1. Changeling; K855. Fatal swinging game; K1930. Treacherous impostors; P210. Husband and wife; P231. Mother and son; P232. Mother and daughter; P233. Father and son; P234. Father and daughter; P250. Brothers and sisters; P252.1. Two sisters; P272. Foster mother; P275. Foster son; Q211.6. Killing an animal revenged; Q262. Impostor punished; Q411. Death as punishment; S110. Murders; T545. Birth from ground

Brothers Killed a *Masalai* from Salamaua
(Wantok 852, November 1, 1990, page 19)

Long, long ago, in Hotec [**Hote**] Village, in the Salamaua area, there lived two brothers [**Morobe** Province, **Hote** People]. The name of the big brother was Habueng and the name of the little brother was Mokloveng. They lived there with the other people of the village.

One day, the big brother spoke about breaking from the village because a *masalai* woman named Sevolok was going around the Salamaua area, killing and eating people.

The people of many other nearby villages tried to fight with Sevolok, but she would win and kill all of them. The *masalai* woman did this for a while, and the number of men in the village became few.

One day, the *masalai* woman discovered that she had killed and eaten many men from the other villages, but that she had not yet become the enemy of Hotek [Hote] Village. So, she sped along the trail towards this village.

When everyone of Hotek Village heard that the *masalai* woman was coming to kill them, they were terrified. Sevolok came and made her camp in a part of the forest that we call Lemkupick Bok Me E.

Everyone was afraid and just stayed in the village. They would go to look for food during the day, then when evening arrived, they would all go inside the houses and shut the doors. Not one of them would come out when the first night bird sang. All of them were afraid together.

One night, the two brothers, Habueng and Mokloveng, argued back and forth, then they came together in thinking of trying to fight with the *masalai* woman. In the very early morning, they awoke, then walked and walked to the place where Sevolok was living. They spied upon the *masalai* woman's camp, then they returned to the house.

They went and cut betel nut palms, and other strong trees, then they made new spears. They made many of them, then they prepared other things for fighting. When the sun was about to set, everything was ready. Afterwards, they ate and went to sleep.

The next day, they awoke and carried all of their fighting equipment to the place where the *masalai* woman was living. At exactly noon, they arrived at Sevolok's camp and walked very quietly towards her. They did not want to make a sound because they knew that the *masalai* woman was sleeping at this time.

The brothers looked up to the house. They saw Sevolok's hair hanging and going beneath the house. When they saw this, Habueng and Mokloveng had the idea that Sevolok's strength came from her long hair. This would be the way to kill her and to save themselves and the people of Salamaua.

They quickly sped into the forest, then cut a tall tree. In the front of this tree, they made a hook for hooking up fruit on trees. They carried the tree away and pulled all of the *masalai* woman's hair with this tree. The brothers then they tied up all of Sevolok's hair very well.

The brothers prepared well, then they pulled a part of the tree on which they had tied the *masalai* woman's hair. All of Sevolok's hair came loose and flew down to the ground. Sevolok got up, looked down and saw the brothers standing there. She shouted, "Too bad, my two nice animals are there. I'm hungry now and I'm going to eat you."

When she approached, Habueng just threw his spear and missed. Then his little brother, Mokloveng, threw a spear directly into Sevolok's breast. Sevolok fell down, then rolled and rolled down the mountain. The brothers followed her down and cut her into tiny pieces. The brothers left her, then walked away. When they arrived at the top of the first mountain, this woman got up and rejoined herself then followed them. When the brother saw this, they stood and waited for her. When Sevolok approached, Habueng missed her again, but Mokloveng's spear stuck to her body.

The brothers killed her and left her there, then they walked away to **Busekom** Village. At this place, the sun was setting and it was becoming dark. The little brother spoke at this place, then the pond swelled and overflowed, surrounding them. They slept at this place until dawn.

In the morning, they left Busekom. Sevolok came and smelled the place where they had slept, and she cried. She said, "Too bad, my two animals, where are you now?" The *masalai* woman shouted loudly again and followed the brothers to **Osavi-Bukom** Village. This was a village where men had died before. The brothers heard birds crying and they knew that it was just Sevolok.

The brothers called the village's name and said, "You're famous, Osavi-Bukom. Hold the ghost of Sevolok, the *masalai* woman, here and we shall kill her." Immediately after they said this, Sevolok arrived. She saw them and shouted, "Aha... my animals." The brothers replied,

"Sevolok, you've killed many thousands of people. Now we'll kill you at Osavi-Bukom Village, then you'll be finished."

The brothers threw two strong spears directly at the *masalai* woman. When the spears stuck to the *masalai* woman's body, they shouted for the ground to open, then Sevolok fell down inside.
The brothers turned their backs, then they broke the news to the village. After this, the people appointed the brothers as the leaders of the village.

Yawising Tekosaki

Box 98

Gerehu

N. C. D. [National Capital District]

A515.1. Culture heroes brothers; A1011. Local deluges; B143.1. Bird gives warning; D1774. Magic results from speaking; D1831. Magic strength resides in hair; E30. Resuscitation by arrangement of members; F490+. Masalai; F555.3. Very long hair; F942.1. Ground opens and swallows up person; G219.4. Witch with very long hair; G221.1. Strength of witches in hair; G275.8. Hero kills witch; G346. Devastating monster; G510.4+. Hero overcomes devastating ogre; G512.1+. Ogre killed with spear/arrow; P251.5. Two brothers; Q211. Murder punished; Q411. Death as punishment; R260. Pursuits; S110. Murders; S139.7. Murder by slicing person into small pieces; Z210. Brothers as heroes

Patfon Originated from a Chicken-Pig

(Wantok 85[3], November 8, 1990, page 19)

This ancestor story comes from Kerasob [**Kevasop**] Village on Karkar Island, **Madang** [Province, **Takia** People]. Long, long ago, our ancestors on Karkar Island made a huge garden in Tapilan [Kevasop] Village. They awoke in the early morning and cleared this area. Afterwards, they made a fence and began planting food.

Many months later, the food was ready and the people went and harvested it. However, at the same time, the pigs also went inside the garden from the other side and ruined the food. The real owner of the garden did not know that this was happening.

One morning, he went around and checked on the food in the garden. He arrived on the other side and was surprised to see that all of the food on this other side was completely ruined. The pigs had broken the earth and cast about the food.

When he checked on the fence, there were no holes. The fence was high, so he did not know how the pigs had gotten inside. The poor man thought hard and returned to the village. He met with all of the strong men of the village then he told them what had happened. All of them made

their decision then prepared their bows and arrows. They thought of going and keeping watch by the garden at night.

At night, they all went to the garden and watched. The sun was completely hidden and the ancestors did not make any noises. They just sat quietly with hands on their bows and arrows as they kept watch.

Before long, they heard crashing. They were shocked to see a big, white chicken flying closer and going inside the garden fence. Quickly, it landed and became a pig. Afterwards, it broke the earth then ate taros and leafy greens inside the garden.

All of the strong men of the village saw this, then [their] bones began to tremble. Not one of them had any more strength. All of them talked pointedly to each other about throwing away the arrows. They did this, then one of them threw his spear. The spear stuck to the side of the pig's leg. The pig felt it immediately and transformed back into the white chicken, then it flew past the fence. It flew and flew, then it landed fairly far from the garden.

The old men followed with their spears, but there was no chicken lying there. They just saw a boulder. They tried to shove the boulder down the mountain, but the boulder did not budge. It was late at night. They all felt hungry and exhausted, so they left this boulder there and went back to the village.

When the men arrived at the village, the story of the chicken and pig broke. All of the villagers heard about it and went to gather at the chief's house. They sent a message to the strong men of the other villages to come and bring sticks to dig the earth at the place where the boulder was located.

They broke the ground by the boulder until evening, then they removed it from the ground. They shoved it down the mountain, but when the boulder fell down the mountain, a tremendous noise came forth. The sound of this noise was like a volcano exploding. A fierce wind also arose. The people of the Madang mainland heard this and thought that a volcano was exploding. However, it was not the case. Everyone was happy and returned to the village. They made a big feast to celebrate the people from the other villages.

In the early morning, the owner of the large garden wanted to go see his garden, but now he saw the boulder lying on top of his place. He sped back breathlessly to the village. The garden owner told everyone, then they went to see.

When they arrived, the women went and dug the earth by the boulder. Afterwards, they planted nice flowers. The news went to all of the parts of the island, and people came to see this boulder. The leaders of the villages gathered and gave the name *Patfon* to this boulder. This means, "The stone came back and is at its place."

This stone is still there, and I have seen it. The name of this village has also changed from Tapilan to Patfon.

Sternmphil K. Balifon
Karkar Island
Madang Province

A977.5. Origin of particular rock; A16.7. Origin of place-name; B872.8K. Giant rooster; D412.3+. Transformation: swine to chicken; D413+. Transformation: chicken to swine; D423.5K2. Transformation: fowl to rock; D931. Magic rock (stone); D1641.2. Stones remove themselves; D2142.1. Wind produced by magic

A Brother-In-Law Was Jealous and Killed a Little Boy

(Wantok 85[4], November 15, 1990, page 19)

Long, long ago, in a small village on top of a mountain, there lived two children whose mother and father had died. The girl was a little older, so she took care of her little brother. They lived well for a while, then the sister thought of marrying. She told her little brother, "I'll leave you and go to a village where I can find a man to marry."

The sister thought of how her little brother could live well until he was big enough to find his own food. She had an idea, then dug a hole and made a small house underground.

Afterwards, she fetched all of the food from inside their garden and gave it to her little brother inside the house. In the early morning, she left her little brother and walked away to the village.

Beginning at this time, his sister forgot completely about him. She lived very happily and forgot about her brother inside the little house.

Her brother lived underground for a while, then the food was finished. At this time, the poor boy had grown up entirely. So when he went outside, he thought of finding food and his big sister.

He did not just think about where his sister had gone. Long ago when his parents were alive, he had seen his father shooting a multi-pronged arrow to find whatever he wanted.

The poor boy thought and thought, then he just thought that he would take a bow and shoot upwards, then wherever the multi-pronged arrow went, he would just follow it.

The little boy did not think of where he was following the arrow, so he found his sister. When his sister saw him, she ran directly to him, then she held him and cried.

His sister thought that the boy must have died, but it was not the case. The boy had lived well in the hole that she had made. His sister was very happy to see him, but his brother-in-law did not like this boy living with them in his house.

One time, the brother-in-law made some preparations to kill the poor little boy. The sister saw the various things that her husband was doing to the little boy were not right in her mind, but what could she do? His brother-in-law often just scolded him and found many malicious things to do to him.

One morning, the brother-in-law took the little boy and went to the garden. In the garden, there was a big hole where he thought of killing the little boy.

He took the boy down to the hole and gave him many sugarcanes to drink. He also sang and danced for a while, then the little boy slept.

When the boy was asleep, he ran up to the top and blocked the opening of the hole. Then he called out for the *masalai*s to come and kill the boy.

Then the *masalai*s came; they killed and ate the boy. A flying fox saw this and told his sister to go and see something in her husband's garden.

When the sister arrived, she saw that her little brother had been eaten by the *masalai*s and that only his head was by the hole. She cried terribly and jumped down into the hole, then she too died.

[Anonymous]

B211.2.11K+. Speaking flying fox; D1314.1. Magic arrow indicates desired place; D1781. Magic results from singing; D1781+. Magic results from dancing; D1964. Magic sleep induced by certain person; F490+. Masalai; F771.3.5. Underground house; G10. Cannibalism; M451.1. Death by suicide; P253+. Sister commits suicide on death of brother; P263. Brother-in-law; R4. Surprise capture; S55+. Cruel brother-in-law; S110. Murders; S146.2. Abandonment in cave; S211. Child sold (promised) to devil (ogre); W181. Jealousy

A Snake Married a Woman from Sialum

(Wantok 855, November 22, 1990, page 19)

In **Gitua** Village, by Sialum Patrol Post, on the Finschhafen Peninsula of **Morobe** Province, there was a big lake [**Gitua** People]. The fish were just packed there, and not one man or woman from the village had found out about this because the lake was a *masalai* place and the people were afraid to go nearby.

In this village, there lived a man and his family. The man's daughter was better than the other young women of the village were, so many young men would keep their eyes on her. One time, the sun had been very bright and all of the streams were nearly desiccated. All of the fish, eels, and crayfish were dying.

The family of this beautiful young woman stayed there for a while, then they thought of hunting for fish, eels, and crayfish in the *masalai* lake. All of the young woman's kin went and she was alone in the house. After two days passed, the woman thought, "I've been here in the house for a long time. I think I'll follow papa and the others to the lake, then I'll bathe too. Afterwards, we can all return together." She took her net bag and cast ahead, following the other family members to the lake.

However, the sun was bright and it baked the trail that she was taking to the other side of the water. She looked around the water and saw that nothing was moving. The water was lying sadly, and the young woman thought again, "No man or woman shall see me here. I think I'll bathe and remove the dirt from my body." (She was menstruating.) "Later, I can go to the house and sleep, waiting for papa and the others." She went to the beach by the water, removed her net bag and "grass" skirt, then she jumped into the water. The water was terribly cold, so the youth did not think of anything else.

After a fairly long time, she felt terribly cold. She jumped up to the beach, tied on her skirt, threw her net bag back on her head, then went back to the village. In the evening, the father, the rest of her family, and the other families of the village returned. They cooked all of the game from the water that they had found, then they exchanged the food with other families and ate happily. A very nice moon was lit and the village was completely clear. So, they did not think that anything bad would happen or that enemies would come.

The beautiful young woman ate crayfish, fish and eels, then she forgot completely about what she had done during the day. The father was very happy to see his wife and daughter eat well. So, he just sat quietly, took out his betel nuts and lime [calcium oxide], then he chewed with gusto. It was late at night now, everyone in the village went to sleep. The mother and children went to sleep, then their father shut the door. Afterwards, he pulled a piece of tobacco from a net bag, lit it, then brought it to where he sat at his sleeping place. He wanted to sleep quietly, so he drew at his tobacco until the strength of the tobacco kicked in and he would sleep until dawn.

When the father's eyes were nearly shut, he heard a noise that sounded like a man walking closer, then standing outside the house door. He got up very quietly, made the fire bigger, and then opened the house door. The leader [father] looked outside and was shocked to see a gigantic python lying there. The head of the snake came and blocked the door while his tail lay on the ground. The middle of the snake was exactly like a python.

The leader saw this and very quietly went back to sit at the place where he slept. He thought hard about why this snake had come to sleep outside the house door like this. Later, he awakened all of his kin inside the house. He told them what had happened, and not to scream or shout. They all looked outside and saw that the snake was still lying there. They made the fire bigger, then the father of the family began asking the snake, "Did you come to destroy this village?" The snake did not reply. He just lay there quietly and turned his head. Then the man asked all of the other questions, such as whether he had come to ruin the family, whether he wanted to eat, and other things. However, to all of these questions, the snake just turned his head and did not speak.

Then the leader told the snake, "I've called out everything that we have here. Now, exactly what do you want?" When the leader said this, the snake shoved his tongue out and stared at the young daughter. The father saw this and asked the snake again, "Do you want my daughter?" Then the snake threw his head, and made a noise with his body from his head all of the way down to his tail to show that he was happy.

The father turned back and asked his daughter, "What did you do during the day?" Then the young woman told the story to her father of what she had done. The father told her, "You made a mistake. You must go with this snake. If you don't go, the snake will destroy the whole village and kill all of us." The woman cried and followed the snake towards the water. At the lake, the snake turned and the woman held tightly onto the snake's tail. They went down into the water and swam towards the center. The woman thought that she would drown, but she did not.

They arrived at the *masalai*'s house, then he changed his body and became a very handsome, young and tall boy. The woman saw this and was no longer afraid. She was elated and married the *masalai*, then they lived together. The next day, everyone from the village came and gathered by the lake to watch. They did not see anything, so they turned back to the village. The woman's mother and the other women of the village cried as they returned to the village. The married couple lived in the lake for a while, then the woman gave birth to a son. The *masalai* was elated, so he gathered various kinds of game, both from the land and the water. After this, he gathered the food from the garden, then took his wife and son to the village. They arrived late at night when everyone was asleep.

They gathered all of the food and game outside the house, then the snake told his wife and son, "You can stay and celebrate with the people of the village. I'm going back home. Afterwards, you can come." Then he left. In the morning, the woman's father awoke and was shocked to see his daughter and grandson sitting outside the house with an enormous amount of food. He called out for everyone of the village to come, then they had a huge feast. Afterwards, his daughter and grandson wanted to return to their underwater home. In return, all of the villagers brought plenty of food and game for them to take. This custom began at this time, and has gone on for very many years.

However, the work of the mission came strongly to the area and stopped this custom, so it is no longer practiced.

Jimmy Lingu
Number 1592, Box 147
Popondetta
Oro Province

B212. Animal understands human speech; B631. Human offspring from marriage to animal; B656.1. Marriage to python in human form; B875.1. Giant serpent; C141. Tabu: going forth during menses; C954. Person carried off to other world for breaking tabu; D391B. Transformation: serpent (snake) to boy; F420.1.3.9. Water-spirit as snake; F421. Lake-spirit; F490+. Masalai; F562.3. Residence in (under) water; P210. Husband and wife; P231. Mother and son; P232. Mother and daughter; P233. Father and son; P234. Father and daughter; P291. Grandfather; T111. Marriage of mortal and supernatural being; T580. Childbirth; V331. Conversion to Christianity

Uiac Found Wild Game
for the People of Kaiapit

(Wantok 856, November 29, 1990, page 17)

Long, long ago, there was a man who lived in a small village in **Morobe** Province. The name of the village is Inzi [**Intsi**], in the Kaiapit District [**Adzera** People].

The man's name was Uiac. Uiac was the best at hunting for wild game in the Kaiapit area at this time. He often killed many animals, such as pigs, and he shared them with the people of the village.

One nice day, Uiac thought of going to hunt for game. He took multi-pronged spears and his dog, then he walked into the forest. He walked and walked, then he climbed a big mountain. He arrived at the top of the mountain and looked around. At this time, the dog left him and went to hunt for game on the other side of the mountain.

Uiac kept looking around, then he walked beneath the mountain. At this time, there was a gigantic snake that was dreaming of Uiac. Poor Uiac did not know this. He approached, then the snake opened its eyes. Uiac saw this and stood directly under the snake. There was nothing he could do. Quickly, the huge snake straightened itself out, then leapt down and wrapped itself around Uiac's neck.

Uiac and the snake fought and fought, then Uiac had no more strength. He gave up and fell down, lying on a big mat. The snake saw this and put its tongue into Uiac's nose. However, Uiac quickly shut off his nose and opened his eyes wide, as if he was dead. At the same time, he found a big stick nearby that he could break.

When the snake squeezed Uiac to break his bones, Uiac broke the big stick. The snake heard this and thought that it was Uiac's bone that had broken.

The snake left Uiac, then went to find wild taro inside the forest. The snake ate the wild taro to make its throat moist, then it returned to swallow Uiac.

When the snake had gone into the forest, Uiac immediately took his axe and knife to his side, then he waited. He waited for the big snake to return, then he would kill it.

The snake thought that it had killed Uiac. After it ate the wild taro, it sped back to the place where it had left Uiac. The snake went back and forth, trying to find Uiac.

Quietly, Uiac went behind the snake and cut it with his axe and knife. The snake broke into two pieces, then rolled about and died.

Uiac was elated and spoke mockingly on top of the snake's body, "I've been coming to hunt for game for a very long time. Then you tried to do the same to me. Your time is over. Now is my time and you're just lying there. Now you're going on top of a fire. It's time for me to eat you."

Uiac walked back to the village to eat the snake. When he arrived at the village, all of the snake meat was gone. He just carried the head into the village. The people were surprised to see him.

They ran to him and asked, "Where's the snake's tail? You just carried the head to the village." Uiac said, "We fought, then I ate its tail. So, I just brought its head for you to see and eat."

At this time, the people of the village understood the good help and support that Uiac had given them. They took a nice young woman and gave her for Uiac to marry. Uiac married this young woman, then they lived happily together.

Alex Wabson
Kaiapit
Lae
Morobe Province

B11.11+. Fight with giant snake; B875.1. Giant serpent; D1810.8.2. Information received through dream; K1860. Deception by feigned death (sleep); P210. Husband and wife; T100. Marriage

Kevasob [Kevasop] Village
in Madang Province

(Wantok 857, December 6, 1990, page 19)

Long, long ago, there lived an excellent wild game hunter. His name was Nges Tamol. He often hunted for game, then he would share it with everyone in a village in Madang [Province]. Everyone of this village was usually very happy with him.

In this village, there also lived an old woman and her two children. Their father had died. The poor threesome often worked very hard at obtaining food and meat. Many times, they slept hungry.

One day, Nges Tamol again traveled in the forest to hunt for game. He began when it was still early morning. When the sun rose, the boy sat right next to a big tree and rested. Before long, he heard his dog barking. Nges Tamol got up and sped away. He was shocked to see a gigantic python lying there.

Nges' eyes popped open when he saw the gigantic python slither and move back slowly into his hole in the tree. When the snake went into the tree hole, the boy blocked it and tied up the tree hole, then he sped away to the village. He arrived and met the leading men and women, then he told them how to kill the snake. In the very early morning, when the first bird of dawn sang, all of the leading men awoke then carried their bows and arrows towards the base of this tree. All of the women shot off to the garden to find food for the party they would have in the afternoon when the men returned with the snake.

The men arrived at the base of the tree, then they began digging the earth, going downwards. They did this for a while, then they encountered a python. However, Nges told them that this was not the one. So, they kept digging down and they encountered many pythons in this hole. Nges told them to keep digging the earth, so they worked diligently and broke their backs. Before long, they met the giant python and grabbed him.

They tied it to a big log with ropes, then they brought him to the village. The men hung him up in a corner of the village, then waited for the food to become ready. However, when all of the men went to check on the women and the food, the giant python immediately turned into a man, then walked into the house of the old woman and her two children. The old woman was shocked and afraid to see this man. However, the man told her, "Don't be afraid of me. I came to help you." He told the old woman to take his head, middle and tail when the people of the village killed him.

After the snake-man said this, he went back into his snake body. In the afternoon, everyone in the village met and killed the python. The old woman went and took a piece of the middle, the tail, and the head of the python, then she went to her house. When the party was almost over, the clouds thundered and broke open at the place where the sun sets. A strong rain fell and the wind blew strongly inside the village.

Before long, a big river flooded and came to sweep everything away with the houses of the village. Not one scrap was left. The village was completely cleared. Only the old woman and her two children were left. There, the tail, middle and head of the snake became a real man again, and married the old woman. They all lived together and raised more children. From this came Kevasob [**Kevasop**] Village in **Madang** [Province], which is still there [**Takia People**].

Sternphil Blaifon [Balifon]
Ulamona
Kimbe
West New Britain Province

A991+. Origin of particular village; A1011. Local deluges; A1018. Flood as punishment; B875.1. Giant serpent; D191M. Transformation: man to serpent (snake); D391M. Transformation: serpent (snake) to man; D2142.1. Wind produced by magic; D2143.1. Rain produced by magic; D2149.1. Thunderbolt magically produced; D2151.8. Magic flood; E30. Resuscitation by arrangement of members; E656+. Reincarnation: snake to man; P210. Husband and wife; P230. Parents and children; P250. Brothers and sisters; P281. Stepfather; Q211.6. Killing an animal revenged; S110. Murders; T100. Marriage

A *Masalai* Man Killed a Mother and Baby

(Wantok 858, December 13, 1990, page 19)

Long, long ago, in the time of the ancestors, there was a village in **Morobe** Province. Inside this village, there lived a *masalai* man.

This *masalai* man would always sharpen a big stone. He did not just sharpen the stone. No, he always whistled while he sharpened the stone.

One day, a woman gave birth to a daughter in another nearby village. Everyone in the village heard about this and went to have a festival at this village. They only left the children back at the village.

Among the children were a young woman and her child. They lived alone in a house because the father and the first child had left to join the other people at the festival.

The children worked at gathering some eggs from trees, then they made little holes on top of them. After they sharpened sticks, they pushed them inside the little eggs or tree fruits. They would roll them on their hands and throw them on the ground. These things would twist on the ground and whistle.

The *masalai* man heard this and thought the children were copying his whistle. He left his home in the tree hole, then he walked to the village.

He arrived in the village and asked the children, "Why are you copying my whistle? Do you think I'm your boy?"

The boys replied, "We didn't copy your whistle. We're just boys. Go and check with the mother and her baby in the house. It would be bad if they copied you."

The *masalai* man went and checked on the mother and baby in the house. The two of them told him that they had not copied his whistle. So, the *masalai* man returned. The boys told him the same thing, sending him back to the mother and baby in the house.

After a while, the *masalai* man was furious. He went up to the house and killed the mother and baby. Afterwards, he removed all of the skin from their bodies. Then he put their bodies on top of the platform for smoking meat. After he did this, he ran back to his home near the village.

The people of the village were still singing and dancing passionately in the other village. However, the father and son thought about the mother and baby, so they walked back to the village.

They walked and walked back, climbing a very tall mountain. They stood on top of the mountain and saw the place where they hung up things.

The father and son saw a big tree in the forest. During yam season, this tree's leaves would all turn red and fall to the ground. They had the idea that the mother and baby must have met some kind of enemy in the village.

However, they did not worry. They sped away and arrived at the village. In the village, they went inside and saw that the mother and baby had died.

Quickly, they took palm leaves [sago or nipa] used for shingling, then they tied their legs and arms. After they tied the mother and baby's bodies well, they looked like very handsome people

They made a big fire and began to smoke the house. The smoke filled the house, then the bodies of the mother and baby awoke and cried. The mother and baby complained about the smoke from the fire, so the father removed it. Then the mother and baby came down from the place for smoking meat, and all of them lived happily together.

That is the end of my story. This stone that the *masalai* sharpened is still there. We boys often just hear this story, and we have not yet seen this big stone. Only the grandfathers and fathers have seen it when they traveled in the forest hunting for game.

Kethy Daunak

[M]orobe Province

A977. Origin of particular stones or groups of stones; D955. Magic leaf; D1812.5. Future learned through omens; E15+. Resuscitation by smoking; F401.6. Spirit in human form; F490+. Masalai; P210. Husband and wife; P231. Mother and son; P232. Mother and daughter; P233. Father and son; P250. Brothers and sisters; R220. Flights; S110. Murders; S139.2.2+. Corpse put into cooking pot or cooked; T580. Childbirth

The Salt Water from Aipidak Village, Enga [Province]
(Wantok 859, December 20, 1990, page 19)

Long, long ago, there were two brothers who lived in Enga Province, in the very deep forest. There were no women who lived with them, nor did they have a father or mother. They had a dog that was named Pete. [*Peté* means "lake" or "pond" in the Enga Language (Lang, 1973: 85).]

The big brother's name was Aipinakale [*aípí* means "salt" and *nakálé* means "door" (Lang, 1973: 1, 73)], and the little brother's name was Aipisai [*sái* means "crooked" or "left" and *saí* means "orchid" (Lang, 1973: 92)]. Every day, they would go into the forest and hunt for wild game to bring back, cook and eat. One day they took their dog to the forest to hunt for game. However, they did not find any. They returned to the house and ate the other meat that they had from before, that they had left there.

One day, Aipinakale wanted to go hunting for game in the very deep forest because all that was nearby was gone. In the afternoon, he revealed his thought to his little brother. When it was still early morning, they awoke and cooked food. Just before the big brother was ready to leave, Aipinakale told his little brother to watch the chickens that were standing by the house, "If you see the chickens hanging around down by the house, you'll know that I'm going around the forest OK. If the chickens hang around outside the house, you'll know that I'm lost in the forest." After he said this, he and the dog walked and walked along the trail into the deep forest.

The little brother waited at the house for two weeks and the big brother had not yet returned. He turned and saw the chicken and her chicks hanging outside their house. He saw this and knew that his big brother was lost in the forest. He cried and before long, their dog came running back. Aipisai knew that his big brother must have died, so he thought about going to find him the next day.

In the early morning, Aipisai prepared food, then he and the dog walked along the trail that his brother had taken. They walked and walked, then they arrived some-where and slept because it was now dark. The next morn-ing, they walked and walked, then arrived at another place. It was dark again, so they slept. The next day, they awoke and went to sleep at a third place. That night, the big brother came in a dream and told Aipisai that he had fallen in a big stony cave and that he had died.

In the morning, Aipisai and the dog arrived at this place, then Aipisai tried to remove his body from this cave, but it was very hard. He worked for a while unsuccessfully, then he began to cry again at the cave entrance. He put a pig on top of this cave, and he cut five of his fingers. The grease from the pig fell down into the cave, filling it com-pletely. Later, it turned into a big lake. The little brother took this water and drank it. It was not like other water be-cause it was tangy like saltwater.

The little brother made his house near the lake and he erected a dam to block the water. This water is still there, and many people come to take the water to cook with their food. This is a true story from **Aipidak** Village in **Enga** Province [**Enga** People].

Itipad Namol
Soasilum Community School
Wabag
Enga Province

A920.1.0.1. Origin of particular lake; B171. Magic chicken (hen, cock); D457+. Transformation: fat to lake; D1810.8.2. Information received through dream; D1812.5. Future learned through omens; E765.2. Life bound up with that of animal; P251.5. Two brothers; P681+. Mourning customs: self-mutilation; S161.1. Mutilation: cutting off fingers

The Brothers Themselves Created Deveperuga [Dereperengwa] Village

(Wantok 860, December 27, 1990, page 21)

Long, long ago, there was a family who lived in **Wegomangi** Village in **Simbu** Province. In this family, there were four children, all male, and their parents. Their names were Nungu, Babine, Sinbe and Nime. One time, their parents went to a very faraway place to hunt for wild game. The parents awoke in the early morning when the children were still sleeping and they left the village. The place where they wanted to go was not nearby. They would take two days to get there, then two days to return.

In the morning, the children awoke and saw that their parents were not there, so they themselves cooked food and prepared to travel during the day. The two elder sons asked them to go watch bird nests to try to find some birds. All of them agreed, then they took their things and walked away. When they arrived at a place for hunting birds, they told the two little brothers to stay and watch one bird's nest, while the two elders watched another. The little brothers watched for a while, then Nime's eyes became sleepy and he slept soundly. Sinbe watched and waited for Nime to take his place so that he could sleep too. Sinbe was completely knocked out by sleepiness, but Nime did not awake. Sinbe waited and waited, then he became completely tired and he beat Nime to waken him. Sinbe was shocked to see that Nime's body was cold and that his eyes had turned white. He cried terribly, then he ran to see his two elder brothers. Nungu and Babine were shocked and came out to find out what was the problem. The three of them ran and went to Nime's side, who was lying there lifelessly. They tried to see what had happened, but it was true that Nime had died in his sleep.

They cried terribly and carried Nime's body back to the village, then they put him inside the house. Their parents had not returned to the village yet. The three brothers just took the body and put it there well, then they tried to find out what was the real cause of their brother's death. They cut some wild sugarcanes (*pitpit*) and some *tanget* plants, then they put them on top of Nime's body.

They shoved a log by the side of Nime's body, then little Sinbe carried him. They carried Nime's body away and called the names of men to find out who it was that had killed Nime. When they called the name of a village leader, Nime's hand threw the *tanget* and wild sugarcane leaves up to show that this was the man's name.

The three brothers now knew, so they carried Nime's body to a bridge, then they went to the other side. When they arrived at the other side, they planted *tanget* plants on the other side of the river. They shouted back, "Now you'll live by yourselves and we'll live by ourselves. We lived well together but you people ruined us, so we'll live by ourselves."

The brothers went to live in this new village, which they called Dereperunga [**Dereperengwa**]. The people from the other village are [called] **Mior-Kipemukondiri** [**Chuave** People]. If you go to this area, you will see that Dereperunga Village does not have many people because many of them had died at this time.

James Miwa Nimo
Suave [Chuave]
Simbu Province

[Mr. Nimo retells this story in *Wantok* #862.]

A991+. Origin of particular village; D965+. Magic *tanget* plant (*Taetsia fructicosa*); D965+. Magic wild sugarcane; D1318.5.2+. Corpse moves when murderer's name announced; D1817.0.3. Magic detection of murder; D2061. Magic murder; P210. Husband and wife; P231. Mother and son; P233. Father and son; P251.6.2. Four brothers; R213. Escape from home

The Sepik River Headwaters in Enga

(Wantok 861, January 3, 1991, page 18)

Long, long ago, a boy and his sister lived in **Gulipyanda** Village, in **Enga** Province. Their father and mother had died when they were still little, so they lived by themselves. The boy's name was Itare Mata [Máta (Lang, 1973: 214)] and the girl's name was Yukyapae.

It was a very good time when Itare Mata told Yukyapae that he would go hunting for wild game in the deep forest. He told his sister to stay and watch the house.

However, the sister did not want to do this. She replied, "If I'm alone here, I'll be afraid. I don't want to stay. I want to come with you." However, Yukyapae's brother persisted and left her in the house, then he walked into the deep forest to hunt for game.

Yukyapae stayed alone in the house for a while. She did not know that a ghost man from the base of large tree near the house was spying upon her. One time, he got up and turned into her brother then came into the clearing. He stood and called out to Yukyapae, "Sister, I've returned. Come and see the game that I've killed." Yukyapae thought that it was really her brother so she said, "Itare Mata, you just left home for the deep forest. How did you kill these animals?"

However the ghost man replied, "I wanted to go into the deep forest, but just by the sword-grass lands of the mountain, there was plentiful game. So, I killed them quickly and turned back towards the village."

The ghost man continued talking and pretended to block one of his eyes. He told Yukyapae, "Sister, come quickly and remove the piece of rubbish from inside my eye." The woman thought that it was true, so she went close to the ghost man. The ghost man just grabbed Itare Mata's sister, then he laid her on the ground and raped her.

When everything was over, Yukyapae thought that it was really her brother who had done that to her, so she cried and said, "Aaah... I'm... your... sister. Aaaand... why... did... youuuuu... do... this... to... meeeee?" The ghost man replied, "I'm very sorry, my sister. After you said that, my thoughts have become clear. Something bad in the forest confused me, so I did this bad thing. So, stay here. I'll return to the forest and find some game, then we'll cook it in an earth oven and forget about what has happened." After the ghost man said this, he left Yukyapae.

However, the woman's thoughts were not clear because she thought it was really her brother who had done this to her, so she kept crying hard.

Before long, Itare Mata arrived. He carried very many animals and called out to his sister. However, Yukyapae did not reply. Itare Mata approached and saw that Yukyapae's face had changed completely, and that she was ashamed to look at him. He asked his sister, "Yukyapae, why are you angry at me? I didn't do anything bad to you."

Itare Mata tried to cheer up his sister, but he was unsuccessful. His sister's face was hardened. Yukyapae's brother tried this for a while, then he became furious and killed a huge pig of his. Itare Mata cooked the pig in an earth oven, then called for his sister to eat. However, Yukyapae replied, "Who cares about eating that rotten pig of yours? You can eat it yourself."

Itare Mata listened to what his sister had said, then he threw it away and was very worried. He thought of leaving his sister and running away to another place. His thoughts were stuck, so he spat out his last words, "Sister, what bad thing did I do to you, that you have done this to me? It's alright, you can live by yourself and I'll go to live by myself. Your small anger towards me has broken apart our good livelihood."

Itare Mata said this, then he took a piece of pig leg and walked down to the trail. The ground broke a little and the grease from the pig fell down, immediately turning into a lake.

Yukyapae slept for a while, then she did not hear any more noises. She knew that her brother had left the village.

She came out of the house and wanted to look down the trail, but at the place where the ground had broken, she saw a lake. In the middle of the lake stood her brother.

Yukyapae cried and sped down to the lake to try to hold Itare Mata. However, the strength of the water pushed her back to the ground. She did this for a while, but she could not reach him.

Then Yukyapae got up and ran back into the house. She gathered all of their belongings, then she brought them into the house. While she was inside, Yukyapae burned the house and everything else. Afterwards, she herself jumped into the fire and burned to a crisp.

This lake is still there and it looks as if it is the source of the Sepik River. We people of Enga usually call this body of water [Lake] Ivea. If you go to Enga Province, you will see this lake directly from the highway near **Sirunki** Police Station [**Enga** People].

Benjamin Yapson

C. I. S. [Corrective Institute Services] Boram

Wewak

East Sepik Province

D457+. Transformation: fat to lake; E425.2. Revenant as man; K1930. Treacherous impostors; M451.1. Death by suicide; P253. Sister and brother; P253+. Hostile sister and brother; R213. Escape from home; S125.1. Self-immolation; T415. Brother-sister incest; T471. Rape

How Did Dereperunga [Dereperengwa] and Mior-Kipemukondiri Break Apart?

(Wantok 862, January 10, 1991, page 18)

In the **Wegomangi** Clan House, in the East Elimbari [Erimbari] area of **Simbu** Province, there lived four brothers. The brothers' names were Yarume Nungu, Goro Babine, Sin Be and Nime. Nungu and Babine were the elder brothers. Sin and Nime were the younger brothers.

One day, their mother and father awoke in the very early morning and went to the area of Mount Elimbari to search for pandanus tree fruits (*karuka*). The mother and father decided to stay in the forest for about two days. Later, they would return to the village.

The children slept for a while, then they awoke in the morning. They saw that their father and mother were not there, so they knew that they must have gone into the forest. The elder brothers cooked sweet potatoes, and they all ate. After they ate, they thought about going to hunt for birds.

They took bows and arrows, then sped away into the forest. They went and went, then they watched nests that birds were building. The birds would come and rest on the nests to drink the water that they would gulp down.

The two elder brothers, Nungu and Babibe [Babine], went to keep watch on their own bird nests. The two little brothers watched just one bird's nest. They all kept watch for a while, then it became noontime.

The two little brothers kept watch, then Nime wanted to sleep. He fell dead asleep while Sin alone kept watch. Sin's eyes were hurting terribly for sleep, so he wanted to wake Nime.

However, he sat a little longer, then his eyes hurt like nothing else. He could not bear it, so he [tried to] wake up Nime. He tried waking him, but Nime did not awake. Then he put his ear close to Nime's chest. He could not hear his heart beating anymore.

He knew that his brother Nime was dead. He left everything and sped away to his big brothers' bird nests. They all went back and saw that the little brother was dead.

Oh my, they cried terribly and carried Nime's body back to the village. At the village, they found out that their father and mother had not yet returned. So, they told everyone from the other clan houses to come together, and they cried.

The three brothers had a great desire to find out who it was that had killed their little brother. Quickly, they cut some [wild sugarcanes (*pitpit*)] and covered the body. They told Sin to carry one end and they hung the other end from a tree hook.

The two elder brothers held a wild sugarcane with *tanget* leaves in their right hands. Then the two brothers called the names of all of the clan houses of the tribe.

Later, they carried the body into a clan house called, "Miyol Kinom." They called this name and beat the wild sugarcanes on top of Nime's body. Then the body began to move very slowly.

Quickly, they let go of the body, then went to the rattan bridge over the Kurubumabunom River. They buried the *tanget* leaves by the water.

They shouted to the other side, "Before, we two tribes [clans] lived together. However, you people performed sorcery and before long you'll finish off all of us. You've killed one of our young with your power, so we're cutting the rope and you can't come to our side."

At this time, the clan of the three [four] brothers, Nungu, Yarume, Babine, and Sin Be lived by themselves. They called themselves, Dereperunga [**Dereperengwa** Village, Chuave People]. The clan on the other side called themselves, **Mior-Kipemukondiri**.

If you travel there, you will see that Dereperunga is not a big clan because the people of Mior-Kipemukondiri had killed many of them by sorcery in the time of the ancestors.

James Miwa Nimo
Chuave
Simbu Province

[Mr. Nimo retells this story in *Wantok* #860.]

A991+. Origin of particular village; D965+. Magic *tanget* plant (*Taetsia fructicosa*); D965+. Magic wild sugarcane; D1318.5.2+. Corpse moves when murderer's name announced; D1817.0.3. Magic detection of murder; D2061. Magic murder; P210. Husband and wife; P231. Mother and son; P233. Father and son; P251.6.2. Four brothers; R213. Escape from home; S110. Murders

Yasa Killed the Old *Masalai* Man

(Wantok 863, January 17, 1991, page 22)

Long, long ago, in the time of the ancestors, there were four brothers who lived in **Kuligalire** Village, in the Ialibu area of **Southern Highlands** Province [**Kewa**, **Wiru** or **Hagen** People]. The names of these brothers were Yasa, Yawa, Kalunda and Mano.

Three of the brothers each had their own work to do. Yasa would just work in the garden. He never went into the forest. Kalunda was a marsupial (*kapul*) hunter. Mano was a man who husbanded pigs. He was also the spokesman for this family.

One time, Mano did not have bark to put on his body, so he went into the forest to search for some. Near Kuligalire Village, there is dense forest. The name of this part of the forest is Raga. Mano went to this forest.

He walked and walked, then he arrived in the middle of the forest. He searched for a kind of tree whose bark is useful, but he did not find one. After a while, he rested on a hill.

He rested for a while, then he heard a very nice song. He went and saw an old man sitting and singing passionately. The old man's skin and hair were red. Also, the man's house and everything else he used were red.

The old man saw Mano and welcomed him, "Hey! I'm happy that you heard my singing. I haven't seen a man for a long time. You're the first man to come here. Where do you live and where did you come from?"

Mano replied that he did not have tree bark, so he had come searching in the forest. The old man was elated and said that he would help Mano, "I have a plantation for tree bark deep inside the forest. Tomorrow, we'll go and you can take some bark. Tonight, you'll sleep with me and hear some nice songs first." Mano listened to what the old man said, then they slept.

Poor Mano did not know that this old man was lying and that he was a cannibal. The next day, they prepared to go to the plantation. The old man told Mano to go first to the house door, then outside. Mano walked away first, then he became hung up on the rope that was ready at the door. Poor Mano died. The old man made an earth oven and ate his body. He threw the bones in a huge hole by the house. He did this so that the other people could not find out about him.

The three brothers waited and waited, but Mano did not arrive. So, Kalunda took an axe and followed the way that Mano had taken. He departed, then he arrived and met the old man.

The old man lied to Kalunda, and later he killed him. Kalunda did not return to the village the next day, so Yawa followed his trail. Yawa followed and followed, then the old man also killed and ate him.

Only the last brother, Yasa, was left. Yasa waited and waited, and the three brothers did not return. He knew that an enemy in the forest must have killed his three brothers. He was furious, so he readied his axe and his bow and arrows.

The next day, he followed the footprints on the ground, then he walked into the forest. He searched for the three brothers for a while, then he arrived at the hill that was near where the old man lived.

He rested for a while, then he heard one of the songs that the old man was singing. The three brothers had heard this same song and they had died.

He walked and walked, then he saw the old man. However, he did not reveal himself quickly to the old man. He saw the big hole in which the old man had hidden the bones of the three brothers.

He looked down and saw their bones. He had the idea that it was just the old man who had killed the three brothers. Oh my, he was completely furious. However, he got an idea of killing the old man, so he cut back to the trail on which he had come. Later, he returned and the old man saw him.

The old man was elated and said, "It's very good that you've come. I know what you're looking for. It's OK, I'll help you. Let's sleep first, then tomorrow morning we'll go farther into the forest and search for your three brothers. I saw them come and go into the forest, but they did not return. They must have encountered some problems in the forest. It's alright, I'll help you."

That night, they slept and the three brothers told Yasa in a dream that the old man was lying and that he was a murderer. They told Yasa that the old man's trick was to send a man to the house door first. Yasa now knew this, so he would wake up first in the morning.

The old man also awoke. He was ready to leave the house and go into the forest. The old man asked Yasa to go out the door first. However, Yasa knew about this and replied that he had left his smoking pipe. So, he went back to get some fire and told the old man to go first.

The old man moved back and Yasa pushed him forward towards the door, then the rope caught him. The old man died and Yasa set fire to the house, burning him with it. Afterwards, he fled back to his village.

Vincent Purigi

Ialibu

Southern Highlands Province

D1810.8.2.3. Murder made known in a dream; D1810.8.3. Warning in dreams; F527.1. Red person; G10. Cannibalism; K810. Fatal deception into trickster's power; K1601. Deceiver falls into his own trap (literally); P251.3.1. Brothers strive to avenge each other; P251.6.2. Four brothers; Q211. Murder punished; Q413.4. Hanging as punishment for murder; R220. Flights; R260. Pursuits; S113.1. Murder by hanging; W157. Dishonesty

How Did Tisgmal and Kup [Villages] Arise?

(Wantok 864, January 24, 1991, page 18)

Long, long ago, in **Simbu** [Province], there was a village called Kuump [**Kup**], by the Wagi [Wahgi] River [**Wahgi** People]. In this part of the earth, there were no people. It was just dense forest with big trees standing there. This place was the home only to big snakes.

On one side of a mountain, there lived a man. He would go to this area to make gardens. He made a huge garden on this side, then he would always go to weed and to bring food back to the house.

When he arrived at the garden, the ripe bananas that he had seen before were no longer hanging from their branches. He was irate and he knew that some group had stolen his bananas, so he went to the house.

The next time, he went to get more bananas and bring them to the house, but the bananas were gone again. The unlucky guy was furious so he went to the house. This thievery happened many times and many more bananas were lost from the poor man's garden.

One time he went to the garden and saw that one banana was ripe. The unlucky guy wanted to find out who it

was that was performing this thievery and he wanted to discover the man's footprints. He went around the garden for a while until he heard a small boy crying.

He was terrified, but he wanted to see the boy who was crying. When he arrived at the clearing, he saw a baby crying. The man saw that there was no one else with this boy. So, he carried the baby and went to his house.

The man took care of the baby for a while, until he became a big man and had the strength to do things. The young boy grew big and married a woman, then they raised many more children.

At this time, many children were still raised there. They fought back and forth, then some broke apart to the area of **Western Highlands** Province called **Tisgmal** and some went to live in Kup Village in Simbu Province. So, these two villages arose from the snake who was their ancestor.

Dani G. Kaman

Minj

Western Highlands Province

A991+. Origin of particular village; D391B. Transformation: serpent (snake) to boy; K420. Thief loses his goods or is detected; P210. Husband and wife; P230. Parents and children; P271. Foster father; P275. Foster son; R131. Exposed or abandoned child rescued; T100. Marriage

Two from Goroka Fought over Bananas

(Wantok 865, January 31, 1991, page 18)

Long, long ago, in the time of the ancestors, there was just one man who lived in **Sengi** Village, by Goroka in **Eastern Highlands** Province. However, at this time there were no houses. The men would just sleep in caves.

One day, the Sengi man traveled to the area of **Timbara** and he tried to see if there was a short banana plant in his old garden. He arrived and saw that the banana plant was ready to bear fruit. So, he weeded the base of the banana plant well and returned to his cave.

However, a man from another nearby village called **Arubong** also often checked on this banana plant. One day, the Arubong man went and saw that a man had weeded the base of this banana plant. Oh my, he was angry and shouted, "You're a real crazy man to have come and weed the base of my banana plant so well! So, you planted it and came to weed the base of the plant! Don't you have shame!" He shouted like this, then he followed the footprints to a part of the trail. He knew that a thief must have come from Sengi Village.

The next day, the Sengi man thought about the banana plant and went to check upon it. He saw that the banana plant was ready to bear fruit, so he weeded the base of the banana plant well again. After he was done, he went farther into the forest and hunted some wild game, then he went back home.

Two days later, the real owner of the garden, the Arubong man, went and saw this. He was furious, so he cut around the grasses and blocked the trail. Later, he returned home. He was burning up inside. He wanted to see who this man was who came to check on his banana plant.

The next day, he went back and cut small trees, then he barricaded the banana plant and strengthened it. When he was done, he returned home.

The next day, the Sengi man went and saw this. He was completely furious. He removed the Arubong man's trees, then he cut his own and re-fenced the banana plant.

The next day, in the early morning, he awoke and went to cut the bananas that he had worked hard at preparing, [but] they were not there. Oh my, he was completely irate.

If there were a man who lived nearby he would kill him and just eat. He followed the footprints, then he arrived at the Sengi man's home.

The Sengi man was fervently cooking the bananas and eating. The poor man did not know that the real owner of the bananas, his enemy, had arrived.

The Arubong man arrived at the cave where the Sengi slept, then he searched for firewood. When he found enough firewood, he blockaded the cave entrance.

Afterwards, he made a bonfire outside the cave, then the Sengi man did not have a way to exit. The poor man was [in pain], and his belly was burning up like a bomb.

Previously, the home of the Sengi did not have water. After this, the Sengi man's blood turned into a stream. This stream is still there, and we often drink from it. However, if you bathe in it, your skin will become scabrous.

Kenny Agab

Goroka

Eastern Highlands Province

A934.11. River from transformation; C721.2. Tabu: bathing in certain place; C941+. Ringworm caused by breaking tabu; D457.1+. Transformation: blood to river; K420. Thief loses his goods or is detected; K812. Victim burned in his own house (or hiding place); Q212. Theft punished; Q414. Punishment: burning alive; S110. Murders; S112.0.2. House (hostel) burned with all inside

A Scabby Man Married a Nice Woman

(Wantok 866, February 7, 1991, page 18)

Long, long ago, in the time of the ancestors, there lived a man at Mount Humito, by Yabiufa [**Yaviyufa**], in **Eastern Highlands** Province [**Yawiyuha** People]. The man's name was Mania. The poor man tried hard to find a girlfriend for himself, but no woman wanted him.

The women did not like him because he was a short man and his skin was just filled with scabies. The women would always spit upon him, so he was ashamed and ran away to make a house by Mount Humito, and there he lived by himself.

One time, everyone went to gather in the place where they lived. Mania heard the singing and noise making. He followed the sound and went to the gathering.

All of the young people went inside a big house where they *karim lek*ed and sang together. Mania went into the house and hid there. He saw the young people having fun together.

He sat for a while, then he saw a nice gorgeous woman sitting at the side of the house. The unlucky guy saw her and did not take his eyes away. He stared and stared, then he began to think that if this woman would become his wife, he would be truly happy.

Mania thought and thought, then he thought of the latrine where everyone would go in the morning. He stayed until it was nearly dawn, then he hid by the toilet.

In the morning, the people lined up very closely by the toilet. Mania, the rotten scab, hid and spied upon them. He waited and waited, then he saw that the nice woman was walking towards the toilet. Mania's heart beat like never before.

He thought of running out and grabbing her, but he thought harder and just sat quietly. She defecated, then she wanted to return to the house. Mania jumped out and held the woman's feces on a stick, then he was about to eat them. She turned and saw him. He told her, "I'll eat your shit because it looks very nice in my eyes."

However, she insisted that Mania could not do this because it would be sick. Mania insisted on eating the woman's feces. They argued back and forth, then she cowered from [the idea of] Mania eating her feces. Finally, she told Mania, "If you don't eat my shit, I'll marry you."

Mania was just waiting for her to give this answer. Oh my, his heart was elated. He married her and they lived in his home by Mount Humito.

So today, if you travel to Humito Village, you will see that only short and scabrous men have married the good women.

Jabuk J. Luana

Megeuka Village

Goroka

Eastern Highlands Province

A1550+. Why ugly and beautiful marry each other; K1380+. Woman agrees to marry rather than watch man eat her feces; L140+. Ugly marries beautiful; P210. Husband and wife; P426.2. Hermit; P600+. Courtship customs: *karim lek*; R213. Escape from home; T100. Marriage; X716H+. The escoumerda

[There was no ancestor story in *Wantok* #867.]

Hoke Fled from His Wife's Ghost

(Wantok 868, February 21, 1991, page 18)

Long, long ago, in the time of the ancestors, there was a man who lived in a village called Kisituwen [**Kisituen**] in **Morobe** Province [**Nabak** People]. The man's name was Hoke. Hoke was married and lived with just his wife in this village.

They lived for a while, then one time the woman told Hoke that she was pregnant. Oh my, Hoke was elated. However one day, Hoke's wife died with the baby inside her. Hoke did not know what to do. He was extremely worried. He cried and [buried] her body, then he lived by himself.

He finished mourning for his wife, then one day he thought about hunting for some wild game. That day, he awoke in the early morning, then he went to the garden to get some food. He took various kinds of food, such as sugarcanes, taros and bananas. After he gathered the food, he brought it back in the afternoon.

He slept that night, then he awoke in the very early morning. He took all of the food that he had taken from the garden, then he walked and walked to a village named **Nademeben**. This village is under and near Mount Suruvaget [Saruwaged].

He arrived at this place, then he put all of the food into a pigsty. The pigsty had been made before by Hoke and was still there. After he put the food inside the hut, he took his dog and went into the forest to hunt for some game. Hoke went into the deep forest and killed very many animals.

When it was about to become dark, he walked back. He walked and walked, then he rested on a mountain. While he was resting, he saw smoke from a fire rising from his pigsty.

He sat for a little longer, then he thought and thought about who it could be that was burning the hut. Quickly, he left the mountain, then he walked close to the pigsty. He walked very quietly and heard the voice of his dead wife.

The woman's spirit went into his mouth, so he felt as if he could not talk. He felt as if his mouth was dry and very heavy. Then the woman's ghost told him to go inside the hut and eat the sweet potatoes that she had cooked.

Hoke was quite afraid, so he went inside and just sat quietly. Her ghost just gave him sweet potatoes, and he did not eat. He sat and thought very hard. Before long, a good idea came to him.

Hoke told his wife's ghost, "I was hunting for game for a while and my throat has become terribly dry. So, I'll go fetch water first, then I'll return to eat the sweet potatoes."

He lied like that, then he took a bamboo tube for fetching water. He walked and walked to the river. At the river, he left the bamboo and sped away as fast as he could to a village called **Kumbakumba**.

The ghost woman waited at the hut for a while and Hoke did not appear. She left the baby there at the hut, then she followed Hoke to the river. She arrived at the river and saw that Hoke had been afraid and had fled.

She returned to the hut to fetch the baby, and then she followed Hoke. She followed and followed, then she called for Hoke to return. Hoke was at Kumbakumba Village, and he heard the ghost woman calling and following him.

Hoke listened and left Kumbakumba Village. He ran and ran to the big village of Kisituwen. However, her ghost and her baby kept following him. Later, the ghost lost Hoke and went away.

Hoke slept and regained his strength, then he awoke in the very early morning. He told this story to the other men of the village, then he killed many pigs and made a huge party.

Mobbi Wamex

Popondetta

Oro Province

E261.4. Ghost pursues man; E221+. Dead wife's malevolent return; E425.1.4. Revenant as woman carrying baby; E425.3. Revenant as child; F406. Spirits propitiated; P210. Husband and wife; P230. Parents and children; R220. Flights; R260. Pursuits; T570. Pregnancy; V12.4.3. Pig as sacrifice; V61.3+. Dead buried; W157. Dishonesty

Why are Spiders and Crabs [or Water Striders] Enemies?

(Wantok 869, February 28, 1991, page 18)

Long, long ago, in the time of the ancestors, Crab and Spider were very good friends. They shared food between themselves, as friends do. If Crab were short of food, Spider would help Crab. If Spider were short of food, Crab would help Spider.

Spider had many thousands of children. So, Spider lived with the children at the source of a stream. They would make a house on a tree branch, above the grasses and stones. Then they would travel to the source of the stream, hunting for wild game. Crab had just two children. Their house was in a hole in the ground. They would only hunt for food underwater.

One day, a very heavy rain fell. This rain stayed for some days, then a big flood came, removing the spiders' house. Spider and the children searched for a place to flee. They were unsuccessful, then they drifted on the surface of the water, down to the crabs' home.

Spider had very many children. So, when they went inside Crab's house, they made much noise and sat by the fire. Spider's children were plentiful and very disobedient. They played around and completely ruined Crab's house.

Crab and its two children did not stay in the house. They all stayed in the garden and searched for food. When it was nearly afternoon, they walked back to the house. They were surprised to hear the tremendous noise coming from the house.

They arrived and saw Spider and its children making noise. Oh my, Crab was completely furious. Crab scolded Spider and its children. However, Spider had an enormous number of children, so they replied jokingly and they all laughed together.

Afterwards, Crab told Spider, "Before, we never argued. This is the very first time that we've done this, so I'm very ashamed. Come and I'll kiss you, then I promise that I won't be angry with you any more."

Spider thought that Crab was telling the truth. Spider went closer, then Crab opened its mouth and put its teeth upon Spider. Oh my, blood spilled like nothing else from Spider's body.

At the same time, Crab jumped into the water and fled. Spider jumped after Crab to fight, but Spider did not see Crab. Crab, you know, is at home in the water. So, Crab went inside and hid with its two children.

Following this story, today, you will see that crabs and spiders do not live together. Whenever you see spiders going on top of the water [possibly water striders (insect family Gerridae), or a diving spider], they are searching for their enemies, the crabs.

Denny Mark
Catholic Mission Mai
P. O. Box 93
Kundiawa
Simbu Province

A1011. Local deluges; A2494.16.5. Enmity between crab and spider; K2021.1. The bitten cheek; P230. Parents and children; P310. Friendship; Q270. Misdeeds concerning property punished; Q453. Punishment: being bitten by animal; R210. Escapes; R310. Refuges; W157. Dishonesty

A Snake Gave Birth to a Boy

(Wantok 870, March 7, 1991, page 18)

Long, long ago, there lived a married couple. They lived together for a long time, but they did not have their own children yet and they had become old.

One time, they went to the garden until the afternoon, then they returned to the house. The old man carried a piece of firewood, and his wife carried food in a net bag.

They arrived at the house in the afternoon, then his old wife went ahead and straightened the trash in the house. She broomed all of the trash and gathered it up. Then she carried it to the place where they usually threw away the trash.

After she threw away the trash, she was about to return to the house when she heard a baby crying. She searched and searched, then she went back to the place where she had thrown the trash, where she heard the crying loudly. Quickly, she ran to the house and told the old man, then they went back together.

The man removed the trash and found a little baby boy crying. Quickly, they took the baby boy to the house and bathed him in water. The old [man] did not wait because [he] was very happy to see this big thing [the baby], and because he had greatly desired a child for a long time.

He took a banana leaf, cooked it, attached it to his old wife's breast, then milk came forth. The baby began to drink the milk.

The baby was not an ordinary boy. His real mother was a snake, and the she-snake had given birth to him in this pile of trash. The snake often ate the old couple's trash. It had the strength to take care of the baby until the old couple had found him.

The she-snake did not forget her son, she always fol-lowed him. When they returned to the house and slept, the snake would also go, then lie in hiding and look at her son.

One time, the boy became a big man. He went to work in the garden with the old couple. They worked there, then he saw his snake mother.

He knew that it was his mother, so he told his old foster mother not to kill the snake. However, the old couple killed the snake, then the man cried terribly.

They lived for a while, then the boy grew up com-pletely and married a woman from this village. He married and raised two children. Later, the children grew up, and many people were raised in this village.

So, the people who came from the snake now live in the Sepik. This ancestor story comes from Mungul [**Mongol**] Village in **East Sepik** Province [**Mongol** People].

William Wanny [Wani]
Wewak
East Sepik Province

D955+. Magic banana leaf; F598. Old woman gives miraculous amount of milk; P210. Husband and wife; P230. Parents and children; P231. Mother and son; P271. Foster father; P272. Foster mother; P275. Foster son; R10.3. Children abducted; R260. Pursuits; S36. Cruel foster father; S36+. Cruel foster mother; T100. Marriage; T566. Human son of animal parents; T611. Suckling of children

Brothers Killed a *Masalai* from Tawambo

(Wantok 871, March 14, 1991, page 16)

Long, long ago, there lived a ghost man. He usually lived in a hole in **Tawambo** Village on the Finschhafen Peninsula of **Morobe** Province [**Kosorong** People].

The name of this *masalai* was Somambo Songoring. He had killed and eaten all of the men, women, children, pigs and dogs of this area. There was not one animal or human left.

When *masalai* Somambo was working hard at killing people, an old woman was lucky to have missed the wrath of the *masalai*, and she went into hiding. The old woman took her little grandson, and the two of them hid very well.

Every day, they would work on things. They watched very carefully so that *masalai* Somambo could not find out about themselves. They did this for a while, then the boy grew to be a young man.

One time, the boy asked his grandmother where all of the other people lived. The old woman told him the story that everyone had died at the hands of a *masalai* man who

was now hiding in a cave. The boy listened and was dis-turbed. He thought about killing the *masalai*.

One time, he prepared his bow and arrows, then he wanted to travel the forest. On the trail, he shot at the little lizards and insects, then he arrived at a bamboo plant. The youth shot an arrow that stuck to the bamboo.

When the spear stuck to the bamboo, the boy heard a little baby crying. He searched and searched, then he went close to the bamboo and saw a little baby boy crying inside the bamboo.

Quickly, he removed the baby from the bamboo and took him to the house. His old granny took care of the baby. They took care of the little baby for a while, then he became a big man.

One time, the two men decided to kill the ghost man, Somambo. So, they sharpened their arrows and spears, and tightened their bowstrings very well, then they were ready to fight.

Before they went to fight, they tried their hands at throwing big spears into things. When they saw that they could take down the ghost man, they were happy and went to the cave to find him.

The two [foster] brothers arrived at Somambo's home, then they called for him to come outside and test his strength. The three of them fought and fought until the brothers prevailed and sent all of the spears into the ghost man's side. *Masalai* Somambo fell down and died at this place, then the brothers were happy and returned to their old grandmother.

K. Saley Meawong
Finschhafen
Morobe Province

E425.2. Revenant as man; E440+. Ghost laid by spear/arrow; F490+. Ma-salai; G11.10. Cannibalistic spirits; G346. Devastating monster; G510.4+. Hero overcomes devastating ogre; G512.1+. Ogre killed with spear/arrow; L111.2. Foundling hero; L111.4.1. Orphan hero lives with grandmother; P272. Foster mother; P273. Foster brother; P275. Foster son; P292.1. Grandmother as foster mother; R310. Refuges; S110. Murders; Z210. Brothers as heroes

[There was no ancestor story in *Wantok* #872.]

A Lazy Man Became the Bird
of Paradise from Kabwum

(Wantok 873, March 28, 1991, page 16)

Long ago, a woman and her brother lived in Hemon [**Hemang**] Village, in the Kabwum District [**Morobe** Province, **Timbe** People]. The sister was talkative and she made everything, but her brother was lazy and he had scabies on his skin. He never helped his sister in the slightest.

When she would ask her brother to go to the garden or to do some work, the young man would not want to do it. He would just sleep in the house. The young brother would do this all of the time. His sister would come to scold him terribly when she returned to the house in the afternoon.

One time, a big festival was about to come to a village, so they called out for everyone to go to this festival. The big sister told her brother to arrange the festive adornments, but he was tired and went to sleep. The big sister scolded her brother, then she took the adornments and went to the festival site.

When his sister had left, the young man ran quickly to his hiding place inside a cave. Then he tried on his adornments. He often hid his festive adornments in the cave. Afterwards, he transformed himself, dancing and singing in the manner that his sister would do for him. When everything was ready, he just went stealthily to the festival site, then he showed his stylishness.

All eyes were fixed upon him. The young women shot towards him cunningly as they lusted for him. The bad boy gave forth, then when his song and dance were almost over, he quickly ran back to the village to his hiding place where he removed all of the adornments. Afterwards, he ran back to the house and slept soundly.

His sister came and saw her young brother sleeping by the fire, then she scolded him terribly, "You're sleeping like a sick dog. Many nice things happened at the festival grounds." His sister spoke angrily for a while, then she threw her "grass" skirt on top of him and went to sleep.

Some months passed, then a village announced a festival again. Later, all of the clans were ready to go. The big sister asked him whether he would go too, but he took his sleeping things and went to sleep by the fire.

The big sister saw this and took her things, then she went to the festival grounds. After she had gone, the bad brother quietly ran to his hiding place, then he dressed for the festival. He again began to sing and dance mournfully, turning [in the manner of his sister], then he walked to the festival grounds.

When he arrived, he showed his style and all of the women were just ruined by him. He did this for a while, then all of the women watched him. His big sister was also just dying for him and she tried to think of ways to pull him towards her.

She took a piece of bamboo and filled it with her lime (calcium oxide), then she hung it on his skirt. When the festival was almost over, he went out and quickly ran to his hiding place. The big sister did not know that he was her brother, so she followed him.

She arrived and was surprised to see her brother changing his body and adornments. Her thoughts were confused, so she went and grabbed her brother's hand. When she did this, they just left and went to a village. The name of this village is **Dolomon**. In this area, her brother turned into a bird and flew away.

His sister stood crying for a while, then she turned into a flower from this place. He had turned into a bird of paradise that lives in the Kabwum area. The place where he hid to adorn himself is there, and so is the big stone [cave].

Mai Ganao
Kimbe
West New Britain Province

D52. Magic change to different appearance; D150+M. Transformation: man to bird of paradise; D212W. Transformation: woman to flower; D1781. Magic results from singing; D1781+. Magic results from dancing; D1860. Magic beautification; N365.3.1. Brother and sister unwittingly in love with each other; P253. Sister and brother; R260. Pursuits; T10. Falling in love; W111. Laziness

A *Masalai* Fish Married a Young Woman
(Wantok 874, April 4, 1991, page 16)

Very long ago, in Kuariangua [**Kwaringia**] Village in **East Sepik** Province, there lived an old woman and her daughter [**Kwasengen** People].

One time, the mother and daughter talked about going to search for sago in the forest in the early morning. They awoke in the early morning, cooked their food, then took some with their sago equipment and went into the forest.

They went into the deep forest and searched until they found a place to cut sago. The mother her young daughter worked diligently at cutting a sago palm tree. The old woman wanted to cut the palm crown too so that she could make a "grass" skirt for herself. She told her young daughter this, then the daughter told the mother to go ahead while she processed the sago.

The mother sat well in her own corner and began to make herself a skirt while the daughter worked hard at making sago. Before long, a fish came by the river and saw the young woman. The fish lusted strongly for her. The fish thought about whether he could marry this young woman.

The fish went back underwater then told his father about this young woman, but his father laughed at him and did not believe what his son had said. The fish's father was a strong *masalai* of this river. A brother of this fish also went up and saw the woman. He looked at the young woman, then returned and told his father, but the father did not believe them.

A turtle went up by itself and saw the young woman, then it went back and told the young fish's father that the story was true. The turtle was the chair for the fish's father in this river.

The fish's father listened to all of the stories, then he knew what to do. He straightened the ginger and pieces of traditionally used leaves, then he went up and saw the young woman working hard at making sago.

By this time, it was afternoon and the water was receding. The *masalai* fish just performed his sorcery, then he pulled the young woman down into the water. She stood and felt as if her legs were stuck and that a power was pulling her very strongly down into the water.

She cried and shouted for her mother who was far from her and who was making her skirt. The old woman wanted to come to help her, but the bad *masalai* pulled her into the water and covered her with a strong current.

The river flooded and came to the old woman, then she held a log to strengthen herself and flee from the big flood. The old woman planted the log on the other side, then the water came to this place and receded.

The poor old woman cried for her daughter, then she returned to the village. At the place where the old woman had erected the log, there is now a lake that has many fish.

Moses Singe

Lae

Morobe Province

A920.1.0.1. Origin of particular lake; A1011. Local deluges; A1015.2. Spirit causes deluge; B211.5. Speaking fish; B211.6.3K. Speaking turtle; B603. Marriage to fish (whale); D2074. Attracting by magic; F420.1.3.2. Water-spirit as fish; F490+. Masalai; P232. Mother and daughter; P233. Father and son; P251.5. Two brothers; R13.4.1K2. Abduction by fish (eel); R220. Flights; T111. Marriage of mortal and supernatural being

A Married Couple Argued
and Clouds Thundered

(Wantok 875, April 11, 1991, page 17)

Before, there was a man and his wife who lived someplace. They lived for a long time, but they did not have children. They lived far away from other people. They never had problems or lacked anything. They had a bounteous garden and plenty of meat to eat.

One time, they wanted to go into the deep forest to hunt for wild game. Quickly, the woman went to the garden and fetched some food, then met [her husband] at the house. They went to the garden, then gathered sweet potatoes, taros, and other food. Afterwards, they were ready to go hunt for game.

In the very early morning, they awoke prepared some food to carry into the forest. When everything was ready, they left home and walked into the deep forest.

They arrived at a faraway place, then the man told his wife to follow a stream while he himself followed the forest. So, she began following the stream while he cut a trail through the forest.

In the forest, he killed many animals and filled his net bag. He found many wildfowl eggs, and cooked them in an earth oven. He hunted for game for a while, then it was becoming dark.

The woman did not fool around with fish, eels, and crayfish, either. She just slaughtered them. She followed the stream until afternoon, then she went to the house first and waited for her husband.

She waited and waited, then it became completely dark. She worried and began to cry for her husband. She cried hysterically when her husband did not show his face. She had the idea that an enemy must have encountered her husband in the deep forest, and that he must have died.

When dawn was about to break, the man's ghost arrived at the house, but she [became] crazy from this sort of thing. She knew that this was a ghost and not a real man. So, she told the ghost man that they would go to the big village.

They walked along the trail for a while, then he told her that he wanted to go urinate. However, she told her husband that they must walk first. They walked and walked, then he said that he [wanted] to go defecate. At this time, she knew that he was a ghost.

The ghost also had the idea that she wanted to test him. So, he told her to go tell the men of the village to carry his body from the forest and bury it by the big village.

She cried and went to tell the village men. They all went to carry his body and bury him by the big village, as the ghost had desired.

Many months passed, then one time, the woman wanted to go give food to her husband's ghost. She walked and walked, then she encountered a ghost along the trail. She was afraid of this ghost, so she gave all of the meat to the ghost.

Afterwards, the ghost asked her what she was searching for that caused her to go into the forest. She said that she was searching for her husband. Then the ghost told her where her husband dwelled. She followed and they met her husband.

They stayed for two weeks, then she wanted to return to the village, but her husband insisted that they must stay. They talked and shouted back and forth until he won and they stayed there.

So when there is a heavy rain, the clouds will thunder and almost break the sky. This is the married couple scolding and arguing back and forth in their new home.

Kay M. Toiyugini
Kauwo Village [**Wiru** People]
Pangia
Southern Highlands Province

A1142+. Origin of thunder: arguing ghosts; E321. Dead husband's friendly return; E425.2. Revenant as man; F81.1.2. Journey to land of dead to visit deceased; P210. Husband and wife; V61.3+. Dead buried

A Dog Listened to the
Simbu Language and Died
(Wantok 876, April 18, 1991, page 16)

Long ago, an old man and his dog lived in a village called **Londota**, among the **Siane** [People] of **Simbu** Province. The name of the old man was Yangure Haviri and the name of the dog was Hulafone. Yangure often left his wife and child, then he and the dog would go fight with their enemies at faraway places.

The two of them would go spring over a big mountain, then go to the other side to a village called **Bomai** where they would kill very many clans [**Golin** and **Mikaru** Peoples]. Afterwards, they would return to the village at night.

They worked like this for a while, then one time, they went to fight. When they returned, they felt tired and rested near a boulder. The name of this boulder is Nimburimana.

Near the boulder, there was a very good place to rest. Men could cook food or sleep there too. So, the old man felt very good. He removed his pipe and drew [smoke] from it.

The old man smoked well, then he called for his dog and they took off. However, he did not think of his pipe. They went far, then he remembered. He was very worried about this pipe, but he did not want to return again because he was far away.

The poor man thought and looked at his dog. Afterwards, he just spoke to his dog. "*Ake* Hulafone *usi nomu ma akaima hevana hinauma furitoto ya onimbo yae,*

henombane ombula mae wenina minangeari uto tanambe kala."

In English, this means, "Oh sorry [Hulafone], I left my pipe at the place where we rested. My dog, you're not a man. Will you go fetch it?"

After he spoke to the dog, he went to the house. However, his dog did not follow him. The dog stood at the place where they had stopped, and it thought.

Later, the dog just got up and sped away like a bird back to the place where they had rested. The dog found the pipe, put it in its mouth, and sped back to its master. The dog carried the pipe all the way to the house.

Oh my, when the old man saw his dog, he was terribly worried for it. He killed a gigantic pig, then he gave it to the dog. The dog ate its fill, then it went directly to its master's bed and slept. When the dog went to sleep, it died. You know, the dog would not have died, but it was ashamed [not] to do something that it could not do.

Andrew Appy
Waigani
Port Moresby [National Capital District]

B212. Animal understands human speech; B421+. Helpful dog dies after task; F610. Remarkably strong man; B871.1.2.1. Giant hog; P210. Husband and wife; P230. Parents and children; S110. Murders

The Mondo [Mando] Clan Houses of Goroka
(Wantok 877, April 25, 1991, page 17)

Long ago, in Mondo [**Mando**] Village in **Eastern Highlands** Province, there lived two brothers and a sister [**Asaro** People]. One time, the big brother told his little brother to take care of their sister. Then he would climb Mount Muwora and go all of the way to Kolepa [**Koreipa** Village] at the base of Daulo Pass [**Siane** People]. Later, he would return.

The little brother asked why it was that he wanted to go to this faraway place. The big brother replied, "I'm going to hunt for marsupials (*kapul*) and birds."

After the big brother said this, he prepared all of the food and his bow and arrows. Later, he followed a river up into the forest. He walked very quietly and killed a marsupial on top of a pandanus tree (*karuka*) by the trail, then he put it in his net bag. He stood and rested a little while, then he saw very many birds flying. They flew to the other side of the mountain. So, the big brother got up and followed the birds. He arrived and saw very many birds coming and filling a tree then eating the tree flowers.

Very quietly, he made a hut under the tree, then he went outside. He looked around and saw a nice bird. Quickly, the big brother put an arrow in the bow and shot it upwards. The arrow stuck to the bird's chest, but the bird did not fall down. The bird flew away to another place where smoke from a fire brought it down. He saw this and followed the bird that had his arrow.

He arrived at this place, then he saw an old woman making fire and burning trash. He asked the old woman about the bird and his arrow. The old woman replied, "Something edible, I ate. Something inedible, I left there." The man listened and did not speak. He just asked the old woman for water. After he quenched himself, he sat and rested.

A little later, the old woman asked him to go sharpen a digging stick for her. He got up and sharpened two very nice sticks for digging the ground, then he spoke about leaving. The old woman gave two nice pandanus (*marita*) fruits to him and said, "When you want to go drink water from the stream, you must leave these pandanus fruits on the trail, then go. Afterwards, you can come and fetch them, then return home." He followed everything that the old woman said. When he drank water, he heard the voices of two women on the trail. Quickly, he went back up and saw two very beautiful women standing at the place where he had left his pandanus fruits. He asked them about his pandanus fruits, but they replied, "Wherever you go, we'll follow you."

The boy listened, he was ecstatic and took the women to Mondo. The little brother and sister saw the three of them coming. They asked the big brother about the two women. The big brother told the story to them about everything that had happened to him. Afterwards, he gave one woman to his little brother, then they married them.

This old woman also transformed her body and became a young man. She married the sister of the two brothers, then they all lived happily together. Afterwards, they broke apart and lived in their own places on top of the mountain. All of them raised very many children. They called their clan houses, Mondo One, Two and Three. The children [also] grew up, broke apart, and married until today.

MXF P.
Jata Village
Goroka
Eastern Highlands Province

A1640+. Origin of Mondo clans; D11. Transformation woman to man; D431.4+W. Transformation: pandanus fruit to woman; D1880. Magic rejuvenation; P210. Husband and wife; P230. Parents and children; P253.0.2. One sister and two brothers; P263. Brother-in-law; P264. Sister-in-law; Q40. Kindness rewarded; T100. Marriage

The Canoes from Bukawa [Bukaua] and Tami Island Came from an Old Man
(Wantok 878, May 2, 1991, page 17)

Long ago, in the area of Bukawa [**Bukaua** Village, **Bukawac** People] and **Tami** Island [**Tami** People] in **Morobe** Province, there lived many little boys in these two places.

In this area, there was also an old man who had a big canoe. He would paddle his canoe and travel to all of the islands, seeing the many children who would be bathing in the sea.

One time, he thought about tricking the little boys, then he would eat them. So, one good day when the sun was hot and it was clear, the little boys filled the sea and bathed with gusto.

The old man saw this and prepared a trick to fool the boys. He went to a garden and took many ripe foods, then returned to the beach. He left some ripe foods in the canoe, then he took some to the beach.

He sat at the base of a big tree where the boys had left their shirts and pants. After the boys had bathed, they went up to change. They saw the old man's ripe foods and they lusted for them. The old man took some and gave them to the boys, but some boys did not eat because there was not enough.

The old man told them to come with him to the canoe, then they could get more food. They went and ate greedily on top of the canoe. The old man paddled the canoe, taking them to an island where he tricked them with more foods.

He left the first group there, then he returned to the beach and took more boys away. When the old man left the boys on the island, he quickly departed for his house. He waited for one hungry boy to die, then he would go eat his body.

The boys traveled to all of the places on the island to find food, but there was none, so they ate tree leaves. Time was up for these boys, and they lost all of their strength.

One time, they decided to kill the old man when he came there. They broke apart into two groups. One group went to the sea and searched for snails and shellfish by the shore. The other group dug two huge holes, one larger than the other. The larger one was very deep. They took the shellfish and other things from the sea then they filled the holes. The sun heated the shellfish.

When the sun heated these things in the holes, a very strong smell arose and the old man smelled it from his house. Quickly, he thought that a boy must have died, so he paddled his canoe and went to this island. When he approached, he saw the boys filling the beach and surrounding the two holes. The old man thought that a boy must have died and that the boys had buried him.

He went down and left the canoe, then he went to gorge on the rotting snails and shellfish that were there. The boys heated two stones until they were red hot along with a taro. The boys pretended to go to the forest, then they cut across stealthily to the old man's canoe and they began to paddle away.

When the old man turned around, he saw that the boys had taken his canoe and were paddling away. He pulled his two ears until they enlarged, then he began to fly towards the boys' canoe. He arrived and stood at the front of the canoe. The boys told him that they did not have a way to escape, so he must eat the two taros that they had cooked before.

The old man took the two red-hot stones and gulped them down. Before long, he jumped about and rolled awkwardly, then he fell into the sea and died. The boys had tricked him. He had eaten the hot stones that had burned his stomach.

The boys were very happy and they paddled the canoe back to their home. Some boys went to their village on Tami Island, and some went to Bukawa. So from this time, you will see that only the Tami People have big canoes. These boys learned about canoes from the old man.

John Yau
Catholic Mission, West Taraka
Lae
Morobe Province

[For a similar story, see *Wantok* #1033.]

A2800+. Origin of canoes; D670+. Magic flight with ears; F542.2+. Pulled ears enlarge; G421. Ogre traps victim; G422. Ogre imprisons victim; G440. Ogre abducts person; G512.3.1+. Ogre tricked into eating hot stones; K710. Victim enticed into voluntary captivity or helplessness; K951.1+. Murder by tricking into eating hot stones; K1860. Deception by feigned death (sleep); R43. Captivity on island; R51.1. Prisoners starved; R210. Escapes; R260. Pursuits; S145. Abandonment on an island; S132. Murder by starvation; S301. Children abandoned (exposed); V61.3+. Dead buried

[There was no ancestor story in *Wantok* #879.]

The Brother Who Married a *Masalai* Woman
(Wantok 880, May 16, 1991, page 16)

Long, long ago, in the time of the ancestors, a man, his sister, and his dog lived by the Wali [Wáli (Lang, 1973: 215)] River in the **Turia** area of Kompiam, in **Enga** Province [**Enga** People]. They lived inside the very deep forest. The sister's house was far away from the brother and dog's house.

The brother planted very much food by his house. They lived for a while, then one day a very heavy rain fell. The brother and sister made a bonfire and they sat in the house.

They sat around the fire and watched the water below them. They watched and saw smoke from a fire rising up from the source of the river. This smoke showed that a *masalai* man was following the smoke and coming to kill them.

The brother stayed alone for a while, then before long a *masalai* man arrived at his house with some pork. He wanted to give the pork to him.

However, their dog quickly smelled the *masalai* man and barked as he approached. The dog went and bit the *masalai* man directly on the leg. The dog just ruined the *masalai* man, but the *masalai* did not show any sign that he would die, absolutely not.

The *masalai* man and the dog fought and fought, then the dog ran out of the breath. The *masalai* man ran towards the house where the brother was.

The brother saw the *masalai* man and was terrified. The *masalai* man went up to the house. He then told the brother that he wanted to give some meat to him and so not to be afraid.

The brother listened and was elated because he knew that now he would have meat to eat during the rainy season. The sister had already fled, and was hiding in her house. However, the brother did not forget her. He cut a piece of pork, then he gave it for his dog to give to his sister at her house.

They did not know that this was not a real man. The *masalai* man gave the meat so that the brother would eat it, then transform and become like his wife. The *masalai* did not know that the brother had a sister who lived in another house.

The brother sped away to his sister's house and changed into a women's "grass" skirt. The *masalai* returned and saw that the brother was like a nice, gorgeous woman.

He was elated and took the brother with him. The dog continued to follow and they arrived at the *masalai* man's house. The *masalai* man's sister also lived inside the house.

The *masalai* man always asked to sleep with the brother who was pretending to be a woman. However, the dog would bite the *masalai* man, preventing him from sleeping with him.

The brother was very happy for his dog because he did not want the *masalai* man to find out that he was not a real woman. They lived for a while, then one day the *masalai* man went to hunt for wild game for themselves in the very deep forest. That day, there was a big festival coming to a village near the *masalai* man's house.

The *masalai* man's sister asked her sister-in-law (the brother) to go to the festival with her. However, her in-law did not want to do this. So, the *masalai* woman went alone. She sang and danced passionately with the women there. While she was singing and dancing, the brother followed her and arrived later.

The brother saw many young women and men singing and dancing very passionately. He went to join them. He sang and danced fervently that night. Many young women saw the brother and became fixed upon him because the brother was a very handsome man.

Before long, the *masalai* man's sister saw him and she too became fixed upon him. She went and grabbed the brother, then the two of them sang and danced passionately.

Near dawn, the brother forgot and returned to the *masalai* man's house where he waited. The *masalai* man's sister was very troubled because the nice young man whom she wanted to marry had just disappeared and she would not see him again.

She cried and walked to the house. The brother who had changed back into the women's skirt saw her and asked, "Why are you crying like that?"

The *masalai* woman told her story to her fake sister-in-law. Her in-law listened and told her not to worry because the next day, they would return to the festival where she would again see the nice man.

The next night, they went to the festival site. Oh my, people filled their desires with jumping, dancing and singing. The *masalai* woman joined them and showed her skills.

Quickly, the brother went and hid in a corner where he removed his sister's skirt. He sped inside and joined the other people at the festival.

When the *masalai* woman saw him, oh my, her heart broke. She ran and grabbed the brother so that she would not lose him again. When dawn was nearly breaking, the brother took the *masalai* woman. They ran away to the brother's real home and [married].

Peale Prange
Enga Province

B421. Helpful dog; D1032. Magic meat; F401.6. Spirit in human form; F490+. Masalai; K1911+. Unwitting marriage to transvestite; P210. Husband and wife; P253. Sister and brother; P264. Sister-in-law; R220. Flights; R260. Pursuits; T111. Marriage of mortal and supernatural being; T192. Marriage by force

The Little Boy and the Rivers of Goroka
(Wantok 881, May 23, 1991, page 16)

Long ago, a woman and her little brother lived in a place on top of Mount Otto, by **Goroka** [**Gahuku** People]. On top of this mountain, there was no water for bathing, drinking or cooking food. They would just eat sweet potatoes with ashes from the fire. One nice morning, they sat and warmed their backs in the sun, then they saw smoke rising from **Lufa** [**Yagaria** People, **Eastern Highlands** Province].

When they saw the smoke, the sister sent her little brother down to see who was making the fire. It was the first time for the brother to walk around, so his sister tied a rope to his hand and told him to walk away. Biu [the brother] put a piece of grass on his head and sped down the mountain. While he jumped ahead, his head turned black. The little boy walked very quietly, then he arrived at the place where the smoke was rising. When he approached, he saw a hole from which the smoke was coming. He jumped down into the hole and walked very quietly inside. Inside the hole, there were many human bones lying about.

Before long, he saw an old woman sitting in the corner. The old woman saw him and asked, "Grandson, what did you come to find here?" The boy told the old woman, "My sister and I do not have water and we saw the smoke from the fire. So, I came to ask you for water."

Quickly, the old woman went and pulled a short and a long bamboo tube of water to give to the boy. She told the little boy to walk away quickly because his grandfather often killed and ate people. She said what he must do with the two bamboos. The long bamboo was filled with insects. The short bamboo was filled with water for the boy to drink with his sister.

Along the trail, the boy finished the water in the short bamboo. The long bamboo was still full. When he approached the house, he was again dying for water, so he opened it to drink. When he opened it, the insects came out and completely ruined the poor little boy's mouth.

He threw away the water and shouted loudly. He ran and ran to his sister, then he told her that the insects had bitten him. At night, the two of them slept and heard the crashing of water by their side. When they awoke in the morning, they saw a big river running by the side of the mountain.

This was not just one stream, because when the little boy had thrown the tube of water, it spilled and broke into five pieces. On Mount Otto, the Hao River is still there. The other four are the Bena Bena River, the Asaro River, the Kotuni River, and the Zogizo River. They were very happy that they had big rivers from which to drink and bathe. Now, these rivers help many people in the Goroka area to bathe, drink, and cook food.

Hani Evati Jomino
Goroka
Eastern Highlands Province

A934.11. River from transformation; D57.4+. Transformation: head turns black; D450+. Transformation: bamboo to river; F562.7K. People live in mountain top; G10. Cannibalism; P253. Sister and brother; P291. Grandfather; P292. Grandmother; S110. Murders

The Music of the Little Brother Attracted His Big Brother's Wife

(Wantok 882, May 30, 1991, page 16)

In the time of yore, in a village by the Melkoi [River] in the Pomio area of **East New Britain** Province, there were two brothers. The parents of these brothers had died, so the little brother lived with his big brother because he was married. They lived very well every day and they worked together at finding food, working on the house, singing, dancing, gardening and such things.

One afternoon, the young brother went to sit outside the house at one corner, then he played music on a bamboo flute. He put the bamboo to his mouth and blew. His fingers blocked the holes of the bamboo, making various kinds of nice music.

Before long, the big brother's wife came and stood by him, listening to her young brother-in-law's music. However, on the side of the house also sat her husband who was listening to his brother's music and watching what his wife was doing.

The big brother was angry now at his young brother because his wife was lusting for him. So, the big brother gathered all of his anger.

One time, a big drought arose and the area was completely dry. The rivers dried, and many people went to the river to hunt for crayfish, fish, eels and other water animals. The two brothers also went down to the river to work hard on one side of the river. The brothers dug a huge hole, and the water went down into it. They did this so that the water would all go into the hole, and they could very easily take the animals from the water.

After they dug the deep hole, the big brother asked the little brother to go down into the hole and straighten the path for the water. The little brother used a rope and slipped down, then the big brother stood on top and held the rope as his brother slid down. The little brother straightened the opening of the hole, then he wanted to ascend. He hung onto the rope and came up a little, then the big brother removed his hands from the rope, and his little brother fell back down into the hole, half dead.

The big brother went to the village in the afternoon. He told people about the accident that his little brother had had in the water. Everyone was sorry and they cried terribly because the young boy was very good. He had often said and done good things for many people.

The young brother lay for a while inside the hole. Then he awoke and he looked for a way to get up, but there was no way to leave. He tried to just follow the water flow inside the hole. He followed the water for a while until he arrived at the mouth of the hole where the light of the sun shot out at him.

Then he went out. He found many tree fruits and ate. Oh my, he was completely famished because he had not eaten when he was following the flow of the water inside the hole.

He took the food, then he walked away. Before long, he arrived at a river and saw two young women preparing to eat a pig. He took a stone and threw it at the women. They saw him and wanted to flee, but he called for them to come back. He told the women that he was a real man and not a ghost. He asked them for food and they gave it to him. He told the story of what had happened to him with his brother. They listened and were terribly sorry for the young man. They took him and went to their home, where the three of them lived. The leading men and the women of the village agreed, then the man married both of the women.

One time, a message went around to all of the villages. The message was that this man's big brother wanted to make a big feast to allow everyone to gather and show concern for the death of the young brother. The big brother asked everyone from the other villages to come with some food and gather to remove the time of sorrow.

The young man heard this, so he prepared his bow and arrows, then he went to his big brother's village. He saw everyone gathered very nicely, preparing food.

The bad man just went and buried an arrow into his big brother's chest, before everyone's eyes. Everyone was shocked and did not do a thing.

The big brother died, so people made a big feast for thinking sorrowfully of him and crying for him. Only the little brother turned back to his two wives, and they lived very well.

In their garden, they often planted cucumbers. These cucumbers grew large and plentiful in the area of the **Mamusi** [People], in the Pomio area of East New Britain Province.

Benedict Lot Oliver
Kimbe
West New Britain Province

K2211.0.1. Treacherous elder brother(s); P210. Husband and wife; P251.5.3. Hostile brothers; P251.5. Two brothers; P263. Brother-in-law; P264. Sister-in-law; Q285. Cruelty punished; Q411. Death as punishment; S73.1. Fratricide; S142. Person thrown into the water and abandoned; S146.2. Abandonment in cave; T100. Marriage; T145.0.1. Polygyny; W181. Jealousy

Two Brothers Fought over Food
(Wantok 883, June 6, 1991, page 13)

Long ago, in the time of the ancestors, there were two brothers and a sister who lived in Wome Village, in the Menyamya area of **Morobe** Province. This place is now where Wauwok [**Wauwoga**] Community School is located [**Menya** People].

The big brother was the best man at hunting for wild game in the forest. Whenever he went to the forest, he would return with game. The little brother and the sister usually stayed in the village. They would just work in the garden.

However, when the big brother returned from the forest, he never shared the meat with his two younger siblings. He alone would eat the all of the meat. So, the little sister and brother often worked very hard at finding food for themselves.

However, these two often packed the house with various kinds of food from the garden such as taros, yams and bananas. They only lacked meat, but they were unconcerned.

One day, the big brother's house was short of meat, so he took his bow and arrows, then he sped into the very deep forest. The little brother and sister went to the garden, as they did every day.

That day was not a good day for the big brother. He hunted for game for a while, but he did not even see small game. When it was nearly afternoon, he felt terribly hungry.

He gave up and walked slowly back to the house. When he arrived at the house, the birds of night had already called. Oh my, he was famished, and he did not even have a little strength to cook some food.

The little sister and brother arrived at the house then they cooked some food. They ate, then the big brother arrived. He saw his little siblings eating. He asked them, "I'm terribly hungry. Please give some food to me."

The little brother and sister did not look at him. They looked down at their food and ate heartily. A little later, the brother shoved his plate to the side and replied, "You always go to the forest to hunt for game and you never think the slightest about garden work. Also, when you kill animals and bring them here, you never think the slightest about us, your little siblings."

The little brother replied like this and did not give any food to his big brother. The two of them looked very angrily at their big brother. The big brother listened and was angry. He went up to the house, pulled the little brother down and began to fight. The sister saw this and tried to stop them, but she was unable to do so.

The big brother took his spear and killed the little brother. Afterwards, he took the same spear and killed himself. His blood fell down and turned into a tree. We call this tree _paindri_.

Their poor sister saw this and cried until morning. She was terribly worried that she no longer had brothers with whom to live. She took everything and walked down to the Wapi River. She wanted to cross the river to the other side, but the river was terribly flooded, and the current was very strong. She stood by the river for a while, then she too became a tree. This tree we call the fig.

Today, if you look at all of the fig trees, none of them grow straight, they only stand crookedly. Also, if you go to Wauwok Community School, you will see the _paindri_ tree standing by the school. When you stand by the school and look down to the Wapi River, you will see fig trees standing crookedly by the river.

Barni Darius
Kokopo
East New Britain Province

D215+W. Transformation: woman to fig tree; D457.1+. Transformation: blood to tree; M451.1. Death by suicide; P251+. Brother commits suicide on brother's death; P251.5.3. Hostile brothers; P253.0.2. One sister and two brothers; S73.1. Fratricide; S110. Murders; W151. Greed

A Nobonob [Nobanob] Headdress Became the Coconut Palm

(Wantok 884, June 13, 1991, page 16)

Long ago, an old man had many granddaughters and just one grandson. The name of the little boy was Roing Roing. He had many scabs on his skin. These children lived in **Nunzen** Village, on a mountain called Wimalau in **Madang** Province.

They lived for a while, then their grandfather died. One time, a big festival came to a village, then all of the sisters dressed and went to the festival.

The sisters of the young boy told him to stay in the house and cook food. It became dark, then the [ghost of the] young boy's grandfather came and removed all of the scabs from his skin. The boy became very nice and handsome. His grandfather adorned him, then told him to follow the sisters to the festival.

The bad boy stood up his headdress, then sped away to the festival. Then everyone's eyes opened when they saw the young boy because his adornments were much better than the others were. The young women fell right for him. Many just waited for morning to get a good look at the face of this young man. However, when it was still late at night, he left the festival and went back to his house.

He was extremely sleepy when he arrived at the house. Also, his skin was full of scabs again. The festival ended in the morning, then the young man's sisters just sped away to the house. They were famished when they arrived and saw that their brother had not cooked food. They woke [him] and scolded him terribly.

On the second night, the festival continued and the sisters went again. They told Roing Roing to stay and cook food. Roing Roing did not listen to what they said. While they were dancing, the bad boy came to sing and dance with them again. They were again extremely hungry.

At the house, they saw Roing Roing dead asleep. They awakened him and asked him what had happened. They said, "You always lie to us and come to the festival too." After they said this, they beat him terribly. At this time, all

of Roing Roing's scabs were gone, and he became a very nice boy.

Some months passed and a festival again came to a village. So, Roing Roing and his sisters dressed and walked away. They arrived at the festival site, then the sisters and their brother went forth.

At this time, all of the women knew about him. Then just after the festival, they all followed him towards his house. Roing Roing saw this and just sped into the house. He arrived and sat singing of trouble and sorrows. His grandfather heard this and flew there like a flying fox.

At the same time, a big fire came and burned Roing Roing inside the house. His headdress was still on his head when he fell directly on top of the arms of his sisters. Quickly, the big sister took Roing Roing's headdress and put it on her head. The big sister then explained to the other sisters that they would go to **Madang** [**Bilbil** People]. At this time too, her face changed into that of a man.

So, she left them and walked to Nobonob [**Nobanob**], then it became dark [**Garuh** People]. She saw a man sitting on the trail. This man looked exactly like her brother, Roing Roing. She asked him, "Brother, can I sleep with you, then tomorrow I'll continue walking?"

The man took her and they went to his house. They ate, then the Nobonob man made a bed for themselves to sleep upon. The man did not notice that he had taken a woman to his house.

They slept, then late at night he wanted to turn. He threw his arm over and it landed directly upon the woman's breast. The boy just woke up and went to tell his mother what had happened in his house.

In the morning, the mother went to his house and saw a very beautiful woman sleeping there. The story broke in Nobonob and everyone came to see this woman. Later, they asked her to marry him.

She told the story of what had happened to her up until that point. She married him and buried her brother's headdress in the ground.

Before long, she gave birth to a baby. At the same time, a very nice tree grew at the place where the woman had buried her brother's headdress. This tree grew and grew large. The child of the Nobonob man and the woman also grew big. Before long, the tree began to bear fruit.

One time, the mother and father went to the garden while the boy stayed with his grandmother. They stayed for a while, then the child became hungry. The old woman just went to get a fruit from this tree. She broke it open, and inside the tree fruit was a very nice juice. The old woman tried it and the juice was delicious, so she gave it to the little boy. Afterwards, the two of them also ate the fruit [pulp].

When the father and mother of the little boy arrived at the house, the old woman told the story of what had happened during the day. The father listened and told the story to all of the clans of the Nobonob Village about this new tree. Everyone came and each took one to plant in his or her own areas. This is the story of how the coconut was distributed to all of the places in Madang [Province].

T. M. T. Nunzen
Sialum
Finschhafen
Morobe Province

A2681.5.1. Origin of coconut tree; D50+. Transformation of woman's face to that of a man; D457.7+. Transformation: feather headdress to tree; D566. Transformation by striking; D1860. Magic beautification; E320+. Dead grandfather's friendly return; E384+. Ghost summoned by singing; F577. Persons identical in appearance; P210. Husband and wife; P231. Mother and son; P233. Father and son; P250. Brothers and sisters; P291. Grandfather; P262. Mother-in-law; P265+. Daughter-in-law; P292. Grandmother; Q325. Disobedience punished; Q458. Flogging as punishment; T100. Marriage; T415.5+. Sister marries man who looks like brother; T580. Childbirth; W126. Disobedience; W157. Dishonesty

[There was no ancestor story in *Wantok* #885.]

How Did Kondiu Village Get Its Name?

(Wantok 886, June 27, 1991, page 16)

Before, there was a woman who lived in **Kondiu** Village in the Kundiawa District of **Simbu** Province [**Kuman** People]. This woman was not married. She lived in her clan's house. Her name was Manambo and she was a very gorgeous woman.

One afternoon, Manambo was in the house and making a fire. She made a very big fire. Afterwards, she left the fire and went to sleep.

Manambo was dead asleep, then late at night a ghost man came to the house. The ghost came and sat near the fire. Before long, the ghost's eyes became drowsy. He fell down by the fire and slept.

Manambo had heard the noise from the ghost man when he had opened the door to go inside the house. She listened and pretended to be dead asleep. The ghost man had thought that Manambo had not heard him.

While the ghost man slept, Manambo got up very quietly. She wanted to see the ghost man's face, but she was surprised to see a gigantic snake sleeping by the fire near her.

Manambo wanted to shout, but she did not, lest the ghost snake awaken and kill her. So, she very quietly ran out of the house and awakened the other people of the village.

Everyone woke up and ran to surround the house with fire in their hands. They burned the house with the snake sleeping inside of it.

As the fire burned the house, the snake found that its time was up and spoke in my language, "*Na ambara o, Kamun pondo sugo, pre na ene kipanara ke simi wa pra we*." [*Na ambara* is "said by a male, means an ineligible marriage partner for him" (Nilles, 1969: 10). *Kamun* means, "area, sky, heaven, large place" (Nilles, 1969: 100). *Pondo* means, "huge" (Nilles, 1969: 197). *Pre* means "lid" or "for the reason/sake of" (Nilles, 1969: 199). *Na* means, "I" (Nilles, 1969: 169). *Ene* means, "you" (Nilles, 1969: 61).]

The snake man shouted like this, then died. Just before the snake died, the people heard a big noise from the snake's head like, "Kon... di... u... u...u."

After this story, my ancestors gave the name Kondiu to this village. This location is where Rosary High School now stands.

Mindima Maugo
Kundiawa
Simbu Province

A1617. Origin of place-name; B875.1. Giant serpent; E423.5. Revenant as snake (serpent); E425.2. Revenant as man; E446.2. Ghost laid by burning body; E568. Revenant lies down and sleeps; K1868. Deception by pretending sleep; S112.0.2. House (hostel) burned with all inside

Where Did the Wild Breadfruit and Wild Taro of Simbu Province Originate?

(Wantok 887, July 4, 1991, page 16)

Long ago, a woman and her daughter lived in Elimbarei [**Erimbari**] Village in southern **Simbu** [Province, **Chuave** People]. The woman's husband had died, so she only lived with her daughter in this village. The name of the girl was Mohari. Mohari was very young and could not do work yet. So, she could not travel too much with her mother to the garden.

One time, Mohari's mother wanted to go to a new garden that was fairly far from the village. The mother cooked some food for the child and told her to just stay in the house. She could not open the door and come outside because many ghosts often traveled, taking children or adults who were alone at home.

The mother departed for the garden, then little Mohari was alone at the house. Since she was alone, she shut the door and stayed inside.

In the middle of the day, a ghost man came to the house. The name of the ghost man was Firuame. He had one leg, one hand, and one ear. There was just one of everything on his body.

He just went and tricked Mahari [Mohari] by calling her like her mother. When Mohari heard this, she quickly jumped from the bed and went to open the house door.

Quickly, the ghost man went inside the house and held the girl, then he cut off a piece of her leg and arm. He took the girl and left her at the top of the house, then he departed for his hiding place.

The girl was in pain and cried on top of the house as she waited for her mother. In the afternoon, her mother arrived at the village and called ahead for her daughter. She shouted and asked Mohari, "Are you in the house or not?"

When the girl heard the voice of her mother, she replied quietly. She was in pain and did not call loudly. She just spoke a little, "I'm missing a leg and an arm, so I can't come to you."

When her mother saw this, she knew that it was the ghost man. The mother cried. She took a knife and some fire to the ghost man's home, then she burned and killed Firuame. After she killed the ghost man, she burned his house with fire, and the ghost was laid completely.

After the fire, the ghost man turned into wild taro, then the mother and daughter turned into wild breadfruit trees. If you go to **Mokuma** Village in southern Simbu [Province], you will see that these are still there.

Andrew Pamundi Monza

Fireman's House

Waigani

National Capital District

D211.7K+G. Transformation: girl to breadfruit; D211.7K+W. Transformation: woman to breadfruit; E425.2. Revenant as man; E446.2. Ghost laid by burning body; E631.5+. Reincarnation as taro plant; F525. Person with half a body; K812. Victim burned in his own house (or hiding place); K1930. Treacherous impostors; P232. Mother and daughter; Q285.3. Cruel mutilation punished; Q411. Death as punishment; S161. Mutilation: cutting off hands (arms); S162. Mutilation: cutting off legs (feet); S112.0.2. House (hostel) burned with all inside

Trouble Concerning Birds Created the Tatemba [Tatumba] River

(Wantok 888, July 11, 1991, page 14)

In Tatemba [**Tatumba**] Village, in the Maprik area of **East Sepik** Province, there lived a woman with just her two sons [**South Arapesh** People]. The woman's husband had died, so she alone cared for the two boys. The name of the elder boy was Bagodo and his brother was Baegelad.

They always went into the forest to hunt birds. When they would return in the afternoon, Baegelad would excel Bagodo at shooting the good birds.

The little brother always excelled the big brother. Their mother was very happy with the little brother for his birds. This made the big brother very angry because the mother loved her young son. None of the birds that the big brother killed were good like his little brother's birds were.

So, Bagodo wanted to redress his anger at his little brother. One morning, he told his little brother that they must go to the forest and wait for the birds to come, then they would shoot them.

Quickly, the little brother took his bow and arrows, then they departed. When they arrived in the deep forest, Bagodo told Baegelad to go to one side, then he would stay and watch from the other side.

The little brother listened and went to the other side of the forest. Then he waited for birds to come. After the little brother had left, the big brother dug the earth and found water to drink. He took insects and small snakes from the area, then he threw them into this drinking hole.

Bagodo went back and waited at the bird place, then before long, Baegelad came to drink water. He asked Bagodo, and Bagodo showed him the place where the water was located.

When the little brother lowered his head to drink water, the big brother just split his two legs then tossed him down into the water where he died.

Bagodo just took Baegelad's birds and carried them to the house. When the mother saw that only her big son was coming, she asked about his little brother. The son lied and told his mother that his little brother had come first to the house.

The mother saw the birds and knew that the birds belonged to the little brother and not to [Bagodo]. So, she knew that her big son must have killed her little son.

The mother cried and she tried to leave, but the big brother killed her too. Then the brother turned into a stone that is by the water where the little brother had died. Now, this stone and the water are still there, and we often go to drink there.

Patrick Nu Linus
Tatemba [Tatumba] Village
Maprik
East Sepik Province

A977. Origin of particular stones or groups of stones; A941.0.1. Origin of a particular spring; D231B. Transformation: boy to stone; P231. Mother and son; P251.5. Two brothers; S22+. Matricide; S73.1. Fratricide; S131. Murder by drowning; W157. Dishonesty; W195. Envy

A Little Baby Became the Birds
on the Gazelle Peninsula Beaches
(Wantok 889, July 18, 1991, page 16)

Long ago, an old man and his wife lived in a small place by the Gezelle [Gazelle] Peninsula of East New Britain Province. They had a young daughter. They lived for a while, then the old man died, and only the old woman and the girl lived there. The daughter grew up and married a man from another place. They had a son.

They lived for a while, then the man chased his wife and son back to the old woman's house. Some months passed, then a great drought arose. All of the rivers and forests just disappeared. Everyone went to the forests and rivers to hunt for wild game.

No one was in the village, so the old woman told her daughter and the little boy that they should stay home while she went to find game for themselves.

The old woman went and arrived at a big river, then she began searching for fish under the boulders. She went up towards the source of the river where she saw an old man sitting on top of a stone. The old man was sharpening a small axe. When he saw her, he wanted to cut her bones. So, he asked the old woman, "Did you catch some fish too or not?" She replied, "There's a drought and everyone is hunting for game, so I came to search for fish for my daughter, my grandson, and myself."

The old man asked her to give him some fish. The old woman said, "I didn't catch many fish, but that's OK, you can take them and I'll search again."

When the old woman passed by him, he sped along the forest trail and sat on top [of a stone, ready to] ask her for more fish. The sun was hot, and the old woman was tired, so she bent down and searched for fish. However, she thought of her daughter and grandson, so she kept fishing.

She did not know that the old man had cut through the forest and that he was sitting and waiting for her to catch more fish. The old woman arrived and he said the same thing. The old woman gave him fish for the second time. The sun was setting and it was becoming dark.

All of the men had left for the village, but the old woman had not arrived at the village yet. At this time, the old man took her to a garden and told her to dig a yam. Afterwards, she could take it and go to the village to eat it.

When she first began to dig the yam, the old man told her, "You must dig it well. Don't break one piece of the yam inside the ground." The poor old woman watched the ground very carefully and she dug the yam. She removed the big yam, but she did not remove it well, so part was stuck inside the ground.

She shouted at the old man, "A small piece broke in the ground." When he heard this, he sped towards her and scolded her terribly. Then he told her to remove the little piece that was still in the ground. She bent down to dig the yam, but no, the old man raised the axe and cut her neck, killing her. He took the old woman's clothes, put them on his body and went to the village. However, before he arrived at the village, the old woman's daughter saw marks on banana leaves indicating that her mother was dead. The old man arrived at the house and went to sit directly by the fire, then he looked at a small stone. The stone was becoming hot, so he told the old woman's daughter to fetch some dry wood and put it on the fire. She went outside to gather some firewood. He took the hot stone and put it in the baby's mouth, then he spilled water into the baby's mouth, killing him.

The woman straightened out the home, then the three of them slept. They slept for a while, then she held the baby's chest. Now, she saw that her baby was dead. She carried the baby quietly and went outside. Then she shut the house door and made a fire around the house. The fire burned down the house with the old man.

She took the baby and went to the baby's father. When the young man saw the dead baby, he was very sorry for her and her baby. He cried, then he dug a hole under a tree and buried the baby. Some months passed, then the man saw two eggs lying on top of the baby's grave. Later, the eggs hatched and two small birds came out. The man took *tanget* leaves and tied them to the two birds' necks.

So now, these two birds have marks on their necks. If you stay in **Rabaul**, you can see that these two little birds have colorful necks. These two birds always fly back and forth on the beaches of the Gazelle Peninsula of **East New Britain** Province [**Tolai** People].

Wesley O. Eko
Rabaul
East New Britain Province

A1970. Creation of miscellaneous birds; A2411.2. Origin of color of bird; E613.0.1. Reincarnation of murdered child as bird; E761.3+. Life token: banana plant; H1100+. Task: digging a long yam without breaking it; K910. Murder by strategy; K1930. Treacherous impostors; P210. Husband and wife; P231. Mother and son; P232. Mother and daughter; P233. Father and son; P234. Father and daughter; P292. Grandmother; Q211. Murder punished; Q325. Disobedience punished; Q411. Death as punishment; Q414.0.12. Burning as punishment for murder; R260. Pursuits; S112. Burning to death; S112.0.2. House (hostel) burned with all inside; S139.4. Murder by mangling with axe; V61.3+. Dead buried; W126. Disobedience

Obena and Huli Created the
Wabeg [Wabag] and Tari People
(Wantok 890, July 25, 1991, page 16)

Long, long ago, in the time of the ancestors, there were two sisters who lived between **Kandep** [**Enga** People, **Enga** Province] and the **Tari** area of **Southern Highlands** Province [**Huli** People]. At this time, the women often hunted for green tree frogs to eat.

One time, the two women decided to hunt for some green frogs by a big river. The sun rose, then they prepared food and wild sugarcane (*pitpii*) stems for hunting frogs at night. In the afternoon, they took everything and walked down towards the big river.

They arrived at the river, then they thought of some good ways that they could find many frogs. The big sister thought of a good idea, then she told the little sister, "Let's do this. I'll hunt for frogs downriver and [you]'ll hunt for frogs up towards the river's source."

It was nearly dark, so the sisters lit the wild sugarcane [torches]. Then, the little sister walked towards the river's source and the big sister walked down towards the river's mouth.

They had decided that whoever found many frogs could go home quickly. Before long, the big sister found many frogs because the mouth of the river had many big trees and very many frogs.

The poor little sister up at the source of the river worked very hard at hunting and grabbing frogs. She kept trying hard, then her torch finished. The poor sister did not have a single tiny frog.

Oh my, her eyes were very heavy with sleep. It was completely dark and she did not have any more wild sugarcanes to light a fire. She gave up and sat in a corner, then slept and waited for dawn.

She sat for a while, then she smelled smoke. At this time, it was nearly dawn, so it was very cold. You know that the Highlands are a cold place.

She thought of searching for the fire and warming her body. She got up, took her things and followed the trail to where the smoke from the fire was originating. She walked and walked, then she saw a hut.

She saw the smoke from the fire coming out of the hut. She walked closer and saw a young boy sleeping by the fire inside the house.

She felt ashamed, but she went by the hut and wanted to go inside. At the same time, the boy woke up and walked out to check on the noise. She saw this and turned back. She sped into part of forest and hid.

The young boy heard the noise and thought that a marsupial (*kapul*) was jumping on the trees. He stood quietly and waited for the "marsupial" to make a noise again, but the girl did not make another sound because she was afraid that he would see her.

The boy waited until dawn. At dawn, he walked to the base of the tree. He looked, then he saw the little sister sleeping inside of it. He took her and carried her to his hut. He asked her how she had come to his area.

Afterwards, he gave her some marsupial meat and other food, then the little sister ate. He wanted to take her back to his village, but she was confused about where his village was located.

They sat there, then the little sister told the story about her big sister and herself, and how she had arrived at the boy's hut. They told stories for a while, then the sun rose.

The little sister strongly wanted to stay and marry the young boy. The young boy also wanted this, so they lived together. They lived for a while, then the little sister gave birth to a son. The name of this baby was Hela Huli. At the same time, the big sister had given birth to a son in the village. The name of this baby was Hela Obena.

These two names, Obena and Huli, signify the people of Tari and Wabeg [**Wabag**] today. Obena [Enga] marks the group of people from Wabeg, and Huli marks the group of people from Tari.

So today, we see that the people of the two places are like brother and sister. This is because they came from these two sisters. When enemies come to the people of Wabeg, the Tari people will quickly come to their assistance. And the same is true for the Tari people. Even today, there is friendship between the youths [lit., "young bloods"] of these two places.

Tabakaua

Tari

Southern Highlands Province

[See *Wantok* #410 for another story about Opena and Huli.]

A1611+. Origin of Enga People; A1611+. Origin of Huli People; P210. Husband and wife; P231. Mother and son; P233. Father and son; P252.1. Two sisters; T100. Marriage; T580. Childbirth

A Ghost Woman Fixed
Three Brothers' Worries

(Wantok 891, August 1, 1991, page 16)

Long, long ago, in the time of the ancestors, there were three brothers who lived in Mulaganni Village [**Muliagani** Island] in the Kombe area of **West New Britain** Province [**Mok** People]. Their names were Sanga, Vava and Ako.

Their father and mother had died, so they lived by themselves in this village. However, there were no other families or people in the village to help them with food. They lived by their own strength.

Many times, they lived with worry. The big brother, Sanga, noticed this and was very sorry for his two little brothers. He would think hard about what to do so that that they would always have enough food in the house.

One time, Sanga told Vava and Ako that he would travel the forest, searching to see whether there was some land for making a garden.

He traveled the deep forest, but he did not find a piece of land. Other people had made all of the good areas into gardens. Some good places where there were not yet any gardens had already been marked as such.

Sanga worked hard looking for a good piece of land from the morning until the afternoon. He felt sorry for his two brothers, so he began to walk slowly back home.

He passed by gardens and thought very hard about what he could do now. Before long, he began to think of their mother and father, then he was very troubled, "If they had not died, my two brothers and I would not be lost like this. We would have had a garden where we could always get food. But, they're gone now and our maternal kin no longer take care of us."

He thought like that, then he walked back home. Before long, he passed a garden and met an old woman. Sanga had never seen this old woman before, so he was terrified. This was because he thought that she was an evil ghost woman who wanted to trick and confuse him.

Sanga had this kind of idea, so he wanted to quickly cut across another trail, but the old woman had seen him. She shouted for him to return.

Sanga was strong and wanted to flee, but the old woman called out again. So, Sanga very slowly walked into the garden. His thoughts were still of fear.

Sanga approached, and the old woman told him to help her plant some taros and bananas. Sanga listened and quickly began planting taros and bananas in the garden.

He thought that it would be bad if he did not listen to what the ghost woman said, lest he become befouled. He worked quickly, planting all of the bananas and taros in the garden.

What had really happened was that his mother had become a ghost woman and had come to help him. However, Sanga did not get this idea.

Sanga planted all of the bananas and taros, then the old woman told him, "Young man, thank you very much for helping me. It's alright, go home. After three days, come to this garden. The food will be ripe. Come back with your two little brothers and gather all of the food. All of the food in the garden is for you."

When Sanga heard this, he felt wonderful inside. He ran home quickly to tell his young brothers, Vava and Aka [Ako]. They all had the idea that their old mother must have arrived as the ghost woman and had come to help them.

They were terribly worried. At the same time, they were happy. Three days later, they awoke in the very early morning. They ate a little food, then they began to walk towards the garden.

They arrived and saw that the garden was packed with bananas and taros. There were also plentiful sweet potatoes. The garden was jammed with various kinds of food. The big brother's worries about themselves were over. They filled their baskets with some food, then they sang and danced and returned home.

They left some food to take later. So today in Mulaganni Village in the Kombe area, the food gardens, such as sweet potatoes, taros and bananas, are abundant.

Ken Kalus

Bialla

West New Britain Province

A2793+. Why garden food is abundant in certain place; D1030.1. Food supplied by magic; E323. Dead mother's friendly return; E425.1. Revenant as woman; P231. Mother and son; P251.6.1. Three brothers; P290+. Maternal kin; W27. Gratitude

The Heron Tricked Some Fish

(Wantok 892, August 8, 1991, page 17)

Long, long ago, in the time of the ancestors, there was a heron that lived in a pond. The name of this pond is Wo. It is located in the **Kaintiba** area of Kerema in the **Gulf** Province [**Hamtai** People].

The heron always tried hard to find food, but it never caught any. It would sit on top of Wo Pond, then watch for a fish to grab and eat, but it never grabbed even a small one.

One afternoon, the heron did not eat anything, so it was completely famished. It went to its home and thought about what it could do. The heron thought and thought, then it had an idea. The idea was to trick the fish of Wo Pond.

In the very early morning, the heron went to the pond and waited for fish to come. The heron sat for a while, then before long, some fish swam towards it. Oh my, the heron was elated.

Quickly, the heron shouted, "My kin, I have a message to tell you."

The fish came and the heron told them, "Last night, I heard that the people of **Yambona** Village decided to dam Wo Pond and catch all of the fish."

When the fish heard the heron's story, they were terrified. The heron told them to go back and to send the message to the other fish.

The next day, all of the fish of the Wo Pond returned and again met the heron. They held a huge meeting. They wanted to come up with a good way to save their lives.

So, they asked the heron whether it had some way to help them. The heron told them, "I have a way that I'll tell you. If you agree, then I'll help you."

The heron told them that it knew of a pond and that it would take them to this pond. The heron also told them that it would carry each of them in its mouth and throw them into the pond.

All of the fish agreed to this idea. The heron told them that it would carry one fish and show the pond first. Then this fish would return and tell the other fish whether it was a good place or not.

The heron did this, then all of the fish pushed themselves to be first. The heron took each fish in its mouth, then went midway and swallowed it.

The heron kept doing this until there were no more fish in the pond. When the heron returned, there were only crabs there. So, the heron asked whether the crabs wanted to go to the new pond.

However, the crabs tricked the heron. They sent their own leader to go with the heron. The leader of the crabs had very big claws. It was quite ready to show the heron something if the heron tried to eat it.

Midway, the heron tried to eat the leader of the crabs, but the crab was at the ready it and put its big claws around the heron's neck. The heron died and the crab returned to Wo Pond. Afterwards, only crabs lived in this pond.

So today in Wo Pond, you never see any herons. Also, you do not see many fish there because they were all sent to be eaten by this heron.

Kikusu W.

Wewak

East Sepik Province

A2584+. Why there are few fish at particular pond; A2584+. Why there are no herons at particular pond; B211.3.10K. Speaking heron; B211.5. Speaking fish; B243+. King of crabs; K815.14. Fish tricked by crane into letting selves be carried from one pond to another; K953.3+. Crab carried by heron, clings round his neck and cuts off his head with pincers; Q211.6. Killing an animal revenged; Q424. Punishment: strangling

A Dog and Marsupial (*Kapul*) Found a Kagua Man's Wife

(Wantok 893, August 15, 1991, page 16)

Long ago, in **Puluparu** Village, in the Kagua area of **Southern Highlands** Province, there lived a man [**Kewa** People]. The man's name was Koteke Paru and he was unmarried.

One very early morning, Paru woke up, took his spears and things, then followed the trail to Mount Poduke to hunt for wild game. He went directly to the base of the mountain and met a wild dog pup that was lying in the tree litter. The boy carried the pup and went to the house.

Paru took care of the pup until it grew up. Then the two of them were very good friends. Whenever Paru and the dog would go to hunt for wild game, they would kill very many animals.

One time, Paru was cleaning his dog's hair and he blurted out, "I'm sorry my friend, we don't have an axe to cut trees." The dog listened and went to kill a she-marsupial (*kapul*). This marsupial was pregnant, so they ate the mother and took care of the baby marsupial.

The marsupial also grew up, so the three of them became very good friends. However, the man was not happy yet so he told his two friends, "We have very plentiful sweet potatoes. However, we don't have pork to garnish the sweet potatoes." So, the marsupial and the dog went into the deep forest and chased a pregnant sow back to the garden fence. The dog began to bark, then Paru walked very quietly and saw what was wrong. Oh my, he was shocked to see the pregnant sow.

So, Paru made a fence, then took care of the pig until she gave birth. Then the boy became a very wealthy man from the pigs. However, he still had a big problem. One afternoon, he sat watching the sun turn red as it set. He got up and blurted out to the dog and marsupial, "Sorry, I always work hard at cooking food, weeding the garden, fetching water, and taking care of us. If there was a woman, all of these things would be very easy."

After he said this, the dog and marsupial went to a very faraway place. They arrived there and saw a big group of women working at burning the forest so as to make a garden. The marsupial jumped up a tree and sat waiting for the dog. The dog sped inside to where the women were and looked around. The dog looked and saw a very nice woman. The woman's entire skin was very light, more so than the color of pig fat.

This woman worked for a while, then she became thirsty and wanted to go down to the stream. Very quietly, the dog followed her. This was at the same place where the marsupial was waiting. At the same time that the woman saw the marsupial on the tree branch, the dog jumped up and pretended to kill the marsupial. The marsupial fell down and when the woman wanted to go grab it, the marsupial went far away towards the stream. The dog and the marsupial kept doing this, and so they enticed the woman to go very far away. Then they arrived at Paru's fence.

When Paru heard his dog barking, he jumped and went outside to the see the woman standing there. There was nothing more to say, so the two of them married and erected a big clan house.

One time, this clan house wanted to kill pigs to make a party. They worked at killing the pigs for a while, then the dog and the marsupial surrounded the pig that they had taken the very first time. Paru did not understand what they said, so he killed this pig. The dog and marsupial were angry, so the dog fled into the deep forest and the marsupial went to hide inside a cave.

Kaua Kondeanea

Lae City

Morobe Province

B212. Animal understands human speech; B421. Helpful dog; B430+. Helpful marsupial; B582.1.1. Animal wins wife for his master (Puss in Boots); F527.7K+. White person; K1860. Deception by feigned death (sleep); P210. Husband and wife; P230. Parents and children; P310. Friendship; R213. Escape from home; T100. Marriage; T570. Pregnancy

The Bimat People Killed a Sorcerer Man from Tawurepat [Turutapa]

(Wantok 894, August 22, 1991, page 16)

Long, long ago, in the time of the ancestors, in Tawurepat [Turutapa] in **Madang** Province, they went around making black magic [**Saki** People]. This story comes from the Almani Council area of Bogia.

One time, a **Bimat** [Village] woman [**Pila** People] went down to the beach of **Suaru** [Pila People] and **Beriwen** to hunt for some shellfish and crabs to eat. She hunted and hunted, then in the late afternoon she wanted to return home. However, a heavy rain fell and she did not have a way to return, so she went inside a garden hut and slept.

Before long, Tawurepat men also came to this hut to hide from the rain. The garden hut was not very nice, so the rain fell inside it too.

One of these men went up to the place where the woman was sleeping and he saw her. He was elated and he grabbed her. Then he went down and lied to the other men that he would just sleep at the place where the rain was falling.

He went up to the woman again. He retired and went close to her. He wanted to sleep with her. However, she lied to him, "Aie-ye-e-e something's poking my side. Wait a minute."

She then shoved her hand into her net bag and took a crab that she had tied. Quietly, she loosened the rope on the crabs two big claws. She put it right upon the sorcerer's testicles.

The crab pinched the sorcerer's testicles strongly. He felt a terrible pain and shouted very loudly. The other sorcerers heard this and sped away into the forest in various directions. They thought that a Bimat man must have grabbed their kinsman. The Bimat woman also ran down and sped off to her village.

Some months passed, then a big party came to Bimat Village. Everyone from Tawurepat went to see this party. At the party, the woman saw the sorcerer, and she laughed to herself. He was completely furious and said, "Ah! So it's you who put the crab on my balls!"

Before long, the woman thought of a pot of food in the house and went back to check on it. The Tawurepat man was already waiting at the house. She went inside the door and he grabbed her.

She just wanted to scream, but he had already put soot from the fire in her mouth and nose. The poor woman did not have any more strength and she died in the house. Immediately, he butchered her like a pig and threw her into the pot on top of the fire. The sorcerer hung her two breasts on top of the house door.

After he did this, he fled back to his house in Tawurepat Village. The woman's husband went up to the house and saw that his wife was dead. He was speechless. Quietly, he put the body together and buried her.

The talk got louder, and everyone shot words back and forth. They all came up with the idea that a Tawurepat man must have killed her.

Some years passed, then everyone forgot this death. One time, the sorcerer wanted to travel to the beach. He walked and walked, then he arrived at Bimat Village.

He slept a little in Bimat, then he wanted to go back. The people of Bimat asked him when he would return. Then they kept watch and the sorcerer returned.

He rested in the village, then some women cooked food and gave it to him. They gave him some fish with betel nuts, and tobacco too.

The man wanted to get up and walk away, but no. The Bimat men grabbed him. They tied his arms and legs with rope, *limbum* palm, and dry coconut palm leaves (used for torches).

On the sorcerer's head, they put the net bag of the woman that he had killed. They finished adorning him, then they lit the torch on top of his head. They let him run down the mountain.

The fire burned the sorcerer's head. His head broke and exploded very loudly. He died and the fire burned his entire body.

Paul Mekiah

Bogia

Madang Province

[For a similar story, see *Wantok* #832.]

D1711. Magician; F547.1.1. Vagina dentata; K914. Murder from ambush; P210. Husband and wife; Q244.1. Punishment for attempted rape; Q411. Death as punishment; Q414.0.12. Burning as punishment for murder; Q451.10.1+. Punishment: attack on testicles; Q583. Fitting bodily injury as punishment; R220. Flights; S112. Burning to death; S139.2. Slain person dismembered; S139.2.2+. Corpse put into cooking pot or cooked; V61.3+. Dead buried; W157. Dishonesty; X712.1H. Female genitals; X712.3.1H. Injury to testicles

[There was no ancestor story in Wantok #895.]

Why Are the Menang [Mengan] People Enemies with the Masalais?

(Wantok 896, September 5, 1991, page 16)

Long ago, in the time of the ancestors, two brothers lived in a village that is now called Menang [**Mengan**]. This village is in the Teptep area of **Madang** Province [**Kewieng** People].

The names of the brothers were Menang and Sowe. Long before, their father and mother had died when they were young, so they lived by themselves.

However, they were never short of food. Inside their house, there was plenty of good food and meat. This was because they made many gardens and because they were the best men at hunting.

The *masalai*s often looked very carefully at what the brothers did. Then one time, all of the *masalai*s gathered and decided to kill them.

Menang was the elder brother and Sowe was the younger. One day, they awoke in the morning and walked off to the garden. They worked and worked, then in the afternoon, they walked back to the house. They cooked some food, then they ate. Afterwards, they thought about what they would do the next day.

Before long, the big brother came up with an idea and told the little brother, "Tonight we must prepare everything for hunting wild game. Tomorrow when it is still morning, we'll go to the forest and hunt for game."

Sowe just followed what the big brother said, so he did everything as the brother wanted. Then they slept. When it was nearly dawn, Menang awakened Sowe to prepare their things. Sowe tied the two dogs with ropes, then they took food and sped away into the forest.

They arrived at a big river, then dawn broke. The birds cried and the sun began to rise. They jumped across a river, then they went up a hill and into the very deep forest.

They arrived in the deep forest, then they let go of the dogs' ropes. The dogs ran into the forest, and they just followed them. The dogs did not smell even the smallest animal. They just smelled the smell of marsupials (*kapul*).

The big brother, Menang, knew this and told the little brother to rest, then they would erect a forest hut for sleeping. That night, Menang killed very many marsupials in this area. However, all of these were just *masalai* marsupials.

The *masalai*s saw the brothers killing many marsupials, so they planned to kill them. The *masalai*s performed a little black magic, then many marsupials hung about from the trees. The brothers saw this and worked hard at killing the marsupials.

Menang did not know that these were *masalai* marsupials. Sowe also did not know. The *masalai*s had confused him. He carried a net bag and followed Menang.

Oh my, he saw very many marsupials that were dying. The big brother, Menang, was still killing more marsupials. Sowe saw this and worked at filling the net bag, but the net bag filled up very quickly.

So, he made a forest hut and filled the hut with the marsupials. He left the marsupials in the hut and followed the big brother.

They thought about the marsupials and they wanted to rest because the sun was setting. They quickly gathered all of the marsupials and carried them back home.

When it was nearly dark, the brothers arrived home. Sowe worked at singeing off the marsupial fur in a fire. Menang worked at cutting their bellies and removing their feces.

Menang completely forgot his little brother. Oh my, the fire grew larger on the marsupial fur then flew over and burned Sowe.

Then the fire burned bigger and Menang saw this. He ran over to stop the fire and he saw his brother. However, the *masalai*s had done this and the fire leapt to Menang too.

Menang fought the fire strongly, trying to extinguish it. But no, the *masalai*s took his strength. The fire finished off the two brothers. The two dogs saw that their masters had died in the fire and they were very troubled. The dogs sped away to a village, then whined at the people of this village.

The people saw this and followed the dogs towards the place where the fire had killed the brothers. When they arrived, they just saw the bones of Menang and Sowe lying there. They sat and cried a little for the two brothers.

Afterwards, they removed tree bark and put all of Menang's and Sowe's bones inside the bark. Then they carried them to the village. The men of the village thought of getting revenge and killing these *masalai*s.

They made a big house, then they carried it to this place. Many good foods, such as pork and dog flesh, were put inside the house. They tied five ropes to all of the corners, so as to kill the *masalai*s if they went inside the house.

They took the house and left it at the place where the brothers had died. Then all of the men went to hide in the forest, waiting for the *masalai*s to come out and eat the food.

Before long, many *masalai*s smelled the food. They came out of the forest and raced into the house. The men [pulled] the ropes on all of the corners and killed the *masalai*s.

Only one woman was not dead. She was still eating the food and nursing her baby. The men cut the ropes on this *masalai* woman. Then she fled into the deep forest with her baby. She ran and went inside, then she shouted back to the men that the Menang people were the enemies of the *masalai*s.

So now still, the Menang people are enemies with the *masalai*s of this place.

Jame Mamage
Tamangke Village

A1617. Origin of place-name; A2800+. Origin of enmity between spirits and humans; D1271. Magic fire; D1402.4. Magic fire kills; D2074.1. Animals magically called; D2000+. Magic confusion; F401.3+. Spirit in marsupial form; F401.6. Spirit in human form; F405+. Spirit killed; F490+. Masalai; K914. Murder from ambush; P230. Parents and children; P251.5. Two brothers; Q211. Murder punished; Q211.6. Killing an animal revenged; Q411. Death as punishment; Q414. Punishment: burning alive; S112.0.2. House (hostel) burned with all inside; T611. Suckling of children; Z356. Unique survivor

Two Men Turned into *Masalai*s and Killed the Others

(Wantok 897, September 12, 1991, page 16)

Long ago in Kandinge [**Kandangai**] Village, in the Pagwi area of the Sepik River, there lived two men [**Iatmul** People, **East Sepik** Province]. The men's names were Kamam and Gawi. Every night, Kaman would turn into a *masalai* crocodile, then kill people who were fishing on the Sepik River.

Gawi often turned into a bird during the day and searched for the skulls and bones of the people that Kamam had eaten and hung up at night. Kamam was a man from Kaninge [Kandinge] Village, but every night he would go first to the water, then turn into a *masalai* crocodile.

His friend Gawi would do the same kind of things during the day. Gawi usually slept at night. In the morning, he would speed off to the Sepik River and search for the heads of the people that Kaman had hung up and eaten.

Many years passed and the two men killed very many people. Every night, Kaman would kill two or three men and eat them. During the day, Gawi would search for the heads and bones then eat. They were very good friends at killing and eating the people of Kandinge Village.

People found it very difficult to see that it was really a crocodile that was killing people at night. One time, the village council called all of the young and old men to give their thoughts about what they could do to see and kill this crocodile.

One time, the council pounded the signal drum and called for everyone to come to a meeting. They talked about killing the crocodile. At this time, Kaman was dead asleep in his house because his belly was filled from men's bodies from the night before.

His friend Gawi flew by the river and was searching for the skulls and bones of the dead men that Kaman had eaten the night before. They did not know what the villagers were talking about. One day, everyone prepared things for killing Kaman.

However, he did not know what the people would do to kill him. He slept and the men paddled the canoes in the river. Kaman was surprised that it was dark.

He went to the river to remove everything, then he changed into a crocodile. However, he did not know that the men had surrounded the water and were ready to kill him. They hid and saw him change his body to become a big crocodile, then swim down in the river.

Every man saw this and was unhappy about Kaman because he had killed many people. They just made a sign, then every man was ready at the place where he was swimming. Then they sent a woman and a man there to pretend to fish by the water.

Kaman saw the two of them. He pretended to swim closer to pull them down into the water and kill them. When the men saw this, they sped closer and planted all of the spears into him. He tried to remove the spears and flee, but many men had already thrown their spears and killed him. They took knives and cut his body into small pieces.

That same night, they all sat and gathered their thoughts about killing the bird who had eaten the skulls and bones of the dead that Kaman had killed and hung. They cut off Kaman's head and went to hang it on a tree.

Afterwards, they went back to the village and said to the other men who lived in the village, "You should go to watch Kaman's head. Kill whichever bird that has eaten our skulls and bones."

In the early morning, they went to hide around the tree. They waited for the bird to come and eat the hanging head. Gawi awoke in the morning and went into the forest, then he quickly changed into a big bird. He flew to the tree where Kaman's head was hanging.

When the men saw the big bird, they were not happy with it. So, when the bird put its mouth to eat Kaman's skull, all of the men held their spears and shot it. They killed the bird and cut its body into small pieces, then they took the pieces to the village to show the other people.

Afterwards, they heard that the families of Kumam [Kamam] and Gawi were crying. All of the men knew that it was just these two men who had turned into *masalai*s and killed people. They took their bodies and went to the mouth of the Sepik River, then buried them.

Even now, the people of Kandinge call the mouth of this river, Kamamgawi Pond. Kamam is the name of the *masalai* crocodile, and Gawi is the name of the *masalai* bird.

Cietus Kura
Hagen
Western Highlands Province

A1617. Origin of place-name; B16.5.2. Devastating crocodile; D150M. Transformation: man to bird; D194M. Transformation: man to crocodile; D350M. Transformation: bird to man; D397+M. Transformation: crocodile to man; F490+. Masalai; G354.2. Crocodile as ogre; G353.1. Cannibal bird as ogre; G512.1+. Ogre killed with spear/arrow; K914. Murder from ambush; P310. Friendship; Q211. Murder punished; Q215. Cannibalism punished; Q411. Death as punishment; S110. Murders; S139.2. Slain person dismembered; V61.3+. Dead buried

An Ordinary Carving Turned into a Crocodile
(Wantok 898, September 19, 1991, page 17)

In the time of yore, in the Sandaun [**West Sepik**] Province area, there was a little trail that went down to the river. At this place, the men knew precisely how to make wooden carvings.

One time, they carved a *galip* tree into the image of a crocodile. They finished carving the wood, then they put it right in the young boys' house.

One morning, everyone traveled in the forest to hunt for wild game to make a feast for this carving. They worked at hunting for game, such as pigs, marsupials (*kapul*), as well as animals from the water. Some went to the gardens to dig up food. This village was near Mount Polosal.

When the men were out at their work, the crocodile carving began to transform itself. It did this until it became a real crocodile. It got up and jumped down, then it searched for a place to flee.

It walked and followed the trail to the beach. When it arrived at the beach, it turned back and saw the mountain from which it had run. The mountain was behind it, in the east.

It left this place and went west. When it arrived at a river called Puian, it turned and looked back again. The mountain was still clear, so it continued to walk farther.

It walked and walked farther, then it arrived at two more rivers, Oweiar and Wiliei. Every time that it walked away, it would turn and look back at the mountain from which it had fled.

It arrived at another river called Chiyipala. When it turned, it no longer saw the mountain. It kept going ahead, then it arrived at the last river, called Yulumula, and it stayed there. Now they call this crocodile, Puai Cholomon. It came from the east and now lives in the west, in **Manus** [Province].

Ignasius Kalal
Lorengau
Manus Province

A2146. Creation of crocodile; D435.1.1. Transformation: statue comes to life; R220. Flights

The Ghosts Ate their Own Friend
(Wantok 899, September 26, 1991, page 17)

Long, long ago, two boys lived with their mother and father in the deep forests of **Kainantu** [**Agarabi** People, **Eastern Highlands** Province]. The four of them lived for a while, then their mother died. They buried her under the house.

The boys lived with their father. Their father never left them by themselves because there were many ghosts that ate boys. They just filled this area.

One time, the father wanted to go to a faraway place to hunt for wild game for themselves. So, he made five fences around the house, then gave a stern lecture to [the boys]. He told them to just stay in the house until he returned.

They sat with their father on the right and he gave them the stern lecture. After sleeping, the father awakened them at dawn and spoke to them again that he was now leaving. He took his multi-pronged spears, his two dogs, and his food, then he went into the forest.

The big brother did not want to scare the little brother, so he talked about various things to distract the little brother's thinking. They stayed and played just outside their house. Then at night they would lock the door, hide themselves in a little room and sleep.

Two days passed, then they wanted their father to return quickly before something happened to them. On the third day, a nice sun rose. The big brother told the little brother that they should go play outside and wait for their father to bring their game back.

They played, then they heard an unusual noise coming from the forest. The big brother told the little brother to run inside the house and look for everything for fighting, then take the things inside the house before the ghost came.

The big brother straightened out the area in front of the door. To shoot the ghost, the little brother took other things and was ready to help his big brother. The ghost went directly to the first fence and tried to break it.

The ghost tried hard, then the big brother pulled back a bow and [shot an arrow] directly into the ghost's mouth. The ghost screamed and then removed the arrow from its mouth. The ghost was angry and gnashed its teeth together [at the thought of] breaking all of the fences and eating the two little brothers.

The ghost broke the first fence, then it arrived at the second. It did the same thing, then removed all of the fences. The boys did not say anything now. They were ready, then the ghost broke the house from the other side. The ghost just jumped onto the big brother and grabbed him. The ghost broke his neck and carried him upon its shoulders, then it ran into the forest.

The little brother was speechless when he saw the ghost kill his big brother. He sat and just thought that his father must return quickly from the forest. Before long, their father saw a rainbow up in the heavens.

This rainbow showed the name of the ghost that must have killed his two boys. So, he left everything there in the forest and ran back to the house. When he arrived, he did not hear a sound. He knew that his two boys must have died.

However, when he opened the door, he saw the little boy sitting there with plenty of blood on the floor. He cried and held his little boy.

Afterwards, he did not talk. He just asked where the ghost had carried his son. When the boy showed him, the father took the fighting gear and followed the ghost.

He arrived exactly when the ghost was [getting ready to] swallow his son. The ghost was putting the body on stones to cook in an earth oven.

The ghost did not see the boy's father standing nearby. When the father saw the ghost, the ghost was closing up the earth oven. Then the ghost saw the boy's father standing there speechless.

The ghost just tried to fight with the father. However, the father was ready and put his knife directly into the ghost's neck, cutting it and causing the ghost to fall down. Afterwards, he removed all of the stones to find his son, but he did not find him quickly, because the ghost had hidden the boy very well, far down in the earth oven. When he found him, he cried terribly, then he carried him to the house to bury him.

He went back to the place where the laid ghost was located and he carried the ghost to the house. He burned the ghost in a big pot, then he carried the pot into the forest and threw the contents around for the ghost's friends to eat.

Even now, the custom of eating the liver (or heart) of dead men and performing sorcery on men is popular in Kainantu. However, they left behind the custom of eating men some years ago because the message of God came strongly to Kainantu when the missionaries came in 1889. [The missionary arrival in Kainantu was actually substantially later, in the late 1920s and early 1930s (Radford, 1987: xv-xvi, 51-52, 97, 133).]

Tise Osneka
Kainantu
Eastern Highlands Province

D1812.5.1+. Rainbow gives bad omens; E440+. Ghost laid by knife; G11.10. Cannibalistic spirits; G70+. Funerary cannibalism; P210. Husband and wife; P231. Mother and son; P233. Father and son; P251.5. Two brothers; Q211. Murder punished; Q411. Death as punishment; R260. Pursuits; S110. Murders; V61.3+. Dead buried; V331. Conversion to Christianity; Z71.3. Formulistic number: five

Two Brothers Made Salt
for the Gumine People

(Wantok 900, October 8, 1991, page 17)

Long, long ago, two young men from **Gunagi** Village in southern Simbu had strong thoughts of marriage. They had already searched for women in the villages of the Gumine area of **Simbu** Province [**Golin** People]. This was why they did not want to marry in their own village of Gunagi. So one time, they decided to search for women in a village called **Deri** in the Gumine area.

One morning, they walked from Gunagi to Deri to search for young women. They arrived at Deri and watched the nice women coming out of the houses, then they shouted to them. Afterwards, they asked them to sleep with them. They watched and saw two sisters walking out of their parents' house.

The two young men shouted for the two sisters to come. When the two women came, they asked them to sit and they would tell stories, then a little later they would go to work with them. The two men said that they would sleep with the women at night. Then the two women sped away, back to the house and explained this to their parents. That same afternoon, the young women returned and took the men to their house.

Their mother and father made a big celebration because the women had found two nice men to help the family with garden work. At night, the two men slept with the two young women.

In the early morning, the two [men] awoke, took their things and walked back towards Gunagi to explain to their parents that they had found two women to marry.

While they were still walking along the trail, they had various thoughts about the women that they had slept with that night. They walked and followed the trail up to the Waghi [Wahgi] River. When they stood on top of the bridge, they saw two young women who were like the sisters that they had slept with that night.

These women had not put on good clothes. They sat looking at the Waghi River. When the men saw them, they tried to take them to Gunagi Village, their home. So, the two of them decided that one would stay on top and the other would go down and bring up the two women.

When the one walked down, he did not see the women, but his friend on top of the bridge saw the women sitting close to him.

The men argued with each other, then the one on top told the one who was down below, "Come up and watch, then I'll go down and bring the women because you're blind." When his friend went down, the same thing happened to him. He did not see the women, but his friend on top of the bridge saw them.

The men greatly wanted to take the women. The sun rose strongly. They were very thirsty for water because the sun was very hot. The Waghi River was far from them, so they searched hard to find good water to drink.

They saw a small hole that a pig had cleared that had clean water in it. They took leaves from forest taro [i.e., wild taro] and drank the water. The water was delicious to them, so they finished all of the water.

Afterwards, they walked towards the village. While they were still walking, they talked about the water and the two young women. They arrived at the house in the late afternoon. They were too tired to do anything because they had walked a long way and they had worked very hard trying to find the women.

They slept that night, then they dreamt of the water hole from which they had drunk, and of the two young women that they had slept with at Deri.

In the early morning, they met again and talked about what their dreams had told them to do late that night. When one of them finished his story, his friend told him, "Brother, I had the same dream as you."

They got up and followed what their dreams had told them to do. They went and took a little of the water that they had drunk along with some firewood and grass for making a fire. They burned these things, then the grass and water made salt.

Later, the two men made this salt, and the Simbu People used the men's salt until the white man's type of salt arrived. However, the people of the Gumine area in Simbu Province still use this salt to cook food.

Peter Kaupa
southern Simbu Province

A1429.4. Acquisition of salt; D1810.8.2. Information received through dream; D2031. Magic illusion; D2095. Magic disappearance; P210. Husband and wife; P231. Mother and son; P232. Mother and daughter; P233. Father and son; P234. Father and daughter; P252.1. Two sisters; P310. Friendship; T90+. Premarital sex; T100. Marriage

A Woman Married a Snake

(Wantok 901, October 10, 1991, page 16)

Long, long ago, in the time of the ancestors, there was a *masalai* snake. The *masalai* snake lived in the deep forests of **Besomang** in **Morobe** Province [**Nabak** People].

The *masalai* snake always looked for young women to marry, but he never had the chance to meet one. So, he always watched people's gardens.

One time when he was watching, a young woman and her family arrived at a garden. Many young men from the village lusted for this young woman.

However when she went to the garden, the *masalai* snake saw [her,] and his arms and legs trembled to grab her. When they arrived at the garden, the woman weeded it very well with her parents. In the afternoon, they removed some taros and sweet potatoes. They filled net bags and took them to the village.

At this time, the young woman forgot entirely about her necklace that was on top of the base of a tree. They lifted all of their things and walked towards the village. They climbed a mountain and they were completely out of breath, so they sat and caught their breaths.

The woman thought of her necklace, then she went to the garden again to find it. She searched everywhere, but there was no necklace.

She held her head and sat in the garden, thinking of where she could have lost her necklace. The snake had known this, so he quickly took her necklace and hid it inside a cave.

The snake looked at the young woman for a while, then he became very angry. He went outside and just grabbed her, taking her into his stone house. The parents waited on top of the mountain until late at night, then they went to the village and explained to the people what had happened.

In the early morning, they beat the signal drum and blew the conch trumpet. Then everyone went to the forest to search for her. They searched for two days, then they forgot her. They believed strongly that the *masalai* snake must have killed and eaten her.

However, some months passed, then the people of the village found out that the *masalai* snake had taken her. The snake and the woman just lived inside the cave. The leaders of the village prevented the young women from going near this place.

One nice day, the young woman and the *masalai* snake went up to look for water to bathe. After the second time, people found out that she was pregnant.

This thing aroused the thoughts of the villagers to get her back. However, all of their hard work was for nothing because the *masalai* snake just hid her inside the cave. They lived for a while, then she gave birth to a baby girl. This girl looked like the young woman.

The *masalai* snake never let the two of them leave. Whenever he went to find food for themselves, he would shut them inside his stone house. They lived for a while, and then the baby grew to be a big woman. Later, her mother became pregnant again. This time, she gave birth to a baby boy who looked like his father.

He had a man's head and a snake's body. The body showed that his father was the *masalai* snake. The mother was a real woman from Besomang Village.

Even now, this family still lives inside a big cave in back of Besomang Village. They married among themselves and raised very many children. So, the forests of Besomang have many snakes. They have various kinds of heads and various kinds of bodies.

Ruma Nonje Joxs
Rabaul
East New Britain Province

A2433.6.8+. Why there are many snakes at particular place; B29.2.1. Serpent with human head; B604.1. Marriage to snake; B631. Human offspring from marriage to animal; B634. Monstrous offspring from animal marriage; B765.23. Snake with legs; F401.3.8. Spirits in form of snake; F490+. Masalai; P210. Husband and wife; P231. Mother and son; P232. Mother and daughter; P233. Father and son; P234. Father and daughter; P253. Sister and brother; R10. Abduction; R45.3. Captivity in cave; T111.

Marriage of mortal and supernatural being; T410. Incest; T192. Marriage by force; T550. Monstrous births; T570. Pregnancy; T580. Childbirth

A Brother Rediscovered His
Sister at the Site of a Festival
(Wantok 902, October 17, 1991, page 18)

Long, long ago, in the time of the ancestors, a little boy and his parents lived in a little place inside the deep forest. The three of them lived for a while, then the mother became pregnant with another child.

The mother was about to give birth when the father thought about walking on a long trail. So, he told his wife to take good care of the baby until he returned. However before the father walked away, he told his wife that she must give birth to a son and to take good care of him until he returned. The man also said that if she gave birth to a daughter, she must kill her before he returned.

The little boy and the mother stayed for a while, then the mother gave birth to a baby girl. She wanted to kill the girl, but she felt sorry. The father did not return quickly, so the girl grew bigger.

The girl, the mother and the little brother lived for a while, then one day the father returned. When the father saw the mother and boy, he was elated.

However, he later saw the little girl come out of the house door. He was discontented. He was angry and told the mother, "I told you to kill this baby if it was a girl. I'm tired of seeing girls before my eyes."

Some days later, the father planned that he, his son and his wife must run away from the girl. So one day, he told the mother and the other child to prepare everything to flee.

In the morning, the father told the mother to cook some food for the girl, then flee. The girl went to play and did not know that her family had fled.

She played until it was dark, then she sped into the house. She did not see a sign of anyone in the house, so she shouted for her little brother and mother, but no one replied to her calls.

She went into her room and saw her little dog sleeping there. She held the dog and cried that her mother and father had abandoned them. In the morning, she awoke and shouted around the house.

When she returned to the house door, she saw that the footprints of her mother, little brother, and father. They had walked away into the forest. She went back to fetch the little dog and she put it in net bag. Afterwards, she went out of the house and followed their footsteps.

She walked until dark, then she slept at the base of a tree. In the morning, she followed their footsteps again. She followed them for four whole days. While her family was walking ahead, the mother would hide some food and leave it at the places where they sat to eat.

So, the girl knew that her mother must have been thinking of her and leaving her food. On the third day, she did not sleep. She used a torch at night to follow them until dawn.

When the sun rose, she kept walking and following them. She arrived at a river and saw her family sitting and eating on the other side.

She carried the dog and sped off to meet them. The little brother saw his sister and he was elated. The father was angry and told the girl, "We're tired of you. Why did you follow us here?" When she heard this, she began to cry. The father grabbed her and threw her down into the river. The water carried her down and cast her up near an old woman.

The old woman saw her and asked, "How did you get here?" She told the story to the old woman about what her mother and father had done. The old woman was sorry and took her to the house where she looked after her.

The girl stayed for a while and grew bigger at the old woman's village. When she was grown, many young men tried to marry her because she had become very beautiful. However, she did not want any man from this village.

She lived for a while, then one time the young people sang and danced at the village. The old woman adorned the young woman very nicely and told her to go to the festival. When the young woman went to the playground [festival grounds] for the dance, many men just went crazy to get her.

However, she caught sight of one man standing in the corner. Quickly, she went to hold him, then she told him to meet her at night. The man did not eat, he just waited eagerly for darkness because he was happy to meet this young woman. Night arrived, then she went to meet him in a house.

They were very happy to meet each other and they *karim lek*ed. They flattered each other skillfully. Afterwards, he told the story of his life with his family. She listened carefully for a while. He told her that he had cut [off a piece of] his hand and that his sister had taken it with a young bitch. She heard this [and] cried. She sped off to the house and took the piece of her brother's hand, then she returned.

The brother saw this and knew that the woman was just his sister. They held each other and cried terribly. Afterwards, he took his sister and went to [his] house.

He did not tell his mother and father that she was his sister. Late at night, he took a knife and killed his father. The mother was happy that her two children had returned, and they all lived happily together.

Mark Minjenga
Banz [Village, **Wahgi** People]
Western Highlands Province

N365.3.1. Brother and sister unwittingly in love with each other; P210. Husband and wife; P231. Mother and son; P232. Mother and daughter; P233. Father and son; P234. Father and daughter; P253. Sister and brother; P272. Foster mother; P275+. Foster daughter; P600+. Courtship customs: *karim lek*; P681+. Mourning customs: self-mutilation; Q285. Cruelty punished; Q411. Death as punishment; R220. Flights; R260. Pursuits; S11.3.6+. Father throws girl into river (sea); S22+. Patricide; S143. Abandonment in forest; S110. Murders; S160.1. Self-mutilation; S161.1. Mutilation: cutting off fingers; S301. Children abandoned (exposed); S142. Person thrown into the water and abandoned; S322.0.1K+. Man instructs pregnant wife to cherish infant if a boy, to kill if a girl; T570. Pregnancy; T580. Childbirth

An Eye for an Eye and a Tooth for a Tooth
(Wantok 903, October 24, 1991, page 18)

Long ago, in a village called Ngariwidi [**Narawiti**], in the Bogio [Bogia] sub-District of **Madang** Province, there lived many people [**Saki** People].

One time, everyone decided to make a big feast for the young people. Everyone prepared the food, then the women filled bamboo tubes with water and brought them back. They worked hard and prepared for three whole days.

On the fourth day, the grand party arose. The chiefs or leaders of the village told all of the young people to go bathe in the river. When they heard the signal drum beating, they should come to the village because it would be time to eat.

All of the youths carried their younger siblings and sped away to wash in the Manag [River]. They sang and danced together in celebration.

They bathed, then they heard a dog barking and chasing a marsupial (*sikau*) towards themselves. Quickly, the young men grabbed the dog and marsupial, then went down to the river. Before long, the dog's master shouted and came to ask about his dog.

The youths lied to him that they had not seen a dog. He was terribly worried for his dog, so he walked down to the river. Before long, he saw his dog lying by the river. The dog was dead.

He knew that it was just the youths of Ngariwidi who had killed his dog. He carried the dog and walked back to his village, **Magumagu**, where he buried the dog.

Afterwards, he met all of the leaders and told them about the bad things that the Ngariwidi youths had done to him. The leaders listened and were completely furious.

They all took spears and left, surrounding the Menag [Manag] River. They made noises, then the youths of Ngariwidi came out of the water and tried to flee. However, they [the Magumagu] took all of them [the youths] as if they were pigs.

Just one boy escaped with his little sister. He just pulled the little sister by the hand, then they arrived at the village. They told everyone that the enemies had come to the other youths.

Oh my, all of the leaders listened and were greatly pained. They were terribly worried. Their leader saw this and took some betel nut clusters. He carried them on a stick and brought them to give to each village that was nearby, such as **Kukurai**, **Gurube**, Turutaba [**Turutapa**] and Pariakanam [**Pariakinam**].

That was it. They decided to go and kill everyone from Magumagu Village. A new moon rose and it was still dark. Before they went to fight, they all gathered at Ngariwidi. A month passed, then all of the men gathered at Ngariwidi. The leaders of Ngariwidi killed a big pig and all of the warriors ate.

After they had eaten, while it was still late at night, they surrounded Magumagu Village. Dawn arrived, then everyone shouted and made noise. The people heard the shouting and tried to go outside.

However, they gave it right to each one of them with their spears. Everyone died, but one mother and her son survived. This woman went and married at another village. She gave birth to more children and they carried forth the story of Magumagu.

Paul Mekiah
Madang
Madang Province

K914. Murder from ambush; P210. Husband and wife; P230. Parents and children; P231. Mother and son; P253. Sister and brother; Q211. Murder punished; Q211.6. Killing an animal revenged; Q411. Death as punishment; Q411.6. Death as punishment for murder; R210. Escapes; S110. Murders; T100. Marriage; T580. Childbirth; Z356. Unique survivor

Mandedagua Fled to Wewak Hill

(Wantok 904, October 31, 1991, page 16)

Long, long ago, in the time of the ancestors, there was a big village by the beaches of **Wewak** Town in **East Sepik** Province [**Kairiru** People]. In this village, there lived many young people

The young people would always go to the mangroves and beaches to search for *kina* shells and other seafood. Sometimes, they would sit together every afternoon and decide to search for *kina* shells and wild game.

The youths were always happy to do this work. When they did it, they often would forget about returning to the village. So, many times they would walk back to the village when darkness had arrived.

They did this sort of thing for a while, then one morning all of the youths gathered and decided to return to the mangroves and beaches.

Two young women left the group and went by the rubbish dump, where they had decided [to meet]. They did not know that a ghost woman had gone there first and was eating the rubbish. The ghost woman kept her ears out and listened carefully to everything that the young women had planned. The young women had decided that in the very early morning one would go wake the other, then they would walk to the big river to hunt for game.

In the early morning, when the two of them were still sleeping, the ghost woman turned into one of the two young women. She walked and walked, then she awakened the other young woman. The young woman woke up, took the things with [her] baby and followed the ghost woman.

They arrived at the river, then pushed down the canoe. They paddled and paddled along the river to the place of the mangroves to search for *kina* shells. They tied the canoe rope to a mangrove tree, then they searched for shells.

The sun had risen, and they saw a *tulip* tree. The ghost woman told the real woman to leave the baby there with her and to climb the *tulip* tree.

The ghost woman was hungry and wanted to just eat the real woman's baby. When the woman was on the tree, the ghost woman began cutting the baby's arms and eating it.

The baby cried, but the ghost woman did not care about it. The baby's mother asked from on top of the tree, "What's making the baby cry?" The ghost woman lied and replied that mosquitoes were biting the baby, causing it to cry.

The ghost woman finished the baby's two arms, then began to eat the legs. The baby began to cry louder now.

Quickly, the ghost woman finished off the baby. Then she just put its bones in a net bag and hung it on the branch of a tree that was near the canoe.

The mother finished taking the *tulip* leaves, then she went down and asked for her baby. The ghost woman lied to the mother that the baby was sleeping in the net bag. So, they took everything and went down to the canoe to paddle back to the village. The ghost woman told the mother that they must paddle far up to the headwaters first. The ghost woman wanted to eat the mother too, so she had lied to her.

They paddled and paddled upwards, then the mother took the net bag to give milk to the baby. She opened the net bag and saw that only the head and skin of the baby were lying there. She was afraid and jumped down into the water. The ghost woman turned the canoe around and followed her. However, the mother swam very quickly and arrived at the village.

She told everyone what had happened. They all waited and waited for the morning, then they lit torches or dry coconut leaves. They went to surround the cave in the mountain where the ghost woman and her baby slept.

Immediately, the ghost woman went to hide her daughter. The name of this ghost girl was Mandedagua. The people arrived and saw the ghost woman crying. They grabbed her and carried her, binding her arms and legs like a pig. Afterwards, they cooked her in a big fire. Mandedagua fled up to the top of a river called Kiring, by Saure [**Sauri Number 2**] Village, and stayed there [**Boiken** People].

Even today, this big cave is still there in back of the mountain called Wewak Hill, by Wewak Town.

Andrew Everlyn and Hellen Waram

Kainantu

Eastern Highlands Province

E261.4. Ghost pursues man; E425.1. Revenant as woman; E425.1.4. Revenant as woman carrying baby; E446.2. Ghost laid by burning body; E541. Revenants eat; G11.10. Cannibalistic spirits; K1930. Treacherous impostors; P230. Parents and children; P232. Mother and daughter; Q211.4. Murder of children punished; Q414. Punishment: burning alive; R210. Escapes; R220. Flights; R260. Pursuits; S110+. Eaten alive; S112. Burning to death; W157. Dishonesty

The Orokolo People Received Yams from the Moon

(Wantok 905, November 7, 1991, page 16)

Long, long ago, in the time of the ancestors, there was an old man who lived in **Orokolo** Village [**Orokolo** People,

Gulf Province]. The name of this man was Aru Aru. Aru Aru was married to a very young woman from this village.

Aru Aru had never heard about menstruation. One time, he found out that his wife was menstruating. He was shocked and angry.

He thought that a man must have slept with her, so he began to scold his wife. However, his wife said, "All women get this kind of illness. Don't get angry with just me."

However, old Aru Aru was not happy with this reply, "I know that a man must have slept with you, causing you to get this kind of illness. This man's name is Papale Mun. I'll kill this man." [*Papare* means "moon" in Orokolo (Brown, 1986: 96). *Mun* means "moon" in Tok Pisin.]

The next morning, he took her and they went to cut sago. She cut sago for a while, then he went to cut a *hapala* tree [fishtail palm tree, *Caryota* spp. (Brown, 1986: 26)] and he sharpened his spear. He prepared the things to go kill Papale Mun.

The next morning, he took the canoe and paddled away to kill Papale Mun. He paddled and paddled to the stream branch where Moon and Sun set. At night, he would follow Moon and during the day he would follow Sun. Moon had heard everything that Aru Aru had said about it to his wife.

He paddled and paddled, then he arrived at an island. He went ashore and saw two boys playing on the beach. He shouted to them, "Where's your papa and mama?" They shouted that their mother and father were coming, so they all pulled up his canoe.

That night, he slept with them. They told stories for a while, and then he told them why he had come. They clarified his thinking, that all women menstruated. However, Aru Aru still strongly desired to kill Moon.

The next morning, he did not eat. He thought that if he ate, he would lose his strength to do whatever work he went to do. Then he sang, "This is an enemy… where Moon and I meet." He sang like this and paddled the canoe downriver. He paddled until he arrived at another island.

This island only had a man and his wife. He saw a child and he asked for its parents. They all pulled his canoe up to the place where all of the canoes were ashore.

That night, he slept with them. Before they slept, old Aru Aru told the story of his journey. They thought that it was very funny and they gave him a lesson. However, Aru Aru did not listen to what they said.

The next morning, Aru Aru awoke and drank some water. Afterwards, he combed his hair, jumped down into the canoe and paddled away. He believed that if he drank water, all of his strength and magic power would leave when he urinated.

He paddled and paddled, then he arrived at a third island. He only saw a boy, so he asked him, "Call for your papa and mama to come here." However, the boy replied that he lived alone on this island. The little boy was Moon. This was the place that Aru Aru was looking for.

The little boy helped Aru Aru and pulled the canoe up to he beach. Afterwards, he took Aru Aru to his house on top of a *hepe* tree [*here* means "betel nut palm tree" (Brown, 1986: 36)].

Moon and Sun lived in this house. They would travel to all of the corners of the earth. Moon would travel at night and Sun would travel during the day.

The house was completely filled with stars. Sun was going around **Kerema** and was not at home [**Uaripi** People]. Moon told Aru Aru that his big brother, Sun, was away, working in the garden.

There were unusual string ropes on this house that joined all of the logs to the ground. Ordinary men could not see these ropes. Moon and Sun used these ropes to travel the earth.

They told stories for a while, and then Sun came. Oh my, Aru Aru saw that Sun's body was very clean and he was surprised. He knew that when a man worked in the garden, he could not come back clean like that.

Afterwards, the young boy went to change and became Moon. He looked very nice, like a strong, young man. He told Aru Aru everything that he had heard. Aru Aru was completely furious.

However, Moon told him, "I never slept with your wife exclusively. Every night I sleep with every woman on the earth, so they menstruate [lit., 'moon sickness']. You can't kill me because it is my wife that you stole."

Old Aru Aru was speechless. Moon gave him a yam and told him to paddle back to the village. Aru Aru jumped into the canoe and just paddled for a few minutes. Before long, he arrived at the village. Everyone shouted and came to meet him.

He told them that he had not killed Moon. However he brought a very good food for them. He planted this yam in the garden, then he stood up his fighting spears. The yam grew large and climbed up the spears.

This story follows the origin of how people now plant yams.

Morea Ua'a
Bomana
National Capital District

A720+. Sun travels across the sky using magical ropes; A726. Daily course of sun across sky; A736.3. Sun and moon as brothers; A750+. Moon travels across the sky using magical ropes; A753.1.2. Moon (man) cohabits with woman; A753.2. Moon has house; A1355+. Origin of menstruation: moon sleeps with all women; A2686.4.3. Origin of yams; D1741. Magic powers lost; D270+B. Transformation: boy to moon; D1655. Invisible objects; D1830. Magic strength; F16. Visit to land of moon; F17. Visit to land of the sun; J1745.2+. Ignorance of menses; P210. Husband and wife; P230. Parents and children; P231. Mother and son; P233. Father and son; P251.5. Two brothers; T481. Adultery; W181. Jealousy

A Scabby Man Married a Beautiful Woman

(Wantok 906, November 14, 1991, page 20)

Long ago, in **Parom** Village, in **East Sepik** Province, there lived a man with scabies [**Boiken** People]. His name was *Yeritoduo*. This name means scabies or scabby man.

People would always make jokes and say various things about him. The poor man just sat in his house and listened to the bad things that the people said about him.

When young women walked past his house, they would say various things to themselves. One woman would say to the other, "Your husband's sitting there." They would say such things and they would die laughing.

They would always do this customarily. The poor scabby man would feel terrible. However, they did not know that he had ancestral powers. He had sorcery to attract women to himself.

One time, the scabby man sat in the house and thought of showing his real powers. He took betel nuts, then he sang, danced, and spoke to himself. Afterwards, he just waited.

Before long, young women walked towards his place. The bad man looked at the women and tried to observe who was really the best of them.

He looked for a while, then he saw a beautiful woman amongst the other women. He took the betel nuts and threw them down in front of her. The young woman saw the betel nuts, then she took them and looked at them.

The betel nuts were good, and she lusted to chew them. Very slowly, she held them, put one in her mouth and chewed. The other women did not know this, so they just walked away into the forest to search for firewood.

The bad man knew this and just waited in his house. He knew that the powers had taken her. She could not be obstinate any longer.

The women worked at cutting firewood, then before long the powers of the scabby man took the woman. The

bad man overtook her head and she very quietly left the other women in the forest, leaving for the village.

She arrived at the bad man's house and told him directly, "I came to live with you."

The bad man had known this, but he lied and pushed the talk back and forth, "Why did you come to my house? You people always joke and laugh hysterically at me."

However, the powers had overtaken her, so she did not want to listen to anything that he said. Her mind was just stuck, so they lived together.

The bad man just laughed quietly and took her inside the house. They married and lived together in the village.

Hanleks Ian

Wewak

East Sepik Province

D985.5. Magic betel-nut; D1774. Magic results from speaking; D1781. Magic results from singing; D1781+. Magic results from dancing; D1900. Love induced by magic; D2000+. Mind control; L140+. Ugly marries beautiful; P210. Husband and wife; T10. Falling in love; T100. Marriage; W157. Dishonesty; W167. Stubbornness

The Yablo Kanom Died from Magic Mangos

(Wantok 907, November 21, 1991, page 16)

Long, long ago, in the time of the ancestors, there were two tribes who lived in a village called **Erimbari** in the Suave area of **Simbu** Province [**Chuave** People]. One tribe was called Yablo Kanom, and the other was called Maina Gol Kama.

The people of these two tribes lived well. However, the ancestors of Maina Gol Kama tribe were a very strong group of fighters, so they argued and liked to smash things about.

One time, they argued terribly, then the people of Yablo Kanom took all of their things and walked away to another village. They crossed the Waghi [Wahgi] River, then they went to live in the Yobai [**Iobai**] area of the Gumini [Gumine sub-District, **Salt-Yui** People]. This area is still in Simbu Province.

One very nice day, everyone in the village wanted to travel the forest to hunt for some food and wild game. The two tribes both did this at the same time.

The people of Maina Gol Kama traveled in the forest and made a new garden, then they hunted for some food. They found a big mango tree, then the feasted on the food.

They ate the mangos for a while, then they threw the mango [pits] to the other side of the Waghi River. Many mangos were quite ripe at this time, so they just gorged themselves.

Before long, the people of Yablo Kanom came around to this place and met them. They asked for some mangos, so the people of Maina Gol Kama asked them to climb the mango tree to fetch them.

The Yablo Kanom people went up the mango tree, then they threw the mangos down to their people. The Maina Gol Kama people told them that they should dig a big hole, cook the mangos in an earth oven, and then eat them.

So, while some of the people took the mangos from above and threw them down, the other men, women and children on the ground worked at digging a hole and preparing firewood to make a fire.

They gathered all of the mangos very carefully, then they made a big fire and cooked the mangos in the earth oven. They ate and finished all of the mangos. Then before long, all of their bellies were in terrible pain. They began to lie at the base of the mango tree. None of them knew that the mangos had a bad magic, so they lay on the ground for a while, then they died.

In the afternoon, two of their kinsmen, who were going around another place in the forest, came and met them. They saw that their kin were dead asleep at the base of the mango tree.

They tried to awaken them, but they did not awake. The two of them knew that they were dead from the bad magic of the mangos. They ran back to the village and told all of the other people about what they had seen. They returned and saw that all of their kin were dead.

So, they just covered them with earth and left them to stay at the hole that they had dug to cook the mangos. The two men who had come first and seen this were still alive. They moved their entire families to live at the place where their kin had died. They founded a very big village at this place.

These two men still carry the name of Yablo Kanom Tribe until this day. They died, but their children and grandchildren still know this ancestor story.

Peter Kaupa

Kimbe

West New Britain Province

A991+. Origin of particular village; D981+. Magic mango; D2061.1.3. Poisoning by magic; R213. Escape from home; V61.3+. Dead buried; P230. Parents and children

[The ancestor story in *Wantok* #908 is the same as the one in #818.]

Women Fought over a Cassowary's Foster Son
(Wantok 909, December 5, 1991, page 19)

Long, long ago, in the time of the ancestors, there lived a woman and her husband. They lived in a village near the area of Gurakor [**Gurukor**] in **Morobe** Province [**Mumeng** People].

One time, the woman was pregnant. However, the man did not always live with his wife. Every day, he would just travel the forest, hunting for wild game.

Every day, he just did the same thing. One day, he awoke in the early morning and told his wife, "Stay in the house. I'm going to hunt for game for us in the deep forest. I'll return in the afternoon." Afterwards, he took a bow and arrows, then he walked into the deep forest. The woman stayed alone in the house.

This time, she began feeling pain because it was nearly time for her to give birth. However, an unusual thought had seized the man, so he lied to his wife and fled completely to another village.

The poor woman did not know that he had lied to her. She waited for a while, then her husband did not return. Some days passed and she thought that a *masalai* of the forest had killed her husband. She cried terribly.

Before long, she gave birth to a handsome baby boy. Oh my, she was elated because she knew that the baby would become strong and take care of her later.

However, she thought hard because she did not have the strength for gardening and hunting for game. Some days later, she left the baby alone in the house, then she followed the man's footsteps into the forest. She thought that he must have found some trouble when he had not return to the village. She walked and walked, but she did not return to the village.

The poor baby boy was alone in the house and began to cry when he was hungry. A cassowary heard this and came to get the boy to take care of him.

Every day, the cassowary would just give ripe bananas to the baby boy. The cassowary would go faraway, to the big gardens near a village, then steal bananas. Every day, the cassowary would steal the ripe bananas in these gardens, then come and give them to the boy to eat.

The cassowary did this for a while, then the baby boy grew bigger. The cassowary returned to the village and stole some men's loincloths and "grass" skirts. The cassowary gave these and the boy wore them.

Some years later, the boy became a big man. Then the cassowary went back to the village and stole some stone axes. The boy used them to cut trees and to make big gardens for themselves.

Now they had their own gardens. The boy planted many foods in the gardens, such as bananas, taros, and yams. Their house was packed with food. They did this, and much food just rotted in the garden [because it was so plentiful].

They lived for a while. Then one day they heard that a huge festival would be coming to **Minduru** Village, by the side of Gurakor Village.

They prepared all of the things for the festival. Then they walked and walked, and arrived at the village at night. At this time, the cassowary had turned into a man.

The cassowary's foster son went to the festival site. He beat the hand drum passionately, singing and dancing with people. The men, women and children of the various nearby villages had gathered at the festival.

The boy sang and his voice went very high, excelling the voices of the other people. The young women noticed this and just died for him. Some danced and went closer, trying to hold him. Before long, the women began to fight jealously amongst themselves.

The fight grew bigger, then the people of the village also joined them. They fought with the boy and his foster father. The cassowary was not an ordinary animal from the deep forest. He also had powers. He fought them, then his foster son took a very beautiful woman whom he desired.

He held the young woman by the hand, then she just followed. They ran away and arrived at their home in the morning. The boy married her and the two of them raised very many children. These children created the small village of Minduru.

James Nari

Lae

Morobe Province

A991+. Origin of particular village; B535.0.7+. Cassowary as nurse for child; D350+M. Transformation: cassowary to man; D1355.1.1. Love-producing song; D1355.1.1+. Love-producing dance; D1830. Magic strength; K300. Thefts and cheats—general; P210. Husband and wife; P230. Parents and children; P231. Mother and son; P271. Foster father; P275. Foster son; R213. Escape from home; R260. Pursuits; S301. Children abandoned (exposed); T10. Falling in love; T100. Marriage; T570. Pregnancy; T580. Childbirth; W157. Dishonesty; W181. Jealousy

[There was no ancestor story in *Wantok* #910.]

Ghosts Killed an Angoram Man

(Wantok 911, December 19, 1991, page 16)

Long, long ago, in Sarapa [**Charapa**] Village, in the Angoram area of **East Sepik** Province, there traveled many ghosts [**Sawos** People]. They would hunt for people to kill, then go eat them.

One time, a man named Wangrukai took his two dogs and the three of them traveled in the forest. He carried his bow and arrows, then he walked into the forest with his two dogs.

They walked and walked, then they arrived in the very deep forest. At this place, Wangrukai saw a huge boar eating sago sprouts. Immediately, he called his dogs, then the dogs fought ferociously with the pig.

However the pig was not a small thing, so the dogs did not win quickly. Wangrukai just stood for a while, then he raised the bow and was about to shoot [an arrow] at the pig.

Surprisingly, the pig turned into a man, then later stood like a huge wooden carving, like those that are made in the Sepik. Wangrukai did not know what to think now. He was terrified and he left all his things there, then he took off briskly for the village. He arrived at the village, then he fell down at the house of the young boys. The boys saw him and asked what had happened to him.

Wangrukai breathlessly told the story of the ghost pig. He told them that he had been about to shoot the pig with an arrow, but something bad happened and the pig turned into a man, then later, into a big, wooden, Sepik-style carving.

At night, Wangrukai went to sleep in his house. Then the ghost pig, who had turned into a wooden carving, came looking for him in the village. He arrived at the village and went directly to Wangrukai's house at night, and then he beat upon the house door.

Wangrukai was sleeping and heard the noise at the door. He thought that it was still the boys of the village, so he went up to the door and opened it. When he opened the door, his eyes popped open, looking at the huge carving standing at his door.

The ghost killed Wangrukai at this time, then carried him back to his home in the deep forest. He called out to the other ghosts to go find garden food, then to come and they would cook it with the wild game [i.e., Wangrukai] in an earth oven.

So, the ghosts made a big earth oven and they held a huge party for Wangrukai's body that night.

Camulus Mori

Angoram

East Sepik Province

B871.1.2. Giant boar; D250+M. Transformation: man to statue; D336.1M. Transformation: pig to man; D1620.1. Automatic statue of man; E261.4. Ghost pursues man; E423.1.5. Revenant as swine; E541. Revenants eat; G11.10. Cannibalistic spirits; R220. Flights; R260. Pursuits

A Worthless Man Married the Best Woman

(Wantok 912, December 16, 1991, page 20)

One time in Pawia [**Pawaiamu**] Village in the **Southern Highlands** Province, there lived a man named Pulupapi [**Kewa** People].

The young women of the village often talked about the poor man behind his back. Women always would see him and tell jokes, then laugh hysterically at him. Poor Pulupapi would be ashamed of himself and would worry terribly.

Not a single woman liked him. He did not have a real chance to marry a woman of the village. However, Pulupapi excelled at hunting for wild game in the forest. When he traveled in the forest, he would kill the marsupials (*kapul*) and other animals of the forest, then he would carry them back to the house in the afternoon.

One day, he traveled in the forest, hunting for game. He traveled the deep forest until afternoon and he only killed three marsupials. So, he filled the net bag, and carried them back to the house.

At this time, he cut the marsupials' bellies and removed their guts. He tied the three marsupials together, and filled his net bag with the marsupials' guts.

While he was walking along the trail to the house, it became afternoon and rain began to fall. He walked a little farther, then it rained heavily. He searched for a place to sleep until dawn, after which he could return to the village.

He searched and searched, then he saw a house near the trail. He walked up to the house and beat on the door. In the house, there lived an old woman with her young daughter. They agreed that he could sleep in their house until morning, then he could go to his village.

Pulupapi went up and removed the three marsupials, giving them to the women to cook for themselves to eat. The two of them cooked them well, then they all sat and ate.

After they ate, they wanted to sleep. The mother made a place for Pulupapi to sleep for the night. While they were sleeping that night, the bad man removed the marsupial feces from the net bag and rubbed them on his face. After he did this, he slept near the young woman's buttocks. Pulupapi's face lay directly next to the young woman's buttocks.

In the morning, they awoke and saw that Pulupapi's face was smashed with feces. So, the mother scolded her daughter about the feces on Pulupapi's face.

The mother told them to go down to the river and wash themselves because the daughter also had feces adhering to her buttocks.

They went down to the river and did not return quickly to the house. The young woman was terribly ashamed about the feces on Pulupapi's face, so she gave herself to Pulupapi. Pulupapi took her back to the village and married her.

Rex P. Nande

Madang

Madang Province

K1350. Woman persuaded (or wooed) by trick; P160. Beggars; P210. Husband and wife; P232. Mother and daughter; T100. Marriage; X716.1H+. Befouling with excrement

A Sister Turned into a Bird of Paradise

(Wantok 913, January 2, 1992, page 21)

Long, long ago, an old couple lived in a village called **Kurubukari**. This village was in the deep forests of **Madang** Province [**Musak** People].

The old couple lived for a while, then they had two children, a boy and a girl. The name of the boy was Angia and the little girl was Moru. The children lived with their old parents for a while, then one time the old couple died.

One morning, Angia told his sister that he would walk to a village called **Musak**. He wanted to see some of their kin. However when he arrived at Musak Village, he saw that no one was there. He did not say anything, he just sat in the spirit house. He sat for a while, then the sun began to set. Before long, he saw many people carrying vines and leaves from the forest towards the village.

It was nearly dark by then, so he just met with the kin, then he walked back to his little village. When Moru saw Angia, she was elated. She thought that some enemy had killed her brother, but this was not the case.

Quickly, Moru cooked food and prepared it to eat. When they were about to eat, Angia told his sister what he had seen in Musak Village when the people returned from the gardens.

He told his sister that the people of Musak Village would be arranging a big festival. So, everyone had gone into the deep forests to search for adornments.

When Moru heard this, she was elated because she knew that she would have a [chance] at singing and dancing, and of doing so with the young men of Musak.

In the early morning, Angia awakened his sister. He told her that they must go into the forest and search for adornments for themselves too. Moru was happy and cooked some yams in the fire. She put them in a net bag, then they went into the forest.

They took all of their adornments, but they did not cut a tree for making a loincloth and "grass" skirt [from its bark]. The next day, they returned to the forest to search for this tree.

Angia saw a good tree, then cut it down. They scraped the tree's bark very well, then they took the bark home. They adorned the tree bark for a while and it became bright white.

However, Angia thought hard because he had one sister. He thought of tricking Moru into staying at the house while he alone went to the festival.

Angia also wanted to marry a young woman of Musak because he wanted a new woman to befriend his sister and live at the house. Then he could go alone to hunt for wild game in the forest.

On the day of the festival, Angia told his sister to try on her adornments. When Moru put on her adornments, Angia saw that his sister was like a morning [angel?] of the sea.

In the early morning, Angia called his sister outside the house, then he lied to her, "Moru, you'll go to the garden and fetch some taros for us to take to Musak and the festival." Moru thought that her brother was telling the truth, so she sped off to the garden. At the same time, Angia went inside the house, put all his adornments in a basket, and walked off to Musak. When he arrived at Musak, people were beating hand drums, singing and dancing passionately.

He removed all of the adornments and he arranged himself, then he beat the hand drum with them. When Angia went outside, his adornments were whiter than were those of all the other people. When it was becoming late at night, Angia cut directly to a young woman's heart.

At the house, sister Moru adorned herself, then waited for her brother Angia. She went outside the house and fixed herself up with various paints.

When it was still afternoon, she ate, then sang and danced. She spun outside the house and waited for her

brother to come out of the forest so that they would go to the festival.

Poor Moru waited and waited in vain, then she slept. It was nearly dawn when the mother's ghost came and transformed Moru, who sat until her big brother returned from the festival. She would ask why he had done this, then she would leave him and go to the festival.

In the very early morning, Angia walked and came with his young wife. When they arrived at the house, they saw a beautiful bird of paradise come outside and sit on the verandah.

Angia went directly inside the house and called for his sister. When he went out, the bird of paradise told him, "Brother, you lied to me and you went alone to the festival. That's OK, you can live with your wife. I'll leave you and go into the deep forest." When her brother heard this, he cried terribly.

So today, there are many birds of paradise by Kurubukari and Musak villages in Madang Province. However, these birds of paradise hide very well among the trees if they see men approaching.

Mathias K. Guyebi

Madang

Madang Province

B211.3+. Speaking bird of paradise; D150+W. Transformation: woman to bird of paradise; E323. Dead mother's friendly return; P210. Husband and wife; P231. Mother and son; P232. Mother and daughter; P233. Father and son; P234. Father and daughter; P253. Sister and brother; Q260. Deceptions punished; R213. Escape from home; T10. Falling in love; T100. Marriage; V112.1. Spirit huts; W157. Dishonesty

A Wild Man Killed and Ate a Woman

(Wantok 914, January 9, 1992, page 20)

One time in **Sirunki** Village, in **Enga** Province, there lived a man and his wife [**Enga** People]. The man's name was Kimala.

Kimala lived in Sirunki Village, and he heard that his sister would go to marry in **Paiala** Village. So, he thought of going to visit his sister.

One day, he sat and thought of going, then he decided to leave the village in the very early morning of the next day. He and his wife prepared all of the food, then they tied up a huge pig and began to walk away to Paiala Village.

They walked and walked until it became dark on the trail, so they made a small pretend-house and slept there. Before they slept, they ate some of the food that they had cooked in the house and had carried in the net bag with them.

At night, they slept and heard the sound of a man approaching. Oh my, their hearts leapt. They were terrified. They woke up, sat down and looked into the deep forest. Before long, a wild man jumped into the place where they had been sleeping.

Kimala and his wife no longer had a way to escape. They just sat and looked to see what the wild man would do to them. The wild man told them that he was completely famished for forest game, so he wanted to eat the big pig that they had tied and brought with them.

Kimala was terrified and agreed that the wild man could eat the pig, but he did not have firewood to cook the pig. However, the wild man had black magic. The wild man shouted, then the firewood and other cooking materials came to the ready.

They wanted to kill the pig but there was no water. So, Kimala told the wild man that there was no water to clean the pig and cook it. Quickly, the wild man shouted again and a little water appeared at this place. They used the water to cook.

Kimala and his wife saw this and were terrified. They just followed whatever the wild man told them to do. They prepared everything and cooked the pig. Before long, the pig was ready, and the wild man gorged himself on the food. The wild man finished off all of the meat and bones of the big pig. He did not leave a scrap.

Kimala saw this and was completely furious. At the same time, he was afraid and did not do anything. They wanted to flee, but the wild man's big eyes did not leave them for a second. So, they just sat quietly and watched the wild man.

Kimala knew that the wild man would kill him or his wife, then eat them. Before long, the wild man finished eating then grabbed Kimala's wife. The wild man was huge, so Kimala could not do anything. He just sat, watched and cried.

The wild man ate Kimala's wife, then he ran away into the deep forest. Poor Kimala sat alone, crying for a while, then he searched for the village through the deep forest late that night.

He cut through the forest for a while, then he arrived at Paiala Village where his sister would marry. The men saw him and were shocked. Afterwards, they listened to Kimala's story and his fury. However, they did not do anything because they could not locate the wild man in the deep forest.

So today in this place, the small stream is still there with the marks of the wild man's feet. The marks from the hole that they dug to make the earth oven for the pig are still there too.

Today, we call this place Mogowalo Teges, in the Wabeg [Wabag] area of Enga Province.

Kepas Tiss [Tiss Kepas Lakoe]
Kimbe
West New Britain Province

A930. Origin of streams; B871.1.2.1. Giant hog; D915.1. River produced by magic; D1774. Magic results from speaking; D2136. Objects magically moved; F531.1.1. Eyes of giant; F541. Remarkable eyes; F567. Wild man; F910. Extraordinary swallowings; G11.2. Cannibal giant; P210. Husband and wife; P253. Sister and brother; R220. Flights; S110. Murders

[There was no ancestor story in *Wantok* #915.]

A Butterfly Created the Auma People
(Wantok 916, January 23, 1992, page 20)

Pipi Korovu was a butterfly-man. [*Pipi* means "butterfly," and *korovu* means "barren" or "childless" in the Orokolo and Toaripi Languages (Brown, 1986: 65, 98).] He lived in **Auma** Village in the Orokoro [Orokolo] area of **Gulf** Province [**Orokolo** People].

Korovu lived alone on his own piece of land. Every afternoon, he would stand on top of a stone. He would stare at the clouds and sing to them.

Sometimes, he would think of seeing where the clouds originated. Many times, he would tell himself that the clouds came from above the sea. However, a piece of land must stay on top of the sea and thus raise the clouds. [Brown (1986: 241) notes that cloudbanks often resemble land in the Coral Sea].

One time, he had a strong thought to see this land. However, he thought hard about what could carry him to this land. He also did not know that a man from this place wanted to go looking around there. "If the enemies are there, they'll kill me," Pipi said.

One time, Pipi was sitting when he had a good idea to make a pretend butterfly. Then he could find where the clouds originated.

One morning, Pipi finished eating, then he walked and walked to his friend, Hilake. He asked for rattan rope to make this butterfly, "Hilake, I want to make a butterfly and fly to the island of the clouds. I wanted to go by canoe, but it was not very good." So, I want to ask you, "Can you give some rattan rope to me for making a butterfly to fly to the island."

Hilake gave him the rattan, then he went to the house. He made a big butterfly that could carry his body and fly to the island. When Pipi flew above the clouds, he looked down to the sea and sang to the clouds, "I'm a butterfly, the butterfly of Auma. I'm flying above the clouds and I'm flying to the land of the dead."

He sang and flew, then he arrived at this island. Pipi saw a big tree and he fell on top of it. When Pipi looked down, he saw two young women. The names of these women were Aro and Pora, the children of Marupi, the owner [or father] of this island [*Aro* means "frigate bird". *Pora* or *para* is a kind of mangrove in the Orokolo and Toaripi Languages (Beehler *et al.*, 1986: 52-53; Brown, 1986: 89, 97, 242)].

Pipi greatly desired the young women and he wanted to marry them. He thought hard about jumping down the tree and meeting them. However, he changed his mind again and threw betel nuts down to them. Pipi said that if they desired him, they would chew the betel nuts.

The betel nuts fell between them, then they looked up. They only saw the body of a butterfly sitting on top of the tree. Then they saw the betel nuts and they chewed them. He saw this and he was happy because the women liked him since they were chewing his betel nuts.

Now he knew that the two women desired him. However, he did not think hard about them, and he flew back to his home. At night, Pipi quickly removed an ancestral spirit [*tanget*?] leaf. He put it under the sleeping place, then he flew back to the island.

When Pipi arrived, he made the two women dream of where they would meet him. In their dream, he told them that they must meet him by the stream where they had first met him as the butterfly. They would see his image in the water, sitting on top of the tree.

In the traditional customs of the Orokoro People, it is forbidden for young women to look directly into the faces of young men. In the morning, Pipi flew back to the tree again. He left the image of the butterfly on top of the tree. He sat on another branch of the tree and watched.

The women noticed the time and they walked towards the stream. They saw the image of a nice butterfly [upon] the water, the same kind that they had dreamt. They asked the butterfly to come down and meet them. However, the butterfly thought hard and asked them, "Which man do you live with on this island?" The women replied that they lived with their father. When Pipi heard this, he quickly went down the tree and met them.

Afterwards, he went back and forth to see them, then they both became pregnant. However, their father was not happy when he saw that they were both pregnant. The father was greatly puzzled about who it was that had impregnated his nice daughters. One morning, he went to hide by the river at the place where the two women usually fetched water. He hid carefully to see who it was that would come and meet the daughters.

When he saw a big butterfly come and land, then talk with them, he shot the butterfly directly in his chest with a stone. Afterwards, the butterfly fell. He sped towards [the butterfly] to cut his head, but the daughters quickly held their father.

Later, the women explained to their father what had happened. They asked him if they could take the butterfly to live with themselves. The father was happy and took the butterfly to the house. All of them lived together for a while, then the women gave birth to two nice children, a boy and a girl.

Later, Pipi told his two wives that they must return to his home. So, in the early morning, he flew back to the village and took more rattans to make butterflies for the two women.

He carefully made two big butterflies for them, they all flew back to his village. Afterwards, Pipi made more butterflies. He took his father-in-law from the island to live with his two daughters in the village. Now, everyone was happy and they lived well together in Pipi's village. This ancestor story shows the true origin and how the butterfly Pipi Korovu received his name at **Kerema** in Gulf Province [**Uaripi** People].

[Anonymous]

[Sir Albert Maori Kiki told a similar story of Pipi Korovu in Brown (1986: 224-247).]

A705.1. Origin of clouds; A991+. Origin of particular village; B211.4.6K. Speaking butterfly; B631+. Human offspring from marriage to butterfly; B643+. Marriage to person in butterfly form; C313. Tabu: woman looking at man; D186.1M. Transformation: man to butterfly; D186.1W. Transformation: woman to butterfly; D380+M. Transformation: butterfly to man; D985.5. Magic betel-nut; D1355.3. Love charm; D1810.8.2. Information received through dream; E481.2.0.1. Island of the dead; F129.3+. Voyage to the land of clouds; F1021.1. Flight on artificial wings; P210. Husband and wife; P231. Mother and son; P232. Mother and daughter; P233. Father and son; P234. Father and daughter; P252.1. Two sisters; P253. Sister and brother; P261. Father-in-law; P265. Son-in-law; P291. Grandfather; P294. Aunt; P297. Nephew; P298. Niece; P310. Friendship; T10. Falling in love; T100. Marriage; T145.0.1. Polygyny; T570. Pregnancy; T580. Childbirth

A Boy Stole a Fish-Woman's Skin

(Wantok 917, January 30, 1992, page 20)

Long, long ago, in the Talasia [Talasea] area of **West New Britain** Province, a man and his wife lived in a village called **Warunegaru** [**Bola** People].

They just had one son. They lived for a while, then the mother and father became old. The boy took care of his parents very well.

One day, the boy left his father and mother, then he went alone to bathe at the beach. No one lived by this beach.

He bathed for a while, then he became famished. So, he searched for a rope to climb a coconut palm tree. He climbed up and drank from the green coconuts on top of the tree.

Before long, a loud sound came from the sea. He heard the voices of women laughing about. The boy was terrified, but he sat quietly and watched.

Oh my, it was not quiet. The young fish-women came out of the sea and went onto the beach. They just came and removed their skins, then they hid them on the sand.

One fish-woman's face was shinier than the others were. She was a very stylish woman. Everything that men searched for, she had. The boy kept a careful watch on the place where this fish-woman hid her skin.

All of the fish-women turned into real women and played on the beach, going upwards. The fish-women turned the corner, then the boy immediately descended the coconut palm. He dug the sand and took the very beautiful fish-woman's skin, then he hid it elsewhere. Afterwards, the boy went to hide and wait for the fish-women to return.

It was nearly afternoon when all of the fish-women returned. They went into their skins, then they swam back to the sea. However, the stylish woman did not find her skin. She searched the place where she had hidden it, but it was not there.

All of the other fish-women went back to the sea. Then she sat alone and was terribly worried. Quickly, the boy went out and held her hand.

The fish-woman was ashamed, but he told her not to be ashamed. He helped her and they searched for her skin. They searched and searched until dark, and they did not see anything. What really happened was that he had hidden it elsewhere.

It was dark, so he told her that they would go to his house. He held the stylish woman's hand and they arrived at the house.

The old father and mother saw them and they were elated. The next morning, everyone gathered and held a big feast and festival. The boy married the fish-woman and they lived in the village.

So today, in Narunegeru Village, when women marry and go to another village, there must be a big festival and feast. This is the custom from long ago until now.

Joshua Koyakia

Vanimo

West Sepik Province

A1550. Origin of customs of courtship and marriage; B654. Marriage to fish in human form; D170W. Transformation: woman to fish; D370W. Transformation: fish to woman; D531+. Transformation by removing skin; K300. Thefts and cheats—general; P210. Husband and wife; P231. Mother and son; P233. Father and son; P261. Father-in-law; P262. Mother-in-law; P265. Son-in-law; P600+. Virilocality; T100. Marriage; T130. Marriage customs

A Sepik Man Married a Sago-Woman

(Wantok 918, February 6, 1992, page 16)

Long, long ago in a village inside **East Sepik** Province, there lived a single man. The man's name was Moiuwahu. One day, he took the tools for cutting sago, then he walked away into the deep forest. He walked and walked into the middle of a group of sago palm trees, then he heard a young woman's voice.

He followed and followed, then he heard her singing from the crown of a sago tree. The name of this woman was Nangurakhua.

Oh my, when Moiuwahu saw this stylish woman, he thought that he was dreaming or hallucinating. He shouted up to her and told her to descend. She replied to him, "How can I come down?"

Moiuwahu thought for a while, then he quickly sped off, cut a tall tree and brought it back. He stood it close to the sago palm, then Nangurakhua held the tree and went down to the ground.

Oh my, Moiuwahu was elated. He took the beautiful woman and they arrived at the village. Everyone in the village gathered and held a huge party. Moiuwahu married this sago-woman and they lived happily together.

However, Moiuwahu did all of the house and garden work. His wife, Nangurakhua, never did the slightest work. This was because Nangurakhua was a sago-woman. If she did any work and she touched water, she would just disappear or turn back into sago food.

Moiuwahu also knew this, so he just let his wife stay there. He alone did all of the work, such as cooking food and working in the garden. This was something that only Moiuwahu and his wife knew. Not one other man or woman of the village knew this.

Moiuwahu and his wife lived for a while. Then some months later, Nangurakgua [Nangurakhua] gave birth to a daughter. Huaniara was the name that they gave to this girl. The work of taking care of the baby was also something that only Moiuwahu would do.

After a while, Moiuwahu was angry with his wife because he alone would always do everything and he felt ill. Moiuwahu scolded his wife terribly that she, Nangurakhua, was just a dead-bodied woman and that she never did the slightest work.

Nangurakhua listened to this and was terribly worried. She took her daughter and they walked away to the river to wash their things. This time, Moiuwahu was angry and went to tell stories with the other men in the spirit house.

Nangurakgua put the baby on top of a stone and washed the things. At the same time, she cried. She knew that it would be time to return to sago and she would leave her daughter.

While she washed the things, the water touched her and she turned back into sago, beginning with her legs and going up to her head. The daughter, Huaniara, cried and cried. Before long, Moiuwahu searched for them and arrived at the river. He saw the baby crying there, then he sped towards her and carried her. Afterwards, he looked in the water and just saw the woman's hair drifting on top of the water.

He cried terribly and carried the baby girl back to the village. Moiuwahu knew that he was wrong, so he would not see his beautiful wife again.

David Pangi
Wewak
East Sepik Province

D215.11K+W. Transformation: woman to sago; D361.1+. Forest Spirit Bride; D431+W. Transformation: sago to woman; D565.6. Transformation by touching water; D681. Gradual transformation; P210. Husband and wife; P232. Mother and daughter; P234. Father and daughter; Q304. Scolding punished; T100. Marriage; T580. Childbirth; V112.1. Spirit huts

[There was no ancestor story in *Wantok* #919.]

A Flood Killed the People of Wurins Village
(Wantok 920, February 20, 1992, page 19)

Long, long ago, there lived a man in **Wurins** village, near Passam [**Boiken** People]. This village was just outside Wewak Town, in **East Sepik** Province.

The man's name was Aru. One day, Aru walked down the mountain to a river to bathe. He walked and walked, then he saw a fallen tree on top of a pond. The name of this pond is Wiruhu. It is near a big river.

The tree was good for catching insects [to eat, because it was rotting (probably beetle grubs)]. Aru cut the tree and worked at taking the insects inside of it. Before long, his axe went loose and fell into the pond.

He went and cut a rattan vine, then he tied it to the tree. He held the rattan, and followed it down into the pond. Slowly, he held the rattan underwater. Before long, he trampled on top of the shingles of a house that was under the pond.

Aru knew that he must have arrived at a big village of the *masalai*s. He walked on top of the house shingles, then he jumped down to the ground.

At the same time, he noticed that a man was looking at him and shouting. Quickly, he turned and looked at two women sitting by the house. He asked them, "Have you seen my axe?" [lit., "It would be bad if you've seen my axe."]

They lied to Aru that they had not seen an axe. What was really the case was that the two women had taken the axe and hidden it under their "grass" skirts.

The women were *masalai*s. Aru left the women and walked away to the *masalai* men's spirit house, where he slept. At this time, all of the *masalai* men had left for the forest.

Aru slept for a while, then he awoke in the evening. He took the wooden neck rest that belonged to the leader of the *masalai* men, then he fled back to Wurins Village. We call this traditional neck rest, _homunku_ [used for sleeping].

In the afternoon, all of the *masalai* men returned and saw that their leader's neck rest was not there. They searched and searched, then they asked the two *masalai* women. The two *masalai* women said, "We saw a man come down around here during the day, then he went back. He must have taken it."

The *masalai*s' leader sent a message to the *masalai*s of all of the other waters for them to come meet. They sniffed around, then they arrived at Wurins Village. That night, a heavy rain and wind arose. The water began to rise.

Aru saw this and had the idea that it was a mistake to have stolen the neck rest. However, he did not carry it back and throw it down into the water.

The water rose and killed everyone in the village. Aru alone was left. So, he climbed a tall coconut palm tree at the village.

He stayed for a while until it was nearly dawn, then the water receded. One-by-one, he took coconuts and threw them down. He did this until he threw the last coconut down, and it hit the ground and broke.

He knew that the water had subsided, and that the *masalai*s must have returned to their home. Slowly, he went down to the ground, then dawn broke. Everyone in the village as well as the pigs, dogs and other animals had died. Slowly, he took the *masalai* man's neck rest and threw it back down into the pond.

So today, the people of the village never cut a tree or anything that is near this pond. The stones that the big flood carried up to the village are still there. Also, no man ever goes to bathe at this pond nowadays.

Clement Wamma

Wewak

East Sepik Province

A977. Origin of particular stones or groups of stones; A1011. Local deluges; A1018. Flood as punishment; C518. Tabu: cutting down tree; C615.1. Forbidden lake (pool); C721.2. Tabu: bathing in certain place; D2126. Magic underwater journey; D2142.1. Wind produced by magic; D2143.1. Rain produced by magic; D2151.8. Magic flood; F401.6. Spirit in human form; F408.3. Spirits dwell at tabu place; F420.1.1. Water-spirit as man; F420.1.2. Water-spirit as woman (water-nymph, water-nix); F420.2.2. Water-spirits live in village under water; F421. Lake-spirit; F490+. Masalai; K420. Thief loses his goods or is detected; Q212. Theft punished; Q428. Punishment: drowning; R311. Tree refuge; V112.1. Spirit huts; W157. Dishonesty; Z356. Unique survivor

Sainaturu Died Because of His Thievery

(Wantok 921, February 27, 1992, page 20)

Long, long ago in Bibiori [**Bibe'ori**] Village, in the Obura District of **Eastern Highlands** Province, there lived a man and his dog [**Tairora** People]. The man's name was Sainaturu and the dog's name was Sapadelu.

Sainaturu was a lazy gardener. So every day, he would go to other men's nearby gardens, steal food and bring it back. However, Sainaturu was a champion at hunting for wild game. He and his dog, Sapadelu, would go to the deep forest, kill many marsupials, cook them and eat them.

One time, the food and other meat were short in the house. So, they decided to wake up in the early morning, then go hunt for some marsupials (*kapul*) in the deep forest.

They woke up in the early morning and cooked some food. They ate, then they walked and walked into the forest. They hunted for marsupials, then a great smoke from a fire rose from their house. They did not know this.

The smoke rose and rose, then went to a particular place. A woman saw this smoke and followed it. She followed the smoke and arrived at Sainaturu's house.

She opened the door and went inside. However, she did not see anyone or hear a sound because the owner of the house, Sainaturu, was still in the deep forest with his dog. She made a fire inside the house, then she waited to see whether anyone would come or not.

Sainaturu slaughtered very many marsupials. He killed the marsupials for a while, then he climbed a mountain. Before long, he looked down and saw smoke rising from part of his house.

Oh my, he thought very hard, "Is my house on fire or who made this fire?" However, there was no one in the house to make a fire. He thought and thought, then he sent his dog, Sapadelu, back to the house to check upon it.

He shouted for Sapedului [Sapadelu] to come, then he told the dog, "You go first to the house and see who made the fire at our house. If you see a man, howl and come back so I'll know. If you don't see a man, then don't howl."

Sapadelu sped off, then arrived at the house and saw the woman. The dog did not waste time. The dog was very knowledgeable. The dog sped back to the mountain and howled loudly.

Sainaturu [heard this] and knew that Sapadelu must have seen a man at the house. He carried the marsupials and they sped to the house. Sainaturu opened the door and went inside to see the woman sitting by the fire.

Sainaturu cooked the marsupials, then they ate together. That night, they slept. Later, Sainaturu found out that she wanted to marry him. They married and lived together.

When they were short of food, Sainaturu would go to the nearby men's gardens from other villages. He would steal their food and bring it back. One time, he told her, "If one time I go stealing and don't return, you'll know that they must have killed me."

One day he went to steal in the gardens of some men. That day, he did not return. She waited and waited until the afternoon. Afterwards, she saw a huge fire coming from near some men's garden.

She knew that the men must have killed her husband. She was terribly saddened and cried. Later, she returned to her home. Sainaturu's dog, Sapadelu, transformed into a stone. This stone is still there, by the place where Sainaturu's house stood.

Naipo Su-uto

Obura District

Eastern Highlands Province

A977.5. Origin of particular rock; B212. Animal understands human speech; D422.2.4K. Transformation: dog to stone; K420. Thief loses his goods or is detected; P210. Husband and wife; Q212. Theft punished; Q411. Death as punishment; S110. Murders; T100. Marriage; W111. Laziness

A Marsupial-Man Exchanged Fire for a Girl
(Wantok 922, March 5, 1992, page 19)

Long ago, a big marsupial (*kapul*) lived on top of Kili Tapalu Mountain in **Enga** Province [**Enga** People]. This marsupial would transform into a young man. Sometimes it would transform into a young woman.

One time, an old woman and her young daughter went fishing in a pond. This pond was below two big mountains. They fished at the mouth of a stream, but they did not [catch] one fish. When they arrived at the source of the stream, a strong wind and rain arose. So, they stayed there because they were terribly wet and cold.

Afterwards, they saw a boulder and went underneath it. The wind ended, but the rain kept falling, so they stayed for a long time underneath the boulder.

Before long, they heard an explosion and the earth trembled near the stone where they were standing. They looked around, but they did not see a thing. They were quite afraid, so they sat and held tightly to the stone.

Before long, they heard a young man walking directly towards them. The old woman saw him and was happy because he would help them make a fire and they could dry their bodies.

When he arrived, the old woman asked him to make a fire for them. However, he did not speak. He just stood and watched them. Afterwards, he asked the old mother, "If I make a fire for you and your daughter, you shall pay me something nice."

The old woman did not reply to him because she was freezing. He stood for a fairly long time, then he asked the old woman again what she would pay him if he made a fire for them.

The old woman turned her eyes and looked at her daughter. Then she told the man, "I don't have anything good to give you because we are far away from my village." However, he kept staring at the girl and he asked the same question. He had strong thoughts for the old woman's daughter. So, he kept standing there and he asked a third time, asking that the old woman must pay him first for him to make a fire.

The old woman looked at the girl and told him, "You must make a fire first for me to give my daughter to you." He was happy and sped off to make a fire. The fire [became] well [lit], so he told the old woman to go dry herself by the fire.

He put his hands to the girl's hands and took her around to the place where he usually hid. The marsupial-man scratched the young woman's body [i.e., had sex with her] and she cried loudly inside the cave. The old woman listened and sped into the cave to see what the marsupial was doing with her daughter. However, the marsupial-man told the old woman that the fire would die.

The old woman was cold too, so she sped off to look at the fire. Before long, she heard her daughter crying again. She sped back again, but the man stopped her. The marsupial-man told her, "If you come inside and look at the girl, your fire will die. It will be the same if you look at the fire, your daughter will die." The old woman was confused and just sat in the heavy rain.

He was sorry for the old woman, so he took the girl outside to her. He sped away into the cave. Afterwards, he shouted, "If you two want to see me, come to Kili Tapali [Tapalu] Mountain. Otherwise, you can come to Mongalo Kemates and see me there." He walked closer to the mountain, then he turned into a marsupial.

They saw this and were terrified. They sped off to the village, then they told everyone what they had encountered at Kili Tapali Mountain. At the same time, all of the men prepared their fighting gear and got ready to find this marsupial.

In the early morning, they beat the signal drum and they walked with the two women to Kili Tapali Mountain. When they arrived, the old woman and her daughter walked and walked, then they sat on top of the stone again.

All of the men hid nearby in the forest. The marsupial watched and quickly changed into a young man, then he walked out towards them.

He walked directly towards the young woman. The men saw this and shouted together to come out of the forest. They threw spears and other things at the man, killing him.

Later, they tied him to a log and carried him to the village. When he arrived near the village, his body became a marsupial. All of the men let go and ran about. They returned later and carried him into the village.

They made a bonfire and burned him. Now, Kili Tapali does not have any ghosts that frighten men or rape young women.

Robson Frank
Bialla
West New Britain Province

D179.6K+M. Transformation: man to marsupial; D310+M. Transformation: marsupial to man; D310+W. Transformation: marsupial to woman; D2142.1. Wind produced by magic; D2143.1. Rain produced by magic; D2148. Earth magically caused to quake; E423.2+. Revenant as marsupial; E425.2. Revenant as man; E446.2. Ghost laid by burning body; F562.7K. People live in mountain top; P232. Mother and daughter; Q244. Punishment for ravisher; Q411. Death as punishment; S110. Murders; T471. Rape

[There was no ancestor story in *Wantok* #923.]

The Newlywed Custom Sent a Little Brother into the Hands of the Enemies

(Wantok 924, March 19, 1992, page 19)

Long, long ago, in our area of **Talasea**, if you were newlywed, it would be completely forbidden for you to eat or talk in front of your wife [**Bola** People, **West New Britain** Province].

There were two brothers who lived by Talasea with many other people in a village. Their names were both Kamun, so when the people wanted to call the big brother, they would say, "Big Kamun." The little brother was "Little Kamun." The Kamun brothers lived very well. Big Kamun married and had some children. However, Little Kamun had just married.

One night, Big Kamun told stories with his little brother. They told stories for a while, then Big Kamun told Little Kamun, "Tomorrow, you'll awake in the very early morning and go to work in the garden. If your new wife comes later to plant taros, you should flee into the forest and search for a *galip* tree. When you find one, climb it and gather the *galip* nuts. I'll come later."

They made this decision and they went to sleep. In the very early morning, Little Kamun awoke and went to the garden first. He arrived in the garden and worked hard.

Before long, the new wife came behind him to plant taro. He thought about staying, but then he thought of the village custom and went to hide in the forest.

He followed Big Kamun's instructions and walked into the deep forest, then he saw a *galip* tree. He climbed the tree, then he gathered *galip* nuts.

Before long, some enemies arrived and saw him. They kept watch underneath and waited for Little Kamun to descend, so that they could see where he was from.

Poor Little Kamun did not know that the enemies were waiting for him at the base of the tree. He worked hard at gathering *galip* nuts, then he waited for Big Kamun to arrive.

It was nearly afternoon and he descended. The enemies completely surrounded him. They grabbed him and killed him. In the garden, Big Kamun took his daughter and Little Kamun's wife back to the house, then he went to check on Little Kamun.

He followed his footsteps, then he arrived at the base of the *galip* tree. Little Kamun's ghost was already waiting there. He saw Big Kamun and told him, "I waited for you for a long time and you didn't come quickly." Big Kamun replied, "Oh, I'm very sorry. I took my daughter and your new wife back to the village, so I didn't come quickly. Let's take the *galip* nuts now and return to the village quickly."

They took the *galip* nuts, then Big Kamun saw blood plastered around the base of the *galip* tree. He knew that something was wrong. Immediately, he asked the Little Kamun's ghost, "Whose blood is this?" Big Kamun did not know that he was talking to his little brother's ghost.

The little brother's ghost replied, "I'm very sorry, Big Kamun. I waited and waited for you, but you did not come quickly. I'll help you and we'll carry my body to the village."

The big brother saw Little Kamun's body and cried terribly. They made a platform, then carried the body back to the village. Close to the village, Little Kamun's ghost just disappeared and Big Kamun carried his little brother's body to the house alone.

Everyone saw this and was shocked. They gathered and cried until dawn. In the morning, they buried Little Kamun's body.

Andrew Taroa
Kimbe
West New Britain Province

C246+. Tabu: husband eating in front of newlywed wife; C400+. Husband speaking in front of newlywed wife; D2095. Magic disappearance; E231

Return from dead to reveal murder; E326. Dead brother's friendly return; K914. Murder from ambush; P210. Husband and wife; P230. Parents and children; P232. Mother and daughter; P234. Father and daughter; P251.5. Two brothers; P263. Brother-in-law; P264. Sister-in-law; P294. Aunt; P298. Niece; S110. Murders; T100. Marriage; V61.3+. Dead buried

The Moon Rose First at Jiki Village

(Wantok 925, March 26, 1992, page 19)

Long ago, in the time of the ancestors, there was just the sun. There was no moon, so at night it was completely dark. At this time, there were two sisters who lived in a small village called **Jiki** in the Bialla area of **West New Britain** Province [**West Nakanai** People]. Their names were Bejo and Biat.

Bejo was the only woman at this time who had the moon. She would hide the moon in a big clay pot inside the house. Every night, when her child was asleep, she would use the moon to work alone in the house. Her sister, Biat, did not know about this either.

One day, the sisters decided to go cut and rinse sago. The sago that they wanted to cut was near the village, by a stream.

The sisters took their things and went to the base of the sago palm tree. They cut the sago tree, then they began to rinse [the pith].

They rinsed and rinsed until the afternoon, but there was still plenty of sago to be rinsed. Bejo thought hard and asked whether Biat had a light for themselves to use and finish the work at night. Biat replied that they would light torches or dry coconut leaves, make a fire and rinse the sago.

They rinsed the sago for a while, then darkness came. Biat thought hard and wanted to go by the house to bring some torches and make a fire. However, Bejo replied, "Sis, don't worry. I have a light. We'll use the light to see well and rinse the sago." Biat asked, "Where's the light? Get it now, it's almost completely dark."

Bejo replied, "I hid it on the ground in a pot inside the house." Then she ran back to the house to check on her child. She arrived at the house and saw the child playing intensely outside the house with the other children. She shouted for the child to come, then she said, "You can't remove that big clay pot on top of the house until your aunt and I return. We haven't finished working yet."

Then she walked back to the stream to rinse the sago. However, the boy sat for a while, thinking of what his mother had said to him. That is how boys are; he really wanted to know what was inside the pot.

He left the other boys and went into the house. He walked closer and removed the cover of the pot. Oh my, he was shocked to see the house lit intensely.

The moon shot right out at his eyes, and then it flew out of the house door. The boy wanted to stop it, but no, the moon's strong wind came forth and the child hung onto the moon's side, going up to the sky.

It started to become dark, but quickly it lightened again because of the moon's light. Everyone ran outside the houses and was surprised to see a big ball that was terribly bright. They saw the child hanging by the moon and flying up to the sky like a balloon. They had never seen anything do this because this was their first time seeing the moon.

Bejo and her sister rinsed the sago for a while, then they were surprised to hear a loud noise from the village. Before long, the area was brightly lit. Bejo looked up and saw her child hanging from the moon. She had the idea that her child must have ignored what she had said and had opened the pot in the house.

Bejo left the sago, then she ran to the house. She went inside and saw that the pot was open and that her child was not there. She ran outside and cried for her child. However, the child was dead and just hanging from the moon. Before long, his body fell down, crashing onto a garden.

Bejo ran and ran, but she did not see the child's body break apart and fly about. Some weeks later, she saw a leaf growing at the place where the child's body had fallen.

This leaf grew and grew. It became like the red yam (*mami*). After this story, the red yam became an important food of the people of Jiki Village.

Today, when the full moon is lit, the people of Jiki will begin to plant yams (*yam* and *mami*) because this is a good time for yams to grow well.

Peter Timan
Bialla
West New Britain Province

A754. Moon kept in box; A2686.4.3. Origin of yams; D1719.9. Magic power at certain time; E631.5+. Reincarnation as yam; F1021. Extraordinary flights through air; P231. Mother and son; P252.1. Two sisters; P294. Aunt; P297. Nephew; Q325. Disobedience punished; Q411. Death as punishment; W126. Disobedience

The Aralkulo Received Fire from Kair Village

(Wantok 926, April 2, 1992, page 19)

Before, in the time of the ancestors, in **Aralkulo** Village, in the Gembogl area of **Simbu** Province, there lived a man and his wife [**Kuman** People].

The couple lived together and would travel together in the forest to hunt for food. However, there was one thing that made their life look bad.

They never cooked their food in a fire. They would eat things [raw], regardless of whether it was meat or leafy greens from the forest.

However, in a nearby village, there lived a woman. She lived in a village called **Kair**, which is also in the Gembogl area. She was not married and she lived alone in Kair Village. By her house, there was a *marita* or other kind of pandanus tree. Under the *marita* tree, she placed bamboos.

When the rain came, the water would fall into the bamboo tubes. Afterwards, she would take the water from the bamboos and drink.

She drank the water from the bamboos and she became pregnant. Afterwards, she gave birth to a baby boy. She lived with her baby and the baby grew to be a big man.

One day, the man stayed in the house and thought about going around the forest. He took his things and began walking into the forest.

While he was going around the forest, he became confused on the trail and arrived at Aralkulo Village. He met the man and his wife. The young boy [man] was terrified when he saw them eating the [raw] food and leafy greens.

Afterwards, the boy found out that the man and woman did not know how to make a fire or how to cook food in a fire. So, he taught them how to make a fire. He took a dry log and broke it a little in the middle. He took a piece of bamboo and broke it into small pieces. Later, he arranged some dry leaves and put the log on top of the leaves.

He took the bamboo pieces and put them among the leaves and the log. Then he began to pull a piece of bamboo back and forth, and fire came forth.

After he did this, he told them to cook the meat in the fire. When he removed the meat from the fire and gave it to them to eat, oh my, they loved it. This was because the food tasted unusual and quite delicious.

Later, the young boy left them and went back to his village, Kair. However before he departed, he told the couple to cook food in the fire and not to just eat it [raw].

The couple lived there and raised children. Now their family lives in **Womkama** Village in the Gembogl area.

Joe Kuil Sundu
Simbu Province

J1813+. Cooking processes misunderstood: eating raw food; P210. Husband and wife; P230. Parents and children; P231. Mother and son; T512.3. Conception from drinking water; T570. Pregnancy; T580. Childbirth

Kerenga Found [Trouble] in the Forest
(Wantok 927, April 9, 1992, page 19)

Long, long ago, in **Simbu** [Province], there was a man who lived in **Gugo** Village. His name was Aundo Kerenga.

One morning, he awoke and went outside the house. He saw that the sky was terribly dark. At the same time, a little rain was falling. Kerenga went back inside the house and warmed his body by the fire. He was also racked with hunger, so he looked for food in the house. However, he did not find any meat or other food.

He thought of a place where there was plenty of pandanus (*marita*) and other fruits. Kerenga left the house and walked away to this place called **Kundire**. When he arrived at Kundire, he gathered the *marita* and other fruits.

Before long, Kerenga heard some kind of sound coming from behind him. He turned and saw plentiful flying foxes in a cave. Oh my, he was elated because now his house would be filled with meat.

The cave was on the other side of the juncture of two waterways, named are the Singa Nigle [Singa] Creek and the Simbu River [**Kuman** People]. So, Kerenga searched very hard and went to the other side.

The poor man sat by the side of the water and looked at the flying foxes flying back and forth. Before long, he saw the sun setting and he thought of returning to the village. However, when he got up to go back to the village, he saw a casuarina tree. This tree was very tall and when the wind blew, the tree moved close to the cave, then back again.

Kerenga was conflicted about climbing the tree so that he could jump to the other side and kill the flying foxes. However, the sun was setting and it was getting dark, so he went back to the village.

Kerenga arrived at the house, and he did not tell his wife or children about the flying foxes. He ate a little, then he very quickly went to sleep.

He awoke in the very early morning. He took his bow and arrows, and a stone axe. The wife and children did not know where Kerenga wanted to go.

The guy walked and walked, then it became light in the forest. Before long, he arrived at this place. He rested, then he prepared things. He tied the bow and arrows to his back, put the axe at one side, and carried a net bag on the other side. He began to climb the casuarina tree. When he arrived at the middle, the tree began to move back and forth. However, Kerenga was not afraid. He kept climbing the tree, then he arrived at the very top.

He lay on top and waited for the wind to come. Before long, he jumped into the cave. He looked around inside, and he saw very many flying foxes. Kerenga did not wait, he began killing them and filling his net bag.

When it was nearly afternoon, he wanted to return to the village. However, the casuarina tree did not move in the slightest. The tree stood straight, and Kerenga did not have a way to get back.

He sat and waited for a while, then it became dark. He shouted, but there was no one to hear him. This was because no one ever went to this place, because the area had bad *masalais*. It was hopeless, so Kerenga slept by the cave.

The next day, no wind came. The tree stood straight, and Kerenga still waited. He was hungry, so he began to eat the flying foxes that he had killed. He did this until one week passed. His poor body looked completely different. He did not look like a man.

One morning, Kerenga sat outside the cave and warmed his body in the sun. When he looked to the other side of the river, he saw a man and his wife. Oh my, he was very happy. Kerenga shouted again, but they did not hear him. He stretched all his bones, then he shouted again. The couple heard him and found him. They told Kerenga to stay quiet while they ran back to the village to bring the men.

The men arrived and they very quickly sent a man to swim the river to the other side. He arrived and he began climbing up the stones. However, when he arrived at the place where Kerenga was staying, he was terrified. This was because Kerenga had stayed in the forest for a long time and he looked exactly like a ghost. He grabbed Kerenga, and they cried terribly.

Kerenga did not have any more strength. He carried Kerenga on his back and he tied himself and Kerenga together with rope. On the other side of the rope, he tied a log. They held the rope, and went down very slowly. When they arrived at the bottom of the stones, the group from the village held Kerenga and cried terribly. This was because if they had not found Kerenga, he would have died after two or three more days.

After they went back to the village, Kerenga told the story of what had happened to him. The villagers gathered food and made a big party to celebrate Kerenga.

Mark Kama Joe
Kimbe
West New Britain Province

F490+. Masalai; P210. Husband and wife; P230. Parents and children; R45.3. Captivity in cave; R110. Rescue of captive

A Kyaka Man Stole a Kaidane Woman
(Wantok 928, April 16, 1992, page 18)

Long, long ago, in **Kyaka** Village, in the Ambum area of Wabag, **Enga** Province, there lived a man [**Kyaka** People]. His name was Kupuni Lapok.

One time, he heard that the people of **Kaidane** were holding a big festival. He left his village and began to walk to Kaidane Village.

When he arrived at the festival site, he began to cast his eyes upon the women. Oh my, Kupuni's eyes were fixed upon Kimala's daughter.

The woman danced with great passion. This made Kupuni's eyes spin around. He just watched her until the festival ended. After the festival, Kupuni followed her to all of the houses. The people in the houses cooked some food and gave it to Kupuni.

They prepared a bed for Kupuni to sleep. However, the rotten scoundrel was not asleep, he was merely pretending to sleep. His eyes were fixed upon Kimala's daughter.

Very late at night, when everyone was dead asleep, Kupuni got up very quietly from his bed and went to her bed. Then he carried her to Kyaka.

She was dead asleep, so she did not know what was happening to her. In the morning, when she awoke, she found that she was in Kyaka Village.

She thought about fleeing from Kupuni, but she felt like her village, Kaidane, was very far away. So, she married Kupuni. They lived for a while, then she gave birth to a baby boy.

However, she had explained to Kupuni not to call the name of her father, Kimala. She told Kupuni, "You can scold me or beat me, but you can't call the name of my father."

One time, she went to fetch water and she left the baby with Kupuni. She did not return quickly and the baby cried terribly.

This made Kupuni furious. When she returned, Kupuni was terribly angry with her. He told her, "You must go see your father, Kimala, at Kaidane Village, so don't come quickly."

She was very troubled when Kopuni called the name of her father. While they slept that night, they saw a light approaching. The light came directly towards them, taking the woman and child away. This light took them away completely to a lake.

In the morning, Kupuni sharpened a log and began digging at the lake. However, some logs (or trees) were stuck at the place where he was digging. So, he returned to the village and killed a pig to make a party to befriend his son.

Even now, this lake is still at **Sirunki**. It is called Lake Ivae [Enga People]. Near this lake, there are some logs (or trees).

Tiss Kepas Lakoe
Kimbe
West New Britain Province

C435.2.1+. Tabu: uttering name of father-in-law; F969.3. Marvelous light; J652. Inattention to warnings; P210. Husband and wife; P230. Parents and children; P231. Mother and son; P233. Father and son; P261. Father-in-law; P265. Son-in-law; R10. Abduction; T192. Marriage by force

The Ancestor of Nokondi
Nama Came from Kosayufa
(Wantok 929, April 23, 1992, page 19)

Long, long ago in **Kosayufa** Village, in the Asaro District, by Goroka, in **Eastern Highlands** Province, there lived a married couple [**Asaro** People]. They did not have children until they became old.

The men of the village never helped them do their work. They were tired of looking at the two of them. The poor old couple took a lot time to do work.

One time, Nosa felt as if she was pregnant, so she told her husband. Old Zombawe was elated when he heard this news. They lived for a while, then old Nosa gave birth to a baby boy and they gave him the name Nokondi. However, this child did not grow well. The child had one leg, one hand and one eye. His body did not look like that of a real person because he only had half a body.

However, the old couple worked very hard at taking care of Nokondi until he grew big. Later, Nokondi's parents became terribly old and they died.

Poor Nokondi cried terribly, then he buried his old parents. After this, he was alone and he found it very difficult to find and gather food.

However, Nokondi lived for a while and became a very big man. He found it difficult to look at and to live with the people of the village because he was ashamed of his body.

So, he lived alone in the forest and hid from the people of the village. Afterwards, he raised very many children and they just lived in the forest.

Even now, if you go to Goroka, you will hear this name, Nokondi Nama. When you go to Kosayufa Village in the Asaro area, you will see the place where Nokondi lived.

Ipson K. Lubahi
Kimbe
West New Britain Province

F490+. Nokondi; F525. Person with half a body; P210. Husband and wife; P230. Parents and children; P231. Mother and son; P233. Father and son; P426.2. Hermit; T570. Pregnancy; T580. Childbirth; V61.3+. Dead buried

[There were no ancestor stories in *Wantok* #930 or 931.]

Hot Water Helped Women
Give Birth to Babies
(Wantok 932, May 7, 1992, page 20)

Long, long ago, in the time of the ancestors, there was a mountain in **Eastern Highlands** Province. The mountain's name is Havuleto. On this mountain, there is a stream that runs and shoots out to a place where the mountain descends deeply.

The stream's name is _Kolasamauvi_ _Abade_ _Ninae_. The meaning of this is, "The Water to Give When Women are Pregnant."

By the side of this place, there are also two streams that meet and shoot downwards. They all meet and form a lake at their junction.

The first stream on the side is called _Veninae_, meaning "Man's Liquid." This is because when the water comes out of the cave, it shoots out like a man's urine.

The strength of this stream dug the sand and stones on the side, then shot them downwards. So at this place, there is a very big hole. Today, the hole is still there.

Another stream runs by the other side and it is called _Abadei_ _Ninae_. This name means "Woman's Liquid." This is because the water jumps in the way that women urinate.

All three of these streams meet and form a big lake. In the middle of this lake, there is a big cave. In the middle of this cave, there is a pond. This pond is always hot.

The name of this hot water is _Abadesamuri_ _Ninae_. This name means, "Women Who Have Just Become Pregnant Shall Put Their Legs into the Water."

In the time of the ancestors, women who were pregnant would go to this place and put their legs down. When they would put their legs inside the hot water, the water would move back and go up their legs until it went to their knees, then it would go down again. If this happened, the woman would give birth to a baby boy.

If the water passed their knees and went all of the way up, this signal would show that the woman would give birth to a baby girl. At the exact same time, she would give birth.

Today, if you go to Mount Havuleto, you will see this hot water, and the other streams there.

Feta Luse
Port Moresby
National Capital District

A983+. Origin of holes in ground; A1617. Origin of place-name; D921. Magic lake (pond); M369.7.3. Prophecy: sex of unborn child; T548. Birth obtained through magic or prayer; T570. Pregnancy

A Marsupial (*Kapul*) Caused the Ground Bury [a Man from] Koray [Karue]

(Wantok 933, May 21, 1992, page 19)

Long ago, five young boys and their two dogs lived in a little village called Koray [**Karue**]. This little village was in the deep forests of Pangia, in **Southern Highlands** Province [**Wiru** People].

The names of the three brothers were, Pakea, Kundipa and Lowale. The other two brothers were Lopa and Yarapea. These young men had two dogs. Two brothers had a dog named Kapene. Wimini was the name of the dog belonging to the three brothers.

The young men and their dogs lived very well in Koray. One night they sat outside the house, and a nice moon rose in the sky. They had various thoughts about the moon. So, they wanted to do something when the moon next hid.

Pakea was the eldest of the five. So, he told the others that the nice moon was good for hunting wild game. He told them to mark a time to arrange their things for going to hunt game.

In the morning, they all awoke and went to the garden. They worked until the afternoon, then Pakea told them to get ready. Afterwards, they would go to the village and arrange things for hunting game. At night, they arranged the bows and arrows, then they gave food to their two dogs.

Later that night, they cooked food and arranged other things to take with them to the forest. That night, they made a fire and slept, waiting for dawn. They became lost in sleep [lit., "sleep-forget"], then dawn arrived. Pakea awoke in the early morning and awakened all of the others.

They took everything with the two dogs, then they walked away into the forest. They walked and walked towards a mountain. The mountain's name is Mirambe [Mamuane]. When they arrived at Mirambe, they let the dogs run loose as they desired.

Before long, they heard the dogs barking at a marsupial (*kapul*). When they heard the dogs barking, they left all of their things and ran after the dogs. They approached and saw the dogs chasing a marsupial into a hole in the ground near a stream.

They helped the two dogs dig the earth. When the marsupial saw that they were digging the earth after it, it went further down into the ground. They saw that the marsupial was not moving [or making noise] anymore, so Pakea was angry. He kept digging the earth to grab the marsupial.

All of the brothers told Pakea to stand on top and let the two dogs dig the earth. However, Pakea was angry and he removed the dogs. He alone dug the earth, still pursuing the marsupial.

All of the brothers stood on top with the two dogs and watched Pakea. Before long, the ground broke and covered Pakea. They saw this and tried to dig the earth to bring Pakea to the surface. However, the ground obstructed all of Pakea's air and he died in the ground with the marsupial.

Everyone was sorry for Pakea because the ground had covered him completely and because they found it hard to help him. They cried until dawn at the place where the ground had covered their big brother.

In the morning, they dug the earth and tried to bring Pakea's body to the village. However, when they spoke, they saw that everything was moving and that the ground was shaking back and forth. Before long, they saw the ground break apart everywhere. So, they left Pakea there inside the earth, and they went back to the village.

They lived for a while, then one time they thought about walking to another village and looking for women to marry. So, one morning they went to a village. They hid and stole four young women, then they took them back to their own village.

Afterwards, they married and raised many children. However, their children did not live well because when it rained, the ground would break apart and chase them around.

[Anonymous]

D1431.1+. Ground pursues person; D2148. Earth magically caused to quake; F960.2.5. Earthquake at death of important person; J561. Intemperance in pursuit; J651. Inattention to danger; J652. Inattention to warnings; P210. Husband and wife; P230. Parents and children; P251.5. Two brothers; P251.6.1. Three brothers; R10. Abduction; R260. Pursuits; T192. Marriage by force

The Sun Came from the Sepik River

(Wantok 934, May 28, 1992, page 18)

Long, long ago, in Koiut [**Koiwat**] Village, in the Timbungke [Timbunke] area of **East Sepik** Province, there lived a man and his wife [**Sawos** People].

The woman's name was Simmei. Simmei lived with her husband, Rimeliwaken. They lived for a while, then one time, Simmei became pregnant. She gave birth to a baby boy. The boy's name was Ampian.

Before, when Simmei had been pregnant, she stayed inside a birthing hut. She gave birth to Ampian, then Rimeliwaken went inside to check on her.

However, she was angry and she pelted Rimeliwaken with the baby's feces. She did this because Rimeliwaken had not helped her deliver the baby.

Simmei then scolded her husband, Rimeliwaken, "You always just think about grabbing. You didn't think about helping me give birth to your son. Your baby won't grow well. He'll become sick. His belly will swell and become large."

Rimeliwaken was ashamed of this and fled to the land of the dead. He stayed there, and Simmei alone took care of Ampian.

Oh my, Ampian grew big very quickly. When baby Ampian slept, the place would become dark. When he would awake, the place would become completely light. After a while, [after] all of the days and nights, Ampian grew and became a big man.

One day, Simmei taught Ampian to beat the signal drum of the spirit house. Father Rimeliwaken heard the sound of the signal drum from the land of the dead, and he was shocked.

"Who's that beating my signal drum? The village has no men. It's just Simmei and the baby who live there. I think I should go back and check," said Rimeliwaken. Then he began to walk back to the village where only Simmei and Ampian lived.

Simmei knew that Rimeliwaken would hear the signal drum and return. So, she told Ampian to wash carefully, then dress himself at night.

In the early morning, Ampian walked and walked to the trail to meet his father. When Ampian left, everything on the trail just died. This was because he went with the heat of the sun.

Rimeliwaken arrived, but he did not approach. He stood far away and he shouted to his son, "Son, remove the bird of paradise that you shot with your head." Ampian removed the bird of paradise and the place began to become cold very quickly.

Afterwards, the father arrived and they exchanged human flesh with sago. Ampian gave sago to his father. The father had come from the land of the dead, so he gave the flesh of the dead to Ampian.

Jerry Masipar

Lae

Morobe Province

A711. Sun as man who left earth; A1170. Origin of night and day; D1890. Magic aging; D2146. Magic control of day and night; F81.1.2+. Journey to land of dead; P210. Husband and wife; P231. Mother and son; P233. Father and son; Q280. Unkindness punished; Q470+. Befouling as punishment; R213. Escape from home; T570. Pregnancy; T580. Childbirth; V112.1. Spirit huts; X716.1H+. Befouling with excrement

A *Masalai* Killed [His] Two Brothers

(Wantok 935, June 4, 1992, page 19)

Long, long ago, in the time of the ancestors, there lived a man at the source of the Karamure River in the Opao area [**Opau** Village] of Kerema, **Gulf** Province [**Opao** People].

He was not a real man. The name of this *masalai* man was Opu. Opu had a wife. Her name was Fairi. Opu had two brothers too. The name of one brother was Ea and the name of the youngest brother was Aboka.

The two little brothers lived well with Opu and his wife, Fairi. The little brothers were farmers. Every day, they would awake in the early morning and go to work in the gardens. In the evening, they would return to the house with food from the gardens, such as bananas, taros, yams, sugarcanes, leafy greens, and many others.

Opu, you know, was a *masalai* man. He often just used his powers to get whatever he wanted. Also, he was a fighting man. Every day, he would just fight and win more powers and renown.

Every day, he alone would go to fight with the warriors of the villages by the beach. This was because he wanted to kill all of them and take their land.

They lived for a while, then Opu's wife, Fairi, became pregnant. One day, Opu took his wife, then they walked and walked towards the beach.

They walked and walked to a faraway place, then Fairi felt that her belly was in pain and stirring. She was about to give birth to the baby, so she told Opu, "I feel like I'm going to give birth to the baby now."

Then they looked for a good place for her to give birth. Opu told his wife, "I'll go directly to my friend's house.

Their house is far away. I'll see my friend, then I'll return and bring you to give birth to the baby at his house."

After Opu spoke, he left her on the trail. He walked and walked to a nearby village to see his friend. However, she waited for a while, then she felt the pain in her belly become very strong.

She cried and cried, then she lay on the trail. It was hopeless, and Fairi turned into a turtle. Opu was a *masalai* man. He walked alone and came from far away. He saw that his wife's time had come and that she had turned into a turtle. He was terribly troubled and sent forth a big flood.

The flood came and carried the woman who had turned into a turtle back to the village where only the two little brothers were staying. The brothers thought that it was a real flood that had come. They saw the turtle and thought that it was a real turtle. Oh my, they were elated that they would have good meat to eat.

They were both happy, so they killed the turtle. Afterwards, they cooked it well in a fire and ate it. What they had really done was to kill and eat their big sister-in-law.

Opu saw this and was completely furious at the little brothers. He sent forth a huge flood with stones and logs, killing the little brothers in the village.

All of the detritus completely covered over the two brothers. After the great flood, Opu went alone and followed the water upwards, where he made a home at the headwaters.

Today, if you go to Kerema, you can take a motor-canoe up to the Opae [Opao] area. You will see that these logs and stones are still in the clearing.

Roy Lahul Keroro

Lae

Morobe Province

A977. Origin of particular stones or groups of stones; A1011. Local deluges; A1015.2. Spirit causes deluge; A1018. Flood as punishment; D193W. Transformation: woman to tortoise (turtle); D642. Transformation to escape difficult situation; D2151.8. Magic flood; F401.6. Spirit in human form; F490+. Masalai; G61. Relative's flesh eaten unwittingly; P210. Husband and wife; F251.6.1. Three brothers; P263. Brother-in-law; P264. Sister-in-law; Q211 Murder punished; Q211.6. Killing an animal revenged; Q552.19.6. Flood as punishment for murder (fratricide); S55+. Brother-in-law kills sister-in-law; S73.1. Fratricide; S110. Murders; T570. Pregnancy

Why are Dog and *Magani* [Kangaroo] Enemies?

(Wantok 936, June 11, 1992, page 20)

Long ago, in the time of the ancestors, *Magani* [Kangaroo] and Dog lived, ate, traveled, and slept well together. However, because of the lie that *Magani* made, they are enemies today.

One nice time, *Magani* told Dog that Dog must take care of their house in the village, while *Magani* would go hunting for wild game for themselves. So, in the early morning, *Magani* awoke and walked off into the forest to hunt for game. However, when *Magani* arrived in the forest, *Magani* saw that there were many breadfruits and *Magani* did not think further of hunting for game.

Magani worked hard at gathering the breadfruits, then *Magani* returned to the village. When *Magani* arrived at the village, *Magani* saw that Dog was not there. So, *Magani* cooked the breadfruits on a fire and ate.

Before long, Dog returned and saw *Magani* eating, so Dog shouted, "My good friend, have you arrived? Did you find some game for us or not?" *Magani* replied, "Good friend, I didn't find any game, but I found these tree fruits for us to eat. Do you eat them too?" Dog replied, "I've never eaten tree fruits."

So *Magani* told Dog, "My good friend, come and try them." Dog approached slowly and sat nearby, then *Magani* gave one to Dog. Dog held it and ate. The breadfruit was delicious, so Dog asked *Magani* to give some more. Afterwards, Dog held another and asked *Magani*, "What should I do with this to eat it?" *Magani* replied, "Hold it in your hand and rub it on your chest. After it cools, eat it."

However, the breadfruit was tasty, so Dog did not think about removing its skin to eat it. Dog rubbed it on its chest, then swallowed it hot with the skin still on it. The breadfruit burned Dog's throat, but Dog did not care because the breadfruit was tasty.

Magani removed the breadfruit skin very slowly, then ate. However, *Magani* did not know that his friend, Dog, was stealing glances. Dog looked and removed the skin quickly, then ate. Dog was angry that it could not do anything, "That's OK. I'll trick *Magani* later," Dog thought.

One time, Dog told *Magani*, "You'll stay in the village. I'll go to the sea and hunt for fish for us." *Magani* was also just famished to eat fish. So, *Magani* was happy when Dog said that it would go to the sea to go fishing.

Dog walked and walked to the beach, then paddled the canoe to the reef. Dog stopped the canoe, then swam in the sea to search for fish. However, Dog was still angry at *Magani*, so Dog did not think about fishing. Dog just took [some giant] clam meat. Dog paddled the canoe back to the shore, then carried the clam meat to the village.

Magani saw this and asked, "Brother, have you arrived?" Dog replied, "Pal, I've returned, but the fish did not stay on the hook, so I just brought some clam meat. Come, we'll cook and eat it."

Magani came and sat nearby, then they cooked the clam on the fire. *Magani* ate the clam meat and lusted to eat more. So, *Magani* asked Dog how it had caught the clam. Dog turned slowly and said what *Magani* must do to catch clams if it wanted to eat them. *Magani* was happy and told Dog that one time, it would go hunting for clam meat in the sea.

They lived for a while, then *Magani* told Dog, "Stay here, I'll go to the sea and hunt for fish for us." *Magani* made preparations in the morning, then walked off to the beach. *Magani* paddled the canoe to the reef, then jumped down into the sea and hunted for fish. *Magani* fished for a while, then saw a big clam open its mouth.

"Now I'll get you, then my friend and I will eat you. I'll put my two hands inside to your flesh and pull you up," *Magani* thought ecstatically. *Magani* swam down and put its two hands into the clam's flesh.

Magani missed at pulling the clam's flesh up and the clam held *Magani*'s two hands. *Magani* ran out of breath inside the sea. *Magani* was near death, so *Magani* pulled its hands hard and the clam cut them off.

When *Magani* returned to the village, it was furious and told Dog, "You lied to me and the clam bit my hands off, shortening them. I'm angry with you. I'll leave you in the village and go into the forest." Dog was angry and told *Magani*, "Before, you lied to me about breadfruits and I was burned. So, I've avenged myself for this. Now, if you want to be angry with me and flee to the forest, that's your problem. But if I find you in the forest, don't think that we're friends and that I can't kill you. No, I'll chase and kill you."

So, dogs and *magani*s are still enemies until now. If a dog sees a *magani* in the forest, it will be angry and chase the *magani*. There is still enmity between them.

Willie Mulai

Hagen

Western Highlands Province

[See the ancestor story in *Wantok* #105 closely resembles this story.]

A2284. Origin of animal characteristics: animal persuaded into self-injury; A2371.2.10. Why kangaroo has short front legs; A2494.4+. Enmity be-

tween dog and kangaroo; B211.1.7. Speaking dog; B211.2.12K. Speaking kangaroo; B874.6. Giant clam; K890+. Deceived into sticking body part into giant clam; K1065+. Kangaroo persuaded into cutting off its front legs; K2297. Treacherous friend; P310. Friendship; R213. Escape from home; S161. Mutilation: cutting off hands (arms); W157. Dishonesty

Turtle Made the Cockatoo Bald

(Wantok 937, June 18, 1992, page 20)

Long ago, in **Morobe** Province, Cockatoo and Turtle were very good friends. They traveled, ate and drank together. However, they later became angry and Cockatoo fled into the forest while Turtle went to the sea in complete confusion.

One nice day, Turtle drifted on top of the sea. Turtle was thinking about seeing its friend, Cockatoo. Turtle swam and arrived at the shore, then walked slowly to the garden. Turtle heard a noise inside a group of banana plants and thought that men were weeding their garden. Turtle hid and watched the bananas. Turtle's eyes shot directly towards something white among the banana leaves. Turtle walked closer and saw Cockatoo with its eyes shut and eating bananas.

Turtle sat and caught its breath, then shouted to Cockatoo, "Brother, what are you doing in the men's garden?" Cockatoo replied, "Stay calm, I want to arrange some banana plant rubbish." However, Turtle thought hard that it would be bad if the men came, so Turtle told Cockatoo to come down and they would run away from the men's garden. Then they would go to find some food for themselves.

Turtle told Cockatoo to come down quickly. This was because the day before, Turtle had seen many breadfruits. So Turtle wanted Cockatoo to come down, then they would go fetch the breadfruits.

When Cockatoo heard this, it immediately descended and walked with Turtle to the base of the breadfruit tree. Turtle sat at the base of the tree, and Cockatoo ascended. Cockatoo worked hard at removing breadfruits. Turtle quickly gathered them below. Afterwards, Turtle searched for and gathered firewood, then prepared it. When Cockatoo descend, they cook the breadfruits. Turtle arranged everything, then waited for Cockatoo to descend. However, Cockatoo was using the breadfruit juice to strengthen the feathers on its head. So, Cockatoo did not hear what Turtle had said. Turtle waited and waited, then it made a fire to cook the breadfruits.

Cockatoo saw the fire getting bigger, so it went down to the ground. They put breadfruits on the fire. However,

Turtle's main thought was to kill its friend, Cockatoo. So, Turtle tried to do various things to trick Cockatoo. They cooked the breadfruits, then Turtle lied to Cockatoo that its body was hot. So, Turtle would go bathe a little in the sea.

Turtle walked and walked to the beach, then dug the ground, so as to hide. Afterwards, Turtle swam quickly into the sea and took its axe. Turtle came up and walked, then Turtle hid it near the place where Turtle would trick and kill Cockatoo. Later, Turtle walked back to the base of the breadfruit tree and saw Cockatoo working hard. They finished eating the breadfruits, then Turtle told Cockatoo, "Look for lice [or fleas] on me, then I'll look for lice on you."

Cockatoo listened to Turtle, then they walked away to sit near the place where Turtle had hidden its axe. Turtle sat and told Cockatoo to search for lice on it. Cockatoo searched for a long time, then told Turtle, "Pal, my hands are in pain."

When Turtle heard this, it told Cockatoo, "My buddy, that's OK. Sit and I'll search for your lice." Cockatoo was happy and lowered its head for Turtle to search for its lice. Cockatoo bowed and waited for Turtle to find its lice. However, Turtle went to the hiding place and took its axe, then approached. Afterwards, Turtle told Cockatoo to go down far. When Cockatoo was far down, Turtle tried to cut Cockatoo's neck. However, Turtle missed, and Cockatoo fled into the forest.

When Turtle saw that it had missed, it sped into the hole and hid. When Cockatoo arrived in the forest, it told all of the birds that all of the sea creatures were ready to fight with them. When all of the birds heard this, they prepared and sent with their leader, Cassowary.

Turtle slept a little, then sped into the sea. Turtle lied to Crocodile, the leader of all of the sea creatures, then Crocodile gathered all of the fish. They met at a place, then all of the birds came. They made a fence, then Cassowary and Crocodile fought. All of them stood watching to see who would win this fight. They fought and fought, then Crocodile took a big stone and broke Cassowary's legs.

All of the birds saw this and fled. Turtle saw that all of the birds had fled, so it took a big stone and broke Cockatoo's head, causing all of the feathers to fly off.

Cockatoo was angry and ran away completely from Turtle. However, the mark from the stone is still on the heads of cockatoos [probably the sulphur-crested cockatoo, which is white (Beehler *et al.*, 117)]. From this origin, cockatoos and turtles are still enemies. The same is true for all of the birds and sea creatures.

Kellyson Wangken

Lae

Morobe Province

A2321.12K. Origin of comb of white cockatoo; A2370+. Why cassowary's legs bend backwards; A2494.13+. Enmity between cockatoo and turtle; A2494.15+. Enmity between sea creatures and birds; B211.3+. Speaking cockatoo; B211.7.3K2. Speaking turtle; B242.1+. Cassowary as king of birds; B243+. Crocodile as king of sea creatures; K2297. Treacherous friend; P310. Friendship; R220. Flights; W157. Dishonesty

A Sepik Woman Gave Birth to Piglets
(Wantok 938, June 25, 1992, page 20)

Long ago, in the time of the ancestors, there were no pigs on the earth. Men would just hunt for other wild game to eat in the forest.

In the deep forests of **East Sepik** Province, there was a small village. Inside this village, there lived an old man who was the champion at hunting game.

One nice day, he prepared all of the food and a multi-pronged spear for game hunting, then he walked into the forest to hunt for pig. The name of the spear was Livatimi. He held this spear and went to hide among the sago leaves.

He saw many pigs going around and trampling the ground. However, he wanted a big pig to test his spear, so he waited. Before long, he saw a big pig walking closer, away from the others, and trampling the ground. He hid behind the sago leaves and went closer, then he threw his spear at the pig.

However, this pig did not fall or squeal because it was not a real pig. The pig was a man who always would transform into a pig, then travel with the other pigs inside the forest. The old man saw this and followed the pig's blood.

The pig ran and ran to his house in the village, and then he told [his] two daughters to remove the spear from his body. The names of the two girls were Kankuto and Kankuposi. After they removed the spear, they carried their father away and laid him by the fire.

They took care of their father, then the old man followed the pig's blood and arrived. When he saw the girls, he shut his mouth and just watched them. Afterwards, the girls asked the old man what he was looking for. He told them that he had shot a big pig, and that the pig had taken his spear and fled there.

The girls stared at the old man. Later, they told the old man to go inside the house. They told him that he had shot their father, so he must become their friend. Whenever they made food for their father and brother, they would make a portion for the old man too. Their brother asked the two of them, "Who lives inside the room and to whom do you bring food in there?"

One time, their brother smelled the old man's body and asked them again, "What is it that smells inside the house?" The girls did not reply to him. However one time, they traveled and the brother opened the door to go inside the house. He saw the old man, and he was unhappy that his two sisters had lied to him.

So, he waited for them to return to the house. When they arrived, he asked them, "That man who lives inside the house, whose husband is he?" The girls did not reply to him.

He told them, "I'll measure you together. If the man is taller or shorter than you, I'll kill him and you'll eat him."

Afterwards, he went inside and told the father that his two sisters had taken a man and hidden him in the house. Their father did not do anything. The brother went out and measured the sisters against the old man.

Then he saw that their three heights were equal. So, he told the sisters to marry the old man. [The man] was happy. He lived with the two of them and took care of their father. They lived for a while, then the old man asked the women's brother to take them to his village to see his kin.

However, the brother did not want to do this. So, he told the younger sister to go with the old man and leave the elder sister there. In the morning, the old man awakened both of the women, then he asked them who would go with him to the village. Kankuposi told Kankuto to stay with her brother and father.

Then she would go with the husband to his village. They arrived at the village, then the man's brothers and sisters were very happy to see Kankuposi. They all lived together for a while, then Kankuposi became pregnant. They lived for a while longer, then Kankuposi felt as if she was about to give birth to a baby, so she cried inside the house.

Kankuposi was about to give birth, but she did not want men to see her give birth. So, she told her husband to go to see her father and brother, and her sister, Kankuto.

The old man left, then Kankuposi walked towards a banana garden. She transformed her body and became a pig, then she gave birth to two piglets. She waited at the base of the banana plants, then her husband came. Kankuposi lay quietly and the old man found her. When the old man approached the base of the banana plants, Kankuposi chased him. She took her two piglets and fled back to her family in the forest.

The old man was not happy because he had lived a long time with Kankuposi. She had changed and become a pig then left him to go crazy.

So, the old man became an enemy of the pigs of the forest. He always wanted to hunt and kill them. So now, we often eat pork.

Jerry Masipar
Sepik River

A1871. Creation of hog (pig); A2585+. Enmity between people and swine; D114.3.2M. Transformation: man to boar; D114.3+W. Transformation: woman to sow (wild); D336.1M. Transformation: pig to man; G10. Cannibalism; H300. Tests connected with marriage; P210. Husband and wife; P234. Father and daughter; P250. Brothers and sisters; P253.0.2+. Two sisters and one brother; P261. Father-in-law; P263. Brother-in-law; P264. Sister-in-law; P265. Son-in-law; P310. Friendship; R220. Flights; R260. Pursuits; T100. Marriage; T145.0.1. Polygyny; T554.16.K2. Woman gives birth to hog; T570. Pregnancy; T587. Birth of twins; W157. Dishonesty

[The ancestor story in *Wantok* #939 is the same as that in #842.]

An Okapa Woman Followed the Smoke from a Fire
(Wantok 940, July 9, 1992, page 19)

Long ago, in the time of the ancestors, there lived an old woman and her daughter in a small place. This place was far away on a big mountain in the Kainantu area of Eastern Highlands Province. There were no other people in this place, only the old woman and her daughter lived there.

The daughter's name was Imandaya, and she often worked very hard. She helped her old mother plant taros, yams, bananas, and sweet potatoes in the garden during the mornings.

When the sun was in the middle of the sky, she would rest under the banana plants and drink sugarcane juice. In the afternoon, she would go to the old garden with her mother and they would search for food to take back to the house.

When they went to the old gardens, Imandaya would see the sun setting behind the mountain. She would always do this. One time, she saw smoke from a fire rising from the other side of the mountain.

Imandaya often saw the smoke and was very troubled. She had a strong belief that a man must live on the other side of the mountain.

One time, Imandaya and her mother went to the garden in the very early morning. They worked hard at planting new foods, then they weeded the garden. In the afternoon, the old mother shouted to Imandaya then they went to find some food in the old garden.

Imandaya looked back to the mountain and saw the smoke. Her thoughts were completely confused now. Imandaya stopped thinking about looking for food. All of her thoughts were about the smoke. She thought of following the smoke and seeing who lived there.

She thought for a while, then her mother shouted to her and they went back home. When they arrived home, Imandaya did all of the housework. The old mother was very happy that she had done this.

Imandaya cooked food, then prepared it to be eaten. They ate, then Imandaya very quickly went to sleep. She slept and only dreamt of the smoke from the fire.

However, she thought of a plan that night. So, in the early morning, she awoke and prepared everything. The old mother was also ready and they went back to the garden.

They worked until the afternoon, then they walked back home very slowly. When they arrived home, Imandaya did the same thing. They ate, then she quickly went to sleep.

Very late at night, Imandaya awoke and cooked sweet potatoes to bring, then she walked away towards the mountain. She went out of the house, broke some *tanget* plants [as a trail marker] and walked to the mountain. She walked and walked, then she approached and saw an old woman weeding her garden.

She hid and watched the old woman shout the name of her child. She hid and watched to see who would reply to the old woman. Before long, she saw a young man walking with his multi-pronged spear and coming out of the forest.

When Imandaya saw him, her heart stopped. She wanted very much to marry him. This man's name was Nufara.

Nufara walked towards his mother. Later he went back into the forest. When Imandaya saw this, she followed Nufara and called his name. Nufara turned and saw Imandaya standing behind him.

Later, Imandaya lied to Nufara that she had seen the nest of a big bird. She wanted Nufara to kill the bird. So, Nufara followed Imandaya and they went very far towards a mountain. When they approached the mountain, Nufara asked about the bird's nest. However, Imandaya did not reply to him.

Later, Nufara saw the smoke from the fire that his mother was making in the garden. Nufara saw this and was very sorry for his mother.

However, Imandaya told him, "Don't worry about your mama. You'll marry me, then we'll go to live with my mama."

When Nufara heard this, he was not in agreement because he had not explained to his mother that he had followed Imandaya. They left the mountain, then Imandaya took Nufara to her home. When Imandaya's mother saw Nufara, she was elated. They made a huge party, and Imandaya married Nufara.

At first, Nufara was not happy with Imandaya's home. However, they lived for a while and Imandaya gave birth to a baby. This made Nufara forget completely about his mother.

Today, all of the families from Nufara and Imandaya in the Kainantu area speak two languages. These two languages are **Tairora** and Awiyana [**Auyana**].

The Tairora Language comes from Imandaya's home in the **Okapa** area [**Fore** People]. The Awiyana Language is from Nufara from the **Kainantu** area [**Agarabi** People]. Nowadays, many people in the **Eastern Highlands** Province speak these two languages.

Daniel Wekas

Kainantu

Eastern Highlands Province

A1616+. Origin of Auyana Language; A1616+. Origin of Tairora Language; P210. Husband and wife; P231. Mother and son; P232. Mother and daughter; P233. Father and son; P262. Mother-in-law; P265. Son-in-law; R260. Pursuits; T10. Falling in love; T100. Marriage; T580. Childbirth; W157. Dishonesty

An Ambunti Man Followed His Axe and Met *Masalais*

(Wantok 941, July 16, 1992, page 20)

Long, long ago, in **Waihos** Village, by Ambunti in **East Sepik** Province, there lived a man [**Manambu** People?].

One time, he awoke in the very early morning and went into the forest. He walked and walked, then he arrived at a big sago palm tree that stood by a pond.

He threw down everything, then he took his stone axe and began cutting the sago palm tree. He worked and worked, but his hands were slippery and the stone axe fell into the pond. Inside the water, there lived a *masalai* woman. The axe went to lie directly at her feet. The *masalai* woman saw this and quickly took the stone axe, then she hid it in her net bag.

The man stood above the pond and thought hard. He was very worried about his stone axe and he did not know what to do. In desperation, the boy [man] threw away everything that was up there, then went into the pond to find the axe. He jumped directly into the pond and met the *masalai* woman.

The *masalai* woman asked him, "Exactly what have you come looking for here?" He replied, "I came to find my axe. I was working at cutting a sago tree above and my hands were slippery, so the axe went into the water. I came to find it."

The *masalai* woman listened to this and took the man to the *masalai*s' spirit house. After she brought him, the *masalai* woman went to bring all of the other *masalai*s to see him. Then they argued about whether or not to kill and eat him. They went on and on, then they crushed the idea of killing him and they spoke about bringing him back home. So, the *masalai* woman who had brought him went back and forth, then told him, "We want you to stay with us of one or two weeks first. After that, we'll make a feast and bring you back to your village."

So, after about two weeks, the *masalai*s of the pond made a huge feast and they prepared to bring him back up to the ground. Before they did this, the *masalai*s gave him some traditional *kina* shell money, and some ring [money] that was used traditionally to purchase a wife or to purchase heavy labor.

They brought him up to the ground. At this time, a heavy rain and wind arose, then the place became completely dark. So, the people in the village did not travel the forest or garden, or go fishing in the little pond. They all stayed in the village. The *masalai*s brought him up and left him by the base of a fig tree, then they returned. At the same time, the wind and rain ended, and it became light again.

The villagers saw this and quickly took their work gear; they were about to go to the forest. Some people wanted to go fishing in the pond; they went there directly and saw the leader [man] standing with various foods, and with traditional shell and ring money. They were surprised, so they asked the leader, "Where did you get these things?" He replied, "You probably thought that I died, but I've returned. Carry the food and things, then we'll go to the village. At the village, I'll tell you a good story."

In the evening, everyone gathered, and he told what had happened to him. The villagers listened and decided to repay the *masalai*s of the pond. After one week, they prepared food and things, then they brought them to the pond.

There, the man went and called for the *masalai*s to come up from the pond and take the things to their home.

Paul Olphant
RMI-BHP [Rabaul Metal Industries-Broken Hill Properties]
Rabaul
East New Britain Province

D2126. Magic underwater journey; D2142.1. Wind produced by magic; D2143.1. Rain produced by magic; D2146.2. Night controlled by magic; F420.2.2. Water-spirits live in village under water; F490+. Masalai; G308.2. Water-monster; G639. Ogress lives in water; G639+. Ogre lives in water; Q45. Hospitality rewarded; V112.1. Spirit huts

Maningulai Came from a Simbian Woman
(Wantok 942, July 23, 1992, page 20)

One time, long, long ago, the young women of Warikum [**Wanabrugu**] Village, near Simbian in **East Sepik** Province, wanted to make new "grass" skirts [**Sawos** People]. So, they found their old-fashioned stone axes and they went to cut new sago palm leaves.

Among these women, there was one whose father and mother had died. This woman went to her grandmother's house and asked to use her stone axe. The old woman told her to return in the morning and take the axe.

In the early morning, the grandmother awoke and transformed herself into a nice axe. Then she hung on top of he front door. When the young woman arrived at her grandmother's house, she saw the axe and was elated. This was because she would cut all of the sago leaves quickly, and then return to the village. She was extremely happy and went to meet the other women. Afterwards, they went into the forest to cut the sago leaves.

They were working at cutting the sago leaves when the young woman's axe became loose and flew down to the swampy water. She searched and searched, but she did not see anything. The axe changed into the old woman again, then she walked quietly back to the village.

All of the women finished cutting the sago leaves, then returned to the village. However, the poor woman kept working hard, still trying to find the axe. She kept at it until it was afternoon, then she thought hard about what she would say to her grandmother.

In the evening, she walked slowly back to the village and told the old woman what happened. However, the grandmother just acknowledged her and said that she would find a new stone axe. Later, they sat and told stories, then the old woman told her that they would go fishing at a lake.

In the early morning, they went to the lake. They paddled the canoe to the middle, then the young woman wanted to defecate. So, the old woman brought the canoe's side to a small, nearby island for the youth to defecate.

However, while she was defecating, her grandmother jumped onto the canoe and paddled back to the village. The young woman came out and saw this, then she shouted to her grandmother. However, the old woman replied, "You lost my stone axe. Now find your own way to get home." After she said this, she went to the village.

The young woman sat crying, then a *masalai* fish heard her. So, the fish sent its child up to check. The bad boy [fish] came and saw the young woman. He wanted to marry her, so he gave her food and did everything to flatter this young woman.

The next afternoon, he returned and slept with her. He always did this and the young woman became pregnant. However, she did not give birth to a human baby, she gave birth to two bird eggs. She was greatly afraid that crocodiles would eat them, so she dug the earth and buried the two eggs.

One morning, she went to check on where she had buried the two eggs. She was surprised to see two nice little birds sitting there. She returned to the house to get food, then she went and gave it to them. Later, she brought them to the house and took care of them until they grew big.

They were not ordinary birds: they could talk. So one time, they asked their mother to tell them how they had come to live on this island. She told the story, then the two birds spoke of taking their mother to her village. However, the mother was afraid and told them to carry a big tree first. The birds did this, but the mother was still afraid. They became stronger, and the mother agreed that they could carry her back to the village. So, they carried her and flew to the village, leaving her directly at the house. The birds went to sit on top of the house.

At this time, the woman's real husband and his friend returned from the garden and saw smoke rising from the house. They sped over there, then looked and went inside. His wife was sitting and cooking sago in the fire. He was elated and began asking her about her entire story. She told the story, then her husband went outside and saw the two birds sitting there. He thought of the sago that his wife was cooking and he wanted to kill the two birds. [ends abruptly]

Avisat Nien
Wewak
East Sepik Province

B211.3. Speaking bird; B211.5. Speaking fish; B542.1+. Bird flies with woman to safety; B552+. Woman carried by bird; B612. Fish paramour; D250+W. Transformation: woman to axe; F420.1.3.2. Water-spirit as fish; D434+W. Transformation: axe to woman; F490+. Masalai; P210. Husband and wife; P230. Parents and children; P292. Grandmother; P310. Friendship; Q270. Misdeeds concerning property punished; Q438+. Punishment: abandonment on island; R130. Rescue of abandoned or lost persons; S41. Cruel grandmother; S145. Abandonment on an island; T10. Falling in love; T481. Adultery; T554.10. Woman gives birth to a bird; T565. Woman lays an egg; T570. Pregnancy; T587. Birth of twins

A Brother Tricked His Sister's Ghost in Kabwum

(Wantok 943, July 30, 1992, page 18)

Long ago, a young woman with her brother and father lived in a small village called **Gimbong** in the Kabwum area of **Morobe** Province [**Selepet** People]. The old man had many food gardens. Often, people from other villages would exchange things with him.

So one time, he told his two children to find food in the gardens, then they would exchange the food with other things from a village called Weliki [**Weleki** Village, **Weleki** People]. Weliki was far away, so they left the house and walked off in the very early morning.

In the afternoon, they arrived at Weliki and exchanged food with the people there. At this time, the daughter saw a young man bring his things and make exchanges with them. She just died for him.

While they were walking along the trail, she still thought of him. However, she was ashamed to tell her father and brother. They arrived home and the young man's face was still on her mind. One afternoon, she told her father and brother that she desired a young man, "I want to say that it's been a long time. I was ashamed, so I didn't say anything."

When the father heard this, he was elated that his daughter had found a young man to marry. So, he told his daughter and son to prepare to return to Weliki. They would leave the daughter with the young man. They walked and arrived at Weliki, then the father went to the young man's house. He spoke to him, "We came to see you. My daughter desires you, so I brought her to give to you. Before I give you my daughter, I'll ask you, 'Do you like my daughter or not?'"

The young man looked at her and he desired her too. So, he told the father to bring his daughter to the house. "I'm happy to marry your daughter and I promise that I'll take care of her," the young man said.

The father and brother sat with the daughter, then they walked back home. Three whole years passed and they had not seen the daughter. So, the father told the son that they should prepare some food to take to Weliki and see his sister.

In the early morning, they took their things and walked off to Weliki. When they arrived, they saw that no one was in the village. It was dark, so they arranged a place inside a house and were about to go to sleep.

Before long, they saw a young woman walk out of the darkness. When the father saw her, he knew that his daughter must have died. So, he told his son, "Look at your sister walking and bringing her own body here."

The son saw this and was terrified at his sister's ghost. However, he did not have a way to escape, so he sat. His sister brought her body and placed it near them. Later, she told her father and brother that everyone had died.

She had seen them sitting in her house, so she came to cook some food for them. They sat, then the ghost carved her own body and placed it in a pot. The father saw this and very quickly told his son to look for leafy greens by the house and to cook the greens for themselves to eat. When the daughter's ghost put food into her mouth. Her brother very quickly put the food into his mouth too.

The ghost woman ate her own corpse for a while, then her belly became full. So, she fell dead asleep that night. However, her father awoke at night and saw his daughter's liver hanging on top of the house, so he ate it. They slept until morning, then the son awakened his father and they fled. When they arrived at the middle of the trail, it was dawn. The ghost woman awoke and did not find them. So, she very quickly smelled them and followed them.

She approached them and the father felt his legs becoming heavy, so he did not walk quickly. His son carried him and they sped away. However, the son's body was in pain, so he walked slowly and his sister's ghost came closer.

The son saw this and left his father on the trail. He jumped up a tall tree. The daughter just looked at her father and killed him. Afterwards, she just ate the head, then looked for her brother to kill and eat his head too. Before long, she looked up and saw her brother sitting on the tree. She shouted for her brother to descend. However, the brother did not listen to her. She jumped up the tree so that she could pull him down to the ground and eat him.

When her brother saw this, he put a bird-of-paradise feather on his head and he flew to Gimbong. When his sister saw this, she went down and completely finished her father.

Anna Kelong
Bialla
West New Britain Province

D670. Magic flight; D1021. Magic feather; D2061.2.1. Death-giving glance; E220+. Dead daughter's malevolent return; E226+. Dead sister's malevolent return; E261.4. Ghost pursues man; E425.1. Revenant as woman; E541.2+. Revenant eats own corpse; E568. Revenant lies down and sleeps; E592.1. Ghost carries own dead body; G11.10. Cannibalistic spirits; G50. Occasional cannibalism; P210. Husband and wife; P233. Father and son; P234. Father and daughter; P253. Sister and brother; R210. Escapes; R260. Pursuits; R311. Tree refuge; S21K. Cruel daughter; S22+. Patricide; S110. Murders; T10. Falling in love; T100. Marriage

The Law Against [Killing] Birds of Paradise Is Still Strong in the Highlands

(Wantok 944, August 6, 1992, page 19)

Long, long ago, in the time of the ancestors, two young men lived in the Awiyana area [**Auyana** People], by Kainantu in the **Eastern Highlands** Province.

The big brother's name was Soh, and the little brother's name was Teh. They made a house under a big cave and lived there. During the day, they would go out near the cave and make a garden. In the afternoon, they would gather food and go into the cave to cook.

They lived for a while, then Teh told his big brother Soh that he was tired of eating dry sweet potatoes and bananas. The big brother asked him, "What do you want to eat?" Teh told him that sometimes they must leave the house and go to the deep forest to hunt for wild game. Soh listened and was sorry that his little brother had said this. He told Teh, "If you want us to eat meat, will you follow everything that I say?" Teh was elated and told Soh that he would follow everything that he said.

One morning, Soh awoke and told Teh to get a stone axe, then to go search for bamboos to make arrows. So, Teh went and cut very many bamboos. He broke them and sharpened all of them, readying them to be made into arrows.

Later, he cut them and brought them to the house, then he arranged them well. Soh also went to the forest to cut *limbum* palms to make bows. They would always awake in the morning and go into the forest. They worked in the garden during the day, then in the afternoon they returned to the house to work on their bows and arrows.

They did this for a while, until a whole month passed. Then the little brother asked Soh exactly when they would go into the forest to hunt for game. Soh told him that they would wait until all of the fruit trees began to flower, then they would go to hunt for game.

One time, Teh went to the garden and he saw that all of the trees were beginning to bear flowers, so he told Soh. In the morning, Soh awakened Teh, then they went into the forest. They traveled, then Soh saw a big tree and told Teh that they would make a hut in which to hide. From there, they would shoot birds on top of the tree.

They went and cut saplings to make a hut. In the afternoon, they gathered all of the saplings at the base of the big tree, then they went to the house. The next morning, they went back again and made two huts on top of the tree. They finished all of the work, then they returned to the house.

They cooked food in the afternoon. They also arranged some food to eat on top of the tree for when they watched birds. When the sun rose the next day, they very quickly went on top of the tree and hid in the two huts. Before long, they saw the little birds come there directly and eat the tree fruits.

Teh saw this and he began to shoot them. The first arrow stuck to two birds, and they fell. This raised an idea in The' mind to kill all of the birds in one day. However, the birds came in a big group and he could not finish off all of them. In the afternoon, they descended the tree and gathered all of the birds, then they took them to the house. They were happy to eat meat now.

Teh was happy to have killed the birds, so every day he wanted to go to the forest and shoot them. However, Soh said that they must put in some days at the garden. One time, they went back again hid. They shot birds until the afternoon, then Teh saw a big bird come and sit close to him. He straightened himself out, then he shot the big bird and shouted, "*Fefalulo*."

The bird fell to the ground. All of the little birds saw this, then they squawked and fled into the deep forest, never to return to this tree. Soh saw this and asked Teh what he had done to cause all of the little birds to flee from them. Teh knew that he was wrong, so he lowered his head and told Soh, "Brother, I saw the nice plumage on that bird, so I forgot everything that you had said. I'm ashamed." Soh told Teh, "I forbade you to shoot the big birds. However, you ignored what I had told you and you shot the king of the birds." So he cast a big tabu upon Teh never to shoot birds of paradise again.

This tabu is still strong in Awiyana Village, near Kainantu in Eastern Highlands Province. Also, many people in the Highlands follow this law against killing birds of paradise in the deep forest.

Deniel [Daniel] Wekas
Kokopo
East New Britain Province

A1587.2. Tabus instituted by culture hero; B242.1+. Bird of paradise as king of birds; C92.1.6+. Tabu: killing bird of paradise; J652. Inattention to warnings; P251.5. Two brothers; W126. Disobedience

[The ancestor story in *Wantok* #945 is the same as the one in #938.]
[There was no ancestor story in *Wantok* #946.]

The Marsupials (*Kapul*) of Pangia Arose from a Man
(Wantok 947, August 27, 1992, page 19)

Long ago, in the time of the ancestors, a young woman and her brother lived in a small village called Kauo [**Kauwo**] in the Pangia District of **Southern Highlands** [Province, **Wiru** People]. The young woman's name was Karue and the man's name was Kali.

They youths were still young when their mother and father had died. So, they took care of themselves until they grew bigger. Before their mother and father had died, they made gardens and planted many foods by their house.

So, when their parents had died, the youths took this food and took care of themselves. They lived quite happily because they had everything such as clothes, meat and other food. They also had a small pig that lived by the house.

One time, Karue told her brother, Kali, that she never ate enough meat and that she wanted some. This went directly to Kali's heart, so he told his sister to prepare some food for themselves, then in the morning he would go hunting for some wild game. Karue prepared things for Kali, then she tied a rope on the little pig and the two of them walked to the garden. When they arrived, Karue tied the pig to a tree, then she went into the garden and searched for food.

Kali went to the forest and hunted for game. When it was almost dark, Kali had killed five marsupials (*kapul*). However, he still had a great desire to kill a pig, so he stayed until it was completely dark.

He walked quickly, then he saw his sister in the garden. Karue took all of the food, then she sat and waited for him. Afterwards, they would go to the village. However, when Kali arrived, he gave the marsupials to his sister and told her to walk behind him while he went first to the village. He went and bathed, then he sat and waited for his sister to come and cook food for themselves to eat. He sat waiting for a long time, then he was angry because he was famished.

When his sister arrived, Kali scolded her terribly. Karue was troubled about his, so she put her head down and cried. She thought back about their mother and father. It was bad that one had done this kind of thing to the other.

Kali got up and counted the marsupials. He discovered that one was not there. So he asked his sister, "Where's that one marsupial? You've only brought four of them here." Karue did not reply, so Kali asked her to bring all of the marsupials to him.

Karue was angry. She threw the marsupials on top of him and told him to eat all of the marsupials, skin and all. Kali listened and did not do anything to his sister because it was just the two of them in this place.

Later, he looked at his sister's body and asked, "Sister, what are those two things hanging from your chest?" Karue told him that they were her breasts.

Kali looked at her body again and asked about all of the other parts of his sister's body. His sister found the words and he very quickly touched her body. When Kali touched his sister's breasts, everything inside the house changed and transformed into a giant he-marsupial.

Then the brother walked into the forest and just left his sister at the house. Now, Papua New Guinea has many marsupials, and many have big arms and legs like people do. They live by Kauo [Kauwo] Village in the Pangia District of Southern Highlands Province.

Inni and Benjamin A.
Voco Point, Lae
Morobe Province

A2582+. Why certain marsupials are plentiful; B871.2+. Giant marsupial; D440+. Transformation house to marsupial; D565. Transformation by touching; P253. Sister and brother; P253+. Hostile sister and brother; R213. Escape from home

Walenge Turned into a Snake

(Wantok 94[8], September 3, 1992, page 18)

Long, long ago, in the time of the ancestors, an old man and his wife lived in a village called Kamannokor [**Kamanakor**], by Maprik, in **East Sepik** Province [**Kwanga** People]. The old man's name was Tunge Walenge. Walenge and his wife had a son who lived with them. On Walenge's leg, there was a huge sore. The sore stank terribly and never dried up or went away.

Every day, Walenge would travel the river to fish. He often caught very many fish. So, every afternoon, he would return to the house, and his wife and child would be very happy to eat fish.

One day, Walenge awoke in the very early morning and told his wife and son to cook some sweet potatoes. The two of them fixed the sweet potatoes, then they all ate.

Before dawn had completely broken, Walenga [Walenge] took his walking stick and walked very slowly into the forest. He was thinking of fishing for more fish for themselves to eat in the afternoon.

After Walenge went into the forest, his wife just sat for a while and a thought came to her. The old woman thought about why Walenge never took his son into the forest, and why he never taught him how to catch fish or to snare other game. She thought this because the boy was big now.

Immediately, she shouted for her son to come, then she told him to quietly follow his father into the forest to see how his father caught fish.

The boy listened to everything that his mother said and he followed his father. He followed and followed, then he saw his father jump on top of a big stone in the middle of the river.

Afterwards, he removed a piece of leaf that he had plastered to the sore on his leg, then he put the leg down into the water. The fish saw Walenge's rotting sore and they swam, quickly filling it.

The fish would gorge themselves upon the rotting flesh of the sore for a while, then Walenge would put a net down and catch them. Walenge would do this al day, catching very many fish.

They boy hid by the river and saw everything. He ran back first to the village and he told everything that he had seen to his mother.

The mother listened to the story and she was completely furious. This was because every day, father Walenge would lie to them that he was catching fish in a net. However, what they ate would be fish that Walenge had caught with his sore.

It was nearly dark when Walenge arrived in the village with a big basket completely filled with fish. He went and chatted to the mother and child, but she was not happy with him.

She did not wait. She stood and shouted at Walenge, "Every day you lie to us, then you catch these rotten fish. You bring them to the kid and me to fill our bellies."

Walenge wanted to be vague, but the old woman revealed everything that the boy had seen. So, Walenge did not have a way to hide the shameful things that he had done.

He was terribly ashamed, as he held the fish and the basket. He turned the basket towards the woman and the boy, then he walked into the forest. He turned and shouted, "You're a lazy boy from my rotting fish. You two stay in the village, and I'll go into the forest."

Old Walenge shut his eyes and walked directly towards the home of a *masalai*. A big snake came and put its tongue to Walenge's skin, then Walenge turned into a huge snake.

Walenge slithered along and arrived in **Madang** [**Madang** Province]. When he arrived at Madang, all of the ghosts and *masalai*s of the area saw him and chased him.

He fled completely into the forests of **Lae** [**Morobe** Province]. However, the same thing happened there. The *masalai*s and ghosts of Lae did not welcome Walenge, they beat him.

So, Walenge cut across the sea and arrived at **Rabaul** [**East New Britain** Province]. At Rabaul, he saw a nice place and he established himself there.

Mark Iso

Kimbe

West New Britain Province

B875.1. Giant serpent; D191M. Transformation: man to serpent (snake); D565. Transformation by touching; D2150+. Catching fish with ulcer as bait; E261.4. Ghost pursues man; F402.1.10. Spirit pursues person; F687. Remarkable fragrance (odor) of person; F490+. Masalai; P210. Husband and wife; P231. Mother and son; P233. Father and son; R213. Escape from home; R260. Pursuits; W157. Dishonesty

[There was no ancestor story in *Wantok* #949.]

The Lesson of Shame Concerning an In-Law

(Wantok 950, September 17, 1992, page 20)

Long, long ago, in the north coast area of **Madang** [Province], there were two brothers who lived in a little village called **Ugere**.

The name of the big brother was Umong, and the little brother was Tinaki. They lived with their old mother. Their father had died when they were still little.

Their mother often taught them various things. She taught them to make gardens, to hunt for wild game in the forest, to make houses, and to fish in the sea. The two of them were very strong men and many of the young women of the village lusted for them.

The brothers lived for a while, then one day, their mother became very sick and died. The brothers were terribly worried and they buried their mother by their house.

Five months after their mother's death, the big brother, Umong, married a woman. He took his things to sleep in his wife's house. Tinaki stayed home alone, watched their things, and tended his mother's grave. Sometimes, he would go to see his big brother.

The woman that Umong had married was not a good woman. When Tinaki would go to see his brother, she would hide food and she would sometimes lie. When she cooked food with meat, she would never put meat on her brother-in-law's plate.

She did this for a while. Then one time, the ghost of Umong and Tinaki's mother turned into a village woman and told stories with Umong's wife. They told stories for a while, and then Tinaki walked towards them. He was racked with hunger because his head hurt and so he had not gone to find food in the garden.

When Umong's wife saw him, she quickly ran into the house and hid the pig and marsupial meat that her husband had killed that night. She covered it well under *limbum* leaves, then she went and sat with the other woman outside.

When she saw Tinaki, she quickly said, "I'm very sorry, brother-in-law, your brother was sick and did not kill any game, so we didn't cook with meat."

When the ghost of Tinake's [Tinake's] old mother heard this, her face immediately changed to that of the brothers' mother. She told Tinake, "Your brother's wife is a liar. She is greedy for her food. She often hides meat and just lies to you. There is plenty of game that your brother had killed last night under the *limbum* leaves." When the ghost said this, she immediately disappeared and they did not see her again.

Umong's wife was terribly ashamed when she heard this. She ran into the house and killed herself with her husband's axe. Umong was lying there and did not know what had happened. When he got up, Tinaki told him the whole story, so he was furious at his wife.

Umong's wife had died, but her blood ran down and became a pond. This pond is there now in the forests of **Karkum** Village on the north coast [**Dimir** People]. The name of this pond is Buyar. Even now, the people of the village often use it for washing and fetching water to cook food.

A lesson that this story gives is that people must treat their in-laws well. They cannot hide things from their in-laws. This custom of respect is important on the north coast of Madang.

Vali Markus Kila
Gerehu Stg. 6
National Capital District

A920.1.0.1. Origin of particular lake; D40.2. Transformation to likeness of another woman; D457.1+. Transformation: blood to lake; D2095. Magic disappearance; D2188. Magic disappearance; E323.2. Dead mother returns to aid persecuted children; E425.1. Revenant as woman; E545. The dead speak; F610. Remarkable strong man; M451.1. Death by suicide; P210. Husband and wife; P231. Mother and son; P251.5. Two brothers; P263. Brother-in-law; P264. Sister-in-law; S55. Cruel sister-in-law; T10. Falling in love; T100. Marriage; V61.3+. Dead buried; W151. Greed; W157. Dishonesty

A Sio Gave Birth to a Crocodile Child

(Wantok 951, September 24, 1992, page 20)

Long ago, in **Nambariwa**, by Sio in **Morobe** Province, there was not a single crocodile [**Sio** People]. There were only people. Then a man married his own cousin [or sister], and they raised a crocodile child. So now, Nambariwa is filled with crocodiles.

The woman came from a family called Sialambu and the man came from another family called Bunowa. In this area, it is forbidden for brothers and sisters [or cousins] to marry each other. However these two broke the tabu and married.

They lived for a while, then the woman became pregnant. Her husband was happy that they would have a baby. However, they waited for a while and she gave birth to a crocodile.

She did not notice this and she slept. However afterwards, her eyes opened and she saw the crocodile baby sleeping on top of her legs. She was speechless because she had given birth to a crocodile baby. She called her husband to come inside the house and she told him what had happened.

They did not want to show the men that she had given birth to a crocodile baby. Because of this, they hid the baby inside the house. They did not want all of the men to know that she had given birth to a crocodile baby.

They always cooked food and brought it into the house to give to the crocodile baby. One time, the men noticed that she was not pregnant, so they asked her husband whether she had given birth or not.

However, the man was ashamed and lied that his wife had just lost blood and had not given birth. All of the men listened and believed him.

They took care of the crocodile baby for a while, and it became larger. They never took it around the village. They would always lock it up, then they would sleep until all of

the men went to the gardens. Afterwards, the crocodile would come down to look for its own food on the ground. If the crocodile did not eat, it would wait for its mother and father.

The crocodile did this, and killed all of the pigs and chickens that belonged to the village men. Often, people would find that their pigs and chickens were lost. However, no one knew that the couple was hiding a crocodile inside their house, a crocodile that was finishing off all of their pigs and chickens.

One time, an old woman thought of finding out exactly what it was that was eating their pigs and chickens. So, she pretended to go the garden, then she returned and hid by the house, keeping watch.

The old woman hid and saw a big crocodile jump down from the couple's house, then kill the pigs and chickens. Afterwards, the crocodile saw the sun setting and the men returning to the houses. The crocodile sped into its parent's house and went to sleep.

Everyone returned, then the old woman went to the middle of the village and made a bonfire. All of the men saw this and ran towards her. The old woman met all of them and told them what she had seen during the day.

She told everyone and they were not happy. This was because many of their pigs and chickens had gone into the crocodile's mouth. They made a decision and told the man and his wife to kill the crocodile. If they did not, they would surround the house in the morning and kill their crocodile.

The couple listened and they made a big feast that night for their crocodile child. They explained to the crocodile that it must run away and live in the river. This was because their kin would kill it because of its killing and eating the pigs and chickens.

In the early morning, when everyone was still asleep, the couple took their crocodile child and went to the river. They said good-bye to the crocodile, and left their child inside the river.

This crocodile lives in the rivers and seas of the Sio area even today. The crocodile goes around and eats all of the pigs and chickens of the Sio area.

Jerry Nonnie [Nonny]
Sio
Morobe Province

A2146. Creation of crocodile; C114. Tabu: incest; C980+. Punishment for breaking tabu: woman bears crocodile; P210. Husband and wife; P230. Parents and children; P295. Cousins; R213. Escape from home; T100. Marriage; T410. Incest; T554.0.3K+. Woman gives birth to crocodile; T570. Pregnancy; W157. Dishonesty

A *Masalai* Snake Married a Kondolop Woman

(Wantok 952, [October] 1, 1992, page 19)

Long, long ago, in **Kondolop** Village, in the Kabwum District of **Morobe** Province, there was a *masalai* snake [**Selepet** People]. This snake and his mother lived inside a big river near Kondolop Village.

One time, the people of Kondolop worked at making a big party. So, the women carried meat and pig guts to the river to wash. When they arrived at the river, they all arranged themselves well, then they washed the meat and pig guts. However, one of them did not sit carefully. So, the *masalai* snake saw this woman and lusted for her.

The women finished all of their work, then they carried the meat and pig guts back to the village. They cooked, ate, and celebrated. Before long, everyone felt the earth tremble, then they searched for a place to flee. However, they soon saw a big snake slithering towards the village.

They all stood and watched the snake to see what it would do. The snake passed them all and slithered directly towards the woman's house. They saw this and took some women to give to him, but he did not want anything. He slithered directly towards the woman's house.

The men saw this and prepared the trail for him. The woman saw the snake coming directly towards her, then she walked slowly forward to meet the snake. Her mother saw the snake grab her daughter, so she filled a net bag with food and took it to her daughter. The woman was afraid of the snake and wanted to flee, but she was terrified that the snake would kill her. So, she told the snake to let her go and she would walk with him to his house.

She walked slowly ahead and the snake slithered behind. They approached the river, then she was afraid to go inside, so she stood on top. The snake slithered forwards and wrapped his tail around her leg, then he carried her into the water. When they arrived at the house, she opened her eyes wide to see the nice house and many nice things at his home.

However, she was not happy because the snake would marry her. The snake left her inside the house, then slithered away to hide and change itself into a young man. When she saw him, she was very happy and she asked him where he had come from. The snake replied, "I'm very sorry, I'm a man. I saw you sitting awkwardly by the river, so I wanted to marry you."

When she heard this, she was happy to marry the nice young man. However, the *masalai* snake's mother did not hear or see that her son had brought a Kondolop woman to marry. Afterwards, she saw the young woman living in their house, so she scolded her son. Later, they all lived happily together for a while, then the woman became pregnant and gave birth to two babies, a boy and a girl.

She was happy and she took care of her two children well until they grew big. One nice day, their mother asked them to go to the garden with her. In the early morning, they ate then walked to the garden. They stayed until the afternoon, then she told them to sit by the garden and she would find food for them.

The two of them saw that it was a nice afternoon, so they did not think about sitting. They went into the garden and played hide-and-seek among the food plants. Their mother returned to get food and to find them. She shouted, but the children did not want to reply to her. This made her burn up inside. She waited for a while, then the children sped out of the garden.

She asked them, "Where did you go when I shouted?" They did not reply to her quickly, so she told them, "Your minds are stubborn like your *masalai* snake father." They heard this and cried terribly because they had thought that their father was a man. However, their mother told them that their father was not a real man, that he was a *masalai* snake from the river.

They left and arrived at the house, then the mother cooked the food. At night, they ate and slept. In the early morning, their mother went to the garden again. The children stayed with their father at home. The children thought of what their mother had told them, so they told their father.

When the father heard this, he was very angry with his wife. He saw that it was afternoon, so he immediately went to transform himself into a big snake. Then he lay at the door of the house. His wife finished in the garden, then she went to the house. When she put her legs into the door, he tackled her and broke her bones.

Then he made a big fire and cooked his wife so that the children would never know about this. However later, the children did not see their mother, so they asked where their mother had gone. The father lied to them that their mother had gone to her village to see her people.

Anna Kelong

Bialla

West New Britain Province

B656.2. Marriage to serpent in human form; B875.1. Giant serpent; D191M. Transformation: man to serpent (snake); D391M. Transformation: serpent (snake) to man; D2126. Magic underwater journey; D2148. Earth magically caused to quake; F420.1.3.9. Water-spirit as snake; F420.2.2. Water-spirits live in village under water; F490+. Masalai; P210. Husband and wife; P231. Mother and son; P232. Mother and daughter; P233. Father and son; P234. Father and daughter; P253. Sister and brother; P262.

Mother-in-law; P265+. Daughter-in-law; Q411. Death as punishment; R10. Abduction; S63+. Husband kills wife; S110. Murders; T10. Falling in love; T100. Marriage; T570. Pregnancy; T587. Birth of twins; T685. Twins; W126. Disobedience; W157. Dishonesty; W167. Stubbornness

Water Came from Okapa

(Wantok 953, October 8, 1992, page 18)

Long, long ago, in the time of the ancestors, in the Okapa area of **Eastern Highlands** Province, there were no streams and no wild animals such as cassowaries and birds in the forest.

At this time, there lived two brothers. They often raced each other to heat stones for making earth ovens for food. They always competed, but the food in the big brother's earth oven would [not] be well cooked and that of the little brother would [be].

This was because the little brother would place water in the ground. When he heated the stones, he would hide them well from his big brother and pour water from the ground.

One day, the brothers raced again to heat the stones in another earth oven. The big brother knew that the little brother was hiding something from him.

So, he heated his stones, then he hid well so that the little brother could not see him. He hid and watched the little brother take a bamboo tube to fetch water.

The big brother did not make a sound. He hid well and saw the little brother remove large leaves from the ground where the water exited, where he alone fetched it. The big brother saw this and his eyes popped open.

When the little brother went fairly far away to find some more firewood for heating the stones well, the big brother immediately ran up to remove the leaves and pour all of the water into his bamboo tube.

The little brother returned and saw that the big brother's bamboo was overflowing. He knew that his big brother must have found out about the water and taken all his water.

Then they began to argue. The little brother accused the big brother of stealing his water. However, the big brother lied to the little brother.

The little brother ran inside the house, then took his bow and arrows. He jumped down from the house and shot his big brother in the shoulder. The big brother screamed loudly and fell dead to the ground.

Everyone in the nearby villages heard this and came. They scolded the little brother, then they buried the big brother's body. Afterwards, they returned to their clan houses.

The little brother lived alone and was terribly troubled about what he had done. He filled a net bag with some food, such as taros, yams, and bananas. He took his bow and arrows, then walked off to the **Fore** [Language] area of Okapa.

He gathered *kina* shells on the trail for a while, then he met an old man. The old man saw the little brother and asked him, "What is it that you want that has caused you to come here?" The little brother told the story of his troubles.

The old man took the little brother to the forest and cut a piece of bamboo. He gave it to the little brother and told him, "When you walk away and arrive at a big river, fill the bamboo completely with water."

The little brother listened and followed everything that the old man had said. Along the trail, he also took various animals such as cassowary, then put them inside his bamboo.

He walked and walked, then he arrived in his forest. He had not yet arrived at the place when the bamboo began to make noises. He thought about what it could be, so he opened the mouth of the bamboo and the various birds and cassowaries flew out of the mouth of the bamboo.

He just shut it a little, then he arrived someplace and broke the bamboo upon a tree, as the old man had told him to do. The water broke out from this mountain and went to the **Henganofi** side [**Kamano** People], then it broke completely and went to **Onumuga** [Fore People?] in the Okapa area. The tree on which the little brother had broken the bamboo is still there.

Kasuku Konomipave

Kainantu

Eastern Highlands Province

A930. Origin of streams; A1900. Creation of birds; A1970+. Creation of cassowary; K420. Thief loses his goods or is detected; P251.5. Two brothers; Q212. Theft punished; Q411. Death as punishment; S73.1. Fratricide; S110. Murders; V61.3+. Dead buried; W157. Dishonesty

Five Ingambilis Men Married *Masalai* Women

(Wantok 954, October 15, 1992, page 18)

In the time of the ancestors, only young men lived in Ingambilis [**Ingambas**] Village in the Maprik area of **East Sepik** Province [**South Arapesh** People].

At this place, there are five rivers. The names of these rivers are Kambul, Wahup, Ambina, Wasafana and Wampau. There were also five women who lived in these rivers. Their names were the same as those of the rivers and they would each take care of a river.

At this place, there was also a fig tree. The tree was the home of a *masalai* woman. Her name was the same as that of the fig tree.

The five women took care of the rivers very well. They would always clean the rivers, so that there was no rubbish drifting about. The *masalai* woman on top of the fig tree also did the same thing. She cleaned her tree. There was not one dry leaf at the base of the tree. A nice cool breeze would always go there.

Every day, when the men wanted to go to work, bathe or do something, the five women at the rivers would spy upon them. However, the clansmen of Ingambilis did not know that there were beautiful women spying upon them.

The men always went and worked hard, making gardens, hunting for wild game, making houses, and other work. Every day, they would work without resting. They did not rest even a little.

The young men also each had a spirit house. Each would do his own work. One time, they met and appointed one of themselves as the leader. They appointed Wamiga.

The leader told them that they must each go to their homes and see what kind of work to do. This would happen every morning. A while later, they found out that some women were hiding and spying upon them. Then they argued about who would marry these five women of the rivers.

After they finished speaking, they went to the houses. One morning, they pretended to go to work, and the five men who would marry went and each hid by the rivers. When the women wanted to leave the rivers and go up to spy on the men, the five men quickly held them and took them to the village.

All of the others had gone to their gardens, they gathered much food and things, then they returned. They also went to the forests to kill many pigs, birds, and other kinds of game. That afternoon, they made a big feast and married the men and women.

Afterwards, the clan lived happily and raised many, many children. Their children also married among themselves and raised more children. They did this until the number of clans in Ingambilis grew and grew, and the village became as it is now.

Staron Wanga
Kavieng
New Ireland Province

F420.1.2. Water-spirit as woman (water-nymph, water-nix); F441.2. Tree-spirit; F490+. Masalai; F566.1. Village of men only; P210. Husband and wife; P230. Parents and children; R10. Abduction; T111. Marriage of mortal and supernatural being; T192. Marriage by force; V112.1. Spirit huts

Two Brothers Killed a *Masalai* Man
(Wantok 955, October 22, 1992, page 15)

Long, long ago, in the time of the ancestors, in **Gumun** Village, in the Kabwum area of **Morobe** Province, there lived a man who killed and ate men [**Komba** People]. His name was Zonggomnining.

People were terribly afraid and they hid from him. Zonggomnining would see smoke from a fire somewhere, then just go there to kill and eat the people.

There was a woman named Toumptop. All of Toumptop's kin had been killed and eaten by the bad man, Zonggomnining. Toumptop was afraid and made a hut among the vines of the forest. In my language, we call this hut a _kiteng_. She hid in this hut.

One time, late at night, she wanted to cut taros and cook them in a bamboo tube. Her blood spilled and she took a taro leaf to cover the blood. Later, she hid it [the blood].

Some days later, she saw two eggs in the taro leaf that she had used to hide her blood. Some months later, the two eggs hatched and two baby boys came out.

Toumptop saw this and was elated. She named them Bokoro and Kawakatik. The boys lived with their mother for a while, then they grew to be big men.

Toumptop made bows and arrows, and taught them how to shoot. The two brothers would go into the forest and return with various kinds of wild game. The mother would cook the edible game, and they would eat it. The mother would throw away the game that was not edible.

One day, Toumptop told her sons the story of Zonggomnining. This bad man lived on Mount Kuuten, by **Upat** Village. Bokoro and Kawakati [Kawakatik] listened, then slept. In the very early morning, the brothers awoke and crossed the big Gwama River, then they went directly up to Zonggomnining's house door.

The brothers challenged the bad man. They fought and went down to the Gwama River. The brothers were winning. They shot Zonggomnining all of the way down to Sios [**Sio** Village, **Sio** People], then the fish of the sea ate him.

Their mother, Toumptop, stood on top of Mount Momging. She looked down to the water and saw that her two sons had killed the bad man. Oh my, she was elated and she cried.

She traveled and descended the mountain, then held her two sons. Afterwards, they returned to the house. Toumptop turned into a *kiteng* vine. Bokoro turned into the *airu* bird that lives on Bokoro Stone, and Kawakatik turned into the *diru* bird that lives on Kawakatik Stone.

Today, men find it very difficult to kill these birds at these two stones. This is because these birds arose from men.

Moses D. Lavagu
Gumum Village
Kabwum
Morobe Province

A515.1.1. Twin culture heroes; A1617. Origin of place-name; A1970. Creation of miscellaneous birds; D150M. Transformation: man to bird; D213.4W. Transformation: woman to vine; D457.1.14K. Transformation: blood to eggs; G346. Devastating monster; G510.4+. Hero overcomes devastating ogre; G512.1+. Ogre killed with spear/arrow; P231. Mother and son; P251.5. Two brothers; Q211. Murder punished; Q411. Death as punishment; R312. Forest as refuge; S110. Murders; T534. Conception from blood; T542. Birth of human being from an egg; T587. Birth of twins; T685. Twins; Z210. Brothers as heroes; Z356. Unique survivor

A Ghost Woman Cut a
Finschhafen Woman's Neck

(Wantok 956, October 29, 1992, page 15)

Long, long ago, in **Siu** Village, in the Finschhafen area of **Morobe** Province, there lived a man with his wife [**Tobo** People]. They had a daughter.

One day, the sun rose very nicely. They sat and told stories for a while, and then the father arranged with the mother to take the daughter and go to hunt for some wild game in the deep forest.

The next day, in the very early morning, the mother prepared food for the father and daughter to take into the forest. The daughter carried the food in a net bag and followed the father. They walked and walked, then they arrived in the forests of Awengu [**Avenggu**]. When they arrived there, the sun was setting and it was nearly dark.

Very quickly, the father cut some saplings and made a forest hut. They slept for a while, then they awoke in the very early morning and walked slowly towards **Tepmarom**. There were some big marsupial (*kapul*) nests by Tepmarom.

The father worked very hard at killing many marsupials. The two of them did not go slowly. They filled a net bag with some marsupials and they tied it some with ropes.

When it was nearly noon, the father saw that they had killed enough marsupials to carry back to the house. They arrived at the forest hut, then [they gathered and cut firewood for a fire]. The father sent the daughter to fetch water in a bamboo tube. The forest hut was near a stream.

The daughter took the bamboo and went by the stream. Then a ghost woman came out of a cave, took an axe and cut the girl's neck.

The father did not know that his daughter had died by the stream. He waited until dark for his daughter to bring water back. Then he got the idea that his daughter must have encountered an enemy.

Quickly, he followed her and went to the stream to see his daughter's body lying by the water. He cried terribly and he found it difficult to do anything. This was because the ghost woman had blocked his thoughts.

He went back and saw his daughter come with the bamboo tube completely filled with water. However, it was really the ghost woman who had turned into his daughter.

The ghost woman helped and the two of them singed off all of the marsupial's fur, then butchered them. After they smoked the marsupials all on the fire, they went to sleep.

In the morning, they carried all of the marsupials and walked back to the village. When they arrived at the village, the mother saw them and was elated, but she did not know that this was not really her daughter.

She wanted to help the girl remove the net bag from her head. At the same time, the ghost woman's head fell. Oh my, she was completely afraid and she fled into the house.

The next day, the father and mother took the ghost woman's body back into the deep forest and burned it in a fire.

Pele [Pelle] M. Levo
BKO [Boroko]
[National Capital District]

D40.2. Transformation to likeness of another woman; D2000+. Mind control; E250. Bloodthirsty revenants; E425.1. Revenant as woman; E422.1.1. Headless revenant; E446.2. Ghost laid by burning body; K1930. Treacherous impostors; P210. Husband and wife; P232. Mother and daughter; P234. Father and daughter; S139.4. Murder by mangling with axe

Women Originated from Bananas

(Wantok 957, November 5, 1992, page 20)

Long, long ago, in the time of the ancestors, there were two brothers who lived in Mumengtaen [**Mumengtein**] Village, in the Mumeng District of **Morobe** Province [**Mumeng** People]. The first brother's name was Bang and the second brother's name was Monkebung.

Bang and his little brother, Monkebung, excelled at gardening. Their garden was better than those of the others in the village. Their garden was just filled with banana plants.

Many of their bananas just rotted in their garden. They would each cook them in their own garden and eat them. They would throw away many by the fire.

Every day, Bang and Monkebung would go to work in the garden. Every afternoon, they would return to the house. However, when they wanted to return, they would hear the voices of women talking and singing about. They would hear this and they would think very hard. They checked around the garden, and they did not see any women.

One afternoon, the same thing happened. They arrived at the house, cooked food, and then told stories. Before they went to sleep, they decided to find out about the women's voices.

The next day, they awoke and went to the garden. They worked until the afternoon, then they cooked some bananas in a fire. Afterwards, they carried some and walked back to the village. However, along the trail, they turned and went back. They hid by the garden and spied out.

When it was nearly dark, they saw beautiful young women come out of the bananas that they had cooked and thrown by the fire. Bang and Monkebung saw this, and their hearts stopped.

They did not wait. They ran into the garden and grabbed two very beautiful women. The other women saw this and they quickly turned back into bananas.

The two women no longer had a chance. Their power to turn back into bananas was gone. This was because the brothers had grabbed them.

The women were ashamed, but the brothers took them to the house, married them and lived with them. Some time later, the women told Bang and his little brother, "We women are plentiful, but the fire in which you cook bananas has burned many of us."

They lived together and raised very many children in Mumengtaen Village. They threw many bananas into the river and the river carried them to the Markham Valley. So today, the Markham Valley has very many bananas.

Sae Gwae
Motupore Island
Central Province

A2794.2+. Why bananas are plentiful in certain place; D213.6+W. Transformation: woman to banana plant; D431.4+W. Transformation: banana to woman; P210. Husband and wife; P230. Parents and children; P251.5. Two brothers; P263. Brother-in-law; P264. Sister-in-law; T100. Marriage

A Tree Blocked an Old Man's Testicles
(Wantok 958, November 12, 1992, page 22)

Long ago in **Kauwo** Village, in the Pangia District, boys were very plentiful [**Wiru** People, **Southern Highlands** Province].

One day, they decided to go hunt for beads by the river. The next day, all of them awoke in the very early morning and walked away. They followed a river up into the very deep forest, then one boy went to defecate. While he was defecating, he heard a very loud noise. He walked towards it to check, then he stood on a boulder. He looked down and saw a big old man down below.

He ran and ran back, then he told the other boys by the river. They returned and looked carefully at the old man. The old man had a big belly, his skin was terribly filthy, and his teeth were broken. The old man used a dirty axe and worked hard at cutting a big tree, so that he could catch the insects [probably beetle grubs] that were inside [to eat].

Before long, the old man bent down and scavenged the insects that were in the tree, then they saw his two big testicles hanging down low to the ground.

They made a decision and they sent two boys down to him. The boys approached and said, "Hello grandfather!" The old man was surprised and asked them, "Where did you come from?" They told him that they were going around the forest when they had heard a noise, then went to look.

The old man told them, "Good. Come hold these two sticks here and there, then I'll break apart the tree and we'll catch many insects."

The two boys were very happy and they held the sticks. The old man bent down to scavenge the insects, then his two testicles went down, hanging clearly by the ground.

The old man moved between the two sticks, then at the same time his testicles went down and lay directly between the two sticks. The boys who were holding the sticks opened the tree up and then back.

Quickly, the boys [left] the sticks and the sticks blocked the old man's testicles. The poor old man felt a terrible pain and screamed. The two boys stole all of the insects, then they ran up to meet the other boys.

However, the old man was strong and he removed his testicles, then he began to chase the boys. The boys ran and ran, going into a tree hole. At the entrance of the hole, they erected a boulder and shut it well.

However, the old man smelled them and arrived at the tree. He knew that the boys must have been hiding inside. He removed his axe from his side and began to cut the tree. The tree fell onto the river and the river carried it away.

The tree followed the river down and went ashore by a man's house. The man saw this and carried the tree up into the hut where he cared for pigs. He wanted the tree to dry so that he could cut it for firewood and make a fire.

However, the next day he went into the forest. The boys inside the tree came out and killed one of his pigs. They carried it into their home inside the tree then they cooked the pig inside an earth oven.

The pigs' owner returned and saw that one pig was not there. He thought that a thief had come and stolen it. The next day, he went back to the forest. Later, he returned and saw that another pig was gone. He thought hard.

The next day, he pretended to return to the forest but he walked back and hid by the pigsty. He saw the boys come out of the tree and kill another of his pigs, then carry it back inside.

He waited and waited until dark, then he made a bonfire. He threw the tree up into the fire. Inside the tree, the boys' bellies broke open and exploded. All of the boys died.

After this story, and today, there is a great enmity between men and boys.

Tolyu Pini
Lae
Morobe Province

A1590+. Origin of enmity between young and old; F529.6. Person with enormous belly; F547.7. Enormous testicles; F562.2. Residence in a tree; K420. Thief loses his goods or is detected; K812. Victim burned in his own house (or hiding place); K1111+. Dupe puts testicles into cleft of tree; Q212. Theft punished; Q414. Punishment: burning alive; R210. Escapes; R260. Pursuits; R311. Tree refuge; S112. Burning to death; W115. Slovenliness; X712.3.1H. Injury to testicles

Two Sirunki Brothers Split Apart

(Wantok 959, November 19, 1992, page 16)

One time, there lived two brothers in **Sirunki** Village, **Enga** Province [**Enga** People]. Where they lived, there were two lakes and they took care of these lakes. They were very good friends. They did everything together.

However one day, they argued. They argued and argued, then the big brother shouted to the little brother, "You're the man who never takes good care of your lake. You live with pigs and with human shit. Pigs and dogs just fill up by your lake and the stench is horrible."

They kept arguing, then the big brother shouted again, "Your lake is making my lake smell too. My lake is ruined [just like yours]. Tomorrow, we'll go to another place and live there because this place smells as if humans, pigs and dogs have ruined it."

The little brother listened and slept. However, he awoke at night and thought very hard, "Big brother said that we'd go find another place to live, but he scolded me terribly during the day. Why should I go with him? I can go my own way."

The little brother thought that when it was still at night, he would run down and follow the river called Lai. He thought that the big brother could run and chase him, so he went first. He just ran and followed the river, then he arrived at **Birip** Village. When he arrived at this village, dawn broke.

Then he ran up a mountain and hid in the deep forest. He looked down and thought that his big brother would shout and follow him there.

However, he did not see or hear a sound coming from behind. He waited until the sun rose completely, then he knew that his big brother had lied to him so that he would run away and so that his big brother would live alone there.

He was not troubled. He arranged this place, then he lived alone in the deep forests of Birip Village and the side towards **Wapenamanda**. The big brother lived alone with the two lakes.

Today, if you travel to Sirunki Village, you will see the lakes there. At night, Sirunki Village is often very cold because of the lakes.

Lawrence Itaitai
Kimbe
West New Britain Province

K2378.3. Enemies deceived through shammed flight; P251.5. Two brothers; P251.5.3. Hostile brothers; R213. Escape from home; W115. Slovenliness; W157. Dishonesty; X716.1H+. Befouling with excrement

Why Do Flying Foxes Steal?

(Wantok 960, November 26, 1992, page 17)

Long, long ago, in the time of the ancestors, there was an old woman and her child who lived in Upa [Uba] Village, in the Mendi area of **Southern Highlands** Province [**Mendi** People]. The child's name was Naiko. Their foods were butterflies and lizards because there was no other food in the area.

One morning, Naiko took its bow and followed the Kerei River to its source. Naiko saw very many butterflies gathering there. Naiko was very happy and shot at a [bee].

All of the butterflies alit and flew about. Naiko followed them and saw that the arrow was stuck to the guts of a pig. Oh my, Naiko was elated and took the pig to the house. The old mother saw this and was elated because they always just ate butterflies and lizards.

Every day, Naiko followed the Kerei River, then Naiko would find pig guts and carry them back to the house. One day, Naiko thought about finding out who killed the pigs and threw their guts in the water.

Naiko followed the Kerek [Kerei] River, and arrived at a village. In the middle of the village, there was a tree. At the base of the tree, there was a place for making earth ovens.

Naiko walked closer and the tree spoke. Naiko was afraid and wanted to flee, but the tree told Naiko to approach and remove the [ginger] at its base, then carry it up the tree to see what would happen.

Before long, the ground trembled and various things fell down to the ground. Then not long afterwards, inside the tree hole, Naiko saw huge pigs. Naiko's eyes popped open.

Later, a *masalai* man came out and killed one of the pigs. He made an earth oven, then he went down to the river to fetch stones. At the same time, Naiko descended, took many pigs and fled home. Every day after that, Naiko and Naiko's mother would only eat pork.

After a while, the *masalai* saw that his pigs were fewer. One day, he kept watch and saw Naiko arrive. He grabbed Naiko and put him inside his rattan house. Later, he made a big fire and smoked Naiko.

Oh my, Naiko became emaciated. The old mother waited and waited in vain, then she knew that her child was dead. She cried and cried, then a flying fox arrived.

She called for the flying fox to go fetch Naiko. The flying fox listened and arrived at the *masalai*'s home. Very late at night, the flying fox carried the *masalai*'s rattan house with Naiko in it, then left it at the house door. The old mother saw this and was elated.

The old mother told the flying fox, "I don't have anything to give you, but in all of the gardens you must take the food first, then we people shall take the food after you."

From this speech until today, flying foxes often eat bananas and papayas in the gardens.

Paul Pei

Kimbe

West New Britain Province

A2455+. Why flying fox is thief; B212. Animal understands human speech; B552+. Person carried by flying fox; B871.1.2.1. Giant hog; D967+. Magic ginger; D1610.2. Speaking tree; D2148. Earth magically caused to quake; F401.6. Spirit in human form; F490+. Masalai; K420. Thief loses his goods or is detected; P230. Parents and children; Q53. Reward for rescue; Q212. Theft punished; Q411. Death as punishment; Q433. Punishment: imprisonment; Q469.5. Punishment: choking with smoke; R4. Surprise capture; R100. Rescues; R220. Flights

[There was no ancestor story in *Wantok* #961.]

Crab Broke Kangaroo

(Wantok 962, December 10, 1992, page 18)

Long, long ago, in the time of the ancestors, Kangaroo and Crab were very good friends. They lived just like blood brothers. They would do everything together.

One day, they decided to take their two dogs and go hunt for wild game in the deep forest. They sharpened their spears and prepared everything.

The dogs thought that the next day would be a time for going around the forest, so they were very happy. They played and ran back and forth. Kangaroo and Crab saw that the dogs were very happy, then they looked each other in the eye and just [laughed] quietly.

They worked on the spears, then they cooked some food. They ate and they became bloated. Afterwards, they got up and whistled for the dogs, then they walked into the forest. The dogs followed them. The names of the dogs were Sampai and Umpum. Sampai and Umpum were dogs that excelled at hunting game.

Kangaroo had long legs, and so walked first with the two dogs. Crab was a man who walked very slowly, so he walked very far behind. Kangaroo and the two dogs did not wait for him.

Kangaroo and the dogs arrived first in the deep forest. Before long, the dogs smelled and chased a huge wild pig.

The dogs chased the pig and surrounded it at the base of a big fig tree.

Kangaroo arrived at the base of the fig tree quickly, then saw the pig fighting with the dogs. Kangaroo went up to a branch of the tree, then threw a spear down to the pig.

The pig twisted about and died. Kangaroo jumped down and removed the spear, then walked back to the trail to meet Crab. Poor Crab was still running along slowly and was terribly winded.

Kangaroo met Crab. Oh my, Crab was furious that Kangaroo had not waited for him. He said all sorts of bad things to Kangaroo. Kangaroo was also angry and they then began to fight in earnest. Before long, Kangaroo was furious and wanted to eat Crab.

Kangaroo shouted at Crab, "You must have a huge shell on your back, so you didn't go quickly. You're rotten, with puny eyes."

Poor Crab was terribly ashamed and replied, "Do you want me to pinch you with my two big claws?" Kangaroo shouted again, "Damn! Do you want me to kill you? You're smaller than I am."

While they were fighting, Crab quickly dug his hole and went down into the ground. Later, he dug and went up again at the place where Kangaroo was sitting. The hole went up directly at the place where Kangaroo's testicles were hanging. Kangaroo did not know this. He was angry while his testicles hung down directly into Crab's hole.

Quickly, Crab went up and fought Kangaroo. Kangaroo went to bite him, Crab immediately ran down his hole. Later, he went up again and pinched Kangaroo's testicles. Poor Kangaroo felt a terrible pain and died.

Max Daniel
Kaiapit [Village, **Adzera** People]
Morobe Province

A2494.16.5+. Enmity between crab and kangaroo; B211.2.12K. Speaking kangaroo; B211.8.1K. Speaking crab; B871.1.2. Giant boar; F547.1.1. Vagina dentata; K914. Murder from ambush; P310. Friendship; Q411. Death as punishment; S110. Murders; X712.1H. Female genitals; X712.3.1H. Injury to testicles

A Boy Tricked a Ghost Man

(Wantok 963, December 1[7], 1992, page 24)

In the time of the ancestors, there was a village in the Finschhafen area of **Morobe** Province. The name of this village was Nasing [**Nasingalatu** Village, **Yabêm** People]. In Nasing Village, there lived a stylish boy.

One morning, he took his bow and arrows, then he traveled in the forest. He walked and walked, then he saw a breadfruit tree. Afterwards, he walked back to the village.

Near the breadfruit tree, there lived a ghost man. The ghost man came and saw that a man had put a mark on the base of the breadfruit tree. Oh my, he was completely furious, "Which man did this to my breadfruit tree? If I see him, he'll be my food." After he said this, he returned to his house.

Some days later, the boy returned and took some breadfruits. The ghost man heard a noise and came. He saw the boy on top of the breadfruit tree, then he shouted up to him, "Hey, kinsman! Is that your breadfruit or mine?" The boy replied, "Who are you? It's my breadfruit."

The ghost man heard this reply and was furious. "You're sitting on top of the breadfruit. Later, you'll look for a way to return home. If you come down, you'll die," the ghost man shouted loudly up to the boy.

However, the boy had various tricks. He shouted down to the ghost man, "I'm very sorry for you. I have many ways to go home." The ghost man's belly was on fire, so he cut all of the forest and cleared the base of the breadfruit tree carefully. He did this so that when the boy came down, he could not escape.

After the ghost man cut all of the forest, he shouted up to the boy again, "Now you don't have a way to escape. I've cut all of the forest. How will you flee now?"

However, the boy played another trick. "You've cut the forest, but you haven't cut it well. I'll come down and hide in the scrub, then go home," the boy replied.

The ghost man thought hard, then he removed all of the trees and grasses that surrounded the breadfruit tree. However, the boy told him, "I have one way left. I'll jump and go hide at that place." However, the *masalai* [ghost] knew that he was lying, "You're lying. You're my food now. I'll ruin your life. Come down."

However, the bad boy had more tricks. He told the *masalai* man, "You have long hair on your head, so I'll go down and hide in your hair, then I'll leave."

The ghost man cut all of the hair on his head. At the same time, the boy took a breadfruit and threw it far away. The breadfruit tumbled and went down the mountain, then the ghost man thought that the boy had descended and run away.

He followed and followed, down the mountain. Then the boy went down, took all of the breadfruits and ran away to the village. The ghost ran and ran, down the mountain. Then he saw the breadfruit and he knew that the boy had tricked him. He was entirely winded and furious. He ran up again to the base of the breadfruit tree, and then he saw that the boy had taken all of the breadfruits and fled.

O. Jhesy
Nasing Village
Finschhafen
Morobe Province

E425.2. Revenant as man; F490+. Masalai; G11.10. Cannibalistic spirits; G501. Stupid ogre; K525+. Escape by substituting breadfruit; R210. Escapes; R311. Tree refuge

The Trick Pig
(Wantok 964, December 23, 1992, page 17)

There were three good friends who lived in a village and they often hunted for wild game in the forest. Once, they set a time, then they prepared their food and spears, and they walked into the forest.

While they were walking into the forest, one of the friends concentrated on his thoughts. He thought of lying to his two friends. So when they were still in the forest, one of the other two friends saw a betel pepper vine and he cut it on top of a tree. When the tree fell down, the friend went into the tree. He squealed like a pig inside the tree.

Afterwards, the other friend heard the pig squeal at the crown of the tree and he thought that it was really a pig. He called out to his friend.

The other friend heard him shout and he sped towards him. When he arrived, he asked his friend, "What did you see that you called me?" His friend told him, "I cut the tree and it fell on top of that pig. It's about to die and it's squealing in the crown of the tree."

Inside the tree, the other friend was using all his breath to squeal like a pig. His two friends tried to find him again and they shouted for him. They gave up after a while, then they tried to shoot the pig. However, it was not a pig. It was their friend who was squealing like a pig and fooling them.

They tried very hard to see the pig and shoot it. However, their friend kept fooling them, circling them, and pretending to bite them. Oh my, they were shaking and terrified. They jumped on top of a tree.

When the two [guys] were on top of the tree, they again stretched and shouted for their friend to come and see the pig. However, the pig was actually their friend who was fooling them. He did this for a very long time.

The two friends retreated a fairly long way, then one told the other, "[Pal], we can't be afraid of the pig's body. We'll just shoot inside of [it] and shoot the pig dead."

When their friend heard this, he was terrified because his two friends would shoot him now. He got up and died laughing inside the tree.

When his two friends heard that it was just their friend laughing, they died laughing with him. They laughed because they were very good hunting friends, and one friend can trick another.

Andrew Taroa
Kimbe
West New Britain Province

[Mr. Taroa wrote the ancestor stories in *Wantok* #924 and 1022. He is from the **Bola** People.]

K1823+. Man disguises as pig; P310. Friendship; W157. Dishonesty

A Crab Bit the Sorcerer's Balls
(Wantok 965, December 30, 1992, page 18)

Long, long ago, in the time of the ancestors, in **Bongos** Village, in the Drekikir [Dreikikir] area of **Sepik** Province, there lived a woman [**Kwanga** People]. The woman's husband had died, so she lived by herself.

One day, she thought about going to work in the garden. She took her basket and left. She worked in the garden until the afternoon. At that time, a very heavy rain fell.

She quickly cut some bananas, filled her net bag, and walked back. However, when she arrived at the river, the water was already flooded. She found that it hard to cross the river at that time.

She followed the river upstream and down, then she saw a crab. She tied the claws of the crab, then she put it inside the basket. However, the water had not receded yet.

She gave up trying on crossing the river, then she walked back to the garden. She thought of sleeping in the garden hut, then returning in the morning.

She arrived at the garden, and she removed some firewood that she had cut before and left there. Afterwards, she made a fire and cooked some bananas.

She ate then sat. Before long, she heard the sounds of sorcerers. The heavy rain had also caused the sorcerers to look for a place to hide.

She heard the sorcerers approaching, then she very quietly removed all of the firewood. She went inside, put the firewood on top of herself and sat quietly.

The sorcerers arrived and saw the fire. Oh my, they were elated. They sat and warmed their bodies. One sorcerer worked at removing firewood and putting it on top of the fire. Before long, his hand went down and touched the woman's body.

He looked carefully and saw her lying there. He did not tell the other men. He wanted all of them to sleep, then he would have sex with [lit., "befriend"] her.

All of the sorcerers slept, then he alone was awake. He removed all of the firewood and tried to hold her. However, she loosened the ropes around the crab's two claws and waited. She placed the crab to the sorcerer's testicles and the sorcerer felt a great pain because the crab was pinching his testicles.

The other sorcerers heard this and awoke. They thought that men had grabbed one of themselves. They ran about and went into the forest. Their friend also rose, shouted, and ran after them with the crab that was still hanging from his testicles.

The woman just slept quietly until dawn. Then in the morning, she returned to the village.

Joseph S. Paulas
Kimbe
West New Britain Province

D1711. Magician; F547.1.1. Vagina dentata; P310. Friendship; Q244.1. Punishment for attempted rape; Q451.10.1+. Punishment: attack on testicles; R220. Flights; X712.1H. Female genitals; X712.3.1H. Injury to testicles

An Old Man Died in a Fire

(Wantok 966, January 7, 1993, page 18)

Long ago, in a village called **Kombole**, in the Kabwum District of **Morobe** Province, there lived five brothers.

One time, they made a big bonfire. The smoke from the fire rose into the sky. An old man saw the smoke and followed it to the brothers' house. He saw the five brothers and he was very happy.

They sat and told stories for a while, and then the old man wanted to return to his village. The brothers took some food from their garden and gave it to him. They took the food, cooked it, and ate it together.

The old man could not carry all of the food, so the big brother helped him carry the food back to his village. The big brother and the old man walked and walked, then they arrived at a bridge. The bridge was not sturdy, so the old man went first and the big brother followed. When the old man arrived at the other side, the big brother was in the middle of the bridge. Immediately, the old man twisted the bridge and the big brother fell down into the river. The old man took off and went to his house.

Some days later, the old man again saw smoke from the fire. He followed it and arrived at the village of the four brothers. The big brother had been left in the river.

The brothers treated the old man well. When it was nearly afternoon, the old man took another brother with him. They arrived at the same bridge and the old man did the same trick to the second brother.

The old man did this to four of the brothers and only the last brother was left. When the old man returned for the fifth time, the little brother asked the old man about his brothers. He asked him, "What is it that my brothers are eating that they are over there?" The old man replied, "Oh my, they are eating various kinds of food and they are bloated, so they do not want to return."

The little brother thought that the old man was telling the truth, so they prepared things and walked away. The little brother took his dog with him, and the two men walked away.

When the old man arrived on the other side of the bridge, he raised the tree [or log]. Then the little brother and his dog fell into the same river where the other brothers had fallen. When they fell down, they arrived at the exact place where the other brothers were. Oh my, their bodies were completely gone. They looked at themselves and cried terribly.

Before long, their dog began digging the earth, then they saw a light arise. They were surprised and saw a ladder to their house. Oh my, they were very happy for their dog.

Four days passed, then they went outside, scrounged all of the rubbish and made a huge bonfire. When the old man saw the smoke, he was very happy and went to their house. He arrived and shouted to them, "Yes, grandsons!" The brothers replied, "Yes grandpa, you've arrived, huh?" They told the old man to sit inside the house. While he was sitting inside the house, the brothers dug a hole and made a platform on top of the hole. Afterwards, they joined the ladder directly to their own house.

They returned and told the old man to go outside of the house. When the old man walked outside, he went directly there and fell into the hole. He shouted for the brothers to help him come outside. However, the brothers took firewood and threw it inside, then they burned the old man. The old man's belly exploded and he died. The brothers were very happy and they lived together again at their house.

[Anonymous]

B421. Helpful dog; F92+. Hole dug in ground leads home; K735. Capture in pitfall; K910. Murder by strategy; P251.6.2+. Five brothers; Q261. Treachery punished; Q285. Cruelty punished; Q414. Punishment: burning alive; S112. Burning to death; S143. Abandonment in forest; W157. Dishonesty

A Ghost Killed a Boy

(Wantok 967, January 14, 1993, page 18)

Long, long ago, in the Susuruga area [**Samo** Village] of **New Ireland** Province, there lived a family [**Susurunga** People].

They lived for a while, then one time the sun rose and stayed for a very long time. Not the slightest rain fell. After a while, every place with water became completely dry.

One day, the father told his wife and child that he would go to the river and hunt for some crayfish. The father arrived at a big river and worked hard at gathering the crayfish. He gathered very many crayfish, then the sun was about to set, so he brought them back to the house.

He arrived at the house, then he gave them to his wife to cook. She cooked them, then the father went to the spirit house and told stories with the other men.

Their son played outside for a while, then he went inside the house. He saw the crayfish and wanted to eat some. However, the mother told him to wait for father first.

This was customary for boys, they become more and more stubborn. He cried and went around the house. So, the mother gave him all of the crayfish. The child ate, then he went back to play with the other boys.

The father told stories for a while, then he thought of his crayfish. He arrived back at the house and asked the wife for food. She gave him the taros, but there were no crayfish. He asked about them and she told him, "Your offspring cried for crayfish and ate all of them." He was furious and said all kinds of bad things about the mother and son.

The child was still playing outside. The mother cried and cried inside the house. Before long, the boy heard his mother's crying and went inside to check on her. "Mama! Mama! Why are you crying?" asked the boy, "Did papa beat you?" The mother told him that his father had cursed them for finishing all of the crayfish, so she was crying. "Mama, don't worry, we'll return papa's crayfish," he said, then he ran outside.

The mother took a torch, a knife and a basket, then her son followed her. They walked and walked, then arrived at a river where the mother thought there were many fish and crayfish. However, this river had a ghost man who often ate people. The poor mother and son did not know this.

It was dark, so the mother lit the torch and hunted for fish. The boy slept in a cave by the river, waiting for his mother. The mother torch-fished for a while, then the boy waited and fell dead asleep. Before long, the ghost man came down and ate him. The ghost just left the bones and jumped on top of the stone [cave], waiting for the mother.

The mother torch-fished for a while, then she went to check on her son. She was surprised to see only the bones there. Surprisingly, the ghost man transformed himself to appear like her husband.

She thought that it really was her husband from the village who had worried about them and had come. She told the ghost that she had cut her hand, so the ghost carried the basket. She carried the lit torch and went first to the river.

She took the crayfish and gave them to the ghost man to put in the basket. However, he was just swallowing the crayfish. After a while, she found out that he was not really her husband.

Quickly, she had an idea, so she told the ghost man to wait for her. She took her lit torch and walked into the middle of the river.

In the middle of the river, there was a vine moving back and forth. We call this vine _susuruga_ in my language. She tied the lit torch on top of this vine, then the river made it go back and forth. The ghost man saw this and thought that she was working and catching fish, but she had already fled to the village.

This ancestor story teaches people of the village the good custom of taking care of the family.

William Baimo

Susuruga [Samo]

New Ireland Province

D42.2. Spirit takes shape of man; E425.2. Revenant as man; E541. Revenants eat; F961.1.5.3.1. Sunset delayed many hours; G11.10. Cannibalistic spirits; K1888. Illusory light; K1930. Treacherous impostors; P210. Husband and wife; P231. Mother and son; P233. Father and son; Q272. Avarice punished; Q411. Death as punishment; R210. Escapes; S110. Murders; V112.1. Spirit huts; W151. Greed; W167. Stubbornness

A Brother-In-Law Was
Tricked into Killing His Wife

(Wantok 968, January 21, 1993, page 18)

Long, long ago, in a village called **Niamat**, in **East Sepik** Province, there lived many people. The livelihood of these villagers was not very good and they often argued among themselves. Also, many men of the village knew how to perform sorcery. They had various black powers to kill others and to win things.

At this time, there were two men who had married two sisters. However, the two in-laws never ate well. They would always argue among themselves. In contrast, the two sisters lived well and never fought.

One day, the big sister and her husband went to the garden. They worked in the garden, then they went into the forest to find some *tulip* leaves and some mushrooms. In the afternoon, they returned to the village. When they arrived at the house, the woman took a pot for cooking food, then she went to fill it with water. When she returned, she made a fire and began to cook the *tulip* leaves and mushrooms.

Oh my, she made excellent soup. When the food was ready, she shared her food with her husband. The husband tried the soup and the soup tasted like nothing else. He ate and took some to the spirit house. He saw his brother-in-law sitting there and he gave some soup to him. His brother-in-law tried the soup and the soup was delicious to his mouth, "How did your wife cook this soup, and with what did she cook it?"

His brother-in-law told him, "I spoke to my wife and I cut one side of her breast to make the soup. So, this soup is quite delicious."

When his friend [brother-in-law] heard this, he left the spirit house and ran to his own house. When he arrived at the house, he was completely out of breath, so his wife asked him why he had come running to the house.

Her husband told her the story of the soup that her big sister had made and given to her husband. He told the story of what his friend had told him. At first, his wife did not believe this story, but her husband spoke sternly to her and she began to believe it.

Her husband told her that he would cut one side of her breasts and make soup. She believed her husband and she began to prepare things to make a fire. When she lit the fire, she put the pot of leafy greens on the fire.

Then her husband told her to lie down and he would cut off her breast. She lay down and he just took a stone axe, then he cut one side of her breast.

However, he was surprised to see that his wife was not moving. At this time, he knew that his brother-in-law had tricked him, and that he had killed his wife. He tried to wake his wife, but she was dead and lifeless. He took his wife's body and cried. Later, he took the body and he went

to bury it. After he buried her body, he began to search his thoughts about avenging the death of his wife.

John Laku Kemat
East Sepik Province

D1711. Magician; D2061. Magic murder; KK940.2K2. Man betrayed into killing his wife; P210. Husband and wife; P252.1. Two sisters; P263. Brother-in-law; P310. Friendship; S55+. Cruel brother-in-law; S139.4. Murder by mangling with axe; S176.1K2+. Murder by cutting off breasts; V61.3+. Dead buried; V112.1. Spirit huts; W157. Dishonesty

Why Dogs and Marsupials (*Sikau*) are Enemies
(Wantok 969, January 28, 1993, page 17)

Long, long ago, the dogs and marsupials (*sikau*) were good friends, and they lived together in one house. When the marsupials hunted for food, they would carry all of the wild game to the house. They would make a fire and cook their food. When they finished cooking, they would share the food with the dogs.

However, the dogs often acted in a very rotten manner. When they went to the forest, they would kill game and they never brought any to the marsupials. The dogs never thought of cooking the good meat in a fire; they would just eat it in the forest. The marsupials tired of the dogs' nasty behavior.

Another thing was that the marsupials would go hunting for food during the day, while the dogs would sleep in the house then go hunting for food at night. When the marsupials made a fire, the dogs would sleep near the fire and make a lot of garbage in the house.

One night, when all of the dogs had gone to the forest, the marsupials gathered and spoke behind their backs. However, they did not know that one mangy dog was sleeping in the house. The dog had not followed the others into the forest.

The leader of the marsupials called all of them and they began to argue. Many of them complained that the dogs never acted nicely. They said that the dogs never cooked food for them. They also complained that the dogs never carried food to give to them. Many also complained that the dogs never made fire and that they waited for them to make a fire. Then they would go to sleep near the fire and make a lot of garbage in the house. The mangy dog heard everything that was said, then the dog just slept quietly and waited for the big group to arrive.

In the morning, all of the marsupials went to the forest and all of the dogs returned to the house. The mangy dog called to all of the other dogs. The dog told them that there was something important to tell them.

All of the dogs came closer and the dog began to tell them the story. The dog told them that the marsupials had said that the dogs never cooked good food or shared with them, that the dogs never made fire. The dog said that when the marsupials made a fire, the dogs would sleep near it and wreck the house with rubbish from the fire.

When the leader of the dogs heard this story, it was furious. The leader told all of the dogs to fight with the marsupials. The leader told them to prepare and wait for the marsupials to return to the house, then they would fight together.

In the afternoon, the marsupials returned from the forest, then all of them went inside the house to prepare to cook the food. All of the dogs went outside then went around, looking at all of the marsupials coming into the house. When they went up into the house, they shut the house door.

Then the dogs began to argue and fight with the marsupials. In this fight, many marsupials were injured and some died. When the marsupials saw that the dogs were beating them, some of them broke the house wall and jumped out, fleeing into the forest. The marsupials were also strong and they had killed some dogs.

Now, you can see that dogs live in villages and that marsupials live in the forest. Dogs also love to sleep by the fire and they often eat raw meat.

Mewari Amibi
Okapa [Village, **Fore** People]
Goroka
Eastern Highlands Province

A2433.2.1+. Why marsupial lives in forest; A2433.3.2+. Why dog lives in village; A2435.3.1+. Why dog eats food raw; A2494.4+. Enmity between dog and marsupial; B211.2.12K+. Speaking marsupial; B211.1.7. Speaking dog; B241.2+. King of marsupials; B241.2.7. King of dogs; B263+. War between dogs and marsupials; P310. Friendship; R210. Escapes; W115. Slovenliness; W151. Greed

A Worthless Man Married
a Gorgeous Woman

(Wantok 970, February 4, 1993, page 16)

Long, long ago, in **Yomakawi** Village, in the Sinasina area of **Simbu** Province, there lived a man named Waipol [**Sinasina** People]. Waipol was a worthless man in the village. Many people never liked him and he was single.

One time, he was in the house and thought of going to hunt for cassowaries in the deep forest. In the very early morning, Waipol left the house and went to the forest. He went all of the way to Talbakul [**Tobakogal**] Village to hunt for cassowaries.

Waipol arrived at a mountain, then he saw cassowary footprints at the base of a tree. The cassowaries had come to eat the fruits of this tree.

On the other side of the mountain, he saw a pond. Then the bad boy put all of his things down and he kept watch for cassowaries. He did not go astray, he just hid there until afternoon.

In the afternoon, he wanted to see, but no, he saw that the cassowaries had filed over to the water. When they arrived at the water, they removed their cassowary skins and became like people.

When Waipol looked over there, he saw that only the women were bathing. Oh my, at this time, his mouth dropped open and all of his bones trembled. Waipol looked and saw one of them come very late and remove her skin. Oh my, she was not just a woman, she was absolutely gorgeous. When she went down to the water to bathe, Waipol went very quietly, took the cassowary skin, and hid it.

The woman came up and looked for the skin, but it was not there. She began to search for it. When Waipol saw this, he went very quietly and grabbed her, then he took her to the village and married her.

They lived very well and they raised two children. However one time, Waipol scolded his wife, then he traveled in the forest. The woman stayed and thought about running away, so she began to search for her skin. She searched and searched, then she saw her skin underneath a clay pot and she put it on.

After she put on the skin, she explained to the children that when their father returned, they must tell him that their mother had put on the cassowary skin and fled.

In the afternoon, Waipol returned from the forest and the two children told him what their mother had done. When Waipol heard this, he was very troubled and he began to search for his wife in the forest. He searched and searched, then he arrived at a big cave where he saw a big man standing there.

He told the man that he was searching for his wife. The man told Waipol to go inside. When Waipol went inside, oh my, he saw very many cassowaries. The man told him that his wife was the third in the line. Waipol just went inside and held his wife who was sitting third in the line.

Waipol grabbed her and she tried to beat Waipol, but she was unable to do so. Waipol was very happy and he carried her to the house, then they lived together again.

Michael Jack
Simbu Province

B222+. Land of cassowaries; D169.4W. Transformation: woman to cassowary; D350+W. Transformation: cassowary to woman; D361.1. Swan Maiden; D531. Transformation by putting on skin; D531+. Transformation by removing skin; K300. Thefts and cheats—general; P160. Beggars; P210. Husband and wife; P230. Parents and children; P250. Brothers and sisters; R10. Abduction; R213. Escape from home; R227. Wife flees from husband; R260. Pursuits; T192. Marriage by force

A Father Lied and Slept with His Daughter

(Wantok 971, February 11, 1993, page 17)

Long, long ago, there lived a man in Mul [Nul] Village, in the Gumine District of Simbu Province [Golin People]. His name was Hmel Kihmel and he excelled at hunting marsupials (*kapul*).

One time, he saw that the moon was quite bright and he thought of going to hunt marsupials in the forest. He sat in the house and spoke with his daughter. The girl's name was Yauri. The father told her, "When you were little, I would go hunting for marsupials and you would eat them. I often hunted for marsupials then."

After he told his daughter this, he told her that they would go together and hunt for marsupials in the forest. Then he told his daughter to go find some sweet potatoes in the garden, afterwards they would travel in the forest, hunting for marsupials.

Yauri agreed to this and told her father, "Tomorrow, we'll go together to the forest. If you kill marsupials, I'll take their fur and make 'grass' skirts and net bags for myself."

The father was very happy for his daughter's thoughts. They prepared all of the food, then the next day, they went into the forest. When they arrived in the forest, the father told her the story that the area where they were located was a *masalai* place. When people traveled in the forest, they could not think badly or say lies, and they must listen to what just one man says. This was not true. The father was lying to his daughter.

Kihmel made a hut and told his daughter to just stay inside the hut. He said, "If you hear something come to you, you must speak out. You must not hide."

The father took his bow and arrows, then he went to the forest, but he had lied. Immediately, he went and stood outside the hut, then he whistled and said, "*Gi* Yauri *ya, ei*

nene kena paio ei nene kena paio." What he said means, "Woman [Yauri], sleep with your own father."

Kihmel pretended to travel in the forest, then he returned to the hut. When he arrived at the hut, he spoke to his daughter but his mouth just opened. He tried to speak, but he could not talk. Then he asked his daughter, "Did you also hear something or not?" The daughter told him that she had not heard anything.

The father told his daughter not to sleep, that she must stay awake and hear what would come. Then he went back to the forest, but before long, the father returned to the hut and did the same thing.

Later, he returned and asked his daughter. He told her that the *masalai*s had opened [their] mouths and that he found it hard to talk, so he did not find any wild game in the forest. He told his daughter to say what had happened.

The father spoke very sternly, then he told his daughter, "If you hide what had happened, then we can't return home. The *masalai*s will kill us."
The poor daughter did not know that her father was lying and that he had said everything that she had heard. The daughter told her father that she had heard a whistle and that she must sleep with him.

When the father heard this story, he immediately told his daughter that the *masalai*s had spoken and that they could not ignore them, "I'll sleep with you. If I don't sleep with you, we'll die together." The father had played a big trick and he slept with his own daughter to fulfill his desires and greediness.

Adof Saku
Kimbe
West New Britain Province

K1315. Seduction by impostor; K1828. Disguise as deity (or spirit); K2214K. Treacherous father; P234. Father and daughter; T411. Father-daughter incest; W151. Greed; W157. Dishonesty

A *Masalai* Finished off
Two Old Men from Libo

(Wantok 972, February 18, 1993, page 21)

Long, long ago, there were two old men who lived in Libo Village, in the Kagua area of Southern Highlands Province [Kewa People?]. Their names were Yole and Liba. They also took care of their dog named Yana. The two men were unmarried.

One time, the sun was very bright where they lived. At this time, the rain had also not fallen. Yoli [Yole] awoke and told his friend, Limba [Liba], that they would go hunting for marsupials (*kapul*) in the forest.

They went to the garden, took some sweet potatoes, cooked them in the fire, and prepared them for the next day. In the early morning, they took their dog and went into the forest.

They went around and around in the very deep forest. Their dog excelled at killing marsupials. Oh my, they killed many marsupials. They saw that it was becoming dark, so they wanted to walk back to the village.

However, they had gone very far from the village and it was hard to return to the house. Yole told Limba, "I came around here before and I saw a cave in that mountain. We should go there."

Limba agreed and they looked for a way to get to the cave. When Limba saw the cave, he was elated because the cave was like a house.

It was very lucky that they still had some sweet potatoes, so they began to eat. Afterwards, they made a fire, cooked two marsupials, and ate them with sweet potatoes.

However, the cave belonged to a *masalai*. The men did not know that a *masalai* dwelled there. The *masalai* was asleep and smelled the marsupials' fur that the old men had singed.

The men ate, then they slept near the fire. The *masalai* sat waiting for them to fall dead asleep, then the *masalai* left where it was and went to the place where the men were sleeping.

The poor men did not know what would happen to them. The *masalai* just went there, then killed and ate both of them. The *masalai* finished all of their flesh and just left their bones there.

At this time, their dog, Yana, had gone into the forest and was hunting for game at night. When the dog returned, it saw the old men's bones. The dog took the bones and carried them to the village.

When the villagers saw the men's bones, they knew that a *masalai* must have killed them. They sat, mourned, cried and rubbed mud on their faces. They did this to show their great sorrow for the two old men.

Peter Fundu and Joshua Koyakia
Kimbe
West New Britain Province

B301.1.1+. Faithful dog retrieves master's corpse; F490+. Masalai; G300. Other ogres; P310. Friendship; P681+. Mourning customs: earth on body; S110. Murders

Two Sisters Argued over Sago then Transformed into the Cockatoos of Pangia

(Wantok 973, February 25, 1993, page 21)

Long, long ago, there were two gorgeous sisters who lived in Kali Village, by Kauwo, in the Pangia District of Southern Highlands Province [Wiru People].

Their names were Aroa and Akoma. Aroa was the big sister and Akoma was the little sister. Their mother and father had died when they were still young.

They searched for their own food. The people of the village never helped them. The two of them lived like this until they grew big. The sisters were very pretty and all of the men of the village often just died for them. All of the young and old men often talked about them.

The big sister was a very strong woman. Men tried to ask [her] desires, but she was uninterested. She always told her sister Akoma not to tremble for men.

The two women were also strong at searching for food. Every day, they would go to the forest and hunt for wild game. They often killed and cooked the game with sweet potatoes.

One time, Aroa told her little sister Akoma that she was tired of eating sweet potatoes. She wanted Akoma and herself to go to the swamp and cut a sago palm tree. The little sister agreed to this idea.

The next day, they took things for scraping and rinsing sago. They arrived at the swamp and began looking for a sago tree to cut down.

They went and saw a good sago tree standing there. They put their things down and made a platform for rinsing the sago pith. Afterwards, the big sister took an axe and began cutting the sago tree.

After they had cut the tree, they began removing the thorns from the sago tree and beating the sago pith. They finished scraping the sago pith, then they carried it to the place for rinsing it. There, Aroa told Akoma to make a fire to cook sweet potatoes and bananas. Then Akoma did this.

Aroa alone took *limbum* palm leaves and made a basket to fetch water for rinsing the sago. Before long, a young boy came to them. He walked and approached Aroa, then he told her that he was sorry for them and that he wanted to help them rinse the sago.

The young man [boy] took the *limbum* basket and went to fetch water, then he began rinsing the sago. The sisters went to eat the sweet potatoes and bananas. They finished eating, then they walked over to see him.

When they arrived there, he was rinsing the sago. They saw that the level of the sago was still low. The little sister was not happy, she wanted the sago to go higher. However, her big sister wanted the sago to just stay at one level.

Because of this, the two of them began to argue. It was the first time that they had argued. Until the little boy had come, they never argued in the slightest.

The little sister was angry and beat the big sister with a sago scraper. Shortly thereafter, the little sister turned into a white cockatoo [sulphur-crested cockatoo (Beehler *et al.*, 1986: 117)] and the big sister turned into a black cockatoo [palm cockatoo (Beehler *et al.*, 1986: 117)]. The yellow on the cockatoo's head shows the place where the little sister had hit her. The young man saw this and turned into a bird.

Rex Manie
Lae
Morobe Province

A1998K. Creation of black cockatoo; A1998K+. Creation of white cockatoo; A2321.12K. Origin of comb of white cockatoo; D150M. Transformation: man to bird; D150+W. Transformation: woman to cockatoo; D566. Transformation by striking; F610.0.1. Remarkably strong woman; P252.1. Two sisters; Q458. Flogging as punishment; T10. Falling in love

The Gokme Mothers Are Afraid of the Bright Moon
(Wantok 974, March 4, 1993, page 20)

Long, long ago, in Gokme [**Gogime**] Village, in **Simbu** Province, there lived a man with his wife and their child [**Kuman** People].

One time, the father left the mother and child in the house. He took things and went alone in the forest to hunt for wild game. The father went around and around, then he went into the very deep forest. Darkness caught up with him before he had returned to the house.

The mother and baby were in the house and saw that it was dark. The mother took their baby and went out of the house, then she saw that the moon was brightly lit. She lifted the baby on top of [herself] and spoke to it. She said, "*Kanibo endo, kanibo endo, paimo kana baumbo kano.*" In my language, this means, "Look up, it's the moon, it's the moon."

While she was showing her baby the moon, a man from another village came and spied upon them. He hid among the wild sugarcanes (*pitpit*) near the house.

Then the mother carried her baby back into the house. She did not know that a man was spying upon them, so they went to sleep.

This man hid until the mother and baby were dead asleep. Then he left his hiding place and walked very quietly to the house. He opened the house door. He went to the room where they were sleeping and he saw that they were completely dead asleep. He went very quietly and took the baby, then he carried it outside. He took the baby and went to a mountain, then he threw it down. However, the baby did not die. It became stuck on top of wild sugarcanes.

Late that night, the mother awoke and tried to get her baby to sleep near her. But no, her baby was not there. The mother worked diligently at finding her baby. The baby was sleeping and felt the fuzz of the wild sugarcanes. The leaves of the wild sugarcanes also began to cut it, and the baby began to cry.

The mother was crying in the house and heard her baby crying outside. She got up, lit a torch and followed the crying. She went and saw her baby lying on top of the wild sugarcane leaves. She cried and brought the baby to the house.

So now, if you go to Gokme Village, you will see that the mothers never take their babies outside at night when the moon is bright.

Joseph Waim
Kimbe
West New Britain Province

C755.8+. Tabu: taking child out at night when the moon is bright; P210. Husband and wife; P230. Parents and children; R10.3. Children abducted; R131. Exposed or abandoned child rescued; R153.4+. Mother rescues child

[The ancestor story in *Wantok* #975 is the same as that in #966.]
[The ancestor story in *Wantok* #976 is the same as that in #964.]

A Dog Gave Water to Mumeng
(Wantok 977, March 25, 1993, page 20)

Long, long ago, there was a village called Mumengtaen [**Mumengtein**] in the Mumeng District of **Morobe** Province [**Mumeng** People]. There was a man and his dog that lived there. The man's name was Mavim and the dog's name was Katekes.

Mavim was a man who went hunting for wild game in the forest. He often liked to travel in the forest with Katekes because the dog had big teeth for hunting marsupials (*kapul*).

One day, they traveled in the forest until they killed about ten marsupials. They would go around and around until the net bag was full, then later they would return to the village.

Mavim would cook marsupials on a fire, then eat some. He would smoke many others. The marsupials that he smoked would last for two weeks, then he and his dog would go hunting again.

One time, his dog Katekes thought of going into the forest. The dog tired of following Mavim because his master often cooked the marsupials that they ate. The dog wanted to just eat them [raw].

Katekes left the village and went to stay for a week in the forest. The dog hunted marsupials and ate them. One time, the dog went around hunting for marsupials and it became terribly thirsty. The dog was just dying for a drink of water. However, it looked around and did not see any water to drink.

The dog sat and began removing dirt to find water. The dog dug the earth and saw that the ground was getting muddy, then it dug in earnest. Before long, water shot up from the ground directly into the dog's face.

When the dog saw the water, oh my, it was elated. The dog drank the water, and its belly became very bloated. Then the dog just slept. When the dog felt its belly loosen a little, it went back to the house to explain this to its master.

Katekes arrived at the house and saw its master there. It went and barked, then the master knew that the dog must have killed some marsupials and left them in the forest. Mavin followed his dog into the forest. They arrived at the place that the dog had dug and filled with drinking water.

This water that Ketekes [Katekes] had dug is still there and the people of Mumeng often call this water, "The Dog Dug It."

Sae Gwae
Port Moresby
National Capital District

A941.0.1. Origin of a particular spring; A1617. Origin of place-name

The Wild Swamp Taro Arose at Mindik
(Wantok 978, April 1, 1993, page 19)

Long, long ago, in **Mindik** Village, in **Morobe** Province, there lived a man and his big sister [**Yaknge** People]. Their names were Tup and Koarup. Tup was the big sister, and Koarup was the little brother. Their father and mother had died before, and they lived alone.

They lived for a while, then Tup went to marry a man. She took her little brother to live with her. However, Koarup's life was never very good because his brother-in-law did not act well. He was argumentative and he was greedy for little things.

Tup always cooked food and would want to give it to her little brother, but the brother-in-law would take the food and finish it. The poor little boy would sleep hungry or go searching about for rubbish to eat. Koarup saw what his brother-in-law did and he was not happy.

One time, he took a long, red cock's comb and poked it into his head. He took a bow and arrows, and pretended to shoot the bananas that were by the house.

He fetched [the arrows] and pretended to shoot repeatedly. While he did this, his sister was in the house, watching him go into the forest. She called for Koarup to return, but he did not want to do so. His sister left the house, crying and following her brother.

Tup followed her brother for a while, then they arrived at a swampy place. Koarup walked and walked, then he sank into the swamp, going deeper and deeper. When his sister saw this, she was terribly worried.

Koarup told his sister to return, but Tup did not want to do so. She said that she would die with her brother. Tup saw that Koarup was going beneath the swamp. Then Koarup's head was completely hidden and the big sister just saw the red cock's comb that the brother had poked into his head.

She watched and watched, then she also jumped into the swamp and they became wild taros. So now, wild taros are often very plentiful in swampy areas.

Holy Lingip Weis
Hagen
Western Highlands Province

A2686.4.2+. Origin of wild taro; D213.8K+M. Transformation: man to wild taro plant; D213.8K+W. Transformation: woman to wild taro plant; D642. Transformation to escape difficult situation; P210. Husband and wife; P253. Sister and brother; P263. Brother-in-law; R213. Escape from home; R260. Pursuits; S55+. Cruel brother-in-law; T100. Marriage; W151. Greed; W188. Contentiousness

Bokol Missed Marrying the Forest Woman
(Wantok 979, April 8, 1993, page 20)

Long ago, on Djaul [**Dyaul**] Island, in **New Ireland** Province, there was a village. The name of this village was Lion [**Leion** Village, **Tigak** People]. Lion was at the far end of the island. It was near another small island called Meit [**Mait**].

Now, if you went to this island, you would see various kinds of sea fish that you could not find elsewhere. If you pulled in fish from this area, you would catch just the head because various kinds of sharks live there and they would take the fish from you very quickly. Because of this, the people of this island are terrified to travel this area.

In this area, there lived a young boy. His name was Tel Bokol. One very early morning, Bokol traveled in the forest to hunt for wild game. Then he went and rested near a small stream, then he chewed betel nuts. There was a nice cool breeze, so he did not think about returning quickly to the village.

Before long, there was a sound like that of a tree branch breaking from above. However, there were no marks that the tree had broken, so the boy thought hard.

At the same time, oh my, the nearby water changed colors, turning completely red, like the blood of someone who has been cut. He checked his legs, but there were no marks on them. The boy continued to think about what would happen next.

Immediately, he felt as if there was a man behind him. Oh my, he got up to look and he saw two women. He had never seen them before. One had had the skin of a crocodile and looked completely awful. Oh my, the other was just like an angel.

Because of this, the boy wanted to run away, but they told him not to be afraid. They had not come to ruin him, not at all, they said. They told him that they were just like him, and that they could see him but he could not see them. They flattered him for a while, then they gave him food and Bokol ate. It was the same kind of food that he ate at the village. They just gave him fish with sago. Later, they gave him betel nuts with betel peppers, and he chewed these. Oh my, he was quite sated.

They treated him for almost three whole hours. Then they explained that they would meet him again at the same place, the next morning. After this, they departed.

From these good words, he was terribly worried and he returned to the village. He wanted to return quickly the next day so that he would see them again. You know, he had chewed betel nuts.

Bokol did not sleep well that night. He awoke in the very early morning and went into the forest. Oh my, when he arrived in the forest, he was shocked to meet just the nice woman. She explained that the other woman had yet to come and find him. She said that she had a great desire

to be friends [i.e., to have sex], then they would marry. Bokol was elated about what she had said.

They flattered each other, then she wanted to know if she could take Bokol to her village to show to her clan. Bokol just agreed.

She told him that he could close his eyes, then Bokol would follow her. She took some lime [calcium oxide] and rubbed it on Bokol's face. Oh my, when Bokol smelled the lime, he smelled something completely unusual. The smell was wonderful, better than the perfumes that we have.

Oh my, when the boy opened his eyes to look, they were inside the woman's food gardens. The gardens were completely weeded. She took him to show to her clan, so that they would marry later. Her clan had purchased shame [i.e., agreed on bride price?], but the boy's clan had not yet done so. Later, they would straighten this out.

The two of them were friends for a long time, then the boy planned to take her to his clan. At this time, there was a great feast at Bokol's village. The feast was to celebrate a canoe that the men of the village had carved and that would be used at sea. At this time, the boy thought of taking his wife[-to-be] to a clearing. He took his wife and her mother, then he put them in his house in the village.

However, Bokol's big brother came to the house at a different time to take his paddle. Oh my, he was shocked to meet the woman and her mother in Bokol's house. Bokol had not explained this situation to his clan.

The brother asked which clan it was that was staying in the house. Because of this, the woman and her mother were terribly ashamed and they cried.

Bokol heard this and tried to stop them, but he was unable to do so. The two of them told him that they had taken time to speak to his brother, so they would leave him now.

Then the two of them shook his hand and they went behind the house to leave. The boy cried and followed them for a while, then he did not see them. He wanted to take the baskets that the woman had given him, but they were no longer there. He wanted to think of the various kinds of tricks that she had shown him, but he could no longer think of them either.

It was too bad, he worried for a while, until the worrying nearly killed him. He had lost his chance to marry the angel of the forest.

John Mays Bonma
Djaul [Dyaul] Island
New Ireland Province

B90+. Woman with crocodile skin; D931.1.4. Magic lime; D492. Color of object changed; D2121.2. Magic journey with closed eyes; F441. Wood-spirit; F715.9. Red river; P251.5. Two brothers; P262. Mother-in-law; P263. Brother-in-law; P264. Sister-in-law; P265. Son-in-law; T50. Wooing; T52. Bride purchased; T75. Man scorned by his beloved; T91.3. Love of mortal and supernatural person; V230. Angels

A Father and Son Snake Fled from the Mother
(Wantok 980, April 15, 1993, page 16)

Long, long ago, in Imom [**Imon** Village], by the Yalumet [River], in the Kabwum District of **Morobe** Province, there lived a man with his wife and child [**Timbe** People].

He was not a real man. Sometimes, he would turn into a snake. They lived for a while, then one time, they felt hungry for wild game. The father told the mother and child that he would go hunting for game. In the very early morning, the father took a bow and arrows, and his dog, then he went to hunt for game.

The father left and killed very many marsupials (*kapul*). He completely filled the net bag with marsupials. He called the dog and they were about to return to the village, but they were still far away, so they searched for a place to sleep. It was fortunate that they had a hut in the forest.

So, the leader [man] and his dog went to get some rest there. He made a fire, then cooked two sweet potatoes and some marsupials in the fire.

They ate, then they slept. In the morning, he took the net bag of marsupials and walked towards the village. The father was still walking far away when he heard his wife scolding their son.

The father hid and heard his wife scolding their son terribly. The mother told the boy that his father was not a real man. She told him that his father was a snake and a *masalai*. The leader heard this and said, "That's OK, I'm not a good man. I'm a snake, so I'll leave you."

The leader called his dog, then they went to the house. When he arrived at the house, he asked his wife to cook food. She cooked food, then let the father and son eat while she walked alone to the garden to fetch taros and leafy greens.

When she went to the garden, the father called the boy and told the story of what he had heard. Then he told the boy to stay quiet, and the two of them would run away.

When the mother returned from the garden, the father went out and killed one of his pigs that was by the fence. They butchered all of the meat and made a huge earth oven. In the afternoon, they uncovered the earth oven and divided the meat among themselves.

In the morning, the father and son awoke very quietly, took some things and ran away, leaving the mother. Before they departed, the father took *tanget* plants and planted them by the house ladder.

The mother awoke and did not see them. She went outside the house and just saw the *tanget* plants. At this time, the mother understood that they had run away from her. She was terribly worried and began to cry, following them.

The mother cried and cried, then she arrived at the crest of a mountain. At this time, the boy heard his mother's crying and told his father that he would wait for her. However, the father did not want him to follow his mother, so he told him to forget her.

He was worried about his mother, so he walked slowly and the mother met them along the trail. The father was angry with his son, so he turned into a tree. The mother came and saw her son, then she asked him about his father.

However, when the boy turned to check on his father, he saw that he had turned into a tree. The boy was troubled about his father, then he turned into a vine that climbed up the tree. She saw this and turned into a stone. Now, if you go to this place, you will see these things.

Robert Simo

Popondetta

Oro Province

A974. Rocks from transformation of people to stone; A977.5. Origin of particular rock; B656.2. Marriage to serpent in human form; D191M. Transformation: man to serpent (snake); D213.4B. Transformation: boy to vine; D215M. Transformation: man to tree; D231W. Transformation: woman to stone; D391M. Transformation: serpent (snake) to man; F490+. Masalai; P210. Husband and wife; P231. Mother and son; P233. Father and son; R213. Escape from home; R227+. Husband flees from wife; R260. Pursuits

Brothers Married Bird [Pandanus] Women
(Wantok 981, April 22, 1993, page 21)

Long, long ago, there were two brothers who lived in **Wangal** Village, by Gembogl, in **Simbu** Province [**Kuman** or **Nagane** People?]. Their names were Dime and Dame. Dime was the elder brother and Dame was the younger brother.

Their father and mother had died when they were still young. The place where they lived did not have other people, so they searched for their own food. They lived there and grew to be big men, but there were no other people near them for them to find women to marry.

They lived for a while, then one time, the big brother told his little brother that he would go to hunt for wild game the next day. He sent his little brother to go prepare a bow and arrows, and some food.

The next day, the big brother, Dime, took these things and went into the forest. Before long, he heard birds calling. He saw one, then he took an arrow, put it to the bowstring, and shot the bird. The bird went down with the arrow, then Dime went to find it.

Dime found it very difficult to find the bird because the vines had thorns and blocked his path. While he was trying to locate the bird, he heard some things making noises behind him.

Oh my, when Dime heard this, his legs and arms began to tremble. He thought that some forest *masalai*s wanted to eat him. He turned and saw an old woman. The woman called out and said to him, "What are you looking for? Whatever you're looking for, I've taken. I took the bird and ate it, but I left the arrow and bird feathers there. Go take them and carry them to your home."

Then the old woman took Dime to the house and gave him food. They told stories for a while, then it became dark and the old woman told Dime to sleep with her. Before they slept, she told him to stay quiet if he heard some noises in the night.

The guy slept for a while, then he heard various noises coming from the house. He heard men talking and he heard some who were laughing hysterically. He heard some people eating at the kitchen house. He followed the instructions of the old woman and he just lay quietly.

In the [early] morning, the old woman went to wake Dime. She said that she was happy that he had slept quietly and followed her instructions. She went to her bed and took two new net bags, two sticks for digging sweet potatoes, and a bamboo flute. She gave these to Dime.

The old woman took Dime back to the pandanus (*marita*) garden. She took two ripe pandanus fruits, and she gave them to him. Then she spoke about the things that Dime must do when he took the pandanus fruits to his home.

She told him to take the two pandanus fruits to the stream near his home, then stand the fruits on both sides of the stream, and not to turn his back to them. [She said that he should] also bury the flute so that [it] cannot "look towards" his home.

He did all of the things that the old woman told him to do. Before long, two gorgeous women came behind him very quietly and said, "You worked at taking us from morning until now, so our legs and arms are tired. You must take us to your home."

Dime felt ashamed, but in his heart, he was elated. Quickly, he told one woman to marry his little brother, Dame. She agreed to marry Dame. He himself married the other woman. They lived together and raised very many children.

Joseph Silku

Lae

Morobe Province

A1461.7+. Origin of flute; D431.4+W. Transformation: pandanus fruit to woman; J1050. Attention to warnings; P210. Husband and wife; P230. Parents and children; P251.5. Two brothers; P263. Brother-in-law; P264. Sister-in-law; T100. Marriage; W31. Obedience

A Boy Tricked His Father about Ghosts
(Wantok 982, April 29, 1993, page 25)

Very long ago, there lived a man and his son. One time, they wanted to go hunting for marsupials (*kapul*) in the forest. They prepared some food, then they went into the forest. They walked and walked, then they arrived at a mountain. The father told his son to put their things down, then they rested.

After they rested, the father began cutting a tree to make a hut for themselves to sleep at night. They made the hut, then they put the things inside. The place where they had made the hut was the home of ghosts.

In the afternoon, the father told a story to the little boy that this place had many ghosts. So at night, he told the boy to sleep in the hut and not to go hunting for marsupials in the forest.

Quietly, the father took the bow and arrows, then went into the forest. When the boy saw his father leave the hut, he began to become afraid. Quickly, he left the hut and followed his father.

The father did not know that his son was following him. The father walked and walked, then saw a marsupial on top of a tree. He climbed the tree, then shot down the marsupial.

The leader [man] did not know that his son was at the base of the tree. The boy saw the marsupial and shouted upwards, "Papa, that's my marsupial."

When the father heard this, he thought that it was a ghost, so he immediately descended the tree. The father just went down then began running and crashing through the forest. The boy also saw this and ran after his father.

The son thought that his father had seen a ghost and was running, so he followed him.

The father ran and shouted at the same time. He did not care that it was dense forest. Oh my, the guy crashed through the forest just like a wild pig. He ran and arrived at the village, then he went directly into the spirit house.

When the father turned around, oh no, he saw a man running and coming behind him. He thought it was a ghost, so he told the clan that there was a ghost chasing him from the forest and coming all of the way into the village.

However, he did not know that it was his son running behind him. The boy approached his father and told him that it was himself who was running behind him, not a ghost man. The whole clan of the house went outside and laughed hysterically at them.

Ben Koi Kawie

Kimbe

West New Britain Province

E261.4+. Imagined ghost pursues man; J652. Inattention to warnings; P233. Father and son; R260. Pursuits; V112.1. Spirit huts; W126. Disobedience

Lust for a Woman Brought Enemies to Kadajiki

(Wantok 983, May 5, 1993, page 20)

Long, long ago, there lived a man. His name was Kadajiki. Kadajiki was not an ordinary man. He had the wherewithal to marry two women. At this time, he also had sex with a married woman from another nearby village.

One time, Kadajiki heard that his [girl]friend had become very sick. At night, he did not tell his two wives and his child that he would go take yams (*yam* and *mami*) from the garden.

In the morning, he left the house and went to the garden. He worked at weeding the garden. When he saw the sun setting, he removed yams to carry to the house.

At this time, he did not know that his girlfriend had died on that same day. Kadajiki carried firewood with the yams and walked back to the village.

While he was walking, he saw the girlfriend walking towards him. However, it was not really his girlfriend. It was woman's ghost who had died.

The scoundrel saw her and was very happy. Kadajiki approached her and said, "Good afternoon," but she did not reply. Kajajiki [Kadajiki] asked her again whether she had run away to him or whether her husband had scolded her. However, the ghost woman did not reply.

Kadajiki asked her to return to the garden and sleep in the garden hut. He told her that this would be a chance for them to sleep together.

So, they turned and went back to the garden. When they arrived at the hut, Kadajiki quickly made a fire and cooked two big yams. When the yams were ready, he took one and gave it to her. However, she did not sit down and Kadajiki told her to sit. "What are you ashamed of? I'm not a new man for you to be ashamed of me. You know me," Kadajiki said.

The ghost woman did not eat her yam. Kadajiki finished his yam, then he made a bed for them to sleep upon. After he made the bed, he told her to go sleep with him.

Late at night, they slept for a while, then all of the ghosts of the dead came and surrounded the hut in which they were sleeping. All of the ghosts called for her to chase Kadajiki outside. They stood with fighting gear, ready to kill Kadajiki.

She heard her fellow ghosts calling, then she pulled Kadajiki outside. However, Kadajiki was a very strong man, so he fought with the ghost woman. They fought and fought, then the ghost woman won and pulled him outside. Then the ghosts who were outside killed him. After they [beat] him, they left him and fled back to their home.

William Wani

Rabaul

East New Britain Province

[Mr. Wani wrote the ancestor stories in *Wantok* #870 and 1040. He is from **Mongol** Village, **Mongol** People, **East Sepik** Province.]

E210. Dead lover's malevolent return; E232. Return from the dead to slay wicked person; E425.1. Revenant as woman; E461. Fight of revenant with living person; E474. Cohabitation of living person and ghost; F610. Remarkably strong man; K2231. Treacherous mistress; P210. Husband and wife; P230. Parents and children; Q241. Adultery punished; Q411. Death as punishment; R220. Flights; S110. Murders; T145.0.1. Polygyny; T481. Adultery

Worrying Caused the Sister to Become a Marsupial (*Kapul*)

(Wantok 984, May 13, 1993, page 18)

Long, long ago, there lived a man and his sister in a place that was far away from the other people. One time, they saw that the moon was brightly lit. The man told his sister, "The moon is nicely lit, let's go hunt for marsupials (*kapul*)."

The sister listened and was very happy with what her brother had said. Before they left, she told her brother that she would bring some food. So, she took some sweet potatoes for her brother and herself to eat in the forest.

Her brother went to the house, took a bow and arrows, then they went into the forest. They walked and walked, then they arrived at a cave.

The place where they went had very many marsupials. The man helped his sister make a fire and cook the sweet potatoes. When the sweet potatoes were done, he told his sister to grate them. Then he left his sister and went to the forest to hunt marsupials.

The sister took a stone axe and grated the sweet potatoes. She was still working at grating a sweet potato when the axe cut her finger. Oh my, the blood shot out and the place where she was sitting was just filled with blood.

The poor woman was in pain and she cried terribly. She cried and screamed, then her brother heard her from the forest and ran quickly to the place where she was.

He arrived and saw the blood, then he told [his] sister that they would return home. They left everything and walked back home. At this time, the moon was brightly lit, so they could see and walk in the forest. They walked and walked, then the big brother held his sister to stop her from crying.

The sister walked along the trail and was worried about her finger. She was not happy about her brother and she was still crying. This was because her brother had told her to grate the sweet potatoes like that, and the axe had cut her finger.

They walked and walked, then they approached a huge tree. This tree had a big hole inside it. The sister walked directly into the tree hole and turned into a marsupial.

Her brother saw this and told his sister to come back, but his sister did not listen. When her brother spoke, she replied, "You told me to grate the sweet potatoes, so the axe cut my finger."

The sister told the brother that she was troubled, so she had turned into a marsupial. Later, she told her brother to return home and not to worry about her. The brother left his sister, but he was terribly worried. He began to cry and he cried all of the way home.

Stella Fabian
Simbu Province

B211.2.12K+. Speaking marsupial; D179.6K+W. Transformation: woman to marsupial; D642. Transformation to escape difficult situation; D950. Magic tree; P253. Sister and brother

Why Food and Game are Plentiful at Wanwan

(Wantok 985, May 20, 1993, page 19)

Long, long ago, in Kaple [**Klaplei**] Village, in the Nuku area of **Sandaun** [Province], there lived a *masalai* [**Mehek** People]. The *masalai* liked to make his home in a little area called Okumborbor. He searched for a stick for a while, then he saw a man and his two wives adorning themselves to go to a festival.

After the festival, the married couple [threesome] returned to their house and the *masalai* man followed them there. When they arrived at the house, the man left his two wives. Then he went back to the festival grounds and his two wives went to hunt for fish and crayfish in the river.

The *masalai* man saw that the women's husband had left, so he transformed himself into their husband, and he went to look for them by the river. The women were surprised to see him, so they asked him whether he had already returned from the festival grounds. The *masalai* lied, telling them that he had become tired of the festival and that he had returned.

Later, he asked the women where they had left the children, so they showed him the place where the children were located . He went to the place where the two children were sleeping and he pretended to [watch] them. The two mothers kept their heads towards the river and worked at hunting for fish and crayfish.

Before long, the *masalai* man began eating the children's fingers and the children cried. So, he shouted for the children's mothers to come and give milk to them.

When the mothers came to give milk to the children, they found out that the children had no fingers. They thought and talked a lot.

Before long, a frog [jumped] across the river, so one mother went to see why the river was dirty. When she arrived there, she saw that it was a frog that had done this. She was angry and just wanted to kill the frog, but the frog told her, "You can't kill me yet. You think that that man is your husband, right? If he eats your two children, then he'll also eat you two mothers."

Then he told one woman to go fetch a kind of tree leaf. The mother put one at the source of the river, and one at the mouth of the river.

The frog performed a song and dance upon the two leaves, then the leaves began fishing in the river. The *masalai* man saw the leaves and thought that the women were still there, but no, they had returned to the [village].

After he swallowed the two children, he shouted down to the river, but there was no reply. So, he went down to check on the two women. He swallowed the two leaves, then he began sniffing the trail that the two women had followed until he also arrived at the village.

When the women saw that the *masalai* was following them, they shut the door and beat the signal drum to call their husband. At this time, the *masalai* surrounded their house.

The men at the festival grounds heard the beating of the signal drum, and they explained this to the women's husband. When he received this message, he took his brother-in-law, and they ran towards the village. The women's husband very quickly went inside the house and took a multi-pronged spear. He told his wives to throw a ripe coconut at the place where he stood.

The *masalai* heard the noise of the coconut and he followed it to where the man was standing. He was shocked when the man buried the spear directly into the *masalai*'s chest. The *masalai* was surprised and tried to turn back, but no, the brother-in-law put another one into his chest.

After they shot him, the *masalai* got up and ran away to a river with the spear pieces. He wanted to hide, but the river was too small, so he walked and walked until he arrived at a big river.

The man and his brother-in-law followed the *masalai* until they arrived at the place where the *masalai* was hiding. Then the two of them returned to the village and explained to the village men what had happened. They returned and removed the water from where the *masalai* was hiding.

At this time, a rat saw the *masalai* man and told him, "Follow me and we'll go along my trail." The *masalai* heard the rat and followed the rat into hiding.

Afterwards, he climbed a tree and sat there. Then he saw two short men with their dogs approaching. The dogs smelled the *masalai* on top of the tree, so they barked from beneath the tree. The men heard this and thought that the dogs were barking at a wild pig. When they arrived, the *masalai* shouted down, telling the men to hold their dogs. The *masalai* descended, then the men made a stretcher and carried him.

They arrived at a river, then the men let the *masalai* down because they wanted to wash. However, the *masalai* told them that one must stay and watch him.

The men were afraid of this, so they both went down to wash. While they were still in the water, their two dogs bit the *masalai*'s balls. The poor *masalai* was in pain and

shouted, then the men ran back up. They took the *masalai*'s balls and sewed [or patched] them back.

Afterwards, they left and arrived at the house belonging to the two men. There, the *masalai* told them to make a big house for himself. When they finished the house, he told them to go hunt for wild game, starting with lizards and going on through wild pigs.

After they had hunted all of the game, the *masalai* took the game and smoked it at the front of the house. Later, he told them again to go search for sago palm trees and bring them there. After they finished the work, he told them again to fetch a pig to garnish the sago, but they had not yet eaten any of these things.

After it became dark, the *masalai* told them, "You two can't listen to anything that happens at night." So, the two of them just followed the *masalai*'s instructions. Before long, a strong wind, rain and earthquake arose and lasted until morning. When the two men awoke, the place had changed entirely.

The *masalai* woke up and told them to take three tree seeds where he threw them into the river, one at the source of the river, another in the middle, and another at the mouth.

After he did this, the *masalai* told them that henceforth, until much later, their forest and river would be completely filled with wild game and sago trees.

Now, they call this place Wanwan, and it is quite full of wild game and various kinds of sago trees.

Caspar Maino

Kimbe

West New Britain Province

A2582+. Why wild game is plentiful at particular place; B177.2. Magic frog; B211.2.9. Speaking rat; B211.7.1. Speaking frog; B130+. Frog gives warning; B437.1. Helpful rat; B493.1. Helpful frog; D40. Transformation to likeness of another person; D955. Magic leaf; D1781. Magic results from singing; D1781+. Magic results from dancing; D2142.1. Wind produced by magic; D2143.1. Rain produced by magic; D2148. Earth magically caused to quake; F490+. Masalai; F547.7+. Severed testicles reattached; G550. Rescue from ogre; K1910. Marital impostors; K1930. Treacherous impostors; P210. Husband and wife; P230. Parents and children; P253. Sister and brother; P263. Brother-in-law; Q53. Reward for rescue; Q141.2. Plentiful game animals (fish) as reward; R100. Rescues; R151. Husband rescues wife; R210. Escapes; R260. Pursuits; R311. Tree refuge; S110+. Eaten alive; S176.1. Mutilation: emasculation; T145.0.1. Polygyny; X712.3.1H. Injury to testicles

The *Masalai* of Sombore Time Came

(Wantok 986, May 27, 1993, page 20)

Long, long ago, the people of **Dengop** Village in the Kabwum area of **Morobe** Province, did not live well [**Selepet** People]. They were often afraid because a *masalai* ate them. The *masalai* dwelled in a place called Sombore, near Dengop village.

The *masalai* always would go to the village and hunt for people, then kill and eat them. The *masalai* would also go to the other villages of the Kabwum area and kill people. This *masalai* did this for a while, then finished off everyone.

At this time, there also lived an old woman, but the *masalai* had not seen her. The old woman saw that the *masalai* had killed everyone in the village, so she fled the village. She found a cave and went to hide in it.

She was terrified to travel, so she would just hide. During the day, she would sleep and rest, but at night, she would go make gardens and search for food.

One night, she left home and went to the garden to fetch food. She took all of the food, filling the net bag, then she brought it back home.

She sat and rested, then she took a cucumber from the net bag and peeled it. While she was peeling it, the knife cut her. Oh my, blood shot out, so the old woman cut two banana leaves and she let the blood fall upon the leaves. Afterwards, she tied up the banana leaves well and buried them by her home.

Two months later, she wanted to go work in the garden when she heard two babies crying by her home. She went to check and she saw two baby boys there. The old woman took them inside her home and gave them names. The name of the big brother was Ningum and the little brother was Sangina.

She took care of them until they grew big, when they knew how to make bows and arrows, and how to hunt for wild game in the forest. The poor old woman would tell them about the story of the *masalai*. She told them not to go near Sombore. Ningum and Sangum [Sangina] followed their old mother's instructions.

One time, they made a plan to kill the *masalai*. The big brother, Ningum, told the little brother, Sangina, that they would make bows and arrows.

The next day, they began making bows and arrows. They made very many, then they gathered them in one place. The next day, they took these arrows and the bows, then arranged them along the trail, beginning at their home and going all of the way to the *masalai*'s home.

They returned home and they did not talk to their old mother about what they would do. They slept, then in the morning, they returned to the *masalai*'s home. When they arrived at the *masalai*'s home, the *masalai* told them, "Oh my grandsons, how did you get here?"

After the *masalai* spoke, it went inside and changed its skin. The *masalai* transformed its skin into stone. The *masalai* walked and approached the two brothers, then began to fight with them.

They fought and fought, then the *masalai* began to win. All of the brothers' arrows were just spent because the *masalai*'s skin had become stone and they could not kill it. They fought and fought, then the *masalai* pushed them all of the way back to the old woman's home.

The old woman went outside. She saw the *masalai* fighting with her two sons and she was furious. "I told you two not to go near that place where the *masalai* dwells and you ignored what I said," the old woman told the two boys.

The poor old woman was furious, so she went inside her home, transformed into a bird and flew outside. She perched upon a stick that was near the home.

At this time, all of the brothers' spears were gone. The *masalai* told the two of them that they would stop fighting because first the *masalai* wanted to kill the bird. They would eat the bird, then later they could fight again. When the *masalai* raised its arm to take the bird, the little brother took his last arrow and shot it directly under the *masalai*'s arm. The arrow entered the *masalai*'s heart and the *masalai* fell down dead. They took the *masalai* and pulled it down to the Pumune [Pumine] River. The old woman had become a bird and she flew away completely, leaving them.

Dekenam Gololok

Mt. Hagen

Western Highlands Province

D150W. Transformation: woman to bird; D231+. Transformation: ogre to stone; F490+. Masalai; F495. Stone-spirit; G346. Devastating monster; G510.4+. Hero overcomes devastating ogre; G512.1+. Ogre killed with spear/arrow; N476.2. Man vulnerable only in armpits shot as he stretches his arms; P231. Mother and son; P251.5. Two brothers; R213. Escape from home; R315. Cave as refuge; S110. Murders; T534. Conception from blood; T587. Birth of twins; T685. Twins; W31. Obedience; W126. Disobedience; Z356. Unique survivor; Z210. Brothers as heroes

Two Brothers Ate Children by the Daee River

(Wantok 987, June 3, 1993, page 20)

Long, long ago, there was a big village that was near a river. The name of the river was Daee. Near this village, there lived two brothers. They made a house for themselves on the other side of the river. One thing that was wrong with the brothers was that they were cannibals.

One time, the villagers made a huge festival. Many clans from other villages came to the festival. These two brothers went to sing and dance fervently at the festival too.

In the morning, everyone traveled to the houses and villages. Then one little boy walked directly to the place where the two brothers lived.

The little boy wanted to defecate, so he had gone into the forest. However, the poor boy did not know that the two bad men were hiding there. The little boy was defecating when the big brother took a stone axe and put it directly to the boy's neck. The brothers took the boy and carried him to the house where they ate him.

His father and mother noticed that he had not returned to the house, so they began asking the other little boys and the other people of the village if they had seen him. When the people of the village discovered that he was lost, they all began searching for him, but they did not find him.

They lived for a while, then all of the little boys of the village disappeared. The two brothers often went to the village and killed each of the boys every day. Before long, the villagers found out that many boys of the village had just disappeared.

One time, the leader of the village beat the signal drum and everyone gathered. At this meeting, everyone revealed his or her worries. They wanted to know who it was that was stealing their children. OK, they planned a way to find out which man was taking their children.

Everyone in the village said that they would put the boys in one house, then shut the door and leave them inside. They planned to hide one old man to see what would happen to the boys.

In the morning, everyone in the village took something and went to work in the gardens. The old man stayed and kept watch on the house where they boys were staying. He stayed and watched the two brothers come and check out the whole house.

Very quietly, the old man left the house and walked towards the place where the signal drum was located. He took a piece of wood and beat the signal drum. When the two brothers heard the signal drum, they fled back to their house.

The villagers heard the signal drum from their gardens, so they ran back to the village. When they arrived at the village, the old man told the story of what he had seen. He called the names of the two brothers.

At this time, everyone in the village was angry and gnashed their teeth. All of the men told the women to cook food, then they would sit and eat. They fetched the fighting gear, then they went to the place where the two brothers lived.

The villagers surrounded the house where the two brothers were sleeping, then they lit the house on fire. The brothers found it very difficult to run outside. One just went underneath, but when he wanted to come up, no, he saw that the men were watching. The men took spears and shot him as the other brother burned with the house.

After this, all of the boys of the village lived well and they were no longer afraid to travel.

Sam Paul

Madang

Madang Province

G10. Cannibalism; G346. Devastating monster; K812. Victim burned in his own house (or hiding place); P210. Husband and wife; P231. Mother and son; P233. Father and son; P251.5. Two brothers; Q211. Murder punished; Q411. Death as punishment; Q414. Punishment: burning alive; R220. Flights; S112.0.2. House (hostel) burned with all inside; S139.4. Murder by mangling with axe

Pig Fat Created Lake Evai

(Wantok 988, June 10, 1993, page 20)

Long, long ago, there lived a young man with his sister in Siruki [**Sirunki**] Village, in **Enga** Province, but they never slept in the same house [**Enga** People]. The brother had his own small house in which to sleep. The sister slept in another house.

They never sat and told stories. It was their custom that it was forbidden for them to look at each other's face. So, they never slept in the same house, and they never sat or ate together.

The sister would work in the garden while the brother would travel in the forest, hunting for wild game. When the sister returned from the garden, she would share some sweet potatoes and put them on top of a table. When the brother returned from the forest, he would carry some game and leave it on the table, then take the sweet potatoes that the sister had left for him.

One morning, the brother left his sister there, then he traveled in the forest, hunting for marsupials (*kapul*). He left the house, then he went into the very deep forest. The brother hunted for marsupials for a while, then he saw a huge marsupial sitting on a tree.

Very quietly, he took an arrow and put it in the bowstring, then he shot down the marsupial. He wanted to hold the marsupial, but no, the marsupial got up again and fled.

The marsupial ran, following the trail that the young boy had taken, going all of the way to the house.

The marsupial approached the house and turned into a man, then he went to the house where the man's sister lived. The sister thought that it was her brother, and asked him why he had come to the house. The marsupial told her that he wanted to marry her.

When she heard this, she was terribly ashamed because she thought that it was her brother asking her to marry. The marsupial stayed and slept with her, then the marsupial left her and fled into the forest.

Her brother did not know what had happened. He returned from the forest and took some marsupials to leave on the table, then he saw that there were no sweet potatoes there.

In the morning, he went to check the table. He saw that there were still no sweet potatoes there and that the marsupials were still there too. He thought that his sister had become unconscious, so he went to check the house.

The sister saw her brother coming, so she went to hide in the corner of the house because she thought that her brother wanted to sleep with her again. The brother asked her what was wrong and why she was angry. However, she did not reply, so the brother just killed a pig and cooked it.

He divided the pig and gave some to his sister, but his sister did not want to take it. The brother was angry and told his sister that he would leave her if she did not eat the pork.

The brother saw that the sister was not eating the pork, so he took his things and fled to Siruki. His sister shouted and said that she would eat the pork, but the brother did not hear her and just walked away.

He went to the top of a mountain and sat there. While he sat, the pig fat went down to the ground. The fat descended and made the place wet.

The pig fat descended until the place became a lake. The sister came and saw that the water had risen and covered her brother. At this time, the sister was very troubled and she became a bird.

Now if you go to Siruki, you will see this lake there. Now, they call this Lake Evai and many birds often fly by the water.

Peter Misinikkail

Londol

Enga Province

A920.1.0.1. Origin of particular lake; B871.2+. Giant marsupial; C312+. Tabu: brother looking at sister; C313+. Tabu: sister looking at brother; D150W. Transformation: woman to bird; D310+M. Transformation: marsupial to man; D476+. Transformation: grease to lake; K1930. Treacherous impostors; P253. Sister and brother; R220. Flights; R260. Pursuits; T415. Brother-sister incest; T471. Rape

The Ghost of Woginara Sent Soup

(Wantok 989, June 17, 1993, page 20)

Long, long ago, there was a ghost woman in Woginara Village, **East Sepik** Province [**Mountain Arapesh** People]. The villagers were often afraid because the ghost woman would kill their children.

One night, the moon was brightly lit and all of the boys of the village went outside to play. Before long, the ghost woman came and took one to go and eat. The ghost returned and took another one. She thought he was delicious, so she returned to take another one away. She did this for a while that night. The ghost killed very many boys.

In the morning, the parents began searching for their children around the village. They went and asked the other children and they said that the ghost had eaten them.

One time, all of the leaders of the village gathered and decided to kill the ghost woman. They thought of digging a hole, then when the ghost came, she would fall inside the hole and then they would shoot her with arrows.

The next day, the leaders gathered all of the big boys and told them to dig a hole. After they dug the hole, they put some dry wood on top of the hole, then they put dry leaves on top of that.

When it was nearly dark, the leaders told the women to heat stones in fires. Afterwards, they called the boys and told them to play far away from the hole lest they fall inside of it.

The villagers stayed and saw the moon rise and shine brightly. The little boys left their houses and went down to play. The ghost woman did not know what the villagers had done.

While the boys were playing, the men took bows and arrows, then they watched by the side. They wanted to see, but no, their eyes were blind to the ghost woman. The ghost saw the boys playing and went to get one of them. However, she missed and went directly down into the hole. Quickly, the men took the arrows and shot her. The women took the hot stones and put them on top of her, killing her.

After this, the parents of Woginara Village were very happy because they were no longer afraid of the ghost. Their children also lived happily.

Philomina Rayson

Kimbe

West New Britain Province

E421.1. Invisible ghosts; E425.1. Revenant as woman; E437.4. Ghost laid under stone; E446.2. Ghost laid by burning body; G11.10. Cannibalistic spirits; K735. Capture in pitfall; P230. Parents and children; Q211. Murder punished; Q414. Punishment: burning alive; S112. Burning to death

Two Sisters Turned into the Stones of Wurup
(Wantok 990, June 24, 1993, page 18)

Long, long ago, there lived two sisters in **Wurup** Village, in the **Western Highlands** Province [**Hagen** People]. Their names were Tikal and Mukal.

One time, they wanted to go search for forest vines for making net bags. OK, they cooked some sweet potatoes, put them in a net bag, and went towards the forest. They arrived in the forest, then they began cutting vines for making net bags.

Oh my, they cut many vines. They did this for a while, then they arrived at a stream. The name of this stream is Kuna. They went to the water, then they put their things down and rested. Afterwards, they went down to the water and bathed to cool their bodies.

The two sisters finished bathing, then they warmed their bodies in the sun. Later, they took their things and went back to the forest to search for more vines. They went and began cutting vines again.

At this time, Tikal and Mukal forgot completely about checking [the position of] the sun. When they looked up, they saw that the sun was setting. Also, the place where they were cutting vines was far away from their house.

They walked and walked, then they saw a boulder. They arrived at the place where the boulder was located, then they put their things down and rested. While they rested, they took the sweet potatoes that they had cooked and they ate.

However, they did not know that this stone was a *masalai* place. They sat well, gorged themselves, and told stories exuberantly. One sister put her back to the stone and looked towards the forest. The other also sat and put her back to the stone. She looked towards the village. They sat like this for a very long time, telling stories and eating.

When they finished the food, they wanted to get up and take their things. But no, something pulled them back to the stone. They felt as if something like the wind was pulling them stuck to the stone.

They tried very hard to get up, but something pulled them back to the stone. They did this for a while, but the power of the *masalai* was stronger and pulled them, making them completely affixed to the stone.

At this time, the sisters felt as if all of their strength was gone, so they began to cry. They knew that they could not return to the village, so they just cried.

Before long, they turned into stones. Now if you go to Wurup Village, you will see that these two stones are still there. The names of the stones are Tikal and Mukal.

Joseph Ten Neringa

Mt. Hagen

Western Highlands Province

[There are similar ancestor stories in *Wantok* #149 and 344. The one in #344 is also from Wurup. Vicedom (1977: 70) reports a similar story with the characters Ndekatl and Mokatl.]

A1617. Origin of place-name; D231W. Transformation: woman to stone; D1412. Magic object pulls person into it; F490+. Masalai; F495. Stone-spirit; P252.1. Two sisters

Brothers Created the Dua Konage Clans
(Wantok 991, July 1, 1993, page 20)

Long, long ago, there lived a man named Konga in Dua Village, **Simbu** Province. One time, he thought of going to hunt for fish in a stream. He went to Erenihle Stream and he fished. He caught fish for a while, then he saw a pandanus (*marita*) fruit in the stream. A flood had carried the fruit down and deposited it on the side of the stream.

Immediately, Konga took it and brought it to the house. When he arrived at the house, Konga took the fruit and put it on top of the house front.

The next day, he wanted to go outside, but no, he saw a little girl at the top of the house front. Old Konga went and took the girl, then he carried her inside the house.

Old Konga took the girl and looked after her. Konga gave her the name Ambu. They lived together for a while, until she became a grown woman.

Ambu found that there were no other marriageable men in Konga. So, they lived together and raised three sons. The names of these children were Giunde, Nuglai, and Pagua. They lived with their parents until they became big men.

When they saw that they could find their own food, they left their parents and went to make their own houses. They each lived in their own house. They made their own gardens and they hunted for their own food.

The three brothers married and they raised very many children. The three brothers created three clans that live in **Dua Konage** Village. The clan created by Nuglai is called **Nuglaikane**. The clan that came from Giunde is called

Giundekane [**Giunakane**], and the clan that came from Pagau is called **Pagaukane** [**Kuman** People].

Today, these three clans usually live in Dua Konage Village. The name Dua Konage comes from the name of father Konga. Now if you go to this village, you will see that there are four entire clans. Another clan came from the side of the three men's mother and it is called **Kongambu**.

Yakson Yaltainde Goiye
Kerowagi High School
Simbu Province

A1617. Origin of place-name; A1640+. Origin of Giundekane Clan; A1640+. Origin of Nuglaikane Clan; A1640+. Origin of Pagaukane Clan; D431.4+G. Transformation: pandanus fruit to girl; P210. Husband and wife; P230. Parents and children; P231. Mother and son; P233. Father and son; P271. Foster father; P251.6.1. Three brothers; P275+. Foster daughter; T100. Marriage; T411+. Foster father-daughter incest

The Old Men's Dispute Created a Pond

(Wantok 992, July 8, 1993, page 19)

Long, long ago, there lived two old men. Their names were Telepe Papeu and Telepe Puhulih. They lived on a mountain that was near the sea. One time, Telepe Puhulih worked at making a net for catching fish. He shouted for Telepe Papeu to come see him.

So, Papeu left his house and walked to the other side of the mountain to see his friend, Telepe Puhulih. When he arrived at Telepe Papeu's house, he saw his friend making the net. Puhulih asked Papeu why he had called for him to see him.

However, Papeu lied and said that he had not called Puhulih to come see him. They talked for a very long time. Papeu completely concealed that he had called Puhulih. So, they forgot about this and began to tell various stories.

OK, they told stories for a long time, then Telepe Puhulih felt thirsty. He asked Telepe Papeu to give him water. At this time, Papeu was reluctant to give good drinking water, so he gave him saltwater to drink.

When Puhulih drank the water, the poor man thought that the water tasted unusual. He tasted the salt and he knew that his friend had given him saltwater to drink.

Puhulih was furious at his friend, but he did not tell him that he was angry. Puhulih knew that his friend had good drinking water, but that he had hidden it.

They told stories for a while, then Papeu told Puhulih that he would go to the sea and catch fish for himself to bring back. He told Papeu to wait until he returned.

When Puhulih saw that Papeu had gone out to sea, he went inside Papeu's house and searched for the place where the drinking water was hidden. He searched and searched, then he saw the water and he carried it away to his house.

His friend worked hard at fishing and he did not know what had happened at the house. He threw a spear at a fish and the spear became completely stuck. Then he knew that something had gone wrong at the house.

Immediately, he ran back to the house. When he arrived at the house, he saw that the water was not there. Papeu knew that his friend had taken it and he was very troubled.

Papeu knew that he was wrong to have lied to his friend, so he tied up a pig and carried it away. However, when Puhulih came, he was not happy. He was still angry because his friend had tricked him and that he had drunk saltwater.

Puhulih asked Papeu to give back the pot of water, but Papeu did not want to do this. They went back and forth, then they began to pull the water pot and the water spilled to the ground.

Judy Lilih
Ramu [Sugar]
Morobe Province

A920.1.0.1. Origin of particular lake; D1084. Magic spear; D1317.16. Magic spear warns of danger; K300. Thefts and cheats—general; K2297. Treacherous friend; N350. Accidental loss of property; P310. Friendship; Q276. Stinginess punished; Q595. Loss or destruction of property as punishment; W157. Dishonesty; W152. Stinginess

Ike's Mistake Stopped the Gulmo People from Hunting for Wild Game at Night

(Wantok 993, July 15, 1993, page 20)

Long, long ago, there lived a man in Gulmo Village in Western Province. The man's name was Ike. He was married and had four children.

One time, Ike went to the forest to hunt for wild game. He took his bow and arrows, a small stone axe, and a taro that his wife had cooked and given him to eat in the forest.

He hunted and hunted for game. He went very far from the village. Ike did not tire, he kept hunting for game. It was nearly dark when he shot a pig. Ike was unconcerned, so he carried the pig, walking back towards the village. At this time, it was completely dark.

Ike walked and walked. He did not know that a snake had its mouth open. He went along and he went inside the snake's mouth. When the snake shut its mouth, Ike felt that the place was wet. So, he cast his hands about to check and he found out that he was inside the snake's belly.

The scoundrel was not worried. He took the piece of taro that he was carrying and began to eat. After he ate, he slept. When dawn was nearly breaking, he took the small stone axe and began to cut the snake's belly.

He worked diligently at cutting the snake's belly. He did not know that the snake was in pain and throwing itself about on the ground. Ike thought of his own life and worked very hard at cutting the snake's belly.

Ike kept at it, then he saw light coming. He knew that he had cut through the snake's skin to the outside. Immediately, he held the snake's liver and cut it, then he went outside.

He ran and ran, up a mountain, then he looked down to the place where the snake was located. He saw that it was perfectly cleared because when Ike had cut the snake's belly, the snake had thrown itself about and broken all of the small trees that were nearby.

OK, he left the snake and the pig there, then he ran back to the village. He told the story to the villagers about what had happened to him. Then he took the villagers and they went to see the place where the snake was located.

The villagers saw the snake and they did not believe it because the snake was gigantic. They carried the snake and the pig towards the village.

When they arrived at the village, they made two bonfires, then cooked the pig and the snake. The villagers did not eat the pig and the snake, they let the fires burn them up completely.

So now, if you go to **Gulmo** Village, in the Tabubil area of **Western** Province, you will not see men going to hunt for wild game at night [**Tifal** or **Ningirrum** People?].

David Kworin
Western Province

B875.1. Giant serpent; C755.6+. Tabu: hunting at night; F911.7. Serpent swallows man; F912.2. Victim kills swallower from within by cutting; P210. Husband and wife; P230. Parents and children

Sons Married Their Mother
and Raised Grandchildren

(Wantok 994, July 22, 1993, page 19)

Long, long ago, in the little village of Annapose [**Ana** and **Posei** Villages], by Morobe Patrol Post in **Morobe** Province, there lived a married couple [**Yekora** People].

The married couple made a big taro garden. The taro garden was bigger than those of all of the other people in the village. One time when the couple was [in the village], a wild pig went into the garden and finished off all of the taros.

They had not made a fence, so the pig went in and ate all of the taros. The next day, they went to the garden and made a trap to kill the pig.

In the very early morning, the woman awakened her husband to go to the garden. He was tired and continued to sleep, so she took a net bag and went to the garden. When she arrived in the garden, she saw that the trap had captured a gigantic pig.

She ran back to the village to fetch her husband. He took his spear and his stone axe, then he followed his wife to the garden. She ran first and he ran after her.

However, when she arrived at the garden, she did not see the pig in the trap. She looked and looked, then she saw a man standing in the garden. The man saw her running and asked her where she was going. He said, "I'm not a pig. I'm a man and I want you to follow me."

She followed the man. The poor woman's real husband did not know what had happened. He arrived afterwards and saw that his wife had followed another man, so he followed them.

The woman and the man walked and walked, then they arrived at a cave. OK, the man took a piece of wood and beat it on the side of the cave. The door opened and they went inside.

The woman's real husband came later and tried to go inside, but he did not see the entrance. He stood and just cried, then he turned and went back to the village. When he arrived at the village, he told everyone about the place, then they went there and tried to break a hole in the stone. However, they were unable to do so and they returned to the village.

The pig who had turned into a man took the woman, then they married then raised two sons. They just lived there, and their father prohibited them from going up the betel palm tree that was near their house.

Whenever the married couple went to work in the garden, their father would prohibit them from climbing the betel palm. The father himself would climb and remove leaves from the betel palm to give to the two of them. The two boys would tie the leaves to their legs and arms, then sing and dance.

However one time, the father forgot about taking leaves to give to them. The brothers stayed there for a while, then the big brother told his little brother that he would climb the betel palm and see what their father had forbidden to them. The big brother went up the betel palm and tried to look down to the Mou River. He saw women and children bathing and playing in the river. He descended and told his little brother what he had seen.

They took hand drums, then they sang and danced. The father and mother returned from the garden, then the father saw the boys singing and dancing fervently. He knew that he had been wrong, so he called to the two children. He told them that the people whom they had seen below in the Mou River were their mother's family.

At night, when they ate, the father took all of the woman's belongings. Then his two sons put them in one place. In the morning, he told them to go to their mother's village.

Before they departed, he told them to tell everyone in the village to make a house for themselves on top of a mountain. This was because the Mou River would flood from the father going to the source of the river and crying for his two sons.

When they arrived at the village, they told the people of the village to make a house on top of a mountain. However, the men told the woman who had married the pig that she was lying. So at night, they slept and a huge flood arose, breaking all of the houses and carrying them away.

The next day, the woman and her two sons went down from the mountain and made a house in the old village. They lived there by themselves, married, and raised many children at Annapose Village.

R. Nirry Mansome

Lae

Morobe Province

A1011. Local deluges; A1012.1. Flood from tears; B631. Human offspring from marriage to animal; B650+. Marriage to pig in human form; B871.1.2. Giant boar; D336.1M. Transformation: pig to man; D1552.1. Mountain opens at blow of divining rod; J652. Inattention to warnings; P210. Husband and wife; P230. Parents and children; P231. Mother and son; P233. Father and son; P251.5. Two brothers; R260. Pursuits; T100. Marriage; T412. Mother-son incest; W126. Disobedience

Trouble Caused the Dogs to Kill a *Masalai* Pig

(Wantok 995, July 29, 1993, page 20)

Long, long ago, in a village, there lived a big *masalai* pig. The *masalai* pig's name was Makrumbi. *Masalai* pig Makrumbi lived in a cave.

Every morning, the pig would wake up and go to all of the villages, then break the villagers' houses. The pig would kill everyone to eat. Makrumbi did this for a while, killing very many people.

To avoid death, people would only cook food and eat at night. In the very early morning, near dawn, they would awake, cook food again, and then eat. Before it became completely light, they would go down to a lake by the village, then turn over their canoes. They would go underneath their canoes and hide.

In the morning, when Makrumbi left the cave and went to a village, the pig would hunt for and kill people, then eat them. In the afternoon, the pig would return to the cave. When the pig arrived at the cave and fell asleep, a tremendous earthquake would arise. Then people would know that Makrumbi was sleeping. They would go outside and to the village, then cook food and eat. Afterwards they would sleep. In the morning [when] Makrumbi would awake, a big earthquake would arise again. Immediately, people would return down to the lake, turn over their canoes and hide underneath the water.

The people of this village always did this. One night, when Makrumbi went to the cave and slept, a woman went to her house and cooked some sago. Her dog slept by the fire and lusted for the sago that she was cooking. She cooked a piece of sago and threw it towards her dog, then she scolded, "You too. You don't want to go fight with that *masalai* pig and kill it. Your work is just to stay there and come look at the food."

After she scolded her dog, the dog took the piece of sago and went to the spirit house. The dog beat the signal drum and sent a message here and there for all of the dogs of the village. All of the dogs came and gathered at the spirit house. The dog repeated what its mistress had said scoldingly. Their leader heard this and told the other dogs, "Don't worry, break that piece of sago into little pieces and we'll eat it. Then we'll all sleep in the spirit house. Tomorrow morning, we'll go block the path of the *masalai* pig Makrumbi, then fight with it."

After their leader spoke, they ate the sago and slept in the spirit house. When it was nearly dawn, they all went and blocked Makrumbi's path then they watched. Makrumbi awoke and a big earthquake arose. When Makrumbi arrived, they fought with the pig. They fought from the morning until the afternoon. Makrumbi killed many of the dogs and also ruined many of their bodies. However, they were unconcerned. They fought with the pig for a while, then a scrawny dog just got up and jumped into Makrumbi's anus. The dog bit Makrumbi's liver and Makrumbi died. All of the dogs returned to the village and barked around. A man heard them and [tossed] his canoe, then he ran to the village. When he arrived at the village, he saw that all of the dogs had blood on their mouths and bodies.

The dogs saw him and barked around, then they ran to the place where Makrumbi had died. He saw this, then he returned to the village and beat the signal drum. Everyone heard the drum, then they left the lake and went to the village. The man told them that the dogs had killed Makrumbi. So, they butchered Makrumbi and made a big feast for the dogs.

After this time, they often lived well in the houses, cooked food and ate. Also, they never scolded their dogs again.

Robin Gawi

Madang

Madang Province

A2850+. Why dogs are not scolded at particular place; B16.1.4.1. Giant devastating boar; B211.1.7. Speaking dog; B241.2.7. King of dogs; B421. Helpful dog; F402.6.4.1. Spirits live in caves; F490+. Masalai; F531.3.8.5. Earthquake as giant falls down; F912.2+. Dog enters giant pig's anus and kills pig by biting liver; G346. Devastating monster; G352.2. Wild boar as ogre; G512.9.1. Ogre killed by helpful dogs; L315+. Scrawny dog overcomes giant pig; Q53. Reward for rescue; R310. Refuges; V112.1. Spirit huts; X740.1H+. Symbolic pedicatory rape

A Father Played a Trick and Slept with His Daughter

(Wantok 996, August 5, 1993, page 19)

Long, long ago, in Tiria [**Tiri**] Village, in the Hagen area of **Western Highlands** Province, there lived a man with his wife and daughter [**Hagen** People].

This family made their house near a mountain that was far away from their big village. The daughter's name was Yara, she was about twenty years old.

Yara was a very stylish woman, and all of the young men of the village just died for her. Many were in love, and spoke about marrying her, and she was agreeable. However, her father did not want Yara to marry. The father was a little jealous of the young men of the village.

One time, the father lied to Yara and her mother that his eyes were about to come out. The father went to fetch leaves from the forest, then he put them on his eyes and he screamed and cried. One time, he asked the two of them to make something to fix his eyes. However, they said that there was nothing to fix them.

The father really pretended that his eyes were coming out, so he screamed terribly. They were sorry for him, and

came closer. Then the father told them to go to the graveyard and to listen to what the dead tell them.

They listened to him and walked away. Quietly, the father left the house and followed a short cut, arriving at the graveyard. He watched and saw them coming.

Then the father changed his voice and began speaking. He said, "*Glapa ne lemin tanga o, glapa ne lemin tanga o.*" In my language, this means, "Father must sleep with child, father must sleep with child."

The two of them listened and returned to the house. The father also followed the trail that he had taken, then he arrived quickly at the house and pretended to sleep. When he heard them arrive at the house, he began crying loudly and screaming terribly.

The mother and daughter were ashamed to reveal what they had heard, and did not want to tell the father. However at this time, the father screamed terribly and said that his eyes were about to come out and that he would die.

OK, the mother told the daughter to tell the father what they had heard at the graveyard. The daughter was ashamed, but she saw her father crying and went closer to him, then she told him what they had heard. The daughter told her father that the dead had said that she must sleep with him.

The father got up and told her that whatever the dead had told them must become true. If it did not, he would die. So the father told the mother to go fetch a taro leaf. The daughter's body would be covered with the leaf, then the father could sleep with her. The mother saw the father sleeping with the daughter, then she left the house, fleeing for good.

Tanu Wati

Nebilyer

Mt. Hagen

Western Highlands Province

K1315. Seduction by impostor; K1833. Disguise as ghost; P210. Husband and wife; P232. Mother and daughter; P234. Father and daughter; R213. Escape from home; R227. Wife flees from husband; T10. Falling in love; T411. Father-daughter incest; V61.3+. Dead buried; W157. Dishonesty; W181. Jealousy

Two Snake Brothers Married Two Sisters

(Wantok 997, August 12, 1993, page 20)

Long, long ago, there where two snakes that lived on top of Mount Temunong. The names of these two snakes were Nang and Mari. They were not real snakes. Sometimes, they would turn into men and go around hunting for food. Nang and Mari were brothers and they lived with their grandfather.

One time, the two of them heard a story that there would be a big festival coming to **Tawambo** [**Kosorong** People, **Morobe** Province]. When they heard that the festival was coming, they vomited adornments for the festival and two hand drums.

When they adorned their bodies, their old grandfather told a rat to dig the earth, then the two of them could go to the other side of the mountain.

The rat just began digging the earth until it arrived at the festival grounds. The people of the village did not know that the rat hole was underground. They sang and danced passionately at the festival.

The old grandfather was not an ordinary man either, he was a man who had much sorcery. At this village, there also lived two sisters. Their names were Zining and Rungu.

The two boys' grandfather took some tree bark, then spat on their hand drums and threw some charms on top of them. Afterwards, the three of them walked swiftly together along the trail that the rat had made.

When they arrived at the festival site, the two scoundrels put their hands on top of the hand drums and began to raise the dust of the festival grounds.

At this time, their hand drums sounded completely unusual. The two sisters sang and danced, then they heard the hand drums calling their names. When the brothers beat the hand drums, one beat and called Zining's name and the other called Rungu's name.

The two sisters arrived and searched for where the drums were beating. When they approached the two brothers, they grabbed Nang and Mari, then they went to their village.

They arrived at the house, then they married and lived together. However, one thing that the brothers had not done was to tell the sisters that sometimes they would turn into snakes.

One time, the brothers went into the forest to hunt for food. They left their grandfather with the two women. They stayed for a while, then the grandfather turned into a snake and lay there.

The sisters wanted to go to the house. They saw the snake lying there and they thought that it was a real snake. Quickly, they held the snake and threw him into the fire, then the fire burned and killed him.

In the afternoon, the brothers returned from the house and saw that their grandfather was on top of the fire. Oh my, they were very troubled, so they hanged the two

women. Later, they took spears and shot each other, then the entire family died together.

Charle [Charles] Meawong
Port Moresby
National Capital District

B212. Animal understands human speech; B437.1. Helpful rat; B656.2. Marriage to serpent in human form; D191M. Transformation: man to serpent (snake); D391M. Transformation: serpent (snake) to man; D952. Magic tree-bark; D1001. Magic spittle; D1355.1.1. Love-producing song; D1355.1.1+. Love-producing dance; D1355.3. Love charm; D1711. Magician; D1900. Love induced by magic; F562.7K. People live in mountain top; F639.1.1. Mighty digger of tunnels; F721.1. Underground passages; F910+. Extraordinary vomitings; M451.1. Death by suicide; P214.1+. Husband commits suicide (dies) on death of wife; P251.5. Two brothers; P252.1. Two sisters; P260. Relations by law; P263. Brother-in-law; P264. Sister-in-law; P291. Grandfather; Q211.6. Killing an animal revenged; Q413. Punishment: hanging; S112. Burning to death; T10. Falling in love; T100. Marriage

Why Dogs and Marsupials Are No Longer Friends

(Wantok 998, August 19, 1993, page 19)

Long, long ago, in the **Kiunga** area of **Western** Province, the dogs and marsupials (*kapul*) lived in one village and were usually good friends [**Awin** People]. They lived and went about very well. They often ate well and fights never came amongst themselves.

One time, the marsupials went hunting for wild game in the forest, then the dogs stayed in the village and watched the house. At this time, the dogs were completely lazy and never did a thing. They just slept until the afternoon.

When the marsupials returned to the village, they let the dogs sleep. When they looked around, they saw that the dogs had not cut any firewood, nor fetched any water. Because of this, the marsupials were completely furious.

At this time, the marsupials were terribly hungry. They thought that the dogs had cooked some food and prepared it. When they found out that there was no food and that the things in the house were not straightened, they were completely irate.

Then the leader of the marsupials began scolding the dogs. The marsupial called the dogs lazy and gluttonous. When the marsupial said this, all of the other marsupials gave their support and scolded the dogs.

The dogs listened to this and were not happy about what the marsupials had done to them. The leader of the dogs went out of the house and began arguing with the leader of the marsupials. They argued heatedly for a while, then the other dogs also supported their leader.

At this time, everyone was agitated and did not waste time. Their thoughts were to shoot directly into fighting. Before long, the two groups began fighting. At this time, the marsupials were terribly afraid and no longer returned to the village.

So now, you can see that the marsupials only live in the deep forest and that the dogs live in the village. This is true until today, you cannot see marsupials and dogs together. When the dogs see the marsupials, they never let them go.

David Kworin

Daru

Western Province

A2433.2.1+. Why marsupial lives in forest; A2433.3.2+. Why dog lives in village; A2494.4+. Enmity between dog and marsupial; B241.2+. King of marsupials; B241.2.7. King of dogs; B263+. War between dogs and marsupials; P310. Friendship; R213. Escape from home; W111. Laziness; W125. Gluttony

The Python's Child Ruined a Village

(Wantok 999, August 26, 1993, page 22)

Long, long ago, the people of a village went into the forest and cut it to make a new garden. After they cut the forest, they saw a big python lying on top of a tree.

Oh my, when they saw this snake, they were very happy and they cut down the tree. They killed the snake, then they carried it to the village. When they arrived at the village, they butchered the snake and divided it for everyone to eat.

They gave the snake's head to an old woman. The old woman lived with her little grandchild. The old woman took the python's head and put it inside a clay pot, then she put it on top of the house.

The old woman took a net bag and went to the garden to fetch taros. She told her little grandchild to watch the snake's head. The old woman wanted to fetch taros so that she could make some nice soup.

At this time, the python's child was searching for its father and went to find him. The snake-child went to all of the places and asked the men whether they had seen its father. The child asked and asked, then the child arrived at this village and saw the boy at the house.

The python's child told the boy that it was searching for its father. The little boy told the snake that the villagers had killed and eaten him. Then he told the snake that he and his grandmother were holding the head.

The snake asked him whether they had eaten the head and the boy said no. He said that he was waiting for his grandmother to return from the garden, then they would eat.

The python's child told the little boy to show the head. When the snake saw the head, it told the boy that it would carry it to the house.

However, before the snake left, the snake told the little boy to take his entire family to the top of the mountain. This was because something would happen at night.

The python's child carried its father's head to the house and called for all of the snakes to gather and meet. The snake-child told them what had happened. They listened to the story and were terribly worried.

The child asked which men would go to the village and fight with the villagers. Very quietly, one snake that often kills rats and small game said that it would go.

Late at night, when everyone in the village was sleeping, the rotten scoundrel left all of the snakes and went to the village. No one in the village knew about this. Everyone was dead asleep. Only the little boy and his family knew and they went to stay on top of the mountain.

The snake went to the middle of the village and broke the earth. Later, the snake leapt again, and water shot up, breaking all of the houses. The people of the village were surprised, but they had no chance to flee. The water carried all of them away and only the little boy's family survived.

Yoso Untsi

Lae

Morobe Province

A1011. Local deluges; B211.6.1. Speaking snake (serpent); D2151.8. Magic flood; J1050. Attention to warnings; P230. Parents and children; P292. Grandmother; Q211.6. Killing an animal revenged; Q428. Punishment: drowning; S131. Murder by drowning

A Child's Worries [Were Caused By] Blame

(Wantok 1000, September 2, 1993, page 22)

Long, long ago, there lived a man with his wife and son. They lived in **Disige** Village, by the Yalumet River, in the Kabwum District of **Morobe** Province [**Selepet** People].

The family usually lived very well. They did not fight among themselves and they never let their troubles collect. They usually just thought about working in the garden and hunting for wild game in the forest.

One time, the father and mother were tired of going to weed their new yam garden. The father called for the son and told him to go weed the garden. The son listened to what his father said and went to the garden.

Before he left or took the garden equipment, the father called to him and told him some things that he must do when he arrived in the garden. The father told the boy to weed all of the young yams. However, he prohibited him from weeding the big yams. He completely forbade this, telling him not to weed the bases of these yams.

The boy listened and took the work equipment, then he took off for the garden. However, in the middle of the trail, he forgot and said that he would go weed the bases of the big yams first.

When he arrived at the garden, he went to the old garden and weeded the bases of the big yams. He missed at weeding and cut the sprout of a big yam, then the yam's leaves dried. When he saw this, he left and went to work in the new garden.

The boy was terrified when he went back to the house. He did not tell his father and mother. In the afternoon, the father went around the garden and saw that the big yam was not there. He saw that the yam's leaves were dry. The father gnashed his teeth and returned to the house.

The father shouted at his son for a while, scolding him strongly. The boy listened to his father's scolding and was terribly worried. He did not want to live with this married couple any more.

The next day, the boy took a bow and arrows, then went to the forest. He told his parents that he would go hunt for birds. The parents stayed and they noticed that the boy did not return quickly to the house. The father then knew that the boy had run away from them, so he followed him. The father went and saw that his son had shot birds and put them along the trail. The father took the birds and followed his footprints.

The boy saw his father approaching, so he turned into a bird. The father saw this, so he too turned into a bird and flew towards the boy. The boy was angry and turned into a wild betel pepper in the forest.

The mother waited for them for a while, then she noticed that they had not returned. She turned into a stone. Now, if you go to this place, you will see a stone there.

Deveyong Navoion

Boroko

National Capital District

A974. Rocks from transformation of people to stone; A977.5. Origin of particular rock; D150B. Transformation: boy to bird; D150M. Transformation: man to bird; D231W. Transformation: woman to stone; D423+. Transformation: bird to betel pepper plant; P210. Husband and wife; P231. Mother and son; P233. Father and son; R213. Escape from home; R260. Pursuits; W126. Disobedience

A Woman Caused the Death of Two Brothers

(Wantok 1001, September 9, 1993, page 20)

Long, long ago, on a small island in the **North Solomons** Province area, there lived two brothers. Their parents had died while they were still there. The two boys did not have a garden and this place had no other people to help them.

One time, they left the house and went around the island. They arrived on the other side of the island and saw a small island in the middle of the sea. The small island had just one house.

The brothers turned back and went to their house to fetch a canoe. They pulled the canoe down to the beach, and then they paddled towards the island. When they arrived at the island, they pulled the canoe ashore. The big brother told his little brother to stay and watch the canoe.

The big brother went to the house and saw an old man there. He told him that he was hungry and searching for food. The old [man] told the young boy to go inside, and then he gave him some sweet potatoes to eat.

Afterwards, the big brother asked him for some meat. The leader [man] said that he had no meat. However, he took the boy's sweet potato and put his mucous on top of it, then he gave it to him to eat.

The young boy did not care and he just gorged on the sweet potato with the old man's mucous. After he finished, he said, "Thank you" to the old man, then he left him.

However, before he left the house, the old man told him that he would meet something along the trail. He told him to take it to the house.

The bad boy left the house, and then he walked back towards his little brother. He was still walking along the trail when he saw a gorgeous woman standing there. The woman looked like nothing else and she was very beautiful. He grabbed her and took her to his little brother.

The little brother saw this and asked where he had gotten her. The big brother was resolute on what he must do when he arrived at the old man's house.

The guy left them and walked to the old man's house. The old man gave him food with mucous. However, when the little brother ate, he threw some down and did not finish all of the food. When he finished eating, he did not say thank you to the old man.

The little brother left the house and walked back towards the beach. While he was still walking, he saw a scabby woman standing on the trail. He shot the woman with a stone, then he ran away.

The little brother arrived at the beach, and then he fought with his big brother. They fought and fought, then the big brother sent his wife back. They kept fighting, and then the big brother killed his little brother. The big brother was troubled about his brother and he killed himself.

This story comes from **Buka** Island [**Petats**, **Solos** or **Halia** People].

[Anonymous]

H1570+. Test: eating disgusting food; J652. Inattention to warnings; M451.1. Death by suicide; P210. Husband and wife; P251+. Brother commits suicide on brother's death; P251.4+. One brother acts wisely, another acts unwisely; P251.5. Two brothers; Q41. Politeness rewarded; S73.1. Fratricide; S110. Murders; W27. Gratitude; W154. Ingratitude

A Father Tricked and Married His Daughter

(Wantok 1002, September 16, 1993, page 18)

Long, long ago, there was a family that lived in **Bimin** Village, in the Oksapmin area of **West Sepik** Province [**Bimin** People]. This family lived together in one place.

There were only three in this family: the mother, the father and their daughter. The father's name was Tum and the mother's name was Aiskori. The name of the daughter was Tumtem.

One time, the mother died. Only the father and daughter remained. They were troubled and just stayed in the house. They never went around the gardens or forests to search for food.

They stayed for a while, then one time Tum told his daughter that they would go to the garden. They arrived at the garden, and then they saw that the forest had covered it.

The father sent his daughter up a mountain, while he himself began to remove the grasses from the base of the mountain, going upwards. They worked and worked, then the father looked up and saw his daughter sitting awkwardly. At this time, the father's head was quite confused and he wanted to rape his daughter.

He thought and thought, then he pretended to put dirt in his eye. He told his daughter Tumtem to check on what was in his eye. Tumtem searched and searched, but she did not see any detritus in his eye.

They finished at the garden, then they returned to the house. The father went to the house and slept. His daughter went to the forest and searched for firewood. The father pretended to sleep, then when he heard Tumtem return to the house, he quickly took ashes from the fire and put it in his eye.

The father pretended to shout and he called for Tumtem to come quickly. Immediately, his daughter came up to the house. Tum told her to go to the place where a stone was, then to ask the stone what he must do to fix his eye. The father lied to her and said that the stone would fix people's illnesses and also fix broken bones.

Tumtem listened and went towards the place where the stone was. Quickly, the father left the house then went first to the place where the stone was. He saw his daughter coming.

The daughter arrived there and spoke to the stone. The father was behind it and replied, telling her to sleep with her father. The father said that if Tumtem slept with him, his eye would become well.

The poor daughter did not know that her father was tricking her. She went back towards the house. Quickly the father returned and pretended to twist around. Oh my, the daughter was quite ashamed to say what she had heard.

Tum asked his daughter what the stone had told her. The daughter was ashamed and lowered her head, then she sat. Afterwards, she got up and told him what she had heard.

There at night, the father went and slept with his daughter. They stayed and married, raising very many children.

Aimi Walson
Oksapmin
West Sepik Province

K1315. Seduction by impostor; P210. Husband and wife; P230. Parents and children; P232. Mother and daughter; P234. Father and daughter; T100. Marriage; T411. Father-daughter incest; T411.1. Lecherous father; W157. Dishonesty

The Little Boys Killed a *Masalai*

(Wantok 1003, September 23, 1993, page 20)

Long, long ago, in Malabaim [**Malapaiem**] Village, in the West Yangoru area of **East Sepik** Province, there dwelled a *masalai* [**Boiken** People]. The *masalai* often ate the boys of the village.

One day, the parents planned to kill this *masalai*. So, in the morning, they gathered all of the boys and told them to follow them to the garden. They told them that they would leave banana skins along the trail, then the boys must follow the trail of banana skins until they arrived at the garden.

However, their plan did not work because the *masalai* went behind and took the banana skins, then put them elsewhere. The *masalai* man took all of the banana skins and put them each of them along the trail that went all of the way to his house.

The boys left the village and wanted to go to the garden to see their parents. They went along the trail and saw the banana skins, then they followed them. They walked and walked, not knowing that they were going to arrive at the *masalai*'s home.

However, the boys did not walk quickly. They walked very slowly and worked at hunting for grasshoppers along the trail. They killed very many, then they wanted to bring them to the garden to cook and eat.

They followed the banana skins, then they arrived at the *masalai*'s home. The *masalai* saw the boys approaching and he was very happy. He took the grasshoppers from the boys and told them that he would go cook them.

The *masalai* left the boys outside the house, then he went inside to cook the grasshoppers. After he cooked the grasshoppers, he did not call the boys to come eat. He himself ate all of the grasshoppers.

While he was still inside the house, the wife met them all and told them that her husband would eat them. She told them to heat stones and prepare to throw them into his mouth.

The rotten scoundrel inside the house was salivating. He was starving to eat the boys. He told the boys to come up into the house. However, the boys said that their eyes were not sleepy, so they would play outside the house.

When their eyes felt tired, they would go up into the house. However, they had lied and instead worked at heating stones. When they saw that the stones were terribly hot, they lied and said that they wanted to go up into the house to sleep.

The *masalai* opened his mouth and stood close to the door. However, the boys already knew this. One of them took a stone up and threw it into the *masalai*'s mouth.

The poor *masalai* found it difficult to escape. He burned completely and died. The boys saw this and fled back to the village.

Mapil Neleson Kumun
Bialla
West New Britain Province

F490+. Masalai; G512.3.1. Ogre killed by throwing hot stones (metal) into his throat; G530.1. Help from ogre's wife (mistress); K951.1. Murder by throwing hot stones in the mouth; K2213. Treacherous wife; P210. Husband and wife; P230. Parents and children; Q211.4. Murder of children punished; Q414. Punishment: burning alive; R220. Flights; S112. Burning to death; W157. Dishonesty

A Butterfly Woman Burned with Her House

(Wantok 1004, September 30, 1993, page 20)

Long, long ago, there lived five brothers in a village called **Tawambo** among the **Kosorong** [People], in the Finschhafen area of **Morobe** Province.

These five brothers were not ordinary men. They excelled at hunting wild game. Every day, they never rested at hunting game. They would go out and hunt in the forest for game such as marsupials (*kapul*), cassowaries, bandicoots, kangaroos, and pigs.

The brothers' house was just filled with game. Every week, they would go into the forest and kill pigs. There was not one week that they just stayed at home. They would eat pork every week.

However, an old woman often came and stole all of the pork guts. When they wanted to butcher a pig, the old woman would come around. When they removed the pig's guts, she would go take them.

The old woman would do this sort of thing every time. However, the five men never saw her. The old woman lived in another village. She would turn into a butterfly and approach the place where they butchered pigs. When they removed the pig's guts, she would immediately go and steal them.

One time, the five brothers went into the forest, killed a pig, and carried it to the village to butcher. When they were butchering the pig, they saw a butterfly flying around.

They removed the pig's guts and put them aside. The butterfly went and perched on top of the pig's guts then carried them away. However, the five brothers did not see anyone.

Quite luckily, they saw blood falling along the trail. OK, they followed the blood until they arrived at the old woman's house.

At this time, they were furious. They went directly inside and pulled the old woman down the house, then they began beating her. They beat her for a while, then they killed her. Afterwards, they threw her into the house and burned her with the house.

Charles Meawong
Boroko
[National Capital District]

D186.1W. Transformation: woman to butterfly; D380+W. Transformation: butterfly to woman; D2087. Theft by magic; K420. Thief loses his goods or is detected; K812. Victim burned in his own house (or hiding place); P251.6.2+. Five brothers; Q212. Theft punished; Q414. Punishment: burning alive; R260. Pursuits; S110. Murders; S112.0.2. House (hostel) burned with all inside

[There was no ancestor story in *Wantok* #1005.]

A Ghost Woman Killed a Real Woman

(Wantok 1006, October 14, 1993, page 18)

Long, long ago, in Werman [**Wereman**] Village, in the Pagwi District of **East Sepik** Province, there lived two sisters-in-law [**Sawos** People].

One time, they decided to go scrape [process] sago. They decided that they should scrape sago in the early morning, before the first cock crowed.

At this time, they did not know that a ghost woman was listening to them. The ghost woman was outside the house and listening to what the sisters-in-law where planning to do the next day.

The sisters-in-law went to sleep, then the ghost woman pretended to call like a cock and one of the sisters-in-law awoke. Quickly, the ghost woman went up to her house and told her that she was ready to go scrape sago. Then the real woman told the ghost woman to wait for her.

When she took everything for processing sago, she went out and followed the ghost woman. They walked and walked, telling stories and laughing along the trail.

The poor real woman did not know that the other woman was a ghost. They walked and walked, then they arrived at the place where the canoe was located. The ghost woman told the real woman to paddle. [However], she was obstinate and told the ghost woman to paddle. After a while, the ghost woman insisted that the real woman take the oar and paddle upriver.

They paddled and paddled, then the ghost woman told her that if she saw a frog, she must give it to her. While they were paddling upstream, she saw a frog. She killed it and gave it to the ghost woman. The ghost woman just took the frog and began to eat it.

The real woman saw this and knew that she was not a real woman. They went upstream and arrived at the place where they would scrape sago.

OK, the woman told the ghost to go remove the sago spines, then she would go to defecate. The ghost agreed and went to remove the sago spines. The woman went to defecate, then she told her feces to reply to the ghost woman if she called out.

Afterwards, she went to the river, took the canoe, and returned to the village. The [ghost] woman waited and waited for a long time, then she called out to [the woman]. The feces replied and said that there was diarrhea, so she

was still defecating. The ghost waited and waited, then she shouted again, getting the same reply.

The ghost was angry and went to check on the place where the woman's voice was originating. When she checked, she only saw the feces there. She was angry and pulverized the feces, then she followed the woman to the village.

Immediately, she arrived at the village, then she saw the woman climbing the house ladder. The ghost took a rattan and snagged her down, then the woman died.

Raphael Sure Suamo

Wewak

East Sepik Province

D1610.6.4. Speaking excrements; E250. Bloodthirsty revenants; E261.4. Ghost pursues man; E425.1. Revenant as woman; E541. Revenants eat; F419.4K. Spirits eat food raw; H46.1+. Revenant recognized when it devours raw flesh; K1930. Treacherous impostors; P264. Sister-in-law; Q411. Death as punishment; R220. Flights; R260. Pursuits; S110. Murders; W167. Stubbornness

[There was no *Wantok* #1007.]
[The ancestor story in *Wantok* #1008 was the same as that in #1006.]

Because of a Mother's Mistake, Her Son Killed Her

(Wantok 1009, October 28, 1993, page 20)

Long, long ago in **Manugoro** Village, by Rigo, in **Central** Province, there lived an old woman with her child [**Humene** People].

The woman's husband had died when their son was still small. However, the poor woman worked hard and took good care of the boy until he grew big.

The little boy's mother taught him to make a garden and to hunt for wild game in the forest. He lived and became a big man. He stayed there and married a gorgeous woman. Many of the young boys of the village just died for his wife, but she never liked them.

One time, they lived there and her husband was to go into the forest to hunt for game. Her mother-in-law asked her to follow her into the forest to search for mangos.

The old woman was jealous. She was also a magician. The old woman would see her daughter-in-law and she would become jealous because she had nice adornments on her head. Also, she was a very beautiful woman.

The old woman and her daughter-in-law went to the forest and saw a mango tree that was just filled with ripe mangos. The old woman told her daughter-in-law to climb and fetch the ripe mangos.

She listened to the old woman. She removed the nice adornments from her head, then she climbed the mango tree. Her old mother-in-law took some forest leaves, then she sang and danced and rubbed them on the base of the mango tree. Then the mango tree began to grow and become taller.

She took her daughter-in-law's adornments and put them on her head, then she went to the house. She [arrived] at the house and saw her son sleeping there, then she went to sleep with him. The son thought that it was really his wife, so he slept with his mother. They slept together, then his mother became pregnant.

One time, he traveled to the forest and heard a sound like a bird calling. He thought that it was a bird, so he tried to find where the bird was located.

He went and arrived at the [mango] tree where [his wife] was located. He looked up and he saw his wife there. Oh my, he was very troubled because his wife had lost weight.

His wife had found it very difficult to descend, so she had just eaten the mangos. When there were no more mangos, she had eaten the mango leaves.

Her husband saw this and was completely furious at his mother. He returned to the village. When he arrived at the village, he saw his mother at the house. He took a spear and killed his mother. Then he told the villagers what had happened.

OK, the people of the village argued, then they planned to call all of the kinds of birds. They asked the birds to help the woman who was on top of the tree. The birds agreed and took her down. The villagers made a big party to show their happiness for them.

Wacz Noga
Central Province

B450. Helpful birds; B542.1+. Bird flies with woman to safety; B552+. Woman carried by bird; D955. Magic leaf; D1576.1. Magic song causes tree to rise to sky; D1711. Magician; D1781. Magic results from singing; D1781+. Magic results from dancing; D2074.1.3. Birds magically called; F54.1. Tree stretches to sky; K300. Thefts and cheats—general; K1910. Marital impostors; P210. Husband and wife; P231. Mother and son;P262.1. Bad relations between mother-in-law and daughter-in-law; P265+. Daughter-in-law; Q53. Reward for rescue; Q285. Cruelty punished; Q411. Death as punishment; R130. Rescue of abandoned or lost persons; S22+. Matricide; S110. Murders; S143.2. Abandonment in tall tree; T10. Falling in love; T100. Marriage; T412. Mother-son incest; T570. Pregnancy; W181. Jealousy

The Short *Masalai* of Mount Kulir also Had Magic Powers

(Wantok 1010, November 4, 1993, page 16)

Long, long ago, in **Nebilyer** [Village], in **Western Highlands** Province, there lived a *masalai* [**Hagen** People]. The name of the *masalai* was Wen Wen and he dwelled on top of a mountain called Kulir.

Wen Wen was a *masalai* who killed men and who also helped them. When he walked around the forest, hunting for food, he would carry a little bow. He looked like a little boy, but he was not an ordinary person. No, he was a *masalai*.

One time, a great drought arose and everything was dry. The rain had not fallen at all there. Many streams and gardens were dry. The villagers found it very difficult to find food in the gardens.

One night, the leader of the village called for everyone to gather together. He told all of the young men and some strong old men to go hunt for wild game. He told the women to cook food for the men to carry into the forest.

They slept, then in the morning, everyone prepared all of the bows, arrows and other things to carry into the forest. The women cooked food and gave it to the men.

When the sun was about to set, the men left the village, leaving the women and small children there. They walked and walked into the forest, then they arrived at Mount Kulir and they saw a cave.

All of them put their things down on the ground, then they told two little boys to watch the things and to cut firewood for cooking food. Then the others went into the forest to hunt for marsupials (*kapul*).

The two boys stayed and saw a little man come out of the cave. This man was *masalai* Wen Wen. He told the boys that he was not happy that they were staying at his home. He told them that when all of the others returned, they must tell them that Wen Wen did not want them to stay there. Afterwards, he left the boys and returned inside the cave.

Late at night, everyone who had gone marsupial hunting returned. The two boys told the story of what had happened. They told everyone to leave the place where they were because Wen Wen would kill them if they did not listen.

No one believed the boys, so they ignored them. They replied that they would kill the little man. The two boys left them and went to sleep outside the cave.

Before long, a strong wind arose and shook the trees, then a heavy rain also fell. The boys were terrified and wanted to return inside the cave.

When they arrived there, they saw that the cave was shut. They saw a small hole there and they spoke with those who were inside. They now knew that it was Wen Wen who had done this.

The poor boys cried and went to the village where they explained to the people what had happened. Everyone was very worried. The people inside the cave took the marsupials that they had shot that night and they began eating them. They stayed some weeks, then there was no more food. They began eating every little thing that they had brought, such as bows and arrows.

All of their food was gone, and one-by-one they began dying. Wen Wen himself would come to check on them, then when he returned, men would die afterwards. After a while, all of them died inside because they did not have a way to go outside again.

Tanu Wati

Mt. Hagen

Western Highlands Province

D1552. Mountains or rocks open and close; D2142.1. Wind produced by magic; D2143.1. Rain produced by magic; F402.6.4.1. Spirits live in caves; F451.4.1.1. Dwarfs live in caves; F490+. Masalai; F562.7K. People live in mountain top; J652. Inattention to warnings; J1050. Attention to warnings; Q270+. Trespassing punished; Q411. Death as punishment; R45.3. Captivity in cave; R51.1. Prisoners starved; S132. Murder by starvation

A Piece of Bamboo Helped Tokinavai

(Wantok 1011, November 11, 1993, page 21)

Long, long ago, in **Malaguna** Village, in the Rabaul area of **East New Britain** Province, there lived a man and his dog [**Tolai** People]. The man's name was Tokinavai [ToKinavai].

Tokinavai was a man who excelled at hunting for wild game in the forest. Whenever he went to the forest, he would not return empty-handed, he would shoot one or two pigs.

One time, he awoke in the very early morning and went to the forest with his dog. They went to a faraway place and his dog began chasing a pig. The pig was also strong and it worked at preventing the dog from biting it.

Before long, Tokinavai approached, took a spear and shot the pig dead. He found it difficult to carry the pig to the village because the village was far away.

So, he took a bamboo [knife] and began to butcher the pig. He finished cutting, then he made a hut and cooked the pig. He and his dog ate some meat, then they smoked the rest in a fire.

Tokinavai and his dog felt tired, so they slept near the fire. At this time, they were passing a lot of gas. Their gas smelled like nothing else.

They slept and they did not know that a huge snake was sleeping near a pond. The snake smelled their gas and the pork that Tokinavai and his dog had smoked.

The snake awoke and went out of the water, then followed the smell upwards. The snake went to the place where the two leaders [the man and dog] were located and it saw them sleeping. The snake left them and went to find grasses. The snake ate the grasses to lubricate its throat, so that it would be easier to swallow them.

Quietly, [its] neck went up and swallowed Tokinavai, then it returned to the pond. The leader did not know that he was lying inside the snake's belly. He slept and wanted to turn, but no, he felt that it was cold. He felt as if he was in a snake's belly.

It was very lucky that he had a piece of bamboo that he had put in his armband. He removed it and began cutting the snake's belly, then he went outside.

He left the snake and went up to get his dog, then they cut through the forest at night, arriving at the village. He told the story to the people of the village. In the morning, everyone in the village cooked the pig, then [he] showed them the huge snake. The people of the village took the snake, then they cooked and ate it.

Michael Joe Lames

Rabaul

East New Britain Province

B871.1.2. Giant boar; B875.1. Giant serpent; F911.7. Serpent swallows man; F912.2. Victim kills swallower from within by cutting; X716.7H. Disastrous breaking wind

How Did the Sea Arise?

(Wantok 101[2], November 18, 1993, page 21)

Long, long ago, the earth did not have a sea. There was only land, and there lived a woman with her two children in a village called **Keleba**, by Rabaul in **East New Britain** Province [**Tolai** People]. Her name was Ya-Letel. Her first son's name was ToDuna and her other son's name was ToMotet.

This family often worked very hard in the garden. Everyday, they never rested at garden work. When they went to the garden, the mother would return quickly to the house when she saw that the sun was about to set. She would go back to the house, then prepare their food.

One time, they worked for a while, then sugarcane leaves cut the mother's finger. The mother went down to a small stream near the garden to wash the blood. When she put her hand inside the water, the water stung her hand and she was greatly pained.

Ya-Letel removed her finger [from the water] and put it into her mouth to try to stop the pain. However instead, she tasted something good in her mouth.

She slowly took a bamboo tube and filled it with this salt water. After she filled the water, she took it and hid it from the children. In the afternoon, she left the children and returned to the house to cook food. She took the water in the bamboo and carried it to the house.

When she cooked food, she did not put salt water on her first son's food. When his brother wanted to eat, he tasted that it was quite delicious. The next day, she cooked food and did not put salt water on the little brother's food.

The mother did the same thing for a very long time. One time, the brothers decided to hide and see what it was that their mother used to cook food.

In the morning, they all went to work in the garden. In the afternoon, the boys hid and saw the mother taking the bamboo and filling it with water. When she left, the boys went and took the water. They put the water to their mouths and it was delicious.

They removed a boulder from which the water originated. When they removed the boulder, the water shot out and came up, carrying them to a lake.

When the mother wanted to check on the water, she saw the water growing very large. She was angry and she became a stone. So now, the sea is all over the earth.

Michael Joe Lames
Rabaul
East New Britain Province

A920. Origin of the seas; A1111. Impounded water; D231W. Transformation: woman to stone; P231. Mother and son; P251.5. Two brothers

A Ringworm Man Married Two Sisters

(Wantok 1013, November 25, 1993, page 21)

Long, long ago, there lived a man with ringworm in a village. His name was Kajenkboom. He lived with his grandmother.

One time, Kajenkboom went to the beach, and climbed a tree that was near the beach. He sat on top and looked out to the sea. He stayed on top of the tree, jumping and singing on the tree.

At this time, two sisters lived in another village, near the village where Kajenkboom and his mother lived. The sisters' names were Meming and Anii.

The two of them heard the ringworm man's singing. Oh my, his singing cut directly to their hearts. Quickly, they left the village and followed the trail towards the singing.

When they left the house, they followed a river called Behainim downstream. Afterwards, they followed another river called Ngedong. However, the river was [difficult], so they followed the Behainim River again.

The leader [Kajenkboom] did not know what was happening. He sang ardently. Mening [Meming] and Anii walked, then arrived at the house of the worthless ringworm man. The two of them went inside the house and saw Kajenkboom's grandmother.

They sat and caught their breaths, then they told the story of why they had come. They told the old woman that they wanted to marry her grandson. The old woman did not speak. She just sat and waited for the scoundrel [Kajenkboom].

They stayed and saw Kajekboom [Kajenkboom] walking towards the house. When he was about to go inside, his scabies smelled and the two women were afraid, so they went to sit in the corner of the house.

Kajekboom told her grandmother to take the women and work in the garden. The three of them took equipment and shot off to the garden.

At this time, Kajekboom took firewood and made a fire. Afterwards, he took a piece of bamboo, shoved himself inside the bamboo and began turning.

All of his scabs came off and he now had a nice skin. He went out and took off towards the house, then he adorned himself and waited for the three of them. His skin shone brightly like glass and was very young looking.

In the afternoon, the grandmother took the women back to the house. The two women went inside the room and saw that Kajekboom had changed. His skin looked completely different.

Oh my, they saw this and just urinated, then they held him. They half-died when they saw the scoundrel.

Bigiding Ian Ork
Finschafen [**Finschhafen**, **Yabêm** People]
Morobe Province

D950.15. Magic bamboo tree; D1355.1.1. Love-producing song; D1866.2. Beautification by removal of skin; F687. Remarkable fragrance (odor) of person; P210. Husband and wife; P252.1. Two sisters; P292. Grandmother; T10. Falling in love; T100. Marriage; T145.0.1. Polygyny

How Did Cockatoos Get Yellow Feathers on their Heads?

(Wantok 1014, December 2, 1993, page 21)

Long, long ago, in a village called **Vunavatikai** in **East New Britain** Province, there lived two friends. The friends were Cockatoo and Flying Fox.

They were excellent friends. They would sleep, eat and travel together. When they traveled and hunted for food, they would eat together. They never argued or fought.

However, there was one thing that made them look unusual. Long ago, Flying Fox had two yellow feathers (or hairs) on its head. At this time, Cockatoo did not have these yellow feathers.

Cockatoo often coveted the yellow feathers on Flying Fox's head. Every day, when they bathed and adorned themselves, Flying Fox would look very handsome with the yellow feathers on his head.

When Cockatoo saw Flying Fox's head, Cockatoo was quite ashamed because Cockatoo did not have any good adornments for its head. Cockatoo's body was entirely white. When Cockatoo looked at its friend, oh my, its eyes would spin. This was because Flying Fox's entire body was black except for its head, which was yellow.

One time, they went and bathed, then they prepared to dress. Cockatoo asked Flying Fox whether it could try putting on the yellow feathers. However, Flying Fox loathed the thought of giving them to Cockatoo. Cockatoo told Flying Fox, "If I put the yellow feathers on top of my head, Vunatikai shall burst into flames." However, Flying Fox was insistent and did not speak

Cockatoo always stayed and thought of what to do to take the feathers from its friend's head. One time, they slept together at night. However, Cockatoo pretended to sleep. Cockatoo spied upon Flying Fox. When Cockatoo saw that its friend was dead asleep, Cockatoo very quietly left its place and walked closer to its friend. Cockatoo removed the yellow feathers from Flying Fox's head and put them on its own head. When Cockatoo finished, it [ran away] into the forest.

Flying Fox slept for a while, then it awoke to check on its friend, but Flying Fox did not see its friend. Flying Fox checked its head and did not see the yellow feathers there.

Oh my, Flying Fox was completely furious and went searching in the forest. Flying Fox searched for its friend until dawn, but it did not find Cockatoo.

Now you often see flying foxes going around at night until dawn. Also, you often see that cockatoos have yellow feathers on their heads [sulphur-crested cockatoo (Beehler et al., 1986: 117)]. These are the feathers that they stole from the flying fox.

Michael Joe Lames
Rabaul
East New Britain Province

[Mr. Lames also wrote the ancestor stories in Wantok #1011 and 1012. The people of Vunavatikai probably speak the **Tolai** Language.]

A2321.12K. Origin of comb of white cockatoo; A2411.2.6.11+. Color of cockatoo; A2500+. Why flying foxes are nocturnal; K331. Goods stolen while owner sleeps; P310. Friendship; R213. Escape from home; W195. Envy

A Family Helped a *Masalai* with Adornments for a Festival

(Wantok 1015, December 9, 1993, page 20)

Long, long ago, in Kumgi [**Konbi**] Village, in **Simbu** Province, there lived a married couple with their two children.

One time, the mother and father thought of going to work in the garden at a place called Daralumno [**Darabumo**] in the Kerowagi area [**Kuman** People]. They left their two sons and told them to take care of the house.

The two boys sat at the house. They heard hand drums beating and men singing. However, at the place where they lived, there were no other people nearby.

They knew that there were no other people near them. However, when they heard the hand drums and the singing, they really believed that there were other people nearby.

However, these were not really men that were singing. No, they were mountain *masalais* singing and dancing fervently. When they heard the hand drums beating and the men singing, their legs trembled. They very much wanted to go to the festival because the beating of the hand drums was very unusual.

The two of them spoke, then a man came to them. He was not a real man. No, he was a *masalai* man. The *masalai* knew that there was a family living at this place, so he went there to find bird feathers.

The *masalai* asked the boys whether they had bird feathers because he wanted to use them for the festival.

They told him that they had them but that their parents had hidden them.

OK, the *masalai* told them that he would leave, but that he would return in the morning. When the parents returned from the garden, the boys told the story of what had happened. The next day, the father showed where the bird feathers were and told them to give them to the man if he returned.

In the morning, the two of them sat at the house and saw the leader [*masalai*] return. They gave him the bird feathers. The *masalai* man carried away the feathers. He dressed and used them for the festival.

When the sun was about to set, the *masalai* carried the bird feathers back. He also brought some pork. This showed his happiness for the family because they had given him adornments for the festival.

He arrived at the house and gave the pork and the bird feathers, then he returned to his home. The boys took the pork and began eating. They gorged on the food, then the parents came and saw them. They also did not wait and they also began eating the pork.

After they ate, they thought that they would become sick. However, they did not become sick because the *masalai* had not done anything to ruin them. He pitied them because they had helped him dress for the festival.

Aker Bernard Meremba
Kundiawa
Simbu Province

F261. Fairies dance; F262.1. Fairies sing; F394. Mortals help fairies; F401.6. Spirit in human form; F460. Mountain-spirits; F490+. Masalai; P210. Husband and wife; P231. Mother and son; P233. Father and son; P251.5. Two brothers; Q40. Kindness rewarded

A *Masalai* [Ghost] Became a Clam and Killed Six Sisters

(Wantok 1016, December 16, 1993, page 26)

Long, long ago, in Payawa [**Paiewa**] Village, in **Morobe** Province, there lived a family [**Guhu-Samane** People]. The family had seven young girls and they lived together in the village.

One night, the young girls sat and told stories in their room. They all decided that in the morning they would go hunting for shells on the beach of an island.

While they were sitting and telling stories, a ghost went to sit under the house. The ghost listened to all of the stories, hearing everything that the sisters planned to do the next day. While it was still night, the ghost went to the island and transformed itself into a [giant] clam.

In the early morning, the seven sisters awoke, took a canoe and paddled to the island. They paddled and approached the island, then they saw a clam under the sea.

The big sister jumped down into the sea. She went and became completely stuck. The others waited for a while, then they thought that the clam was heavy, so another sister jumped down to help her. The other five waited for a while, then another jumped down into the sea.

They did this for a while, then six sisters became stuck by the side of the clam. Their little sister was in the canoe. She looked down and saw all six of her sisters sitting around the clam. She watched and cried.

The clam closed its mouth and swallowed all six sisters. At the same time, it dirtied the water and the little sister on the canoe saw what had happened. The ghost also made the sea rough and brought the canoe with the sister to the beach.

The little sister left the canoe and cried as she went up to the house. When the parents saw her, she cried and they asked her whether her big sisters had scolded and beat her.

She said that this was not the case and she told the story of what had happened when they went asea. She told her father that a clam held her six sisters.

The next day, the father and the other people of the village went to the island. They saw the clam there, so they took strong ropes and tried to remove the clam.

However, this was not a real clam, so they found very difficult to remove it. They tried and tried, then they tired and returned to the village. When they arrived at the village, everyone in the village wailed and cried.

Wangkeng Nimorem
Lae
Morobe Province

B874.6. Giant clam; D911.1. Magic wave; E423.2+. Revenant as clam; F911.4.1.1+. Person swallowed by great clam; G11.10. Cannibalistic spirits; P210. Husband and wife; P232. Mother and daughter; P234. Father and daughter; P252.3. Seven sisters; Z356. Unique survivor

How Did Manubada Island Arise?

(Wantok 1017, December 23, 1993, page 17)

Long, long ago, in **Port Moresby** [**National Capital District**] there lived a huge bird on top of a mountain near **Sogeri** [Village, **Central** Province]. The bird would travel and descend to Ela Beach to hunt for people, then it would eat them when it was hungry.

At this time, there was not one white person who had trampled Papua yet. Only the **Rigo** and the **Koiari** Peoples lived there. At this time, they would go to Ela Beach, to **Pari** Village, to Kilakila Village, and then go farther. They would return and go to **Hanuabada** Village [**Motu** People], **Baruni** and **Tatana**, then go farther to other villages.

When they heard the bird's cry on the mountaintop, they knew that the bird was hungry and that it wanted to descend to find wild game (i.e., people) to eat. Afterwards, people would hide in a huge cave where the bird could not find them.

One day, the people decided to leave their village at the beach and go very far away to a place where they would hide. The day arrived, then all of the men, women, children, dogs and pigs together left their village at the beach. They went to a place that was very far away from the huge bird.

When they departed, they had forgotten a blind girl who was sleeping and did not know that everyone had left the village.

In the morning, she awoke and searched for the villagers. There was not the slightest sound in the village. There were no pigs or dogs either. The poor girl was very worried. She was alone for a while, then she gave birth to twin boys.

She took care of them, and they grew to be very big and strong men. They taught themselves how to throw multi-pronged spears and to shoot bows. They went hunting for game and they took care of their mother.

One day, the brothers told their mother that they had never seen anyone in the village and that they had heard the cries of the huge bird on top of the mountain.

The mother told them that she did not know where the villagers had gone. She told them that she had never seen this thing, but that she had heard its cries and noises when it came down to the beach, "I would be afraid and hide from that thing."

Then the boys told their mother that they would go hunt the huge bird and kill it. Afterwards, they would search for their people and bring them back to their village.

The poor mother was very worried, but the boys told her that it was all right and that they would leave. The two of them walked to the top of the mountain near Sogeri, then they rested near a river that was falling from the mountain. (This is now called Rouna Falls.) They caught their breaths there.

They drank from the clean, cold water, then they heard the cries of the huge bird again. However this time, the bird was very close to them.

The first brother ran up to a boulder, looked out and saw the huge bird bathing in a lake (which is now called Sirinumu Dam). He immediately called to the second brother to hide on the other side of the lake and to wait there.

The first brother shouted loudly. The bird heard him, turned its head, and saw him standing there. The bird alit and flew towards the first brother, so as to eat him.

On the other side, the second brother aligned his multi-pronged spear and shot it at the bird's neck. The spear shot directly into the huge bird's neck. The bird felt pained and was furious. It left the first brother and turned to the second brother. At the same time, the first brother jumped on top of the bird's leg and hung from there.

When the second brother saw the bird coming, he jumped down into the lake and hid beneath it. The bird came and missed the second brother, then when it wanted to fly away, the second brother went out of the water and threw up his hands. He grabbed the first brother's legs and they flew away with the huge bird.

The huge bird shot down Sogeri's mountain and arrived at Ela Beach. Then it flew out to sea with the boys still hanging from its legs.

The first brother removed his spear and shoved it into the bird's chest, directly into the bird's heart. The bird screamed awkwardly and shook its head to remove the brothers, but they held fast, like ants. Then the second brother climbed the bird's leg and went up to the bird's head. He took his spear and shot it into the bird's eye. The bird went about crazily, then it went headfirst towards the sea.

The brothers jumped when they approached the sea, then the huge bird descended. Its own weight caused it to break straight down the middle. Its head went to lie near Koki Point and its body went to lie in the middle of the sea. Then the two pieces of the bird's body transformed and became islands. At this time, they called the islands, *Manubada*, meaning "Huge Bird." Now they lay sadly near Ela Beach.

Jada Wilson

Rigo-Gaba 2

Central Province

A515.1.1. Twin culture heroes; A955.10. Islands from transformed object or person; A1617. Origin of place-name; B31.6. Other giant birds; B33. Man-eating birds; B552. Man carried by bird; D423+. Transformation: bird to island; P231. Mother and son; P251.5. Two brothers; R213. Escape from home; R315. Cave as refuge; S140+. Abandonment of blind; S371+. Abandoned woman's son becomes hero; T587. Birth of twins; T685. Twins; Z210. Brothers as heroes

[Because of] Sama's Mistake,
the Forest Woman Left Him

(Wantok 1018, December 30, 1993, page 20)

Long, long ago, in **Sumi** Village, in the Kagua area of **Southern Highlands** Province, there lived a man [**Kewa** People]. His name was Sumi Sama.

Sama was a completely worthless man in the village. He did not have anything, and the women of the village did not like to speak with him. He would always ask women, but they were tired of him.

One time, he traveled to the forest to hunt for wild game. He arrived at a place where there was red earth. Sama saw human foot and handprints.

Sama knew that the villagers never went to this place. At this time, Sama thought very hard because real people had taken the red earth [to make body paint]. He returned to the village. He did not tell the villagers what he had seen.

The next day, Sama awoke in the early morning and went into the forest. However, when he arrived at this place, the people who had taken the red earth had already taken it and left.

The scoundrel went and hid by a tree buttress and watched. The people who had taken the red earth were wild women. The women lived on top of a tree.

When the women went in the early morning, only one stayed. She asked the others to take some for her too. However, when they returned, not one of them had felt sorry for her and taken some to her.

So, she left the others there and went down to fetch some earth. At the same time, Sama was hiding and watching. When she descended, Sama saw her. His arms and legs began to tremble. She was quite gorgeous. Sama watched for a while and he urinated. His heart shot out like a rocket.

She did not know that Sama was hiding. She worked diligently at gathering the earth. Sama went behind and grabbed her. She tried to remove Sama's hands, but he was stronger.

After a while, she turned into a snake. However, this did not scare Sama. He had seen her nice face and he held very tightly. After a while, she told Sama to let go and they would go to the village. However, Sama kept holding her and she turned back to a woman. Then they walked towards the village.

However, while they were walking, she told Sama to make a house for her in the forest and not to take her to the village. Sama carried her away. He made a small house for her in the forest.

Sama's thoughts were carefree now, he was happy and he walked towards the village. He would cook food and bring it to her, then go to sleep with her during the day.

At this time, Sama also gained her power and he worked harder. He would make big gardens, and the house was bigger than were those of the villagers.

One time, the villagers decided to fight him. After a while, one man went and argued with him. Everyone in the village supported this other man.

When Sama had first taken the woman away, she had told Sama that he could not tell the other people of the village about them. He could not say that he had married a forest woman.

When Sama argued with the other man, he forgot completely about what she had told him. After a while, Sama told him, "If you were like me, you would have married a forest woman."

After he said this, his thoughts quickly returned. He said that he was wrong. Sama left everyone in the village, then he ran into the forest, to the place where the woman lived. When he arrived at the house, he saw that she was not there. He was terribly worried and he shouted into the forest. She was on top of the tree and she replied. She told Sama that he was wrong and that he had not kept his promise. Afterwards, he went and forgot completely about their [life in the forest].

Luke Tua

Kagua

Southern Highlands Province

D191W. Transformation: woman to serpent (snake); D361.1+. Forest Spirit Bride; D391W. Transformation: serpent (snake) to woman; D1720. Acquisition of magic powers; D1830. Magic strength; F567.1. Wild woman; F811.10+. Tree in which people live; P210. Husband and wife; P160. Beggars; Q266. Punishment for breaking promise; T10. Falling in love; T192. Marriage by force

[The ancestor story in *Wantok* #1019 is the same as that in #841.]

A Little Boy Caused the
Death of His Brother-In-Law

(Wantok 1020, January 13, 1994, page 17)

Long, long ago, there lived a girl with her brother. The sister was grown, so she took good care of her little brother. They lived together and made a big garden, then they planted various kinds of foods. They lived for a while, then the sister noticed that her breasts had grown, so she thought of finding a man to marry.

One time, the sister went to the garden and dug a hole in the ground. She dug and dug, then she made it like a house. Afterwards, she went to the garden, took all of the food from the garden, and put it underground.

Later, she went to the house, took her little brother, and carried him underground, leaving him there. The sister told the brother to just stay in the ground.

She told her little brother that she would go to find a man to marry. They held each other and cried terribly because she would leave her brother.

The little boy stayed and ate the food that his sister had left. He stayed for a while, then there was no more food. At this time, he had become a big man, so he felt that he could hunt for his own food.

There was no more food except for just one stalk of bananas. He ate and thought of hunting for some food in the afternoon. He went above ground and began making a bow and arrows. He took an arrow and shot it. After he shot the arrow, he saw where it went and followed it.

The arrow had traveled and stuck directly to his sister's breast. The boy followed and followed, then he arrived directly at his sister's house. His sister was surprised when she saw her brother.

In the afternoon, his sister's husband returned to the house and saw him. However, this man was not very happy to see his brother-in-law. OK, he told his brother-in-law to follow him to the garden to get some sugarcane.

The man's garden was far below a mountain. They went to the garden, then the boy's brother-in-law cut sugarcanes to give to him. The boy did not wait and he gorged on the sugarcanes. His brother-in-law began singing and dancing. He wanted to try to make the boy sleep, then he would kill him.

The boy ate the sugarcanes, then he went to sleep. His brother-in-law went up the bamboo ladder, then he took the ladder and put it elsewhere. When he went up, he shouted to the _nokondi_ men, or ghost men who only had one-sided bodies, to kill the boy. He told them that he had tied up a wild animal for them.

At this time, a flying fox was also inside a cave. The flying fox heard this and flew over. It took the boy and hid him.

When the _nokondi_s came, they did not find the boy. His brother-in-law went and wanted to check. He took the bamboo ladder, then he went down [to] the boy [and] saw that he was in hiding.

Immediately, he climbed the ladder. When he arrived at the top of the mountain, he took the ladder and hid it elsewhere. Later, he called out to the _nokondi_s. The _nokondi_s came and ate him. The boy ran and went to the house, then he told his sister. They took their things and fled back to their home.

Quila Kokena and Jethro Raporo
Rabaul
East New Britain Province

[See the ancestor stories in *Wantok* #315, 633, and 708 for other _nokondi_ stories. This story is probably from the **Eastern Highlands** Province.]

B212. Animal understands human speech; B449.3+. Helpful flying fox; B540+. Flying fox rescuer; D1314.1. Magic arrow indicates desired place; D1781. Magic results from singing; D1781+. Magic results from dancing; D1960. Magic sleep; E380. Ghost summoned; E425.2. Revenant as man; F490+. Nokondi; F525. Person with half a body; G11.10. Cannibalistic spirits; G411. Person aids ogre and is captured; K1600. Deceiver falls into own trap; K2211.1. Treacherous brother-in-law; P253. Sister and brother; P263. Brother-in-law; R100. Rescues; R220. Flights; R310. Refuges; S55+. Cruel brother-in-law; S211. Child sold (promised) to devil (ogre)

A Marsupial (*Kapul*) Helped Parents Get their Baby Back

(Wantok 1021, January 20, 1994, page 20)

Long, long ago, in Gajengan [**Ganzegan**] Village, in the Boana District of **Morobe** Province, there lived a man, his wife, and their child [**Nek** People].

They lived for a while, then one time, they went to work in the garden. When they arrived in the garden, the mother put the baby inside a net bag and hung him on the branch of a tree.

Then she and the father left the baby and worked diligently. Before long, a flying fox flew by and saw the baby sleeping in the net bag. The flying fox flew close to the baby and clapped its two wings. This raised a nice cool breeze towards the baby, and he became dead asleep.

When the flying fox saw that that baby was dead asleep, it just carried him to its home. In the afternoon, the baby's parents finished working and wanted to return home. They went to check the place where the mother had hung the baby and they saw that the baby was not there. They thought that some of their kin had carried the baby away, so they walked towards the village.

However, when they arrived at the village, they did not see the baby. They asked everyone in the village, but they said that they had not taken their baby.

The flying fox had taken the baby to its home, and it took very good care of him. They lived together and the flying fox would go hunting for food in the garden of the little boy's parents. Then the flying fox would give the food to the little boy.

One time, the flying fox went to the village and pulled off chicken feathers, then brought them to the little boy. The next time, it went all of the way to his parent's house and took his father's hand drum. The flying fox carried the hand drum away and beat it. The flying fox dressed the boy, then when the flying fox beat the drum, the little boy shook his head.

One time, the little boy's mother and his female cousin went fishing in the river. They fished and went upstream, then the cousin sat by the river.

While she sat, she saw a cave. She checked and saw the shadow of someone shaking their head when the sun caught the side of the cave. The cousin shouted to the boy's mother, then she came and they went to check. They looked and saw the little boy shaking his head fervently.

The mother cried terribly and they went to the village. The next day, everyone in the village went to try to get the boy. When they arrived, the little boy's male cousin went up to try to get him. However, the flying fox called all of the birds and they beat him down. The flying fox took the boy and carried him up to the top of a tree. They tried unsuccessfully [to get him], then went to the village.

At night, the little boy's father slept and dreamt. In the dream, some people told him that the next day, he must cook five sweet potatoes, then carry them into the forest. Afterwards, he must call the marsupials (*kapul*) to come. They would help him get his son.

The next day, the father cooked five sweet potatoes, and carried them to the forest. Then he called the marsupials. However, they did not want to come and eat the five sweet potatoes. The little boy's father walked and walked, then he saw a tree hole. He placed the five sweet potatoes and a marsupial came out to eat them. Afterwards, the father told the marsupial to help him get his son on top of the tree. The marsupial finished the five sweet potatoes, then it went directly to the tree where the little boy was located and it began to make a hole. The marsupial worked on the hole, going up to near where the boy was located, then it left.

The father went to the village and fetched everyone, then they went to the tree where the baby was located. The flying fox saw that many people from the village had come, so the flying fox called for all of them to watch. However,

they did not know that there was a big hole directly under the place where the little boy was located.

When everyone in the village was ready, the marsupial went up and fetched the baby. The flying fox saw this and tried to grab the marsupial, but the marsupial just sped down to the ground. The marsupial gave the baby to his father. The flying fox tried to take the baby from the father's hands. However, the father held his baby and was very strong. He carried him to the village.

Tomas Mota

Rabaul

East New Britain Province

B430+. Helpful marsupial; B450. Helpful birds; B535+. Flying fox as nurse for child; B540+. Marsupial rescuer; B552+. Person carried by flying fox; D1810.8.2. Information received through dream; P210. Husband and wife; P231. Mother and son; P233. Father and son; P295. Cousins; R13.1+. Abduction by flying fox; R45.3. Captivity in cave; R49.1. Captivity in tree; R110. Rescue of captive; Z71.3. Formulistic number: five

A Little Boy Killed an Ancestral Ghost that Lived by a Tree
(Wantok 1022, January 27, 1994, page 21)

Long, long ago, there lived two brothers in a village. Their parents had died. They lived by themselves and searched for their own food. The villagers never gave them food.

One time, the brothers saw that everyone in the village had gone into the forest to hunt for food. The big brother spoke to his little brother and they went to the forest to hunt for food. They took sand, filled a basket, and carried it away.

They went and the big brother saw an *ela* [*aila*] tree that was bearing many fruits. The big brother told the little brother to stay below and he would climb the tree.

However, they did not know that an ancestral ghost was watching them by the *ela* tree. This was because the ghost's house was nearby. The big brother climbed the tree and gathered the *ela* fruits. One fell down and touched the ghost's leg. The ghost asked the *ela* fruit, "Who took you, a man or a bird?" When the ghost spoke, oh my, the *ela* fruit began to move.

The ghost was furious and walked towards the base of the tree, then the ghost shouted upwards. When the boy heard the ghost, he immediately took the sand and threw it on the tree leaves. The ghost heard the sound of the leaves and thought that it was a bird eating, so the ghost returned to the house.

The young boy finished taking the *ela* fruits, then he went back towards the house. He took the *ela* fruits and carried them to his brother, then they returned to the village.

They stayed for a while, then the little brother said that he would go into the forest and gather *ela* fruits. However, the big brother told him to watch carefully because the *ela* tree belonged to an ancestral ghost.

The little brother did not worry. He took some sand and filled a basket. He climbed the *ela* tree, then he gathered the *ela* fruits in earnest.

He did not know that an *ela* fruit had fallen down and touched the ancestral ghost's arm. The ancestral ghost saw this and asked the *ela* fruit who had picked it, then the *ela* fruit made a sound when the ghost said, "Man."

The *masalai* [ghost] was furious and walked towards the base of the tree, then the ghost shouted upwards. He said that he would eat whoever was up there. However, the little boy was not afraid of the *masalai* [ghost]. He said that he would kill the *masalai*.

The *masalai* was angry and went up to kill him, but the little boy was not afraid. He took an *ela* fruit and threw it directly at the *masalai*'s head, then the *masalai* fell down and died.

The little brother went to the village and told the story to his big brother about what had happened. They lived there and they were no longer afraid of ancestral ghosts when they gathered *ela* fruits in the forest.

Andrew Taroa

Kimbe

[**West New Britain** Province]

[Mr. Taroa wrote the ancestor stories in *Wantok* #924 and 964. He is probably from the **Bola** People.]

D981. Magic fruit; D1311+. Divination by fruit; E446.3+. Ghost laid by blow to head; E545. The dead speak; F490+. Masalai; G11.10. Cannibalistic spirits; G512.8. Ogre killed by striking; K500. Escape from death or danger by deception; L111.4.3. Orphan brothers as heroes; P251.5. Two brothers; R210. Escapes; S110. Murders

A Log Gave Songs and Dances to Siar Village

(Wantok 1023, February 3, 1994, page 20)

Siar is a small village in **New Ireland** Province [**Siar** People]. This place is one of the very last places to receive development work because the people there often believe very strongly in traditional things. People who go to this place usually see the various things that they do. The masked dancers can sing above the leaves of the wild *paragum*, above the sea, where some people from other provinces never do.

The origin of this is a small village on Lavangai [**New Hanover**] Island that was renowned long ago [**Lavongai** People]. The small village is **Luan**. However Luan does not have this kind of custom now and the people of Siar have the fame.

Long ago, in Luan Village, there was a tree. This tree was a man. The tree was named Toluan. One time, he went out to sea. Then he drifted to the shore of a small place on the west coast of New Ireland. The name of this place is **Lamusmus** [People]. He was fairly far from Luan.

This place had one man. He was sleeping and catching his breath by the beach. At this time, the tree went ashore and he lay upon it. When he saw the log arrive there, he looked at it. He was furious. He shoved the log back down to the sea. He was stupid and did not think of holding onto the log. No, he thought that it was an ordinary log and he shoved it back towards the sea.

So, the tree went away and arrived at Siar Village. It turned and turned. This time, there was an old woman there. The old woman was preparing to go to the house and she saw a log turning and turning. So, she went to get this log and carry it to the house to make a fire. She thought that it was a log for firewood.

It was not. At night, she dreamt. She was surprised that the tree turned into a man and showed her the various kinds of songs and dances such as, *limbung*, *paraparik*, *liu* and *tumbuan* (masked dance). These songs and dances came from the hard work of the old woman and her children. So at this time, Siar gained great fame from these songs and dances in New Ireland Province.

John Mays Bonma

New Ireland Province

A1464.2.1. Origin of particular song; A1542.2. Origin of particular dance; D431.2M. Transformation: tree to man; D1810.8.2. Information received through dream; P230. Parents and children

An Ugly Bird Married the Bird-of-Paradise Woman

(Wantok 1024, February 10, 1994, page 20)

Long ago, there was a young bird-of-paradise woman who lived with her parents. The young bird-of-paradise woman lived for a while, then her parents told her, "You're the only beautiful woman on the earth and all of the men are just dying to marry you. You know that we're old.

Who'll take care of us? You must find a handsome man, so that you can marry him and take care of us."

One day, all of the ground-dwelling birds gathered and held a meeting so that the bird-of-paradise woman could choose her husband. Before this day arrived, the bird-of-paradise woman's parents told her that she must dress well and style her hair (or feathers). This was because many kinds of men would come to see her. They slept that night and the bird-of-paradise woman arranged her thoughts. She thought that if she married a handsome man, he would probably not take care of her well afterwards. If she married a man regardless of whether his face was handsome or ugly, then he would take care of her well. So, in the very early morning, her parents awoke and prepared all her adornments. After they prepared the adornments, they dressed her and told her that many handsome men would come to see her, men such as Cassowary, Victoria Crowned Pigeon [*Goura victoria*], Hornbill, Black Cockatoo [palm cockatoo (Beehler et al., 1986: 117)], Wildfowl, White Cockatoo [sulphur-crested cockatoo (Beehler et al., 1986: 117)], and many other handsome men.

The bird-of-paradise woman had not chosen a man yet, but the birds just spoke strongly. The cassowary told the other birds that he would marry the bird-of-paradise woman because he had strength and was the king of the ground birds. He had big muscles to fight the other birds.

The bird-of-paradise woman's parents beat the signal drum, then all of the birds arrived and stood in a row. The bird-of-paradise woman came and began walking the entire line, examining the men. Cassowary was the king of all of the birds, so he stood in the very front.

When the bird-of-paradise woman walked the entire line, examining the birds, all of them made various poses, standing and waiting for her to choose them. However the bird-of-paradise woman did not choose one, so she said that the next day, she would reexamine all of the men. Afternoon arrived, then they all returned to the village. Along the trail, they talked back-and-forth, saying that all of the men were gone and that she had some kind of man to marry.

So the next day, they went again. However, the bird-of-paradise woman examined the entire line and she could not find a man to marry. So, they all returned to their village. They talked back-and-forth, then a small brown bird with big eyes, long feathers and a short beak, heard them shouting. The bird came and asked them, "Has the bird-of-paradise woman found a husband or not?" The birds told him, "Not yet," and that the next day would be the last, that she would probably find a man to marry. So, the brown

bird listened and told them that the next day, he too would try. [Perhaps] the bird-of-paradise woman would like him.

When he said this, the other birds listened and laughed hysterically, just humiliating him. The birds told him that the strong men had already tried and that she would [not] like an ugly man such as this brown bird. They defamed the little bird terribly, then they departed.

The third day arrived, then all of the birds returned to the bird-of-paradise woman. The brown bird also stood in the line. He was terribly ashamed and went to hide in a corner, at the very end of the line.

The bird-of-paradise woman went and examined the line again. She went to the corner, saw the little brown bird and carried him outside. She told the other birds that she had found her husband. Then she told the other birds that they must return to their village. When the other birds saw this, they began a big fight. However, the bird-of-paradise woman told them that it would be bad if she married a handsome man, because this lifestyle would last a very long time.

Beautiful men and women will marry themselves and the ugly-faced people will marry themselves, then many people will not be able to marry a good person. The bird-of-paradise woman said this, then they complained back-and-forth and returned to their village.

So from this time, you can see that some men marry beautiful women, and handsome men can marry [ugly] women. The birds of paradise in our country showed us this marriage custom.

Judas M'hue
Portion 81
Gavien
East Sepik Province

[Female bird-of-paradise species are generally more drab than male of the same species. Gender in folklore does not necessarily correspond with biological gender.]

A1550+. Why ugly and beautiful marry each other; B211.3. Speaking bird; B211.3+. Speaking bird of paradise; B211.3.17K. Speaking cassowary; B242.1+. Cassowary as king of birds; L140+. Ugly marries beautiful; L213.2+. Choice of ugliest for marriage; P210. Husband and wife; P232. Mother and daughter; P234. Father and daughter; T100. Marriage

Two Blood Brothers Killed an Evil Thing
(Wantok 1025, February 17, 1994, page 20)

Long, long ago [near] Finschafen [Finschhafen], there was a small island called **Tami** [**Tami** People, **Morobe**

Province]. There was also a woman who was pregnant and who lived with her clan.

They always lived well. However, they never cooked during the day. They only cooked at night because there was a huge bird that lived in their area. If they cooked during the day, the bird would see the smoke from the fire and it would come down to eat them.

They never ate well during the day, so they decided to flee to the mainland, then they would be able to cook and eat well during the day.

All of the men made canoes for themselves, then they were ready to flee to the mainland. They took all of their belongings, such as pigs, dogs, cats, and supplies. They took their children, then they paddled towards the mainland.

When they fled, they forgot the pregnant woman and they left her there. This was because when she wanted to jump into a canoe, the canoe sank. She tried unsuccessfully, so she remained at the island while everyone else went to the mainland.

The poor woman was alone on the island for a while, then one time she wanted to go check on her garden. She went to cut sugarcanes, then a sugarcane leaf cut her hand. When the blood flowed down her hand, she dug a hole and put the blood inside the hole. She did this until the hole was full. Then she dug another hole and did the same thing again. When the holes were both full, she covered them and returned to the village.

She stayed for two days in the village, then she wanted to go check on her garden again. However when she arrived at the garden, she saw that her bananas looked as if men had eaten them.

It was not men who ate the bananas; it was her two children who ate them. The children had originated from her blood when she had buried it in the ground. The children's mother had a good idea, so she covered herself with banana leaves and stood there until the afternoon. That afternoon, the two boys were hungry and wanted to look for food.

They came out and when they saw their mother standing there, they thought that she was a tree [banana plant]. They ran directly up there and jumped on top of their mother. The mother saw this and grabbed them.

When she grabbed them, they screamed terribly. They screamed for a while, then the elder brother told the younger that they must shut up and listen to their mother.

Their mother told them that all of their kin had fled to the mainland and that only they were there. She told them that she was alone and that she had wanted to remove sugarcane leaves when a leaf had cut her. She told them that

she had buried her blood and that the boys originated from the blood. After she told them this, they agreed to follow her to her house.

They went and stayed with their mother for a while, but they never cooked and ate during the day. They did this for a while, then one time they asked their mother why they never cooked and ate during the day.

The mother told them that before they were born, everyone who had fled lived like this and that they only cooked at night. She told them that when they cooked during the day, a bad bird would see the smoke from the fire then descend to snatch people and eat them. So, they never cooked during the day. After a while, everyone fled, leaving only herself there. After the boys heard this, they began to make things for fighting, such as bows, arrows, and axes.

One day, they told their mother that she must sweep the rubbish and burn it, then she must go hide in the forest. The mother listened to them and followed their instructions, then she hid in the forest.

Before long, the bad bird saw the smoke and went down to kill the two of them. However, they were exceptionally strong and they stood at the ready. When the bird was about to descend, the little brother tightened his bow and shot the bird directly in its brain. The big brother took an axe and cut its neck, then the bird was dead. Their mother came and they lived happily together. They sent a message to the mainland, then everyone came and lived well together again.

Kaliu Jacob

Finschafen [Finschhafen]

Morobe Province

A515.1.1. Twin culture heroes; B31.6. Other giant birds; B33.1. Other devastating birds; F610. Remarkably strong man; G510.4. Hero overcomes devastating animal; P231. Mother and son; P251.5. Two brothers; S145. Abandonment on an island; S371+. Abandoned woman's son becomes hero; T534. Conception from blood; T570. Pregnancy; T587. Birth of twins; T685. Twins; Z210. Brothers as heroes

A Boy Scared His Father, then They Ran Away from Each Other

(Wantok 1026, February 24, 1994, page 22)

Long, long ago, there lived an old man. His name was Koma Bomonu and his child was Gorabe Gora. They lived in a village called **Famulei Yalimegoli** in the Chuave District of **Simbu** Province.

One time, they saw that there was a nice, bright moon. The father told his son, "There's a nice, bright moon. Let's prepare some food, then we'll go to the forest and hunt for wild game."

The son was agreed with the father's idea, so they prepared food. The next day, they awoke and went into the very deep forest, near a place called **Mobikapugumam**. Darkness arrived and they made a sleeping hut for themselves.

They cooked some food, then they sat and ate. After they ate, the son wanted to sleep and the father said, "Son, go to sleep. I'll walk very quietly in the area and hunt for game." After he said this, he walked away to hunt for game.

However, his son was terrified to sleep alone because he knew that this area was very deep forest. He knew that it would be bad if a ghost came and carried him away, or if one killed and ate him.

The boy pretended to sleep. He saw his father get up, take the bow, arrows and axe, then walk off to hunt for game. When the father was fairly far away, the boy noticed this and followed his father. He went quietly behind him. The father did not know that his son was following him.

The father walked and walked, then he saw a marsupial (*kapul*) lying on top of a tree. When he saw the marsupial, he noted which branch the marsupial was lying upon. Then he prepared his arrows and axe, and went up the tree. He followed the tree directly towards the branch where the marsupial was lying.

While the father was still climbing the tree, his son arrived and stood directly at the base of the tree. The father did not know that his son was under the tree.

The father got ready and drew back his bow, then he shot the marsupial. When the marsupial fell down, his son stood under the tree and asked him, "Did you shoot it?" When his father heard this, oh my, he felt quite odd.

The father thought that a ghost man had come and was at the base of the tree, talking to him. Oh my, he just got up while he was still on top of the tree, then he jumped down. He fell very badly directly onto the ground. He immediately stood again, then he sped off to the place where his son had been sleeping.

However, the boy came behind him. When the father fled from the base of the tree, the boy thought that a *masalai* man must have been chasing his father. However, he did not know that it was himself that had caused his father to flee. He also ran, following his father. However, his father thought that a *masalai* was coming behind him.

They ran and ran. Rattan thorns and sharp grasses completely ruined both of them. They kept running until dawn came and they arrived at the village.

The father ran into his house, completely breathless. He shouted loudly, "Oi! A *masalai* man chased me all of the way to the village."

The villagers awoke and saw the boy coming behind his father. They were both completely out of breath. They saw this and asked them why they had been running. When the two of them saw that they had been chasing each other, the father was terribly ashamed. Everyone in the village came and laughed hysterically at them.

Ben Koibo

Kimbe

West New Britain Province

E261.4+. Imagined ghost pursues man; P233. Father and son; R260. Pursuits

[There was no ancestor story in *Wantok* #1027.]

A *Masalai* Eel Killed the People of Butam
(Wantok 1028, March 10, 1994, page 18)

Long, long ago, there were three places in the Gazelle Peninsula of **East New Britain**. The places were [where] the **Butam** [People], the **Tolai** [People] and the **Taulil** [People lived]. The language of Taulil was unusual because it was inferior.

OK, the story goes as follows. In the very beginning, there were no people at Taulil. The men at Butam were men who hunted for wild game in the forest and who [had] various foods in the gardens. They always awoke in the early morning and did this sort of work.

When the people of Taulil would go into the forest, they would leave an old woman in the village. The old woman never walked at all and her skin was like that of a frog. Her eyes were also shut and she was blind. It was fortunate that the old woman had a son. He would watch after his mother and carry his mother's food to the house.

One time, everyone finished working and returned to the village. They cooked food and brought it from the forest. When they arrived at the village, a leader searched for his bow. He searched and searched, but did not see it. A woman told the leader that the bad old woman had taken it, "She just sleeps in the village and steals our things."

The old woman just sat quietly and the villagers berated her. They asked her for the things that she had taken. They asked where she had put them.

The old woman told them that she did not know anything. She told them that she stayed in the cookhouse in the mornings, then she would go to sleep at noon. However, the men did not believe her and they continued to berate her.

Everyone scolded the old woman and her son, saying that they had stolen and eaten their things. The poor old woman and her son wailed because of the terrible things said to them.

One day, the old woman and her son stayed in the village. They wanted to find out who it really was that was stealing things. By their village, there was a big river. In the river, there lay a huge eel. The eel was huge and its skin was pitch black.

While the mother and son were [lying] and watching, there was no one in the village. Then they saw the big eel come above the water and slither through all of the houses, taking their food and things. They saw this and were terrified. They hid and stayed quiet. In the afternoon when people arrived, the two of them told them what had happened during the day.

OK, all of the men arranged their spears. In the early morning, they dug through the water, searching for the eel. They searched for the eel until the afternoon. In the afternoon, they saw something nasty lying at the base of a big tree. So, all of the men threw their spears together, piercing the eel. When they shot, the old woman's son stood with them. He ran away and hid in the house.

Everyone cut the eel, then they gave its head to the old woman and her son. They cooked all of the pieces with meat. When the old woman and her son took the eel's head, they cooked it in a fire for four whole days. On the fourth day, when they removed it, something was terribly strong, so the old woman spilled some water on eel's head to cool it.

When she spilled the water on the eel's head, the eel said, "I'm cold. I'm cold." Oh my, the old woman was terrified and she just stood there.

The eel told her that when her son returned from the forest, they must flee quickly. This was because [the eel] would make rain and kill everyone in Butam because they had killed it and eaten its flesh. The mother and son had not eaten its flesh at all, so the eel would let them flee. Before they were to flee, they had to put the eel's head back in the water.

When the son returned to the village, his mother told him to hurry and prepare to leave the village. That night, they went to the water and returned the eel's head . Then they ran away to a place fairly far from Butam.

When it was still that night, a heavy rain and flood arose, finishing off everyone in Butam. The mother and

son had fled and found **Taulil** Village. So, now you will hear that the languages of Butam and Taulil are similar.

Joseph B. Tokuravinau

Kokopo

East New Britain Province

[There are no longer people who speak the Butam Language (Wurm, 1975: 789).]

A991+. Origin of particular village; A1011. Local deluges; A1015.2. Spirit causes deluge; A1018. Flood as punishment; A1616+. Origin of Taulil Language; B98. Frog-skinned person; B211.6.3K. Speaking eel; B874.2. Giant eel; D1610.5. Speaking head; D2143.1. Rain produced by magic; D2151.8. Magic flood; E168. Cooked animal comes to life; E783.5. Vital head speaks; F420.1.3.2+. Water-spirit as eel; F490+. Masalai; F655. Extraordinary perception of blind men; J1050. Attention to warnings; K420. Thief loses his goods or is detected; K2127. False accusation of theft; P231. Mother and son; Q150.1. Rescue from deluge as reward; Q211.6. Killing an animal revenged; Q212. Theft punished; Q411.13. Death as punishment for thievery; Q428. Punishment: drowning; R213. Escape from home

Yams Arose in Buang from a Man's Bones
(Wantok 1029, March 17, 1994, page 16)

Long, long ago, in the time of the ancestors of the Buang [**Mapos Buang**] People of **Morobe** Province, there lived two brothers. The big brother's name was Ali and the little brother's name was Gho.

The brothers always noticed that the other people of Buang ate meat. However these people never gave any meat to the brothers.

This sort of thing happened many times, then Ali told his little brother, Gho, that people never gave them meat. So, the next day in the very early morning, when the others were sleeping, they would awake and go hunt for wild game in the forest. The little brother listened and agreed that they would go hunt for game in the forest.

At night, they prepared everything for hunting game. They arranged the bows, arrows and food. Then in the early morning, when the people of the village were still asleep, the brothers awoke, left the village, and walked into the forest.

They walked and walked into the very deep forest, then they began to hunt for game such as pigs, cassowaries, marsupials (*kapul*) and birds. They hunted and hunted. Only Ali shot game such as birds and marsupials. After he shot one, he would call to his little brother, then call his own name. Ali did this for a while, then his little brother, Gho, was upset because he had not shot a single animal.

Ali and Gho hunted game for a while, then they arrived at a big mountain. The name of this mountain is Risne and it is a *masalai* mountain. They saw a marsupial on top of a tree. However, this marsupial was not a real marsupial, it was a *masalai* man tricking the brothers.

Ali and Gho stood on the ground and tried to shoot the marsupial, but their arrows did not reach it. They were unsuccessful, so Ali told Gho to climb the tree and make a noise. The marsupial would then descend and he would kill it. However, Gho told Ali that he had not yet killed a marsupial and he named this marsupial as his own. So, he asked Ali to climb and make a noise. The marsupial would come down, then Gho would kill the marsupial and call his name upon it.

However, Ali was persistent and told Gho to climb. This was because it would be bad if he went up and made a noise and Gho stood below. The marsupial would come down, Gho would not be able to kill the marsupial and the marsupial would escape. So, the little brother listened to his big brother and climbed the tree.

Gho climbed the tree and arrived near the *masalai* marsupial. The *masalai* marsupial caused Gho's arms and legs to go completely numb and weak. Then his arms and legs began to tremble. He shouted down and told Ali, "Ali, my arms and legs are completely numb and trembling. So, I'm going down and you're coming up." However Ali shouted up to Gho, "You still have some strength, so climb. The marsupial is not far away. If you come down, I'll beat you." Gho was afraid of Ali beating him, so he went a little higher, then his arms and legs went completely dead and he fell down to the ground.

When Gho fell to the ground, the *masalai* marsupial tricked them and shouted, "That's it Ali, it's falling down. Kill it or it'll escape." Ali listened and thought that Gho had made a noise and that the marsupial was falling. So, he told him that he would kill the marsupial lest it escape. Ali listened and watched very carefully, then Gho fell down, breaking his head. He did not know this, so he killed Gho. Later, he saw that he had killed his little brother.

Ali cried over his brother's body, then he ran to the village. He blew the conch trumpet and called everyone to meet in the village. He told them what had happened in the forest. Then he took the village men to the *masalai* mountain. They took Gho's body and the animals that they had killed back to the village. They buried his little brother's body.

After some months had passed, Ali traveled to the place where they had buried Gho and he saw the sprouts of something growing there. He finished looking at Gho's grave, then he returned to the house. At night, he dreamt that he must return and cut tall trees and erect them near these things. This was because these things grew from Gho's body and he must clean and take care of them. He must take care of them until he saw the leaves become big, then he must dig and remove the food from them. He would share them with everyone, then they could plant them in their gardens.

The next day, Ali followed his dream and returned to the place where they had buried Gho. He did what he had dreamt and seen. After some months, he saw that the leaves were becoming large. He dug and removed this thing's underground food. He took these things back to the village and shared them with each family. They cooked some food and felt that this was unusually delicious.

Later, he told them to plant some in their gardens. Ali told them to clean and take care of these things until their leaves appeared mature and large. Then they could dig them and remove the food from them. Afterwards, he told them to call these things, "*Gho*." This was because they originated from the body of his little brother, Gho.

So now, the Buang People call yams, "*gho*" [[sup]N[/sup]*goH* (Hooley, 1970: 254)] in their language. Because of this, the Buang People often plant many yams in their gardens. This cannot cease because *gho* originated from Gho's bones.

A. P. Stiven
Port Moresby
National Capital District

A2686.4.3. Origin of yams; B211.2.12K+. Speaking marsupial; D179.6K+M. Transformation: man to marsupial; D457.12+. Transformation: bone to yam; D1810.8.2. Information received through dream; D1837. Magic weakness; F401.3+. Spirit in marsupial form; F401.6. Spirit in human form; F402.1.11. Spirit causes death; F490+. Masalai; P251.5. Two brothers; S110. Murders; V61.3+. Dead buried

A Little Boy Tricked Two *Masalais*

(Wantok 1030, March 24, 1994, page 23)

Long, long ago, in the time of the ancestors, there dwelled two *masalai* men in the **Kabwum** area of **Morobe** Province [**Selepet** People]. There were also two villages there called **Konimdo** and **Dengop**.

The two *masalai* men dwelled in Konimdo. One was deaf and had good eyesight. The other had good hearing and was blind. Between the two villages, there was a big river named Pumune.

One time, the *masalai* men decided to dam the Pumune River. They dammed the river, then they went to their house. At this time, a little boy was hiding and saw that the *masalai* men had dammed the river. When they went to their house, the boy went to Dengop Village. He met the other little boys and told them what the *masalai* men had done.

The next day, the boys went to bathe in the river. One boy jumped down first and the others followed him down to bathe in the river.

The boy who had jumped down and bathed first felt cold, so he went up and sat in the sun. He sat on top of a stone. While he was sitting on the stone, he became completely stuck.

In the afternoon, the *masalai* men finished working and wanted to go bathe in the river. The little boys saw them coming, so they fled to the village.

The poor boy who was stuck to the stone could not get up and run away. The *masalai*s came and saw him. They were terribly happy to see their food [i.e., the boy] there. So, they took ropes and logs, then they tied the boy like a pig and carried him to their house.

The one with good eyesight told the blind one that he would walk behind. However, the blind one told him that he had bad eyesight and that he must walk behind. So, the one with good eyesight went first and they carried the boy towards the house.

While they were walking, the *masalai* man with good eyesight did not turn back to look. He just sped ahead. When they arrived at the house, the one with good eyesight turned to look, but the boy was not there. They were furious and walked back along the trail to find the boy. They followed the trail and saw the boy sitting on top of a tree.

Then the good-eyed one told the blind one that he must stay underneath, prepare a boulder and wait. The good-eyed one climbed the tree and he fought with the little boy. They fought and fought and fought, then the little boy's strength was completely gone. He took a tree fruit and shot it directly at the good-eyed *masalai*, then the *masalai* fell down the tree.

When he fell down, the blind good-for-nothing thought that it was the boy falling. He took the huge boulder and finished his friend's breath. The boy went down and killed the blind one too, then he fled to his village.

Dekenam Olep

Hagen

Western Highlands Province

D931. Magic rock (stone); D2171. Magic adhesion; F490+. Masalai; G370+. Blind ogre; G370+. Deaf ogre; G440. Ogre abducts person; G512. Ogre killed; G519. Ogre killed through other tricks; K841. Substitute for execution obtained by trickery; P310. Friendship; Q213. Abduction punished; Q411. Death as punishment; R10.3. Children abducted; R210. Escapes; R220. Flights; R260. Pursuits; R311. Tree refuge; S110. Murders

The Ancestors Brought Forth Salt in Sinasina
(Wantok 1031, March 31, 1994, page 18)

Long, long ago, in the time of the ancestors of the people of Gunange [**Gunakane**] and **Sinasina** villages of **Simbu** Province, there lived two men [**Sinasina** People]. Their names were Keraga and Kamasua. They were very young men and they were very stylish. When they went along the trails, young women would just die for them.

One time, the men went to a mountain called Kuirima. They decided to go to the **Gumine** [**Golin** People] area, to villages such as Mul [**Nul**] and **Kone** [Sinasina People]. Their two girlfriends lived in this village.

The two of them went to bathe in the river, then they went towards the house, dressed well in their traditional adornments. They put oil on their bodies, so they were very shiny. They walked slowly across the mountain.

When they arrived at the village, they went directly to the house and knocked on the house door where their two girlfriends lived. The two women opened the door and saw their boyfriends. The men went inside the house, sat and told stories. They finished telling stories, then they went to sleep.

In the early morning, they awoke and wanted to walk back to their village. They walked and walked, then they arrived at the Waghi [Wahgi] River. The river did not have a bridge, so they wanted to jump across on stones.

While they were jumping on stones, they heard something like the sound of women calling behind them. When they turned to look, they saw two young women standing by the river and calling. They turned to go back and see the women, but when they arrived, neither was there. They tried to listen for them calling, but they heard nothing. They crossed the river again, but when they were in the middle, they heard them calling again.

So, one stayed and the other went back. However, when he arrived there, there were no women. The one who stayed in the river saw his buddy standing with the two women. He went there too, but when he arrived, there were no women. He told his buddy that when he was still in the river, he saw the women standing with him. However, his buddy said that there were no women there.

They began to check the nearby forests and grasslands. They checked everything, but to no avail. However, when they raised the grasses, they saw a white liquid arising. They took it and tasted it. When they tasted it, the liquid was as satisfying as salt. They took their bamboo tubes and filled some, then they carried it to the village. At the village, they told everyone that they had found salt. Everyone went to see the water and make salt. This water is still there in the Sinasina area and the people still gather salt there.

Kelly Wamiel
Port Moresby
National Capital District

A942.2. Origin of salt springs; D2095. Magic disappearance; P310. Friendship; T50. Wooing

Mondogo [Scabby] Used a Trick
to Marry a Gorgeous Woman
(Wantok 1032, April 7, 1994, page 20)

Long, long ago, in the Tarox Clan House in **Kainantu**, in **Eastern Highlands** Province, there lived a scabby boy [**Agarabi** People]. At this clan house, there also lived a young woman who was just like an angel. Many nice and handsome young men also lived there. They would put their bodies against the young woman.

They often mocked the scabby boy, saying that the young woman would like him and that he must ask whether she wanted to marry him. However, the crocodile-skinned boy did not care. He would tell them that they could joke about him. So, the young boys always joked about him. He was ashamed and always just stayed in Tairox [Tarox].

One time when the sun was very bright, all of the men and women of Tairox went into the forest to hunt for wild game. All of the young men also went and the crocodile-skinned boy followed them.

The young men went and killed a wild pig, then they wanted to cook it in an earth oven in the forest. They did not have fire to cook it, so they sent the crocodile-skinned boy back to the clan house to fetch a fire to bring back for them to make a big fire. The scabby boy listened to them and he sped towards the village. When he arrived at the village, he saw that all of the doors were shut. Only one house door was open. This was the house of the sharp-looking woman.

The crocodile-skinned boy ran to look inside the house, then he saw that the sharp-looking woman was terribly sick and lying inside the house. He saw that no one else was there. He went inside the house and sat by her.

He thought to himself that this was the young woman whom the boys had joked about to him, that she was terribly sick and that no one else was there, "That's it, it's just me. What should I do now?" He thought like that, then a thought came into his head. Quickly, the scoundrel approached her.

He sat by her and raised her "grass" skirt, then he looked at her buttocks. The rotten scoundrel put his buttocks by her, then he laid a huge turd. She was sick and she did not notice. After he defecated, he rubbed it on her buttocks.

He went back outside the house and searched for leaves, then he came and cleaned the feces from her. He raised her legs up and down, then she felt as if there was a man holding her. She opened her eyes and he told her, "Sister, you're terribly sick and you shat. I had wanted to light a fire when I noticed this, so I went to remove it. You were just sleeping, so I came to clean it."

She was terribly sick and she did not speak. She just slept. The bad boy cleaned her well and spied upon her private parts. He looked at all of the places on her body.

The scoundrel cleaned the feces, then the woman's father and mother arrived. They saw him and shouted loudly, then they scolded him, "What are you doing?" When the girl heard this, she awoke and told them that she was sick had defecated. She told them that the scabby boy had wanted to light a fire, and that he had seen her and cleaned her. The father and mother did not say any more. They shut their mouths and stayed quiet.

The bad boy finished cleaning the feces, then he took the fire and went into the forest. He and the other boys made a fire, then they made a huge earth oven and they ate.

After one month passed, she told her parents that she must marry the scabby boy because he had seen every part of her body. So, she married the young crocodile-skinned boy. The marriage came from just the little trick that the ringworm boy had performed. All of his friends were completely ashamed that what they had jested had actually happened.

Lapun R. [Reuben K.] Nassoh
Kainantu
Eastern Highlands Province

K1200. Deception into humiliating position; K1372. Woman engaged to marry by trick; L161. Lowly hero marries princess; P210. Husband and wife; P232. Mother and daughter; P234. Father and daughter; P310. Friendship; T100. Marriage; X716.1H+. Befouling with excrement; X743H+. Voyeurism

Children Tricked and Killed
a *Masalai* from Tami Island

(Wantok 1033, April 14, 1994, page 16)

Long, long ago, in the time of the ancestors, there was a *masalai* who dwelled on an island near Finsafen [Finschhafen] in **Morobe** Province. This island is called **Tami** [**Tami** People].

The *masalai* just stayed and waited. When the islanders made parties or big festivals, the *masalai* would go out of his hole and steal their children, then he would carry them away and eat them. The *masalai*'s name was Wentin.

One time, the men made a huge feast. They celebrated, sang and danced. However, they did not know that Wentin was coming. When he arrived, he enticed the children to try sailing on his new canoe. They would go out to the deep sea, then later they would return. However, when they went out, they sailed all of the way out to an island near **Siassi** [**Mutu** People].

When they arrived on the island, the *masalai* left them there and fled to another island. The *masalai* wanted to stay and wait until the boys were dead, then he would come eat them. However, the boys did not die. They lived well for a while and had a strong belief that Wentin was a *masalai* man.

The boys dug three big holes, then they went out to the beach. They cooked sea cucumbers in an earth oven, then they filled the holes. Afterwards, they covered the holes and went to hide in the forest.

Wentin stayed for a while, then he went to check on the boys. When he arrived, he smelled the sea cucumbers and thought that the boys had died. He was elated because he thought that they had died and that the smell was coming from them.

Slowly, he paddled his canoe up to the shore, then he went directly to one hole and gorged himself. When the boys saw him gorging on the sea cucumbers, they took a stone and shot his canoe. Wentin was surprised. He looked around to see what had made the noise. However, he did not see anything. The scoundrel did not care, he still kept at the sea cucumbers. After a while, he finished two holes and he jumped into the last hole.

When he went inside and ate, the boys ran to his canoe and paddled it seaward, fleeing from Wentin. When Wentin finished the last hole, he looked towards the beach and his canoe was not there.

The scoundrel was completely irate. He pulled his two ears up, enlarging them like sails and he followed the boys away. He went and saw the boys, then he was elated and said, "From whom are you fleeing? I'm coming to eat you now." Then the boys were afraid and cried.

However, it was quite fortunate that the boys had heated two stones in the earth oven until they were red hot. The stones were lying upon the canoe platform. When Wentin came, they said "Good morning" to him, then they shouted for him to come and eat his two "taros" first. Afterwards, he could eat them. When Wentin opened his mouth, the boys threw the two stones into his mouth. The stones burned his insides and he died, falling into the sea, lost forever. The boys were elated and they arrived back at their village. Their kin made a huge party.

Jacob Kaliu
Tami Island
Finchafen [Finschhafen]
Morobe Province

[For a similar story, see *Wantok* #878.]

D670+. Magic flight with ears; F490+. Masalai; F542.2+. Pulled ears enlarge; G421. Ogre traps victim; G422. Ogre imprisons victim; G440. Ogre abducts person; G512.3.1+. Ogre tricked into eating hot stones; K710. Victim enticed into voluntary captivity or helplessness; K951.1+. Murder by tricking into eating hot stones; K1860. Deception by feigned death (sleep); R210. Escapes; R260. Pursuits; S110. Murders; S145. Abandonment on an island; S301. Children abandoned (exposed)

An Old Person Enticed Two Brothers and
the Little Brother Became a Snake-Man

(Wantok 1034, April 21, 1994, page 16)

Long, long ago, in a small village called Lakukun [**Lakungkung**], in **West New Britain** Province, two little brothers lived with their mother [**Kaulong** People]. Their father had died, so they lived with their mother.

The little brothers were very good friends. They never fought with each other or with their mother, they just lived well.

One time, their mother told them that she would leave them to go to the garden. She told them that if an old person came and gave them food covered with leaves, they could not take it and eat it. They must tell the old person that they were full. Their mother finished speaking to them, then she left them in the village and went to the garden.

Before long, an old person came to the two brothers. The old person gave them a bundle of food. However, the big brother told the old person that they were full and not [hungry]. However, the old man was quite insistent that they just take the food bundle and eat it. The big brother persisted and told the old person that they were not [hungry]. The old person spoke insistently for a while, then the little brother took the food bundle and ate it. The old person saw this, left them, and walked away. The little brother ate the food bundle for a while, then he finished it.

In the afternoon, the mother left the garden and walked to the village. The big brother told their mother what had happened. The mother was worried about her little son, so she cooked some taros and other food. That night, they went inside the house and slept. The big brother slept on one bed. The little brother and his mother slept on another bed. The mother thought about her little boy and she did not go to sleep quickly. She stayed there until her little boy slept, then she also slept.

Late that night, the little boy turned into a big python. His head looked human, but from his legs up to his neck, he looked like a snake.

In the morning, the big brother and his mother saw what had happened to the little boy. They were very sorry for him. The little boy was ashamed for his mother and big brother, so he told them to make a house for himself. The big brother made a small house and put his little brother inside of it.

They lived for a while, then the big brother married a woman. He prohibited his wife from going inside or even near the small house.

One time, the big brother and his mother went to the garden. Then the big brother's wife went and looked into the little house to see why her husband had prohibited her from going near it or inside it. When she looked inside, she saw her husband's little brother. The head was like that of a man. From the neck to the legs, it was like a snake.

In the afternoon, the big brother and his mother went back to the village. They heard a [boy] crying inside the little house. Then they went to check and they saw the little boy crying there. They asked him why he was crying. He told them that he was crying because he was ashamed that his sister-in-law had seen him.

The little boy told them that he would no longer live with them and that he would leave them. Before long, he left the little house and fled. The two of them followed him. The little boy fled and went down to a river called Akse. He went underwater, then he [raised] his head above the water and said good-bye to them. He went underwater, leaving forever. The big brother and his mother were troubled and cried terribly for him, then they returned to the village.

[Anonymous]

B29.2.1. Serpent with human head; C172+. Brother-in-law tabu; D191B. Transformation: boy to serpent (snake); D551. Transformation by eating;

D682. Partial transformation; D696. Transformation during sleep; D1030. Magic food; J652. Inattention to warnings; J1050. Attention to warnings; P210. Husband and wife; P231. Mother and son; P251.4+. One brother acts wisely, another acts unwisely; P251.5. Two brothers; P262. Mother-in-law; P263. Brother-in-law; P264. Sister-in-law; P265+. Daughter-in-law; Q325. Disobedience punished; Q551.3.2+. Punishment: transformation into snake; R213. Escape from home; R260. Pursuits; T100. Marriage; W31. Obedience; W126. Disobedience

Because of the Father's Mistake, the Mother Left Him and the Two Children
(Wantok 1035, April 28, 1994, page 18)

In the Pagwi area of **East Sepik** Province, there was a village called Werman [**Wereman**, **Sawos** People]. Long, long ago, all of the cassowaries of this area would go and bathe in a river where no humans went.

However one time, a man traveled in the forest. He went and went, to all of the places where no one had ever gone. The man went around and around, then arrived at the river where the cassowaries bathed. When he arrived there, he saw many cassowaries filing down, about to bathe in the river. He hid nearby, then he watched them.

He saw a nice, sweet, gorgeous woman go down and remove her feathers, then she jumped into the water. The guy trembled quietly, then he went to fetch her feathers and hide them.

After all of the cassowary women finished bathing, they jumped up and searched for their feathers then they went back to their home. However, the one young woman came up and searched for her feathers, but they were not there. She worked very hard, searching and searching. All of the others put on their feathers, becoming cassowaries, then they fled.

She worked hard at searching for her feathers, then the man came out of his hiding place. She saw this and was terribly ashamed, but he told her not to be ashamed. They would go to his village and he would marry her. So, she followed him to his village.

They married and lived in his village, raising two children. Many years passed, then the children grew big. One time, one of the children followed the mother to make sago. The other child stayed with the father in the village.

The father told the story to this child about his marriage with his mother. The father showed him a bundle on top of the house and told him that it was his mother's "grass" skirt. He had taken this and married his mother. The child said that he wanted this skirt, so the father removed it and brought it down, then he showed it to him and put it back.

In the afternoon, the mother and the other child returned to the village, then the mother arranged things to eat. After she finished cooking and they had eaten, the father went to the spirit house. Only the mother and the children stayed back at their house.

The mother washed them, then she told them stories. Afterwards, the child who had stayed with their father during the day told their mother the story that the father had told him. The mother listened and asked the child to show her where the father had hidden her skirt. The boy showed his mother, then she took it and held it.

In the early morning, she awakened her children and cooked their food. Then she taught them the things that they would do to become big men and to live with their father. After she finished speaking to them, she took her skirt and held it.

The boys' father awoke at the spirit house, then he walked back to the house. When he arrived, he saw a cassowary fleeing into the forest, then he knew that his wife and run away. He went and spoke to the children, then they just cried because their mother could not return again.

Solah Suanomo

Lae

Morobe Province

D169.4W. Transformation: woman to cassowary; B290+. Cassowary removes skirt or skin to bathe; D350+W. Transformation: cassowary to woman; D361.1. Swan Maiden; D530+. Transformation by removing skirt; D531+. Transformation by removing feathers; K300. Thefts and cheats—general; K1350. Woman persuaded (or wooed) by trick; P210. Husband and wife; P230. Parents and children; P231. Mother and son; P233. Father and son;P250. Brothers and sisters; R213. Escape from home; T100. Marriage; V112.1. Spirit huts

[The ancestor story in *Wantok* #1036 is the same as that in #1020.]
[There was no ancestor story in *Wantok* #1037.]
[The ancestor story in *Wantok* #1038 is the same as that in #999.]
[The ancestor story in *Wantok* #1039 is the same as that in #988.]

A *Masalai* Marsupial Helped a Woman Return to Her Two Children

(Wantok 1040, June 2, 1994, page 20)

Before, in the time of the ancestors, there was a married couple who lived in a village. They lived for a while, then one time, they had no food in the house. The woman told her husband that they would go into the forest to beat sago pith. However, the man said that he was tired, so he went and cut the sago palm tree down, then he returned to the village. He told his wife to take the two children and they themselves could go beat the sago pith.

She took the two little children and they went into the forest to scrape sago. They went and scraped sago until the afternoon. In the late afternoon, a heavy rain fell and it became dark very quickly. She noticed this and was sorry for the children because they were not yet grown. There was a small garden hut near the place where they were scraping sago.

So, she took her children and they went into the hut, then she told them that they would sleep there because they were too far away and they could not walk back. They went inside the hut, then the mother made a fire and just cooked sago in the fire. They ate and slept.

A heavy rain fell that night, showering the mother and making her terribly cold. However, she awoke and made a good fire, then they fell dead asleep. The mother did not give sleep a chance: she slept just like a dead person.

Late that night, a big python that lived in the river came up and smelled them. It knew that there was game nearby. It went and saw the three of them sleeping there. It saw the mother and began to open its mouth, then it swallowed her. The mother was completely dead asleep and she did not know that the python was swallowing her. The python swallowed the mother then it went back into the river to its home.

The children's mother slept and slept, then she needed to urinate so she awoke. However, when she opened her eyes, it was completely dark. She tried to move back and forth, but she could not do so. Quickly, she realized that she was inside the belly of a big snake. The children awoke in the early morning, searched for their mother, then shouted.

Their mother was inside the snake's belly for a while. Later, she thought of her *kina* shell that was inside of her armband. When she would cook foods in the fire, she would take this *kina* shell and scrape the foods. She removed the *kina* shell from her armband and began to cut the big python's belly. She cut and cut, then the snake died and she leapt outside.

When she came out, she saw that she was in the middle of the water. She swam and swam to the side where her children were searching for her.

She swam and went nearby. She tried to hold a tree branch to get up to the ground, but when she was about to go up, the tree branch broke and she fell back into the water. She did not have a way to get up. She tried to swim, then a rat came and saw her. The rat said, "Hold my tail and I'll lift you." She listened to what the rat said and she held its tail. When the rat was about to pull her straight up, the rat's tail broke and she went back into the water. Then a marsupial (*sikau*) came and the same thing happened. After a while, she was completely out of breath.

At this time, a ghost woman that lived on top of a tree saw her and was sorry for her. The ghost turned into a marsupial (*kapul*), descended the tree, and told the woman to hold her tail. The woman said, "No," but the marsupial was insistent. So, the woman held the marsupial's tail and the marsupial told her that she must close her eyes. When she closed her eyes, the marsupial [raised] her, and the two children were very happy to see their mother.

The ghost asked the woman to pay for her hard work. She told the woman to bring a pig and food, then leave them at the big tree. So, she went to the village and followed the *masalai*'s [ghost's] instructions. She brought the things there, then she returned to the village.

William Wani
Wewak
East Sepik Province

[Mr. Wani wrote the ancestor story in *Wantok* #983. He wrote the ancestor story in *Wantok* #870. He is probably from the **Mongol** People, **East Sepik** Province.]

B211.2.9. Speaking rat; B211.2.12K+. Speaking marsupial; D310+W. Transformation: marsupial to woman; B430+. Helpful marsupial; B437.1. Helpful rat; B540+. Marsupial rescuer; B875.1. Giant serpent; D179.6K+W. Transformation: woman to marsupial; E379.1. Return from dead to rescue from drowning; E423.2+. Revenant as marsupial; E425.1. Revenant as woman; F401.3+. Spirit in marsupial form; F490+. Masalai; F911.7. Serpent swallows man; F912.2. Victim kills swallower from within by cutting; P210. Husband and wife; P230. Parents and children; P250. Brothers and sisters; Q53. Reward for rescue; R100. Rescues; W111. Laziness

The *Masalai* of Urin Village

(Wantok 1041, June 9, 1994, page 18)

[There was] a village near Kimbe called **Urin** that had a forest where most women never traveled [**Pulie** People, **West New Britain** Province]. This has been true from the time of the ancestors until now. Even nowadays, women never travel to this area. The story of this place goes as follows.

Long, long ago, two women of Urin Village followed a river upstream. They hunted for crayfish in the river because the river had slowly dried and the crayfish had found hiding places, just from lying on top of the water.

The two women had awoken in the very early morning, then prepared things for walking upstream. They would follow the river, then arrive at another village where people still spoke the same language.

The two of them left their Urin village and began following the river up to the other village. While they went upriver, they grabbed crayfish and filled their net bags. They carried them with them up towards the river's headwaters.

They just did this for a while, then they arrived someplace and sat to rest for a short while. They made a fire to cook some crayfish, then they ate. Later, they would walk up to the headwaters, then down to the village.

The women did not know that the place where they were sitting was a *masalai* place. They made the fire, then they cooked the crayfish. One of them saw a huge wild sugarcane (*pitpit*) plant by the river. She saw this and told the other that they must take it, cook it with the crayfish and other food, and then eat.

The women got up and went to break the wild sugarcane, then they returned, cooked it in the fire and ate it with the crayfish. They finished eating then they wanted to walk away.

However, when they went just a little farther, a big earthquake shook the ground. They went up a little more and the earthquake became even stronger. The clouds also thundered and lightning came from the sky in the [middle of the day]. A strong rain and wind also arose, blanketing them completely.

The woman who had cut the wild sugarcane told the other woman that they must have done something wrong. This was because the cane that they had cut and cooked had been taken from a *masalai* place. She said that this place must be a *masalai* place, so the *masalai* would follow them and try to catch them.

The other one scolded her that she alone had done this and that the *masalai* would take both of them now. They talked for a while, then a strong wind and rain arose. The *masalai* also came.

The *masalai* went directly up to them and told them that they had ruined the nice [wild sugarcane] flower at his house, so he would take them and marry them.

The *masalai* had more powers and took them to his home, then they lived with him. So, from that time until now, not one woman has traveled to this place lest the *masalai* would take them too.

Mr. and Mrs. Rigita
Kimbe
West New Britain Province

C181. Tabu confined to women; C612. Forbidden forest; D2142.1. Wind produced by magic; D2143.1. Rain produced by magic; D2148. Earth magically caused to quake; D2149.1. Thunderbolt magically produced; F408.3. Spirits dwell at tabu place; F424. River-spirit; F460. Mountain-spirits; F490+. Masalai; P210. Husband and wife; T111. Marriage of mortal and supernatural being; T145.0.1. Polygyny; T192. Marriage by force

[The ancestor story in *Wantok* #1042 is the same as that in #1019.]

How Lime (Calcium Oxide) Came to Yangoru
(Wantok 1043, June 23, 1994, page 20)

This is the story of how lime (calcium oxide) for chewing betel nut really came to **Yangoru** [Village], **East Sepik** [Province, **Boiken** People]. It is also the story of how the people of **Kairiru** Island often poured water from a lake at Kairiru, and washed taros before they planted them [**Kairiru** People].

Long, long ago, in the time of the ancestors of **Wewak**, there were two *masalai*s from two big mountains in the area, so they were friends. The mountains were the big mountain of Kairiru and the big mountain of Yangoru, called Turu. The name of the Kairiru *masalai* was Tau and the name of the Mount Turu *masalai* was Rurun. OK, the story of the *masalai*s goes as follows.

One time, *masalai* Tau sent a message to Rurun that he would travel and see him. They would tell a few stories about positioning, then he would go back home. He sent the message to Rurun, then Rurun replied to him, saying that he would just wait for him there.

One time, in the very early morning, Tau took his baskets, some fish, some betel nuts, and some tobacco leaves. He carried them and went to see his friend in Yangoru.

He arrived at the place where his friend lived, then Rurun and his *masalai* kin made a huge party to celebrate his friend. They partied for a while, then they went to sleep.

However, one thing that Tau had forgotten to carry with him was his lime. In the morning, Tau awoke and wanted to chew betel nuts. He checked the basket for his lime, but it was not there. He thought and thought, then he knew that he had left the lime in his house at Kairiru. There was none now, so he sat and waited for Rurun to awake, then he would ask him for lime.

Rurun awoke in bed, made a cigarette for himself and went to see Tau. They argued about positioning. Tau's eyes were sleepy, so he asked Rurun for Rurun's lime, then he would chew betel nuts.

When he asked Rurun, Rurun shouted to [his] wife to bring forth some lime. Rurun's wife walked forward and raised her "grass" skirt upwards, then she lay between Tau and Rurun.

Oh my, when Tau saw this, he was shocked. He scolded Rurun about why he had done this kind of thing to his wife before his very eyes.

Then Rurun told Tau, "You spoke of lime, so I told my wife to bring lime. The lime is there." Then Rurun pointed to his wife's genitals. Rurun took betel nuts and betel peppers. He rubbed them on his wife's genitals and then he chewed them.

Oh my, when Tau saw this, he was shocked and sorry for his friend Rurun because his betel nut mixture did not become bright red [as it should].

Tau told Rurun that this was not real lime. He told Rurun that he would send a message for his own wife to bring real lime there, then he would chew betel nuts.

Tau sent a message back to the village. The next day, his wife carried a huge shell for making lime and two *limbum* baskets of *kina* shells.

When his wife arrived, she brought the baskets forth and gave them to Tau, then Tau gave them to Rurun and told him that this was [for] lime. When Rurun chewed betel nuts, his mouth became bright red and he spat very well. He was happy for the real lime and he told Tau to teach him the method for making lime. So, Tau took the *kina* shells, burned them in a sago palm container, making lime. Rurun saw this and he now knew the method for making lime for himself.

Rurun and his wife gave the power to plant taros to Tau and his wife in return. They took this to their village at Kairiru. Rurun would always travel to see Tau at Kairiru and take *kina* shells from him.

Petrus Pepeku
Kairiru Island
East Sepik Province

A978+. Origin of lime (calcium oxide); A2686.4.2. Origin of taro; F460. Mountain-spirits; F490+. Masalai; P210. Husband and wife; P310. Friendship; X712.1.1H+. Origin of lime (calcium oxide): woman's genitals; X736.3H+. Symbolic cunnilinctus; X743H. Humor concerning exhibitionism

Anger and Scolding Gave a Mondogo
[Scabrous] Woman to a Young Man

(Wantok 1044, June 30, 1994, page 20)

Long, long ago, in **Namatung** Village, in **Morobe** Province, there lived a young man who stayed in the village with the other young men. The young man was a very stubborn man, and he never listened to people.

One time, he went into the forest to make a hut for watching birds, then he would shoot them. He arrived there, then he wanted to make the hut, so he made a small hut for himself in which to hide.

He went inside the hut that he had made and he hid. He waited for the birds to come, then he would shoot them with his bow. He watched, then a huge dove (or pigeon) came and ate tree fruits. He took his bow and pulled it far back, then he shot down the big dove. However, the dove did not fall directly to the ground. The dove carried the young man's arrow and flew directly to an old woman's house, where it died. The old woman saw this and took the bird, then she cooked it very well and just waited. This was because she knew that the man who had shot the bird would follow it to get it.

The man saw that the dove had departed, so he walked and followed the bird's blood. He followed and followed, then he arrived directly at the old woman's house. He asked whether she had seen his bird with the arrow or not.

The old woman told him that she had cooked the bird and had been waiting for him there. The old woman had placed his arrow with the bird.

However, the young man scolded the old woman terribly. He beat her and called her various kinds of bad names. He scolded her and told her that he could not return to the village. He would sleep in her house.

The young man slept with the old woman, then in the early morning he wanted to depart. When he was about to leave, the old woman told him that he would see a pandanus (*marita*) fruit along the trail. He could not remove it with a stick. He must remove it with his hands.

However, the stubborn man went and ignored what the old woman said. He took a stick and removed the pandanus fruit. The pandanus fruit fell and broke into pieces. When he saw this, he wanted to go urinate. When he returned to get his arrow [stick], a scabby woman was waiting for him. He scolded the woman. However, she told him that this was because of his mistake, so he took her.

So, the young man did not do anything else and he carried his wife to the village. When he took her to the village, the others saw them. One of his pals asked him why he was taking this woman. He told the story to his pal, and then his pal wanted to do what he had done.

However, his friend was a good boy and he did the same thing that his pal had done. When his pal shot a bird and the bird fled to the old woman's house, he did not scold the old woman. He told her that she could eat the bird and he would sleep. However, in the morning he would take his arrow and return to the village.

In the very early morning, he awoke and wanted to leave. The old woman told him that there was a pandanus fruit in the middle of the trail. He must take this pandanus fruit by hand. He followed the old woman's instructions and when he took it, the pandanus became a gorgeous, copper-colored woman. He took her to the village.

When his friend heard the story, he was furious because he had not followed the instructions well and he had taken a rotten woman. His pal had listened and received a good woman.

Charles Maewong
Port Moresby
National Capital District
[Mr. Meawong also wrote the ancestor stories in *Wantok* #997 and 1004. He is from the **Kosorong** People.]

B31.6+. Giant pigeon; D431.4+W. Transformation: pandanus fruit to woman; J652. Inattention to warnings; J1050. Attention to warnings; P210. Husband and wife; P310. Friendship; P310+. One friend acts wisely, the other does not; Q40. Kindness rewarded; Q270. Misdeeds concerning property punished; Q280. Unkindness punished; T100. Marriage; W10. Kindness; W167. Stubbornness

[The ancestor story in *Wantok* #1045 is the same as that in #1004.]

Tantanu Gave Various Kinds
of Foods to the Siwai People

(Wantok 1046, July 14, 1994, page 15)

This is an ancestor story from the **Siwai** People of Bougainville Island about the origin of good food [**North Solomons** Province].

Long, long ago, in the time of the ancestors, there was not any good food at Siwai. The parents would leave the village every morning, then they would go into the forest to search for food. In the village, they would just leave the elderly with the children. Later, in the afternoon, they would carry the food that they had found in the forest back to the village.

One day, when all of the parents went into the forest, the boys saw a tall and handsome man walking towards their village. He walked and stood directly in the middle of the village where the signal drum was located.

The man asked the boys where their parents had gone. The children told him that their parents had gone to search for food in the forest. He also asked them which food they were searching for and the boys gave the name of this food as *kuhro*. This is a tree fruit.

Sometimes, their parents would be lucky and would kill marsupials (*kapul*), bandicoots, or pigs, then they would have plenty of meat to eat. When the parents would arrive, it would be almost night time.

This man was Meka Tantanu, but he did not want to tell the boys his name. Meka Tantanu was a man like God, or an important spirit in whom the people of Siwai believed.

OK, Tantanu told the little boys to go fetch a huge pot and to boil water. The boys just listened to what he told them to do because they wanted to see what he would do.

When the water in the pot was boiling, he told the boys to remove the lid. He told them that he would jump inside, then they would again shut the lid of the pot. When the water was boiling, Tantanu jumped inside and the boys shut the lid of the pot again.

The boys waited a very long time, then they knew that the man must have died, so they opened the pot. However, when they opened it, they saw various kinds of good foods inside the pot. Tantanu had gotten up and walked away to his home. He washed well, then he returned.

When the boys saw him coming, they thought that it was the man's ghost returning. They were terrified and they wanted to flee, but he told them that he was not a ghost.

So, the boys returned to him and he told them to try the foods that he had given them. The boys tried them, and they were delicious, so they put some aside. Tantanu told them the names of these foods, such as taro, banana, and the other kinds that he gave them. He told them that they must plant some of their foods.

However, the boys asked him what they should say when their parents arrived. He told the boys that when their kin came, they must say that Meka Tantanu gave the foods. When he said this, he disappeared.

When the boys' parents returned, they heard what had happened and saw the food. They were elated that their god had given food to them.

[Anonymous]

A1420.1+. Origin of food from boiled god; A2686.4.2. Origin of taro; A2687.5. Origin of banana; D2095. Magic disappearance; F490. Other spirits and demons; P230. Parents and children

A Crab Pinched a Sorcerer
(Wantok 1047, July 21, 1994, page 17)

Long, long ago, in the time of the ancestors, there was a man and a young woman who lived in a small place in the Finschhafen area of **Morobe** Province.

The woman's name was Kama and the man's name was Gumi. Only the two of them lived in this place. Not one man or woman lived with them.

They lived for a while, then one time, the woman went to the garden to get some food. She arrived at the garden, then she saw that the grasses were too big. She thought of removing some grasses, then she went to the garden hut.

Kama left her net bag and began removing some grasses. She worked and worked, then she saw that the clouds were filling the sky. She knew that a very heavy rain would fall.

Immediately, she took some food to carry back towards the house. She prepared everything and was about to return to the house.

She walked and walked, then she was about to cross a stream. However, a great downpour had fallen at the source of the stream, so the water was greatly flooded and she could not cross to the other side.

Kama sat and waited for a while for the water to recede, then darkness approached. The water did not recede, so she walked back to the garden hut. A heavy rain was also falling now. Along the trail, she encountered a crab. She tied its claws and took it with her.

When she arrived at the garden hut, she made a bonfire and slept. Before long, some sorcerer men, who were fleeing from the rain, came all of the way to the garden hut.

Kama heard their noises, so she went to hide under the firewood. The sorcerers arrived and wanted to take the firewood to make more fire. Before long, a sorcerer saw Kama under the firewood.

He pretended to the other sorcerers that he was sleepy, so he alone went to sleep. Late that night, he put a hand inside and tried to have sex with Kama. Immediately, Kama freed one of the crab's claws and put it to his genitals.

The crab gave it directly to his genitals. The sorcerer was in pain and he screamed. He ran and ran towards the fire, then the other sorcerers awoke. They thought that men from the village had found them.

The sorcerers fled in various directions. Kama also got up and fled back to her home. She told her husband and they laughed hysterically.

John Simogah
Lae
Morobe Province

D1711. Magician; F547.1.1. Vagina dentata; P210. Husband and wife; Q244.1. Punishment for attempted rape; Q451.10.1+. Punishment: attack on testicles; R220. Flights; X712.1H. Female genitals; X712.3.1H. Injury to testicles

Ignoring Instructions Killed the Little Brother

(Wantok 1048, July 28, 1994, page 17)

Long, long ago, there lived two brothers someplace. There were no other people there. One time, the big brother went down to the river and worked at fishing. He saw much rubbish coming downriver. He followed the river upstream to find out the origin of the rubbish.

He met an old man cutting a tree. He approached and looked at the old man. The old man asked him to go sit and help him. The old man asked him to gather the insects [probably beetle grubs] from the tree into a bamboo tube. The old man told him to put the good insects in one place and the bad insects in another. He followed the old man's instructions and gathered the insects until the old man had taken enough insects.

The old man asked the brother [about his intentions]. The old man said that they should sleep, then the next day he could return to his home. The brother was in agreement and they departed.

They went and arrived at a boulder. The old man struck the boulder with a stick, then a door opened. They went inside and the old man made a fire. He cooked the insects and they ate.

That night, the old man told the brother that when they slept, many noises would arise. He could not be afraid and open his eyes to see. He must just sleep and listen to the noises. That night, these things happened. The brother followed the old man's instructions and he just lay quietly, listening to the noises.

At dawn, the old man went outside the house and killed a big pig, then they filled two bamboo tubes. The old man asked the brother to climb a tree and to cut two branches. He told him that he must cut the good branches of the tree.

The brother climbed the tree and cut a good tree branch, then he wanted to cut another, but the knife missed and he cut it awkwardly. He carried down the two branches together. The old man put the pork into two net bags and hung the bags on the two branches.

After he did this, he told the brother that when he carried the bags of pork along the trail, that if a big bird came and pulled a bag, he must use the branches to chase the bird away.

After he said this, the brother carried his two bags of pork and walked away on the trail. Before long, a big bird came and tried to pull the bags. However, the brother thought of what the old man had said. He put the bags down on the ground, then he fought the bird with the branches until the bird noticed him and departed.

When the bird departed, the brother was surprised to see two very nice women standing with the bags of pork. One of them had only one leg. This was because the brother had not cut the branch well. The man's eyes popped out. He pulled the women and they went home.

At home, the little brother had become terribly worried for his big brother, so he had not eaten. When he saw his big brother arrive home, he jumped and went outside the house to hold him. When he saw the two nice women, he lusted for them.

The little brother asked the big brother to give one of the women to him, but the big brother did not agree with this. The little brother spoke sternly for a while, then he asked if he could take the bad-legged one and the big brother could take good woman. However, the big brother said, "No," to his question.

So, the little brother asked where he had found the two women, because he wanted to go find his own. The big brother told him that he would meet an old man, that he must listen to everything that he says, and that he must follow the instructions. The big brother finished speaking to him, then in the morning, he awoke and followed the river. When he arrived, he met the old man. The old man asked him to help him gather insects from the tree. However, the little brother spoke strongly that he wanted to follow his big brother's footsteps.

The old man queried him sternly, then they stayed and later went to his stone home. They went inside and the old man told him not to wake up and look if noises arose at night while they were sleeping.

That night, the various noises arose. The little brother was afraid and screamed, then he killed the old man. In the morning, he did not have a way to get outside the cave. He was stuck there inside the cave.

The big brother and his two wives waited for the little brother for a while. The little brother did not return. Then they went to the cave and called him. The little brother heard them and said that he had killed the old man and that he did not have a way to escape. The big brother heard this and knew that there was no way that he could help his little brother. So, the little brother stayed in the cave for a while. He became hungry and began to eat himself until he died inside the cave.

Jossie Manuo
Goroka
Eastern Highlands Province

[Jossie Manuo also wrote the ancestor stories in *Wantok* #372, 725, 747, and 799. He is probably from the **Kamano** People of **Eastern Highlands** Province.]

D431.2+W. Transformation: stick to woman; D1552.1. Mountain opens at blow of divining rod; G51.1. Person eats self up; J652. Inattention to warnings; J2130+. Fool kills only person who can free him; P210. Husband and wife; P251.5. Two brothers; P251.4+. One brother acts wisely, another acts unwisely; P263. Brother-in-law; P264. Sister-in-law; Q72K2. Obedience rewarded; Q211. Murder punished; Q325. Disobedience punished; Q411. Death as punishment; R45.3. Captivity in cave; R51.1. Prisoners starved; S110. Murders; T100. Marriage; T145.0.1. Polygyny; W31. Obedience; W126. Disobedience; W181. Jealousy

[The ancestor story in *Wantok* #1049 is the same as that in #434.]

Why Do Crocodiles Live in Ponds?

(Wantok 1050, August 11, 1994, page 19)

Long, long ago, the crocodiles traversed the big mountains and lived inside the very deep forest, like lizards and goannas. At this time, they were strong and all of the wild game was afraid of them. When a crocodile was hungry, it would chase all of the animals in the forest.

Whichever animals were not lucky enough to flee would go directly into the crocodile's mouth. These animals were just the poor bandicoots.

One day, the bandicoots decided to kill this crocodile or to remove it from the area. They made their decision, then they hid at the place where this crocodile slept.

The crocodile ate one of the bandicoots' kin, then its stomach was quite bloated and it slept quietly and panted. Quietly, the bandicoots went down and pulled tightly on its mouth, arms and legs.

Then they took a long rope and pulled the crocodile's tail. Very slowly, they pulled the crocodile down the mountain. They arrived at a huge lake where the water ran very strongly all of the way down to all of the big lakes that were far below, near the sea.

The crocodile did not know this. It was still sleeping and panting. Quickly, the bandicoots threw the crocodile down into the lake.

The water carried it down to the big lake, then the crocodile opened its eyes and found out that it was in a lake. It wanted to open its mouth to shout, but the rope was fastened around its mouth. The poor crocodile drank much water and died there.

All of the animals were very happy that the crocodile was far below and could not come up to eat them. So now, crocodiles live below in the lakes. They often just wait for animals because the animals become confused and approach [the crocodile], then they eat them.

Jada Wilson
Gordens
National Capital District

[Jada Wilson also wrote the ancestor story in *Wantok* #1017. He or she is probably from the **Motu** or **Koiari** People, **Central** Province.]

A2433.6+. Why crocodile lives in lakes; B211.2.12K+. Speaking bandicoot; R13.1+. Abduction by bandicoot; S131. Murder by drowning

A *Masalai* Man Stole Food

(Wantok 1051, August 18, 1994, page 2)

This ancestor story tells of a *masalai* man who lusted for other people's food. If people cooked food somewhere, he would change and become a man. Then he would go place [his] body by their food. This story comes from **Salata** Village, near Maprik, in **East Sepik** Province [**Bumbita Arapesh** People]. The story goes as follows.

Long, long ago, in the time of the ancestors, there was a *masalai* man. The *masalai* man's name was Ohenim. Ohenim lived by himself.

He lived for a while, then he heard rumors that they would kill a pig at **Omunibil** Village. He planned to go up there, turn into a real man, then cook with them.

The men asked, "Who will carry the food down to **Suhapuneb** Village? Our siblings live at this nearby village and we must think of them, otherwise they will make a big feast later and not think of us."

The *masalai* man agreed to do this, so they sent him with the food down to Suhapuneb Village. However along the way, *masalai* Ohenim removed his two eyes and put them on the side of the trail. Then he swallowed all of the meat and other food.

Later, he would go up to the village and tell the men that he had brought the food. The men would say, "Good man." The bad boy [*masalai*] would then return to his home.

He went there and heard the Suhapuneb Village men talking about making a feast again. He went down and placed himself among them. He would help them cut firewood, cut leaves, and prepare the feast.

After the food was [ready], they would divide it. The men would ask who would carry food to give to their siblings up at Omunibil Village. The bad boy would say, "Me." Then he would carry the food and do the same thing.

He went back to the village and told the men that he had carried the food and given it to the men, women and children of the other village. Then he went back to his home.

Some time later, the men of Omunibil made another feast. The men heard their kin's complaints from Suhapuneb, that they were greedy about food. They knew that Ohenim would befoul the food on the trail.

They ate, then they sent Ohenim to carry the food to Suhapuneb. One man followed the trail and saw what Ohenim did. Ohenim saw a man spying upon him. He was terribly ashamed, so he ran down to a nearby river and turned into crushed coral.

Kalsen Sailen
Maprik
East Sepik Province

D237. Transformation: man to coral; F401.6. Spirit in human form; F490+. Masalai; K420. Thief loses his goods or is detected; F541.11. Removable eyes; W151. Greed

The Last Brother Was Angry and Killed the Bad Man

(Wantok 1052, August 25, 1994, page 2)

One time, five brothers lived in **Kewe** Village, in **Southern Highlands** Province [**Kewa** People?]. These brothers lived very well. They made big gardens and had plenty of food to eat.

One time, the big brother told his four brothers that he would go somewhere to make a new garden. The other brothers prepared food and his bow and arrows for him to bring.

In the very early morning, the big brother awoke and carried the food and his things, then he walked away. He walked and walked to somewhere in the forest, then he saw a big bird. The big brother readied the bow and an arrow to shoot the bird. However, the bird heard a noise and jumped to another tree branch.

While he was searching for the bird, he saw a little boy cutting a tree. The big brother walked closer and asked him why he was cutting the tree.

The little boy said that he was cutting the tree to get the insects [probably beetle grubs] inside it [to eat]. He said that his parents had gone somewhere to make a big feast, that he had not wanted to go, and so he had come to cut the tree and get the insects.

Then the little boy asked the big man to help him by shoving his hand inside the tree hole and holding the insects. The big brother listened and shoved his hand into the tree hole. However, the little boy was quick and loosened the axe from the tree, then the tree came back and trapped the big brother's hand.

The boy went and turned into a giant man, then the big brother saw this and was completely confused. The man just held the axe and broke open the big brother's head, killing him. He carried the big brother's body, then he ate him.

The other four brothers were at the house, waiting for the big brother. However, he did not come, so they sent the second brother to find their big brother. The second brother went and arrived at the place where the boy was cutting the tree, searching for insects.

Then the boy saw the man's second brother. He asked him to help him by putting his hand into the tree hole, then to pull out the insects. The second brother listened and did this. When he put his hand inside the tree, the boy immediately loosened the axe and the tree came back, trapping the second brother's hand inside the tree.

The boy had tricked him, then he went fairly far away and turned into a giant man. He returned and took the axe, then he broke open the second brother's head. He killed him, then he took his body and ate it.

Three brothers were at home for a while, then they sent the third brother to find their two elder brothers. He went and arrived at the place where the boy was pretending to search for insects. Before long, the boy had tricked the third brother in the same way, killing him. Then he ate his body.

The fourth brother left the village and went to find the three elder brothers, then the same thing also happened to him. He too died and only the last brother was left at the village. He waited for his brothers in vain, then he planned to go find them on the next day.

In the very early morning of the next day, he left the village and walked away to find his brothers. He walked and walked, then he heard a noise. He walked closer and saw a giant cutting a tree. This time, the man did not hear the sound of the last brother walking towards him. So, he had not turned into a little boy.

The last brother walked very quietly, then he went up to the man. Then the last brother asked the giant what he was doing. The giant told him that he was cutting the tree and getting the insects. He asked the last brother to help him and to shove his hand into the tree, then to pull out the insects. However, the last brother said that he was too small of a boy and that his hand could not reach inside the tree.

The man spoke sternly, that he must help him. However, the last brother was insistent, so the big man shoved his own hand inside. The giant's hand passed one part of the tree, then the tree came down and blocked his hand. He stretched and pulled his hand, but he could not withdraw it, so he asked the boy to help him. However, the boy was short and he could not help shove the axe inside and wedge the tree. This was because the tree was big and terribly heavy.

The giant turned into a little boy so that the last brother could help him. At this time, the last brother saw him turn into a little boy. He had the idea that it was just this man who had tricked and killed his brothers. The last brother just took the axe and broke his head open, killing him. He left his body there and ran away to the village.

Nelson Goyana

Lae

Morobe Province

D28B. Transformation: boy to giant; D28+B. Transformation: giant to boy; D94B. Transformation: boy to ogre; D94+B. Transformation: ogre to boy; G100. Giant ogre; K1111. Dupe puts hand (paws) into cleft of tree (wedge, vise); K1601. Deceiver falls into his own trap (literally); P251.6.2+. Five brothers; Q211. Murder punished; Q411. Death as punishment; Q582. Fitting death as punishment; R220. Flights; S139.4. Murder by mangling with axe

[The ancestor story in *Wantok* #1053 is the same as that in #1019.]

Why Banana Plants Grow
Well and Bear Large Fruits

(Wantok 1054, September 8, 1994, page 16)

Long, long ago, there lived a man in **Timini** Village, in **Morobe** Province [**Mumeng** People]. He had many huge gardens.

Every day, he and his wife and children would go to all of the gardens, to weed and to gather the food. Then they would return to the house.

One time, the man made a new garden, then he planted taros, bananas, and wild sugarcanes (*pitpit*) there. The soil was very good and the taros grew very well. However, the bananas did not grow well.

One day, he went around the new garden in the very early morning. He was [surprised] to hear some men talking in the middle of the garden. So, he walked quietly to find out who was speaking inside his garden.

He looked around, but he did not see anyone. He heard the men's talking grow louder. He approached the place, then he heard the talking coming directly from the banana plants.

The banana plants were complaining to the wild sugarcanes that the canes must go far away from them because they were not getting good food. The bananas said that they were jam packed with wild sugarcanes, standing close to them, and that they could not grow well.

When the garden owner heard this, he quickly returned to the house and brought back a bush knife. He returned and cut all of the wild sugarcanes down to the ground, letting the bananas remain standing. After this, the bananas grew very well and bore very large fruits.

However, if you look closely at banana skins, you will see that some fuzz from the wild sugarcanes is still stuck to the banana skins.

These are the marks where wild sugarcanes adhered to the bananas from the time when the bananas complained, before the garden owner came and fixed the bananas' troubles.

John Punda

Enga Province

A2771.4+. Why banana bears large fruits; D1610.10.2. Speaking bananas; P210. Husband and wife; P230. Parents and children

A Ghost Woman Killed the Mother, But the Two Children in Her Belly Did Not Die

(Wantok 1055, September 15, 1994, page 16)

One time, there was a man named Emmai who lived with his wife. Emmai's wife was pregnant and they were waiting for the time when she would give birth.

One time, they went into the forest to hunt for *galip* nuts. They arrived at one tree that was bearing very many nuts, so Emmai climbed the tree and removed the nuts, throwing them down to his wife.

He worked at harvesting the *galip* nuts from the tree for a while, then he became thirsty for water. He asked his wife to go fetch water and bring it to him.

Emmai's wife went down to find water. A ghost woman had been hiding and watching them, so she climbed a mountain, then crossed over it. She went down and covered Emmai's wife, then she killed her.

The ghost woman urinated in a bamboo tube and brought it back to give to Emmai. The ghost woman knew [about] the *galip* nuts and she ate all of them, then she made her belly enlarge so that Emmai would not know that she was another woman.

When the woman gave the bamboo to Emmai to drink, Emmai noticed that it was not water because it smelled like urine. Emmai thought hard about what he would do because the ghost woman would kill him.

Emmai spilled the urine, then she saw this and asked him about it. However, Emmai said that he had drunk plenty of water in the morning, so he was not too thirsty for water.

Emmai descended the *galip* tree, then he began to gather the galip nuts in a net bag and to prepare to go back to the village. He told her to follow another trail to the village because he would travel the forest for a little while to check on some things first.

However, Emmai had lied to her and he arrived at the village first. He told all of his clan in the village, then they heated a stone in a fire and made a big earth oven. They dug a big hole, then above it they made a platform and put a mat for the woman to sit upon.

When the woman arrived at the village, Emmai took her to the platform, then he told her to sit. She sat with the other women of the village, then they ate there. Before long, she wanted to stand for a little because her legs were stiff. She got up and stood, then the place where she was sitting broke and she fell down the big hole where the hot stone had been readied. She shouted for the clan to help

her, but they threw more hot stones on top of her, burning her completely.

After the ghost woman died, the belly of Emmai's old wife had two boys underground. They had not died. One time, they worked their way up, breaking through the ground, up to their father's garden. They got up, then played and sang back and forth.

At this time, Emmai was weeding the garden and he heard the two boys singing. They were singing a song that Emmai loved to sing. In the song, they also sang the name of their father.

The boys sang, "Emmai, Emmai *mara mukoirong, mara nahingiron rori, singi rukuru, kururuki rukuru,* Emmai *ne* Emmai *ne.*"

Oh my, when Emmai heard his name, he knew that it must be his children. So, he went and hid, then spied upon his two children who were singing and dancing.

He saw that the two boys had his face exactly, so he went to talk with the clan in the village. They came and hid at this place so as to hold them.

The next day, when the two boys came out to sing, their father jumped out and grabbed them both. The clan from the village also came and aided Emmai. They held the two boys, then brought them to the village. They made a huge feast and celebrated Emmai's good sons.

This story comes from the **Siwai** [People] of Bougainville [**North Solomons** Province].

[Anonymous]

E250. Bloodthirsty revenants; E425.1. Revenant as woman; E446.2. Ghost laid by burning body; E541. Revenants eat; K735.1. Mats over holes as pitfall; K1044.1+. Dupe nearly induced to drink urine; K1930. Treacherous impostors; P210. Husband and wife; P233. Father and son; P251.5. Two brothers; Q211. Murder punished; Q414. Punishment: burning alive; S112. Burning to death; T545. Birth from ground; T570. Pregnancy; T584.2.1. Child born of dead mother in grave; T587. Birth of twins; T685. Twins; X717H+. Urine as gift; W157. Dishonesty

A Young Boy Killed a Ghost Pig, Then the Tribe Returned Home

(Wantok 1056, September 22, 1994, page 22)

One time, on an island called **Wutulim**, there lived many people. On this island, the people were often quite afraid because there was a big ghost pig that came and ate them. It had killed many people.

One time, everyone decided to flee the island and go to another place. This was because the ghost pig had eaten people for a while and few remained.

OK, one day, everyone prepared [their] canoes and other things, then they began to paddle away to find a new place to live. When everyone departed, they left just one woman on the island. This was because she was pregnant and her husband was dead.

The poor woman lived by herself and did not have anyone to talk to, so she made a big hole and went to hide inside of it. Every afternoon, the big wild pig would come to search for people, but there were no people, so it would return to its home.

One time, after she had lived there for a while, she gave birth. When everyone from the village had left her, she had been pregnant, so she had been unable to help herself find a place on top of a canoe to go with them. She lived for a while, then she gave birth to a boy. She took care of her baby very well until he grew to be a big man.

One day, the boy asked his mother why only they lived there and why no other people lived with them on the island. Then his mother told the story of what had happened. The boy listened for a while, then he became angry. He told his mother that he would try to kill the ghost pig and to save the island.

So, his mother began to teach him how to make bows and arrows to kill wild game. He learned from his mother until his arms were strong, then he pulled the bow and shot wild game with arrows.

One time, he was ready to fight with the wild pig, then he and his mother prepared everything to kill the ghost pig. The boy and his mother heated stones. They made seven big pyres for the boy to stand near and to fight with the ghost pig.

When they made the bonfires, the ghost pig smelled them and left its home. It took off and went down to the village. The boy went to stand at the first pyre, then he waited for the ghost pig to arrive. When the ghost pig arrived, it wanted to fight with him. He jumped over the first pyre, then he shot an arrow that stuck to the ghost pig's body.

The ghost went closer, then the boy jumped over the second pyre. He did this until he arrived at the seventh pyre. At this time, many of his arrows were stuck to the ghost pig's body and the pig fell down on top of the bonfire.

The boy went down and cut off the ghost pig's head. Afterwards, he made a canoe. He put the head on top of the canoe, then he put it towards the sea.

The ghost pig's head drifted on the sea until it arrived at the island where the people of this island had fled. When they saw the ghost pig's head arrive, they were all sur-prised. They wanted to return to the island and see who it was that had killed the big ghost pig.

So, they sent the leaders off, then they gathered the young boys with their mothers. They went back and told everyone, then they took their belongings and returned to their old island. They cooked a huge feast and made a big party to celebrate the woman and her son.

Konzil Ray

Lae

Morobe Province

B16.1.4.1. Giant devastating boar; B871.1.2. Giant boar; E423.1.5. Revenant as swine; E440+. Ghost laid by spear/arrow; E446.2. Ghost laid by burning body; E446.3. Ghost laid by decapitating body; G512.1+. Ogre killed with spear/arrow; G512.1.2. Ogre decapitated; G512.3. Ogre burned to death; G510.4. Hero overcomes devastating animal; P230. Parents and children; P231. Mother and son; R213. Escape from home; R315. Cave as refuge; R316.1. Refuge on island; S145. Abandonment on an island; S185. Cruelty to pregnant woman; S371+. Abandoned woman's son becomes hero; T570. Pregnancy; T580. Childbirth; Z71.5. Formulistic number: seven

A Bird and a Turtle Brought a Young Woman Back from the Forest

(Wantok 1057, September 29, 1994, page 22)

Long ago on **Tami** Island, in the Finschhafen area of **Morobe** Province, the villagers would lock the first daughter in the house when she was about to become a big woman [**Tami** People].

So, one time they locked a young woman in a house. Inside this house, there was also an ancestral stone axe that was used to cut trees and to carve canoes and statues.

At this time, everyone departed and the village was empty. The stone axe turned into a woman, then she jumped down to the floor of the house and asked the young woman to go fishing in the sea with her.

The woman was afraid that the other people of the village would see her. However, the fake woman was persistent and said that it was time for fishing and that everyone had gone to the sea. She said that they must go, or else they would not have fish to eat in the house.

The woman agreed, so they pulled a canoe down to the sea and paddled away. They paddled towards the middle of the sea, then the fake woman saw a big tree branch drifting towards them. She asked the young woman to go sit upon it, then she would paddle towards the reef and fish there.

The young woman listened and followed her instructions. However, the fake woman had tricked her and she paddled the canoe back to the beach. Then she turned back into a stone axe in the house.

The young woman drifted on the sea for a while and the woman did not return. She looked around and waited to see whether some people would paddle by, then she would ask them for help.

She drifted on the sea, then she held a small turtle. She put it inside a hole in the tree on which she was drifting. She grabbed small fish and gave them to the turtle to eat.

She did this for a while, then she found a bird feather. She held it and tied it to a coconut husk, then the bird feather transformed into a very young bird. Before long, she drifted to an island. She stayed on the island and took care of the turtle and bird until they grew big.

One time, the turtle and the bird asked their mother about her home. She said that her home was Tami Island. So, they asked their mother to prepare things, then they would go to her home.

In the morning, she went to sit on the back of the turtle, then they swam in the sea and the bird flew up in the sky until they arrived at Tami Island.

She went into her parents' house and they were very happy to see her return. They had thought that she was dead, but she had returned and they were happy.

She told people not to throw rubbish from the fire into the sea or to shoot birds on trees. She did this because her turtle lived in the sea and her bird also flew in the village.

However, people did not do what she had told them to do. They threw ashes into the sea that burned the turtle's eyes. So, the turtle told its mother that it could no longer live there because its eyes were ruined. After it said this, it swam in the sea, back to the island where it had lived before.

The bird was also afraid to live on Tami Island because boys shot it with stones. So, it told its mother about this problem, and then it also flew back. The bird and the turtle lived on their island.

So now, when men hunt for turtles and find one with red eyes, they let it go back to the sea.

[Anonymous]

A1520+. Why red-eyed turtles are released back to the sea; B211.3. Speaking bird; B211.6.3K. Speaking turtle; B551.5. Turtle (tortoise) carries person across river (ocean); D250+W. Transformation: woman to axe; D434+W. Transformation: axe to woman; D447+. Transformation: feather to bird; P272. Foster mother; P600+. Customs associated with menarche; S141.3+. Abandonment on log floating in sea; W157. Dishonesty

Why There Is Plentiful
Taro at Alkena [Atkena]
(Wantok 1058, October 6, 1994, page 22)

In a village called Alkena [**Atkena**] in the Hagen [area] of **Western Highlands** Province, there lived a bad man [**Hagen** People]. Everyone in this village was afraid of him because he was a very strong man. His name was Ona Glame. He often fought many men in the village and he also killed them because he had a great strength. He had more strength than all of the other people of the village had.

Ona Glame never slept well in his house because he knew that the men of the village would follow him to get revenge for the deaths of their kin whom he had killed.

One time, Ona did not want to sleep in the village, so he carried his things and traveled into the forest. He went and saw a big tree, then thought of setting a trap there.

He made a trap on top of the tree, then he wanted to descend and make a sleeping hut for himself to watch the trap. Before long, he heard the trap make a noise and the trap rope was loose. He ran and went to see it. Oh my, it was not a small cassowary stuck in the trap. He went and removed the cassowary, but the cassowary was not dead yet. So, they fought and fought until Ona killed the cassowary. Then he tied it with rope and hung it from his garden hut.

He returned and prepared the trap again, then he slept until the very early morning. He awoke and saw a huge marsupial (*kapul*) stuck in the trap. So, he climbed the tree and began to remove the marsupial. He went down, put it with the cassowary and carried them back to the village.

At night, he slept and dreamt that his trap held a giant bird, a bird like a dove (or pigeon). When he awoke in the morning, he thought of the dream and looked up to the trap. His dream was true. The largest of birds was stuck in the trap.

He climbed and cut the rope from the tree, then the bird fell down to the ground. He gathered all of the wild game, then he thought of going to the village and telling his family to come and carry the game.

So, he went to the village and took his brothers and maternal cousins back to the forest. They carried the three big animals to the village to make an earth oven, or [heated] stones to cook the game with taros and bananas.

All of his kin gathered the food and things like leafy greens, then they began to heat the stones to make an earth oven. Many people in the village were afraid of Ona, so they did not help him much.

However, Ona thought of making this feast and fixing people's worries so that they could forget all of their unease. Then everyone would be in harmony again.

They had gathered the food for the earth oven, but they were short of taro. This was because this village did not have good land for planting taro.

Ona took water and spilled it on the earth oven when they were about to cover it. Before long, a great downpour fell, then a big flood came to the village.

The river flooded tremendously and went into the village, ruining things and breaking houses apart. It also killed many people at this time. The river rose as a great flood, higher than the village.

Since this time, the village has had water and was good for planting taro. So now, this village had very many taros to eat.

Simon Nonga
Mount Hagen
Western Highlands Province

A1011. Local deluges; A2730+. Why taro grows well in one place; B31.6+. Giant pigeon; B871.2+. Giant marsupial; B872+. Giant cassowary; D1810.8.2. Information received through dream; D2143.1. Rain produced by magic; D2151.8. Magic flood; F610. Remarkably strong man; P251. Brothers; P295. Cousins; S110. Murders

[The ancestor story in *Wantok* #1059 is the same as that in #835.]

Why Cats and Rats are Enemies

(Wantok 1060, October 20, 1994, page 22)

Long, long ago, in the time of the ancestors, Cat and Rat were very good friends. They lived together, worked together, ate together, and traveled together. Cat's food was birds, and Rat's foods were taros and sweet potatoes.

One time, they wanted to go to the other side of a river. The river was too big and they could not cross it. They wanted to make a canoe, then they would drift to the other side.

They went to a garden, then they saw a huge taro. They worked hard at digging the ground, then it became dark. The next day, they returned to the garden and removed the giant taro. They pulled it back to the river, then they began to make it into a canoe. They worked and worked, then it became dark. They stopped working, then they went to sleep. The next day, they worked on the canoe and it was ready.

They were very happy and pulled the canoe down to the river. They went inside the canoe, then they drifted downriver and it became dark. They were very hungry, so Cat told Rat, "Hey friend, what should we eat now?" Rat knew that its food was there (the taro that formed their boat). So, Rat told Cat, "Sorry, we don't have real food." Cat told its friend Rat, "We must fall dead asleep, then we won't feel hungry."

Cat was dead asleep, but Rat could not sleep. Rat felt terribly hungry and thought very hard. Rat thought that the boat that they had made of taro was its food. So, Rat worked at eating the boat. Cat was sleeping and heard a noise, then told Rat, "I hear a noise there, do you hear it too?" Rat Replied, "There's no noise. Sleep."

Cat slept for a while, then it heard a noise coming closer. This time, Rat ate the taro and went closer to where Cat was sleeping. Then because of that, the water began to enter the boat that they had made of taro.

"I think you've eaten the boat and the water's coming inside now," [said Cat]. Then Rat told Cat that the boat was breaking and the water was now entering. Cat told Rat, "You're lying. It was just you who broke the boat and caused the water to enter."

They argued like that, then dawn arrived and Cat told Rat, "When we arrive on the other side, I'll kill and eat you." They arrived on the other side, then Cat wanted to eat Rat. Rat told Cat, "I think you're not someone who would eat something dirty. So, I must go bathe first, then you can eat me. Wait here. I'll go bathe first in that hole, then I'll return."

Rat tricked Cat, then went into the hole. Rat went to the other side and ran away. Cat waited at the hole for a while, then it became dark. Cat knew that Rat had tricked it and Cat was quite furious. Cat began to search for Rat to kill it.

So, after this story, today, cats are enemies with rats.

Kikusu Kopeo
Kaintiba [Village, **Hamtai** People]
Kerema
Gulf Province

A2494.1.4. Enmity between cat and rat; B211.1.8. Speaking cat; B211.2.9. Speaking rat; B295.2.1K. Animals make voyage in canoe; B295.2K. Animals build canoe; J2119.4+. Rat eats hole in boat made of tuber; K550. Escape by false plea; P310. Friendship; R210. Escapes; W157. Dishonesty

Why Snakes and Frogs are Enemies

(Wantok 1061, October 27, 1994, page 22)

Long, long ago, in the time of the ancestors, Snake and Frog were very good friends. They lived, worked and did everything together, just as good friends would do.

One time, they decided to travel in the forest. Frog asked Snake where it would go the next day. Snake replied to Frog that it would travel and hunt for wild game for themselves to eat in the afternoon. Frog also told Snake that it would travel along the river and hunt for fish or small insects for themselves to eat in the afternoon.

Snake was very happy because in its mind, they would be quite full of food from their hunting. They thought of their plans for a while, then their eyes shut and they went to sleep.

However, we know that night is like day for frogs and snakes. They would travel and hunt for food at night. At the time that they made their decision, it was daylight. After that, they went to sleep.

When it was about to become dark, they awoke and went outside. They each followed a trail. They traveled and hunted for food. The snake worked hard and hunted very many animals. The snake carried them to the house, then waited for its pal, Frog.

However when Frog came, it did not carry any food. Frog came with nothing. So, Snake asked Frog, "Pal, did you hunt for game too?" Frog said, "No." Snake told Frog not to worry because they would eat the food that Snake had hunted.

Starting from this time, only Snake hunted for their food. Frog never hunted for any food. No, never. Frog just waited for Snake to hunt for their food.

What was really happening was that Frog pretended to travel. Frog instead went in the river to play and not to hunt for food. Frog would croak and jump, or just bathe in the river, then later it would return to the house.

After a while, Snake wanted to find out why it was that Frog did not hunt for food for themselves. This was because Snake was tired of being the only one to find food.

One night, Snake awoke and pretended to go hunt for game in the forest. Snake went to hide near the place in the river where Frog usually bathed.

Then Snake's pal, Frog, appeared at the river. When Frog saw the river, it croaked, jumped and went inside. Frog did not do anything to find food.

When Snake saw its friend do this, it was terribly angry. Immediately, Snake jumped down into the river and they began to fight. Then Frog escaped. However, Snake told Frog that it would kill and eat Frog if Frog met it somewhere.

Starting from this time, Snake and Frog were no longer friends. They became enemies. So today, when frogs see snakes, they usually flee and hide. If a snake sees a frog, the snake will just chase and kill it.

Albert Humblara
Bialla [Village, **West Nakanai** People]
West New Britain Province

A2494.16.1. Enmity between frog and snake; B211.6.1. Speaking snake (serpent); B211.7.1. Speaking frog; P310. Friendship; R210. Escapes; W111. Laziness

[The ancestor story in *Wantok* #1062 is the same as that in #1046.]
[The ancestor story in *Wantok* #1063 is the same as that in #434.]
[The ancestor story in *Wantok* #1064 is the same as that in #854.]
[The ancestor story in *Wantok* #1065 is the same as that in #848.]
[The ancestor story in *Wantok* #1066 is the same as that in #797.]

A *Masalai* Snake Married a Gorgeous Woman

(Wantok 1067, December 8, 1994, page 21)

Long, long ago, in the time of the ancestors, there was a village called **Bainduang** in **Morobe** Province [**Nabak** People]. This village has a story because of a big *masalai* snake that lived there.

In this village, there were many young men who they lusted for a young woman. The woman was very beautiful, and she drew the attention of many young men in her own village as well as from the other nearby villages.

The snake also had the same kinds of thoughts that the young men had. The snake often looked at the young woman and had much lust for her.

One time, the young woman and her mother went to the garden. They walked and walked, then they arrived at the garden and began to gather garden foods, filling their net bags.

They did this for a while, then the young woman felt hungry. So, she looked around for something that she could take and eat. The snake was hiding in the forest and spying upon her. So, the snake knew that she was feeling hungry.

The snake quickly performed a love spell upon a cucumber, then the cucumber looked nice and very beautiful. She saw the cucumber and went to fetch it, then she began to eat it. After she ate, her thoughts were confused. She removed her necklace and she put it at the place where she had taken the cucumber.

She returned and joined her mother, then they began to fill the net bags with food. Afterwards, they carried them back to the village. They arrived at a river, then the woman thought of her necklace. So, she quickly told her mother that she had left her necklace in the garden.

Her mother sat by the river and waited for her daughter to return to the garden to find her necklace. When she arrived back at the garden, the snake was lying there and holding the young woman's necklace. The snake just quickly held her, then carried her into a cave where the snake lived.

The woman's mother stayed all night at the river, waiting for her daughter. However, the daughter did not return. So, the mother ran and ran to the village, then she told everyone in the village. The men formed a line and went to the garden to search for the woman, but they did not find her.

The snake took her and married her, then they raised many children. When she gave birth to boys, they would become snakes like their father. When she gave birth to girls, they would be real women like their mother.

At this time, in the area of Besoma [**Besomang**] and **Kwalangoma** Villages, people knew that it was completely forbidden to gather food from the garden that had their marks.

If there were marks, such as from rats or birds eating the food of the garden, we could not take this food because it was the mark of the *masalai* snake.

If people took the food that had been eaten and marked by the bad snake, they would be completely ruined. People have forbidden this sort of thing, even now.

Buma Nonje Tukambuk
Kimbe
West New Britain Province

B604.1. Marriage to snake; B631.9. Human offspring of marriage of person and snake; B632+. Snake offspring from marriage to snake; B633. Human and animal offspring from marriage to animal; B875.1. Giant serpent; C241+. Tabu: eating food chewed by spirit; D1365.3. Food causes magic forgetfulness; D1900. Love induced by magic; D2000. Magic forgetfulness; F401.3.8. Spirits in form of snake; F402.6.4.1. Spirits live in caves; F490+. Masalai; P210. Husband and wife; P231. Mother and son; P232. Mother and daughter; P233. Father and son; P234. Father and daughter; R13.4.1. Abduction by snake; R45.3. Captivity in cave; T10. Falling in love; T111. Marriage of mortal and supernatural being; T192. Marriage by force

A *Masalai* Couple Killed a Little Boy

(Wantok 1068, December 15, 1994, page 23)

Long, long ago, in **Dengop** Village, in the Kabwum District of **Morobe** Province, there lived six brothers [**Selepet** People]. The place where they lived was a big boulder called Niot. This was a place that was terrible for finding food.

The poor brothers would eat black soot and they would defecate only black feces. The youngest brother was just a young boy. He would follow a big vine and descend into a garden that belonged to a *masalai* married couple, and then he would eat ripe bananas. After he would eat, he would follow the same vine and return to the village. The little brother kept this secret, so he alone ate ripe bananas.

One time, all of the brothers defecated black feces, except for the little brother who defecated yellow ripe bananas. The big brothers saw this and they took it to eat.

Oh my, they thought that it tasted delicious. The little brother told them that he often stole ripe bananas from a garden that belonged to a *masalai* couple. So on the next day, all of the brothers went to the garden and collected all of the ripe bananas.

The *masalai* couple came and saw that all of the ripe bananas were gone. They were furious, so they made a trap at the base of some ripe bananas, then they returned to their house.

One time, all of the brothers followed the vine. In the afternoon they returned to the village. However, the little brother was held fast by the trap. Only the big brothers had returned to their village.

In the early morning, the *masalai* couple went and saw the boy. They killed him and carried him to the house. They cooked the boy with some garden food, and then they ate. They only left the head, which was to be eaten on the next day.

The five brothers saw that the little brother had not followed them back. They searched for him, but they did not find him. They followed the vine down to the garden and searched further. Before long, they saw smoke from a fire rising from the *masalai* couple's house. The *masalai* couple had gone into the deep forest to hunt for some wild game.

The brothers arrived at the house and only saw the *masalai* couple's child there. They asked whether the child had seen their little brother or not. Later, they saw their little brother's head hanging there.

They held the *masalai* child and threw it inside the house. Later, they burned the house and ran with their little brother's head back to their home.

M. Yorks Samson
Port Moresby
[National Capital District]

F490+. Masalai; G421. Ogre traps victim; K420. Thief loses his goods or is detected; K730. Victim trapped; P210. Husband and wife; P230. Parents and children; P251.6.3+. Six brothers; Q212. Theft punished; Q402. Punishment of children for parents' offenses; Q411. Death as punishment; Q414. Punishment: burning alive; R4. Surprise capture; R155+. Brothers recovers brother's bones; R220. Flights; S112.0.2. House (hostel) burned with all inside; S139.2.2+. Corpse put into cooking pot or cooked; X716H+. The escoumerda

[The ancestor story in *Wantok* #1069 is the same as that in #844.]

Dog Slept with Insect's Sister

(Wantok 1070, December 29, 1994, page 17)

A long time ago, they were terrified of Dog. This was because Dog barked fiercely and gnashed his teeth, so this scared many wild animals of the deep forest.

Every time that Dog gave an order, the animals would follow it and do whatever Dog asked for. At this time of the animals, Dog was the king of the community in which the animals lived.

All of the animals were terrified of Dog, so they appointed Dog to be king because they knew that Dog was strong and that he could kill whichever enemy approached them or wanted to frighten them.

Dog made strong laws for the village and all of the animals followed them. One of their laws was that all of the young female animals had to go to Dog first, then the others could see them later.

When this law was made, many animals were unhappy, so they would speak angrily in secret where Dog could not hear them.

At times of war with the enemies, Dog would go in front as the commander. This was because at this time, Dog's tail stood up. All of the animals would follow the tail and obtain their strength from Dog as they walked into battle.

One time, Insect was not happy that Dog had taken his young sister and slept with her. He thought hard for a while, then he became angry. He thought of what he could do to kill Dog, so that all of the animals could be free and never again be afraid.

One time, Insect asked his sister for something. Because she had slept with Dog, she would know how strong Dog's limbs were.

Insect's sister said, "Dog's hands are very strong, like hooks that can snare things that pass near his chest where his mouth can devour them. His legs are also very strong. They are like trees that he can plant at the base of fig trees and remove them. Dog's tail contains his power because his tail stands up and all of the animals respect it like a flag. They see it and follow it."

Then insect had a clear idea about what he would do. So one time, he told his sister that she should go flatter dog and go down to the river with him, then they would bathe.

Insect's young sister listened and went to flatter dog. Afterwards, they went down to the river and bathed vigorously, playing by the beach.

Before long, Insect came out of the water and shouted to the two of them that his sister must return to the house because the water would flood soon and carry her away.

When Dog heard this, he saw the woman's brother laughing hysterically at him, saying, "Do you know me well or not?"

However, Insect said, "You can't save my sister if a river enemy comes. So, listen to what I said and let her go to the house."

Insect said this for a while, then he muttered, "It would be bad if I bit you." When Dog heard this, he let his anger come forth quickly. He stood close by the water, where some of his legs were standing inside the water.

Insect told Dog, "You often think that you're strong and that everyone in the village bends their knees before you every day. However, I will never go down before a rubbish man."

Dog said, "Exactly how many people have you killed? Do you want to show your strength to me? I never see your face during times of war."

So, Insect said, "OK, I'll show you that I'm the kind of person that you can believe." Insect rose and flew upwards, then circled Dog's head and sat on top of Dog's tail.

Insect just rose and bit Dog's tail so that the pain and swelling became terrible. Dog's tail swelled greatly, such that its weight caused it go fall down.

At this time, Dog was terribly ashamed because his tail had fallen down, so he fled into the deep forest and hid. Afterwards, all of the animals were happy and they were never again afraid of stubborn people such as Dog.

Sonny Sandre
Plu Viles
Morobe [Province]

A2378.1.7+. How dog's tail fell; B210. Speaking animals; B211.1.7. Speaking dog; B211.4. Speaking insects; B240.9. Dog as king of animals; B754.0.1. Unusual sexual union of animals; D1029.2. Magic tail of animal; D1830. Magic strength; L315.6. Insects worry large animal to despair or death; L410. Proud ruler (deity) humbled; P253. Sister and brother; Q240. Sexual sins punished; Q453.1+ Punishment: being bitten by insect; R220. Flights; T161. Jus primae noctis; W167. Stubbornness

[The ancestor story in *Wantok* #1071 is the same as that in #817.]

How the Forest Cockatoo and
the Beach Cockatoo Originated

(Wantok 1072, January 12, 1995, page 19)

Long ago, somewhere in **Morobe** Province, there lived two brothers. They often killed many animals and ate them.

One time, they thought of going to hunt for wild game. They took sharp stones and some ripe mangos, and then they walked into the forest.

They arrived at a place in the deep forest where there were many wild pig footprints. They placed the sharp stones into the mangos, and then they put them on the pig trail. The brothers sat on top of a big tree and watched.

Before long, a big pig arrived and started eating the mangos. The pig gorged itself for a while. Then the sharp stones inside the mangos cut its throat and the pig fell dead. The brothers descended the tree and butchered the pig, preparing it to be cooked.

However there was no fire to cook the pig, so they went back up the tree and looked around for smoke. Before long, they saw smoke from a big fire coming from one side of a mountain, so they began to walk towards there.

They arrived at the place of the fire, and they met a woman and her daughter working in the garden. This was not an ordinary woman. She was a *masalai* without a doubt.

They went and told her that they wanted a fire to cook the pig. The woman told them to carry the girl and she would hold the fire, and then all of them together would go to the place where the pig was located.

The brothers agreed, and then they walked away and arrived at the place where the dead pig was lying. The brothers went ahead and butchered the pig well. After they cut the pig, they gave the pig guts to the woman to wash in a stream.

She went to the stream and did not return quickly, so the big brother sent the little brother to the stream to check on her. When the little brother approached the stream, he spied upon her and saw that she was arranging the pig guts and eating them. So, he quickly ran back and told his big brother what he had seen.

The brothers cooked their pig, and then they took it up the tree. They also killed the *masalai*'s daughter and cooked her in bamboo tubes, and then they readied them [to be eaten].

When the *masalai* woman returned, she saw the brothers on top of the tree and asked them for some pork to eat. They gave her the flesh of her daughter and she gorged herself.

Afterwards, she asked about her daughter. The brothers told her that she had eaten her own daughter. She cried terribly, and then she ran and told many other *masalai*s to come and kill the brothers.

The *masalai*s came and gathered under the base of the tree, and then they began to climb it. One strong *masalai* man stood at the base of the tree, then the others stood on top of him, going upwards.

Before long, a black ant came out of the tree and bit the testicles of the strong *masalai* man who was standing at the base of the tree and supporting the others above himself.

When the *masalai* flinched a little, all of the *masalai*s above him spilled down to the ground and fell about [lit., "caught time about"]. They went to the front again and made a ladder of themselves going upwards. However, the ant bit the man at the base of the tree and they fell upon themselves.

The brothers sat on top of the tree for a while, then they took bird feathers and fastened them to their arms. They became like cockatoos and flew away.

One flew to the forest and the other flew to the beach. So now, you can see that there are two kinds of cockatoos, one that lives in the forest and the other at the beach. Also, cockatoos often fly near people because cockatoos came from men.

Anna Kelong
Morobe Province

[Anna Kelong wrote the ancestor stories in *Wantok* #943 and 952. She is from the **Selepet** People.]

A2433.4+. Haunt of cockatoo; B481.1. Helpful ant; D150+M. Transformation: man to cockatoo; D531. Transformation by putting on skin; D642.7. Transformation to elude pursuers; D671. Transformation flight; F401.6. Spirit in human form; F473.6.4. Spirit eats food; F490+. Masalai; G61. Relative's flesh eaten unwittingly; H46.1+. Spirit recognized when it devours raw flesh; K1043.2. Dupe persuaded to eat stones; P232. Mother and daughter; P251.5. Two brothers; R210. Escapes; R260. Pursuits; R311. Tree refuge; S110. Murders; X712.3.1H. Injury to testicles

Two Dogs Helped Their
Owner Kill the *Masalai*s
(Wantok 1073, January 19, 1995, page 20)

Long, long ago, there lived an old man on **Tami** Island [**Tami** People, **Morobe** Province]. The old man's name was Nalit. He often lived on another island called **Kalal**. By that island, he would paddle the canoe around and fish in the sea.

Once, he saw that it was a good time for fishing. The sea was dead still and there was a nice breeze blowing. So, he pulled his big canoe down to the sea. Afterwards, he took the canoe mast and he erected it, and then he hoisted the sail.

When he first pulled out, he thought of his baskets, so he quickly jumped down again and fetched the four baskets. He put them onto the canoe platform and sailed towards the deep sea.

When he left the island and went towards the deep sea, the wind went into the sail and his canoe ran like a speedboat. Old Nalit sat happily and just held the canoe tiller. He voyaged and pulled in fish from the sea.

When he went ashore on the mainland at Busega [**Busiga**], in the Finschhafen area, he pulled up the canoe [**Yabêm** People]. He carried the baskets of fish to give to his friends to celebrate them.

When he gave the fish to them, they were very happy to see him, so they cooked food and gave it to him. Later, he slept with them that night. At dawn, his friends took him around the gardens and found sweet potatoes, taros, and bananas for him. He filled up his food to take to the island.

He was still on the mainland and he wanted to walk around. So, he walked and walked, arriving at a point where he saw a big breadfruit tree.

The old man lusted for the breadfruits, so he climbed the tree. He worked at gathering the breadfruits, throwing them down to the ground.

Before long, the *masalai*s of this place became jealous and wanted to ruin him. They came and surrounded the base of the breadfruit tree, and then they prepared to cut it down.

Old Nalit saw this, so he climbed to the tree crown. Then he looked towards his island. He shouted to his two dogs on the island.

The two dogs heard their names, so they knew that their old owner was in difficulty. Immediately, the dogs just jumped down into the sea and they began to swim towards the mainland at Busega.

When the dogs arrived, they saw the *masalai*s standing around the base of the breadfruit tree. They began to fight with them. The dogs fought with them and killed all of them.

Old Nalit was very happy and he descended the tree. He took his dogs and went up to the canoe. He filled up his food on the canoe, and then he pulled it to the sea and returned to his island.

Aniu Ephraim

Bukawa

Lae

Morobe Province

B421. Helpful dog; B524.1.1. Dogs kill attacking cannibal (dragon); F490+. Masalai; F641+. Dog with remarkable hearing; F696. Marvelous swimmer; P310. Friendship; Q411. Death as punishment; R311. Tree refuge; S110. Murders; W181. Jealousy

A *Masalai* Tricked a Woman and Ate the Baby
(Wantok 1074, January 26, 1995, page 19)

Long, long ago, in the time of the ancestors, before the missions came to Papua New Guinea, there was a *masalai* man who dwelled in **Wutung** Village, Sandaun [**West Sepik**] Province [**Wutung** People].

The *masalai* man tricked very many people, then he killed and ate them. He would perform his various tricks upon the people of the village, then he would kill them. Many people did not know that this was happening. However, they saw that men, women and children were disappearing one-by-one.

One time, the *masalai* man was staying in his house. The *masalai*'s house was a big tree in the middle of the village. He heard two women saying that in the very early morning they would go fishing at the beach.

After the *masalai* heard this, he thought that it was his chance to trick and eat one of these women. In the very early morning, the *masalai* woke up first, then he went to call one of the two women who had a baby. The *masalai* became like her friend.

He called her, then she thought that it was her friend who had come to call for her. So, she got up very quietly and carried her baby, then she followed the *masalai* man who had transformed into her friend.

They walked and walked, then they arrived at the beach. The *masalai* said to the real woman, "Go put your net in the sea first, then I'll watch your baby on the beach. Go fishing until dawn, then I can go and you'll watch your baby." The real woman did not know that the *masalai* was fooling her. She thought that it was her friend.

She left the *masalai* with the baby there, then she went fishing by the beach. When the *masalai* saw her go into the sea, he began to eat the baby's first finger. The baby was in pain and cried. Its mother, who was in the sea, heard this and she asked why the baby was crying. The *masalai* said that mosquitoes were biting it and that it was crying. The mother just kept quiet and fished. The *masalai* kept doing this until the baby was dead and entirely eaten. When it was nearly dawn, the *masalai* knew that it was his time to return home. So, the *masalai* called her to come up, then they would leave.

The woman thought for a while, then she knew that this was a *masalai* woman who had tricked her and she knew that her baby was dead. The woman told [the *masalai*] that she must wait a little, then she would go into the forest and find bamboo to cut the fish bellies. However, when she went into the forest, she began to flee. She ran and ran, then went up a very tall tree and hid.

The *masalai* woman waited in vain for a while, then she smelled that she had left. She went to the trail, then she saw the woman on top of the tree, and she was elated that she would kill her.

However, the woman knew this. She took a fish from the basket and threw it far down into the forest. The *masalai* thought that it was the woman who had jumped down. She followed and ate the fish. The two of them did this for a while.

At this same time, the real friend in the village was searching for her friend and knew that a *masalai* had confused her. She told everyone in the village, then they searched for her. They went and shouted, then the woman heard them and replied. The *masalai* knew that people were coming, so the *masalai* fled. Immediately, the woman's clan came and took her to the village.

The woman arrived in the village, then she said that it had just been the *masalai* who lived in the big tree in the village. Everyone decided to cut the tree down and break it in the middle. They did this from the base of the tree to the crown. At the very top, they found the woman, then they cut her into little pieces and burned her in a fire.

Even now, the people of Wutung Village in Sandaun [Province] never make decisions at night, nor do they make decisions by the big trees or stones because something would happen the next day.

Thomas Kulak

Wutung

Vanimo

West Sepik Province

C401+. Tabu: making decision during certain time; C490+. Tabu: making decision near boulder; C490+. Tabu: making decision near big tree; D12. Transformation: man to woman; F490+. Masalai; G346. Devastating monster; K1930. Treacherous impostors; P230. Parents and children; P310. Friendship; Q211. Murder punished; Q411. Death as punishment; R100. Rescues; R220. Flights; R260. Pursuits; R311. Tree refuge; S110. Murders; S139.7. Murder by slicing person into small pieces; S110+. Eaten alive

[The ancestor story in *Wantok* #1075 is the same as that in #834.]
[The ancestor story in Wantok #1076 is the same as that in #665.]
[The ancestor story in Wantok #1077 is the same as that in #403.]
[The ancestor story in *Wantok* #1078 is the same as that in #339.]
[The ancestor story in *Wantok* #1079 is the same as that in #400.]
[The ancestor story in *Wantok* #1080 is the same as that in #308.]
[The ancestor story in *Wantok* #1081 is the same as that in #343.]
[The ancestor story in *Wantok* #1082 is the same as that in #346.]
[The ancestor story in *Wantok* #1083 is the same as that in #306.]
[The ancestor story in *Wantok* #1084 is the same as that in #309.]
[The ancestor story in *Wantok* #1085 is the same as that in #305.]
[The ancestor story in *Wantok* #1086 is the same as that in #298.]
[The ancestor story in *Wantok* #1087 is the same as that in #303.]
[The ancestor story in *Wantok* #1088 is the same as that in #312.]
[The ancestor story in *Wantok* #1089 is the same as that in #311.]

A Big Sore Removed the Kombe [Kimbe] Woman from a Man

(Wantok 1090, May 18, 1995, page 19)

Long, long ago, in the time of the ancestors, an old woman and her son lived in a village in **West New Britain** Province. The old woman's husband had died, so she alone took care of their son.

The boy had a huge sore, so he never did any work. He would just stay in the house. His mother took care of him for many years and she was very tired of her son.

They lived for a while, then one time his mother scolded him. She told him, "Son, I've taken care of you for many years and I'm tired now. So, it would be good if you found a wife. She could take care of you and give you food."

When the young boy heard his mother tell him this, he was overcome with worry and he cried terribly.

He sat and worried about what his mother had said. Later, he went and asked her, "Mama, do you know how to carve a canoe?" His mother told him, "Yes, I know how." Later, he asked his mother, "Mama, do you know how to carve a canoe paddle?" His mother said that she knew how.

After a week, his mother carved a canoe and paddle for him. The young boy saw this and he was elated. When darkness covered the village, he told his mother to prepare his food because on the next day he would take the canoe down to the sea. He would paddle it out to sea and wash his sore.

They slept for a while. Before it was very light, the young boy awoke and took his things. He walked down to the sea. Later, he jumped inside the canoe and paddled out to sea.

He paddled and paddled, and then he arrived on an island called Bali [**Unea** Island, **Vitu** People]. The young women of Bali saw him and shouted at him, "Come drink some water and eat some food. Later, you can paddle away." However, he told them, "Never mind that. It would be bad if your fathers became angry and fought me."

He told them this, and then he paddled to Bulu Point [**Bulumuri** Village, **Bulu** People]. The Bulu women were fishing in the sea and they saw him. They told him to chew some betel nuts, but he told them the same thing that he had told the Bali women.

The bad boy paddled off to Kombe [**Kimbe**, **Xarua** People]. He saw the young women working at washing in the sea. Then they saw him and they lusted for him, then mucus fell from him. Before long, a young woman jumped into his canoe. They paddled back to his village.

The two of them arrived on the beach by the village and the boy told the woman to walk to the house first, then he would come afterwards. This was because he was ashamed of the sore on his leg and because the Kombe woman did not know that he had this sore.

When the woman went to the house of the boy's mother, the boy quietly walked to his house. He hid by his house. The woman did not see his face at all.

The woman just followed the boy's old mother to the garde, and she also did other work. They did this for a while, and then the woman asked herself, "Why does the old woman's son never follow me with his mother to work in the garden? Why doesn't he do other work? He brought me here and left me with his mother. Then he ran and hid in his house. I should find out why he did this to me."

So one day, the woman told the boy's old mother that they would go to the garden. When they arrived in the garden, the woman tricked the old woman and returned to the village. She hid in a small forest by the village. Before

long, she saw the boy leave the house and come outside. The woman saw the big sore on his leg.

The woman returned to the garden. She told her old mother-in-law that they would return to the village. She took a pot to fill with water, but she was really playing a trick to run away. She arrived at the place for fetching water, and then she threw away the pot and fled to her parents.

She arrived there and her father scolded her. However, the woman explained to her father why she had left the old woman's son and fled.

Andrew Taboa

Kimbe

West New Britain Province

K1372. Woman engaged to marry by trick; L140+. Ugly marries beautiful; P210. Husband and wife; P231. Mother and son; P232. Mother and daughter; P234. Father and daughter; P262. Mother-in-law; P265+. Daughter-in-law; R220. Flights; T10. Falling in love; T100. Marriage; W111. Laziness

[The ancestor story in *Wantok* #1091 is the same as that in #319.]
[The ancestor stories in *Wantok* #1092 and 1093 are the same as that in #314.]
[The ancestor story in *Wantok* #1094 is the same as that in #811.]
[The ancestor story in *Wantok* #1095 is the same as that in #820.]
[The ancestor story in *Wantok* #1096 is the same as that in #803.]
[The ancestor story in *Wantok* #1097 is the same as that in #836.]
[The ancestor story in *Wantok* #1098 is the same as that in #866.]
[The ancestor story in *Wantok* #1099 is the same as that in #811.]
[The ancestor story in *Wantok* #1100 is the same as that in #791.]
[The ancestor story in *Wantok* #1101 is the same as that in #839.]
[The ancestor story in *Wantok* #1102 is the same as that in #853.]

A Crab and a Turtle Destroyed Fekifuk Village

(Wantok 1103, August 17, 1995, page 19)

Long, long ago, there was a village called Fekifuk in **East Sepik** Province, near the Passam Highway. In this village, there lived a man named Jamiliwolo. He was a fisherman.

He saw a pond and never told anyone in the village about it. One time, he tried fishing at the pond. He was surprised that he caught very many fish in there, so he kept the existence of this pond to himself and he would always go there to fish.

One time, a crab and a turtle saw that all of the fish were disappearing from the pond, so they tried to think of a way to save some fish for themselves.

The turtle and the crab both thought that when the man came and threw the hook into the water, the crab would wait for the first, second and then third fish that the man caught. Then the fourth time, the crab would pull the hook and tie it to a tree or sturdy place, then fasten the man's hook.

The crab and turtle decided this, then they waited for Jamiliwolo to come and throw the hook into the water. When Jamiliwolo threw the hook down, the crab saw the fish take the hook. Then the man pulled the fish up.

When the man threw the hook for the fourth time, the crab went very slowly and pulled the hook away, then he fastened it to the base of a tree. The man did not feel that his hook was moving.

He waited for the fish to pull the hook, but none did. So he wanted to pull up the hook. When he pulled the hook, oh my, the hook was stuck. He pulled the hook hard, but he was afraid because it was his only fishhook.

So, he removed his clothing and he walked down to the water to remove the hook. He went, but the water was deep, so he jumped down and swam to find the hook.

While he was swimming, the turtle just came and put its beak to the man's testicles, then he screamed inside the water. He just went up and took off towards the village.

The turtle had planted its beak on the man's testicles and was hanging with him as he went to the village. The man's maternal kin came and just put a knife to the turtle's head, killing it and removing the beak from the man's testicles.

When the people of the village made an earth oven with the turtle, blood flowed from the man's testicles and flowed freely. At this time, the blood filled and became a lake, and then everyone in the village carried their belongings and things. They fled to another village, then the lake took the village and it has been there until now.

This lake is near Pasam [**Passam**] 2 and it has very many fish. If you swim inside it, you will see that house posts are underneath it [**Boiken** People]. This is because the water had broken the village of Jamiliwolo's people and had also killed them, taking down the houses. This lake is there now and we can show it to you if you want to see it.

David Kosy
Passam Village
Wewak
East Sepik Province

A920.1.0.1. Origin of particular lake; A1011. Local deluges; A1018. Flood as punishment; D457.1+. Transformation: blood to lake; K770+. Victim caught by luring with stuck fishing hook; P290+. Maternal kin; Q272. Avarice punished; Q411. Death as punishment; Q211.6. Killing an animal revenged; Q285. Cruelty punished; Q428. Punishment: drowning; R220. Flights; W151. Greed; X712.3.1H. Injury to testicles

[The ancestor story in *Wantok* #1104 is the same as that in #841.]
[The ancestor story in *Wantok* #1105 is the same as that in #843.]
[The ancestor story in *Wantok* #1106 is the same as that in #819.]
[The ancestor story in *Wantok* #1107 is the same as that in #840.]
[The ancestor story in *Wantok* #1108 is the same as that in #845.]
[The ancestor story in *Wantok* #1109 is the same as that in #833.]

A *Masalai* Confused Two Sisters
(Wantok 1110, October 5, 1995, page 19)

Long, long ago, there was a village near Rawot [**Rauit**] Village, in the Yankok [East Au] sub-District of **West Sepik** Province [**Gnau** People]. There lived many people in this village.

There was one man in this village who had a very long penis [lit., "urinating penis"]. His name was Marki. Marki often lusted for two young, stylish sisters. The names of the sisters were Meitu, the big sister, and Samatu, the little sister.

One morning, Meitu and Samatu awoke. They began cleaning the house and cooking yams to eat. So, Marki planted his penis upon the ground and arrived at the sisters' house. He wanted to have sex with one of the two sisters.

The big sister was fetching water and cleaning by the house. The little sister, Samatu, was inside the house. She was sitting on the ground and peeling yam skins.

Before long, she felt something coming under the ground where she was sitting. It felt very good, so she did not move to another place. She just sat at this place and peeled the yams.

The big sister finished cleaning outside. She saw Samatu working and sitting in just one position. She saw that she was feeling happy and that she had not peeled many yams.

The big sister, Meitu, looked carefully and saw something bad there. Quickly, she took a sago thorn that they had been using as a spade and she removed the rubbish near the house. Quickly, she threw away and cut in two Marki's penis. Blood spilled from the penis and flowed down by a stream that was near the village.

Marki's *masalai* friend was in the stream. When the *masalai* saw that his friend had encountered an enemy and had died in the village, he made all of the village people go completely bad. The *masalai* turned some people into stones. Part of Marki's penis also became a stone.

The people who had awoken in the early morning and gone into the forest went crazily about. Some became birds of paradise and flew to faraway places. Afterwards, then they turned into real people again.

The *masalai* completely confused the thoughts of the two sisters. They followed Marki's blood and went down to the place where the *masalai* dwelled. The sisters had left everything in the house. They only took a big *limbum* basket and some yams.

They followed the stream down, cutting each yam until they arrived at a big river. They went down a little farther, and then they arrived at a big bay. By this time, the sisters were completely confused.

Before they had approached the bay, they had left their basket with the yams. They went down into the bay and never came up again.

At this time, no one goes down into the bay. The yams that the sisters had left by the river grew until the time when the grandparents gave birth to the parent's generation. Then a big flood removed them. On top of old **Moru** Village, there is a mark where the sago thorn cut Marki's penis, where it turned to stone.

Paul Wurwai
West Sepik Province

A974. Rocks from transformation of people to stone; C615. Forbidden body of water; D150+. Transformation: person to bird of paradise; D231. Transformation: man to stone; D350+. Transformation: bird of paradise to person; D457+. Transformation: cut off penis to stone; D2000+. Magic confusion; F424. River-spirit; F490+. Masalai; F547.3. Extraordinary penis; F547.3.1. Long penis; P252.1. Two sisters; P310. Friendship; Q211. Murder punished; Q240. Sexual sins punished; Q411. Death as punishment; Q428. Punishment: drowning; Q451.10. Punishment: genitalia cut off; Q551.3. Punishment: transformation; Q551.3.4. Transformation to stone as punishment; S118. Murder by cutting; S131. Murder by drowning; S176.1. Mutilation: emasculation; T475. Unknown (clandestine) paramour; X712.2H. Male genitals

[The ancestor story in *Wantok* #1111 is the same as that in #800.]

Two Brothers Died in an Earth Oven

(Wantok 1112, October 19, 1995, page 19)

In the time of the ancestors, there were only two brothers who lived in an area called **Kumin** Village, in **Southern Highlands** Province [**Mendi** or **Kewa** People]. Their parents had died when they were still boys.

The big brother became an excellent worker. He made very many gardens and the brothers had plentiful garden food. The little brother excelled at hunting wild game in the deep forest. Every day, their house would be just filled with game.

One day, all of the food in the big brother's garden was very ripe. So, they wanted to make an earth oven and eat. The big brother went into the garden. The little brother went into the deep forest and checked his traps. He went to where he knew that they would be holding marsupials (*kapul*) and then he killed them.

The big brother arrived in the garden and saw that the bananas and other garden food were good and ready. He took the food and put it in a net bag. Later, he returned to the village. He removed the banana skins and cooked them on stones.

The little brother was still in the deep forest, checking on the traps. Before long, he arrived at a trap and saw something very unusual. There was no marsupial hanging from this trap. He saw an old woman with long teeth taking the place of the marsupial.

He left his bow and all of his arrows, and then he ran back to the village. He was completely out of breath when he arrived at the front gate to their clan house. However, he missed and [bumped] his head on the fence post. He fell down dead.

At the same time, the big brother climbed a tree whose leaves they used for earth ovens. He took a leaf and heard a noise from the front of the fence that surrounded their clan house. He thought that his little brother had arrived, so he wanted to help him carry the marsupials.

He wanted to speed down the tree, but he missed and fell down on top of the big fire, burning himself. The fire burned him terribly. He twisted and turned for a while, and then he died.

At the same time, smoke from the fire rose very high, going directly up to the sky. The brother's maternal kin were in another clan house. They saw the smoke and thought that the two brothers must have been making an earth oven for a pig. Quickly, a kinsman took some things and walked to see the two brothers.

He arrived and just saw the big brother's belly on fire amongst the earth oven stones. He thought that it was a pig's belly. He shouted for the two brothers, but he did not hear any reply.

Later, he checked the front gate of the fence that surrounded the clan house and he saw the little brother's body. He went inside again. He saw the belly and gathered his thoughts. He cried terribly for his two maternal kinsmen. He removed the big brother's belly from the fire and buried it with his little brother's body in the same place.

Later, he returned to his clan house and made a big mourning party. Today, there are no people who live in the area where the two brothers encountered their deaths.

Mescy Blue
Kumin Village
Mendi
Southern Highlands Province

F544.3.5. Remarkably long teeth; N330. Accidental killing or death; P251.5. Two brothers; P290+. Maternal kin; R220. Flights; V61.3+. Dead buried

Crocodiles and Lizards Came from the Ramu River

(Wantok 1113, October 26, 1995, page 21)

Long, long ago, in the Ramu River, there were no crocodiles or lizards. Everyone lived well there. In a village called Nodubu [**Nodabu**], there lived a man, his wife and their two sons [**Nokopo** People, **Madang** Province]. The boys' names were Nronari and Mambokuri.

One time, a big famine arose on the Ramu and everyone was hungry. Nronari and Mambokuri's parents thought hard. They thought that it would be bad if the two children died from hunger.

One day, the boys' parents decided to put them inside baskets to sleep and drift along the Ramu River.

While the boys were playing outside the house, their parents carefully arranged their sleeping baskets so that the water would not enter.

Late at night, when everyone in the village was asleep, the parents took the boys and their baskets. They went down to the Ramu River and put them in the water. The water carried the boys downstream.

In the morning, the boys' baskets stuck to a tree by the river. Nronari felt very cold, so he awoke. He went out of the basket and saw that Mambokuri's basket was nearby. He awakened his little brother. Then they followed the tree and went up by the side of the water.

Mambokuri asked Nronari, "Where are we now?" Nronari replied, "I don't know, but I think that Papa and Mama did this to us."

The little boys sat by the side of the water for a long time, until the sun rose completely. Later, Mambokuri said, "Hey Nronari, go back down and get [your] rattan sleeping basket." He fetched it and came up. Then he rubbed it in the middle of a tree and a fire arose.

Mambokuri took some wood and they made a big fire. Later, Nronari climbed a breadfruit tree. He gathered many breadfruits. He brought them down, and then they cooked and ate them.

Many breadfruits were ripe, so they did not finish eating them. The two boys began play fighting, shooting each other with the breadfruits.

Nronari jumped down to the Ramu River and Mambokuri stayed up by the side of the water. They played at shooting each other, and then their bodies began to change. Nronari's legs became like that of a crocodile. His buttocks lengthened and became like that of a crocodile's tail.

The same thing also happened to Mambokuri. His legs and buttocks became like the legs and tail of the lizard used for hand drums. After they had shot each other with all of the ripe breadfruits, Nronari told Mambokuri, "That's good. You can stay up there and I'll stay in the water."

Mambokuri replied, "That's alright. You can watch from the river and I can watch from the trees."

After they finished speaking, their bodies changed completely and they became a crocodile and lizard entirely. Now we can see many crocodiles and lizards that are used for hand drums in the Ramu River. This is because they came from these two brothers, Nronari and Mambokuri.

Jimbegim of **Viutobua** Village, by the Ramu River, told this story to me.

Otto G. Ume
Kwalakessi Village
Hoskins
West New Britain Province

A2146. Creation of crocodile; A2148. Creation of lizard; A2433.6+. Why crocodile lives in river; A2433.6+. Why lizard lives in tree; D194B. Transformation: boy to crocodile; D197B. Transformation: boy to lizard; D566. Transformation by striking; D681. Gradual transformation; F969.7. Famine; P210. Husband and wife; P231. Mother and son; P233. Father and son; P251.5. Two brothers; S141. Exposure in boat

Two Brothers Killed *Masalai* Kuakua

(Wantok 1114, November 2, 1995, page 19)

Long, long ago, in the time of the ancestors, there was a *masalai* man named Kuakua. This *masalai* man lived on an island named **Vokeo**, by Wewak, **East Sepik** Province [**Wogeo** People]. The *masalai* man lived on a mountain named Yam, which is close to the beach. Just by the beach, there was a village named **Ga**.

The *masalai* man was not a little man. He was gigantic, so whenever he would hold a stick and walk down to the village, the ground would tremble.

He always killed and ate the men, women and children of the village. He did this for a while, and then all of the people of the island were [almost] completely gone.

Because he did this, the people of the village were afraid and they searched for a place to which to flee. However, when they tried to escape, there was not any way out. Some days later, the *masalai* began to kill men and eat them again.

Then the people held a big meeting to find a way to escape. They met and spoke, saying that beginning on the next day each family would go carve a wooden canoe to use to escape. So the next day, they cut a tree and worked together making a big canoe. They erected a sail and prepared to go far away to the mainland, in the area of Turubu [**Terebu**, **Kaiep** People].

However, there was one woman who was pregnant who did not have a husband to ask her to take her in the canoe, so everyone sailed away, leaving the poor woman alone on the island. The woman saw this, so she went to hide in a cave in Mount Yam. The cave was above where the *masalai* lived. The woman stayed inside the cave until she gave birth to two boys. She named them Fitfit and Lolo.

They lived there until they were only about four years old, then their mother taught them to shoot bows and arrows. She also told them that everyone had fled because there was a giant *masalai* who had eaten them, so they had fled to the mainland long ago.

The mother just did this until the boys became big. Then the mother herself prepared the boys to fight with the *masalai* man.

OK, the day for two men to fight with the *masalai* arrived and the mother prepared everything. The two of them told the mother that when the reef became dry, the mother should go searching for shells. When the *masalai* would see her, she would run back to the cave in which they lived.

When the mother did this, the *masalai* man looked down and thought, "I thought they had fled, but there's just one still there. Now's my chance to eat her." So, the *masalai* sped directly down the mountain to grab her. However, she saw this and ran back directly to the cave where she hid with her sons. The sons just waited for the *masalai* at the cave entrance.

When the *masalai* was directly at the cave entrance, the two bad boys just came out and shot him with arrows. They pummeled him until he was dead. Then the two of

them made a canoe, put the body in, put up a sail, and sent it to the mainland. When the people of the mainland saw this, they were elated. They took their canoes and paddled back to Vokeo Island, where they now live.

Jimmy Sakie
Wokiplel Village
Vokeo Island
East Sepik Province

A515.1.1. Twin culture heroes; F490+. Masalai; F531.3+. Giant's walking causes earthquake; G100. Giant ogre; G346. Devastating monster; G510.4+. Hero overcomes devastating ogre; G512.1+. Ogre killed with spear/arrow; K914. Murder from ambush; P231. Mother and son; P251.5. Two brothers; R213. Escape from home; R315. Cave as refuge; S110. Murders; S145. Abandonment on an island; S185. Cruelty to pregnant woman; T570. Pregnancy; S371+. Abandoned woman's son becomes hero; T587. Birth of twins; T685. Twins; Z210. Brothers as heroes

A Father Ignored a Warning and a Child Was Lost

(Wantok 1115, November 9, 1995, page 19)

Long, long ago, there lived a man and his wife on an island. No other people lived on this island. They made very many gardens and they had very plentiful food. The food just went to waste in their gardens. They did not have children to whom they could give this food.

Some days, the woman's husband would take his fishing gear and he would go out to sea to look for fish. He would go and sit on a stone that was very far out at sea and he would fish. The name of this stone is Matit. On top of this *masalai* stone is a very tall tree. The name of this tree is Pandanus.

The married couple lived for a while, and then they had a daughter. Whenever the mother went to work in the gardens, the father would stay in the house and watch their only child. When the father wanted to go hook fishing, he would take his daughter with him and they would go out to the stone. Then they would fish. He would leave his daughter on top of the stone. Then he would take his canoe, paddle out a short distance, and go fishing. After he had taken many fish, he would paddle back again by the stone and take his daughter. Then they would paddle to their home on the beach.

The father did this for years, and then the girl grew to be about twelve years old. However, the father still took the daughter out to sea to fish. His wife often watched this and she would scold him, "Daughter's grown, so sometimes you must leave her at home with me."

However, the father would reply to the mother that there was nothing that would ruin the girl. He told his wife, "You're just an ordinary woman and you don't know anything." The father never listened to her and he made his daughter like a son, so he always brought her out to go fishing. He just did this, and then one day the father took the daughter back to the stone where they always fished.

The father left the girl on top of the *masalai* stone again and he went out to fish. While he was out, the girl had her menses. Her father did not know this.

Oh my, when she menstruated, the *masalai* of the stone smelled the nearby seawater, then the big *masalai* stone began to break apart, tremble and sink slowly into the sea. When the girl saw this, she just cried and shouted for her father. Her father was still far away and he did not hear her shouts.

The stone was hidden underwater and only the tree was still above water. The girl shouted and shouted to no avail. Then she climbed the tree on the *masalai* stone at the same time that her father returned. When the father saw that his daughter was about to go under the sea, he paddled the canoe rapidly over there. However, when her father wanted to hold her, the sea rose completely. The father cried terribly for losing his daughter. Then the poor father cried and returned to the village.

When he arrived at the village, he argued terribly with the mother about what to do. The mother told him, "You didn't listen to me. Now see what happened."

Jimmy Sakie
Waix Village, **Vokeo** [Island, **Wogeo** People]
Wewak
East Sepik Province

C141. Tabu: going forth during menses; C923. Death by drowning for breaking tabu; D2148. Earth magically caused to quake; F490+. Masalai; F495. Stone-spirit; J652. Inattention to warnings; P210. Husband and wife; P232. Mother and daughter; P234. Father and daughter; W126. Disobedience

A Man with Scabies Married a Nice Woman

(Wantok 1116, November 16, 1995, page 19)

Long, long ago, in the time of the ancestors, there was a man who lived on Mount Iugu in the **Kandep** area of **Enga** Province [**Enga** People].

The man's name was Apalakia and the poor guy very much wanted to find himself a girlfriend. However, none of the women of the Kandep area liked him because he was a tall and skinny man. His skin was completely filled with scabies.

He often wanted to go to the house to *karim lek*, but the women did not want to do this and they would spit upon him. The women spat upon him every time, so he was ashamed of this and he fled to make a house on Mount Iugu, where he made his home.

One time, he heard that a big festival would arise at **Poketamanda** Village one week later. When Apalaki [Apalakia] heard this, he did not eat or sleep that day. He thought hard about doing something for this festival.

Late at night, he had an idea about what to do for the festival. In the very early morning, he took his bow and arrows, and he went into the forest to hunt for marsupials (*kapul*).

He killed three marsupials, carried them to his house, and then he singed their fur. After he singed off their fur, he took all of the marsupial guts and filled all of the feces into the stomach of one of the marsupials.

He looked for a good place and he put the stomach there. He cooked the three marsupials in an earth oven and he ate them.

In the early morning, he stayed in his house and saw people [going] to the festival. He followed them and arrived at the festival grounds. He carried the marsupial feces in his small net bag.

He watched the festival until the afternoon. Then everyone went to the houses to find food and to sleep. Apalaki followed them and arrived at one house. This house was packed with young people singing and *karim lek*ing.

He went inside and sat in a corner. He sat and sat, then he saw a nice, very beautiful woman sitting there. The unlucky guy watched and did not keep his eyes off of her for even a little while. He stared and stared. Then he thought, "If this woman becomes my wife, I'll be very happy."

Apalaki thought and thought. Then he told the old woman of the house that he wanted to sleep. The old woman told Apalaki to sleep in the house where the women usually sleep. He did not sleep in there, he kept thinking.

He slept until when it was nearly dawn and everyone was in the houses. The nice woman walked and came inside. Then her old mother told her to sleep on the other side.

The pretty woman just fell dead asleep. At this time, Apalaki's heart was beating like mad. He thought about running over and just grabbing her, but he thought hard and he just lay quietly. He stayed until it was nearly dawn. Then the old mother, the mother of this woman, awoke and went outside to make a fire to cook food.

Then, Apalaki jumped towards the woman. He lay by her and held her. The woman did not feel him holding her. She was dead asleep. Apalaki took the marsupial's stomach that was full of feces. He lifted the feces onto her buttocks and onto his face. Apalaki went and slept by her buttocks.

They slept, and then the old mother shouted for her daughter to come eat. However, she did not hear her mother's shouts. Her mother broke off a piece of firewood and carried it inside to see the two of them sleeping there. She cut the light and saw the man sleeping under her buttocks.

She saw the feces all over her buttocks and also over his face. The old woman thought that the woman had had diarrhea and defecated over his face. The old woman just went quietly and awakened the young woman. She told her, "You had diarrhea and you shat upon that man's face." The man heard the mother and daughter talking back and forth, but he pretended that he was dead asleep.

Then he awoke and said, "Mama, what did you say to your daughter?" The old woman told Apalaki, "Good man, the woman had diarrhea and she shat upon your face. The two of us were ashamed to wake you, so we're here." Then Apalaki put a hand to his face and felt the feces on it. The old woman told the woman, "You ruined the man's face, so you two can leave." Apalaki listened and his heart was very happy. He married the woman and they went to live at his home in the Mount Iugu area. So, today if you go around Kandep Village, to the top of Kandep airfield, the men in that area are called the Ima Clan. *Ima* in the Enga Language means, "Feces."

Altip Kipan Kongom
Patull Village
Kandep
Enga Province

A1640+. Origin of Ima Clan; K1350. Woman persuaded (or wooed) by trick; L140+. Ugly marries beautiful; P210. Husband and wife; P232. Mother and daughter; P262. Mother-in-law; P265. Son-in-law; P426.2. Hermit; R220. Flights; T50. Wooing; T100. Marriage; X716.1H+. Befouling with excrement

Two Coconuts Became Two Young Women

(Wantok 1117, November 23, 1995, page 19)

Long, long ago, by the Sepik River in **East Sepik** Province, there lived two brothers in a village. They did not have parents or kin. They lived alone. They hunted and they cooked. After a while, the big brother found a woman drifting by on a canoe. They the two of them had a chance to rest, so the woman cooked food. However, the big brother was jealous of the little brother because of the big brother's wife.

Before long, the big brother told his little brother, "Hurry and make your own spirit house over there. It's bad that all of us sleep and eat in just one house." The big brother helped him and they quickly finished a house. The little brother would sleep alone in the spirit house.

One morning, the big brother told his wife to befriend his little brother and go to process sago. So, he took another canoe and went alone to hunt wild game at the headwaters of the river.

The little brother worked at quickly scraping sago. The big brother's wife worked at rinsing the sago by the river. The little brother finished scraping the sago and he went up to the headwaters, where he bathed and played. He also worked on cutting [sago leaves], making a nice color on the sago leaves. This was the mark used for cutting men's skin at the time of [ritually] entering the spirit house.

The sister-in-law rinsed the sago and saw a picture or marking on top of a sago leaf that was drifting down the river to the place where she was rinsing sago. She very much wanted it, so she told her little brother-in-law, "I want you to cut this mark on my buttocks." The little brother said, "No. You're not my wife that I could do that. It would be bad if big brother saw this and scolded me."

However, the sister-in-law was persistent. The sister-in-law told the little brother that if he did not cut the mark on her buttocks, she would kill him. Her saying this frightened the little brother. He cut the mark on his sister-in-law's buttocks. Later, he told his sister-in-law to carefully hide the mark, so that his big brother could not see it. In the afternoon, they took the sago, put it in the canoe and paddled back to the house. The big brother had killed very many kinds of game and had also arrived at the house. They made a huge feast and ate it with the sago. However, before long, the big brother found out about the marking on his wife's buttocks.

He was furious and he shouted for his little brother to come. Then he accused him. The little brother argued that his sister-in-law had insisted upon it. The little brother was extremely ashamed and went to sleep in the spirit house. In the very early morning, he awoke and told his big brother, "If I return, you'll see smoke from a fire. If I leave entirely, you won't see smoke."

Then he took a canoe and sail, [and] fire for cooking food and smoking. Then he paddled down the river branch, going very far away. The next day, the sun rose and he kept paddling until dusk came. However, he continued to paddle until he arrived at a place that had a small house by the river. There were many kinds of coconut palms that surrounded the house, which belonged to an old woman. Quietly, the boy paddled down by the river and the shore near the house. He saw various kinds of game, such as pigs, cassowaries and crocodiles that were near the house. He stood and watched the animals, and then a woman went outside of the house. The woman was terribly old. Large amounts of mucus ran from her nose.

The woman asked the boy, "Why have you come here? Men never come to my house. You are the first man to have come here." The boy told the old woman, "No, I had not meant to come here. I'm angry with my big brother, so I went to live somewhere else."

The old woman was sorry for the little brother and she told him to sleep with her for just one night. In the morning, the little brother could paddle away and find a good place for himself to live. At night, the little brother told her about everything that had happened to him. Oh my, the old woman was terribly sorry for the boy.

Before they slept, the old woman told the boy, "At night when you're sleeping, if you hear some noises or if the ground trembles, you must not get up. Never mind if you need to urinate. Hold it until morning, and then you can go."

The little brother listened, and then he fell dead asleep. When it was nearly dawn, the little brother felt the ground tremble. The house moved, and the smell of grass skirts and dance decorations filled the air. Women's voices spilled out. The little brother's bones trembled terribly. He did not know that he was on the shores of the land of women and that the old woman was the women's leader. Every morning, the coconuts would become women. They would descend, sing, dance and make noises. During the day, they would climbed the coconut palms again and sleep.

In the morning, the boy awoke and went out of the house. He did not see the women. Oh my, he was quite confused. He thought that he had been dreaming at night. The old woman also came outside of the house. She talked to the boy, "I don't have food. Climb up and take two coconuts, then return. Never mind if you're hungry. Stop your hunger with your thoughts and then leave. [After you leave and arrive at the border], stop the canoe and go down into the water to bathe. However, don't turn to look at the two coconuts in the canoe. After you finish washing, cut the two coconuts and eat."

The boy was never stubborn about what his big brother would say. He would listen and just follow. So, when the old woman told him to fetch coconuts, he just listened and followed what she said.

He climbed a coconut tree and took two coconuts, one green-skinned and one red-skinned. He did not throw them down to the ground. He held them together with his teeth and carried them down.

He listened to everything that the old woman had said. He paddled back towards home. Then he stopped the canoe at the border and went down to bathe. While he was bathing, he heard the voices of two women on top of the canoe. He turned and saw two very beautiful women on top of the canoe smiling at him.

The green coconut had become a black-skinned woman, and the red-skinned coconut had become a white-skinned woman or moon-[colored woman]. The women pulled the little brother into the canoe. Later, they all jumped down into the water and bathed.

The little brother was elated. He put down all his troubles and returned to the village with the two women. He approached and put some [lighted] wild sugarcane (*pitpit*) by the river. The smoke from the fire rose and the big brother saw this. He had known that his little brother had not left for good. One day, he would return. He thought that it was just his little brother who had returned.

However, alongside the little brother were the two women in the canoe. All of them were happy and they made a feast that night. The little brother told the big brother what had happened after he had met the old woman.

The big brother listened to his entire story and he started getting ideas. One morning, the big brother took off in a canoe and arrived at the old woman's home. He followed everything that the little brother had told him. However, he was too impatient and did [not] listen to the old woman.

When he went up and took two coconuts like the old woman had said, he threw the young coconut down and it broke. He only took the ripe coconut and carried it down carefully.

When he paddled back to the village, the ripe coconut became an old woman. The big brother was furious, but he could not do anything more. His luck was shot.

Patrick Gambia

Wewak

East Sepik Province

D222+W. Transformation: woman to coconut; D431.11+W. Transformation: coconut to woman; F112. Journey to Land of Women; F527.7K+. White person; J652. Inattention to warnings; J1050. Attention to warnings; P210. Husband and wife; P251.4+. One brother acts wisely, another acts unwisely; P251.5. Two brothers; P251.5.3. Hostile brothers P263. Brother-in-law; P264. Sister-in-law; P600+. Initiation of boys: scarification; R213. Escape from home; T145.0.1. Polygyny; V112.1. Spirit huts; W31. Obedience; W126. Disobedience; W181. Jealousy

[The ancestor story in *Wantok* #1118 is the same as that in #824.]
[The ancestor story in *Wantok* #1119 is the same as that in #455.]
[The ancestor story in *Wantok* #1120 is the same as that in #374.]

Two Men Ignored What the Woman Said and they Died

(Wantok 1121, December 21, 1996, page 19)

Long, long ago, in the year 1941, my grandfather and his brother had [difficult] names! Tibionsep and Dangkalengim lived together in **Inangtigin** Village, in the Telefomin District of **West Sepik** Province [**Telefol** People].

One sunny morning, there were no clouds obscuring the mountains. So the big brother, Tibionsep, told the little brother, Dangkalengim, "I'm going to hunt marsupials (*kapul*) on my favorite mountain, the mountain that we call Bugulkot." That bad boy, Tibionsep Tuya! He was newly married and he wanted to walk with his new wife. The dust just flew in the forest and they went rapidly, arriving at Mount Bugulkot. Then it became terribly dark.

Quickly, they made a hut. They cut some big pieces of firewood and the wife began cooking taro. Tibionsep was ready to go in the moon[light]. While they were busy, their dog was barking in the forest. Tibionsep told his wife not to worry, "Stay here. I'll kill marsupials and when I return, we'll roast them well. We'll eat and later we'll go and find more."

Tibionsep followed the dog's barking and arrived at a place where he was confused by many marsupials. Dawn arrived. His poor bride waited and waited. Her eyes became heavy. She slept and she began to dream about her husband. In the dream, the woman saw Tibionsep arrive at a village and fight with the villagers. She herself cried and cried inside this village, which had two giant brothers and Tibionsep Toya [Tuya]. He was a strong man too, so he won the fight and he killed the two brothers. All of the people of this village cried and cried. Then she awoke and it was dawn.

She waited for her husband. Oh my, Tibionsep had killed only huge marsupials. He brought them and told his wife, "I went to watch the marsupials, but I missed them and used up all of my arrows. So, I just killed two." She said not to chase the marsupials. [She told him that she had dreamt that he had fought] with a village and killed two

brother. [She asked him] how many marsupials he had killed. He told her just two. Then she said, "Let's throw away the marsupials." Her husband told her that it was just a dream.

They carried them to a village called **Bonokbil** and met Dangkalengim there. They cooked the marsupials in an earth oven and ate them. The next morning, the enemies came and waited on Atbalmin Trail. Tibionsep and Dangkalengim both wanted to go to Atbalmin to find vines to make traditional rope. So, they took off before the woman getting back her thoughts from her dream and stopping them from going. They ignored what she had said and they crossed the Sepik River. They wanted to go, but enemies blocked their path and killed them. They butchered them and carried them to their village, where they cooked them in an earth oven and ate them. Tibionsep's wife heard this story and just cried and cried. Later, she died.

[Anonymous]

B871.2+. Giant marsupial; D179.6K+. Transformation: person to marsupial; D310+. Transformation: marsupial to person; D1810.8.2. Information received through dream; J652. Inattention to warnings; G11.18. Cannibal tribe; K914. Murder from ambush; M300. Prophecies; P210. Husband and wife; P251.5. Two brothers; P263. Brother-in-law; P264. Sister-in-law; Q211.6. Killing an animal revenged; Q411. Death as punishment; S110. Murders

A Rat Helped Seven Brothers Escape from a *Masalai*

(Wantok 1122, December 28, 1996, page 21)

Long, long ago, in the time of the ancestors, a man and his wife lived in **Kararau** Village, in the Middle Sepik area [**Iatmul** People, **East Sepik** Province]. They had seven children.

One day, the parents sent all of the children to remove grasses in the garden. The garden was near a big river.

They were removing the grasses when they saw a rat. They wanted to kill it, but the little brother took it and said that he would take care of it.

They worked hard for a while. In the afternoon they found their way back towards the village. They sat and rested, and then they saw a big tree drifting down the river.

Quickly, they all swam to the tree and drifted down the river. They drifted and drifted. They thought that the village was still far away. However, they had actually already passed the village.

They drifted down and arrived at the mouth of the river at the sea. By then it was dark, so they could not search for the village anymore.

They clung to the tree and went towards the deep sea. Near dawn, they saw an island nearby. They swam and swam until they arrived at the island. The little brother was still holding the rat that he had taken from the garden.

This island had a *masalai* man. When the seven brothers went ashore, the *masalai* man cam and said hello to them, "I'm very happy that you've come to this island. I don't have any children. I live alone here."

So, the masalai man gave them a house and some food. They ate, then they slept in the house. The little brother had not lost his rat. He held his rat and they slept until dawn.

In the morning, the *masalai* man came and told the brothers, "I want the first and second brothers to go into the forest and hunt for some pig or other wild game for us to eat. Number three and number four brothers, you go work in the garden and fetch some food. Number five and six brothers, you remove the grasses by my house. You, the little brother and your rat, come and cook food in my house."

This was the work that the *masalai* man gave to the brothers. So, the brothers would do their work every day. They lived there for a while, then one night they were all dead asleep. The *masalai* man sat and talked to himself, "That's it. Tomorrow morning, I'll kill all of you and eat you. The time for my belly to be full has arrived."

The *masalai* man thought that all of the brothers were dead asleep and that they had not heard him. However, the first and second brothers were not asleep. They had listened carefully and heard everything that he said.

Oh my, they were surprised that he was not a real man and that he was a *masalai*. However, they were not afraid. They were now thinking of a way to escape and return to their real home.

Quickly, they awakened all of the brothers and they thought. They thought and thought. Then they thought of the rat that the little brother carried around with him. They told the little rat to help them.

The rat listened to them and began digging a big tunnel down under the house towards the sea. All of them quietly followed the tunnel and arrived at the beach.

It was lucky that the *masalai* man's canoe was there. They pulled it down from the island and paddled away. When they left the island, dawn was breaking.

The *masalai* man awoke and went to check on the brothers. He saw the big hole and he was furious. He fol-lowed the tunnel, going underground and arriving at the beach.

He arrived at the beach and saw that his canoe was not there. He looked in the middle of the sea and saw the brothers paddling away. He was irate.

He sped back to the house and took a long rope. You know *masalai* men. They have great powers. He went back to the beach, threw the rope and hooked the bow of the canoe.

When he tried to pull the brothers back, the rat quickly chewed on the rope and broke it. The *masalai* man fell down very badly on the beach. He threw the rope again and hooked the middle of the canoe. However, the rat did the same thing and the *masalai* man fell down again.

This time, the *masalai* man was completely furious. He threw the rope again and hooked the rudder of the canoe. He tried to pull, but the rat cut the rope again. The *masalai* man again fell down badly.

The *masalai* man threw the rope and jumped into the sea, swimming behind the brothers. The brothers paddled and paddled. They arrived close to their village where they lived on the beach. However, the *masalai* man was also approaching.

The brothers shouted and shouted to the village. The warriors came with bows and arrows. They danced belligerently and jumped on the beach. When the brothers went ashore, the *masalai* man also went ashore.

Quickly, the village warriors grabbed the *masalai* man and killed him. Later, they also killed two pigs and cooked them with the *masalai* man. They danced and sang passionately until dawn. The parents saw their seven children again and they were elated.

Bots Kelly
Kararau Village
Middle Sepik
East Sepik Province

B212. Animal understands human speech; B437.1. Helpful rat; F490+. Masalai; F636. Remarkable thrower; F639.1.1. Mighty digger of tunnels; F843. Extraordinary rope; G82. Cannibal fattens victim; G512. Ogre killed; G661. Ogre's secret overheard; P210. Husband and wife; P231. Mother and son; P233. Father and son; P251.6.3+. Seven brothers; Q215. Cannibalism punished; Q411. Death as punishment; R210. Escapes; R260. Pursuits; S110. Murders; S139.2.2+. Corpse put into cooking pot or cooked

Two Children Became Male and Female Sago Trees

(Wantok 1123, January 4, 1996, page 19)

Long, long ago, in the time of the ancestors, a man and his wife lived on Mount Bosavi in the Komo area of **Southern Highlands** Province.

This forested mountain did not have any other people. The man and woman lived only with their two children. The first child was a boy and the second was a girl.

The boy's name was Kumayia and the girl's name was Yia. Kumayia and Yia lived very well and played together. They never fought with each other. Their parents loved them and took very good care of them.

Every day, the parents would go into the deep forest. They would hunt for wild game to eat in the afternoon and at night. The children would stay alone in the house and play around.

The children stayed for a while. Then they went fairly far away where they could work in a garden. While the parents were hunting game in the deep forest, the children were going by Mount Bosavi and making a garden for themselves.

The boy, Kumayia, made a garden for himself. His garden was on the side of the mountain that looked towards Kutubu, Kerema and Central Province. Kumayia's sister, Yia, also made a garden for herself. Hers was on the side of the mountain that looked towards Daru and the Sepik.

Oh my, they made huge gardens, but their parents did not know that their children had big gardens. This was because during the day, the parents would go into the deep forest and the children would go to work in their two gardens.

One early morning, the parents awoke and took all of their things. They went into the deep forest to hunt for game. Kumayia and Yia slept. They awoke some hours later.

They took work tools and arrived in the garden. They worked very hard until it was nearly noon. Then their bodies were pained. They rested and slept in the gardens.

They slept and slept, and they did not awake. They were completely dead asleep in each of their gardens. Late at night, their brains transformed and grew like trees in each of their gardens.

The parents did not know that the two children had changed in the gardens. They returned from the deep forest in the afternoon and tried to find the two children. The father and mother searched everywhere, but the children were no longer there.

In the very early morning, the parents awoke and followed the children's footprints, arriving at the two gardens. Oh my, they were shocked.

They walked slowly inside the gardens and saw the two sago trees standing there. The parents were troubled and they cried terribly at this place. Later, they returned home.

The two sago trees grew white and red. The white sago came from Kumayia (male sago). It fills the side facing Kutubu and Kerema, where Kumayia had made his garden. The red sago fills the Daru, Kiunga and Sepik side, where the girl (Yia) had made her garden.

Yukari Talipe
Para Village-Komo [**Huli** People]
Southern Highlands Province

A2681+. Origin of sago; D447.10+. Transformation: brain to sago palm tree; D696. Transformation during sleep; P210. Husband and wife; P231. Mother and son; P232. Mother and daughter; P233. Father and son; P234. Father and daughter; P253. Sister and brother

A Jimi Man Married a *Masalai* Woman

(Wantok 1124, January 11, 1996, page 21)

In the time of the ancestors, there was a village called **Anmep-Kap**. This village was in the Jimi District of **Western Highlands** Province.

In this village, there was a man who slept by a big river. His name was Kundunga Tok. Kundunga Tok was an excellent hunter of wild game.

One night, the young man took his bow and arrows. He walked away to keep watch on tree fruits at night. On this night, the moon was brightly lit.

These tree fruits were being eaten by marsupials (*kapul*) at night. The man sat on a tree branch and kept very careful watch.

He sat until late a night. Before long, he heard women's voices making jokes and laughing in the deep forest and approaching. He listened and listened, then the noise came directly to the tree where he was keeping watch. He shut his mouth and sat very quietly with his bow and arrows.

He stayed quietly and saw five young women climb the tree. They gorged themselves on the tree fruits, just like marsupials. He watched and he had goosebumps [lit., "his skin rose"]. This was because he had not seen a woman for a very long time.

He looked at each of the women and he saw that one was very beautiful, more so than the others were. He thought of getting up and grabbing her. He did not know that this was not a real woman. It was a *masalai* woman.

He let his bow and arrows fall to the ground. Quickly, he jumped and grabbed the gorgeous woman. The other *masalai* women saw this and they fled. They did not think of helping their friend.

The man and the woman fell down to the ground and began to wrestle. You know that the *masalai* woman used all her strength, but the scoundrel kept holding her.

She could not get free, so she turned into a snake. However, the scoundrel was not afraid. He kept holding onto the snake.

The woman tried turning into various kinds of animals to frighten the man and escape from him, but the man thought that now was his chance. He would not have another chance later.

He held onto her until she had no more strength. She changed and became the beautiful woman by the tree fruits. Then he talked to her about marrying him. She replied that he was stronger, so they could marry. They went back to together to the village and lived together. He gave the name Kunongsaun to her.

They lived for a while and raised two children, a boy and a girl. The boy's name was Bekalo and the girl's name was Moleambo. That is the story of how a *masalai* woman became a real woman.

Alphonse Anda

Jimi District

Western Highlands

D191W. Transformation: woman to serpent (snake); D610. Repeated transformation; F401.6. Spirit in human form; F490+. Masalai; P210. Husband and wife; P231. Mother and son; P232. Mother and daughter; P233. Father and son; P234. Father and daughter; P253. Sister and brother; P310. Friendship; R4. Surprise capture; R220. Flights; T111. Marriage of mortal and supernatural being; T192. Marriage by force

[The ancestor story in *Wantok* #1125 is the same as that in #465.]

Two *Masalai*s Helped the Fathers Make a House

(Wantok 1126, January 25, 1996, page 19)

Long, long ago, in the time of the ancestors, there lived an old man with his three daughters. They lived in a village in **East Sepik** Province called **Kandamaik**. The old man did not have a son. He only had the three daughters. The old man's wife was dead.

They lived very well and they carried out their work, such as gardening, cutting and scraping sago, hunting for wild game, and other work. The old man worked very hard, so he and his three daughters were never short of meat or food. They had meat and food every day.

The old man's dogs also hunted game. When the old man took the dogs with him into the forest to hunt for game, they did not give a chance to game such as pig, cassowary or bandicoot.

They lived for a while, then one time, the old man's brother-in-law went around looking for them. The old man's brother-in-law arrived in their village and saw the old man with his three daughters. He was terribly worried for them. This was because only the old man and his three daughters were there. So, he thought of his sister (the old man's wife) and was worried for them.

The other thing that made the old man's brother-in-law worry was that his old brother-in-law and his three nieces lived in an old house. So, he knew that his brother-in-law was alone and that he could not make a new house. This was because the village was on top of a mountain and he alone could not cut the trees, *limbum* palms, posts and other things for the house, and then carry them up to build a house.

In the afternoon, the three sisters cooked food. Their uncle ate, and then he walked back towards his village. He arrived at the village and shouted for his two brothers to come meet. He revealed his concerns about what he had seen. Then the three of them decided that they would make a new house for the old brother-in-law and the three nieces.

Another day, the three brothers went to a place where their *masalai* dwelled. They told their *masalai* that the next day, they would go to see it. The *masalai* would remove a big tree with the roots and leaves still on it. The *masalai* would then carry it to their brother-in-law's village and build a house for him (the brother-in-law). They explained this, and then they returned to the village. One of them went to the brother-in-law's village and explained what would happen on the next day.

He explained that the next day, when they and their *masalai* approached the village, one of them would whistle. When their three nieces heard the whistling, they must leave the village and hide. They could not stay in the village. Only their old brother-in-law should stay in the village. The old man's brother-in-law explained everything, and then he returned to the village.

In the very early morning of the next day, the three brothers went to their *masalai*. They told the *masalai* that they had arrived for the work that they had talked about on the previous day. A great wind arose and their *masalai* rose from its hiding place. The *masalai* removed an ironwood tree with its roots, leaves and vines still intact. The three brothers saw this and walked in front, while their *masalai* carried the tree and followed them. The three brothers and their *masalai* arrived near the old brother-in-law's village and one of them whistled. The three brothers and their *masalai* brought the tree into the village. They sat and rested. Then they ate and told stories with their old brother-in-law.

In the afternoon, they returned to their village and the three sisters returned to their village. They saw the tree and they just could not believe it. They could not believe it because they thought that *masalai*s could not remove entire trees and carry them to other places.

Later, the three brothers returned and cut the tree, then they carved the posts. They also cut other trees and erected a large house for the old brother-in-law and their nieces. They finished building the house. Then they put on the roof [using sago or nipa palm fronds].

When the three sons of the [three brothers] heard what the three brothers had done with their *masalai*, they were not happy. They told themselves, "Why did we just stay and watch while they showed the strength and power of their *masalai*? Is it just them who have a *masalai*?"

So on another day, the three brothers awoke in the very early morning. They went to their *masalai*. They took the *masalai* and went to a place near the old man's village, where there were trees standing. Their *masalai* removed the *limbum* palm trees with the roots intact and carried them up to the village. The old man and his three daughters saw this and were surprised.

Then the old man's three brothers-in-law and his three nephews met and finished the house for the old man and his three daughters.

This old man has since died. Of his three daughters, the youngest, died. The two eldest are still alive. Of the old man's three brothers-in-law, the two eldest are dead and the youngest is still alive.

Klewia Duowing

Wewak

East Sepik Province

D2142.1. Wind produced by magic; F403.2. Spirits help mortal; F490+. Masalai; J1050. Attention to warnings; P233. Father and son; P234. Father and daughter; P251.6.1. Three brothers; P252.2. Three sisters; P263. Brother-in-law; P293. Uncle; P295. Cousins; P297. Nephew; P298. Niece; W195. Envy

[The ancestor story in *Wantok* #1127 is the same as that in #299.]

928

[The ancestor story in *Wantok* #1128 is the same as that in #302.]
[The ancestor story in *Wantok* #1129 is the same as that in #300.]
[The ancestor story in *Wantok* #1130 is the same as that in #358.]
[The ancestor story in *Wantok* #1131 is the same as that in #393.]
[The ancestor story in *Wantok* #1132 is the same as that in #330.]

The Little Brother Left the Village because the Big Brother Wanted to Kill Him

(Wantok 1133, March 14, 1996, page 20)

Long, long ago, in the time of the ancestors, in a village in the Nembi area of **Southern Highlands** Province, called **Pipilex**, there lived two brothers. Their names were Nakone and Napope.

Nakone, the elder, was a hunter. The second brother, Napope, was a farmer. Nakone's skin was red and Napope's was black. They were very good friends and they lived in their village of Pipilex.

Nakone went into the forest every day to hunt for game. He would make traps to catch game such as cassowaries, bandicoots, marsupials (*kapul*), and birds.

However, there was a problem. Nakone always went to the forest to check the traps that he had laid and he never took one animal back to the village. Never. He would just work hard for nothing. So, the little brother, Napope, would work very hard in the garden, cook food, fetch water, and also do other work.

This happened for a very long time, so the little brother thought that he must find out about his big brother. The little brother wanted to find out why his big brother never brought one animal to the village.

One time, the little brother made his plan that he would follow his big brother into the forest. He did not tell his big brother. He just thought of doing this.

OK, the next day, Napope, the little brother, lied that he would go work in the garden. Then he hid by the side of the trail and kept watch for Nakone. When Nakone walked by him and went into the forest, Napope left the place where he was sitting and hiding, then he followed Nakone very quietly. Napope followed Nakone quietly into the deep forest. He climbed a hill and sat at the summit, then looked down at his brother.

Napope saw his brother walking away. He arrived at his trap, then he removed a cassowary from the trap. Napope was surprised to see Nakone cut one of the cassowary's legs, then begin eating it with the blood. Nakone gorged himself on the leg, then he said, "I'll eat Napope's leg like this." The little brother heard his big brother say this. The fear was killing him, so he got up and left the hiding spot where he was sitting. He ran back to the village. He killed a pig that the two of them had husbanded, then he made an earth oven. Napope finished making the earth oven. Then he put a piece of the pig's ear, a piece of the leg, the snout, and a little liver there for his big brother Nakone. Nakone carried all of the pig meat with him in a big bamboo tube, then he walked on a long trail. Napope also took one of each of all of the kinds of foods, and he carried them with him.

Napope walked and walked, then he heard Nakone's shouts. Nakone shouted, "Where are you? Now I'm going to eat you. Don't make me angry."

When Napope heard this, he poured all of the food and pork into the big bamboo tube that he was carrying. He himself also went into the bamboo. After he went inside the bamboo, he rolled the bamboo down to a river. The big river carried the bamboo away.

Nakone shouted and followed Napope, then arrived at the big river. When he was about to cross the river to go to the other side, the water crossed his legs and arms, then he went into the river. He did not come up again.

The river carried Napope's bamboo downstream, arriving at a place along the river where some young women were fishing. One of the women saw the bamboo and thought that it was an ordinary bamboo, so she took it. Later, she [thought that she] would put fish inside of it and cook the fish. She put the bamboo in a net bag, then she carried it to the village.

She brought the bamboo to the village, then she wanted to clean the rubbish and put the fish in, but no. A young man jumped out of the bamboo. She was surprised and asked him, "What are you, a *masalai* or a real man?" Napope revealed the story about his brother Nakone. She was sorry for Napope, so they married and lived in the woman's village, raising children.

Simon Komel

Mendi

Southern Highlands Province

[Mr. Komel wrote a similar story in Wantok #1211.]

D950.15. Magic bamboo tree; F527.1. Red person; F527.5. Black man; G10. Cannibalism; P210. Husband and wife; P230. Parents and children; P251.5. Two brothers; P251.5.3. Hostile brothers; P310. Friendship; R213. Escape from home; R260. Pursuits; T100. Marriage; W151. Greed

[The ancestor story in *Wantok* #1134 is the same as that in #473.]
[The ancestor stories in *Wantok* #1135 and 1136 are the same as that in #1114.]
[The ancestor story in *Wantok* #1137 is the same as that in #748.]
[Issue #1138 of *Wantok* could not be located.]

[The ancestor story in *Wantok* #1139 is the same as that in #536.]
[The ancestor story in *Wantok* #1140 is the same that in #501.]
[The ancestor story in *Wantok* #1141 is the same that in #640.]
[The ancestor story in *Wantok* #1142 is the same that in #641.]

A Brother and Sister Became Birds

(Wantok 1143, May 23, 1996, page 19)

Long, long ago, in a village called **Amungem**, there lived a young woman with her scrawny [lit., "chicken-boned"] brother. They were still young when their parents had died. The father died first, then the mother.

Before their mother had died, she gave a last message to them. She told them, "My two children, you must take good care of yourselves. Don't argue or fight between yourselves. When you want to leave the house and go to the garden, it would be best if you carefully tended the fire. Don't let the fire die."

When their mother died, they followed their mother's instructions well. They lived very well in the village. After they cooked food and ate, they never let the fire die. No, they would make the fire keep burning. They would shove the embers under the ashes and keep the fire lit.

They lived for a while, then one time a bad thing happened to them at night. They were completely dead asleep and not thinking of the fire, then the fire died. It was too bad for them, when they awoke in the morning, the sister wanted to start the fire. But no, the fire was dead. They could not revive the fire and she did not cook food at sunrise. Then the sister told the brother, "I'm very sorry my brother, I don't know how we'll find fire. It would be best if we kept watch and looked for a place where smoke is rising."

They began to look around everywhere. Before long, they saw smoke from a fire rising from a place inside the deep forest. The sister cut a flower and gave it to her brother, then she told him, "Brother, you must look at this flower. I'll try to bring the fire here. If men kill me, you'll see this flower dry up. If men don't kill me, this flower will not dry up."

After she told her brother this, she left the village and walked towards the place in the deep forest where they had seen smoke rising. She went and went, then she arrived at the place where the smoke was rising. She was surprised to see an old bald man knocking himself out, working in a garden. He was making a gigantic garden near his existing garden.

The sister was not afraid. She walked quietly behind the old bald man to take the fire. She walked slowly forward and took the fire. When she was about to turn and go back, the old bald man turned and saw her holding the fire and standing there. Then the old man left his work and ran towards her to grab her.

It was too bad, but when she saw the old man running to grab her, a great fear took her and she also wanted to escape. The old bald man saw that she wanted to escape, so he told her, "If you run away, I'll kill you."

The young woman listened and just stood quietly. The old bald man went and grabbed her. He took her to his village. They married and lived together.

Before they married, he asked her if she had parents or brothers or sisters. She told him that her parents had died and that she was alone. So, she had followed the smoke there to get the fire when she had met him. She had lied and hid the existence of her little brother.

It was too bad for the woman's little brother. The flower that his sister had cut and given to him died. He thought that men had killed his sister. So, he worried and cried for his sister. He was alone and lived in their house in the village.

He lived there all of the time and he would only eat ripe foods, such as papayas and bananas. He lived for a while, then he became a big man and he could do big and difficult work.

One time, he thought about following his sister's footsteps. So in the very early morning of the next day, he awoke and wanted to walk and see the place where his sister had gone. He [saw] smoke from a fire rising in the middle of the deep forest. Then the bad boy followed the smoke. He followed the same path that his sister had followed. He arrived at the place where the smoke was rising and he saw a garden. He hid by the garden and watched. Before long, he saw an old bald man and his young wife knocking themselves out, working in the garden.

They worked and their baby cried for a drink of milk, so the mother left work and walked to the garden fence to give milk to the baby. This was the place where the woman's brother was standing and hiding.

When she wanted to give milk to the baby, the bad boy pretended to cough. She heard this, so she stood and saw her brother. The brother gave her a big smile. She knew that it was her brother, so she screamed and shouted. She forgot about giving milk to the baby. She left the baby, then she ran to hold her brother and to rub their bodies together.

Her old bald husband saw this and thought that his wife wanted to marry this young man. Quietly, the bald man ran to the house and took his spear to kill him. He held the spear and ran to shoot them. He arrived and drew back his arm, then shot the spear. When the brother and sister saw the spear approaching their bodies, they turned into two birds. They flew up and perched upon a tree, then they shouted and cried.

It was too bad. What would the old man do? The woman had left with her brother. He cried terribly for a while, then he took his baby and they went to the house.

Handom Gumuseng

Hagen

Western Highlands Province

D150M. Transformation: man to bird; D150W. Transformation: woman to bird; D642.2. Transformation to escape death; D671. Transformation flight; E761.3. Life token: tree (flower) fades; J652. Inattention to warnings; J1050. Attention to warnings; P210. Husband and wife; P230. Parents and children; P231. Mother and son; P232. Mother and daughter; P253. Sister and brother; P263. Brother-in-law; R210. Escapes; R213. Escape from home; T192. Marriage by force; T611. Suckling of children; W157. Dishonesty

[The ancestor story in *Wantok* #1144 is the same as that in #376.]
[The ancestor story in *Wantok* #1145 is the same as that in #352.]
[The ancestor story in *Wantok* #1146 is the same as that in #433.]
[The ancestor story in *Wantok* #1147 is the same as that in #419.]
[The ancestor stories in *Wantok* #1148 and 1149 are the same as in #545.]
[The ancestor story in *Wantok* #1150 is the same as that in #474.]
[The ancestor story in *Wantok* #1151 is the same as that in #520.]
[The ancestor story in *Wantok* #1152 is the same as that in #518.]
[The ancestor story in *Wantok* #1153 is the same as that in #284.]
[The ancestor story in *Wantok* #1154 is the same as that in #295.]
[The ancestor story in *Wantok* #1155 is the same as that in #419.]
[The ancestor story in *Wantok* #1156 is the same as that in #285.]
[The ancestor story in *Wantok* #1157 is the same as that in #292.]

Brother and Sister Killed the Bad Snake
(Wantok 1158, September 5, 1996, page 16)

Long, long ago, in the time of the ancestors, in the **Kimil** area of **Western Highlands** Province, there lived a big and strong snake [**Nii** People]. The name of the snake was Wani Muming and it lived inside of a big cave.

Every night, Wani Muming would hunt for things to eat. If it did not find things to eat, it would become angry and go to the village to eat men, women, children and animals. After it killed and ate them, it would be elated and return to its home.

Wani Muming did this for a while, then the people of this area became terrified. So, at night the women and children slept while the men sat and watched them. They never slept [at night]. They would sit and watch the women and children until dawn. When the men slept during the day, the women would go to the gardens to gather food and other things for the night. When the men went to the forest to hunt for wild game at night and they did not return to the village, the women and children knew that the snake had eaten them.

The years came and went, the months came and went, the weeks came and went, then the days and nights came and went. The bad snake Wani Muming worked diligently at hunting for food at night, and when it did not find food, it would go the village and kill the men, women, children and animals. The people of the village were very troubled about their kin who had been eaten by Wani Muming. The poor villagers had it very difficult and they did not know what to do. After a while, the numbers of men, women and children became few in the village.

One time, the village leader held a big meeting with the other people of the village. Everyone supported their leader's ideas that they must leave the village and go to another place. Everyone was in agreement, so they prepared all of their belongings.

They prepared everything at night and waited for dawn. In the very early morning, they took their belongings and walked away to another village. The name of this village is **Bunum Wo**. Everyone left the village except for one woman. Her husband had died and she was alone. She could not follow the other people because she was pregnant and she found it difficult to carry her belongings and follow them to the new village.

The poor woman was afraid of Wani Muming, so she dug a hole by her house. She went into the hole and hid. After a while, she gave birth to two babies, a boy and a girl.

The woman took care of her babies and after a while they began to walk. They lived for a while, then the babies began to talk and they knew about things. When they grew bigger, about five or six years old, she taught the girl how to take care of spears. She taught the boy how to make spears and also how to kill the bad snake. She also told them clearly why they were the only ones who lived in the village. She told them about the bad snake who had devastated the men, women and children, and about the clans of the village leaving to another place.

She and her children lived for a while, then the children became bigger and stronger. The boy went to the forest, carried things, and made bows and arrows. His sister would help him. One day, after they had prepared everything, they told their mother that they were ready to kill Wani Muming.

One day, their mother prepared their food. Her children arranged and prepared things for the next day when they would go to kill the bad snake.

In the very early morning of the next day, the mother awoke and cooked food for them. She tied up some for them to carry away with themselves. After she prepared the food, she awakened them up and the two of them ate. After they ate, she took the spears and food, then she tied them and put them inside a net bag. She told the girl to carry this. When it was almost completely light, her children left the hole where they hid, then they began to walk away to the place where Wani Muming lived.

They walked and walked, then they arrived at the cave where Wani Muming lived. When they arrived, the bad snake smelled them, left the cave and went outside. When they saw this, the sister removed the spears from the net bag and gave them to her brother. When Wani Muming was about to put its head completely outside, the brother was already prepared. Quickly, he threw his first spear and shot Wani Muming's head. The sister gave him more spears, then the brother let the bad snake have it until he killed the snake.

Afterwards, they brought the good news back home and told their mother that they had killed Wani Muming. Their mother was elated for them. They lived happily together in the village until their mother died, leaving just the two of them there.

Johanna Ding and Jennifer Kiap
Fatima Primary School
Banz
Western Highlands Province

B11.11+. Fight with giant snake; B16.5.1. Giant devastating serpent; B875.1. Giant serpent; G510.4. Hero overcomes devastating animal; P210. Husband and wife; P230. Parents and children; P231. Mother and son; P232. Mother and daughter; P253. Sister and brother; R213. Escape from home; R310. Refuges; R315. Cave as refuge; S140. Cruel abandonments and exposures; S371+. Abandoned woman's daughter becomes hero; S371+. Abandoned woman's son becomes hero; T570. Pregnancy; T587. Birth of twins; T685. Twins

Black Magic Helped to Kill Two *Masalai* Birds
(Wantok 1159, September 12, 1996, page 15)

Long, long ago, in the time of the ancestors of Werman [**Wereman**] Village, in the Burui sword-grass area of **East Sepik** Province, there lived two birds [**Sawos** People]. The name of this type of bird is *gawi*, and they were *masalai* birds. They lived in their house on top of a big tree, which stood by a pond. This pond was near Werman Village.

The two *masalai* birds would fly and go down to the village. They would then take people up to their house in the big tree. Later, they would kill and eat them.

The *masalai* birds would did this all of the time and the ancestors of Werman Village found it very difficult. The ancestors would work, find food and go around only at night. During the day, from morning until afternoon when the sun set, the two birds would walk around. So, the ancestors were afraid and they would hide. They never went outside into clearings.

The ancestors lived like this for a while. Then one night, the old and powerful sorcerer men of the village met and argued about how they would kill the two *masalai* birds. They argued for a while, then they found a way. They forbade themselves from eating and drinking water, so that they could create black magic to kill the *masalai gawi* birds.

After, the performed the black magic, they began to make a hand drum that could sleep two men inside of it. The hand drum that they made looked like a big fish. After they finished, they carved two pieces of wild betel nut palm and they made spears for the two men to use to fight the *masalai* birds. Later, they shut the openings of the hand drum with coconut shells. They made these things under the name of *supukundi* black magic.

The poor ancestors used stone axes to do this work. When it was nearly morning, they pushed the drum down to the water. They kept at it until morning. Then the *masalai gawi* birds saw the hand drum and they thought that it was a big fish. They flew down and brought it up to their house. Before long, it became dark and they slept.

When the two ancestors inside the hand drum heard the *masalai* birds snoring, they removed the coconut shells from the openings of the drum very quietly and went outside. They each pointed to a *masalai* bird and approached them. They shot them with spears and they fell down to the ground dead.

After they killed the *masalai* birds, they found it very difficult to get down to the ground. They sat on top of the *masalai* birds' house until dawn when the sun rose.

When the people of the village looked up the tree, they saw the two men sitting there. They understood that they were finding it difficult to come down to the ground. Then the leaders performed black magic again. They asked the green lizard, which is used for hand drum skins, to climb up the tree and bring them down. They tried, and their hard work failed. They asked various kinds of birds, but they could not do it. They asked various kinds of things to help the two men, but they could not do it. They tried all kinds

of things, until they had done everything they knew. They leaders of the village thought, and then a vine that we call *dumakua* came and told them that it would try.

At night, when the people of the village were asleep, the vine climbed the big tree that held the *masalai* birds' house. The vine went up and met the two men. Then it told them that it would take them down to the ground. However, the two men were terrified and did not want to do this. Dumakua was persistent, so the two of them jumped onto it and it took them down to the ground. Before long, dawn broke. The villagers awoke and saw the two men standing in the middle of the village.

The villagers were elated. They made a big feast and festival to show their happiness for their killing the two *masalai* birds.

Ray Alan
Burui Sword Grass
Pagwi
East Sepik Province

[There is a similar story in *Wantok* #503.]

B16.3+. Devastating bird killed; B33. Man-eating birds; B212. Animal understands human speech; B552. Man carried by bird; D1084. Magic spear; D1211. Magic drum; D1610.3+. Speaking vine; D1711. Magician; D1733.3.1. Magic power by fasting; D1733.3.1+. Magic power by abstaining from drinking water; D2074.1.3. Birds magically called; D2074.1.3+. Reptiles magically called; F490+. Masalai; F815.7. Extraordinary vine; G353. Bird as ogre; G510.4. Hero overcomes devastating animal; K753. Capture by hiding in disguised objects; N815.0.1+. Helpful vine-spirit; Q10. Deeds rewarded; R49.1. Captivity in tree; R100. Rescues

Mothers Became Flying Foxes
(Wantok 1160, September 19, 1996, page 16)

Long, long ago, when the earth was still new, the people of Nasuapum [**Ngasawampum**] Village, **Wampar** [People] (number 1 Markham), **Morobe** Province, would make big feasts, parties, festivals and celebrations every day. The men were very hard workers at hunting for wild game and the women were very hard workers at gardening, planting yams, taros, bananas, sweet potatoes, and various kinds of fruits and leafy greens that are good to eat.

Every afternoon when the men came out of the forest and the mothers came out of the gardens, they would make a big party. At night, they would sit by the fire, scrape lime (calcium oxide), chew betel nuts, and then talk and tell stories. From this manner, their life became good and very happy until one time when the men stopped bringing game out to the village. The men's habits changed. They tired and they were greedy. They would hunt game only for themselves. They would cook it in the forest and finish it, and then walk back to the village empty-handed.

The poor mothers were still the same as before. Every morning, they would go to the gardens and work until the afternoon. Then they would take some food from the gardens, fill net bags and carry it back to the houses. When they arrived at the houses, they would very quickly cook food, and then they would sit and watch the trail to see what animals their husbands would bring for them to make soup with the other food. When their husbands arrived in the village, they walked empty-handed and they had no meat. The poor mothers just shared the food with fruits and leafy greens. Then everyone together ate the food. So, every afternoon the mothers and the children would do this, and they became just skin-and-bones. However, their husbands stayed strong and fat because they would eat meat every day.

Among this group of men, there was a young man named Bruno. He was married to a young woman named Mantik. Bruno loved Mantik as his wife, so he was very sorry when he saw that Mantik was losing weight, becoming skin and bones. When the men were killing animals and finishing them, Bruno alone would pretend that he was cooking a piece of meat for himself. He would cover it with a ginger (*gorgor*) leaf, and then hide it well where the other men could not see it. He would bring it to give to his wife in the village, telling her, "After you eat this meat, don't say that you ate it."

One time, all of the men went into the forest to hunt for game and the village leader's wife met with all of the other women of the village. They held a meeting and talked about finding out why their husbands were strong and fat, and why the poor mothers and children were losing weight and becoming skin and bones. The meeting started and the village leader's wife spoke, "I don't think that our husbands have told us the truth when they said that they have not found any game. Why do we women work hard in the gardens and carry food to the village, when the greedy and lazy men come just to eat?"

Then Mantik spoke, "My husband's a good man. He brings pieces of meat to the village. What you said is true, that when our husbands go to hunt for game, they do not miss. No, they kill, cook and eat in the forest, then they come empty-handed to the village."

When the other mothers heard this, they were furious and they said, "What have we done, that they have lied to us? The poor children cry for meat. Who will give meat to them?"

Then the village leader's wife spoke, "Now today, let us mothers not go to the gardens. Instead of going to the gardens, let us all go into the forests and find black bird feathers. We must scavenge many bird feathers."

So, the mothers began to follow the instructions of the village leader's wife. They did not have a single question because they knew that the village leader's wife was wise and that she had wrinkles [lit., "tree bark"]. She was the leader of the village women.

That day, the mothers and fathers came out of the forest empty-handed. The men began to complain when they saw that there was no food or fruit to eat. The village leader angrily said, "You're very lazy mothers. Exactly what did you do today that you didn't fetch food?"

Then the village leader's wife replied, "To plant food takes six months."

The next day, the village leader's wife and the other women went to the banana gardens. They lined up the bird feathers that they had gathered. After they finished putting them up, each mother began putting their feathers on themselves. Then they made noises and tried to fly. The village leader's wife made noises on the ground with her legs and said, "Hard-working mothers of Nasuapum, our greedy husbands have lied to us many times. Now we must forget them. Let's go and live by ourselves in another place. Let the men take care of our children henceforth. Come follow me. Let's fly into the deep forest. Then we'll find our husbands and say goodbye to them. Afterwards, let's leave forever."

There were three noises when they mothers began to raise their big black wings and fly away. It was very dark and one could not see the sun at this time. The flying fox mothers flew very high, missing all of the treetops. Before long, they saw their husbands watching. The husbands were shocked and they asked, "What's that? These birds look like they're our wives." Then the flying-fox mothers said, "You lied to us all of the time. Now we're no longer your wives. We're leaving you now. Go back to the village. Your children are waiting."

While they were speaking, the flying fox mothers flew and perched on the trees [upside down]. They spoke, "Listen. From this time onwards, you'll never see us during the day. However, you will see us in the late afternoon and at night."

This was the last thing that the mothers said. They flew into the very deep forest and lived in their hiding places. Very quickly, the men left the forest and ran into the village. They were shocked to see the children crying as if they were dying. Then they met Mantik, Bruno's wife.

She told the story to them that the mothers had transformed into flying foxes and had flown away from the village.

Today, flying foxes stay in their hiding places during the [day]. They come out only at night.

[Anonymous]

A1895. Creation of bat; A2260+. Why flying fox flies at dusk; B211.2.11K+. Speaking flying fox; D117.5KW. Transformation: woman to flying fox; D531. Transformation by putting on skin; D671. Transformation flight; P210. Husband and wife; P230. Parents and children; Q272. Avarice punished; R213. Escape from home; S11+. Cruel father refuses children food; S62+. Cruel husband refuses wife food; T10. Falling in love; W111. Laziness; W151. Greed; W157. Dishonesty

An Eagle Married a Girl

(Wantok 1161, September 26, 1996, page 16)

Long, long ago, there lived a man. The man's name was Alitap Kimal and he had two wives. One was named Tari and one was named Kandep. They lived in a **Patuli** Village, in the Kandep area of **Enga** Province [**Enga** People].

The two women would work together in the sweet potato garden. Then they would go to the house where they would cook and eat.

One time, Kandep dug sweet potatoes. Then she cooked and ate them. The two women were never angry. They just lived happily.

However, their husband would scold them all of the time. He would tell them to do something or to fetch something, and they would follow his instructions. If they did not do so, he would quickly get angry and beat them. So, the women would follow their husband's instructions.

After a while, the women both became pregnant. One time, the man heard that they would be killing pigs at a clan house in his mother's home at **Wakwak** Village, by Mendi [**Mendi** People, **Southern Highlands** Province].

After he heard this, he went to his house and told his wives that he would go to his mother's village by Mendi. Then he would bring back some pork.

He could not return quickly. He said that if one of them gave birth to a girl, they must kill it. If it was a boy, then they must take good care of him.

Their husband said that if they did not listen to him and they did take care of a girl, then he could not see her. Later, he would leave them.

The two women listened and became very worried. It was nearly time for them to give birth, in only about one month.

Night and day, they never ate or slept well. They became terribly worried. After a while, they gave birth one night. They gave birth, lighted torches and looked. It was too bad, Tari gave birth to a girl and Kandep gave birth to a boy. They became very worried. They did not kill the girl; they both took care of her. They cared for them for a while. Then one year, their two children were talking. Their husband had still not returned. They lived for a while and three years had passed. However, the children's father had not returned to the village. The women told the two children that their father had gone to eat pork in Mendi, but that he had not returned.

The mothers would talk to the two children, but they never talked about what their husband had spoken of doing. So, sometimes people would say that they had just finished killing pigs and were now going home. They heard this, so the two women told the children to go stay on the road and wait for their father bringing pork.

Tari thought very hard and she worried. She thought about what her husband would come and do. The two children waited for their father. People carrying pork passed by them. They gave them a piece of meat and told the two children that their father was coming from very far behind.

They ate some pork and they gave some to their two mothers in the house. They waited, then much later, their father came. Along the trail, he saw the two children; he saw a girl and a boy. So, he was unhappy. He just came and gave a piece of pig's leg to the boy. He passed the girl who came later. He went inside the house and took the boy, and then he held and kissed him. When the girl wanted to go to her father, he told her to go stay by her two mothers. The girl's mother saw the man's face and many tears came down from her face. The man did not speak. He heated stones and cooked all of the pork in an earth oven. Then he brought the pork.

After the earth oven was ready, he took a bamboo tube of water. In the base of the bamboo tube, he made a hole. He told the little girl to go fill the tube with water. He uncovered the earth oven when the little girl was down at the river. He told the two women and the boy to take all of their things and go outside of the house. He shut the house door and they departed.

The poor little girl thought that the bamboo tube was good, so she worked at filling it with water. However, the base of the tube had a hole and she did not see that the water was exiting the hole.

Much later, when the water had still not filled the tube, she saw that it had a hole. She took it to the house, but the house door was shut and her parents were not there. The poor girl cried and saw their footsteps. She followed them and went quietly. The poor girl thought about what she had done and that they had left her. She thought very hard and she became very troubled.

Along the trail, she saw a piece of meat with some sweet potato. She took it and ate. Then she continued to follow them. She went and went. She arrived at a big river and she saw people on the other side of the river. She looked at them, then she shouted and cried. Her mother wanted to come get her, but her father wanted to take the girl's hand in the river. He pulled her up slowly and let her fall. The poor little girl fell down in the river and the water carried her away. Her mother saw this and cried. The water carried the little girl away. Afterwards, an eagle snatched her and looked after her.

The eagle took care of the little girl for a while. When she grew up, the eagle married her. She gave birth to many children. The eagle family lives in **Wapim** Village in the Tari area [**Huli** People, Southern Highlands Province]. This woman gave birth to the ancestors of the Tari People. The Enga People are the boy's descendants. So, the Tari People call the Enga People, *Avi*, which means, "Ankle."

Komai Kipan Kongom
Kandep
Enga Province

[See *Wantok* #531 for a similar story.]

A1611+. Origin of Enga People; A1611+. Origin of Huli People; B535.0.7+. Eagle as nurse for child; B602.1. Marriage to eagle; B631. Human offspring from marriage to animal; H1023.2.4. Task: filling a bottomless water tube; P210. Husband and wife; P231. Mother and son; P232. Mother and daughter; P233. Father and son; P234. Father and daughter; Q325. Disobedience punished; R131. Exposed or abandoned child rescued; R220. Flights; R260. Pursuits; S11.3.6+. Father throws girl into river (sea); S62. Cruel husband; S142. Person thrown into the water and abandoned; S301. Children abandoned (exposed); S322.0.1K+. Man instructs pregnant wife to cherish infant if a boy, to kill if a girl; T145.0.1. Polygyny; T570. Pregnancy; T589.7. Simultaneous births; W31. Obedience; W126. Disobedience

[The ancestor story in *Wantok* #1162 is the same as that in #1161.]

A Man Thought that it Was a Frog
and He Killed His First Wife

(Wantok 1163, October 10, 1996, page 18)

Long, long ago, in the time of my ancestors, there lived a man and his wife. They had two children. One time, the man thought about marrying another woman, so he had sex with her. After some months passed, he married his new wife. They lived well for just a short time.

Once, the man's first wife went to purchase sorcery to ruin her husband's mind. She purchased it, and then she brought and put it inside the house.

One time, the man and his second wife went into the forest to check on the wild game traps that he had placed some days before. They walked and walked, and then they entered the very deep forest where he had set the traps. They arrived there and he told his second wife to go on another trail and to wait for him at a small men's house in the forest where he usually slept.

His second wife listened to him and went along the trail. She walked and walked, and then she saw a big frog sitting on a big tree leaf. When she saw the frog, she took it, bound it with leaves and put it in her net bag. Then she walked away.

Before too long, she felt a pain in her back. She removed the net bag and she began to scratch her back. The pain became greater and she felt terrible. She shouted for her husband to come to her. When he heard his wife shouting, you know new wives, he ran very quickly. He asked his second wife, "Why are you shouting for me?" His second wife said, "Something is on my back and touching me." When he looked, it was too bad. He saw a big frog making a hole inside her back as it lay there.

He told his wife, "A frog is inside of you." He laid his wife down. Very quickly, he made a fire and singed the marsupial (*kapul*) fur from the marsupials that he had taken from the traps.

Quickly, he cut the belly of a big marsupial and removed the guts. Then he cooked it on top of the fire. When the marsupial guts were well cooked, he hung them on a stick and held it close to the frog that was in the hole in his wife's back.

The man told the frog, "If you're a real man, come outside of my wife's body and take this meat."

The frog listened and the good smell of the meat also influenced it, so it came outside of his wife's back. When the frog came out, the man took a piece of firewood and just bashed the frog. The frog kicked out its legs and died.

Afterwards, his wife felt like her back was completely ruined. He carried his wife and they began to walk to the house. He carried his wife and cried until arriving at the village. He wanted to look, but no, the house door was shut. He opened the door and went inside. He saw much blood spilled about, near the door and inside his first wife's room.

Quickly, he went and checked inside the room, but no, he held something cold. He lit a fire and looked carefully, then he saw that his wife was dead inside of the room. The [first] wife's two little children went to live with her clan in her village. The man explained what had happened to some of people in the village and they took his first wife to be buried.

What really had happened was that the first wife had performed malignant sorcery and she had wanted to kill the second wife. So, she became a frog and made a hole inside the back of the man's second wife. However, her husband killed her.

Mescy Blue
Kumin Village [**Mendi** People]
Mendi
Southern Highlands Province

[Mescy Blue retells this story in *Wantok* #1208.]

D195W. Transformation: woman to frog; D572. Transformation by magic object; D651.1. Transformation to kill enemy; K910. Murder by strategy; P210. Husband and wife; P230. Parents and children; P290+. Hostile co-wives; Q261. Treachery punished; Q411. Death as punishment; S63+. Husband kills wife; S110. Murders; T100. Marriage; T145.0.1. Polygyny; V61.3+. Dead buried; W181. Jealousy

An Old Couple Saw a Dead Man and They Ran Crazily

(Wantok 1164, October 17, 1996, page 18)

Long, long ago, there was a clan house in **Okapa**, in **Eastern Highlands** Province [**Fore** People]. The name of this clan house was Ke-efu. There was an old couple who lived in this clan house. They lived for a while. Then one time, a man in **Lufa** died [**Yagaria** People].

The people of Lufa sent a message to the old couple at Ke-efu in Okapa because the man who had died was their maternal relative. The old couple thought that the maternal relative was important, so they would have much food at their maternal relative's [funeral] party.

You know that before, there were no roads for automobiles. The old couple did not fool around with taking net bags — the old man took five and the old woman took five.

They began to walk towards Lufa by themselves. When they approached the village where the man had died, they threw themselves into the mud [a sign of mourning]. They walked and cried as they entered the village.

The people of the village held them and cried until it was nighttime, and then until the morning of the next day. During the day, they began to make fires to heat stones and make food for the deceased. The people gathered food and cooked a huge feast until it was afternoon. In the afternoon, the villagers gave a huge amount of food to the old couple.

The old couple filled their net bags with food. Then they took them and departed. They slept again. On the morning of the next day, they carried the net bags and walked towards the village. The woman put three net bags hanging down from her head and two on top of her head. Her husband followed her. He put [three] on top of his head and he carried two. It was too bad that the bags of food were terribly heavy and they could not raise their heads. The weight of the pork, with the grease and skins, made them walk very slowly. In the afternoon, they arrived at a village called Nupuru [Yagaria Pipel].

They went to rest at Nupuru and they talked until the end of the afternoon. They said that they would sleep there until the next morning. They looked around and they saw a small house that was near the trail. It was dark, so they put all of their things inside the small house and they made a fire. In their net bags, they had bamboo tubes of pork. A light rain was falling, so they were cold and they made a fire.

Some people had put a dead man on top of the house in which they were staying, but the two of them did not know this. The two of them sat well. The old man took four tubes of pork and put them on the fire. The old woman also did the same thing.

They gorged on the pork, but they did not know what was on top of the house. They did not look up. When the man had died, his clan had dressed him with various kinds of ancestral ornaments, such as bird feathers, pig's tusks, bows, and other things.

The old couple began to eat their pork. While they were eating, the dead man's ghost speared the old man's meat and ate it, but they did not see this. The ghost did this many times, but they did not see it. The ghost descended and shot it again. Then the ghost went up and ate. The juices from the pork fell down on the old man's leg. He thought that it was water from the rain.

The ghost shot another piece, and then the juices fell down again on the old man's leg. The old man looked up to the top of the house because the liquid that was falling had grease and was very hot.

The man's throat was blocked. He whispered to his old wife that he wanted to urinate. When he went outside the house, it was too bad. He took off running with his [legs] hitting his buttocks. He did not care that it was dark, he just left.

His poor old wife was waiting and waiting, but her husband did not go back into the house. She waited and went outside, and she did not go back into the house. She waited and waited, then she thought about what her husband had seen on top of the house to cause him to leave the house and not return.

When the old woman cast her eyes up to the top of the house, she saw something bad lying there. The poor old woman urinated and left the house, running outside. She too did not care that it was dark. She sped away like an airplane. She did not care where she went; she just left.

She fled and met her husband. Her old husband thought that she was the ghost of the dead man, so he got up and sped away again. When the old man took off again like an airplane, the old woman thought that he was the ghost of the bad thing that she had seen. She too sped away again, like a wild pig runs.

The two of them kept running. Wild sugarcanes (*pit-pit*) made noises [cutting them], and they cried out. When they fell, they thought that the ghost was holding them, so they screamed and shouted together.

They were both short of breath when they approached the village and shouted. The villagers heard their voices and wondered what it was. The couple told them not to talk. They told them to light a fire and to go fetch the two of them.

The villagers lit a fire and went to get them. Their poor bodies had many abrasions. They took the couple and they went to sleep. In the morning, the couple told the villagers what had happened to them.

Later, the couple and the men of the village walked back to fetch their things at the house. They explained to the men of Nupuru that they must bury the man in the ground.

Rodney Ogutna Uwema
Okapa
Eastern Highlands Province

E261.4+. Imagined ghost pursues man; E541. Revenants eat; P210. Husband and wife; P290+. Maternal kin; R220. Flights; R260. Pursuits; V61.3+. Dead buried

[The ancestor story in *Wantok* #1165 is the same as that in #1164.]
[The ancestor story in *Wantok* #1166 is the same as that in #419.]
[The ancestor story in *Wantok* #1167 is the same as that in #1143.]

A Real Man Turned into a Bird

(Wantok 1168, November 14, 1996, [page 19)

Long, long ago, we had a bird that stole children. His name was Masiahagai. He was a real [bird], like an eagle. He was a man who had turned into a bird.

One day, a newlywed couple had a new baby. The two of them worked in the garden and they hung up [the newborn in a net bag] near where they were kneeling down and working hard.

While they were kneeling and working in the garden, a big bird very quietly came and removed the baby with the net bag. The bird very quickly removed the baby and flew away. The married couple saw this and they cried and shouted, "Hey, you're carrying our baby. Come back." However, the bird did not listen to them. The bird flew up to a big *talis* tree. The couple shouted and shouted until they lost their voices. They just stood and began to throw up their arms. After a while, their arms also became tired. They stayed until darkness arrived, and then they went to the village to sleep. The baby cried for milk. The bird fooled the baby by giving it various kinds of food, but the baby did not stop crying.

Later, he gave his balls to the baby and the baby stopped crying. The baby sat quietly and babbled. The two of them lived for a while. Some years later, the baby became a huge young man. When he finished growing, he asked his father, "Hey Papa, where's mama?" His father said, "Your mama died when you were still little." He again asked his father, "Papa, what did I eat that made me grow?" His father said, "Look over there. That's my garden over there. You think that you're just big?" The man was very happy for his father. He followed the branches of the *talis* tree and went towards the real ground.

Later, he asked his father, "Hey Papa, where will I sit and comb myself?" His father said, "Follow this tree branch. Go there and comb your hair." When he wanted to go down and comb himself, he saw two young women drawing water. He did not know that his reflection came up in the water. The big sister saw the man's reflection in the water and the man looked very handsome. So, the first sister quickly rose and made the water dirty. She was afraid that her little sister would see him too. The little sister helped the big sister make the water dirty. After a while, they let the water clear. Then they both saw the man sitting and laughing. The two of them ran and ran to the village. Then they told their father about what they had seen. They asked their father, "Papa, can you send a message for your clan to come and cut down a tree for us? We saw something nice. We'll marry a good man." Their father killed pigs and he tied up betel nuts and tobacco. Then he sent these to his clan. The people from his village marked a day that they would come and cut down the tree. That day arrived and they went to cut it. They cut and cut the tree for some weeks. When the tree was broken, the man jumped under the tree leaves and hid. The men tried and tried to find him, but they were unable to do so. They left and went to their village. The two women hid near the base of the tree. They stayed for a while. Then when it was nearly the afternoon, the man thought that everyone had left for the village. He got up from his hiding place and went outside. He sat directly at the base of the tree where the women were hiding from him. When he sat down, the women came very quietly and grabbed him. He said, "Please let me go." However, the women said, "Please come with us to our village." He listened to them and went with them. They walked along the trail. Then the big sister asked the little sister, "Who will marry him, me or you?" The little sister said, "Never mind, we both saw him at the same time. OK, we must both marry him." They argued for a while and they went to their father. Their father judged what they said for a while. Then he said, "You, the big sister, will marry him." So, the big sister married him and the little sister did not.

[Anonymous]

B211.3.11K. Speaking eagle; B535.0.7+. Eagle as nurse for child; D152.2M. Transformation: man to eagle; P210. Husband and wife; P231. Mother and son; P232. Mother and daughter; P233. Father and son; P234. Father and daughter; P252.1. Two sisters; P271. Foster father; P275. Foster son; R13.3.2. Eagle carries off youth; T100. Marriage; W157. Dishonesty; X712.3H. Testicles; X736.2H+. Symbolic fellatio

[The ancestor stories in *Wantok* #1169 and 1170 are the same as that in #1123.]
[The ancestor story in *Wantok* #1171 is the same as that in #284.]

A Man Became Onou, the Snake Sorcerer

(Wantok 1172, December 12, 1996, page 19)

Long, long ago, in the time of the ancestors, there lived an ancestral couple and there also lived a *masalai* snake. One very early morning, the ancestral man awoke and went to hunt for wild game in the very deep forest. The ancestral woman awoke, cried and shouted for the ancestral man.

While she was crying, she thought of going to gather grass on a mountain. While she was getting the grass on the mountain, she worked at cutting it. The *masalai* snake was going around, hunting for wild game and approaching her.

The snake heard the ancestral woman crying for her husband. Then the snake removed the rattan [bowstring] from its bow. The snake put it on the ground, and then it became a poisonous snake. The snake began to go into the grass that the ancestor was cutting in the garden.

The poor ancestral woman was very busy gathering the grass. The snake went very quietly. It went directly into the ancestral woman's body. It was too bad that before long, the ancestral [woman] became terribly fat. She looked as if a bow was on her side, so men began to have sex with her. When they had sex with her, they began to die off. This was because [the] snake sorcerer was inside the ancestor's body.

Then the snake began to talk a little about itself, "Eat the food that I cook. Don't eat the [food that I don't cook]. Look at all of the men who came to me and die." Afterwards, the snake killed the insects that were in the crown of a sago tree [probably sago beetles]. When the snake killed them, a knife cut them. It did not take them and leave them. Then Pakasia [the snake] left the ancestor woman's body and wanted to eat the insects.

It looked as if it had come to talk a little to her, "You must go and make a cut on the sago that I scraped. Then cut some wild taro and put it on the sago spines with wooden plates. When you are ready, send a message for everyone to come. Tell them that you saw this [cut] me. We'll go sit at the base of the sago. Then spill the insects onto the plate."

Then the snake sorcerer left the ancestor's body and ate the insects for a while. When it left the ancestor's body, [the men came and killed it]. [They] broke it, held it, cut it and burned all of it in a fire.

So, if you go to **Yile** Village, you will see that **Yiki 1** holds the middle, **Yihi 2** holds the neck of snake, and **Yili 3** holds the tail. This is the story from my village, Yili, about Onou, the snake sorcerer.

John Nelen
Catholic Mission Yili Yanmok

B191.7. Serpent as magician; B211.6.1. Speaking snake (serpent); D191M. Transformation: man to serpent (snake); D2061. Magic murder; F401.3.8. Spirits in form of snake; F490+. Masalai; P210. Husband and wife; Q211. Murder punished; Q241. Adultery punished; Q411. Death as punishment; S110. Murders; T481. Adultery; X1723.3+. Snake enters woman's body

[There was no ancestor story in *Wantok* #1173.]

A Sister and Brother Became Two Lakes

(Wantok 1174, December 24, 1996, page 19)

Long, long ago, in **Kisip** Village, among the **Mendi** [People], there lived a brother and sister [**Southern Highlands** Province]. They often made gardens and planted sugarcanes. They worked and lived very well.

They husbanded a pig and the pig became huge. It never went out of the house. It just lay inside the house and they would only give it sweet potatoes. Oh my! The boy often hunted much wild game.

He [excelled] at catching marsupials (*kapul*) and other wild game. One time, the boy went to hunt game and he told his sister to stay there. The boy went into the forest and looked for a huge tree. He approached one, but no, small insects had eaten much of the tree. He thought of taking the insects.

He removed his clothes and put them near another tree. Then he went to fetch the insects at the tree. He worked diligently at gathering the insects for about five or ten minutes. Then a trick marsupial was in the forest.

The trick marsupial saw him putting his things under a tree. Very quietly, the marsupial put on the man's clothes and sped away in flash down to the house where the sister was staying. The sister was making a garden when the marsupial man sped up to a fruit-bearing tree that was there. The marsupial took a fruit and threw it close to her. She stood up and looked at the tree.

The marsupial wanted the woman who was under the tree. Later, the marsupial took another fruit and threw it directly onto the woman's breast. She thought that her brother had done this, so she raced directly to the house. The trick marsupial descended the tree and sped back to the boy. The marsupial removed all of the clothing and put the clothing back carefully.

[The author apparently omitted part of this story, which follows a tale-type formed by the ancestor stories in *Wantok* #154, 803 and 988. Omitted was: the real brother's return home, the sister's refusal to talk to the brother, the brother killing the pig and dividing the pork, the brother leaving home, and the sister pursuing the brother.]

The boy followed a trail and the sister followed him. The boy climbed a mountain and the woman went around below the mountain. The two of them kept racing. Then the woman shouted, "Brother, brother, I'm still coming. Wait for me." However, the boy did not to do this. He kept going. They went and went, and then they arrived at a place called Ekari [**Egari**]. The boy went down a small trail. The woman missed him and went up a forest trail.

Then the boy stood still. A tremendous downpour came and he thought that until the rain stopped, he would stand at the base of a tree. He kept standing and the rain kept pouring, then water came from everywhere. The boy still stood there and a little water came up to his legs. He still stood there with his pork. The grease from the pork also came down, making a puddle at his legs. The rain kept coming, and then the water rose and flooded, going higher and higher. It kept rising, up to his belly. The boy thought that it was a trick, so he kept standing and the rain kept coming. The water rose to his breast and then it rose to his [neck]. At the last minute, the water swallowed him and a [huge] lake arose.

The woman did the same thing and became another lake in the forest. The name of the lake that the man became is called Ekari and it is terribly cold. The name of the lake that the woman became is called Pipyaka. This lake is hot because it is from the woman's tears.

If you want to see these two lakes, then you can go to Mogo High School and you will see them.

Jerry Nolpi and Benuth Buru

Tabubil

Western Province

[Jerry Nolpi wrote a similar story in *Wantok* #1177.]

A920.1.0.1. Origin of particular lake; B871.1.2.1. Giant hog; D283.1+B. Transformation: boy to lake; D310+M. Transformation: marsupial to man; D457.18.2+. Transformation: tears to lake; K1930. Treacherous impostors; P253. Sister and brother; P253+. Hostile sister and brother; R213. Escape from home; R220. Flights; R260. Pursuits

[The ancestor story in *Wantok* #1175 is the same as that in #1124.]

An Unmarried Man Took
Out a Beautiful Woman

(Wantok 1176, January 9, 1997, page 18)

Long, long ago, in the time of the ancestors, there lived a man named Konge Yawa. He lived in **Kauwo** Village, near Pangia, in **Southern Highlands** Province [**Wiru** People]. One time, he took his two dogs and went to Komuene, a place in the forest. He hunted for marsupials (*kapul*), but a heavy rain came, so he sat under a big tree with his two dogs.

While he was sitting and waiting for the rain to end, the rain became even heavier. So, he continued to sit. He sat and sat, and then it became dark. At this time, he heard the voices of many people approaching. He listened carefully to the voices. He was terrified because he thought that these were forest spirits who were coming to kill him. He tried to hide at the base of the tree. Oh my, these were not men's voices. These were only the voices of women that he heard.

He had been trying hard to find a wife for himself, so now was his big chance to try to find one. He listened carefully to what the women were saying, but when he did this, he noticed that they were hidden from him. He wanted to look carefully. He saw a big tree hole and the women were searching for red earth.

He tried to find a chance to pull out one of the women. All of the women that he saw were beautiful. He watched and watched, then he saw a very beautiful woman, more so than all of the women in Papua New Guinea, who was searching the earth by the side. The scoundrel hid and followed the woman who went far away from the other women. Then he just jumped and grabbed her.

Oh my, she was very strong. She was extremely strong, and the two of them fought back and forth. However, you know, Yawa was ready and he took her. He did not care about her strength. He used his strength and overpowered her. They fought and fought, breaking all kinds of things. She held snakes and fought Yawa, but Yawa did not flinch from the snakes. He grabbed the snakes and killed them. He jumped on top of her and then they fought on the ground, twisting and turning. They crashed through things such as trees, stones, streams and everything else. The place was completely cleared, as if the wind had blown down the trees and forest. They fought and fought until the afternoon. Their strength was gone and they were both completely weakened.

The woman told Yawa, "I have no more strength, so what do you think that we should do?"

Oh my, the scoundrel did not waste time. When he heard her, he spoke to her like this. He had been searching for a woman to marry for a long time and now was his real chance. He could not let her go easily. He still had a little strength, so the scoundrel held her and put her on top of his shoulders. He brought her to his village. She did not have any more strength, so she just lay quietly on top of Yawa's shoulders. They went to the leader's house. They married and lived entirely in the village. Now, there are many people who have come from there.

That is the end of my short story from **Kali** Village in the Pangia District of Southern Highlands Province.

Paulus Tung
Voco Point Trading
Lae
Morobe Province

B491.1. Helpful serpent; B524.3+. Helpful snake aids woman from attack; F610.0.1. Remarkably strong woman; P210. Husband and wife; R311. Tree refuge; T192. Marriage by force

A Brother and Sister Became Lakes
(Wantok 1177, January 16, 1997, page 18)

Once upon a time, there was a young boy and his big sister who lived in **Makura** Village, among the **Mendi** [People] of **Southern Highlands** Province. Their parents had died and they lived by themselves in the forest where no people lived. They planted food and their food just rotted in their garden.

They took very good care of a pig. The pig grew and grew, becoming very large, so that it could no longer stand. It just lay and ate.

The boy excelled at hunting wild game. When he went around the forest, he would kill very many marsupials (*kapul*). He would also kill cassowaries and bring them back to their house. They lived very well.

One time, the boy wanted to hunt for game in the forest, so he went into the forest. He saw a marsupial sleeping on top of a big tree. The boy thought of going to kill the marsupial, so he removed some of his nice adornments and put them near the base of the tree. Very quietly, he went over and climbed the tree. Before long, a trick marsupial that lived in the forest saw the boy putting the adornments by the tree. The trick marsupial came and put on the boy's adornments, then the marsupial transformed into the boy and went to the house of the boy's sister. At this time, the boy's sister was working hard in the garden.

The marsupial very quietly went to a tree that was near the garden. The marsupial took a fruit and pretended to throw it at the woman. She turned and stood up, then her eyes moved towards the tree. The marsupial took another fruit. Oh my, he threw it directly at the woman's breast. The woman was shocked and looked at the tree. She saw her brother's clothes on the tree. She was very troubled. She ran quickly as she cried and she went inside the house.

The trick marsupial also ran. He ran back to the place where the boy was hunting marsupials. The marsupial removed all of the boy's clothes and put them close to the tree.

The boy found four marsupials on top of the big tree, and then he returned. He wore his clothing and carried his marsupials. He held his bow and ran towards the house. When he was fairly far away, he saw that smoke was not rising from the house, so he thought that his sister must have encountered a problem or something.

When he went into the house, he saw his sister crying. He asked what her what the problem was, but his sister did not reply. She just cried. The brother tired of this and he went to make a fire. He cooked the marsupials and he ate. He left two marsupials for his sister to eat. The boy's sister was still crying because she thought that her brother had tricked her. She thought that he had shot her with a stone and fled into the forest.

Late at night, the boy awoke and saw that his sister was still crying and that she had not eaten anything. In the morning, the boy was tired of his sister's crying. He wanted to leave the house and go to some other place because his sister had not stopped her crying.

That morning, he took the pig and cooked it in an earth oven. When the earth oven was ready, he divided the food. He put his in a net bag and he left half for this sister. He took his bow and clothes, and then he departed.

The sister saw this and quickly got up to eat and to shout for her brother. She shouted that she had stopped crying and that she wanted to follow him. However, her brother did not care and did not want to wait. He kept walking and his sister ran behind his footsteps.

They walked a very long distance, passing big mountains, many trees and the deep forest. They crossed many rivers and kept going. The boy went first and his sister cried behind him. In the middle of Ekari [**Egari**] Village, a great downpour fell. The boy stood and hid under a big tree. His sister came and passed him, going along another trail. The boy thought that the rain would finish and he would walk away, but it did not finish. The rain came even harder and a big river rose. The water gathered, rising and rising, coming up to his footprints. He thought that the rain would end after this, but he kept waiting. The water filled and came to his knees. Before long, the water came to his belly. He wanted to leave, but the trail that he had followed had been covered by water and he was confused about the trail.

The boy stayed there, but it was too late and the water covered his chest. The downpour kept falling and the water covered him completely, killing him. His sister met the same fate. The flood also drowned her as she cried trying to find her brother.

So in the Upper Mendi area today, you will see two big lakes. One arose from the man, called Lake Ekari. It is a little cold because it is from rainwater and pig fat. It is close to the road.

The lake in the forest arose from the woman. This lake is named Pipiyeka. It is hot because it is from the woman's tears and rainwater. It is inside the forest. If you are a student of Mogol National High School, you can talk to your friends about this ancestor story from the Upper Mendi in Southern Highlands Province.

Jerry Nolpi
Simburubu
Mogol Cold Village
[Western Province?]

[Jerry Nolpi and Benuth Buru wrote a similar story in *Wantok* #1174.]

A920.1.0.1. Origin of particular lake; B871.1.2.1. Giant hog; D310+B. Transformation: marsupial to boy; D457.18.2+. Transformation: tears to lake: D476+. Transformation: grease to lake; K1930. Treacherous impostors; M451.2. Death by drowning; P253. Sister and brother; R213. Escape from home; R220. Flights; R260. Pursuits

Two Marsupials (*Kapul*) Became Enemies
(Wantok 1178, January 23, 1997, pages 22)

Very long ago, there lived a little bird named Ambramenenga near **Mt. Hagen** Town [**Hagen** People, **Western Highlands** Province]. One time, the bird perched and thought of making a house for itself.

The bird slept in the morning, and then it went to cut a tree to make posts and nails. After this was completed, on the next morning, the bird took a knife and went into the forest to Mount Hagen to fetch vines. The bird carefully tied the vines together and threw them into a river, which carried them away. The bird thought that it would follow them and get them later.

However, a heavy rain came and stopped the bird. The bird sat near the base of a tree. The bird slept, then big Cassowary came looking for food. Cassowary saw the little bird and thought that it was a tree fruit, so Cassowary just took the bird in its mouth and swallowed it. After a little while, Cassowary defecated out the bird. The little bird straightened its wings and tail. Then it walked back and took the vines that were stuck to a tree. It brought them back towards home.

The bird arrived home. In the morning, it dug the ground and thought of making a house for itself. It arranged the earth, then it placed the posts that were planed and sharpened. On the next morning, the bird sent a message for the other birds and rats of the village to come. They met and the bird told the story of the bad thing that

Cassowary had done to it. The bird told them that it wanted to trick the birds and marsupials (*kapul*) of the forest to cut and bring sword grass for the bird's house. The bird told them that it would try to kill Cassowary and afterwards, they would have a party. They decided that they would first go to their homes. They sent a message to the birds and marsupials of the forest to come. They said that Ambramenenga had made a men's house and they said that they would come cut sword grass for Ambramenenga. Afterwards, they would eat sweet potatoes and tell stories.

All of the named marsupials and all of the named birds came and cut sword grass, and they worked on the Ambramenenga's house. They put the sword grass up. They removed sweet potatoes, dividing them among the marsupials and the birds. They put some for other villages on another pile. They took the sweet potatoes and ate. Then Ambramenenga stood and spoke, "I want to make a statement, so listen carefully." Cassowary did not know that he had done something bad to Ambramenenga, so Cassowary sat in front and listened. Ambramenenga brought a spear and said, "You, my friends, came and we're happy that you helped me make my house." Ambramenenga went down and then went up a little. Ambramenenga raised the spear and sent it directly towards Cassowary. However, Cassowary had long legs, you know. So, Cassowary jumped up and the spear missed. The other marsupials and birds of the forest followed Cassowary. The rats and birds of the village ran and arrived at a village called **Tuma**. Many of them died from injuries. Those of the village [left] and went all of the way to the mountain. Two big marsupials called *kumugl* and *alti* threw sticks and fought them. "So I've broken my tail and fought them. You must break your tail and fight them too." Marsupial Kumugl thought that this was true, so Kumugl broke its tail and fought them. After they finished fighting, they went to each of their homes. Some died along the trails. Some were injured and went slowly home.

Then Marsupial Alti spoke, "Brother, let's go to the mountain or the trees." Then Alti climbed a tree. Marsupial Kumugl tried to climb a tree, but it had no tail, so it told Alti, "Brother, you tricked me. I broke my tail and fought them. You tied up your tail and you climbed the tree. So now, I won't see your face. You can go around the trees and I must go down on the ground." Kumugl then dug the earth and went underground. Marsupial Alti went up on the trees and into the forest. The *alti* marsupials now live in the forest and boulders.

Dickson L. Mel
Mt. Hagen
Western Highlands Province

[There are similar ancestor stories in *Wantok* #112 and 731.]

A2433.2.1+. Why marsupial lives in forest; A2433.2.1+. Why marsupial lives underground; B211.2.12K+. Speaking marsupial; B211.3. Speaking bird; B263. War between other groups of animals; F911.2+. Cassowary swallows bird and defecates it alive; K1000. Deception into self-injury; P310. Friendship; R220. Flights; S160.1. Self-mutilation

The Story of the Bird-of-Paradise Woman
(Wantok 1179, January 30, 1997, page 18)

Long, long ago, there was a woman who was menstruating. Her husband had gone to the garden. When her husband went to the garden, she said, "I'm hungry. Give me some food and I'll eat."

Her husband told her, "Eat your menses." She was ashamed of what he had said, so she sat and cried. She worried about what her husband had told her.

She sat crying and twisted a string down into a traditional clay pot. She took the string and pot, and then she departed. She broke off a yellow *tanget* plant.

She carried it and put it down. Then she sat on top of it. The *tanget* [transformed] her into a bird. Her whole body except for her head had turned into a bird. She told her husband, "Hey, look at me. You went into the forest and you hunted for food to bring home. Then I told you to give me some food for me to cook and eat. What did you tell me? I'm menstruating and eating now. Later, I going to leave." Her husband spoke, "Hey, don't go. Come back. She flew up and perched on a tree.

Then she told her husband, "When I called you for food, you told me to eat my menses, so I'm leaving you now." Then she turned into a bird of paradise and flew away for good. Now, our bird of paradise is the yellow bird of paradise of East and West Sepik Provinces [possibly the twelve-wired bird of paradise (Beehler *et al.*, 1986: 226)].

Kalsen Sellen [Sailen]
Salata Village [**Bumbita Arapesh** People]
Maprik
East Sepik Province

A1970+. Creation of bird of paradise; D150+W. Transformation: woman to bird of paradise; D671. Transformation flight; D681. Gradual transformation; D965+. Magic *tanget* plant (*Taetsia fructicosa*); P210. Husband and wife; R213. Escape from home; S62+. Cruel husband refuses wife food

Hunting for Wild Game in the Forest

(Wantok 1180, February 6, 1997, page 16)

One afternoon, Kihana told his wife, Ohiyame, to prepare food for him and to also tie up and prepare the dogs. He did not want the dogs to escape in the morning when he was ready to walk away.

In the early morning, the leader [Kihana] prepared food and his things. Then he wanted to call his dogs. No dogs came. These were not his dogs; they belonged to his maternal relative.

He shouted and shouted, but to no avail. He was angry and tried to grab a dog. He grabbed the dog, then he carried it and they began to walk. They walked and walked into the forest. They arrived at a place called, "Man's Bones." In my language, it is called, _Kono Aumau_. Kihana had carried the dog to this place in the forest for five or six kilometers. He let go of the dog and at the same time the dog went down from Kahana's [Kihana's] shoulders. Afterwards, the dog smelled a marsupial (_kapul_), so Kihana went into the middle of the forest and shouted for the dog, Komoguli. The dog barked from above in the middle of the forest. Kihana went into the forest and shouted at Komoguli. Then the dog climbed Mount Ukahaka, still barking and barking. Kihana arrived at Mount Ukahaka and met Komoguli. When he met the dog, he saw that the dog was scraping and digging the ground. Before long, a big hole opened up where the dog had been digging. When the hole opened, the dog jumped inside of it completely.

Kihana waited at the hole entrance for a while, but nothing happened. The dog did not sound like it was coming back to him. He cut a tall tree and shoved it into the hole. He walked quietly around the middle of the trail, and then he met a wild man inside a cave. The two of them fought, but Kihana was stronger and he chased the ghost [wild man] away. The ghost had only one leg. It was Nokondi. Nokondi took some feces from his one leg, then he rubbed it on his body and searched for the dog, but the dog did not see Nokondi. Nokondi cried for the dog, then Nokondi cut a piece of his ear and returned home. The man was short and his name was Duvaba. However, he went into the cave that they call Kihana Duava [Duvaba]. In my language, this means the names of the men who went into various caves. The poor man left his maternal kin's dog and went into the cave. Then he returned to the village.

Aila Handiya

Korepa Fove [**Koreipa**] Village [**Siane** People]

Goroka

Eastern Highlands Province

E461. Fight of revenant with living person; F451. Dwarf; F525. Person with half a body; F490+. _Nokondi_; F567. Wild man; P210. Husband and wife; P290+. Maternal kin; R210. Escapes; R260. Pursuits; S160.1. Self-mutilation; X716.1H. Befouling with one's own excrement

[There was no ancestor story in _Wantok_ #1181.]

The Cassowary Woman Fled from Her Family

(Wantok 1182, February 20, 1997, page 16)

Long, long ago, there lived a man. He often saw cassowary women carrying yams (_yam_ and _mami_) from the forest and bringing them home.

The poor man watched and then he went to a river where the cassowary women were bathing. One time, he went to watch the cassowary women's river. He watched and saw the cassowary women carrying yams to their house. The cassowary women removed the yams, and then the removed their "grass" skirts and went down to bathe.

He saw a beautiful woman, so he immediately jumped up and took the gorgeous woman's skirt and necklace. Then he went and hid in the forest. Afterwards, all of the cassowary women came out of the water, took their skirts, and put them on. The woman searched for her skirt and necklace, but she could not find them. They tried to find them for a while, but the women tired. All of the cassowary women told her to stay and search, and then to come later. All of the cassowary women brought yams to the house. The woman was the only one searching. Later, the man came out of the forest and asked her, "What are you searching for?" She told him that she was searching for her skirt and necklace. Then the two of them searched for her necklace. He lied to her because, you know, [he] had no loincloth and they were bare-assed. He took her and they went back to his house. They married and lived together.

They lived very well together. He watched very carefully that she would not flee. So, he could not make her angry or fret because she was from another place and also because she was very beautiful in his heart.

One time, the woman told her husband that she was menstruating. She asked where the women's house [menstrual hut] was located. He told her where the house was located, "Take things such as a mat, a loincloth and a net bag, then go to the women's house."

She departed. Later, she went with her husband. Some time later, she was pregnant. Afterwards, she gave birth. The baby saw its father take its mother's necklace and try to hide it from the baby. The baby saw where the father had hidden it. One time, the parents took the baby to the forest to gather breadfruits. They gathered a lot of breadfruits. Then the brought them back to the village and cooked them.

They ate and the baby thought that the breadfruit was very tasty, so the baby wanted more. The baby told its mother to give it some more. However, the mother was firm. The baby said that if the mother gave it some breadfruit, it would show her something very nice. The mother gave breadfruit to the baby, and then the baby went to get its mother's skirt and necklace. When the woman saw this, she quietly hid and dressed. When she dressed, her strength returned. She sped down to the house and took off for her home inside the forest. Before the mother did this, she hid the skirt and necklace, and then she lied to the father that she was going outside the house. They asked her to go fetch water. The baby and the mother made a decision, and then the mother took off and went all of the way back to her home.

Fex Richard
Bandagel Village
[**Balangabadanga** Village, **South Arapesh** People; or
Belangel Village, **Mountain Arapesh** People]
Maprik
East Sepik Province

B290+. Cassowary removes skirt or skin to bathe; D361.1. Swan Maiden; D1052. Magic garment (robe, tunic); D1073. Magic necklace; D1335. Object gives magic strength; D1830. Magic strength; K300. Thefts and cheats—general; K1350. Woman persuaded (or wooed) by trick; P210. Husband and wife; P230. Parents and children; R213. Escape from home; T100. Marriage; T570. Pregnancy; T580. Childbirth; W157. Dishonesty

Because of Eagle's Anger, It Is Still Searching for Food

(Wantok 1183, February 20, 1997, page 16)

Long, long ago, in the time of the ancestors, there were some wild animals who were very good friends with each other. Among these animals, there was one named Eagle who was a very large bird and who was the leader of the animals. Eagle made the law for all of the animals. Eagle would sent them to keep watch, to hold other animals, and to search for their food to eat in the afternoon. When it was nearly night, if each of them did not return with wild game, their leader would be very angry with them.

After they ate all of the food, they would sleep and then they would do the same thing the next day. They would do this every day.

One time, they all decided to go steal [food] at a garden that was near a river. However before long, they heard Chicken laughing. They went to see Chicken. When they approached, they saw Chicken holding three fish that Chicken had caught on the shore. All of the wild animals were happy that Chicken had followed them. They cooked the fish and they sent Chicken to go find more fish that hey could cook and eat.

When all of the animals were eating fish, they no longer thought about going out and hunting game for the leader. They became bloated from eating, and only Chicken was catching fish.

In the afternoon, the leader came and checked on all of the animals. They were celebrating and having a party with the fish. When Eagle saw this, Eagle was furious and began to ask for food for the afternoon. However, they all said that Chicken would find food in the sea. Then the leader, Eagle, became irate and flew to see poor Chicken working hard and throwing the hook into the sea. Eagle saw that there were no other animals nearby, so Eagle just went down and snatched Chicken's neck, killing Chicken.

The leader carried Chicken and hid. After Eagle finished eating Chicken, Eagle returned and hid in the house. When everyone came in the afternoon, Eagle pretended to berate and scold the animals.

Eagle tricked them and killed all of the animals gradually, eating them until all of the animals were gone. Afterwards, there were no more animals and Eagle flew alone into the sky, searching for animals and food all over. Now, you can see eagles still flying and searching for food and animals as they circle around.

Graham Rambin
Madang
Madang Province

A2471.3+. Why eagle flies in circles; B210. Speaking animals; B211.3.11K. Speaking eagle; B214.3. Laughing animal; B240+. Eagle as king of animals; K2246.1. Treacherous king; P310. Friendship; S110. Murders

Cassowary Played a Trick and Killed Crab

(Wantok 1184, March 6, 1997, page 13)

Long, long ago, Cassowary and Chicken were very good friends. One time, they talked about going to find *galip* nuts by the beach.

They went and Cassowary wanted to eat a *galip* nut quickly, so Cassowary searched for other trees and asked Chicken, "Have we arrived by the *galip* trees now or not?"

Chicken said, "There are no *galip* trees yet. They're elsewhere." They kept going, and before long Cassowary again asked, "Have we arrived at the *galip* trees?" Chicken said, "Not yet." They arrived at a point that was very high. They kept going and they arrived at the *galip* trees. Then Cassowary asked, "Have we arrived now?" Chicken said, "Yes." Then they pushed a canoe onto the beach. Chicken climbed a *galip* tree and Cassowary stood at the base of the *galip* tree.

Chicken worked and removed *galip* nuts, putting some in its net bag. *Galip* nuts fell down and Cassowary worked at breaking and eating them for a while. Then all of Cassowary's *galip* nuts were gone. Chicken came down to the ground. They tied the canoe down by the sea. Chicken told Cassowary, "Let's go." Cassowary paddled the canoe. Cassowary saw that Chicken was breaking and holding its *galip* nuts, and then eating them.

Chicken told Cassowary, "You broke them on the shore and ate them." Cassowary said, "Give me one to eat or I'll break the canoe and we'll sink in the water." Chicken said, "OK, go ahead and break it. Then we'll sink in the water." Cassowary spoke for a while, and then he became furious at Chicken.

Cassowary just got up and broke the canoe. Then Chicken just went to the shore, while Cassowary went into the water. Cassowary saw small fish and told them, "Can you take me closer to the beach?" They said, "We have work to do." Cassowary sat and saw a huge fish approaching. Cassowary asked it, "Can you bring me to the beach?" The fish spoke, "Sorry, I have work to do." Cassowary asked all of the fish and they said no.

Poor Cassowary sat for a while. When Cassowary was about to lose its life, Cassowary saw a crab approaching. Cassowary asked the crab, "Can you bring me to the beach?"

The crab said, "OK." Cassowary went on top of the crab and the crab brought Cassowary by the beach. The crab asked Cassowary, "Should I put you here?" Cassowary said, "Go up the mountain a little! Leave me there."

The crab carried Cassowary up a little ways. The crab asked Cassowary, "Shall I leave [you] here?" Cassowary said, "Yes." Then Crab left Cassowary on top of the mountain. Cassowary told the crab, "Let's play hide and seek (*beng-beng*)." Crab agreed. Cassowary said, "I'll close my eyes and you go hide." The crab said, "[You] go first, then I'll go hide." They spoke for a while, and then the crab won and Cassowary went to hide at the base of a tree. Cassowary was big, so the crab found Cassowary very quickly. Later, it was the crab's turn to hide. The poor crab did not know that Cassowary would mangle the crab. The crab cut a fallen tree leaf and hid underneath it.

Cassowary tried to find the crab everywhere, but to no avail. Cassowary wanted to return, but Cassowary missed and its leg went on top of the crab. Oh my, the crab was completely smashed. Now, this place is called, "*Qera Haruc*" [Cassowary and Crab] in the **Kâte** Language. This place is in the Finschhafen area of **Morobe** Province.

Bilda Bilsco

Finschhafen

Morobe Province

[See the stories in *Wantok* #249, 289 and 676, which are similar.]

A1617. Origin of place-name; B211.3.2.1. Speaking chicken; B211.3.17K. Speaking cassowary; B211.5. Speaking fish; B211.8.1K. Speaking crab; B295.2.1K. Animals make voyage in canoe; B296.2K. Animal (who is land-dweller) crosses water on back of another animal; B336+. Helpful crab killed by ungrateful cassowary; B495.1. Helpful crab; B874. Giant fish; J2133.11+. Cassowary destroys boat in anger, but almost drowns while chicken flies away; P310. Friendship; S110. Murders; W125. Gluttony; W154. Ingratitude

The Snake Descendants
(Wantok 1185, March 13, 1997, page 16)

Long, long ago, there lived a couple in Kerowagi. They only had one daughter who lived with them. One time, there was a great dry season, so the daughter took some ripe bananas and went to search for forest greens along the Wahgi River. She gathered the greens, and then she felt hungry. She saw a large fallen tree, so she sat on top of it. She ate the bananas and threw the peels down.

Later, she looked and saw a short snake come and eat the banana skins. The woman saw that some bananas were still there. She put them near the snake and said, "If you're a man, then come and eat. I've put some bananas there. Later, I'll come and look."

After two days, she returned and saw that there was a snake's head and tail. Between them, there was a human body. She took a large banana leaf and she put it in her net bag. Then she put the snake in the bag. She cut across to the house. She put it on top of the roof and made a fire.

She finished cooking, then she ate and she heard a noise from within the net bag. She slept and in the morning, she removed the net bag and saw a big baby boy inside the net bag.

Her father and mother saw this and were shocked. She was also elated. They cared for the baby and he grew to be a big man.

Then one time, the woman's mother heated stones and wanted to make an earth oven. So, she sent the two of them to fetch water. The mother finished the earth oven and waited for the water. The two of them played and played. They did not return to the house quickly. Her mother was angry and told her two brothers about the woman and the snake-child. She said that the married couple was living elsewhere. The [man] and the woman approached the house and heard the mother talking about them. They were worried and they did not eat. They cried and slept that night. In the morning, they awoke and packed all of their clothes and belongings. They removed garden food and seeds for planting. They departed and camped somewhere. The man was a snake and the woman had fetched him. They made a house, and then they married and became man and wife.

The couple lived there. They called their first son Manda. They called the second son Konu. They called the third son Wemin. They called the fourth son Vipe, the fifth Gelpi, the sixth Kop, and the last son Pawa.

The woman gave birth to seven sons and gave them these names. The seven men lived as brothers, but they each created a clan house. One old man takes care of the snakeskin that is now in the village. I am also a descendant of this snake. Our seven clan houses originated from this snake.

This story comes from **Kup** Village, in the Kerowagi District of **Simbu** Province [**Wahgi** People].

Jacob Kai

Kerowagi

Simbu Province

A1640. Origin of tribal subdivisions; B604.1. Marriage to snake; B631.9. Human offspring of marriage of person and snake; D191M. Transformation: man to serpent (snake); D391B. Transformation: serpent (snake) to boy; D551.1. Transformation by eating fruit; D681. Gradual transformation; P210. Husband and wife; P231. Mother and son; P232. Mother and daughter; P233. Father and son; P234. Father and daughter; P251.6.3+. Seven brothers; P253.0.2. One sister and two brothers; P262. Mother-in-law; P265. Son-in-law; P271. Foster father; P272. Foster mother; P275. Foster son; R213. Escape from home; R225. Elopement; T100. Marriage; T580. Childbirth; V140. Sacred relics

A Brother and Sister Became a [Bird and a] Lake

(Wantok 1186, March 20, 1997, page 17)

Long, long ago, in Bilimon Hobuturon [**Bolimang**] Village, by Yatumei, in the Kabwum District of **Morobe** Province, there lived a sister and brother and their grandparents. They lived in Hobuturon Village. The sister and [brother] lived with their grandparents [**Timbe** People].

Their grandfather had a big yam garden. One time everyone went to the garden. Their grandfather told their grandmother, "Come remove the grass from the garden." Then she told the grandfather, "We'll go cut sticks for the yam vines [to grow on]." At the same time that we plant [the yams], we'll put in the sticks." They arranged the yam sprouts and tied them to strings on the sticks. Then the grandson broke the yam sprouts.

His grandparents saw this and scolded him terribly, and then he went to the house. He cried and cried. He took an axe and knife. Then he went into the forest. He cut and knocked over wild sugar canes (*pitpit*), then he went to the house.

The young man sharpened a bow, and then he drew the bowstring. He made a fire and cooked the wild sugarcane. At the same time, he made many arrows, including multi-pronged arrows. The next day, his grandparents sent the two of them to the garden, and only the grandmother went.

The grandmother went the garden and the grandson did not want to go with his sister. He stayed at the house and he wanted his sister to go to the garden. He took his bow and arrows. Then he went out behind the house and told his grandfather, "I'm going bird hunting." He shot a bird and he stood it up with an arrow by the trail. Then he shot a *kep* bird in the forest.

He stood it up with an arrow on the trail. He did the same thing, going and going into the deep forest. [The name] of this place is Yawanholiholi [**Yawan**]. It is in the **Halimon** area. She slept with her grandfather. The next day, she searched for her brother and she [cried] terribly. She found a bird on top of an arrow on the trail. She cried and took the arrow. She removed the bird and put it into her net bag. She went into the deep forest and met her [brother], and they kept going. They shot many birds and the sister's net bag became filled with birds. Her brother cooked one bird, by a small tree that we call *sombe*.

At the same time, he climbed the tree and told his sister, "Stay there. I'll climb the tree and shoot birds." When he climbed the tree, he shot at birds, but he did not hit any. The arrows [missed] and the tree grew very tall.

The sister's tears fell and all of the birds rotted, becoming a lake. This lake is not very big. The brother became a bird and flew away. His sister cried and became Witwit Lake. This lake is big in the Buliman [Bolimang] area. Yams are in the very deep forest.

The brother became a bird that we call, _supmanga_. We often call it _korongan_. The Yatumet [Komba People] call it _kotingon_ [_ningon kotingon_] if you go over there. If you cook this bird, you will be sated. The _sombe_ tree is in the middle of the lake, and only in this lake. If you go around this area, you will see that the tree is still there.

Chris Masm and Toworuk Nange

Kimbe

West New Britain Province

A920.1.0.1. Origin of particular lake; A1900. Creation of birds; D150B. Transformation: boy to bird; D457.18.2+. Transformation: tears to lake; F54.1. Tree stretches to sky; P210. Husband and wife; P253. Sister and brother; P291.1. Grandfather as foster father; P292.1. Grandmother as foster mother; R213. Escape from home; R260. Pursuits

A Giant Snake Discovered an Island

(Wantok 1187, March 27, 1997, page 15)

Long, long ago, near my village on **Siassi** Island, there was a place called **Lablab** Station, where there were three caves [**Mangap** People, **Morobe** Province]. These caves are still there and we say that spirits or dead people's ghosts go to dwell in these places.

In these caves, there lived a huge snake. The snake's head was a man and from the buttocks downward it was a snake. They called this snake Bobogara.

One time, when the sun was bright, everyone went to the gardens to look for their food. At this time, there were no people in the village. However, one woman put her baby in a net bag and hung it up. She told an old woman to watch the baby.

The old woman sat inside the room and just kept her eyes on the baby in the net bag because she could not walk. The baby in the net bag was hung far from her on the verandah. Before long, she saw the huge snake come up on the verandah, and then remove the net bag and baby.

When the old woman saw the snake, she just shut her mouth. She saw that the snake's head was that of a man and that the rest was a snake. She just sat quietly. She thought, "If I make a noise, he'll kill me too. Who knows where he'll go." He carried the baby into his home in the cave. Before long, the baby's mother returned. She threw down a net bag of food, and then she ran towards where the

old woman was. She asked about her baby in the net bag. The old woman told her everything that she had seen. The mother went to the middle of the village, shouting and crying

Everyone heard her crying, so they gathered and the asked her why. She told them, "A huge snake with a man's head took my baby away." They told her, "We know about this snake. It sleeps inside a huge cave at the top of a river."

All of the men of Yangla Village carried axes, machetes and spears, and then they departed [Mangap People]. They arrived at the entrance of the cave.

Immediately, the men gathered dry firewood and made a huge fire. They heated six big stones on top of the fire. When the six stones were red hot, they took them and shoved them down into the cave where the snake lived. The hot stones fell on top of the snake. The snake was terribly pained.

Quickly, the snake took the baby in the net bag and went up to the cave entrance. He saw that the men were not fooling around. He told them, "Good men, I didn't take this baby to kill or to eat. I just took the baby to take care of it." After he said this, he gave the baby back to them.

The men took the baby and returned to the village. They gave the baby back to its mother. They were happy, so that night they sang and danced until dawn. Bobogara slept and thought hard, "The men came and ruined my house. I must go to another village."

One early morning, he awoke and left this place. He went to a place called Gunn. Later, he went down to a big river called Siban [Simban]. Then he left the Siban River and went to a place called Bunjil by the sea.

He followed along the seashore, and then he arrived at a village called **Barim** [**Barim** People]. He sat at this point and he looked towards the sword grass at Sialum and Finschhafen. He jumped down into the water and began to sail away.

He arrived at an island called Tuwam [**Tuam**, **Mutu** People]. He sat by Tuwam Island. His body became stiff and he did not want to sail further. [He thought,] "It would be better if I went just a little farther and lived at Finschhafen or Siassi."

He did this and then he lived over there. He lived there for a while and he still lives there now. When you take a ship, it takes a while to get to this place. Sometimes there is no wind [going to] Bobogara's home.

They say in Siassi that this is a true story, but I wrote it as if it was an ancestor story and I sent it to _Wantok Newspaper_.

Robert Kupul
Mendi
Southern Highlands Province

B29.2.1. Serpent with human head; B875.1. Giant serpent; E278+. Ghosts haunt cave; P230. Parents and children; Q213. Abduction punished; Q414. Punishment: burning alive; R10.3. Children abducted; R13.4.1. Abduction by snake; R110. Rescue of captive; R213. Escape from home

A Female Snake Gave Birth to a Boy

(Wantok 1188, April 3, 1997, page 20)

Long, long ago, in the time of the ancestors, there lived a married couple. They had been married for a very long time and they did not have children. They had become old. One morning, they worked in the garden. In the afternoon, they returned to the village. The old woman took a broom and swept the garbage from the house. When she finished, she removed the soot from the fire. She brought it out and was about to throw it away.

She heard a baby crying from underneath the garbage. She stood quietly and continued to hear the baby crying. The old woman ran and told her old husband that she had heard a little baby crying. The old couple ran and stood near the garbage. Then they heard the baby cry in earnest. They listened and were a slightly afraid. They thought that it was an evil spirit or black magic that was tricking them. The old man took a stick and removed the garbage. They removed the garbage for a while, and then they saw a snake lying there. The snake had entirely encircled the baby boy's body and the two of them were underneath the garbage. The old couple saw this and was very happy. They removed the snake from the baby and they took the baby to their house.

They watched the baby very carefully, and the old woman gave the baby her breast. The snake followed its baby and went into the house, where it slept near the fire.

When the old couple took the baby to the garden, the snake would follow them. When they went to search for food in the forest, the snake would also follow them. The snake went wherever the baby went because this was the snake's baby.

The little boy lived for a while, and then he became a big boy. He would see things and he would be afraid of them. Then he saw the snake and he was afraid. However, the old woman told him, "Don't be afraid, that's your mother." The boy became a big man and he married. He began to clear a huge garden. He planted yams (*yam* and *mami*), taros, bananas, and other foods.

One time, he went into the garden and removed some garden food. He carried the food and piled it up somewhere. Then he cut firewood to put with the food. He made a big fire, and then he killed his real mother, the snake. All of the food and the snake were in the fire. Then he cried for his mother, the snake who had given birth to him and raised him as a real human.

My short ancestor story came from Sepik **Mangul** No. 2 Village, in the Maprik area, **East Sepik** Province [**Abelam** People].

William Saut

B631.9+. Human offspring of snake; P210. Husband and wife; P231. Mother and son; P271. Foster father; P272. Foster mother; P275. Foster son; S22+. Matricide; S112. Burning to death; T100. Marriage; T580. Childbirth; T611. Suckling of children

A Child Came from a Snake

(Wantok 1189, April 10, 1997, page 13)

Long, long ago, in the time of the ancestors, there lived a married couple. They were married and they had no children, although they had become old.

One morning, they went to work in the garden and in the forest. In the afternoon, they returned to the village. The old woman took a broom and swept the garbage from inside the house. She brought the garbage out and was about to throw it away, when she heard a baby crying from underneath the garbage. She put the garbage on the trail and she quietly ran to tell her husband.

They went and stood close to the garbage. They thought that it was a ghost or a *masalai*. They removed the garbage slowly, and then the man carried a nice baby boy. They saw this and were very happy. They brought the boy into the house. The old man ran to fetch some fresh banana leaves. He carried them and ran to the fire.

When the leaves were very hot, he put them on the old mother's breasts, and then her breasts ran like water. Afterwards, the baby nursed. The snake who had given birth to the baby is called *kuj* in my language. The old couple took care of the baby and the baby grew.

They paid bride price for him and he married. They raised many children, and the children also married and raised many children in the Sepik.

This ancestor story comes from **Maprik** [**Abelam** People, **East Sepik** Province].

Willam [William] Gawi

B631.9+. Human offspring of snake; P210. Husband and wife; P230. Parents and children; P231. Mother and son P271. Foster father; P272. Foster mother; P275. Foster son; T52. Bride purchased; T100. Marriage; T580. Childbirth; T611.6+. Nursing induced

Revenge

(Wantok 1190, April 17, 1997, page 12)

Long, long ago, two brothers fought over a woman. The woman was the little brother's wife. The big brother desired her and he fought with his little brother. One time, the two brothers wanted to hunt for flying foxes in a cave, so they departed.

They went along a trail, and then they cut some long rattans. They went to a very high place. Then they went down from the high place to a place where there was a cave. They stopped and they argued about who should go down first. They argued and argued. The big brother was stronger, so he sent the little brother down. The little brother was about to go, so he thought, "I should go quickly." He went quickly and entered the cave. Then he held the stone and left the rattan [which he was using as a rope]. At the same time, the big brother cut the rattan and the rattan went down into a bad place.

Afterwards, the big brother went to the village and married his little brother's wife. The little brother stayed in the cave in the bad place. There was no easy way for him to leave, so he just cried and shouted. No one heard him, so he slept angrily and he killed all of the flying foxes. He dried them during the day and ate them. His clan tried to find him. The men asked about him, so his brother said, "I don't know about him." He also went with them to try to find him.

The men searched for him for a while, until one month passed. One time, his sister and her husband went to a garden that was near the very high place. They heard a noise coming from somewhere. She heard the noise come again, then she tried searching and searching. She looked around the bad place. Something white [?] was making the noise, so she told her husband. The two of them brought some ripe bananas, some sugarcanes and some sweet potatoes, and then they just ran. They cut some long rattans, and then they looked at the place where the two brothers had fastened rattans. The couple said that they must just tie the rattans and send them down to the bad place. The rattans made noises and they sent some bananas down. He ate and made a noise [?]. Then they gave him some bananas and sugarcanes. He took these and ate. Then he regained his strength and climbed up. They saw that he was emaciated,

as if he had been sick. His sister held him and cried, then his sister's husband carried him and they went to a pigsty. They killed a pig and gave it for him to eat. [He became well again]. He took his brother-in-law's bow and he saw the married couple in the garden. The man [his brother] was on top of sugar canes and removing taro leaves. The woman [his wife] was digging sweet potatoes. Then he just shot [his brother]. [His brother] took the spear and fell down. The woman saw this and cried. Then she went to hold him. He went and killed her too, and then he went to the village. He told the men of the village that he had killed a pig [his brother] in the garden as his revenge. They said that they would take the married couple and bury them in a grave.

Whoever likes this story and wants to see this very high place, then you are welcome to come. I live in Wau, in Block 7.

Bonny Netti and Blaru Emay
Morobe Province

P210. Husband and wife; P251.5.3. Hostile brothers; P253.0.2. One sister and two brothers; P263. Brother-in-law; P264. Sister-in-law; Q285. Cruelty punished; Q411. Death as punishment; R158. Sister rescues brother(s); S63+. Husband kills wife; S73.1.4. Fratricide motivated by love-jealousy; S110. Murders; S146.2. Abandonment in cave; T92.10. Rival in love killed; T100. Marriage; V61.3+. Dead buried; W157. Dishonesty; W181. Jealousy

A Snake Became the Fly River

(Wantok 1191, April 24, 1997, page 16)

Long, long ago, in the time of the ancestors, there was a big village where many people lived. This village was **Fultumtem** in the **Bimin** area [People] of Oksapmin, by Telefomin [**West Sepik** Province].

One day, all of the villagers decided to go into the deep forest to look for pandanus (*karuka*) nuts. That night, everyone prepared food and their belongings to carry into the forest.

In the very early morning, everyone awoke and walked into the deep forest that is called Gukombangsel. They went there and found very plentiful *karuka* nuts. They cooked some in an earth oven and they dried some to carry back to the village. One of the leaders whose name was Aismitankil Ubolokmun also had gone with this big group to find *karuka* nuts.

When everyone had gathered *karuka* nuts and wild game, such as marsupials (*kapul*) that they had killed, they prepared to go back to the village. When they were about to leave, the leader, Aismitanikil [Aismitankil], said that he would stay a little while longer in the forest. So, he brought his dog and they took off to go deeper into the forest. The other people returned to the village. They told their family that their father would return in about a week.

The leader and his dog went and went until they arrived at the border with **Western** Province. Oh my, they [found] many *karuka* nuts and they also killed much wild game, such as marsupials. Their net bags were packed, exceeding expectations.

They wanted to return, but his dog barked and made much noise, running even deeper into the forest. Before long, the dog barked loudly. The leader left the net bags of marsupials and *karuka* nuts, and he followed the dog.

When he arrived, he saw that the dog was shoving its snout into the ground and barking. The leader stood nearby and watched the dog. Before long, the dog had made a big hole.

Oh my, Aismitankil's eyes opened wide when he saw a gigantic python lying there.

The leader just slowly pulled his dog. They carried their net bags of food and took off. It became dark, so they arrived at a village. They slept with some of his kin there.

He gave food to his kin and he slept with them. He thought that in the morning, he would go to his village. While he slept, it thundered loudly and a great earthquake arose. Oh my, when Aismitankil wanted to look up, he saw that the big snake that he had seen in the forest had come again. The snake had followed him and had come to get him.

Oh my, the snake tore apart and ruined everything in the village. The snake finished wrecking things when it smelled Aismitanikl [Aismitankil], and then it swallowed him.

The leader was inside the snake's belly for a while. Then he twisted and turned inside the snake's belly. This caused the snake to also twist and turn on the outside. Slowly, the leader checked his net bag and found a piece of bamboo. He held the bamboo and cut inside the snake towards its cloaca. Oh my, the snake's cloaca opened up and the snake's feces fell upon him. He went out and fell on top of Mount Aseltikin. The snake twisted and turned, then went down. So now, we have the river that we call the Fly.

[Anonymous]
Oksapmin
Telefomin
West Sepik Province

A930.1.1. Snake as creator of rivers and lakes; A934.11. River from transformation; B875.1. Giant serpent; D2148. Earth magically caused to quake; D2149.1. Thunderbolt magically produced; E691.1+. Reincarnation: snake into river; F911.7. Serpent swallows man; F912.2. Victim kills swallower from within by cutting; P230. Parents and children; R260. Pursuits; X716.1H+. Befouling with excrement

[The ancestor story in *Wantok* #1192 is the same as that in #419.]
[The ancestor story in *Wantok* #1193 is the same as that in #1164.]

A *Masalai* Man Married a Village Woman
(Wantok 1194, May 15, 1997, page 16)

Long, long ago, there was a *masalai* man who lived somewhere. He was unmarried. He lived for a while, and then one time the villagers went to cut the forest that was near where [he lived]. They [wanted to make] a new garden and begin to plant. The men dug the earth and the women went ahead, planting yams (*yam* and *mami*).

They worked in the garden for a while, and then this ghost [*masalai*] man sat and watched the women. Then one woman looked very beautiful in his mind. He looked for a way to get her. He turned into a little stone, and then he flew and went on top of her back.

When she felt the stone fall on her back, she was surprised. She turned and searched for it. However at the same time, the *masalai* took her spirit and locked it. Also at this time, the woman began to menstruate and her body was not able to work well. She tired and just rested.

In the afternoon, she wanted to return to the village with the other people. However along the trail, her thoughts changed and she wanted to return to the garden. This was because her spirit was still in the garden.

She insisted on returning to the new garden alone. The *masalai* man was waiting for her there. When she arrived, the *masalai* took her and they jumped into a big hole in the ground where the *masalai* hid. They married and lived at this place.

Some years later, the woman and her *masalai* husband had three sons. The three of them came out of the hole in the ground. They went around to all of the places in the forests and mountains, searching for food and wild game.

They tired of living in the hole in the ground, so they always went around outside. After a while, the brothers left completely for somewhere. They lived there, made a garden, married and began a new life. One of the brothers lived back at the place where his parents lived.

This village is called Amahup [**Amahop**], in **East Sepik** Province [**South Arapesh** People]. If someone goes around the lake, searching for fish or sago there, they can see this boy who has become a man. This story comes from Maprik in East Sepik Province.

Joe Tonny and Buki Mangi
Imahup [Amahop] Viles No. 2
East Sepik Province

D231M. Transformation: man to stone; D2000+. Mind control; E278+. Ghosts haunt cave; E425.2. Revenant as man; E720. Soul leaves or enters the body; F490+. Masalai; K1350. Woman persuaded (or wooed) by trick; P210. Husband and wife; P231. Mother and son; P233. Father and son; P251.6.1. Three brothers; T100. Marriage; T111. Marriage of mortal and supernatural being

[There was no ancestor story in *Wantok* #1195.]

Two Sisters Founded a Large Family
(Wantok 1196, May 29, 1997, page 20)

Long ago, there lived two young sisters. One time, the sisters were bathing in a river when they saw the river carrying sugarcane peels downstream. They quickly thought that there must be some people at the head of the river, so they followed the river upstream.

As they followed the river upstream, they continued to see the sugarcanes coming down. So, they kept following the river.

When the women arrived at small tributaries, they checked them, but there were no sugarcane peels on those. When they checked the main river, the sugarcanes were still coming. So, they kept following the river upstream.

The sisters followed the river for a while, and then they came close to the place where it was very cold because it was the headwaters. [They] saw that a fire was lit.

The young women hid and went close to the fire. Then they saw that the fire was cooking some food. They checked the fire and they saw that there was a cassowary on top of the fire.

Very quietly, they gathered all of the wild game, and then they began to eat. They gorged themselves on the food. Before long, the owner of the food returned. It was a big man who came. He saw the two women there. He did not say anything at that time. He was happy because he now had some people with whom he could talk. He knew that the good spirits of the earth must have discovered them and brought them to live with him.

He looked after the women and they married. At this time, the women had children and they all lived together. However at this time, there were no other villagers that

were near them. The women's children married each other at this time. They continued their families and multiplied.

Many children grew up. They married each other and the community became bigger. Some of the children took their girls and continued to make camps in the area, making the number of families grow larger.

Now, many villages have arisen because of these families each living in areas and creating villages. However, the important thing is that all of them have the same language that is clear to people in all parts. Now, very many villages have arisen and people live where they desire. However, they come from just one family and one ancestor.

This story comes from the **Veyangta** People [Village] of the **Mumeng** [People] in **Morobe** Province.

Mr. Wai
Mumeng
Morobe Province

A1611+. Origin of Mumeng People; F403.2. Spirits help mortal; F494.3. Earth spirit; P210. Husband and wife; P230. Parents and children; P252.1. Two sisters; P295. Cousins; T100. Marriage; T145.1.3. Man married to several sisters; T580. Childbirth

[There was no ancestor story in *Wantok* #1197.]

Crabs and Ants Are Good Friends from Before
(Wantok 1198, June 12, 1997, page 16)

Long, long ago, there were two very good friends. One was Ant and the other was Crab. They were friends and they met together to make things. They shared every kind of thing and they went around together, like two very good brothers. They were never angry with each other. They were always happy.

Crab said, "I have a good idea to tell you. If you agree, then we'll do it. If you don't want to, then we can forget about it."

Then Crab told its friend, "I want us to go around and see what kinds of places there are on earth. We just live in one place. We don't see changes, villages, rivers, mountains, or young women in other places. So, we should go see these things."

Ant agreed with this idea, so they decided to go at a certain time. They made a good plan. Then they began to prepare food and things to take with them on their journey.

While it was still very early in the morning, when Ant was asleep, Crab awoke. Crab took its belongings and went to sleep at Ant's door. Ant slept very soundly. When Ant awoke and opened the door, Ant saw Crab sleeping against the door. Then Ant awakened its friend, Crab. They cooked food and ate. Then they began to walk away.

They walked and walked. They crossed a big river. They climbed a mountain. They entered the very deep forest and they kept going. While they were walking, they stood and saw something new, such as a bird or other thing that they had never seen before. Crab chattered a lot about all of the kinds of things that Ant could see and do.

While they were walking, they arrived at the base of a big breadfruit tree. They sat and caught their breaths and rested. They removed their food and they gorged themselves. They ate and ate. Then a cool breeze made them sleepy, so they began to fall asleep. They slept and slept. The wind blew and blew. It blew the breadfruit leaves sailing downward.

They slept and slept, and then their eyes opened. When they awoke, their eyes opened wide to see the breadfruit leaves blowing wildly above and the wind causing them to sail downwards.

Oh my, Crab's and Ant's eyes were wide open, and they died laughing. This was because they had never seen this before. They laughed and laughed without letting up at all. They continued to laugh until they were out of breath. More breadfruit leaves continued to fall down. They stopped laughing and they had lost their strength. They were completely exhausted.

At this time, Ant deflated and became very small. So now, you can see that ants are very small things. You can see that crabs have spittle on the sides of their mouths. This is because at this time, Crab laughed and laughed until spit spilled from Crab's mouth. Now, crabs live in caves or by the water. They must come up sometimes to find their good friends, the ants.

[Anonymous]

A2213.1+. Ant shrunk in size from exhaustion; A2341+. Why crab's mouth is wet; A2493.19+. Friendship between crab and ant; B211.8.1K. Speaking crab; B214.3. Laughing animal; D491.1. Compressible magic animals; D1773. Magic results from laughing; P310. Friendship

Two Mountains Became Enemies

(Wantok 1199, June 19, 1997, page 16)

Long, long ago, there were three wild men who lived on the border of Mendi and Ialibu, inside Southern Highlands Province. Their names were Kiluwe, Yalipu and Koraipe. At this time, there lived an old man named Yombi.

The old man did not know that there were three wild men living there, but they knew about him. The three wild men liked him, so they watched him very carefully. When the old man made traps in the forest, they would catch rats and marsupials (*kapul*). The three wild men decided that they would not ruin the traps.

They did this for a while. Then one time, Yombi made a big garden of leafy greens. He cut trees and cleaned the area, until the garden was nearly finished. Then the old man cut the last tree. The tree fell down on top of the house of the three wild men.

At this time, they had gone to search for their food. When they returned, they saw that their house was completely ruined. However, Koraipe's and Yalipu's rooms were not too badly damaged.

Kiluwe saw this and he was furious. He threw everything around. Slowly, he turned his back to the house and saw that the old man had cut the forest, so he went to kill and eat him. In the morning, the two of them thought that they would see old man Yombi, but there was no sound of axe chopping.

Yalipu was very sorry and he cried until morning. He buried all of the bones, and then he walked and walked to the house. He took a piece of wood and cracked Kiluwe's head. A great fight arose between the two of them. Poor Koraipe was between them and tried to stop them, but they pushed him away. They fought and fought until the morning, when they were half-dead. Koraipe mumbled, "Kiluwe, you ate a man, so it looks like you will continue to eat men. You live here. Yalipu, you're sorry for men, so you will take care of them and live over there."

Koraipe had stopped the fight and he was between the two of them. He turned into a mountain. Now we call these mountains, Mount Kiluwe [Giluwe], Mount Yalipu [Ialibu], and Mount Koraipe. In Yalipu's home, where Yombi is buried, there is now a village called **Yombi** [**Hagen** People]. His crying became a lake called Bune.

When you go to Mendi in **Southern Highlands** Province on the Highlands Highway, you will see Mount Yalipu, Mount Koraipe, Mount Kiluwe, Lake Bune, and Yombi Village.

Michael A. Kokem

Bomana

National Capital District

A920.1.0.1. Origin of particular lake; A965. Origin of mountain chain; A1617. Origin of place-name; D291M. Transformation: man to mountain;

D457.18.2+. Transformation: tears to lake; F567. Wild man; G10. Cannibalism; Q211. Murder punished; Q270. Misdeeds concerning property punished; Q411. Death as punishment V61.3+. Dead buried

A Dog Found Yams (*Mami*) from the *Masalai* River

(Wantok 1200, June 26, 1997, page 18)

Long, long ago, there were no yams (*yam* or *mami*) in **Buki** [**Bukinara**] Village [**Boiken** People, **East Sepik** Province]. All of the men, women and children ate wild taros and bananas. After they ate, their bodies would itch. There was not one place in Buki that had good food.

Their food was only wild taros and wild bananas. They lived for a while. One day, a dog went around the river. This was a *masalai* river.

The name of this river is Asisira. The dog wanted the *mami*s that were on top of the water. The dog pulled a *mami*, and then it began to eat. The dog ate it and it was delicious. After the dog ate, the dog brought the top of the *mami* to its mistress. The woman looked at the top of the *mami*. In the morning, she and her dog went to the river. The dog showed her these *mami*s.

She fetched the *mami*s and she filled a net bag, then she brought them to the village. She ate good food and she slept well, while the poor other people ate wild taros and wild bananas.

One day, her little granddaughter went to the old woman's house. She saw the old woman eating *mami*s. The granddaughter told her father that her old grandmother was eating *mami*s and that she had seen her. Her father listened and said that he would go to see his old mother.

Her son told her, "You eat good food and sleep well. The children and grandchildren eat wild taros and wild bananas, while they scratch their bodies." He continued to say that his mother ate *mami*s and slept well. Everyone heard this, so everyone went to meet at the old woman's house.

The old woman gave each of them a *mami*. They brought them to their houses and cooked them. After they cooked them, they tried eating them and they were delicious. They also slept well; they no longer itched. One morning, everyone brought net bags and went to this river. They brought *mami*s to the village and they were happy to eat *mami*s.

Taitus Iso and Kamsco Velly
Maprik
East Sepik Province

A2686.4.3. Origin of yams; B421. Helpful dog; F424. River-spirit; F490+. Masalai; P231. Mother and son; P234. Father and daughter; P292. Grandmother

How Sugarcane Arose

(Wantok 1201, July 3, 1997, page 16)

Long, long ago, there lived an old man, his wife and their daughter. They lived on an island.

One time, the old couple's daughter wanted to go bathe. She walked and walked, towards a stream on the island. When she arrived at the stream, she saw that just one side had a nice pond. The water looked completely clean, so she did not think of anything. Quickly, she jumped down to bathe. While she was bathing, a big snake came out of the water and grabbed her. She began to scream.

The father heard his daughter screaming, so he ran and ran to see what was happening to his daughter. He saw that the snake had grabbed his daughter.

The old man quickly ran to the house, took a knife, and then ran to kill the snake. After they killed the snake, they took the snake's head to the house and they just buried it by the side of the house.

When they awoke in the morning, they saw that a new kind of "tree", which they had not seen before, growing from the head of the snake. Its base was red.

They cut the new "tree" and they tried eating it. It was delicious. They called this tree, "sugarcane."

Ronald A. Wamaivali
Maprik
East Sepik Province

A2684.4K. Origin of sugar cane; E691.1+. Reincarnation: snake into sugar cane; P210. Husband and wife; P232. Mother and daughter; P234. Father and daughter; R153.5. Father rescues daughter

A Marsupial (*Sikau*) Took a Woman Named Nakoko [Makoko] Up a Mountain

(Wantok 1202, July 10, 1997, page 19)

Long, long ago, in the time of the ancestors, in the Mamusi area of Pomio District, there lived a man and his family in a village called **Huning Bubuna** [**Mamusi** People, **East New Britain** Province]. Near this village, there was a big mountain.

The man had one daughter named Merry Makono [Nakoko]. One time, her parents and brothers went to the garden. The young woman stayed. During the day, Marsupial (*Sikau*) brought the young woman up to the mountain where Marsupial lived. This mountain was very tall. Its peak was near the clouds.

The woman's parents were terribly worried. They made a big feast. They killed pigs and called all of the birds to gather. The woman's father said, "This food is for you to eat. I want you to go up and get my daughter from Marsupial." All of the men and women and all of the different birds gathered at the base of the mountain. Then they sent each bird up the mountain.

They sent Pigeon up and up. Pigeon reached halfway up, lost its breath and returned. They sent Cockatoo. Cockatoo went and went, but halfway, Cockatoo returned. They tried all of the birds of the earth. They went up, but they could not conquer the mountain.

Then Fly said that it would try. Fly also knew that it had boils and other things on its back. These were not affixed to its hand drum. Also, Fly had a fishing line that was exceptionally long.

Fly put the line on the sides of its mouth. Fly told the birds and all of the people, "Stand there and look at me try." Fly took two hard and yellow betel nuts with it. Then Fly told the men that it would fly upwards and go into a hole.

Fly flew away. When it went up, it put the fishing line on the middle of the mountain. The men stood and watched from behind. Fly kept going, arriving at the place where the birds had gone, and then Fly returned.

Fly kept putting the fishing line on the tall mountain. The men still stood below, at the base of the mountain. They watched Fly pass the place where the birds had turned back.

Fly went and went, approaching the mountaintop. There was a small hole, like a window, that was at the peak of the mountain. Fly went directly inside this hole.

The men could no longer see Fly. Fly arrived at the place where Marsupial and the woman were located. Fly went up to a tree that stood close to their home. Fly stood on one part of the tree.

Marsupial was vigorously clearing a garden by burning while the woman was in the house. Marsupial shouted for water and the woman went to give it to him. This was because Marsupial's garden was near home. Before long, Marsupial shouted again, "Makoko [Nakoko] *hara sive hara veo*."

So, the woman brought betel peppers to him. She gave him betel peppers and betel nuts, and then she returned to the house. Fly threw a yellow betel nut at Makoko. Makoko saw this and said, "That's the kind of betel nut from near our home."

Marsupial shouted again, "Makoko *hara sive hara veo*." (Bring the betel peppers and nuts.) She took these things and gave them to Marsupial. Marsupial spoke, "Bring everything because you've often made me tired of shouting for these things."

She returned to the house. Fly again threw a betel nut. Then she stared at this. She looked up to see Fly lying there. Fly told her to come and take it.

She quickly went there. Fly took her and they descended. They went and went, approaching the base of the mountain. Then Marsupial shouted, "Makoko *hara sive hara veo*." This meant that he wanted her to bring betel peppers and nuts.

However, she was not there because she had gone to her people. Marsupial shouted again, but she did not reply. Marsupial went to the house, but she was not there.

Briwo K. Awalesa
Viosepuna [Viosipuna] Village
Mamusi No. 1, Pomio District
East New Britain Province

B211.4.4K2. Speaking fly; B211.2.12K+. Speaking marsupial; B212. Animal understands human speech; B483.1. Helpful fly; B540+. Fly rescues person; D2074.1.3. Birds magically called; F55. Mountain reaches to sky; P210. Husband and wife; P231. Mother and son; P232. Mother and daughter; P233. Father and son; P234. Father and daughter; P250. Brothers and sisters; R13.1+. Abduction by marsupial; R111.2.2. Rescue of princess from mountain

A Moluhis [Malahun] Ancestor Story
(Wantok 1203, July 17, 1997, page 17)

Long, long ago, there lived some musicians in **Bibriweh** Village, in the area of Warelih [**Wareli**]. They sang and danced until dawn. Then the people went down to bathe in the Muegite Ulabena River and in the big Amuk River.

They bathed and bathed, and then a heavy rain fell. They ran inside a big casuarina tree. In my language, this tree is called *moluh*. They fell dead asleep there.

They did not know that that rain was continuing to fall and that a big flood was following the Amuk River downstream. When the flood came, it took them downstream without turning the tree. No, it just took them. The flood took them to the shores of a village called Lehigeh [**Lehinga**, **South Arapesh** People, **East Sepik** Province]. This is the village of Sir Peter Lus [Member of Parliament].

At dawn of the next morning, a man awoke and took a dog around the forest. They went and went. Afterwards, they heard a child slowly approaching, then hiding and watching them.

They saw the child and the child wanted to flee. The man spoke, "You can't flee. Stay there."

Then he took all of the people to the village and put them in a village called Maluhum [**Malahun**]. This is the name that the people of Werelih [Wareli] Village used to call Embih. They took the name Maluhum and Maluhum grew until today.

Those of you who are from Maluhum and see this story, try to return to your own village, Maluhis [Maluhum].

Jim Aisak

Werelih [Wareli] Village

Maprik

East Sepik Province

A527.4. Culture hero as poet (musician); A991+. Origin of particular village; D2121. Magic journey; R311. Tree refuge

Two Brothers Worked Hard and the Younger Brother Married

(Wantok 1204, July 24, 1997, page 15)

Long, long ago, in Mialaulop Village, in the Kandrian District of **West New Britain** Province, there lived two brothers with their parents. The big brother's name was Sutna and the little brother's name was Aplim.

One time the two [brothers] decided to go into the deep forest to cut a big tree that they could use to carve [spears] for fighting with the enemies. This tree is called _pamu_ [the coral tree?]

In the very early morning, they took their food and walked into the deep forest to cut the tree. They walked and walked. Then they arrived at the tree. They began to cut the tree. When the tree broke and fell to the ground, the big brother began to cut small trees to make a fire to cook food for themselves.

It was nearly dark, so they made a hut in which to sleep until morning. They began cutting trees again. When the little brother, Aplim, wanted to stand carefully to cut one side of a tree, he stood on top of a small tree buttress that broke. A small piece hit his leg. At the same time, Aplim's leg began to swell considerably. They finished cutting tree sat about three o'clock. The big brother tied their two bundles for when they would leave the forest and return to the village.

The little brother could not walk because his leg was completely ruined and swollen. So, the big brother left him

and he went to the village. The little brother slept another night in the forest. The small amount of food was gone, so he just slept hungry in the forest. He slept until about one o'clock that night, and then he heard a noise near the hut. The noise was a young woman in the forest. The woman took green coconuts, taros and cooked pig legs. She put them together.

When Aplim saw her, he was terrified. He thought that she was a ghost who wanted to eat him. However, she told Aplim not to be afraid, "I'm human just like you. I know that you'll coconut milk and _kaiz_ [?] because you're hungry." When he was about to eat, he felt that the taro and pork was warm and recently cooked.

The poor woman took a kind of tree leaf. She gathered water and put it on the boy's sore. Then all of the fluids on his leg went out. In the morning, he began to walk back again to **Misaulop** Village.

The two of them arrived at the village. The mother and father and the first son saw the woman, their [prospective] in-law, and they were elated. Then the little brother married her. They had many children, and they lived together in the village. Now, if you go to Misaulop Village, you will see that the woman's family is still in the forest and that some of them died in the First [Second] World War. However, many of them are still alive.

Thomas Tare

PNGBC [Papua New Guinea Banking Corporation]

Kimbe

West New Britain Province

D1500.1.4.2. Magic healing leaves; D1500.1.18. Magic healing water; D2161. Magic healing power; P210. Husband and wife; P230. Parents and children; P231. Mother and son; P233. Father and son; P251.5. Two brothers; P261. Father-in-law; P262. Mother-in-law; P263. Brother-in-law; P264. Sister-in-law; T100. Marriage

Gapal-Ku and a Wildman

(Wantok 1205, July 31, 1997, page 23)

Long, long ago, there lived a man named Kaula Kopoina. He lived by a small mountain called Gapal-Ku.

One time, there was a nice and very bright moon. The guy took his axe, bow and arrows, and then he departed. He wanted to watch tree fruits.

He kept [watch] on a tree that was at a small place called **Kusum-Kalo**, by **Mokap**. The guy went quietly and he saw something moving in the tree. The bad boy looked up and saw a man with a long "grass" skirt sitting on a tree branch and eating tree fruits.

The guy thought that it was a marsupial (*kapul*). Then he saw that it was not a marsupial and that it was a wild man perched high upon the casuarina tree. He saw that his skirt went all of the way down to the base of the tree, so he went to hide in the forest.

The wild man on the tree branch wanted to jump to another casuarina tree. He missed and he fell down. He banged his head directly upon a stone and his head broke open completely.

Koka Kaula [Kaula Kopoina] left and went to his home at Gapal-Ku. Then he went to sleep. In the early morning, he went and saw that the bad guy was dead.

He carried the wild man to his house and buried him near it. After the body rotted, he removed the bones. When he fought, he would win fights using the bones of the wild man. They called the wild man Minjaya Talpale.

Mr. Alphones Yangule
Waro Community School
Jimi District, Tabibuga
Western Highlands Province

D1007. Magic bone (human); D2163. Magic defense in battle; F567. Wild man; F820. Extraordinary clothing and ornaments; N339+. Person falls to death from tree; V61.3+. Dead buried; V61.3+. Bones exhumed

Mawo's Story Is the Ancestor
Story of How the Sea Arose

(Wantok 1206, August 7, 1997, page 13)

Long, long ago, in a village among the **Siwai** [People], there lived a woman and her child [**North Solomons** Province]. The child was not human. No, it was a snake child whose name was Mawo. The mother and child lived by themselves. They were near a village that had many people living in it. Many of the villagers were in Mavo's [Mawo's] clan and so was her mother.

In this village, people would eat a vegetable that many people in Papua New Guinea eat. The name of this leafy green is *tulip*. The Siwai People call this vegetable *mareuwa*. These vegetables have spines and when people eat them, they pile the spines in coconut shells and put them aside.

Whenever a young woman who was not in Mawo's [clan] would see these *tulip* spines, she would say, "Oh my, you're very greedy because you ate flying fox and you didn't leave any for me." [Flying foxes have very fine bones.]

Mawo's clanswomen would reply, "It's from the flying fox that your lazy husband killed and that we ate. He's going to kill more every night."

This sort of thing happened many times.

One time, all of the clans of the village went to the garden, and only the young woman stayed back in the village. She put on traditional adornments. She put shell money around her neck and her body. She put adornments on her arms and legs. She walked to the village where the man who had been arranged to marry her lived.

When she arrived in the village, Mawo's mother saw her and sent her back to her parents. She told her that the boy that had been chosen to marry her was not a man, but a snake. However, the young woman did not want to go back to her family. At this time, Mawo was not living in the village because he had gone hunting for marsupials (*kapul*), flying foxes and other animals. Mawo's mother told her to find a place in the house and to stay there. This was a place where Mawo could not see her.

She went to hide carefully in a corner of the house. The mother showed her a hole in the house that was like a door where Mawo would enter. She also told her that if the house shook, it was a sign that Mawo was returning home.

Not much later, Mawo came home. The young woman hid and saw the snake. She was afraid and she cried. Mawo knew that something was in the house, so he asked his mother. The mother did not want to say anything, but it was too late. One of the woman's tears fell on top of Mawo. He looked up and saw her.

The mother told Mawo not to do anything to the woman because her parents did not know that she had come to visit them. She also told him that the woman had heard other people's gossip and that she had gone to her.

Mawo was happy and showed his tongue. The woman stood up with fright, but the snake went to her and encircled her body. He also ruined her clothing.

The woman stayed with Mavo and his mother as the snake's wife. She lost her fear. She lived well as the snake's wife.

Her family and clan began to worry about her, but it was very lucky that at this time Mawo had told her that they were married and that they should see her family. Afterwards, he killed a pig. He smoked it to bring to her family.

In the very early morning of the next day, the couple brought the smoked pork with other foods to the woman's village. Her clan did not recognize her because she looked different. The snake's semen had filled her body [i.e., she became pregnant?]. When they saw that their friend's child was a woman, they were very sorry but they did not say anything. They treated Mawo well and they let them sleep one night. After that, they returned.

Her clan house made a plan to kill Mawo. They cut trees and put them down on the trail that went to Mawo's home. Then they hid nearby.

After some days, her clan sent a message with a man that her father had died and that the two of them should come to see him. Quickly, they prepared their things and they departed. However, Mawo's mother was afraid and worried about her son because Mawo had not left home much before this.

So to look after him, Mawo's mother tied a piece of rope to his tail and held it. If the rope broke, it would mean that they had killed him.

When then two of them walked away from her home, he performed a sad song and dance for his father-in-law who had died, as they approached the village. Before Mawo sat down, the men who were at the ready took their axes and cut Mawo's body. Quickly, his mother knew that her poor son had been killed. She took the piece of his tail that was attached to the rope. She held it [and it] fell down. She cried for a long time. She took the small piece of Mawo's tail, put it inside a coconut shell and hid it.

The tail rotted in the coconut shell. Mawo's mother used this like salt to flavor food when she cooked. She had a daughter. She always asked her mother what it was that she put in the food that she cooked to make it taste so good. The mother would tell her that it was the last small piece of salt that they were using (They used the traditional method of making salt with things from the forest.) The Siwai People call this _mio_.

The young woman did not believe her mother and she really wanted to know what it was that her mother used to flavor the food so well.

One time, she hid and watched her mother cooking. After a while, when the food pot was boiling, she saw her mother take a coconut shell and spill a little liquid into the pot. When she put down the coconut shell with the rotting liquefied tail, the mother spoke to herself, "If your sister used you, a small piece must fall on the ground. If she wants to remove it, she can't because I know of this."

When the mother checked on the pot, she looked directly into it and she knew that the sister was holding her brother's decayed flesh. The mother and girl stood and watched, and then a small amount of liquid from Mawo's decayed flesh spilled onto the ground. It began to become bigger.

The mother took a fan that was made of coconut leaves, called _heuheu_ in the Siwai Language. She fanned the liquid in all directions, from east to west. The liquid grew when the mother fanned it. It covered everything and everywhere. This is the water that today we call the sea.

When the sea was about to cover everywhere, Mawo's mother said, "Son, leave a small piece of dry land for the children and grandchildren to live and make their gardens." From this, came the origin of islands and the mainland.

This is Mawo's true story. It is the story of how the sea, the islands and the mainland arose. The ancestors of the Siwai People believe this.

[Anonymous]

[For a related tale from the nearby Mono-Alu People of the Solomon Islands, see Wheeler (1972: 182-183).]

A924.2. Origin of sea from rotting snakes; A955. Origin of islands; B211.6.1. Speaking snake (serpent); B604.1. Marriage to snake; D1171.1. Magic pot; E761.7+. Life token: string slackens; K914. Murder from ambush; P231. Mother and son; P232. Mother and daughter; P234. Father and daughter; P253. Sister and brother; P261. Father-in-law; P262. Mother-in-law; P265. Son-in-law; P265+. Daughter-in-law; S139.4. Murder by mangling with axe; T570. Pregnancy; T131. Arranged marriage; W157. Dishonesty

Today, Cat and Rat Are Enemies
(Wantok 1207, August 14, 1997, page 17)

Long, long ago, Cat and Rat were very good friends. They would always work together and do everything together. Whatever kind of food they found, they would share. Rat and Cat were true friends, more so than the other animals. This was because many other animals were still enemies with each other.

One time, Rat went around the garden to find food for themselves to eat at the house in the afternoon. Rat dug the ground for a while. Then a small bird arrived in the garden and shouted at Rat. Oh my, Rat's soul just leapt. Rat thought that an enemy was about to arrive. Rat turned and saw the little bird shouting, "Do you have something to give me or something good to say to me?"

The bird said, "Friend, I've seen you do much hard work. Your friend, Cat, never does the slightest amount of work. Cat always just sits while you prepare food and things. Then Cat just eats." Rat said that they never fought and that they never had a problem about this. So, their life was always good.

The bird spoke again, "Friend, when you go around the garden or do other work, Cat finishes all of the food in the house. Later, Cat goes with the other animals and tells them that you're Cat's indentured servant. Cat will eat you.

Cat's just waiting for a good time, and then Cat will kill and eat you."

When Rat heard this, it was not very happy. At first, Rat did not believe this gossip. Later, Rat thought that it must be true.

The bird spoke, "I always fly and perch on top of your house where I see what the two of you are doing. When Cat goes to meet with the other animals, I fly there too and I listen to them speak."

When Rat returned to the house, Rat began to make a plan to kill Cat. Rat thought and thought, then a good plan came to Rat.

One time, Rat told Cat that the other side of the island had much food. So, the two of them should go there to find it.

Cat asked, "How can we cut across the sea to get there?" Rat replied, "We must make a canoe, and then we can paddle it across the sea to the other side of the island."

They searched for things to make a canoe. Rat said, "If we make a canoe of wood, the wood will sink in the water and we'll drown. So, we must make a canoe out of sweet potato. Then they searched for a huge sweet potato in the garden and they began to make a hole in the middle of it. They carved the sides of the sweet potato and made it into a small canoe.

On the side of the sweet potato, Rat made a small room in which to go. Rat took a long piece of bamboo for poling.

In the morning, they paddled in the water. Midway, they became hungry. Rat told Cat to look in front and see whether there was a nearby island where they could quickly find food. When Cat looked in front, Rat began to eat the sides of the sweet potato. Rat ate and ate. Then the sweet potato opened up and the sea came inside the canoe. When Cat saw this, Cat shouted, "Hey, the water's coming inside the canoe!" However, it was too late. The sea swelled and the canoe went under. However, Rat had made a plan, so Rat jumped inside the little hole [room] in the sweet potato and hid. Rat took the long bamboo pole, and then breathed deep. The sea carried Rat slowly to the beach. Rat was happy and alive. Poor Cat went down in the sea and died.

So from this time, cats and rats are terrible enemies. When a cat sees a rat, it will jump and kill it quickly, and then eat it. If the rat sees the cat from faraway, it will hide or take off.

[Anonymous]

A2494.1.4. Enmity between cat and rat; B143.1. Bird gives warning; B211.1.8. Speaking cat; B211.2.9. Speaking rat; B211.3. Speaking bird; B295.2.1K. Animals make voyage in canoe; ; B295.2K. Animals build canoeJ2119.4+. Rat eats hole in boat made of tuber; K910. Murder by strategy; K958. Murder by drowning; P310. Friendship; Q210.1. Criminal intent punished; Q428. Punishment: drowning; R210. Escapes; S131. Murder by drowning; W111. Laziness

The First Wife Performed Black Magic on the Second Wife

(Wantok [12]08, August 21, 1997, page 17)

One time, there lived a married couple. They had two children and they lived very well together. Once, the man thought of marrying another woman. Some months passed. He married a second wife and they lived together.

Some time later, the man's first wife went to purchase black magic to ruin her husband's mind. She bought it and went to put it in the house.

One time, the man and his second wife went into the forest to remove some traps that he had set to catch wild game.

The two of them walked and walked, and then they arrived in the forest where he had set traps. He told his wife to go on another trail and to wait for him in a hut that he had slept in before when he had gone around the forest. His wife listened and went on the trail to her husband's open-air house.

Along the trail, she saw a gigantic frog sitting on top of a big tree leaf. She took the frog and bound it with leaves. Then she put it into her net bag and walked away.

Before long, she felt the skin on her back itch. She removed her net bag and her "grass" skirt. Then she scratched her back. She scratched diligently and felt terrible, so she shouted for her husband to come. You know how newly married women are. The man ran to her and quickly told her, "Why are you shouting for me?" She said, "Something is in my back and eating me." The man looked there and he saw a huge frog making a hole inside her back. He told her that there was a big frog inside her back.

He quickly laid her down and made a fire. He singed the fur from [a big] marsupial (*kapul*), and then he cooked it on top of the fire. He cooked the marsupial and when it was done, he hung it above the woman's back where the frog was hiding.

He told the frog, "If you're a real man, then leave from her back, come outside, and eat this meat." After he said this, the marsupial's smell made the frog jump and come out of her back.

When the frog jumped out, the leader [man] held a big piece of firewood on top of the frog until the frog died completely. He took the frog and threw it into the fire, obliterating it.

His wife had a huge sore on her back, so he tied all of the net bags together and filled them with meat. Then he himself carried everything on his back, including his second wife, and he walked back to the village.

He carried his wife on his shoulders and he walked to the village. He went and went, then he arrived at the house.

He looked, but no, the house door was shut. He opened the door and he saw that blood was all over the house door and inside his first wife's room.

Immediately, he went to check inside the room, but no, he held something cold. He lit a fire and looked carefully. He saw that his wife was dead in the room. The two little children left to live with their [mother's] family in her village.

The man told some people in a nearby village to take the woman's body and bury it. Then he brought his other wife to his clan to fix the wound on her back.

He buried his first wife and they began to cry. The first wife had taken black magic and turned herself into a frog in order to kill the second wife. However, their husband tempted her with the smell of meat, and then he killed her. He had thought that he was just killing a frog, but this was not the case. He had killed his first wife.

The man and his second wife lived with his clan until her wound healed. Then they returned to their mountaintop home and began a new life for themselves.

This is a true story from Mop [**Map**] Village, **Mendi** [People], **Southern Highlands** Province.

Mescy Blue
Kumin Village
Mendi
Southern Highlands Province

[Mescy Blue retold this story in *Wantok* #1163.]

B876.1. Giant frog; D195W. Transformation: woman to frog; D572. Transformation by magic object; D651.1. Transformation to kill enemy; K910. Murder by strategy; P210. Husband and wife; P230. Parents and children; P290+. Hostile co-wives; Q261. Treachery punished; Q411. Death as punishment; S63+. Husband kills wife; S116. Murder by crushing; T100. Marriage; T145.0.1. Polygyny; V61.3+. Dead buried; W181. Jealousy

Fish Eggs Became *Galip* Nuts

(Wantok [12]09, August 28, 1997, page 17)

Long, long ago, in the time of the ancestors, there lived a man named Pilag. Pilag was excelled at hunting wild game. Pilag lived in a small village in the mountains called **Bosavek**. In Bosaek Village, he was the best hunter.

Whenever Pilag would kill animals, he would divide the meat among everyone in the village. Everyone wanted the meat and they were very happy for Pilag's generosity.

One time, Pilag went to hunt game, but he did not kill the smallest animal. He just went around until the sun was about to set and darkness began to fall. He was famished, so he made an open-air hut by a pond and he slept there. Pilag slept until it was late at night. Then he felt a great hunger. He was wracked with hunger and he could not sleep well, so Pilag awoke late at night and began fishing in the pond. Before long, he caught a big fish. He wanted to put the fish on top of the fire. When Pilag was about to put the fish on the fire, he was shocked to hear the fish speak. The fish said, "Please good man, don't cook me." Pilag was afraid, so he put the fish down and he slept a little until dawn broke. When Pilag awoke in the morning, he was shocked to see that the fish had laid eggs and that some of the eggs had hatched and become tree nuts. Pilag took the eggs that had become tree nuts to the village. He planted them by his house.

Before long, the trees grew large and bore much food. When the food was ripe, Pilag tried it. He tried breaking one of them open and it tasted delicious in his mouth. Pilag beat the signal drum and everyone gathered. He told them about this new thing. Then Pilag broke open the nuts and shared them with everyone. They ate and it tasted wonderful to them. The men asked Pilag where he had gotten the tree nuts.

Everyone returned to the homes and they told stories until late. Whenever they would get game, dog's teeth [used as valuables], and other presents, they would give them to Pilag. In return, Pilag would give them tree nuts. They would take them back to their homes and each of them would plant them. Everyone ate these tree nuts and they were delicious. So, they began to plant them and they became plentiful on **Karkar** Island in **Madang** Province [**Takia** or **Waskia** People]. Later, people gathered to make big feasts and huge parties with their new food.

This tree became plentiful and it fills Karkari [Karkar] Island in Madang Province. This is the tree nut that is called *galip*. It is a delicious food, so Karkar Island is filled with *galip* trees today.

[Anonymous]

A2681.13K. Origin of Tahitian chestnuts; B211.5. Speaking fish; D469.1+. Transformation: egg to nut; Q55. Reward for sparing life when in animal form

A Lake Arose and Saved Many People

(Wantok 1210, September 4, 1997, page 14)

Long, long ago, there were two clans. The clans often made very large gardens. However at this time, there was no good water for drinking or for the food plants to grow.

The clans lived well and were very happily. They always worked happily together in the gardens. They shared food and other things.

One time, they decided to make a large garden. At this garden, they would only plant leafy greens. The next day, everyone in the clans stood in a row and began cutting the forest and trees. They made a huge garden, and then they planted the leafy greens from the top of the garden to the bottom.

After they planted the greens, they began to divide the garden into halves. One side belonged to Pawaw Kobeya Clan and the other side belonged to Pombo Wareya Clan. After this, then they always went back and forth, weeding and taking care of the big vegetable garden.

One time, everyone in the clans went to weed the garden. The sun was terribly hot and they worked diligently, weeding the garden for a while. Before long, they heard a man speaking. They stopped working, then listened carefully to hear exactly what it was. They went closer, then heard a voice say, "Part of the garden belongs to you and part belongs to me." They only heard the voice. There was no one to be seen.

They were all terrified of this, and then they quickly gathered the belongings and fled back to their village. They began to tell stories. They revealed all of the various stories and customary beliefs about the ancestors and the various forest spirits.

In the morning, they sent just one strong man back to see whether something had happened at the garden. They sent some men away to hide and watch from a distance to try to see whether something had happened. They watched carefully, then they arrived at the border of where they had divided the garden between the clans. They saw that a lake had arisen. They approached and saw that the lake was rising and becoming larger. They quickly went back to the village and told of what they had seen. When everyone had returned to see it, they tried to touch it, but no, something happened to them. They went inside and felt that it was very cold. They tasted it and it was delicious, cooling their bodies very nicely.

This lake arose and everyone in the clans used it. The lake is still there. It enlarged because of this story. They now call this Lake Bune. It is near **Lepiti**, by Ialibu, **Southern Highlands** Province [**Hagen** People].

Bembo Maka

East Taraka

Lae

Morobe Province

A920.1.0.1. Origin of particular lake; F420.1.5. Water-spirits invisible; F421. Lake-spirit; F441. Wood-spirit

Nepope and His Ghost Brother, Nakone

(Wantok 1211, September 11, 1997, page 18)

Long, long ago, in a village called **Pipilex** by Nembi Mountain, in **Southern Highlands** Province, there lived two brothers. Their names were Nakone and Nepope. The first brother grew to become a hunter of wild game. The second brother became a gardener. Nakone's skin was red and Nepope's was black. The brothers were good friends and they lived in Pipilex.

The hunter would always go into the forest and put traps along the trails of marsupials (*kapul*), cassowaries, birds and other animals of the forest. He would place traps inside the forest for a whole month. After he had finished placing the traps, he would go to watch the traps. He never brought meat to their home, not even a little. Poor Nepope worked very hard in the garden. He would cook food and fetch water for themselves. He worked very hard at various tasks. The red-skinned man would work in the deep forest. He never brought any meat to their house, none at all.

One time, the gardener made a plan to follow the hunter. He never explained this; he just thought it to himself. He pretended that he was going to the garden, but no, he hid in the forest near their house and he watched Nakone. When the red-skinned man took off for the forest, he followed him quietly. Napope [Nepope] stood on a mountain. Then it became dark and he saw that the red-skinned man was cutting a cassowary's leg. He was eating it raw with the blood. The hunter had trapped this cassowary and he had grabbed it.

He worked at eating the cassowary's leg. Then he got up and said that he would eat Neipope's [Nepope's] leg just as he was devouring the cassowary. Oh my, the boy trembled fiercely. He had followed him and gone a long way. He turned and walked directly back to the village, kicking up dust as he went.

Immediately upon arrival, he killed their pig and cooked it in an earth oven. He put down a piece of leg, the snout and a small piece of pig liver for the man who had eaten raw cassowary. He carried the rest and put it in a big bamboo tube for himself. He walked away on a long trail. He carried some sweet potatoes, taros and each of every kind of food. He arrived at a big river.

While he was still walking along the trail, he heard the shouts of his brother's ghost. He said, "Where are you now? I'll eat you. Don't make me angry at you, my brother." Quickly, he went inside the bamboo tube and put all of the food inside of it too.

You know that this is an ancestor story, so he rolled himself in the bamboo down into the river and the river carried the bamboo away, as he had wanted. He ate the pork inside of his bamboo home and he was very happy.

Afterwards, the ghost wanted to follow him, but no, it was a big river. It broke Nakone's limbs and the ghost died in the middle of the river, where he stayed.

So, when you go around big rivers, you will see giant lakes through which the rivers run. These are houses of Nakone, the ancestral ghost brother.

Poor Napope, the river brought him downstream. Some young and beautiful women were fishing by the river when one of them found the bamboo. She thought that she would cook fish in the bamboo tube, so she carried it in her net bag. They caught enough fish and then they went to their village. The woman who had taken the bamboo wanted to cook fish, so she removed the rubbish from inside the tube. But no, a handsome young man shot out of the tube. The woman was shocked and she shouted awkwardly, "What are you, a man or a ghost?" Nepope told his whole story and she was very sorry for him. She married him and they raised many children. Now, we live there. We're the grandchildren of this married couple.

Simon Komel
Mendi
Southern Highlands Province

[Mr. Komel wrote a similar story in Wantok #1133.]

D950.15. Magic bamboo tree; E226. Dead brother's return; E261.4. Ghost pursues man; E278+. Ghosts haunt lake; E446. Ghost killed and thus finally laid; F527.1. Red person; F527.5. Black man; G11.10. Cannibalistic spirits; P210. Husband and wife; P230. Parents and children; P251.5. Two brothers; P310. Friendship; P251.5.3. Hostile brothers; R260. Pursuits; R213. Escape from home; T100. Marriage; W151. Greed

An Old Man Turned into a Baby and Drank from the Sister's Breasts

(Wantok 1212, September 18, 1997, page 16)

Long, long ago in **Kamung** Village, in the Finschhafen area of **Morobe** Province, there were only two gorgeous sisters who lived there. There were no other people with them.

One day, they were famished and they had no more food in the house. So, they followed the Kamung River and killed many crayfish and fish, traveling all of the way to the headwaters. Oh my, their baskets were packed with fish and crayfish.

Before long, they arrived at a pond. They looked and saw an old man sitting there. When the old man saw them, he quickly jumped into the pond, turning into a fish.

The little sister quickly grabbed the fish and gave it to her big sister. The big sister held the fish and put it in her mouth in order to break its head. However, she missed and the fish slipped into her mouth, going down into her belly.

When it was nearly dark, they returned to the house. At the house, they cooked the fish and crayfish, making a great feast. They gorged on the food until their bellies were swollen. Then they went to sleep.

In the morning, the big sister felt as if she were pregnant. They lived for some days. Later, the big sister gave birth to a baby. Oh my, they were very happy that they had a baby boy.

One day, they brought the baby in a net bag to the garden. They hung the baby on a tree branch, and then they went to the garden. While they were working, the baby went outside of the net bag and turned into the man that they had seen by the pond. Later, he called for the pig to come. He killed and ate it. After he ate, he went inside the net bag, turned into a baby and slept.

Afterwards, the baby defecated and cried. The mother came and cleaned the feces, and then gave the baby her breast. However, the mother saw that baby's feces had pig hair.

Every day, the same thing happened. The big sister (the baby's mother) thought hard. One day, she told her little sister. They hid and saw the baby come outside of the net bag. He killed another pig and ate it. Later, he went back inside the net bag, turned into a baby and slept.

The sisters were completely furious. The big sister shouted, "Damn! That huge old man has been tricking me and drinking my milk. I've worked hard at cleaning his shit as if it were my own hair."

They went back home and just stayed there quietly. One day, they planned everything. They made ten net bags and they began to put the baby into the ten bags. They took the baby to the house and hung him up there.

They ran quietly outside of the house. Then they began to gather firewood. They gathered plenty of firewood and they began to make a fire. A great fire arose and burned the *masalai* baby inside the house. The baby was in great pain. He cried and then he died.

Today because of this story, the people of Kamung Village are pork eaters.

V. Zafirio

Lae

Morobe Province

A1681.2+. Origin of pork eating; D170M. Transformation: man to fish; D1880. Magic rejuvenation; D1890. Magic aging; F321.1. Changeling; F490+. Masalai; K1930. Treacherous impostors; P231. Mother and son; P252.1. Two sisters; P294. Aunt; P297. Nephew; Q262. Impostor punished; Q414. Punishment: burning alive; S112.0.2. House (hostel) burned with all inside; T511.5.1. Conception from eating fish; T580. Childbirth; T611. Suckling of children; Z71.16.2. Formulistic number: ten

[The ancestor story in *Wantok* #1213 is the same as that in #1207.]

A Young Boy Saved His Village
(Wantok 1214, October 2, 1997, page 17)

Long, long ago, there was a big village. The people there were very happy because they had plenty of food and all of the good things in life.

However, in this village, there lived a poor woman. Her husband had died and she did not have children to help her or to take care of her. Many people joked and laughed about her.

One night, the old woman went out to look for firewood. She went into the forest near the village. She cut firewood and she gathered it. She did this for a while, and then she approached the graveyard. She cut firewood for a while, close to the graveyard. Then before long she heard a cry. She stopped work and she listened closely to try to hear the cry. She did not hear it well, so she walked closer and listened. When she went very close, she heard the voice of a small baby crying.

Quickly, the old woman went closer to look. She saw a little baby breaking the ground in the graveyard and coming upwards. She stood closer and she saw that it was a boy breaking the ground, coming out and gathering pieces of dirt do eat.

Quickly, the old woman held him and took him to her house that night where she hid him. She took care of the baby very well. She watched him eat and eat. The baby was a boy who had come from his dead mother's pregnant belly. The boy had grown inside his mother's belly. He became strong and broke through the ground, rising to the surface.

The old woman did not want anyone in the village to know about this, so she hid the boy in the house and took very good care of him. She quickly gave him food and bathed him. She quickly stopped him from crying lest people in the village hear him and check on the noise.

At this time, a great battle arose between this village and the enemies from another village. It was a huge fight. Many people fled and many died. Everyone fled and left the poor old woman there. The old woman hid the boy in a net bag and carried him like her belongings. She wanted to jump into a canoe with the other people, but they prevented her from doing so. She stood on the beach, holding her boy and crying.

The old woman took the boy back to the house. They moved to hide at the base of a boulder, where they made a small house and hid. The old woman never made a fire during the daytime. This was because it would be bad if the enemies saw smoke from the fire. She would only cook at night. She would prepare food for the morning for themselves when they would awake and eat. They lived for a while, and then the boy became a big and strong man. His mother taught him to carve bows and arrows, and to shoot arrows to kill wild game. She taught him to swim in the sea to catch fish. She also taught him to make traps and to fight the enemies.

One night, the old woman told the boy what had happened. She told him that the people had fled and left them there. The boy listened and was very worried about his mother. So, he began to make a plan to kill the enemies and to take over their village.

The boy began to make traps everywhere near the village. Later, he made a kind of black magic with a tree vine. He threw it in the water, and they began to die. When they went around by the village, the traps caught them and killed them. At this time, they knew that someone was being hostile towards them. So, they began to search for him. They went around and met the boy when he was crossing a mountain and preparing to loose a boulder down into the village. They wanted to fight with him, but it was too late. The bad boy took away his hands and the giant boulder slipped downwards. Then, all of the stones followed this one and went down, breaking all of the houses and killing people in the village. The bad boy went down and killed a small group of men. Later, he lit a fire and burned all of the houses, creating a great blaze. He found the [bodies] of ten warriors from this village. He sent them to sea in a canoe.

When his mother's clan saw the big fire, they knew that it was now time for their village. Before long, they saw the ten bodies drifting in the sea and coming towards them. They knew that some people must have killed all of their enemies and that the village was now free. Some men paddled a canoe. They went to meet the old woman and her son who were standing on the beach, waiting for their clan.

They sent the story back and all of the people began to return. They were very happy for the young man and his mother. They made the boy the leader of the village. Everyone was happy.

Nonimo Kenau

Port Moresby

National Capital District

D965. Magic plant; D2061. Magic murder; K730. Victim trapped; K910. Murder by strategy; L111.4. Orphan hero; P272. Foster mother; P275. Foster son; R213. Escape from home; R310. Refuges; Q53. Reward for rescue; Q211. Murder punished; Q411. Death as punishment; Q486.1.1. Sinful city burnt as punishment; S111. Murder by poisoning; S116. Murder by crushing; S140.1. Abandonment of aged; T570. Pregnancy; T584.2.1. Child born of dead mother in grave; V61.3+. Dead buried; Z71.16.2. Formulistic number: ten

Dog and Marsupial (*Kapul*) Are Enemies Now

(Wantok 1215, October 9, 1997, page 21)

Long, long ago, Dog and Marsupial (*Kapul*) were very good friends. They went around together, hunting for food and wild game. Whatever food one of them found, they would share and eat together.

Their good friendship was very strong and other animals thought jealously of them. Whenever they went around, all of the other animals, such as Cat, Bird and Rat, would take off because they did not want to talk with the two friends.

One time, the animals began to search for ideas to ruin the good friendship between Dog and Marsupial. Cat called a big meeting and shouted for all of the kinds of animals to gather. Cat was an animal who had good knowledge and ideas. So, the other animals listened to what Cat said. In the big meeting, they came up with various ideas and plans to ruin the two friends.

Crab said that it had strong teeth. Crab said that it could twist their necks and kill them. Bird said that it could trick them into going to the sea to the swallow water and die. Eagle said that it could trick them and carry them around. Then Eagle could loosen its claws and let them drop; they would fall and die. Crocodile said that it could trick them and carry them around. Then Crocodile could shake its tail and throw them into a bad place. All of the kinds of animals came up with their ideas and plans.

Cat listened to all of the talking and then it came up with an idea. The first thing to do would be to make the two of them angry with each other. When they were angry with each other, then the animals could meet again and come up with another plan to make them argue and fight each other. So, the animals agreed and made this plan.

One time, Cat called a big meeting and shouted for all of the forest animals. All of the animals heard this news and they were afraid. However, Dog spoke, "I'm not afraid. Let's stand up strong and fight against the enemies. Let's fence in our food and land and forests." What Dog said made all of the other animals agree that they must stand up and fight. So, Cat spoke again, "Let's make an army." Dog went first as their captain.

In the times of yore, Dog's tail stood up tall. So, all of the animals said that this would be their flag. When Dog went in front, the animals would see their flag standing and they could follow it.

So in the morning, all of the animals gathered and marched to the place of battle. When they arrived at a pond, Insect quickly flew back and bit Dog's tail, which then fell down. When all of the animals saw this, they ran about. They shouted that the flag had fallen, so they would lose the battle. They took off and ran about. Marsupial left everyone and wanted leave completely, but Marsupial thought hard about its friend, so it stood for a little while again.

Dog had the idea that it would leave the battle because the enemies had ruined Dog's tail. Dog's tail was in terrible pain, so Dog went down and stood in the water, trying to soothe the tail with the water's coolness. Marsupial stood by the water and watched. Dog was cooling its tail when Cat and the other animals returned. They arrived and saw Dog standing in the river and Marsupial standing on the side of the river. All of them spoke to Dog, "We walked a long way behind you and we saw with our own eyes that it wasn't an enemy that ruined you. We saw with our own eyes that it was someone right behind you. It was your own good friend, Mr. Marsupial. He hit your tail with a big, sharp piece of bamboo. So now, your tail can no longer stand. It will fall down and lie low from now onwards." When Marsupial heard this, Marsupial was terribly ashamed because Marsupial knew that this was a lie. Marsupial had not done this, but all of the animals were in agreement, so Dog believed them and became very angry with its friend, Marsupial. It was too late. Marsupial jumped up onto a tree branch. Then Marsupial jumped on top of the tree and disappeared into the deep forest. Dog tried to find Marsupial, but was unable to do so. Dog left and tried to find Marsupial to seek revenge for his anger. Today, you will see that dogs and marsupials are enemies because dogs are still trying to find marsupials to avenge their pain from yore.

Mr. Wai
Port Moresby
National Capital District

A2378.1.7+. Why some dog's tail droops; A2494.4+. Enmity between dog and marsupial; B211.1.7. Speaking dog; B211.1.8. Speaking cat; B211.3. Speaking bird; B211.3.11K. Speaking eagle; B211.6.4K. Speaking crocodile; B211.8.1K. Speaking crab; B263. War between other groups of animals; K2295. Treacherous animals; P310. Friendship; R220. Flights; W157. Dishonesty; W181. Jealousy

Two Boys Came from a Water Family
(Wantok 1216, October 16, 1997, page 17)

One time, two brothers lived in a village. None of the people of this village liked them because they said that their mother was a *masalai* woman. Their mother did not have any friends or family in this village. She had come from somewhere, met their father and married him. Then she had given birth to them. Later, she just left for a place where no one lived. When the boys' father went to look for their mother, he did not return to the village either. Their father's clan never worried about the brothers and they never cared for them well.

The brothers lived in the house that their father had built for them. However because they were too little [to repair them], the sago leaves on the roof of the house had become old and the rain fell down on them at night. The walls of the house were also old and becoming broken. People could look inside at the two boys. They would joke and laugh at them.

One time, there was a shortage of their garden food because they had no parents to plant new gardens and raise new food. So, the two boys did not have food and they began to feel hungry.

One night, they decided to go find their parents because their father's siblings never helped them with food or anything. When it was still late at night, they gathered their belongings and prepared one last taro on the fire. Afterwards, they departed.

In the very early morning, they awoke and ate their last piece of taro. Then they began to walk away. They walked and walked, arriving in the very deep forest. They climbed a mountain, and then went down the mountain. They arrived at a beach and they followed the seashore. They arrived at a place where the water fell from the mountain and formed a pond. The little brother cried and shouted for their mother. He did not have any more strength because hunger was ruining him. His legs and body were completely stiff. So, he felt bad and he cried for their parents.

While he was crying, the big brother was also sad. He cried for his little brother. While they held hands and cried, a tremendous noise arose from the pond. The water exploded and flew up and down. Before long, much water was coming from the mountain and the pond quickly grew bigger down below. A bright light flashed and various images arose with singing, dancing and large groups of people on the water. The water opened and the place became a huge village.

Then a woman walked and came to explain what was happening to the two boys. She told them that they must come with her. The boys looked and were afraid. However, she threw out her hands. She put a hand towards them and held their hands. Then the boys held her hands and she pulled them in front. She told them, "I'm your mother. I came from the water family, so I'm not fit to live on land all of the time. I must return to my family and leave you with your father."

She said that their father had searched for her. He had wanted her to return, but the water had drowned him.

The boys' mother was angry that their father's clan had not taken care of them well, so she promised to punish the people in this village for the bad things that they had done to her children. One day, she stopped the water and everyone in the village found it difficult to obtain water for drinking, cooking food and washing things. The area was completely dry for six months, and then everyone died from the drought. After that, she let the water run again. She was happy with her two sons and they lived happily as a water family.

[Anonymous]

D2143.2. Drought produced by magic; F401.6. Spirit in human form; F420.2.2. Water-spirits live in village under water; F421.1. Lady of the Lake; F490+. Masalai; P210. Husband and wife; P231. Mother and son; P233. Father and son; P250. Brothers and sisters; P251.5. Two brothers; P260. Relations by law; Q285. Cruelty punished; Q411. Death as punishment; Q552.3.3. Drought as punishment; R260. Pursuits; S70+. Cruel paternal kin; T111. Marriage of mortal and supernatural being; T580. Childbirth

The Big Sister Fled and the
Masalai Killed the Little Sister
(Wantok 1217, October 23, 1997, page 19)

Long, long ago, there lived a woman whose name was Oiluso Fero. One time, everyone went into the forest and searched for wild game. The old woman, Oruso Felo [Oiluso Fero], told her two daughters that they must go to the garden and search for sweet potatoes to bring and cook. She said that there was a frog in the garden that they could not take.

However, the sisters ignored their mother. They took the frog and they went to the house. They said, "Quick, let's cook the frog and eat it because mama's coming now." The women cooked the frog, but the fire died down. They tried cooking again and the fire died completely. So, the big sister told the little sister, "Stay here and I'll go find firewood and bring it back." She went to get fire[wood] from an old *masalai* man who lived on a mountain named Kiwi Hogoderu. He was cooking some of his wild game when the young woman went and stole firewood from the old *masalai*. She brought it to her little sister and they made a fire. They cooked the food and ate it with the frog. The big sister told the little sister, "Cook all of the sweet potatoes and I'll check on the big hole that is close to [us]." She went inside the hole and arrived on the other side of the mountain where she had already been.

The young sister was cooking and not thinking of the time. Because her big sister hand not returned, she cooked very slowly, waiting until the afternoon when many of people who had gone to the forest would return.

A long time had passed when the old *masalai* came and looked for his firewood. He shouted and screamed. People heard this angry talking. They asked who had stolen the old *masalai* man's firewood from Kiwi Hogotor [Hogoderu]. No one had cooked. They left their houses and went into two big holes that were near the village. The people fled because the *masalai* would come to look for people who had stolen from him and he would kill them. So, everyone took off and went to hide inside these two big caves that were near the village. When the *masalai* came, he searched and searched for the culprit. While he was there, he just swallowed whatever kind of meat that was there and anything else that was in the village.

The *masalai* was angry. He searched for people until he arrived at the place where the young woman was cooking sweet potatoes. Immediately, he went and grabbed her, then he killed and ate her whole. He was happy that he had eaten someone, so he returned to his hiding place. Afterwards, everyone returned and stayed in their homes. The young woman's big sister also returned. She knew that she had offended the *masalai* and that the *masalai* had killed her sister. However, she did not say anything.

Their mother always lived with worry, thinking that her daughter was gone and that everyone had fled to the cave. She always cried and went inside the cave, screaming and crying. She would call the name of her young daughter. She did not know that the *masalai* had killed and eaten her daughter.

Oruso Felo Wayasa
Lae City
Morobe Province

F721.1. Underground passages; F490+. Masalai; F911.6. All-swallowing monster; G642K. Ogres eat raw flesh; K420. Thief loses his goods or is detected; P232. Mother and daughter; P252.1. Two sisters; Q212. Theft punished; Q411.3. Death of father (son, etc.) as punishment; R213. Escape from home; R315. Cave as refuge; S110. Murders; W126. Disobedience

A Young Woman Killed a *Masalai* Bird
(Wantok 1218, October 30, 1997, page 17)

Once there was a village. This village was a place that was frightful to go near because there were strong *masalai*s who dwelled there. Birds would fly there, perch on trees and watch you. However, something would eat at your liver. This would cause you to die immediately when the birds got up to fly away.

There was a huge bird that was called the father of all of the other *masalai*s of this village. He was the father of all of the spirit birds. When he came, it would become pitch black and the wind and sea would rise. People would flee and hide in the forest or in tree holes. Many of them took canoes and paddled to faraway islands to live until the wind and sea died down. After that, they would return.

The villagers held big meetings in the village to come up with ideas and methods to make the *masalai* bird content and to not come ruin the village and kill them. There were many meetings. Then one time, they decided to give the bird a young girl when he came. They would give him the first daughter of a family when he came. Everyone was in agreement and decided to do this.

When the *masalai* bird was about to come, the people gathered and pointed to the village leader's first daughter. They took her to the mountain and tied her to a tree. They adorned her very well and they stood her up with some food and adornments. When the bird arrived at the mountain, he looked down and saw the woman standing there and he was very happy. Immediately, he flew down and lifted her with all of the food and things into his mouth, carrying her away. After he departed, he did not return again.

When the people saw this, they knew that this was the way to save the village. So, the leader appointed another woman and prepared her. Later, the bird came and removed many young women from the village.

In the village, there lived one young woman and her mother. Her mother was always afraid that they would appoint her daughter. She was afraid because this was her only daughter.

One time, there were no other first daughters. So, the village leader came and took this young woman. The poor woman and her mother cried terribly. The old mother wanted to kill herself. However, the men did not listen to her or feel sorry for her.

When the leader carried the woman to the mountain, they wanted to bind her arms and legs. However, the young woman said that she would not be stubborn and flee. She told them that they could leave her there until the *masalai* bird arrived and took her.

When the men returned to the village, she sat and worried terribly for her mother. She wanted to do something to return and live with her mother.

She sat and worried for a while, and then she put her hand on her necklace. Her mother had made this necklace and given it to her when she was still a young girl. She had made the necklace from cassowary bones from a cassowary that her father had killed. She felt that the bones were sharp on her head, so she took them and held them tightly in her hand. She covered her hand with them and held them. Before long, a strong wind arose and the sea began to swell. She raised her head and looked up to see something big and black coming from the clouds. It was like a big black cloud. She knew that this was the bad *masalai* flying towards her. She held tightly onto the cassowary bones in her hand. The bird flew and thew out its two [wings], covering the young woman. The bird wanted to carry her away. Quickly, she shoved the cassowary bones directly into the *masalai* bird's neck. The bird screamed terribly and flew upwards. The bird threw out his [wings]. He fell down on top of a house, breaking the house and other things.

She held the tightly on to the cassowary bones. She kept shoving it, cutting the *masalai* bird's neck even further. Her hand felt the bird's heart and she shoved one cassowary bone in, cutting around until the bird's heart broke and blood spurted about. The bird was almost dead and it flew upwards towards the sea, falling with her. She died with the bird and they drifted in the sea. Then the big bird's body turned into an island and the woman became a nice river that flows on this island. All of the villagers go to fetch nice cold water and drink it there. They are no longer afraid of anything.

Kandre Tobias
Sialum [Village, **Sialum** People]
Morobe Province

A500+. Heroine dies while slaying devastating bird; B16.3. Devastating birds; B31.6. Other giant birds; B552. Man carried by bird; D2061. Magic murder; E636+. Reincarnation as river; E691+. Reincarnation: bird to island; F401.3.7. Spirit in form of a bird; F490+. Masalai; P232. Mother and daughter; P234. Father and daughter; Q211. Murder punished; Q411. Death as punishment; R213. Escape from home; R311. Tree refuge; R312. Forest as refuge; R316.1. Refuge on island; S115. Murder by stabbing; S260.1. Human sacrifice; V11.7. Sacrifice to animal

The Friendship of Dogs and Marsupials (*Kapul*) Ended
(Wantok 1219, November 6, 1997, page 17)

Long, long ago, there was a man who lived near Mount Giluwe. The man took care of many dogs. He would cook sweet potatoes in an earth oven to feed them every day. After the dogs would eat the sweet potatoes, they would go to drink water and run near the house. At this time, dogs were very good friends with the marsupials (*kapul*) of the forest, so they played around with them.

When dogs and marsupials were good friends, the poor man who owned the dogs was angry at the dogs because they did not kill marsupials. He thought hard about finding a way to teach the dogs to kill marsupials.

One time, he went into the forest to make traps for killing marsupials. Then in one trap, a huge marsupial became caught and died. However, the man had not gone to check this trap, so the marsupial was about to rot when he finally arrived. Very slowly, he removed the marsupial from the trap and carried it to bury at the headwaters of a river from which the dogs always drank after eating sweet potatoes.

After the man buried the marsupial at the headwaters, he returned to the house and cooked plenty of sweet potatoes for the dogs to eat. After the sweet potatoes were ready, he gave them to the dogs to eat.

After the dogs finished all of the sweet potatoes, the dogs ran to the river where it flowed by the house, the river in which the man had buried the marsupial.

Oh my, when then dogs drank the water, it was delicious to them and not like it had been before. When the dogs tasted how good the water was, they followed the river upstream.

They went to the headwaters, where the rotting marsupial was located. When the dogs passed this place, the water was no longer tasty.

When they tasted that the water was no longer delicious, they returned to where the rotting marsupial was located. The dogs pulled and pulled the rotting marsupial out, and then they ate it.

From this time that dogs tasted the deliciousness of marsupials, dogs began to kill them. Also at this time, the friendship of dogs and marsupials ended and they became enemies.

Vincent Doa
Kaupena [**Hagen** People]
Ialibu
Southern Highlands Province

A2494.4+. Enmity between dog and marsupial; B871.2+. Giant marsupial; P310. Friendship; S110. Murders

A *Masalai* Killed All of the Brothers Except the Little Brother

(Wantok 1220, November 13, 1997, page 18)

Long, long ago, there lived twelve brothers. Eleven were strong and fit to fight, but the last brother was not strong and he was not fit for doing many things. So, his brothers never liked him. They would fight with him and scold him. Sometimes, they did not give him food.

One night, all of them went to hunt for wild game in the deep forest. The little brother stayed by himself in the house. Theirs was [not] a real house. They would just sleep in a cave.

A full moon was lit and a strong wind arose. The mountains exploded and the cave door shut. So, it was completely dark inside.

The young boy sat and sat. He was very lucky that the cave door reopened. Very slowly, he took his belonging and he went outside of their fake house. Then he slept outside.

Later, his big brothers returned to the house with wild game and food to cook and eat. The little brother sped over and told his brothers what had happened at the cave. They told him to shut up and they cursed him. They said, "If you want to, you can sleep outside in the cold wind."

However, the young brother was persistent and told the brothers what had happened to shut the cave entrance. He told them not to go inside to sleep.

They ignored him. They took the game and food inside their home in the cave. They cooked, gorged themselves and slept. All of the brothers were very happy except the little brother who was afraid and who did not want to go inside the cave. So, he alone slept outside.

Late at night, when they were all dead asleep, a deafening noise arose from the mountain. Clouds and the mountain thundered. All of the brothers inside the cave were surprised and they tried to run outside. However, the big stone door of the cave shut and all of the brothers were locked inside.

The little brother who was sleeping outside ran to the door and shouted, "I told you so. You should have listened to me and slept outside, but all of you ignored me. You're strong, so come outside now."

He just stood and watched because there was nothing he could do to save the lives of his eleven brothers. All of the eleven brothers died inside the cave.

Now, if you go to this part of Mount Ilu in the **Tari** area of **Southern Highlands** Province, you will see this big cave [**Huli** People].

Buddy Boli
Igiri
Hagen
Western Highlands Province

D1552. Mountains or rocks open and close; D2149.1. Thunderbolt magically produced; F460. Mountain-spirits; F490+. Masalai; J652. Inattention to warnings; P251.5.3. Hostile brothers; P251.6.7. Twelve brothers; S110. Murders

[The ancestor story in *Wantok* #1221 is the same as that in #1209.]

A Girl Tricked a Ghost Woman and Fled

(Wantok 1222, November 27, 1997, page 17)

Long, long ago, there lived a woman and her daughter. One night, the girl's mother asked her if she wanted to go around together and hunt frogs. The girl agreed and they prepared their things to carry to the river.

The mother said that she would stay, so she asked her daughter if she could go ask her maternal aunt to go instead. The girl quickly went to talk to her maternal aunt. However that night, a ghost woman was listening. She changed her face to be that of the maternal aunt and she met the girl along the trail. When the woman told her that her mother wanted them to go frog hunting in the river, the ghost woman agreed. She pretended to go back to the house and prepare things. She returned and met the girl and her mother. They prepared bamboos to light torches and net bags to fill with frogs. Then the two of them began to walk away to the big river to hunt for frogs.

They arrived at the river and the girl told the fake woman that they should split up and hunt for frogs. She told her fake maternal aunt to go to the other side of the river and she would walk on the opposite side. They could follow the river upstream and catch frogs. However, the ghost aunt insisted that they must work together. Because she insisted, the girl agreed with her and they began to follow the river upstream to catch frogs.

When the girl grabbed frogs, she would put them in the net bag, but the ghost woman did not do this. When she grabbed frogs, she would eat their legs and throw their heads down on the ground. She did this as they continued upriver.

Then the girl asked the ghost woman how many frogs she had taken. The ghost told her that she had not taken any frogs. However, the girl had spied upon her and seen that she had eaten two frogs. So, she thought that the woman was not her real aunt. She must be a ghost woman.

The ghost woman said that they should stop and prepare a place to sleep. Then at dawn, they would return to the village. So, they went to a corner of the river. They prepared to sleep and they made a fire. When things were ready, the fake woman told the girl that she would go to drink some water first. Then she took off. However, the girl had an idea. She followed her and spied upon her. She saw her go and swallow rocks. This made her strong so that she could fight with the girl, and then kill and eat her.

The girl ran back to their camp after she saw this. She took her net bag, and then she performed a magic song and dance. A big lizard arose. She put the lizard aside and told it, "If a woman comes back and asks for me, tell her that you don't know anything." The girl performed a magic song and dance again, and then she followed the river upstream. She found a very tall *limbum* palm tree. She climbed it and sat on the crown of the tree.

Later, the ghost woman returned and searched for the girl. She did not find her so she was angry and she shouted

around the place. She said, "Hey! I didn't want to eat her quickly on the river. Why did I waste time?" She spoke angrily and she saw the green lizard. She asked the lizard, "Did you see a girl or not?" The lizard said, "No. She followed you down to the river."

The ghost woman was even angrier. She drank water from the big river to taste whether the water was delicious, to see if the girl had gone upstream. She drank the water, but the water was not tasty, so she turned around and told the lizard, "I know that you lied to me." She grabbed the green lizard and swallowed it down into her belly, devouring it completely. Then the ghost followed the river upstream.

When she arrived at the *limbum* tree, she rubbed her tongue on the *limbum* and it was tasty. So, she laughed and was elated. She looked up and saw the girl sitting up there. She was happy and jumped around, trying to go up. However, the *limbum* was too slick, so she slid and came down again.

The ghost woman shouted for all of the ghosts of the forest to come. They sat on top of each other, going very high. At the top of them was a huge man who approached the girl. However, the girl saw this and defecated, and then threw the feces on the old ghost's head. The ghost man held the feces and he fell down. When all of the ghosts smelled this, they said, "Oh my, our meat is falling down." They all went like ants on the ghost father's body and ate him. It was nearly dawn, so all of the ghosts turned into lizards and frogs. They jumped around and slept by the rivers and trees. Then the girl slowly descended and ran to the village.

When she arrived in the village, the mother asked her why she had wasted time and arrived in the morning. The girl told her the story that the woman was not her aunt. She was a ghost woman and she had nearly killed and eaten her, but she was strong and she returned.

Bonny Yalei
Kupuom Village
[**Kupoam** Village, **Olo** People]
Lumi
West Sepik Province

B211.6.2K. Speaking lizard; B491.2. Helpful lizard; D931. Magic rock (stone); D1335. Object gives magic strength; D1793. Magic results from eating or drinking; D1781. Magic results from singing; D1781+. Magic results from dancing; D2074.1. Animals magically called; E380. Ghost summoned; E422.3.2. Revenant as a very large man (giant); E423.4. Revenant as frog; E423.5+. Revenant as lizard; E425.2. Revenant as man; E425.1. Revenant as woman; E541. Revenants eat; E587.3. Ghosts walk from curfew to cockcrow; G11.10. Cannibalistic spirits; G61. Relative's flesh eaten unwittingly; G100. Giant ogre; H46.1+. Revenant recognized when it devours raw flesh; H46.1+. Revenant recognized when it devours rocks; K1930. Treacherous impostors; N338. Death as result of mistaken identity: wrong person killed; P232. Mother and daughter; P294. Aunt; P298. Niece; Q263. Lying (perjury) punished; Q429.1. Punishment: culprit eaten by cannibals; R220. Flights; R311. Tree refuge; W157. Dishonesty; X716H+. Feces as gift

A Bird Took Care of a
Poor Girl until She Grew

(Wantok 1223, December 4, 1997, page 1[5])

Long, long ago, there was a village called Was Kambeep [Kambirip in the Upper Karinge side of the Mendi area [**Mendi** People, **Southern Highlands** Province]. There lived three young women. Their parents had died and they lived by themselves. Two were grown women but one was still little. She received her support and strength from her two big sisters. They lived there and worked in gardens, planting food and taking care of two big pigs with big tusks.

One time, the two big sisters made a plan and decided that they wanted to runaway to another place on the other side of the Mendi River, where they would find men to marry. So, they concealed their plan. They killed the two big pigs and wanted to cook them. They took a long bamboo tube and gave it to the little sister. They asked her to go fill it with water, but the place for fetching water was very far away. Afterwards, the little sister left.

When the little sister departed, the big sisters quickly made a big earth oven and cooked the two pigs. They gorged themselves and they left some for their little sister. They went and adorned themselves very nicely. Then they quickly took off to find their boyfriends.

While the little sister was fetching water from the deep forest, a bird came and cried above her, "*Nongo, tipi duli dli*." When she heard this, she knew that her big sisters were no longer in the village. She cried and ran back. She shouted and cried as she went towards their house. She saw that the two sisters were gone, so she cried and tied her "grass" skirt. Then she took off behind them. She arrived at the other side of the Mendi River where she saw the sisters standing and telling stories with their [boy]friends.

The little sister watched and jumped in the river. She almost crossed the river to the other side, but the current was strong and it carried her away just like a big leaf. The water carried her away and threw her on a stone that was in the middle of the river. She was out of breath and she vomited water.

Before long, a big eagle was flying in the sky. It came and saw her. It cast its talons downwards and snatched her, carrying her away. The bird left her in a cave on a big mountain called Mount Mila. The bird went around, searching for and gathering food, which it gave to her.

The bird took care of her for a while, and then she became a big and beautiful woman. One time, there was a big festival and party in a village. So, the eagle told her to dress and go to the party. She dressed very stylishly and departed. When everyone saw her coming, oh my, their eyes were glued to her. She was exceptionally stylish.

She walked and went to watch from the side. Oh my, her two big sisters were also standing on the side and holding their children as they stared. However, the two sisters recognized her. They grabbed her and cried terribly. After that, she lived with them. She married in the village and they lived happily together.

Samson Ariyako
Humbra Village
Mendi
Southern Highlands Province

B143.1. Bird gives warning; B211.3.11K. Speaking eagle; B535.0.7+. Eagle as nurse for child; B552. Man carried by bird; P210. Husband and wife; P230. Parents and children; P252.2. Three sisters; P294. Aunt; R100. Rescues; R213. Escape from home; R260. Pursuits; S140. Cruel abandonments and exposures; T100. Marriage

[The ancestor story in *Wantok* #1224 is the same as that in #1214.]
[The ancestor story in *Wantok* #1225 is the same as that in #1215.]

A Man Had a Snake Family

(Wantok 1226, December 25, 1997, page 14)

One time, there lived a man from the **Pangia** area. He married in a place that was called the last **Wiru** [People, **Southern Highlands** Province]. However, the man's sister married very far away from their village.

One time, he wanted to go see his sister. He prepared food and things to carry in his hands. He walked and walked until he arrived at the village where his sister had married. He asked the people there and they showed him where her house was located.

The leader arrived at his sister's house. He knocked on the house door and he went inside. His sister was sitting inside the house, but near her sister were many small children and some huge snakes, which filled the house. His sister carried [or gave birth to] two young snakes on her legs as she was sitting there.

When he saw this, his eyes popped open. He wanted to ask her about this, but she already knew and she told him, "These are my children." When the snakes heard this, they began to make noises and they began to call their uncle.

The man sat in the house and they prepared food to eat. In the afternoon, the father snake came. He had come from far away. He was a gigantic snake and he carried a big wild pig to the house. When he arrived at the house and met his brother-in-law, he changed his body and turned into a man. Then they told stories and made a huge feast in the afternoon.

In the morning, the brother-in-law wanted to return to his village. So, he carried two of his sister's young snake children in a basket and hid them. He carried them back to his village.

When he arrived in his village, he went directly to his garden and he hid the two snakes there. At the house, he told his wife that she could not go cutting in the garden or moving it to the side. As you know, this was because he had hidden the two snakes there.

Whenever his wife went to the garden, she never cut the forest or moved the garden around. Her husband had forbidden her to do so.

However one time, his wife very much wanted to know what it was that was in the garden that had been forbidden to her. She went to the garden without telling her husband. She pretended to work in the garden near where her husband had forbidden her to go. When she arrived there, she saw that the grass in the area was completely dead. She thought that wild game and camped there. So, she went inside and looked directly at the two big pythons. When the two snakes saw her, they immediately became afraid and they jumped into the forest, fleeing for good. When they had gone far away, they shouted back, "Send a message to our uncle that we've gone away now." They shouted like that and they left completely for the deep forest.

Chris Mari

Kimbe

West New Britain Province

B211.6.1. Speaking snake (serpent); B631.9. Human offspring of marriage of person and snake; B633. Human and animal offspring from marriage to animal; B604.1. Marriage to snake; B875.1. Giant serpent; D191M. Transformation: man to serpent (snake); P210. Husband and wife; P230. Parents and children; P253. Sister and brother; P263. Brother-in-law; P293. Uncle; P294. Aunt; R10.3. Children abducted; R220. Flights; T100. Marriage; W31. Obedience; W126. Disobedience

[The ancestor story in *Wantok* #1227 is the same as that in #1210.]

Author Index

This is an index of author names as published in *Wantok* newspaper. Numbers refer to the issue number of *Wantok* newspaper. To find the page number, see the table of contents.

L

M

X

Y

Z

Village Index

This is an index of village names as published in *Wantok* newspaper. Villages appear in this index if they are mentioned in a folktale. If no village is mentioned in the folktale, then the village in the author's address is indexed. Urban areas are not indexed unless the folktale is clearly situated there. Numbers refer to the issue number of *Wantok* newspaper. To find the page number, see the table of contents.

C

D

E

F

G

L

M

N

Y

Z

Zumanggurun. 844
Zumangorum. *See* Zumanggurun

Language Index

Rather than index culture group, which is not well standardized in Papua New Guinea, the name of the local language used in the village from which each story originates is indexed. The names for the language index are primarily based on Dutton (1973), Laycock (1973), Wurm (1975), Wurm (1976), Wurm and Hattori (1983), and Z'graggen (1975). Generally, only distinct languages are indexed, not dialects. In some cases, there is ambiguity or linguistic gradation as to what constitutes a distinct language. In these cases, I have chosen to be more specific. The count of languages in this index is 273; the actual count of languages in the book may be slightly lower because of uncertainty of village location for some stories. This represents 39% of Papua New Guinea's total language count (about 700, according to Wurm, 1985).

This is an index of language names as published in *Wantok* newspaper. Numbers refer to the issue number of *Wantok* newspaper. To find the page number, see the table of contents.

Province Index

This is an index of provinces as published in *Wantok* newspaper. Numbers refer to the issue number of *Wantok* newspaper. To find the page number, see the table of contents.

Index of Flora and Fauna

This index roughly follows a biological system. Entries for the larger groups of biota are in **bold**. Fauna are grouped by: mammals, amphibians, birds, reptiles, crustaceans, mollusks (including octopus, and mollusk products such as lime and *ring*), and insects. Miscellaneous fauna (e.g., centipedes and spiders) are listed individually. Within mammals, marsupials are grouped together.

Flora are grouped into three categories: trees, grasses (including bamboo, corn, rice, and sugarcane) gourds (including cucumber, melon and pumpkin), and vines. "Tree" and "vine" are physical forms, rather than a biologically related groups of plants, but trees and vines are each grouped together here for convenience. All palm trees are grouped within "tree" even though some occur as vines (e.g., rattan). "Fig" is always listed under "tree", even though it can occur either as a tree or a vine. Miscellaneous flora are listed separately (e.g., shrubs). Banana is an herbaceous plant, not a tree, and so it is listed separately. "Leafy green" (*kumu*) is listed separately since this can be from many unrelated types of plants.

Tok Pisin words are in *italics*. Words in local languages are in *underlined italics*. For definitions of all Tok Pisin words and some English words, see the glossary.

Numbers in this index refer to the issue number of *Wantok* newspaper. To find the page number, see the table of contents.

C

N

O

P

R

S

T

Motif Index

This index is based primarily on Thompson's *Motif-Index of Folk-Literature* (1993), with supplemental motifs from Kirtley (1955, 1971) and Hoffmann (1973). Motif classifications that end in "K" or "K+" refer to Kirtley (1955). Those that end in "K2" or "K2+" refer to Kirtley (1971). Those that end in "H" or "H+" refer to Hoffmann (1973). All others refer to Thompson (1993). Those classifications that end in "+" are new motifs, which are categorized to the closest classification in Thompson (1993), Kirtley (1955, 1971) or Hoffmann (1973).

In PNG, animals are often mono-gendered (e.g., cassowaries, marsupials). By implication, folk tales with transformations between animals and humans, may imply such a gender. Consequently, motif classifications have been refined hereto indicate gender (and age): man (M), woman (W), child (C), boy (B), girl (G) for the transformation motifs (D10-D499). When a story does not specify gender and it is not a child, or when transformation involves both genders, the classification is not specified.

Numbers in this index refer to the issue number of *Wantok* newspaper. To find the page number, see the table of contents.

A: Mythological Motifs

A0-A99. Creator

A15.1. Female creator. 330

A100-A499. Gods

A132.13. Fish-god. 622
A162.1.0.1. Recurrent battle (everlasting fight). 458b, 460
A200. God of the upper world. 459
A284+. Cloud-man falls from sky, people aid his return. 421
A287. Rain-god. 525
A310+. Ancestral spirit who lives in fiery underworld. 397
A493.1. Goddess of fire. 449, 450
A493. God of fire. 449

A500-A599. Demigods and culture heroes

A500+. Heroine dies while slaying devastating bird. 1218
A511.1.9+. Culture hero born from fruit. 400
A515.1. Culture heroes brothers. 630, 644, 721, 756, 845, 846, 852
A515.1.1.Twin culture heroes. 248, 271, 479, 520, 629, 955, 1017, 1025, 1114
A515.1.1+. Quintuplet culture heroes. 680
A522.3+. Flying fox as culture hero. 269
A523. Giant as culture hero. 527
A527.4. Culture hero as poet (musician). 825, 1203
A530. Culture hero establishes law and order. 169
A536. Demigods fight as allies of mortals. 213

A600-A699. Cosmogony and cosmology

A605.1. Primeval darkness. 366
A705.1. Origin of clouds. 916
A711. Sun as man who left earth. 54, 366, 748, 934
A711.2. Sun as a cannibal. 168
A715.3. Moon as ogre. 431
A720+. Moon travels across the sky using magical ropes. 905
A720+. Sun in form of man. 66
A720+. Sun travels across the sky using magical ropes. 905
A721.6K. Hero kills the sun. 66
A722.5.1+. Sun bathes. 66
A726. Daily course of sun across sky. 905
A726+. Why sun shines at particular point first. 748
A736.3. Sun and moon as brothers. 905
A741+. Moon thrown into sky by person. 53
A741+. Moon from object brought by birds into sky. 431
A747. Person transformed to moon. 254
A750+. Moon beneath the earth. 397
A750+. Moon escapes to sky from captivity in pot. 646
A750+. Moon escapes to sky when man does not let it drink blood of pig that he killed using moon's light. 326
A751.8. Woman in the moon. 265-7
A751.11. Other marks on the moon. 431
A753.1.2. Moon (man) cohabits with woman. 905
A753.2. Moon has house. 905
A753. Moon as a person. 431
A754. Moon kept in box. 326, 646, 925
A754.1. Moon buried in pit. 326
A755.9K+. Causes of moon's phases: hidden by woman's loincloth. 53

A755+. Moon's phases caused by being hit. 326
A758. Theft of moon. 326, 53
A759.5. Formerly moon was larger. 431
A759+. Moon comes to earth. 431
A759+. Moon killed by people. 431
A762.2 Mortal marries star-girl. 49
A767. Stars sing together. 265-7
A769. Origin of stars' shining. 614
A770. Origin of particular stars. 404, 56
A771.1. Origin of the Southern Cross. 214
A781.1. Origin of morning star. 56

A900-A999. Topographical features of the earth

A901. Topographical features caused by experiences of primitive hero (demigod, deity). 209
A920.1.0.1. Origin of particular lake. 78, 154, 205, 210, 217, 226, 291a, 297, 335, 338, 339, 539, 541, 557, 596, 650, 713, 727, 743, 746, 769, 798, 801, 803, 817, 859, 874, 950, 988, 992, 1103, 1174, 1177, 1186, 1199, 1210
A920. Origin of the seas. 268, 1012
A920.1+. Origin of swampy area. 237
A924+. Ocean from corpse. 444
A924.2. Origin of sea from rotting snakes. 1206
A930. Origin of streams. 914, 953
A930.1.1. Snake as creator of rivers and lakes. 1191
A933+. River from urine of deity/spirit. 418
A934.4+. Origin of river: magic stick. 262
A934.9. Stream unexpectedly bursts from side of mountain. 216
A934.11. River from transformation. 252, 297, 368, 497, 783, 811, 849, 865, 881, 1191
A935.1K+. Origin of particular current. 712

A1000-A1099. World calamities

A1100-A1199. Establishment of natural order

A1200-1699. Creation and ordering of human life

A1700-A2199. Creation of animal life

A2200-A2599. Animal characteristics

A2494.16+. Enmity between lizard and ant. 309, 661

A2494.16+. Enmity between snake and chicken. 791

A2494.16+. Enmity between snake and marsupial. 280

A2494.16.1. Enmity between frog and snake. 1061

A2494.16.1+. Enmity between frog and bat. 585

A2494.16.5. Enmity between crab and spider. 869

A2494.16.5+. Enmity between crab and kangaroo. 962

A2500+. Why flying foxes are nocturnal. 1014

A2500+. Why marsupials are nocturnal. 94

A2500+. Why rats are nocturnal. 94

A2513.3. How pig was domesticated. 404

A2520+. Why crocodile hides from people. 660

A2533.6+. Why lizard lives in leaf litter. 309

A2582+. Why certain marsupials are plentiful. 947

A2582+. Why wild game is plentiful at particular place. 301, 985

A2584+. Why there are few fish at particular pond. 892

A2584.1+. How mosquito arrived on certain island. 490

A2584+. Why there are no herons at particular pond. 892

A2585+. Enmity between marsupial and man. 94

A2585+. Enmity between rat and man. 94

A2585+. Enmity between people and swine. 938

A2600-A2699. Origin of trees and plants

A2611.3.1K. Coconut tree from head of human. 57, 62, 196, 406, 711

A2611.3.1K+. _Pimates_ tree from head of human. 656

A2611.3+. Origin of coconut: sun's head. 168

A2680. Origin of other plant forms. 474

A2681+. Origin of sago. 209, 508b, 1123

A2681.5.1. Origin of coconut tree. 474, 884

A2681.13K. Origin of Tahitian chestnuts. 1209

A2681.15K2. Origin of pandanus tree. 109, 651, 829

A2683. Origin of grass. 516

A2684.4K. Origin of sugar cane. 58, 468, 584, 1201

A2685.1.1. Origin of maize. 332

A2686.1. Origin of mushroom. 76

A2686.4.1. Origin of sweet potato. 332, 474

A2686.4.1+. Origin of cassava. 567

A2686.4.2. Origin of taro. 332, 508b, 567, 1043, 1046

A2686.4.2+. Origin of wild taro. 978

A2686.4.3. Origin of yams. 86, 191, 263, 332, 461, 502, 508b, 622, 905, 925, 1029, 1200

A2686.6. Origin of beans. 332

A2686.6+. Origin of winged bean. 253

A2687.2. Origin of melons. 332

A2687.2+. Cucumber from head of ogre. 215

A2687.2+. Origin of cucumber. 142, 332

A2687.5. Origin of banana. 332, 474, 567, 584, 1046

A2687.5+. Distribution of kind of banana. 624

A2691+. Lime (calcium oxide) initially hidden by women. 290

A2691.2. Origin of tobacco. 320

A2700-A2799. Origin of plant characteristics

A2730+. Why coconuts do not grow well in one area. 396

A2730+. Why taro grows well in one place. 1058

A2760+. Why certain tree has red leaves. 720

A2770+. Why bamboo is plentiful. 613

A2771.4+. Why banana bears large fruits. 1054

A2778+. Why coconuts grow in hot places. 168

A2791+. Why sago pith turns red when rinsed. 356

A2793+. Why garden food is abundant in certain place. 891

A2794.2+. Why bananas are plentiful in certain place. 957

A2800-A2899. Miscellaneous explanations

A2800+. Origin of canoes. 878

A2800+. Origin of enmity between spirits and humans. 896

A2800+. Origin of marks on particular trees. 78

A2800+. Why certain plants grow in certain place. 287

A2800+. Why it is now safe to travel in the forest unmolested by ghosts. 92

A2824. Origin of drum. 766, 376

A2850+. Why there are more males than females: fathers no longer kill sons. 445-6

A2850+. Why younger brothers are stubborn. 510

A2850+. Why dogs are not scolded at particular place. 995

A2872+. Why reefs are sharp. 291b

B: Animals

B0-B99. Mythical animals

B2+. Marsupial totem. 761

B11.11+. Fight with giant snake. 337, 436, 856, 1158

B15.1.1+. Headless snake. 210

B15.1.2.1+. Two-headed lizard. 219

B15.1.2.1+. Two-headed pig. 699

B15.1.2.1.1. Two-headed serpent. 504

B15.1.2.2.2. Three-headed serpent. 58

B15.1.2.2.2+. Four-headed serpent: snake, dog, pig and man. 756

B16.1.4. Devastating swine. 271

B16.1.4.1. Giant devastating boar. 466, 680, 995, 1056

B16.3. Devastating birds. 257-8, 378, 479, 1218

B16.3+. Devastating bird killed. 503, 1159

B16.3+. Devastating eagle killed. 630

B16.4.2K. Man-eating eel. 440

B16.5.1. Giant devastating serpent. 58, 269, 504, 756, 1158

B16.5.2. Devastating crocodile. 897

B16.5.3. Devastating shell-fish. 295, 466

B16.5.3+. Devastating octopus. 466

B16.6. Devastating insects. 545

B17.2.1.2. Hostile eel attacks hero. 373

B17.2.3+. Hostile bird. 779

B19.4.2+. Glowing lizard. 784

B20+. Man-flying fox. 530

B20+. Marsupial-faced woman. 514

B29+. Crocodile-person. 797

B29.1+. Body of snake, face and arms of human. 325

B29.2.1. Serpent with human head. 93, 165, 325, 901, 1034, 1187

B29.3. Man-hog. 563

B29.3+. Man-hog makes sound of drum when touched. 376

B31.4+. Giant flying fox. 472

B31.6. Other giant birds. 235, 311, 359, 530, 551, 737, 1017, 1025, 1218

B31.6+. Giant pigeon. 538, 1044, 1058

B33.0.2K. Man-eating eagle (osprey). 378

B33.1. Other devastating birds. 1025

B33. Man-eating birds. 257-8, 479, 503, 630, 1017, 1159

B40+. Bird-flying fox. 530

B40+. Flying marsupial. 647

B50. Bird-men. 530

B81.2. Mermaid marries man. 700

B81.13.11.1. Mermaid caught by fishermen. 458a

B81.13.4+. Mermaid gives mortals wealth. 458a

B90+. Frog-faced bandicoot. 645

B90+. Woman with crocodile skin. 979

B91.4. Sky-traveling snake. 269, 679

B91.5. Sea-serpent. 554

B91.6. Serpent causes flood. 210, 226, 575

B91+. Man-eating snake destroys houses. 190

B91+. Serpent with dog's head. 529

B94.1+. Crab-person. 457

B98. Frog-skinned person. 1028

B100-B199. Magic animals

B130+. Frog gives warning. 985
B143.1. Bird gives warning. 730, 815, 839, 852, 1207, 1223
B154. Animal as soothsayer. 740
B170+. Flight on bee. 504
B170+. Flight on butterfly. 709
B171. Magic chicken (hen, cock). 859
B172. Magic bird. 518
B176.1. Magic serpent. 696
B177.2. Magic frog. 985
B182.1. Magic dog. 205
B184.3.1. Magic boar. 649
B191.7. Serpent as magician. 1172
B191.7+. Lizard as magician. 219

B200-B299. Animals with human traits

B210.3. Formerly animals and man spoke the same language. 772
B210. Speaking animals. 1070, 1183
B211+. Speaking dugong. 318
B211.5.2K. Speaking eel. 51, 72
B211.1.4. Speaking hog. 772, 817
B211.1.7. Speaking dog. 89, 94, 105, 106, 147, 157, 174, 189, 205, 212, 330, 357, 455, 459, 462, 521b, 538, 544, 571, 587, 657, 696, 701, 714, 724, 772, 781, 787, 791, 793, 810, 847, 936, 969, 995, 1070, 1215
B211.1.8. Speaking cat. 605, 1060, 1207, 1215
B211.2.11K. Speaking bats. 585
B211.2.11K+. Speaking flying fox. 76, 269, 382, 507, 638, 763-4a, 771, 854, 1160
B211.2.12K. Speaking kangaroo. 89, 105, 313, 462, 657, 787, 936, 962
B211.2.12K+. Speaking bandicoot. 1050
B211.2.12K+. Speaking marsupial. 52, 94, 221, 228, 231, 292, 293, 314, 514, 594, 647, 659, 666, 693, 701, 724, 772, 781, 823, 969, 984, 1029, 1040, 1178, 1202
B211.2.9. Speaking rat. 80, 94, 156, 228, 307, 985, 1040, 1060, 1207
B211.2+. Speaking boar. 649, 563
B211.3. Speaking bird. 49, 88, 112, 201, 216, 271, 311, 313, 339, 345, 351, 355, 423, 443, 468, 518, 521a, 525, 551, 597, 653, 670, 682, 688, 730, 731, 737, 772, 815, 824, 839, 942, 1024, 1057, 1178, 1207, 1215
B211.3+. Speaking bird of paradise. 913, 1024
B211.3+. Speaking cockatoo. 95, 131, 279, 402, 507, 670, 745, 937
B211.3+. Speaking hornbill. 71, 684
B211.3.10K. Speaking heron. 207, 350, 892
B211.3.11K. Speaking eagle. 67, 162, 204, 211, 481, 507, 531, 791, 1168, 1183, 1215, 1223
B211.3.17K. Speaking cassowary. 71, 88, 138, 164, 191, 249, 263, 289, 295, 305, 313, 470, 515, 676, 684, 822, 847, 1024, 1184

B211.3.19K2. Speaking duck. 174
B211.3.2.1. Speaking chicken. 164, 292, 575, 676, 1184
B211.4. Speaking insects. 65, 684, 1070
B211.4+. Speaking grasshopper. 581
B211.4.1. Speaking ant. 309, 433, 661, 793
B211.4.2. Speaking bee. 504
B211.4.4K2. Speaking fly. 793, 1202
B211.4.6K. Speaking butterfly. 916
B211.5. Speaking fish. 67, 207, 292, 541, 874, 892, 942, 1184, 1209
B211.6.1. Speaking snake (serpent). 52, 58, 111, 152, 172, 183, 190, 210, 210, 269, 307, 321, 453-4, 468, 529, 554, 579, 655, 722, 740, 767, 769, 775, 791, 999, 1061, 1172, 1206, 1226
B211.6.2K. Speaking lizard. 122, 202, 219, 237, 309, 310, 660, 661, 784, 1222
B211.6.3K. Speaking eel. 1028
B211.6.3K. Speaking turtle. 207, 292, 513, 744, 745, 874, 1057
B211.6.4K. Speaking crocodile. 187, 478, 541, 797, 1215
B211.7.1. Speaking frog. 585, 772, 985, 1061
B211.7.3K2. Speaking turtle. 937
B211.8.1K. Speaking crab. 80, 207, 249, 289, 457, 485, 676, 688, 709, 962, 1184, 1198, 1215
B211.8K+. Speaking crayfish. 433, 541
B211.9K+. Speaking clam. 295
B212. Animal understands human speech. 138, 194, 198, 211, 284, 450, 498, 508a, 517, 535, 604, 671, 741, 842, 855, 876, 893, 921, 960, 997, 1020, 1122, 1159, 1202
B214.1+. Singing fish. 349
B214.1+. Singing kangaroo. 657
B214.1+. Singing marsupial. 292, 521b, 587, 835
B214.1.10. Singing snake. 655, 764b
B214.1.10+. Singing lizard. 833
B214.1.4. Singing dog. 521b, 538, 835
B214.3. Laughing animal. 1183, 1198
B214+. Singing bird. 427
B215+. Pig language. 649
B216. Knowledge of animal languages. 649
B221+. Dog society. 203, 544
B221+. Kingdom of swine. 549
B222+. Land of cassowaries. 470, 970
B224. Kingdom of insects. 545
B225+. Kingdom of crocodiles. 797
B225.1. Kingdom of serpents. 321
B225.1.1+. Snake kingdom underwater. 655
B226+. Kingdom of turtles. 513
B240. King of animals. 52
B240+. Eagle as king of animals. 791, 1183
B240.9. Dog as king of animals. 1070
B240.15. Crocodile as king of animals. 541
B240.15+. Crocodile as king of river animals. 652
B241.2+. King of marsupials. 781, 823, 835, 969, 998

B241.2.7. King of dogs. 544, 714, 781, 969, 995, 998
B242+. Serpent as king of birds. 579
B242.1+. Bird of paradise as king of birds. 944
B242.1+. Cassowary as king of birds. 313, 937, 1024
B242.1+. Cockatoo as king of birds. 670
B242.1.1. Eagle king of birds. 652
B242.2+. Leader of cassowaries. 470
B243.2.2. King of eels. 72
B243.2.2+. Queen of eels. 373
B243+. King of crabs. 892
B243+. Crocodile as king of sea creatures. 937
B244.1. King of serpents (snakes). 321
B246. King of insects. 545
B263. War between other groups of animals. 1178, 1215
B263+. War between ants and lizards. 661
B263+. War between dogs and marsupials. 521b, 835, 969, 998
B263.4+. War between cockatoos and turtles. 745
B263.5. War between groups of birds. 731
B266. Animals fight. 544
B290+. Animal's dream. 80
B290+. Bird of paradise removes skirt or skin to bathe. 74
B290+. Cassowary removes skirt or skin to bathe. 110, 304, 1035, 1182
B290+. Dog as tattler/gossip. 212
B290+. Fish that chews betel nut. 349
B290+. Fish that smokes. 349
B290+. Flying fox kills snake with axe. 269
B290+. Serpents' hospital. 321
B291.1. Bird as messenger. 216
B293+. Dance of dogs. 521b, 835
B293+. Dance of marsupials. 521b, 835
B293.5+. Dance of lizards. 833
B293.5+. Dance of snakes. 655
B293.6K. Dance of birds. 835
B293.7K2. Dancing fish. 349
B295.2.1K. Animals make voyage in canoe. 88, 164, 249, 289, 670, 676, 1060, 1184, 1207
B295.2K. Animals build canoe. 88, 164, 1060, 1207
B296.2K. Animal (who is land-dweller) crosses water on back of another animal. 88, 164, 249, 289, 676, 1184
B296. Animals go a-journeying. 684
B298+. Dogs play sports. 203
B299.1+. Animal takes revenge for animal friend. 207
B299.7. Festival of animals. 112
B299.7.1K. Birds hold a feast. 731
B299.9+. Dove/pigeon processes sago. 95
B299.12K. Animals go hunting. 208, 309
B299.14K. Animals build house. 112, 684, 731

B646.1. Marriage to person in snake form. 325, 775

B650+. Marriage to dugong in human form. 318

B650+. Marriage to marsupial in human form. 514

B650+. Marriage to pig in human form. 994

B650+. Marriage to flying fox in human form. 631, 763-4a

B652. Marriage to bird in human form. 74, 298, 392, 473, 850

B652+. Marriage to cassowary in human form. 110, 304, 470

B652.2+. Man marries heron in human form. 350

B654. Marriage to fish in human form. 300, 349, 917

B654.1K. Marriage to eel in human form. 750-1

B655+. Marriage to frog in human form. 333

B655+. Marriage to turtle in human form. 513

B656.1. Marriage to python in human form. 494, 516, 769, 855

B656.2. Marriage to serpent in human form. 199, 328, 453-4, 468, 641, 722, 767, 952, 980, 997

B656.3K+. Marriage to crocodile in human form. 478

B700-B799. Fanciful traits of animals

B720+. Eel with two tails. 456b

B720+. Luminous snake. 328

B750+. Cassowary lives in sea. 295

B750+. Eel rejoins itself. 720

B754.0.1. Unusual sexual union of animals. 1070

B754.6.1. Unusual impregnation of animal. 183, 370, 740

B765+. Lizard drinks milk from woman's breasts. 353

B765+. Snake eats leaves. 240

B765+. Snake uses net bag. 240

B765.5+. Snake kills by entering person's ulcer. 227

B765.7.2. Snake grows back together after it has been severed. 136, 190, 321, 328

B765.7.3K. Snake is immortal. 307

B765.20. Snake kills man who has killed its prey. 316

B765.23. Snake with legs. 901

B770+. Dog removes tail. 203

B770+. Turtle climbs tree. 75a

B770+. Turtle shoots out one of moon's eyes. 75a

B784+. Pig lives in tree. 238

B800-B899. Miscellaneous animal motifs

B800+. Marriage of spirit to snake. 388

B857+. Dog avenges master by helping kill unfaithful dog. 69

B871.1.2. Giant boar. 396, 494, 534, 563, 639, 649, 657, 680, 681, 763-4a, 793, 819, 911, 962, 994, 1011, 1056

B871.1.2.1. Giant hog. 138, 376, 505, 531, 633, 699, 759, 810, 876, 914, 960, 1174, 1177

B871.1.7. Giant dog (hound). 634

B871.2+. Giant bandicoot. 645, 833

B871.2+. Giant marsupial. 293, 502, 594, 693, 739, 816, 823, 947, 988, 1058, 1121, 1219

B871. Giant beasts. 367

B872. Giant bird. 343

B872+. Giant cassowary. 728, 729, 1058

B872.1. Giant eagle. 257-8, 378, 479, 630

B872.8K. Giant rooster. 575, 853

B873. Giant insects. 65

B873+. Giant bee. 504

B873+. Giant centipede. 573

B874+. Giant fish, child of woman. 339

B874.2. Giant eel. 51, 373, 440, 550, 720, 1028

B874.6. Giant clam. 105, 165, 295, 533, 936, 1016

B874. Giant fish. 1184, 642, 426, 352, 300, 287

B875.1. Giant serpent. 208, 239, 240, 297, 316, 321, 328, 337, 389, 436, 437, 494, 504, 516, 529, 557, 573, 575, 579, 583, 592, 643, 687, 740, 756, 762, 767, 769, 775, 784, 807, 855, 856, 857, 886, 948, 952, 993, 1011, 1040, 1067, 1158, 1187, 1191, 1226

B875.2. Giant crocodile. 496, 535, 541

B875.3. Giant turtle. 513

B875.5K2. Giant lizard. 237

B876.1. Giant frog. 1208

B876.2.1. Giant crab. 676

C: Tabu

C0-C99. Tabu connected with supernatural beings

C92.1.6+. Tabu: killing bird of paradise. 224, 944

C100-C199. Sex tabu

C114. Tabu: incest. 951

C141. Tabu: going forth during menses. 481, 564, 666, 673, 800, 855, 1115

C172+. Brother-in-law tabu. 1034

C181. Tabu confined to women. 100, 137, 814, 1041

C181+. Taboo against women fishing at night. 145

C181+. Women may not enter men's house. 481

C181.2+. Tabu: man not to sleep in same house as women or children prior to hunting. 757

C181.2+. Tabu: women hunting in the forest. 235

C182. Tabu confined to men. 86

C182. Uninitiated men may not enter men's house. 481

C200-C299. Eating and drinking tabu

C200+. Cooking taboos. 169

C200+. Tabu: cutting wrong animals with special knife. 761

C200+. Tabu: eating during menstruation. 800

C221.1.1.5. Tabu: eating pork. 563

C221.1.2. Tabu: eating bird. 323

C221.1.3.2. Tabu: eating eel. 550

C221.1+. Tabu: eating flying fox. 284, 530

C221.1+. Tabu: eating snake's skin. 529

C221.1+. Tabu for children: eating flesh of bandicoot. 744

C224+. Tabu concerning taro. 137

C226. Tabu: eating certain plant. 347

C241+. Tabu: eating food chewed by spirit. 1067

C246+. Tabu: husband eating in front of newlywed wife. 924

C260. Tabu: drinking at certain place. 607

C265K2. Tabu: to drink from a certain brook. 323

C280+. Tabu: coveting food given by wife to brother-in-law. 577

C300-C399. Looking tabu

C300+. Looking at yams. 86

C300. Looking tabu. 172

C310+. Tabu: looking at sacred flute. 814

C311.1.8. Tabu: looking at deity. 539, 642

C312. Tabu: man looking at woman. 841

C312+. Tabu: brother looking at sister. 988

C313. Tabu: woman looking at man. 916

C313+. Tabu: sister looking at brother. 988

C400-C499. Speaking tabu

C400. Speaking tabu. 287, 459, 541, 769

C400+. Husband speaking in front of newlywed wife. 924

C401+. Tabu: making decision during certain time. 1074

C401+. Tabu: speaking of plans at night. 598

C430+. Tabu: uttering name of mountain. 506

C435.2.1+. Tabu: uttering name of father-in-law. 928

C435+. Tabu: uttering parent's name. 784

D127.5M. Transformation: man to dolphin. 73

D136+M. Transformation: man to sow. 842

D136B. Transformation: boy to swine. 623

D136M. Transformation: man to swine. 103,
376, 519, 842

D141M. Transformation: man to dog. 269, 810

D141W. Transformation: woman to dog. 821

D142B. Transformation: boy to cat. 463

D150B. Transformation: boy to bird. 104, 238,
283, 359, 459, 497, 735, 761, 777, 838,
1000, 1186

D150G. Transformation: girl to bird. 359, 459

D150M. Transformation: man to bird. 241,
297, 311, 439, 518, 574, 626, 635, 681, 817,
897, 955, 973, 1000, 1143

D150W. Transformation: woman to bird. 104,
439, 443, 750-1, 808, 844, 986, 988, 1143

D150.0.1K. Transformation: ogre to bird. 443

D150.0.1K+. Transformation: spirit to bird.
522

D150+.W. Transformation: woman to bird of
paradise. 669

D150+. Transformation: person to bird of
paradise. 1110

D150+. Transformation: spirit to cockatoo. 402

D150+B. Transformation: boy to bird of
paradise. 244, 294, 612, 827

D150+B. Transformation: boy to cockatoo.
256, 83, 77

D150+C. Transformation: child to cockatoo.
279

D150+M. Transformation: man to bird of
paradise. 224, 639, 808, 873

D150+M. Transformation: man to cockatoo.
1072, 639, 508a

D150+W. Transformation: woman to bird of
paradise. 74, 405, 523, 673, 703, 828, 850,
913, 1179

D150+W. Transformation: woman to cockatoo.
77, 451, 838, 973

D152.2M. Transformation: man to eagle. 565,
1168

D154.2+W. Transformation: woman to
Victoria crowned pigeon. 405, 669

D154.4M. Transformation: man to gull. 632

D157B. Transformation: boy to parrot. 314

D157M. Transformation: man to parrot. 733

D162+W. Transformation: woman to heron.
350

D169.4M. Transformation: man to cassowary.
763-4a

D169.4W. Transformation: woman to
cassowary. 110, 263, 304, 970, 1035

D170B. Transformation: boy to fish. 359, 632

D170M. Transformation: man to fish. 62, 574,
660, 808, 1212

D170W. Transformation: woman to fish. 137,
300, 574, 917

D170+M. Transformation: man to herring. 615

D173M. Transformation: man to eel. 72, 456b,
691, 750-1

D175W. Transformation: woman to crab. 709

D179K+. Transformation: person to marsupial.
1121

D179.6K+B. Transformation: boy to marsupial.
463

D179K+C. Transformation: child to marsupial.
419

D179K+G. Transformation: girl to marsupial.
778

D179K+M. Transformation: man to marsupial.
397, 419, 627, 752, 794, 922, 1029

D179K+W. Transformation: woman to
marsupial. 158, 419, 514, 627, 739, 761,
794, 803, 984, 1040

D179+W. Transformation: woman to trevally
fish. 735

D180M. Transformation: man to insect. 65

D183.2+M. Transformation: man to
grasshopper. 540

D183.2M. Transformation: man to cricket. 540

D185.1+B. Transformation: boy to mosquito.
260

D185.1+M. Transformation: man to mosquito.
308

D186.1G. Transformation: girl to butterfly. 442

D186.1M. Transformation: man to butterfly.
691, 709, 916

D186.1W. Transformation: woman to butterfly.
1004, 916

D191+. Transformation: spirit to serpent
(snake). 522, 402

D191B. Transformation: boy to serpent
(snake). 210, 467, 1034

D191M. Transformation: man to serpent
(snake). 1226, 1185, 1172, 997, 980, 952,
948, 857, 820, 775, 769, 722, 712, 633, 609,
590, 568, 568, 557, 554, 494, 468, 457, 325,
232, 194, 166

D191W. Transformation: woman to serpent
(snake). 1124, 1018, 773, 767, 750-1, 641,
573, 568, 477, 402, 245

D192.2W. Transformation: woman to
centipede. 573, 568

D193M. Transformation: man to tortoise
(turtle). 513

D193W. Transformation: woman to tortoise
(turtle). 935, 744, 735

D194B. Transformation: boy to crocodile. 1113

D194M. Transformation: man to crocodile.
897, 187

D194W. Transformation: woman to crocodile.
477

D195W. Transformation: woman to frog. 1208,
1163

D197+. Transformation: spirit to lizard. 522

D197B. Transformation: boy to lizard. 1113,
122

D197M. Transformation: man to lizard. 237

D197W. Transformation: woman to lizard. 195

D199.4K2W. Transformation: woman to
mermaid. 274

D200-D299. Transformation: man to object

D210+M. Transformation: man to yam. 622

D210+W. Transformation: woman to
mushroom. 76

D211.7K+G. Transformation: girl to breadfruit.
887

D211.7K+M. Transformation: man to
breadfruit. 765

D211.7K+W. Transformation: woman to
breadfruit. 750-1, 887

D211+W. Transformation: woman to
cucumber. 282

D211B. Transformation: boy to fruit. 400

D211W. Transformation: woman to fruit. 451

D212W. Transformation: woman to flower.
873

D213+B. Transformation: boy to tanget plant
(*Taetsia fructicosa*). 314

D213+M. Transformation: man to tanget plant
(*Taetsia fructicosa*). 453-4

D213+M. Transformation: man to yam. 851

D213.6+M. Transformation: man to banana
plant. 765

D213.6+W. Transformation: woman to banana
plant. 957

D213.8K+M. Transformation: man to wild taro
plant. 978

D213.8K+W. Transformation: woman to wild
taro plant. 978

D213.4B. Transformation: boy to vine. 980

D213.4W. Transformation: woman to vine.
396, 955

D213.5W. Transformation: woman to thorns.
245

D213.8KM. Transformation: man to taro plant.
765

D215.10KM. Transformation: man to pandanus
tree. 829

D215.10KW. Transformation: woman to
pandanus tree. 305

D215.10K+W. Transformation: woman to
pandanus fruit. 319

D215.11K+B. Transformation: boy to sago
tree. 352

D215.11K+G. Transformation: girl to rattan
root. 386

D215.11K+M. Transformation: man to sago.
757

D215.11K+W. Transformation: woman to
rattan. 477

D215.11K+W. Transformation: woman to
sago. 327, 918

D215+B. Transformation: boy to fig plant. 252

D215+W. Transformation: woman to fig tree.
296, 883

D215B. Transformation: boy to tree. 232, 748

D215M. Transformation: man to tree. 633, 656,
980

D215W. Transformation: woman to tree. 223,
372, 394, 473, 477, 725, 748

D216M. Transformation: man to log. 196, 272

D222+W. Transformation: woman to coconut. 1117, 665, 185

D223B. Transformation: boy to grass. 516

D230+. Transformation: ogre's corpse to calcium oxide (lime). 194

D230+M. Transformation: man to clay. 806

D230C. Transformation: child to stone. 51

D231. Transformation: man to stone. 1110

D231+. Transformation: mermaid to stone. 458a

D231+. Transformation: ogre to stone. 635, 986

D231B. Transformation: boy to stone. 257-8, 591, 888

D231M. Transformation: man to stone. 72, 279, 296, 467, 524, 593, 627, 737, 770, 812, 824, 1194

D231W. Transformation: woman to stone. 51, 113, 167, 222, 257-8, 252, 279, 340, 427, 473, 477, 516, 627, 667, 706, 738, 770, 812, 980, 990, 1000, 1012

D237. Transformation: man to coral. 1051

D237+M. Transformation: man to reef. 291b

D250+M. Transformation: man to axe. 481

D250+M. Transformation: man to statue. 911

D250+W. Transformation: woman to axe. 942, 1057

D270+B. Transformation: boy to moon. 905

D270+M. Transformation: man to ball. 447

D270+M. Transformation: man to drum. 625

D270+M. Transformation: man to tree's shadow. 195

D270+W. Transformation: person to love-charm. 172

D281.1M. Transformation: man to wind. 104

D281.3M. Transformation: man to thunder. 425

D281+M. Transformation: man to hail. 415

D281+W. Transformation: woman to rain. 415

D283W. Transformation: woman to water. 223, 477

D283.1+B. Transformation: boy to lake. 1174

D283.1+M. Transformation: man to river. 252

D283.1+. Transformation: person to lake. 297

D283.1M. Transformation: man to pool of water. 352

D283.1W. Transformation: woman to pool of water. 335

D283.3. Transformation: watersprite to flood. 712

D283+. Transformation: spirit to river. 368

D287+W. Transformation: woman to dirt. 223

D291M. Transformation: man to mountain. 297, 588, 1199

D291W. Transformation: woman to mountain. 149, 473

D293B. Transformation: boy to star. 214, 56

D293C. Transformation: child to star. 404

D293G. Transformation: girl to star. 214

D293M. Transformation: man to star. 214

D293W. Transformation: woman to star. 214

D300-D399. Transformation: animal to person

D310+. Transformation: marsupial to person. 1121

D310+B. Transformation: marsupial to boy. 463

D310+C. Transformation: marsupial to child. 419

D310+M. Transformation: flying fox to man. 622, 631, 673

D310+M. Transformation: marsupial to man. 154, 419, 627, 803, 922, 988, 1174, 1177

D310+W. Transformation: flying fox to woman. 763-4a

D310+W. Transformation: marsupial to woman. 181, 417, 419, 514, 627, 922, 1040

D327.4K+W. Transformation: dugong to woman. 318

D336.1M. Transformation: pig to man. 348, 376, 441, 519, 549, 911, 938, 994

D336.1W. Transformation: pig to woman. 156

D341. Transformation: dog to person. 324

D341M. Transformation: dog to man. 198, 234, 810

D341W. Transformation: dog to woman. 821

D342B. Transformation: cat to boy. 463

D342W. Transformation: cat to woman. 493

D350G. Transformation: bird to girl. 617, 459

D350M. Transformation: bird to man. 897, 635, 525

D350W. Transformation: bird to woman. 844

D350+. Transformation: bird of paradise to person. 1110

D350+B. Transformation: bird of paradise to boy. 97

D350+M. Transformation: cassowary to man. 175, 909

D350+M. Transformation: cockatoo to man. 402, 508a

D350+W. Transformation: bird of paradise to woman. 74, 298, 392, 850

D350+W. Transformation: cassowary to woman. 110, 304, 470, 970, 1035

D350+W. Transformation: cockatoo to woman. 451

D350+W. Transformation: heron to woman. 350

D350B. Transformation: bird to boy. 761, 459, 238

D357B. Transformation: parrot to boy. 314

D361.1. Swan Maiden. 74, 110, 304, 970, 1035, 1182

D361.1+. Forest Spirit Bride. 296, 298, 300, 327, 427, 473, 477, 918, 1018

D370. Transformation: fish to person. 349

D370B. Transformation: fish to boy. 520

D370C. Transformation: fish to child. 675, 689

D370M. Transformation: fish to man. 601, 642, 675, 808

D370W. Transformation: fish to woman. 137, 300, 675, 917

D373M. Transformation: eel to man. 72, 750-1

D380+G. Transformation: butterfly to girl. 442

D380+M. Transformation: butterfly to man. 916

D380+W. Transformation: butterfly to woman. 1004

D380W. Transformation: centipede to woman. 573

D390+M. Transformation: turtle to man. 513, 601

D390+W. Transformation: turtle to woman. 513

D391+M. Transformation: python to man. 516

D391B. Transformation: serpent (snake) to boy. 210, 855, 864, 1185

D391M. Transformation: serpent (snake) to man. 190, 199, 328, 457, 468, 494, 575, 609, 712, 722, 748, 769, 775, 784, 820, 857, 952, 980, 997

D391W. Transformation: serpent (snake) to woman. 573, 641, 767, 1018

D395. Transformation: frog to person. 218

D395G. Transformation: frog to girl. 161

D395M. Transformation: frog to man. 61

D395W. Transformation: frog to woman. 333, 170

D397+B. Transformation: crocodile to boy. 509

D397+G. Transformation: crocodile to girl. 509

D397+M. Transformation: crocodile to man. 897

D397+W. Transformation: crocodile to woman. 478

D397C. Transformation: lizard to child. 353

D397M. Transformation: lizard to man. 237

D400-D499. Other forms of transformation

D410+. Transformation: eel to swine. 440, 720

D411+. Transformation: bandicoot to lizard. 833

D411+. Transformation: marsupial to bird. 235

D412.3.2+. Transformation: swine to eel. 440, 720

D412.3.5+. Transformation: pig to lizard. 237

D412.3+. Transformation: swine to chicken. 853

D412.3+. Transformation: swine to rat. 792

D413+. Transformation: beautiful bird to ugly bird. 518

D413+. Transformation: chicken to swine. 853

D413+. Transformation: one kind of bird to another. 355

D413+. Transformation: ugly bird to beautiful bird. 518

D415. Transformation: insect to snake. 457

D418+. Transformation: lizard to crocodile. 660

D418+. Transformation: lizard to snake. 784

D420+. Transformation: marsupial to stone. 835

D422.2+. Transformation: dog to spear. 634

D422.2.4K. Transformation: dog to stone. 835, 921

D422.3+. Transformation: pig to drum. 376

D422.3.2K. Transformation: pig to stone. 341

D423.5K2. Transformation: fowl to rock. 853

D423+. Transformation: bird to betel pepper plant. 1000

D423+. Transformation: bird to island. 1017

D425.1+. Transformation: snake to lake. 297

D425.1+. Transformation: snake to pond. 775

D425.2K+. Transformation: lizard to drum. 237

D426.1+. Transformation: eel to moon. 51

D430+W. Transformation: rain to woman. 415

D431+M. Transformation: sago to man. 757

D431+W. Transformation: sago to woman. 393, 918

D431.2+W. Transformation: stick to woman. 471, 524, 802, 1048

D431.4+G. Transformation: banana to girl. 624

D431.4+G. Transformation: pandanus fruit to girl. 991

D431.4+M. Transformation: breadfruit to man. 765

D431.4+W. Transformation: banana to woman. 957

D431.4+W. Transformation: cucumber to woman. 152, 282

D431.4+W. Transformation: pandanus fruit to woman. 877, 981, 1044

D431.4+W. Transformation: mango to woman. 85, 438

D431.6+B. Transformation: tanget plant (*Taetsia fructicosa*) to boy. 314

D431.9+C. Transformation: yam to child. 851

D431.9+W. Transformation: yam to woman. 158

D431.11+W. Transformation: coconut to woman. 185, 391, 483, 573, 682, 815, 844, 1117

D431.1W. Transformation: flower to woman. 389

D431.2M. Transformation: tree to man. 1023

D431.2W. Transformation: tree to woman. 347

D431.3W. Transformation: leaf (of tree) to woman. 296

D431.4G. Transformation: fruit to girl. 709

D431.4W. Transformation: fruit to woman. 451

D431.10M. Transformation: sections of bamboo to man. 570

D432.1M. Transformation: stone to man. 737, 241

D432.1+. Transformation: stone to mermaid. 458a

D434+M. Transformation: axe to man. 481

D434+W. Transformation: axe to woman. 942, 1057

D434+W. Transformation: love-charm to person. 172

D435.1.1. Transformation: statue comes to life. 234, 806, 898

D437.4W. Transformation: excrements to woman. 427

D439.5.2. Transformation: star to person. 265-7

D439.5.2W. Transformation: star to woman. 49

D440+. Transformation house to marsupial. 947

D440+. Transformation: cloud to pig. 331

D440+. Transformation: excrement to fish. 626

D440+. Transformation: skirt to bandicoot. 744

D440+. Transformation: spear to dog. 634

D440+. Transformation: tree to fish. 689

D441.1+. Transformation: tree to bird. 394

D441.2+W. Transformation: cucumber to woman. 215

D441.4+. Transformation: yam to snake. 199

D442.1+. Transformation: stone to swine. 441

D445+. Transformation: image of crocodile vivified. 498

D447+. Transformation: feather to bird. 1057

D447+. Transformation: finger to snake. 395

D447+. Transformation: testicles to frog. 161

D447.3+. Transformation: blood to fish. 269, 503, 520

D447.8+. Transformation: bone to fish. 675

D447.10+. Transformation: brain to sago palm tree. 1123

D450+. Transformation: bamboo to river. 881

D450+. Transformation: bamboo to tooth. 618

D450+. Transformation: breast to mountain. 811

D450+. Transformation: breast to stone. 748

D450+. Transformation: excrement to mushroom. 831

D450+. Transformation: fat to lake. 154

D450+. Transformation: head to mountain. 811

D450+. Transformation: house to tree. 497

D450+. Transformation: mushroom to excrement. 831

D450+. Transformation: soup to rain. 497

D450+. Transformation: soup to wind. 497

D451.1+. Transformation: log to bananas. 272

D451.1+. Transformation: log to taro. 272

D451.1+. Transformation: log to yam. 272

D451.1+. Transformation: tree to excrement. 427

D451.9+. Transformation: taro juice to lake. 339

D451.9+. Transformation: taro to mountain. 339

D452.1+. Transformation: stone to tree. 427

D452.1.1. Transformation: rock to hut. 748

D452.1.13K. Transformation: stone to boat. 511

D452.3+. Transformation: sand to rock. 514

D457+. Transformation: cut off penis to stone. 1110

D457+. Transformation: fat to lake. 859, 861

D457.1+. Transformation: blood to lake. 667, 950, 1103

D457.1+. Transformation: blood to river. 811, 865

D457.1+. Transformation: blood to tree. 883

D457.1.14K. Transformation: blood to eggs. 225, 600, 955

D457.4+. Transformation: beard hair to yam. 461

D457.7+. Transformation: feather headdress to tree. 884

D457.9+. Transformation: finger to egg. 360

D457.12+. Transformation: bone to yam. 1029

D457.18.2. Transformation: tears to river. 811, 849

D457.18.2+. Transformation: tears to lake. 743, 777, 1174, 1177, 1186, 1199

D457.18+. Transformation: tears to mountains. 740

D469.1+. Transformation: egg to nut. 1209

D471+. Transformation: drum to stone. 497

D476+. Transformation: grease to lake. 96, 803, 988, 1177

D480+. Transformation: stream to river. 497

D482.1. Transformation: stretching tree. 391

D489. Objects made larger—miscellaneous. 467

D489+. Boulder gets larger. 441

D491.1. Compressible magic animals. 1198

D491.2.1. Compressible magic box. 512

D492. Color of object changed. 352, 979

D492+. Clouds turn blue. 255

D492+. Trees turn blue. 255

D500-D599. Means of transformation

D516. Transformation through excessive grief. 296

D520. Transformation through power of the word. 282

D521. Transformation through wish. 287

D522. Transformation through magic word (charm). 453-4, 713

D530+. Transformation by removing skirt. 1035, 641, 110

D531. Transformation by putting on skin. 457, 459, 549, 618, 673, 763-4a, 767, 970, 1072, 1160

D531+. Transformation by removing skin. 167, 175, 234, 282, 333, 416, 444, 478, 544, 561, 641, 705, 767, 917, 970

D531+. Transformation by removing feathers. 1035

D551. Transformation by eating. 513, 518, 1034

D551.1. Transformation by eating fruit. 1185

D551.2+. Transformation by eating sago. 700

D551.2.7+. Transformation by eating yam. 521a

D551.3. Transformation by eating flesh. 297, 521a, 700, 842

D551.3+. Transformation by eating fat. 554

D551.3+. Transformation by eating lizard. 187

D551.3+. Transformation by eating snake. 687

D551.6+. Transformation by eating excrement. 103

D560+. Transformation by application of paint. 224

D560+. Transformation by cutting. 768

D560+. Transformation by falling. 761

D560+. Transformation from defecation. 765

D560+. Transformation from urination. 765

D562.1. Transformation by application of water. 51, 806

D562. Transformation by bathing. 748

D564. Transformation by smelling. 389

D565. Transformation by touching. 609, 947, 948

D565.6. Transformation by touching water. 918

D566. Transformation by striking. 83, 748, 838, 884, 973, 1113

D566+. Transformation by cutting. 354

D566.4+. Transformation by cutting or dismemberment. 402

D572. Transformation by magic object. 1163, 1208

D576. Transformation by being burned. 274

D595+. Transformation by application of ashes. 130

D600-D699. Miscellaneous transformation incidents

D610. Repeated transformation. 222, 223, 245, 359, 427, 458a, 473, 477, 522, 633, 750-1, 773, 1124

D615. Transformation combat. 439

D642. Transformation to escape difficult situation. 703, 733, 735, 763-4a, 828, 935, 978, 984

D642.1. Transformation to escape from captivity. 107

D642.2. Transformation to escape death. 639, 681, 744, 1143

D642.6. Transformation to escape ogress. 681

D642.7. Transformation to elude pursuers. 341, 1072

D651.1. Transformation to kill enemy. 1208, 1163

D670. Magic flight. 107, 237, 464, 663, 684, 796, 943

D670+. Magic flight with ears. 878, 1033

D671. Transformation flight. 224, 232, 252, 274, 283, 291b, 296, 516, 639, 631, 733, 735, 744, 828, 1072, 1143, 1160, 1179

D681. Gradual transformation. 279, 325, 353, 518, 612, 675, 842, 918, 1113, 1179, 1185

D682. Partial transformation. 563, 1034

D683.2. Transformation by witch (sorceress). 512, 543

D683.7. Transformation by fairy. 254

D683. Transformation by magician. 387

D688. Transformed mother suckles child. 744

D696. Transformation during sleep. 842, 1034, 1123

D700-D799. Disenchantment

D791.2. Disenchantment by only one person. 549

D793.2. Disenchantment made permanent by burning cast-off skin. 167, 333, 478, 561, 705, 733, 767

D793.2+. Killing by burning detached skin. 175

D800-D1699. Magic objects

D800. Magic object. 370, 538

D817. Magic object received from grateful person. 447

D821. Magic object received from old woman. 447

D863. Magic object mysteriously disappears. 525

D906. Magic wind. 509, 800

D908. Magic darkness. 168, 287, 529, 543

D911.1. Magic wave. 620, 1016

D915.1. River produced by magic. 914

D915.6. Magic flood. 448, 461, 655

D921. Magic lake (pond). 448, 473, 508a, 932

D921.1. Lake (pond) produced by magic. 713

D928. Magic water-hole. 713

D931.1.2. Magic ashes. 346, 511, 785

D931.1.4. Magic lime. 733, 822, 979

D931. Magic rock (stone). 149, 312, 336, 344, 420, 458a, 575, 853, 1030, 1222

D935.2. Magic clay. 504

D941. Magic forest. 773

D941.1. Forest produced by magic. 512, 773

D950. Magic tree. 449, 757, 984

D950+. Magic tree seedling. 476

D950+. Magic ironwood tree. 733

D950.8. Magic fig tree. 677

D950.15. Magic bamboo tree. 474, 1013, 1133, 1211

D950.19+. Magic *limbum* palm tree (*Caryota* spp.). 673

D952. Magic tree-bark. 997

D955. Magic leaf. 536, 694, 696, 780, 858, 985, 1009

D955+. Magic banana leaf. 870

D956. Magic stick of wood. 262, 500, 524, 536, 715

D956+. Magic house post. 609

D958. Magic thorn. 761

D965. Magic plant. 1214

D965+. Magic *tanget* plant (*Taetsia fructicosa*). 860, 862, 1179

D965+. Magic vine. 683

D965+. Magic wild sugarcane. 860, 862

D965.12. Magic grass. 573

D967+. Magic ginger. 298, 492, 550, 572, 627, 630, 758, 960

D974. Magic plant-sap. 570

D981. Magic fruit. 142, 1022

D981+. Magic mango. 907

D983.2. Magic yam. 747

D983.2+. Fight with magic taro. 339

D985+. Magic *galip* nut. 191

D985.5. Magic betel-nut. 449, 474, 572, 627, 822, 906, 916

D985.5+. Magic betel-pepper. 572, 627, 822

D993. Magic eye. 568

D996.1. Magic finger. 123, 639

D1001. Magic spittle. 449, 474, 492, 511, 541, 550, 572, 630, 683, 822, 997

D1001+. Magic sexual secretions. 191

D1001+. Magic mucus. 590

D1002.1. Magic urine. 461, 467, 568

D1002. Magic excrements. 332

D1002+. Magic flatulence. 796

D1005. Magic breath. 504, 597

D1007. Magic bone (human). 453-4, 477, 818, 1205

D1011.0.1+. Woman puts on heron head to go fishing. 350

D1013+. Magic cassowary bone. 244

D1015.4. Magic liver of animal. 798

D1016. Magic blood of animal. 799

D1021. Magic feather. 459, 943

D1029.2. Magic tail of animal. 1070

D1030. Magic food. 513, 529, 1034

D1030.1. Food supplied by magic. 573, 891

D1032. Magic meat. 261, 522, 880

D1034+. Magic taro. 138

D1039. Magic sweet potato. 798

D1041. Blood as magic drink. 736, 758

D1052. Magic garment (robe, tunic). 1182

D1067.4. Magic mask. 757

D1073. Magic necklace. 1182

D1084. Magic spear. 992, 1159

D1091. Magic bow. 64, 251

D1092. Magic arrow. 702

D1121. Magic boat. 541

D1133.1. House created by magic. 773

D1151.2. Magic chair. 420

D1162. Magic light. 294

D1171.1. Magic pot. 1206

D1181. Magic needle. 372

D1184.2. Magic string. 477, 557, 773

D1184. Magic thread. 123

D1203. Magic rope. 98, 255

D1211. Magic drum. 237, 497, 1159

D1221. Magic trumpet. 122, 610

D1223.1. Magic flute. 217, 255, 496, 543, 705

D1241. Magic medicine (= charm). 684

D1242.1. Magic water. 80, 516, 596, 788

D1242.4+. Magic coconut oil. 618

D1246. Magic powder. 515

D1254.1. Magic wand. 788

D1271. Magic fire. 80, 691, 896

D1271+. Magic smoke. 572, 627

D1273. Magic formula (charm). 432

D1275. Magic song. 285, 449, 461, 642

D1275+. Magic dance. 642

D1275.1+. Magic music travels great distance. 705

D1298. Magic firewood. 677

D1700-D2199. Magic powers and manifestations

642, 647, 669, 700, 741, 747, 776, 780, 798, 806, 821, 833, 846, 854, 873, 906, 985, 1009, 1020, 1222

D1782. Sympathetic magic. 123

D1787. Magic results from burning. 696

D1792. Magic results from curse. 142

D1793. Magic results from eating or drinking. 1222

D1810.8.2. Information received through dream. 49, 80, 196, 250, 350, 522, 529, 532, 600, 634, 642, 709, 719, 722, 728, 729, 739, 748, 756, 813, 833, 856, 859, 900, 916, 1021, 1023, 1029, 1058, 1121

D1810.8.2.3. Murder made known in a dream. 773, 863

D1810.8.3. Warning in dreams. 776, 863

D1810.8.3.1. Warning in dream fulfilled. 250

D1810.11. Magic knowledge from mythical ancestor. 460

D1812.3.3. Future revealed in dream. 739

D1812.5. Future learned through omens. 464, 858, 859

D1812.5.1+. Rainbow gives bad omens. 899

D1817.0.3. Magic detection of murder. 860, 862

D1825.2. Magic power to see distant objects. 524

D1830. Magic strength. 91, 439, 464, 492, 524, 630, 905, 909, 1018, 1070, 1182

D1830+. Cripple walks by magic. 690

D1831. Magic strength resides in hair. 852

D1835.5. Magic strength results from songs. 557

D1835.5+. Magic strength results from dances. 557

D1835+. Magic strength from spittle. 511

D1837. Magic weakness. 557, 1029

D1860. Magic beautification. 444, 492, 761, 822, 873, 884

D1862.1. Magic beauty bestowed by supernatural wife. 700

D1866.1. Beautification by bathing. 602

D1866.2. Beautification by removal of skin. 602, 733, 1013

D1880. Magic rejuvenation. 851, 877, 1212

D1880+. Transformation to young man to escape recognition. 615, 669, 733

D1881. Magic self-rejuvenation. 282, 403, 405, 594, 615, 669

D1889.6. Rejuvenation by changing skin. 124, 733

D1890. Magic aging. 403, 543, 615, 622, 761, 822, 851, 934, 1212

D1891. Transformation to old man to escape recognition. 457

D1900. Love induced by magic. 496, 522, 627, 647, 733, 794, 906, 997, 1067

D1908. Love lost by magic. 737

D1935+. Work magically multiplied. 474

D1960. Magic sleep. 138, 698, 700, 1020

D1964.3. Magic sleep induced by abductor. 831, 846

D1964.6. Magic sleep induced by deity. 642

D1964. Magic sleep induced by certain person. 198, 854

D1964+. Magic sleep induced by twin brother's ghost. 171

D1976.1. Transportation during magic sleep. 813

D1980. Magic invisibility. 564, 572

D1981+. Woman visible only to husband. 172

D1983. Invisibility conferred on person. 543

D2000. Magic forgetfulness. 515, 519, 562, 1067

D2000+. Magic confusion. 417, 543, 572, 612, 642, 754, 760, 896, 1110

D2000+. Mind control. 514, 525, 737, 756, 906, 956, 1194

D2031. Magic illusion. 900

D2035. Magic heaviness. 400

D2061.1.3. Poisoning by magic. 907

D2061.2.1. Death-giving glance. 943

D2061.2.2. Murder by sympathetic magic. 569, 715

D2061.2.2.7. Animals abused or destroyed to cause death of person. 69

D2061.2.2.8+. Death from ensorcelled tobacco. 139

D2061. Magic murder. 219, 408-9, 399, 538, 694, 776, 816, 860, 862, 968, 1172, 1214, 1218

D2062.2. Blinding by magic. 578, 659, 799

D2069. Death or bodily injury by magic — miscellaneous. 109, 464

D2071. Evil Eye. 109

D2074.1. Animals magically called. 120, 582, 679, 744, 896, 1222

D2074.1.3. Birds magically called. 416, 539, 1009, 1159, 1202

D2074.1.3+. Reptiles magically called. 1159

D2074.1+. Insects magically called. 417

D2074.1+. Snake magically called. 554

D2074.2.3. Summoning by wish. 287

D2074. Attracting by magic. 874

D2087. Theft by magic. 1004

D2095. Magic disappearance. 51, 622, 639, 756, 780, 824, 900, 924, 950, 1031, 1046

D2100. Magic wealth. 298, 458a

D2105.7. Fruit obtained from tree by magic. 285

D2106.1.2. Animals miraculously multiplied. 773, 812

D2120. Magic transportation. 261, 477

D2121.2. Magic journey with closed eyes. 979

D2121. Magic journey. 213, 215, 531, 1203

D2122. Journey with magic speed. 408-9, 439, 464, 511, 572, 795, 797

D2125.1.1. Magic transportation by waves. 620

D2126. Magic underwater journey. 750-1, 920, 941, 952

D2136.1. Rocks moved by magic. 427

D2136.4+. Lake magically appears. 338

D2136.9. Magic house removed. 773

D2136. Objects magically moved. 512, 914

D2142.1. Wind produced by magic. 143, 217, 360, 378, 388, 428, 429, 456b, 467, 468, 509, 515, 525, 529, 554, 563, 575, 588, 625, 756, 796, 846, 853, 857, 920, 922, 941, 985, 1010, 1041, 1126

D2142.1+. Tornado produced by magic. 181, 496

D2142. Wind produced by magic. 726

D2143.1. Rain produced by magic. 143, 144, 181, 217, 242, 250, 261, 262, 268, 331, 360, 378, 396, 421, 428, 429, 441, 456b, 467, 468, 509, 512, 515, 525, 529, 539, 554, 563, 575, 588, 686, 720, 726, 756, 796, 817, 839, 857, 920, 922, 941, 985, 1010, 1028, 1041, 1058

D2143.1.2. Rain produced by singing. 388, 461, 543, 625

D2143.1.2+. Rain produced by dancing. 388, 461, 543, 625

D2143.1+. Rain produced by cutting trees in certain part of forest. 637

D2143.2. Drought produced by magic. 543, 1216

D2144.3. Heat produced by magic. 255

D2146.1.1. Day magically lengthened. 432

D2146.2. Night controlled by magic. 941

D2146.2.2. Night magically lengthened. 432

D2146. Magic control of day and night. 934

D2147. Magic control of clouds. 529

D2148. Earth magically caused to quake. 122, 168, 429, 467, 468, 539, 550, 557, 563, 748, 756, 829, 922, 933, 952, 960, 985, 1041, 1115, 1191

D2149.1. Thunderbolt magically produced. 143, 217, 261, 268, 331, 378, 388, 414, 421, 429, 441, 468, 525, 539, 550, 588, 625, 679, 720, 770, 817, 857, 1041, 1191, 1220

D2150+. Catching fish by removing one's head and letting fish enter body. 62, 196, 425, 711

D2150+. Magic associated with planting yams. 527

D2150+. Catching fish with ulcer as bait. 291b, 498, 948

D2151.2. Magic control of rivers. 291a

D2151.2.3. Rivers magically made dry. 366

D2151.3. Magic control of waves. 554

D2151.8. Magic flood. 143, 217, 234, 287, 388, 396, 429, 461, 539, 550, 575, 588, 596, 707, 720, 726, 796, 839, 857, 920, 935, 999, 1028, 1058

D2152+. Magic control of volcanoes. 449

D2156+. Magic control over snakes. 679

D2158.1. Magic kindling of fire. 453-4

D2161.3.1.1. Eyes torn out magically replaced. 435, 467, 597, 799

D2161. Magic healing power. 464, 1204

D2163. Magic defense in battle. 1205

D2165. Escapes by magic. 690

D2171. Magic adhesion. 149, 241, 344, 1030

D2174+. Dancer removes one leg and smokes it on fire while dancing with other leg. 265-7

D2176.3. Evil spirit exorcised. 679, 692

D2188.3. Village vanishes. 512

D2188. Magic disappearance. 950

D2188+. Objects magically appear and disappear inside cooking pot. 237

D2198. Magic control of spirits (angels). 265-7

E: The Dead

E0-E199. Resuscitation

E3. Dead animal comes to life. 104, 812

E10. Resuscitation by rough treatment. 138

E12+. Resuscitation by decapitation in otherworld. 715

E15. Resuscitation by burning. 696

E15+. Resuscitation by smoking. 858

E30+. Resuscitation by being pieced back together by ants. 485

E30. Resuscitation by arrangement of members. 215, 504, 852, 857

E32.0.2K. Eel cooked and eaten comes to life. 440, 720, 742

E32. Resuscitated eaten animal. 823

E35. Resuscitation from fragments of body. 138

E50. Resuscitation by magic. 685

E55.1. Resuscitation by song. 741, 741, 747, 833

E55.1+. Resuscitation by dance. 741, 747, 833

E55.2. Resuscitation by playing flute. 255

E64.18. Resuscitation by leaf. 696

E64. Resuscitation by magic object. 453-4

E79+. Resuscitation by saying victim's name. 453-4

E80. Water of life. 99

E100+. Resuscitation by ginger. 242

E113. Resuscitation by blood. 104

E114. Resuscitation by spittle. 242

E122.2. Resuscitation by snake. 696

E150+. Snake survives burial. 227

E168. Cooked animal comes to life. 51, 440, 720, 742, 799, 823, 1028

E200-E599. Ghosts and other revenants

E210. Dead lover's malevolent return. 983

E217. Fatal kiss from dead. 96

E220+. Dead daughter's malevolent return. 943

E221+. Dead husband's malevolent return. 505

E221+. Dead wife's malevolent return. 153, 607, 868

E222. Dead mother's malevolent return. 452

E222+. Dead father's malevolent return. 505

E226. Dead brother's return. 92, 356, 410, 758, 1211

E226+. Dead sister's malevolent return. 943

E230. Return from dead to inflict punishment. 505, 530

E231. Return from dead to reveal murder. 356, 410, 528, 728, 753, 924

E231+. Return from dead to reveal suicide. 382

E232. Return from the dead to slay wicked person. 382, 983

E234. Ghost punishes injury received in life. 382, 452

E234.3. Return from dead to avenge death (murder). 61

E235.2+. Ghost returns because of improper mourning. 92

E238.1. Dance with the dead. 698

E250. Bloodthirsty revenants. 98, 145, 760, 956, 1006, 1055

E253+. Ghost mother tries to kill daughter. 351

E259+. Ghost seals people in cave, killing them. 380

E261.4. Ghost pursues man. 382, 398, 408-9, 480, 493, 495, 505, 528, 553, 562, 574, 581, 598, 616, 698, 727, 732, 747, 758, 780, 785, 786, 805, 817, 849, 868, 904, 911, 943, 948, 1006, 1211

E261.4+. Imagined ghost pursues man. 276, 381, 413, 517, 982, 1026, 1164

E262. Ghost rides on man's back. 452, 510

E262+. Spirit rides on man's back. 90

E262+. Presumed ghost rides on man's back. 385

E265.1. Meeting ghost causes sickness. 514, 528

E266. Dead carry off living. 114

E271. Sea-ghosts. 782

E276. Ghosts haunt tree. 184, 547, 692, 698, 766, 822

E276+. Ghosts haunt forest. 567, 607

E278+. Ghosts haunt cave. 1187, 1194

E278+. Ghosts haunt lake. 1211

E279.2. Ghost disturbs sleeping person. 115

E293. Ghosts frighten people (deliberately). 677

E299.4+. Ghost breaks objects. 351

E299.5+. Ghost causes person to be lost at sea. 782

E300. Friendly return from the dead. 720

E300+. Ghost arranges marriage. 385

E320. Dead relative's friendly return. 166, 426, 547, 771

E320+. Dead relative's friendly return to adopt child. 565

E320+. Dead grandfather's friendly return. 884

E321. Dead husband's friendly return. 99, 600, 728, 875

E322. Dead wife's friendly return. 555

E323.1.1. Dead mother returns to suckle child. 489

E323.1.1+. Dead (transformed) mother returns to suckle child. 394

E323.2. Dead mother returns to aid persecuted children. 950

E323.2+. Dead mother returns to aid child. 776

E323. Dead mother's friendly return. 488, 532, 632, 639, 891, 913

E325. Dead sister's friendly return. 648

E326. Dead brother's friendly return. 171, 384, 410, 529, 728, 753, 924

E327. Dead father's friendly return. 127

E327+. Dead father returns to prevent son from learning of his death. 489, 556

E327+. Dead father returns to aid child. 489, 776

E332.1+. Ghost haunts stream. 252

E341.1.1+. Corpse grateful for being buried. 155

E352. Dead returns to restore stolen goods. 698

E363.1. Ghost aids living in emergency. 756, 757

E363.2. Ghost returns to protect the living. 600

E363.3. Ghost warns the living. 127, 529, 648

E379.1. Return from dead to rescue from drowning. 1040

E379.1+. Return from dead to rescue someone from an ogre. 488

E380. Ghost summoned. 382, 555, 780, 1020, 1222

E384+. Ghost summoned by singing. 757, 884

E390+. Ghost transports women to friend who marries them. 108

E400+. Man puts hand in dead wife's mouth and he himself dies. 153

E402.1.1.1. Ghost calls. 574

E402.1.1.4. Ghost sings. 416, 495, 528

E402.1.11.2+. Evil spirit kills and eats domestic animals. 272

E402.4. Sound of ethereal music. 217

E410. The unquiet grave. 505, 528

E421.1. Invisible ghosts. 989

E421.2.1+. Ghost leaves unusual footprints. 384

E421.3.3+. Ghost/corpse with glowing eyes. 413

E421.3+. Fire shoots from ghost. 343

E421.3+. Ghost/corpse with glowing groin. 413

E421.4+. Ghost's skin as shadow. 416

E422.1.1. Headless revenant. 956

E422.1.11.4. Revenant as skeleton. 581

E422.1.3. Revenant with ice-cold hands. 677

E422.1.3+. Cold revenants. 572

E422.1.8+. Revenant with long nails. 484, 805

E422.2.1. Revenant red. 145, 153, 581

E422.3.1. Revenant as small man. 730

E422.3.2. Revenant as a very large man (giant). 286, 306, 1222

E422.4.4. Revenant in female dress. 380

E422.4.5. Revenant in male dress. 380

E423. Revenant in animal form. 510

E423+. Revenant as flying fox. 530

E765.3.3. Life bound up with tree. 339
E783.1. Head cut off and successfully replaced. 574
E783.5. Vital head speaks. 440, 574, 1028
E783. Vital head. 210

F: Marvels

F0-F199. Otherworld journeys

F1. Journey to otherworld as dream or vision. 715
F6. Departure to otherworld (fairyland) attributed to death. 715
F12.1. Journey to sky-god. 525
F15. Visit to star-world. 485
F16. Visit to land of moon. 265-7, 905
F17. Visit to land of the sun. 168, 709, 719, 905
F51. Sky-rope. 50, 431, 485
F52. Ladder to upper world. 245, 477, 525, 614
F52.2. Columns of smoke as ladder to upper world. 49
F54. Tree to upper world. 619
F54.1. Tree stretches to sky. 56, 75a, 250, 352, 443, 477, 503, 523, 610, 630, 773, 789, 1009, 1186
F54.2+. Sugarcane grows to sky. 404
F55. Mountain reaches to sky. 795, 1202
F55.1. Mountain stretches to sky. 307
F56.2+. Birds fly to sky. 431
F58. Tower (column) to upper world. 55
F60+. Ascent to upper world by climbing. 404
F60+. Person falls from sky. 421
F61. Person wafted to sky. 251, 366, 412, 421, 425
F81. Descent to lower world of dead (Hell, Hades). 79, 766
F81.1.2. Journey to land of dead to visit deceased. 875
F81.1.2+. Journey to land of dead. 547, 934
F81.5. Journey to lower world to get treasures. 766
F87. Journey to otherworld to secure bride. 766
F91. Door (gate) entrance to lower world. 766
F92.3 Visit to lower world through opening rocks. 79
F92+. Hole dug in ground leads home. 966
F112. Journey to Land of Women. 299, 469, 499, 644, 1117
F112.2. City of women. 204
F113. Land of men. 327
F121. Journey to world of spirits. 522, 677
F123. Journey to land of little men (pygmies). 656
F124. Journey to land of demons. 536
F127.1. Journey to serpent kingdom. 321
F127.4K. Journey to land of turtles. 513
F129.3+. Voyage to the land of clouds. 916

F129.4. Journey to otherworld island. 426
F141.1. River as barrier to otherworld. 715
F166.11. Abundant food in otherworld. 709

F200-F699. Marvelous Creatures

F205+. People from the sky. 245
F215. Fairies live in star-world. 265-7, 477, 485
F216.1+. Blind and mute man who lives in tree. 284
F238. Fairies are naked. 230, 268
F252.1. Fairy king. 674
F261. Fairies dance. 334, 1015
F262.1. Fairies sing. 334, 1015
F321.1. Changeling. 615, 637, 662, 851, 1212
F321.1.4.3. Changeling thrown on fire and thus banished. 403
F349.2. Fairy aids mortal in battle. 708
F350. Theft from fairies. 194
F387. Fairy captured. 553
F389.4. Fairy killed by mortal. 194, 674
F394. Mortals help fairies. 1015
F401+. Spirit in cave form. 430
F401.3+. Spirit in bandicoot form. 645, 833
F401.3+. Spirit in crocodile form. 535, 593, 797
F401.3+. Spirit in flying fox form. 76
F401.3+. Spirit in marsupial form. 419, 739, 803, 823, 896, 1029, 1040
F401.3.10K. Spirit in form of boar. 331, 441, 629, 680, 812
F401.3.13K2. Spirit in form of lizard. 241, 821, 833
F401.3.7. Spirit in form of a bird. 241, 351, 839, 850, 1218
F401.3.7+. Spirit in form of an eagle. 479
F401.3.7+. Spirit in form of cassowary. 263, 295, 728, 812
F401.3.7+. Spirit in form of cockatoo. 402, 508a
F401.3.8. Spirits in form of snake. 165, 210, 321, 402, 468, 554, 641, 740, 756, 901, 1067, 1172
F401.6. Spirit in human form. 75b, 90, 210, 241, 268, 283, 305, 332, 368, 419, 641, 642, 795, 804, 821, 824, 858, 880, 896, 920, 935, 960, 1015, 1029, 1051, 1072, 1124, 1216
F401.8. Gigantic spirit. 268
F402.1.10. Spirit pursues person. 548, 713, 727, 804, 948
F402.1.10+. Imagined spirit pursues person. 180, 310, 458b
F402.1.11. Spirit causes death. 76, 287, 712, 713, 800, 1029
F402.1.2. Spirit blocks person's road. 108
F402.6.4.1. Spirits live in caves. 805, 995, 1010, 1067
F403.2. Spirits help mortal. 1196, 1126
F405+. Snake spirit killed by burial and propitiation. 321

F405+. Spirit killed by axe. 283
F405+. Spirit killed by poisoning. 720
F405+. Spirit killed by pushing it into water. 90
F405+. Spirit killed by spear/arrow. 268, 331, 433, 771
F405+. Spirit killed. 305, 435, 896
F405.12+. Spirit killed by fire. 481
F406. Spirits propitiated. 840, 868
F408.3. Spirits dwell at tabu place. 368, 406, 419, 430, 553, 564, 566, 798, 920, 1041
F419.2. Thieving spirit. 697, 792
F419.4K. Spirits eat food raw. 123, 581, 608, 610, 720, 732, 747, 1006
F420. Water-spirits. 713
F420.1.1. Water-spirit as man. 920
F420.1.2. Water-spirit as woman (water-nymph, water-nix). 90, 332, 920, 954
F420.1.3.2. Water-spirit as fish. 287, 536, 642, 874, 942
F420.1.3.2+. Water-spirit as clam. 295
F420.1.3.2+. Water-spirit as eel. 72, 440, 550, 720, 1028
F420.1.3.9. Water-spirit as snake. 194, 679, 712, 820, 855, 952
F420.1.5. Water-spirits invisible. 1210
F420.2.2. Water-spirits live in village under water. 677, 920, 941, 952, 1216
F420.5.3+. Water spirit takes woman away. 820
F420.6.1.6. Offspring of marriage between mortal and water-spirit. 67
F420.7.1+. Living underwater with water-spirit. 67
F421.1. Lady of the Lake. 1216, 824
F421. Lake-spirit. 1210, 920, 855, 820, 664, 448
F424. River-spirit. 67, 68a, 90, 240, 677, 824, 839, 843, 1041, 1110, 1200
F431. Cloud-spirit. 331, 421
F434. Spirit of thunder. 421
F438+. Spirit of earthquake: black with wings, long nose, and tail. 367
F441.2. Tree-spirit. 230, 789, 796, 799, 954
F441.6.3. Sexual relations with wood-spirit fatal. 548
F441. Wood-spirit. 177, 390, 435, 820, 821, 979, 1210
F450. Underground-spirits. 673
F451.4.1.1. Dwarfs live in caves. 1010
F451.4.1.11. Dwarfs live in hills and mountains. 843
F451. Dwarf. 656, 662, 730, 1180
F460. Mountain-spirits. 522, 572, 795, 800, 843, 1015, 1041, 1043, 1220
F471.2. Incubus. 564
F473.6.4. Spirit eats food. 331, 788, 1072
F490. Other spirits and demons. 1046
F490+. Masalai. 67, 68a, 75b, 78, 90, 113, 117, 122, 123, 143, 150, 150, 155, 165, 167, 177, 184, 194, 209, 210, 220, 230, 233, 240, 241, 243, 244, 254, 268, 273, 281, 283, 287, 295,

305, 321, 329, 332, 334, 339, 340, 364, 367, 368, 378, 386, 388, 390, 395, 399, 402, 406, 417, 418, 419, 428, 429, 430, 433, 435, 439, 440, 441, 443, 444, 453-4, 449, 450, 468, 479, 481, 485, 488, 496, 504, 508a, 509, 515, 520, 521a, 522, 529, 535, 536, 543, 548, 550, 553, 554, 556, 557, 558, 563, 564, 566, 568, 571, 575, 575, 578, 582, 588, 591, 593, 596, 604, 608, 611, 613, 614, 615, 619, 623, 625, 629, 635, 637, 641, 645, 650, 664, 668, 672, 673, 674, 677, 679, 680, 681, 685, 690, 697, 702, 703, 712, 719, 720, 721, 727, 728, 734, 740, 741, 743, 754, 756, 771, 772, 786, 788, 789, 792, 795, 796, 797, 798, 799, 800, 803, 804, 807, 808, 809, 812, 820, 821, 823, 824, 833, 839, 840, 843, 850, 852, 854, 855, 858, 871, 874, 880, 896, 897, 901, 920, 927, 935, 941, 942, 948, 952, 954, 960, 963, 972, 980, 985, 986, 990, 995, 1003, 1010, 1015, 1022, 1028, 1029, 1030, 1033, 1040, 1041, 1043, 1051, 1067, 1068, 1072, 1073, 1074, 1110, 1114, 1115, 1122, 1124, 1126, 1159, 1172, 1194, 1200, 1212, 1216, 1217, 1218, 1220

F490+. Masumura. 520, 635, 672, 721

F490+. Nokondi. 315, 399, 633, 703, 708, 741, 929, 1020, 1180

F494.3. Earth spirit. 1196

F495. Stone-spirit. 167, 241, 430, 441, 575, 986, 990, 1115

F495+. Stone-axe spirit. 481

F497. Fire-spirits. 449

F501. Person consisting only of head. 102, 552

F501+. Man consisting only of head attaches to woman's breast. 569

F511.0.4+. Person with removable head. 62, 196, 350, 425, 711

F511.1.0.1. Person without features (with flat face). 638

F511.1.3+. Human-snake-pig face. 629

F511.1+. Faceless person. 120

F511.2.4. Person without ears. 638

F512+. Person has plants growing from eye sockets. 597

F512+. Person with pumpkins growing out of eye-sockets. 435

F512+. Unusually large eyes. 529, 564, 732

F512.2.1. Persons (animals) with four (six) eyes. 564

F512.5. Person without eyes. 77, 362, 638

F513.0.3. Mouthless people. 77, 362, 638

F513.0.3+. Mouth cut open for mouthless person. 434

F513.1. Person unusual as to his teeth. 255

F513.1+. Baby born with teeth. 445-6

F513.1+. Removable teeth. 588, 635

F513+. Person with mouth on top of head. 434, 638

F515.1+. Remarkably long fingers. 421, 821

F515.2.2. Person with very long fingernails. 230, 484, 566, 588, 590, 805

F516.3+. Long-armed person. 590

F517+. Person with one large leg. 537

F517+. Person with four legs. 542

F517+. Removable legs. 657, 542

F517.0.1. Person with one leg. 741

F517.0.2+. Short-legged people. 709

F517.0.3K. Person without legs. 542

F521.5K+. Spirit with human front, tree backside. 754

F525. Person with half a body. 315, 633, 703, 708, 887, 929, 1020, 1180

F527.1. Red person. 107, 439, 500, 602, 626, 768, 863, 1133, 1211

F527.5. Black man. 421, 500, 768, 1133, 1211

F527.7K+. White person. 213, 218, 304, 428, 473, 719, 893, 1117

F529.2. People without anuses. 236, 354, 500, 573

F529.3+. Man with grass growing on body. 754

F529.6. Person with enormous belly. 443, 808, 958

F531. Giant. 61, 79, 107, 169, 527, 780

F531.0.4. Giant woman. 90

F531.1.1. Eyes of giant. 914

F531.1.1.3. Blind giant. 638

F531.1.2.2.1. Two-headed giant. 360

F531.1.6.3.1. Giant (giantess) with particularly long hair. 177

F531.1.6.4. Giant with long beard. 177

F531.3.8.5. Earthquake as giant falls down. 995

F531.3+. Giant's walking causes earthquake. 591, 613, 629, 680, 1114

F531.3+. Giant's walking causes thunder. 591, 613, 680

F531.6.12.6. Giant slain by man. 638

F535. Pygmy. 61, 808, 843

F535.6. Kingdom of pygmies. 335

F540+. Person fishes using own flesh as bait. 718

F541. Remarkable eyes. 914

F541.1.1. Eyes flash fire. 702, 799

F541.6.2. Person has red eye. 529

F541.11. Removable eyes. 374, 467, 723, 1051

F542. Remarkable ears. 559

F542.2+. Pulled ears enlarge. 878, 1033

F543.1. Remarkably long nose. 660, 804

F544.3. Remarkable teeth. 681

F544.3.5. Remarkably long teeth. 421, 566, 574, 588, 637, 674, 721, 817, 1112

F545.1. Remarkable beard. 447

F545.1.0.1. Beardless man. 81

F545.1.5. Bearded woman. 81, 229

F545.1+. Unusually long beard. 81

F547.1.1. Vagina dentata. 832, 894, 962, 965, 1047

F547.3. Extraordinary penis. 1110

F547.3.1. Long penis. 1110

F547.3.3+. Thorny penis. 484

F547.6.1. Remarkably long pubic hair. 588

F547.7. Enormous testicles. 958

F547.7+. Severed testicles reattached. 985

F547.7+. Thorny testicles. 484

F548. Remarkable legs. 443

F551.2+. Crooked toes. 421

F555.3. Very long hair. 177, 421, 447, 659, 674, 735, 805, 821, 852

F555+. Hair with snakes and lizards in it. 355

F555+. Exceptionally hairy man. 662

F556. Remarkable voice. 323

F561+. People only eat tubers. 256

F562+. Children live inside father's belly. 443

F562.1+. Person who never walks. 789

F562.2. Residence in a tree. 109, 789, 958

F562.2+. Residence in a bamboo. 453-4

F562.3. Residence in (under) water. 855

F562.4+. Women live in banana. 678

F562.7K. People live in mountain top. 61, 132, 256, 656, 716, 759, 800, 834, 843, 881, 922, 997, 1010

F564+. Person sleeps in bamboo tube. 115, 135, 159

F564+. Person sleeps in hollow log. 173

F565.2. Remarkably strong women. 644, 648

F566.1. Village of men only. 354, 794, 806, 954

F566.1+. Island of women only. 499

F566.1+. Village of women only. 115, 569, 742

F567. Wild man. 178, 233, 360, 401, 419, 457, 506, 633, 662, 708, 914, 1180, 1199, 1205

F567.1. Wild woman. 109, 130, 419, 442, 487, 621, 1018

F570+. Person with part of body on fire. 459

F577. Persons identical in appearance. 884

F585.2. Magic phantom army. 674

F598. Old woman gives miraculous amount of milk. 870

F610. Remarkably strong man. 54, 99, 286, 406, 416, 419, 453-4, 656, 736, 876, 950, 983, 1025, 1058

F610.0.1. Remarkably strong woman. 299, 489, 494, 496, 589, 590, 627, 642, 737, 838, 848, 973, 1176

F614.8+. Tree split in two by arrow/spear. 257-8

F628.1.3. Strong man kills great serpent. 807

F628.2.1. Strong man kills many men at once. 139

F636. Remarkable thrower. 1122

F639.1.1. Mighty digger of tunnels. 671, 674, 826, 997, 1122

F641+. Dog with remarkable hearing. 1073

F652. Marvelous sense of smell. 817

F655. Extraordinary perception of blind men. 488, 1028

F682.0.1+. Person only one leg. 225

F687. Remarkable fragrance (odor) of person. 561, 681, 698, 705, 948, 1013

F696. Marvelous swimmer. 1073

G: Ogres

G352.2. Wild boar as ogre. 156, 563, 680, 995

G352+. Marsupial as ogre. 417

G352+. Insect as ogre. 545

G353.1. Cannibal bird as ogre. 897

G353. Bird as ogre. 1159

G354.1. Snake as ogre. 457, 504, 529, 557, 756

G354.2. Crocodile as ogre. 797, 897

G354.3. Lizard as ogre. 219

G361.1.1. Two-headed ogre. 360

G361.1.5. Ten-headed ogre. 429

G361.2. Great head as ogre. 102

G363+. Ogre with enormous mouth. 558

G370+. Ogre eats pregnant woman, fetus survives. 244

G370+. Blind ogre. 340, 1030

G370+. Deaf ogre. 1030

G371+. Stone ogre. 840

G400-G499. Falling into ogre's power

G400. Person falls into ogre's power. 496

G405. Man on hunt falls into ogre's (witch's) power. 604

G411. Person aids ogre and is captured. 1020, 281, 107

G413. Ogre disguises voice to lure victim. 255

G413+. Ogre disguises self to lure victim. 395

G421. Ogre traps victim. 1068, 1033, 878

G422. Ogre imprisons victim. 1033, 878, 509, 443, 340

G440. Ogre abducts person. 1033, 1030, 878, 845, 839, 719, 718, 488, 443, 378, 122

G441. Ogre carries victim in bag (basket). 846, 663, 614, 590, 586, 574, 340, 306, 281

G500-G599. Ogre defeated

G501. Stupid ogre. 963, 488

G510.4. Hero overcomes devastating animal. 58, 257-8, 269, 271, 295, 378, 466, 479, 503, 504, 630, 680, 756, 1025, 1056, 1158, 1159

G510.4+. Hero overcomes devastating ogre. 220, 343, 453-4, 488, 635, 644, 672, 694, 721, 756, 852, 871, 955, 986, 1114

G512. Ogre killed. 219, 255, 277, 339, 401, 431, 509, 556, 566, 608, 614, 650, 718, 741, 1030, 1122

G512+. Ogre killed with yam. 281

G512+. Ogre eaten alive by insects. 417

G512+ Ogre killed by entrapment. 178, 496

G512+. Ogre killed by snakes. 582

G512.1. Ogre killed with knife (sword). 121, 582, 613

G512.1+. Ogre killed with axe. 399, 443, 488, 623

G512.1+. Ogre killed with spear/arrow. 220, 233, 281, 340, 343, 520, 566, 604, 629, 635,

672, 741, 797, 809, 852, 871, 897, 955, 986, 1056, 1114

G512.1.2. Ogre decapitated. 360, 721, 756, 1056

G512.2. Ogre stoned to death. 578, 582

G512.3. Ogre burned to death. 230, 414, 578, 845, 1056

G512.3+. Ogre boiled to death. 457

G512.3.1. Ogre killed by throwing hot stones (metal) into his throat. 558, 1003

G512.3.1+. Ogre tricked into eating hot stones. 808, 878, 1033

G512.8. Ogre killed by striking. 1022

G512.8+. Ogre killed by striking with shield. 123

G512.8.1. Ogre killed by striking with club. 82

G512.9.1. Ogre killed by helpful dogs. 995

G514. Ogre captured. 613

G519. Ogre killed through other tricks. 1030

G519.1. Ogre's wife killed through other tricks. 121

G519.2+. Ogre killed with own weapon. 846

G530+. Help from ogre's assistant. 635

G530.1. Help from ogre's wife (mistress). 610, 1003

G530.1+. Help from ogress' husband. 123, 590

G550. Rescue from ogre. 985, 797, 703, 590

G550+. Rescue from ogre by star women. 485

G551.1. Rescue of sister from ogre by brother. 122

G560. Ogre deceived into releasing prisoner. 123, 485

G570. Ogre overawed. 122, 406, 796

G572. Ogre overawed by trick. 243, 306, 611, 702

G572+. Ogre immobilized by stuffing with food. 613

G580+. Ogres frightened away by screaming. 571

G580+. Ogres chased away by dog. 685

G600-G99. Other ogre motifs

G610. Theft from ogre. 121, 406, 772, 809

G632. Ogre who cannot endure daylight. 406

G636. Ogres powerless after cockcrow. 702

G639. Ogress lives in water. 941

G639+. Ogre lives in water. 941

G641K. Ogres live in cave(s). 496, 520

G642K. Ogres eat raw flesh. 123, 608, 610, 720, 1217

G650+. Ogre duped into eating spouse. 82

G661. Ogre's secret overheard. 1122

H: Tests

H0-H199. Identity tests: recognition

H46.1+. Cannibal recognized when it devours raw flesh. 608, 610, 720

H46.1+. Ogre recognized when it devours raw flesh. 485

H46.1+. Revenant recognized when it devours raw flesh. 559, 572, 598, 732, 747, 1006, 1222

H46.1+. Revenant recognized when it devours rocks. 1222

H46.1+. Spirit recognized when it devours raw flesh. 332, 1072

H75.6. Recognition by missing hair. 659

H300-H499. Marriage tests

H300. Tests connected with marriage. 594, 660, 938

H310+. Suitor tests: kindness. 688

H310+. Suitor test: dancing. 794

H310+. Suitor test: singing. 794

H335.3.4+. Suitor task: kill man-eating snake. 58

H360. Bride test. 633

H360+. Bride test: fetching clean water. 422

H383.4. Bride test: cooking. 131

H900-H1199. Tests of prowess: tasks

H1023.2.4. Task: filling a bottomless water tube. 445-6, 478, 747, 1161

H1100+. Task: digging a long yam without breaking it. 134, 747, 889

H1115.1. Task: cutting down huge tree which magically regrows. 733

H1115.1+. Task: cutting down forest, which is magically replanted. 75b, 130, 397, 673

H1118.3+. Task: counting trees near village. 169

H1118+. Task: counting snakes. 169

H1118+. Task: counting stones in a river. 169

H1144.5K+. Task: counting the grains of sand. 63

H1144.7K. Task: counting the stars. 63

H1200-H1399. Tests of prowess: quests

H1256. Journey to other world to obtain a wife. 168

H1400-H1599. Other tests

H1400. Fear test. 633

H1500+. Speaking contest. 80

H1543. Contest in remaining under water. 309

H1562.2.2+. Before undertaking rescue, bird tests strength by lifting stone. 521a, 737

H1562.2.2+. Before undertaking rescue, eagle tests strength by lifting stone. 481

H1562.5.2K. Contest to determine who can throw (toss) the highest. 243

H1570+. Contest to see which tree dies first that will cause the corresponding twin brother to die. 171

H1570+. Test: eating disgusting food. 1001

H1596. Beauty contest. 660

J: The Wise and the Foolish

J0-J199. Acquisition and possession of wisdom (knowledge)

J157.0.1. Deity appears in dream and gives instructions or advice. 642

J200-J1099. Wise and unwise conduct

J200+. Choices: eat the food contaminant or face more jail time. 363

J561. Intemperance in pursuit. 933

J651. Inattention to danger. 933, 841

J652. Inattention to warnings. 72, 129, 141, 165, 186, 210, 237, 245, 250, 293, 312, 319, 336, 352, 430, 441, 538, 575, 578, 665, 666, 682, 685, 688, 691, 704, 716, 718, 730, 806, 815, 823, 839, 840, 842, 928, 933, 944, 982, 994, 1001, 1010, 1034, 1044, 1048, 1115, 1117, 1121, 1143, 1220

J1050. Attention to warnings. 72, 123, 127, 129, 166, 210, 237, 250, 312, 319, 430, 440, 441, 493, 591, 594, 648, 665, 682, 688, 699, 707, 719, 776, 815, 840, 844, 981, 999, 1010, 1028, 1034, 1044, 1117, 1126, 1143

J1100-J1699. Cleverness

J1110. Clever persons. 341, 408-9, 482, 486, 542, 580, 695, 730, 749

J1146. Detection by strewing ashes (sand). 742

J1485. Mistaken identity. 365, 368

J1700-J2749. Fools (and other unwise persons)

J1745.2+. Ignorance of childbirth. 499

J1745.2+. Ignorance of menses. 905

J1770+. Airplane misunderstood. 376

J1770+. Bomb misunderstood. 376

J1770+. Net bag mistaken for woman. 759

J1772+. Soap thought to be food. 361

J1772.9+. Excrement thought to be food and therefore eaten. 462, 657

J1772.9+. Man eats someone else's feces, believing that they are his own. 281

J1782+. Floating tree thought to be ghost. 381

J1795+. Image in mirror mistaken for ghost. 383

J1806+. Flashlight mistaken for torch. 340

J1813+. Cooking processes misunderstood: cooking with the sun. 80, 131, 264, 285, 670, 709, 734

J1813+. Cooking processes misunderstood: eating partly cooked food. 236

J1813+. Cooking processes misunderstood: eating raw food. 926

J1813+. Cooking processes misunderstood: using animal flesh as firewood. 236, 633, 775

J1820+. Person drowns trying to catch fish in underwater cage. 119

J1850+. Radio thought to contain humans. 371

J1856. Food given to object. 375

J1856+. Food given to body part. 375

J1867. Man punishes offending part of his body. 375

J1880+. Flashlight spoken to as if human. 340

J1971+. Legs used as knife to cut sugarcane. 236

J2030. Absurd inability to count. 253

J2050+. Mosquitoes purchased to distribute on island to keep people awake at night. 490

J2100+. Pregnant woman becomes stuck climbing tree. 146

J2119.4+. Numskull puts hole in boat. 88

J2119.4+. Rat eats hole in boat made of tuber. 1207, 1060

J2130+. Numskull has wife put hole in his head to attach feathers. 303

J2130+. Fool kills only person who can free him. 1048

J2132.1+. Man ties himself to cassowary and is dragged to death. 729

J2133.11+. Cassowary destroys boat in anger, but almost drowns while chicken flies away. 1184, 676, 289, 249, 164

J2134. Numskull makes himself sick (uncomfortable). 320

J2183.6. Short-sightedness in case of fire. 555

J2244+. Climb up tree feet first. 395

J2244+. Climb down tree head first. 82, 620

J2700+. Hunter paralyzed with fear by dead marsupial. 129

K: Deceptions

K0-K99. Contests won by deception

K16.2+. Diving match: trickster eats food while pretending to be underwater. 309

K16. Diving match won by deception. 661

K18.3. Throwing contest: bird substituted for stone. 243

K90+. Contest won by opening eyes and cheating. 388

K100-K299. Deceptive bargains

K140.1+. Trick exchange of feathers. 275

K300-K499. Thefts and cheats

K300. Thefts and cheats—general. 71, 94, 95, 315, 326, 432, 442, 450, 456a, 467, 496, 531, 551, 591, 647, 658, 663, 698, 707, 772, 909, 917, 970, 992, 1009, 1035, 1182

K300+. Cassowary steals kangaroo's legs after exchange. 313

K301.2. Family of thieves. 408-9

K307. Thieves betray each other. 408-9

K311.6.5. Thief disguised as pig. 237

K311. Thief in disguise. 229

K330+. Thief escapes punishment by feeding owner his own stolen food. 749

K330+. Thief poisons guard. 455

K331. Goods stolen while owner sleeps. 709, 1014

K333. Theft from blind person. 77, 120, 187, 284, 362, 638, 717

K333.1. Blind Dupe. 488

K335. Thief frightens owner from goods. 695, 730

K341. Owner's interest distracted while goods are stolen. 595

K343.1. Owner sent on errand and goods stolen. 301

K360+. Man exchanges pig for game meat with boys, then dupes boys and takes all. 447

K400. Thief escapes detection. 251, 754, 763-4a, 763-4a, 809

K401.1.1. Trail of stolen goods made to lead to dupe. 357, 459, 605

K419+. Thief escapes detection through transformation. 656

K420. Thief loses his goods or is detected. 133, 141, 160, 193, 194, 212, 228, 259, 283, 284, 341, 362, 376, 392, 397, 406, 464, 497, 690, 709, 717, 749, 754, 763-4a, 780, 813, 864, 865, 920, 921, 953, 958, 960, 1004, 1028, 1051, 1068, 1217

K423. Stolen object magically returns to owner. 655

L: Reversal of Fortune

L113.1. Menial hero. 58, 649
L114.1. Lazy hero. 826
L116. Insane hero (heroine). 818
L123. Pauper hero. 825, 826
L140+. Ugly marries beautiful. 296, 866, 866, 906, 1090, 1116
L143. Poor man surpasses rich. 458a
L160. Success of the unpromising hero (heroine). 245, 482, 580
L161. Lowly hero marries princess. 726, 1032
L161+. Deformed man marries beautiful woman. 627
L161.1. Marriage of poor boy and rich girl. 826

L200-L299. Modesty brings reward
L213.2+. Choice of ugliest for marriage. 1024

L300-L399. Triumph of the weak
L300. Triumph of the weak. 518, 557, 649
L310. Weak overcomes strong in conflict. 458b, 598, 708
L315+. Small bird slays cassowary. 112
L315+. Small bird overcomes cassowary. 423
L315+. Scrawny dog overcomes giant pig. 995
L315.6. Insects worry large animal to despair or death. 1070

L400-L499. Pride brought low
L410. Proud ruler (deity) humbled. 1070

M: Ordaining the Future

M300-M399. Prophecies
M300. Prophecies. 1121
M300+. Contest: whoever shoots the other's eye out will be a good hunter. 374
M341. Death prophesied. 312, 336, 740
M359.9. Prophecy of famine. 829
M364.8+. Prophesy: resuscitation by disposition of bones. 242
M369.7.3. Prophecy: sex of unborn child. 932

M400-M499. Curses
M411.1. Curse by parent. 551
M451. Curse: death. 459
M451.1. Death by suicide. 57, 259, 314, 327, 353, 382, 407, 424, 433, 448, 456a, 483, 489, 499, 507, 628, 692, 743, 766, 789, 834, 854, 861, 883, 950, 997, 1001
M451.2. Death by drowning. 119, 448, 789, 1177

N: Chance and Fate

N300-N399. Unlucky accidents
N320.1+. Man unwittingly causes death of sister. 626
N330. Accidental killing or death. 82, 811, 1112
N331+. Killed by treefall. 659, 681
N332. Accidental poisoning. 429
N333. Aiming at fly has fatal results. 357
N337. Accidental death through misdirected weapon. 659
N338. Death as result of mistaken identity: wrong person killed. 1222
N339+. Accidental drowning. 619, 688, 801
N339+. Death from slipping. 753
N339+. Man dies after falling into fire. 476
N339+. Person falls to death from tree. 671, 1205
N339.13+. Accidental death by striking head against tree. 476
N340. Hasty killing or condemnation (mistake). 476, 488
N340+. Dogs kill owner, mistaking his sleep for death. 486
N343.4. Lover commits suicide on finding beloved dead. 483
N350. Accidental loss of property. 992
N365.2. Unwitting father-daughter incest. 365
N365.3.1. Brother and sister unwittingly in love with each other. 873, 902

N400-N699. Lucky accidcents
N476.2. Man vulnerable only in armpits shot as he stretches his arms. 986

N700-N799. Accidental encounters
N730+. Relative accidentally killed when intervening in fight. 366
N741. Unexpected meeting of husband and wife. 439

N800-N899. Helpers
N812. Giant or ogre as helper. 117
N813. Helpful genie (spirit). 788
N815.0.1. Helpful tree-spirit. 91, 757
N815.0.1+. Helpful vine-spirit. 1159
N825.1. Childless old couple adopt hero. 400, 400, 707

P: Society

P0-P99. Royalty and nobility
P14.13+. Chief gives his own daughter as reward. 450
P16.4.1. Suttee. 483
P17.0.2. Son succeeds father as king. 169
P17.3. Dying king names successor. 169

P100-P199. Other social orders
P160. Beggars. 144, 219, 245, 270, 308, 375, 616, 912, 970, 1018

P200-P299. Family
P210. Husband and wife. 48, 49, 50, 56, 57, 58, 66, 67, 70, 74, 75a, 76, 78, 79, 82, 83, 85, 86, 90, 91, 92, 93, 97, 99, 104, 107, 108, 109, 110, 111, 115, 117, 121, 123, 124, 127, 128, 130, 131, 132, 133, 135, 137, 138, 139, 144, 145, 146, 150, 153, 156, 157, 158, 159, 161, 162, 163, 165, 166, 168, 169, 170, 172, 173, 174, 175, 176, 181, 182, 185, 187, 190, 191, 193, 194, 195, 197, 199, 200, 202, 204, 208, 209, 211, 214, 215, 216, 220, 222, 223, 224, 226, 228, 230, 231, 232, 233, 234, 235, 240, 241, 242, 245, 246, 247, 248, 250, 251, 252, 253, 254, 255, 265-7, 259, 260, 261, 263, 268, 270, 271, 274, 277, 278, 279, 281, 282, 285, 287, 288, 291a, 293, 294, 296, 298, 299, 300, 301, 303, 304, 305, 308, 310, 311, 312, 315, 318, 319, 323, 325, 326, 327, 328, 333, 334, 335, 336, 339, 345, 346, 347, 348, 349, 350, 351, 352, 353, 354, 355, 357, 359, 365, 366, 368, 369, 370, 371, 373, 376, 378, 381, 385, 386, 387, 389, 390, 391, 392, 393, 394, 396, 397, 398, 400, 401, 402, 403, 404, 405, 407, 410, 412, 414, 415, 416, 417, 421, 422, 426, 427, 428, 429, 436, 438, 445-6, 439, 441, 442, 444, 447, 448, 453-4, 451, 456b, 456a, 457, 459, 461, 463, 465, 467, 468, 469, 470, 471, 472, 473, 474, 475, 476, 477, 478, 479, 481, 482, 483, 484, 486, 487, 489, 490, 491, 492, 493, 494, 495, 496, 498, 499, 501, 504, 505, 507, 508b, 509, 511, 512, 513, 514, 515, 516, 517, 518, 519, 521a, 522, 523, 524, 525, 526, 527, 528, 531, 532, 533, 534, 535, 537, 538, 539, 542, 543, 545, 546, 547, 548, 549, 550, 551, 554, 555, 556, 560, 561, 563, 565, 566, 567, 568, 570, 573, 574, 578, 579, 580, 582, 583, 584, 586, 589, 590, 592, 594, 595, 596, 599, 600, 601, 602, 603, 604, 605, 607, 608, 610, 611, 612, 617, 619, 620, 622, 624, 625, 626, 627, 628, 631, 632, 633, 635, 636, 639, 640, 641, 642, 644, 645, 646, 647, 648, 653, 654, 658,

804, 836, 844, 851, 864, 870, 871, 909, 1168, 1185, 1188, 1189, 1214

P281. Stepfather. 857

P282. Stepmother. 351

P290+. Half-brother. 445-6, 494

P290+. Half-sister. 445-6

P290+. Hostile co-wives. 79, 463, 1163, 1208

P290+. Maternal kin. 57, 59, 79, 91, 98, 101, 104, 181, 195, 230, 236, 242, 339, 350, 365, 366, 426, 448, 476, 505, 517, 521a, 549, 750-1, 763-4a, 767, 805, 818, 891, 1103, 1112, 1164, 1180

P291. Grandfather. 123, 192, 286, 308, 412, 464, 481, 525, 554, 557, 636, 647, 699, 758, 855, 881, 884, 916, 997

P291.1. Grandfather as foster father. 440, 830, 1186

P291.1+. Foster grandfather. 620

P292. Grandmother. 123, 241, 265-7, 294, 404, 412, 441, 464, 481, 525, 554, 556, 647, 763-4a, 761, 775, 805, 822, 827, 881, 884, 889, 942, 999, 1013, 1200

P292.1. Grandmother as foster mother. 81, 179, 187, 210, 243, 271, 333, 362, 415, 451, 533, 582, 663, 830, 871, 1186, 1200

P293. Uncle. 79, 123, 129, 156, 159, 252, 310, 407, 474, 491, 522, 624, 648, 707, 719, 722, 750-1, 836, 1126, 1226

P293+. Maternal uncle. 505, 511

P293+. Paternal uncle. 505

P294. Aunt. 104, 204, 355, 407, 479, 491, 522, 527, 615, 624, 644, 808, 836, 916, 924, 925, 1212, 1222, 1226

P294+. Aunt as foster mother. 836

P294+. Maternal aunt. 505, 511

P295. Cousins. 439, 511, 624, 648, 951, 1021, 1058, 1126, 1196

P297. Nephew. 104, 129, 474, 479, 491, 511, 527, 624, 644, 836, 916, 925, 1126, 1212

P298. Niece. 407, 491, 648, 707, 836, 916, 924, 1126, 1222

P300-P399. Other social relationships

P310. Friendship. 52, 65, 71, 88, 89, 93, 94, 103, 105, 106, 108, 157, 164, 170, 189, 200, 201, 207, 211, 228, 248, 249, 251, 264, 268, 275, 280, 289, 292, 300, 301, 302, 307, 309, 326, 350, 354, 361, 413, 416, 455, 462, 475, 476, 485, 488, 490, 492, 495, 500, 505, 508b, 521b, 525, 526, 540, 543, 544, 546, 552, 568, 575, 585, 587, 598, 601, 602, 621, 660, 661, 664, 676, 683, 684, 701, 702, 724, 745, 755, 764b, 766, 768, 779, 781, 784, 787, 799, 810, 811, 814, 825, 847, 850, 869, 893, 897, 900, 916, 936, 937, 938, 942, 962, 964, 965, 968, 969, 972, 992, 998, 1014, 1030, 1031, 1032, 1043, 1044, 1060, 1061, 1073, 1074, 1110, 1124, 1133, 1178, 1183, 1184, 1198, 1207, 1211, 1215, 1219

P310+. Friend scorns friend's wise counsel. 391

P310+. One friend acts wisely, the other does not. 1044

P311.0.1+. Friends share same name. 581

P400-P499. Trades and professions

P426.2. Hermit. 356, 375, 447, 634, 800, 866, 929, 1116

P428. Musician. 825

P500-P599. Government

P551.5. Boy corps. 774

P555. Defeat in battle. 160, 774

P600-P699. Customs

P600+. Babies secluded after birth. 465

P600+. Cane swallowing as purgative. 715

P600+. Corpses buried away from houses. 351

P600+. Courtship customs: *karim lek*. 333, 382, 445-6, 482, 580, 866, 902

P600+. Courtship customs: *kukim nus*. 726

P600+. Courtship customs: *tanim het*. 344, 726

P600+. Custom of hanging oneself. 146

P600+. Custom of retaliation. 127

P600+. Custom: birth payment. 805

P600+. Customs associated with menarche. 109, 666, 822, 1057

P600+. Initiation of boys: scarification. 217, 1117

P600+. Payment of goods to kin as recompense for murder. 674

P600+. Special seats for teaching customs. 420

P600+. Stick put at top of garden for protection. 500

P600+. Tooth filing. 763-4a

P600+. Virilocality. 261, 285, 589, 917

P634.0.1+. Custom of exchanging food after reconciliation. 500

P681+. Mourning customs: earth on body. 92, 204, 294, 526, 529, 534, 648, 693, 972

P681+. Mourning customs: feast. 407

P681+. Mourning customs: growing beard. 491

P681+. Mourning customs: self-mutilation. 135, 149, 211, 373, 407, 445-6, 628, 692, 696, 761, 778, 859, 902

Q: Rewards and Punishments

Q2. Kind and unkind. 596

Q10-Q99. Deeds rewarded

Q10+. Obedience rewarded. 355

Q10. Deeds rewarded. 138, 716, 1159

Q40. Kindness rewarded. 558, 570, 596, 620, 688, 759, 802, 815, 821, 844, 877, 1015, 1044

Q41. Politeness rewarded. 262, 1001

Q42. Generosity rewarded. 99, 189, 447, 671

Q45. Hospitality rewarded. 234, 941

Q53. Reward for rescue. 58, 77, 120, 152, 285, 305, 345, 521a, 601, 614, 638, 653, 694, 717, 723, 757, 771, 784, 799, 960, 985, 995, 1009, 1040, 1214

Q53+. Reward for retrieval of body. 760

Q55. Reward for sparing life when in animal form. 1209

Q55+. Reward for sparing life. 578

Q72K2. Obedience rewarded. 1048

Q86. Reward for industry. 497

Q93. Reward for supernatural help. 594, 788

Q100-Q199. Nature of rewards

Q111.2. Riches as reward (for hospitality). 269

Q114. Gifts as reward. 635

Q141.2. Plentiful game animals (fish) as reward. 578, 985

Q150.1. Rescue from deluge as reward. 1028

Q151.6. Life spared as reward for hospitality. 234

Q151. Life spared as reward. 156, 467, 821

Q190+. People rewarded with good weather after aiding cloud-man. 421

Q200-Q399. Deeds punished

Q200+. Exogamy punished. 648

Q200+. Feeding excrement punished. 626

Q200+. Nagging punished. 626

Q200+. Revealing secret punished. 290

Q210.1. Criminal intent punished. 127, 1207

Q210+. Trespassing punished. 435

Q211. Murder punished. 61, 138, 139, 142, 145, 160, 186, 198, 219, 230, 255, 310, 343, 380, 419, 429, 432, 457, 460, 463, 486, 495, 504, 514, 517, 533, 550, 558, 577, 578, 582, 604, 616, 635, 662, 673, 674, 680, 689, 704, 721, 721, 735, 736, 741, 747, 756, 758, 775, 809, 818, 845, 849, 852, 863, 889, 896, 897, 899, 903, 935, 955, 987, 989, 1048, 1052, 1055, 1074, 1110, 1172, 1199, 1214, 1218

Q211.4. Murder of children punished. 156, 395, 431, 652, 808, 904, 1003

Q211.4+. Punishment for not killing son. 162

Q211.6. Killing an animal revenged. 72, 136, 157, 189, 190, 202, 207, 210, 226, 237, 250, 293, 314, 331, 440, 534, 575, 666, 687, 696, 699, 720, 722, 728, 741, 752, 783, 812, 821, 851, 857, 892, 896, 903, 935, 997, 999, 1028, 1103, 1121

Q400-Q599. Kinds of punishment

Q438. Punishment: abandonment in forest. 159, 162, 256, 298, 512, 678, 777, 798

Q438+. Punishment: abandonment on island. 942

Q450+. Punishment by withholding food. 162

Q451.1. Hands cut off as punishment. 560

Q451.3. Loss of speech as punishment. 459

Q451.7. Blinding as punishment. 435, 467, 597, 723, 799

Q451.10. Punishment: genitalia cut off. 1110

Q451.10.1. Punishment: castration. 768

Q451.10.1+. Punishment: attack on testicles. 776, 832, 894, 965, 1047

Q451.12. Lips sewed together as punishment for slander. 212

Q451. Mutilation as punishment. 105

Q453.1+. Punishment: being bitten by insect. 1070

Q453. Punishment: being bitten by animal. 869

Q456+. Punishment: trapped in grave with corpse/ghost. 408-9

Q458. Flogging as punishment. 72, 75a, 139, 180, 211, 224, 253, 276, 368, 369, 374, 424, 459, 511, 533, 537, 703, 709, 742, 755, 771, 808, 820, 824, 884, 973

Q461. Impalement as punishment. 310, 362

Q467K+. Abandonment in river as punishment. 481

Q467K. Marooning at sea as punishment. 481, 601

Q469.5. Punishment: choking with smoke. 77, 960

Q469.7. Punishment: twisting entrails from body. 819

Q469.10. Scalding as punishment. 744

Q469.10.3. Scalding as punishment for insult. 274

Q470+. Befouling as punishment. 831, 934

Q470+. Public excoriation. 461

Q478+. Punishment: eating dead relative. 678

Q478+. Punishment: eating excrement. 626

Q486.1. Criminal's house burned down. 160, 565

Q486.1.1. Sinful city burnt as punishment. 1214

Q486. Criminal's property destroyed as punishment. 160

Q550+. Punishment: male impregnation. 626

Q551. Magic manifestations as punishments. 780

Q551.3. Punishment: transformation. 293, 447, 554, 645, 687, 765, 792, 1110

Q551.3+. Punishment: transformation to woman. 768

Q551.3.2+. Punishment: transformation into marsupial. 689

Q551.3.2+. Punishment: transformation into pig. 549, 842

Q551.3.2+. Punishment: transformation into snake. 1034

Q551.3.2.2+. Punishment: transformation into bird. 83, 297, 497, 518

Q551.3.4. Transformation to stone as punishment. 79, 635, 770, 812, 1110

Q551.5+. End of reincarnation as punishment. 78

Q551.8.7. Punishment: face distorted. 745

Q552.2.3.2.3+. Island sinks for offense. 331

Q552.3.1. Famine as punishment. 829

Q552.3.3. Drought as punishment. 1216

Q552.11. Punishment: meeting frightful apparition. 679

Q552.19.6. Flood as punishment for murder (fratricide). 935

Q552.25. Earthquake as punishment. 550

Q553.4. Death of children as punishment. 565, 574

Q580. Punishment fitted to crime. 81

Q580+. Murderer forced to eat corpse. 735

Q580+. Person must eat food contaminant that was served to another. 363

Q580+. Punishment for not sharing food: tricked into cannibalism. 317

Q582. Fitting death as punishment. 464, 465, 538, 1052

Q582+. Fitting death as punishment: burning. 419

Q583. Fitting bodily injury as punishment. 656, 832, 894

Q584.2. Transformation of a man to animal as fitting punishment. 497, 500, 518

Q585. Fitting destruction (disappearance) of property as punishment. 298

Q595.4. Loss of money as punishment. 338, 511

Q595. Loss or destruction of property as punishment. 247, 298, 563, 674, 773, 849, 992

R: Captives and Fugitives

R0-R99. Captivity

R1+. Wild woman captured. 130

R4. Surprise capture. 88, 104, 106, 107, 120, 122, 164, 200, 222, 228, 230, 255, 415, 468, 473, 477, 484, 508a, 590, 597, 638, 709, 797, 809, 845, 854, 960, 1068, 1124

R9+. Spirit captured. 754

R10.3. Children abducted. 200, 484, 487, 519, 563, 572, 586, 590, 644, 789, 804, 805, 836, 849, 870, 974, 1030, 1187, 1226

R10. Abduction. 74, 108, 115, 130, 173, 378, 386, 397, 410, 422, 488, 501, 537, 541, 545, 683, 727, 785, 824, 831, 839, 850, 901, 928, 933, 952, 954, 970

R10+. Abductee returned. 631

R11. Abduction by monster (ogre). 281, 306, 340, 519, 521a, 574, 586, 590, 614, 644, 663, 718, 719, 846

R13.0.1. Children carried off by animals. 202

R13.1+. Abduction by bandicoot. 1050

R13.1+. Abduction by flying fox. 631, 1021

R13.1+. Abduction by marsupial. 84, 231, 647, 1202

R13.3. Person carried off by bird. 235, 530, 551

R13.3.2. Eagle carries off youth. 128, 204, 211, 311, 507, 531, 1168

R13.4+. Abduction by crocodile. 797

R13.4+. Abduction by frog. 161

R13.4+. Abduction by turtle. 513

R13.4K+. Cassowary abducts person. 515

R13.4.1. Abduction by snake. 1067, 1187

R13.4.1K2. Abduction by fish (eel). 874

R14. Deity (demigod) abducts person. 525

R14+. Abduction by spirit. 428, 789, 795

R16+. Abduction by stone-person. 737

R24. Abductor in disguise. 805

R40+. Entrapment by sitting on shoulders/back. 90, 152, 510

R43. Captivity on island. 878

R45.1. Man confined under roots of tree. 771

R45.3. Captivity in cave. 315, 340, 378, 380, 430, 443, 509, 526, 543, 666, 685, 795, 846, 901, 927, 1010, 1021, 1048, 1067

R49+. Captivity in pigsty. 534

R49+. Captivity in bag. 77. 638, 717

R49.1. Captivity in tree. 120, 284, 345, 417, 426, 472, 547, 638, 653, 717, 813, 1021, 1159

R50+. Whole village captured by ghost(s). 308

R51.1. Prisoners starved. 120, 284, 345, 380, 417, 430, 526, 638, 653, 685, 717, 813, 878, 1010, 1048

R100-R199. Rescues

R100. Rescues. 101, 106, 148, 164, 198, 231, 289, 292, 305, 485, 495, 504, 631, 687, 703, 705, 720, 758, 764b, 765, 784, 786, 960, 985, 1020, 1040, 1074, 1159, 1223, 1223

R100+. Person buried in excrement rescued. 355

R110. Rescue of captive. 77, 88, 120, 152, 164, 200, 228, 284, 345, 417, 426, 443, 521a, 536, 590, 638, 653, 717, 771, 797, 927, 1021, 1187

R111.2.2. Rescue of princess from mountain. 1202

R130. Rescue of abandoned or lost persons. 373, 481, 682, 737, 825, 844, 942, 1009

R131. Exposed or abandoned child rescued. 864, 974, 1161

R150+. Rescue by pauper. 308

R150+. Animal rescues woman from cruel husband. 631

R151. Husband rescues wife. 985, 175

R151.1. Husband rescues stolen wife. 683, 844

S: Unnatural Cruelty

S55. Cruel sister-in-law. 407, 632, 950

S55+. Cruel brother-in-law. 577, 659, 758, 854, 968, 978, 1020

S56. Cruel son-in-law. 444, 775

S62. Cruel husband. 274, 402, 427, 512, 523, 554, 560, 626, 631, 635, 675, 678, 686, 703, 704, 723, 735, 746, 755, 771, 820, 1161

S62+. Cruel husband refuses wife food. 565, 1160, 1179

S62.1. Bluebeard. 678

S63+. Wife kills husband. 165, 299, 499, 523, 538, 577, 686, 742, 744, 775

S63+. Husband kills wife. 153, 310, 385, 407, 467, 498, 517, 628, 678, 769, 818, 952, 1163, 1190, 1208

S70+. Murder of kin. 104

S70+. Wife betrays her kin to her husband. 230

S70+. Cruel nephew. 407

S70+. Cruel niece. 407

S70+. Cruel co-mother. 463

S70+. Cruel co-wife. 463

S70+. Cruel cousin. 407, 511

S70+. Cruel brother. 663, 682, 765, 767

S70+. Cruel maternal kin. 767

S70+. Cruel paternal kin. 1216

S70+. Cruel sister. 224, 703, 767

S71.1+. Murderous uncle. 722

S71. Cruel uncle. 511, 836

S72. Cruel aunt. 407, 491, 511

S73.1. Fratricide. 85, 127, 157, 186, 189, 325, 387, 682, 696, 802, 810, 819, 844, 882, 883, 888, 935, 953, 1001

S73.1.4. Fratricide motivated by love-jealousy. 345, 438, 451, 470, 483, 653, 1190

S73.2. Person banishes brother (sister). 358

S75.1K2. Sororicide. 722, 739, 836

S100-S199. Revolting murders or mutilations

S100+. Murder by putting hot stones up rectum. 565

S110. Murders. 54, 61, 64, 76, 82, 85, 87, 99, 101, 104, 111, 112, 122, 123, 140, 142, 152, 153, 157, 160, 162, 164, 165, 175, 175, 177, 178, 189, 190, 198, 202, 213, 219, 220, 233, 237, 244, 249, 251, 265-7, 278, 281, 289, 294, 299, 310, 321, 332, 339, 340, 373, 384, 385, 387, 396, 399, 401, 404, 407, 417, 419, 435, 438, 445-6, 444, 453-4, 451, 456a, 457, 461, 463, 465, 475, 476, 483, 484, 499, 505, 507, 521a, 523, 528, 529, 533, 537, 540, 556, 566, 577, 580, 582, 586, 589, 590, 595, 597, 604, 608, 615, 628, 629, 635, 636, 639, 644, 646, 647, 648, 650, 663, 672, 674, 676, 678, 680, 681, 682, 685, 687, 689, 692, 694, 696, 697, 700, 707, 718, 719, 730, 732, 733, 735, 736, 739, 741, 742, 744, 750-1, 758, 766, 769, 771, 772, 774, 781, 783, 785, 789, 797, 798, 801, 802, 808, 809, 814, 816, 817, 821, 823, 835, 836, 839, 840, 843, 844, 846, 849, 851, 854, 857, 858, 863, 865, 871, 876, 881, 882, 883, 897, 899, 902, 903, 911, 914, 921, 922, 924, 935, 943, 952, 953, 955, 962, 967, 972, 983, 986, 1001, 1004, 1006, 1009, 1022, 1029, 1030, 1033, 1048, 1058, 1072, 1073, 1074, 1114, 1121, 1122, 1163, 1172, 1183, 1184, 1190, 1217, 1219, 1220

S110+. Eaten alive. 104, 227, 395, 495, 510, 562, 652, 775, 798, 904, 985, 1074

S110+. Eaten alive by insects. 417

S111. Murder by poisoning. 429, 1214

S111.8+. Murder by feeding poisonous invertebrates. 310, 517

S112. Burning to death. 215, 239, 242, 284, 335, 414, 483, 558, 567, 569, 578, 638, 727, 747, 775, 818, 834, 845, 889, 894, 904, 958, 966, 989, 997, 1003, 1055, 1188

S112+. Murder by putting hot stones up rectum. 553

S112+. Murder by throwing hot stones down throat. 775

S112.0.2. House (hostel) burned with all inside. 130, 142, 161, 183, 218, 230, 380, 397, 403, 419, 574, 675, 686, 704, 737, 740, 809, 810, 841, 865, 886, 887, 889, 896, 987, 1004, 1068, 1212

S112.1. Boiling to death. 156, 351, 433, 457

S113. Murder by strangling. 207, 659

S113.1. Murder by hanging. 863

S113.2. Murder by suffocation. 98

S115. Murder by stabbing. 86, 110, 263, 268, 1218

S115.2.1+. Murder by driving spear through head. 310

S116.4. Murder by crushing head. 356, 453-4

S116. Murder by crushing. 1208, 1214

S118. Murder by cutting. 121, 1110

S118.1. Murder by cutting adversary in two. 269, 378, 520

S118.2. Murder by cutting throat. 58, 127, 134, 138, 277, 385, 574, 613

S122. Flogging to death. 215, 290, 390, 432

S125.1. Self-immolation. 861

S127. Murder by throwing from height. 302, 406, 407, 614

S131. Murder by drowning. 410, 514, 535, 538, 699, 712, 713, 720, 888, 999, 1050, 1110, 1207

S132. Murder by starvation. 358, 878, 1010

S133. Murder by beheading. 394, 545, 662, 721, 722, 747, 756

S139.1. Murder by twisting out intestines. 819

S139.2. Slain person dismembered. 70, 138, 145, 255, 306, 495, 496, 505, 566, 574, 577, 595, 604, 678, 689, 697, 730, 894, 897

S139.2.1.1. Head of murdered man taken along as trophy. 343

S139.2.2. Other indignities to corpse. 61

S139.2.2.1+. Corpse impaled. 610

S139.2.2+. Corpse put into cooking pot or cooked. 70, 194, 255, 482, 565, 580, 604, 639, 673, 678, 681, 858, 894, 1068, 1122

S139.4. Murder by mangling with axe. 186, 210, 255, 269, 283, 314. 343, 353, 385, 399, 443, 482, 488, 616, 623. 656, 678, 715, 889, 956, 968, 987, 1052, 1206

S139.7. Murder by slicing person into small pieces. 215, 230, 269, 395, 399, 431, 474, 510, 621, 673, 704, 852, 1074

S140. Cruel abandonments and exposures. 1158, 1223

S140+. Abandonment of blind. 1017

S140.1. Abandonment of aged. 187, 271, 635, 1214

S141. Exposure in boat. 1113

S141.3+. Abandonment on log floating in sea. 481, 1057

S142. Person thrown into the water and abandoned. 445-6, 459, 478, 601, 652, 882, 902, 1161

S143.2. Abandonment in tall tree. 345, 391, 653, 682, 765, 844, 1009

S143. Abandonment in forest. 159, 256, 259, 296, 445-6, 456a, 512, 515, 531, 597, 619, 663, 678, 707, 737, 777, 798, 819, 902, 966

S145. Abandonment on an island. 433, 670, 878, 942, 1025, 1033, 1056, 1114

S146.2. Abandonment in cave. 380, 854, 882, 1190

S160. Mutilations. 104

S160+. Anus sewn up. 585

S160.1. Self-mutilation. 89, 135, 161, 211, 373, 407, 445-6, 462, 628, 718, 761, 778, 787, 902, 1178, 1180

S161. Mutilation: cutting off hands (arms). 105, 462, 560, 761, 787, 887, 936

S161.1. Mutilation: cutting off fingers. 135, 149, 373, 445-6, 692, 696, 778, 859, 902

S162. Mutilation: cutting off legs (feet). 89, 761, 887

S162.3. Mutilation: cutting off toes. 158

S165. Mutilation: putting out eyes. 104, 230, 435, 574, 597, 799

S168. Mutilation: tearing off ears. 373, 407, 628

S176+. Mutilation: breasts cut off. 194, 310, 402, 517, 662

S176.1. Mutilation: emasculation. 161, 598, 656, 674, 741, 768, 985, 1110

S176.1K2+. Murder by cutting off breasts. 463, 508a, 968

S180+. Smoking person over fire. 574

S180+. Torture by whipping. 305

S183.1. Person forced to eat hearts (flesh) of relatives (draw blood). 678

S185. Cruelty to pregnant woman. 1114, 1056, 832, 820

S186. Torturing by beating. 718

S200-S299. Cruel sacrifices

S211. Child sold (promised) to devil (ogre). 703, 854, 1020

S260.1. Human sacrifice. 1218

S300-S399. Abandoned or murdered children

S301. Children abandoned (exposed). 478, 878, 902, 909, 1033, 1161

S322.0.1K+. Man instructs pregnant wife to cherish infant if a boy, to kill if a girl. 902, 1161

S322.3. Jealous co-wife kills woman's children. 463

S326.1. Disobedient child burned. 358

S371+. Abandoned woman's daughter becomes hero. 1158

S371+. Abandoned woman's son becomes hero. 271, 635, 1017, 1025, 1056, 1114, 1158

S400-S499. Cruel persecutions

S401. Unsuccessful attempts to kill person in successive reincarnations (transformations). 215

S430. Disposal of cast-off wife. 560

S433. Cast-off wife abandoned on island. 635

S441. Cast-off wife and child abandoned in forest. 678

T: Sex

T0-T99. Love

T10. Falling in love. 58, 108, 172, 211, 244, 248, 259, 285, 288, 300, 311, 327, 328, 333, 350, 372, 378, 382, 389, 405, 410, 445-6, 459, 494, 496, 501, 512, 522, 551, 570, 602, 627, 640, 647, 648, 653, 668, 669, 705, 725, 733, 735, 812, 816, 820, 825, 841, 873, 906, 909, 913, 916, 940, 942, 943, 950, 952, 973, 996, 997, 1009, 1013, 1018, 1067, 1090, 1160

T15. Love at first sight. 531, 99

T24.1. Love-sickness. 668

T50. Wooing. 262, 333, 344, 382, 445-6, 482, 580, 627, 726, 838, 979, 1031, 1116

T52. Bride purchased. 92, 202, 248, 269, 285, 288, 298, 318, 333, 357, 445-6, 477, 507, 551, 603, 659, 664, 759, 979, 1189

T52+. Groom purchased. 507

T52.6+. Father pays for bride rather than suitor. 826

T56.1.1. Bride attracted by flute. 594

T75. Man scorned by his beloved. 979

T75.2. Scorned lover kills successful one. 685, 692

T75.2.1. Rejected suitors' revenge. 382

T80. Tragic love. 568, 640, 648

T81.2. Death from unrequited love. 382

T81.2.1. Scorned lover kills self. 382

T81. Death from love. 533

T86. Lovers buried in same grave. 382

T90+. Premarital sex. 900

T91.3. Love of mortal and supernatural person. 394, 622, 820, 979

T92.10. Rival in love killed. 345, 438, 451, 470, 483, 653, 816, 1190

T100-T199. Marriage

T100. Marriage. 58, 91, 92, 93, 97, 99, 104, 108, 110, 111, 111, 127, 128, 132, 135, 157, 159, 163, 166, 170, 173, 176, 182, 185, 187, 197, 199, 202, 204, 224, 234, 242, 247, 248, 252, 253, 265-7, 259, 260, 263, 269, 271, 278, 279, 282, 285, 288, 294, 298, 299, 300, 303, 304, 311, 314, 319, 325, 328, 333, 335, 336, 347, 350, 351, 352, 354, 355, 357, 370, 378, 385, 388, 389, 392, 393, 400, 407, 410, 415, 416, 422, 438, 445-6, 442, 453-4, 456a, 459, 463, 468, 469, 470, 474, 478, 479, 482, 487, 491, 492, 494, 499, 507, 512, 512, 514, 516, 524, 527, 528, 531, 532, 534, 535, 538, 545, 551, 555, 556, 561, 572, 575, 577, 580, 582, 589, 594, 595, 596, 602, 605, 611, 617, 620, 624, 625, 627, 631, 633, 640, 642, 644, 648, 654, 658, 659, 665, 666, 667, 670, 671, 672, 673, 677, 678, 682, 685, 687, 688, 692, 693, 694, 700, 703, 704, 705, 707, 709, 721, 722, 726, 728, 729, 734, 741, 742, 747, 748, 755, 763-4a, 759, 761, 765, 767, 768, 769, 773, 775, 776, 779, 784, 790, 795, 799, 802, 810, 812, 816, 820, 825, 826, 830, 831, 841, 844, 856, 857, 864, 866, 870, 877, 882, 884, 890, 893, 900, 903, 906, 909, 912, 913, 916, 917, 918, 921, 924, 938, 940, 943, 950, 951, 952, 957, 978, 981, 991, 994, 997, 1002, 1009, 1013, 1024, 1032, 1034, 1035, 1044, 1048, 1090, 1116, 1133, 1163, 1168, 1182, 1185, 1188, 1189, 1190, 1194, 1196, 1204, 1208, 1211, 1223, 1226

T111. Marriage of mortal and supernatural being. 67, 78, 165, 181, 241, 339, 364, 386, 402, 439, 441, 451, 468, 477, 496, 522, 619, 641, 664, 692, 700, 773, 795, 804, 805, 824, 850, 855, 874, 880, 901, 954, 1041, 1067, 1124, 1194, 1216

T111.2. Woman from sky-world marries mortal man. 49, 50, 245

T111.2.3+. Marriage of man to sun's daughter. 168

T111.2+. Mortal marries person in sky. 525

T115. Man marries ogre's daughter. 414, 556

T115+. Man marries ogress. 230

T117+. Marriage to stone. 323

T117.5+. Marriage to sago woman. 327

T117.7+. Marriage to a fruit. 85, 533

T117.10. Coconut wife (in form of a woman). 185

T126+. Marriage between lizard and tree's shadow. 195

T126+. Marriage of ogre and eagle. 378

T130. Marriage customs. 917

T130+. How to find a wife: light a fire at the base of a mountain. 182

T131. Arranged marriage. 1206

T145.0.1. Polygyny. 79, 108, 111, 153, 158, 167, 172, 191, 197, 202, 204, 233, 242, 265-7, 260, 305, 323, 366, 370, 391, 394, 405, 429, 432, 445-6, 444, 447, 456a, 463, 468, 469, 471, 479, 483, 492, 498, 499, 523, 525, 527, 531, 533, 538, 545, 555, 573, 577, 584, 619, 641, 644, 647, 654, 669, 673, 675, 678, 682, 683, 692, 716, 735, 742, 755, 763-4a, 765, 815, 816, 844, 882, 916, 938, 983, 985, 1013, 1041, 1048, 1117, 1161, 1163, 1208

T145.1.1+. Man marries nine women. 173

T145.1.3+. Man married to two sisters. 162, 299, 667, 1196

T145.7+. Man's first wife beautiful but lazy, his second ugly but diligent. 602

T146. Polyandry. 672

T161. Jus primae noctis. 1070

T182+. Death from witnessing parents' intercourse. 461

T192. Marriage by force. 74, 111, 211, 222, 223, 230, 245, 327, 346, 349, 422, 427, 441, 473, 477, 501, 513, 525, 537, 545, 664, 750-1, 773, 795, 850, 880, 901, 928, 933, 954, 970, 1018, 1041, 1067, 1124, 1143, 1176

T200-T299. Married life

T201. Marriage destroys friendship. 755

T211.9.2+. Man dies in dead wife's arms. 732

T253. The nagging wife. 626

T298. Reconciliation of separated couple. 512

T400-T499. Illicit sexual relations

T410. Incest. 901, 951

T411. Father-daughter incest. 365, 726, 971, 996, 1002

T411+. Foster father-daughter incest. 991

T411.1. Lecherous father. 1002

T412. Mother-son incest. 204, 994, 1009

T415.2. Brother repels incestuous sister. 626

T412+. Foster mother-son incest. 478

T412+. Mother-son marriage. 776

T415. Brother-sister incest. 154, 349, 499, 722, 752, 837, 861, 988

T415.5. Brother-sister marriage. 166, 445-6, 596, 658, 728, 848

T415.5+. Foster brother-sister marriage. 386, 442

T415.5+. Man marries brother in form of woman. 282

T415.5+. Sister marries man who looks like brother. 884

T421. Man marries his aunt (mother's sister). 204

T425. Brother-in-law seduces (seeks to seduce) sister-in-law. 742, 802

T471. Rape. 154, 305, 365, 391, 622, 683, 722, 752, 861, 922, 988

T471+. Gang rape. 832

T475.2.1. Intercourse with sleeping girl. 194, 564

T475. Unknown (clandestine) paramour. 1110

T481. Adultery. 190, 299, 394, 468, 501, 535, 653, 735, 784, 905, 942, 983, 1172

T500-T599. Conception and birth

T510. Miraculous conception. 257-8, 269

T511.1+. Conception from eating cucumber. 135

T511.5.1. Conception from eating fish. 615, 1212

T511.5.3+. Conception from eating insects. 626

T511.5.3+. Pregnancy from swallowing mosquito. 260, 308

T511.7.2. Pregnancy from eating an egg. 204

T511.7.3. Conception from eating meat. 116

T511.8.4+. Conception from eating nut. 191

T511. Conception from eating. 370

T511+. Male conception from eating woman's loincloth. 626

T512.2.1. Child develops from man's urine. 183, 461, 740

T512.3. Conception from drinking water. 926

T518+. Impregnation from spirit. 625

T534. Conception from blood. 225, 422, 466, 479, 520, 527, 600, 629, 955, 986, 1025

T538. Unusual conception in old age. 257-8

T541.1. Birth from blood. 635, 776

T541.5. Birth from man's thigh. 677

T541.8.1. Birth from excrement. 192

T542. Birth of human being from an egg. 191, 225, 360, 600, 955

T543.1. Birth from a tree. 675

T543.3. Birth from fruit. 132, 442, 453-4

T545. Birth from ground. 182, 466, 527, 635, 851, 1055

T548. Birth obtained through magic or prayer. 932

T549.4. Child born from miscarried fetus. 244

T550. Monstrous births. 901

T554.0.2K+. Woman gives birth to flying fox. 269

T554.0.3K+. Woman gives birth to crocodile. 465, 680, 951

T554.0.3K+. Woman gives birth to lizard. 516

T554.0.4K. Woman gives birth to fish. 625

T554.7. Woman gives birth to a snake. 241, 516, 583, 722, 775

T554.16.K2. Woman gives birth to hog. 938

T554.10. Woman gives birth to a bird. 942

T554.10+. Woman bears cockatoo. 680

T554.10+. Woman gives birth to an eagle. 67, 481

T555+. Woman gives birth to a vine. 680

T565. Woman lays an egg. 67, 481, 652, 942

T566. Human son of animal parents. 128, 563, 740, 870

T570. Pregnancy. 78, 124, 146, 162, 173, 183, 204, 220, 242, 244, 248, 257-8, 259, 260, 278, 288, 290, 312, 314, 318, 327, 334, 357, 366, 378, 386, 398, 408-9, 400, 402, 445-6, 456a, 465, 466, 468, 469, 489, 494, 499, 505, 512, 519, 528, 531, 547, 580, 607, 615, 624, 625, 626, 659, 680, 707, 732, 733, 740, 748, 775, 782, 808, 820, 830, 837, 868, 893, 901, 902, 909, 916, 926, 929, 932, 934, 935, 938, 942, 951, 952, 1009, 1025, 1055, 1056, 1114, 1158, 1161, 1182, 1206, 1214

T570+. Pregnancy without intercourse. 93

T573. Short pregnancy. 116, 135, 260, 308, 834

T574. Long pregnancy. 583

T578. Pregnant man. 626, 794

T580. Childbirth. 78, 93, 104, 108, 116, 124, 135, 162, 169, 187, 204, 220, 223, 241, 260, 278, 288, 291a, 298, 299, 308, 318, 327, 354, 357, 364, 370, 386, 398, 401, 445-6, 441, 442, 453-4, 456a, 468, 469, 474, 482, 489, 494, 499, 512, 519, 525, 528, 531, 542, 547, 556, 560, 580, 607, 615, 622, 624, 625, 626, 627, 644, 647, 664, 665, 680, 690, 692, 693, 707, 722, 732, 735, 748, 761, 782, 794, 795, 805, 808, 824, 825, 834, 855, 858, 884, 890, 901, 902, 903, 909, 916, 918, 926, 929, 934, 940, 1056, 1182, 1185, 1188, 1189, 1196, 1212, 1216

T580+. Stillbirth. 832

T581.1. Birth of child in forest. 314, 312, 269, 259

T581.3. Child born in tree. 334

T581.9. Child born on beach. 257-8, 334

T584.2. Child removed from body of dead mother. 314, 659

T584.2.1. Child born of dead mother in grave. 1055, 1214

T584.3. Cesarean operation upon a woman at childbirth as a custom. 278

T586.1. Many children at a birth. 775

T587. Birth of twins. 67, 171, 183, 248, 271, 466, 479, 520, 629, 635, 652, 740, 769, 830, 837, 938, 942, 952, 955, 986, 1017, 1025, 1055, 1114, 1158

T587+. Birth of twins: one human, one snake. 583

T589.7. Simultaneous births. 445-6, 492, 1161

T589.7.1. Simultaneous birth of (domestic) animal and child. 128

T590+. Woman gives birth to revenant. 625

T596. Naming of children. 707

T600-T699. Care of children

T611. Suckling of children. 124, 128, 137, 353, 394, 395, 403, 448, 489. 495, 563, 744, 747, 761, 836, 870, 896, 1143, 1188, 1212

T611.6+. Nursing induced. 1189

T615. Supernatural growth. 527

T676. Childless couple adopt animal as substitute for child. 353

T685. Twins. 67, 183, 248. 271, 466, 479, 520, 629, 635, 652, 740, 769, 830, 952, 955, 986, 1017, 1025, 1055, 1114, 1158

V: Religion

V0-V99. Religious services

V1.8.11. Fish worship. 622

V1.11.2. Worship of stone idols. 273

V1.11.3. Worship of wooden idol. 539

V11.7. Sacrifice to animal. 1218

V12+. Food as sacrifice. 430

V12+. Tobacco as sacrifice. 430

V12+. Tree leaves as sacrifice. 430

V12.1. Blood as sacrifice. 321

V12.4.11+. Chicken as sacrifice. 321, 367

V12.4.3. Pig as sacrifice. 166, 236, 321, 430, 529, 558, 692, 868

V12.4+. Marsupial as sacrifice. 100, 558

V50. Prayer. 449

V52.3. Prayer before battle brings victory. 54

V61.2. Dead burned on pyre. 401, 432, 475, 483

V61.3+. Bones exhumed. 1205

V61.3+. Dead buried. 54, 57, 92, 98, 101, 123, 134, 136, 139, 155, 156, 168, 171, 186, 194, 215, 226, 303, 314, 316, 317, 343, 348, 351, 380, 382, 384, 389, 390, 398, 408-9, 399, 401, 402, 407, 414, 417, 452, 459, 463, 486, 488, 489, 493, 505, 526, 528, 532, 540, 546, 592, 617, 623, 626, 639, 640, 656, 662, 678, 711, 712, 728, 729, 732, 736, 739, 743, 747, 753, 756, 758, 766, 800, 810, 816, 837, 868, 875, 878, 889, 894, 897, 899, 907, 924, 929, 950, 953, 968, 996, 1029, 1112, 1163, 1164, 1190, 1199, 1205, 1208. 1214

V61.10. Corpses exposed in tree. 414, 648

V61+. Dead placed in garden hut. 414

V70. Religious feasts and fasts. 558

V100-V199. Religious edifices and objects

V112.1. Spirit huts. 64, 130, 161, 175, 217, 224, 234, 242, 330, 354, 380, 397, 407, 420, 450, 497, 503, 541, 545, 565, 630, 649, 662, 673, 683, 687, 704, 707, 737, 757, 766, 780,

785, 803, 814, 820, 913, 918, 920, 934, 941,
954, 967, 968, 982, 995, 1035, 1117
V140. Sacred relics. 1185
V140+. Sacred bones. 840
V150+. Discovery of sacred flute. 814

V200-V299. Sacred persons

V230. Angels. 979

V300-V399. Religious beliefs

V331+. Sacred flute destroyed upon conversion
to Christianity. 814
V331. Conversion to Christianity. 257-8, 679,
692, 855, 899

V400-V499. Religious orders

V450+. Cargo cult. 213, 840

W: Traits of Character

W0-W99. Favorable traits of character

W10. Kindness. 596, 844, 1044
W11. Generosity. 99, 189, 595, 596, 747, 759
W27. Gratitude. 77, 92, 106, 148, 155, 187,
305, 431, 443, 447, 558, 598, 653, 682, 756,
784, 793, 802, 891, 1001
W28.2+. Man sacrifices life for son's honor.
659
W31. Obedience. 166, 218, 244, 259, 282, 355,
391, 396, 455, 483, 523, 716, 738, 815, 981,
986, 1034, 1048, 1117, 1161, 1226

W100-W199. Unfavorable traits of character

W111. Laziness. 69, 88, 95, 164, 341, 405, 444,
496, 517, 538, 602, 626, 657, 669, 578, 697,
733, 776, 791, 800, 826, 836, 873, 921, 998,
1040, 1061, 1090, 1160, 1207
W115. Slovenliness. 272, 381, 958, 959, 969
W116. Vanity. 80, 173, 679, 701, 847
W117. Boastfulness. 602
W121. Cowardice. 784
W125. Gluttony. 90, 94, 95, 103, 111, 156,
309, 322, 407, 423, 496, 571, 998, 1184
W126. Disobedience. 78, 83, 90, 116, 124, 134,
152, 157, 162, 179, 214, 216, 218, 230, 245,
253, 256, 259, 261, 283, 297, 322, 338, 352,
355, 358, 391, 396, 428, 456a, 474, 477,
483, 505, 510, 515, 533, 638, 644, 546, 651,
654, 663, 687, 696, 703, 709, 716, 718, 739,

742, 747, 773, 791, 798, 800, 815, 827, 829,
884, 889, 925, 944, 952, 982, 986, 994,
1000, 1034, 1048, 1115, 1117, 1161, 1217,
1226
W141. Talkativeness. 95
W151. Greed. 48, 57, 60, 98, 129, 150, 228,
247, 254, 355, 423, 445-6, 447, 448, 452,
462, 464, 475, 491, 514, 609, 611, 651, 659,
675, 686, 688, 753, 768, 777, 780, 783, 806,
819, 883, 950, 967, 969, 971, 978, 1051,
1103, 1133, 1160, 1211
W152. Stinginess. 103, 146, 174, 317, 329,
369, 433, 474, 565, 571, 723, 992
W154. Ingratitude. 164, 249, 289, 433, 472,
485, 497, 571, 676, 1001, 1184
W157. Dishonesty. 71, 89, 90, 101, 105, 168,
196, 221, 271, 272, 281, 309, 310, 330, 360,
376, 380, 382, 391, 394, 396, 408-9, 407,
414, 416, 417, 424, 425, 462, 464, 467, 475,
491, 492, 499, 503, 517, 528, 537, 538, 540,
560, 574, 577, 601, 604, 616, 644, 657, 658,
660, 681, 684, 689, 720, 723, 724, 728, 735,
741, 742, 745, 746, 747, 748, 749, 770, 777,
787, 801, 819, 836, 845, 863, 868, 869, 884,
888, 894, 904, 906, 909, 913, 920, 936, 937,
938, 940, 948, 950, 951, 952, 953, 959, 964,
966, 968, 971, 992, 996, 1002, 1003, 1055,
1057, 1060, 1143, 1160, 1168, 1182, 1190,
1206, 1215, 1222
W158. Inhospitality. 103, 407
W167. Stubbornness. 63, 83, 99, 107, 173, 271,
312, 314, 316, 428, 450, 457, 484, 510, 513,
516, 570, 578, 602, 687, 704, 771, 906, 952,
967, 1006, 1044, 1070
W181. Jealousy. 68b, 79, 85, 110, 275, 304,
345, 350, 394, 432, 438, 448, 451, 470, 471,
483, 484, 501, 511, 514, 515, 518, 569, 601,
625, 631, 640, 648, 653, 671, 673, 682, 685,
688, 692, 705, 755, 765, 794, 802, 806, 816,
826, 844, 854, 882, 905, 909, 996, 1009,
1048, 1073, 1117, 1163, 1190, 1208, 1215
W188. Contentiousness. 978
W195. Envy. 201, 244, 251, 277, 376, 380,
420, 577, 602, 642, 655, 676, 699, 711, 847,
888, 1014, 1126
W196. Lack of patience. 246

X: Humor

X700-X799. Humor concerning sex

X712.1H. Female genitals. 354, 687, 707, 818,
832, 894, 962, 965, 1047
X712.1H+. Origin of lime (calcium oxide):
woman's genitals. 508b, 1043
X712.2H. Male genitals. 687, 808, 1110
X712.3H. Testicles. 161, 226, 747, 1168

X712.3.1H. Injury to testicles. 102, 484, 598,
656, 674, 697, 741, 776, 832, 894, 958, 962,
965, 985, 1047, 1072, 1103
X716H+. Feces as gift. 121, 298, 355, 637,
831, 1222
X716H+. The escoumerda. 103, 228, 275, 281,
457, 462, 502, 626, 657, 787, 866, 1068
X716.1H. Befouling with one's own
excrement. 1180
X716.1H+. Befouling with excrement. 152,
164, 433, 482, 500, 580, 604, 640, 831, 912,
934, 959, 1032, 1116, 1191
X716.1H+. Birds and beasts (animal excretion).
88, 423, 462
X716.4H. Fastidiousness regarding excrement.
801
X716.6H. Smell of breaking wind. 114, 502,
674
X716.6H+. Humor concerning breaking wind.
730
X716.7H. Disastrous breaking wind. 114, 832,
1011
X716.8H. Fortuitous breaking wind. 502, 796
X717H+. Urine as gift. 301, 452, 463, 1055
X717.1H+. Urination on animal. 183, 295, 740
X736.2H+. Symbolic fellatio. 1168
X736.3H+. Symbolic cunnilinctus. 508b, 1043
X740.1H+. Symbolic pedicatory rape. 565,
573, 995
X740.1H+. Symbolic pedicatory rape while at
stool. 236, 354, 500
X743H+. Humor concerning voyeurism. 841
X743H+. Voyeurism. 1032
X743H. Humor concerning exhibitionism. 501,
683, 743, 770, 1043

X800-X99. Humor based on drunkenness

X800. Humor based on drunkenness. 369

X900-X1899. Humor of lies and exaggeration

X1303.1. Big fish pulls man or boat. 426
X1723.3+. Snake enters woman's body. 1172

Z: Miscellaneous Groups of Motifs

Z0-Z99. Formulas

Z41.1K. The mangrove and the crab. 80
Z49.13+. Chain of deaths. 476
Z71.1. Formulistic number: three. 135, 220,
316, 426, 430, 442, 453-4, 449, 466, 551,
553, 622, 630, 721, 735

Z71.2. Formulistic number: four. 108, 250,
253, 493, 563, 635
Z71.3. Formulistic number: five. 79, 392, 899,
1021
Z71.4. Formulistic number: six. 520
Z71.5. Formulistic number: seven. 169, 784,
1056
Z71.16.1. Formulistic number: eight. 169, 418,
507
Z71.16.2. Formulistic number: ten. 253, 680,
1212, 1214
Z71.16.11. Formulistic number: fifteen. 215
Z71.16+. Formulistic number: one hundred
ninety-nine. 649

Z200-Z299. Heroes

Z210. Brothers as heroes. 248, 271, 479, 520,
629, 630, 635, 644, 680, 721, 756, 852, 871,
955, 986, 1017, 1025

Z300-Z399. Unique exceptions

Z311.4. Man can be injured only in armpits.
817
Z356. Unique survivor. 61, 269, 453-4, 520,
672, 685, 687, 775, 896, 903, 920, 955, 986,
1016

Glossary

Words from the text are listed here that may not be familiar to a typical reader in the United States. Also explained here are items of material culture that have non-obvious meanings. The Tok Pisin equivalent of the English word is listed in the Helvetica font, scientific nomenclature is given in *italics*. Elevations are given for species, when known, to assist in determining the provenance of a story.

aibika: two plants (sunset hibiscus or *Abelmoschus manihot*, and Chinese amaranth or *Amaranthus tricolor* [a.k.a. aupa]) with edible leaves (Mihilic, 1971: 58, 62; May, 1984: 56-57; Rehm & Espig, 1991: 139, 159; Siemonsma & Piluek, 1993: 82). *A. manihot* is also used medicinally (Woodley, 1991: 89-90). *A. manihot* mainly occurs up to 1200 meters elevation (Siemonsma & Piluek, 1993: 61).

aila: a tree (*Inocarpus fagifer*) with edible nuts that grows near water at up to 500 meters elevation (Hanum & van der Maesen, 1997: 285-286)

ancestral spirit [tambaran]: see **spirit**

bamboo [mambu]: is used for containers, **fire making**, and **flutes**

bandicoot [mumut, sikau]: The bandicoots of Australia and **New Guinea** are rat-like marsupials from the family Peroryctidae (Figure 1). The word sikau conflates bandicoot with **kangaroo**.

bean, winged: see **winged bean**

betel nut [buai]: an addictive and mildly psychoactive nut from the palm tree *Areca catechu* (Figure 2). It is widely consumed in parts of the tropics from Africa to the Pacific islands. In **PNG** it is often consumed with a kind of pepper (daka, *Piper betle*) and calcium oxide (kambang) derived from seashells (Oliver, 1989: 305-307). Ash from certain plants is sometimes substituted for lime (Powell, 1976: 135). Chewing betel nut turns one's saliva blood red, and after many years it turns one's teeth black. *A. catechu* grows at elveations as high as 100 meters (Powell, 1976: 135), or 900 meters under heavy rainfall (Twohig, 1986: 105). *P. betle* grows up to 1000 meters elevation (Twohig, 1986: 106). *A. catechu* and *P. betle* are also used medicinally (Woodley, 1991: 109, 112-114). *A. catechu* and lime are used in magic, and betel chewing is an important part of ceremonial life (Powell, 1976: 148; May, 1984: 97).

Figure 1. Striped bandicoot, *Microperoryctes longicauda* (Krieger, 1899: 85; Flannery,

Figure 2. Betel nut chewing by Bukawac Men, Morobe Province (Neuhauss, 1911: 113)

betel nut, wild [kawiwi]: a nut from the palm tree that is chewed in place of betel nut, *Howea belmoreana* according to Mihalic (1971: 108). *H. belmoreana* is not indigenous to New Guinea however, so perhaps kawiwi actually refers to *Areca macrocalyx*, which is cultivated (Essig, 1977: 24).

bikman: The Tok Pisin term bikman can be translated as either "leader" or the more specific anthropological term "big man." A big man is a village leader who has acquired his personal power via his own merits, such as oratory, magic, courage, hunting, farming, animal husbandry, and exchange of wealth. From this personal power, the big man develops a faction of supporters. The concept of "big man" is not applicable to all of **PNG**, so the term bikman is translated as "leader" throughout this book.

bird of paradise [kumul]: various species of birds (family Paradisaeidae), often with beautiful, elongated and highly coveted feathers, used by Papua New Guineans for ornamentation (Figure 3). The birds are sexually dimorphic; the males have special plumage during mating season to attract females. Male birds assemble in a communal area (called a "lek") to attract females during mating season. The lek is also where they are primarily hunted by men in bird blinds.

breadfuit tree [kapiak]: a tree (*Artocarpus altilis*) with a bland, starchy fruit that can be eaten raw or cooked (Figure 4). It is found in many parts of Micronesia and Polynesia. The fruit is approximately the size of a head and is sometimes symbolically associated with the head in folktales. Parts of the breadfruit tree are also used for medicine and magic (Powell, 1976: 144, 148). The tree is found at up to 1500 meters elevation (Verheij & Coronel, 1991: 85).

bride price [pe bilong marit]: Throughout **New Guinea** and other parts of Oceania, it was customary for a groom's family to give a gift of valuables to the prospective bride's family. This gift was considered part of an exchange, because the future-wife was considered a source of wealth from her skills at gardening and animal husbandry. This is not universal though. For example, some New Guinean cultures practice sister-exchange instead.

Figure 3. Raggiana bird of paradise, *Paradisaea raggiana* (D'Albertis, 1880, vol. 1, 222)

Figure 4. Breadfruit (Krieger 1899: 56)

callophyllum [kalopilum]: a hardwood tree (*Callophyllum* spp.): *C. bicolor* is found in rainforest at up to 250 meters elevation; *C. collinum* is found in forest at up to 500 meters; *C. euryphyllum* is found in rainforest at up 600 meters; *C. goniocarpum* is found at up to 800 meters; *C. inophyllum* (a.k.a. Alexandrian laurel and Borneo mahogany) hardwood, common on sandy beaches, but found up to 200 meters; *C. laticostatum* is found in rainforest at up to 1400 meters elevation; *C. leleanii* is found in forests at up to 900 meters; *C. neo-ebudicum* is found in New Britain and Bougainville at up to 800 meters; *C. papuanum* is found in forests at up to 1850 meters; *C. pauciflorum* is found at 1550-2900 meters; *C. peekelii* is found in rainforest at up to 300 meters; *C. persimile* is found in western **PNG** at up to 550 meters; *C. sil* is found in northern **New Guinea** at up to 650 meters; *C. suberosum* is found in southern New Guinea in wetlands at up to 50 meters; *C. vexans* is found in forest at 900-1450 meters

(Soerianegara & Lemmens, 1993: 114-132). Callophyllum is used for spear- and canoe-making (Powell, 1976: 152, 158).

cargo cult [kago kal, kago bilong ol tumbuna]: A cargo cult is a millenarian and millenialist religion that is often short lived.The premise of cargo cults is usually that material goods were erroneously given to the white people rather than Papua New Guineans, and that by performing certain rituals these goods will be returned to the Papua New Guineans.Such beliefs were sometimes reinforced by similar traditional beliefs (e.g., see the ancestor story in *Wantok* #213 and Berndt, 1992: 74-75).For a contextualization of the cargo cult concept, see Lindstrom (1993).

cassowary [muruk]: huge, fierce, flightless birds (*Casuarius* spp.).The feathers and meat are prized, and the bones are used as daggers.Males care for the eggs and chicks, but there is a widespread folk belief that it is the females that do this.The dwarf cassowary (*C. bennetti*) occus at sea level to 3000 meters elevation; the southern cassowary (*C. casuarius*) occus at sea level to 500 meters; and the northern cassowary (*C. unappendiculatus*) occurs from sea level to 700 meters.The three species are all found on mainland **New Guinea** and *C. bennetti* is also found on New Britain Island (Beehler *et al.*, 1986: 45-46).

Figure 5. Boy blowing a conch trumpet (Riley, 1925: 216)

casuarina [yar]: a tree found in Australia and **New Guinea** (*Casuarina* spp.).The inner bark of *C. equistifolia* is used medicinally (Woodley, 1991: 31-32).Casuarina is used for magic, arrowheads and digging sticks (Powell, 1976: 148, 152).*C. equisetifolia* grows naturally up to 100 meters elevation, but can be planted up to 1200 meters (Hanum & van der Maesen, 1997: 86-89).*C. oligodon* grows between 1500-1800 meters (Hanum & van der Maesen, 1997: 271-272).

changeling: A changeling is a child substituted at birth by fairies for the real child (folk motif F321.1).In this book, the concept of changeling is considered more broadly as any child that is not what it seems to be. Typically in Papua New Guinea, an old man transforms himself into a baby and abuses his (foster) mother's hospitality.

cockatoo [koki]: **New Guinea** has two species.The black one is the palm cockatoo (*Probosciger aterrimus*), which usually occurs at less than 750 meters elevation.The white one is the sulphur-crested cockatoo (*Cacatua galerita*), which has a yellow crest.It usually occurs at less than 1000 meters (Beehler *et al.*, 1986: 117).

charm, love [marila]: see **sorcery**

conch trumpet [taur]: a trumpet made from the spiral conch shell (*Charonia tritonis*; Figure 5).It is widespread in coastal areas, but is also found in some inland locations (McLean, 1994: 45-47).

coral tree [balbal, palpal]: a quick-growing, soft-wooded tree used for fences (*Erythrina variegata*), canoes (Powell, 1976: 158), medicine (Woodley, 1991: 83-84), spears, shields, and perfume (Hanum & van der Maesen, 1997: 130).The tree grows in coastal areas and in cultivated areas at up to 1200 meterselevation (Hanum & van der Maesen, 1997: 130-132). The leaves were traditionally eaten with human flesh in parts of the **Sepik** and Madang provinces (May, 1984: 59, 88).

Figure 6. Southern common cuscus, *Phalanger intercastellanus* (D'Albertis, 1880, vol 1., 124)

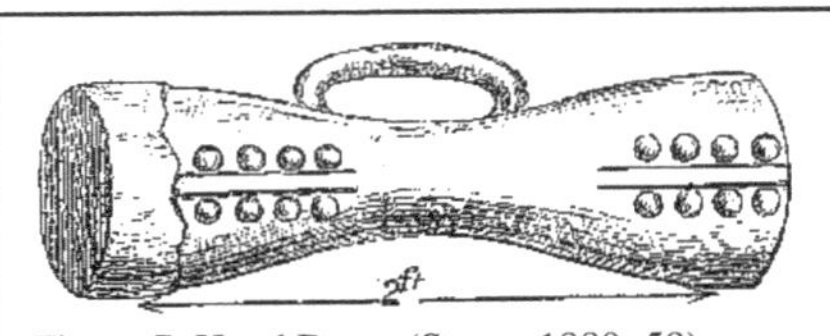
Figure 7. Hand Drum (Stone, 1880: 59)

crab: see **vagina dentata**

cuscus [kuskus, kapul]: marsupials of the family Phalangeridae (Figure 6). The white (spotted) cuscus is *Spilocuscus maculatus maculatus*. The word kapul conflates cuscus with **possum** and **kangaroo**.

dancing: see **festival**

drum, hand [kundu]: a small, wooden, hourglass-shaped drum often used in traditional singing and dancing (Figure 7). The top of the drum is covered with lizard, snake or **marsupial** skin with an adhesive of either tree gum or blood mixed with lime (McLean, 1994: 4). The hand drum is widespread in New Guinea, but is absent from Manus Province as well as parts of southern Eastern Highlands Province and interior Gulf and Morobe provinces (McLean, 1994: 4-6). See also **festival**.

drum, signal [garamut]: a canoe-shaped hardwood log (often from *Vitex cofassus*), hollowed out with only a slit opening, that produces a loud sound when struck (Mihalic, 1971: 86-87; McLean, 1994: 52; Figure 8). The signal drum is also known as the slit-gong or slit-drum (McLean, 1994: 52). *V. cofassus* is found at up to 2000 meters elevation (Lemmens *et al.*, 1995: 507). The slit-drum is found primarily with maritime and riverine peoples of the **Sepik**, Madang, Morobe, Manus and New Ireland provinces, as

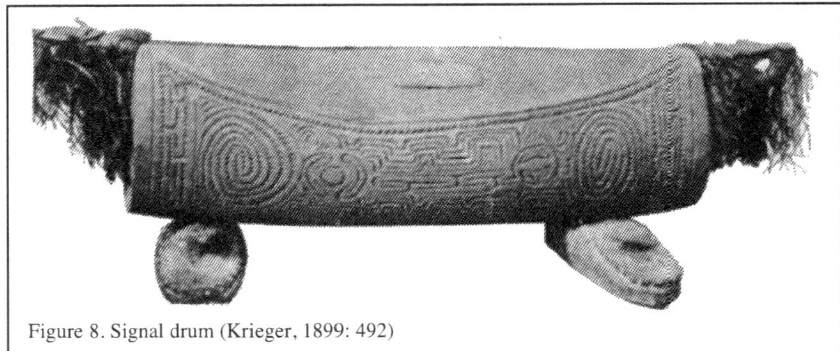
Figure 8. Signal drum (Krieger, 1899: 492)

well as in northern New Britain Province (McLean, 1994: 52-54). Use of signal drums is primarily restricted to men (McLean, 1994: 52). See also Gourlay (1975).

earth oven [mumu]: An earth oven is made as follows. Heated stones are placed at the bottom of a pit. On top of this is placed food wrapped in leaves (often banana, fig or **breadfruit**). The pit is sealed with branches and leaves (May, 1984: 31-33).

escoumerda: coprophagist (e.g., see Legman, 1975: 937-956); folk motif X115.52 in this book

Fee-fi-fo-fum: A cannibal returns home and makes an exclamation (folk motif G84).

Figure 9. Two methods of fire-making (Neuhauss, 1911: 256)

festival [singsing]: Singsing is translated herein as any of "festival", "dancing", and/or "singing", as contextually appropriate. Festivals often include singing, dancing and drumming which usually occur simultaneously.

fig [fikus]: Fig fruits (*Ficus* spp.) are widely eaten throughout the world. Certain species in **PNG** also have edible leaves (kumu mosong; *F. copiosa*, *F. cynaroides*, *F. dammaropsis*, *F. iodotricha*, *F. nodosa*, *F. pachyrachis*, *F. pungens*, *F. robusta*, *F. wassa*) [May, 1984: 59, 74].

fire making [mekim paia]: Two fire making methods were generally used in **New Guinea**: the twirl method (rapidly rotating a hardwood stick on a piece of bamboo or softwood) and making sparks from iron pyrite (Figure 9).

flute [mambu]: a flute made out of **bamboo** ("bamboo" is also called mambu in Tok Pisin). Two main types of flutes are played in

Figure 10. Pan pipes, Buka Island, North Solomons Province (Thurnwald, 1912, plate 13)

New Guinea: the panpipe (Figure 10) and single-tube flute (McLean, 1994: 17-24). Panpipes are widely distributed in the **Highlands**, but are also found in many other locales (McLean, 1994: 17-19). Single-tube flutes are divided into two categories: side-blown and end-blown. In **New Guinea**, side-blown flutes are primarily associated with sacred rituals. Sacred flutes were used mainly in maritime and riverine parts of the **Sepik**, as well as large parts of Morobe, Eastern Highlands and Simbu provinces (McLean, 1994: 20-24). The sacred flute often has a phallic association. It was traditionally hidden from women, and it was associated with ritual homosexuality and initiation rites (e.g., see Herdt, 1984). See also Gourlay (1975).

flying fox [blakbokis]: large, frugivorous bats (*Pteropus* spp., probably conflated with other species in the Pteropodidae family) [Flannery, 1995a: 347-402]

fowl, wild [wel paul, paul bilong bus]: 1. The bush hen (*Amaurornis olivaceus*) is found from sea level to 1500 meters elevation (Beehler *et al.*, 1986: 78) 2. The common scrubfowl (*Megapodius freycinet*) is found from sea level to 500 meters. It builds nests of leaves with soil or sand. Decomposition of the organic matter generates heat that incubates the eggs (Beehler *et al.*, 1986: 72-74).

forest spirit bride: see **Swan Maiden**

galip nut: a small oval nut from any of the following trees: *Canarium indicum* (Tahitian chestnut), *Terminalia kaernbachii* (a.k.a. okari), or *T. impediens* [Mihalic, 1971: 86; Verheij & Coronel, 1991: 301-302, 322]. *C. indicum* is widespread in coastal and island areas and is found at up to 600 meters elevation (Powell, 1976: 123; Verheij & Coronel, 1991: 322) or 2000 meters (Twohig, 1986: 93). *T. kaernbachii* grows at up to 1000 meters (Verheij & Coronel, 1991: 301-302). *C. indicum* is used medicinally (Powell, 1976: 137).

gam: see **shell, gam**

garamut: see **drum, signal**

ghost [dewel, tewel]: see **spirit**

ginger [kawawar, gorgor]: Ginger is used for food, medicine (Woodley, 1991: 135-136; Powell, 1976: 136-45) and magic (Powell, 1976: 148-149). Kawawar (*Zingiber oficinale*) is ordinary ginger. Gorgor (galangal, *Alpinia* spp.) is also used for wrapping and for counting days (Mihalic, 1971: 89; Rehm & Espig, 1991: 302). *Z. oficinale* grows at up to 1500 meters elevation in areas of high rainfall (Twohig, 1986: 116).

gourd: see **kambang**

"grass" skirt: see **purpur**

grubs, sago: see **sago**

Highlands [Hailans]: the central mountain range of **New Guinea**, consisting in **PNG** principally of the following provinces: Eastern Highlands, Western Highlands, Southern Highlands, Enga, and Simbu, as well as southern West **Sepik** Province. People of the Highlands are almost entirely speakers of trans-New Guinea phylum languages (thought this phylum is much more extensive than just these provinces) [Wurm & Hattori, 1983]. People of the Highlands share cultural features, such as "primary dependence on **sweet potato** cultivation, pig husbandry and pork prestations… patrilineal-descent ideology, nonhereditary big-man [**bikman**] political leadership, endemic warfare, and male domination of public affairs." (Hays & Hays, 1982: 202) See also Brown (1978).

hornbill [kokomo]: a large bird with a huge beak. The **New Guinea** species (*Rhyticeros plicatus*) is usually found at less than 500 meters elevation (Beehler *et al.*, 1986: 145).

ironwood tree [kwila, tor]: a hardwood tree with edible leaves (May, 1984: 63). *Intsia bijuga* is found mostly in coastal areas; *I. palembanica* is found at up to 600 meters elevation (Mihalic, 1971: 117, 196; Soerianegara & Lemmens, 1993: 69, 269). The ironwood tree is used for house posts (Powell, 1976: 163).

Jus primae noctis: a custom in which a leader claims the right to sleep with a subject's wife on the first night of marriage (motif T161)

kambang/sel kambang: 1. edible gourds (bottle gourd or *Lagenaria siceraria* [Rehm & Espig, 1991: 148; Siemonsma & Piluek, 1993: 190-191], snake gourd or *Trichosanthes cucumerina*, and *T. ovigera* [May, 1984: 64; Rehm & Espig, 1991: 149]) *L. siceraria* grows at up to 1600 meters elevation, and *Trichosanthes* spp. grow at up to 1500 meters. They are used traditionally in some parts of **New Guinea** for covering the penis (mostly the western **Highlands** of **PNG** and the Highlands of Irian Jaya). In some cultures, this was virtually the only clothing that a man wore. The gourd also has many other uses; it is edible when young, and it is often used as a container (Eastburn, 1989, Siemonsma & Piluek, 1993: 190-191). 2. lime (calcium oxide); see **betel nut**

kangaroo [kapul, sikau]: In Tok Pisin, there is no unambiguous word for kangaroo (family Macropodidae, which includes the wallaby and dorcopsis [Figure 11]). The word kapul conflates kangaroo with **possum** and **cuscus**. The word sikau conflates kangaroo with **bandicoot**. Most species of kangaroo in **PNG** are arboreal.

karim lek: Literally, "to carry the leg(s)." This is "a Middle Wahgi Valley courtship practice where a girl sits on a boy's lap or alongside a boy with both her legs across one of his thighs. Both parties rub noses for hours." (Mihalic, 1971: 107) They sing songs and are chaperoned (Lobban, 1985: 31-33). The Middle Wahgi Valley includes the Wahgi, Kuman, and Golin languages in the Western Highlands and Simbu provinces. The custom of **karim lek** was car-

Figure 11. Grey dorcopsis, *Dorcopsis luctuosa* (D'Albertis, 1880, vol. 1, 295)

ried to the South Fore of Eastern Highlands Province by Simbu policemen, but was apparently short-lived (Alpers, 1992: 318). See also **kukim nus, tanim het** (Lobban, 1985: 31-33).

kina: see **shell money**

kongkong: see **taro**

kukim nus: to rub noses in courtship (lit., "to heat up noses"), practiced in the **Highlands**. See also **karim lek, tanim het**.

leader: see **bikman**

Figure 12. Men's house, original round form, Sissano People, West Sepik Province (Neuhauss, 1911: 215)

limbum: a kind of palm tree (*Kentiopsis archontophoenix*) used for making houses, spears, arrows, bows, mats, buckets and for tying (Mihalic, 1971: 122; Murphy, 1985: 88)

limbum, wild: The fishtail palm tree (*Caryota rumphiana* and/or *C. mitis* in **PNG** [Flach & Rumawas, 1996: 66]) is used for bows and floors in PNG (Powell, 1976: 152, 162; Brown, 1986: 26). It occurs at up to 2000 meters elevation (Flach & Rumawas, 1996: 68).

lime: see kambang

Llewellyn and his dog: a folk motif (B331.2) in which a dog saves a child's life by killing a serpent, the dog's master returns to see the bloodied dog, who then kills the dog thinking instead that the dog killed the child (e.g. see Thompson, 1993)

Malay apple [aiai, laulau]: trees that bears small, red edible fruits (*Syzygium jambos* [rose apple], *S. malaccense* [Malay apple], and probably *Eugenia* spp.). The trees are found at 1200 meters elevation or less (May, 1984: 76-77; Verheij and Coronel, 1991: 292-294). The trees are also used for medicine, magic, axes, digging sticks, construction, and cooking (Powell, 1976: 138, 143-145, 149, 153, 164-169).

mangas: a tree (*Hibiscus tileaceus*) used for cigarette paper, rope making (Mihalic, 1971: 129), medicine, house posts, and weaving (Powell, 1976: 136, 138-139, 143-144, 163, 169). It is found along sandy shores and tidal creeks (Sosef, *et al.*, 1998: 291).

marsupial [kapul, kuskus, mumut, sikau]: nonplacental mammals of the order Marsupialia. See individual entries for **bandicoot**, **cuscus**, **kangaroo**, and **possum**.

masalai: 1. a malevolent **spirit** associated with a specific location (such as a mountain) or a specific natural feature (such as a whirlpool), generally folk motifs F400-499 2. In a human-like (anthropomorphic) form, this is often a large and/or ugly cannibal, similar to an ogre. For purposes of the folk-motif index, a masalai is considered an ogre if associated with cannibalism or cannibalistic intent (folk motifs G300-G699). Sometimes this meaning of masalai is conflated with **spirit**.

maternal relative [kandere]: any relative on one's mother's side of the family

men's house [haus man]: men's sleeping quarters. Men sleep separately from women in many parts of **New Guinea** (Figure 12). See also **spirit house**.

mosquito bag [moskito net]: a cylindrical bag made of plaited **sago**-shoots or bast that were used throughout the Middle **Sepik**. Families slept inside them for protection against the fierce mosquitos (Gewertz, 1983: 3).

mukmuk: "a mottled black and white stone, round and flat, about the size of a saucer or smaller with a sharpened perimeter and pierce through the centre. The larger ones are the badge or mark of rank amongst the natives of south-west New Britain. The smaller ones were used as currency." (Murphy, 1985: 91). See also **shell money**.

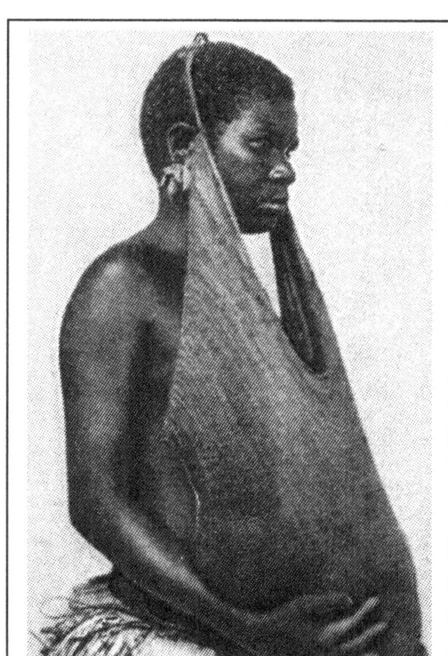
Figure 13. Woman with baby asleep in net bag (Thompson, 1892: 80)

net bag [bilum]: a bag made from string that is found throughout mainland **New**

Guinea. It is used for carrying bundles as well as babies (Figure 13). The string is made from a variety of plants (Powell, 1976: 167, 169).

New Guinea: The island of New Guinea was divided into three parts during colonial times: Dutch New Guinea, German New Guinea, and British New Guinea (**Papua**). Administration of British New Guinea was transferred to Australia between 1901-1906 (Souter, 1963: 91). German New Guinea became the Australian Mandated Territory of New Guinea after the 1919 Treaty of Versailles, following World War I (Souter, 1963: 124). German New Guinea consisted of what is now the **Sepik**, Manus, New Britain, New Ireland, and North Solomon provinces as well as parts of the **Highlands**. Administration of Papua and the mandated territory was merged in 1949. Dutch New Guinea became the Indonesian province of Irian Jaya in 1969. The territories of Papua and New Guinea became the independent nation of **Papua New Guinea** in 1975.

New Guinea walnut tree [mon]: The tree (*Dracontomelon edule*) bears "edible but inferior fruits" and grows at low altitudes (Verheij & Coronel, 1991: 329-330).

nokondi: a mythical figure who has half of a body. The *nokondi* apears in myths from various parts of the **Highlands** (e.g. Asaro, Fore, and Gahuku peoples), and is depicted on the flag of Eastern Highlands Province (Rannells, 1990: 36).

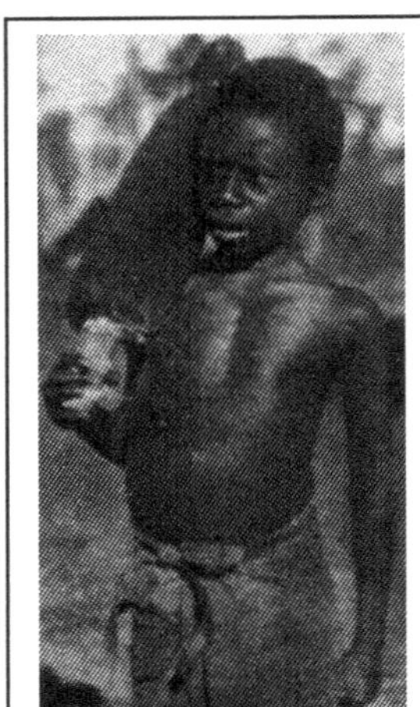

Figure 14. A boy carrying marita fruit, Ogeramnang Village, Morobe Province (Lane-Poole, 1925: 177)

okari: see **galip nut**

pandanus 1. [karuka]: a high-elevation palm tree with edible nutty fruits (*Pandanus julianetti* and *P. brosimus*). The oil from the fruits is used by some cultures as body adornment. *P. brosimos* is mostly cultivated between 1700-3300 meters elevation and rarely below 2000 meters (Powell, 1976: 132; Verheij and Coronel, 1991: 242). 2. [aran, marita]: a palm tree with pulpy fruits that usually have red flesh (*P. conoideus*). It grows up to 2300 meters (Figure 14; Powell, 1976: 132).

Papua: British **New Guinea**, later an Australian colony, now Western, Gulf, Central, Oro and Milne Bay provinces as well as parts of the **Highlands**

Papua New Guinea (PNG): the independent country formed in 1975 from **Papua** and **New Guinea**

penis gourd: see **kambang**

PNG: see **Papua New Guinea**

possum [kapul]: marsupials from various families: Acrobatidae, Burramyidae, Petauridae, and possibly Pseudocheiridae. The word kapul conflates possum with **cuscus** and **kangaroo**.

purpur: 1. a shrub (*Codiaeum variegatum*) used for personal adornment, medicine and magic (Powell, 1976: 137, 142, 145, 147-148, 172) 2. a fibrous skirt made of **sago** palm leaves or special kinds of reeds. It is called a "grass" skirt in English but it is not made of grass.

python [moran]: **Papua New Guinea** has eight species of python (subfamily Pythoninae of family Boidae) as well as two species of boa (subfamily Boinae) [O'Shea, 1996: 56-87]. Boas might also be referred to as moran.

rat [rat]: 1) rat 2) mouse (liklik rat) 3) small, rat-like marsupials

ring money [ring mani]: see **shell money**

ringworm [grile, pukpuk grile, kaskas]: a skin disease (a.k.a. tinea or scabies) caused by fungi, it results in scaly patches covering the skin. People with ringworm were often regarded as ugly and treated as outcasts. The symptomatic scaly skin caused people to analogize the sufferers with crocodiles (pukpuk) or fish.

rose apple: see **Malay apple**

sago [saksak]: a palm tree (*Metroxylon sagu* and *M. rumphii*) from which a starchy foodstuff is made. The process entails chopping down the tree, cutting off the bark, mashing the pith (Figure 15) and straining the pith repeatedly in water (Figure 16). The resultant substance can be made into pudding or flour. It is low in nutrition but high in calories (Powell, 1976: 116-117; May, 1984: 52-55, 182-183). It can be kept for a long time in tropical climates. Parts of the plant are also used for medicine, spathes, canoes and construction (Powell, 1976: 140, 153, 158, 163, 165, 169). Usually, sago processing is traditionally women's work except for felling

Figure 15. Pounding sago pith (Hurley, 1925: 107)

the trees. Sago grows in low-lying, swampy areas. In **PNG**, this is primarily Western, Gulf and **Sepik** provinces, but also western Manus Province, New Hanover Island, and some low-altitude areas of the **Highlands** provinces (Vasey, 1982: 50-51).

sago beetle [binatang bilong saksak]: Sago beetles (*Rhyncophorus ferringinlus papuanus*) are often encouraged to grow inside fallen sago trees. The beetle grubs eat the pith of the tree. The grubs are eaten by humans with relish since they are high in nutrition (May, 1984: 95).

sago, wild [wel saksak]: Parts of the nipa palm (*Nypa fruticans*) are used for food and houses (Powell, 1976: 111, 163). The nipa palm thrives only in brackish water but it is rarely seen at seashores, so it is mainly seen in the estuarine tidal floodplains of rivers (Flach & Rumawas, 1996: 135).

salat: various plants used as as counter-irritants and for revivification: 1. stinging nettle (*Dendrocnidae* spp.) 2. the "poison oak" tree (*Semecarpus cassuvium*). The sap of *S. cassuvium* is poisonous, although the swollen pedicel is eaten as a fruit and the young leaves can be eaten raw (Verheij & Coronel, 1991: 359). *S. cassuvium* grows up to 2000 meters (Sosef, *et al.*, 1998: 521)

salt [sol]: Salt was an important trade item. One common method of salt manufacture was to soak banana stems in a brine pool, followed by drying and burning. The salt-infused ashes would then be used as a seasoning. Sometimes the salt was further purified by leaching. Salt was also made from the ashes of various plants (Powell, 1976: 133-134; May, 1984: 102; Woodley, 1991: 108).

scabies: see **ringworm**

Figure 16. Washing and filtering sago (Thurnwald, 1912: plate 8)

sea cucumber/sea slug/trepang [pislama]: an edible invertebrate often found in reefs (*Holothuria* spp.)

sel kambang: see **kambang**

Sepik: 1. the Sepik River 2. West Sepik (Sandaun) and East Sepik provinces

shaman [tambaranman]: a spirit intermediary (Figure 17). In some cases, shamans are associated with the men's secret society. Shaman is equated with folk motif D1711, "magician", for this book. See also **sorcery, spirit**

shell, gam: 1. bailer shell (*Melo aethiopicus* and *M. umbilicatus*) [Mihalic, 1971: 86; Hinton, 1977: 50] 2. large cowrie shell (*Cypraea* spp.) [Mihalic, 1971: 86; Hinton, 1977: 11-16]

shell money [gam, girigiri, kina, ring, tambu]: Shell valuables were traded traditionally in many parts of **PNG**. The most valuable in the **Highlands** was the kina (*Pinctada maxima*) which was also used for ornamentation and prestige. Use of cowrie shells (girigiri, *Cypraea* spp.) as money was widespread. Tambu shells are *Columbella* spp. or *Acrularia jonasi* (Mihalic, 1971: 191). See also **mukmuk**

singing, singsing: see **festival**

singapo: see **taro**

snake: see **python**

Figure 17. Orokaiva sorcerer, Oro Province (Hurley, 1924: 123)

Figure 18. Spirit house, Sissano, West Sepik Province (Neuhauss, 1911: 231)

sorcery [marila, posin, puripuri, sanguma]: Malevolent sorcery and traditional warfare are often intimately related. Malevolent sorcery often uses body exuviae of the person to be ensorcelled. A specific, murderous form of sorcery, sanguma, involves mesmerization of the victim followed by insertion of thorns dipped in poison (Murphy, 1985: 100). Another form of magic is marila, the making of love charms or spells (Murphy, 1985: 89).

sorcerer: see **shaman**

spirit 1. [masalai] a spirit belonging to a location, usually feared (generally folk motifs F400-F499) 2. [dewel, tewel] the spirit of a dead person (i.e., a ghost), located near the place of its death. It may be benign or malevolent depending on proper observation of mortuary rites [see folk motifs E200-

E599]. 3. [tambaran] ancestral spirits, often associated with special functions and with sacred masks (also called tambaran). See also **shaman**

spirit house [haus tambaran, haus boi]: a house where men conduct secret cermonies, where the ancestor's spirits reside. This may or may not be the same house where the men live (Figure 18). See also **men's house**.

sugarcane [suga]: Sugarcane (*Saccharum officinarum*) probably originated on the island of **New Guinea** since New Guinea is the center of sugar diversity. Sugarcane with banana is a traditional, refreshing welcoming gift in many New Guinea societies.

sugarcane, wild [pitpit, pitpit moi, tiktik]: Wild sugarcane is not truly wild, nor is it particularly sweet. 1. Pitpit (*Saccharum spontaneum*) is used for fences and food. It grows near rivers and wetlands in lowland areas. The edible part resembles an unripe ear of corn (maize). 2. Pitpit moi (*Setaria palmaefolia*) is grown in the **Highlands** (Powell, 1976: 130-131). 3. Tiktik (*Saccharum* spp.) is used for fences, spear shafts, arrows, and roofing (Mihalic, 1971: 194).

Swan Maiden: The Swan Maiden is a diverse and worldwide tale type (also motif D361.1) in which a female animal (typically a **cassowary** or **bird of paradise** in New Guinea) removes its skin to become a woman, then bathes and is caught and married by a man who hides her skin. Typically, the husband later angers the wife who then flees and changes back into an animal. See Tuzin (1997: 68-95) for a discussion of the cassowary as Swan Maiden among the Ilahita Arapesh and neighboring peoples of East **Sepik** Province. In this book, there are also stories that resemble the Swan Maiden, but which are not necessarily genetically related. These stories contain the following sequential elements: man captures supernatural woman in the forest, man marries woman, husband breaks promise or wife becomes angered, wife departs. These stories are given the new motif, "D361.1+. Forest Spirit Bride."

sweet potato [kaukau]: an important staple food crop in the **Highlands** (*Ipomoea batata*), often grown in raised mounds to encourage water drainage. The sweet potato is able to grow at higher elevations than other **New Guinea** root crops, up to 2800 meters (May, 1984: 46). It is a relatively recent introduction (400-1600 A. D. [Olivier, 1989: 98]), hence it is responsible for population expansion into previously unpopulated or sparsely populated areas of the Highlands. Sweet potatoes are grown primarily in the Highlands and also in the mountainous areas of New Ireland and Bougainville islands (Vasey, 1985: 50-51). Young leaves are also eaten (May, 1984: 58).

sword grass [kunai]: a tough, tall grass (*Miscanthus floridulus*) that grows in burned-over, infertile areas (Figure 19). It grows with *Imperata arundinacea* in the **Highlands** (Paijmans, 1976: 92).

talis: a tree with edible nuts (Indian almond, *Terminalia catappa*). Parts of the tree are also used medicinally. It is typically a coastal tree (Womersley, 1978: 72; Woodley, 1991: 33-34; Rehm & Espig, 1991: 242).

taboo sign [mak bilong tambu]: a sign that indicates ownership. It often consists of leaves tied together, indicating that the object or area is off-limits to others.

Figure 19. "The empty lands" (sword grass lands) [Grimshaw, 1911: 170]

tambu: see **shell money**

tanget: a shrub (*Cordyline fruticosa*, a.k.a. *Taetsia fructicosa*). It is known as "ti" in Hawaii. It is used variously in sorcery; in ceremonies, to mark areas as off-limits, as mnemonic devices, for other messages; and as a male buttocks covering in the **Highlands**. Strathern (1982: 120) reports that in several Melanesian cultures, it "marks the boundary betwen life and death."

tanim het: a courtship custom (lit., "turning heads") that is restricted to the Hagen People of the Southern and Western **Highlands** provinces. "Boys and girls line up face-to-face. The boy's left ear is placed on the girl's right ear. The faces roll until the boy's right ear touches the girl's left ear." (Lobban, 1985: 31) See also **karim lek, kukim nus**.

taro: 1. Taro or taro tru (*Colocasia esculenta*) grows at up to 2700 meters elevation (Flach & Rumawas, 1996: 70). *C. esculenta* is also used medicinally and for magic (Powell, 1976: 137, 143-145, 148). 2. Swamp taro (taro bilong tais, *Cyrtosperma merkusii*) grows in swamps at up to 150 meters elevation (May, 1984: 46; Flach & Rumawas, 1996: 82-84). 3. Taro kongkong or taro singapo (*Xanthosoma sagittifolium*) grows at up to 2000 meters elevation (Flach & Rumawas, 1996: 163). Both corms and leaves are eaten.

taro, wild [wel taro]: wild taro (*Amorphophallus paeoniifolius*, a.k.a. *A. campanulatus*) is neither truly wild nor truly taro since it is sometimes grown domestically and is not closely related to true taro. Both corms and leaves are eaten. It is common in grassland areas of Madang, Morobe and Oro provinces, but it is also found in the **Highlands** at up to 900 meters elevation (Powell, 1976: 144; Twohig, 1986: 65; Flach & Rumawas, 1996: 48). Wild taro is also used medicinally (Powell, 1976: 144).

tigaso: see tree oil

Tok Pisin: the Pidgin English of ex-German **New Guinea**. It is now also spoken in the **Highlands** and in the capital, Port Moresby (Dutton, 1982)

ton tree [diwai ton, diwai taun]: a hardwood tree with edible fruit (*Pometia pinnata*), generally found below 500 meters elevation, but also up to 1700 meters (Mihalic, 1971: 196; Soerianegara & Lemmens, 1993: 362). The ton tree is used for medicine and construction (Powell, 1976: 137, 164).

tree oil [wel gris]: tree oil (or tigaso oil) is dervied from *Campnosperma* spp. tree wood (Mihalic, 1971: 204). The oil is used as a body adornment, as a medicine, and in cooking (Powell, 1976: 174). *Campnosperma* spp. are often found in swampy, lowland forests. *C. brevipetiolatum* occurs at up to 500 meters elevation; *C. coriaceum* occurs at up to 1000 meters; *C. montanum* occurs at up to 1500 meters (Soerianegara & Lemmens, 1993: 133-138).

trepang: see **sea cucumber**

tulip tree [tulip]: a kind of tree with paired, edible leaves, seeds and fruit (joint fir, *Gnetum gnemon*), unrelated to the tulip flower, found at up to 1200 meters elevation (Verheij & Coronel, 1991: 182-184; Rehm & Espig, 1991: 240). The flowers and fruits can also be eaten (May, 1984: 58).

vagina dentata: the toothed vagina (folk motif F547.1.1). In **PNG**, *katu* means "shell" or "crab" in **Tok Pisin** (Mihalic, 1971: 108) and "cunt" metaphorically (Mosel, 1980: 29). This folk motif apparently occurs in PNG as a woman wielding a "crab" to attack a man's genitals.

walnut: see **New Guinea walnut tree**

wildfowl: see **fowl, wild**

wild man/wild woman [welman, welmeri]: a person who lives alone, away from villages; a hermit (folk motif F567)

winged bean [asbin]: a high-protein bean that is grown in the **Highlands** (*Psophocarpus tetragonolobus*). Most of the plant is edible. It is generally grown below 1800 meters elevation (Powell, 1976: 116-117; Twohig, 1986: 73).

yam: 1. the greater yam (yam, *Dioscorea alata*) 2. the lesser yam (mami, *D. esculenta*) 3. less common species of yams (sand yam or *D. pentaphylla*, *D. nummularia*, and aerial yam or *D. bulbifera*) [Rehm & Espig, 1991: 50-51]. The yam is frequently associated with religious activities in **PNG**, especially mami which is grown for length (May, 1984: 48-49). Parts of the yam are used for medicine and magic (Powell, 1976: 140, 143, 148). The yam is generally a lowland crop, but it can grow at high elevations, up to 2500 meters for *D. alata*, up to 900 meters for *D. esculenta*, and up to 2700 meters for *D. bulbifera* and *D. pentaphylla* (Flach & Rumawas, 1996: 89, 92, 94).

Bibliography

Allen, Gerald R. & Swainston, Roger (1992). *Reef Fishes of New Guinea*. Madang, Papua New Guinea: Christensen Research Institute.

Allen, Jerry & Hurd, Conrad (1963). *Languages of the Bougainville District*. [Ukarumpa, Papua New Guinea]: Summer Institute of Linguistics.

Alpers, Michael P. (1992). Kuru. In: *Human Biology in Papua New Guinea: The Small Cosmos*, Robert D. Attenborough & Michael P. Alpers, eds. Research Monographs on Human Population Biology 10. New York: Clarendon Press, pp. 313-334.

Anonymous (1943). *Gazetteer to Maps of New Guinea. Map Series AMS T401. Scale 1:500,000*. Washington, DC: War Department.

— (1952). "Ethnological reconnaissance in New Guinea." *University [of Pennsylvania] Museum Bulletin* 17(1): 5-37.

— (1973). *Papua New Guinea Village Directory*. Konedobu, Papua New Guinea: Department of the Chief Minister and Development Administration.

— (1990). *UBD Map of Papua New Guinea*. Macquarie Park, New South Wales: UBD.

— (1992). *Papua New Guinea* [map]. Springwood, Australia: Hema Maps.

Barry, Glen (1995). *Utilizing Informational Technologies for Forest Advocacy and Management: A Biodiversity Conservation Support Program for the Country of Papua New Guinea*. Master's Thesis. Madison: University of Wisconsin.

Beehler, Bruce M.; Pratt, Thane K.; and Zimmerman, Dale A. (1986). *Birds of New Guinea*. Princeton, NJ: Princeton University Press.

Berndt, Ronald Murray (1952). "A cargo movement in the Eastern Central Highlands of New Guinea." *Oceania* 23: 40-65.

— (1962). *Excess and Restraint: Social Control among a New Guinea Mountain People*. Chicago: University of Chicago Press.

— (1992). Into the unknown! In: *Ethnographic Presents: Pioneering Anthropoligsts in the Papua New Guinea Highlands*, Terence E. Hays, ed. Berkeley: University of California Press, pp. 68-97.

Brookfield, H. C. & Brown, Paula (1963). *Struggle for Land: Agriculture and Group Territories among the Chimbu of the New Guinea Highlands*. New York: Oxford University Press.

Brown, Paula (1978). *Highland Peoples of New Guinea*. New York: Cambridge University Press.

Brown, H[erbert] A. (1968). "A dictionary of Toaripi with English-Toaripi index." *Oceania Linguistic Monographs*, volume 11.

— (1986). *A Comparative Dictionary of Orokolo, Gulf of Papua*. Canberra: Australian National University. Pacific Linguistics Series C, No. 84.

Browne, Bob [1991?]. *The Grass Roots Guide to Papua New Guinea Pidgin*. Port Moresby, Papua New Guinea: Grass Roots Comic.

Buick, W. G. (1970). *An Alphabetical List of Villages in Papua New Guinea*. Waigani: University of Papua New Guinea.

Busse, Mark; Turner, Susan; and Araho, Nick (1993). *The People of Lake Kutubu and Kikori: Changing Meanings of Daily Life*. Port Moresby: Papua New Guinea National Museum.

Capell, A. (1962). *A Linguistic Survey of the South-Western Pacific. South Pacific Commission Technical Paper*. No. 136.

Cavalli-Sforza, Luigi Luca & Cavalli-Sforza, Francesco (1995). *The Great Human Diasporas: The History of Diversity and Evolution*. New York: Addison-Wesley.

—; Menozzi, Paolo; and Piazza, Alberto (1996). *The History and Geography of Human Genes*. Princeton, NJ: Princeton University Press. Abridged edition.

Chinnery, E. W. Pearson (1924a). *Natives of the Waria, Williams and Bialolo Watersheds*. Territory of New Guinea Anthropological Report 4. Canberra: Government Printer.

— (1924b). *Notes on the Natives of South Bougainville and Mortlocks (Taku)*. Territory of New Guinea Anthropological Report 5. Canberra: Government Printer.

Crowley, Terry (1990). *Beach-la-Mar to Bislama: The Emergence of a National Language in Vanuatu*. New York: Oxford University Press.

— (1995). *A New Bislama Dictionary*. Suva, Fiji: Institute of Pacific Studies.

D'Albertis, L. M. (1880). *New Guinea: What I Did and What I Saw*. London: Sampson Low, Marston, Searle & Rivington, 2 volumes.

Deibler, Ellis & Trefry, David (1963). *Languages of the Chimbu Sub-District.* Port Moresby: Department of Information and Extension Services.

Department of Anthropology and Sociology, Australian National University (1968). *An Ethnographic Bibliography of New Guinea. Volume 1. Author Index.* Canberra: Australian National University Press.

— (1968). *An Ethnographic Bibliography of New Guinea. Volume 3. Proper Names Index.* Canberra: Australian National University Press.

Diamond, Jared (1993). New Guineans and their natural world. In: *The Biophilia Hypothesis*, Stephen R. Kellert & Edward O. Wilson, eds. Washington, DC: Island Press, pp. 251-271.

Dutton, T[om] E. (1973). *A Checklist of Languages and Present-Day Villages of Central and South-East Mainland Papua.* Pacific Linguistics, Series B, Number 24. Canberra: Australian National University.

— (1982). Languages of wider communication (or lingua francas). In: *Papua New Guinea Atlas: A Nation in Transition*, David King and Stephen Ranck, eds. Bathrust, Australia: Robert Brown, pp. 36-37.

— & Thomas, Dicks (1985). *A New Course in Tok Pisin (New Guinea Pidgin).* Pacific Linguistics, Series D, Number 67. Canberra: Australian National University.

Eastburn, David (1989). Sel kambang. In: *Paradise Faces: A Selection of Stories from Air Niugini's In-Flight Magazines.* McLaughlin, Geoff, ed. Port Moresby: Geoff McLaughlin, pp. 46-48.

Essig, Frederick B. (1977). *The Palm Flora of New Guinea: A Preliminary Analysis.* Lae: Office of Forests, Division of Botany. Papua New Guinea Botany Bulletin #9.

Feil, D. K. (1984). *Ways of Exchange: The Enga Tee of Papua New Guinea.* St. Lucia: University of Queensland Press.

Fitz-Patrick, David G. & Kimbuna, John (1983). *Bundi: The culture of a Papua New Guinea people.* Nerang, Queensland: Ryebuck.

Flach, M. & Rumawas, F., eds. (1996). *Plant Resources of South-East Asia: Plants Yielding Non-seed Carbohydrates.* Wageningen, Netherlands: Pudoc. Prosea Volume 9.

Flannery, Timothy F. (1995a). *Mammals of New Guinea.* Ithaca, NY: Cornell University Press.

— (1995b). *Mammals of the South-West Pacific & Moluccan Islands.* Ithaca, NY: Cornell University Press.

Foley, William A. (1991). *The Yimas Language of New Guinea.* Stanford, CA: Stanford University Press.

— (1992). Language and identity in Papua New Guinea. In: *Human Biology in Papua New Guinea: The Small Cosmos*, Robert D. Attenborough & Michael P. Alpers, eds. Research Monographs on Human Population Biology 10. New York: Clarendon Press, pp. 136-149.

Franklin, Karl J. & Franklin, Joice (1978). *A Kewa Dictionary: With Supplementary Grammatical and Anthropological Materials.* Pacific Linguistics, Series C, Number 53. Canberra: Australian National University.

Franklin, Karl J.; Kerr, Harland B. & Beaumont, Clive H. (1974) *Tolai Language Course.* Huntington Beach, CA: Summer Institute of Linguistics. Asian-Pacific Series #7.

Franklin, Karl J. & Z'graggen, John (1975). "Comparative wordlists of the Gulf District and adjacent areas." *Workpapers in Papua New Guinea Languages* 14: 5-116.

Gagné, W. C. (1982). Staple crops in subsistence agriculture: Their major insect pests, with emphasis on biogeographical and ecological aspects. In: *Biogeography and Ecology of New Guinea*, J. L. Gressitt, ed. Hague: Junk, pp. 229-259.

Gewertz, Deborah B. (1983). *Sepik River Societies: A Historical Ethnography of the Chambri and their Neighbors.* New Haven, CT: Yale University Press.

— and Errington, Frederick K. (1991). *Twisted Histories, Altered Contexts: Representing the Chambri in a World System.* New York: Cambridge University Press.

Goodale, Jane C. (1995). *To Sing with Pigs Is Human: The Concept of Person in Papua New Guinea.* Seattle: University of Washington Press.

Gourlay, K. A. (1975). *Sound-Producing Instruments in Traditional Society: A Study of Esoteric Instruments and their Role in Male-Female Relations.* Port Moresby & Canberra: New Guinea Research Unit, The Australian National University. New Guinea Research Bulletin 60.

Gressitt, J. L. & Hornabrook, R. W. (1977). *Handbook of Common New Guinea Beetles.* Wau, Papua New Guinea: Wau Ecology Institute.

Grimshaw, Beatrice (1911). *The New New Guinea*. London: Hutchinson.

Hanum, I. Faridah & van der Maesen, L. J. G., eds. (1997). *Plant Resources of South-East Asia: Timber Trees: Auxiliary Plants*. Leiden, Netherlands: Backhuys. Prosea Volume 11.

Hays, Terense E. & Hays, Patricia H. (1982). Opposition and complementarity of the sexes in Ndumba initiation. In: *Rituals of Manhood: Male Initiation in Papua New Guinea*. Herdt, Gilbert H., ed. Berkeley, University of California Press, pp. 201-238.

Herdt, Gilbert, H., ed. (1984). *Ritualized Homosexuality in Melanesia*. Berkeley: University of California Press.

Hinton, Alan ([1977]). *Guide to Shells of Papua New Guinea*. Port Moresby: Robert Brown.

Hoffmann, Frank (1973). *Analytical Survey of Anglo-American Traditional Erotica*. Bowling Green, OH: Bowling Green University Popular Press.

Hölldobler, Bert & Wilson, Edward O. (1990). *The Ants*. Cambridge, MA: The Belknap Press of Harvard.

Holzknecht, Susanne (1989). *The Markham Languages of Papua New Guinea*. Pacific Linguistics, Series C, Number 115. Canberra: Australian National University.

Hooley, Bruce Arthur (1970). *Mapos Buang — Territory of New Guinea*. Ph.D. Thesis, University of Pennsylvania.

Hurley, Frank (1924). *Pearls and Savages: Adventures in the Air, on Land and Sea — in New Guinea*. New York: G. P. Putnam's Sons.

Jackson, Richard (1985). Secondary industries. In: *Papua New Guinea Atlas*, King & Ranck, eds. Port Moresby: University of Papua New Guinea, pp. 66-67.

Jukes, J. Beete (1847). *Narrative of the Surveying Voyage of H. M. S. Fly, Commanded by Captain F. P. Blackwood, R. N. in Torres Strait, New Guinea, and Other Islands of the Eastern Archipelago, During the Years 1842-1846: Together with an Excursion into the Interior of the Eastern Part of Java*. London: T. & W. Boone, volume 1.

Kirk, Malcolm & Strathern, Andrew (1981). *Man as Art: New Guinea*. San Francisco: Chronicle Books.

Kirtley, Bacil Fleming (1955). *A Motif-Index of Polynesian, Melanesian, and Micronesian Narratives*. Bloomington: Indiana University, Ph. D. Thesis.

— (1971). *A Motif-Index of Traditional Polynesian Narratives*. Honolulu: University of Hawaii Press.

Krieger, Maximilian (1899). *Neu-Guinea*. Berlin: Alfred Schall.

Kulick, Don & Stroud, Christopher (1990). "Christianity, cargo and ideas of self: Patterns of literacy in a Papua New Guinean Village." *Man: The Journal of the Royal Athropological Society* 25: 286-304.

Kundama, J.; Wilson, P. & Sapai, A. (1987). *Kudi Kupuk Ambulas (Maprik Dialect) Tok Pisin English*. Ukarumpa, Papua New Guinea: Summer Institute of Linguistics.

Kunze, Georg (1896). "Karkar- oder Dampier-Insel." *Petermanns Geographische Mitteilungen* 42: 193-195 (with map).

Lane-Poole, C. E. (1925). *The Forest Resources of the Territories of Papua and New Guinea*. Victoria: Parliament of the Commonwealth of Australia.

Lang, Adrianne (1973). *Enga Dictionary with English Index*. Pacific Linguistics, Series C, Number 20. Canberra: Australian National University.

Lawrence, Peter (1986). *Rot bilong Kago*. Port Moresby: Institute of Papua New Guinea Studies. Translated by Bil Tomaseti.

Laycock, D. C. (1965). *The Ndu Language Family (Sepik District, New Guinea)*. Pacific Linguistics, Series C, Number 1. Canberra: Australian National University.

— (1973). *Sepik Languages — Checklist and Preliminary Classification*. Pacific Linguistics, Series B, Number 25. Canberra: Australian National University.

Legman, G[ershon] (1975). *No Laughing Matter. Rationale of the Dirty Joke: An Analysis of Sexual Humor*. Second Series. New York: Bell.

Lemmens, R. H. M. J., Soerianegara, I. & Wong, W. C., eds. (1995). *Plant Resources of South-East Asia: Timber Trees: Minor Commercial Timbers*. Leiden, Netherlands: Backhuys. Prosea Volume 5(2).

LeRoy, John, ed. (1985a). *Kewa Tales*. Vancouver: University of British Columbia Press.

— (1985b). *Fabricated World: An Interpretation of Kewa Tales*. Vancouver: University of British Columbia Press.

Lindstrom, Lamont (1993). *Cargo Cult: Strange Stories of Desire from Melanesia and Beyond*. Honolulu: University of Hawaii Press.

Lithgow, David & Claassen, Oren (1968). *Languages of the New Ireland District*. Port Moresby: Department of Information and Extension Services.

Lobban, William D. (1985). "A collection of children's singing games of Papua New Guinea." *Oral History* 13(2).

Lutkehaus, Nancy; Kaufmann, Christian; Mitchell, William E.; Newton. Douglas; Osmundsen, Lita; & Schuster, Meinhard, eds. (1990). *Sepik Heritage: Tradition and Change in Papua New Guinea.* Durham, North Carolina: Carolina Academic Press.

Mager, John F. (1952). *Gedaged-English Dictionary.* Columbus, OH: American Lutheran Church.

May, Ronald James (1984). *Kaikai Aniani: A Guide to Bush Foods, Markets and Culinary Arts of Papua New Guinea.* Bathurst, New South Wales: Robert Brown.

McElhanon, K. A. (1984). *A Linguistic Field Guide to the Morobe Province, Papua New Guinea.* Series D, No. 57. Canberra: Pacific Linguistics, The Australian National University.

McGregor, Donald E. & McGregor, Aileen R. F. (1982). *Olo Language Materials.* Series D, No. 42. Canberra: Pacific Linguistics, The Australian National University.

McLean, Mervyn (1994). *Diffusion of Musical Instruments and their Relation to Language Migrations in New Guinea.* Kulele: Occasional Papers on Pacific Music and Dance 1. Boroko, Papua New Guinea: Cultural Studies Division, National Research Institute.

Mead, Margaret (1970). *The Mountain Arapesh II: Arts and Supernaturalism.* Garden City, NY: Natural History Press.

Mihalic, F. (1971). *The Jacaranda Dictionary and Grammar of Melanesian Pidgin.* Milton, Queensland, Australia: Jacaranda Press.

Mosel, Ulrike (1980). *Tolai and Tok Pisin: The Influence of the Substratum on the Development of New Guinea Pidgin,* Series B, No. 73. Canberra: Pacific Linguistics, The Australian National University.

Murphy, John J. (1985). *The Book of Pidgin English.* Revised Edition. Bathurst, New South Wales, Australia: Robert Brown.

Nash, Jill & Ogan, Eugene (1990). "The red and the black: Bougainvillean perceptions of other Papua New Guineans." *Pacific Islands* 13(2): 1-17.

Neuhauss R. (1911). *Deutsch Neu-Guinea.* Berlin: Dietrich Reimer (Ernst Vohsen), volume 1.

Neumann, Klaus (1992). *Not the Way It Really Was: Constructing the Tolai Past.* Honolulu: University of Hawaii Press. Pacific Islands Monograph Series 10.

Newton, Henry (1914). *In Far New Guinea: A Stirring Record of Work and Observations Amongst the People of New Guinea, with a Description of their Manners, Customs, & Religions.* London: Seeley, Service.

Nilles, J. (1969). *The Kuman-English Dictionary.* Mimeograph copy stored at the University of Hawaii.

O'Hanlon, Michael (1989). *Reading the Skin: Adornment, Display and Society among the Wahgi.* London: British Museum Publications.

Oliver, Douglas (1967 [1955]). *A Solomon Island Society: Kinship and Leadership among the Siuai of Bougainville.* Boston: Beacon.

— (1989). Oceania: *The Native Cultures of Australia and the Pacific Islands.* Honolulu: University of Hawaii Press, 2 volumes.

— (1991). *Black Islanders: A Personal Perspective of Bougainville 1937-1991.* Honolulu: University of Hawaii Press.

O'Shea, Mark (1996). A Guide to the Snakes of Papua New Guinea. Port Moresby: Independent Publishing.

Paijmans, K. (1976). Vegetation. In: *New Guinea Vegetation,* K. Paijmans, ed., New York: Elsevier Scientific, pp. 106-183.

Pataki-Schweizer, K. J. (1980). *A New Guinea Landscape: Community, Space, and Time in the Eastern Highlands.* Seattle: University of Washington Press.

Peterson, Boyd D., Garren, William R., and Heyda, Charles M. (1982). *Gazetteer of Papua New Guinea: Names Approved by the United States Board on Geographical Names.* Washington, DC: Defense Mapping Agency.

Powell, J. M. (1976). "Ethnobotany." In: *New Guinea Vegetation,* K. Paijmans, ed., New York: Elsevier Scientific, pp. 106-183.

Powell, Jerry A. & Hogue, Charles L. (1979). *California Insects.* Berkeley: University of California.

Purseglove, John William (1972). *Tropical Crops: Monocotyledons.* New York: Longman Scientific & Technical.

Radford, Robin (1987). *Highlanders and Foreigners in the Upper Ramu: The Kainantu Area 1919-1942.* Melbourne: Melbourne University Press.

Ramsey, E. M. (1975). *Middle Wahgi Dictionary.* Mount Hagen: Church of the Nazarene.

Randolph, Vance (1992). *Roll Me in Your Arms: "Unprintable" Ozark Folksongs and Folklore.*

Volume 1. Folksongs and Music. Fayetteville: University of Arkansas Press.

Rannells, Jackson (1990). *PNG: A Fact Book on Modern Papua New Guinea.* New York: Oxford University Press.

Rehm, Sigmund & Espig, Gustav (1991). *The Cultivated Plants of the Tropics and Subtropics.* Weikersheim, Germany: Verlag Josef Margraf.

Riley, E. Baxter (1925). *Among Papuan Headhunters: An Account of the Manners & Customs of the Old Fly River Headhunters, with a Description of the Secrets of the Initiation Ceremonies Divulged by Those Who Have Passed through All the Different Orders of the Craft, by One Who Has Spent Many Years in Their Midst.* London: Seeley, Service.

Ross, M. D. (1988). *Proto Oceanic and the Austronesian Languages of Western Melanesia.* Pacific Linguistics Series C, No. 98. Canberra, Australia: Australian National University.

Ryan, D'Arcy (1992). "Meeting the Mendi." In: *Ethnographic Presents: Pioneering Anthropoligists in the Papua New Guinea Highlands*, Terence E. Hays, ed. Berkeley: University of California Press, pp. 199-231.

Ryan, Peter, ed. (1972). *Encyclopaedia of Papua and New Guinea.* Carlton, Victoria: Melbourne University Press, 3 volumes.

Ryan, Erica (1995) "Publishing in Papua New Guinea: The National Library of Australia Acquisitions Trip, 1994." *Australian Academic & Research Libraries* 26: 157-162.

Schooling, Stephen & Schooling, Janice [1980]. *A Preliminary Sociolinguistic and Linguistic Survey of Manus Province, Papua New Guinea.* [Ukarumpa]: Summer Institute of Linguistics.

Schwimmer, Eric (1984). "Male couples in New Guinea." In: *Ritualized Homosexuality in Melanesia*, Gilbert H. Herdt, ed. Berkeley, CA: University of California Press, pp. 248-291.

Scorza, David & Franklin, Karl J. (1989). *An Advanced Course in Tok Pisin.* Ukarumpa, Papua New Guinea: Summer Institute of Linguistics.

Sekhran, N. & Miller, S., eds. (1995). *Papua New Guinea Country Study on Biological Diversity.* Waigani, Papua New Guinea: Department of Environment and Conservation.

Shnukal, Anna (1988). *Broken: An Introduction to the Creole Language of Torres Strait.* Series C, No. 107. Canberra: Pacific Linguistics, The Australian National University.

Siegel, Lee (1987). *Laughing Matters: Comic Tradition in India.* Chicago: University of Chicago Press.

Siemonsma, J. S. & Piluek, Kasem, eds. (1993). *Plant Resources of South-East Asia: Vegetables.* Wageningen, Netherlands: Pudoc. Prosea Volume 8.

Sillitoe, Paul (1993). "Forest and demons in the Papua New Guinea Highlands." *The Australian Journal of Anthropology* 4: 220-232.

Slone, Thomas H. (1996). Tok nogut: An Introduction to malediction in Papua New Guinea. *Maledicta: The International Journal of Verbal Aggression* 11: 75-104.

Smith, Geoff P. (1990). "Idiomatic Tok Pisin and referential adequacy." In: *Melanesian Pidgin and Tok Pisin: Proceedings of the First International Conference of Pidgins and Creoles in Melanesia*, John W. M. Verhaar, ed. Studies in Language Companion Series, Volume 20. Philadelphia: John Benjamins Publishing, pp. 275-287.

Soerianegara, I. & Lemmens, R. H. M. J., eds. (1993). *Plant Resources of South-East Asia: Timber Trees: Major Commercial Timbers.* Wageningen, Netherlands: Pudoc. Prosea Volume 5(1).

Sosef, M. S. M., Hong, L. T. & Prawirohatmodjo, S., eds. (1998). *Plant Resources of South-East Asia: Timber Trees:Lesser-Known Timbers.* Leiden, Netherlands: Backhuys. Prosea Volume 5(3).

Souter, Gavin (1963). *New Guinea: The Last Unknown.* New York: Taplinger.

Steinbauer, Friedrich (1969). *Concise Dictionary of New Guinea Pidgin (Neo-Melanesian).* Madang, Papua New Guinea: Kristen Pres.

Strathern, Andrew (1982). "Witchcraft, greed, cannibalism an death: Some related themes from the New Guinea Highlands." In: *Death and the Regeneration of Life*, Maurice Bloch and Jonathan Parry, eds. Cambridge: Cambridge University Press.

— (1984). *A Line of Power.* New York: Tavistock.

Strickert, Frederick (1978). *Diksenari bilong Nupela Testamen.* Madang, Papua New Guinea: Kristen Press.

Stone, Octavius C. (1880). *A Few Months in New Guinea.* London: Sampson Low, Marston, Searle & Rivington.

Swainston, Roger (1992). *Reef Fishes of New Guinea.* Madang, Papua New Guinea: Christensen Research Institute.

Tawali, Kumalau, ed. (1971). *Nansei: An Anthology of Original Pidgin Poems*. Port Moresby: Papua Pocket Poets.

Thomson, J. P. (1892). *British New Guinea*. London: George Philip & Son.

Thompson, Stith (1946 [1977]). *The Folktale*. Berkeley: University of California Press.

— (1993). *Motif-Index of Folk-Literature: A Classification of Narrative Elements in Folk Tales, Ballads, Myths, Fables, Mediaeval Romances, Exempla, Fabliaux, Jest-Books, and Local Legends*. Bloomington: Indiana University Press, CD-ROM editon.

Thurnwald, Richard (1912). *Forschungen auf den Salomo-Inseln und dem Bismarck-Achipel: Mit Unterstützung der Baessler Stiftung Herausgegeben im Auftrage der General Verwaltung der Königlichen Museen zu Berlin. Volume 1. Lieder und Sagen aus Buin: Nebst einem Anhang: Die Musik auf den Salomo-Inseln von E. M. V. Hornbostel*. Berlin: Dietrich Reimer (Ernst Vohsen).

Tuzin, Donald F. (1980). *The Voice of the Tambaran: Truth and Illusion in Ilahita Arapesh Religion*. Berkeley, CA: University of California Press.

— (1997). *The Cassowary's Revenge: The Life and Death of Masculinity in a New Guinea Society*. Chicago: University of Chicago Press.

Twohig, Amanda, ed. (1986). *Liklik Buk: A Sourcebook for Development Workers in Papua New Guinea*. Lae: Liklik Buk Information Centre, 2nd edition.

Valentine, C. A. (1965). "The Lakalai of New Britain." In: *Gods, Ghosts and Men in Melanesia: Some Religions of Australian New Guinea and the New Hebrides*. P. Lawrence and M. J. Meggitt, eds. New York: Oxford University Press, pp. 162-197.

Vasey, D. (1982). "Subsistence crop systems." In: *Papua New Guinea Atlas: A Nation in Transition*, David King and Stephen Ranck, eds. Bathrust, Australia: Robert Brown, pp. 50-51.

Verheij, E. W. M. & Coronel, R. E., eds. (1991). *Plant Resources of South-East Asia: Edible Fruits and Nuts*. Wageningen, Netherlands: Pudoc. Prosea Volume 2.

Vicedom, Georg F. (1977). *Myths and Legends from Mt. Hagen*. [Port Moresby]: Institute of Papua New Guinea Studies. Translated by Andrew Strathern.

Vormann, Franz (1909). "Dorf- und Hausanlage bei den Monumbo." *Anthropos* 4: 660-668.

Walsh, A. Crosbie (1985). *Inter-Provincial Migration in Papua New Guinea*. Papua New Guinea Research Monograph no. 3. Port Moresby: National Statistical Office.

— (1987). *Migration and Urbanization in Papua New Guinea: The 1980 Census*. Papua New Guinea Research Monograph No. 5. Port Moresby: National Statistical Office.

Watson, James B. (1983). *Tairora Culture: Contingency and Pragmatism*. Seattle: University of Washington Press.

— (1992). "Kainantu: Recollections of a First Encounter." In: *Ethnographic Presents: Pioneering Anthropoligists in the Papua New Guinea Highlands*, Terence E. Hays, ed. Berkeley: University of California Press, pp. 167-198.

Weeks, Sheldon & Guthrie, Gerard (1985). "Second and third level education: High school and beyond." In: *Papua New Guinea Atlas: A Nation in Transition*, David King and Stephen Ranck, eds. Bathrust, Australia: Robert Brown, pp. 28-29.

Wheeler, Gerald Camden (1972 [1926]). *Mono-Alu Folklore (Bougainville Strait, Western Solomon Islands)*. New York: Benjamin Blom.

Wheeler, Tony & Murray, Jon (1993). *Papua New Guinea: A Travel Survival Kit*. Berkeley, California: Lonely Planet.

Wilbert, Johannes & Simoneau, Karin (1992). *Folk Literature of South American Indians: General Index*. UCLA Latin American Studies #80. Los Angeles: UCLA Latin American Center.

Williams, F. E. (1924). *The Natives of the Purari Delta*. Anthropology Report 5. Port Moresby: Government Printer.

— (1933). *Population and Education in Papuaf*. Anthropology Reports 13-14. Depopulation of the Suau District and Practical Education: The Reform of Native Horticulture. Port Moresby: Government Printer.

— (1936). *Bull-Roarers in the Papuan Gulf*. Anthropology Report 17. Port Moresby: Government Printer.

Womersley, John S. (1978). *Handbooks of the Flora of Papua New Guinea*. Melbourne, Australia: Melbourne University Press, Volume 1.

Woodley, Ellen, ed. (1991). *Medicinal Plants of Papua New Guinea. Part 1: Morobe Province*. Weikersheim, Germany: Verlag Josef Margraf/Wau, Papua New Guinea: Wau Ecology Institute.

Wurm, S. A. (1975). *New Guinea Area Languages and Language Study. Volume 1. Papuan Languages and the New Guinea Linguistic Scene*. Pacific Linguistics Series C, No. 38. Canberra, Australia: Australian National University.

— (1976). *New Guinea Area Languages and Language Study. Volume 2. Austronesian Languages*. Pacific Linguistics Series C, No. 39. Canberra, Australia: Australian National University.

— & Harris, J. B., eds. (1963). *Police Motu: An Introduction to the Trade Language of Papua (New Guinea) for Anthropologists and Other Fieldworkers*. Pacific Linguistics Series B, No. 1. Canberra, Australia: Australian National University.

— (1982). "Indigenous languages." In: *Papua New Guinea Atlas: A Nation in Transition*, David King and Stephen Ranck, eds. Bathrust, Australia: Robert Brown, pp. 34-35.

Wurm, S. A. & Hattori, Shirô, eds. (1983). *Language Atlas of the Pacific Area. Part I. New Guinea Area, Oceania, Australia*. Pacific Linguistics, Series C, No. 67. Canberra: Australian Academy of the Humanities.

Wurm, S. A., Voorhoeve, C. L., & Laycock, D. C. (1983). "Southern Highlands Provinc, with Enga, Western, Gulf and Sepik Provinces (Papua New Guinea)." In: S. A. Wurm, & Shirô Hattori, eds. (1983). *Language Atlas of the Pacific Area. Part I. New Guinea Area, Oceania, Australia*. Pacific Linguistics, Series C, No. 67. Canberra: Australian Academy of the Humanities.

Z'graggen, John A. (1975). *The Languages of the Madang District, Papua New Guinea*. Pacific Linguistics Series B, No. 41. Canberra, Australia: Australian National University.

Gazetteer of Villages

The following latitude and longitude positions are taken primarily from the *Gazetteer of Papua New Guinea* (Peterson, 1982). Positions are given for all villages and small islands that are in **boldface** in the ancestor stories when they are known. Approximate locations are given when a village or island is associated with a known location. These positions can be used to find villages in conjunction with the assigned map numbers on the maps that follow. Map numbers are shared when village locations are only known approximately. Latitudes are in the southern hemisphere; longitudes are in the eastern hemisphere.

Village	Lat.°		Long.°		Map #	Village	Lat.°		Long.°		Map #
Abauia	3°	42´	143°	26´	539	Bainduang (approx.)	6°	39´	147°	1´	226
Aboba	6°	21´	143°	44´	169	Bainings	4°	15´	151°	45´	393
Abua (approx.)	3°	25´	142°	25´	469	Bainyik	3°	40´	143°	3´	524
Aibom	4°	17´	143°	12´	399	Baiyer River	5°	25´	144°	4´	275
Aimaga (approx.)	5°	30´	148°	26´	286	Bakupa	6°	28´	155°	29´	210
Airote (approx.)	3°	1´	142°	4´	446	Balaia	5°	32´	145°	39´	290
Ais	6°	13´	149°	33´	131	Balangabadangal	3°	38´	142°	56´	510
Aitape	3°	8´	142°	21´	451	Baluan Island	2°	33´	147°	17´	577
Aiwo	6°	6´	149°	34´	87	Bangasav	4°	41´	145°	4´	432
Aiyap	5°	17´	145°	42´	258	Baniara	9°	47´	149°	45´	15
Alexishafen	5°	5´	145°	48´	243	Banz	5°	47´	144°	37´	321
Ali Island	3°	8´	142°	28´	452	Barim	5°	39´	147°	50´	304
Amahop	3°	36´	142°	59´	498	Bedum (approx.)	5°	43´	145°	11´	316
Amaki	4°	4´	142°	40´	369	Belagel	3°	37´	143°	12´	505
Ambang (approx.)	5°	47´	144°	37´	321	Bendam (approx.)	5°	53´	145°	5´	335
Amboin	4°	37´	143°	29´	425	Besomang (approx.)	6°	39´	147°	1´	226
Ambunti	4°	14´	142°	50´	391	Biak	1°	0´	136°	0´	586
Amdi (approx.)	5°	51´	144°	51´	328	Bibe'ori	6°	36´	145°	54´	222
Amia (approx.)	4°	16´	144°	58´	398	Bibriweh (approx.)	3°	35´	142°	52´	493
Ampaonga (approx.)	6°	17´	145°	52´	149	Bieng	4°	3´	145°	1´	367
Ana	7°	50´	147°	32´	50	Bilbil	5°	18´	145°	47´	260
Angisi	4°	40´	144°	17´	429	Biliau Island (approx.)	5°	13´	145°	48´	249
Angoram	4°	4´	144°	4´	370	Bimat	4°	22´	145°	5´	402
Apan (approx.)	4°	14´	142°	52´	392	Bimbienye	6°	11´	144°	0´	113
Apanaipi	8°	24´	146°	22´	24	Bimin	5°	22´	142°	7´	268
Aralkulo (approx.)	5°	54´	145°	3´	339	Birip	5°	33´	143°	47´	291
Arili	6°	18´	150°	4´	154	Blupblup	3°	31´	144°	36´	487
Aris Island	4°	0´	144°	58´	363	Boana	6°	26´	146°	49´	201
Arkosame (approx.)	3°	49´	142°	39´	564	Bogai	5°	41´	145°	10´	307
Arumut Island (approx.)	5°	56´	148°	3´	347	Bogia	4°	16´	144°	58´	398
Aseki	7°	21´	146°	12´	40	Bokure	4°	3´	145°	4´	368
Asip (approx.)	7°	2´	147°	4´	31	Bolen (approx.)	6°	1´	144°	58´	64
Atkena (approx.)	5°	54´	144°	0´	337	Bolim	5°	17´	141°	27´	254
Auma	7°	55´	145°	24´	56	Bolimang	6°	8´	147°	2´	102
Aupik	3°	39´	142°	59´	515	Bomai (approx.)	6°	27´	144°	41´	203
Avenggu	6°	22´	147°	23´	183	Bomai Kiari	6°	27´	144°	41´	203
Awiyana (approx.)	6°	17´	145°	52´	149	Bongos	3°	44´	142°	40´	545
Aying (approx.)	6°	51´	146°	48´	237	Bonkiman	5°	54´	146°	40´	340
Bagabag Island	4°	48´	146°	14´	438	Bonokbil (approx.)	5°	8´	141°	35´	245
Bagasin	5°	23´	145°	27´	271	Boroman	4°	43´	145°	56´	434
Baia	4°	56´	151°	32´	444	Bovera	8°	5´	147°	44´	19

Village	Lat.°		Long.°		Map #	Village	Lat.°		Long.°		Map #
Bualibual (approx.)	4°	25′	145°	4′	407	Fultumtem (approx.)	3°	22′	142°	7′	461
Buanaputa (approx.)	4°	25′	145°	4′	407	Ga (approx.)	3°	14′	144°	2′	457
Buin	6°	50′	155°	44′	236	Gabsonkek	6°	34′	146°	46′	217
Buka Island	5°	15′	154°	38′	253	Gaikarobi	4°	6′	143°	18′	376
Bukaua	6°	44′	147°	22′	233	Galai 1	5°	38′	150°	22′	301
Bukinaru	3°	38′	143°	14′	514	Ganzegan	6°	22′	146°	51′	182
Bulbul (approx.)	10°	7′	142°	7′	4	Garaina	7°	53′	147°	8′	55
Bulolo	7°	12′	146°	39′	34	Garu	5°	25′	149°	58′	276
Bulumuri	5°	1′	150°	9′	239	Garua Island	5°	18′	150°	5′	262
Bumatu (approx.)	7°	2′	147°	4′	31	Gavien	3°	54′	144°	7′	570
Bunam	4°	39′	144°	15′	428	Gemaheng	6°	24′	147°	30′	194
Bundi	5°	44′	145°	14′	318	Gembogl	5°	53′	145°	5′	335
Burauta (approx.)	6°	21′	145°	53′	174	Gena	6°	8′	144°	56′	96
Busekom (approx.)	7°	3′	146°	56′	32	Genana (approx.)	10°	5′	150°	5′	3
Busiga	6°	42′	147°	46′	230	Gereglkane	5°	52′	145°	7′	333
Butam	4°	26′	152°	9′	411	Gi (approx.)	5°	28′	148°	22′	281
Buvasi	5°	38′	150°	23′	302	Gial	4°	32′	145°	58′	422
Charapa	4°	1′	143°	39′	365	Gievi (approx.)	5°	44′	145°	14′	318
Chuave	6°	8′	145°	8′	99	Gila Gila	4°	24′	152°	15′	405
Chuimondo	4°	12′	144°	8′	387	Gimbong (approx.)	6°	9′	147°	11′	106
Dalugilomon	6°	8′	147°	3′	103	Ginam	5°	35′	145°	16′	295
Dami	5°	18′	149°	57′	261	Giraku (approx.)	6°	8′	144°	56′	96
Darabumo	5°	50′	144°	54′	323	Giri	4°	16′	144°	43′	397
Dengop (approx.)	6°	9′	147°	11′	106	Gitua	6°	1′	147°	29′	66
Dereperengwa	6°	17′	145°	12′	148	Giunakane	5°	55′	144°	55′	342
Deri	6°	12′	144°	58′	123	Giviseveka	9°	55′	150°	55′	17
Disige (approx.)	6°	5′	147°	2′	80	Gogime	5°	56′	145°	2′	345
Dolomon (approx.)	6°	10′	147°	4′	109	Gohikave	6°	2′	145°	20′	68
Dowaeta (approx.)	3°	42′	142°	58′	536	Gomia	6°	7′	145°	8′	89
Droia	2°	7′	147°	2′	573	Goodenough Island	9°	22′	150°	16′	6
Dua Konage (approx.)	5°	51′	145°	5′	329	Gope People [Gauri]	7°	29′	144°	30′	43
Dumad	4°	55′	145°	45′	443	Goroka	6°	5′	145°	23′	78
Dumun (approx.)	6°	5′	145°	0′	76	Goru (approx.)	4°	40′	149°	18′	430
Dunuabanma (approx.)	5°	17′	144°	31′	257	Guala (approx.)	5°	42′	142°	45′	309
Dyaul Island	2°	56′	150°	53′	581	Gueibi	5°	40′	145°	9′	306
Egari	6°	1′	143°	42′	62	Gugo	5°	59′	145°	0′	358
Eglem (approx.)	6°	18′	143°	50′	151	Gulipyanda (approx.)	5°	24′	143°	27′	272
Elimbara (approx.)	6°	12′	145°	9′	125	Gulmo (approx.)	5°	14′	141°	14′	250
Emegari	5°	43′	145°	11′	316	Gumine	6°	12′	144°	57′	122
Erap	6°	32′	146°	42′	214	Gumun	6°	14′	147°	12′	135
Erave	6°	39′	143°	53′	225	Gunagi (approx.)	6°	12′	144°	58′	123
Erima	5°	24′	145°	44′	273	Gunakane	6°	8′	144°	59′	98
Erimbari	6°	12′	145°	9′	125	Gunazaking	6°	35′	147°	37′	220
Esianda	6°	24′	147°	32′	195	Gurube	4°	27′	145°	6′	417
Etesena	6°	26′	145°	37′	200	Gurukor	6°	50′	146°	38′	235
Fairu (approx.)	3°	25′	142°	1′	466	Gusap	5°	59′	146°	5′	360
Fatima	3°	27′	142°	6′	472	Gwalip	3°	41′	143°	11′	529
Fergusson Island	9°	30′	150°	40′	11	Hagen	5°	52′	144°	13′	330
Finschhafen	6°	36′	147°	51′	224	Halimon (approx.)	6°	8′	147°	2′	102
Finungwa	6°	20′	146°	37′	165	Hamberauri	3°	39′	143°	36′	520
Firigano	6°	20′	145°	27′	162	Handara	3°	41′	143°	27′	530

Village	Lat.°		Long.°		Map #
Hanjiri	8°	55´	147°	55´	27
Hanuabada	9°	27´	147°	8´	9
Hanyak	3°	44´	143°	30´	549
Hauabongo	7°	23´	146°	0´	41
Haumbugwe	3°	43´	143°	27´	543
Haumbugwe	3°	43´	143°	27´	543
Hemang	6°	10´	147°	4´	109
Henganofi	6°	14´	145°	38´	134
Horon Keban (approx.)	6°	0´	147°	12´	59
Hoskins	5°	27´	150°	24´	277
Hote	7°	3´	146°	56´	32
Huasufawu (approx.)	3°	41´	143°	38´	534
Huning Bubuna (approx.)	5°	41´	151°	8´	308
Huwa	6°	22´	145°	27´	180
Ialibu	6°	17´	143°	59´	147
Iamanda	6°	14´	143°	39´	132
Iame	6°	23´	143°	51´	187
Iaro	6°	25´	144°	5´	197
Ibusa	6°	27´	145°	37´	204
Ibwananio	9°	38´	150°	27´	13
Ikana	6°	21´	145°	56´	175
Ilahita	3°	41´	142°	56´	528
Ilakia	6°	20´	145°	30´	164
Ilesa	6°	41´	145°	40´	228
Imon	6°	7´	147°	1´	92
Imonda	3°	20´	141°	10´	460
Impep (approx.)	3°	44´	142°	28´	544
Inangtigin (approx.)	5°	8´	141°	35´	245
Indagen	6°	14´	147°	15´	136
Ingambas	3°	42´	142°	56´	535
Inkiap (approx.)	3°	44´	142°	28´	544
Inolo	4°	12´	152°	29´	389
Intsi (approx.)	6°	7´	146°	11´	91
Iobai	6°	13´	145°	6´	128
Irafo (approx.)	6°	23´	145°	42´	188
Isale (approx.)	6°	19´	143°	42´	156
Isontenu	6°	17´	145°	55´	150
Isung	4°	27´	144°	49´	415
Iumielo	6°	11´	149°	31´	118
Iwam (approx.)	4°	16´	141°	53´	395
Japanaut	4°	5´	143°	3´	371
Japandai	4°	9´	142°	59´	380
Japuain	3°	29´	143°	16´	482
Josephstaal	4°	44´	145°	1´	435
Kabari	6°	20´	145°	8´	160
Kabwum	6°	9´	147°	11´	106
Kadep (approx.)	5°	31´	143°	29´	256
Kafe	6°	18´	145°	44´	153
Kafle	3°	45´	142°	35´	553
Kagua	6°	26´	143°	48´	199
Kaiap (approx.)	5°	29´	143°	42´	282
Kaidane (approx.)	5°	29´	144°	4´	283
Kainantu	6°	17´	145°	52´	149
Kainde	3°	34´	143°	37´	491
Kaintiba	7°	30´	146°	2´	44
Kair (approx.)	5°	54´	145°	3´	339
Kairiru	3°	37´	143°	13´	506
Kakemuto (approx.)	6°	20´	145°	18´	161
Kakoro	7°	51´	146°	31´	51
Kalabu	3°	38´	143°	6´	512
Kalal	6°	46´	147°	54´	234
Kalalo (approx.)	6°	0´	147°	12´	59
Kalem	3°	44´	142°	28´	544
Kali (approx.)	6°	24´	144°	6´	192
Kalo Kalo	10°	3´	147°	47´	2
Kamanakor	3°	43´	142°	56´	542
Kamano (approx.)	6°	17´	145°	52´	149
Kamatatopemandak (approx.)	5°	51´	143°	31´	325
Kambaram (approx.)	5°	22´	143°	57´	269
Kambirip	6°	3´	143°	38´	70
Kambuntina	5°	55´	147°	20´	343
Kamuar (approx.)	4°	25´	145°	4´	407
Kamus	5°	57´	145°	22´	350
Kandangai	4°	7´	143°	5´	378
Kandep	5°	51´	143°	31´	325
Kandoka	5°	30´	149°	50´	287
Kandrian	6°	13´	149°	33´	131
Kanganaman	4°	11´	143°	16´	384
Kanomi	6°	11´	147°	40´	116
Kapu (approx.)	3°	41´	142°	28´	527
Kapuri	8°	14´	146°	12´	22
Karamukei	5°	43´	145°	7´	314
Kararau	4°	12´	143°	21´	385
Karimui	6°	30´	144°	51´	212
Karkar Island	4°	38´	145°	58´	426
Karkum	4°	46´	145°	40´	437
Kasokasa	6°	36´	145°	39´	221
Kasumandaka (approx.)	5°	51´	143°	31´	325
Katumani	7°	2´	146°	42´	30
Kaupena	6°	6´	144°	9´	84
Kauwo	6°	24´	144°	6´	192
Kefeya, Mount (approx.)	6°	5´	145°	13´	77
Keloa (approx.)	6°	19´	143°	42´	156
Kendagl	6°	16´	143°	58´	142
Kerema	7°	58´	145°	46´	57
Keresau	3°	24´	143°	27´	464
Kerum	6°	21´	145°	3´	173
Kesawaka	6°	10´	145°	41´	108
Kevasop	4°	42´	145°	55´	433
Kilenge	5°	28´	148°	22´	281
Kimbe	5°	33´	150°	9´	293
Kimil	5°	43´	144°	32´	313

Village	Lat.°		Long.°		Map #	Village	Lat.°		Long.°		Map #
Kiminibis	3°	35′	143°	3′	494	Kulubob	4°	44′	146°	0′	436
Kindarupa	5°	38′	145°	5′	299	Kumbakumba (approx.)	6°	21′	147°	1′	177
Kindogokevi	5°	43′	145°	9′	315	Kumbip	6°	7′	147°	18′	95
Kiniambu	3°	51′	143°	19′	565	Kumbuhum	3°	37′	143°	14′	507
Kira	6°	25′	143°	49′	196	Kumdi	5°	42′	144°	9′	311
Kiripia	5°	57′	144°	0′	348	Kumin (approx.)	6°	5′	143°	37′	74
Kisip (approx.)	6°	1′	143°	42′	62	Kundire	5°	59′	145°	0′	358
Kisituen	6°	21′	147°	1′	177	Kunjip (approx.)	5°	51′	144°	34′	326
Kiunga	6°	7′	141°	18′	88	Kup	5°	58′	144°	48′	353
Klaplei	3°	45′	142°	34′	552	Kupoam	3°	27′	142°	7′	473
Klelbuf	3°	30′	142°	2′	483	Kuraini (approx.)	5°	43′	145°	11′	316
Koen (approx.)	6°	6′	143°	41′	83	Kurubukari (approx.)	5°	20′	145°	15′	264
Kofena	5°	59′	145°	16′	359	Kurumuil	5°	51′	144°	36′	327
Kogaru (approx.)	6°	6′	145°	29′	85	Kutiga	5°	42′	144°	9′	311
Kogoga	6°	15′	144°	0′	137	Kutubu	6°	24′	143°	20′	190
Kogrikargo (approx.)	4°	41′	145°	4′	432	Kwagaga	7°	18′	146°	5′	35
Koiwat	4°	6′	143°	33′	377	Kwaringia	3°	54′	142°	52′	569
Kokopo	5°	29′	148°	41′	284	Kwenzenzeng	6°	28′	147°	29′	209
Komban	6°	14′	147°	15′	136	Kwikane	6°	12′	145°	0′	124
Kombilinye	6°	11′	143°	57′	112	Kyaka (approx.)	5°	29′	144°	4′	283
Kombio	3°	26′	142°	44′	471	Lababia	7°	18′	147°	8′	37
Komo	6°	4′	142°	52′	71	Lablab	5°	42′	148°	3′	312
Kompiam	5°	22′	143°	57′	269	Labogai (approx.)	6°	20′	145°	18′	161
Konbi	5°	3′	144°	54′	240	Labutina (approx.)	5°	55′	147°	20′	343
Kondeali (approx.)	6°	19′	143°	42′	156	Lae	6°	44′	147°	0′	232
Kondiu	5°	59′	144°	52′	356	Lagaip sub-Province	5°	30′	143°	20′	285
Kondolop	6°	7′	147°	14′	94	Lagira	6°	22′	143°	39′	178
Kone (approx.)	6°	8′	144°	57′	97	Laiagam	5°	31′	143°	29′	256
Kongambu (approx.)	5°	51′	145°	5′	329	Laitaro (approx.)	6°	50′	155°	44′	236
Kongibugl	6°	12′	144°	1′	121	Lakungkung	6°	5′	149°	35′	82
Konimbo	6°	10′	147°	13′	110	Lalang	6°	22′	147°	26′	185
Konoboyufa	5°	56′	145°	15′	346	Lebam (approx.)	3°	34′	142°	48′	490
Kopar	3°	52′	144°	32′	567	Lega	6°	21′	144°	5′	171
Koray (approx.)	6°	21′	144°	7′	172	Lehinga	3°	40′	142°	58′	523
Koreipa	6°	2′	145°	17′	67	Leion	2°	57′	150°	46′	583
Korikunu (approx.)	6°	20′	154°	40′	168	Leitre	2°	50′	141°	38′	580
Korogo	4°	6′	143°	9′	374	Lenke (approx.)	5°	29′	143°	42′	282
Koromasarik (approx.)	5°	13′	145°	46′	248	Lepiti (approx.)	6°	10′	144°	1′	107
Kosayufa (approx.)	5°	57′	145°	16′	349	Leyalam	5°	14′	143°	37′	251
Kovu	7°	59′	146°	20′	58	Litipinaga	6°	15′	145°	23′	138
Kowa Lalo Muli (approx.)	3°	29′	142°	2′	480	Loloho (approx.)	6°	2′	155°	24′	69
Kozaga (approx.)	6°	6′	145°	36′	86	Loneim	3°	37′	143°	6′	503
Kranket Island	5°	12′	145°	49′	247	Lossu #1	3°	3′	151°	37′	447
Kremending	3°	36′	143°	38′	500	Lou Island	2°	25′	147°	22′	574
Kuare	6°	27′	143°	59′	202	Luan (approx.)	2°	31′	150°	28′	576
Kudjip	5°	51′	144°	34′	326	Lufa	6°	20′	145°	18′	161
Kuimbu (approx.)	4°	30′	152°	15′	419	Lumi	3°	29′	142°	2′	480
Kukurai	4°	27′	145°	5′	416	Lutu Busama (approx.)	7°	2′	147°	4′	31
Kulavi	5°	58′	147°	15′	354	Luwi (approx.)	6°	24′	143°	20′	190
Kulefu (approx.)	6°	5′	145°	13′	77	Madang	5°	13′	145°	48′	249
Kuli	5°	52′	144°	26′	331	Maer Island (approx.)	9°	56′	144°	0′	18

Village	Lat.°		Long.°		Map #
Magumagu (approx.)	4°	27′	145°	5′	416
Mai (approx.)	5°	33′	150°	20′	294
Maiamsariang (approx.)	6°	11′	146°	13′	115
Maibana (approx.)	5°	44′	145°	14′	318
Maipanai	8°	11′	143°	44′	21
Mait Island	2°	59′	150°	43′	585
Maiwara School	5°	5′	145°	47′	242
Makada Island	4°	7′	152°	25′	379
Makura (approx.)	6°	1′	143°	42′	62
Malaguna (also 4°23′ 152°21′)	4°	13′	152°	9′	390
Malapaiem	3°	39′	143°	12′	516
Malin	3°	24′	142°	58′	463
Malol Mission	3°	6′	142°	13′	449
Malu	4°	14′	142°	52′	392
Mambauro	3°	42′	143°	12′	537
Manam Island	4°	5′	145°	2′	373
Mando	6°	1′	145°	17′	65
Mangul	3°	52′	143°	9′	566
Manu	4°	27′	144°	3′	414
Manu	4°	27′	144°	3′	414
Manubada Island	9°	31′	147°	10′	12
Manugoro	9°	42′	147°	28′	14
Map	6°	5′	143°	37′	74
Mapor	4°	33′	146°	1′	423
Maprik	3°	38′	143°	3′	511
Marawaka	6°	59′	145°	52′	238
Margarima	5°	59′	143°	22′	355
Marili (approx.)	5°	56′	148°	3′	347
Marmar	4°	27′	152°	20′	418
Masandenai	4°	25′	143°	32′	406
Masingara	9°	7′	142°	56′	5
Matakiripa (approx.)	6°	15′	145°	23′	138
Matiu 2 (approx.)	4°	55′	145°	55′	443
Maui	3°	29′	142°	2′	480
May River	4°	16′	141°	53′	395
Megan Kobu (approx.)	6°	12′	145°	9′	125
Meiwhak	3°	36′	142°	44′	497
Meki	6°	16′	143°	39′	141
Melandum	6°	10′	147°	19′	111
Mendi	6°	9′	143°	39′	105
Mengan	5°	59′	146°	33′	361
Menihegororo (approx.)	6°	12′	145°	20′	126
Mensuat	4°	27′	143°	45′	413
Meregese (approx.)	3°	39′	143°	49′	521
Mili	5°	21′	151°	23′	267
Min (approx.)	5°	23′	141°	32′	270
Mindik	6°	28′	147°	26′	208
Minduru (approx.)	6°	50′	146°	38′	235
Minimb (approx.)	5°	42′	144°	9′	311
Minj	5°	54′	144°	41′	338
Mior-Kipemukondiri (approx.)	6°	17′	145°	12′	148

Village	Lat.°		Long.°		Map #
Mis	5°	13′	145°	46′	248
Misim	3°	34′	142°	48′	490
Miwa	7°	8′	141°	32′	33
Mnamgimgi (approx.)	4°	41′	145°	4′	432
Moa Island (approx.)	10°	7′	142°	7′	4
Mogom	6°	20′	146°	55′	166
Mokuma (approx.)	6°	12′	145°	9′	125
Mongol	4°	16′	143°	55′	396
Moriuari (approx.)	8°	14′	146°	12′	22
Moru (approx.)	3°	37′	142°	14′	501
Moubus (approx.)	7°	48′	147°	40′	49
Moveave	8°	10′	146°	10′	20
Muap (approx.)	4°	25′	145°	4′	407
Mugil Mission	4°	50′	145°	47′	440
Mukili	3°	41′	142°	22′	526
Muli Mission	6°	20′	143°	55′	158
Muliagani	5°	33′	149°	24′	292
Mumengtein	7°	0′	146°	34′	28
Mundjiharanji	3°	45′	143°	26′	556
Mungoro	6°	21′	143°	53′	170
Munum	6°	34′	146°	51′	219
Muri (approx.)	5°	42′	142°	45′	309
Musak	5°	20′	145°	15′	264
Nademeben (approx.)	6°	21′	147°	1′	177
Nagara Island (approx.)	4°	38′	149°	18′	427
Naiama	3°	5′	151°	26′	448
Nakamito	6°	6′	145°	36′	86
Nambaga	5°	44′	144°	18′	317
Nambariwa	5°	57′	147°	22′	351
Nanduo	6°	27′	147°	42′	206
Narawapum	6°	11′	146°	13′	115
Narawiti	4°	26′	145°	4′	410
Nasingalatu	6°	40′	147°	50′	227
Nebilyer Valley (approx.)	6°	1′	144°	7′	63
Negri	3°	40′	143°	19′	525
Nengan (approx.)	6°	8′	144°	57′	97
New Hanover Island	2°	30′	150°	15′	575
Ngasawapum	6°	34′	146°	49′	218
Nguzi	7°	47′	146°	52′	47
Niglguma (approx.)	5°	50′	146°	6′	324
Ningaumbi	3°	42′	142°	58′	536
Nissan Islad	4°	30′	154°	14′	420
Nobanob	5°	10′	149°	32′	246
Nodabu	4°	54′	144°	40′	442
Nokolakolato (approx.)	6°	5′	145°	13′	77
Nondugl	5°	52′	144°	46′	332
Nubia	4°	10′	144°	51′	382
Nuglaikane (approx.)	5°	51′	145°	5′	329
Nuku	3°	41′	142°	28′	527
Nul	6°	8′	144°	57′	97
Numamaka	3°	45′	143°	0′	555

Village	Lat.°		Long.°		Map #
Numindogum (approx.)	3°	42′	143°	27′	540
Numoirum	3°	41′	143°	36′	533
Nungori	3°	41′	143°	28′	531
Nupuru	6°	20′	145°	29′	163
Ok Tedi Mine (approx.)	5°	7′	141°	2′	244
Okapa	6°	32′	145°	37′	213
Olen Numugu (approx.)	6°	22′	145°	27′	180
Ologuangin (approx.)	6°	25′	146°	25′	198
Olsobip	5°	23′	141°	32′	270
Omai	6°	14′	143°	46′	133
Omaura	6°	5′	145°	25′	79
Omkalai	6°	11′	144°	57′	114
Omunibil (approx.)	3°	37′	142°	53′	502
Onumuga (approx.)	6°	32′	145°	37′	213
Opau	7°	52′	145°	42′	54
Orokolo	7°	52′	145°	19′	53
Osavi-Bukom (approx.)	7°	3′	146°	56′	32
Pagaukane	5°	51′	145°	5′	329
Pahang (approx.)	3°	31′	142°	42′	485
Paiala (approx.)	5°	24′	143°	27′	272
Paiewa	7°	31′	147°	22′	45
Palagao (approx.)	5°	20′	154°	34′	266
Pangal	6°	5′	143°	39′	75
Pangia	6°	21′	144°	7′	172
Papayuku (approx.)	5°	24′	143°	27′	272
Par	5°	28′	143°	45′	280
Para	6°	1′	142°	48′	60
Pari	5°	59′	144°	59′	357
Pariakinam	4°	25′	145°	4′	407
Parina	3°	39′	143°	21′	518
Parom	3°	28′	143°	29′	478
Passam	3°	41′	143°	38′	534
Patuli (approx.)	5°	51′	143°	31′	325
Paup	3°	14′	142°	35′	455
Pawaiamu	6°	20′	143°	46′	157
Pembi	6°	1′	143°	36′	61
Pependaug (approx.)	6°	27′	147°	31′	205
Perepe (approx.)	6°	19′	143°	42′	156
Pes	3°	11′	142°	16′	453
Petats Island	5°	20′	154°	33′	265
Pilelo	6°	11′	149°	3′	117
Pindiu	6°	27′	147°	31′	205
Pipilex (approx.)	6°	17′	143°	33′	145
Piritop (approx.)	4°	12′	152°	29′	389
Pobung	6°	10′	147°	4′	109
Poketamanda (approx.)	5°	51′	143°	31′	325
Polu (approx.)	3°	25′	142°	25′	469
Pomberd (approx.)	6°	12′	143°	56′	119
Pomio	5°	31′	151°	31′	288
Ponam Island	1°	54′	146°	54′	587
Popoaitave (approx.)	8°	10′	146°	10′	20

Village	Lat.°		Long.°		Map #
Popondetta	8°	46′	148°	14′	26
Porgera	5°	28′	143°	12′	279
Port Moresby	9°	29′	147°	11′	10
Posei	7°	51′	147°	29′	52
Puleng	6°	15′	147°	18′	139
Pumakos (approx.)	5°	38′	143°	55′	298
Pupuk (approx.)	6°	16′	146°	16′	143
Rabaul	4°	12′	152°	11′	388
Radava	10°	1′	149°	53′	1
Rakili (approx.)	6°	19′	143°	42′	156
Rauit	3°	37′	142°	14′	501
Raungwe (approx.)	3°	41′	142°	22′	526
Rauwetei	3°	25′	142°	6′	467
Rempi	4°	58′	145°	46′	445
Rigo	9°	48′	147°	33′	16
Rintebe	6°	7′	145°	34′	90
Riwi (approx.)	6°	19′	143°	42′	156
Ropore (approx.)	6°	19′	143°	42′	156
Rupiali (approx.)	6°	19′	143°	42′	156
Sagasi	3°	44′	143°	9′	548
Sagasi	3°	44′	143°	9′	548
Saidor	5°	38′	146°	28′	300
Saikuare (approx.)	3°	44′	143°	9′	548
Salamaua	7°	2′	147°	4′	31
Salata	3°	37′	142°	53′	502
Samaran (approx.)	6°	13′	146°	19′	129
Sambori	6°	8′	147°	17′	104
Samo	3°	56′	152°	50′	571
Sangriman	4°	27′	143°	17′	412
Sara	3°	42′	143°	16′	538
Sasaura	6°	22′	146°	1′	181
Sassoia	3°	41′	143°	30′	532
Sattelberg Mission	6°	29′	147°	47′	211
Saulaku (approx.)	3°	31′	142°	1′	484
Sauri 1	3°	36′	143°	36′	499
Sauri 2	3°	37′	143°	36′	509
Sawetmove (approx.)	7°	2′	146°	1′	29
Seigu	6°	5′	145°	25′	79
Selni	3°	33′	142°	53′	488
Semamur	4°	48′	146°	15′	439
Semin	6°	13′	143°	29′	127
Serai	2°	58′	141°	57′	584
Siago (approx.)	5°	38′	145°	5′	299
Sialum	6°	5′	147°	36′	81
Siang	5°	59′	146°	58′	362
Siar	4°	36′	153°	4′	424
Siassi Islands	5°	37′	147°	50′	297
Sibilanga	3°	27′	142°	30′	475
Sikindiwai (approx.)	5°	38′	145°	5′	299
Sima	3°	37′	143°	19′	508
Simpok (approx.)	6°	21′	146°	25′	176

Village	Lat.°		Long.°		Map #
Sinasina	6°	5′	145°	0′	76
Sio Island	5°	55′	147°	20′	343
Siriwai (approx.)	5°	38′	146°	28′	300
Sirowai (approx.)	6°	18′	155°	25′	155
Sirunki	5°	24′	143°	27′	272
Siu	6°	22′	147°	24′	184
Sogeri	9°	25′	147°	25′	7
Sokelen	6°	20′	146°	56′	167
Soloku	3°	29′	142°	14′	481
Songgin	6°	7′	147°	6′	93
Sua	6°	18′	145°	12′	152
Suambukum	3°	44′	143°	8′	547
Suap (approx.)	6°	24′	146°	43′	193
Suaru	4°	23′	145°	5′	403
Sugu	6°	24′	146°	43′	193
Suhapuneb (approx.)	3°	37′	142°	53′	502
Sumi	6°	24′	143°	44′	191
Suninga	3°	25′	142°	25′	469
Suwena (approx.)	7°	42′	147°	32′.1′	46
Tabar Island	2°	56′	152°	0′	582
Tabibuga	5°	36′	144°	41′	296
Taikopini (approx.)	6°	28′	144°	13′	207
Talasea	5°	17′	150°	2′	259
Talbakul	6°	5′	145°	0′	76
Talbipi	3°	31′	142°	1′	484
Talwat	4°	15′	152°	13′	394
Tamanairik (approx.)	4°	17′	152°	6′	400
Tambanum	4°	12′	143°	36′	386
Tambul	5°	54′	143°	54′	336
Tami Island	6°	46′	147°	54′	234
Tamoni (approx.)	3°	1′	142°	4′	446
Tanga Island	3°	28′	153°	14′	479
Tangu	4°	26′	144°	55′	409
Tarara	6°	2′	155°	24′	69
Tararan	6°	25′	146°	25′	198
Tarawai Island	3°	13′	143°	15′	454
Tari	5°	42′	142°	57′	310
Tarobi	5°	27′	150°	48′	278
Tatana	9°	26′	147°	7′	8
Tatumba	3°	45′	142°	58′	554
Taulil	4°	25′	152°	5′	408
Tavui	4°	9′	152°	9′	381
Telefomin	5°	8′	141°	35′	245
Teobuhin	5°	38′	155°	1′	303
Tepmarom (approx.)	6°	22′	147°	24′	184
Terebu	3°	39′	143°	49′	521
Termes (approx.)	3°	44′	142°	28′	544
Tibinini	5°	25′	143°	12′	274
Tigina (approx.)	5°	44′	145°	14′	318
Tindua	6°	22′	144°	2′	179
Tiri	6°	18′	143°	50′	151

Village	Lat.°		Long.°		Map #
Tisawe (approx.)	5°	43′	145°	11′	316
Tisgmal (approx.)	5°	58′	144°	48′	353
Toanumbu	3°	46′	143°	28′	558
Tobua	6°	17′	143°	31′	144
Tofungu	3°	25′	142°	1′	466
Togoba	5°	54′	149°	9′	341
Tohatsi	5°	4′	154°	39′	241
Tomba	5°	50′	144°	1′	322
Torembi	4°	1′	143°	8′	364
Toroambuna	5°	50′	146°	6′	324
Tororo	8°	15′	146°	56′	23
Trobriand	8°	40′	150°	55′	25
Tsak	5°	40′	143°	50′	305
Tuam Island	5°	56′	148°	3′	347
Tubum	3°	36′	141°	58′	495
Tuma (approx.)	5°	52′	144°	13′	330
Tumleo Island	3°	7′	142°	24′	450
Tungili (approx.)	6°	20′	144°	2.′5′	159
Turia (approx.)	5°	22′	143°	57′	269
Turutapa	4°	27′	145°	5′	416
Uba	6°	17′	143°	33′	145
Udaha Island (approx.)	4°	40′	149°	18′	430
Ugere (approx.)	4°	46′	145°	40′	437
Ulau	3°	18′	142°	48′	459
Ulaulatava	4°	23′	152°	13′	404
Ulga	5°	56′	144°	10′	344
Undangokam (approx.)	4°	25′	145°	4′	407
Unea Island	4°	53′	149°	9′	441
Upat	6°	13′	147°	11′	130
Urika	7°	48′	145°	4′	48
Urin (approx.)	5°	57′	149°	9′	352
Urindogum (approx.)	3°	39′	143°	34′	519
Usino	5°	32′	145°	23′	289
Utai	3°	23′	141°	35′	462
Utamup	3°	44′	142°	57′	546
Vambu Island	4°	38′	149°	18′	427
Vanimo	2°	40′	141°	16′	579
Vokeo Island	3°	14′	144°	2′	457
Wabag	5°	29′	143°	42′	282
Wabinama	6°	17′	143°	37′	146
Wabindumga	3°	47′	142°	55′	559
Wabutei	3°	26′	142°	6′	470
Wagi (approx.)	4°	26′	144°	55′	409
Wagri (approx.)	5°	43′	145°	9′	315
Waihos (approx.)	4°	14′	142°	50′	391
Wait Ston (approx.)	5°	43′	145°	11′	316
Waix (approx.)	3°	14′	144°	2′	457
Wakua (approx.)	6°	19′	143°	42′	156
Wakunai	5°	52′	155°	13′	334
Walingai	6°	15′	147°	42′	140
Walis Island	3°	14′	143°	18′	456

Village	Lat.°		Long.°		Map #
Waluaperepa (approx.)	6°	19′	143°	42′	156
Wama (approx.)	6°	19′	143°	42′	156
Wambiu	3°	43′	142°	28′	541
Wampit	6°	36′	146°	45′	223
Wamu	3°	40′	141°	14′	522
Wanabrugu	3°	59′	143°	31′	572
Wanali	3°	36′	142°	27′	496
Wanepap (approx.)	5°	31′	143°	29′	256
Wantenda (approx.)	6°	4′	143°	39′	72
Wantini (approx.)	7°	18′	146°	28′	36
Waolong (approx.)	6°	42′	147°	40′	229
Wapenamanda	5°	38′	143°	55′	298
Waragelu (approx.)	6°	8′	144°	59′	98
Warapu	3°	1′	142°	4′	446
Warekam	4°	21′	144°	52′	401
Wareli	3°	35′	142°	52′	493
Warimbi	4°	6′	143°	13′	375
Warom (approx.)	6°	43′	146°	25′	231
Warunegaru (approx.)	5°	17′	150°	2′	259
Wasemi	6°	23′	143°	17′	186
Waskuk	4°	11′	142°	45′	383
Watabung	6°	5′	145°	13′	77
Wau	7°	20′	146°	43′	39
Wauwoga	7°	19′	146°	5′	38
Wedau	10°	5′	150°	5′	3
Wegior	3°	48′	143°	1′	561
Wegomangi (approx.)	6°	17′	145°	12′	148
Wela (approx.)	3°	33′	142°	53′	488
Weliki (approx.)	6°	4′	147°	4′	73
Wempangu	7°	24′	146°	3′	42
Wereman	4°	2′	143°	7′	366
Wewak	3°	33′	143°	38′	489
Wilbeite	3°	25′	142°	8′	468
Witu Islands	4°	40′	149°	18′	430
Witupe Number 1	3°	46′	143°	14′	557
Witupe Number 2	3°	48′	143°	13′	563
Wobima (approx.)	6°	59′	145°	52′	238
Woginara	3°	28′	143°	18′	477
Wom	3°	31′	143°	36′	486
Womisis	3°	27′	142°	57′	476
Womkama	5°	54′	145°	3′	339
Wongat	6°	21′	146°	25′	176
Wosan (approx.)	5°	57′	145°	22′	350
Wosera	3°	48′	143°	2′	562
Wurins	3°	41′	143°	38′	534
Wuruf	6°	43′	146°	25′	231
Wurup (approx.)	5°	45′	144°	2′	319
Wutung	2°	37′	141°	1′	578
Yabob	5°	15′	145°	47′	252
Yahang	3°	45′	142°	26′	551
Yakalu (approx.)	3°	41′	142°	28′	527

Village	Lat.°		Long.°		Map #
Yakamul	3°	16′	142°	42′	458
Yakeltim	3°	48′	142°	5′	560
Yamben	3°	44′	143°	42′	550
Yambi	3°	53′	143°	1′	568
Yambil	3°	35′	142°	28′	492
Yambona (approx.)	7°	30′	146°	2′	44
Yamil	3°	38′	143°	9′	513
Yaminbot	4°	31′	143°	8′	421
Yamofe (approx.)	6°	5′	145°	13′	77
Yamok	4°	5′	143°	13′	372
Yampu (approx.)	5°	17′	143°	45′	255
Yandapo (approx.)	5°	19′	143°	17′	263
Yandugen (approx.)	3°	41′	142°	28′	527
Yangla	5°	45′	148°	3′	320
Yango (approx.)	6°	21′	143°	53′	170
Yangoru	3°	39′	143°	18′	517
Yapunda	3°	27′	142°	28′	474
Yarika (approx.)	5°	28′	143°	12′	279
Yaro (approx.)	6°	30′	144°	51′	212
Yassa (approx.)	4°	5′	145°	2′	373
Yassip	3°	31′	142°	42′	485
Yasubi	6°	33′	145°	34′	216
Yaubul (approx.)	3°	37′	143°	8′	504
Yaviyufa	6°	12′	145°	20′	126
Yawan	6°	8′	146°	52′	101
Yimas	4°	41′	143°	33′	431
Yomakawi (approx.)	6°	5′	145°	0′	76
Yombaliyi (approx.)	6°	22′	145°	27′	180
Yombi	6°	12′	143°	59′	120
Yopbukan (approx.)	6°	8′	146°	29′	100
Yopopaus (approx.)	5°	51′	143°	31′	325
Yuka (approx.)	5°	38′	143°	55′	298
Yuo	3°	24′	143°	29′	465
Yuro (approx.)	6°	30′	144°	51′	212
Zamolo (approx.)	6°	22′	147°	23′	183
Zengaren	6°	32′	147°	26′	215
Zumanggurun	6°	23′	146°	22′	189

Map Number Index

The following map numbers give the names of villages and small islands that are displayed on the maps that follow. Map numbers are shared when village locations are only known approximately.

1	Radava	46	Suwena	87	Aiwo	127	Semin
2	Kalo Kalo	47	Nguzi	88	Kiunga	128	Iobai
3	Genana	48	Urika	89	Gomia	129	Samaran
3	Wedau	49	Moubus	90	Rintebe	130	Upat
4	Bulbul	50	Ana	91	Intsi	131	Ais
4	Moa Island	51	Kakoro	92	Imon	131	Kandrian
5	Masingara	52	Posei	93	Songgin	132	Iamanda
6	Goodenough Island	53	Orokolo	94	Kondolop	133	Omai
7	Sogeri	54	Opau	95	Kumbip	134	Henganofi
8	Tatana	55	Garaina	96	Gena	135	Gumun
9	Hanuabada	56	Auma	96	Giraku	136	Indagen
10	Port Moresby	57	Kerema	97	Kone	136	Komban
11	Fergusson Island	58	Kovu	97	Nengan	137	Kogoga
12	Manubada Island	59	Horon Keban	97	Nul	138	Litipinaga
13	Ibwananio	59	Kalalo	98	Gunakane	138	Matakiripa
14	Manugoro	60	Para	98	Waragelu	139	Puleng
15	Baniara	61	Pembi	99	Chuave	140	Walingai
16	Rigo	62	Egari	100	Yopbukan	141	Meki
17	Giviseveka	62	Kisip	101	Yawan	142	Kendagl
18	Maer Island	62	Makura	102	Bolimang	143	Pupuk
19	Bovera	63	Nebilyer Valley	102	Halimon	144	Tobua
20	Moveave	64	Bolen	103	Dalugilomon	145	Pipilex
20	Popoaitave	65	Mando	104	Sambori	145	Uba
21	Maipanai	66	Gitua	105	Mendi	146	Wabinama
22	Kapuri	67	Koreipa	106	Dengop	147	Ialibu
22	Moriuari	68	Gohikave	106	Gimbong	148	Dereperengwa
23	Tororo	69	Loloho	106	Kabwum	148	Mior-Kipemukondiri
24	Apanaipi	69	Tarara	107	Lepiti	148	Wegomangi
25	Trobriand	70	Kambirip	108	Kesawaka	149	Ampaonga
26	Popondetta	71	Komo	109	Dolomon	149	Awiyana
27	Hanjiri	72	Wantenda	109	Hemang	149	Kainantu
28	Mumengtein	73	Weliki	109	Pobung	149	Kamano
29	Sawetmove	74	Kumin	110	Konimbo	150	Isontenu
30	Katumani	74	Map	111	Melandum	151	Eglem
31	Asip	75	Pangal	112	Kombilinye	151	Tiri
31	Bumatu	76	Dumun	113	Bimbienye	152	Sua
31	Lutu Busama	76	Sinasina	114	Omkalai	153	Kafe
31	Salamaua	76	Talbakul	115	Maiamsariang	154	Arili
32	Busekom	76	Yomakawi	115	Narawapum	155	Sirowai
32	Hote	77	Kefeya, Mount	116	Kanomi	156	Isale
32	Osavi-Bukom	77	Kulefu	117	Pilelo	156	Keloa
33	Miwa	77	Nokolakolato	118	Iumielo	156	Kondeali
34	Bulolo	77	Watabung	119	Pomberd	156	Perepe
35	Kwagaga	77	Yamofe	120	Yombi	156	Rakili
36	Wantini	78	Goroka	121	Kongibugl	156	Riwi
37	Lababia	79	Omaura	122	Gumine	156	Ropore
38	Wauwoga	79	Seigu	123	Deri	156	Rupiali
39	Wau	80	Disige	123	Gunagi	156	Wakua
40	Aseki	81	Sialum	124	Kwikane	156	Waluaperepa
41	Hauabongo	82	Lakungkung	125	Elimbara	156	Wama
42	Wempangu	83	Koen	125	Erimbari	157	Pawaiamu
43	Gauri	84	Kaupena	125	Megan Kobu	158	Muli Mission
44	Kaintiba	85	Kogaru	125	Mokuma	159	Tungili
44	Yambona	86	Kozaga	126	Menihegororo	160	Kabari
45	Paiewa	86	Nakamito	126	Yaviyufa	161	Kakemuto

333	Gereglkane	383	Waskuk	429	Angisi	477	Woginara
334	Wakunai	384	Kanganaman	430	Goru	478	Parom
335	Bendam	385	Kararau	430	Udaha Island	479	Tanga Island
335	Gembogl	386	Tambanum	430	Witu Islands	480	Kowa Lalo Muli
336	Tambul	387	Chuimondo	431	Yimas	480	Lumi
337	Atkena	388	Rabaul	432	Bangasav	480	Maui
338	Minj	389	Inolo	432	Kogrikargo	481	Soloku
339	Aralkulo	389	Piritop	432	Mnamgimgi	482	Japuain
339	Kair	390	Malaguna	433	Kevasop	483	Klelbuf
339	Womkama	391	Ambunti	434	Boroman	484	Saulaku
340	Bonkiman	391	Waihos	435	Josephstaal	484	Talbipi
341	Togoba	392	Apan	436	Kulubob	485	Pahang
342	Giunakane	392	Malu	437	Karkum	485	Yassip
343	Kambuntina	393	Bainings	437	Ugere	486	Wom
343	Labutina	394	Talwat	438	Bagabag Island	487	Blupblup
343	Sio Island	395	Iwam	439	Semamur	488	Selni
344	Ulga	395	May River	440	Mugil Mission	488	Wela
345	Gogime	396	Mongol	441	Unea Island	489	Wewak
346	Konoboyufa	397	Giri	442	Nodabu	490	Lebam
347	Arumut Island	398	Amia	443	Dumad	490	Misim
347	Marili	398	Bogia	443	Matiu 2	491	Kainde
347	Tuam Island	399	Aibom	444	Baia	492	Yambil
348	Kiripia	400	Tamanairik	445	Rempi	493	Bibriweh
349	Kosayufa	401	Warekam	446	Airote	493	Wareli
350	Kamus	402	Bimat	446	Tamoni	494	Kiminibis
350	Wosan	403	Suaru	446	Warapu	495	Tubum
351	Nambariwa	404	Ulaulatava	447	Lossu 1	496	Wanali
352	Urin	405	Gila Gila	448	Naiama	497	Meiwhak
353	Kup	406	Masandenai	449	Malol Mission	498	Amahop
353	Tisgmal	407	Bualibual	450	Tumleo Island	499	Sauri 1
354	Kulavi	407	Buanaputa	451	Aitape	500	Kremending
355	Margarima	407	Kamuar	452	Ali Island	501	Moru
356	Kondiu	407	Muap	453	Pes	501	Rauit
357	Pari	407	Pariakinam	454	Tarawai Island	502	Omunibil
358	Gugo	407	Undangokam	455	Paup	502	Salata
358	Kundire	408	Taulil	456	Walis Island	502	Suhapuneb
359	Kofena	409	Tangu	457	Ga	503	Loneim
360	Gusap	409	Wagi	457	Vokeo Island	504	Yaubul
361	Mengan	410	Narawiti	457	Waix	505	Belagel
362	Siang	411	Butam	458	Yakamul	506	Kairiru
363	Aris Island	412	Sangriman	459	Ulau	507	Kumbuhum
364	Torembi	413	Mensuat	460	Imonda	508	Sima
365	Charapa	414	Manu	461	Fultumtem	509	Sauri 2
366	Wereman	414	Manu	462	Utai	510	Balangabadangal
367	Bieng	415	Isung	463	Malin	511	Maprik
368	Bokure	416	Kukurai	464	Keresau	512	Kalabu
369	Amaki	416	Magumagu	465	Yuo	513	Yamil
370	Angoram	416	Turutapa	466	Fairu	514	Bukinaru
371	Japanaut	417	Gurube	466	Tofungu	515	Aupik
372	Yamok	418	Marmar	467	Rauwetei	516	Malapaiem
373	Manam Island	419	Kuimbu	468	Wilbeite	517	Yangoru
373	Yassa	420	Nissan Islad	469	Abua	518	Parina
374	Korogo	421	Yaminbot	469	Polu	519	Urindogum
375	Warimbi	422	Gial	469	Suninga	520	Hamberauri
376	Gaikarobi	423	Mapor	470	Wabutei	521	Meregese
377	Koiwat	424	Siar	471	Kombio	521	Terebu
378	Kandangai	425	Amboin	472	Fatima	522	Wamu
379	Makada Island	426	Karkar Island	473	Kupoam	523	Lehinga
380	Japandai	427	Nagara Island	474	Yapunda	524	Bainyik
381	Tavui	427	Vambu Island	475	Sibilanga	525	Negri
382	Nubia	428	Bunam	476	Womisis	526	Mukili

526	Raungwe	576	Luan
527	Kapu	577	Baluan Island
527	Nuku	578	Wutung
527	Yakalu	579	Vanimo
527	Yandugen	580	Leitre
528	Ilahita	581	Dyaul Island
529	Gwalip	582	Tabar Island
530	Handara	583	Leion
531	Nungori	584	Serai
532	Sassoia	585	Mait Island
533	Numoirum	586	Biak
534	Huasufawu	587	Ponam Island
534	Passam		
534	Wurins		
535	Ingambas		
536	Dowaeta		
536	Ningaumbi		
537	Mambauro		
538	Sara		
539	Abauia		
540	Numindogum		
541	Wambiu		
542	Kamanakor		
543	Haumbugwe		
544	Impep		
544	Inkiap		
544	Kalem		
544	Termes		
545	Bongos		
546	Utamup		
547	Suambukum		
548	Sagasi		
548	Sagasi		
548	Saikuare		
549	Hanyak		
550	Yamben		
551	Yahang		
552	Klaplei		
553	Kafle		
554	Tatumba		
555	Numamaka		
556	Mundjiharanji		
557	Witupe Number 1		
558	Toanumbu		
559	Wabindumga		
560	Yakeltim		
561	Wegior		
562	Wosera		
563	Witupe Number 2		
564	Arkosame		
565	Kiniambu		
566	Mangul		
567	Kopar		
568	Yambi		
569	Kwaringia		
570	Gavien		
571	Samo		
572	Wanabrugu		
573	Droia		
574	Lou Island		
575	New Hanover Island		

Provinces of Papua New Guinea

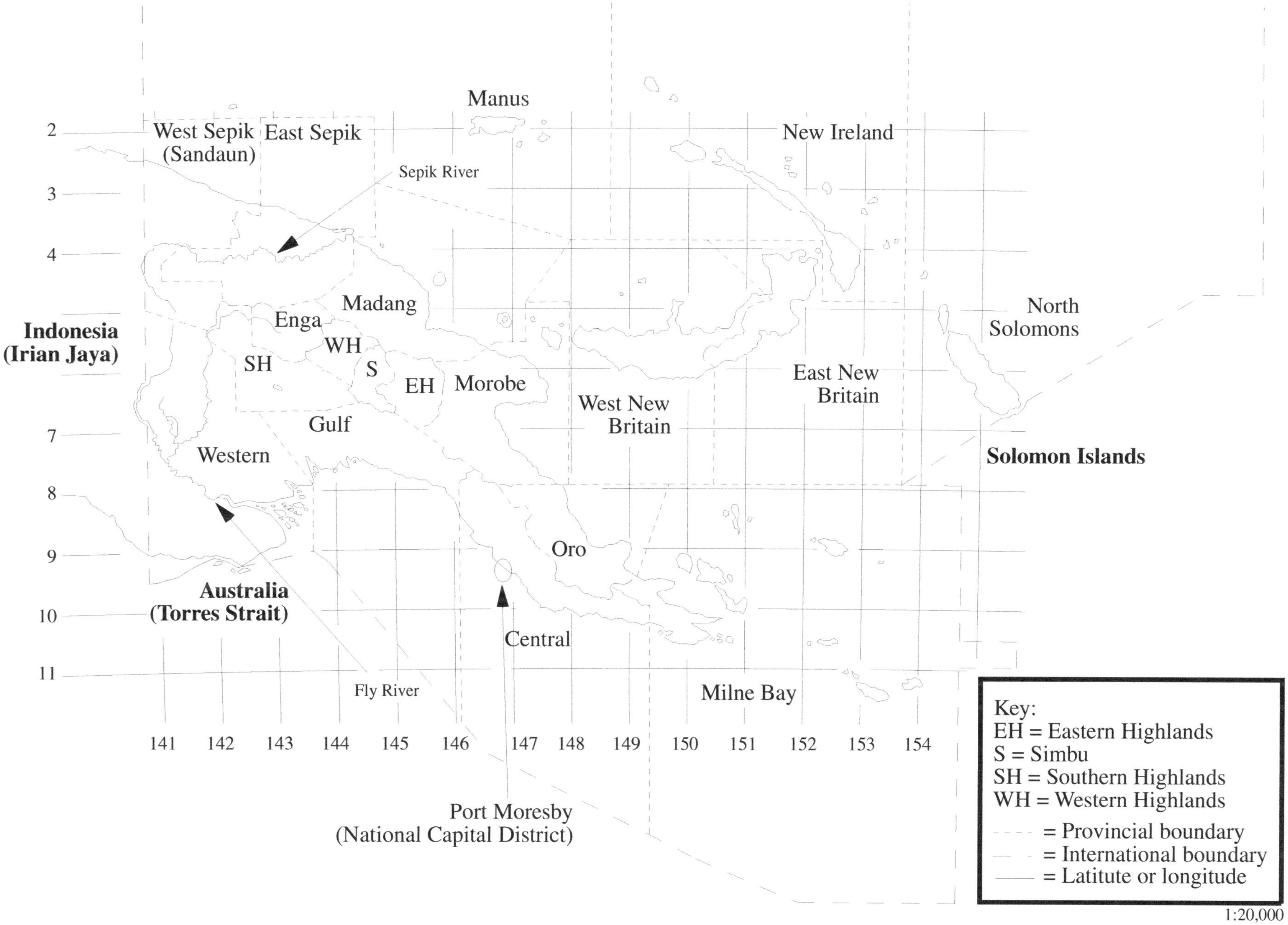

West Sepik Province

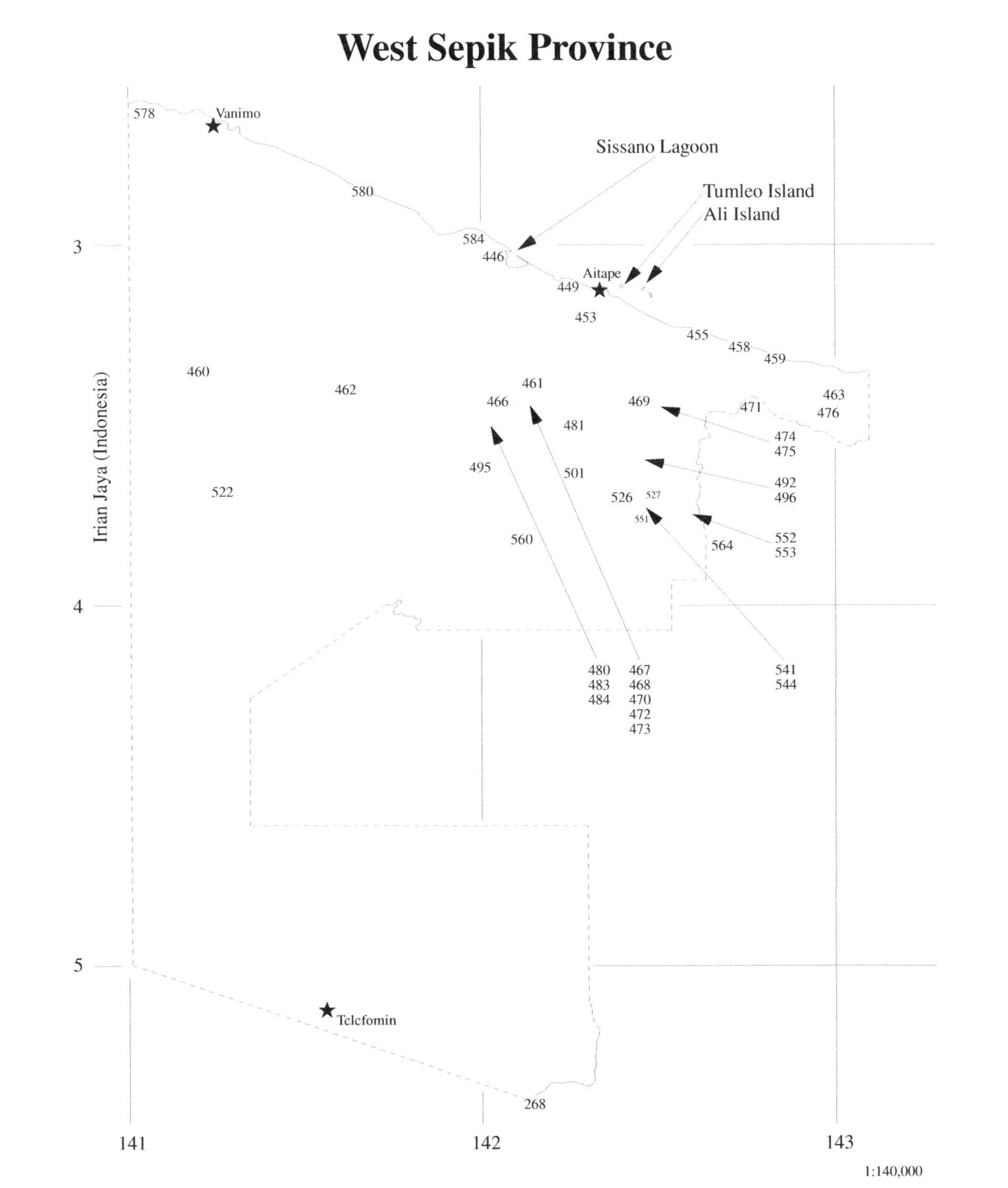

East Sepik Province

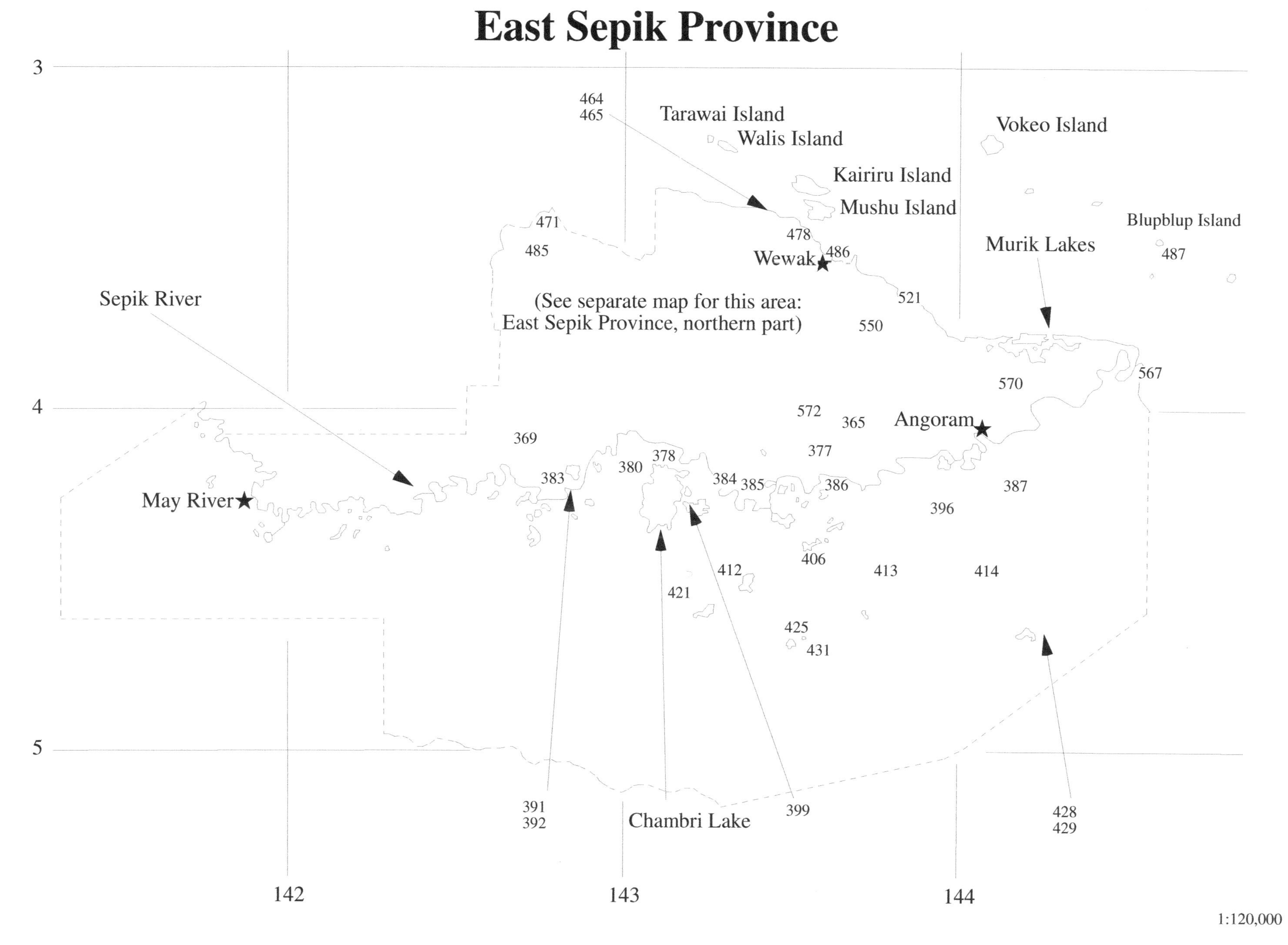

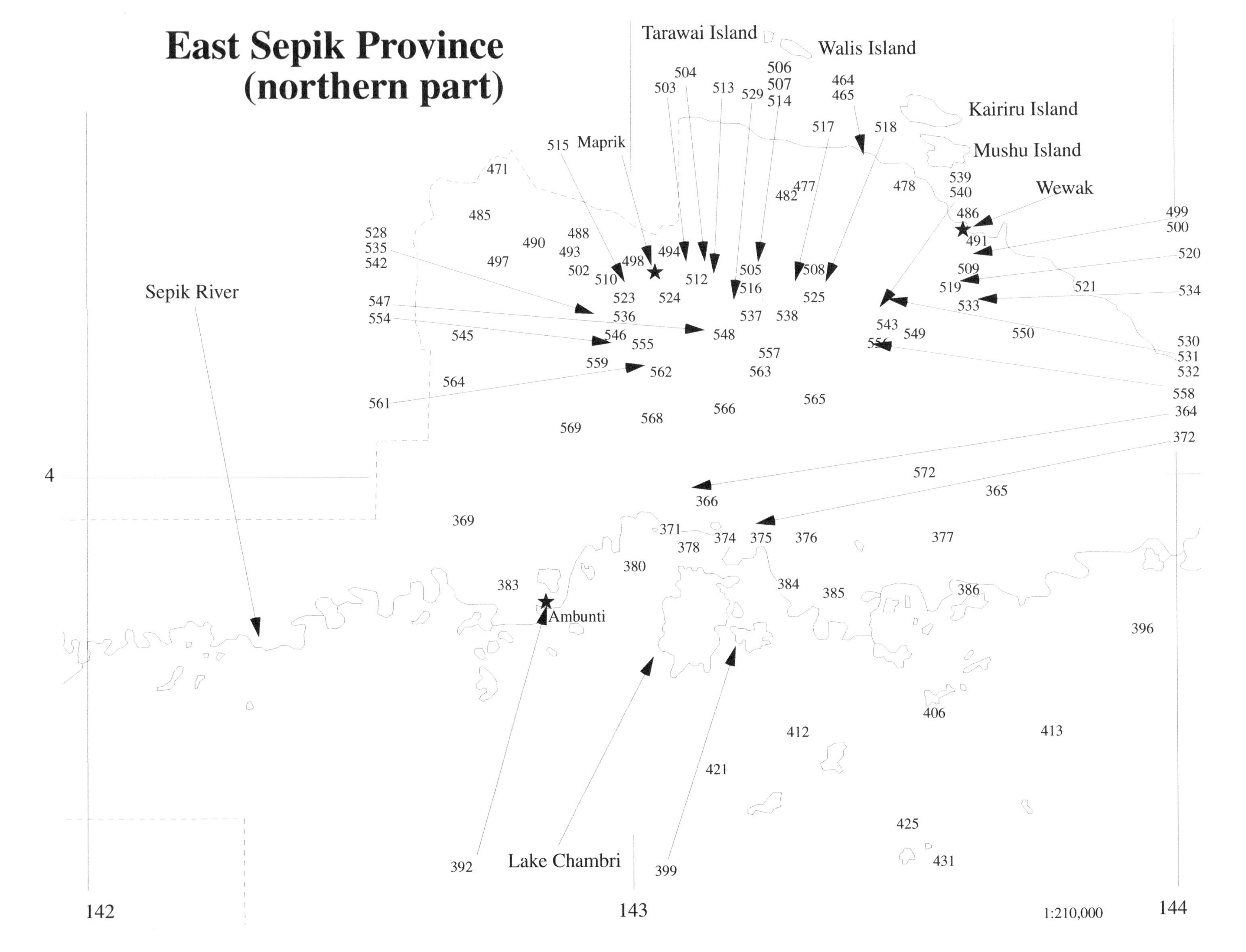

East Sepik Province (northern part)

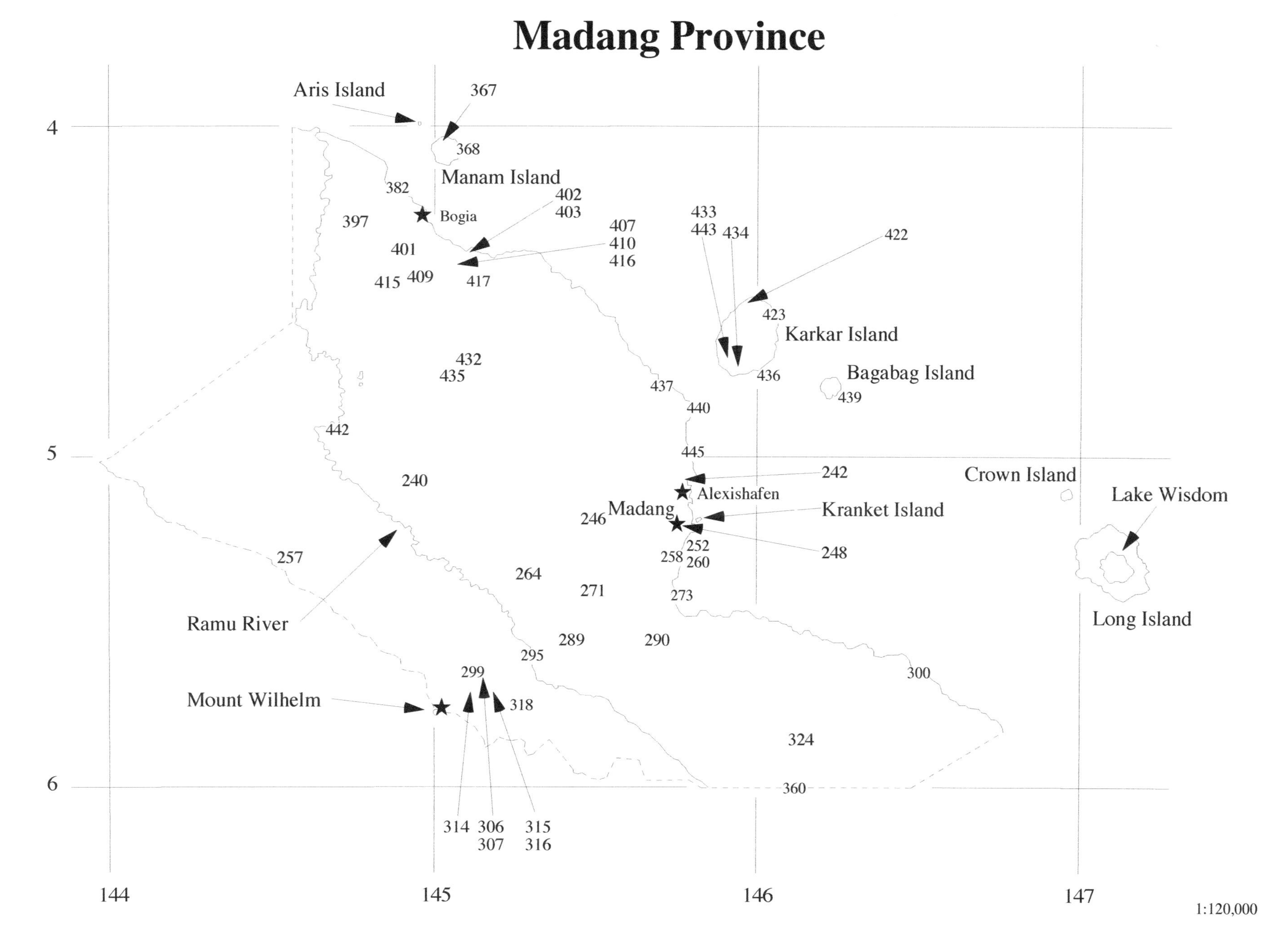

Madang Province
Aris Island
367
4
368
Manam Island
382
402
403
397
Bogia
407
410
416
433
443 434
422
401
415 409 417
423
Karkar Island
432
435
Bagabag Island
437
439
440
442
5
445
240
242
Crown Island
Alexishafen
Lake Wisdom
246 Madang
Kranket Island
257
252
248
258 260
264
273
Ramu River
271
289 290
295
300
299
Mount Wilhelm
318
Long Island
324
6
360
314 306 315
307 316
144
145
146
147
1:120,000

Morobe Province

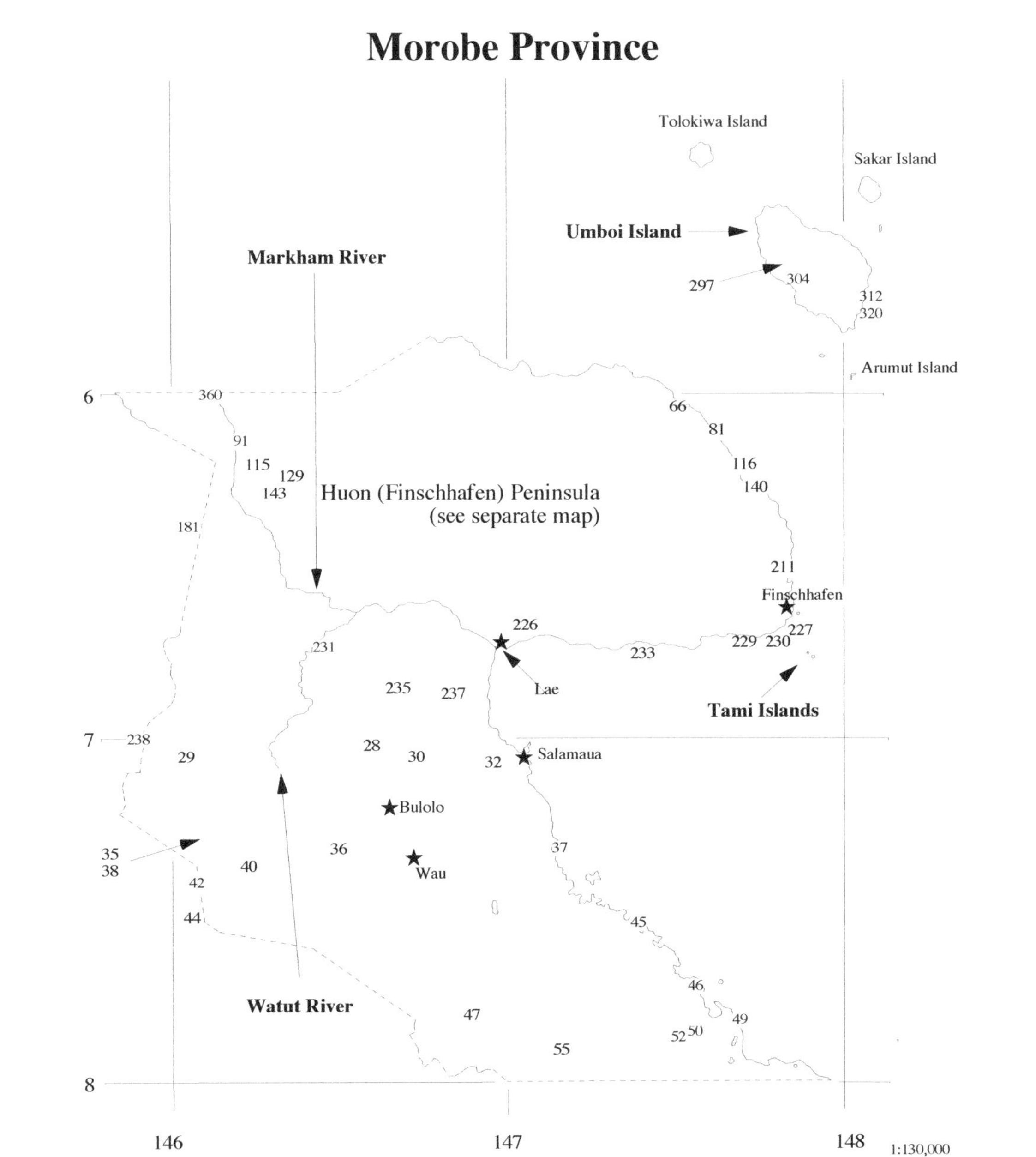

Huon (Finschhafen) Peninsula and Environs

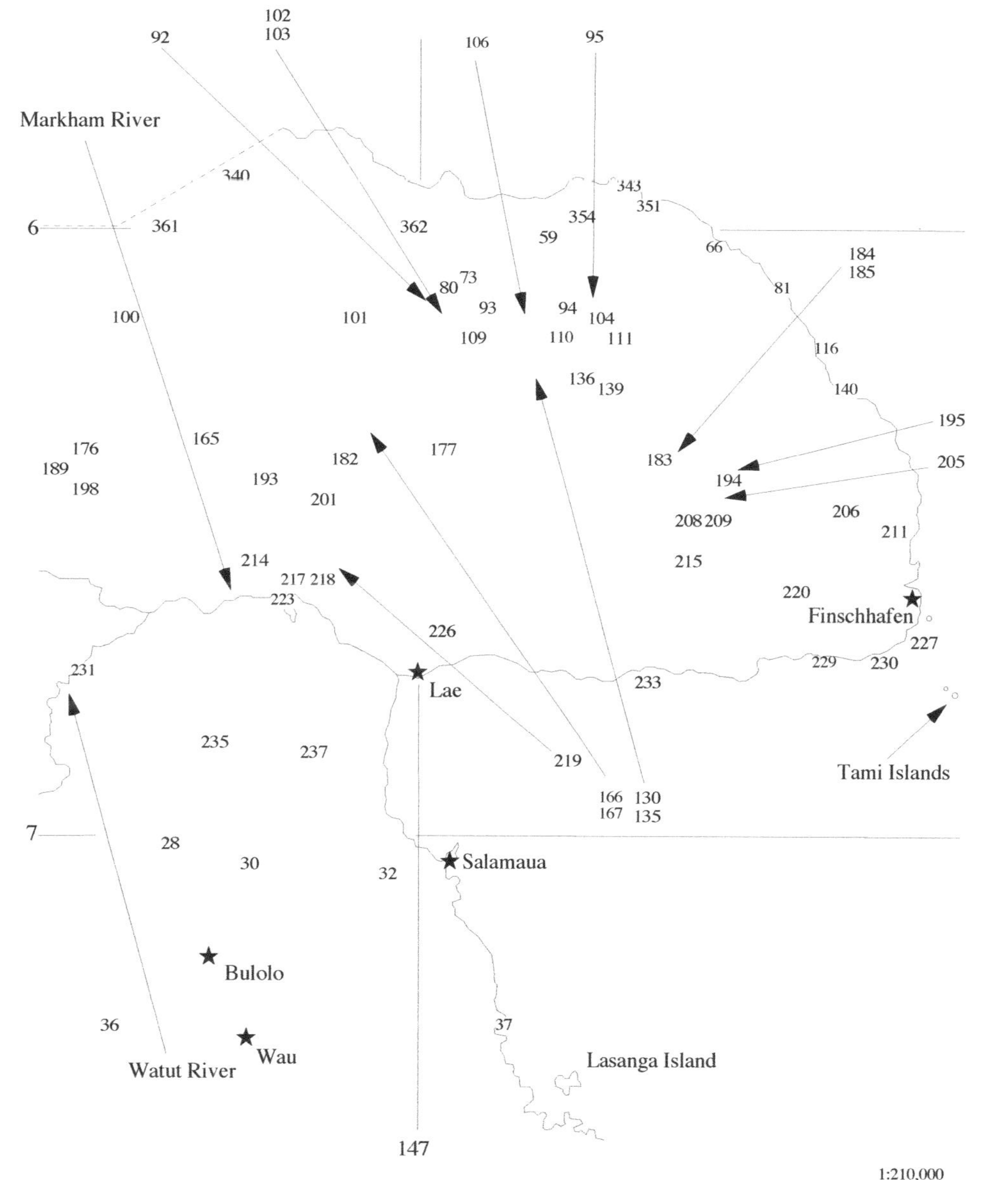

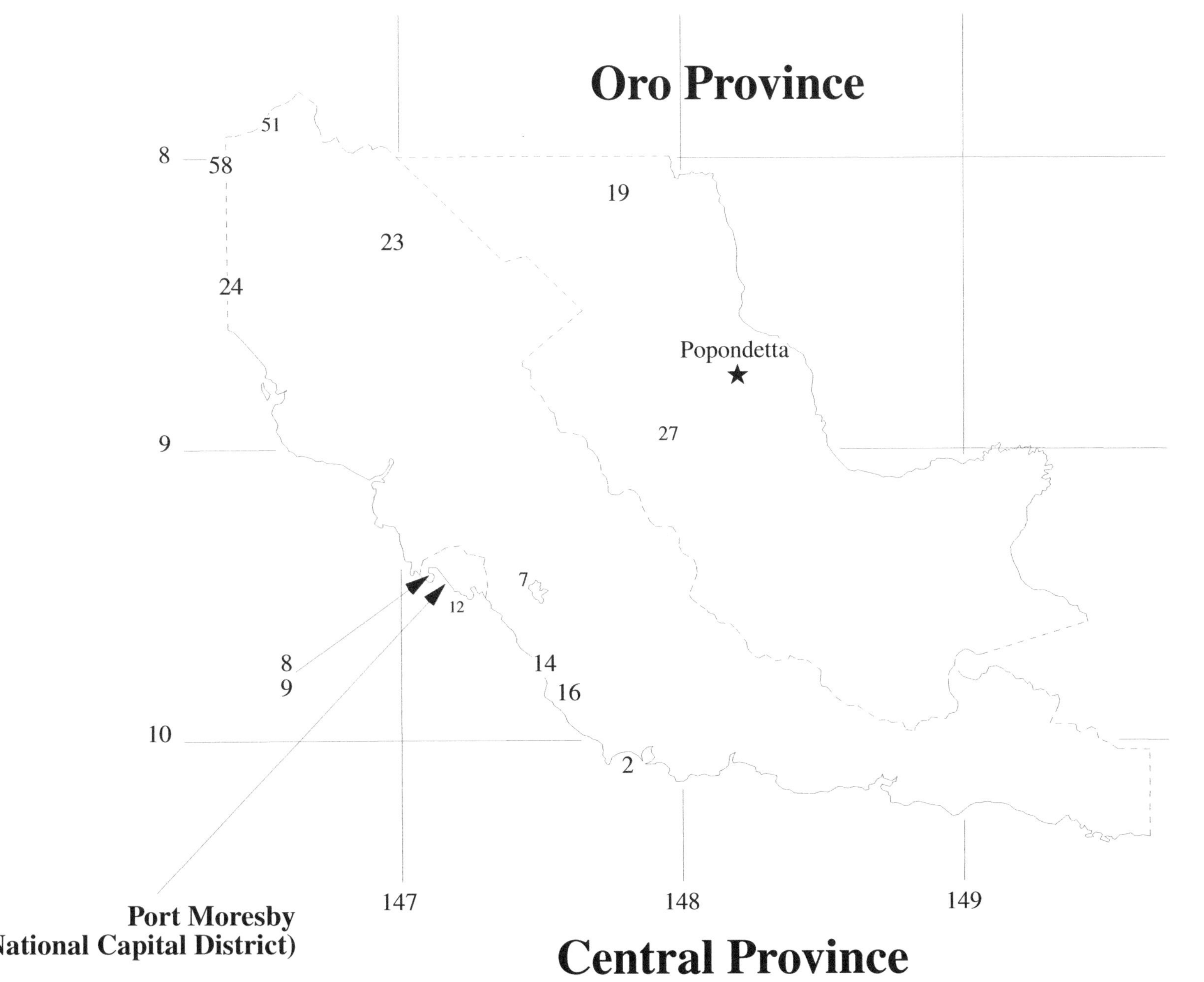

Oro Province
51
8
58
19
23
24
Popondetta
27
9
7
8
12
8
9
14
16
10
2
Port Moresby
(National Capital District)
147
148
149
Central Province
1:90,000

Milne Bay Province

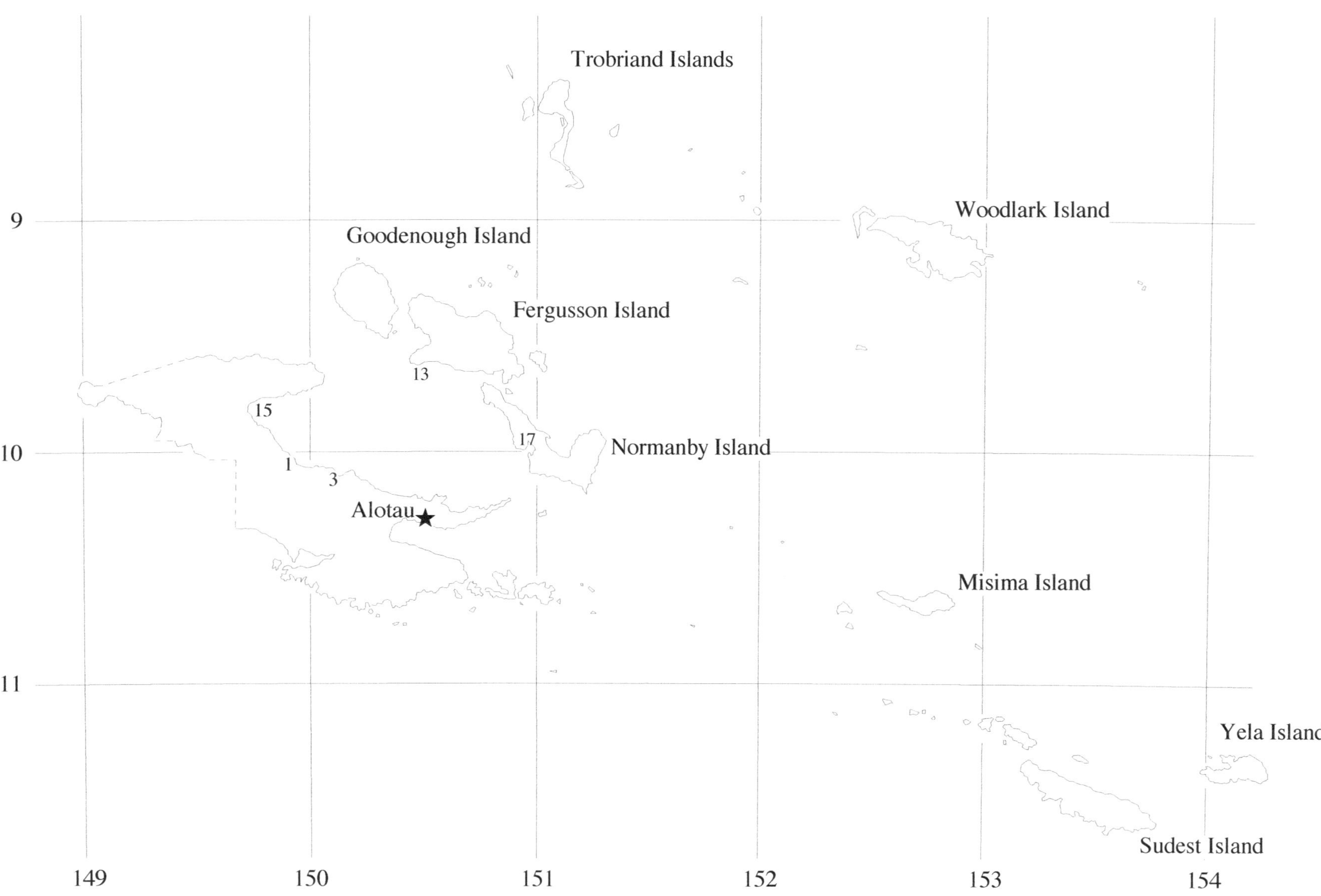

Gulf Province

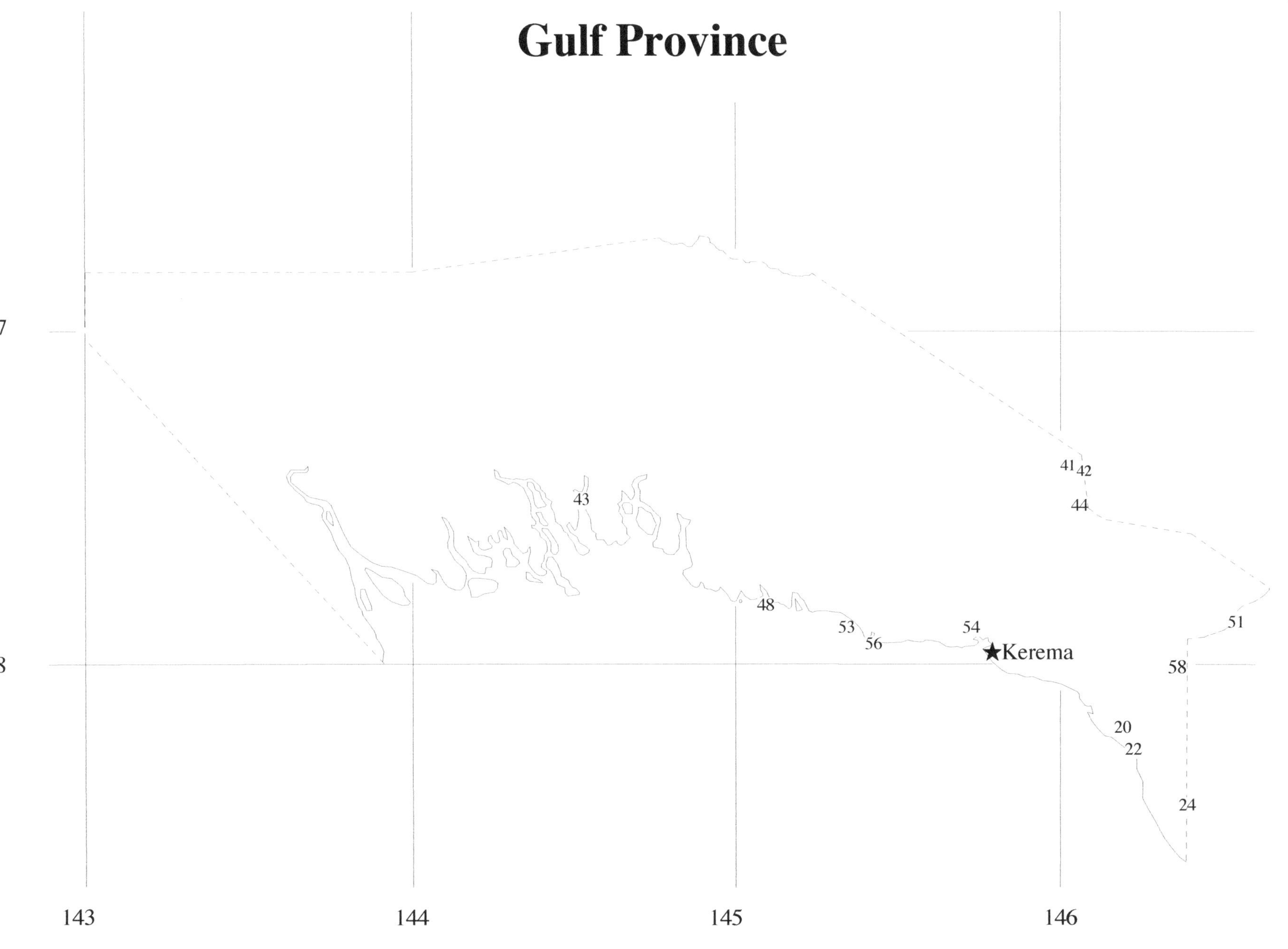

Western Province

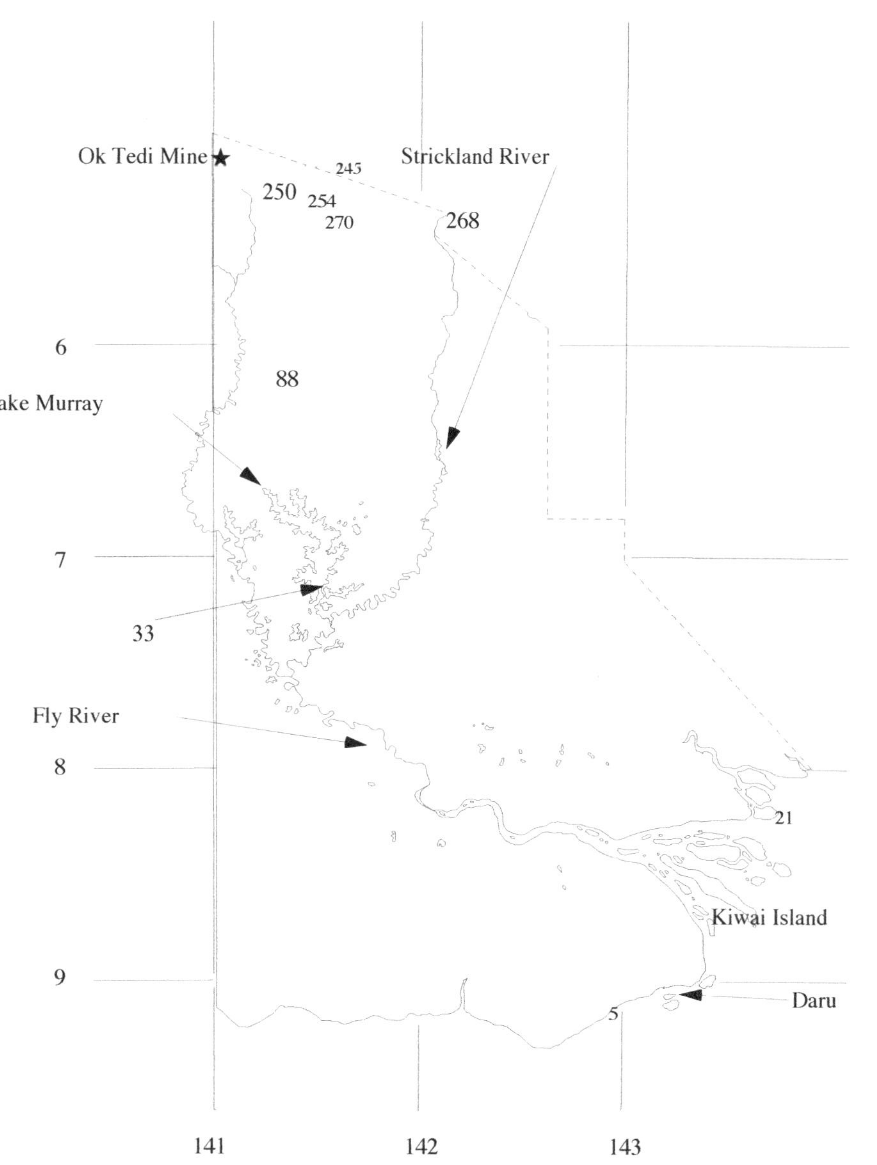

Eastern Highlands Province

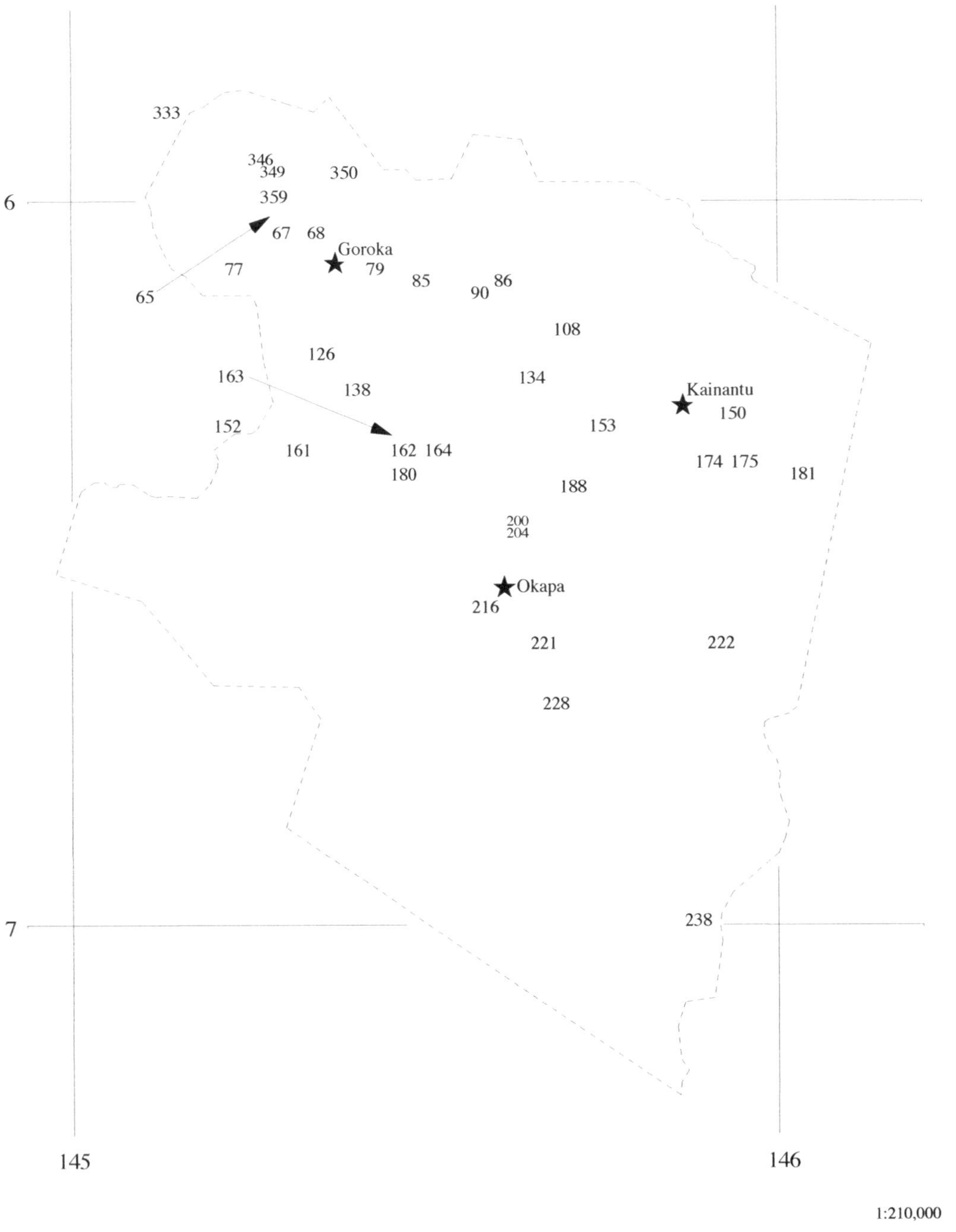

Simbu Province

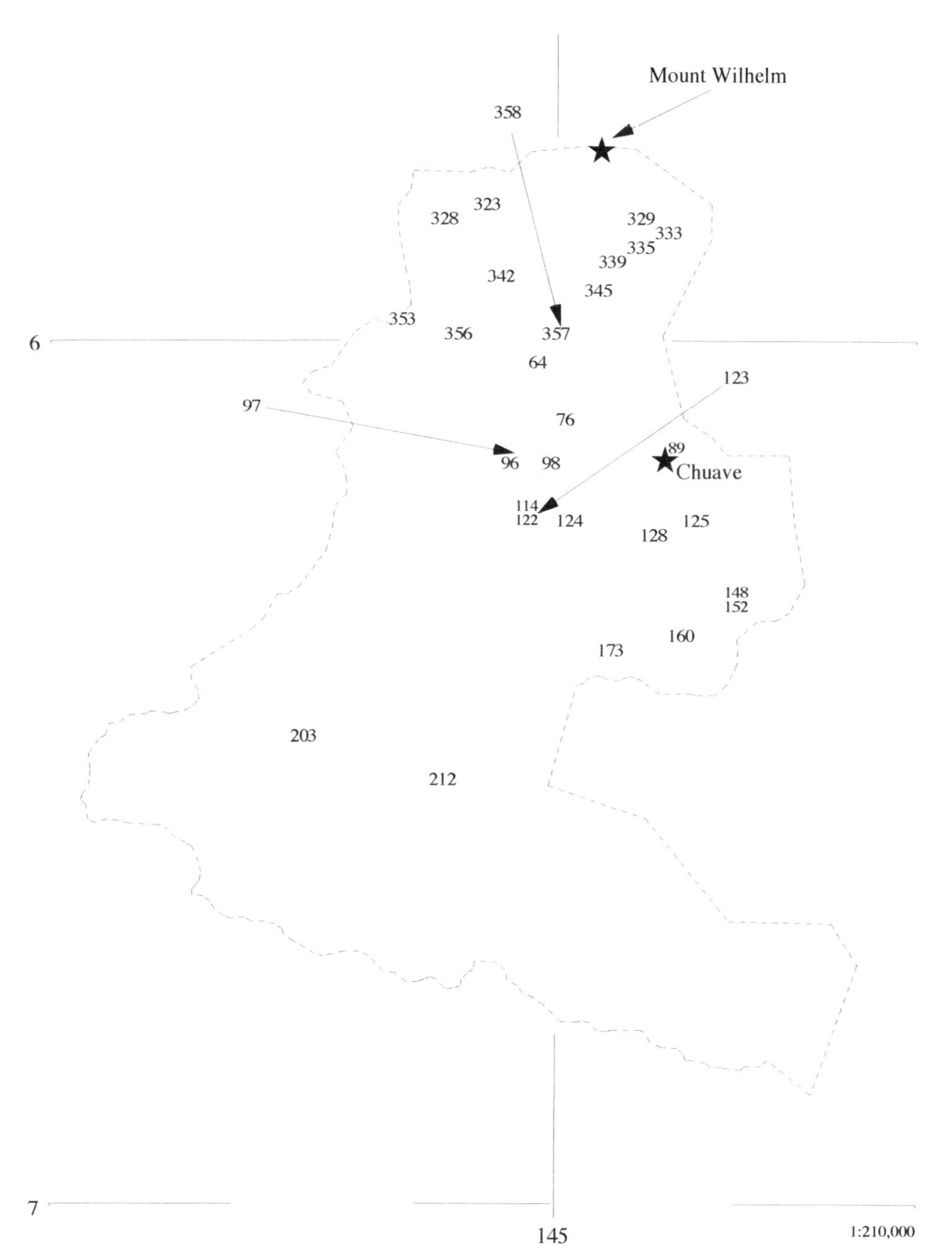

Western Highlands Province

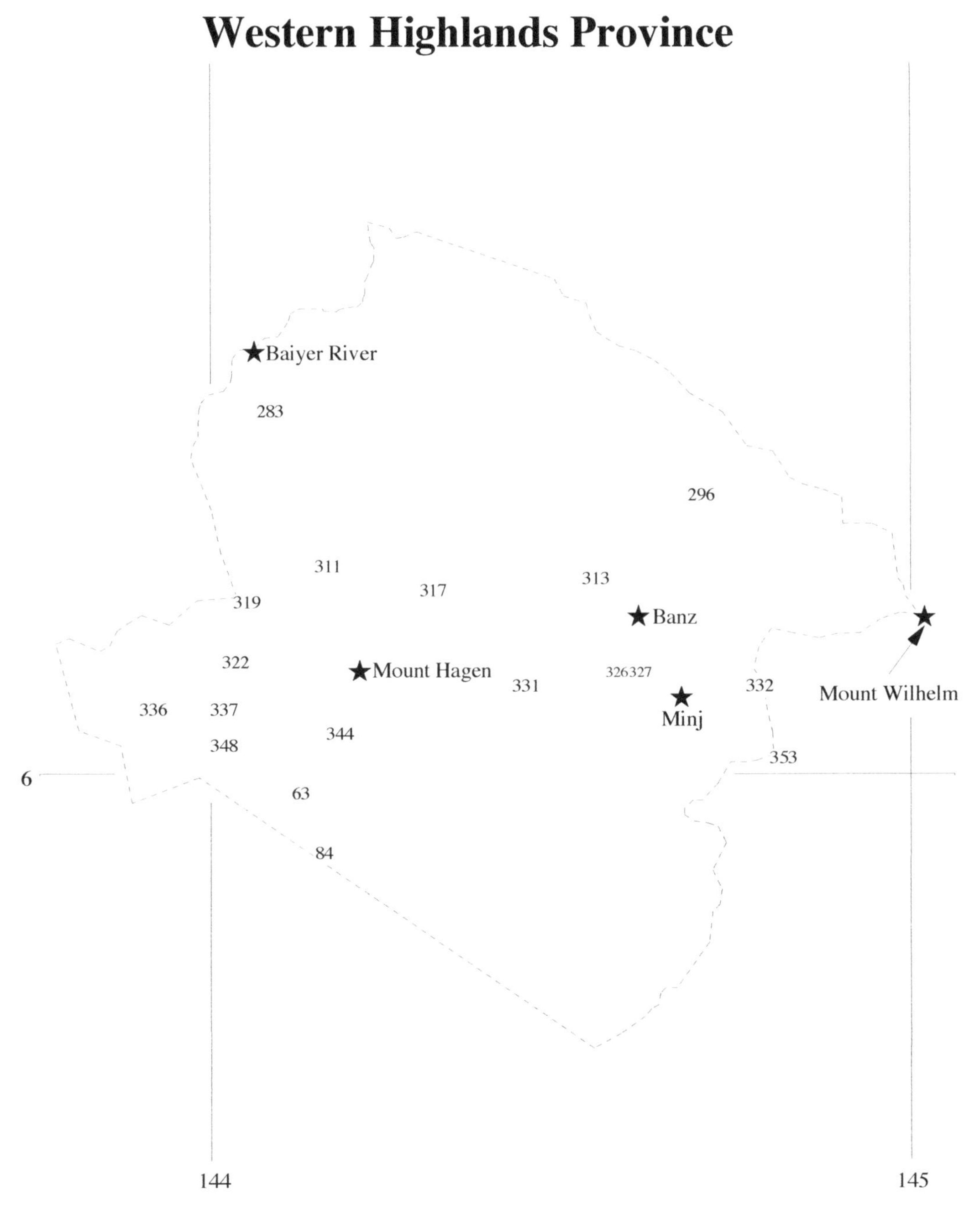

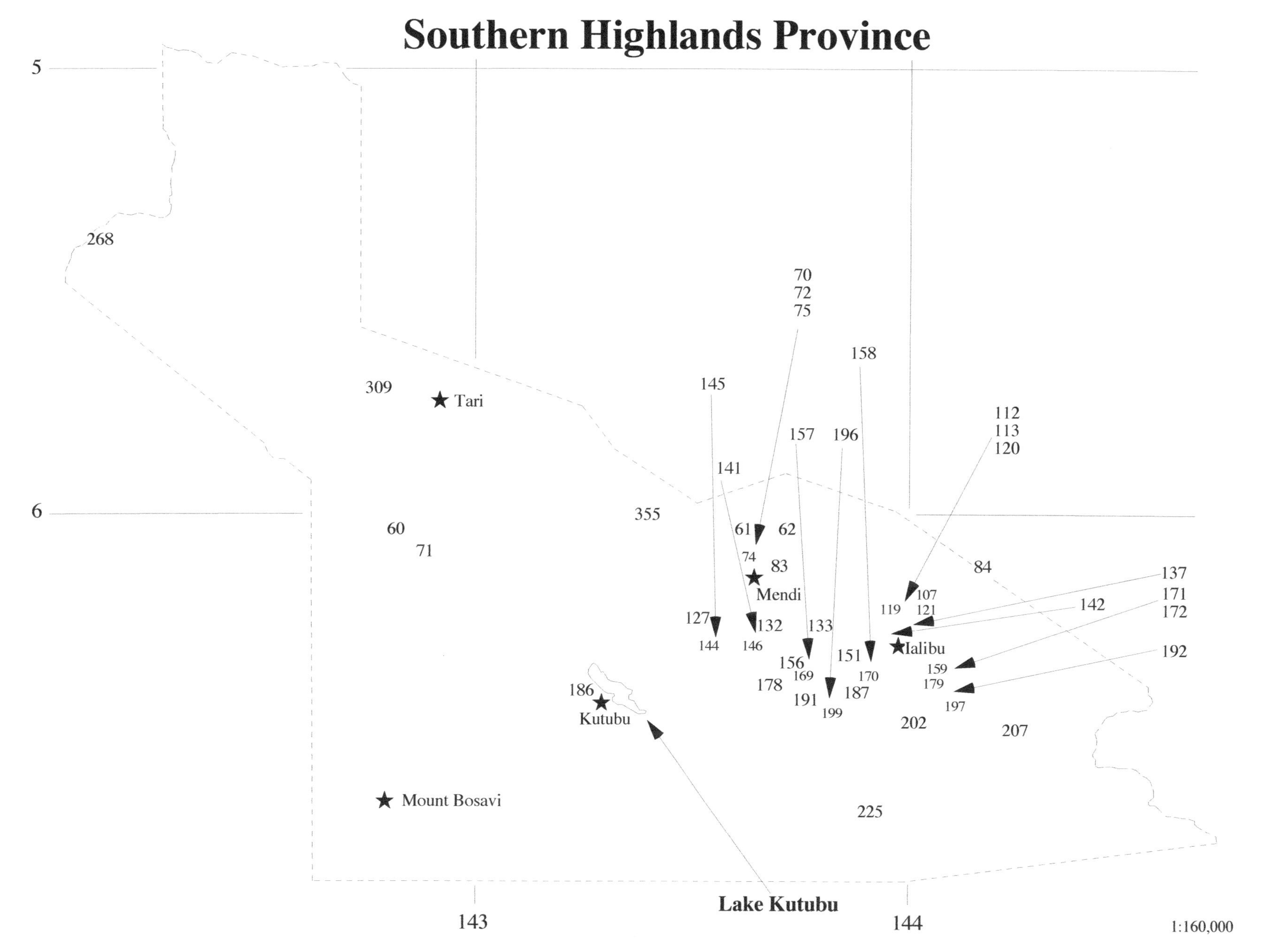

Southern Highlands Province
1:160,000
5
6
143
144
309
★ Tari
268
60
71
355
70
72
75
145
141
157
196
158
112
113
120
61
74
83
★ Mendi
62
84
137
171
172
142
127
144
132
146
156
178
133
169
191
151
170
187
199
202
107
119
121
★ Ialibu
159
179
197
207
192
225
186
★ Kutubu
★ Mount Bosavi
Lake Kutubu

Enga Province

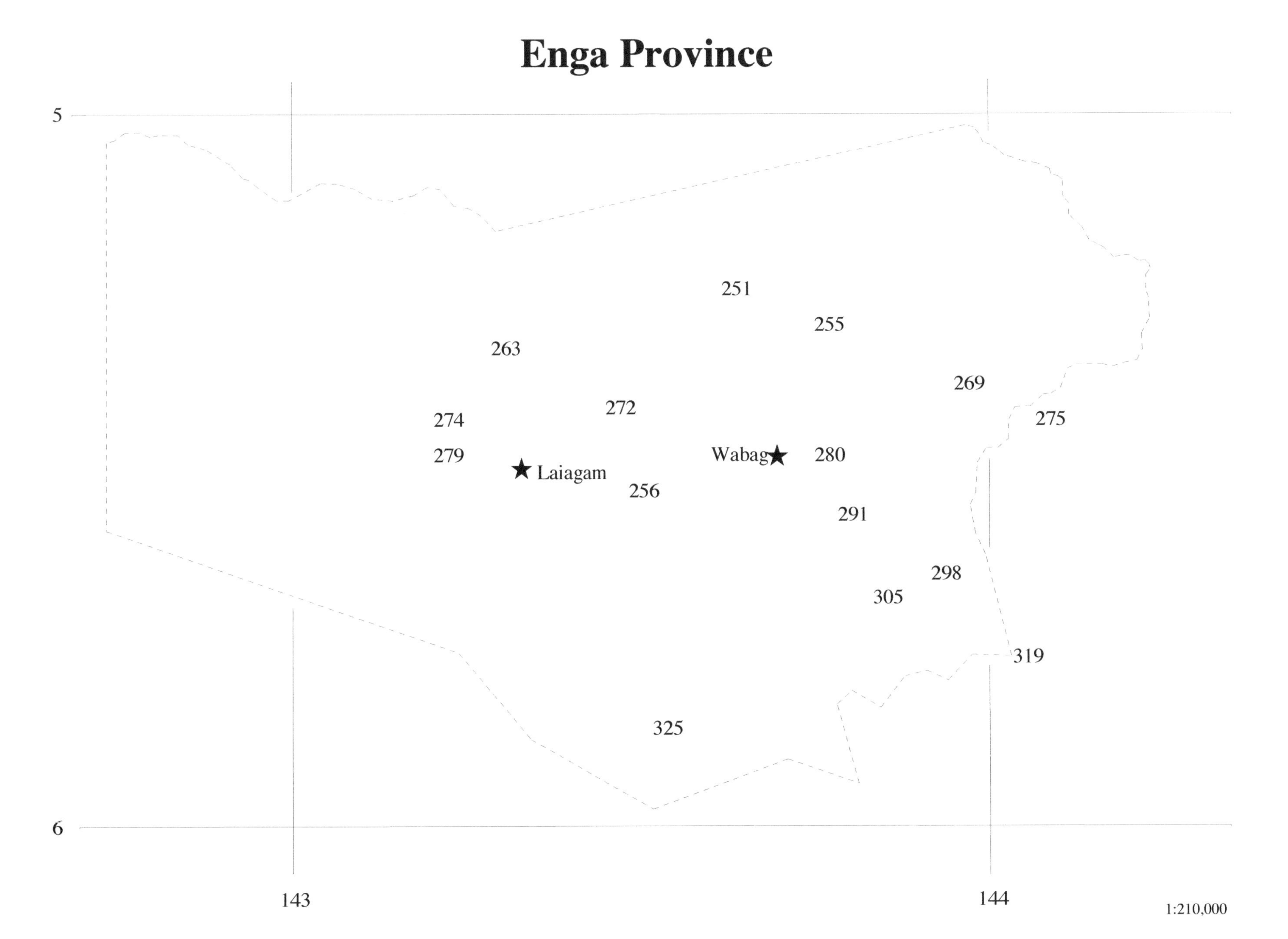

Manus Province

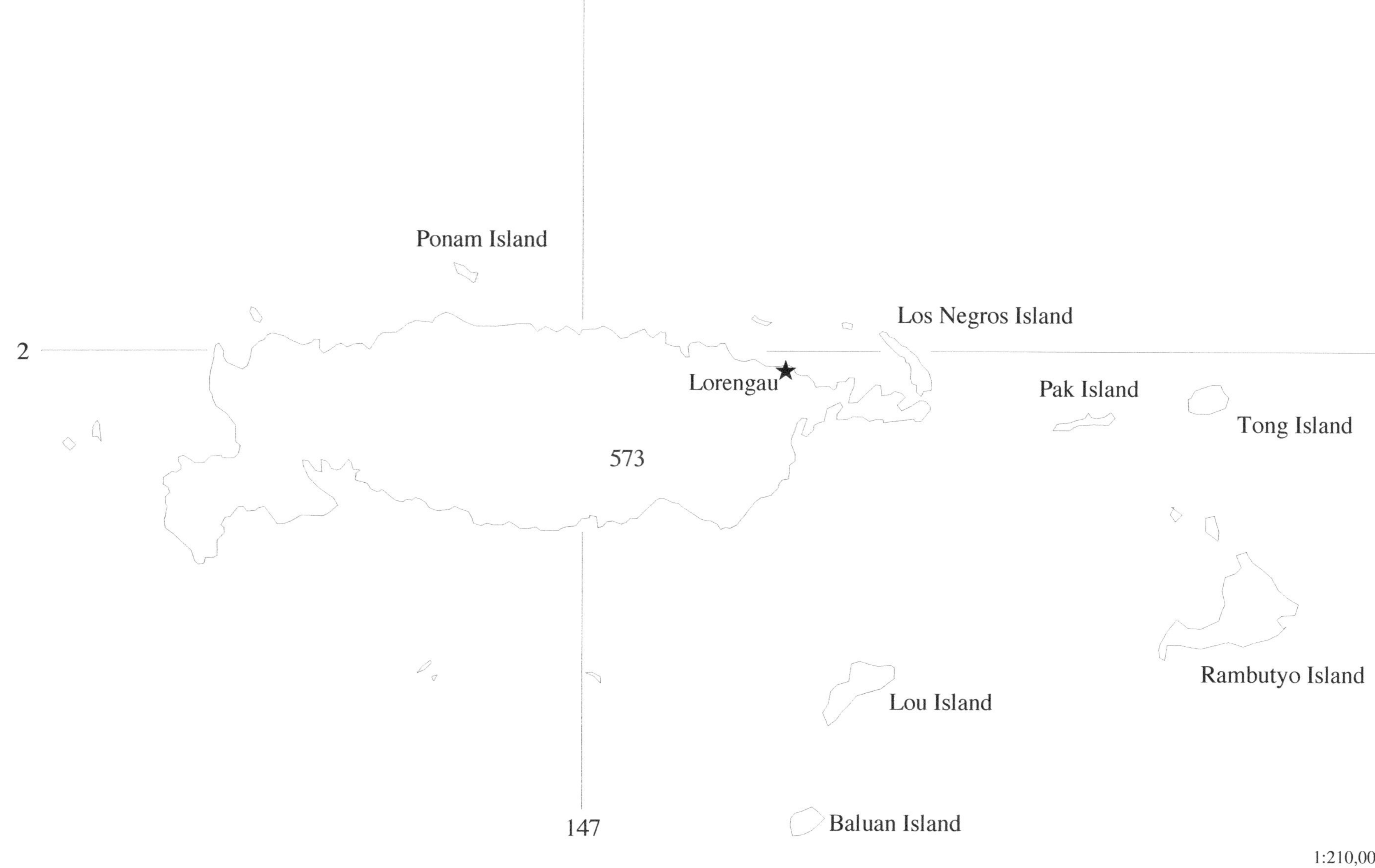

New Ireland Province

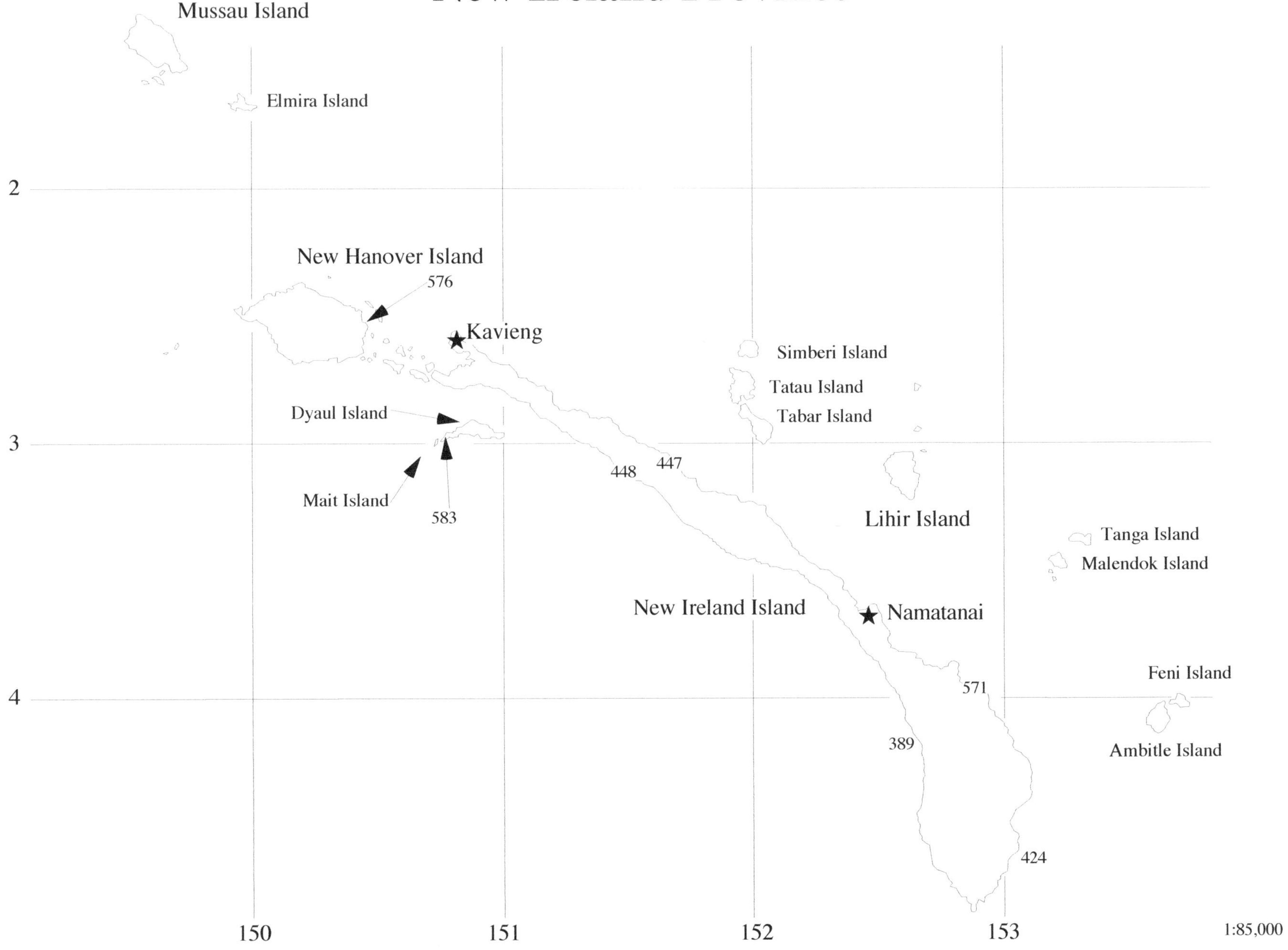

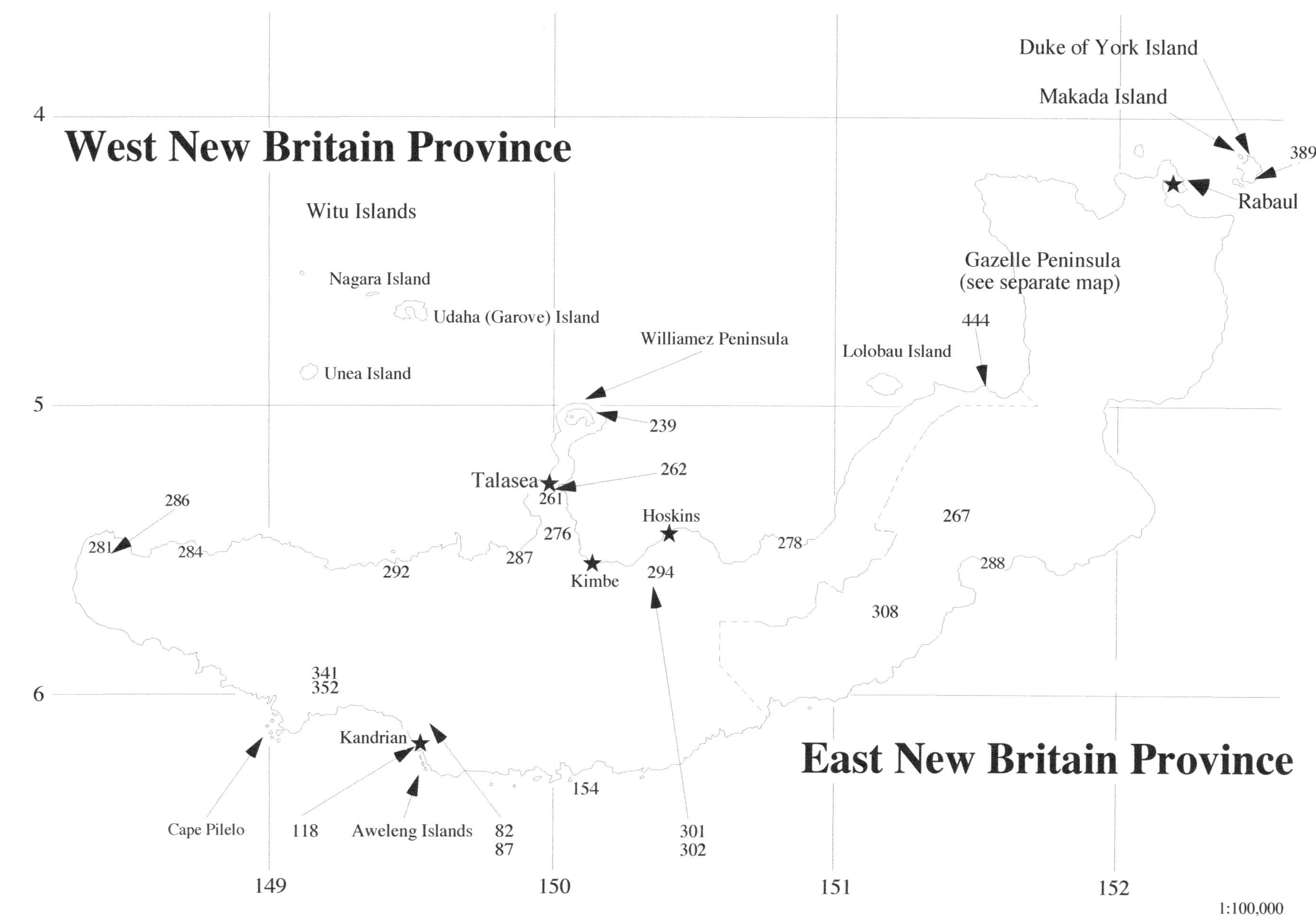

West New Britain Province
East New Britain Province
Duke of York Island
Makada Island
389
Rabaul
Witu Islands
Nagara Island
Udaha (Garove) Island
Unea Island
Williamez Peninsula
Gazelle Peninsula
(see separate map)
444
Lolobau Island
239
Talasea
261
262
Hoskins
267
276
278
288
287
Kimbe
294
308
292
286
281
284
341
352
Kandrian
Cape Pilelo
118
Aweleng Islands
82
87
154
301
302
4
5
6
149
150
151
152
1:100,000

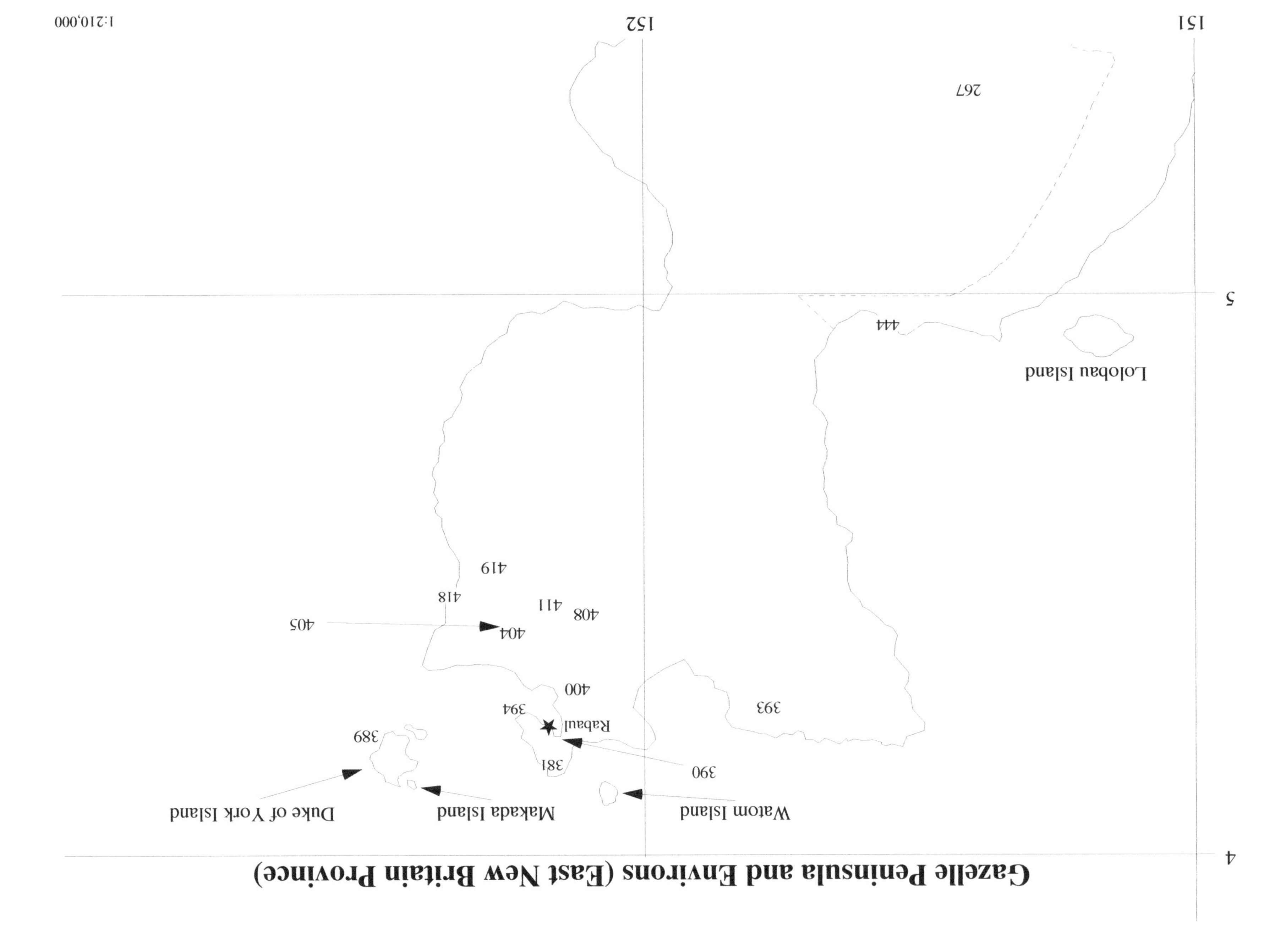

Gazelle Peninsula and Environs (East New Britain Province)
Duke of York Island
Makada Island
Watom Island
Rabaul
Lolobau Island
389
405
418
404
419
394
381
400
408 411
390
393
444
267
1:210,000
4
5
151
152

North Solomons Province

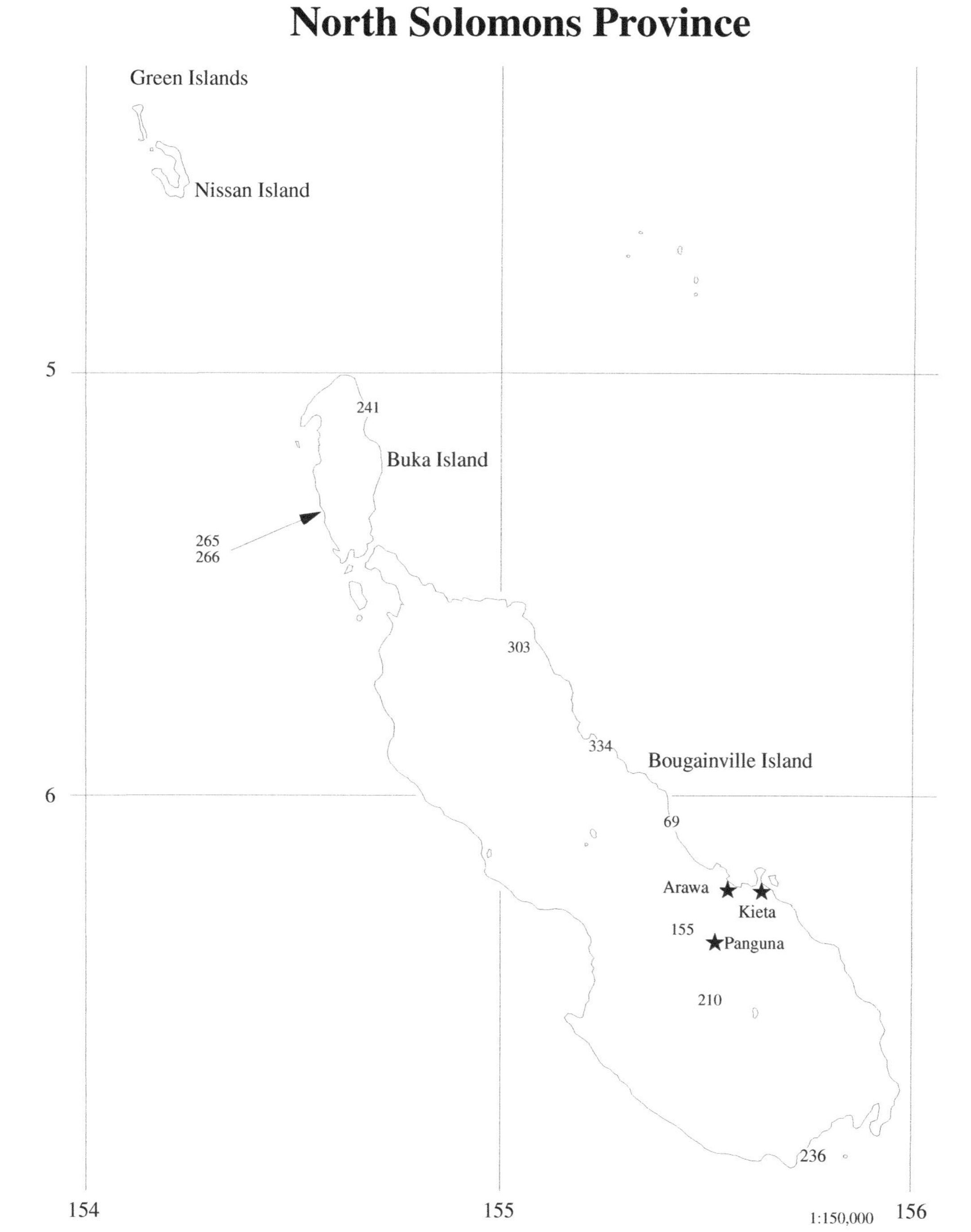